CLASSIC GHOST STORIES

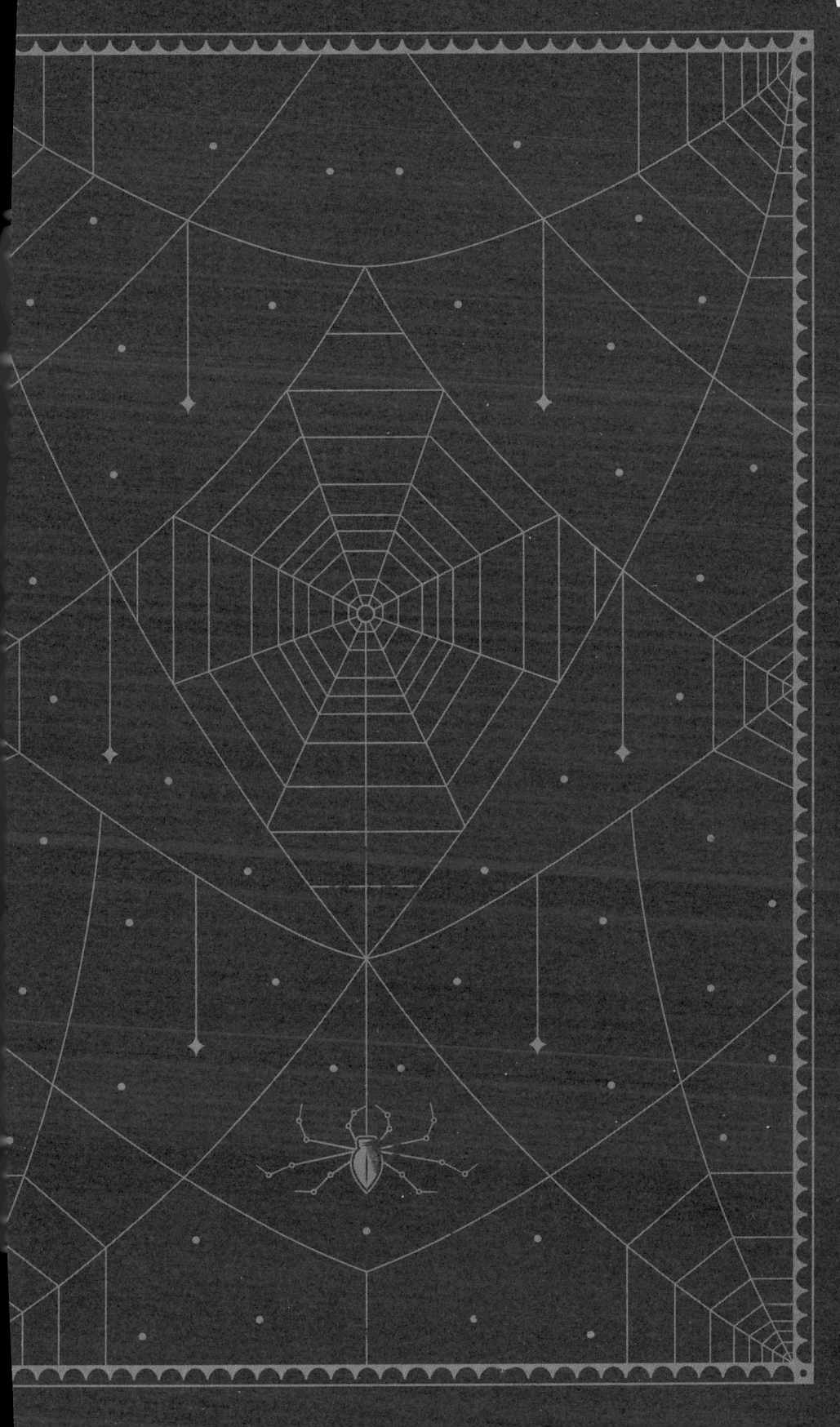

Compilation and Introduction © 2017 by Sterling Publishing Co., Inc.
Cover and endpaper design © 2017 by Sterling Publishing Co., Inc.

All rights reserved. No part of this publication may be reproduced,
stored in a retrieval system, or transmitted in any form or by any means
(including electronic, mechanical, photocopying, recording, or otherwise)
without prior written permission from the publisher.

This 2017 edition printed for Barnes & Noble by Sterling Publishing Co., Inc.

ISBN: 978-1-4351-6507-6

Barnes & Noble, Inc.
122 Fifth Avenue
New York, NY 10011

Manufactured in China

1 3 5 7 9 10 8 6 4 2

sterlingpublishing.com

Cover design and endpapers by Raphael Geroni

Contents

Introduction ix

EDGAR ALLAN POE
    Eleonora 1

CHARLES DICKENS
    No. 1 Branch Line—The Signal-Man 6

WILKIE COLLINS
    Mad Monkton 17

ELIZABETH GASKELL
    The Old Nurse's Story 68

AMELIA B. EDWARDS
    The North Mail 85

MRS. J. H. RIDDELL
    A Terrible Vengeance 96

EDWARD BULWER-LYTTON
    The Haunted and the Haunters; or, The House and the Brain 131

JOHN BUCHAN
    Fullcircle 161

VERNON LEE
    Amour Dure 173

BERNARD CAPES
    An Eddy on the Floor 200

J. Sheridan Le Fanu
The Haunted Baronet 233

Robert S. Hichens
How Love Came to Professor Guildea 338

Rudyard Kipling
The Phantom 'Rickshaw 377

W. W. Jacobs
The Three Sisters 395

Richard Middleton
The Ghost-Ship 402

Arthur Quiller-Couch
The Roll-Call of the Reef 410

Arthur Conan Doyle
The Captain of the *Pole-Star* 423

Oliver Onions
The Cigarette Case 442

Mrs. Henry Wood
A Curious Experience 453

H. G. Wells
The Story of the Inexperienced Ghost 470

Lord Dunsany
The Ghosts 481

Ralph Adams Cram
In Kropfsberg Keep 485

J. Meade Falkner
The Lost Stradivarius 493

CONTENTS

Algernon Blackwood
    Keeping His Promise 588

Ambrose Bierce
    The Moonlit Road 600

E. F. Benson
    The House with the Brick-Kiln 608

Mary E. Wilkins Freeman
    The Wind in the Rose-Bush 617

M. R. James
    An Episode of Cathedral History 632

Perceval Landon
    Thurnley Abbey 646

William Hope Hodgson
    The Searcher of the End House 659

Ellen Glasgow
    The Shadowy Third 679

Edith Wharton
    Kerfol 699

Henry James
    The Turn of the Screw 718

Original Sources 804

Introduction

IN THE INTRODUCTION TO HIS ANTHOLOGY *LOST SOULS*, GHOST-STORY SCHOLAR Jack Sullivan states unequivocally that "the first modern short stories in English were ghost stories." By way of illustration, he points to American author Edgar Allan Poe and his Irish contemporary J. Sheridan Le Fanu, both of whom were publishing fiction in the 1830s, and notes that in their tales of the supernatural one found "the unity of mood and economy of means" that we associate with the short stories of their distinguished literary successors. "There are more ghost stories with unity of tone than any other kinds of early stories," Sullivan continues, "precisely because mood is so basic to the genre." It's not that ghost-story writers were trying consciously to invent a new literary form, but that they were doing what they knew intuitively was the best way to tell their stories for maximum effect.

The ghost story is, of course, one of the oldest types of fiction, and variations on it can be found in the literature of every nation around the world. As the popular fiction subgenre we consider it today, it was present in nascent form during the era of the gothic novel at the end of the eighteenth century and became a full-blown literary phenomenon in the first few decades of the nineteenth century. The ghost stories selected for *Classic Ghost Stories* represent some of the best ghost stories written in the late-nineteenth and early-twentieth centuries, as well as some of the best ghost stories ever written in the English language. Many of them established the ground rules for ghostly fiction of their day, and they continue to influence the ghost story as it is written today.

M. R. James, the leading exponent of the antiquarian ghost story and the writer who is regarded as having laid down the rules for modern ghost fiction maintained that ghosts had to be "malevolent or odious." That description certainly fits the being whose recrudescence from the past haunts the cathedral setting of his tale "An Episode of Cathedral History," but then what are we to make of the ghostly presence in Robert Hichens's "How Love Came to Professor Guildea," whose behavior is comparatively benign but whose persistence drives his victim to a nervous breakdown (and worse). James's definition of malevolence is more open to interpretation than its narrowness would suggest, and it is in that expanded definition that the thirty-three stories in this volume comfortably fit.

The truth is, the ghosts in James's own fiction are far from orthodox. Few represent the ghost or spirit of someone who has shuffled off his or her mortal coil. Rather, they tend to be hellish survivals from less enlightened times that embody the direst superstitions of what people feared back then. And so, again, the stories in this book are not constrained by narrow parameters for what form they should manifest or how they should express themselves. There are more traditionally insubstantial ghosts in E. F. Benson's "The House with the Brick-Kiln" and Mary E. Wilkins-Freeman's "The Wind in the Rose-Bush," and ghosts with considerably less insubstantiality in Ralph Adams Cram's "In Kropfsberg Keep" and Perceval Landon's gruesome masterpiece "Thurnley Abbey." The flamboyant haunting presence in Edward Bulwer-Lytton's "The Haunted and the Haunters; or, The House and the Brain" virtually defies the traditional definition of a ghost, but then so does the specter in Charles Dickens's "No. 1 Branch Line—The Signal-Man," which might be called a precognitive ghost rather than a post-mortem specter. William Hope Hodgson works an imaginative variation on the classic haunted house theme in "The Searcher of the End House" by having his ghostly presence "hunted" by his character Carnacki, a sort of occult detective with scientific tools at his disposal.

James's dictum notwithstanding, the stories in this volume feature several ghosts that are not odious. The spirit that haunts the home that is the setting for John Buchan's "Fullcircle" is far from malevolent, while those found in H. G. Wells's "The Story of the Inexperience Ghost" and Richard Middleton's "The Ghost-Ship" are downright whimsical. The book concludes with Edith Wharton's "Kerfol" and Henry James's short novel *The Turn of the Screw*. Wharton and James were both literary writers who frequently turned their hands to ghost stories and the common unities they acknowledged in both their supernatural and non-supernatural fiction bears out Sullivan's contention that "the birth of the modern ghostly tale and the modern short story are virtually synonymous."

The foregoing commentary notwithstanding, it is perhaps not a good idea to analyze the tales in *Classic Ghost Stories* at great length or ponder the categories of ghostly fiction to which they are best slotted. By its nature the well-told ghost story should catch us by surprise, and present us with improbabilities that, no matter how irrational, encourage us to suspend our disbelief in them and thrill to their *possibility*. Thrills of this sort, as perfected by the best practitioners of the ghost story as it was written over one hundred years ago, await you in the pages that follow.

—Stefan Dziemianowicz
New York, 2017

Eleonora

Edgar Allan Poe

Sub conservatione formae specificae salva anima.
RAYMOND LULLY

I AM COME OF A RACE NOTED FOR VIGOR OF FANCY AND ARDOR OF PASSION. MEN HAVE called me mad; but the question is not yet settled, whether madness is or is not the loftiest intelligence—whether much that is glorious—whether all that is profound—does not spring from disease of thought—from *moods* of mind exalted at the expense of the general intellect. They who dream by day are cognizant of many things which escape those who dream only by night. In their gray visions they obtain glimpses of eternity, and thrill, in awaking, to find that they have been upon the verge of the great secret. In snatches, they learn something of the wisdom which is of good, and more of the mere knowledge which is of evil. They penetrate, however, rudderless or compassless, into the vast ocean of the "light ineffable"; and again, like the adventures of the Nubian geographer, "*agressi sunt mare tenebrarum, quid in eo esset exploraturi.*"

We will say, then, that I am mad. I grant, at least, that there are two distinct conditions of my mental existence—the condition of a lucid reason, not to be disputed, and belonging to the memory of events forming the first epoch of my life—and a condition of shadow and doubt, appertaining to the present, and to the recollection of what constitutes the second great era of my being. Therefore, what I shall tell of the earlier period, believe; and to what I may relate of the later time, give only such credit as may seem due; or doubt it altogether; or, if doubt it ye cannot, then play unto its riddle the Oedipus.

She whom I loved in youth, and of whom I now pen calmly and distinctly these remembrances, was the sole daughter of the only sister of my mother long departed. Eleonora was the name of my cousin. We had always dwelled together, beneath a tropical sun, in the Valley of the Many-Colored Grass. No unguided footstep ever came upon that vale; for it lay far away up among a range of giant hills that hung beetling around about it, shutting out the sunlight from its sweetest recesses. No path was trodden in its vicinity; and, to reach our happy home, there was need of putting back, with force, the foliage of many thousands of forest trees, and of crushing to death the glories of many millions of fragrant flowers. Thus it was that we lived all alone, knowing nothing of the world without the valley,—I, and my cousin, and her mother.

From the dim regions beyond the mountains at the upper end of our encircled domain, there crept out a narrow and deep river, brighter than all save the eyes of Eleonora; and, winding stealthily about in mazy courses, it passed away, at length, through a shadowy gorge, among hills still dimmer than those whence it had issued. We called it the "River of Silence"; for there seemed to be a hushing influence in its flow. No murmur arose from its bed, and so gently it wandered along, that the pearly pebbles upon which we loved to gaze, far down within its bosom, stirred not at all, but lay in a motionless content, each in its own old station, shining on gloriously forever.

The margin of the river, and of the many dazzling rivulets that glided through devious ways into its channel, as well as the spaces that extended from the margins away down into the depths of the streams until they reached the bed of pebbles at the bottom,—these spots, not less than the whole surface of the valley, from the river to the mountains that girdled it in, were carpeted all by a soft green grass, thick, short, perfectly even, and vanilla-perfumed, but so besprinkled throughout with the yellow buttercup, the white daisy, the purple violet, and the ruby-red asphodel, that its exceeding beauty spoke to our hearts in loud tones, of the love and of the glory of God.

And, here and there, in groves about this grass, like wildernesses of dreams, sprang up fantastic trees, whose tall slender stems stood not upright, but slanted gracefully towards the light that peered at noon-day into the centre of the valley. Their bark was speckled with the vivid alternate splendor of ebony and silver, and was smoother than all save the cheeks of Eleonora; so that but for the brilliant green of the huge leaves that spread from their summits in long, tremulous lines, dallying with the Zephyrs, one might have fancied them giant serpents of Syria doing homage to their Sovereign the Sun.

Hand in hand about this valley, for fifteen years, roamed I with Eleonora before Love entered within our hearts. It was one evening at the close of the third lustrum of her life, and of the fourth of my own, that we sat, locked in each other's embrace, beneath the serpent-like trees, and looked down within the waters of the River of Silence at our images therein. We spoke no words during the rest of that sweet day; and our words even upon the morrow were tremulous and few. We had drawn the God Eros from that wave, and now we felt that he had enkindled within us the fiery souls of our forefathers. The passions which had for centuries distinguished our race, came thronging with the fancies for which they had been equally noted, and together breathed a delirious bliss over the Valley of the Many-Colored Grass. A change fell upon all things. Strange, brilliant flowers, star-shaped, burst out upon the trees where no flowers had been known before. The tints of the green carpet deepened; and when, one by one, the white daisies shrank away, there sprang up in place of them, ten by ten of the ruby-red asphodel. And life arose in our paths; for the tall flamingo, hitherto unseen, with all gay glowing birds, flaunted his scarlet plumage before us. The golden and silver fish haunted the river, out of the bosom of which issued, little by little, a murmur that swelled, at length, into a lulling melody more divine than that of the harp of Æolus—sweeter than all save the voice of Eleonora. And now, too, a voluminous cloud, which we had long watched in the regions of Hesper, floated out thence, all gorgeous in crimson and gold, and settling in peace above us, sank, day by day, lower and lower, until its edges rested upon the tops of the mountains, turning all their dimness into magnificence, and shutting us up, as if forever, within a magic prison-house of grandeur and of glory.

The loveliness of Eleonora was that of the Seraphim; but she was a maiden artless and innocent as the brief life she had led among the flowers. No guile disguised the fervor of love which animated her heart, and she examined with me its inmost recesses as we walked together in the Valley of the Many-Colored Grass, and discoursed of the mighty changes which had lately taken place therein.

At length, having spoken one day, in tears, of the last sad change which must befall Humanity, she thenceforward dwelt only upon this one sorrowful theme, interweaving it into all our converse, as, in the songs of the bard of Schiraz, the same images are found occurring, again and again, in every impressive variation of phrase.

She had seen that the finger of Death was upon her bosom—that, like the ephemeron, she had been made perfect in loveliness only to die; but the terrors of the grave to her, lay solely in a consideration which she revealed to me, one evening at twilight, by the banks of the River of Silence. She grieved to think that, having entombed her in the Valley of the Many-Colored Grass, I would quit forever its happy recesses, transferring the love which now was so passionately her own to some maiden of the outer and every-day world. And, then and there, I threw myself hurriedly at the feet of Eleonora, and offered up a vow, to herself and to Heaven, that I would never bind myself in marriage to any daughter of Earth—that I would in no manner prove recreant to her dear memory, or to the memory of the devout affection with which she had blessed me. And I called the Mighty Ruler of the Universe to witness the pious solemnity of my vow. And the curse which I invoked of *Him* and of her, a saint in Helusion, should I prove traitorous to that promise, involved a penalty the exceeding great horror of which will not permit me to make record of it here. And the bright eyes of Eleonora grew brighter at my words; and she sighed as if a deadly burthen had been taken from her breast; and she trembled and very bitterly wept; but she made acceptance of the vow, (for what was she but a child?) and it made easy to her the bed of her death. And she said to me, not many days afterwards, tranquilly dying, that, because of what I had done for the comfort of her spirit, she would watch over me in that spirit when departed, and, if so it were permitted her return to me visibly in the watches of the night; but, if this thing were, indeed, beyond the power of the souls in Paradise, that she would, at least, give me frequent indications of her presence; sighing upon me in the evening winds, or filling the air which I breathed with perfume from the censers of the angels. And, with these words upon her lips, she yielded up her innocent life, putting an end to the first epoch of my own.

Thus far I have faithfully said. But as I pass the barrier in Time's path, formed by the death of my beloved, and proceed with the second era of my existence, I feel that a shadow gathers over my brain, and I mistrust the perfect sanity of the record. But let me on.—Years dragged themselves along heavily, and still I dwelled within the Valley of the Many-Colored Grass; but a second change had come upon all things. The star-shaped flowers shrank into the stems of the trees, and appeared no more. The tints of the green carpet faded; and, one by one, the ruby-red asphodels withered away; and there sprang up, in place of them, ten by ten, dark, eye-like violets, that writhed uneasily and were ever encumbered with dew. And Life departed from our paths; for the tall flamingo flaunted no longer his scarlet plumage before us, but flew sadly from the vale into the hills, with all the gay glowing birds that had arrived in his company. And the golden and silver fish swam down through the gorge at the lower end of our domain and bedecked the sweet river never again. And the lulling melody that had been softer than the wind-harp of Æolus, and more divine than all save the voice of Eleonora, it died little by little away, in murmurs growing lower and lower, until the stream returned, at length, utterly, into the solemnity of its original silence. And then, lastly, the voluminous cloud uprose, and, abandoning the tops of the mountains to the dimness of old, fell back into the regions of Hesper, and took away all its manifold golden and gorgeous glories from the Valley of the Many-Colored Grass.

Yet the promises of Eleonora were not forgotten; for I heard the sounds of the swinging of the censers of the angels; and streams of a holy perfume floated ever and ever about the valley; and at lone hours, when my heart beat heavily, the winds that bathed my brow came unto me laden with soft sighs; and indistinct murmurs filled often the night air; and once—oh, but once only! I was awakened from a slumber, like the slumber of death, by the pressing of spiritual lips upon my own.

But the void within my heart refused, even thus, to be filled. I longed for the love which had before filled it to overflowing. At length the valley *pained* me through its memories of Eleonora, and I left it forever for the vanities and the turbulent triumphs of the world.

I found myself within a strange city, where all things might have served to blot from recollection the sweet dreams I had dreamed so long in the Valley of the Many-Colored Grass. The pomps and pageantries of a stately court, and the mad clangor of arms, and the radiant loveliness of woman, bewildered and intoxicated my brain. But as yet my soul had proved true to its vows, and the indications of the presence of Eleonora were still given me in the silent hours of the night. Suddenly, these manifestations they ceased; and the world grew dark before mine eyes; and I stood aghast at the burning thoughts which possessed—at the terrible temptations which beset me; for there came from some far, far distant and unknown land, into the gay court of the king I served, a maiden to whose beauty my whole recreant heart yielded at once—at whose footstool I bowed down without a struggle, in the most ardent, in the most abject worship of love. What indeed was my passion for the young girl of the valley in comparison with the fervor, and the delirium, and the spirit-lifting ecstasy of adoration with which I poured out my whole soul in tears at the feet of the ethereal Ermengarde?—Oh, bright was the seraph Ermengarde! and in that knowledge I had room for none other.—Oh, divine was the angel Ermengarde! and as I looked down into the depths of her memorial eyes, I thought only of them—and *of her*.

I wedded;—nor dreaded the curse I had invoked; and its bitterness was not visited upon me. And once—but once again in the silence of the night, there came through my lattice the soft sighs which had forsaken me; and they modelled themselves into familiar and sweet voice, saying—

"Sleep in peace!—for the Spirit of Love reigneth and ruleth, and, in taking to thy passionate heart her who is Ermengarde, thou art absolved, for reasons which shall be made known to thee in Heaven, of thy vows unto Eleonora."

No. 1 Branch Line—
The Signal-Man

Charles Dickens

"Halloa! Below there!" When he heard a voice thus calling to him, he was standing at the door of his box, with a flag in his hand, furled round its short pole. One would have thought, considering the nature of the ground, that he could not have doubted from what quarter the voice came; but, instead of looking up to where I stood on the top of the steep cutting nearly over his head, he turned himself about, and looked down the Line. There was something remarkable in his manner of doing so, though I could not have said for my life what. But, I know it was remarkable enough to attract my notice, even though his figure was foreshortened and shadowed, down in the deep trench, and mine was high above him, so steeped in the glow of an angry sunset, that I had shaded my eyes with my hand before I saw him at all.

"Halloa! Below!"

From looking down the Line, he turned himself about again, and, raising his eyes, saw my figure high above him.

"Is there any path by which I can come down and speak to you?"

He looked up at me without replying, and I looked down at him without pressing him too soon with a repetition of my idle question. Just then, there came a vague vibration in the earth and air, quickly changing into a violent pulsation, and an oncoming rush that caused me to start back, as though it had force to draw me down. When such vapour as rose to my height from this rapid train had passed me, and was skimming away over the landscape, I looked down again, and saw him refurling the flag he had shown while the train went by.

I repeated my inquiry. After a pause, during which he seemed to regard me with fixed attention, he motioned with his rolled-up flag towards a point on my level, some two or three hundred yards distant. I called down to him, "All right!" and made for that point. There, by dint of looking closely about me, I found a rough zigzag descending path notched out, which I followed.

The cutting was extremely deep, and unusually precipitate. It was made through a clammy stone that became oozier and wetter as I went down. For these reasons, I found the way long enough to give me time to recall a singular air of reluctance or compulsion with which he had pointed out the path.

When I came down low enough upon the zigzag descent to see him again, I saw that he was standing between the rails on the way by which the train had lately passed, in an attitude as if he were waiting for me to appear. He had his left hand at his chin, and that left elbow rested on his right hand, crossed over his breast. His attitude was one of such expectation and watchfulness that I stopped a moment, wondering at it.

I resumed my downward way, and stepping out upon the level of the railroad, and drawing nearer to him, saw that he was a dark sallow man, with a dark beard and rather heavy eyebrows. His post was in as solitary and dismal a place as ever I saw. On either side, a dripping-wet wall of jagged stone, excluding all view but a strip of sky; the perspective one way only a crooked prolongation of this great dungeon; the shorter perspective in the other direction terminating in a gloomy red light, and the gloomier entrance to a black tunnel, in whose massive architecture there was a barbarous, depressing, and forbidding air. So little sunlight ever found its way to this spot, that it had an earthy, deadly smell; and so much cold wind rushed through it, that it struck chill to me, as if I had left the natural world.

Before he stirred, I was near enough to him to have touched him. Not even then removing his eyes from mine, he stepped back one step, and lifted his hand.

This was a lonesome post to occupy (I said), and it had riveted my attention when I looked down from up yonder. A visitor was a rarity, I should suppose; not an unwelcome rarity, I hoped? In me, he merely saw a man who had been shut up within narrow limits all his life, and who, being at last set free, had a newly-awakened interest in these great works. To such purpose I spoke to him; but I am far from sure of the terms I used; for, besides that I am not happy in opening any conversation, there was something in the man that daunted me.

He directed a most curious look towards the red light near the tunnel's mouth, and looked all about it, as if something were missing from it, and then looked it me.

That light was part of his charge? Was it not?

He answered in a low voice: "Don't you know it is?"

The monstrous thought came into my mind, as I perused the fixed eyes and the saturnine face, that this was a spirit, not a man. I have speculated since, whether there may have been infection in his mind.

In my turn, I stepped back. But in making the action, I detected in his eyes some latent fear of me. This put the monstrous thought to flight.

"You look at me," I said, forcing a smile, "as if you had a dread of me."

"I was doubtful," he returned, "whether I had seen you before."

"Where?"

He pointed to the red light he had looked at.

"There?" I said.

Intently watchful of me, he replied (but without sound), "Yes."

"My good fellow, what should I do there? However, be that as it may, I never was there, you may swear."

"I think I may," he rejoined. "Yes; I am sure I may."

His manner cleared, like my own. He replied to my remarks with readiness, and in well-chosen words. Had he much to do there? Yes; that was to say, he had enough responsibility to bear; but exactness and watchfulness were what was required of him, and of actual work—manual labour—he had next to none. To change that signal, to trim those lights, and to turn this iron handle now and then, was all he had to do under that head. Regarding those many long and lonely hours of which I seemed to make so much, he could only say that the routine of his life had shaped itself into that form, and he had grown used to it. He had taught himself a language down here,—if only to know it by sight, and to have formed his own crude ideas of its pronunciation, could be called learning it. He had also worked at fractions and decimals, and tried a little algebra; but he was, and had been as a boy, a poor hand at figures. Was it necessary for him when on duty always to remain in that channel of damp air, and could he never rise into the sunshine from between those high stone walls? Why, that depended upon times and circumstances. Under some conditions there would be less upon the Line than under others, and the same held good as to certain hours of the day and night. In bright weather, he did choose occasions for getting a little above these lower shadows; but, being at all times liable to be called by his electric bell, and at such times listening for it with redoubled anxiety, the relief was less than I would suppose.

He took me into his box, where there was a fire, a desk for an official book in which he had to make certain entries, a telegraphic instrument with its dial, face, and needles, and the little bell of which he had spoken. On my trusting that he would excuse the remark that he had been well educated, and (I hoped I might say without offence) perhaps educated above that station, he observed that instances of slight incongruity in such wise would rarely be found wanting among large bodies of men; that he had heard it was so in workhouses, in the police force, even in that last desperate resource, the army;

and that he knew it was so, more or less, in any great railway staff. He had been, when young (if I could believe it, sitting in that hut;—he scarcely could), a student of natural philosophy, and had attended lectures; but he had run wild, misused his opportunities, gone down, and never risen again. He had no complaint to offer about that. He had made his bed, and he lay upon it. It was far too late to make another.

All that I have here condensed he said in a quiet manner, with his grave dark regards divided between me and the fire. He threw in the word "Sir," from time to time, and especially when he referred to his youth, as though to request me to understand that he claimed to be nothing but what I found him. He was several times interrupted by the little bell, and had to read off messages, and send replies. Once he had to stand without the door, and display a flag as a train passed, and make some verbal communication to the driver. In the discharge of his duties, I observed him to be remarkably exact and vigilant, breaking off his discourse at a syllable, and remaining silent until what he had to do was done.

In a word, I should have set this man down as one of the safest of men to be employed in that capacity, but for the circumstance that while he was speaking to me he twice broke off with a fallen colour, turned his face towards the little bell when it did NOT ring, opened the door of the hut (which was kept shut to exclude the unhealthy damp), and looked out towards the red light near the mouth of the tunnel. On both of those occasions, he came back to the fire with the inexplicable air upon him which I had remarked, without being able to define, when we were so far asunder.

Said I, when I rose to leave him, "You almost make me think that I have met with a contented man."

(I am afraid I must acknowledge that I said it to lead him on.)

"I believe I used to be so," he rejoined, in the low voice in which he had first spoken; "but I am troubled, sir, I am troubled."

He would have recalled the words if he could. He had said them, however, and I took them up quickly.

"With what? What is your trouble?"

"It is very difficult to impart, sir. It is very, very difficult to speak of. If ever you make me another visit, I will try to tell you."

"But I expressly intend to make you another visit. Say, when shall it be?"

"I go off early in the morning, and I shall be on again at ten tomorrow night, sir."

"I will come at eleven."

He thanked me, and went out at the door with me. "I'll show my white light, sir," he said, in his peculiar low voice, "till you have found the way up. When you have found it, don't call out! And when you are at the top, don't call out!"

His manner seemed to make the place strike colder to me, but I said no more than, "Very well."

"And when you come down to-morrow night, don't call out! Let me ask you a parting question. What made you cry, 'Halloa! Below there!' to-night?"

"Heaven knows," said I. "I cried something to that effect—"

"Not to that effect, sir. Those were the very words. I know them well."

"Admit those were the very words. I said them, no doubt, because I saw you below."

"For no other reason?"

"What other reason could I possibly have?"

"You had no feeling that they were conveyed to you in any supernatural way?"

"No."

He wished me good night, and held up his light. I walked by the side of the down Line of rails (with a very disagreeable sensation of a train coming behind me) until I found the path. It was easier to mount than to descend, and I got back to my inn without any adventure.

Punctual to my appointment, I placed my foot on the first notch of the zigzag next night, as the distant clocks were striking eleven. He was waiting for me at the bottom, with his white light on. "I have not called out," I said, when we came close together; "may I speak now?" "By all means, sir." "Good night, then, and here's my hand." "Good night, sir, and here's mine." With that we walked side by side to his box, entered it, closed the door, and sat down by the fire.

"I have made up my mind, sir," he began, bending forward as soon as we were seated, and speaking in a tone but a little above a whisper, "that you shall not have to ask me twice what troubles me. I took you for some one else yesterday evening. That troubles me."

"That mistake?"

"No. That some one else."

"Who is it?"

"I don't know."

"Like me?"

"I don't know. I never saw the face. The left arm is across the face, and the right arm is waved. Violently waved. This way."

I followed his action with my eyes, and it was the action of an arm gesticulating, with the utmost passion and vehemence, "For God's sake, clear the way!"

"One moonlight night," said the man, "I was sitting here, when I heard a voice cry, 'Halloa! Below there!' I started up, looked from that door, and saw this some one else standing by the red light near the tunnel, waving as I just now showed you. The voice seemed hoarse with shouting, and it cried, 'Look out! Look out!' And then again, 'Halloa! Below there! Look out!' I caught up my lamp, turned it on red, and ran towards the figure, calling, 'What's wrong? What has happened? Where?' It stood just outside the blackness of the tunnel. I advanced so close upon it that I wondered at its keeping the sleeve across its eyes. I ran right up at it, and had my hand stretched out to pull the sleeve away, when it was gone."

"Into the tunnel?" said I.

"No. I ran on into the tunnel, five hundred yards. I stopped, and held my lamp above my head, and saw the figures of the measured distance, and saw the wet stains stealing down the walls and trickling through the arch. I ran out again faster than I had run in (for I had a mortal abhorrence of the place upon me), and I looked all round the red light with my own red light, and I went up the iron ladder to the gallery atop of it, and I came down again, and ran back here. I telegraphed both ways, 'An alarm has been given. Is anything wrong?' The answer came back, both ways, 'All well.'"

Resisting the slow touch of a frozen finger tracing out my spine, I showed him how that this figure must be a deception of his sense of sight; and how that figures, originating in disease of the delicate nerves that minister to the functions of the eye, were known to have often troubled patients, some of whom had become conscious of the nature of their affliction, and had even proved it by experiments upon themselves. "As to an imaginary cry," said I, "do but listen for a moment to the wind in this unnatural valley while we speak so low, and to the wild harp it makes of the telegraph wires."

That was all very well, he returned, after we had sat listening for a while, and he ought to know something of the wind and the wires, he who so often passed long winter nights there, alone and watching. But he would beg to remark that he had not finished.

I asked his pardon, and he slowly added these words, touching my arm:—

"Within six hours after the Appearance, the memorable accident on this Line happened, and within ten hours the dead and wounded were brought along through the tunnel over the spot where the figure had stood."

A disagreeable shudder crept over me, but I did my best against it. It was not to be denied, I rejoined, that this was a remarkable coincidence, calculated deeply to impress his mind. But it was unquestionable that remarkable coincidences did continually occur, and they must be taken into account in dealing with such a subject. Though to be sure I must admit, I added (for I thought I saw that he was going to bring the objection to bear upon me), men of common sense did not allow much for coincidences in making the ordinary calculations of life.

He again begged to remark that he had not finished.

I again begged his pardon for being betrayed into interruptions.

"This," he said, again laying his hand upon my arm, and glancing over his shoulder with hollow eyes, "was just a year ago. Six or seven months passed, and I had recovered from the surprise and shock, when one morning, as the day was breaking, I, standing at the door, looked towards the red light, and saw the spectre again." He stopped, with a fixed look at me.

"Did it cry out?"

"No. It was silent."

"Did it wave its arm?"

"No. It leaned against the shaft of the light, with both hands before the face. Like this."

Once more I followed his action with my eyes. It was an action of mourning. I have seen such an attitude in stone figures on tombs.

"Did you go up to it?"

"I came in and sat down, partly to collect my thoughts, partly because it had turned me faint. When I went to the door again, daylight was above me, and the ghost was gone."

"But nothing followed? Nothing came of this?"

He touched me on the arm with his forefinger twice or thrice giving a ghastly nod each time:—

"That very day, as a train came out of the tunnel, I noticed, at a carriage window on my side, what looked like a confusion of hands and heads, and something waved. I saw it just in time to signal the driver, Stop! He shut off, and put his brake on, but the train drifted past here a hundred and fifty yards or more. I ran after it, and, as I went along, heard terrible screams and cries. A beautiful young lady had died instantaneously in one of the compartments, and was brought in here, and laid down on this floor between us."

Involuntarily I pushed my chair back, as I looked from the boards at which he pointed to himself.

"True, sir. True. Precisely as it happened, so I tell it you."

I could think of nothing to say, to any purpose, and my mouth was very dry. The wind and the wires took up the story with a long lamenting wail.

He resumed. "Now, sir, mark this, and judge how my mind is troubled. The spectre came back a week ago. Ever since, it has been there, now and again, by fits and starts."

"At the light?"

"At the Danger-light."

"What does it seem to do?"

He repeated, if possible with increased passion and vehemence, that former gesticulation of, "For God's sake, clear the way!"

Then he went on. "I have no peace or rest for it. It calls to me, for many minutes together, in an agonised manner, 'Below there! Look out! Look out!' It stands waving to me. It rings my little bell—"

I caught at that. "Did it ring your bell yesterday evening when I was here, and you went to the door?"

"Twice."

"Why, see," said I, "how your imagination misleads you. My eyes were on the bell, and my ears were open to the bell, and if I am a living man, it did NOT ring at those times. No, nor at any other time, except when it was rung in the natural course of physical things by the station communicating with you."

He shook his head. "I have never made a mistake as to that yet, sir. I have never confused the spectre's ring with the man's. The ghost's ring is a strange vibration in the bell that it derives from nothing else, and I have not asserted that the bell stirs to the eye. I don't wonder that you failed to hear it. But *I* heard it."

"And did the spectre seem to be there, when you looked out?"

"It WAS there."

"BOTH times?"

He repeated firmly: "Both times."

"Will you come to the door with me, and look for it now?"

He bit his under-lip as though he were somewhat unwilling, but arose. I opened the door, and stood on the step, while he stood in the doorway. There was the Danger-light. There was the dismal mouth of the tunnel. There were the high, wet stone walls of the cutting. There were the stars above them.

"Do you see it?" I asked him, taking particular note of his face. His eyes were prominent and strained, but not very much more so, perhaps, than my own had been when I had directed them earnestly towards the same spot.

"No," he answered. "It is not there."

"Agreed," said I.

We went in again, shut the door, and resumed our seats. I was thinking how best to improve this advantage, if it might be called one, when he took up the conversation in such a matter-of-course way, so assuming that there could be no serious question of fact between us, that I felt myself placed in the weakest of positions.

"By this time you will fully understand, sir," he said, "that what troubles me so dreadfully is the question, What does the spectre mean?"

I was not sure, I told him, that I did fully understand.

"What is its warning against?" he said, ruminating, with his eyes on the fire, and only by times turning them on me. "What is the danger? Where is the danger? There is danger overhanging somewhere on the Line. Some dreadful calamity will happen. It is not to be doubted this third time, after what has gone before. But surely this is a cruel haunting of *me*. What can *I* do?"

He pulled out his handkerchief, and wiped the drops from his heated forehead.

"If I telegraph Danger, on either side of me, or on both, I can give no reason for it," he went on, wiping the palms of his hands. "I should get into trouble, and do no good. They would think I was mad. This is the way it would work,—Message: 'Danger! Take care!' Answer: 'What Danger? Where?' Message: 'Don't know. But, for God's sake, take care!' They would displace me. What else could they do?"

His pain of mind was most pitiable to see. It was the mental torture of a conscientious man, oppressed beyond endurance by an unintelligible responsibility involving life.

"When it first stood under the Danger-light," he went on, putting his dark hair back from his head, and drawing his hands outward across and across his temples in an extremity of feverish distress, "why not tell me where that accident was to happen,—if it must happen? Why not tell me how it could be averted,—if it could have been averted? When on its second coming it hid its face, why not tell me, instead, 'She is going to die. Let them keep her at home'? If it came, on those two occasions, only to show me that its warnings were true, and so to prepare me for the third, why not warn me plainly now? And I, Lord help me! A mere poor signal-man on this solitary station! Why not go to somebody with credit to be believed, and power to act?"

When I saw him in this state, I saw that for the poor man's sake, as well as for the public safety, what I had to do for the time was to compose his mind. Therefore, setting aside all question of reality or unreality between us, I represented to him that whoever thoroughly discharged his duty must do well, and that at least it was his comfort that he understood his duty, though he did not understand these confounding Appearances. In this effort I succeeded far better than in the attempt to reason him out of his conviction. He became calm; the occupations incidental to his post as the night advanced began to make larger demands on his attention; and I left him at two in the morning. I had offered to stay through the night, but he would not hear of it.

That I more than once looked back at the red light as I ascended the pathway, that I did not like the red light, and that I should have slept but poorly if my bed had been under it, I see no reason to conceal. Nor did I like the two sequences of the accident and the dead girl. I see no reason to conceal that, either.

But what ran most in my thoughts was the consideration how ought I to act, having become the recipient of this disclosure? I had proved the man to be intelligent, vigilant, painstaking, and exact; but how long might he remain so, in his state of mind? Though in a subordinate position, still he held a most important trust, and would I (for instance) like to stake my own life on the chances of his continuing to execute it with precision?

Unable to overcome a feeling that there would be something treacherous in my communicating what he had told me to his superiors in the Company, without first being plain with himself and proposing a middle course to him, I ultimately resolved to offer to accompany him (otherwise keeping his secret for the present) to the wisest medical practitioner we could hear of in those parts, and to take his opinion. A change in his time of duty would come round next night, he had apprised me, and he would be off an hour or two after sunrise, and on again soon after sunset. I had appointed to return accordingly.

Next evening was a lovely evening, and I walked out early to enjoy it. The sun was not yet quite down when I traversed the field-path near the top of the deep cutting. I would extend my walk for an hour, I said to myself, half an hour on and half an hour back, and it would then be time to go to my signal-man's box.

Before pursuing my stroll, I stepped to the brink, and mechanically looked down, from the point from which I had first seen him. I cannot describe the thrill that seized upon me, when, close at the mouth of the tunnel, I saw the appearance of a man, with his left sleeve across his eyes, passionately waving his right arm.

The nameless horror that oppressed me passed in a moment, for in a moment I saw that this appearance of a man was a man indeed, and that there was a little group of other men, standing at a short distance, to whom he seemed to be rehearsing the gesture he made. The Danger-light was not yet lighted. Against its shaft, a little low hut, entirely new to me, had been made of some wooden supports and tarpaulin. It looked no bigger than a bed.

With an irresistible sense that something was wrong—with a flashing self-reproachful fear that fatal mischief had come of my leaving the man there, and causing no one to be sent to overlook or correct what he did—I descended the notched path with all the speed I could make.

"What is the matter?" I asked the men.

"Signal-man killed this morning, sir."

"Not the man belonging to that box?"

"Yes, sir."

"Not the man I know?"

"You will recognise him, sir, if you knew him," said the man who spoke for the others, solemnly uncovering his own head, and raising an end of the tarpaulin, "for his face is quite composed."

"O! how did this happen, how did this happen?" I asked, turning from one to another as the hut closed in again.

"He was cut down by an engine, sir. No man in England knew his work better. But somehow he was not clear of the outer rail. It was just at broad day. He had struck the light, and had the lamp in his hand. As the engine came out of the tunnel, his back was toward her, and she cut him down. That man drove her, and was showing how it happened. Show the gentleman, Tom."

The man, who wore a rough dark dress, stepped back to his former place at the mouth of the tunnel.

"Coming round the curve in the tunnel, sir," he said, "I saw him at the end, like as if I saw him down a perspective-glass. There was no time to check speed, and I knew him to be very careful. As he didn't seem to take heed of the whistle, I shut it off when we were running down upon him, and called to him as loud as I could call."

"What did you say?"

"I said, 'Below there! Look out! Look out! For God's sake, clear the way!'"

I started.

"Ah! it was a dreadful time, sir. I never left off calling to him. I put this arm before my eyes not to see, and I waved this arm to the last; but it was no use."

Without prolonging the narrative to dwell on any one of its curious circumstances more than on any other, I may, in closing it, point out the coincidence that the warning of the Engine-Driver included, not only the words which the unfortunate signal-man had repeated to me as haunting him, but also the words which I myself—not he—had attached, and that only in my own mind, to the gesticulation he had imitated.

Mad Monkton

WILKIE COLLINS

I

THE MONKTONS OF WINCOT ABBEY BORE A SAD CHARACTER FOR WANT OF SOCIAbility in our county. They never went to other people's houses, and, excepting my father, and a lady and her daughter living near them, never received anybody under their own roof.

Proud as they all certainly were, it was not pride, but dread, which kept them thus apart from their neighbors. The family had suffered for generations past from the horrible affliction of hereditary insanity, and the members of it shrank from exposing their calamity to others, as they must have exposed it if they had mingled with the busy little world around them. There is a frightful story of a crime committed in past times by two of the Monktons, near relatives, from which the first appearance of the insanity was always supposed to date, but it is needless for me to shock any one by repeating it. It is enough to say that at intervals almost every form of madness appeared in the family, monomania being the most frequent manifestation of the affliction among them. I have these particulars, and one or two yet to be related, from my father.

At the period of my youth but three of the Monktons were left at the Abbey—Mr. and Mrs. Monkton and their only child Alfred, heir to the property. The one other member of this, the elder branch of the family, who was then alive, was Mr. Monkton's younger brother, Stephen. He was an unmarried man, possessing a fine estate in Scotland; but he lived almost entirely on the Continent, and bore the reputation of being a shameless profligate. The family at Wincot held almost as little communication with him as with their neighbors.

I have already mentioned my father, and a lady and her daughter, as the only privileged people who were admitted into Wincot Abbey.

My father had been an old school and college friend of Mr. Monkton, and accident had brought them so much together in later life that their continued intimacy at Wincot was quite intelligible. I am not so well able to account for the friendly terms on which

Mrs. Elmslie (the lady to whom I have alluded) lived with the Monktons. Her late husband had been distantly related to Mrs. Monkton, and my father was her daughter's guardian. But even these claims to friendship and regard never seemed to me strong enough to explain the intimacy between Mrs. Elmslie and the inhabitants of the Abbey. Intimate, however, they certainly were, and one result of the constant interchange of visits between the two families in due time declared itself—Mr. Monkton's son and Mrs. Elmslie's daughter became attached to each other.

I had no opportunities of seeing much of the young lady; I only remember her at that time as a delicate, gentle, lovable girl, the very opposite in appearance, and apparently in character also, to Alfred Monkton. But perhaps that was one reason why they fell in love with each other. The attachment was soon discovered, and was far from being disapproved by the parents on either side. In all essential points except that of wealth, the Elmslies were nearly the equals of the Monktons, and want of money in a bride was of no consequence to the heir of Wincot. Alfred, it was well known, would succeed to thirty thousand a year on his father's death.

Thus, though the parents on both sides thought the young people not old enough to be married at once, they saw no reason why Ada and Alfred should not be engaged to each other, with the understanding that they should be united when young Monkton came of age, in two years' time. The person to be consulted in the matter, after the parents, was my father, in his capacity of Ada's guardian. He knew that the family misery had shown itself many years ago in Mrs. Monkton, who was her husband's cousin. The *illness*, as it was significantly called, had been palliated by careful treatment, and was reported to have passed away. But my father was not to be deceived. He knew where the hereditary taint still lurked; he viewed with horror the bare possibility of its reappearing one day in the children of his friend's only daughter; and he positively refused his consent to the marriage engagement.

The result was that the doors of the Abbey and the doors of Mrs. Elmslie's house were closed to him. This suspension of friendly intercourse had lasted but a very short time when Mrs. Monkton died. Her husband, who was fondly attached to her, caught a violent cold while attending her funeral. The cold was neglected, and settled on his lungs. In a few months' time he followed his wife to the grave, and Alfred was left master of the grand old Abbey and the fair lands that spread all around it.

At this period Mrs. Elmslie had the indelicacy to endeavor a second time to procure my father's consent to the marriage engagement. He refused it again more positively than before. More than a year passed away. The time was approaching fast when Alfred would be of age. I returned from college to spend the long vacation at home, and made some advances toward bettering my acquaintance with young Monkton. They were evaded—certainly with perfect politeness, but still in such a way as to prevent me from offering my friendship to him again. Any mortification I might have felt at this petty repulse under ordinary circumstances was dismissed from my mind by the occurrence of a real misfortune in our household. For some months past my father's health had been failing, and, just at the time of which I am now writing, his sons had to mourn the irreparable calamity of his death.

This event, through some informality or error in the late Mr. Elmslie's will, left the future of Ada's life entirely at her mother's disposal. The consequence was the immediate ratification of the marriage engagement to which my father had so steadily refused his consent. As soon as the fact was publicly announced, some of Mrs. Elmslie's more intimate friends, who were acquainted with the reports affecting the Monkton family, ventured to mingle with their formal congratulations one or two significant references to the late Mrs. Monkton and some searching inquiries as to the disposition of her son.

Mrs. Elmslie always met these polite hints with one bold form of answer. She first admitted the existence of these reports about the Monktons which her friends were unwilling to specify distinctly, and then declared that they were infamous calumnies. The hereditary taint had died out of the family generations back. Alfred was the best, the kindest, the sanest of human beings. He loved study and retirement; Ada sympathized with his tastes, and had made her choice unbiased; if any more hints were dropped about sacrificing her by her marriage, those hints would be viewed as so many insults to her mother, whose affection for her it was monstrous to call in question. This way of talking silenced people, but did not convince them. They began to suspect, what was indeed the actual truth, that Mrs. Elmslie was a selfish, worldly, grasping woman, who wanted to get her daughter well married, and cared nothing for consequences as long as she saw Ada mistress of the greatest establishment in the whole county.

It seemed, however, as if there was some fatality at work to prevent the attainment of Mrs. Elmslie's great object in life. Hardly was one obstacle to the ill-omened marriage removed by my father's death before another succeeded it in the shape of anxieties and difficulties caused by the delicate state of Ada's health. Doctors were consulted in all directions, and the result of their advice was that the marriage must be deferred, and that Miss Elmslie must leave England for a certain time, to reside in a warmer climate—the south of France, if I remember rightly. Thus it happened that just before Alfred came of age Ada and her mother departed for the Continent, and the union of the two young people was understood to be indefinitely postponed.

Some curiosity was felt in the neighborhood as to what Alfred Monkton would do under these circumstances. Would he follow his lady-love? would he go yachting? would he throw open the doors of the old Abbey at last, and endeavor to forget the absence of Ada and the postponement of his marriage in a round of gayeties? He did none of these things. He simply remained at Wincot, living as suspiciously strange and solitary a life as his father had lived before him. Literally, there was now no companion for him at the Abbey but the old priest (the Monktons, I should have mentioned before, were Roman Catholics) who had held the office of tutor to Alfred from his earliest years. He came of age, and there was not even so much as a private dinner-party at Wincot to celebrate the event. Families in the neighborhood determined to forget the offense which his father's reserve had given them, and invited him to their houses. The invitations were politely declined. Civil visitors called resolutely at the Abbey, and were as resolutely bowed away from the doors as soon as they had left their cards. Under this combination of sinister and aggravating circumstances people in all directions took to shaking their heads mysteriously when the name of Mr. Alfred Monkton was mentioned, hinting at the family calamity, and wondering peevishly or sadly, as their tempers inclined them, what he could possibly do to occupy himself month after month in the lonely old house.

The right answer to this question was not easy to find. It was quite useless, for example, to apply to the priest for it. He was a very quiet, polite old gentleman; his replies were always excessively ready and civil, and appeared at the time to convey a reasonable amount of information; but when they were tested by after-reflection, it was universally observed that nothing tangible could be extracted from them. The housekeeper, a weird old woman, with a very abrupt and repelling manner, was too fierce and taciturn to be safely approached. The few indoor servants had all been long enough in the family to have learned to hold their tongues in public as a regular habit. It was only from the farm-servants who supplied the table at the Abbey that any information could be obtained, and vague enough it was when they came to communicate it.

Some of them had observed the "young master" walking about the library with heaps of dusty papers in his hands. Others had heard odd noises in the uninhabited parts of the Abbey, had looked up, and had seen him forcing open the old windows, as if to let light and air into the rooms supposed to have been shut close for years and years; or had discovered him standing on the perilous summit of one of the crumbling turrets, never ascended before within their memories, and popularly considered to be inhabited by the ghosts of the monks who had once possessed the building. The result of these observations and discoveries, when they were communicated to others, was of course to impress every one with a firm belief that "poor young Monkton was going the way that the rest of the family had gone before him," which opinion always appeared to be immensely strengthened in the popular mind by a conviction—founded on no particle of evidence—that the priest was at the bottom of all the mischief.

Thus far I have spoken from hearsay evidence mostly. What I have next to tell will be the result of my own personal experience.

II

About five months after Alfred Monkton came of age I left college, and resolved to amuse and instruct myself a little by traveling abroad.

At the time when I quitted England young Monkton was still leading his secluded life at the Abbey, and was, in the opinion of everybody, sinking rapidly, if he had not already succumbed, under the hereditary curse of his family. As to the Elmslies, report said that Ada had benefited by her sojourn abroad, and that mother and daughter were on their way back to England to resume their old relations with the heir of Wincot. Before they returned I was away on my travels, and wandered half over Europe, hardly ever planning whither I should shape my course beforehand. Chance, which thus led me everywhere, led me at last to Naples. There I met with an old school friend, who was one of the *attachés* at the English embassy, and there began the extraordinary events in connection with Alfred Monkton which form the main interest of the story I am now relating.

I was idling away the time one morning with my friend the *attaché*, in the garden of the Villa Reale, when we were passed by a young man, walking alone, who exchanged bows with my friend.

I thought I recognized the dark, eager eyes, the colorless cheeks, the strangely-vigilant, anxious expression which I remembered in past times as characteristic of Alfred Monkton's face, and was about to question my friend on the subject, when he gave me unasked the information of which I was in search.

"That is Alfred Monkton," said he; "he comes from your part of England. You ought to know him."

"I do know a little of him," I answered; "he was engaged to Miss Elmslie when I was last in the neighborhood of Wincot. Is he married to her yet?"

"No; and he never ought to be. He has gone the way of the rest of the family; or, in plainer words, he has gone mad."

"Mad! But I ought not to be surprised at hearing that, after the reports about him in England."

"I speak from no reports; I speak from what he has said and done before me, and before hundreds of other people. Surely you must have heard of it?"

"Never. I have been out of the way of news from Naples or England for months past."

"Then I have a very extraordinary story to tell you. You know, of course, that Alfred had an uncle, Stephen Monkton. Well, some time ago this uncle fought a duel in the Roman States with a Frenchman, who shot him dead. The seconds and the Frenchman (who was unhurt) took to flight in different directions, as it is supposed. We heard nothing here of the details of the duel till a month after it happened, when one of the French journals published an account of it, taken from the papers left by Monkton's second, who died at Paris of consumption. These papers stated the manner in which the duel was fought, and how it terminated, but nothing more. The surviving second and the Frenchman have never been traced from that time to this. All that anybody knows, therefore, of the duel is that Stephen Monkton was shot; an event which nobody can regret, for a greater scoundrel never existed. The exact place where he died, and what was done with the body are still mysteries not to be penetrated."

"But what has all this to do with Alfred?"

"Wait a moment, and you will hear. Soon after the news of his uncle's death reached England, what do you think Alfred did? He actually put off his marriage with Miss Elmslie, which was then about to be celebrated, to come out here in search of the burial-place of his wretched scamp of an uncle; and no power on earth will now induce him to return to England and to Miss Elmslie until he has found the body, and can take it back with him, to be buried with all the other dead Monktons in the vault under Wincot Abbey Chapel. He has squandered his money, pestered the police, and exposed himself to the ridicule of the men and the indignation of the women for the last three months in trying to achieve his insane purpose, and is now as far from it as ever. He will not assign to anybody the smallest motive for his conduct. You can't laugh him out of it or reason him out of it. When we met him just now, I happen to know that he was on his way to the office of the police minister, to send out fresh agents to search and inquire through the Roman States for the place where his uncle was shot. And, mind, all this time he professes to be passionately in love with Miss Elmslie, and to be miserable at his separation from her. Just think of that! And then think of his self-imposed absence from her here, to hunt after the remains of a wretch who was a disgrace to the family, and whom he never saw but once or twice in his life. Of all the 'Mad Monktons,' as they used to call them in England, Alfred is the maddest. He is actually our principal excitement in this dull opera season; though, for my own part, when I think of the poor girl in England, I am a great deal more ready to despise him than to laugh at him."

"You know the Elmslies then?"

"Intimately. The other day my mother wrote to me from England, after having seen Ada. This escapade of Monkton's has outraged all her friends. They have been entreating her to break off the match, which it seems she could do if she liked. Even her mother, sordid and selfish as she is, has been obliged at last, in common decency, to side with the rest of the family; but the good, faithful girl won't give Monkton up. She humors his insanity; declares he gave her a good reason in secret for going away; says she could always make him happy when they were together in the old Abbey, and can make him still happier when they are married; in short, she loves him dearly, and will therefore believe in him to the last. Nothing shakes her. She has made up her mind to throw away her life on him, and she will do it."

"I hope not. Mad as his conduct looks to us, he may have some sensible reason for it that we cannot imagine. Does his mind seem at all disordered when he talks on ordinary topics?"

"Not in the least. When you can get him to say anything, which is not often, he talks like a sensible, well-educated man. Keep silence about his precious errand here, and you would fancy him the gentlest and most temperate of human beings; but touch the subject of his vagabond of an uncle, and the Monkton madness comes out directly. The other night a lady asked him, jestingly of course, whether he had ever seen his uncle's ghost. He scowled at her like a perfect fiend, and said that he and his uncle would answer her question together some day, if they came from hell to do it. We laughed at his words, but the lady fainted at his looks, and we had a scene of hysterics and hartshorn in consequence. Any other man would have been kicked out of the room for nearly frightening a pretty woman to death in that way; but 'Mad Monkton,' as we have christened him, is a privileged lunatic in Neapolitan society, because he is English, good-looking, and worth thirty thousand a year. He goes out everywhere under the impression that he may meet with somebody who has been let into the secret of the place where the mysterious duel was fought. If you are introduced to him he is sure to ask you whether you know anything about it; but beware of following up the subject after you have answered him, unless you want to make sure that he is out of his senses. In that case, only talk of his uncle, and the result will rather more than satisfy you."

A day or two after this conversation with my friend the *attaché*, I met Monkton at an evening party.

The moment he heard my name mentioned, his face flushed up; he drew me away into a corner, and referring to his cool reception of my advance years ago toward making his acquaintance, asked my pardon for what he termed his inexcusable ingratitude with an earnestness and an agitation which utterly astonished me. His next proceeding was to question me, as my friend had said he would, about the place of the mysterious duel.

An extraordinary change came over him while he interrogated me on this point. Instead of looking into my face as they had looked hitherto, his eyes wandered away, and fixed themselves intensely, almost fiercely, either on the perfectly empty wall at our side, or on the vacant space between the wall and ourselves, it was impossible to say which. I had come to Naples from Spain by sea, and briefly told him so, as the best way of satisfying him that I could not assist his inquiries. He pursued them no further; and, mindful of my friend's warning, I took care to lead the conversation to general topics. He looked back at me directly, and, as long as we stood in our corner, his eyes never wandered away again to the empty wall or the vacant space at our side.

Though more ready to listen than to speak, his conversation, when he did talk, had no trace of anything the least like insanity about it. He had evidently read, not generally only, but deeply as well, and could apply his reading with singular felicity to the illustration of almost any subject under discussion, neither obtruding his knowledge absurdly, nor concealing it affectedly. His manner was in itself a standing protest against such a nickname as "Mad Monkton." He was so shy, so quiet, so composed and gentle in all his actions, that at times I should have been almost inclined to call him effeminate. We had a long talk together on the first evening of our meeting; we often saw each other afterward, and never lost a single opportunity of bettering our acquaintance. I felt that he had taken a liking to me, and, in spite of what I had heard about his behavior to Miss Elmslie, in spite of the suspicions which the history of his family and his own conduct had arrayed against him, I began to like "Mad Monkton" as much as he liked me. We took many a quiet ride together in the country, and sailed often along the shores of the Bay on either side. But for two eccentricities in his conduct, which I could not at all understand, I should soon have felt as much at my ease in his society as if he had been my own brother.

The first of these eccentricities consisted in the reappearance on several occasions of the odd expression in his eyes which I had first seen when he asked me whether I knew anything about the duel. No matter what we were talking about, or where we happened to be, there were times when he would suddenly look away from my face, now on one side of me, now on the other, but always where there was nothing to see, and always with the same intensity and fierceness in his eyes. This looked so like madness—or hypochondria, at the least—that I felt afraid to ask him about it, and always pretended not to observe him.

The second peculiarity in his conduct was that he never referred, while in my company, to the reports about his errand at Naples, and never once spoke of Miss Elmslie, or of his life at Wincot Abbey. This not only astonished me, but amazed those who had noticed our intimacy, and who had made sure that I must be the depositary of all his secrets. But the time was near at hand when this mystery, and some other mysteries of which I had no suspicion at that period, were all to be revealed.

I met him one night at a large ball, given by a Russian nobleman, whose name I could not pronounce then, and cannot remember now. I had wandered away from reception-room, ballroom, and card-room, to a small apartment at one extremity of the palace, which was half conservatory, half boudoir, and which had been prettily illuminated for the occasion with Chinese lanterns. Nobody was in the room when I got there. The view over the Mediterranean, bathed in the bright softness of Italian moonlight, was so lovely that I remained for a long time at the window, looking out, and listening to the dance music which faintly reached me from the ballroom. My thoughts were far away with the relations I had left in England, when I was startled out of them by hearing my name softly pronounced.

I looked round directly, and saw Monkton standing in the room. A livid paleness overspread his face, and his eyes were turned away from me with the same extraordinary expression in them to which I have already alluded.

"Do you mind leaving the ball early to-night?" he asked, still not looking at me.

"Not at all," said I. "Can I do anything for you? Are you ill?"

"No, at least nothing to speak of. Will you come to my rooms?"

"At once, if you like."

"No, not at once. *I* must go home directly; but don't you come to me for half an hour yet. You have not been at my rooms before, I know, but you will easily find them out; they are close by. There is a card with my address. I *must* speak to you to-night; my life depends on it. Pray come! for God's sake, come when the half hour is up!"

I promised to be punctual, and he left me directly.

Most people will be easily able to imagine the state of nervous impatience and vague expectation in which I passed the allotted period of delay, after hearing such words as those Monkton had spoken to me. Before the half hour had quite expired I began to make my way out through the ballroom.

At the head of the staircase my friend, the *attaché*, met me.

"What! going away already?" Said he.

"Yes; and on a very curious expedition. I am going to Monkton's rooms, by his own invitation."

"You don't mean it! Upon my honor, you're a bold fellow to trust yourself alone with 'Mad Monkton' when the moon is at the full."

"He is ill, poor fellow. Besides, I don't think him half as mad as you do."

"We won't dispute about that; but mark my words, he has not asked you to go where no visitor has ever been admitted before without a special purpose. I predict that you will see or hear something to-night which you will remember for the rest of your life."

We parted. When I knocked at the courtyard gate of the house where Monkton lived, my friend's last words on the palace staircase recurred to me, and, though I had laughed at him when he spoke them, I began to suspect even then that his prediction would be fulfilled.

III

The porter who let me into the house where Monkton lived directed me to the floor on which his rooms were situated. On getting upstairs, I found his door on the landing ajar. He heard my footsteps, I suppose, for he called to me to come in before I could knock.

I entered, and found him sitting by the table, with some loose letters in his hand, which he was just tying together into a packet. I noticed, as he asked me to sit down, that his expression looked more composed, though the paleness had not yet left his face. He thanked me for coming; repeated that he had something very important to say to me; and then stopped short, apparently too much embarrassed to proceed. I tried to set him at his ease by assuring him that, if my assistance or advice could be of any use, I was ready to place myself and my time heartily and unreservedly at his service.

As I said this I saw his eyes beginning to wander away from my face—to wander slowly, inch by inch, as it were, until they stopped at a certain point, with the same fixed stare into vacancy which had so often startled me on former occasions. The whole expression of his face altered as I had never yet seen it alter; he sat before me looking like a man in a death-trance.

"You are very kind," he said, slowly and faintly, speaking, not to me, but in the direction in which his eyes were still fixed. "I know you can help me; but—"

He stopped; his face whitened horribly, and the perspiration broke out all over it. He tried to continue—said a word or two—then stopped again. Seriously alarmed about him, I rose from my chair with the intention of getting him some water from a jug which I saw standing on a side table.

He sprang up at the same moment. All the suspicions I had ever heard whispered against his sanity flashed over my mind in an instant, and I involuntarily stepped back a pace or two.

"Stop," he said, seating himself again; "don't mind me; and don't leave your chair. I want—I wish, if you please, to make a little alteration, before we say anything more. Do you mind sitting in a strong light?"

"Not in the least."

I had hitherto been seated in the shade of his reading-lamp, the only light in the room.

As I answered him he rose again, and, going into another apartment, returned with a large lamp in his hand; then took two candles from the side-table, and two others from the chimney-piece; placed them all, to my amazement, together, so as to stand exactly between us, and then tried to light them. His hand trembled so that he was obliged to give up the attempt, and allow me to come to his assistance. By his direction, I took the shade off the reading lamp after I had lit the other lamp and the four candles. When we sat down again, with this concentration of light between us, his better and gentler manner began to return, and while he now addressed me, he spoke without the slightest hesitation.

"It is useless to ask whether you have heard the reports about me," he said; "I know that you have. My purpose to-night is to give you some reasonable explanation of the conduct which has produced those reports. My secret has been hitherto confided to one person only; I am now about to trust it to your keeping, with a special object which will appear as I go on. First, however, I must begin by telling you exactly what the great difficulty is which obliges me to be still absent from England. I want your advice and your help; and, to conceal nothing from you, I want also to test your forbearance and your friendly sympathy, before I can venture on thrusting my miserable secret into your keeping. Will you pardon this apparent distrust of your frank and open character—this apparent ingratitude for your kindness toward me ever since we first met?"

I begged him not to speak of these things, but to go on.

"You know," he proceeded, "that I am here to recover the body of my Uncle Stephen, and to carry it back with me to our family burial-place in England; and you must also be aware that I have not yet succeeded in discovering his remains. Try to pass over, for the present, whatever may seem extraordinary and incomprehensible in such a purpose as mine is; and read this newspaper article where the ink-line is traced. It is the only evidence hitherto obtained on the subject of the fatal duel in which my uncle fell; and I want to hear what course of proceeding the perusal of it may suggest to you as likely to be best on my part."

He handed me an old French newspaper. The substance of what I read there is still so firmly impressed on my memory that I am certain of being able to repeat correctly at this distance of time all the facts which it is necessary for me to communicate to the reader.

The article began, I remember, with editorial remarks on the great curiosity then felt in regard to the fatal duel between the Count St. Lo and Mr. Stephen Monkton, an English gentleman. The writer proceeded to dwell at great length on the extraordinary secrecy in which the whole affair had been involved from first to last; and to express a hope that the publication of a certain manuscript, to which his introductory observations referred, might lead to the production of fresh evidence from other and better-informed quarters. The manuscript had been found among the papers of Monsieur Foulon, Mr. Monkton's second, who had died at Paris of a rapid decline shortly after returning to his home in that city from the scene of the duel. The document was unfinished, having been left incomplete at the very place where the reader would most wish to find it continued. No reason could be discovered for this, and no second manuscript bearing on the all-important subject had been found, after the strictest search among the papers left by the deceased.

The document itself then followed.

It purported to be an agreement privately drawn up between Mr. Monkton's second, Monsieur Foulon, and the Count St. Lo's second, Monsieur Dalville, and contained a statement of all the arrangements for conducting the duel. The paper was dated "Naples, February 22d," and was divided into some seven or eight clauses. The first clause described the origin and nature of the quarrel—a very disgraceful affair on both sides, worth neither remembering nor repeating. The second clause stated that, the challenged man having chosen the pistol as his weapon, and the challenger (an excellent swordsman), having, on his side, thereupon insisted that the duel should be fought in such a manner as to make the first fire decisive in its results, the seconds, seeing that fatal consequences must inevitably follow the hostile meeting, determined, first of all, that the duel should be kept a profound secret from everybody, and that the place where it was to be fought should not be made known beforehand, even to the principals themselves. It was added that this excess of precaution had been rendered absolutely necessary in consequence of a recent address from the Pope to the ruling powers in Italy commenting on the scandalous frequency of the practice of dueling, and urgently desiring that the laws against duelists should be enforced for the future with the utmost rigor.

The third clause detailed the manner in which it had been arranged that the duel should be fought.

The pistols having been loaded by the seconds on the ground, the combatants were to be placed thirty paces apart, and were to toss up for the first fire. The man who won was to advance ten paces marked out for him beforehand—and was then to discharge his pistol. If he missed, or failed to disable his opponent, the latter was free to advance, if he chose, the whole remaining twenty paces before he fired in his turn. This arrangement insured the decisive termination of the duel at the first discharge of the pistols, and both principals and seconds pledged themselves on either side to abide by it.

The fourth clause stated that the seconds had agreed that the duel should be fought *out* of the Neapolitan States, but left themselves to be guided by circumstances as to the exact locality in which it should take place. The remaining clauses, so far as I remember them, were devoted to detailing the different precautions to be adopted for avoiding discovery. The duelists and their seconds were to leave Naples in separate parties; were to change carriages several times; were to meet at a certain town, or, failing that, at a certain post-house on the high road from Naples to Rome; were to carry drawing-books, color boxes, and camp-stools, as if they had been artists out on a sketching-tour; and were to proceed to the place of the duel on foot, employing no guides, for fear of treachery. Such general arrangements as these, and others for facilitating the flight of the survivors after the affair was over, formed the conclusion of this extraordinary document, which was signed, in initials only, by both the seconds.

Just below the initials appeared the beginning of a narrative, dated "Paris," and evidently intended to describe the duel itself with extreme minuteness. The handwriting was that of the deceased second.

Monsieur Foulon, the gentleman in question, stated his belief that circumstances might transpire which would render an account by an eyewitness of the hostile meeting between St. Lo and Mr. Monkton an important document. He proposed, therefore, as one of the seconds, to testify that the duel had been fought in exact accordance with the terms of the agreement, both the principals conducting themselves like men of gallantry and honor (!). And he further announced that, in order not to compromise any one, he should place the paper containing his testimony in safe hands, with strict directions that it was on no account to be opened except in a case of the last emergency.

After this preamble, Monsieur Foulon related that the duel had been fought two days after the drawing up of the agreement, in a locality to which accident had conducted the dueling party. (The name of the place was not mentioned, nor even the neighborhood in which it was situated.) The men having been placed according to previous arrangement, the Count St. Lo had won the toss for the first fire, had advanced his ten paces, and had shot his opponent in the body. Mr. Monkton did not immediately fall, but staggered forward some six or seven paces, discharged his pistol ineffectually at the count, and dropped to the ground a dead man. Monsieur Foulon then stated that he tore a leaf from his pocketbook, wrote on it a brief description of the manner in which Mr. Monkton had died, and pinned the paper to his clothes; this proceeding having been rendered necessary by the peculiar nature of the plan organized on the spot for safely disposing of the dead body. What this plan was, or what was done with the corpse, did not appear, for at this important point the narrative abruptly broke off.

A foot-note in the newspaper merely stated the manner in which the document had been obtained for publication, and repeated the announcement contained in the editor's introductory remarks, that no continuation had been found by the persons intrusted with the care of Monsieur Foulon's papers. I have now given the whole substance of what I read, and have mentioned all that was then known of Mr. Stephen Monkton's death.

When I gave the newspaper back to Alfred he was too much agitated to speak, but he reminded me by a sign that he was anxiously waiting to hear what I had to say. My position was a very trying and a very painful one. I could hardly tell what consequences might not follow any want of caution on my part, and could think at first of no safer plan than questioning him carefully before I committed myself either one way or the other.

"Will you excuse me if I ask you a question or two before I give you my advice?" said I.

He nodded impatiently.

"Yes, yes—any questions you like."

"Were you at any time in the habit of seeing your uncle frequently?"

"I never saw him more than twice in my life—on each occasion when I was a mere child."

"Then you could have had no very strong personal regard for him?"

"Regard for him! I should have been ashamed to feel any regard for him. He disgraced us wherever he went."

"May I ask if any family motive is involved in your anxiety to recover his remains?"

"Family motives may enter into it among others—but why do you ask?"

"Because, having heard that you employ the police to assist your search, I was anxious to know whether you had stimulated their superiors to make them do their best in your service by giving some strong personal reasons at head-quarters for the very unusual project which has brought you here."

"I give no reasons. I pay for the work I want done, and, in return for my liberality, I am treated with the most infamous indifference on all sides. A stranger in the country, and badly acquainted with the language, I can do nothing to help myself. The authorities, both at Rome and in this place, pretend to assist me, pretend to search and inquire as I would have them search and inquire, and do nothing more. I am insulted, laughed at, almost to my face."

"Do you not think it possible—mind, I have no wish to excuse the misconduct of the authorities, and do not share in any such opinion myself—but do you not think it likely that the police may doubt whether you are in earnest?"

"Not in earnest!" he cried, starting up and confronting me fiercely, with wild eyes and quickened breath. "Not in earnest! *You* think I'm not in earnest, too. I know you think it, though you tell me you don't. Stop; before we say another word, your own eyes shall convince you. Come here—only for a minute—only for one minute!"

I followed him into his bed-room, which opened out of the sitting-room. At one side of his bed stood a large packing-case of plain wood, upward of seven feet in length.

"Open the lid, and look in," he said, "while I hold the candle so that you can see."

I obeyed his directions, and discovered to my astonishment that the packing-case contained a leaden coffin, magnificently emblazoned with the arms of the Monkton family, and inscribed in old-fashioned letters with the name of "Stephen Monkton," his age and the manner of his death being added underneath.

"I keep his coffin ready for him," whispered Alfred, close at my ear. "Does that look like earnest?"

It looked more like insanity—so like that I shrank from answering him.

"Yes! yes! I see you are convinced," he continued quickly; "we may go back into the next room, and may talk without restraint on either side now."

On returning to our places, I mechanically moved my chair away from the table. My mind was by this time in such a state of confusion and uncertainty about what it would be best for me to say or do next, that I forgot for the moment the position he had assigned to me when we lit the candles. He reminded me of this directly.

"Don't move away," he said, very earnestly; "keep on sitting in the light; pray do! I'll soon tell you why I am so particular about that. But first give me your advice; help me in my great distress and suspense. Remember, you promised me you would."

I made an effort to collect my thoughts, and succeeded. It was useless to treat the affair otherwise than seriously in his presence; it would have been cruel not to have advised him as I best could.

"You know," I said, "that two days after the drawing up of the agreement at Naples, the duel was fought out of the Neapolitan States. This fact has of course led you to the conclusion that all inquiries about localities had better be confined to the Roman territory?"

"Certainly; the search, such as it is, has been made there, and there only. If I can believe the police, they and their agents have inquired for the place where the duel was fought (offering a large reward in my name to the person who can discover it) all along the high road from Naples to Rome. They have also circulated—at least, so they tell me—descriptions of the duelists and their seconds; have left an agent to superintend investigations at the post-house, and another at the town mentioned as meeting-points in the agreement; and have endeavored, by correspondence with foreign authorities, to trace the Count St. Lo and Monsieur Dalville to their place or places of refuge. All these efforts, supposing them to have been really made, have hitherto proved utterly fruitless."

"My impression is," said I, after a moment's consideration, "that all inquiries made along the high road, or anywhere near Rome, are likely to be made in vain. As to the discovery of your uncle's remains, that is, I think, identical with the discovery of the place where he was shot; for those engaged in the duel would certainly not risk detection by carrying a corpse any distance with them in their flight. The place, then, is all that we want to find out. Now let us consider for a moment. The dueling-party changed carriages; traveled separately, two and two; doubtless took roundabout roads; stopped at the post-house and the town as a blind; walked, perhaps, a considerable distance unguided. Depend upon it, such precautions as these (which we know they must have employed) left them very little time out of the two days—though they might start at sunrise and not stop at nightfall—for straightforward traveling. My belief therefore is, that the duel was fought somewhere near the Neapolitan frontier; and, if I had been the police agent who conducted the search, I should only have pursued it parallel with the frontier, starting from west to east till I got up among the lonely places in the mountains. That is my idea; do you think it worth anything?"

His face flushed all over in an instant. "I think it an inspiration!" he cried. "Not a day is to be lost in carrying out our plan. The police are not to be trusted with it. I must start myself to-morrow morning; and you—"

He stopped; his face grew suddenly pale; he sighed heavily; his eyes wandered once more into the fixed look at vacancy; and the rigid, deathly expression fastened again upon all his features.

"I must tell you my secret before I talk of to-morrow," he proceeded, faintly. "If I hesitated any longer at confessing everything, I should be unworthy of your past kindness, unworthy of the help which it is my last hope that you will gladly give me when you have heard all."

I begged him to wait until he was more composed, until he was better able to speak; but he did not appear to notice what I said. Slowly, and struggling as it seemed against himself, he turned a little away from me, and, bending his head over the table, supported it on his hand. The packet of letters with which I had seen him occupied when I came in lay just beneath his eyes. He looked down on it steadfastly when he next spoke to me.

IV

"You were born, I believe, in our county," he said; "perhaps, therefore, you may have heard at some time of a curious old prophecy about our family, which is still preserved among the traditions of Wincot Abbey?"

"I have heard of such a prophecy," I answered, "but I never knew in what terms it was expressed. It professed to predict the extinction of your family, or something of that sort, did it not?"

"No inquiries," he went on, "have traced back that prophecy to the time when it was first made; none of our family records tell us anything of its origin. Old servants and old tenants of ours remember to have heard it from their fathers and grandfathers. The monks, whom we succeeded in the Abbey in Henry the Eighth's time, got knowledge of it in some way, for I myself discovered the rhymes, in which we know the prophecy to have been preserved from a very remote period, written on a blank leaf of one of the Abbey manuscripts. These are the verses, if verses they deserve to be called:

> "When in Wincot vault a place
> Waits for one of Monkton's race;
> When that one forlorn shall lie
> Graveless under open sky,
> Beggared of six feet of earth,
> Though lord of acres from his birth—
> That shall be a certain sign
> Of the end of Monkton's line.
> Dwindling ever faster, faster,
> Dwindling to the last-left master;
> From mortal ken, from light of day,
> Monkton's race shall pass away.

"The prediction seems almost vague enough to have been uttered by an ancient oracle," said I, observing that he waited, after repeating the verses, as if expecting me to say something.

"Vague or not, it is being accomplished," he returned. "I am now the 'last-left master'—the last of that elder line of our family at which the prediction points; and the corpse of Stephen Monkton is not in the vaults of Wincot Abbey. Wait before you exclaim against me. I have more to say about this. Long before the Abbey was ours, when we lived in the ancient manor-house near it (the very ruins of which have long since disappeared), the family burying-place was in the vault under the Abbey chapel. Whether in those remote times the prediction against us was known and dreaded or not, this much is certain: every one of the Monktons (whether living at the Abbey or on the smaller estate in Scotland) was buried in Wincot vault, no matter at what risk or what sacrifice. In the fierce fighting days of the olden time, the bodies of my ancestors who fell in foreign places were recovered and brought back to Wincot, though it often cost not heavy ransom only, but desperate bloodshed as well, to obtain them. This superstition, if you please to call it so, has never died out of the family from that time to the present day; for centuries the succession of the dead in the vault at the Abbey has been unbroken—absolutely unbroken—until now. The place mentioned in the prediction as waiting to be filled is Stephen Monkton's place, the voice that cries vainly to the earth for shelter is the spirit-voice of the dead. As surely as if I saw it, I know that they have left him unburied on the ground where he fell!"

He stopped me before I could utter a word in remonstrance by slowly rising to his feet, and pointing in the same direction toward which his eyes had wandered a short time since.

"I can guess what you want to ask me," he exclaimed, sternly and loudly; "you want to ask me how I can be mad enough to believe in a doggerel prophecy uttered in an age of superstition to awe the most ignorant hearers. I answer" (at those words his voice sank suddenly to a whisper), "I answer, because *Stephen Monkton himself stands there at this moment confirming me in my belief.*"

Whether it was the awe and horror that looked out ghastly from his face as he confronted me, whether it was that I had never hitherto fairly believed in the reports about his madness, and that the conviction of their truth now forced itself upon me on a sudden, I know not, but I felt my blood curdling as he spoke, and I knew in my own heart, as I sat there speechless, that I dare not turn round and look where he was still pointing close at my side.

"I see there," he went on, in the same whispering voice, "the figure of a dark-complexioned man standing up with his head uncovered. One of his hands, still clutching a pistol, has fallen to his side; the other presses a bloody handkerchief over his mouth. The spasm of mortal agony convulses his features; but I know them for the features of a swarthy man who twice frightened me by taking me up in his arms when I was a child at Wincot Abbey. I asked the nurses at the time who that man was, and they told me it was my uncle, Stephen Monkton. Plainly, as if he stood there living, I see him now at your side, with the death-glare in his great black eyes; and so have I ever seen him, since the moment when he was shot; at home and abroad, waking or sleeping, day and night, we are always together wherever I go!"

His whispering tones sank into almost inaudible murmuring as he pronounced these last words. From the direction and expression of his eyes, I suspected that he was speaking to the apparition. If I had beheld it myself at that moment, it would have been, I think, a less horrible sight to witness than to see him, as I saw him now, muttering inarticulately at vacancy. My own nerves were more shaken than I could have thought possible by what had passed. A vague dread of being near him in his present mood came over me, and I moved back a step or two.

He noticed the action instantly.

"Don't go! pray—pray don't go! Have I alarmed you? Don't you believe me? Do the lights make your eyes ache? I only asked you to sit in the glare of the candles because I could not bear to see the light that always shines from the phantom there at dusk shining over you as you sat in the shadow. Don't go—don't leave me yet!"

There was an utter forlornness, an unspeakable misery in his face as he spoke these words, which gave me back my self-possession by the simple process of first moving me to pity. I resumed my chair, and said that I would stay with him as long as he wished.

"Thank you a thousand times! You are patience and kindness itself," he said, going back to his former place and resuming his former gentleness of manner. "Now that I have got over my first confession of the misery that follows me in secret wherever I go, I think I can tell you calmly all that remains to be told. You see, as I said, my Uncle Stephen,"—he turned away his head quickly, and looked down at the table as the name passed his lips—"my Uncle Stephen came twice to Wincot while I was a child, and on both occasions frightened me dreadfully. He only took me up in his arms and spoke to me—very kindly, as I afterward heard, for *him*—but he terrified me, nevertheless. Perhaps I was frightened at his great stature, his swarthy complexion, and his thick black hair and mustache, as other children might have been; perhaps the mere sight of him had some strange influence on me which I could not then understand and cannot now explain. However it was, I used to dream of him long after he had gone away, and to fancy that he was stealing on me to catch me up in his arms whenever I was left in the dark. The servants who took care of me found this out, and used to threaten me with my Uncle Stephen whenever I was perverse and difficult to manage. As I grew up,

I still retained my vague dread and abhorrence of our absent relative. I always listened intently, yet without knowing why, whenever his name was mentioned by my father or my mother—listened with an unaccountable presentiment that something terrible had happened to him, or was about to happen to me. This feeling only changed when I was left alone in the Abbey; and then it seemed to merge into the eager curiosity which had begun to grow on me, rather before that time, about the origin of the ancient prophecy predicting the extinction of our race. Are you following me?"

"I follow every word with the closest attention."

"You must know, then, that I had first found out some fragments of the old rhyme in which the prophecy occurs quoted as a curiosity in an antiquarian book in the library. On the page opposite this quotation had been pasted a rude old woodcut, representing a dark-haired man, whose face was so strangely like what I remembered of my Uncle Stephen that the portrait absolutely startled me. When I asked my father about this—it was then just before his death—he either knew, or pretended to know, nothing of it; and when I afterward mentioned the prediction he fretfully changed the subject. It was just the same with our chaplain when I spoke to him. He said the portrait had been done centuries before my uncle was born, and called the prophecy doggerel and nonsense. I used to argue with him on the latter point, asking why we Catholics, who believed that the gift of working miracles had never departed from certain favored persons, might not just as well believe that the gift of prophecy had never departed either? He would not dispute with me; he would only say that I must not waste time in thinking of such trifles; that I had more imagination than was good for me, and must suppress instead of exciting it. Such advice as this only irritated my curiosity. I determined secretly to search throughout the oldest uninhabited part of the Abbey, and to try if I could not find out from forgotten family records what the portrait was, and when the prophecy had been first written or uttered. Did you ever pass a day alone in the long-deserted chambers of an ancient house?"

"Never; such solitude as that is not at all to my taste."

"Ah! what a life it was when I began my search. I should like to live it over again. Such tempting suspense, such strange discoveries, such wild fancies, such enthralling terrors, all belonged to that life! Only think of breaking open the door of a room which no living soul had entered before you for nearly a hundred years! think of the first step forward into a region of airless, awful stillness, where the light falls faint and sickly through closed windows and rotting curtains! think of the ghostly creaking of the old floor that cries out on you for treading on it, step as softly as you will! think of arms, helmets, weird tapestries of bygone days, that seem to be moving out on you from the walls as you first walk up to them in the dim light! think of prying into great cabinets and iron-clasped chests, not knowing what horrors may appear when you tear them open! of poring over their contents till twilight stole on you and darkness grew terrible in the lonely place! of trying to leave it, and not being able to go, as if something held you; of wind wailing at you outside; of shadows darkening round you, and closing you up in obscurity within—only think of these things, and you may imagine the fascination of suspense and terror in such a life as mine was in those past days!"

(I shrank from imagining that life: it was bad enough to see its results, as I saw them before me now.)

"Well, my search lasted months and months; then it was suspended a little; then resumed. In whatever direction I pursued it I always found something to lure me on. Terrible confessions of past crimes, shocking proofs of secret wickedness that had been hidden securely from all eyes but mine, came to light. Sometimes these discoveries were associated with particular parts of the Abbey, which have had a horrible interest of their own for me ever since; sometimes with certain old portraits in the picture-gallery, which I actually dreaded to look at after what I had found out. There were periods when the results of this search of mine so horrified me that I determined to give it up entirely; but I never could persevere in my resolution; the temptation to go on seemed at certain intervals to get too strong for me, and then I yielded to it again and again. At last I found the book that had belonged to the monks with the whole of the prophecy written in the blank leaf. This first success encouraged me to get back further yet in the family records. I had discovered nothing hitherto of the identity of the mysterious portrait; but the same intuitive conviction which had assured me of its extraordinary resemblance to my Uncle Stephen seemed also to assure me that he must be more closely connected with the prophecy, and must know more of it than any one else. I had no means of holding any communication with him, no means of satisfying myself whether this strange idea of mine were right or wrong, until the day when my doubts were settled forever by the same terrible proof which is now present to me in this very room."

He paused for a moment, and looked at me intently and suspiciously; then asked if I believed all he had said to me so far. My instant reply in the affirmative seemed to satisfy his doubts, and he went on:—

"On a fine evening in February I was standing alone in one of the deserted rooms of the western turret at the Abbey, looking at the sunset. Just before the sun went down I felt a sensation stealing over me which it is impossible to explain. I saw nothing, heard nothing, knew nothing. This utter self-oblivion came suddenly; it was not fainting, for I did not fall to the ground, did not move an inch from my place. If such a thing could be, I should say it was the temporary separation of soul and body without death; but all description of my situation at that time is impossible. Call my state what you will, trance or catalepsy, I know that I remained standing by the window utterly unconscious—dead, mind and body—until the sun had set. Then I came to my senses again; and then, when I opened my eyes, there was the apparition of Stephen Monkton standing opposite to me, faintly luminous, just as it stands opposite me at this very moment by your side."

"Was this before the news of the duel reached England?" I asked.

"*Two weeks before* the news of it reached us at Wincot. And even when we heard of the duel, we did not hear of the day on which it was fought. I only found that out when the document which you have read was published in the French newspaper. The date of that document, you will remember, is February 22d, and it is stated that the duel was fought two days afterward. I wrote down in my pocketbook, on the evening when I saw the phantom, the day of the month on which it first appeared to me. That day was the 24th of February."

He paused again, as if expecting me to say something. After the words he had just spoken, what could I say? what could I think?

"Even in the first horror of first seeing the apparition," he went on, "the prophecy against our house came to my mind, and with it the conviction that I beheld before me, in that spectral presence, the warning of my own doom. As soon as I recovered a little, I determined, nevertheless, to test the reality of what I saw; to find out whether I was the dupe of my own diseased fancy or not. I left the turret; the phantom left it with me. I made an excuse to have the drawing-room at the Abbey brilliantly lighted up; the figure was still opposite me. I walked out into the park; it was there in the clear starlight. I went away from home, and traveled many miles to the sea-side; still the tall dark man in his death agony was with me. After this I strove against the fatality no more. I returned to the Abbey, and tried to resign myself to my misery. But this was not to be. I had a hope that was dearer to me than my own life; I had one treasure belonging to me that I shuddered at the prospect of losing, and when the phantom presence stood a warning obstacle between me and this one treasure, this dearest hope—then my misery grew heavier than I could bear. You must know what I am alluding to; you must have heard often that I was engaged to be married?"

"Yes, often. I have some acquaintance myself with Miss Elmslie."

"You never can know all that she has sacrificed for me—never can imagine what I have felt for years and years past"—his voice trembled, and the tears came into his eyes—"but I dare not trust myself to speak of that: the thought of the old happy days in the Abbey almost breaks my heart now. Let me get back to the other subject. I must tell you that I kept the frightful vision which pursued me, at all times and in all places, a secret from everybody; knowing the vile reports about my having inherited madness from my family, and fearing that an unfair advantage would be taken of any confession that I might make. Though the phantom always stood opposite to me, and therefore always appeared either before or by the side of any person to whom I spoke, I soon schooled myself to hide from others that I was looking at it except on rare occasions, when I have perhaps betrayed myself to you. But my self-possession availed me nothing with Ada. The day of our marriage was approaching."

He stopped and shuddered. I waited in silence till he had controlled himself.

"Think," he went on, "think of what I must have suffered at looking always on that hideous vision whenever I looked on my betrothed wife! Think of my taking her hand, and seeming to take it through the figure of the apparition! Think of the calm angel-face and the tortured specter-face being always together whenever my eyes met hers! Think of this, and you will not wonder that I betrayed my secret to her. She eagerly entreated to know the worst—nay, more, she insisted on knowing it. At her bidding I told all, and then left her free to break our engagement. The thought of death was in my heart as I spoke the parting words—death by my own act, if life still held out after our separation. She suspected that thought; she knew it, and never left me till her good influence had destroyed it forever. But for her I should not have been alive now—but for her, I should never have attempted the project which has brought me here."

"Do you mean that it was at Miss Elmslie's suggestion that you came to Naples?" I asked, in amazement.

"I mean that what she said suggested the design which has brought me to Naples," he answered. "While I believed that the phantom had appeared to me as the fatal messenger of death, there was no comfort—there was misery, rather, in hearing her say that no power on earth should make her desert me, and that she would live for me, and for me only, through every trial. But it was far different when we afterward reasoned together about the purpose which the apparition had come to fulfill—far different when she showed me that its mission might be for good instead of for evil, and that the warning it was sent to give might be to my profit instead of to my loss. At those words, the new idea which gave the new hope of life came to me in an instant. I believed then, what I believe now, that I have a supernatural warrant for my errand here. In that faith I live; without it I should die. *She* never ridiculed it, never scorned it as insanity. Mark what I say! The spirit that appeared to me in the Abbey—that has never left me since—that stands there now by your side, warns me to escape from the fatality which hangs over our race, and commands me, if I would avoid it, to bury the unburied dead. Mortal loves and mortal interests must bow to that awful bidding. The specter-presence will never leave me till I have sheltered the corpse that cries to the earth to cover it! I dare not return—I dare not marry till I have filled the place that is empty in Wincot vault."

His eyes flashed and dilated; his voice deepened; a fanatic ecstasy shone in his expression as he uttered these words. Shocked and grieved as I was, I made no attempt to remonstrate or to reason with him. It would have been useless to have referred to any of the usual common-places about optical delusions or diseased imaginations—worse than useless to have attempted to account by natural causes for any of the extraordinary coincidences and events of which he had spoken. Briefly as he had referred to Miss Elmslie, he had said enough to show me that the only hope of the poor girl who loved him best and had known him longest of any one was in humoring his delusions to the last. How faithfully she still clung to the belief that she could restore him! How resolutely was she sacrificing herself to his morbid fancies, in the hope of a happy future that might never come! Little as I knew of Miss Elmslie, the mere thought of her situation, as I now reflected on it, made me feel sick at heart.

"They call me 'Mad Monkton!'" he exclaimed, suddenly breaking the silence between us during the last few minutes, "Here and in England everybody believes I am out of my senses except Ada and you. She has been my salvation, and you will be my salvation too. Something told me that when I first met you walking in the Villa Peale. I struggled against the strong desire that was in me to trust my secret to you; but I could resist it no longer when I saw you to-night at the ball—the phantom seemed to draw me on to you as you stood alone in the quiet room. Tell me more of that idea of yours about finding the place where the duel was fought. If I set out to-morrow to seek for it myself, where must I go to first? where?" He stopped; his strength was evidently becoming exhausted, and his mind was growing confused. "What am I to do? I can't remember. You know everything—will you not help me? My misery has made me unable to help myself!"

He stopped, murmured something about failing if he went to the frontier alone, and spoke confusedly of delays that might be fatal, then tried to utter the name of "Ada"; but, in pronouncing the first letter, his voice faltered, and, turning abruptly from me, he burst into tears.

My pity for him got the better of my prudence at that moment, and without thinking of responsibilities, I promised at once to do for him whatever he asked. The wild triumph in his expression as he started up and seized my hand showed me that I had better have been more cautious; but it was too late now to retract what I had said. The next best thing to do was to try if I could not induce him to compose himself a little, and then to go away and think coolly over the whole affair by myself.

"Yes, yes," he rejoined, in answer to the few words I now spoke to try and calm him, "don't be afraid about me. After what you have said, I'll answer for my own coolness and composure under all emergencies. I have been so long used to the apparition that I hardly feel its presence at all except on rare occasions. Besides, I have here in this little packet of letters the medicine for every malady of the sick heart. They are Ada's letters; I read them to calm me whenever my misfortune seems to get the better of my endurance. I wanted that half hour to read them in to-night, before you came, to make myself fit to see you; and I shall go through them again after you are gone. So, once more, don't be afraid about me. I know I shall succeed with your help, and Ada shall thank you as you deserve to be thanked when we get back to England. If you hear the fools at Naples talk about my being mad, don't trouble yourself to contradict them; the scandal is so contemptible that it must end by contradicting itself."

I left him, promising to return early the next day.

When I got back to my hotel, I felt that any idea of sleeping after all that I had seen and heard was out of the question; so I lit my pipe, and, sitting by the window—how it refreshed my mind just then to look at the calm moonlight!—tried to think what it would be best to do. In the first place, any appeal to doctors or to Alfred's friends in England was out of the question. I could not persuade myself that his intellect was sufficiently disordered to justify me, under existing circumstances, in disclosing the secret which he had intrusted to my keeping. In the second place, all attempts on my part to induce him to abandon the idea of searching out his uncle's remains would be utterly useless after what I had incautiously said to him. Having settled these two conclusions, the only really great difficulty which remained to perplex me was whether I was justified in aiding him to execute his extraordinary purpose.

Supposing that with my help he found Mr. Monkton's body, and took it back with him to England, was it right in me thus to lend myself to promoting the marriage which would most likely follow these events—a marriage which it might be the duty of every one to prevent at all hazards? This set me thinking about the extent of his madness, or, to speak more mildly and more correctly, of his delusion. Sane he certainly was on all ordinary subjects; nay, in all the narrative parts of what he had said to me on this very evening he had spoken clearly and connectedly. As for the story of the apparition, other men, with intellects as clear as the intellects of their neighbors had fancied themselves pursued by a phantom, and had even written about it in a high strain of philosophical speculation. It was plain that the real hallucination in the case now before me lay in Monkton's conviction of the truth of the old prophecy, and in his idea that the fancied apparition was a supernatural warning to him to evade its denunciations; and it was equally clear that both delusions had been produced, in the first instance, by the lonely life he had led acting on a naturally excitable temperament, which was rendered further liable to moral disease by an hereditary taint of insanity.

Was this curable? Miss Elmslie, who knew him far better than I did, seemed by her conduct to think so. Had I any reason or right to determine off-hand that she was mistaken? Supposing I refused to go to the frontier with him, he would then most certainly depart by himself, to commit all sorts of errors, and perhaps to meet with all sorts of accidents; while I, an idle man, with my time entirely at my own disposal, was stopping at Naples, and leaving him to his fate after I had suggested the plan of his expedition, and had encouraged him to confide in me. In this way I kept turning the subject over and over again in my mind—being quite free, let me add, from looking at it in any other than a practical point of view. I firmly believed, as a derider of all ghost stories, that Alfred was deceiving himself in fancying that he had seen the apparition of his uncle before the news of Mr. Monkton's death reached England, and I was on this account, therefore, uninfluenced by the slightest infection of my unhappy friend's delusions when I at last fairly decided to accompany him in his extraordinary search. Possibly my harum-scarum fondness for excitement at that time biased me a little in forming my resolution; but I must add, in common justice to myself, that I also acted from motives of real sympathy for Monkton, and from a sincere wish to allay, if I could, the anxiety of the poor girl who was still so faithfully waiting and hoping for him far away in England.

Certain arrangements preliminary to our departure, which I found myself obliged to make after a second interview with Alfred, betrayed the object of our journey to most of our Neapolitan friends. The astonishment of everybody was of course unbounded, and the nearly universal suspicion that I must be as mad in my way as Monkton himself, showed itself pretty plainly in my presence. Some people actually tried to combat my resolution by telling me what a shameless profligate Stephen Monkton had been—as if I had a strong personal interest in hunting out his remains! Ridicule moved me as little as any arguments of this sort; my mind was made up, and I was as obstinate then as I am now.

In two days' time I had got everything ready, and had ordered the traveling carriage to the door some hours earlier than we had originally settled. We were jovially threatened with "a parting cheer" by all our English acquaintances, and I thought it desirable to avoid this on my friend's account; for he had been more excited, as it was, by the preparations for the journey than I at all liked. Accordingly, soon after sunrise, without a soul in the street to stare at us, we privately left Naples.

Nobody will wonder, I think, that I experienced some difficulty in realizing my own position, and shrank instinctively from looking forward a single day into the future, when I now found myself starting, in company with "Mad Monkton," to hunt for the body of a dead duelist all along the frontier line of the Roman States!

V

I had settled it in my own mind that we had better make the town of Fondi, close on the frontier, our headquarters, to begin with, and I had arranged, with the assistance of the embassy, that the leaden coffin should follow us so far, securely nailed up in its packing-case. Besides our passports, we were well furnished with letters of introduction to the local authorities at most of the important frontier towns, and, to crown all, we had money enough at our command (thanks to Monkton's vast fortune) to make sure of the services of any one whom we wanted to assist us all along our line of search. These various resources insured us every facility for action—provided always that we succeeded in discovering the body of the dead duelist. But, in the very probable event of our failing to do this, our future prospects—more especially after the responsibility I had undertaken—were of anything but an agreeable nature to contemplate. I confess I felt uneasy, almost hopeless, as we posted, in the dazzling Italian sunshine, along the road to Fondi.

We made an easy two days' journey of it; for I had insisted, on Monkton's account, that we should travel slowly.

On the first day the excessive agitation of my companion a little alarmed me; he showed, in many ways, more symptoms of a disordered mind than I had yet observed in him. On the second day, however, he seemed to get accustomed to contemplate calmly the new idea of the search on which we were bent, and, except on one point, he was cheerful and composed enough. Whenever his dead uncle formed the subject of conversation, he still persisted—on the strength of the old prophecy, and under the influence of the apparition which he saw, or thought he saw always—in asserting that the corpse of Stephen Monkton, wherever it was, lay yet unburied. On every other topic he deferred to me with the utmost readiness and docility; on this he maintained his strange opinion with an obstinacy which set reason and persuasion alike at defiance.

On the third day we rested at Fondi. The packing-case, with the coffin in it, reached us, and was deposited in a safe place under lock and key. We engaged some mules, and found a man to act as guide who knew the country thoroughly. It occurred to me that we had better begin by confiding the real object of our journey only to the most trustworthy people we could find among the better-educated classes. For this reason we followed, in one respect, the example of the fatal dueling-party, by starting, early on the morning of the fourth day, with sketch-books and color-boxes, as if we were only artists in search of the picturesque.

After traveling some hours in a northerly direction within the Roman frontier, we halted to rest ourselves and our mules at a wild little village far out of the track of tourists in general.

The only person of the smallest importance in the place was the priest, and to him I addressed my first inquiries, leaving Monkton to await my return with the guide. I spoke Italian quite fluently, and correctly enough for my purpose, and was extremely polite and cautious in introducing my business, but in spite of all the pains I took, I only succeeded in frightening and bewildering the poor priest more and more with every fresh word I said to him. The idea of a dueling-party and a dead man seemed to scare him out of his senses. He bowed, fidgeted, cast his eyes up to heaven, and piteously shrugging his shoulders, told me, with rapid Italian circumlocution, that he had not the faintest idea of what I was talking about. This was my first failure. I confess I was weak enough to feel a little dispirited when I rejoined Monkton and the guide.

After the heat of the day was over we resumed our journey.

About three miles from the village, the road, or rather cart-track, branched off in two directions. The path to the right, our guide informed us, led up among the mountains to a convent about six miles off. If we penetrated beyond the convent we should soon reach the Neapolitan frontier. The path to the left led far inward on the Roman territory, and would conduct us to a small town where we could sleep for the night. Now the Roman territory presented the first and fittest field for our search, and the convent was always within reach, supposing we returned to Fondi unsuccessful. Besides, the path to the left led over the widest part of the country we were starting to explore; and I was always for vanquishing the greatest difficulty first—so we decided manfully on turning to the left. The expedition in which this resolution involved us lasted a whole week, and produced no results. We discovered absolutely nothing, and returned to our headquarters at Fondi so completely baffled that we did not know whither to turn our steps next.

I was made much more uneasy by the effect of our failure on Monkton than by the failure itself. His resolution appeared to break down altogether as soon as we began to retrace our steps. He became first fretful and capricious, then silent and desponding.

Finally, he sank into a lethargy of body and mind that seriously alarmed me. On the morning after our return to Fondi he showed a strange tendency to sleep incessantly, which made me suspect the existence of some physical malady in his brain. The whole day he hardly exchanged a word with me, and seemed to be never fairly awake. Early the next morning I went into his room, and found him as silent and lethargic as ever. His servant, who was with us, informed me that Alfred had once or twice before exhibited such physical symptoms of mental exhaustion as we were now observing during his father's lifetime at Wincot Abbey. This piece of information made me feel easier, and left my mind free to return to the consideration of the errand which had brought us to Fondi.

I resolved to occupy the time until my companion got better in prosecuting our search by myself. That path to the right hand which led to the convent had not yet been explored. If I set off to trace it, I need not be away from Monkton more than one night, and I should at least be able, on my return, to give him the satisfaction of knowing that one more uncertainty regarding the place of the duel had been cleared up. These considerations decided me. I left a message for my friend in case he asked where I had gone, and set out once more for the village at which we had halted when starting on our first expedition.

Intending to walk to the convent, I parted company with the guide and the mules where the track branched off, leaving them to go back to the village and await my return.

For the first four miles the path gently ascended through an open country, then became abruptly much steeper, and led me deeper and deeper among thickets and endless woods. By the time my watch informed me that I must have nearly walked my appointed distance, the view was bounded on all sides and the sky was shut out overhead by an impervious screen of leaves and branches. I still followed my only guide, the steep path; and in ten minutes, emerging suddenly on a plot of tolerably clear and level ground, I saw the convent before me.

It was a dark, low, sinister-looking place. Not a sign of life or movement was visible anywhere about it. Green stains streaked the once white façade of the chapel in all directions. Moss clustered thick in every crevice of the heavy scowling wall that surrounded the convent. Long lank weeds grew out of the fissures of roof and parapet, and, drooping far downward, waved wearily in and out of the barred dormitory windows. The very cross opposite the entrance-gate, with a shocking life-sized figure in wood nailed to it, was so beset at the base with crawling creatures, and looked so slimy, green, and rotten all the way up, that I absolutely shrank from it.

A bell-rope with a broken handle hung by the gate. I approached it—hesitated, I hardly knew why—looked up at the convent again, and then walked round to the back of the building, partly to gain time to consider what I had better do next, partly from an unaccountable curiosity that urged me, strangely to myself, to see all I could of the outside of the place before I attempted to gain admission at the gate.

At the back of the convent I found an outhouse, built on to the wall—a clumsy, decayed building, with the greater part of the roof fallen in, and with a jagged hole in one of its sides, where in all probability a window had once been. Behind the outhouse the trees grew thicker than ever. As I looked toward them I could not determine whether the ground beyond me rose or fell—whether it was grassy, or earthy, or rocky. I could see nothing but the all-pervading leaves, brambles, ferns, and long grass.

Not a sound broke the oppressive stillness. No bird's note rose from the leafy wilderness around me; no voices spoke in the convent garden behind the scowling wall; no clock struck in the chapel-tower; no dog barked in the ruined outhouse. The dead silence deepened the solitude of the place inexpressibly. I began to feel it weighing on my spirits—the more, because woods were never favorite places with me to walk in. The sort of pastoral happiness which poets often represent when they sing of life in the woods never, to my mind, has half the charm of life on the mountain or in the plain. When I am in a wood, I miss the boundless loveliness of the sky, and the delicious softness that distance gives to the earthly view beneath. I feel oppressively the change which the free air suffers when it gets imprisoned among leaves, and I am always awed, rather than pleased, by that mysterious still light which shines with such a strange dim luster in deep places among trees. It may convict me of want of taste and absence of due feeling for the marvelous beauties of vegetation, but I must frankly own that I never penetrate far into a wood without finding that the getting out of it again is the pleasantest part of my walk—the getting out on to the barest down, the wildest hill-side, the bleakest mountain-top—the getting out anywhere, so that I can see the sky over me and the view before me as far as my eye can reach.

After such a confession as I have now made, it will appear surprising to no one that I should have felt the strongest possible inclination, while I stood by the ruined outhouse, to retrace my steps at once, and make the best of my way out of the wood. I had, indeed, actually turned to depart, when the remembrance of the errand which had brought me to the convent suddenly stayed my feet. It seemed doubtful whether I should be admitted into the building if I rang the bell; and more than doubtful, if I were let in, whether the inhabitants would be able to afford me any clew to the information of which I was in search. However, it was my duty to Monkton to leave no means of helping him in his desperate object untried; so I resolved to go round to the front of the convent again, and ring at the gate-bell at all hazards.

By the merest chance I looked up as I passed the side of the outhouse where the jagged hole was, and noticed that it was pierced rather high in the wall.

As I stopped to observe this, the closeness of the atmosphere in the wood seemed to be affecting me more unpleasantly than ever.

I waited a minute and untied my cravat.

Closeness?—surely it was something more than that. The air was even more distasteful to my nostrils than to my lungs. There was some faint, indescribable smell loading it—some smell of which I had never had any previous experience—some smell which I thought (now that my attention was directed to it) grew more and more certainly traceable to its source the nearer I advanced to the outhouse.

By the time I had tried the experiment two or three times, and had made myself sure of this fact, my curiosity became excited. There were plenty of fragments of stone and brick lying about me. I gathered some of them together, and piled them up below the hole, then mounted to the top, and, feeling rather ashamed of what I was doing, peeped into the outhouse.

The sight of horror that met my eyes the instant I looked through the hole is as present to my memory now as if I had beheld it yesterday. I can hardly write of it at this distance of time without a thrill of the old terror running through me again to the heart.

The first impression conveyed to me, as I looked in, was of a long, recumbent object, tinged with a lightish blue color all over, extended on trestles, and bearing a certain hideous, half-formed resemblance to the human face and figure. I looked again, and felt certain of it. There were the prominences of the forehead, nose, and chin, dimly shown as under a veil—there, the round outline of the chest and the hollow below it—there, the points of the knees, and the stiff, ghastly, upturned feet. I looked again, yet more attentively. My eyes got accustomed to the dim light streaming in through the broken roof, and I satisfied myself, judging by the great length of the body from head to foot, that I was looking at the corpse of a man—a corpse that had apparently once had a sheet spread over it, and that had lain rotting on the trestles under the open sky long enough for the linen to take the livid, light-blue tinge of mildew and decay which now covered it.

How long I remained with my eyes fixed on that dread sight of death, on that tombless, terrible wreck of humanity, poisoning the still air, and seeming even to stain the faint descending light that disclosed it, I know not. I remember a dull, distant sound among the trees, as if the breeze were rising—the slow creeping on of the sound to near the place where I stood—the noiseless whirling fall of a dead leaf on the corpse below me, through the gap in the outhouse roof—and the effect of awakening my energies, of relaxing the heavy strain on my mind, which even the slight change wrought in the scene I beheld by the falling leaf produced in me immediately. I descended to the ground, and, sitting down on the heap of stones, wiped away the thick perspiration which covered my face, and which I now became aware of for the first time. It was something more than the hideous spectacle unexpectedly offered to my eyes which had shaken my nerves, as I felt that they were shaken now. Monkton's prediction that, if we succeeded in discovering his uncle's body, we should find it unburied, recurred to me the instant I saw the trestles and their ghastly burden. I felt assured on the instant that I had found the dead man—the old prophecy recurred to my memory—a strange yearning sorrow, a vague foreboding of ill, an inexplicable terror, as I thought of the poor lad who was awaiting my return in the distant town, struck through me with a chill of superstitious dread, robbed me of my judgment and resolution, and left me when I had at last recovered myself, weak and dizzy, as if I had just suffered under some pang of overpowering physical pain.

I hastened round to the convent gate and rang impatiently at the bell—waited a little while and rang again—then heard footsteps.

In the middle of the gate, just opposite my face, there was a small sliding panel, not more than a few inches long; this was presently pushed aside from within. I saw, through a bit of iron grating, two dull, light gray eyes staring vacantly at me, and heard a feeble husky voice saying:—

"What may you please to want?"

"I am a traveler—" I began.

"We live in a miserable place. We have nothing to show travelers here."

"I don't come to see anything. I have an important question to ask, which I believe some one in this convent will be able to answer. If you are not willing to let me in, at least come out and speak to me here."

"Are you alone?"

"Quite alone."

"Are there no women with you?"

"None."

The gate was slowly unbarred, and an old Capuchin, very infirm, very suspicious, and very dirty, stood before me. I was far too excited and impatient to waste any time in prefatory phrases; so, telling the monk at once how I had looked through the hole in the outhouse, and what I had seen inside, I asked him, in plain terms, who the man had been whose corpse I had beheld, and why the body was left unburied?

The old Capuchin listened to me with watery eyes that twinkled suspiciously. He had a battered tin snuff-box in his hand; and his finger and thumb slowly chased a few scattered grains of snuff round and round the inside of the box all the time I was speaking. When I had done, he shook his head and said: "That was certainly an ugly sight in their outhouse; one of the ugliest sights, he felt sure, that ever I had seen in all my life!"

"I don't want to talk of the sight," I rejoined, impatiently; "I want to know who the man was, how he died, and why he is not decently buried. Can you tell me?"

The monk's finger and thumb having captured three or four grains of snuff at last, he slowly drew them into his nostrils, holding the box open under his nose the while, to prevent the possibility of wasting even one grain, sniffed once or twice luxuriously—closed the box—then looked at me again with his eyes watering and twinkling more suspiciously than before.

"Yes," said the monk, "that's an ugly sight in our outhouse—a very ugly sight, certainly!"

I never had more difficulty in keeping my temper in my life than at that moment. I succeeded, however, in repressing a very disrespectful expression on the subject of monks in general, which was on the tip of my tongue, and made another attempt to conquer the old man's exasperating reserve. Fortunately for my chances of succeeding with him, I was a snuff-taker myself, and I had a box full of excellent English snuff in my pocket, which I now produced as a bribe. It was my last resource.

"I thought your box seemed empty just now," said I; "will you try a pinch out of mine?"

The offer was accepted with an almost youthful alacrity of gesture. The Capuchin took the largest pinch I ever saw held between any man's finger and thumb—inhaled it slowly without spilling a single grain—half closed his eyes—and, wagging his head gently, patted me paternally on the back.

"Oh! my son!" said the monk, "what delectable snuff! Oh, my son and amiable traveler, give the spiritual father who loves you yet another tiny, tiny pinch!"

"Let me fill your box for you. I shall have plenty left for myself."

The battered tin snuff-box was given to me before I had done speaking; the paternal hand patted my back more approvingly than ever—the feeble, husky voice grew glib and eloquent in my praise. I had evidently found out the weak side of the old Capuchin; and, on returning him his box, I took instant advantage of the discovery.

"Excuse my troubling you on the subject again," I said, "but I have particular reasons for wanting to hear all that you can tell me in explanation of that horrible sight in the outhouse."

"Come in," answered the monk.

He drew me inside the gate, closed it, and then leading the way across a grass-grown courtyard, looking out on a weedy kitchen-garden, showed me into a long room with a low ceiling, a dirty dresser, a few rudely-carved stall seats, and one or two grim, mildewed pictures for ornaments. This was the sacristy.

"There's nobody here, and it's nice and cool," said the old Capuchin. It was so damp that I actually shivered. "Would you like to see the church?" said the monk; "a jewel of a church, if we could keep it in repair; but we can't. Ah! malediction and misery, we are too poor to keep our church in repair!"

Here he shook his head and began fumbling with a large bunch of keys.

"Never mind the church now," said I. "Can you, or can you not, tell me what I want to know?"

"Everything, from beginning to end—absolutely everything. Why, I answered the gate-bell—I always answer the gate-bell here," said the Capuchin.

"What, in heaven's name, has the gate-bell to do with the unburied corpse in your house?"

"Listen, son of mine, and you shall know. Some time ago—some months—ah! me, I'm old; I've lost my memory; I don't know how many months—ah! miserable me, what a very old, old monk I am!" Here he comforted himself with another pinch of snuff.

"Never mind the exact time," said I. "I don't care about that."

"Good," said the Capuchin. "Now I can go on. Well, let us say it is some months ago—we in this convent are all at breakfast—wretched, wretched breakfasts, son of mine, in this convent!—we are at breakfast, and we hear *bang! bang!* twice over. 'Guns,' says I. 'What are they shooting for?' says Brother Jeremy. 'Game,' says Brother Vincent. 'Aha! game,' says Brother Jeremy. 'If I hear more, I shall send out and discover what it means,' says the father superior. We hear no more, and we go on with our wretched breakfasts."

"Where did the report of firearms come from?" I inquired.

"From down below—beyond the big trees at the back of the convent, where there's some clear ground—nice ground, if it wasn't for the pools and puddles. But, ah! misery, how damp we are in these parts! how very, very damp!"

"Well, what happened after the report of fire-arms?"

"You shall hear. We are still at breakfast, all silent—for what have we to talk about here? What have we but our devotions, our kitchen-garden, and our wretched, wretched bits of breakfasts and dinners? I say we are all silent, when there comes suddenly such a ring at the bell as never was heard before—a very devil of a ring—a ring that caught us all with our bits—our wretched, wretched bits!—in our mouths, and stopped us before we could swallow them. 'Go, brother of mine,' says the father superior to me, 'go; it is your duty—go to the gate.' I am brave—a very lion of a Capuchin. I slip out on tiptoe—I wait—I listen—I pull back our little shutter in the gate—I wait, I listen again—I peep through the hole—nothing, absolutely nothing that I can see. I am brave—I am not to be daunted. What do I do next? I open the gate. Ah! sacred Mother of Heaven, what do I behold lying all along our threshold? A man—dead!—a big man; bigger than you, bigger than me, bigger than anybody in this convent—buttoned up tight in a fine coat, with black eyes, staring, staring up at the sky, and blood soaking through and through the front of his shirt. What do I do? I scream once—I scream twice—and run back to the father superior!"

All the particulars of the fatal duel which I had gleaned from the French newspaper in Monkton's room at Naples recurred vividly to my memory. The suspicion that I had felt when I looked into the outhouse became a certainty as I listened to the old monk's last words.

"So far I understand," said I. "The corpse I have just seen in the outhouse is the corpse of the man whom you found dead outside your gate. Now tell me why you have not given the remains decent burial?"

"Wait—wait—wait," answered the Capuchin. "The father superior hears me scream and comes out; we all run together to the gate; we lift up the big man and look at him close. Dead! dead as this (smacking the dresser with his hand). We look again, and see a bit of paper pinned to the collar of his coat. Aha! son of mine, you start at that. I thought I should make you start at last."

I had started, indeed. That paper was doubtless the leaf mentioned in the second's unfinished narrative as having been torn out of his pocketbook, and inscribed with the statement of how the dead man had lost his life. If proof positive were wanted to identify the dead body, here was such proof found.

"What do you think was written on the bit of paper?" continued the Capuchin "We read and shudder. This dead man has been killed in a duel—he, the desperate, the miserable, has died in the commission of mortal sin; and the men who saw the killing of him ask us Capuchins, holy men, servants of Heaven, children of our lord the Pope—they ask *us* to give him burial! Oh! but we are outraged when we read that; we groan, we wring our hands, we turn away, we tear our beards, we—"

"Wait one moment," said I, seeing that the old man was heating himself with his narrative, and was likely, unless I stopped him, to talk more and more fluently to less and less purpose—"wait a moment. Have you preserved the paper that was pinned to the dead man's coat; and can I look at it?"

The Capuchin seemed on the point of giving me an answer, when he suddenly checked himself. I saw his eyes wander away from my face, and at the same moment heard a door softly opened and closed again behind me.

Looking round immediately, I observed another monk in the sacristy—a tall, lean, black-bearded man, in whose presence my old friend with the snuff-box suddenly became quite decorous and devotional to look at. I suspected I was in the presence of the father superior, and I found that I was right the moment he addressed me.

"I am the father superior of this convent," he said, in quiet, clear tones, and looking me straight in the face while he spoke, with coldly attentive eyes. "I have heard the latter part of your conversation, and I wish to know why you are so particularly anxious to see the piece of paper that was pinned to the dead man's coat?"

The coolness with which he avowed that he had been listening, and the quietly imperative manner in which he put his concluding question, perplexed and startled me. I hardly knew at first what tone I ought to take in answering him. He observed my hesitation, and attributing it to the wrong cause, signed to the old Capuchin to retire. Humbly stroking his long gray beard, and furtively consoling himself with a private pinch of the "delectable snuff," my venerable friend shuffled out of the room, making a profound obeisance at the door just before he disappeared.

"Now," said the father superior, as coldly as ever, "I am waiting, sir, for your reply."

"You shall have it in the fewest possible words," said I, answering him in his own tone. "I find, to my disgust and horror, that there is an unburied corpse in an outhouse attached to your convent. I believe that corpse to be the body of an English gentleman of rank and fortune, who was killed in a duel. I have come into this neighborhood with the nephew and only relation of the slain man, for the express purpose of recovering his remains; and I wish to see the paper found on the body, because I believe that paper will identify it to the satisfaction of the relative to whom I have referred. Do you find my reply sufficiently straightforward? And do you mean to give me permission to look at the paper?"

"I am satisfied with your reply, and see no reason for refusing you a sight of the paper," said the father superior; "but I have something to say first. In speaking of the impression produced on you by beholding the corpse, you used the words 'disgust' and 'horror.' This license of expression in relation to what you have seen in the precincts of a convent proves to me that you are out of the pale of the Holy Catholic Church. You have no right, therefore, to expect any explanation; but I will give you one, nevertheless, as a favor. The slain man died, unabsolved, in the commission of mortal sin. We infer so much from the paper which we found on his body; and we know, by the evidence of our own eyes and ears, that he was killed on the territories of the Church, and in the act of committing direct violation of those special laws against the crime of dueling, the strict enforcement of which the Holy Father himself has urged on the faithful throughout his dominions by letters signed with his own hand. Inside this convent the ground is consecrated, and we Catholics are not accustomed to bury the outlaws of our religion, the enemies of our Holy Father, and the violators of our most sacred laws in consecrated ground. Outside this convent we have no rights and no power; and, if we had both, we should remember that we are monks, not grave-diggers, and that the only burial with which *we* can have any concern is burial with the prayers of the Church. That is all the explanation I think it necessary to give. Wait for me here, and you shall see the paper." With those words the father superior left the room as quietly as he had entered it.

I had hardly time to think over this bitter and ungracious explanation, and to feel a little piqued by the language and manner of the person who had given it to me, before the father superior returned with the paper in his hand. He placed it before me on the dresser, and I read, hurriedly traced in pencil, the following lines:—

> This paper is attached to the body of the late Mr. Stephen Monkton, an Englishman of distinction. He has been shot in a duel, conducted with perfect gallantry and honor on both sides. His body is placed at the door of this convent, to receive burial at the hands of its inmates, the survivors of the encounter being obliged to separate and secure their safety by immediate flight. I, the second of the slain man, and the writer of this explanation, certify, on my word of honor as a gentleman that the shot which killed my principal on the instant was fired fairly, in the strictest accordance with the rules laid down beforehand for the conduct of the duel.
>
> (Signed) "F."

"F." I recognized easily enough as the initial letter of Monsieur Foulon's name, the second of Mr. Monkton, who had died of consumption at Paris.

The discovery and the identification were now complete. Nothing remained but to break the news to Alfred, and to get permission to remove the remains in the outhouse. I began almost to doubt the evidence of my own senses when I reflected that the apparently impracticable object with which we had left Naples was already, by the merest chance, virtually accomplished.

"The evidence of the paper is decisive," said I, handing it back. "There can be no doubt that the remains in the outhouse are the remains of which we have been in search. May I inquire if any obstacles will be thrown in our way should the late Mr. Monkton's nephew wish to remove his uncle's body to the family burial-place in England?"

"Where is this nephew?" asked the father superior.

"He is now awaiting my return at the town of Fondi."

"Is he in a position to prove his relationship?"

"Certainly; he has papers with him which will place it beyond a doubt."

"Let him satisfy the civil authorities of his claim, and he need expect no obstacle to his wishes from any one here."

I was in no humor for talking a moment longer with my sour-tempered companion than I could help. The day was wearing on me fast; and, whether night overtook me or not, I was resolved never to stop on my return till I got back to Fondi. Accordingly, after telling the father superior that he might expect to hear from me again immediately, I made my bow and hastened out of the sacristy.

At the convent gate stood my old friend with the tin snuff-box, waiting to let me out.

"Bless you, may son," said the venerable recluse, giving me a farewell pat on the shoulder, "come back soon to your spiritual father who loves you; and amiably favour him with another tiny, tiny pinch of the delectable snuff."

VI

I returned at the top of my speed to the village where I had left the mules, had the animals saddled immediately, and succeeded in getting back to Fondi a little before sunset.

While ascending the stairs of our hotel, I suffered under the most painful uncertainty as to how I should best communicate the news of my discovery to Alfred. If I could not succeed in preparing him properly for my tidings, the results, with such an organization as his, might be fatal. On opening the door of his room, I felt by no means sure of myself; and when I confronted him, his manner of receiving me took me so much by surprise that, for a moment or two, I lost my self-possession altogether.

Every trace of the lethargy in which he was sunk when I had last seen him had disappeared. His eyes were bright, his cheeks deeply flushed. As I entered, he started up, and refused my offered hand.

"You have not treated me like a friend," he said, passionately; "you had no right to continue the search unless I searched with you—you had no right to leave me here alone. I was wrong to trust you; you are no better than all the rest of them."

I had by this time recovered a little from my first astonishment, and was able to reply before he could say anything more. It was quite useless, in his present state, to reason with him or to defend myself. I determined to risk everything, and break my news to him at once.

"You will treat me more justly, Monkton, when you know that I have been doing you good service during my absence," I said. "Unless I am greatly mistaken, the object for which we have left Naples may be nearer attainment by both of us than—"

The flush left his cheeks almost in an instant. Some expression in my face, or some tone in my voice, of which I was not conscious, had revealed to his nervously-quickened perception more than I had intended that he should know at first. His eyes fixed themselves intently on mine; his hand grasped my arm; and he said to me in an eager whisper:

"Tell me the truth at once. Have you found him?"

It was too late to hesitate. I answered in the affirmative.

"Buried or unburied?"

His voice rose abruptly as he put the question, and his unoccupied hand fastened on my other arm.

"Unburied."

I had hardly uttered the word before the blood flew back into his cheeks; his eyes flashed again as they looked into mine, and he burst into a fit of triumphant laughter, which shocked and startled me inexpressibly.

"What did I tell you? What do you say to the old prophecy now?" he cried, dropping his hold on my arms, and pacing backward and forward in the room. "Own you were wrong. Own it, as all Naples shall own it, when once I have got him safe in his coffin!"

His laughter grew more and mere violent. I tried to quiet him in vain. His servant and the landlord of the inn entered the room, but they only added fuel to the fire, and I made them go out again. As I shut the door on them, I observed lying on a table near at hand the packet of letters from Miss Elmslie, which my unhappy friend preserved with such care, and read and re-read with such unfailing devotion. Looking toward me just when I passed by the table, the letters caught his eye. The new hope for the future, in connection with the writer of them, which my news was already awakening in his heart, seemed to overwhelm him in an instant at sight of the treasured memorials that reminded him of his betrothed wife. His laughter ceased, his face changed, he ran to the table, caught the letters up in his hand, looked from them to me for one moment with an altered expression which went to my heart, then sank down on his knees at the table, laid his face on the letters, and burst into tears. I let the new emotion have its way uninterruptedly, and quitted the room without saying a word. When I returned after a lapse of some little time, I found him sitting quietly in his chair, reading one of the letters from the packet which rested on his knee.

His look was kindness itself; his gesture almost womanly in its gentleness as he rose to meet me, and anxiously held out his hand.

He was quite calm enough now to hear in detail all that I had to tell him. I suppressed nothing but the particulars of the state in which I had found the corpse. I assumed no right of direction as to the share he was to take in our future proceedings, with the exception of insisting beforehand that he should leave the absolute superintendence of the removal of the body to me, and that he should be satisfied with a sight of M. Foulon's paper, after receiving my assurance that the remains placed in the coffin were really and truly the remains of which we had been in search.

"Your nerves are not so strong as mine," I said, by way of apology for my apparent dictation, "and for that reason I must beg leave to assume the leadership in all that we have now to do, until I see the leaden coffin soldered down and safe in your possession. After that I shall resign all my functions to you."

"I want words to thank you for your kindness," he answered. "No brother could have borne with me more affectionately, or helped me more patiently than you."

He stopped and grew thoughtful, then occupied himself in tying up slowly and carefully the packet of Miss Elmslie's letters, and then looked suddenly toward the vacant wall behind me with that strange expression the meaning of which I knew so well. Since we had left Naples I had purposely avoided exciting him by talking on the useless and shocking subject of the apparition by which he believed himself to be perpetually followed. Just now, however, he seemed so calm and collected—so little likely to be violently agitated by any allusion to the dangerous topic, that I ventured to speak out boldly.

"Does the phantom still appear to you," I asked, "as it appeared at Naples?"

He looked at me and smiled.

"Did I not tell you that it followed me everywhere?" His eyes wandered back again to the vacant space, and he went on speaking in that direction as if he had been continuing the conversation with some third person in the room. "We shall part," he said, slowly and softly, "when the empty place is filled in Wincot vault. Then I shall stand with Ada before the altar in the Abbey chapel, and when my eyes meet hers they will see the tortured face no more."

Saying this, he leaned his head on his hand, sighed, and began repeating softly to himself the lines of the old prophecy:—

> "When in Wincot vault a place
> Waits for one of Monkton's race;
> When that one forlorn shall lie
> Graveless under open sky,
> Beggared of six feet of earth,
> Though lord of acres from his birth—
> That shall be a certain sign
> Of the end of Monkton's line.
> Dwindling ever faster, faster,
> Dwindling to the last-left master;
> From mortal ken, from light of day,
> Monkton's race shall pass away."

Fancying that he pronounced the last lines a little incoherently, I tried to make him change the subject. He took no notice of what I said, and went on talking to himself.

"Monkton's race shall pass away," he repeated, "but not with *me*. The fatality hangs over *my* head no longer. I shall bury the unburied dead; I shall fill the vacant place in Wincot vault; and then—then the new life, the life with Ada!" That name seemed to recall him to himself. He drew his traveling desk toward him, placed the packet of letters in it, and then took out a sheet of paper. "I am going to write to Ada," he said, turning to me, "and tell her the good news. Her happiness, when she knows it, will be even greater than mine."

Worn out by the events of the day, I left him writing and went to bed. I was, however, either too anxious or too tired to sleep. In this waking condition, my mind naturally occupied itself with the discovery at the convent and with the events to which that discovery would in all probability lead. As I thought on the future, a depression for which I could not account weighed on my spirits. There was not the slightest reason for the vaguely melancholy forebodings that oppressed me. The remains, to the finding of which my unhappy friend attached so much importance, had been traced; they would certainly be placed at his disposal in a few days; he might take them to England by the first merchant vessel that sailed from Naples; and, the gratification of his strange caprice thus accomplished, there was at least some reason to hope that his mind might recover its tone, and that the new life he would lead at Wincot might result in making him a happy man. Such considerations as these were, in themselves, certainly not calculated to exert any melancholy influence over me; and yet, all through the night, the same inconceivable, unaccountable depression weighed heavily on my spirits—heavily through the hours of darkness—heavily, even when I walked out to breathe the first freshness of the early morning air.

With the day came the all-engrossing business of opening negotiations with the authorities.

Only those who have had to deal with Italian officials can imagine how our patience was tried by every one with whom we came in contact. We were bandied about from one authority to the other, were stared at, cross-questioned, mystified—not in the least because the case presented any special difficulties or intricacies, but because it was absolutely necessary that every civil dignitary to whom we applied should assert his own importance by leading us to our object in the most roundabout manner possible. After our first day's experience of official life in Italy, I left the absurd formalities, which we had no choice but to perform, to be accomplished by Alfred alone, and applied myself to the really serious question of how the remains in the convent outhouse were to be safely removed.

The best plan that suggested itself to me was to write to a friend in Rome, where I knew that it was a custom to embalm the bodies of high dignitaries of the Church, and where, I consequently inferred, such chemical assistance as was needed in our emergency might be obtained. I simply stated in my letter that the removal of the body was imperative, then described the condition in which I had found it, and engaged that no expense on our part should be spared if the right person or persons could be found to help us. Here, again, more difficulties interposed themselves, and more useless formalities were to be gone through, but in the end patience, perseverance, and money triumphed, and two men came expressly from Rome to undertake the duties we required of them.

It is unnecessary that I should shock the reader by entering into any detail in this part of my narrative. When I have said that the progress of decay was so far suspended by chemical means as to allow of the remains being placed in the coffin, and to insure their being transported to England with perfect safety and convenience, I have said enough. After ten days had been wasted in useless delays and difficulties, I had the satisfaction of seeing the convent outhouse empty at last; passed through a final ceremony of snuff-taking, or rather, of snuff-giving, with the old Capuchin, and ordered the traveling carriages to be ready at the inn door. Hardly a month had elapsed since our departure ere we entered Naples successful in the achievement of a design which had been ridiculed as wildly impracticable by every friend of ours who had heard of it.

The first object to be accomplished on our return was to obtain the means of carrying the coffin to England—by sea, as a matter of course. All inquiries after a merchant vessel on the point of sailing for any British port led to the most unsatisfactory results.

There was only one way of insuring the immediate transportation of the remains to England, and that was to hire a vessel. Impatient to return, and resolved not to lose sight of the coffin till he had seen it placed in Wincot vault, Monkton decided immediately on hiring the first ship that could be obtained. The vessel in port which we were informed could soonest be got ready for sea was a Sicilian brig, and this vessel my friend accordingly engaged. The best dock-yard artisans that could be got were set to work, and the smartest captain and crew to be picked up on an emergency in Naples were chosen to navigate the brig.

Monkton, after again expressing in the warmest terms his gratitude for the services I had rendered him, disclaimed any intention of asking me to accompany him on the voyage to England. Greatly to his surprise and delight, however, I offered of my own accord to take passage in the brig. The strange coincidences I had witnessed, the extraordinary discovery I had hit on since our first meeting in Naples, had made his one great interest in life my one great interest for the time being as well. I shared none of his delusions, poor fellow; but it is hardly an exaggeration to say that my eagerness to follow our remarkable adventure to its end was as great as his anxiety to see the coffin laid in Wincot vault. Curiosity influenced me, I am afraid, almost as strongly as friendship, when I offered myself as the companion of his voyage home.

We set sail for England on a calm and lovely afternoon.

For the first time since I had known him, Monkton seemed to be in high spirits. He talked and jested on all sorts of subjects, and laughed at me for allowing my cheerfulness to be affected by the dread of seasickness. I had really no such fear; it was my excuse to my friend for a return of that unaccountable depression under which I had suffered at Fondi. Everything was in our favor; everybody on board the brig was in good spirits. The captain was delighted with the vessel; the crew, Italians and Maltese, were in high glee at the prospect of making a short voyage on high wages in a well-provisioned ship. I alone felt heavy at heart. There was no valid reason that I could assign to myself for the melancholy that oppressed me, and yet I struggled against it in vain.

Late on our first night at sea, I made a discovery which was by no means calculated to restore my spirits to their usual equilibrium. Monkton was in the cabin, on the floor of which had been placed the packing-case containing the coffin, and I was on deck. The wind had fallen almost to a calm, and I was lazily watching the sails of the brig as they flapped from time to time against the masts, when the captain approached, and, drawing me out of hearing of the man at the helm, whispered in my ear:

"There's something wrong among the men forward. Did you observe how suddenly they all became silent just before sunset?"

I had observed it, and told him so.

"There's a Maltese boy on board," pursued the captain, "who is a smart enough lad, but a bad one to deal with. I have found out that he has been telling the men there is a dead body inside that packing-case of your friend's in the cabin."

My heart sank as he spoke. Knowing the superstitious irrationality of sailors—of foreign sailors especially—I had taken care to spread a report on board the brig, before the coffin was shipped, that the packing-case contained a valuable marble statue which Mr. Monkton prized highly, and was unwilling to trust out of his own sight. How could this Maltese boy have discovered that the pretended statue was a human corpse? As I pondered over the question, my suspicions fixed themselves on Monkton's servant, who spoke Italian fluently, and whom I knew to be an incorrigible gossip. The man denied it when I charged him with betraying us, but I have never believed his denial to this day.

"The little imp won't say where he picked up this notion of his about the dead body," continued the captain. "It's not my place to pry into secrets; but I advise you to call the crew aft, and contradict the boy, whether he speaks the truth or not. The men are a parcel of fools who believe in ghosts, and all the rest of it. Some of them say they would never have signed our articles if they had known they were going to sail with a dead man; others only grumble; but I'm afraid we shall have some trouble with them all, in case of rough weather, unless the boy is contradicted by you or the other gentleman. The men say that if either you or your friend tell them on your words of honor that the Maltese is a liar, they will hand him up to be rope's-ended accordingly; but that if you won't, they have made up their minds to believe the boy."

Here the captain paused and awaited my answer. I could give him none. I felt hopeless under our desperate emergency. To get the boy punished by giving my word of honor to support a direct falsehood was not to be thought of even for a moment. What other means of extrication from this miserable dilemma remained? None that I could think of. I thanked the captain for his attention to our interests, told him I would take time to consider what course I should pursue, and begged that he would say nothing to my friend about the discovery he had made. He promised to be silent, sulkily enough, and walked away from me.

We had expected the breeze to spring up with the morning, but no breeze came. As it wore on toward noon the atmosphere became insufferably sultry, and the sea looked as smooth as glass. I saw the captain's eye turn often and anxiously to windward. Far away in that direction, and alone in the blue heaven, I observed a little black cloud, and asked if it would bring us any wind.

"More than we want," the captain replied, shortly; and then, to my astonishment, ordered the crew aloft to take in sail. The execution of this maneuver showed but too plainly the temper of the men; they did their work sulkily and slowly, grumbling and murmuring among themselves. The captain's manner, as he urged them on with oaths and threats, convinced me we were in danger. I looked again to windward. The one little cloud had enlarged to a great bank of murky vapor, and the sea at the horizon had changed in colour.

"The squall will be on us before we know where we are," said the captain. "Go below; you will be only in the way here."

I descended to the cabin, and prepared Monkton for what was coming. He was still questioning me about what I had observed on deck when the storm burst on us. We felt the little brig strain for an instant as if she would part in two, then she seemed to be swinging round with us, then to be quite still for a moment, trembling in every timber. Last came a shock which hurled us from our seats, a deafening crash, and a flood of water pouring into the cabin. We clambered, half drowned, to the deck. The brig had, in the nautical phrase, "broached to," and she now lay on her beam-ends.

Before I could make out anything distinctly in the horrible confusion except the one tremendous certainty that we were entirely at the mercy of the sea, I heard a voice from the fore part of the ship which stilled the clamoring and shouting of the rest of the crew in an instant. The words were in Italian, but I understood their fatal meaning only too easily. We had sprung a leak, and the sea was pouring into the ship's hold like the race of a mill-stream. The captain did not lose his presence of mind in this fresh emergency. He called for his ax to cut away the foremast, and, ordering some of the crew to help him, directed the others to rig out the pumps.

The words had hardly passed his lips before the men broke into open mutiny. With a savage look at me, their ringleader declared that the passengers might do as they pleased, but that he and his messmates were determined to take to the boat, and leave the accursed ship, and *the dead man in her,* to go to the bottom together. As he spoke there was a shout among the sailors, and I observed some of them pointing derisively behind me. Looking round, I saw Monkton, who had hitherto kept close at my side, making his way back to the cabin. I followed him directly, but the water and confusion on deck, and the impossibility, from the position of the brig, of moving the feet without the slow assistance of the hands, so impeded my progress that it was impossible for me to overtake him. When I had got below he was crouched upon the coffin, with the water on the cabin floor whirling and splashing about him as the ship heaved and plunged. I saw a warning brightness in his eyes, a warning flush on his cheek, as I approached and said to him:

"There is nothing left for it, Alfred, but to bow to our misfortune, and do the best we can to save our lives."

"Save yours," he cried, waving his hand to me, "for *you* have a future before you. Mine is gone when this coffin goes to the bottom. If the ship sinks, I shall know that the fatality is accomplished, and shall sink with her."

I saw that he was in no state to be reasoned with or persuaded, and raised myself again to the deck. The men were cutting away all obstacles so as to launch the longboat placed amidships over the depressed bulwark of the brig as she lay on her side, and the captain, after having made a last vain exertion to restore his authority, was looking on at them in silence. The violence of the squall seemed already to be spending itself, and I asked whether there was really no chance for us if we remained by the ship. The captain answered that there might have been the best chance if the men had obeyed his orders, but that now there was none. Knowing that I could place no dependence on the presence of mind of Monkton's servant, I confided to the captain, in the fewest and plainest words, the condition of my unhappy friend, and asked if I might depend on his help. He nodded his head, and we descended together to the cabin. Even at this day it costs me pain to write of the terrible necessity to which the strength and obstinacy of Monkton's delusion reduced us in the last resort. We were compelled to secure his hands, and drag him by main force to the deck. The men were on the point of launching the boat, and refused at first to receive us into it.

"You cowards!" cried the captain, "have we got the dead man with us this time? Isn't he going to the bottom along with the brig? Who are you afraid of when we get into the boat?"

This sort of appeal produced the desired effect; the men became ashamed of themselves, and retracted their refusal.

Just as we pushed off from the sinking ship Alfred made an effort to break from me, but I held him firm, and he never repeated the attempt. He sat by me with drooping head, still and silent, while the sailors rowed away from the vessel; still and silent when, with one accord, they paused at a little distance off, and we all waited and watched to see the brig sink; still and silent, even when that sinking happened, when the laboring hull plunged slowly into a hollow of the sea—hesitated, as it seemed, for one moment, rose a little again, then sank to rise no more.

Sank with her dead freight—sank, and snatched forever from our power the corpse which we had discovered almost by a miracle—those jealously-preserved remains, on the safe-keeping of which rested so strangely the hopes and the love-destinies of two living beings! As the last signs of the ship in the depths of the waters.

I felt Monkton trembling all over as he sat close at my side, and heard him repeating to himself, sadly, and many times over, the name of "Ada."

I tried to turn his thoughts to another subject, but it was useless. He pointed over the sea to where the brig had once been, and where nothing was left to look at but the rolling waves.

"The empty place will now remain empty forever in Wincot vault."

As he said these words, he fixed his eyes for a moment sadly and earnestly on my face, then looked away, leaned his cheek on his hand, and spoke no more.

We were sighted long before nightfall by a trading vessel, were taken on board, and landed at Cartagena in Spain. Alfred never held up his head, and never once spoke to me of his own accord the whole time we were at sea in the merchantman. I observed, however, with alarm, that he talked often and incoherently to himself—constantly muttering the lines of the old prophecy—constantly referring to the fatal place that was empty in Wincot vault—constantly repeating in broken accents, which it affected me inexpressibly to hear, the name of the poor girl who was awaiting his return to England. Nor were these the only causes for the apprehension that I now felt on his account. Toward the end of our voyage he began to suffer from alternations of fever-fits and shivering-fits, which I ignorantly imagined to be attacks of ague. I was soon undeceived. We had hardly been a day on shore before he became so much worse that I secured the best medical assistance Cartagena could afford. For a day or two the doctors differed, as usual, about the nature of his complaint, but ere long alarming symptoms displayed themselves. The medical men declared that his life was in danger, and told me that his disease was brain fever.

Shocked and grieved as I was, I hardly knew how to act at first under the fresh responsibility now laid upon me. Ultimately I decided on writing to the old priest who had been Alfred's tutor, and who, as I knew, still resided at Wincot Abbey. I told this gentleman all that had happened, begged him to break my melancholy news as gently as possible to Miss Elmslie, and assured him of my resolution to remain with Monkton to the last.

After I had dispatched my letter, and had sent to Gibraltar to secure the best English medical advice that could be obtained, I felt that I had done my best, and that nothing remained but to wait and hope.

Many a sad and anxious hour did I pass by my poor friend's bedside. Many a time did I doubt whether I had done right in giving any encouragement to his delusion. The reasons for doing so which had suggested themselves to me after my first interview with him seemed, however, on reflection, to be valid reasons still. The only way of hastening his return to England and to Miss Elmslie, who was pining for that return, was the way I had taken. It was not my fault that a disaster which no man could foresee had overthrown all his projects and all mine. But, now that the calamity had happened and was irretrievable, how, in the event of his physical recovery, was his moral malady to be combated?

When I reflected on the hereditary taint in his mental organization, on that first childish fright of Stephen Monkton from which he had never recovered, on the perilously-secluded life that he had led at the Abbey, and on his firm persuasion of the reality of the apparition by which he believed himself to be constantly followed, I confess I despaired of shaking his superstitious faith in every word and line of the old family prophecy. If the series of striking coincidences which appeared to attest its truth had made a strong and lasting impression on *me* (and this was assuredly the case), how could I wonder that they had produced the effect of absolute conviction on *his* mind, constituted as it was? If I argued with him, and he answered me, how could I rejoin? If he said, "The prophecy points at the last of the family: *I* am the last of the family. The prophecy mentions an empty place in Wincot vault; there is such an empty place there at this moment. On the faith of the prophecy I told you that Stephen Monkton's body was unburied, and you found that it was unburied"—if he said this, what use would it be for me to reply, "These are only strange coincidences after all?"

The more I thought of the task that lay before me, if he recovered, the more I felt inclined to despond. The oftener the English physician who attended on him said to me, "He may get the better of the fever, but he has a fixed idea, which never leaves him night or day, which has unsettled his reason, and which will end in killing him, unless you or some of his friends can remove it"—the oftener I heard this, the more acutely I felt my own powerlessness, the more I shrank from every idea that was connected with the hopeless future.

I had only expected to receive my answer from Wincot in the shape of a letter. It was consequently a great surprise, as well as a great relief, to be informed one day that two gentlemen wished to speak with me, and to find that of these two gentlemen the first was the old priest, and the second a male relative of Mrs. Elmslie.

Just before their arrival the fever symptoms had disappeared, and Alfred had been pronounced out of danger. Both the priest and his companion were eager to know when the sufferer would be strong enough to travel. They had come to Cartagena expressly to take him home with them, and felt far more hopeful than I did of the restorative effects of his native air. After all the questions connected with the first important point of the journey to England had been asked and answered, I ventured to make some inquiries after Miss Elmslie. Her relative informed me that she was suffering both in body and in mind from excess of anxiety on Alfred's account. They had been obliged to deceive her as to the dangerous nature of his illness in order to deter her from accompanying the priest and her relation on their mission to Spain.

Slowly and imperfectly, as the weeks wore on, Alfred regained something of his former physical strength, but no alteration appeared in his illness as it affected his mind.

From the very first day of his advance toward recovery, it had been discovered that the brain fever had exercised the strangest influence over his faculties of memory. All recollection of recent events was gone from him. Everything connected with Naples, with me, with his journey to Italy, had dropped in some mysterious manner entirely out of his remembrance. So completely had all late circumstances passed from his memory that, though he recognized the old priest and his own servant easily on the first days of his convalescence, he never recognized me, but regarded me with such a wistful, doubting expression, that I felt inexpressibly pained when I approached his bedside. All his questions were about Miss Elmslie and Wincot Abbey, and all his talk referred to the period when his father was yet alive.

The doctors augured good rather than ill from this loss of memory of recent incidents, saying that it would turn out to be temporary, and that it answered the first great healing purpose of keeping his mind at ease. I tried to believe them—tried to feel as sanguine, when the day came for his departure, as the old friends felt who were taking him home. But the effort was too much for me. A foreboding that I should never see him again oppressed my heart, and the tears came into my eyes as I saw the worn figure of my poor friend half helped, half lifted into the traveling-carriage, and borne away gently on the road toward home.

He had never recognized me, and the doctors had begged that I would give him, for some time to come, as few opportunities as possible of doing so. But for this request I should have accompanied him to England. As it was, nothing better remained for me to do than to change the scene, and recruit as I best could my energies of body and mind, depressed of late by much watching and anxiety. The famous cities of Spain were not new to me, but I visited them again and revived old impressions of the Alhambra and Madrid. Once or twice I thought of making a pilgrimage to the East, but late events had sobered and altered me. That yearning, unsatisfied feeling which we call "homesickness" began to prey upon my heart, and I resolved to return to England.

I went back by way of Paris, having settled with the priest that he should write to me at my banker's there as soon as he could after Alfred had returned to Wincot. If I had gone to the East, the letter would have been forwarded to me. I wrote to prevent this; and, on my arrival at Paris, stopped at the banker's before I went to my hotel.

The moment the letter was put into my hands, the black border on the envelope told me the worst. He was dead.

There was but one consolation—he had died calmly, almost happily, without once referring to those fatal chances which had wrought the fulfillment of the ancient prophecy. "My beloved pupil," the old priest wrote, "seemed to rally a little the first few days after his return, but he gained no real strength, and soon suffered a slight relapse of fever. After this he sank gradually and gently day by day, and so departed from us on the last dread journey. Miss Elmslie (who knows that I am writing this) desires me to express her deep and lasting gratitude for all your kindness to Alfred. She told me when we brought him back that she had waited for him as his promised wife, and that she would nurse him now as a wife should; and she never left him. His face was turned toward her, his hand was clasped in hers when he died. It will console you to know that he never mentioned events at Naples, or the shipwreck that followed them, from the day of his return to the day of his death."

Three days after reading the letter I was at Wincot, and heard all the details of Alfred's last moments from the priest. I felt a shock which it would not be very easy for me to analyze or explain when I heard that he had been buried, at his own desire, in the fatal Abbey vault.

The priest took me down to see the place—a grim, cold, subterranean building, with a low roof, supported on heavy Saxon arches. Narrow niches, with the ends only of coffins visible within them, ran down each side of the vault. The nails and silver ornaments flashed here and there as my companion moved past them with a lamp in his hand. At the lower end of the place he stopped, pointed to a niche, and said, "He lies there, between his father and mother." I looked a little further on, and saw what appeared at first like a long dark tunnel. "That is only an empty niche," said the priest, following me. "If the body of Mr. Stephen Monkton had been brought to Wincot, his coffin would have been placed there."

A chill came over me, and a sense of dread which I am ashamed of having felt now, but which I could not combat then. The blessed light of day was pouring down gayly at the other end of the vault through the open door. I turned my back on the empty niche, and hurried into the sunlight and the fresh air.

As I walked across the grass glade leading down to the vault, I heard the rustle of a woman's dress behind me, and turning round, saw a young lady advancing, clad in deep mourning. Her sweet, sad face, her manner as she held out her hand, told me who it was in an instant.

"I heard that you were here," she said, "and I wished—" Her voice faltered a little. My heart ached as I saw how her lip trembled, but before I could say anything she recovered herself and went on: "I wished to take your hand, and thank you for your brotherly kindness to Alfred; and I wanted to tell you that I am sure in all you did you acted tenderly and considerately for the best. Perhaps you may be soon going away from home again, and we may not meet any more. I shall never, never forget that you were kind to him when he wanted a friend, and that you have the greatest claim of any one on earth to be gratefully remembered in my thoughts as long as I live."

The inexpressible tenderness of her voice, trembling a little all the while she spoke, the pale beauty of her face, the artless candor in her sad, quiet eyes, so affected me that I could not trust myself to answer her at first except by gesture. Before I recovered my voice she had given me her hand once more and had left me.

I never saw her again. The chances and changes of life kept us apart. When I last heard of her, years and years ago, she was faithful to the memory of the dead, and was Ada Elmslie still for Alfred Monkton's sake.

The Old Nurse's Story

Elizabeth Gaskell

You know, my dears, that your mother was an orphan, and an only child; and I dare say you have heard that your grandfather was a clergyman up in Westmoreland, where I come from. I was just a girl in the village school, when, one day, your grandmother came in to ask the mistress if there was any scholar there who would do for a nurse-maid; and mighty proud I was, I can tell ye, when the mistress called me up, and spoke to my being a good girl at my needle, and a steady honest girl, and one whose parents were very respectable, though they might be poor. I thought I should like nothing better than to serve the pretty young lady, who was blushing as deep as I was, as she spoke of the coming baby, and what I should have to do with it. However, I see you don't care so much for this part of my story, as for what you think is to come, so I'll tell you at once. I was engaged and settled at the parsonage before Miss Rosamond (that was the baby, who is now your mother) was born. To be sure, I had little enough to do with her when she came, for she was never out of her mother's arms, and slept by her all night long; and proud enough was I sometimes when missis trusted her to me. There never was such a baby before or since, though you've all of you been fine enough in your turns; but for sweet, winning ways, you've none of you come up to your mother. She took after her mother, who was a real lady born; a Miss Furnivall, a granddaughter of Lord Furnivall's, in Northumberland. I believe she had neither brother nor sister, and had been brought up in my lord's family till she had married your grandfather, who was just a curate, son to a shopkeeper in Carlisle—but a clever, fine gentleman as ever was—and one who was a right-down hard worker in his parish, which was very wide, and scattered all abroad over the Westmoreland Fells. When our mother, little Miss Rosamond, was about four or five years old, both her parents died in a fortnight—one after the other. Ah! that was a sad time. My pretty young mistress and me was looking for another baby, when my master came home from one of his long rides, wet, and tired, and took the fever he died of; and then she never held up her head again, but just lived to see her dead baby, and have it laid on her breast before she sighed away her life. My mistress had asked me, on her death-bed, never to leave Miss Rosamond; but if she had never spoken a word, I would have gone with the little child to the end of the world.

The next thing, and before we had well stilled our sobs, the executors and guardians came to settle the affairs. They were my poor young mistress's own cousin, Lord Furnivall, and Mr. Esthwaite, my master's brother, a shopkeeper in Manchester; not so well to do then, as he was afterwards, and with a large family rising about him. Well! I don't know if it were their settling, or because of a letter my mistress wrote on her death-bed to her cousin, my lord; but somehow it was settled that Miss Rosamond and me were to go to Furnivall Manor House, in Northumberland, and my lord spoke as if it had been her mother's wish that she should live with his family, and as if he had no objections, for that one or two more or less could make no difference in so grand a household. So, though that was not the way in which I should have wished the coming of my bright and pretty pet to have been looked at—who was like a sunbeam in any family, be it never so grand—I was well pleased that all the folks in the Dale should stare and admire, when the heard I was going to be young lady's maid at my Lord Furnivall's at Furnivall Manor.

But I made a mistake in thinking we were to go and live where my lord did. It turned out that the family had left Furnivall Manor House fifty years or more. I could not hear that my poor young mistress had ever been there, though she had been brought up in the family; and I was sorry for that, for I should have liked Miss Rosamond's youth to have passed where her mother's had been.

My lord's gentleman, from whom I asked as man questions as I durst, said that the Manor House was at the foot of the Cumberland Fells, and a very grand place; that an old Miss Furnivall, a great-aunt of my lord's, lived there, with only a few servants; but that it was a very healthy place, and my lord had thought that it would suit Miss Rosamond very well for a few years, and that her being there might perhaps amuse his old aunt.

I was bidden by my lord to have Miss Rosamond's things ready by a certain day. He was a stern proud man, as they say all the Lords Furnivall were; and he never spoke a word more than was necessary. Folk did say he had loved my young mistress; but that, because she knew that his father would object, she would never listen to him, and married Mr. Esthwaite; but I don't know. He never married at any rate. But he never took much notice of Miss Rosamond; which I thought he might have done if he had cared for her dead mother. He sent his gentleman with us to the Manor House, telling him to join him at Newcastle that same evening; so there was no great length of time for him to make as known to all the strangers before he, too, shook us off; and we were left, two lonely young things (I was not eighteen), in the great old Manor House. It seems like yesterday that we drove there. We had left our own dear parsonage very early, and we had both cried as if our hearts would break, though we were travelling in my lord's carriage, which I thought so much of once. And now it was long past noon on a September day, and we stopped to change horses for the last time at a little smoky town, all full of colliers and miners. Miss Rosamond had fallen asleep, but Mr. He told me to waken her, that she might see the park and the Manor House as we drove up. I thought it rather a pity; but I did what he bade me, for fear he should complain of me to my lord. We had left all signs of a town, or even a village, and were then inside the gates of a large wild park—not like the parks here in the south, but with rocks, and the noise of running water, and gnarled thorn-trees, and old oaks, all white and peeled with age.

The road went up about two miles, and then we saw a great and stately house, with many trees close around it, so close that in some places their branches dragged against the walls when the wind blew; and some hung broken down; for no one seemed to take much charge of the place,—to lop the wood, or to keep the moss-covered carriage-way in order. Only in front of the house all was clear. The great oval drive was without a weed; and neither tree nor creeper was allowed to grow over the long, many-windowed front; at both sides of which a wing projected, which were each the ends of other side fronts; for the house, although it was so desolate, was even grander than I expected. Behind it rose the Fells, which seemed unenclosed and bare enough; and on the left hand of the house, as you stood facing it, was a little, old-fashioned flower-garden, as I found out afterwards. A door opened out n on it from the west front; it had been scooped out of the thick ark wood for some old Lady Furnivall; but the branches of the great forest trees had grown and overshadowed it again, and there were very few flowers that would live there at that time.

When we drove up to the great front entrance, and went into the hall I thought we should be lost—it was so large, and vast, and grand. There was a chandelier all of bronze, hung down from the middle of the ceiling; and I had never seen one before, and looked at it all in amaze. Then, at one end of the hall, was a great fire-place, as large as the sides of the houses in my country, with massy andirons and dogs to hold the wood; and by it were heavy old-fashioned sofas. At the opposite end of the hall, to the left as you went in—on the western side—was an organ built into the wall, and so large that it filled up the best part of that end. Beyond it, on the same side, was a door; and opposite, on each side of the fire-place, were also doors leading to the east front; but those I never went through as long as I stayed in the house, so I can't tell you what lay beyond.

The afternoon was closing in and the hall, which had no fire lighted in it, looked dark and gloomy, but we did not stay there a moment. The old servant, who had opened the door for us bowed to Mr. Henry, and took us in through the door at the further side of the great organ, and led us through several smaller halls and passages into the west drawing-room, where he said that Miss Furnivall was sitting. Poor little Miss Rosamond held very tight to me, as if she were scared and lost in that great place, and as for myself, I was not much better. The west drawing-room was very cheerful-looking, with a warm fire in it, and plenty of good, comfortable furniture about. Miss Furnivall was an old lady not far from eighty, I should think, but I do not know. She was thin and tall, and had a face as full of fine wrinkles as if they had been drawn all over it with a needle's point. Her eyes were very watchful to make up, I suppose, for her being so deaf as to be obliged to use a trumpet. Sitting with her, working at the same great piece of tapestry, was Mrs. Stark, her maid and companion, and almost as old as she was. She had lived with Miss Furnivall ever since they both were young, and now she seemed more like a friend than a servant; she looked so cold and grey, and stony, as if she had never loved or cared for any one; and I don't suppose she did care for any one, except her mistress; and, owing to the great deafness of the latter, Mrs. Stark treated her very much as if she were a child. Mr. Henry gave some message from my lord, and then he bowed good-bye to us all—taking no notice of my sweet little Miss Rosamond's out-stretched hand—and left as standing there, being looked at by the two old ladies through their spectacles.

I was right glad when they rung for the old footman who had shown us in at first, and told him to take us to our rooms. So we went out of that great drawing-room, and into another sitting-room, and out of that, and then up a great flight of stairs, and along a broad gallery—which was something like a library, having books all down one side, and windows and writing-tables all down the other—till we came to our rooms, which I was not sorry to hear were just over the kitchens; for I began to think I should be lost in that wilderness of a house. There was an old nursery, that had been used for all the little lords and ladies long ago, with a pleasant fire burning in the grate, and the kettle boiling on the hob, and tea things spread out on the table; and out of that room was the night-nursery, with a little crib for Miss Rosamond close to my bed. And old James called up Dorothy, his wife, to bid us welcome; and both he and she were so hospitable and kind, that by and by Miss Rosamond and me felt quite at home; and by the time tea was over, she was sitting on Dorothy's knee, and chattering away as fast as her little tongue could go. I soon found out that Dorothy was from Westmoreland, and that bound her and me together or, as it were; and I would never wish to meet with kinder people than were old James and his wife. James had lived pretty nearly all his life in my lord's family, and thought there was no one so grand as they. He even looked down a little on his wife; because, till he had married her, she had never lived in any but a farmer's household. But he was very fond of her, as well he might be. They had one servant under them, to do all the rough work. Agnes they called her; and she and me, and James and Dorothy, with Miss Furnivall and Mrs. Stark, made up the family; a ways remembering my sweet little Miss Rosamond! I used to wonder what they had done before she came, they thought so much of her now. Kitchen and drawing-room, it was all the same. The hard, sad Miss Furnivall, and the cold Mrs. Stark, looked pleased when she came fluttering in like a bird, playing and pranking hither and thither, with a continual murmur, an pretty prattle of gladness. I am sure, they were sorry many a time when she flitted away into the kitchen, though they were too proud to ask her to stay with them, and were a little surprised at her taste; though to be sure, as Mrs. Stark said, it was not to be wondered at, remembering what stock her father had come of. The great, old rambling house, was a famous place for little Miss Rosamond. She made expeditions all over it, with me at her heels; all, except the east wing, which was never opened, and whither we never thought of going. But in the western and northern part was many a pleasant room; full of things that were curiosities to us, though they might not have been to people who had seen more. The windows were darkened by the sweeping boughs of the trees, and the ivy which had overgrown them: but, in the green gloom, we could manage to see old China jars and carved ivory boxes, and great heavy books, and, above all, the old pictures!

Once, I remember, my darling would have Dorothy go with us to tell us who the all were; for the were all portraits of some of my lord's family, though Dorothy could not tell us the names of every one. We had gone through most of the rooms, when we came to the old state drawing-room over the hall, and there was a picture of Miss Furnivall; or, as she was called in those days, Miss Grace, for she was the younger sister. Such a beauty she must have been! but with such a set, proud look, and such scorn looking out of her handsome eyes, with her eyebrows just a little raised, as if she wondered how any one could have the impertinence to look at her; and her lip curled at us, as we stood there gazing. She had a dress on, the like of which I had never seen before, but it was all the fashion when she was young: a hat of some soft white stuff like beaver, pulled a little over her brows, and a beautiful plume of feathers sweeping round it on one side; and her gown of blue satin was open in front to a quilted white stomacher.

"Well, to be sure!" said I, when I had gazed my fill. "Flesh is grass, they do say; but who would have thought that Miss Furnivall had been such an out-and-out beauty, to see her now?"

"Yes," said Dorothy. "Folks change sadly. But if what my master's father used to say was true, Miss Furnivall, the elder sister, was handsomer than Miss Grace. Her picture is here somewhere; but, if I show it you, you must never let on, even to James, that you have seen it. Can the little lady hold her tongue, think you?" asked she.

I was not so sure, for she was such a little sweet, bold, open-spoken child, so I set her to hide herself; and then I helped Dorothy to turn a great picture, that leaned with its face towards the wall, and was not hung up as the others were. To be sure, it beat Miss Grace for beauty; and, I think, for scornful pride, too, though in that matter it might be hard to choose. I could have looked at it an hour, but Dorothy seemed half frightened at having shown it to me, and hurried it back again, and bade me run and find Miss Rosamond, for that there were some ugly places about the house, where she should like ill for the child to go. I was a brave, high-spirited girl, and thought little of what the old woman said, for I liked hide-and-seek as well as any child in the parish; so off I ran to find my little one.

As winter drew on, and the days grew shorter, I was sometimes almost certain that I heard a noise as if some one was playing on the great organ in the hall. I did not hear it every evening; but, certainly, I did very often; usually when I was sitting with Miss Rosamond, after I had put her to bed, and keeping quite still and silent in the bedroom. Then I used to hear it booming and swelling away in the distance. The first night, when I went down to my supper, I asked Dorothy who had been playing music, and James said very shortly that I was a going to take the wind soughing among the trees for music: but I saw Dorothy look at him very fearfully, and Bessy, the kitchen-maid, said something beneath her breath, and went quite white. I saw they did not like my question, so I held my peace till I was with Dorothy alone, when I knew I could get a good deal out of her. So, the next day, I watched my time, and I coaxed and asked her who it was that played the organ; for I knew that it was the organ and not the wind well enough, for all I had kept silence before James. But Dorothy had had her lesson I'll warrant, and never a word could I get from her. So then I tried Bessy, though I had always held my head rather above her, as I was evened to James and Dorothy, and she was little better than their servant. So she said must never, never tell; and if I ever told, I was never to say *she* had told me; but it was a very strange noise, and she had heard it many a time, but most of all on winter nights, and before storms; and folks did say, it was the old lord playing on the great organ in the hall, just as he used to do when he was alive; but who the old lord was, or why he played, and why he played on stormy winter evenings in particular, she either could not or would not tell me. Well! I told you I had a brave heart; and I thought it was rather pleasant to have that grand music rolling about the house, let who would be the player; for now it rose above the great gusts of wind, and wailed and triumphed just like a living creature, and then it fell to a softness most complete; only it was always music, and tunes, so it was nonsense to call it the wind. I thought at first, that it might be Miss Furnivall who played, unknown to Bessy; but, one day when I was in the hall by myself, I opened the organ and peeped all about it and around it, as I had done to the organ in Crosthwaite Church once before, and I saw it was all broken and destroyed inside, though it looked so brave and fine; and then, though it was noon-day, my flesh began to creep a little, and I shut it up, and run away pretty quickly to my own bright nursery; and I did not like hearing the music for some time after that, any more than James and Dorothy did. All this time Miss Rosamond was making herself more, and more beloved. The old ladies liked her to dine with them at their early dinner; James stood behind Miss Furnivall's chair, and I behind Miss Rosamond's all in state; and, after dinner, she would play about in a corner of the great drawing-room, as still as any mouse, while Miss Furnivall slept, and I had my dinner in the kitchen. But she was glad enough to come to me in the nursery afterwards; for, as she said, Miss Furnivall was so sad, and Mrs. Stark so dull; but she and I were merry enough; and, by-and-by, I got not to care for that weird rolling music, which did one no harm, if we did not know where it came from.

That winter was very cold. In the middle of October the frosts began, and lasted many, many weeks. I remember, one day at dinner, Miss Furnivall lifted up her sad, heavy eyes and said to Mrs. Stark, "I am afraid we shall have a terrible winter," in a strange kind of meaning way. But Mrs. Stark pretended not to hear, and talked very loud of something else. My little lad, and I did not care for the frost; not we! As long as it was dry we climbed up the steep brows, behind the house, and went up on the Fells, which were bleak, and bare enough, and there we ran races in the fresh, sharp air; and once we came down by a new path that took us past the two old gnarled holly-trees, which grew about half-way down by the east side of the house. But the days grew shorter, and shorter; and the old lord, if it was he, played away more, and more stormily and sadly on the great organ. One Sunday afternoon,—it must have been towards the end of November—I asked Dorothy to take charge of little Missey when she came out of the drawing-room, after Miss Furnivall had had her nap; for it was too cold to take her with me to church, and yet I wanted to go. And Dorothy was glad enough to promise, and was so fond of the child that all seemed well; and Bessy and I set off very briskly, though the sky hung heavy and black over the white earth, as if the night had never fully gone away; and the air, though still, was very biting and keen.

"We shall have a fall of snow," said Bessy to me. And sure enough, even while we were in church, it came down thick, in great large flakes, so thick it almost darkened the windows. It had stopped snowing before we came out, but it lay soft, thick and deep beneath our feet, as we tramped home. Before we got to the hall the moon rose, and I think it was lighter then,—what with the moon, and what with the white dazzling snow—than it had been when we went to church, between two and three o'clock. I have not told on that Miss Furnivall and Mrs. Stark never went to church: they used to read the prayers together, in their quiet gloomy way; they seemed to feel the Sunday very long without their tapestry-work to be busy at. So when went to Dorothy in the kitchen, to fetch Miss Rosamond and take her up-stairs with me, I did not much wonder when the old woman told me that the ladies had kept the child with them, and that she had never come to the kitchen, as I had bidden her, when she was tired of behaving pretty in the drawing-room. So I took off my things and went to find her, and bring her to her supper in the nursery. But when I went into the best drawing-room, there sat the two old ladies, very still and quiet, dropping out a word now and then, but looking as if nothing so bright an merry as Miss Rosamond had ever been near them. Still I thought she might be hiding from me; it was one of her pretty ways; and that she had persuaded them to look as if they knew nothing about her; so I went softly peeping under this sofa, and behind that chair, making believe I was sadly frightened at not finding her.

"What's the matter, Hester?" said Mrs. Stark sharply. I don't know if Miss Furnivall had seen me, for, as I told you, she was very deaf, and she sat quite still, idly staring into the fire, with her hopeless face. "I'm only looking for my little Rosy-Posy," replied I, still thinking that the child was there, and near me, though I could not see her.

"Miss Rosamond is not here," said Mrs. Stark. "She went away more than an hour ago to find Dorothy." And she too turned and went on looking into the fire.

My heart sank at this, and I began to wish I had never left my darling. I went back to Dorothy and told her. James was gone out for the day, but she and me and Bessy took lights and went up into the nursery first, and then we roamed over the great large house, calling and entreating Miss Rosamond to come out of her hiding place, and not frighten us to death in that way. But there was no answer; no sound.

"Oh!" said I at last, "Can she have got into the east wing and hidden there?"

But Dorothy said it was not possible, for that she herself had never been in there; that the doors were always looked, and my lord's steward had the keys, she believed; at any rate, neither she, nor James had ever seen them: so, I said I would go back, and see if, after all, she was not hidden in the drawing-room, unknown to the old ladies; and if I found her there, I said, I would whip her well for the fright she had given me;

but I never meant to do it. Well, I went back to the west drawing-room, and I told Mrs. Stark we could not find her anywhere, and asked for leave to look all about the furniture there, for I thought now, that she might have fallen asleep in some warm hidden corner; but no! we looked, Miss Furnivall got up and looked, trembling all over, and she was no where there; then we set off again, every one in the house, and looked in all the places we had searched before, but we could not find her. Miss Furnivall shivered and shook so much, that Mrs. Stark took her back into the warm drawing-room; but not before they had made me promise to bring her to them when she was found. Well-a-day! I began to think she never would be found, when I bethought me to look out into the great front court, all covered with snow. I was up-stairs when I looked out; but, it was such clear moonlight, I could see quite plain two little footprints, which might be traced from the hall door, and round the corner of the east wing. I don't know how I got down, but I tugged open the great, stiff hall door; and, throwing the skirt of my gown over my head for a cloak, I ran out. I turned the east corner, and there a black shadow fell on the snow; but when I came again into the moonlight, there were the little footmarks going up—up to the Fells. It was bitter cold; so cold that the air almost took the skin off my face as I run, but I ran on, crying to think how my poor little darling must be perished, and frightened. I was within sight of the holly-trees, when I saw a shepherd coming down the hill, bearing something in his arms wrapped in his maud. He shouted to me, and asked me if I had lost a bairn; and, when I could not speak for crying, he bore towards me, and I saw my wee bairnie lying still, and white, and stiff, in his arms, as if she had been dead. He told me he had been up the Fells to gather in his sheep, before the deep cold of night came on, and that under the holly-trees (black marks on the hill-side, where no other bush was for miles around) he had found my little lady—my lamb—my queen—my darling—stiff, and cold, in the terrible sleep which is frost-begotten. Oh! the joy, and the tears of having or in my arms once again! for I would not let him carry her; but took her, maud and all, into my own arms, and held her near my own warm neck, and heart, and felt the life stealing slowly back again into her little gentle limbs. But she was still insensible when we reached the gall, and I had no breath for speech. We went in by the kitchen door.

"Bring the warming-pan," said I; and I carried her up-stairs and began undressing her by the nursery fire, which Bess had kept up. I called my little lammie all the sweet and playful names I could think of,—even while my eyes were blinded by my tears; and at last, oh! at length she opened her large blue eyes. Then I put her into her warm bed, and sent Dorothy down to tell Miss Furnivall that all was well; and I made up my mind to sit by my darling's bedside the live-long night. She fell away into a soft sleep as soon as her pretty head had touched the pillow, and I watched by her till morning light; when she wakened up bright and clear—or so I thought at first—and, my dears, so I think now.

She said, that she had fancied that she should like to go to Dorothy, for that both the old ladies were asleep, and it was very dull in the drawing-room; and that, as she was going throng the west lobby, she saw the snow through the high window falling—falling—soft and steady; but she wanted to see it lying pretty and white on the ground; so she made her way into the great hall; and then, going to the window, she saw it bright and soft upon the drive; but while she stood there, she saw a little girl, not so old as she was, "but so pretty," said my darling, "and this little girl beckoned to me to come out; and oh, she was so pretty and so sweet, I could not choose but go." And then this other little girl had taken her by the hand, and side by side the two had gone round the east corner.

"Now you are a naughty little girl, and telling stories," said I. "What would your good mamma, that is in heaven, and never told a story in her life, say to her little Rosamond, if she heard her—and I dare say she does—telling stories!"

"Indeed, Hester," sobbed out my child, "I'm telling you true. Indeed I am."

"Don't tell me!" said I, very stern. "I tracked you by your foot-marks through the snow; there were only yours to be seen: and if on had had a little girl to go hand-in-hand with you up the hill, don't you think the foot-prints would have gone along with yours?"

"I can't help it, dear, dear Hester," said she, crying, "if they did not; I never looked at her feet, but she held my hand fast and tight in her little one, and it was very, very cold. She took me up the Fell-path, up to the holly trees; and there I saw a lady weeping and crying; but when she saw me, she hushed her weeping, and smiled very proud and grand, and took me on her knee, and began to lull me to sleep; and that's all, Hester—but that is true; and my dear mamma knows it is," said she, crying. So I thought the child was in a fever, and pretended to believe her, as she went over her story—over and over again, and always the same. At last Dorothy knocked at the door with Miss Rosamond's breakfast; and she told me the old ladies were down in the eating parlour, and that they wanted to speak to me. They had both been into the night-nursery the evening before, but it was after Miss Rosamond was asleep; so they had only looked at her—not asked me any questions.

"I shall catch it," thought I to myself, as I went along the north gallery. "And yet," I thought, taking courage, "it was in their charge I left her; and it's they that's to blame for letting her steal away unknown and unwatched." So I went in boldly, and told my story. I told it all to Miss Furnivall, shouting it close to her ear; but when I came to the mention of the other little girl out in the snow, coaxing and tempting her out, and wiling her up to the grand and beautiful lady by the holly-tree, she threw her arms up—her old and withered arms—and cried aloud, "Oh! Heaven, forgive! Have mercy!"

Mrs. Stark took hold of her; roughly enough, I thought; but she was past Mrs. Stark's management, and spoke to me, in a kind of wild warning and authority.

"Hester! keep her from that child! It will lure her to her death! That evil child! Tell her it is a wicked, naughty child." Then, Mrs. Stark hurried me out of the room; where, indeed, I was glad enough to go; but Miss Furnivall kept shrieking out, "Oh! have mercy! Wilt Thou never forgive! It is many a long year ago—"

I was very uneasy in my mind after that. I durst never leave Miss Rosamond, night or day, for fear lest she might slip off again, after some fancy or other; and all the more, because I thought I could make out that Miss Furnivall was crazy, from their odd ways about her; and I was afraid lest something of the same kind (which might be in the family, you know) hung over my darling. And the great frost never ceased all this time; and, whenever it was a more stormy night than usual, between the gusts, and through the wind, we heard the old lord playing on the great organ. But, old lord, or not, wherever Miss Rosamond went, there I followed; for my love for her, pretty helpless orphan, was stronger than my fear for the grand and terrible sound. Besides, it rested with me to keep her cheerful and merry, as beseemed her age. So we played together, and wandered together, here and there, and everywhere; for I never dared to lose sight of her again in that large and rambling house. And so it happened, that one afternoon, not long before Christmas day, we were playing together on the billiard-table in the great hall (not that we knew the right way of playing, but she liked to roll the smooth ivory balls with her pretty hands, and I liked to do whatever she did); and, by-and-by, without our noticing it, it grew dusk indoors, though it was still light in the open air, and I was thinking of taking her back into the nursery, when, all of a sudden, she cried out:

"Look, Hester! look! there is my poor little girl out in the snow!"

I turned towards the long narrow windows, and there, sure enough, I saw a little girl, less than to Miss Rosamond—dressed all unfit to be out-of-doors such a bitter night—crying, and beating against the window-panes, as if she wanted to be let in. She seemed to sob and wail, till Miss Rosamond could bear it no longer, and was flying to the door to open it, when, all of a sudden, and close upon us, the great organ pealed out so loud and thundering, it fairly made me tremble; and all the more, when I remembered me that, even in the stillness of that dead, cold weather, I had heard no sound of little battering hands upon the window-glass, although the Phantom Child had seemed to put forth all its force; and, although I had seen it wail and cry, no faintest touch of sound had fallen upon my ears. Whether I remembered all this at the very moment, do not know; the great organ sound had so stunned me into terror; but this I know, I caught up Miss Rosamond before she got the hall-door opened, and clutched her, and carried her away, kicking and screaming, into the large bright kitchen, where Dorothy and Agnes were busy with their mince-pies.

"What is the matter with my sweet one?" cried Dorothy, as I bore in Miss Rosamond, who was sobbing as if her heart would break.

"She won't let me open the door for my little girl to come in; and she'll die if she is out on the Fells all night. Cruel, naughty Hester," she said, slapping me; but she might have struck harder, for I had seen a look of ghastly terror on Dorothy's face, which made my very blood run cold.

"Shut the back kitchen door fast, and bolt it well," said she to Agnes. She said no more; she gave me raisins and almonds to quiet Miss Rosamond: but she sobbed about the little girl in the snow, and would not touch any of the good things. I was thankful when she cried herself to sleep in bed. Then I stole down to the kitchen, and told Dorothy I had made up my mind. I would carry my darling back to my father's house in Applethwaite; where, if we lived humbly, we lived at peace. I said I had been frightened enough with the old lord's organ-playing; but now, that I had seen for myself this little moaning child, all decked out as no child in the neighbourhood could be, beating and battering to get in, yet always without any sound or noise—with the dark wound on its right shoulder; and that Miss Rosamond had known it again for the phantom that had nearly lured her to her death (which Dorothy knew was true); I would stand it no longer.

I saw Dorothy change colour once or twice. When I had done, she told me she did not think I could take Miss Rosamond with me, for that she was my lord's ward, and I had no right over her; and she asked me, would I leave the child that I was so fond of, just for sounds and sights that could do me no harm; and that they had all had to get used to in their turns? I was all in a hot, trembling passion; and I said it was very well for her to talk, that knew what these sights and noises betokened, and that had, perhaps, had something to do with the Spectre-Child while it was alive. And I taunted her so, that she told me all she knew, at last; and then I wished I had never been told, for it only made me more afraid than ever.

She said she had heard the tale from old neighbours, that were alive when she was first married; when folks used to come to the hall sometimes, before it had got such a bad name on the country side: it might not be true, or it might, what she had been told.

The old lord was Miss Furnivall's father—Miss Grace, as Dorothy called her, for Miss Maude was the elder, and Miss Furnivall by rights. The old lord was eaten up with pride. Such a proud man was never seen or heard of; and his daughters were like him. No one was good enough to wed them, although they had choice enough; for they were the great beauties of their day, as I had seen by their portraits, where they hung in the state drawing-room. But, as the old saying is, "Pride will have a fall"; and these two haughty beauties fell in love with the same man, and he no better than a foreign musician, whom their father had down from London to play music with him at the Manor House. For, above all things, next to his pride, the old lord loved music. He could play on nearly every instrument that ever was heard of: and it was a strange thing it did not soften him; but he was a fierce dour old man, and had broken his poor wife's heart with his cruelty, they said. He was mad after music, and would pay any money for it. So he got this foreigner to come; who made such beautiful music, that they said the very birds on the trees stopped their singing to listen. And, by degrees, this foreign gentleman got such a hold over the old lord, that nothing would serve him but that he must come ever year; and it was he that had the great organ brought from Holland, and built up in the hall, where it stood now. He taught the old lord to play on it; but many and many a time, when Lord Furnivall was thinking of nothing but his fine organ, and his finer music, the dark foreigner was walking abroad in the woods with one of the young ladies; now Miss Maude, and then Miss Grace.

Miss Maude won the day and carried off the prize, such as it was; and he and she were married, all unknown to any one; and before he made his next yearly visit, she had been confined of a little girl at a farm-house on the Moors, while her father and Miss Grace thought she was away at Doncaster Races. But though she was a wife and a mother, she was not a bit softened, but as haughty and as passionate as ever; and perhaps more so, for she was jealous of Miss Grace, to, whom her foreign husband paid a deal of court-by way of blinding her—as he told his wife. But Miss Grace triumphed over Miss Maude, and Miss Maude grew fiercer and fiercer, both with her husband and with her sister; and the former—who could easily shake off what was disagreeable, and hide himself in foreign countries—went away a month before his usual time that summer, and half-threatened that he would never come back again. Meanwhile, the little girl was left at the farm-house, and her mother used to have her horse saddled and galloped wildly over the hills to see her once every week, at the very east—for where she loved, she loved; and where she hated, she hated. And the old lord went on playing—playing on his organ; and the servants thought the sweet music he made had soothed down his awful temper, of which (Dorothy said) some terrible tales could be told. He grew infirm too, and had to walk with a crutch; and his son—that was the present Lord Furnivall's father—was with the army in America, and the other son at sea; so Miss Maude had it pretty much her own way, and she and Miss Grace grew colder and bitterer to each other every day; till at last they hardly ever spoke, except when the old lord was by. The foreign musician came again the next summer, but it was or the last time; for they led him such a life with their jealousy and their passions, that he grew weary, and went away, and never was heard of again. And Miss Maude, who had always meant to have her marriage acknowledged when her father should be dead, was left now a deserted wife—whom nobody knew to have been married—with a child that she dared not own, although she loved it to distraction; living with a father whom she feared, and a sister whom she hated. When the next summer passed over and the dark foreigner never came, both Miss Maude and Miss Grace grew gloomy and sad; they had a haggard look about them, though they looked handsome as ever. But by-and-by Miss Maude brightened; for her father grew more and more infirm, and more than ever carried away by his music; and she and Miss Grace lived almost entirely apart, having separate rooms, the one on the west side, Miss Maude on the east—those very rooms which were now shut up. So she thought she might have her little girl with her, and no one need ever know except those who dared not speak about it, and were bound to believe that it was, as she said, a cottager's child she had taken a fancy to. All this, Dorothy said, was pretty well known; but what came afterwards no one knew, except Miss Grace, and Mrs. Stark, who was even then her maid, and much more of a friend to her than ever her sister had been. But the servants supposed, from words that were dropped, that Miss Maude had triumphed over Miss Grace, and told her that all the time the dark foreigner had been mocking her with pretended love—he was her own husband; the colour left Miss Grace's cheek and lips that very day for ever, and she was heard to say many a time that sooner or later she would have her revenge; and Mrs. Stark was for ever spying about the east rooms.

One fearful night, just after the New Year had come in, when the snow was lying thick and deep, and the flakes were still falling—fast enough to blind any one who might be out and abroad—there was a great and violent noise heard, and the old lord's voice above all, cursing and swearing awfully,—and the cries of a little child,—and the proud defiance of a fierce woman,—and the sound of a blow,—and a dead stillness,—and moans and wailing away on the hill-side! Then the old lord summoned all his servants, and told them, with terrible oaths, and words more terrible, that his daughter had disgraced herself, and that he had turned her out of doors,—her, and her child,—and that if ever they gave her help, or food—or shelter,—he prayed that they might never enter Heaven. And, all the while, Miss Grace stood by him, white and still as any stone; and when he had ended she heaved a great sigh, as much as to say her work was done, and;

her end was accomplished. But the old lord never touched his organ again, and died within the year; and no wonder! for, on the marrow of that wild and fearful night, the shepherds, coming down the Fell side, found Miss Maude sitting, all crazy and smiling, under the holly-trees, nursing a dead child,—with a terrible mark on its right shoulder. "But that was not what killed it," said Dorothy; "it was the frost and the cold;—every wild creature was in its hole, and every beast in its fold,—while the child and its mother were turned out to wander on the Fells! And now you know all! and I wonder if you are less frightened now?"

I was more frightened than ever; but I said I was not. I wished Miss Rosamond and myself well out of that dreadful house for ever; but I would not leave her, and I dared not take her away. But oh! How I watched her, and guarded her! We bolted the doors, and shut the window-shutters fast, an hour or more before dark, rather than leave them open five minutes too late. But my little lady still heard the weird child crying and mourning; and not all we could do or say, could keep her from wanting to go to her, and let her in from the cruel wind and the snow. All this time, I kept away from Miss Furnivall and Mrs. Stark, as much as ever I could; for I feared them—I know no good could be about them, with their grey hard faces, and their dreamy eyes, looking back into the ghastly years that were gone. But, even in my fear, I had a kind of pity—for Miss Furnivall, at least. Those gone down to the pit can hardly have a more hopeless look than that which was ever on her face. At last I even got so sorry for her—who never said a word but what was quite forced from her—that I prayed for her; and I taught Miss Rosamond to pray for one who had done a deadly sin; but often when she came to those words, she would listen, and start up from her knees, and say, "I hear my little girl plaining and crying very sad—Oh! let her in, or she will die!"

One night—just after New Year's Day had come at last, and the long winter had taken a turn, as I hoped—I heard the west drawing-room bell ring three times, which was the signal for me. I would not leave Miss Rosamond alone, for all she was asleep— for the old lord had been playing wilder than ever—and I feared lest my darling should waken to hear the spectre child; see her I knew she could not. I had fastened the windows too well for that. So, I took her out of her bed and wrapped her up in such outer clothes as were most handy, and carried her down to the drawing-room, where the old ladies sat at their tapestry work as usual. They looked up when I came in, and Mrs. Stark asked, quite astounded, "Why did I bring Miss Rosamond there, out of her warm bed?" I had begun to whisper, "Because I was afraid of her being tempted out while I was away, by the wild child in the snow," when she stopped me short (with a glance at Miss Furnivall), and said Miss Furnivall wanted me to undo some work she had done wrong, and which neither of them could see to unpick. So, I laid my pretty dear on the sofa, and sat down on a stool by them, and hardened my heart against them, as I heard the wind rising and howling.

Miss Rosamond slept on sound, for all the wind blew so; and Miss Furnivall said never a word, nor looked round when the gusts shook the windows. All at once she started up to her full height, and put up one hand, as if to bid us listen.

"I hear voices!" said she. "I hear terrible screams—I hear my father's voice!"

Just at that moment, my darling wakened with a sudden start: "My little girl is crying, oh, how she is crying!" and she tried to get up and go to her, but she got her feet entangled in the blanket, and I caught her up; for my flesh had begun to creep at these noises, which they heard while we could catch no sound. In a minute or two the noises came, and gathered fast, and filled our ears; we, too, heard voices and screams, and no longer heard the winter's wind that raged abroad. Mrs. Stark looked at me, and I at her, but we dared not speak. Suddenly Miss Furnivall went towards the door, out into the ante-room, through the west lobby, and opened the door into the great hall. Mrs. Stark followed, and I durst not be left, though my heart almost stopped beating for fear. I wrapped my darling tight in my arms, and went out with them. In the hall the screams were louder than ever; the sounded to come from the east wing—nearer and nearer—close on the other side of the locked-up doors—close behind them. Then I noticed that the great bronze chandelier seemed all alight, though the hall was dim, and that a fire was blazing in the vast hearth-place, though it have no heat; and I shuddered up with terror, and folded my darling closer to me. But as I did so, the east door shook, and she, suddenly struggling to get free from me, cried, "Hester! I must go. My little girl is there; I hear her; she is coming! Hester, I must go!"

I held her tight with all my strength; with a set will, I held her. If I had died, my hands would have grasped her still, I was so resolved in my mind. Miss Furnivall stood listening, and paid no regard to my darling, who had got down to the ground, and whom I, upon my knees now, was holding with both my arms clasped round her neck; she still striving and crying to get free.

All at once, the east door gave way with a thundering crash, as if torn open in a violent passion, and there came into that broad and mysterious light, the figure of a tall old man, with grey hair and gleaming eyes. He drove before him, with many a relentless gesture of abhorrence, a stern and beautiful woman, with a little child clinging to her dress.

"Oh Hester! Hester!" cried Miss Rosamond. "It's the lady! the lady below the holly-trees; and my little girl is with her. Hester. Hester! let me go to her; they are drawing me to them. I feel them—I feel them. I must go!"

Again she was almost convulsed by her efforts to et away; but I held her tighter and tighter, till I feared I should do her a hurt; but rather that than let her go towards those terrible phantoms. They passed along towards the great hall-door, where the winds howled and ravened for their prey; but before they reached that, the lady turned; and I could see that she defied the old man with a fierce and proud defiance; but then she quailed—and then she threw up her arms wildly and piteously to smile her child—her little child—from a blow from his uplifted crutch.

And Miss Rosamond was torn as by a power stronger than mine, and writhed in my arms, and sobbed (for by this time the poor darling was growing faint).

"They want me to go with them on to the Fells—they are drawing me to them. Oh, my little girl! I would come, but cruel, wicked Hester holds me very tight." But when she saw the uplifted crutch she swooned away, and I thanked God for it. Just at this moment—when the tall old man, his hair streaming as in the blast of a furnace, was going to strike the little shrinking child—Miss Furnivall, the old woman by my side, cried out, "Oh, father! father! spare the little innocent child!" But just then I saw—we all saw—another phantom shape itself, and grow clear out of the blue and misty light that filled the hall; we had not seen her till now, for it was another lady who stood by the old man, with a look of relentless hate and triumphant scorn. That figure was very beautiful to look upon, with a soft white hat drawn down over the proud brows, and a red and curling lip. It was dressed in an open robe of blue satin. I had seen that figure before. It was the likeness of Miss Furnivall in her youth; and the terrible phantoms moved on, regardless of old Miss Furnivall's wild entreaty,—and the uplifted crutch fell on the right shoulder of the little child, and the younger sister looked on, stony and deadly serene. But at that moment, the dim lights, and the fire that gave no heat, went out of themselves, and Miss Furnivall lay at our feet stricken down by the palsy—death-stricken.

Yes! she was carried to her bed that night never to rise again. She lay with her face to the wall, muttering low but muttering alway: "Alas! alas! what is done in youth can never be undone in age! What is done in youth can never be undone in age!"

The North Mail

Amelia B. Edwards

THE CIRCUMSTANCES I AM ABOUT TO RELATE TO YOU HAVE TRUTH TO RECOMMEND them. They happened to myself, and my recollection of them is as vivid as if they had taken place only yesterday. Twenty years, however, have gone by since that night. During those twenty years I have told the story to but one other person. I tell it now with a reluctance which I find it difficult to overcome. All I entreat, meanwhile, is that you will abstain from forcing your own conclusions upon me. I want nothing explained away. I desire no arguments. My mind on this subject is quite made up; and, having the testimony of my own senses to rely upon, I prefer to abide by it.

Well! It was just twenty years ago, and within a day or two of the end of the grouse season. I had been out all day with my gun, and had had no sport to speak of. The wind was due east; the month, December; the place, a bleak wide moor in the far north of England. And I had lost my way. It was not a pleasant place in which to lose one's way, with the first feathery flakes of a coming snow-storm just fluttering down upon the heather, and the leaden evening closing in all around. I shaded my eyes with my hand, and stared anxiously into the gathering dark- ness, where the purple moor-land melted into a range of low hills, some ten or twelve miles distant. Not the faintest smoke-wreath, not the tiniest cultivated patch, or fence, or sheep-track, met my eyes in any direction. There was nothing for it but to walk on, and take my chance of finding what shelter I could, by the way. So I shouldered my gun again, and pushed wearily forward; for I had been on foot since an hour after daybreak, and had eaten nothing since breakfast.

Meanwhile, the snow began to come down with ominous steadiness, and the wind fell. After this, the cold grew more intense, and the night came rapidly up. As for me, my prospects darkened with the darkening sky, and my heart grew heavy as I thought how my young wife was already watching for me through the window of our little inn parlour, and imagined all the suffering in store for her throughout this weary night. We had been married four months, and, having spent our autumn in the Highlands, were now lodging in a remote little village situated just on the verge of the great English moorlands. We were very much in love, and, of course, very happy. This morning, when we parted, she had implored me to return before dusk, and I had promised her that I would. What would I not have given to keep my word!

Even now, weary as I was, I felt that with a supper, an hour's rest, and a guide, I might still get back to her before midnight, if only guide and shelter could be found.

And all this time the snow fell, and the night thickened. I stopped and shouted every now and then, but my shouts seemed only to make the silence deeper. Then a vague sense of uneasiness came upon me, and I began to remember stories of travellers who had walked on and on in the falling snow until, wearied out, they were fain to lie down and sleep their lives away. Would it be possible, I asked myself, to keep on thus through all the long dark night? Would there not come a time when my limbs must fail, and my resolution give way? When I, too, must sleep the sleep of death. Death! I shuddered. How hard to die just now, when life lay all so bright before me! How hard for my darling, whose whole loving heart . . . but that thought was not to be borne! To banish it, I shouted again, louder and longer, and then listened eagerly. Was my shout answered, or did I only fancy that I heard a far-off cry? I halloed again, and again the echo followed. Then a wavering speck of light came suddenly out of the dark, shifting, disappearing, growing momentarily nearer and brighter. Running towards it at full speed, I found myself, to my great joy, face to face with an old man and a lantern.

"Thank God!" was the exclamation that burst involuntarily from my lips.

Blinking and frowning, he lifted the lantern and peered into my face.

"What for?" growled he, sulkily.

"Well—for you. I began to fear I should be lost in the snow."

"Eh, then, folks do get cast away hereabouts fra' time to time, an' what's to hinder you from bein' cast away likewise, if the Lord's so minded?"

"If the Lord is so minded that you and I shall be lost together, friend, we must submit," I replied; "but I don't mean to be lost without you. How far am I now from Dwolding?"

"A gude twenty mile, more or less."

"And the nearest village?"

"The nearest village is Wyke, an' that's twelve mile t'other side."

"Where do you live, then?"

"Out yonder," said he, with a vague jerk of the lantern.

"You're going home, I presume?"

"Maybe I am."

"Then I'm going with you."

The old man shook his head, and rubbed his nose reflectively with the handle of the lantern.

"It ain't o' no use," growled he. "He 'ont let you in—not he."

"We'll see about that," I replied, briskly. "Who is He?"

"The master."

"Who is the master?"

"That's now't to you," was the unceremonious reply.

"Well, well; you lead the way, and I'll engage that the master shall give me shelter and a supper to-night."

"Eh, you can try him!" muttered my reluctant guide; and, still shaking his head, he hobbled, gnome-like, away through the falling snow.

A large mass loomed up presently out of the darkness, and a huge dog rushed out barking furiously.

"Is this the house?" I asked.

"Ay, it's the house. Down, Bey!" And he fumbled in his pocket for the key.

I drew up close behind him, prepared to lose no chance of entrance, and saw in the little circle of light shed by the lantern that the door was heavily studded with iron nails, like the door of a prison. In another minute he had turned the key, and I had pushed past him into the house.

Once inside, I looked round with curiosity, and found myself in a great raftered hall, which served, apparently, a variety of uses. One end was piled to the roof with corn, like a barn. The other was stored with flour-sacks, agricultural implements, casks, and all kinds of miscellaneous lumber; while from the beams overhead hung rows of hams, flitches, and bunches of dried herbs for winter use. In the centre of the floor stood some huge object gauntly dressed in a dingy wrapping-cloth, and reaching halfway to the rafters. Lifting a corner of this cloth, I saw, to my surprise, a telescope of very considerable size, mounted on a rude moveable platform with four small wheels. The tube was made of painted wood, bound round with bands of metal rudely fashioned; the speculum, so far as I could estimate its size by the dim light, measured at least fifteen inches in diameter. While I was yet examining the instrument, and asking myself whether it was not the work of some self-taught optician, a bell rang sharply.

"That's for you," said my guide, with a malicious grin. "Yonder's his room."

He pointed to a low black door at the opposite side of the hall. I crossed over, rapped somewhat loudly, and went in, without waiting for an invitation. A huge, white-haired old man rose from a table covered with books and papers, and confronted me sternly.

"Who are you?" said he. " How came you here? What do you want?"

"James Murray, barrister-at-law. On foot across the moor. Meat, drink, and sleep."

He bent his bushy brows in a portentous frown.

"Mine is not a house of entertainment," he said, haughtily. "Jacob, how dared you admit this stranger?"

"I didn't admit him," grumbled the old man. "He followed me over the muir, and shouldered his way in before me. I'm no match for six foot two."

"And pray, sir, by what right have you forced an entrance into my house?"

"The same by which I should have clung to your boat, if I were drowning. The right of self-preservation."

"Self-preservation?"

"There's an inch of snow on the ground already," I replied briefly; "and it will be deep enough to cover my body before daybreak."

He strode to the window, pulled aside a heavy black curtain, and looked out.

"It is true," he said. "You can stay, if you choose, till morning. Jacob, serve the supper."

With this he waved me to a seat, resumed his own, and became at once absorbed in the studies at which I had disturbed him.

I placed my gun in a corner, drew a chair to the hearth, and examined my quarters at leisure. Smaller and less incongruous in its arrangements than the hall, this room contained, nevertheless, much to awaken my curiosity. The floor was carpetless. The whitewashed walls were in parts scrawled over with strange diagrams, and in others covered with shelves crowded with philosophical instruments, the uses of many of which were unknown to me. On one side of the fireplace stood a bookcase filled with dingy folios; on the other, a small organ, fantastically decorated with painted carvings of mediaeval saints and devils. Through the half-opened door of a cupboard at the further end of the room, I saw a long array of geological specimens, surgical preparations, crucibles, retorts, and jars of chemicals; while on the mantelshelf beside me, amid a number of small objects, stood a model of the solar system, a small galvanic battery, and a microscope. Every chair had its burden. Every corner was heaped high with books. The very floor was littered over with maps, casts, papers, tracings, and learned lumber of all conceivable kinds.

I stared about me with an amazement increased by every fresh object upon which my eyes chanced to rest. So strange a room I had never seen; yet seemed it stranger still to find such a room in a lone farmhouse, amid these wild and solitary moors! Over and over again, I looked from my host to his surroundings, and from his surroundings back to my host, asking myself who and what he could be? His head was singularly fine; but it was more the head of a poet than a philosopher. Broad in the temples, prominent over the eyes, and clothed with a rough profusion of perfectly white hair, it had all the ideality and much of the ruggedness that characterises the head of Louis von Beethoven. There were the same deep lines about the mouth, and the same stern furrows in the brow. There was the same concentration of expression. While I was yet observing him, the door opened, and Jacob brought in the supper. His master then closed his book, rose, and with more courtesy of manner than he had yet shown, invited me to the table.

A dish of ham and eggs, a loaf of brown bread, and a bottle of admirable sherry, were placed before me.

"I have but the homeliest farmhouse fare to offer you, sir," said my entertainer. "Your appetite, I trust, will make up for the deficiencies of our larder."

I had already fallen upon the viands, and now protested, with the enthusiasm of a starving sportsman, that I had never eaten anything so delicious.

He bowed stiffly, and sat down to his own supper, which consisted, primitively, of a jug of milk and a basin of porridge. We ate in silence, and, when we had done, Jacob removed the tray. I then drew my chair back to the fireside. My host, somewhat to my surprise, did the same, and turning abruptly towards me said:—

"Sir, I have lived here in strict retirement for three-and-twenty years. During that time, I have not seen as many strange faces, and I have not read a single newspaper. You are the first stranger who has crossed my threshold for more than four years. Will you favour me with a few words of information respecting that outer world from which I have parted company so long?"

"Pray interrogate me," I replied. "I am heartily at your service."

He bent his head in acknowledgment; leaned forward, with his elbows resting on his knees, and his chin supported in the palms of his hands; stared fixedly into the fire, and proceeded to question me.

His inquiries related chiefly to scientific matters with the later progress of which, as applied to the practical purposes of life, he was almost wholly unacquainted. No student of science myself, I replied as well as my slight information permitted; but the task was far from easy, and I was much relieved when, passing from interrogation to discussion, he began pouring forth his own conclusions upon the facts which I had been attempting to place before him. He talked, and I listened spell-bound. He talked till I believe he almost forgot my presence, and only thought aloud. I had never heard anything like it then; I have never heard anything like it since. Familiar with all systems of all philosophies, subtle in analysis, bold in generalisation, he poured forth his thoughts in an uninterrupted stream, and, still leaning forward in the same moody attitude with his eyes fixed upon the fire, wandered from topic to topic, from speculation to speculation, like an inspired dreamer. From practical science to mental philosophy; from electricity in the wire to electricity in the nerve; from Watts to Mesmer, from Mesmer to Reichenbach, from Reichenbach to Swedenborg, Spinoza, Condillac, Descartes, Berkeley, Aristotle, Plato, and the Magi and Mystics of the East, were transitions which, however bewildering in their variety and scope, seemed easy and harmonious upon his lips as sequences in music. By-and-by—I forget now by what link of conjecture or illustration—he passed on to that field which lies beyond the boundary line of even conjectural philosophy, and reaches no man knows whither. He spoke of the soul and its aspirations; of the spirit and its powers; of second sight; of prophecy; of those phenomena which, under the names of ghosts, spectres, and supernatural appearances, have been denied by the sceptics and attested by the credulous, of all ages.

"The world," he said, "grows hourly more and more sceptical of all that lies beyond its own narrow radius; and our men of science foster the fatal tendency. They condemn as fable all that resists experiment. They reject as false all that cannot be brought to the test of the laboratory or the dissecting-room. Against what superstition have they waged so long and obstinate a war, as against the belief in apparitions? And yet what superstition has maintained its hold upon the minds of men so long and so firmly? Show me any fact in physics, in history, in archaeology, which is supported by testimony so wide and so various. Attested by all races of men, in all ages, and in all climates, by the soberest sages of antiquity, by the rudest savages of to-day, by the Christian, the Pagan, the Pantheist, the Materialist, this phenomenon is treated as a nursery tale by the philosophers of our century. Circumstantial evidence weighs with them as a feather in the balance. The comparison of causes with effects, however valuable in physical science, is put aside as worthless and unreliable. The evidence of competent witnesses, however conclusive in a court of justice, counts for nothing. He who pauses before he pronounces, is condemned as a trifler. He who believes, is a dreamer or a fool."

He spoke with bitterness, and, having said thus, relapsed for some minutes into silence. Presently he raised his head from his hands, and added, with an altered voice and manner—

"I, sir, paused, investigated, believed, and was not ashamed to state my convictions to the world. I, too, was branded as a visionary, held up to ridicule by my contemporaries, and hooted from that field of science in which I had laboured with honour during all the best years of my life. These things happened just three-and-twenty years ago. Since then, I have lived as you see me living now, and the world has forgotten me, as I have forgotten the world. You have my history."

"It is a very sad one," I murmured, scarcely knowing what to answer.

"It is a very common one," he replied. "I have only suffered for the truth, as many a better and wiser man has suffered before me."

He rose, as if desirous of ending the conversation, and went over to the window.

"It has ceased snowing," he observed, as he dropped the curtain, and came back to the fireside.

"Ceased!" I exclaimed, starting eagerly to my feet. "Oh, if it were only possible—but no! it is hopeless. Even if I could find ray way across the moor, I could not walk twenty miles to-night."

"Walk twenty miles to-night!" repeated my host. "What are you thinking of?"

"Of my wife," I replied, impatiently. "Of my young wife, who does not know that I have lost my way, and who is at this moment breaking her heart with suspense and terror."

"Where is she?"

"At Dwolding, twenty miles away."

"At Dwolding;" he echoed, thoughtfully. "Yes, the distance, it is true, is twenty miles; but—are you so anxious to save the next six or eight hours?"

"So anxious, that I would give ten guineas at this moment for a guide and a horse."

"Your wish can be gratified at a less costly rate," said he, smiling. "The night mail from the north, which changes horses at Dwolding, passes within five miles of this spot, and will be due at a certain cross-road in about an hour and a quarter. If Jacob were to go with you across the moor, and put you into the old coach road, you could find your way, I suppose, to where it joins the new one?"

"Easily—gladly."

He smiled again, rang the bell, gave the old servant his directions, and, taking a bottle of whisky and a wine-glass from the cupboard in which he kept his chemicals, said—

"The snow lies deep, and it will be difficult walking to-night on the moor. A glass of usquebaugh before you start."

I would have declined the spirit, but he pressed it on me, and I drank it. It went down my throat like liquid flame, and almost took my breath away.

"It is strong," he said; "but it will help to keep out the cold. And now you have no moments to spare. Good night!"

I thanked him for his hospitality, and would have shaken hands, but that he had turned away before I could finish my sentence. In another minute I had traversed the hall, Jacob had locked the outer door behind me, and we were out on the wide white moor.

Although the wind had fallen, it was still bitterly cold. Not a star glimmered in the black vault overhead. Not a sound, save the rapid crunching of the snow beneath our feet, disturbed the heavy stillness of the night. Jacob, not too well pleased with his mission, shambled on before in sullen silence, his lantern in his hand, and his shadow at his feet. I followed, with my gun over my shoulder, as little inclined for conversation as himself.

My thoughts were full of my late host. His voice yet rang in my ears. His eloquence yet held my imagination captive. I remember to this day, with surprise, how my over-excited brain retained whole sentences and parts of sentences, troops of brilliant images, and fragments of splendid reasoning, in the very words in which he had uttered them. Musing thus over what I had heard, and striving to recall a lost link here and there, I strode on at the heels of my guide, absorbed and unobservant. Presently—at the end, as it seemed to me, of only a few minutes—he came to a sudden halt, and said:

"Yon's your road. Keep the stone fence to your right hand, and you can't fail of the way."

"This, then, is the old coach-road?"

"Ay, 'tis the old coach-road."

"And how far do I go, before I reach the cross-roads?"

"Nigh upon three miles."

I pulled out my purse, and he became more communicative.

"The road's a fair road enough," said he, "for foot passengers; but 'twas over steep and narrow for the northern traffic. You'll mind where the parapet's broken away, close again the sign-post. It's never been mended since the accident."

"What accident?"

"Eh, the night mail pitched right over into the valley below—a gude sixty feet an' more—just at the worst bit o' road in the whole county."

"Horrible! Were many lives lost?"

"All. Four were found dead, and t'other two died next morning."

"How long is it since this happened?"

"Just nine year."

"Near the sign-post, you say? I will bear it in mind. Good night."

"Gude night, sir, and thankee."

Jacob pocketed his half-crown, made a faint pretence of touching his hat, and trudged back by the way he had come.

I watched the light of his lantern till it quite disappeared, and then turned to pursue my way alone. This was no longer a matter of the slightest difficulty, for, despite the dead darkness overhead, the line of stone fence showed distinctly enough against the pale gleam of the snow. How silent it seemed now, with only my own footsteps to listen to; how silent and how solitary! A strange disagreeable sense of loneliness stole over me. I walked faster. I hummed a fragment of a tune. I cast up enormous sums in my head, and accumulated them at compound interest. I did my best, in short, to forget the startling speculations to which I had but just been listening, and, to some extent, I succeeded.

Meanwhile the night air seemed to become colder and colder, and though I walked fast, I found it impossible to keep myself warm. My feet were like ice. I lost sensation in my hands, and grasped my gun mechanically. I even breathed with difficulty, as though, instead of traversing a quiet north country highway, I were scaling the uppermost heights of some gigantic Alp. This last symptom became presently so distressing, that I was forced to stop for a few minutes, and lean against the stone fence. As I did so, I chanced to look back up the road, and there, to my infinite relief, I saw a distant point of light, like the gleam of an approaching lantern. I at first concluded that Jacob had retraced his steps and followed me; but even as the conjecture presented itself, a second light flashed into sight—a light evidently parallel with the first, and approaching at the same rate of motion. It needed no second thought to show me that these must be the carriage-lamps of some private vehicle; though it seemed strange that any private vehicle should take a road professedly disused and dangerous.

There could be no doubt, however, of the fact, for the lamps grew larger and brighter every moment, and I even fancied I could already see the dark outline of the carriage between them. It was coming up very fast, and quite noiselessly; the snow being nearly a foot deep under the wheels.

And now the body of the vehicle became distinctly visible behind the lamps. It looked strangely lofty. A sudden suspicion flashed upon me. Was it possible that I had passed the cross roads in the dark without observing the sign-post, and could this be the very coach which I had come to meet?

No need to ask myself that question a second time, for here it came round the bend of the road, guard and driver, one outside passenger, and four steaming greys, all wrapped in a soft haze of light, through which the lamps blazed out like a pair of fiery meteors.

I jumped forward, waved my hat, and shouted. The mail came down at full speed, and passed me. For a moment I feared that I had not been seen or heard, but it was only for a moment. The coachman pulled up; the guard, muffled to the eyes in capes and comforters, and apparently sound asleep in the rumble, neither answered my hail nor made the slightest effort to dismount; the outside passenger did not even turn his head. I opened the door for myself, and looked in. There were but three travellers inside, so I stepped in, shut the door, slipped into the vacant corner, and congratulated myself on my good fortune.

The atmosphere of the coach seemed, if possible, colder than that of the outer air, and was pervaded by a singularly damp and disagreeable smell. I looked round at my fellow passengers. They were all three men; and all silent. They did not seem to be asleep, but each leaned back in his corner of the vehicle, as if absorbed in his own reflections. I attempted to open a conversation.

"How intensely cold it is to-night," I said, addressing my opposite neighbour.

He lifted his head, looked at me, but made no reply.

"The winter," I added, "seems to have begun in earnest."

Although the corner in which he sat was so dim that I could distinguish none of his features very clearly, I saw that his eyes were still turned full upon me. And yet he answered never a word.

At any other time I should have felt, and perhaps expressed, some annoyance; but at that moment I felt too ill to do either. The icy coldness of the night air had struck a chill to my very marrow, and the strange smell inside the coach was affecting me with an intolerable nausea. I shivered from head to foot, and, turning to my left-hand neighbour, asked if he had any objection to an open window.

He neither spoke nor stirred.

I repeated the question somewhat more loudly, but with the same result. Then I lost patience, and let the sash down. As I did so, the leather strap broke in my hand, and I observed that the glass was covered with a thick coat of mildew, the accumulation, apparently, of years. My attention being thus drawn to the condition of the coach, I examined it more narrowly, and saw by the uncertain light of the outer lamps that it was in the last state of dilapidation. Every part of it was not only out of repair, but in a state of actual decay. The sashes splintered at a touch. The leather fittings were crusted over with mould, and literally rotting from the woodwork. The floor was almost breaking away beneath my feet. The whole machine, in short, was foul with damp, and had evidently been dragged from some outhouse in which it had been mouldering away for years, to do another day or two of duty on the road.

I turned to the third passenger, whom I had not yet addressed, and hazarded one more remark.

"This coach," I said, "is in a deplorable condition. The regular mail, I suppose, is under repair?"

He moved his head slowly, and looked me in the face, without speaking a word. I shall never forget that look while I live. I turned cold at heart under it. I turn cold at heart even now when I recall it. His eyes glowed with a fiery unnatural lustre. His face was livid as the face of a corpse. His bloodless lips were drawn back as if in the agony of death, and showed the gleaming teeth between.

The words that I was about to utter died upon my lips, and a strange horror came upon me. My sight had by this time become used to the gloom of the coach, and I could see with tolerable distinctness. I turned to my opposite neighbour. He, too, was looking at me, with the same startling pallor in his face, and the same stony glitter in his eyes. I passed my hand across my brow. I turned to the passenger on the seat beside my own, and saw—oh Heaven! how shall I describe what I saw? I saw that he was no living man—that none of them were living men, like myself! A pale phosphorescent light—the light of putrefaction—played upon their awful faces; upon their hair, dank with the dews of the grave; upon their clothes, earth-stained and dropping to pieces; upon their hands, which were as the hands of corpses long buried. Only their eyes, their terrible eyes, were living; and those eyes were all turned menacingly upon me!

A shriek of terror, a wild unintelligible cry for help and mercy, burst from my lips as I flung myself against the door, and strove in vain to open it.

In that single instant, brief and vivid as a landscape beheld in the flash of summer lightning, I saw the moon shining down through a rift of stormy cloud—the ghastly sign-post rearing its warning finger by the wayside—the broken parapet—the plunging horses—the black gulf below. Then the coach reeled like a ship at sea. Then came a mighty crash—a sense of crushing pain—and then, darkness.

It seemed as if years had gone by, when I awoke one morning from a deep sleep, and found my wife watching by my bedside. I will pass over the scene that ensued, and give you, in half a dozen words, the tale she told me with tears of thanksgiving. I had fallen over a precipice, close against the junction of the old coach-road and the new, and had only been saved from certain death by lighting upon a deep snowdrift that had accumulated at the foot of the rock beneath. In this snowdrift I was discovered at daybreak by a couple of shepherds, who carried me to the nearest shelter, and brought a surgeon to my aid. The surgeon found me in a state of raving delirium, with a broken arm and a compound fracture of the skull. The letters in my pocket-book showed my name and address; my wife was summoned to nurse me; and, thanks to youth and a fine constitution, I came out of danger at last. The place of my fall, I need scarcely say, was precisely that at which a frightful accident had happened to the north mail nine years before.

I never told my wife the fearful events which I have just related to you. I told the surgeon who attended me; but he treated the whole adventure as a mere dream born of the fever in my brain. We discussed the question over and over again, until we found that we could discuss it with temper no longer, and then we dropped it. Others may form what conclusions they please—I know that twenty years ago I was the fourth inside passenger in that Phantom Coach.

A Terrible Vengeance

Mrs. J. H. Riddell

I. Very Strange

Round Dockett Point and over Dumsey Deep the water-lilies were blooming as luxuriantly as though the silver Thames had been the blue Mummel Lake.

It was the time for them. The hawthorn had long ceased to scent the air; the wild roses had shed their delicate leaves; the buttercups and cardamoms and dog-daises that had dotted the meadows were garnered into hay. The world in early August needed a fresh and special beauty, and here it was floating in its matchless green bark on the bosom of the waters.

If those fair flowers, like their German sisters, ever at nightfall assumed mortal form, who was there to tell of such vagaries? Even when the moon is at her full there are few who care to cross Chertsey Mead, or face the lonely Stabbery.

Hard would it be, indeed, so near life, railways, civilization, and London, to find a more lonely stretch of country, when twilight visits the landscape and darkness comes brooding down over the Surrey and Middlesex shores, than the path which winds along the river from Shepperton Lock to Chertsey Bridge. At high noon for months together it is desolate beyond description—silent, save for the rippling and sobbing of the currents, the wash of the stream, the swaying of the osiers, the trembling of an aspen, the rustle of the withies, or the noise made by a bird, or rat, or stoat, startled by the sound of unwonted footsteps. In the warm summer nights also, when tired holiday-makers are sleeping soundly, when men stretched on the green sward outside their white tents are smoking, and talking, and planning excursions for the morrow; when in country houses young people are playing and singing, dancing or walking up and down terraces over-looking wellkept lawns, where the evening air is laden with delicious perfumes—there falls on that almost uninhabited mile or two of riverside a stillness which may be felt, which the belated traveller is loth to disturb even by the dip of his oars as he drifts down with the current past objects that seem to him unreal as fragments of a dream.

It had been a wet summer—a bad summer for the hotels. There had been some fine days, but not many together. The weather could not be depended upon. It was not a season in which young ladies were to be met about the reaches of the Upper Thames, disporting themselves in marvellous dresses, and more marvellous headgear, unfurling brilliant parasols, canoeing in appropriate attire, giving life and colour to the streets of old-world villages, and causing many of their inhabitants to consider what a very strange sort of town it must be in which such extraordinarily-robed persons habitually reside.

Nothing of the sort was to be seen that summer, even as high as Hampton. Excursions were limited to one day; there were few tents, few people camping-out, not many staying at the hotels; yet it was, perhaps for that reason, an enjoyable summer to those who were not afraid of a little, or rather a great deal, of rain, who liked a village inn all the better for not being crowded, and who were not heart-broken because their women-folk for once found it impossible to accompany them.

Unless a man boldly decides to outrage the proprieties and decencies of life, and go off by himself to take his pleasure selfishly alone, there is in a fine summer no door of escape open to him. There was a time—a happy time—when a husband was not expected to sign away his holidays in the marriage articles. But what boots it to talk of that remote past now? Everything is against the father of a family at present. Unless the weather help him, what friend has he? and the weather does not often in these latter days prove a friend.

In that summer, however, with which this story deals, the stars in their courses fought for many an oppressed paterfamilias. Any curious inquirer might then have walked ankle-deep in mud from Penton Hook to East Moseley, and not met a man, harnessed like a beast of burden, towing all his belongings up stream, or beheld him rowing against wind and tide as though he were a galley-slave chained to the oar, striving all the while to look as though enjoying the fun.

Materfamilias found it too wet to patronize the Thames. Her dear little children also were conspicuous by their absence. Charming young ladies were rarely to be seen—indeed, the skies were so treacherous that it would have been a mere tempting of Providence to risk a pretty dress on the water; for which sufficient reasons furnished houses remained unlet, and lodgings were left empty; taverns and hotels welcomed visitors instead of treating them scurvily; and the river, with its green banks and its leafy airs, its white swans, its water-lilies, its purple loosestrife, its reeds, its rushes, its weeping willows, its quiet backwaters, was delightful.

One evening two men stood just outside the door of the Ship, Lower Halliford, looking idly at the water, as it flowed by more rapidly than is usually the case in August. Both were dressed in suits of serviceable dark grey tweed; both wore round hats; both evidently belonged to that class which resembles the flowers of the field but in the one respect that it toils not, neither does it spin; both looked intensely bored; both were of rather a good appearance.

The elder, who was about thirty, had dark hair, sleepy brown eyes, and a straight capable nose; a heavy moustache almost concealed his mouth, but his chin was firm and well cut. About him there was an indescribable something calculated to excite attention, but nothing in his expression to attract or repel. No one looking at him could have said offhand, "I think that is a pleasant fellow," or "I am sure that man could make himself confoundedly disagreeable."

His face revealed as little as the covers of a book. It might contain interesting matter, or there might be nothing underneath save the merest commonplace. So far as it conveyed an idea at all, it was that of indolence. Every movement of his body suggested laziness; but it would have been extremely hard to say how far that laziness went. Mental energy and physical inactivity walk oftener hand in hand than the world suspects, and mental energy can on occasion make an indolent man active, while mere brute strength can never confer intellect on one who lacks brains.

In every respect the younger stranger was the opposite of his companion. Fair, blue-eyed, light-haired, with soft moustache and tenderly cared-for whiskers, he looked exactly what he was—a very shallow, kindly, good fellow, who did not trouble himself with searching into the depths of things, who took the world as it was, who did not go out to meet trouble, who loved his species, women included, in an honest way; who liked amusement, athletic sports of all sorts—dancing, riding, rowing, shooting; who had not one regret, save that hours in a Government office were so confoundedly long, "eating the best part out of a day, by Jove"; no cause for discontent, save that he had very little money, and into whose mind it had on the afternoon in question been forcibly borne that his friend was a trifle heavy—"carries too many guns," he considered—"and not exactly the man to enjoy a modest dinner at Lower Halliford."

For which cause, perhaps, he felt rather relieved when his friend refused to partake of any meal.

"I wish you could have stayed," said the younger, with that earnest and not quite insincere hospitality people always assume when they feel a departing guest is not to be overpersuaded to stay.

"So do I," replied the other. "I should have liked to stop with *you*, and I should have liked to stay here. There is a sleepy dullness about the place which exactly suits my present mood, but I must get back to town. I promised Travers to look in at his chambers this evening, and to-morrow as I told you, I am due in Norfolk."

"What will you do, then, till train-time? There is nothing up from here till nearly seven. Come on the river for an hour with me."

"Thank you, no. I think I will walk over to Staines."

"Staines! Why Staines in heaven's name?"

"Because I am in the humour for a walk—a long, lonely walk; because a demon has taken possession of me I wish to exorcise; because there are plenty of trains from Staines; because I am weary of the Thames Valley line, and any other reason you like. I can give you none better than I have done."

"At least let me row you part of the way."

"Again thank you, no. The eccentricities of the Thames are not new to me. With the best intentions, you would land me at Laleham when I should be on my (rail) way to London. My dear Dick, step into that boat your soul has been hankering after for the half-hour, and leave me to return to town according to my own fancy."

"I don't half like this," said genial Dick. "Ah! here comes a pretty girl—look."

Thus entreated, the elder man turned his head and saw a young girl, accompanied by a young man, coming along the road, which leads from Walton Lane to Shepperton.

She was very pretty, of the sparkling order of beauty, with dark eyes, rather heavy eye-brows, dark thick hair, a ravishing fringe, a delicious hat, a coquettish dress, and shoes which by pretty gestures she seemed to be explaining to her companion were many—very many—sizes too large for her. Spite of her beauty, spite of her dress, spite of her shoes so much too large for her, it needed but a glance from one conversant with subtle social distinctions to tell that she was not quite her "young man's" equal.

For, in the parlance of Betsy Jane, as her "young man" she evidently regarded him, and as her young man he regarded himself. There could be no doubt about the matter. He was over head and ears in love with her; he was ready to quarrel—indeed, had quarrelled with father, mother, sister, brother on her account. He loved her unreasonably—he loved her miserably, distractedly; except at odd intervals, he was not in the least happy with her. She flouted, she tormented, she maddened him; but then, after having nearly driven him to the verge of distraction, she would repent sweetly, and make up for all previous shortcomings by a few brief minutes of tender affection. If quarrelling be really the renewal of love, theirs had been renewed once a day at all events, and frequently much oftener.

Yes, she was a pretty girl, a bewitching girl, and arrant flirt, a scarcely well-behaved coquette; for as she passed the two friends she threw a glance at them, one arch, piquant, inviting glance, of which many would instantly have availed themselves, venturing the consequences certain to be dealt out by her companion, who, catching the look, drew closer to her side, not too well pleased, apparently. Spite of a little opposition, he drew her band through his arm, and walked on with an air of possession infinitely amusing to onlookers, and plainly distasteful to his lady-love.

"A clear case of spoons," remarked the younger of the two visitors, after the pair.

"Poor devil!" said the other compassionately.

His friend laughed, and observed mockingly paraphrasing a very different speech,—

"But for the grace of God, there goes Paul Murray."

"You may strike out the 'but,'" replied the person so addressed, "for that is the very road Paul Murray is going, and soon."

"You are not serious!" asked the other doubtfully.

"Am I not? I am though, though not with such a vixen as I dare swear that little baggage is. I told you I was due to-morrow in Norfolk. But see, they are turning back; let us go inside."

"All right," agreed the other, following his companion into the hall. "This is a great surprise to me, Murray: I never imagined you were engaged."

"I am not engaged yet, though no doubt I shall soon be," answered the reluctant lover. "My grandmother and the lady's father have arranged the match. The lady does not object, I believe, and who am I, Savill, that I should refuse good looks, a good fortune, and a good temper?"

"You do not speak as though you liked the proposed bride, nevertheless," said Mr. Savill dubiously.

"I do not dislike her, I only hate having to marry her. Can't you understand that a man wants to pick a wife for himself-that the one girl he fancies seems worth ten thousand of a girl anybody else fancies? But I am so situated—Hang it, Dick! what are you staring at that darkeyed witch for?"

"Because it is so funny. She is making him take a boat at the steps, and he does not want to do it. Kindly observe his face."

"What is his face to me?" retorted Mr. Murray savagely.

"Not much, I daresay, but it is a good deal to him. It is black as thunder, and hers is not much lighter. What a neat ankle, and how you like to show it, my dear. Well, there is no harm in a pretty ankle or a pretty foot either, and you have both. One would not wish one's wife to have a hoof like an elephant. What sort of feet has your destined maiden, Paul?"

"I never noticed."

"That looks deucedly bad," said the younger man, shaking his head. "I know, however, she has a pure, sweet face," observed Mr. Murray gloomily.

"No one could truthfully make the same statement about our young friend's little lady," remarked Mr. Savill, still gazing at the girl, who was seating herself in the stem. "A termagant, I'll be bound, if ever there was one. Wishes to go up stream, no doubt because he wishes to go d own. Any caprice about the Norfolk 'fair'?"

"Not much, I think. She is good, Dick—too good for me," replied the other, sauntering out again.

"That is what we always say about the things we do not know. And so your grandmother has made up the match?"

"Yes: there is money, and the old lady loves money. She says she wants to see me settled—talks of buying me an estate. She will have to do something, because I am sure the stern parent on the other side would not allow his daughter to marry on expectations. The one drop of comfort in the arrangement is that my aged relative will have to come down, and pretty smartly too. I would wed Hecate, to end this state of bondage, which I have not courage to flee from myself. Dick, how I envy you who have no dead person's shoes to wait for!"

"You need not envy me," returned Dick, with conviction, "a poor unlucky devil chained to a desk. There is scarce a day of my life I fail to curse the service, the office, and Fate—"

"Curse no more, then," said the other; "rather go down on your knees and thank Heaven you have, without any merit of your own, a provision for life. I wish Fate or anybody had coached me into the Civil Service-apprenticed me to a trade—sent me to sea—made me enlist, instead of leaving me at the mercy of an old lady who knows neither justice nor reason—who won't let me do anything for myself, and won't do anything for me—who ought to have been dead long ago, but who never means to die—"

"And who often gives you in one cheque as much as the whole of my annual salary," added the other quietly.

"But you know you will have your yearly salary as long as you live. I never know whether I shall have another cheque."

"It won't do, my friend," answered Dick Savill; "you feel quite certain you can get money when you want it."

"I feel certain of no such thing," was the reply. "If I once offended her—" he stopped, and then went on: "And perhaps when I have spent twenty years in trying to humour such caprices as surely woman never had before, I shall wake one morning to find she has left every penny to the Asylum for Idiots."

"Why do you not pluck up courage, and strike out some line for yourself?"

"Too late, Dick, too late. Ten years ago I might have tried to make a fortune for myself, but I can't do that now. As I have waited so long, I must wait a little longer. At thirty a man can't take pick in hand and try to clear a road to fortune."

"Then you had better marry the Norfolk young lady."

"I am steadily determined to do so. I am going down with the firm intention of asking her."

"And do you think she will have you?"

"I think so. I feel sure she will. And she is a nice girl—the sort I would like for a wife, if she had not been thrust upon me."

Mr. Savill stood silent for a moment, with his hands plunged deep in his pockets.

"Then when I see you next?" he said tentatively.

"I shall be engaged, most likely—possibly even married," finished the other, with as much hurry as his manner was capable of. "And now jump into your boat, and I will go on my way to—Staines—"

"I wish you would change your mind, and have some dinner."

"I can't, it is impossible. You see I have so many things to do and to think of. Good-bye, Dick. Don't upset yourself-go down stream, and don't get into mischief with those dark eyes you admired so much just now."

"Make your mind easy about that," returned the other, colouring, however, a little as he spoke. "Good-bye, Murray. I wish you well through the campaign." And so, after a hearty hand-shake, they parted, one to walk away from Halliford, and past Shepperton Church, and across Shepperton Range, and the other, of course, to row up stream, through Shepperton Lock, and on past Dockett Point.

In the grey of the summer's dawn, Mr. Murray awoke next morning from a terrible dream. He had kept his appointment with Mr. Travers and a select party, played heavily, drank deeply, and reached home between one and two, not much the better for his trip to Lower Halliford, his walk, and his carouse.

Champagne, followed by neat brandy, is not perhaps the best thing to insure a quiet night's rest; but Mr. Murray had often enjoyed sound repose after similar libations; and it was, therefore, all the more unpleasant that in the grey dawn he should wake suddenly from a dream in which he thought some one was trying to crush his head with a heavy weight.

Even when he had struggled from sleep, it seemed to him that a wet dead hand lay across his eyes, and pressed them so hard he could not move the lids. Under the weight he lay powerless, while a damp, icecold hand felt burning into his brain, if such a contradictory expression may be permitted.

The perspiration was pouring from him; he felt the drops falling on his throat, and trickling down his neck; he might have been lying in a bath, instead of on his own bed, and it was with a cry of horror he at last flung the hand aside, and, sitting up, looked around the room, into which the twilight of morning was mysteriously stealing.

Then, trembling in every limb, he lay down again, and fell into another sleep, from which he did not awake till aroused by broad daylight and his valet.

"You told me to call you in good time, sir," said the man.

"Ah, yes, so I did," yawned Mr. Murray. "What a bore! I will get up directly. You can go, Davis. I will ring if I want you."

Davis was standing, as his master spoke, looking down at the floor. "Yes, sir." he answered, after the fashion of a man who has something on his mind,—and went.

He had not, however, got to the bottom of the first flight when peal after peal summoned him back.

Mr. Murray was out of bed, and in the middle of the room, the ghastly pallor of his face brought into full prominence by the crimson dressing-gown he had thrown round him on rising.

"What is that?" he asked. "What the in world is that, Davis?" and he pointed to the carpet, which was covered, Mrs. Murray being an old-fashioned lady, with strips of white drugget.

"I am sure I do not know, sir," answered Davis. "I noticed it the moment I came into the room. Looks as if some one with wet feet had been walking round and round the bed."

It certainly did. Round and round, to and fro, backwards and forwards, the feet seemed to have gone and come, leaving a distinct mark wherever they pressed.

"The print is that of a rare small foot, too," observed Davis, who really seemed half stupefied with astonishment.

"But who would have dared—" began Mr. Murray.

"No one in this house," declared Davis stoutly. "It is not the mark of a boy or woman inside these doors"; and then the master and the man looked at each other for an instant with grave suspicion.

But for that second they kept their eyes thus occupied; then, as by common consent, they dropped their glances to the floor. "My God!" exclaimed Davis. "Where have the footprints gone?"

He might well ask. The drugget, but a moment before wet and stained by the passage and repassage of those small restless feet, was now smooth and white, as when first sent forth from the bleach-green. On its polished surface there could not be discerned a speck or mark.

II. Where Is Lucy?

In the valley of the Thames early hours are the rule. There the days have an unaccountable way of lengthening themselves out which makes it prudent, as well as pleasant, to utilize all the night in preparing for a longer morrow.

For this reason, when eleven o'clock p.m. strikes, it usually finds Church Street, Walton, as quiet as its adjacent graveyard, which lies still and solemn under the shadow of the old grey tower hard by that ancient vicarage which contains so beautiful a staircase.

About the time when Mr. Travers' friends were beginning their evening, when talk had abated and play was suggested, the silence of Church Street was broken and many a sleeper aroused by a continuous knocking at the door of a house as venerable as any in that part of Walton. Rap—rap—rap—rap awoke the echoes of the old-world village street, and at length brought to the window a young man, who, flinging up the sash, inquired,—

"Who is there?"

"Where is Lucy? What have you done with my girl?" answered a strained woman's voice from out the darkness of that summer night.

"Lucy?" repeated the young man; "is not she at home?"

"No; I have never set eyes on her since you went out together."

"Why, we parted hours ago. Wait a moment, Mrs. Heath; I will be down directly."

No need to tell the poor woman to "wait." She stood on the step, crying softly and wringing her hands till the door opened, and the same young fellow who with the pretty girl had taken boat opposite the Ship Hotel bade her "Come in."

Awakened from some pleasant dream, spite of all the trouble and hurry of that unexpected summons, there still shone the light of a reflected sunshine in his eyes and the flush of happy sleep on his cheek. He scarcely understood yet what had happened, but when he saw Mrs. Heath's tear-stained face, comprehension came to him, and he said abruptly,—

"Do you mean that she has never returned home?"

"Never!"

They were in the parlour by this time, and looking at each other by the light of one poor candle which he had set down on the table.

"Why, I left her," he said, "I left her long before seven."

"Where?"

"Just beyond Dockett Point. She would not let me row her back. I do not know what was the matter with her, but nothing I did seemed right."

"Had you any quarrel?" asked Mrs. Heath anxiously.

"Yes, we had; we were quarrelling all the time—at least she was with me; and at last she made me put her ashore, which I did sorely against my will."

"What had you done to my girl, then?"

"I prayed of her to marry me—no great insult, surely, but she took it as one. I would rather not talk of what she answered. Where can she be? Do you think she can have gone to her aunt's?"

"If so, she will be back by the last train. Let us get home as fast as possible. I never thought of that. Poor child! she will go out of her mind if she finds nobody to let her in. You will come with me. O, if she is not there, what shall I do—what ever shall I do?"

The young man bad taken his hat, and was holding the door open for Mrs. Heath to pass out.

"You must try not to fret yourself," he said gently, yet with a strange repression in his voice. "Very likely she may stay at her aunt's all night."

"And leave me in misery, not knowing where she is? Oh, Mr. Grantley, I could never believe that."

Mr. Grantley's heart was very hot within him; but he could not tell the poor mother he believed that when Lucy's temper was up she would think of no human being but herself.

"Won't you take my arm, Mrs. Heath?" he asked with tender pity. After all, though everything was over between him and Lucy, her mother could not be held accountable for their quarrel; and he had loved the girl with all the romantic fervour of love's young dream.

"I can walk faster without it, thank you," Mrs. Heath answered. "But Mr. Grantley, whatever you and Lucy fell out over, you'll forget it, won't you? It isn't in you to be hard on anybody, and she's only a spoiled child. I never had but the one, and I humoured her too much; and if she is wayward, it is all my own fault—all my own."

"In case she does not return by this train," said the young man, wisely ignoring Mrs. Heath's inquiry, "had I not better telegraph to her aunt directly the office opens?"

"I will be on my way to London long before that," was the reply.

"But what makes you think she won't come? Surely you don't imagine she has done anything rash?"

"What do you mean by rash?" he asked evasively.

"Made away with herself."

"*That!*" he exclaimed. "No, I feel very sure she has done nothing of the sort."

"But she might have felt sorry when you left her—vexed for having angered you—heartbroken when she saw you leave her."

"Believe me, she was not vexed or sorry or heartbroken; she was only glad to know she had done with me," he answered bitterly.

"What has come to you, Mr. Grantley?" said Mrs. Heath, in wonder. "I never heard you speak the same before."

"Perhaps not; I never felt the same before. It is best to be plain with you," he went on. "All is at an end between us; and that is what your daughter has long been trying for."

"How can you say that, and she so fond of you?"

"She has not been fond of me for many a day. The man she wants to marry is not a poor fellow like myself, but one who can give her carriages and horses, and a fine house, and as much dress as she cares to buy."

"But where could she ever find a husband able to do that?"

"I do not know, Mrs. Heath. All I do know is that she considers I am no match for her; and now my eyes are opened, I see she was not a wife for me. We should never have known a day's happiness."

It was too dark to see his face, but his changed voice and words and manner told Lucy's mother the kindly lad, who a couple of years before came courting her pretty daughter, and offended all his friends for her sake, was gone away for ever. It was a man who walked by her side—who had eaten of the fruit of the tree, and had learned to be as a god, knowing good from evil.

"Well, well," she said brokenly, "you are the best judge, I suppose; but O, my child, my child!"

She was so blinded with tears she stumbled, and must have fallen had he not caught and prevented her. Then he drew her hand within his arm, and said,—

"I am so grieved for you. I never received anything but kindness from you."

"And indeed," she sobbed, "you never were anything except good to me. I always knew we couldn't be considered your equals, and I often had my doubts whether it was right to let you come backwards and forwards as I did, parting you from all belonging to you. But I thought, when your mother saw Lucy's pretty face for Mr. Grantley—"

"There never was a prettier," assented the young man, though, now his eyes were opened, he knew Lucy's beauty would scarcely have recommended her to any sensible woman.

"I hoped she might take to her, and I'd never have intruded. And I was so proud and happy, and fond of you—I was indeed; and I used to consider how, when you came down, I could have some little thing you fancied. But that's all over now. And I don't blame you; only my heart is sore and troubled about my foolish girl."

They were on Walton Bridge by this time, and the night air blew cold and raw down the river, and made Mrs. Heath shiver.

"I wonder where Lucy is," she murmured, "and what she'd think if she knew her mother was walking through the night in an agony about her? Where was it you said you left her?"

"Between Dockett Point and Cherrsey. I shouldn't have left her had she not insisted on my doing so."

"Isn't that the train?" asked Mr. Heath, stopping suddenly short and listening intently.

"Yes; it is just leaving Sunbury Station. Do not hurry; we have plenty of time."

They had: they were at Lucy's home, one of the small houses situated between Battlecreese Hill and the Red Lion in Lower Halliford before a single passenger came along The Green, or out of Nannygoat Lane.

"My heart misgives me that she has not come down," said Mrs. Heath.

"Shall I go up to meet her?" asked the young man; and almost before the mother feverishly assented, he was striding through the summer night to Shepperton Station, where he found the lights extinguished and every door closed.

III. Poor Mrs. Heath

By noon the next day every one in Shepperton and Lower Halliford knew Lucy Heath was "missing."

Her mother had been up to Putney, but Lucy was not with her aunt, who lived not very far from the Bridge on the Fulham side, and who, having married a fruiterer and worked up a very good business, was inclined to take such bustling and practical views of life and its concerns as rather dismayed her sister-in-law, who had spent so many years in the remote country, and then so many other years in quiet Shepperton, that Mrs. Pointer's talk flurried her almost as much as the noise of London, which often maddens middle-aged and elderly folk happily unaccustomed to its roar.

Girt about with a checked apron which lovingly enfolded a goodly portion of her comfortable figure, Mrs. Pointer received her early visitor with the sportive remark, "Why, it's never Martha Heath! Come along in; a sight of you is good for sore eyes."

But Mrs. Heath repelled all such humorous observations, and chilled those suggestions of hospitality the Pointers were never backward in making by asking in a low choked voice,—

"Is Lucy here?"

"Lor! What put such a funny notion into your head?"

"Ah! I see she is," trying to smile. "After all, she spent the night with you."

"Did what?" exclaimed Mrs. Pointer. "Spent the night—was that what you said? No, nor the day either, for this year nearly. Why, for the last four months she hasn't set foot across that doorstep, unless it might be to buy some cherries, or pears, or apples, or grapes, or suchlike, and then she came in with more air than any lady; and after paying her money and getting her goods went out again, just as if I hadn't been her father's sister and Pointer my husband. But there! for any sake, woman, don't look like that! Come into the parlour and tell me what is wrong. You never mean she has gone away and left you?"

Poor Mrs. Heath was perfectly incapable at that moment of saying what she did mean. Seated on a stool, and holding fast by the edge of the counter for fear of falling, the shop and its contents, the early busses, the people going along the pavement, the tradesmen's carts, the private carriages, were, as in some terrible nightmare, gyrating before her eyes. She could not speak, she could scarcely think, until that wild whirligig came to a stand. For a minute or two even Mrs. Pointer seemed multiplied by fifty; while her checked apron, the bananas suspended from hooks, the baskets of fruit, the pine-apples, the melons, the tomatoes, and the cob-nuts appeared and disappeared, only to reappear and disappear like the riders in a maddening giddy-go-round.

"Give me a drop of water," she said at last; and when the water was brought she drank a little and poured some on her handkerchief and dabbed her face, and finally suffered herself to be escorted into the parlour, where she told her tale interrupted by many sobs. It would have been unchristian in Mrs. Pointer to exult; but it was only human to remember she had remarked to Pointer, in that terrible spirit of prophecy bestowed for some inscrutable reason on dear friends and close relations, she knew some such trouble must befall her sister-inlaw.

"You made an idol of that girl, Martha," she went on, "and now it is coming home to you. I am sure it was last August as ever was that Pointer— But here he is, and he will talk to you himself."

Which Mr. Pointer did, being very fond of the sound of his own foolish voice. He stated how bad a thing it was for people to be above their station or to bring children up above that rank of life in which it had pleased God to place them. He quoted many pleasing saws uttered by his father and grandfather; remarked that as folks sowed they were bound to reap; reminded Mrs. Heath they had the word of Scripture for the fact— than, which, parenthetically, no fact could be truer, as he knew—that a man might not gather grapes from thorns or even figs from thistles. Further he went on to observe generally—the observation having a particular reference to Lucy—that it did not do to judge things by their looks. Over and over again salesmen had tried to "shove off a lot of foreign fruit on him, but he wasn't a young bird to be taken in by that chaff."

No; what he looked to was quality; it was what his customers expected from him, and what he could honestly declare his customers got. He was a plain man, and he thought honesty was the best policy. So as Mrs. Heath had seen fit to come to them in her trouble he would tell her what he thought, without beating about the bush. He believed Lucy had "gone off."

"But where?" asked poor Mrs. Heath.

"That I am not wise enough to say; but you'll find she's gone off. Girls in her station don't sport chains and bracelets and brooches for nothing—"

"But they did not cost many shillings," interposed the mother.

"She might tell you that," observed Mrs. Pointer, with a world of meaning.

"To say nothing," went on Mr. Pointer, "of grey gloves she could not bear to be touched. One day she walked in when I was behind the counter, and, not knowing she had been raised to the peerage, I shook hands with her as a matter of course; but when I saw the young lady look at her glove as if had dirtied it, I said 'O, I beg your pardon, miss'—jocularly, you know. 'They soil so easily,' she lisped."

"I haven't patience with such ways!" interpolated Mrs. Pointer, without any lisp at all. "Yes, it's hard for you, Martha, but you may depend Pointer's right. Indeed, I expected how it would be long ago. Young women who are walking in the straight road don't dress as Lucy dressed, or dare their innocent little cousins to call them by their Christian names in the street. Since the Spring, and long before, Pointer and me has been sure Lucy was up to no good."

"And you held your tongues and never said a word to me!" retorted Mrs. Heath, goaded and driven to desperation.

"Much use it would have been saying any word to you," answered Mrs. Pointer. "When you told me about young Grantley, and I bid you be careful, how did you take my advice? Why, you blared out at me, went on as if I knew nothing and had never been anywhere. What I told you then, though, I tell you now: young Grantleys, the sons of rectors and the grandsons of colonels, don't come after farmer's daughters with any honest purpose."

"Yet young Grantley asked her last evening to fix a day for their marriage," said Mrs. Heath, with a little triumph.

"O, I daresay!" scoffed Mrs. Pointer.

"Talk is cheap," observed Mr. Pointer.

"Some folks have more of it than money," supplemented his wife.

"They have been, as I understand, keeping company for some time now," said the fruiterer, with what he deemed a telling and judicial calmness. "So if he asked her to name the day, why did she not name it?"

"I do not know. I have never seen her since."

"O, then you had only his word about the matter," summed up Mr. Pointer. "Just as I thought—just as I thought."

"What did you think?" inquired the poor troubled mother.

"Why, that she has gone off with this Mr. Grantley."

"Ah, you don't know Mr. Grantley, or you wouldn't say such a thing."

"It is true," observed Mr. Pointer, "that I do not know the gentleman, and, I may add, I do not want to know him; but speaking as a person acquainted with the world—"

"I'll be getting home," interrupted Mrs. Heath. "Most likely my girl is there waiting for me, and a fine laugh she will have against her poor old mother for being in such a taking. Yes, Lucy will have the breakfast ready. No, thank you; I'll not wait to take anything. There will be a train back presently; and besides, to tell you the truth, food would choke me till I sit down again with my girl, and then I won't be able to eat for joy."

Husband and wife looked at each other as Mrs. Heath spoke, and for the moment a deep pity pierced the hard crust of their worldly egotism.

"Wait a minute," cried Mrs. Pointer, "and I'll put on my bonnet and go with you."

"No," interrupted Mr. Pointer, instantly seizing his wife's idea, and appropriating it as his own. "I am the proper person to see this affair out. There is not much doing, and if there were, I would leave everything to obtain justice for your niece. After all, however wrong she may have gone, she is your niece, Maria."

With which exceedingly nasty remark, which held a whole volume of unpleasant meaning as to what Mr. Pointer might expect from that relationship in the future, Mr. Pointer took Mrs. Heath by the arm, and piloted her out into the street, and finally to Lower Halliford, where the missing Lucy was not, and no tidings of her had come.

IV. Mr. Gage on Portents

About the time when poor distraught Mrs. Heath, having managed to elude the vigilance of that cleverest of men, Maria Pointer's husband, had run out of her small house, and was enlisting the sympathies of gossip-loving Shepperton in Lucy's disappearance, Mr. Paul Murray arrived at Liverpool Street Station, where his luggage and his valet awaited him.

"Get tickets, Davis," he said; "I have run it rather close"; and he walked towards Smith's stall, while his man went into the bookingoffice.

As he was about to descend the stairs, Davis became aware of a very singular fact. Looking down the steps, he saw precisely the same marks that had amazed him so short a time previously, being printed hurriedly off by a pair of invisible feet, which ran to the bottom and then flew as if in the wildest haste to the spot where Mr. Murray stood.

"I am not dreaming, am I?" thought the man; and he shut his eyes and opened them again.

The footprints were all gone!

At that moment his master turned from the bookstall and proceeded towards the train. A porter opened the door of a smoking carriage, but Murray shook his head and passed on. Mr. Davis, once more looking to the ground saw still following. There were not very many passengers, and it was quite plain to him that wherever his master went, the quick, wet prints went too. Even on the step of the compartment Mr. Murray eventually selected the man beheld a mark, as though some one had sprung in after him. He secured the door, and then walked away, to find a place for himself, marvelling in a dazed state of mind what it all meant; indeed, he felt so much dazed that, after he had found a seat to his mind, he did not immediately notice an old acquaintance in the opposite corner, who affably inquired,—

"And how is Mr. Davis?"

Thus addressed, Mr. Davis started from his reverie, and exclaimed, "Why, bless my soul, Gage, who'd have thought of seeing you here?" after which exchange of courtesies the pair shook hands gravely and settled down to converse.

Mr. Davis explained that he was going down with his governor to Norwich; and Mr. Gage stated that he and the old general had been staying at Thorpe, and were on their way to Lowestoft. Mr. Gage and his old general had also just returned from paying a round of visits in the West of England. "Pleasant enough, but slow," finished the gentleman's gentleman. "After all, in the season or out of it, there is no place like London."

With this opinion Mr. Davis quite agreed, and said he only wished he had never to leave it, adding,—

"We have not been away before for a long time; and we should not be going where we are now bound if we had not to humour some fancy of our grandmother's."

"Deuced rough on a man having to humour a grandmother's fancy," remarked Mr. Gage.

"No female ought to be left the control of money," said Mr. Davis with conviction. "See what the consequences have been in this case—Mrs. Murray outlived her son, who had to ask her for every shilling he wanted, and she is so tough she may see the last of her grandson."

"That is very likely," agreed the other. "He looks awfully bad."

"You saw him just now, I suppose?"

"No; but I saw him last night at Chertsey Station, and I could but notice the change in his appearance."

For a minute Mr. Davis remained silent. "Chertsey Station!" What could his master have been doing at Chertsey? That was a question he would have to put to himself again, and answer for himself at some convenient time; meanwhile he only answered,—

"Yes, I observe an alteration in him myself. Anything fresh in the paper?"

"No," answered Mr. Gage, handing his friend over the *Daily News*—the print he affected: "everything is as dull as ditchwater."

For many a mile Davis read or affected to read; then he laid the paper aside, and after passing his case, well filled with a tithe levied on Mr. Murray's finest cigars, to Gage, began solemnly,—

"I am going to ask you a curious question, Robert, as from man to man."

"Ask on," said Mr. Gage, striking a match. "Do you believe in warnings?"

The old General's gentleman burst out laughing. He was so tickled that he let his match drop from his fingers unapplied.

"I am afraid most of us have to believe in them, whether we like it or not," he answered, when he could speak. "Has there been some little difference between you and your governor, then?"

"You mistake," was the reply. "I did not mean warnings in the sense of notice, but warnings as warnings, you understand."

"Bother me if I do! Yes, now I take you. Do I believe in 'coming events casting shadows before,' as some one puts it? Has any shadow of a coming event been cast across you?"

"No, nor across anybody, so far as I know; but I've been thinking the matter over lately, and wondering if there can be any truth in such notions."

"What notions?"

"Why, that there are signs and suchlike sent when trouble is coming to any one."

"You may depend it is right enough that signs and tokens are sent. Almost every good family has its special warning: one has its mouse, another its black dog, a third its white bird, a fourth its drummer-boy, and so on. There is no getting over facts, even if you don't understand them."

"Well, it is very hard to believe."

"There wouldn't be much merit in believing if everything were as plain as a pikestaff. You know what the Scotch minister said to his boy: 'The very devils believe and tremble.' You wouldn't be worse than a devil, would you?"

"Has any sign ever appeared to you?" asked Davis.

"Not exactly; but lots of people have told me they have to them; for instance, old Seal, who drove the Dowager Countess of Ongar till the day of her death, used to make our hair stand on end talking about phantom carriages that drove away one after another from the door of Hainault House, and wakened every soul on the premises, night after night till the old Earl died. It took twelve clergymen to lay the spirit."

"I wonder one wasn't enough!" ejaculated Davis.

"There may have been twelve spirits, for all I know," returned Gage, rather puzzled by this view of the question; "but anyhow, there were twelve clergymen, with the bishop in his lawn sleeves chief among them. And I once lived with a young lady's-maid, who told me when she was a girl she made her home with her father's parents. On a winter's night, after everybody else had gone to bed, she sat up to make some girdle-bread—that is a sort of bread the people in Ireland, where she came from, bake over the fire on a round iron plate; with plenty of butter it is not bad eating. Well, as I was saying, she was quite alone; she had taken all the bread off, and was setting it up on edge to cool, supporting one piece against the other, two and two, when on the table where she was putting the cakes she saw one drop of blood fall, and then another, and then another, like the beginning of a shower.

"She looked to the ceiling, but could see nothing, and still the drops kept on falling slowly, slowly; and then she knew something had gone wrong with one dear to her; and she put a shawl over her head, and without saying a word to anybody, went through the loneliness and darkness of night all by herself to her father's."

"She must have been a courageous girl," remarked Mr. Davis.

"She was, and I liked her well. But to the point. When she reached her destination she found her youngest brother dead. Now what do you make of that?"

"It's strange, but I suppose he would have died all the same if she had not seen the blood-drops, and I can't see any good seeing them did her. If she had reached her father's in time to bid brother good-bye, there would have been some sense in such a sign. As it is, it seems to me a lot of trouble thrown away." Mr. Gage shook his head.

"What a sceptic you are, Davis! But there! London makes sceptics of the best of us. If you had spent a winter, as I did once, in the Highlands of Scotland, or heard the Banshee wailing for the General's nephew in the county of Mayo, you wouldn't have asked what was the use of second sight or Banshees. You would just have stood and trembled as I did many and many a time."

"I might," said Davis doubtfully, wondering what his friend would have thought of those wet little footprints. "Hillo, here's Peterborough! Hadn't we better stretch our legs? and a glass of something would be acceptable."

Of that glass, however, Mr. Davis was not destined to partake.

"If one of you is Murray's man," said the guard as they jumped out, "he wants you."

"I'll be back in a minute," observed Mr. Murray's man to his friend, and hastened off. But he was not back in a minute; on the contrary, he never returned at all.

V. Kiss Me

The first glance in his master's face filled Davis with a vague alarm. Gage's talk had produced an effect quite out of proportion to its merit, and a cold terror struck to the valet's heart as he thought there might, spite of his lofty scepticism, be something after all in the mouse, and the bird, and the drummer-boy, in the black dog, and the phantom carriages, and the spirits it required the united exertions of twelve clergymen (with the bishop in lawn sleeves among them) to lay; in Highland second sight and Irish Banshees; and in little feet paddling round and about a man's bed and following wherever he went. What awful disaster could those footprints portend? Would the train be smashed up? Did any river lie before them? and if so, was the sign to die? All these thoughts, and many more, passed through Davis' mind as he stood looking at his master's pallid face and waiting for him to speak.

"I wish you to come in here," said Mr. Murray after a pause, and with a manifest effort. "I am not quite well."

"Can I get you anything, sir?" asked the valet. "Will you not wait and go by another train?"

"No; I shall be better presently; only I do not like being alone."

Davis opened the door and entered the compartment. As he did so, he could not refrain from glancing at the floor, to see if those strange footsteps had been running races there.

"What are you looking for?" asked Mr. Murray irritably. "Have you dropped anything?"

"No, sir; O, no! I was only considering where I should be most out of the way."

"There," answered his master, indicating a seat next the window, and at the same time moving to one on the further side of the carriage. "Let no one get in; say I am ill—mad; that I have scarlet fever—the plague—what you please." And with this wide permission Mr. Murray laid his legs across the opposite cushion, wrapped one rug round his shoulders and another round his body, turned his head aside, and went to sleep or seemed to do so.

"If he is going to die, I hope it will be considered in my wages, but I am afraid it won't. Perhaps it is the old lady; but that would be too good fortune," reflected Davis;

and then he fell "a-thinkynge, a thinkynge," principally of Gage's many suggestions and those mysterious footprints, for which he kept at intervals furtively looking. But they did not appear; and at last the valet, worn out with vain conjections, dropped into a pleasant doze, from which he did not awake till they were nearing Norwich.

"We will go to an hotel till I find out what Mrs. Murray's plans are," said that lady's grandson when he found himself on the platform; and as if they had been only waiting this piece of information, two small invisible feet instantly skipped out of the compartment they had just vacated, and walked after Mr. Murray, leaving visible marks at every step.

"Great heavens! what is the meaning of this?" mentally asked Davis, surprised by fright after twenty prayerless and scheming years into an exclamation which almost did duty for a prayer. For a moment he felt sick with terror; then clutching his courage with the energy of desperation, he remembered that though wet footprints might mean death and destruction to the Murrays, his own ancestral annals held no record of such a portent.

Neither did the Murrays', so far as he was aware, but then he was aware of very little about that family. If the Irish girl Gage spoke of was informed by drops of blood that her brother lay dead, why should not Mr. Murray be made aware, through the token of these pattering footsteps, that he would very soon succeed to a large fortune?

Then any little extra attention Mr. Davis showed his master now would be remembered in his wages.

It was certainly unpleasant to know these damp feet had come down from London, and were going to the hotel with them; but "needs must" with a certain driver, and if portents and signs and warnings were made worth his while, Mr. Davis conceived there might be advantages connected with them.

Accordingly, when addressing Mr. Murray, his valet's voice assumed a more deferential tone than ever, and his manner became so respectfully tender, that onlookers rashly imagined the ideal master and the faithful servant of fiction had at last come in the flesh to Norwich. Davis' conduct was, indeed, perfect: devoted without being intrusive, he smoothed away all obstacles which could be smoothed, and even, by dint of a judicious two minutes alone with the doctor for whom he sent, managed the introduction of a useful sedative in some medicine, which the label stated was to be taken every four hours.

He saw to Mr. Murray's rooms and Mr. Murray's light repast, and then he waited on Mr. Murray's grandmother, and managed that lady so adroitly, she at length forgave the offender for having caught a chill. "Your master is always doing foolish things," she said. "It would have been much better had he remained even for a day or two in London rather than risk being laid up. However, you must nurse him carefully, and try to get him well enough to dine at Losdale Court on Monday. Fortunately to-morrow is Sunday, and he can take complete rest. Now Davis, remember I trust to you."

"I will do my best, ma'am," Davis said humbly, and went back to tell his master the interview had gone off without any disaster.

Then after partaking of some mild refreshment, he repaired to bed in a dressing-room opening off Mr. Murray's apartment, so that he might be within call and close at hand to administer those doses which were to be taken at intervals of four hours.

"I feel better to-night," said Mr. Murray last thing.

"It is this beautiful air, sir," answered Davis, who knew it was the sedative. "I hope you will be quite well in the morning."

But spite of the air, in the grey dawn Mr. Murray had again a dreadful dream—a worse dream than that which laid its heavy hand on him in London. He thought he was by the riverside beyond Dockett Point—beyond where the water-lilies grow. To his right was a little grove of old and twisted willows guarding a dell strewed in dry seasons with the leaves of many autumns, but, in his dream, wet and sodden by reason of heavy rain. There in June wild roses bloomed; there in winter hips and haws shone ruddy against the snow. To his left flowed a turbid river—turbid with floods that had troubled its peace. On the other bank lay a stagnant length of Surrey, while close at hand the Middlesex portion of Chertsey Mead stretched in a hopeless flat on to the bridge, just visible in the early twilight of a summer's evening that had followed after a dull lowering day.

From out of the gathering gloom there advanced walking perilously near to Dumsey Deep, a solitary female figure, who, when they met, said, "So you've come at last"; after which night seemed to close around him, silence for a space to lay its hands upon him.

About the same time Davis was seeing visions also. He bad lain long awake, trying to evolve order out of the day's chaos, but in vain. The stillness fretted him; the idea that even then those mysterious feet might in the darkness be printing their impress about his master's bed irritated his brain. Twice he got up to give that medicine ordered to be taken every four hours, but finding on each occasion Mr. Murray sleeping quietly, be forbore to arouse him.

He heard hour after hour chime, and it was not till the first hint of dawn that he fell into a deep slumber. Then he dreamt about the subject nearest his heart—a public house.

He thought he bad saved or gained enough to buy a roadside inn on which he had long cast eyes of affectionate regard—not in London, but not too far out: a delightful inn, where holiday-makers always stopped for refreshment, and sometimes for the day; at an inn with a pretty old-fashioned garden filled with fruit trees and vegetables, with a grass-plot around which were erected little arbours, where people could have tea or stronger stimulants; a skittle-ground, where men could soon make themselves very thirsty; and many other advantages tedious to mention. He had purchases money in his pocket, and, having paid a deposit, was proceeding to settle the affair, merely diverging from his way to call on a young widow he meant to make Mrs. Davis—a charming woman, who, having stood behind a bar before, seemed the very person to make the Wheatsheaf a triumphant success. He was talking to her sensibly, when suddenly she amazed him by saying, in a sharp, hurried voice. "Kiss me, kiss me, kiss me!" three times over.

The request seemed so strange that he stood astounded, and then awoke to hear the same words repeated.

"Kiss me, kiss me, kiss me!" some one said distinctly in Mr. Murray's room, the door of which stood open, and then all was quiet.

Only half awake, Davis sprang from his bed and walked across the floor, conceiving, so far as his brain was in a state to conceive anything, that his senses were playing him some trick.

"You won't?" said the voice again, in a tone which rooted him to the spot where he stood; "and yet, as we are never to meet again, you might *Kiss me once,*" the voice added caressingly, *"only once more."*

"Who the deuce has he got with him now?" thought Davis; but almost before the question was shaped in his mind there came a choked, gasping cry of "Unloose me, tigress, devil!" followed by a sound of desperate wrestling for life.

In a second, Davis was in the room. Through the white blinds light enough penetrated to show Mr. Murray in the grip apparently of some invisible antagonist, who seemed to be strangling him.

To and fro from side to side the man and the unseen phantom went swaying in that awful struggle. Short and fast came Mr. Murray's breath, while, making one supreme effort, he flung his opponent from him and sank back across the bed exhausted.

Wiping the moisture from his forehead, Davis, trembling in every limb, advanced to where his master lay, and found *he was fast asleep!*

Mr. Murray's eyes were wide open, and he did not stir hand or foot while the man covered him up as well as he was able, and then looked timidly around, dreading to see the second actor in the scene just ended.

"I can't stand much more of this," Davis exclaimed, and the sound of his own voice made him start.

There was brandy in the room which had been left over-night, and the man poured himself out and swallowed a glass of the liquor. He ventured to lift the blind and look at the floor, which was wet, as though buckets of water had been thrown over it, while the prints of little feet were everywhere.

Mr. Davis took another glass of brandy. *That* had not been watered.

"Well, this is a start!" he said in his own simple phraseology. "I wonder what the governor has been up to?"

For it was now borne in upon the valet's understanding that this warning was no shadow of any event to come, but the tell-tale ghost of some tragedy which could never be undone.

VI. Found Drowned

After such a dreadful experience it might have been imagined that Mr. Murray would be very ill indeed; but what we expect rarely comes to pass, and though during the whole of Sunday and Monday Davis felt, as he expressed the matter, "awfully shaky," his master appeared well and in fair spirits.

He went to the Cathedral, and no attendant footsteps dogged him. On Monday he accompanied his grandmother to Losdale Court, where he behaved so admirably as to please even the lady on whose favour his income depended. He removed to a furnished house Mrs. Murray had taken, and prepared to carry out her wishes. Day succeeded day and night to night, but neither by day nor night did Davis hear the sound of any ghostly voices or trace the print of any phantom foot.

Could it be that nothing more was to come of it—that the mystery was never to be elucidated but fade away as the marks of dainty feet had vanished from floor, pavement, steps, and platform?

The valet did not believe it; behind those signs made by nothing human lay some secret well worth knowing, but it had never been possible to know much about Mr. Murray.

"He was so little of a gentleman" that he had no pleasant, careless ways. He did not leave his letters lying loose for all the world to read. He did not tear up papers, and toss them into a waste-paper basket. He had the nastiest practice of locking up and burning; and though it was Mr. Davis's commendable custom to collect and preserve unconsidered odds and ends as his master occasionally left in his pockets, these, after all, were trifles light as air.

Nevertheless, as a straw shows how the wind blows, so that chance remark anent Chertsey Station made by Gage promised to provide a string on which to thread various little beads in Davis' possession.

The man took them out and looked at them: a woman's fall-white tulle, with black spots, smelling strongly of tobacco-smoke and musk; a receipt for a bracelet, purchased from an obscure jeweller; a Chertsey Lock ticket; and the return half of a first-class ticket from Shepperton to Waterloo, stamped with the date of the day before they left London.

At these treasures Davis looked long and earnestly.

"We shall see," he remarked as he put them up again; "there I think the scent lies hot."

It could not escape the notice of so astute a servant that his master was unduly anxious for a sight of the London papers, and that he glanced through them eagerly for something he apparently failed to find—more, that he always laid the print aside with a sigh of relief. Politics did not seem to trouble him, or any public burning question.

"He has some burning question of his own," thought the valet, though he mentally phrased his notion in different words.

Matters went on thus for a whole week. The doctor came and went and wrote prescriptions, for Mr. Murray either was still ailing or chose to appear so. Davis caught a word or two which had reference to the patient's heart, and some shock. Then he considered that awful night, and wondered how he, who "was in his sober senses, and wide awake, and staring," had lived through it.

"My heart, and a good many other things, will have to be considered," he said to himself. "No wages could pay for what has been put upon me this week past. I wonder whether I ought to speak to Mr. Murray now?"

Undecided on this point, he was still considering it when he called his master on the following Sunday morning. The first glance at the stained and polished decided him. Literally it was interlaced with footprints. The man's hand shook as he drew up the blind, but he kept his eyes turned on Mr. Murray while he waited for orders, and walked out of the room when dismissed as though such marks had been matters of customary occurrence in a nineteenth century bedroom.

No bell summoned him back on this occasion. Instead of asking for information, Mr. Murray dropped into a chair and nerved himself to defy the inevitable.

Once again there came a pause. For three days nothing occurred; but on the fourth a newspaper and a letter arrived, both of which Davis inspected curiously. They were addressed in Mr. Savill's handwriting, and they bore the postmark "SHEPPERTON."

The newspaper was enclosed in an ungummed wrapper, tied round with a piece of string. After a moment's reflection Davis cut that string, spread out the print, and beheld a column marked at top with three blue crosses, containing the account of an inquest held at the King's Head on a body found on the previous Sunday morning, close by the "Tumbling Bay."

It was that of a young lady who had been missing since the previous Friday week, and could only be identified by the clothes.

Her mother, who, in giving evidence, frequently broke down, told how her daughter on the evening in question went out for a walk and never returned. She did not wish to go, because her boots were being mended, and her shoes were too large. No doubt they had dropped off. She had very small feet, and it was not always possible to get shoes to fit them. She was engaged to be married to the gentleman with whom she went out. He told her they bad quarrelled. She did not believe he could have anything to do with her child's death; but she did not know what to think. It had been said her girl was keeping company with somebody else, but that could not be true. Her girl was a good girl.

Yes; she had found a bracelet hidden away among her girl's clothes, and she could not say bow she got the seven golden sovereigns that were in the purse, or the locket taken off the body; but her girl was a good girl, and she did not know whatever she would do without her, for Lucy was all she had.

Walter Grantley was next examined, after being warned that anything he said might be used against him.

Though evidently much affected, he gave his evidence in a clear and straightforward manner. He was a clerk in the War Office. He had, against the wishes of all his friends, engaged himself to the deceased, who, after having so.me time professed much affection, had latterly treated him with great coldness. On the evening in question she reluctantly came out with him for a walk; but after they passed the Ship she insisted he should take a boat. They turned and got into a boat. He wanted to go down the river, because there was no lock before Sunbury. She declared if he would not row her up the river, she would go home.

They went up the river, quarrelling all the way. There had been so much of this sort of thing that after they passed through Shepperton Lock he tried to bring matters to a conclusion, and asked her to name a day for their marriage. She scoffed at him and asked if he thought she meant to marry a man on such a trumpery salary. Then she insisted he should land her; and after a good deal of argument he did land her; and rowed back alone to Halliford. He knew no more.

Richard Savill deposed he took a boat at Lower Halliford directly after the last witness, with whom he was not acquainted, and rowed up towards Chertsey, passing Mr. Grantley and Miss Heath, who were evidently quarrelling. He went as far as Dumsey Deep, where, finding the stream most heavily against him, he turned, and on his way back saw the young lady walking slowly along the bank. At Shepperton Lock he and Mr. Grantley exchanged a few words, and rowed down to Halliford almost side by side. They bade each other good-evening, and Mr. Grantley walked off in the direction of Walton where it was proved by other witnesses he arrived at eight o'clock, and did not go out again till ten, when he went to bed.

All efforts to trace what had become of the unfortunate girl proved unavailing, till a young man named Lemson discovered the body on the previous Sunday morning close by the Tumbling Bay. The coroner wished to adjourn the inquest, in hopes some further light might be thrown on such a mysterious occurrence; but the jury protested so strongly against any proceeding of the sort, that they were directed to return an open verdict.

No one could dispute that the girl had been "found drowned," or that there was "no evidence to explain how she came to he drowned." At the close of the proceedings, said the local paper, an affecting incident occurred. The mother wished the seven pounds to be given to the man "who brought her child home," but the man refused to accept a penny. The mother said she would never touch it, when a relation stepped forward and offered to take charge of it for her.

The local paper contained also a leader on the tragedy, in the course of which it remarked how exceedingly fortunate it was that Mr. Savill chanced to be staying at the Ship Hotel, so well known to boating-men, and that he happened to go up the river and see the poor young lady after Mr. Grantley left her, as otherwise the latter gentleman might have found himself in a most unpleasant position. He was much to be pitied, and the leader-writer felt confident that every one who read the evidence would sympathize with him. It was evident the inquiry had failed to solve the mystery connected with Miss Heath's untimely fate, but it was still competent to pursue the matter if any fresh facts transpired.

"I must get to know more about all this," thought Davis as he refolded and tied up the paper.

VII. Davis Speaks

If there be any truth in old saws, Mr. Murray's wooing was a very happy one. Certainly it was very speedy. By the end of October he and Miss Ketterick were engaged, and before Christmas the family lawyers had their hands full drawing settlements and preparing deeds. Mrs. Murray disliked letting any money slip out of her own control, but she had gone too far to recede, and Mr. Ketterick was not a man who would have tolerated any proceeding of the sort.

Perfectly straightforward himself, he compelled straightforwardness in others, and Mrs. Murray was obliged to adhere to the terms proposed when nothing seemed to her less probable than that the marriage she wished ever would take place. As for the bridegroom, he won golden opinions from Mr. Ketterick. Beyond the income to be insured to his wife and himself, he asked for nothing. Further he objected to nothing. Never before, surely, had a man been so easily satisfied.

"All I have ever wanted," he said, "was some settled income, so that I might not feel completely dependent on my grandmother. That will now be secured, and I am quite satisfied."

He deferred to Mr. Ketterick's opinions and wishes. He made no stipulations.

"You are giving me a great prize," he told the delighted father, "of which I am not worthy, but I will try to make her happy."

And the gentle girl was happy: no tenderer or more devoted lover could the proudest beauty have desired. With truth he told her he "counted the days till she should be his." For he felt secure when by her side. The footsteps had never followed him to Losdale Court. Just in the place that of all others he would have expected them to come, he failed to see that tiny print. There were times when he even forgot it for a season; when he did remember it, he believed, with the faith born of hope, that he should never see it again.

"I wonder he has the conscience," muttered Mr. Davis one morning, as he looked after the engaged pair. The valet had the strictest ideas concerning the rule conscience should hold over the doings of other folks, and some pleasingly lax notions about the sacrifices conscience had a right to demand from himself. "I suppose he thinks he is safe now that those feet are snugly tucked up in holy ground," proceeded Davis, who, being superstitious, faithfully subscribed to all the old formulæ. "Ah! he doesn't know what I know—yet"; which last word, uttered with much gusto, indicated a most unpleasant quarter of an hour in store at some future period for Mr. Murray.

It came one evening a week before his marriage. He was in London, in his grandmother's house, writing to the girl he had grown to love with the great, entire, remorseful love of his life, when Davis, respectful as ever, appeared, and asked if he might speak a word. Mr. Murray involuntarily put his letter beneath some blotting-paper, and, folding his hands over both, answered, unconscious of what was to follow, "Certainly."

Davis had come up with his statement at full-cock, and fired at once.

"I have been a faithful servant to you, sir."

Mr. Murray lifted his eyes and looked at him. Then he knew what was coming. "I have never found fault with you, Davis," he said, after an almost imperceptible pause.

"No, sir, you have been a good master—a master I am sure no servant who knew his place could find a fault with."

If he had owned an easy mind and the smallest sense of humour—neither of which possessions then belonged to Mr. Murray—he might have felt enchanted with such a complete turning of the tables; but as matters stood, he could only answer, "Good master as I have been, I suppose you wish to leave my service. Am I right, Davis?"

"Well, sir, you are right and you are wrong. I do not want to leave your service just yet. It may not be quite convenient to you for me to go now; only I want to come to an understanding."

"About what?" Mr. Murray asked, quite calmly, though he could feel his heart thumping hard against his ribs, and that peculiar choking sensation which is the warning of what in such cases must come some day.

"Will you cast your mind back, sir, to a morning in last August, when you called my attention to some extraordinary footprints on the floor of your room?"

"I remember the morning," said Mr. Murray, that choking sensation seeming to suffocate him. "Pray go on."

If Davis had not been master of the position, this indifference would have daunted him; as it was, he again touched the trigger, and fired this: "*I know all!*"

Mr. Murray's answer did not come so quick this time. The waters had gone over his head, and for a minute he felt as a man might if suddenly flung into a raging sea, and battling for his life. He was battling for his life with a wildly leaping heart. The noise of a hundred billows seemed dashing on his brain. Then the tempest lulled, the roaring torrent was stayed, and then he said interrogatively, "Yes?"

The prints of those phantom feet had not amazed Davis more than did his master's coolness.

"You might ha' knocked me down with a feather," he stated, when subsequently relating this interview. "I always knew he was a queer customer, but I never knew how queer till then."

"Yes?" said Mr. Murray, which reply quite disconcerted his valet.

"I wouldn't have seen what I have seen, sir," he remarked, "not for a king's ransom."

"No?"

"No, sir, and that is the truth. What we both saw has been with me at bed and at board, as the saying is, ever since. When I shut my eyes I still feel those wet feet dabbling about the room; and in the bright sunshine I can't help shuddering, because there seems to be a cold mist creeping over me."

"Are you not a little imaginative, Davis?" asked his master, himself repressing a shudder.

"No, sir, I am not; no man can be that about which his own eyes have seen and his own ears have heard; and I have heard and seen what I can never forget, and what nothing could pay me for going through."

"Nevertheless?" suggested Mr. Murray.

"I don't know whether I am doing right in holding my tongue, in being so faithful, sir; but I can't help it. I took to you from the first, and I wouldn't bring harm on you if any act of mine could keep it from you. When one made the remark to me awhile ago it was a strange thing to see a gentleman attended by a pair of wet footprints, I said they were a sign in your family that some great event was about to happen."

"Did you say so?"

"I did, sir, Lord forgive me!" answered Davis, with unblushing mendacity. "I have gone through more than will ever be known over this affair, which has shook me, Mr. Murray. I am not the man I was before ghosts took to following me, and getting into trains without paying any fare, and waking me in the middle of the night, and rousing me out of my warm bed to see sights I would not have believed I could have seen if anybody had sworn it to me I have aged twenty-five years since last August—my nerves are destroyed; and so, sir, before you got married, I thought I would make bold to ask what I am to do with a constitution broken in your service and hardly a penny put by"; and, almost out of breath with his pathetic statement, Davis stopped and waited for an answer.

With a curiously hunted expression in them, Mr. Murray raised his eyes and looked at Davis.

"You have thought over all this," he said. "How much do you assess them at?"

"I scarcely comprehend, sir—assess what at?"

"Your broken constitution and the five-and-twenty years you say you have aged."

His master's face was so gravely serious that Davis could take the question neither as a jest nor a sneer. It was a request to fix a price and he did so.

"Well, sir," he answered, "I have thought it all over. In the nightwatches, when I could get no rest, I lay and reflected what I ought to do. I want to act fair. I have no wish to drive a hard bargain with you, and, on the other hand, I don't think I would be doing justice by a man that has worked hard if I let myself be sold for nothing. So, sir, to cut a long story short, I am willing to take two thousand pounds."

"And where do you imagine I am to get two thousand pounds?" Mr. Davis modestly intimated he knew his place better than to presume to have any notion, but no doubt Mr. Murray could raise that sum easily enough.

"If I could raise such a sum for you, do you not think I should have raised it for myself long ago?"

Davis answered that he did; but, if he might make free to say so, times were changed.

"They are, they are indeed," said Mr. Murray bitterly; and then there was silence. Davis knocked the conversational ball the next time.

"I am in no particular hurry, sir," he said. "So, long as we understand one another I can wait till you come back from Italy, and have got the handling of some cash of your own. I daresay even then you won't be able to pay me off all at once; but if you would insure your life—"

"I can't insure my life: I have tried, and been refused."

Again there ensued a silence, which Davis broke once more.

"Well, sir," he began, "I'll chance that. If you will give me a line of writing about what you owe me, and make a sort of a will, saying I am to get two thousand, I'll hold my tongue about what's gone and past. And I would not be fretting, sir, if I was you: things are quiet now, and, please God, you might never have any more trouble."

Mr. Davis, in view of his two thousand pounds, his widow, and his wayside public, felt disposed to take an optimistic view of even his master's position; but Mr. Murray's thoughts were of a different hue. "If I do have any more," he considered, "I shall go mad"; a conclusion which seemed likely enough to follow upon even the memory of the phantom feet coming dabbling out of an unseen world to follow him with their accursed print in this.

Davis was not going abroad with the happy pair. For sufficient reason Mr. Murray had decided to leave him behind, and Mrs. Murray, ever alive to her own convenience, instantly engaged him to stay on with her as butler, her own being under notice to leave.

Thus, in a semi-official capacity, Davis witnessed the wedding, which people considered a splendid affair.

What Davis thought of it can never be known, because when he left Losdale Church his face was whiter than the bride's dress; and after the newly-wedded couple started on the first stage of their life-journey he went to his room, and stayed in it till his services were required.

"There is no money would pay me for what I've seen," he remarked to himself. "I went too cheap. But when once I handle the cash I'll try never to come anigh him or them again."

What was he referring to? Just this. As the bridal group moved to the vestry he saw, if no one else did, those wet, wet feet softly and swiftly threading their way round the bridesmaids and the groomsman, in front of the relations, before Mrs. Murray herself, and hurry on to keep step with the just wed pair.

For the last time the young wife signed her maiden name. Friends crowded around, uttering congratulations, and still through the throng those unnoticed feet kept walking in and out, round and round, backward and forward, as a dog threads its way through the people at a fair. Down the aisle, under the sweeping dresses of the ladies, past courtly gentlemen, Davis saw those awful feet running gleefully till they came up with bride and bridegroom.

"She is going abroad with them," thought the man; and then for a moment he felt as if could endure the ghastly vision no longer, but must faint dead away. "It is a vile shame," he reflected, "to drag an innocent girl into such a whirlpool"; and all the time over the church step the feet were dancing merrily.

The clerk and the verger noticed them at last.

"I wonder who has been here with wet feet?" said the clerk; and the verger wonderingly answered he did not know.

Davis could have told him, had he been willing to speak or capable of speech.

Conclusion: He'd Have Seen Me Righted

It was August once again—August, fine, warm, and sunshiny—just one year after that damp afternoon on which Paul Murray and his friend stood in front of the Ship at Lower Halliford. No lack of visitors that season. Hotels were full, and furnished houses at a premium. The hearts of lodging-house keepers were glad. Ladies arrayed in rainbow hues flashed about the quiet village streets; boatmen reaped a golden harvest; all sorts of crafts swarmed on the river. Men in flannels gallantly towed their feminine belongings up against a languidly flowing stream. Pater- and materfamilias, and all the olive branches, big and little, were to be met on the Thames, and on the banks of Thames, from Richmond to Staines, and even higher still. The lilies growing around Dockett Point floated with their pure cups wide open to the sun; no close folding of the white wax-leaves around the golden centre that season. Beside the water purple loosestrife grew in great clumps of brilliant colour dazzling to the sight. It was, in fact, a glorious August, in which pleasure-seekers could idle and sun themselves and get tanned to an almost perfect brown without the slightest trouble.

During the past twelvemonth local tradition had tried hard to add another ghost at Dumsey Deep to that already established in the adjoining Stabbery; but the unshrinking brightness of that glorious summer checked belief in it for the time. No doubts when the dull autumn days came again, and the long winter nights, full of awful possibilities, folded water and land in fog and darkness, a figure dressed in grey silk and black velvet fichu, with a natty grey hat trimmed with black and white feathers on its phantom head, with small feet covered by the thinnest of openwork stockings, from which the shoes, so much too large, had dropped long ago, would reappear once more, to the terror of all who heard, but for the time being, snugly tucked up in holy ground the girl whose heart had rejoiced in her beauty, her youth, her admirers, and her finery, was lying quite still and quiet, with closed eyes, and ears that heard neither the church bells nor the splash of oars nor the murmur of human voices.

Others, too, were missing from—though not missed by—Shepperton (the Thames villages miss no human being so long as other human beings, with plenty of money, come down by rail, boat, or carriage to supply his place). Paul Murray, Dick Savill, and Walter Grantley were absent. Mrs. Heath, too, had gone, a tottering, heartbroken woman, to Mr. Pointer's, where she was most miserable, but where she and her small possessions were taken remarkably good care of.

"Only a year agone," she said one day, "my girl was with me. In the morning she wore her pretty cambric with pink spots; and in the afternoon, that grey silk in which she was buried—for we durst not change a thread, but just wrapped a winding-sheet round what was left. O! Lucy, Lucy, Lucy! to think I bore you for that!" and then she wept softly; and nobody heeded or tried to console her, for "what," as Mrs. Pointer wisely said, "was the use of fretting over a daughter dead a twelvemonth, and never much of a comfort neither."

Mr. Richard Savill was still "grinding away," to quote his expression. Walter Gramley had departed, so reported his friends, for the diamond-fields; his enemies improved on this by carelessly answering,—

"Grantley! O, he's gone to the devil"; which latter statement could not have been quite true, since he has been back in England for a long time, and is now quite well to do and reconciled to his family.

As for Paul Murray, there had been all sorts of rumours floating about concerning him.

The honeymoon had been unduly protracted; from place to place the married pair wandered—never resting, never staying; alas! for him there was no rest—there could be none here.

It mattered not where he went—east, west, south, or north—those noiseless wet feet followed; no train was swift enough to outstrip them; no boat could cut the water fast enough to leave them behind; they tracked him with dogged persistence; they were with him sleeping, walking, eating, drinking, praying—for Paul Murray in those days often prayed after a desperate heathenish fashion—and yet the plague was not stayed; the accursed thing still dogged him like a Fate.

After a while people began to be shy of him, because the footsteps were no more intermittent; they were always where he was. Did he enter a cathedral, they accompanied him; did he walk solitary through the woods or pace the lake-side, or wander by the sea, they were ever and always with the man.

They were worse than any evil conscience, because conscience often sleeps, and they from the day of his marriage never did. They had waited for that—waited till he should raise the cup of happiness to his lips, in order to fill it with gall—waited till his wife's dream of bliss was perfect, and then wake her to the knowledge of some horror more agonizing than death.

There were times when he left his young wife for days and days, and went, like those possessed of old, into the wilderness, seeking rest and finding none; for no legion of demons could have cursed a man's life more than those wet feet, which printed marks on Paul Murray's heart that might have been branded by red-hot irons.

All that had gone before was as nothing to the trouble of having involved another in the horrible mystery of his own life—and that other a gentle, innocent, loving creature he might just as well have killed as married.

He did not know what to do. His brain was on fire; he had lost all hold upon himself, all grip over his mind. On the sea of life he tossed like a ship without a rudder, one minute taking a resolve to shoot himself, the next turning his steps to seek some priest, and confess the whole matter fully and freely, and, before he had walked a dozen yards, determining to go away into some savage and desolate land, where those horrible feet might, if they pleased, follow him to his grave.

By degrees this was the plan which took firm root in his dazed brain; and accordingly one morning he started for England, leaving a note in which he asked his wife to follow him. He never meant to see her sweet face again, and he never did. He had determined to go to his father-in-law and confess to him; and accordingly, on the anniversary of Lucy's death, he found himself at Losdale Court, where vague rumours of some unaccountable trouble had preceded him.

Mr. Ketterick was brooding over these rumours in his library, when, as if in answer to his thoughts, the servant announced Mr. Murray.

"Good God!" exclaimed the older man, shocked by the white, haggard face before him, "what is wrong?"

"I have been ill," was the reply.

"Where is your wife?"

"She is following me. She will be here in a day or so."

"Why did you not travel together?"

"That is what I have come to tell you."

Then he suddenly stopped and put his hand to his heart. He had voluntarily come up for execution, and now his courage failed him. His manhood was gone, his nerves unstrung. He was but a poor, weak, wasted creature, worn out by the ceaseless torment of those haunting feet, which, however, since he turned his steps to England had never followed him. Why had he travelled to Losdale Court? Might he not have crossed the ocean and effaced himself in the Far West, without telling his story at all?

Just as he had laid down the revolver, just as he had turned from the priest's door, so now he felt he could not say that which he had come determined to say.

"I have walked too far," he said, after a pause. "I cannot talk just yet. Will you leave me for half an hour? No; I don't want anything, thank you—except to be quiet." Quiet!—ah, heavens!

After a little he rose and passed out on to the terrace. Around there was beauty and peace and sunshine. He—he—was the only jarring element, and even on him there seemed falling a numbed sensation which for the time being simulated rest.

He left the terrace and crossed the lawn till he came to a great cedar tree, under which there was a seat, where he could sit a short time before leaving the Court.

Yes, he would go away and make no sign. Dreamily he thought of the wild lone lands beyond the sea, where there would be none to ask whence he came or marvel about the curse which followed him. Over the boundless prairie, up the mountain heights, let those feet pursue him if they would. Away from his fellows he could bear his burden. He would confess to no man—only to God, who knew his sin and sorrow; only to his Maker, who might have pity on the work of his hands, and some day bid that relentless avenger be still.

No, he would take no man into his confidence; and even as he so decided, the brightness of the day seemed to be clouded over, warmth was exchanged for a deadly chill, a horror of darkness seemed thrown like a pall over him, and a rushing sound as of many waters filled his ears.

An hour later, when Mr. Ketterick sought his son-in-law, he found him lying on the ground, which was wet and trampled, as though by hundreds of little feet.

His shouts brought help, and Paul Murray was carried into the house, where they laid him on a couch and piled rugs and blankets over his shivering body.

"Fetch a doctor at once," said Mr. Ketterick.

"And a clergyman," added the housekeeper.

"No, a magistrate," cried the sick man, in a loud voice.

They had thought him insensible, and, startled, looked at each other. After that he spoke no more, but turned his head away from them and lay quiet.

The doctor was the first to arrive. With quick alertness he stepped across the room, pulled aside the coverings, and took the patient's hand; then after gently moving the averted face, he said solemnly, like a man whose occupation has gone,—

"I can do nothing here; he is dead."

It was true. Whatever his secret, Paul Murray carried it with him to a country further distant than the lone land where he had thought to hide his misery.

"It is of no use talking to me," said Mr. Davis, when subsequently telling his story. "If Mr. Murray had been a gentleman as was a gentleman, he'd have seen me righted, dead or not. *She* was able to come back—at least, her feet were; and he could have done the same if he'd liked. It was as bad as swindling not making a fresh will after he was married. How was I to know that will would turn out so much waste paper? And then when I asked for my own, Mrs. Murray dismissed me without a character, and Mr. Ketterick's lawyers won't give me anything either; so a lot I've made by being a faithful servant, and I'd have all servants take warning by me."

Mr. Davis is his own servant now, and a very bad master he finds himself.

The Haunted and the Haunters; or, The House and the Brain

Edward Bulwer-Lytton

A FRIEND OF MINE, WHO IS A MAN OF LETTERS AND A PHILOSOPHER, SAID TO ME one day, as if between jest and earnest,—"Fancy! since we last met, I have discovered a haunted house in the midst of London."

"Really haunted?—and by what?—ghosts?"

"Well, I can't answer these questions; all I know is this—six weeks ago I and my wife were in search of a furnished apartment. Passing a quiet street, we saw on the window of one of the houses a bill, 'Apartments Furnished.' The situation suited us: we entered the house—liked the rooms—engaged them by the week—and left them the third day. No power on earth could have reconciled my wife to stay longer; and I don't wonder at it."

"What did you see?"

"Excuse me—I have no desire to be ridiculed as a superstitious dreamer—nor, on the other hand, could I ask you to accept on my affirmation what you would hold to be incredible without the evidence of your own senses. Let me only say this, it was not so much what we saw or heard (in which you might fairly suppose that we were the dupes of our own excited fancy, or the victims of imposture in others) that drove us away, as it was an undefinable terror which seized both of us whenever we passed by the door of a certain unfurnished room, in which we neither saw nor heard anything. And the strangest marvel of all was, that for once in my life I agreed with my wife, silly woman though she be—and allowed, after the third night, that it was impossible to stay a fourth in that house. Accordingly, on the fourth morning I summoned the woman who kept the house and attended on us, and told her that the rooms did not quite suit us, and we would not stay out our week. She said dryly, 'I know why; you have staid longer than any other lodger. Few ever staid a second night; none before you a third. But I take it they have been very kind to you.'

"'They—who?' I asked, affecting a smile.

"'Why, they who haunt the house, whoever they are. I don't mind them; I remember them many years ago, when I lived in this house, not as a servant; but I know they will be the death of me some day. I don't care—I'm old, and must die soon anyhow; and then I shall be with them, and in this house still.' The woman spoke with so dreary a calmness, that really it was a sort of awe that prevented my conversing with her farther. I paid for my week, and too happy were I and my wife to get off so cheaply."

"You excite my curiosity," said I; "nothing I should like better than to sleep in a haunted house. Pray give me the address of the one which you left so ignominiously."

My friend gave me the address: and when we parted, I walked straight towards the house thus indicated.

It is situated on the north side of Oxford Street, in a dull but respectable thoroughfare. I found the house shut up—no bill at the window, and no response to my knock. As I was turning away, a beer-boy, collecting pewter pots at the neighbouring areas, said to me, "Do you want any one at that house, sir?"

"Yes, I heard it was to be let."

"Let!—why, the woman who kept it is dead—has been dead these three weeks, and no one can be found to stay there, though Mr. J—— offered ever so much. He offered mother, who chars for him, £1 a-week just to open and shut the windows, and she would not."

"Would not!—and why?"

"The house is haunted; and the old woman who kept it was found dead in her bed, with her eyes wide open. They say the devil strangled her."

"Pooh!—you speak of Mr. J——. Is he the owner of the house?"

"Yes."

"Where does he live?"

"In G—— Street, No. ——."

"What is he?—in any business?"

"No, sir—nothing particular; a single gentleman."

I gave the pot-boy the gratuity earned by his liberal information, and proceeded to Mr. J——, in G—— Street, which was close by the street that boasted the haunted house. I was lucky enough to find Mr. J—— at home—an elderly man, with intelligent countenance and prepossessing manners.

I communicated my name and my business frankly. I said I heard the house was considered to be haunted—that I had a strong desire to examine a house with so equivocal a reputation—that I should be greatly obliged if he would allow me to hire it, though only for a night. I was willing to pay for that privilege whatever he might be inclined to ask. "Sir," said Mr. J———, with great courtesy, "the house is at your service, for as short or as long a time as you please. Kent is out of the question—the obligation will be on my side should you be able to discover the cause of the strange phenomena which at present deprive it of all value. I cannot let it, for I cannot even get a servant to keep it in order or answer the door. Unluckily the house is haunted, if I may use that expression, not only by night, but by day; though at night the disturbances are of a more unpleasant and sometimes of a more alarming character. The poor old woman who died in it three weeks ago was a pauper whom I took out of a workhouse, for in her childhood she had been known to some of my family, and had once been in such good circumstances that she had rented that house of my uncle. She was a woman of superior education and strong mind, and was the only person I could ever induce to remain in the house. Indeed, since her death, which was sudden, and the coroner's inquest, which gave it a notoriety in the neighbourhood, I have so despaired of finding any person to take charge of it, much more a tenant, that I would willingly let it rent-free for a year to any one who would pay its rates and taxes."

"How long is it since the house acquired this sinister character?"

"That I can scarcely tell you, but very many years since. The old woman I spoke of said it was haunted when she rented it between thirty and forty years ago. The fact is that my life has been spent in the East Indies, and in the civil service of the Company. I returned to England last year, on inheriting the fortune of an uncle, amongst whose possessions was the house in question, found it shut up and uninhabited. I was told that it was haunted, that no one would inhabit it. I smiled at what seemed to me so idle a story. I spent some money in repainting and roofing it—added to its old-fashioned furniture a few modern articles—advertised it, and obtained a lodger for a year. He was a colonel retired on half-pay. He came in with his family, a son and a daughter, and four or five servants: they all left the house the next day, and although they deponed that they had all seen something different, that something was equally terrible to all I really could not in conscience sue, or even blame, the colonel for breach of agreement. Then I put in the old woman I have spoken of, and she was empowered to let the house in apartments. I never had one lodger who stayed more than three days. I do not tell you their stories—to no two lodgers have there been exactly the same phenomena repeated. It is better that you should judge for yourself, than enter the house with an imagination influenced by previous narratives; only be prepared to see and to hear something or other, and take whatever precautions you yourself please."

"Have you never had a curiosity yourself to pass a night in that house?"

"Yea. I passed not a night, but three hours in broad daylight alone in that house. My curiosity is not satisfied, but it is quenched. I have no desire to renew the experiment. You cannot complain, you see, sir, that I am not sufficiently candid; and unless your interest be exceedingly eager and your nerves unusually strong, I honestly add, that I advise you *not* to pass a night in that house."

"My interest *is* exceedingly keen," said I, "and though only a coward will boast of his nerves in situations wholly unfamiliar to him, yet my nerves have been seasoned in such variety of danger that I have the right to rely on them—even in a haunted house."

Mr. J—— said very little more; he took the keys of the house out of his bureau, gave them to me,—and thanking him cordially for his frankness, and his urbane concession to my wish, I carried off my prize.

Impatient for the experiment, as soon as I reached home, I summoned my confidential servant—a young man of gay spirits, fearless temper, and as free from superstitious prejudice as any one I could think of.

"F——," said I, "you remember in Germany how disappointed we were at not finding a ghost in that old castle, which was said to be haunted by a headless apparition?—well, I have heard of a house in London which, I have reason to hope, is decidedly haunted. I mean to sleep there to-night. From what I hear, there is no doubt that something will allow itself to be seen or to be heard—something, perhaps, excessively horrible. Do you think, if I take you with me, I may rely on your presence of mind, whatever may happen?"

"Oh, sir! pray trust me," answered F——, grinning with delight.

"Very well,—then here are the keys of the house—this is the address. Go now,—select for me any bedroom you please; and since the house has not been inhabited for weeks, make up a good fire—air the bed well—see, of course, that there are candles as well as fuel. Take with you my revolver and my dagger —so much for my weapons—arm yourself equally well; and if we are not a match for a dozen ghosts, we shall be but a sorry couple of Englishmen."

I was engaged for the rest of the day on business so urgent that I had not leisure to think much on the nocturnal adventure to which I had plighted my honour. I dined alone, and very late, and while dining, read, as is my habit. The volume I selected was one of Macaulay's Essays. I thought to myself that I would take the book with me; there was so much of healthfulness in the style, and practical life in the subjects, that it would serve as an antidote against the influences of superstitious fancy.

Accordingly, about half-past nine, I put the book into my pocket, and strolled leisurely towards the haunted house. I took with me a favourite dog,—an exceedingly sharp, bold, and vigilant bull-terrier,—a dog fond of prowling about strange ghostly corners and passages at night in search of rats—a dog of dogs for a ghost.

It was a summer night, but chilly, the sky somewhat gloomy and overcast. Still there was a moon—faint and sickly, but still a moon—and if the clouds permitted, after midnight it would be brighter.

I reached the house, knocked, and my servant opened with a cheerful smile.

"All right, sir, and very comfortable."

"Oh!" said I, rather disappointed; "have you not seen nor heard anything remarkable?"

"Well, sir, I must own I have heard something queer."

"What?—what?"

"The sound of feet pattering behind me; and once or twice small noises like whispers close at my ear—nothing more."

"You are not at all frightened?"

"I! not a bit of it, sir"; and the man's bold look reassured me on one point—viz. that, happen what might, he would not desert me.

We were in the hall, the street-door closed, and my attention was now drawn to my dog. He had at first ran in eagerly enough, but had sneaked back to the door, and was scratching and whining to get out. After patting him on the head, and encouraging him gently, the dog seemed to reconcile himself to the situation and followed me and F—— through the house, but keeping close at my heels instead of hurrying inquisitively in advance, which was his usual and normal habit in all strange places. We first visited the subterranean apartments, the kitchen and other offices, and especially the cellars, in which last there were two or three bottles of wine still left in a bin, covered with cobwebs, and evidently, by their appearance, undisturbed for many years. It was clear that the ghosts were not winebibbers. For the rest we discovered nothing of interest. There was a gloomy little back-yard, with very high walls. The stones of this yard were very damp,—and what with the damp, and what with the dust and smoke-grime on the pavement, our feet left a slight impression where we passed. And now appeared the first strange phenomenon witnessed by myself in this strange abode. I saw, just before me, the print of a foot suddenly form itself, as it were. I stopped, caught hold of my servant, and pointed to it. In advance of that footprint as suddenly dropped another. We both saw it. I advanced quickly to the place; the footprint kept advancing before me, a small footprint—the foot of a child: the impression was too faint thoroughly to distinguish the shape, but it seemed to us both that it was the print of a naked foot. This phenomenon ceased when we arrived at the opposite wall, nor did it repeat itself on returning. We remounted the stairs, and entered the rooms on the ground floor, a dining parlour, a small back-parlour, and a still smaller third room that had been probably appropriated to a footman—all still as death. We then visited the drawing-rooms, which seemed fresh and new. In the front room I seated myself in an arm-chair. F—— placed on the table the candlestick with which he had lighted us. I told him to shut the door. As he turned to do so, a chair opposite to me moved from the wall quickly and noiselessly, and dropped itself about a yard from my own chair, immediately fronting it.

"Why, this is better than the turning-tables," said I, with a half laugh—and as I laughed, my dog put back his head and howled.

F——, coming back, had not observed the movement of the chair. He employed himself now in stilling the dog. I continued to gaze on the chair, and fancied I saw on it a pale blue misty outline of a human figure, but an outline so indistinct that I could only distrust my own vision. The dog now was quiet. "Put back that chair opposite to me," said I to F——; "put it back to the wall."

F—— obeyed. "Was that you, sir?" said he, turning abruptly.

"I—what!"

"Why, something struck me. I felt it sharply on the shoulder—just here."

"No," said I. "But we have jugglers present, and though we may not discover their tricks, we shall catch *them* before they frighten *us*."

We did not stay long in the drawing-rooms—in fact, they felt so damp and so chilly that I was glad to get to the fire up-stairs. We locked the doors of the drawing-rooms—a precaution which, I should observe, we had taken with all the rooms we had searched below. The bedroom my servant had selected for me was the best on the floor—a large one, with two windows fronting the street. The four-posted bed, which took up no inconsiderable space, was opposite to the fire, which burned clear and bright; a door in the wall to the left, between the bed and the window, communicated with the room which my servant appropriated to himself. This last was a small room with a sofa-bed, and had no communication with the landing-place—no other door but that which conducted to the bedroom I was to occupy. On either side of my fire-place was a cupboard, without locks, flushed with the wall, and covered with the same dull-brown paper. We examined these cupboards—only hooks to suspend female dresses—nothing else; we sounded the walls— evidently solid—the outer walls of the building. Having finished the survey of these apartments, warmed myself a few moments, and lighted my cigar, I then, still accompanied by F——, went forth to complete my reconnoitre. In the landing-place there was another door; it was closed firmly. "Sir," said my servant in surprise, "I unlocked this door with all the others when I first came; it cannot have got locked from the inside for it is a—"

Before he had finished his sentence, the door, which neither of us then was touching, opened quietly of itself. We looked at each other a single instant. The same thought seized both—some human agency might be detected here. I rushed in first, my servant followed. A small blank dreary room without furniture—a few empty boxes and hampers in a corner—a small window—the shutters closed—not even a fire-place—no other door but that by which we had entered—no carpet on the floor, and the floor seemed very old, uneven, worm-eaten, mended here and there, as was shown by the whiter patches on the wood; but no living being, and no visible place in which a living being could have hidden. As we stood gazing round, the door by which we had entered closed as quietly as it had before opened: we were imprisoned.

For the first time I felt a creep of undefinable horror. Not so my servant. "Why, they don't think to trap us, sir; I could break that trumpery door with a kick of my foot."

"Try first if it will open to your hand," said I, shaking off the vague apprehension that had seized me, "while I open the shutters and see what is without."

I unbarred the shutters—the window looked on the little back-yard I have before described; there was no ledge without—nothing but sheer descent. No man getting out of that window would have found any footing till he had fallen on the stones below.

F——, meanwhile, was vainly attempting to open the door. He now turned round to me, and asked my permission to use force. And I should here state, in justice to the servant, that, far from evincing any superstitious terrors, his nerve, composure, and even gaiety amidst circumstances so extraordinary compelled my admiration, and made me congratulate myself on having secured a companion in every way fitted to the occasion. I willingly gave him the permission he required. But though he was a remarkably strong man, his force was as idle as his milder efforts; the door did not even shake to his stoutest kick. Breathless and panting, he desisted. I then tried the door myself, equally in vain. As I ceased from the effort, again that creep of horror came over me; but this time it was more cold and stubborn. I felt as if some strange and ghastly exhalation were rising up from the chinks of that rugged floor, and filling the atmosphere with a venomous influence hostile to human life. The door now very slowly and quietly opened as of its own accord. We precipitated ourselves into the landing-place. We both saw a large pale light—as large as the human figure, but shapeless and unsubstantial—move before us, and ascend the stairs that led from the landing into the attics. I followed the light, and my servant followed me. It entered, to the right of the landing, a small garret, of which the door stood open. I entered in the same instant. The light then collapsed into a small globule, exceedingly brilliant and vivid; rested a moment on a bed in the corner, quivered, and vanished. We approached the bed and examined it—a half-tester, such as is commonly found in attics devoted to servants. On the drawers that stood near it we perceived an old faded silk kerchief, with the needle still left in a rent half repaired. The kerchief was covered with dust; probably it had belonged to the old woman who had last died in that house, and this might have been her sleeping-room. I had sufficient curiosity to open the drawers: there were a few odds and ends of female dress, and two letters tied round with a narrow ribbon of faded yellow. I took the liberty to, possess myself of the letters. We found nothing else in the room worth noticing—nor did the light reappear; but we distinctly heard, as we turned to go, a pattering footfall on the floor—just before us. We went through the other attics (in all four), the footfall still preceding us. Nothing to be seen—nothing but the footfall heard. I had the letters in my hand: just as I was descending the stairs I distinctly felt my wrist seized, and a faint, soft effort made to draw the letters from my clasp. I only held them the more tightly, and the effort ceased.

We regained the bedchamber appropriated to myself, and I then remarked that my dog had not followed us when we had left it. He was thrusting himself close to the fire, and trembling. I was impatient to examine the letters; and while I read them, my servant opened a little box in which he had deposited the weapons I had ordered him to bring; took them out, placed them on a table close at my bed-head, and then occupied himself in soothing the dog, who, however, seemed to heed him very little.

The letters were short—they were dated; the dates exactly thirty-five years ago. They were evidently from a lover to his mistress, or a husband to some young wife. Not only the terms of expression, but a distinct reference to a former voyage indicated the writer to have been a seafarer. The spelling and handwriting were those of a man imperfectly educated, but still the language itself was forcible. In the expressions of endearment there was a kind of rough wild love; but here and there were dark unintelligible hints at some secret not of love—some secret that seemed of crime. "We ought to love each other," was one of the sentences I remember, "for how every one else would execrate us if all was known." Again: "Don't let any one be in the same room with you at night—you talk in your sleep." And again: "What's done can t be undone; and I tell you there's nothing against us unless the dead could come to life." Here there was underlined in a better handwriting (a female's), "They do!" At the end of the letter latest in date the same female hand had written these words: "Lost at sea the 4th of June, the same day as—"I put down the letters, and began to muse over their contents.

Fearing, however, that the train of thought into which I fell might unsteady my nerves, I fully determined to keep my mind in a fit state to cope with whatever of marvellous the advancing night might bring forth. I roused myself—laid the letters on the table—stirred up the fire, which was still bright and cheering—and opened my volume of Macaulay. I read quietly enough till about half-past eleven. I then threw myself dressed upon the bed, and told my servant he might retire to his own room, but must keep himself awake. I bade him leave open the door between the two rooms. Thus alone, I kept two candles burning on the table by my bed-head. I placed my watch beside the weapons, and calmly resumed my Macaulay. Opposite to me the fire burned clear; and on the hearth-rug, seemingly asleep, lay the dog. In about twenty minutes I felt an exceedingly cold air pass by my cheek, like a sudden draught. I fancied the door to my right, communicating with the landing-place, must have got open; but no—it was closed. I then turned my glance to my left, and saw the flame of the candles violently swayed as by a wind. At the same moment the watch beside the revolver softly slid from the table—softly, softly—no visible hand—it was gone. I sprang up, seizing the revolver with the one hand, the dagger with the other: I was not willing that my weapons should share the fate of the watch. Thus armed, I looked round the floor—no sign of the watch. Three slow, loud, distinct knocks were now heard at the bed-head; my servant called out, "Is that you, sir?"

"No; be on your guard."

The dog now roused himself and sat on his haunches, his ears moving quickly backwards and forwards. He kept his eyes fixed on me with a look so strange that he concentred all my attention on himself. Slowly he rose up, all his hair bristling, and stood perfectly rigid and with the same wild stare. I had no time, however, to examine the dog. Presently my servant emerged from his room; and if ever I saw horror in the human face, it was then. I should not have recognised him had we met in the streets, so altered was every lineament. He passed by me quickly, saying in a whisper that seemed scarcely to come from his lips, "Run—run! it is after me!" He gained the door to the landing, pulled it open, and rushed forth. I followed him into the landing involuntarily, calling to him to stop; but, without heeding me, he bounded down the stairs, clinging to the balusters, and taking several steps at a time. I heard, where I stood, the street door open—heard it again clap to. I was left alone in the haunted house.

It was but for a moment that I remained undecided whether or not to follow my servant; pride and curiosity alike forbade so dastardly a flight. I re-entered my room, closing the door after me, and proceeded cautiously into the interior chamber. I encountered nothing to justify my servant's terror. I again carefully examined the walls, to see if there were any concealed door. I could find no trace of one—not even a seam in the dull-brown paper with which the room was hung. How, then, had the THING, whatever it was, which had so scared him, obtained ingress except through my own chamber?

I returned to my room, shut and locked the door that opened upon the interior one, and stood on the hearth, expectant and prepared. I now perceived that the dog had slunk into an angle of the wall, and was pressing himself close against it, as if literally striving to force his way into it. I approached the animal and spoke to it; the poor brute was evidently beside itself with terror. It showed all its teeth, the slaver dropping from its jaws, and would certainly have bitten me if I had touched it. It did not seem to recognise me. Whoever has seen at the Zoological Gardens a rabbit fascinated by a serpent, cowering in a corner, may form some idea of the anguish which the dog exhibited. Finding all efforts to soothe the animal in vain, and fearing that his bite might be as venomous in that state as if in the madness of hydrophobia, I left him alone, placed my weapons on the table beside the fire, seated myself, and recommenced my Macaulay. Perhaps, in order not to appear seeking credit for a courage, or rather a coolness, which the reader may conceive I exaggerate, I may be pardoned if I pause to indulge in one or two egotistical remarks.

As I hold presence of mind, or what is called courage, to be precisely proportioned to familiarity with the circumstances that lead to it, so I should say that I had been long sufficiently familiar with all experiments that appertain to the Marvellous. I had witnessed many very extraordinary phenomena in various parts of the world—phenomena that would be either totally disbelieved if I stated them, or ascribed to supernatural agencies. Now, my theory is that the Supernatural is the Impossible, and that what is called supernatural is only a something in the laws of nature of which we have been hitherto ignorant. Therefore, if a ghost rise before me, I have not the right to say, "So, then, the supernatural is possible," but rather, "So, then, the apparition of a ghost is, contrary to received opinion, within the laws of nature—*i.e.*, not supernatural."

Now, in all that I had hitherto witnessed, and indeed in all the wonders which the amateurs of mystery in our age record as facts, a material living agency is always required. On the Continent you will find still magicians who assert that they can raise spirits. Assume for the moment that they assert truly, still the living material form of the magician is present: and he is the material agency by which, from some constitutional peculiarities, certain strange phenomena are represented to your natural senses.

Accept, again, as truthful, the tales of Spirit Manifestation in America—musical or other sounds—writings on paper, produced by no discernible hand—articles of furniture moved without apparent human agency—or the actual sight and touch of hands, to which no bodies seem to belong—still there must be found the MEDIUM or living being, with constitutional peculiarities capable of obtaining these signs. In fine, in all such marvels, supposing even that there is no imposture, there must be a human being like ourselves, by whom, or through whom, the effects presented to human beings are produced. It is so with the now familiar phenomena of mesmerism or electro-biology; the mind of the person operated on is affected through a material living agent. Nor, supposing it true that a mesmerised patient can respond to the will or passes of a mesmeriser a hundred miles distant, is the response less occasioned by a material being; it may be through a material fluid—call it Electric, call it Odic, call it what you will—which has the power of traversing space and passing obstacles, that the material effect is communicated from one to the other. Hence all that I had hitherto witnessed, or expected to witness, in this strange house, I believed to be occasioned through some agency or medium as mortal as myself; and this idea necessarily prevented the awe with which those who regard as supernatural things that are not within the ordinary operations of nature, might have been impressed by the adventures of that memorable night.

As, then, it was my conjecture that all that was presented, or would be presented, to my senses, must originate in some human being gifted by constitution with the power so to present them, and having some motive so to do, I felt an interest in my theory which, in its way, was rather philosophical than superstitious. And I can sincerely say that I was in as tranquil a temper for observation as any practical experimentalist could be in awaiting the effects of some rare, though perhaps perilous, chemical combination. Of course, the more I kept my mind detached from fancy, the more the temper fitted for observation would be obtained; and I therefore riveted eye and thought on the strong daylight sense in the page of my Macaulay.

I now became aware that something interposed between the page and the light— the page was overshadowed: I looked up, and I saw what I shall find it very difficult, perhaps impossible, to describe.

It was a Darkness shaping itself out of the air in very undefined outline. I cannot say it was of a human form, and yet it had more resemblance to a human form, or rather shadow, than anything else. As it stood, wholly apart and distinct from the air and the light around it, its dimensions seemed gigantic, the summit nearly touching the ceiling. While I gazed, a feeling of intense cold seized me. An iceberg before me could not more have chilled me: nor could the cold of an iceberg have been more purely physical. I feel convinced that it was not the cold caused by fear. As I continued to gaze, I thought—but this I cannot say with precision—that I distinguished two eyes looking down on me from the height. One moment I seemed to distinguish them clearly, the next they seemed gone; but still two rays of a pale-blue light frequently shot through the darkness, as from the height on which I half believed, half doubted, that I had encountered the eyes.

I strove to speak—my voice utterly failed me; I could only think to myself, " Is this fear? it is *not* fear!" I strove to rise—in vain; I felt as if weighed down by an irresistible force. Indeed, my impression was that of an immense and overwhelming Power opposed to my volition;—that sense of utter inadequacy to cope with a force beyond men's, which one may feel *physically* in a storm at sea, in a conflagration, or when confronting some terrible wild beast, or rather, perhaps, the shark of the ocean, I felt *morally*. Opposed to my will was another will, as far superior to its strength as storm, fire, and shark are superior in material force to the force of men.

And now, as this impression grew on me, now came, at last, horror—horror to a degree that no words can convey. Still I retained pride, if not courage; and in my own mind I said, "This is horror, but it is not fear; unless I fear, I cannot be harmed; my reason rejects this thing; it is an illusion—I do not fear." With a violent effort I succeeded at last in stretching out my hand towards the weapon on the table: as I did so, on the arm and shoulder I received a strange shock, and my arm fell to my side powerless. And now, to add to my horror, the light began slowly to wane from the candles—they were not, as it were, extinguished, but their flame seemed very gradually withdrawn: it was the same with the fire—the light was extracted from the fuel; in a few minutes the room was in utter darkness. The dread that came over me, to be thus in the dark with that dark Thing, whose power was so intensely felt, brought a reaction of nerve. In fact, terror had reached that climax, that either my senses must have deserted me, or I must have burst through the spell. I did burst through it. I found voice, though the voice was a shriek. I remember that I broke forth with words like these—"I do not fear, my soul does not fear"; and at the same time I found the strength to rise. Still in that profound gloom I rushed to one of the windows—tore aside the curtain—flung open the shutters; my first thought was—LIGHT. And when I saw the moon high, clear, and calm, I felt a joy that almost compensated for the previous terror. There was the moon, there was also the light from the gas-lamps in the deserted slumberous street. I turned to look back into the room; the moon penetrated its shadow very palely and partially—but still there was light. The dark Thing, whatever it might be, was gone—except that I could yet see a dim shadow, which seemed the shadow of that shade, against the opposite wall.

My eye now rested on the table, and from under the table (which was without cloth or cover—an old mahogany round table) there rose a hand, visible as far as the wrist. It was a hand, seemingly, as much of flesh and blood as my own, but the hand of an aged person—lean, wrinkled, small too—a woman's hand. That hand very softly closed on the two letters that lay on the table: hand and letters both vanished. There then came the same three loud measured knocks I had heard at the bed-head before this extraordinary drama had commenced.

As those sounds slowly ceased, I felt the whole room vibrate sensibly; and at the far end there rose, as from the floor, sparks or globules like bubbles of light, many-coloured—green, yellow, tire-red, azure. Up and down, to and fro, hither, thither, as tiny Will-o'-the-wisps, the sparks moved, slow or swift, each at its own caprice. A chair (as in the drawing-room below) was now advanced from the wall without apparent agency, and placed at the opposite side of the table. Suddenly, as forth from the chair, there grew a Shape—a woman's shape. It was distinct as a shape of life—ghastly as a shape of death. The face was that of youth, with a strange mournful beauty; the throat and shoulders were bare, the rest of the form in a loose robe of cloudy white. It began sleeking its long yellow hair, which fell over its shoulders; its eyes were not turned towards me, but to the door; it seemed listening, watching, waiting. The shadow of the shade in the background grew darker; and again I thought I beheld the eyes gleaming out from the summit of the shadow—eyes fixed upon that shape.

As if from the door, though it did not open, there grew out another shape, equally distinct, equally ghastly—a man's shape—a young man's. It was in the dress of the last century, or rather in a likeness of such dress; for both the male shape and the female, though defined, were evidently unsubstantial, impalpable—simulacra—phantasms; and there was something incongruous, grotesque, yet fearful, in the contrast between the elaborate finery, the courtly precision of that old-fashioned garb, with its ruffles and lace and buckles, and the corpse-like aspect and ghost-like stillness of the flitting wearer. Just as the male shape approached the female, the dark Shadow started from the wall, all three for a moment wrapped in darkness. When the pale light returned, the two phantoms were as if in the grasp of the Shadow that towered between them; and there was a blood-stain on the breast of the female; and the phantom-male was leaning on its phantom-sword, and blood seemed trickling fast from the ruffles, from the lace; and the darkness of the intermediate Shadow swallowed them up—they were gone. And again the bubbles of light shot, and sailed, and undulated, growing thicker and thicker and more wildly confused in their movements.

The closet-door to the right of the fire-place now opened, and from the aperture there came the form of a woman, aged. In her hand she held letters—the very letters over which I had seen *the* Hand close; and behind her I heard a footstep. She turned round as if to listen, and then she opened the letters and seemed to read; and over her shoulder I saw a livid face, the face as of a man long drowned—bloated, bleached—seaweed tangled in its dripping hair; and at her feet lay a form as of a corpse, and beside the corpse there cowered a child, a miserable squalid child, with famine in its cheeks and fear in its eyes. And as I looked in the old woman's face, the wrinkles and lines vanished, and it became a face of youth—hard-eyed, stony, but still youth; and the Shadow darted forth, and darkened over these phantoms as it had darkened over the last.

Nothing now was left but the Shadow, and on that my eyes were intently fixed, till again eyes grew out of the Shadow—malignant, serpent eyes. And the bubbles of light again rose and fell, and in their disordered, irregular, turbulent maze, mingled with the wan moonlight. And now from these globules themselves, as from the shell of an egg, monstrous things burst out; the air grew filled with them; larvae so bloodless and so hideous that I can in no way describe them except to remind the reader of the swarming life which the solar microscope brings before his eyes in a drop of water—things transparent, supple, agile, chasing each other, devouring each other—forms like nought ever beheld by the naked eye. As the shapes were without symmetry, so then-movements were without order. In their very vagrancies there was no sport; they came round me and round, thicker and faster and swifter, swarming over my head, crawling over my right arm, which was outstretched in involuntary command against all evil beings. Sometimes I felt myself touched, but not by them; invisible hands touched me. Once I felt the clutch as of cold soft fingers at my throat. I was still equally conscious that if I gave way to fear I should be in bodily peril; and I concentred all my faculties in the single focus of resisting, stubborn will. And I turned my sight from the shadow—above, all from those strange serpent eyes—eyes that had now become distinctly visible. For there, though in nought else around me, I was aware that there was a WILL, and a will of intense, creative, working evil, which might crush down my own.

The pale atmosphere in the room began now to redden as if in the air of some near conflagration. The larvae grew lurid as things that live in fire. Again the room vibrated; again were heard the three measured knocks; and again all things were swallowed up in the darkness of the dark Shadow, as if out of that darkness all had come, into that darkness all returned.

As the gloom receded, the Shadow was wholly gone. Slowly as it had been withdrawn, the flame grew again into the candles on the table, again into the fuel in the grate. The whole room came once more calmly, healthfully into sight.

The two doors were still closed, the door communicating with the servant's room still locked. In the corner of the wall, into which he had so convulsively niched himself, lay the dog. I called to him—no movement; I approached—the animal was dead; his eyes protruded: his tongue out of his mouth; the froth gathered round his jaws. I took him in my arms; I brought him to the fire; I felt acute grief for the loss of my poor favourite—acute self-reproach; I accused myself of his death; I imagined he had died of fright. But what was my surprise on finding that his neck was actually broken—actually twisted out of the vertebrae. Had this been done in the dark?—must it not have been by a hand human as mine?—must there not have been a human agency all the while in that room f Good cause to suspect it. I cannot tell. I cannot do more than state the fact fairly; the reader may draw his own inference.

Another surprising circumstance—my watch was restored to the table from which it had been so mysteriously withdrawn; but it had stopped at the very moment it was so withdrawn: nor, despite all the skill of the watchmaker, has it ever gone since—that is, it will go in a strange erratic way for a few hours, and then comes to a dead stop—it is worthless.

Nothing more chanced for the rest of the night. Nor, indeed, had I long to wait before the dawn broke. Not till it was broad daylight did I quit the haunted house. Before I did so, I revisited the little blind room in which my servant and myself had been for a time imprisoned. I had a strong impression—for which I could not account—that from that room had originated the mechanism of the phenomena—if I may use the term—which had been experienced in my chamber. And though I entered it now in the clear day, with the sun peering through the filmy window, I still felt, as I stood on its floor, the creep of the horror which I had first there experienced the night before, and which had been so aggravated by what had passed in my own chamber. I could not, indeed, bear to stay more than half a minute within those walls. I descended the stairs, and again I heard the footfall before me; and when I opened the street door, I thought I could distinguish a very low laugh. I gained my own home, expecting to find my runaway servant there. But he had not presented himself; nor did I hear more of him for three days, when I received a letter from him, dated from Liverpool, to this effect:—

> HONOURED SIR,—I humbly entreat your pardon, though I can scarcely hope that you will think I deserve it, unless—which Heaven forbid!—you saw what I did. I feel that it will be years before I can recover myself; and as to being fit for service, it is out of the question. I am therefore going to my brother-in-law at Melbourne. The ship sails to-morrow. Perhaps the long voyage may set me up. I do nothing now but start and tremble, and fancy It is behind me. I humbly beg you, honoured sir, to order my clothes, and whatever wages are due to me, to be sent to my mother's, at Walworth,—John knows her address.

The letter ended with additional apologies, somewhat incoherent, and explanatory details as to effects that had been under the writer's charge.

This flight may perhaps warrant a suspicion that the man wished to go to Australia, and had been somehow or other fraudulently mixed up with the events of the night. I say nothing in refutation of that conjecture; rather, I suggest it as one that would seem to many persons the most probable solution of improbable occurrences. My own theory remained unshaken. I returned in the evening to the house, to bring away in a hack cab the things I had left there, with my poor dog's body. In this task I was not disturbed, nor did any incident worth note befall me, except that still, on ascending and descending the stairs, I heard the same footfall in advance. On leaving the house, I went to Mr. J's. He was at home. I returned him the keys, told him that my curiosity was sufficiently gratified, and was about to relate quickly what had passed, when he stopped me, and said, though with much politeness, that he had no longer any interest in a mystery which none had ever solved.

I determined at least to tell him of the two letters I had read, as well as of the extraordinary manner in which they had disappeared, and I then inquired if he thought they had been addressed to the woman who had died in the house, and if there were anything in her early history which could possibly confirm the dark suspicions to which the letters gave rise. Mr. J—— seemed startled, and, after musing a few moments, answered, "I know but little of the woman's earlier history, except, as I before told you, that her family were known to mine. But you revive some vague reminiscences to her prejudice. I will make inquiries, and inform you of their result. Still, even if we could admit the popular superstition that a person who had been either the perpetrator or the victim of dark crimes in life could revisit, as a restless spirit, the scene in which those crimes had been committed, I should observe that the house was infested by strange sights and sounds before the old woman died—you smile—what would you say?"

"I would say this, that I am convinced, if we could get to the bottom of these mysteries, we should find a living human agency."

"What! you believe it is all an imposture? for what object?"

"Not an imposture in the ordinary sense of the word. If suddenly I were to sink into a deep sleep, from which you could not awake me, but in that sleep could answer questions with an accuracy which I could not pretend to when awake—tell you what money you had in your pocket —nay, describe your very thoughts—it is not necessarily an imposture, any more than it is necessarily supernatural. I should be, unconsciously to myself, under a mesmeric influence, conveyed to me from a distance by a human being who had acquired power over me by previous *rapport*."

"Granting mesmerism, so far carried, to be a fact, you are right. And you would infer from this that a mesmeriser might produce the extraordinary effects you and others have witnessed over inanimate objects fill the air with sights and sounds?"

"Or impress our senses with the belief in them—we never having been *en rapport* with the person acting on us? No. What is commonly called mesmerism could not do this; but there may be a power akin to mesmerism, and superior to it—the power that in the old days was called Magic. That such a power may extend to all inanimate objects of matter, I do not say; but if so, it would not be against nature, only a rare power in nature which might be given to constitutions with certain peculiarities, and cultivated by practice to an extraordinary degree. That such a power might extend over the dead—that is, over certain thoughts and memories that the dead may still retain—and compel, not that which ought properly to be called the SOUL, and which is far beyond human reach, but rather a phantom of what has been most earth-stained on earth, to make itself apparent to our senses—is a very ancient though obsolete theory, upon which I will hazard no opinion. But I do not conceive the power would be supernatural. Let me illustrate what I mean from an experiment which Paracelsus describes as not difficult, and which the author of the *Curiosities of Literature* cites as credible:—A flower perishes; you burn it. Whatever were the elements of that flower while it lived are gone, dispersed, you know not whither; you can never discover nor re-collect them. But you can, by chemistry, out of the burnt dust of that flower, raise a spectrum of the flower, just as it seemed in life. It may be the same with the human being. The soul has as much escaped you as the essence or elements of the flower. Still you may make a spectrum of it. And this phantom, though in the popular superstition it is held to be the soul of the departed, must not be confounded with the true soul; it is but the eidolon of the dead form. Hence, like the best-attested stories of ghosts or spirits, the thing that most strikes us is the absence of what we held to be soul—that is, of superior emancipated intelligence. They come for little or no object—they seldom speak, if they do come; they utter no ideas above that of an ordinary person on earth. These American spirit-seers have published volumes of communications in prose and verse, which they assert to be given in the names of the most illustrious dead—Shakespeare, Bacon— heaven knows whom. Those communications, taking the best, are certainly not a whit of higher order than would be communications from living persons of fair talent and education; they are wondrously inferior to what Bacon, Shakespeare, and Plato said and wrote when on earth. Nor, what is more notable, do they ever contain an idea that was not on the earth before. Wonderful, therefore, as such phenomena may be (granting them to be truthful), I see much that philosophy may question, nothing that it is incumbent on philosophy to deny—viz. nothing supernatural. They are but ideas conveyed somehow or other (we have not yet discovered the means) from one mortal brain to another. Whether, in so doing, tables walk of their own accord, or fiend-like shapes appear in a magic circle, or bodyless hands rise and remove material objects, or a Thing of Darkness, such as presented itself to me, freeze our blood—still am I persuaded that these are but agencies conveyed, as by electric wires, to my own brain from the brain of another. In some constitutions there is a natural chemistry, and those may produce chemic wonders—in others a natural fluid, call it electricity, and these produce electric wonders. But they differ in this from Normal Science—they are alike objectless, purposeless, puerile, frivolous. They lead on to no grand results; and therefore the world does not heed, and true sages have not cultivated them. But sure I am, that of all I saw or heard, a man, human as myself, was the remote originator; and I believe unconsciously to himself as to the exact effects produced, for this reason: no two persons, you say, have ever told you that they experienced exactly the same thing. Well, observe, no two persons ever experience exactly the same dream. If this were an ordinary imposture, the machinery would be arranged for results that would but little vary; if it were a supernatural agency permitted by the Almighty, it would surely be for some definite end. These phenomena belong to neither class; my persuasion is, that they originate in some brain now far distant; that that brain had no distinct volition in anything that occurred; that what does occur reflects but its devious, motley, ever-shifting, half-formed thoughts; in short, that it has been but the dreams of such a brain put into action and invested with a semi-substance. That this brain is of immense power, that it can set matter into movement, that it is malignant and destructive, I believe: some material force must have killed my dog; it might, for aught I know, have sufficed to kill myself, had I been as subjugated by terror as the dog—had my intellect or my spirit given me no countervailing resistance in my will."

"It killed your dog! that is fearful! indeed it is strange that no animal can be induced to stay in that house; not even a cat. Rats and mice are never found in it."

"The instincts of the brute creation detect influences deadly to their existence. Man's reason has a sense less subtle, because it has a resisting power more supreme. But enough; do you comprehend my theory?"

"Yes, though imperfectly—and I accept any crotchet (pardon the word), however odd, rather than embrace at once the notion of ghosts and hobgoblins we imbibed in our nurseries. Still, to my unfortunate house the evil is the same. What on earth can I do with the house?"

"I will tell you what I would do. I am convinced from my own internal feelings that the small unfurnished room at right angles to the door of the bedroom which

I occupied, forms a starting-point or receptacle for the influences which haunt the house; and I strongly advise you to have the walls opened, the floor removed—nay, the whole room pulled down. I observe that it is detached from the body of the house, built over the small back-yard, and could be removed without injury to the rest of the building."

"And you think, if I did that—"

"You would cut off the telegraph wires. Try it. I am so persuaded that I am right, that I will pay half the expense if you will allow me to direct the operations."

"Nay, I am well able to afford the cost; for the rest, allow me to write to you."

About ten days afterwards I received a letter from Mr. J——, telling me that he had visited the house since I had seen him; that he had found the two letters I had described, replaced in the drawer from which I had taken them; that he had read them with misgivings like my own; that he had instituted a cautious inquiry about the woman to whom I rightly conjectured they had been written. It seemed that thirty-six years ago (a year before the date of the letters), she had married, against the wish of her relatives, an American of very suspicious character; in fact, he was generally believed to have been a pirate. She herself was the daughter of very respectable tradespeople, and had served in the capacity of a nursery governess before her marriage. She had a brother, a widower, who was considered wealthy, and who had one child of about six years old. A month after the marriage, the body of this brother was found in the Thames, near London Bridge: there seemed some marks of violence about his throat, but they were not deemed sufficient to warrant the inquest in any other verdict than that of "found drowned."

The American and his wife took charge of the little boy, the deceased brother having by his will left his sister the guardian of his only child—and in event of the child's death, the sister inherited. The child died about six months afterwards—it was supposed to have been neglected and ill-treated. The neighbours deposed to have heard it shriek at night. The surgeon who had examined it after death, said that it was emaciated as if from want of nourishment, and the body was covered with livid bruises. It seemed that one winter night the child had sought to escape—crept out into the back-yard—tried to scale the wall—fallen back exhausted, and been found at morning on the stones in a dying state. But though there was some evidence of cruelty, there was none of murder; and the aunt and her husband had sought to palliate cruelty by alleging the exceeding stubbornness and perversity of the child, who was declared to be half-witted. Be that as it may, at the orphan's death the aunt inherited her brother's fortune. Before the first wedded year was out, the American quitted England abruptly, and never returned to it. He obtained a cruising vessel, which was lost in the Atlantic two years afterwards. The widow was left in affluence; but reverses of various kinds had befallen her: a bank broke—an investment failed—she went into a small business and became insolvent—then she entered into service, sinking lower and lower, from housekeeper down to maid-of-all-work—never long retaining a place, though nothing peculiar against her character was ever alleged. She was considered sober, honest, and peculiarly quiet in her ways; still nothing prospered with her. And so she had dropped into the workhouse, from which Mr. J—— had taken her, to be placed in charge of the very house which she had rented as mistress in the first year of her wedded life.

Mr. J—— added that he had passed an hour alone in the unfurnished room which I had urged him to destroy, and that his impressions of dread while there were so great, though he had neither heard nor seen anything, that he was eager to have the walls bared and the floors removed as I had suggested. He had engaged persons for the work, and would commence any day I would name.

The day was accordingly fixed. I repaired to the haunted house—we went into the blind dreary room, took up the skirting, and then the floors. Under the rafters, covered with rubbish, was found a trap-door, quite large enough to admit a man. It was closely nailed down, with clamps and rivets of iron. On removing these we descended into a room below, the existence of which had never been suspected. In this room there had been a window and a flue, but they had been bricked over, evidently for many years. By the help of candles we examined this place; it still retained some mouldering furniture—three chairs, an oak settle, a table—all of the fashion of about eighty years ago. There was a chest of drawers against the wall, in which we found, half-rotted away, old-fashioned articles of a man's dress, such as might have been worn eighty or a hundred years ago by a gentleman of some rank—costly steel buckles and buttons, like those yet worn in court-dresses—a handsome court sword—in a waistcoat which had once been rich with gold-lace, but which was now blackened and foul with damp, we found five guineas, a few silver coins, and an ivory ticket, probably for some place of entertainment long since passed away. But our main discovery was in a kind of iron safe fixed to the wall, the lock of which it cost us much trouble to get picked.

In this safe were three shelves and two small drawers. Ranged on the shelves were several small bottles of crystal, hermetically stopped. They contained colourless volatile essences, of what nature I shall say no more than that they were not poisons—phosphor and ammonia entered into some of them. There were also some very curious glass tubes, and a small pointed rod of iron, with a large lump of rock-crystal, and another of amber—also a loadstone of great power.

In one of the drawers we found a miniature portrait set in gold, and retaining the freshness of its colours most remarkably, considering the length of time it had probably been there. The portrait was that of a man who might be somewhat advanced in middle life, perhaps forty-seven or forty-eight.

It was a most peculiar face—a most impressive face. If you could fancy some mighty serpent transformed into man, preserving in the human lineaments the old serpent type, you would have a better idea of that countenance than long descriptions can convey: the width and flatness of frontal—the tapering elegance of contour disguising the strength of the deadly jaw—the long, large, terrible eye, glittering and green as the emerald—and withal a certain ruthless calm, as if from the consciousness of an immense power. The strange thing was this—the instant I saw the miniature I recognised a startling likeness to one of the rarest portraits in the world—the portrait of a man of a rank only below that of royalty, who in his own day had made a considerable noise. History says little or nothing of him; but search the correspondence of his contemporaries, and you find reference to his wild daring, his bold profligacy, his restless spirit, his taste for the occult sciences. While still in the meridian of life he died and was buried, so say the chronicles, in a foreign land. He died in time to escape the grasp of the law, for he was accused of crimes which would have given him to the headsman. After his death, the portraits of him, which had been numerous, for he had been a munificent encourager of art, were bought up and destroyed—it was supposed by his heirs, who might have been glad could they have razed his very name from their splendid line. He had enjoyed a vast wealth; a large portion of this was believed to have been embezzled by a favourite astrologer or soothsayer—at all events, it had unaccountably vanished at the time of his death. One portrait alone of him was supposed to have escaped the general destruction; I had seen it in the house of a collector some months before. It had made on me a wonderful impression, as it does on all who behold it—a face never to be forgotten; and there was that face in the miniature that lay within my hand. True, that in the miniature the man was a few years older than in the portrait I had seen, or than the original was even at the time of his death. But a few years!—why, between the date in which flourished that direful noble and the date in which the miniature was evidently painted, there was an interval of more than two centuries. While I was thus gazing, silent and wondering, Mr. J—— said,

"But is it possible? I have known this man."

"How—where?" cried I.

"In India. He was high in the confidence of the Rajah of ——, and well-nigh drew him into a revolt which would have lost the Rajah his dominions. The man was a Frenchman—his name de V——, clever, bold, lawless. We insisted on his dismissal and banishment: it must be the same man —no two faces like his—yet this miniature seems nearly a hundred years old."

Mechanically I turned round the miniature to examine the back of it, and on the back was engraved a pentacle; in the middle of the pentacle a ladder, and the third step of the ladder was formed by the date 1765. Examining still more minutely, I detected a spring; this, on being pressed, opened the back of the miniature as a lid. Within-side the lid were engraved "Mariana to thee— Be faithful in life and in death to ———." Here follows a name that I will not mention, but it was not unfamiliar to me. I had heard it spoken of by old men in my childhood as the name borne by a dazzling charlatan, who had made a great sensation in London for a year or so, and had fled the country on the charge of a double murder within his own house—that of his mistress and his rival. I said nothing of this to Mr. J———, to whom reluctantly I resigned the miniature.

We had found no difficulty in opening the first drawer within the iron-safe; we found great difficulty in opening the second: it was not locked, but it resisted all efforts, till we inserted in the chinks the edge of a chisel. When we had thus drawn it forth, we found a very singular apparatus in the nicest order. Upon a small thin book, or rather tablet, was placed a saucer of crystal; this saucer was filled with a clear liquid—on that liquid floated a kind of compass, with a needle shifting rapidly round, but instead of the usual points of a compass were seven strange characters, not very unlike those used by astrologers to denote the planets. A very peculiar, but not strong nor displeasing odour, came from this drawer, which was lined with a wood that we afterwards discovered to be hazel. Whatever the cause of this odour, it produced a material effect on the nerves. We all felt it, even the two workmen who were in the room—a creeping tingling sensation from the tips of the fingers to the roots of the hair. Impatient to examine the tablet, I removed the saucer. As I did so the needle of the compass went round and round with exceeding swiftness, and I felt a shock that ran through my whole frame, so that I dropped the saucer on the floor. The liquid was spilt—the saucer was broken—the compass rolled to the end of the room—and at that instant the walls shook to and fro, as if a giant had swayed and rocked them.

The two workmen were so frightened that they ran up the ladder by which we had descended from the trap-door; but seeing that nothing more happened, they were easily induced to return.

Meanwhile I had opened the tablet: it was bound in a plain red leather, with a silver clasp; it contained but one sheet of thick vellum, and on that sheet were inscribed, within a double pentacle, words in old monkish Latin, which are literally to be translated thus:—"On all that it can reach within these walls—sentient or inanimate, living or dead—as moves the needle, so work my will! Accursed be the house, and restless be the dwellers therein."

We found no more. Mr. J—— burnt the tablet and its anathema. He razed to the foundations the part of the building containing the secret room with the chamber over it. He had then the courage to inhabit the house himself for a month, and a quieter, better-conditioned house could not be found in all London. Subsequently he let it to advantage, and his tenant has made no complaints.

But my story is not yet done. A few days after Mr. J—— had removed into the house, I paid him a visit. We were standing by the open window and conversing. A van containing some articles of furniture which he was moving from his former house was at the door. I had just urged on him my theory, that all those phenomena regarded as supermundane had emanated from a human brain; adducing the charm or rather curse we had found and destroyed in support of my philosophy. Mr. J—— was observing in reply, "That even if mesmerism, or whatever analogous power it might be called, could really thus work in the absence of the operator, and produce effects so extraordinary, still could those effects continue when the operator himself was dead? and if the spell had been wrought, and, indeed, the room walled up, more than seventy years ago the probability was, that the operator had long since departed this life"; Mr. J——, I say, was thus answering, when I caught hold of his arm and pointed to the street below.

A well-dressed man had crossed from the opposite side, and was accosting the carrier in charge of the van. His face, as he stood, was exactly fronting our window. It was the face of the miniature we had discovered; it was the face of the portrait of the noble three centuries ago.

"Good heavens!" cried Mr. ——J, "that is the face of de V——, and scarcely a day older than when I saw it in the Rajah's court in my youth!"

Seized by the same thought, we both hastened down stairs. I was first in the street; but the man had already gone. I caught sight of him, however, not many yards in advance, and in another moment I was by his side.

I had resolved to speak to him, but when I looked into his face I felt as if it were impossible to do so. That eye—the eye of the serpent—fixed and held me spellbound. And withal, about the man's whole person there was a dignity, an air of pride and station and superiority, that would have made any one, habituated to the usages of the world, hesitate long before venturing upon a liberty or impertinence. And what could I say? what was it I would ask? Thus ashamed of my first impulse, I fell a few paces back, still, however, following the stranger, undecided what else to do. Meanwhile he turned the corner of the street; a plain carriage was in waiting, with a servant out of livery dressed like a *valet-de-place* at the carriage-door. In another moment he had stepped into the carriage, and it drove off. I returned to the house. Mr. J—— was still at the street door. He had asked the carrier what the stranger had said to him.

"Merely asked whom that house now belonged to."

The same evening I happened to go with a friend to a place in town called the Cosmopolitan Club, a place open to men of all countries, all opinions, all degrees. One orders one's coffee, smokes one's cigar. One is always sure to meet agreeable, sometimes remarkable persons.

I had not been two minutes in the room before I beheld at a table, conversing with an acquaintance of mine, whom I will designate by the initial G——, the man—the Original of the Miniature. He was now without his hat, and the likeness was yet more startling, only I observed that while he was conversing there was less severity in the countenance; there was even a smile, though a very quiet and very cold one. The dignity of mien I had acknowledged in the street was also more striking; a dignity akin to that which invests some prince of the East—conveying the idea of supreme indifference and habitual, indisputable, indolent, but resistless power.

G—— soon after left the stranger, who then took up a scientific journal, which seemed to absorb his attention.

I drew G—— aside—"Who and what is that gentleman?"

"That? Oh, a very remarkable man indeed. I met him last year amidst the caves of Petra—the scriptural Edom. He is the best oriental scholar I know. We joined company, had an adventure with robbers, in which he showed a coolness that saved our lives; afterwards he invited me to spend a day with him in a house he had bought at Damascus—a house buried amongst almond-blossoms and roses—the most beautiful thing! He had lived there for some years, quite as an Oriental, in grand style. I half suspect he is a renegade, immensely rich, very odd; by the by, a great mesmeriser. I have seen him with my own eyes produce an effect on inanimate things. If you take a letter from your pocket and throw it to the other end of the room, he will order it to come to his feet, and you will see the letter wriggle itself along the floor till it has obeyed his command. 'Pon my honour 'tis true: I have seen him affect even the weather, disperse or collect clouds, by means of a glass tube or wand. But he does not like talking of these matters to strangers. He has only just arrived in England; says he has not been here for a great many years; let me introduce him to you."

"Certainly! He is English then? What is his name?"

"Oh!—a very homely one—Richards."

"And what is his birth—his family?"

"How do I know? What does it signify?—no doubt some parvenu, but rich—so infernally rich!"

G—— drew me up to the stranger, and the introduction was effected. The manners of Mr. Richards were not those of an adventurous traveller. Travellers are in general constitutionally gifted with high animal spirits; they are talkative, eager, imperious. Mr. Richards was calm and subdued in tone, with manners which were made distant by the loftiness of punctilious courtesy—the manners of a former age. I observed that the English he spoke was not exactly of our day. I should even have said that the accent was slightly foreign. But then Mr. Richards remarked that he had been little in the habit for many years of speaking in his native tongue. The conversation fell upon the changes in the aspect of London since he had last visited our metropolis. G—— then glanced off to the moral changes—literary, social, political—the great men who were removed from the stage within the last twenty years—the new great men who were coming on. In all this Mr. Richards evinced no interest. He had evidently read none of our living authors, and seemed scarcely acquainted by name with our younger statesmen. Once and only once he laughed; it was when G—— asked him whether he had any thoughts of getting into Parliament. And the laugh was inward—sarcastic—sinister—a sneer raised into a laugh. After a few minutes G—— left us to talk to some other acquaintances who had just lounged into the room, and I then said quietly—

"I have seen a miniature of you, Mr. Richards, in the house you once inhabited, and perhaps built, if not wholly, at least in part, in —— street. You passed by that house this morning."

Not till I had finished did I raise my eyes to his, and then his fixed my gaze so steadfastly that I could not withdraw it—those fascinating serpent eyes. But involuntarily, and as if the words that translated my thought were dragged from me, I added in a low whisper, "I have been a student in the mysteries of life and nature; of those mysteries I have known the occult professors. I have the right to speak to you thus." And I uttered a certain pass-word.

"Well," said he dryly, "I concede the right—what would you ask?"

"To what extent human will in certain temperaments can extend?"

"To what extent can thought extend? Think, and before you draw breath you are in China!"

"True. But my thought has no power in China."

"Give it expression, and it may have: you may write down a thought which, sooner or later, may alter the whole condition of China. What is a law but a thought? Therefore thought is infinite—therefore thought has power; not in proportion to its value—a bad thought may make a bad law as potent as a good thought can make a good one."

"Yes; what you say confirms my own theory. Through invisible currents one human brain may transmit its ideas to other human brains with the same rapidity as a thought promulgated by visible means. And as thought is imperishable—as it leaves its stamp behind it in the natural world even when the thinker has passed out of this world—so the thought of the living may have power to rouse up and revive the thoughts of the dead—such as those thoughts *were in life*—though the thought of the living cannot reach the thoughts which the dead *now* may entertain. Is it not so?"

"I decline to answer, if, in my judgment, thought has the limit you would fix to it; but proceed. You have a special question you wish to put."

"Intense malignity in an intense will, engendered in a peculiar temperament, and aided by natural means within the reach of science, may produce effects like those ascribed of old to evil magic. It might thus haunt the walls of a human habitation with spectral revivals of all guilty thoughts and guilty deeds once conceived and done within those walls; all, in short, with which the evil will claims *rapport* and affinity,—imperfect, incoherent, fragmentary snatches at the old dramas acted therein years ago. Thoughts thus crossing each other hap-hazard, as in the nightmare of a vision, growing up into phantom sights and sounds, and all serving to create horror, not because those sights and sounds are really visitations from a world without, but that they are ghastly monstrous renewals of what have been in this world itself, set into malignant play by a malignant mortal. And it is through the material agency of that human brain that these things would acquire even a human power—would strike as with the shock of electricity, and might kill, if the thought of the person assailed did not rise superior to the dignity of the original assailer—might kill the most powerful animal if unnerved by fear, if not injure the feeblest man, if, while his flesh crept, his mind stood out fearless. Thus, when in old stories we read of a magician rent to pieces by the fiends he had evoked—or still more, in Eastern legends, that one magician succeeds by arts in destroying another—there may be so far truth, that a material being has clothed, from its own evil propensities, certain elements and fluids, usually quiescent or harmless, with awful shape and terrific force;—just as the lightning that had lain hidden and innocent in the cloud becomes by natural law suddenly visible, takes a distinct shape to the eye, and can strike destruction on the object to which it is attracted."

"You are not without glimpses of a very mighty secret," said Mr. Richards, composedly. "According to your view, could a mortal obtain the power you speak of, he would necessarily be a malignant and evil being."

"If the power were exercised as I have said, most malignant and most evil—though I believe in the ancient traditions that he could not injure the good. His will could only injure those with whom it has established an affinity, or over whom it forces unresisted sway. I will now imagine an example that may be within the laws of nature, yet seem wild as the fables of a bewildered monk.

"You will remember that Albertus Magnus, after describing minutely the process by which spirits may be invoked and commanded, adds emphatically, that the process will instruct and avail only to the few—that a *man must be born a magician!*—that is, born with a peculiar physical temperament, as a man is born a poet. Rarely are men in whose constitution lurks this occult flower of the highest order of intellect;—usually in the intellect there is some twist, perversity, or disease. But, on the other hand, they must possess, to an astonishing degree, the faculty to concentrate thought on a single object—the energic faculty that we call WILL. Therefore, though their intellect be not sound, it is exceedingly forcible for the attainment of what it desires. I will imagine such a person, pre-eminently gifted with this constitution and its concomitant forces. I will place him in the loftier grades of society. I will suppose his desires emphatically those of the sensualist—he has, therefore, a strong love of life. He is an absolute egotist—his will is concentred in himself—he has fierce passions—he knows no enduring, no holy affections, but he can covet eagerly what for the moment he desires—he can hate implacably what opposes itself to his objects—he can commit fearful crimes, yet feel small remorse—he resorts rather to curses upon others, than to penitence for his misdeeds. Circumstances, to which his constitution guides him, lead him to a rare knowledge of the natural secrets which may serve his egotism. He is a close observer where his passions encourage observation, he is a minute calculator, not from love of truth, but where love of self sharpens his faculties,—therefore he can be a man of science. I suppose such a being, having by experience learned the power of his arts over others, trying what may be the power of will over his own frame, and studying all that in natural philosophy may increase that power. He loves life, he dreads death; *he wills to live on.* He cannot restore himself to youth, he cannot entirely stay the progress of death, he cannot make himself immortal in the flesh and blood; but he may arrest for a time so prolonged as to appear incredible, if I said it—that hardening of the parts which constitutes old age. A year may age him no more than an hour ages another. His intense will, scientifically trained into system, operates, in short, over the wear and tear of his own frame. He lives on. That he may not seem a portent and a miracle, he *dies* from time to time, seemingly, to certain persons. Having schemed the transfer of a wealth that suffices to his wants, he disappears from one corner of the world, and contrives that his obsequies shall be celebrated. He reappears at another corner of the world, where he resides undetected, and does not revisit the scenes of his former career till all who could remember his features are no more. He would be profoundly miserable if he had affections,—he has none but for himself. No good man would accept his longevity, and to no men, good or bad, would he or could he communicate its true secret. Such a man might exist; such a man as I have described I see now before me!—Duke of ———, in the court of ———, dividing time between lust and brawl, alchemists and wizards;—again, in the last century, charlatan and criminal, with name less noble, domiciled in the house at which you gazed to-day, and flying from the law you had outraged, none knew whither;—traveller once more revisiting London, with the same earthly passions which filled your heart when races now no more walked through yonder streets;—outlaw from the school of all the nobler and diviner mystics;—execrable Image of Life in Death and Death in Life, I warn you back from the cities and homes of healthful men; back to the ruins of departed empires; back to the deserts of nature unredeemed!"

There answered me a whisper so musical, so potently musical, that it seemed to enter into my whole being, and subdue me despite myself. Thus it said—

"I have sought one like you for the last hundred years. Now I have found you, we part not till I know what I desire. The vision that sees through the Past, and cleaves through the veil of the Future, is in you at this hour; never before, never to come again. The vision of no puling fantastic girl, of no sick-bed somnambule, but of a strong man, with a vigorous brain. Soar and look forth!"

As he spoke I felt as if I rose out of myself upon eagle wings. All the weight seemed gone from air,—roofless the room, roofless the dome of space. I was not in the body—where I knew not—but aloft over time, over earth.

Again I heard the melodious whisper,—"You say right. I have mastered great secrets by the power of Will;—true, by Will and by Science I can retard the process of years: but death comes not by age alone. Can I frustrate the accidents which bring death upon the young?"

"No; every accident is a providence. Before a providence snaps every human will."

"Shall I die at last, ages and ages hence, by the slow, though inevitable, growth of time, or by the cause that I call accident?"

"By a cause you call accident."

"Is not the end still remote?" asked the whisper, with a slight tremor.

"Regarded as my life regards time, it is still remote."

"And shall I, before then, mix with the world of men as I did ere I learned these secrets, resume eager interest in their strife and their trouble—battle with ambition, and use the power of the sage to win the power that belongs to kings?"

"You will yet play a part on the earth that will fill earth with commotion and amaze. For wondrous designs have you, a wonder yourself, been permitted to live on through the centuries. All the secrets you have stored will then have their uses—all that now makes you a stranger amidst the generations will contribute then to make you their lord. As the trees and the straws are drawn into a whirlpool—as they spin round, are sucked to the deep, and again tossed aloft by the eddies, so shall races and thrones be plucked into the charm of your vortex. Awful Destroyer—but in destroying, made, against your own will, a Constructor!"

"And that date, too, is far off?"

"Far off; when it comes, think your end in this world is at hand!"

"How and what is the end? Look east, west, south, and north."

"In the north, where you never yet trod—towards the point whence your instincts have warned you, there a spectre will seize you. 'Tis Death! I see a ship—it is haunted—'tis chased—it sails on. Baffled navies sail after that ship. It enters the region of ice. It passes a sky red with meteors. Two moons stand on high, over ice-reefs. I see the ship locked between white defiles—they are ice-rocks. I see the dead strew the decks—stark and livid, green mould on their limbs. All are dead but one man—it is you! But years, though so slowly they come, have then scathed you. There is the coming of age on your brow, and the will is relaxed in the cells of the brain. Still that will, though enfeebled, exceeds all that man knew before you, through the will you live on, gnawed with famine: And nature no longer obeys you in that death-spreading region;—the sky is a sky of iron, and the air has iron clamps, and the ice-rocks wedge in the ship. Hark how it cracks and groans. Ice will imbed it as amber imbeds a straw. And a man has gone forth, living yet, from the ship and its dead; and he has clambered up the spikes of an iceberg, and the two moons gaze down on his form. That man is yourself; and terror is on you—terror; and terror has swallowed your will. And I see swarming up the steep ice-rock, grey griesly things. The bears of the north have scented their quarry—they come near you and nearer, shambling and rolling their bulk. And in that day every moment shall seem to you longer than the centuries through which you have passed. And heed this—after life, moments continued make the bliss or the hell of eternity."

"Hush," said the whisper; "but the day, you assure me, is far off—very far! I go back to the almond and rose of Damascus!—sleep!"

The room swam before my eyes. I became insensible. When I recovered, I found G—— holding my hand and smiling. He said, "You who have always declared yourself proof against mesmerism, have succumbed at last to my friend Richards."

"Where is Mr. Richards?"

"Gone, when you passed into a trance—saying quietly to me, 'Your friend will not wake for an hour.'"

I asked, as collectedly as I could, where Mr. Richards lodged.

"At the Trafalgar Hotel."

"Give me your arm," said I to G——, "let us call on him; I have something to say."

When we arrived at the hotel, we were told that Mr. Richards had returned twenty minutes before, paid his bill, left directions with his servant (a Greek) to pack his effects, and proceed to Malta on the steamer that should leave Southampton the next day. Mr. Richards had merely said of his own movements, that he had visits to pay in the neighbourhood of London, and it was uncertain whether he should be able to reach Southampton in time for that steamer; if not, he should follow in the next one.

The waiter asked me my name. On my informing him, he gave me a note that Mr. Richards had left for me, in case I called.

The note was as follows:—"I wished you to utter what was in your mind. You obeyed. I have therefore established power over you. For three months from this day you can communicate to no living man what has passed between us—you cannot even show this note to the friend by your side. During three months, silence complete as to me and mine. Do you doubt my power to lay on you this command?—try to disobey me. At the end of the third month, the spell is raised. For the rest I spare you. I shall visit your grave a year and a day after it has received you."

So ends this strange story, which I ask no one to believe. I write it down exactly three months after I received the above note. I could not write it before, nor could I show to G——, in spite of his urgent request, the note which I read under the gas-lamp by his side.

Fullcircle

JOHN BUCHAN

> Between the Windrush and the Colne
> I found a little house of stone—
> A little wicked house of stone.

I

THE OCTOBER DAY WAS BRIGHTENING TOWARD LATE AFTERNOON WHEN LEITHEN and I climbed the hill above the stream and came in sight of the house. All morning a haze with the sheen of pearl in it had lain on the folds of downland, and the vision of far horizons, which is the glory of Cotswold, had been veiled, so that every valley seemed as a place enclosed and set apart. But now a glow had come into the air, and for a little the autumn lawns stole the tints of summer. The gold of sunshine was warm on the grasses, and only the riot of color in the berry-laden edges of the fields and the slender woodlands told of the failing year.

We were looking into a green cup of the hills, and it was all a garden. A little place, bounded by slopes that defined its graciousness with no hint of barrier, so that a dweller there, though his view was but half a mile on any side, would yet have the sense of dwelling on uplands and commanding the world. Round the top edge ran an old wall of stones, beyond which the October bracken flamed to the skyline. Inside were folds of ancient pasture, with here and there a thorn-bush, falling to rose gardens and, on one side, to the smooth sward of a terrace above a tiny lake. At the heart of it stood the house like a jewel well set. It was a miniature, but by the hand of a master. The style was late seventeenth century, when an agreeable classic convention had opened up to sunlight and comfort the dark magnificence of the Tudor fashion. The place had the spacious air of a great mansion, and was furnished in every detail with a fine scrupulousness. Only when the eye measured its proportions with the woods and the hillside did the mind perceive that it was a small dwelling. The stone of Cotswold takes curiously the color of the weather. Under thunderclouds it will be as dark as basalt; on a gray day it will be gray like lava; but in sunshine it absorbs the sun. At the moment the little house was pale gold, like honey.

Leithen swung a long leg across the stile.

"Pretty good, isn't it?" he said. "It's pure, authentic Sir Christopher Wren. The name is worthy of it, too. It is called Fullcircle."

He told me its story. It had been built after the Restoration by the Carteron family, whose wide domains ran into these hills. The Lord Carteron of the day was a friend of the Merry Monarch; but it was not as a sanctuary for orgies that he built the house. Perhaps he was tired of the gloomy splendor of Minster Carteron, and wanted a home of his own and not of his ancestors' choosing. He had an elegant taste in letters, as we can learn from his neat imitations of Martial, his pretty *Bucolics* and the more than respectable Latin hexameters of his *Ars Vivendi*. Being a great nobleman, he had the best skill of the day to construct his hermitage, and thither he would retire for months at a time, with like-minded friends, to a world of books and gardens. He seems to have had no ill-wishers; contemporary memoirs speak of him charitably, and Dryden spared him four lines of encomium. "A selfish old dog," Leithen called him. "He had the good sense to eschew politics and enjoy life. His soul is in that little house. He only did one rash thing in his career—he anticipated the King, his master, by some years in turning Papist."

I asked about its later history.

"After his death it passed to a younger branch of the Carterons. It left them in the eighteenth century, and the Applebys got it. They were a jovial lot of hunting squires and let the library go to the dogs. Old Colonel Appleby was still alive when I came to Borrowby. Something went wrong in his inside when he was nearly seventy, and the doctors knocked him off liquor. Not that he drank too much, though he did himself well. That finished the poor old boy. He told me that it revealed to him the amazing truth that during a long and, as he hoped, publicly useful life he had never been quite sober. He was a good fellow and I missed him when he died. . . . The place went to a remote cousin called Giffen."

Leithen's eyes as they scanned the prospect, seemed amused.

"Julian and Ursula Giffen . . . I dare say you know the names. They always hunt in couples, and write books about sociology and advanced ethics and psychics—books called either 'The New This or That' or 'The Truth about Something or Other.' You know the sort of thing. They're deep in all the pseudo-sciences. They're decent souls, but you can guess the type. I came across them in a case I had at the Old Bailey—defending a ruffian who was charged with murder. I hadn't a doubt he deserved hanging on twenty counts, but there wasn't enough evidence to convict him on this one. Dodderidge was at his worst,—it was just before they induced him to retire,—and his handling of the jury was a masterpiece of misdirection. Of course, there was a shindy. The thing was a scandal, and it stirred up all the humanitarians till the murderer was almost forgotten in the iniquities of old Dodderidge. You must remember the case. It filled the papers for weeks. Well, it was in that connection that I fell in with the Giffens. I got rather to like them, and I've been to see them at their house in Hampstead. Golly, what a place! Not a chair fit to sit down on, and colors that made you want to howl. I never met people whose heads were so full of feathers."

I said something about that being an odd *milieu* for him.

"Oh, I like human beings—all kinds. It's my profession to study them, for without that the practice of the law would be a lean affair. There are hordes of people like the Giffens—only not so good, for they really have hearts of gold. They are the rootless stuff in the world to-day,—in revolt against everything and everybody with any ancestry. A kind of innocent self-righteousness—wanting to be the people with whom wisdom begins and ends. They are mostly sensitive and tender-hearted, but they wear themselves out in an eternal dissidence. Can't build, you know, for they object to all tools, but very ready to crab. They scorn any form of Christianity, but they'll walk miles to patronize some wretched sect that has the merit of being brand-new. 'Pioneers' they call themselves—funny little unclad people adventuring into the cold desert with no maps. Giffen once described himself and his friends to me as 'forward-looking,' but that, of course, is just what they are not. To tackle the future you must have a firm grip of the past, and for them the past is only a pathological curiosity. They're up to their necks in the mud of the present—but good, after a fashion; and innocent—sordidly innocent. Fate was in an ironical mood when she saddled them with that wicked little house."

"Wicked" did not seem to me to be a fair word. It sat honey-colored among its gardens with the meekness of a dove. The sound of a bicycle on the road behind made us turn round, and Leithen advanced to meet a dismounting rider.

He was a tallish fellow, some forty years old, perhaps, with one of those fluffy blond beards that have never been shaved. Short-sighted, of course, and wore glasses. Biscuit-colored knickerbockers and stockings clad his lean limbs.

Leithen introduced me. "We are walking to Borrowby and stopped to admire your house. Could we have just a glimpse inside? I want Jardine to see the staircase."

Mr. Giffen was very willing. "I've been over to Clyston to send a telegram. We have some friends for the week-end who might interest you. Won't you stay to tea?"

He had a gentle, formal courtesy about him, and his voice had the facile intonations of one who loves to talk. He led us through a little gate, and along a shorn green walk among the bracken, to a postern which gave entrance to the garden. Here, though it was October, there was still a bright show of roses, and the jet of water from the leaden Cupid dripped noiselessly among fallen petals. And then we stood before the doorway above which the old Carteron had inscribed a line of Horace.

I have never seen anything quite like the little hall. There were two, indeed, separated by a staircase of a wood that looked like olive. Both were paved with black and white marble, and the inner was oval in shape, with a gallery supported on slender walnut pillars. It was all in miniature, but it had a spaciousness which no mere size could give. Also it seemed to be permeated by the quintessence of sunlight. Its air was of long-descended, confident, equable happiness.

There were voices on the terrace beyond the hall. Giffen led us into a little room on the left. "You remember the house in Colonel Appleby's time, Leithen. This was the chapel. It had always been the chapel. You see the change we have made. . . . I beg your pardon, Mr. Jardine. You're not by any chance a Roman Catholic?"

The room had a white paneling and, on two sides, deep windows. At one end was a fine Italian shrine of marble, and the floor was mosaic, blue and white, in a quaint Byzantine pattern. There was the same air of sunny cheerfulness as in the rest of the house. No mystery could find a lodgment here. It might have been a chapel for three centuries, but the place was pagan. The Giffens' changes were no sort of desecration. A green baize table filled most of the floor, surrounded by chairs like a committee room. On new raw-wood shelves were files of papers and stacks of bluebooks and those desiccated works into which reformers of society torture the English tongue. Two typewriters stood on a side-table.

"It is our workroom," Giffen explained. "We hold our Sunday moots here. Ursula thinks that a week-end is wasted unless it produces some piece of real work. Often a quite valuable committee has its beginning here. We try to make our home a refuge for busy workers, where they need not idle but can work under happy conditions."

"'A college situate in a clearer air,'" Leithen quoted. But Giffen did not respond except with a smile; he had probably never heard of Lord Falkland.

A woman entered the room, a woman who might have been pretty if she had taken a little pains. Her reddish hair was drawn tightly back and dressed in a hard knot, and her clothes were horribly incongruous in a remote manor-house. She had bright eager eyes, like a bird, and hands that fluttered nervously. She greeted Leithen with warmth.

"We have settled down marvelously," she told him. "Julian and I feel as if we had always lived here, and our life has arranged itself so perfectly. My mothers' cottages in the village will soon be ready, and the Club is to be opened next week. Julian and I will carry on the classes ourselves for the first winter. Next year we hope to have a really fine programme. . . . And then it is so pleasant to be able to entertain one's friends. Won't you stay to tea? Dr. Swope is here, and Mary Elliston, and Mr. Percy Blaker—you know, the Member of Parliament. Must you hurry off? I'm so sorry. . . . What do you think of our workroom? It was utterly terrible when we first came here—a sort of decayed chapel, like a withered tuberose. We have let the air of heaven into it."

I observed that I had never seen a house so full of space and light.

"Ah, you notice that? It is a curiously happy place to live in. Sometimes I'm almost afraid to feel so light-hearted. But we look on ourselves as only trustees. It is a trust we have to administer for the common good. You know, it's a house on which you can lay your own impress. I can imagine places which dominate the dwellers, but Fullcircle is plastic, and we can make it our own as much as if we had planned and built it. That's our chief piece of good fortune."

We took our leave, for we had no desire for the company of Dr. Swope and Mr. Percy Blaker. When we reached the highway we halted and looked back on the little jewel. Shafts of the westering sun now caught the stone and turned the honey to ripe gold. Thin spires of amethyst smoke rose into the still air. I thought of the well-meaning, restless couple inside its walls, and somehow they seemed out of the picture. They simply did not matter. The house was the thing, for I had never met in inanimate stone such an air of gentle masterfulness. It had a personality of its own, clean-cut and secure, like a high-born old dame among the females of profiteers. And Mrs. Giffen claimed to have given it her impress!

That night, in the library at Borrowby, Leithen discoursed of the Restoration. Borrowby, of which, by the expenditure of much care and a good deal of money, he had made a civilized dwelling, is a Tudor manor of the Cotswold type, with its high-pitched narrow roofs and tall stone chimneys, rising sheer from the meadows with something of the massiveness of a Border keep. He nodded toward the linen-fold paneling and the great carved chimney-piece.

"In this kind of house you have the mystery of the elder England. What was Raleigh's phrase? 'High thoughts and divine contemplations.' The people who built this sort of thing lived close to another world, and thought bravely of death. It doesn't matter who they were,—Crusaders or Elizabethans or Puritans,—they all had poetry in them and the heroic and a great unworldliness. They had marvelous spirits, and plenty of joys and triumphs; but they had also their hours of black gloom. Their lives were like our weather—storm and sun. One thing they never feared—death. He walked too near them all their days to be a bogey.

"But the Restoration was a sharp break. It brought paganism into England; paganism and the art of life. No people have ever known better the secret of bland happiness.

Look at Fullcircle. There are no dark corners there. The man that built it knew all there was to be known about how to live. . . . The trouble was that they did not know how to die. That was the one shadow on the glass. So they provided for it in a pagan way. They tried magic. They never become true Catholics—they were always pagan to the end, but they smuggled a priest into their lives. He was a kind of insurance premium against unwelcome mystery."

II

It was not till nearly two years later that I saw the Giffens again. The May-fly season was about at its close, and I had snatched a day on a certain limpid Cotswold river. There was another man on the same beat, fishing from the opposite bank, and I watched him with some anxiety, for a duffer would have spoiled my day. To my relief I recognized Giffen. With him it was easy to come to terms, and presently the water was parceled out between us.

We foregathered for luncheon, and I stood watching while he neatly stalked, rose, and landed a trout. I confessed to some surprise—first that Giffen should be a fisherman at all, for it was not in keeping with my old notion of him; and second, that he should cast such a workmanlike line. As we lunched together, I observed several changes. He had shaved his fluffy beard, and his face was notably less lean, and had the clear even sunburn of the countryman. His clothes, too, were different. They also were workmanlike, and looked as if they belonged to him—he no longer wore the uneasy knickerbockers of the Sunday golfer.

"I'm desperately keen," he told me. "You see it's only my second May-fly season, and last year I was no better than a beginner. I wish I had known long ago what good fun fishing was. Isn't this a blessed place?" And he looked up through the canopy of flowering chestnuts to the June sky.

"I'm glad you've taken to sport," I said, "even if you only come here for the week-ends. Sport lets you into the secrets of the countryside."

"Oh, we don't go much to London now," was his answer. "We sold our Hampstead house a year ago. I can't think how I ever could stick that place. Ursula takes the same view. . . . I wouldn't leave Oxfordshire just now for a thousand pounds. Do you smell the hawthorn? Last week this meadow was scented like Paradise. . . . D'you know, Leithen's a queer fellow?"

I asked why.

"He once told me that this countryside in June made him sad. He said it was too perfect a thing for fallen humanity. I call that morbid. Do you see any sense in it?"

FULLCIRCLE

I knew what Leithen meant, but it would have taken too long to explain.

"I feel warm and good and happy here," he went on. "I used to talk about living close to nature. Rot! I didn't know what nature meant. Now—" He broke off. "By Jove, there's a kingfisher. That is only the second I've seen this year. They're getting uncommon with us."

"With us"—I liked the phrase. He was becoming a true countryman.

We had a good day,—not extravagantly successful, but satisfactory,—and he persuaded me to come home with him to Fullcircle for the night, explaining that I could catch an early train next morning at the junction. So we extricated a little two-seater from the midst of a clump of lilacs, and drove through four miles of sweet-scented dusk, with nightingales shouting in every thicket. I changed into a suit of his flannels in a room looking out on the little lake where trout were rising, and I remember that I whistled from pure lightheartedness. In that adorable house one seemed to be still breathing the air of the spring meadows.

Dinner was my first big surprise. It was admirable—plain, but perfectly cooked, and with that excellence of basic material which is the glory of a well-appointed country house. There was wine, too, which I am certain was a new thing. Giffen gave me a bottle of sound claret, and afterwards some more than decent port. My second surprise was my hostess. Her clothes, like her husband's, must have changed, for I did not notice what she was wearing, and I had noticed it only too clearly the last time we met. More remarkable still was the difference in her face. For the first time I realized that she was a pretty woman. The contours had softened and rounded, and there was a charming well-being in her eyes, very different from the old restlessness. She looked content, infinitely content.

I asked about her mothers' cottages. She laughed cheerfully.

"I gave them up after the first year. They didn't mix well with the village people. I'm quite ready to admit my mistake, and it was the wrong kind of charity. The Londoners didn't like it—felt lonesome and sighed for the fried-fish shop; and the village women were shy of them—afraid of infectious complaints, you know. Julian and I have decided that our business is to look after our own people."

It may have been malicious, but I said something about the wonderful scheme of village education.

"Another relic of Cockneyism," laughed the lady, but Giffen looked a trifle shy.

"I gave it up because it didn't seem worth while. What is the use of spoiling a perfectly wholesome scheme of life by introducing unnecessary complications? Medicine is no good unless a man is sick, and these people are not sick. Education is the only cure for certain diseases the modern world has engendered, but if you don't find the disease, the remedy is superfluous. The fact is, I hadn't the face to go on with the thing. I wanted to be taught rather than to teach. There's a whole world round me of which I know very little, and my first business is to get to understand it. Any village poacher can teach me more of the things that matter than I have to tell him."

"Besides, we have so much to do," his wife added. "There's the house and the garden and the home farm and the property. It isn't large, but it takes a lot of looking after."

The dining-room was long and low-ceilinged, and had a white paneling in bold relief. Through the deep windows came odors of the garden and a faint tinkle of water. The dusk was deepening and the engravings in their rosewood frames were dim, but sufficient light remained to reveal the picture above the fireplace. It showed a middle-aged man in the clothes of the later Stuarts. The plump tapering fingers of one hand held a book; the other was hidden in the folds of a flowered waistcoat. The long curled wig framed a delicate face with something of the grace of youth left to it. There were quizzical lines about the mouth, and the eyes smiled pleasantly yet very wisely. It was the face of a man I should have liked to dine with. He must have been the best of company. Giffen answered my question.

"'That's the Lord Carteron who built the house. No. No relation. Our people were the Applebys, who came in 1753. We've both fallen so deep in love with Fullcircle that we wanted to see the man who conceived it. I had some trouble getting it. It came out of the Minster Carteron sale, and I had to give a Jew dealer twice what he paid for it. It's a jolly thing to live with."

It was indeed a curiously charming picture. I found my eyes straying to it till the dusk obscured the features. It was the face of one wholly at home in a suave world, learned in all the urbanities. A good friend, I thought, the old lord must have been, and a superlative companion. I could imagine neat Horatian tags coming ripely from his lips. Not a strong face, but somehow a dominating one. The portrait of the long-dead gentleman had still the atmosphere of life. Giffen raised his glass of port to him as we rose from table, as if to salute a comrade. We moved to the room across the hall which had once been the Giffens' workroom, the cradle of earnest committees and weighty memoranda. This was my third surprise. Baize-covered table and raw-wood shelves had disappeared. The place was now half smoking-room, half library. On the walls hung a fine collection of colored sporting prints, and below them were ranged low Hepplewhite bookcases. The lamplight glowed on the ivory walls, and the room, like everything else in the house, was radiant. Above the mantelpiece was a stag's head—a fair eleven-pointer.

Giffen nodded proudly toward it. "I got that last year at Machray. My first stag."

There was a little table with an array of magazines and weekly papers. Some amusement must have been visible in my face, as I caught sight of various light-hearted sporting journals, for he laughed apologetically. "You mustn't think that Ursula and I take in that stuff for ourselves. It amuses our guests, you know."

I dared say it did, but I was convinced that the guests were no longer Dr. Swope and Mr. Percy Blaker.

One of my many failings is that I can never enter a room containing books without scanning the titles. Giffen's collection won my hearty approval. There were the very few novelists I can read myself—Miss Austen and Sir Walter and the admirable Marryat; there was a shelf full of memoirs, and a good deal of seventeenth- and eighteenth-century poetry; there was a set of the classics in fine editions, Bodonis and Baskervilles and such like; there was much county history and one or two valuable old Herbals and Itineraries. I was certain that two years earlier Giffen would have had no use for literature except some muddy Russian oddments, and I am positive that he would not have known the name of Surtees. Yet there stood the tall octavos recording the unedifying careers of Mr. Jorrocks, Mr. Facey Romford, and Mr. Soapy Sponge.

I was a little bewildered as I stretched my legs in a very deep arm-chair. Suddenly I had a strong impression of looking on at a play. My hosts seemed to be automata, moving docilely at the orders of a masterful stage manager, and yet with no sense of bondage. And as I looked on, they faded off the scene, and there was only one personality—that house so serene and secure, smiling at our modern antics, but weaving all the while an iron spell around its lovers. For a second I felt an oppression as of something to be resisted. But no. There was no oppression. The house was too well-bred and disdainful to seek to captivate. Only those who fell in love with it could know its mastery, for all love exacts a price. It was far more than a thing of stone and lime: it was a creed, an art, a scheme of life—older than any Carteron, older than England. Somewhere far back in time, in Rome, in Attica, or in an Ægean island—there must have been such places; and then they called them temples, and gods dwelt in them.

I was roused by Giffen's voice discoursing of his books. "I've been rubbing up my classics again," he was saying. "Queer thing, but ever since I left Cambridge I have been out of the mood for them. And I'm shockingly ill-read in English literature. I wish I had more time for reading, for it means a lot to me."

"There is such an embarrassment of riches here," said his wife. "The days are far too short for all there is to do. Even when there is nobody staying in the house I find every hour occupied. It's delicious to be busy over things one really cares for."

"All the same I wish I could do more reading," said Giffen. "I've never wanted to so much before."

"But you come in tired from shooting and sleep sound till dinner," said the lady, laying an affectionate hand on his shoulder.

They were happy people, and I like happiness. Self-absorbed, perhaps, but I prefer selfishness in the ordinary way of things. We are most of us selfish dogs, and altruism makes us uncomfortable. But I had somehow in my mind a shade of uneasiness, for I was the witness of a transformation too swift and violent to be wholly natural. Years, no doubt, turn our eyes inward and abate our heroics, but not a trifle of two or three. Some agency had been at work here, some agency other and more potent than the process of time. The thing fascinated and partly frightened me. For the Giffens—though I scarcely dared to admit it—had deteriorated. They were far pleasanter people, I liked them infinitely better, I hoped to see them often again. I detested the type they used to represent, and shunned it like the plague. They were wise now, and mellow, and most agreeable human beings. But some virtue had gone out of them. An uncomfortable virtue, no doubt, but still a virtue; something generous and adventurous. In the earlier time, their faces had had a sort of wistful kindness. Now they had geniality—which is not the same thing.

What was the agency of this miracle? It was all around me: the ivory paneling, the olive-wood staircase, the lovely pillared hall. I got up to go to bed with a kind of awe on me. As Mrs. Giffen lit my candle, she saw my eyes wandering among the gracious shadows.

"Isn't it wonderful," she said, "to have found a house which fits us like a glove? No! Closer. Fits us as a bearskin fits the bear. It has taken our impress like wax."

Somehow I didn't think that impress had come from the Giffens' side.

III

A November afternoon found Leithen and myself jogging homeward from a run with the Heythrop. It had been a wretched day. Twice we had found and lost, and then a deluge had set in which scattered the field. I had taken a hearty toss into a swamp, and got as wet as a man may be, but the steady downpour soon reduced everyone to a like condition. When we turned toward Borrowby the rain ceased, and an icy wind blew out of the east which partially dried our sopping clothes. All the grace had faded from the Cotswold valleys. The streams were brown torrents, the meadows lagoons, the ridges bleak and gray, and a sky of scurrying clouds cast leaden shadows. It was a matter of ten miles to Borrowby; we had long ago emptied our flasks, and I longed for something hot to take the chill out of my bones.

"Let's look in at Fullcircle," said Leithen, as we came out on the highroad from a muddy lane. "We'll make the Giffens give us tea. You'll find changes there."

I asked what changes, but he only smiled and told me to wait and see.

My mind was busy with surmises as we rode up the avenue. I thought of drink or drugs, and promptly discarded the notion. Fullcircle was, above all things, decorous and wholesome. Leithen could not mean the change in the Giffens' ways which had so impressed me a year before, for he and I had long ago discussed that. I was still puzzling over his words when we found ourselves in the inner hall, with the Giffens making a hospitable fuss over us.

The place was more delectable than ever. Outside was a dark November day, yet the little house seemed to be transfused with sunshine. I do not know by what art the old builders had planned it; but the airy pilasters, the perfect lines of the ceiling, the soft coloring of the wood seemed to lay open the house to a clear sky. Logs burned brightly on the massive steel andirons, and the scent and the fine blue smoke of them strengthened the illusion of summer.

Mrs. Giffen would have us change into dry things, but Leithen pleaded a waiting dinner at Borrowby. The two of us stood by the fireplace, drinking tea, the warmth drawing out a cloud of vapor from our clothes to mingle with the wood-smoke. Giffen lounged in an arm-chair and his wife sat by the tea-table. I was looking for the changes of which Leithen had spoken.

I did not find them in Giffen. He was much as I remembered him on the June night when I had slept here—a trifle fuller in the face, perhaps, a little more placid about the mouth and eyes. He looked a man completely content with life. His smile came readily, and his easy laugh. Was it my fancy, or had he acquired a look of the picture in the dining-room? I nearly made an errand to go and see it. It seemed to me that his mouth had now something of the portrait's delicate complacence. Lely would have found him a fit subject, though he might have boggled at his lean hands.

But his wife! Ah, there the changes were unmistakable. She was comely now rather than pretty, and the contours of her face had grown heavier. The eagerness had gone from her eyes and left only comfort and good humor. There was a suspicion, ever so slight, of rouge and powder. She had a string of good pearls—the first time I had seen her wear jewels. The hand that poured out the tea was plump, shapely, and well cared for. I was looking at a most satisfactory mistress of a country house, who would see that nothing was lacking to the part.

She talked more and laughed oftener. Her voice had an airy lightness which would have made the silliest prattle charming.

"We are going to fill the house with young people and give a ball at Christmas," she announced. "This hall is simply clamoring to be danced in. You must come, both of you. Promise me. And, Mr. Leithen, it would be very nice if you brought a party from

Borrowby. Young men, please. We are overstocked with girls in these parts. . . . We must do something to make the country cheerful in winter-time."

I observed that no season could make Fullcircle other than cheerful.

"How nice of you!" she cried. "To praise a house is to praise the householders, for a dwelling is just what its inmates make it. Borrowby is you, Mr. Leithen, and Fullcircle us."

"Shall we exchange?" Leithen asked.

She made a mouth. "Borrowby would crush me, but it suits a Gothic survival like you. Do you think you would be happy here?"

"Happy?" said Leithen thoughtfully. "Happy? Yes, undoubtedly. But it might be bad for my soul. . . . There's just time for a pipe, Giffen, and then we must be off."

I was filling my pipe as we crossed the outer hall, and was about to enter the smoking-room that I so well remembered, when Giffen laid a hand on my arm.

"We don't smoke there now," he said hastily.

He opened the door and I looked in. . . . The place had suffered its third metamorphosis. The marble shrine which I had noticed on my first visit had been brought back, and the blue mosaic pavement and the ivory walls were bare. At the eastern end stood a little altar, with, above it, a copy of a Correggio Madonna.

A faint smell of incense hung in the air, and the fragrance of hothouse flowers. It was a chapel, but, I swear, it was a more pagan place than when it had been workroom or smoking-room.

Giffen gently shut the door. "Perhaps you may not have heard, but some months ago my wife became a Catholic. It is a good thing for women, I think. It gives them a regular ritual for their lives. So we restored the chapel, which had always been there in the days of the Carterons and the Applebys."

"And you?" I asked.

He shrugged his shoulders. "I don't bother much about that sort of thing. But I propose to follow suit. It will please Ursula and do no harm to anybody."

We halted on the brow of the hill and looked back on the garden valley. Leithen's laugh, as he gazed, had more awe than mirth in it.

"That wicked little house! I'm going to hunt up every scrap I can find about old Tom Carteron. He must have been an uncommon clever fellow. He's still alive down there and making people do as he did. In that kind of place you may expel the priest and sweep it and garnish it, but he always returns."

The wrack was lifting before the wind, and a shaft of late watery sun fell on the gray walls. It seemed to me that the little house wore an air of gentle triumph.

Amour Dure
Passages from the Diary of Spiridion Trenka

VERNON LEE

I

URBANIA, AUGUST 20TH, 1885.—I HAD LONGED, THESE YEARS AND YEARS, TO be in Italy, to come face to face with the Past; and was this Italy, was this the Past? I could have cried, yes cried, for disappointment when I first wandered about Rome, with an invitation to dine at the German Embassy in my pocket, and three or four Berlin and Munich Vandals at my heels, telling me where the best beer and sauerkraut could be had, and what the last article by Grimm or Mommsen was about.

Is this folly? Is it falsehood? Am I not myself a product of modern, northern civilization; is not my coming to Italy due to this very modern scientific vandalism, which has given me a traveling scholarship because I have written a book like all those other atrocious books of erudition and art-criticism? Nay, am I not here at Urbania on the express understanding that, in a certain number of months, I shall produce just another such book? Dost thou imagine, thou miserable Spiridion, thou Pole grown into the semblance of a German pedant, doctor of philosophy, professor even, author of a prize essay on the despots of the fifteenth century, dost thou imagine that thou, with thy ministerial letters and proof-sheets in thy black professorial coat-pocket, canst ever come in spirit into the presence of the Past?

Too true, alas! But let me forget it, at least, every now and then; as I forgot it this afternoon, while the white bullocks dragged my gig slowly winding along interminable valleys, crawling along interminable hill-sides, with the invisible droning torrent far below, and only the bare grey and reddish peaks all around, up to this town of Urbania, forgotten of mankind, towered and battlemented on the high Apennine ridge. Sigillo, Penna, Fossombrone, Mercatello, Montemurlo—each single village name, as the driver pointed it out, brought to my mind the recollection of some battle or some great act of treachery of former days. And as the huge mountains shut out the setting sun, and the valleys filled with bluish shadow and mist, only a band of threatening smoke-red remaining behind the towers and cupolas of the city on its mountain-top, and the sound of church bells floated across the precipice from Urbania, I almost expected, at every turning of the road, that a troop of horsemen, with beaked helmets and clawed shoes, would emerge, with armor glittering and pennons waving in the sunset. And then, not two hours ago, entering the town at dusk, passing along the deserted streets, with only a smoky light here and there under a shrine or in front of a fruit-stall, or a fire reddening the blackness of a smithy; passing beneath the battlements and turrets of the palace.... Ah, that was Italy, it was the Past!

August 21st.—And this is the Present! Four letters of introduction to deliver, and an hour's polite conversation to endure with the Vice-Prefect, the Syndic, the Director of the Archives, and the good man to whom my friend Max had sent me for lodgings....

August 22nd–27th.—Spent the greater part of the day in the Archives, and the greater part of my time there in being bored to extinction by the Director thereof, who today spouted Æneas Sylvius' Commentaries for three-quarters of an hour without taking breath. From this sort of martyrdom (what are the sensations of a former racehorse being driven in a cab? If you can conceive them, they are those of a Pole turned Prussian professor) I take refuge in long rambles through the town. This town is a handful of tall black houses huddled on to the top of an Alp, long narrow lanes trickling down its sides, like the slides we made on hillocks in our boyhood, and in the middle the superb red brick structure, turreted and battlemented, of Duke Ottobuono's palace, from whose windows you look down upon a sea, a kind of whirlpool, of melancholy grey mountains. Then there are the people, dark, bushy-bearded men, riding about like brigands, wrapped in green-lined cloaks upon their shaggy pack-mules; or loitering about, great, brawny, low-headed youngsters, like the parti-colored bravos in Signorelli's frescoes; the beautiful boys, like so many young Raphaels, with eyes like the eyes of bullocks, and the huge women, Madonnas or St. Elizabeths, as the case may be, with their clogs firmly poised on their toes and their brass pitchers on their heads, as they go up and down the steep black alleys. I do not talk much to these people; I fear my illusions being dispelled. At the corner of a street, opposite Francesco di Giorgio's beautiful little portico, is a great blue and red advertisement, representing an angel descending to crown Elias Howe, on account of his sewing-machines; and the clerks of the Vice-Prefecture, who dine at the place where I get my dinner, yell politics, Minghetti, Cairoli, Tunis, ironclads, &c., at each other, and sing snatches of *La Fille de Mme. Angot,* which I imagine they have been performing here recently.

No; talking to the natives is evidently a dangerous experiment. Except indeed, perhaps, to my good landlord, Signor Notaro Porri, who is just as learned, and takes considerably less snuff (or rather brushes it off his coat more often) than the Director of the Archives. I forgot to jot down (and I feel I must jot down, in the vain belief that some day these scraps will help, like a withered twig of olive or a three-wicked Tuscan lamp on my table, to bring to my mind, in that hateful Babylon of Berlin, these happy Italian days)—I forgot to record that I am lodging in the house of a dealer in antiquities. My window looks up the principal street to where the little column with Mercury on the top rises in the midst of the awnings and porticoes of the market-place. Bending over the chipped ewers and tubs full of sweet basil, clove pinks, and marigolds, I can just see a corner of the palace turret, and the vague ultramarine of the hills beyond. The house, whose back goes sharp down into the ravine, is a queer up-and-down black place, whitewashed rooms, hung with the Raphaels and Francias and Peruginos, whom mine host regularly carries to the chief inn whenever a stranger is expected; and surrounded by old carved chairs, sofas of the Empire, embossed and gilded wedding-chests, and the cupboards which contain bits of old damask and embroidered altar-cloths scenting the place with the smell of old incense and mustiness; all of which are presided over by Signor Porri's three maiden sisters—Sora Serafina, Sora Lodovica, and Sora Adalgisa—the three Fates in person, even to the distaffs and their black cats.

Sor Asdrubale, as they call my landlord, is also a notary. He regrets the Pontifical Government, having had a cousin who was a Cardinal's train-bearer, and believes that if only you lay a table for two, light four candles made of dead men's fat, and perform certain rites about which he is not very precise, you can, on Christmas Eve and similar nights, summon up San Pasquale Baylon, who will write you the winning numbers of the lottery upon the smoked back of a plate, if you have previously slapped him on both cheeks and repeated three Ave Marias. The difficulty consists in obtaining the dead men's fat for the candles, and also in slapping the saint before he has time to vanish.

"If it were not for that," says Sor Asdrubale, "the Government would have had to suppress the lottery ages ago—eh!"

Sept. 9th.—This history of Urbania is not without its romance, although that romance (as usual) has been overlooked by our Dryasdusts. Even before coming here I felt attracted by the strange figure of a woman, which appeared from out of the dry pages of Gualterio's and Padre de Sanctis' histories of this place. This woman is Medea, daughter of Galeazzo IV Malatesta, Lord of Carpi, wife first of Pierluigi Orsini, Duke of Stimigliano, and subsequently of Guidalfonso II, Duke of Urbania, predecessor of the great Duke Robert II.

This woman's history and character remind one of that of Bianca Cappello, and at the same time of Lucrezia Borgia. Born in 1556, she was affianced at the age of twelve to a cousin, a Malatesta of the Rimini family. This family having greatly gone down in the world, her engagement was broken, and she was betrothed a year later to a member of the Pico family, and married to him by proxy at the age of fourteen. But this match not satisfying her own or her father's ambition, the marriage by proxy was, upon some pretext, declared null, and the suit encouraged of the Duke of Stimigliano, a great Umbrian feudatory of the Orsini family. But the bridegroom, Giovanfrancesco Pico, refused to submit, pleaded his case before the Pope, and tried to carry off by force his bride, with whom he was madly in love, as the lady was most lovely and of most cheerful and amiable manner, says an old anonymous chronicle. Pico waylaid her litter as she was going to a villa of her father's, and carried her to his castle near Mirandola, where he respectfully pressed his suit; insisting that he had a right to consider her as his wife. But the lady escaped by letting herself into the moat by a rope of sheets, and Giovanfrancesco Pico was discovered stabbed in the chest, by the hand of Madonna Medea da Carpi. He was a handsome youth only eighteen years old.

The Pico having been settled, and the marriage with him declared null by the Pope, Medea da Carpi was solemnly married to the Duke of Stimigliano, and went to live upon his domains near Rome.

Two years later, Pierluigi Orsini was stabbed by one of his grooms at his castle of Stimigliano, near Orvieto; and suspicion fell upon his widow, more especially as, immediately after the event, she caused the murderer to be cut down by two servants in her own chamber; but not before he had declared that she had induced him to assassinate his master by a promise of her love. Things became so hot for Medea da Carpi that she fled to Urbania and threw herself at the feet of Duke Guidalfonso II, declaring that she had caused the groom to be killed merely to avenge her good fame, which he had slandered, and that she was absolutely guiltless of the death of her husband. The marvelous beauty of the widowed Duchess of Stimigliano, who was only nineteen, entirely turned the head of the Duke of Urbania. He affected implicit belief in her innocence, refused to give her up to the Orsinis, kinsmen of her late husband, and assigned to her magnificent apartments in the left wing of the palace, among which the room containing the famous fireplace ornamented with marble Cupids on a blue ground. Guidalfonso fell madly in love with his beautiful guest. Hitherto timid and domestic in character, he began publicly to neglect his wife, Maddalena Varano of Camerino, with whom, although childless, he had hitherto lived on excellent terms; he not only treated with contempt the admonitions of his advisers and of his suzerain the

Pope, but went so far as to take measures to repudiate his wife, on the score of quite imaginary ill-conduct. The Duchess Maddalena, unable to bear this treatment, fled to the convent of the barefooted sisters at Pesaro, where she pined away, while Medea da Carpi reigned in her place at Urbania, embroiling Duke Guidalfonso in quarrels both with the powerful Orsinis, who continued to accuse her of Stimigliano's murder, and with the Varanos, kinsmen of the injured Duchess Maddalena; until at length, in the year 1576, the Duke of Urbania, having become suddenly, and not without suspicious circumstances, a widower, publicly married Medea da Carpi two days after the decease of his unhappy wife. No child was born of this marriage; but such was the infatuation of Duke Guidalfonso, that the new Duchess induced him to settle the inheritance of the Duchy (having, with great difficulty, obtained the consent of the Pope) on the boy Bartolommeo, her son by Stimigliano, but whom the Orsinis refused to acknowledge as such, declaring him to be the child of that Giovanfrancesco Pico to whom Medea had been married by proxy, and whom, in defense, as she had said, of her honor, she had assassinated; and this investiture of the Duchy of Urbania on to a stranger and a bastard was at the expense of the obvious rights of the Cardinal Robert, Guidalfonso's younger brother.

In May 1579 Duke Guidalfonso died suddenly and mysteriously, Medea having forbidden all access to his chamber, lest, on his deathbed, he might repent and reinstate his brother in his rights. The Duchess immediately caused her son, Bartolommeo Orsini, to be proclaimed Duke of Urbania, and herself regent; and, with the help of two or three unscrupulous young men, particularly a certain Captain Oliverotto da Narni, who was rumored to be her lover, seized the reins of government with extraordinary and terrible vigor, marching an army against the Varanos and Orsinis, who were defeated at Sigillo, and ruthlessly exterminating every person who dared question the lawfulness of the succession; while, all the time, Cardinal Robert, who had flung aside his priest's garb and vows, went about in Rome, Tuscany, Venice—nay, even to the Emperor and the King of Spain, imploring help against the usurper. In a few months he had turned the tide of sympathy against the Duchess-Regent; the Pope solemnly declared the investiture of Bartolommeo Orsini worthless, and published the accession of Robert II, Duke of Urbania and Count of Montemurlo; the Grand Duke of Tuscany and the Venetians secretly promised assistance, but only if Robert were able to assert his rights by main force. Little by little, one town after the other of the Duchy went over to Robert, and Medea da Carpi found herself surrounded in the mountain citadel of Urbania like a scorpion surrounded by flames. (This simile is not mine, but belongs to Raffaello Gualterio, historiographer to Robert II.) But, unlike the scorpion, Medea refused to commit suicide. It is perfectly marvelous how, without money or allies, she could so long keep her enemies at bay; and Gualterio attributes this to those fatal fascinations which had brought Pico and Stimigliano to their deaths, which had turned the once honest Guidalfonso into a villain, and which were such that, of all her lovers, not one but preferred dying for her, even after he had been treated with ingratitude and ousted by a rival; a faculty which Messer Raffaello Gualterio clearly attributed to hellish connivance.

At last the ex-Cardinal Robert succeeded, and triumphantly entered Urbania in November 1579. His accession was marked by moderation and clemency. Not a man was put to death, save Oliverotto da Narni, who threw himself on the new Duke, tried to stab him as he alighted at the palace, and who was cut down by the Duke's men, crying, "Orsini, Orsini! Medea, Medea! Long live Duke Bartolommeo!" with his dying breath, although it is said that the Duchess had treated him with ignominy. The little Bartolommeo was sent to Rome to the Orsinis; the Duchess, respectfully confined in the left wing of the palace.

It is said that she haughtily requested to see the new Duke, but that he shook his head, and, in his priest's fashion, quoted a verse about Ulysses and the Sirens; and it is remarkable that he persistently refused to see her, abruptly leaving his chamber one day that she had entered it by stealth. After a few months a conspiracy was discovered to murder Duke Robert, which had obviously been set on foot by Medea. But the young man, one Marcantonio Frangipani of Rome, denied, even under the severest torture, any complicity of hers; so that Duke Robert, who wished to do nothing violent, merely transferred the Duchess from his villa at Sant' Elmo to the convent of the Clarisse in town, where she was guarded and watched in the closest manner. It seemed impossible that Medea should intrigue any further, for she certainly saw and could be seen by no one. Yet she contrived to send a letter and her portrait to one Prinzivalle degli Ordelaffi, a youth, only nineteen years old, of noble Romagnole family, and who was betrothed to one of the most beautiful girls of Urbania. He immediately broke off his engagement, and, shortly afterwards, attempted to shoot Duke Robert with a holster-pistol as he knelt at mass on the festival of Easter Day. This time Duke Robert was determined to obtain proofs against Medea. Prinzivalle degli Ordelaffi was kept some days without food, then submitted to the most violent tortures, and finally condemned. When he was going to be flayed with red-hot pincers and quartered by horses, he was told that he might obtain the grace of immediate death by confessing the complicity of the Duchess; and the confessor and nuns of the convent, which stood in the place of execution outside Porta San Romano, pressed Medea to save the wretch, whose screams reached her, by confessing her own guilt. Medea asked permission to go to a balcony, where she could see Prinzivalle and be seen by him. She looked on coldly, then threw down her embroidered kerchief to the poor mangled creature. He asked the executioner to wipe his mouth with it, kissed it, and cried out that Medea was innocent. Then, after several hours of torments, he died. This was too much for the patience even of Duke Robert. Seeing that as long as Medea lived his life would be in perpetual danger, but unwilling to cause a scandal (somewhat of the priest-nature remaining), he had Medea strangled in the convent, and, what is remarkable, insisted that only women—two infanticides to whom he remitted their sentence—should be employed for the deed.

"This clement prince," writes Don Arcangelo Zappi in his life of him, published in 1725, "can be blamed only for one act of cruelty, the more odious as he had himself, until released from his vows by the Pope, been in holy orders. It is said that when he caused the death of the infamous Medea da Carpi, his fear lest her extraordinary charms should seduce any man was such, that he not only employed women as executioners, but refused to permit her a priest or monk, thus forcing her to die unshriven, and refusing her the benefit of any penitence that may have lurked in her adamantine heart."

Such is the story of Medea da Carpi, Duchess of Stimigliano Orsini, and then wife of Duke Guidalfonso II of Urbania. She was put to death just two hundred and ninety-seven years ago, December 1582, at the age of barely seven and twenty, and having, in the course of her short life, brought to a violent end five of her lovers, from Giovanfrancesco Pico to Prinzivalle degli Ordelaffi.

Sept. 20th.—A grand illumination of the town in honor of the taking of Rome fifteen years ago. Except Sor Asdrubale, my landlord, who shakes his head at the Piedmontese, as he calls them, the people here are all Italianissimi. The Popes kept them very much down since Urbania lapsed to the Holy See in 1645.

Sept. 28th.—I have for some time been hunting for portraits of the Duchess Medea. Most of them, I imagine, must have been destroyed, perhaps by Duke Robert II's fear lest even after her death this terrible beauty should play him a trick. Three or four I have, however, been able to find—one a miniature in the Archives, said to be that which she sent to poor Prinzivalle degli Ordelaffi in order to turn his head; one a marble bust in the palace lumber-room; one in a large composition, possibly by Baroccio, representing Cleopatra at the feet of Augustus. Augustus is the idealized portrait of Robert II, round cropped head, nose a little awry, clipped beard and scar as usual, but in Roman dress. Cleopatra seems to me, for all her Oriental dress, and although she wears a black wig, to be meant for Medea da Carpi; she is kneeling, baring her breast for the victor to strike, but in reality to captivate him, and he turns away with an awkward gesture of loathing.

None of these portraits seem very good, save the miniature, but that is an exquisite work, and with it, and the suggestions of the bust, it is easy to reconstruct the beauty of this terrible being. The type is that most admired by the late Renaissance, and, in some measure, immortalized by Jean Goujon and the French. The face is a perfect oval, the forehead somewhat over-round, with minute curls, like a fleece, of bright auburn hair; the nose a trifle over-aquiline, and the cheek-bones a trifle too low; the eyes grey, large, prominent, beneath exquisitely curved brows and lids just a little too tight at the corners; the mouth also, brilliantly red and most delicately designed, is a little too tight, the lips strained a trifle over the teeth. Tight eyelids and tight lips give a strange refinement, and, at the same time, an air of mystery, a somewhat sinister seductiveness; they seem to take, but not to give. The mouth with a kind of childish pout, looks as if it could bite or suck like a leech. The complexion is dazzlingly fair, the perfect transparent rosette lily of a red-haired beauty; the head, with hair elaborately curled and plaited close to it, and adorned with pearls, sits like that of the antique Arethusa on a long, supple, swan-like neck. A curious, at first rather conventional, artificial-looking sort of beauty, voluptuous yet cold, which, the more it is contemplated, the more it troubles and haunts the mind. Round the lady's neck is a gold chain with little gold lozenges at intervals, on which is engraved the posy or pun (the fashion of French devices is common in those days), "Amour Dure—Dure Amour." The same posy is inscribed in the hollow of the bust, and, thanks to it, I have been able to identify the latter as Medea's portrait. I often examine these tragic portraits, wondering what this face, which led so many men to their death, may have been like when it spoke or smiled, what at the moment when Medea da Carpi fascinated her victims into love unto death—"Amour Dure—Dure Amour," as runs her device—love that lasts, cruel love—yes indeed, when one thinks of the fidelity and fate of her lovers.

Oct. 13th.—I have literally not had time to write a line of my diary all these days. My whole mornings have gone in those Archives, my afternoons taking long walks in this lovely autumn weather (the highest hills are just tipped with snow). My evenings go in writing that confounded account of the Palace of Urbania which Government requires, merely to keep me at work at something useless. Of my history I have not yet been able to write a word. . . . By the way, I must note down a curious circumstance mentioned in an anonymous MS. life of Duke Robert, which I fell upon today. When this prince had the equestrian statue of himself by Antonio Tassi, Gianbologna's pupil, erected in the square of the *Corte*, he secretly caused to be made, says my anonymous MS., a silver statuette of his familiar genius or angel—"familiaris ejus angelus seu genius, quod a vulgo dicitur *idolino*"—which statuette or idol, after having been consecrated by the astrologers—"ab astrologis quibusdam ritibus sacrato"—was placed in the cavity of the chest of the effigy by Tassi, in order, says the MS., that his soul might rest until the general Resurrection. This passage is curious, and to me somewhat puzzling; how could the soul of Duke Robert await the general Resurrection, when, as a Catholic, he ought to have believed that it must, as soon as separated from his body, go to Purgatory? Or is there some semi-pagan superstition of the Renaissance (most strange, certainly, in a man who had been a Cardinal) connecting the soul with a guardian genius, who could be compelled, by magic rites ("ab astrologis sacrato," the MS. says of the little idol), to remain fixed to earth, so that the soul should sleep in the body until the Day of Judgment? I confess this story baffles me. I wonder whether such an idol ever existed, or exists nowadays, in the body of Tassi's bronze effigy?

Oct. 20th.—I have been seeing a good deal of late of the Vice-Prefect's son: an amiable young man with a love-sick face and a languid interest in Urbanian history and archaeology, of which he is profoundly ignorant. This young man, who has lived at Siena and Lucca before his father was promoted here, wears extremely long and tight trousers, which almost preclude his bending his knees, a stick-up collar and an eyeglass, and a pair of fresh kid gloves stuck in the breast of his coat, speaks of Urbania as Ovid might have spoken of Pontus, and complains (as well he may) of the barbarism of the young men, the officials who dine at my inn and howl and sing like madmen, and the nobles who drive gigs, showing almost as much throat as a lady at a ball. This person frequently entertains me with his *amori*, past, present, and future; he evidently thinks me very odd for having none to entertain him with in return; he points out to me the pretty (or ugly) servant-girls and dressmakers as we walk in the street, sighs deeply or sings in falsetto behind every tolerably young-looking woman, and has finally taken me to the house of the lady of his heart, a great black-mustachioed countess, with a voice like a fish-crier; here, he says, I shall meet all the best company in Urbania and some beautiful women—ah, too beautiful, alas! I find three huge half-furnished rooms, with bare brick floors, petroleum lamps, and horribly bad pictures on bright washball-blue and gamboge walls, and in the midst of it all, every evening, a dozen ladies and gentlemen seated in a circle, vociferating at each other the same news a year old; the younger ladies in bright yellows and greens, fanning themselves while my teeth chatter, and having sweet things whispered behind their fans by officers with hair brushed up like a hedgehog. And these are the women my friend expects me to fall in love with! I vainly wait for tea or supper which does not come, and rush home, determined to leave alone the Urbanian *beau monde*.

It is quite true that I have no *amori*, although my friend does not believe it. When I came to Italy first, I looked out for romance; I sighed, like Goethe in Rome, for a window to open and a wondrous creature to appear, "welch mich versengend erquickt." Perhaps it is because Goethe was a German, accustomed to German *Fraus*, and I am, after all, a Pole, accustomed to something very different from *Fraus*; but anyhow, for all my efforts, in Rome, Florence, and Siena, I never could find a woman to go mad about, either among the ladies, chattering bad French, or among the lower classes, as 'cute and cold as money-lenders; so I steer clear of Italian womankind, its shrill voice and gaudy toilettes. I am wedded to history, to the Past, to women like Lucrezia Borgia, Vittoria Accoramboni, or that Medea da Carpi, for the present; some day I shall perhaps find a grand passion, a woman to play the Don Quixote about, like the Pole that I am; a woman out of whose slipper to drink, and for whose pleasure to die; but not here! Few things strike me so much as the degeneracy of Italian women. What has become of the race of Faustinas, Marozias, Bianca Cappellos? Where discover nowadays (I confess she haunts me) another Medea da Carpi? Were it only possible to meet a woman of that extreme distinction of beauty, of that terribleness of nature, even if only potential, I do believe I could love her, even to the Day of Judgment, like any Oliverotto da Narni, or Frangipani or Prinzivalle.

Oct. 27th.—Fine sentiments the above are for a professor, a learned man! I thought the young artists of Rome childish because they played practical jokes and yelled at night in the streets, returning from the Caffè Greco or the cellar in the Via Palombella; but am I not as childish to the full—I, melancholy wretch, whom they called Hamlet and the Knight of the Doleful Countenance?

Nov. 5th.—I can't free myself from the thought of this Medea da Carpi. In my walks, my mornings in the Archives, my solitary evenings, I catch myself thinking over the woman. Am I turning novelist instead of historian? And still it seems to me that I understand her so well; so much better than my facts warrant. First, we must put aside all pedantic modern ideas of right and wrong. Right and wrong in a century of violence and treachery does not exist, least of all for creatures like Medea. Go preach right and wrong to a tigress, my dear sir! Yet is there in the world anything nobler than the huge creature, steel when she springs, velvet when she treads, as she stretches her supple body, or smooths her beautiful skin, or fastens her strong claws into her victim?

Yes; I can understand Medea. Fancy a woman of superlative beauty, of the highest courage and calmness, a woman of many resources, of genius, brought up by a petty princelet of a father, upon Tacitus and Sallust, and the tales of the great Malatestas, of Caesar Borgia and such-like!—a woman whose one passion is conquest and empire—fancy her, on the eve of being wedded to a man of the power of the Duke of Stimigliano, claimed, carried off by a small fry of a Pico, locked up in his hereditary brigand's castle, and having to receive the young fool's red-hot love as an honor and a necessity! The mere thought of any violence to such a nature is an abominable outrage; and if Pico chooses to embrace such a woman at the risk of meeting a sharp piece of steel in her arms, why, it is a fair bargain. Young hound—or, if you prefer, young hero—to think to treat a woman like this as if she were any village wench! Medea marries her Orsini. A marriage, let it be noted, between an old soldier of fifty and a girl of sixteen. Reflect what that means: it means that this imperious woman is soon treated like a chattel, made roughly to understand that her business is to give the Duke an heir, not advice; that she must never ask "wherefore this or that?" that she must courtesy before the Duke's counselors, his captains, his mistresses; that, at the least suspicion of rebelliousness, she is subject to his foul words and blows; at the least suspicion of infidelity, to be strangled or starved to death, or thrown down an oubliette. Suppose that she knew that her husband has taken it into his head that she has looked too hard at this man or that, that one of his lieutenants or one of his women have whispered that, after all, the boy Bartolommeo might as soon be a Pico as an Orsini. Suppose she knew that she must strike or be struck? Why, she strikes, or gets some one to strike for her. At what price? A promise of love, of love to a groom, the son of a serf! Why, the dog must be mad or drunk to believe such a thing possible; his very belief in anything so monstrous makes him worthy of death. And then he dares to blab! This is much worse than Pico. Medea is bound to defend her honor a second time; if she could stab Pico, she can certainly stab this fellow, or have him stabbed.

Hounded by her husband's kinsmen, she takes refuge at Urbania. The Duke, like every other man, falls wildly in love with Medea, and neglects his wife; let us even go so far as to say, breaks his wife's heart. Is this Medea's fault? Is it her fault that every stone that comes beneath her chariot-wheels is crushed? Certainly not. Do you suppose that a woman like Medea feels the smallest ill-will against a poor, craven Duchess Maddalena? Why, she ignores her very existence. To suppose Medea a cruel woman is as grotesque as to call her an immoral woman. Her fate is, sooner or later, to triumph over her enemies, at all events to make their victory almost a defeat; her magic faculty is to enslave all the men who come across her path; all those who see her, love her, become her slaves; and it is the destiny of all her slaves to perish. Her lovers, with the exception of Duke Guidalfonso, all come to an untimely end; and in this there is nothing unjust. The possession of a woman like Medea is a happiness too great for a mortal man; it would turn his head, make him forget even what he owed her; no man must survive long who conceives himself to have a right over her; it is a kind of sacrilege. And only death, the willingness to pay for such happiness by death, can at all make a man worthy of being her lover; he must be willing to love and suffer and die. This is the meaning of her device—"Amour Dure—Dure Amour." The love of Medea da Carpi cannot fade, but the lover can die; it is a constant and a cruel love.

Nov. 11th.—I was right, quite right in my idea. I have found—Oh, joy! I treated the Vice-Prefect's son to a dinner of five courses at the Trattoria La Stella d'Italia out of sheer jubilation—I have found in the Archives, unknown, of course, to the Director, a heap of letters—letters of Duke Robert about Medea da Carpi, letters of Medea herself! Yes, Medea's own handwriting—a round, scholarly character, full of abbreviations, with a Greek look about it, as befits a learned princess who could read Plato as well as Petrarch. The letters are of little importance, mere drafts of business letters for her secretary to copy, during the time that she governed the poor weak Guidalfonso. But they are her letters, and I can imagine almost that there hangs about these moldering pieces of paper a scent as of a woman's hair.

The few letters of Duke Robert show him in a new light. A cunning, cold, but craven priest. He trembles at the bare thought of Medea—"la pessima Medea"—worse than her namesake of Colchis, as he calls her. His long clemency is a result of mere fear of laying violent hands upon her. He fears her as something almost supernatural; he would have enjoyed having had her burnt as a witch. After letter on letter, telling his crony, Cardinal Sanseverino, at Rome his various precautions during her lifetime—how he wears a jacket of mail under his coat; how he drinks only milk from a cow which he has milked in his presence; how he tries his dog with morsels of his food, lest it be poisoned; how he suspects the wax-candles because of their peculiar smell; how he fears riding out lest some one should frighten his horse and cause him to break his neck—after all this, and when Medea has been in her grave two years, he tells his correspondent of his fear of meeting the soul of Medea after his own death, and chuckles over the ingenious device (concocted by his astrologer and a certain Fra Gaudenzio, a Capuchin) by which he shall secure the absolute peace of his soul until that of the wicked Medea be finally "chained up in hell among the lakes of boiling pitch and the ice of Caina described by the immortal bard"—old pedant! Here, then, is the explanation of that silver image—*quod vulgo dicitur idolino*—which he caused to be soldered into his effigy by Tassi. As long as the image of his soul was attached to the image of his body, he should sleep awaiting the Day of Judgment, fully convinced that Medea's soul will then be properly tarred and feathered, while his—honest man!—will fly straight to Paradise. And to think that, two weeks ago, I believed this man to be a hero! Aha! my good Duke Robert, you shall be shown up in my history; and no amount of silver idolinos shall save you from being heartily laughed at!

Nov. 15th.—Strange! That idiot of a Prefect's son, who has heard me talk a hundred times of Medea da Carpi, suddenly recollects that, when he was a child at Urbania, his nurse used to threaten him with a visit from Madonna Medea, who rode in the sky on a black he-goat. My Duchess Medea turned into a bogey for naughty little boys!

Nov. 20th.—I have been going about with a Bavarian Professor of mediaeval history, showing him all over the country. Among other places we went to Rocca Sant' Elmo, to see the former villa of the Dukes of Urbania, the villa where Medea was confined between the accession of Duke Robert and the conspiracy of Marcantonio Frangipani, which caused her removal to the nunnery immediately outside the town. A long ride up the desolate Apennine valleys, bleak beyond words just now with their thin fringe of oak scrub turned russet, thin patches of grass seared by the frost, the last few yellow leaves of the poplars by the torrents shaking and fluttering about in the chill Tramontana; the mountaintops are wrapped in thick grey cloud; tomorrow, if the wind continues, we shall see them round masses of snow against the cold blue sky. Sant' Elmo is a wretched hamlet high on the Apennine ridge, where the Italian vegetation is already replaced by that of the North. You ride for miles through leafless chestnut woods, the scent of the soaking brown leaves filling the air, the roar of the torrent, turbid with autumn rains, rising from the precipice below; then suddenly the leafless chestnut woods are replaced, as at Vallombrosa, by a belt of black, dense fir plantations. Emerging from these, you come to an open space, frozen blasted meadows, the rocks of snow clad peak, the newly fallen snow, close above you; and in the midst, on a knoll, with a gnarled larch on either side, the ducal villa of Sant' Elmo, a big black stone box with a stone escutcheon, grated windows, and a double flight of steps in front. It is now let out to the proprietor of the neighboring woods, who uses it for the storage of chestnuts, faggots, and charcoal from the neighboring ovens. We tied our horses to the iron rings and entered: an old woman, with disheveled hair, was alone in the house. The villa is a mere hunting-lodge, built by Ottobuono IV, the father of Dukes Guidalfonso and Robert, about 1530. Some of the rooms have at one time been frescoed and paneled with oak carvings, but all this has disappeared. Only, in one of the big rooms, there remains a large marble fireplace, similar to those in the palace at Urbania, beautifully carved with Cupids on a blue ground; a charming naked boy sustains a jar on either side, one containing clove pinks, the other roses. The room was filled with stacks of faggots.

We returned home late, my companion in excessively bad humor at the fruitlessness of the expedition. We were caught in the skirt of a snowstorm as we got into the chestnut woods. The sight of the snow falling gently, of the earth and bushes whitened all round, made me feel back at Posen, once more a child. I sang and shouted, to my companion's horror. This will be a bad point against me if reported at Berlin. A historian of twenty-four who shouts and sings, and that when another historian is cursing at the snow and the bad roads! All night I lay awake watching the embers of my wood fire, and thinking of Medea da Carpi mewed up, in winter, in that solitude of Sant' Elmo, the firs groaning, the torrent roaring, the snow falling all round; miles and miles away from human creatures. I fancied I saw it all, and that I, somehow, was Marcantonio Frangipani come to liberate her—or was it Prinzivalle degli Ordelaffi? I suppose it was because of the long ride, the unaccustomed pricking feeling of the snow in the air; or perhaps the punch which my professor insisted on drinking after dinner.

Nov. 23rd.—Thank goodness, that Bavarian professor has finally departed! Those days he spent here drove me nearly crazy. Talking over my work, I told him one day my views on Medea da Carpi; whereupon he condescended to answer that those were the usual tales due to the mythopoeic (old idiot!) tendency of the Renaissance; that research would disprove the greater part of them, as it had disproved the stories current about the Borgias, &c.; that, moreover, such a woman as I made out was psychologically and physiologically impossible. Would that one could say as much of such professors as he and his fellows!

Nov. 24th.—I cannot get over my pleasure in being rid of that imbecile; I felt as if I could have throttled him every time he spoke of the Lady of my thoughts—for such she has become—*Metea*, as the animal called her!

Nov. 30th.—I feel quite shaken at what has just happened; I am beginning to fear that that old pedant was right in saying that it was bad for me to live all alone in a strange country, that it would make me morbid. It is ridiculous that I should be put into such a state of excitement merely by the chance discovery of a portrait of a woman dead these three hundred years. With the case of my uncle Ladislas, and other suspicions of insanity in my family, I ought really to guard against such foolish excitement.

Yet the incident was really dramatic, uncanny. I could have sworn that I knew every picture in the palace here; and particularly every picture of Her. Anyhow, this morning, as I was leaving the Archives, I passed through one of the many small rooms—irregular-shaped closets—which fill up the ins and outs of this curious palace, turreted like a French château. I must have passed through that closet before, for the view was so familiar out of its window; just the particular bit of round tower in front, the cypress on the other side of the ravine, the belfry beyond, and the piece of the line of Monte Sant' Agata and the Leonessa, covered with snow, against the sky. I suppose there must be twin rooms, and that I had got into the wrong one; or rather, perhaps some shutter had been opened or curtain withdrawn. As I was passing, my eye was caught by a very beautiful old mirror-frame let into the brown and yellow inlaid wall. I approached, and looking at the frame, looked also, mechanically, into the glass. I gave a great start, and almost shrieked, I do believe—(it's lucky the Munich professor is safe out of Urbania!). Behind my own image stood another, a figure close to my shoulder, a face close to mine; and that figure, that face, hers! Medea da Carpi's! I turned sharp round, as white, I think, as the ghost I expected to see. On the wall opposite the mirror, just a pace or two behind where I had been standing, hung a portrait. And such a portrait!—Bronzino never painted a grander one. Against a background of harsh, dark blue, there stands out the figure of the Duchess (for it is Medea, the real Medea, a thousand times more real, individual, and powerful than in the other portraits), seated stiffly in a high-backed chair, sustained, as it were, almost rigid, by the stiff brocade of skirts and stomacher, stiffer for plaques of embroidered silver flowers and rows of seed pearl. The dress is, with its mixture of silver and pearl, of a strange dull red, a wicked poppy-juice color, against which the flesh of the long, narrow hands with fringe-like fingers; of the long slender neck, and the face with bared forehead, looks white and hard, like alabaster. The face is the same as in the other portraits: the same rounded forehead, with the short fleece-like, yellowish-red curls; the same beautifully curved eyebrows, just barely marked; the same eyelids, a little tight across the eyes; the same lips, a little tight across the mouth; but with a purity of line, a dazzling splendor of skin, and intensity of look immeasurably superior to all the other portraits.

    She looks out of the frame with a cold, level glance; yet the lips smile. One hand holds a dull-red rose; the other, long, narrow, tapering, plays with a thick rope of silk and gold and jewels hanging from the waist; round the throat, white as marble, partially confined in the tight dull-red bodice, hangs a gold collar, with the device on alternate enameled medallions, "AMOUR DURE—DURE AMOUR."

    On reflection, I see that I simply could never have been in that room or closet before; I must have mistaken the door. But, although the explanation is so simple, I still, after several hours, feel terribly shaken in all my being. If I grow so excitable I shall have to go to Rome at Christmas for a holiday. I feel as if some danger pursued me here (can it be fever?); and yet, and yet, I don't see how I shall ever tear myself away.

    Dec. 10th.—I have made an effort, and accepted the Vice-Prefect's son's invitation to see the oil-making at a villa of theirs near the coast. The villa, or farm, is an old fortified, towered place, standing on a hillside among olive-trees and little osier-bushes, which look like a bright orange flame. The olives are squeezed in a tremendous black cellar, like a prison: you see, by the faint white daylight, and the smoky yellow flare of resin burning in pans, great white bullocks moving round a huge millstone;

vague figures working at pulleys and handles: it looks, to my fancy, like some scene of the Inquisition. The Cavaliere regaled me with his best wine and rusks. I took some long walks by the seaside; I had left Urbania wrapped in snow-clouds; down on the coast there was a bright sun; the sunshine, the sea, the bustle of the little port on the Adriatic seemed to do me good. I came back to Urbania another man. Sor Asdrubale, my landlord, poking about in slippers among the gilded chests, the Empire sofas, the old cups and saucers and pictures which no one will buy, congratulated me upon the improvement in my looks. "You work too much," he says; "youth requires amusement, theatres, promenades, *amori*—it is time enough to be serious when one is bald"—and he took off his greasy red cap. Yes, I am better! and, as a result, I take to my work with delight again. I will cut them out still, those wiseacres at Berlin!

Dec. 14th.—I don't think I have ever felt so happy about my work. I see it all so well—that crafty, cowardly Duke Robert; that melancholy Duchess Maddalena; that weak, showy, would-be chivalrous Duke Guidalfonso; and above all, the splendid figure of Medea. I feel as if I were the greatest historian of the age; and, at the same time, as if I were a boy of twelve. It snowed yesterday for the first time in the city, for two good hours. When it had done, I actually went into the square and taught the ragamuffins to make a snowman; no, a snow-woman; and I had the fancy to call her Medea. "La pessima Medea!" cried one of the boys—"the one who used to ride through the air on a goat?" "No, no," I said; "she was a beautiful lady, the Duchess of Urbania, the most beautiful woman that ever lived." I made her a crown of tinsel, and taught the boys to cry "Evviva, Medea!" But one of them said, "She is a witch! She must be burnt!" At which they all rushed to fetch burning faggots and tow; in a minute the yelling demons had melted her down.

Dec. 15th.—What a goose I am, and to think I am twenty-four, and known in literature! In my long walks I have composed to a tune (I don't know what it is) which all the people are singing and whistling in the street at present, a poem in frightful Italian, beginning "Medea, mia dea," calling on her in the name of her various lovers. I go about humming between my teeth, "Why am I not Marcantonio? or Prinzivalle? or he of Narni? or the good Duke Alfonso? that I might be beloved by thee, Medea, mia dea," &c. &c. Awful rubbish! My landlord, I think, suspects that Medea must be some lady I met while I was staying by the seaside. I am sure Sora Serafina, Sora Lodovica, and Sora Adalgisa—the three Parcae or *Norns*, as I call them—have some such notion. This afternoon, at dusk, while tidying my room, Sora Lodovica said to me, "How beautifully the Signorino has taken to singing!" I was scarcely aware that I had been vociferating, "Vieni, Medea, mia dea," while the old lady bobbed about making up my fire. I stopped; a nice reputation I shall get! I thought, and all this will somehow get to Rome, and thence to Berlin. Sora Lodovica was leaning out of the window, pulling in the iron hook of the shrine-lamp which marks Sor Asdrubale's house. As she was trimming the lamp previous to swinging it out again, she said in her odd, prudish little way, "You are wrong to stop singing, my son" (she varies between calling me Signor Professore and such terms of affection as "Nino," "Viscere mie," &c.); "you are wrong to stop singing, for there is a young lady there in the street who has actually stopped to listen to you."

I ran to the window. A woman, wrapped in a black shawl, was standing in an archway, looking up to the window.

"Eh, eh! the Signor Professore has admirers," said Sora Lodovica.

"Medea, mia dea!" I burst out as loud as I could, with a boy's pleasure in disconcerting the inquisitive passer-by. She turned suddenly round to go away, waving her hand at me; at that moment Sora Lodovica swung the shrine-lamp back into its place. A stream of light fell across the street. I felt myself grow quite cold; the face of the woman outside was that of Medea da Carpi!

What a fool I am, to be sure!

II

Dec. 17th.—I fear that my craze about Medea da Carpi has become well known, thanks to my silly talk and idiotic songs. That Vice-Prefect's son—or the assistant at the Archives, or perhaps some of the company at the Contessa's, is trying to play me a trick! But take care, my good ladies and gentlemen, I shall pay you out in your own coin! Imagine my feelings when, this morning, I found on my desk a folded letter addressed to me in a curious handwriting which seemed strangely familiar to me, and which, after a moment, I recognized as that of the letters of Medea da Carpi at the Archives. It gave me a horrible shock. My next idea was that it must be a present from some one who knew my interest in Medea—a genuine letter of hers on which some idiot had written my address instead of putting it into an envelope. But it was addressed to me, written to me, no old letter; merely four lines, which ran as follows:—

> To SPIRIDION.—A person who knows the interest you bear her will be at the Church of San Giovanni Decollato this evening at nine. Look out, in the left aisle, for a lady wearing a black mantle, and holding a rose.

By this time I understood that I was the object of a conspiracy, the victim of a hoax. I turned the letter round and round. It was written on paper such as was made in the sixteenth century, and in an extraordinarily precise imitation of Medea da Carpi's characters. Who had written it? I thought over all the possible people. On the whole, it must be the Vice-Prefect's son, perhaps in combination with his lady-love, the Countess. They must have torn a blank page off some old letter; but that either of them should have had the ingenuity of inventing such a hoax, or the power of committing such a forgery, astounds me beyond measure. There is more in these people than I should have guessed. How pay them off? By taking no notice of the letter? Dignified, but dull. No, I will go; perhaps some one will be there, and I will mystify them in their turn. Or, if no one is there, how I shall crow over them for their imperfectly carried out plot! Perhaps this is some folly of the Cavalier Muzio's to bring me into the presence of some lady whom he destines to be the flame of my future *amori*. That is likely enough. And it would be too idiotic and professorial to refuse such an invitation; the lady must be worth knowing who can forge sixteenth-century letters like this, for I am sure that languid swell Muzio never could. I will go! By Heaven! I'll pay them back in their own coin! It is now five—how long these days are!

Dec. 18th.—Am I mad? Or are there really ghosts? That adventure of last night has shaken me to the very depth of my soul.

I went at nine, as the mysterious letter had bid me. It was bitterly cold, and the air full of fog and sleet; not a shop open, not a window unshuttered, not a creature visible; the narrow black streets, precipitous between their high walls and under their lofty archways, were only the blacker for the dull light of an oil-lamp here and there, with its flickering yellow reflection on the wet flags. San Giovanni Decollato is a little church, or rather oratory, which I have always hitherto seen shut up (as so many churches here are shut up except on great festivals); and situate behind the ducal palace, on a sharp ascent, and forming the bifurcation of two steep paved lanes. I have passed by the place a hundred times, and scarcely noticed the little church, except for the marble high relief over the door, showing the grizzly head of the Baptist in the charger, and for the iron cage close by, in which were formerly exposed the heads of criminals; the decapitated, or, as they call him here, decollated, John the Baptist, being apparently the patron of axe and block.

A few strides took me from my lodgings to San Giovanni Decollato. I confess I was excited; one is not twenty-four and a Pole for nothing. On getting to the kind of little platform at the bifurcation of the two precipitous streets, I found, to my surprise, that the windows of the church or oratory were not lighted, and that the door was locked! So this was the precious joke that had been played upon me; to send me on a bitter cold, sleety night, to a church which was shut up and had perhaps been shut up for years! I don't know what I couldn't have done in that moment of rage; I felt inclined to break open the church door, or to go and pull the Vice-Prefect's son out of bed (for I felt sure that the joke was his). I determined upon the latter course; and was walking towards his door, along the black alley to the left of the church, when I was suddenly stopped by the sound as of an organ close by, an organ, yes, quite plainly, and the voice of choristers and the drone of a litany. So the church was not shut, after all! I retraced my steps to the top of the lane. All was dark and in complete silence. Suddenly there came again a faint gust of organ and voices. I listened; it clearly came from the other lane, the one on the right-hand side. Was there, perhaps, another door there? I passed beneath the archway, and descended a little way in the direction whence the sounds seemed to come. But no door, no light, only the black walls, the black wet flags, with their faint yellow reflections of flickering oil-lamps; moreover, complete silence. I stopped a minute, and then the chant rose again; this time it seemed to me most certainly from the lane I had just left. I went back—nothing. Thus backwards and forwards, the sounds always beckoning, as it were, one way, only to beckon me back, vainly, to the other.

At last I lost patience; and I felt a sort of creeping terror, which only a violent action could dispel. If the mysterious sounds came neither from the street to the right, nor from the street to the left, they could come only from the church. Half-maddened, I rushed up the two or three steps, and prepared to wrench the door open with a tremendous effort. To my amazement, it opened with the greatest ease. I entered, and the sounds of the litany met me louder than before, as I paused a moment between the outer door and the heavy leathern curtain. I raised the latter and crept in. The altar was brilliantly illuminated with tapers and garlands of chandeliers; this was evidently some evening service connected with Christmas. The nave and aisles were comparatively dark, and about half-full. I elbowed my way along the right aisle towards the altar. When my eyes had got accustomed to the unexpected light, I began to look round me, and with a beating heart. The idea that all this was a hoax, that I should meet merely some acquaintance of my friend the Cavaliere's, had somehow departed: I looked about. The people were all wrapped up, the men in big cloaks, the women in woolen veils and mantles. The body of the church was comparatively dark, and I could not make out anything very clearly, but it seemed to me, somehow, as if, under the cloaks and veils, these people were dressed in a rather extraordinary fashion. The man in front of me, I remarked, showed yellow stockings beneath his cloak; a woman, hard by, a red bodice, laced behind with gold tags. Could these be peasants from some remote part come for the Christmas festivities, or did the inhabitants of Urbania don some old-fashioned garb in honor of Christmas?

As I was wondering, my eye suddenly caught that of a woman standing in the opposite aisle, close to the altar, and in the full blaze of its lights. She was wrapped in black, but held, in a very conspicuous way, a red rose, an unknown luxury at this time of the year in a place like Urbania. She evidently saw me, and turning even more fully into the light, she loosened her heavy black cloak, displaying a dress of deep red, with gleams of silver and gold embroideries; she turned her face towards me; the full blaze of the chandeliers and tapers fell upon it. It was the face of Medea da Carpi! I dashed across the nave, pushing people roughly aside, or rather, it seemed to me, passing through impalpable bodies. But the lady turned and walked rapidly down the aisle towards the door. I followed close upon her, but somehow I could not get up with her. Once, at the curtain, she turned round again. She was within a few paces of me. Yes, it was Medea. Medea herself, no mistake, no delusion, no sham; the oval face, the lips tightened over the mouth, the eyelids tight over the corner of the eyes, the exquisite alabaster complexion! She raised the curtain and glided out. I followed; the curtain alone separated me from her. I saw the wooden door swing to behind her. One step ahead of me! I tore open the door; she must be on the steps, within reach of my arm!

I stood outside the church. All was empty, merely the wet pavement and the yellow reflections in the pools: a sudden cold seized me; I could not go on. I tried to re-enter the church; it was shut. I rushed home, my hair standing on end, and trembling in all my limbs, and remained for an hour like a maniac. Is it a delusion? Am I too going mad? O God, God! am I going mad?

Dec. 19th.—A brilliant, sunny day; all the black snow-slush has disappeared out of the town, off the bushes and trees. The snow-clad mountains sparkle against the bright blue sky. A Sunday, and Sunday weather; all the bells are ringing for the approach of Christmas. They are preparing for a kind of fair in the square with the colonnade, putting up booths filled with colored cotton and woolen ware, bright shawls and kerchiefs, mirrors, ribbons, brilliant pewter lamps; the whole turn-out of the peddler in "Winter's Tale." The pork-shops are all garlanded with green and with paper flowers, the hams and cheeses stuck full of little flags and green twigs. I strolled out to see the cattle-fair outside the gate; a forest of interlacing horns, an ocean of lowing and stamping: hundreds of immense white bullocks, with horns a yard long and red tassels, packed close together on the little piazza d'armi under the city walls. Bah! Why do I write this trash? What's the use of it all? While I am forcing myself to write about bells, and Christmas festivities, and cattle-fairs, one idea goes on like a bell within me: Medea, Medea! Have I really seen her, or am I mad?

AMOUR DURE

Two hours later.—That Church of San Giovanni Decollato—so my landlord informs me—has not been made use of within the memory of man. Could it have been all a hallucination or a dream—perhaps a dream dreamed that night? I have been out again to look at that church. There it is, at the bifurcation of the two steep lanes, with its bas-relief of the Baptist's head over the door. The door does look as if it had not been opened for years. I can see the cobwebs in the windowpanes; it does look as if, as Sor Asdrubale says, only rats and spiders congregated within it. And yet—and yet; I have so clear a remembrance, so distinct a consciousness of it all. There was a picture of the daughter of Herodias dancing, upon the altar; I remember her white turban with a scarlet tuft of feathers, and Herod's blue caftan; I remember the shape of the central chandelier; it swung round slowly, and one of the wax lights had got bent almost in two by the heat and draught.

Things, all these, which I may have seen elsewhere, stored unawares in my brain, and which may have come out, somehow, in a dream; I have heard physiologists allude to such things. I will go again: if the church be shut, why then it must have been a dream, a vision, the result of over-excitement. I must leave at once for Rome and see doctors, for I am afraid of going mad. If, on the other hand—pshaw! there *is no other hand* in such a case. Yet if there were—why then, I should really have seen Medea; I might see her again; speak to her. The mere thought sets my blood in a whirl, not with horror, but with... I know not what to call it. The feeling terrifies me, but it is delicious. Idiot! There is some little coil of my brain, the twentieth of a hair's-breadth out of order—that's all!

Dec. 20th.—I have been again; I have heard the music; I have been inside the church; I have seen Her! I can no longer doubt my senses. Why should I? Those pedants say that the dead are dead, the past is past. For them, yes; but why for me?—why for a man who loves, who is consumed with the love of a woman?—a woman who, indeed—yes, let me finish the sentence. Why should there not be ghosts to such as can see them? Why should she not return to the earth, if she knows that it contains a man who thinks of, desires, only her?

A hallucination? Why, I saw her, as I see this paper that I write upon; standing there, in the full blaze of the altar. Why, I heard the rustle of her skirts, I smelt the scent of her hair, I raised the curtain which was shaking from her touch. Again I missed her. But this time, as I rushed out into the empty moonlit street, I found upon the church steps a rose—the rose which I had seen in her hand the moment before—I felt it, smelt it; a rose, a real, living rose, dark red and only just plucked. I put it into water when I returned, after having kissed it, who knows how many times? I placed it on the top of the cupboard; I determined not to look at it for twenty-four hours lest it should be a delusion. But I must see it again; I must. . . . Good Heavens! this is horrible, horrible; if I had found a skeleton it could not have been worse! The rose, which last night seemed freshly plucked, full of color and perfume, is brown, dry—a thing kept for centuries between the leaves of a book—it has crumbled into dust between my fingers. Horrible, horrible! But why so, pray? Did I not know that I was in love with a woman dead three hundred years? If I wanted fresh roses which bloomed yesterday, the Countess Fiammetta or any little sempstress in Urbania might have given them me. What if the rose has fallen to dust? If only I could hold Medea in my arms as I held it in my fingers, kiss her lips as I kissed its petals, should I not be satisfied if she too were to fall to dust the next moment, if I were to fall to dust myself?

Dec. 22nd, Eleven at night.—I have seen her once more!—almost spoken to her. I have been promised her love! Ah, Spiridion! you were right when you felt that you were not made for any earthly *amori*. At the usual hour I betook myself this evening to San Giovanni Decollato. A bright winter night; the high houses and belfries standing out against a deep blue heaven luminous, shimmering like steel with myriads of stars; the moon has not yet risen. There was no light in the windows; but, after a little effort, the door opened and I entered the church, the altar, as usual, brilliantly illuminated. It struck me suddenly that all this crowd of men and women standing all round, these priests chanting and moving about the altar, were dead—that they did not exist for any man save me. I touched, as if by accident, the hand of my neighbor; it was cold, like wet clay. He turned round, but did not seem to see me: his face was ashy, and his eyes staring, fixed, like those of a blind man or a corpse. I felt as if I must rush out. But at that moment my eye fell upon Her, standing as usual by the altar steps, wrapped in a black mantle, in the full blaze of the lights. She turned round; the light fell straight upon her face, the face with the delicate features, the eyelids and lips a little tight, the alabaster skin faintly tinged with pale pink. Our eyes met.

I pushed my way across the nave towards where she stood by the altar steps; she turned quickly down the aisle, and I after her. Once or twice she lingered, and I thought I should overtake her; but again, when, not a second after the door had closed upon her, I stepped out into the street, she had vanished. On the church step lay something white. It was not a flower this time, but a letter. I rushed back to the church to read it; but the church was fast shut, as if it had not been opened for years. I could not see by the flickering shrine-lamps—I rushed home, lit my lamp, pulled the letter from my breast. I have it before me. The handwriting is hers; the same as in the Archives, the same as in that first letter:—

To Spiridion.—Let thy courage be equal to thy love, and thy love shall be rewarded. On the night preceding Christmas, take a hatchet and saw; cut boldly into the body of the bronze rider who stands in the Corte, on the left side, near the waist. Saw open the body, and within it thou wilt find the silver effigy of a winged genius. Take it out, hack it into a hundred pieces, and fling them in all directions, so that the winds may sweep them away. That night she whom thou lovest will come to reward thy fidelity.

On the brownish wax is the device—

Amour Dure—Dure Amour.

Dec. 23rd.—So it is true! I was reserved for something wonderful in this world. I have at last found that after which my soul has been straining. Ambition, love of art, love of Italy, these things which have occupied my spirit, and have yet left me continually unsatisfied, these were none of them my real destiny. I have sought for life, thirsting for it as a man in the desert thirsts for a well; but the life of the senses of other youths, the life of the intellect of other men, have never slaked that thirst. Shall life for me mean the love of a dead woman? We smile at what we choose to call the superstition of the past, forgetting that all our vaunted science of today may seem just such another superstition to the men of the future; but why should the present be right and the past wrong? The men who painted the pictures and built the palaces of three hundred years ago were certainly of as delicate fiber, of as keen reason, as ourselves, who merely print calico and build locomotives. What makes me think this, is that I have been calculating my nativity by help of an old book belonging to Sor Asdrubale—and see, my horoscope tallies almost exactly with that of Medea da Carpi, as given by a chronicler. May this explain? No, no; all is explained by the fact that the first time I read of this woman's career, the first time I saw her portrait, I loved her, though I hid my love to myself in the garb of historical interest. Historical interest indeed!

I have got the hatchet and the saw. I bought the saw of a poor joiner, in a village some miles off; he did not understand at first what I meant, and I think he thought me mad; perhaps I am. But if madness means the happiness of one's life, what of it? The hatchet I saw lying in a timber-yard, where they prepare the great trunks of the fir-trees which grow high on the Apennines of Sant' Elmo. There was no one in the yard, and I could not resist the temptation; I handled the thing, tried its edge, and stole it. This is the first time in my life that I have been a thief; why did I not go into a shop and buy a hatchet? I don't know; I seemed unable to resist the sight of the shining blade. What I am going to do is, I suppose, an act of vandalism; and certainly I have no right to spoil the property of this city of Urbania. But I wish no harm either to the statue or the city, if I could plaster up the bronze, I would do so willingly. But I must obey Her; I must avenge Her; I must get at that silver image which Robert of Montemurlo had made and consecrated in order that his cowardly soul might sleep in peace, and not encounter that of the being whom he dreaded most in the world. Aha! Duke Robert, you forced her to die unshriven, and you stuck the image of your soul into the image of your body, thinking thereby that, while she suffered the tortures of Hell, you would rest in peace, until your well-scoured little soul might fly straight up to Paradise;—you were afraid of Her when both of you should be dead, and thought yourself very clever to have prepared for all emergencies! Not so, Serene Highness. You too shall taste what it is to wander after death, and to meet the dead whom one has injured.

What an interminable day! But I shall see her again to-night.

Eleven o'clock.—No; the church was fast closed; the spell had ceased. Until tomorrow I shall not see her. But tomorrow! Ah, Medea! did any of thy lovers love thee as I do?

Twenty-four hours more till the moment of happiness—the moment for which I seem to have been waiting all my life. And after that, what next? Yes, I see it plainer every minute; after that, nothing more. All those who loved Medea da Carpi, who loved and who served her, died: Giovanfrancesco Pico, her first husband, whom she left stabbed in the castle from which she fled; Stimigliano, who died of poison; the groom who gave him the poison, cut down by her orders; Oliverotto da Narni, Marcantonio Frangipani, and that poor boy of the Ordelaffi, who had never even looked upon her face, and whose only reward was that handkerchief with which the hangman wiped the sweat off his face, when he was one mass of broken limbs and torn flesh: all had to die, and I shall die also.

The love of such a woman is enough, and is fatal—"Amour Dure," as her device says. I shall die also. But why not? Would it be possible to live in order to love another woman? Nay, would it be possible to drag on a life like this one after the happiness of tomorrow? Impossible; the others died, and I must die. I always felt that I should not live long; a gipsy in Poland told me once that I had in my hand the cut-line which signifies a violent death. I might have ended in a duel with some brother-student, or in a railway accident. No, no; my death will not be of that sort! Death—and is not she also dead? What strange vistas does such a thought not open! Then the others—Pico, the Groom, Stimigliano, Oliverotto, Frangipani, Prinzivalle degli Ordelaffi—will they all be *there?* But she shall love me best—me by whom she has been loved after she has been three hundred years in the grave!

Dec. 24th.—I have made all my arrangements. Tonight at eleven I slip out; Sor Asdrubale and his sisters will be sound asleep. I have questioned them; their fear of rheumatism prevents their attending midnight mass. Luckily there are no churches between this and the Corte; whatever movement Christmas night may entail will be a good way off. The Vice-Prefect's rooms are on the other side of the palace; the rest of the square is taken up with state-rooms, archives, and empty stables and coach-houses of the palace. Besides, I shall be quick at my work.

I have tried my saw on a stout bronze vase I bought of Sor Asdrubale; and the bronze of the statue, hollow and worn away by rust (I have even noticed holes), cannot resist very much, especially after a blow with the sharp hatchet. I have put my papers in order, for the benefit of the Government which has sent me hither. I am sorry to have defrauded them of their "History of Urbania." To pass the endless day and calm the fever of impatience, I have just taken a long walk. This is the coldest day we have had. The bright sun does not warm in the least, but seems only to increase the impression of cold, to make the snow on the mountains glitter, the blue air to sparkle like steel. The few people who are out are muffled to the nose, and carry earthenware braziers beneath their cloaks; long icicles hang from the fountain with the figure of Mercury upon it; one can imagine the wolves trooping down through the dry scrub and beleaguering this town. Somehow this cold makes me feel wonderfully calm—it seems to bring back to me my boyhood.

As I walked up the rough, steep, paved alleys, slippery with frost, and with their vista of snow mountains against the sky, and passed by the church steps strewn with box and laurel, with the faint smell of incense coming out, there returned to me—I know not why—the recollection, almost the sensation, of those Christmas Eves long ago at Posen and Breslau, when I walked as a child along the wide streets, peeping into the windows where they were beginning to light the tapers of the Christmas-trees, and wondering whether I too, on returning home, should be let into a wonderful room all blazing with lights and gilded nuts and glass beads. They are hanging the last strings of those blue and red metallic beads, fastening on the last gilded and silvered walnuts on the trees out there at home in the North; they are lighting the blue and red tapers; the wax is beginning to run on to the beautiful spruce green branches; the children are waiting with beating hearts behind the door, to be told that the Christ-Child has been. And I, for what am I waiting? I don't know; all seems a dream; everything vague and unsubstantial about me, as if time had ceased, nothing could happen, my own desires and hopes were all dead, myself absorbed into I know not what passive dreamland. Do I long for tonight? Do I dread it? Will tonight ever come? Do I feel anything, does anything exist all round me? I sit and seem to see that street at Posen, the wide street with the windows illuminated by the Christmas lights, the green fir-branches grazing the window-panes.

Christmas Eve, Midnight.—I have done it. I slipped out noiselessly. Sor Asdrubale and his sisters were fast asleep. I feared I had waked them, for my hatchet fell as I was passing through the principal room where my landlord keeps his curiosities for sale; it struck against some old armor which he has been piecing. I heard him exclaim, half in his sleep; and blew out my light and hid in the stairs. He came out in his dressing-gown, but finding no one, went back to bed again. "Some cat, no doubt!" he said. I closed the house door softly behind me. The sky had become stormy since the afternoon, luminous with the full moon, but strewn with grey and buff-colored vapors; every now and then the moon disappeared entirely. Not a creature abroad; the tall gaunt houses staring in the moonlight.

I know not why, I took a roundabout way to the Corte, past one or two church doors, whence issued the faint flicker of midnight mass. For a moment I felt a temptation to enter one of them; but something seemed to restrain me. I caught snatches of the Christmas hymn. I felt myself beginning to be unnerved, and hastened towards the Corte. As I passed under the portico at San Francesco I heard steps behind me; it seemed to me that I was followed. I stopped to let the other pass. As he approached his pace flagged; he passed close by me and murmured, "Do not go: I am Giovanfrancesco Pico." I turned round; he was gone. A coldness numbed me; but I hastened on.

Behind the cathedral apse, in a narrow lane, I saw a man leaning against a wall. The moonlight was full upon him; it seemed to me that his face, with a thin pointed beard, was streaming with blood. I quickened my pace; but as I grazed by him he whispered, "Do not obey her; return home: I am Marcantonio Frangipani." My teeth chattered, but I hurried along the narrow lane, with the moonlight blue upon the white walls.

At last I saw the Corte before me: the square was flooded with moonlight, the windows of the palace seemed brightly illuminated, and the statue of Duke Robert, shimmering green, seemed advancing toward me on its horse. I came into the shadow. I had to pass beneath an archway. There started a figure as if out of the wall, and barred my passage with his outstretched cloaked arm. I tried to pass. He seized me by the arm, and his grasp was like a weight of ice. "You shall not pass!" he cried, and, as the moon came out once more, I saw his face, ghastly white and bound with an embroidered kerchief; he seemed almost a child. "You shall not pass!" he cried; "you shall not have her!

She is mine, and mine alone! I am Prinzivalle degli Ordelaffi." I felt his ice-cold clutch, but with my other arm I laid about me wildly with the hatchet which I carried beneath my cloak. The hatchet struck the wall and rang upon the stone. He had vanished.

I hurried on. I did it. I cut open the bronze; I sawed it into a wider gash. I tore out the silver image, and hacked it into innumerable pieces. As I scattered the last fragments about, the moon was suddenly veiled; a great wind arose, howling down the square; it seemed to me that the earth shook. I threw down the hatchet and the saw, and fled home. I felt pursued, as if by the tramp of hundreds of invisible horsemen.

Now I am calm. It is midnight; another moment and she will be here! Patience, my heart! I hear it beating loud. I trust that no one will accuse poor Sor Asdrubale. I will write a letter to the authorities to declare his innocence should anything happen. . . . One! the clock in the palace tower has just struck. . . . "I hereby certify that, should anything happen this night to me, Spiridion Trepka, no one but myself is to be held . . ." A step on the staircase! It is she! it is she! At last, Medea, Medea! Ah! AMOUR DURE—DURE AMOUR!

NOTE—Here ends the diary of the late Spiridion Trepka. The chief newspapers of the province of Umbria informed the public that, on Christmas morning of the year 1885, the bronze equestrian statue of Robert II had been found grievously mutilated; and that Professor Spiridion Trepka of Posen, in the German Empire, had been discovered dead of a stab in the region of the heart, given by an unknown hand.

An Eddy on the Floor

Bernard Capes

PART I OF POLYHISTOR'S NARRATIVE
Written for, but never Inserted in, the —— Family Magazine

THE EYES OF POLYHISTOR—AS HE SAT BEFORE THE FIRE AT NIGHT—TOOK IN THE tawdry surroundings of his lodging-house room with nothing of that apathy of resignation to his personal ἀνάγκη which of all moods is to Fortune, the goddess of spontaneity, the most antipathetic. Indeed, he felt his wit, like Romeo's, to be of cheveril; and his conviction that it needed only the pull of circumstance to stretch it "from an inch narrow to an ell broad" expressed but the very wooing quality of a constitutional optimism.

Now this inherent optimism is at least a serviceable weapon when it takes the form of self-reliance. It is always at hand in an emergency—a guard of honour to the soul. The loneliness of individual life must learn self-respect from within, not without; and were all creeds to be mixed, that truism should be found their precipitate.

Therefore Polyhistor was content to draw grass-green rep curtains across window-panes sloughed with wintry sleet; to place his feet upon a rug flayed of colour to it dusty sinews; to admit to his close fellowship—and find a familiar comfort in them, too—three separate lithographs of affected babies inviting any canine confidences but the bite one desired for them, and a dismal daguerreotype of his landlady's deceased husband, slowly perishing in pegtops and a yellow fog of despondency, out of which only his boots and a very tall hat frowned insistent, the tabernacles of enduring respectability:—he was content, because he knew these were only incidents in his career—the slums to be first traversed on a journey before the rounding breadths of open country were reached,—and the station in life he purposed stopping at eventually was the terminus of prosperity, intellectual and material.

AN EDDY ON THE FLOOR

With no present good fortune but the capacity for desiring it; with the right to affix a letter or so—like grace after skilly—to his name; with the consciousness that, having overcome theoretical pharmaceutics masterfully, he was now combatting practical dispensing slavishly; with full confidence in his social position (he stood under the shadow of "high connections," like the little winged "Victory" in a conqueror's hand, he chose to think) to help him to eventual distinction, he toasted his toes that sour winter evening and reviewed in comfort an army of prospects.

Also his thoughts reverted indulgently to the incidents and experiences of the previous night.

He had had the pleasure of an invitation to one of those reunions or séances at the house, in a fashionable quarter, of his distant connection, Lady Barbara Grille, whereat it was his hostess's humour to gather together those many birds of alien feather and incongruous habit that will flock from the hedgerows to the least little flattering crumb of attention. And scarce one of them but thinks the simple feast is spread for him alone. And with so cheap a bait may a title lure.

Lady Barbara, to do her justice, trades upon her position only in so far as it shapes itself the straight road to her desires. She is a carpet adventurer—an explorer amongst the nerves of moral sensation, to whom the discovery of an untrodden mental tract is a pure delight, and the more delightful the more ephemeral. She flits from guest to guest, shooting out to each a little proboscis, as it were, and happy if its point touches a speck of honey. She gathers from all, and stores the sweet agglomerate, let us hope, to feed upon it in the winter of her life, when the hive of her busy brain shall be thatched with snow.

That reference to so charming a personality should be in this place a digression is Polyhistor's unhappiness. She affects his narrative only inasmuch as he happened to meet at her house a gentleman who for a time exerted a considerable influence over his fortunes.

Here Polyhistor's narrative must give place to certain editorial marginalia by Miss Lucy ——, who "runs" the —— Family Magazine:—

"Polyhistor, indeed!" she writes. "The conceit of some people! He seems to take himself for a sort of *Admirable Crichton*, and all because his chance meeting with the gentleman referred to (a very *interesting* person, who is, I understand, reforming our prisons) brought him the offer of an appointment quite beyond his deserts. I was very glad to hear of it, however, and I asked the creature to contribute a paper recording his first impressions of *this notable man*; instead of which he begins with an opinionated rigmarole about himself, and goes on from bad to worse by describing a long conversation he had about prison reform with that horrid, masculine Mrs. C———, whom all the officers call 'Charlie,' and who thinks that for men to grow humane is a sign of their *decadence*. *Of course* I shall 'cut' the whole of their talk together (it is a blessed privilege to be an editor), and jump to the part where *Polyhistor* (!) describes the *notable person's* visit to him, which was due to his (the N.P.'s) having the night before overheard some of the conversation *between those two*."

Polyhistor's Narrative (continued)

Now as Polyhistor sat, he humoured his recollection (in the intervals of scribbling verses to the *beaux yeux* of a certain Miss L———) with some of "Charlie's" characteristic last-night utterances.

She had dated man's decadence from the moment when he began to "poor-fellow" irreclaimable savagery on the score of heredity.

She had repudiated the old humbug of sex superiority because she had seen it fall on its face to howl over a trodden worm, with the result that it discovered itself hollow behind, like the elf-maiden.

She had said: "Once you taught us divinely—*argumentum baculinum*," said she; "(for you are the sons of God, you know). But you have since so insisted upon the Rights of Humanity that we have learned ourselves in the phrase, and that the earthy have the best right to precedence on the earth."

And thereupon Charlie had launched into abuse of what she called the latest masculine fad—prison reform, to wit—and a heated discussion between her and Polyhistor had ensued, in the midst of which she had happened to glance behind her, to find that very notable person who is the subject of this narrative vouchsafing a silent attention to her diatribe. And then—

But at this period to his cogitations Polyhistor's landlady entered with a card, which she presented to his consideration:—

Major Jame Shrike
H. M. Prison, D———

All astonishment, Polyhistor bade his visitor up.

He entered briskly, fur-collared, hat in hand, and bowed as he stood on the threshold. He was a very short man—snub-nosed; rusty-whiskered; indubitably and unimpressively a cockney in appearance. He might have walked out of a Cruikshank etching.

Polyhistor was beginning, "May I inquire—" when the other took him up with a vehement frankness that he found engaging at once.

"This is a great intrusion. Will you pardon me? I heard some remarks of yours last night that deeply interested me. I obtained your name and address of our hostess, and took the liberty of—"

"Oh! pray be seated. Say no more. My kinswoman's introduction is all-sufficient. I am happy in having caught your attention in so motley a crowd."

"She doesn't—forgive the impertinence—take herself seriously enough."

"Lady Barbara? Then you've found her out?"

"Ah!—you're not offended?"

"Not in the least."

"Good. It was a motley assemblage, as you say. Yet I'm inclined to think I found my pearl in the oyster. I'm afraid I interrupted—eh?"

"No, no, not at all. Only some idle scribbling. I'd finished."

"You are a poet?"

"Only a lunatic. I haven't taken my degree."

"Ah! it's a noble gift—the gift of song; precious through its rarity."

Polyhistor caught a note of emotion in his visitor's voice, and glanced at him curiously.

"Surely," he thought, "that vulgar, ruddy little face is transfigured."

"But," said the stranger, coming to earth, "I am lingering beside the mark. I must try to justify my solecism in manners by a straight reference to the object of my visit. That is, in the first instance, a matter of business."

"Business!"

"I am a man with a purpose, seeking the hopefullest means to an end. Plainly: if I could procure you the post of resident doctor at D—— gaol, would you be disposed to accept it?"

Polyhistor looked his utter astonishment.

"I can affect no surprise at yours," said the visitor, attentively regarding Polyhistor. "It is perfectly natural. Let me forestall some unnecessary expression of it. My offer seems unaccountable to you, seeing that we never met until last night. But I don't move entirely in the dark. I have ventured in the interval to inform myself as to the details of your career. I was entirely one with much of your expression of opinion as to the treatment of criminals, in which you controverted the crude and unpleasant scepticism of the lady you talked with." (Poor New Charlie!) "Combining the two, I come to the immediate conclusion that you are the man for my purpose."

"You have dumbfounded me. I don't know what to answer. You have views, I know, as to prison treatment. Will you sketch them? Will you talk on, while I try to bring my scattered wits to a focus?"

"Certainly I will. Let me, in the first instance, recall to you a few words of your own. They ran somewhat in this fashion: Is not the man of practical genius the man who is most apt at solving the little problems of resourcefulness in life? Do you remember them?"

"Perhaps I do, in a cruder form."

"They attracted me at once. It is upon such a postulate I base my practice. Their moral is this: To know the antidote the moment the snake bites. That is to have the intuition of divinity. We shall rise to it some day, no doubt, and climb the hither side of the new Olympus. Who knows? Over the crest the spirit of creation may be ours."

Polyhistor nodded, still at sea, and the other went on with a smile:—

"I once knew a world-famous engineer with whom I used to breakfast occasionally. He had a patent egg-boiler on the table, with a little double-sided ladle underneath to hold the spirit. He complained that his egg was always undercooked. I said, 'Why not reverse the ladle so as to bring the deeper cup uppermost?' He was charmed with my perspicacity. The solution had never occurred to him. You remember, too, no doubt, the story of Coleridge and the horse collar. We aim too much at great developments. If we cultivate resourcefulness, the rest will follow. Shall I state my system *in nuce*? It is to encourage this spirit of resourcefulness."

"Surely the habitual criminal has it in a marked degree?"

"Yes; but abnormally developed in a single direction. His one object is to out-manoeuvre in a game of desperate and immoral chances. The tactical spirit in him has none of the higher ambition. It has felt itself in the degree only that stops at defiance."

"That is perfectly true."

"It is half self-conscious of an individuality that instinctively assumes the hopelessness of a recognition by duller intellects. Leaning to resentment through misguided vanity, it falls 'all oblique.' What is the cure for this? I answer, the teaching of a divine egotism. The subject must be led to a pure devotion to self. What he wishes to respect he must be taught to make beautiful and interesting. The policy of sacrifice to others has so long stunted his moral nature because it is an hypocritical policy. We are responsible to ourselves in the first instance; and to argue an eternal system of blind self-sacrifice is to undervalue the fine gift of individuality. In such he sees but an indefensible policy of force applied to the advantage of the community. He is told to be good—not that he may morally profit, but that others may not suffer inconvenience."

Polyhistor was beginning to grasp, through his confusion, a certain clue of meaning in his visitor's rapid utterance. The stranger spoke fluently, but in the dry, positive voice that characterizes men of will.

"Pray go on," Polyhistor said; "I am digesting in silence."

"We must endeavour to lead him to respect of self by showing him what his mind is capable of. I argue on no sectarian, no religious grounds even. Is it possible to make a man's self his most precious possession? Anyhow, I work to that end. A doctor purges before building up with a tonic. I eliminate cant and hypocrisy, and then introduce self-respect. It isn't enough to employ a man's hands only. Initiation in some labour that should prove wholesome and remunerative is a redeeming factor, but it isn't all. His mind must work also, and awaken to its capacities. If it rusts, the body reverts to inhuman instincts."

"May I ask how you—?"

"By intercourse—in my own person or through my officials. I wish to have only those about me who are willing to contribute to my designs, and with whom I can work in absolute harmony. All my officers are chosen to that end. No doubt a dash of constitutional sentimentalism gives colour to my theories. I get it from a human tract in me that circumstances have obliged me to put a hoarding round."

"I begin to gather daylight."

"Quite so. My patients are invited to exchange views with their guardians in a spirit of perfect friendliness; to solve little problems of practical moment; to acquire the pride of self-reliance. We have competitions, such as certain newspapers open to their readers, in a simple form. I draw up the questions myself. The answers give me insight into the mental conditions of the competitors. Upon insight I proceed. I am fortunate in private means, and I am in a position to offer modest prizes to the winners. Whenever such an one is discharged, he finds awaiting him the tools most handy to his vocation. I bid him go forth in no pharisaical spirit, and invite him to communicate with me. I wish the shadow of the gaol to extend no further than the road whereon it lies. Henceforth, we are acquaintances with a common interest at heart. Isn't it monstrous that a state-fixed degree of misconduct should earn a man social ostracism? Parents are generally inclined to rule extra tenderness towards a child whose peccadilloes have brought him a whipping. For myself, I have no faith in police supervision. Give a culprit his term and have done with it. I find the majority who come back to me are ticket-of-leave men.

"Have I said enough? I offer you the reversion of the post. The present holder of it leaves in a month's time. Please to determine here and at once."

"Very good. I have decided."

"You will accept?"

"Yes."

So far wrote Polyhistor in the bonny days of early manhood—an attempt made in a spasm of enthusiasm inspired in him and humoured by his most engaging Mentor, to record his first impressions of a notable personality not many days after its introduction to him. He has never taken up the tale again until now, when an insistent sense, as of a task left unfinished, compels him to the effort. Over his sweet Mentor the grass lies thick, and flowers of aged stalk bloom perennially, and "Oh, the difference to me!"

To *me*, for it is time to drop the poor conceit, the pseudonym that once served its little purpose to awaken tender derision.

I take up the old and stained manuscript, with its marginalia, that are like the dim call from a far-away voice, and I know that, so I am driven to record the sequel to that gay introduction, it must be in a spirit of sombreness most deadly by contrast. I look at the faded opening words. The fire of the first line of the narrative is long out; the grate is cold some forty years—forty years!—and I think I have been a little chill during all that time. But, though the room rustle with phantoms and menace stalk in the retrospect, I shall acquit my conscience of its burden, refusing to be bullied by the counsel of a destiny that subpœna'd me entirely against my will.

PART II OF POLYHISTOR'S NARRATIVE
Continued and Finished after a Lapse of Forty Years

With my unexpected appointment as doctor to D—— gaol, I seemed to have put on the seven-league boots of success. No doubt it was an extraordinary degree of good fortune, even to one who had looked forward with a broad view of confidence; yet, I think, perhaps on account of the very casual nature of my promotion, I never took the post entirely seriously.

At the same time I was fully bent on justifying my little cockney patron's choice by a resolute subscription to his theories of prison management.

Major James Shrike inspired me with a curious conceit of impertinent respect. In person the very embodiment of that insignificant vulgarity, without extenuating circumstances, which is the type in caricature of the ultimate cockney, he possessed a force of mind and an earnestness of purpose that absolutely redeemed him on close acquaintanceship. I found him all he had stated himself to be, and something more.

He had a noble object always in view—the employment of sane and humanitarian methods in the treatment of redeemable criminals, and he strove towards it with completely untiring devotion. He was of those who never insist beyond the limits of their own understanding, clear-sighted in discipline, frank in relaxation, an altruist in the larger sense.

His undaunted persistence, as I learned, received ample illustration some few years prior to my acquaintance with him, when—his system being experimental rather than mature—a devastating endemic of typhoid in the prison had for the time stultified his efforts. He stuck to his post; but so virulent was the outbreak that the prison commissioners judged a complete evacuation of the building and overhauling of the drainage to be necessary. As a consequence, for some eighteen months—during thirteen of which the Governor and his household remained sole inmates of the solitary pile (so sluggishly do we redeem our condemned social bog-lands)—the "system" stood still for lack of material to mould. At the end of over a year of stagnation, a contract was accepted and workmen put in, and another five months saw the prison reordered for practical purposes.

The interval of forced inactivity must have sorely tried the patience of the Governor. Practical theorists condemned to rust too often eat out their own hearts. Major Shrike never referred to this period, and, indeed, laboriously snubbed any allusion to it.

He was, I have a shrewd notion, something of an officially petted reformer. Anyhow, to his abolition of the insensate barbarism of crank and treadmill in favour of civilizing methods no opposition was offered. Solitary confinement—a punishment outside all nature to a gregarious race—found no advocate in him. "A man's own suffering mind," he argued, "must be, of all moral food, the most poisonous for him to feed on. Surround a scorpion with fire and he stings himself to death, they say. Throw a diseased soul entirely upon its own resources and moral suicide results."

To sum up: his nature embodied humanity without sentimentalism, firmness without obstinacy, individuality without selfishness; his activity was boundless, his devotion to his system so real as to admit no utilitarian sophistries into his scheme of personal benevolence. Before I had been with him a week, I respected him as I had never respected man before.

One evening (it was during the second month of my appointment) we were sitting in his private study—a dark, comfortable room lined with books. It was an occasion on which a new characteristic of the man was offered to my inspection.

A prisoner of a somewhat unusual type had come in that day—a spiritualistic medium, convicted of imposture. To this person I casually referred.

"May I ask how you propose dealing with the new-comer?"

"On the familiar lines."

"But, surely—here we have a man of superior education, of imagination even?"

"No, no, no! A hawker's opportuneness; that describes it. These fellows would make death itself a vulgarity."

"You've no faith in their—"

"Not a tittle. Heaven forfend! A sheet and a turnip are poetry to their manifestations. It's as crude and sour soil for us to work on as any I know. We'll cart it wholesale."

"I take you—excuse my saying so—for a supremely sceptical man."

"As to what?"

"The supernatural."

There was no answer during a considerable interval. Presently it came, with deliberate insistence:—

"It is a principle with me to oppose bullying. We are here for a definite purpose—his duty plain to any man who wills to read it. There may be disembodied spirits who seek to distress or annoy where they can no longer control. If there are, mine, which is not yet divorced from its means to material action, declines to be influenced by any irresponsible whimsey, emanating from a place whose denizens appear to be actuated by a mere frivolous antagonism to all human order and progress."

"But supposing you, a murderer, to be haunted by the presentment of your victim?"

"I will imagine that to be my case. Well, it makes no difference. My interest is with the great human system, in one of whose veins I am a circulating drop. It is my business to help to keep the system sound, to do my duty without fear or favour. If disease—say a fouled conscience—contaminates me, it is for me to throw off the incubus, not accept it, and transmit the poison. Whatever my lapses of nature, I owe it to the entire system to work for purity in my allotted sphere, and not to allow any microbe bugbear to ride me roughshod, to the detriment of my fellow drops."

I laughed.

"It should be for you," I said, "to learn to shiver, like the boy in the fairy tale."

"I cannot," he answered, with a peculiar quiet smile; "and yet prisons, above all places, should be haunted."

Very shortly after his arrival I was called to the cell of the medium, F———. He suffered, by his own statement, from severe pains in the head.

I found the man to be nervous, anemic; his manner characterized by a sort of hysterical effrontery.

"Send me to the infirmary," he begged. "This isn't punishment, but torture."

"What are your symptoms?"

"I see things; my case has no comparison with others. To a man of my super-sensitiveness close confinement is mere cruelty."

I made a short examination. He was restless under my hands.

"You'll stay where you are," I said.

He broke out into violent abuse, and I left him.

Later in the day I visited him again. He was then white and sullen; but under his mood I could read real excitement of some sort.

"Now, confess to me, my man," I said, "what do you see?"

He eyed me narrowly, with his lips a little shaky.

"Will you have me moved if I tell you?"

"I can give no promise till I know."

He made up his mind after an interval of silence.

"There's something uncanny in my neighbourhood. Who's confined in the next cell—there, to the left?"

"To my knowledge it's empty."

He shook his head incredulously.

"Very well," I said, "I don't mean to bandy words with you"; and I turned to go.

At that he came after me with a frightened choke.

"Doctor, your mission's a merciful one. I'm not trying to sauce you. For God's sake have me moved! I can see further than most, I tell you!"

The fellow's manner gave me pause. He was patently and beyond the pride of concealment terrified.

"What do you see?" I repeated stubbornly.

"It isn't that I see, but I know. The cell's not empty!"

I stared at him in considerable wonderment.

"I will make inquiries," I said. "You may take that for a promise. If the cell proves empty, you stop where you are."

I noticed that he dropped his hands with a lost gesture as I left him. I was sufficiently moved to accost the warder who awaited me on the spot.

"Johnson," I said, "is that cell—"

"Empty, sir," answered the man sharply and at once.

Before I could respond, F—— came suddenly to the door, which I still held open.

"You lying cur!" he shouted. "You damned lying cur!"

The warder thrust the man back with violence.

"Now you, 49," he said, "dry up, and none of your sauce!" and he banged to the door with a sounding slap, and turned to me with a lowering face. The prisoner inside yelped and stormed at the studded panels.

"That cell's empty, sir," repeated Johnson.

"Will you, as a matter of conscience, let me convince myself? I promised the man."

"No, I can't."

"You can't?"

"No, sir."

"This is a piece of stupid discourtesy. You can have no reason, of course?"

"I can't open it—that's all."

"Oh, Johnson! Then I must go to the fountain-head."

"Very well, sir."

Quite baffled by the man's obstinacy, I said no more, but walked off. If my anger was roused, my curiosity was piqued in proportion.

I had no opportunity of interviewing the Governor all day, but at night I visited him by invitation to play a game of piquet.

He was a man without "incumbrances"—as a severe conservatism designates the *lares* of the cottage—and, at home, lived at his ease and indulged his amusements without comment.

I found him "tasting" his books, with which the room was well lined, and drawing with relish at an excellent cigar in the intervals of the courses.

He nodded to me, and held out an open volume in his left hand.

"Listen to this fellow," he said, tapping the page with his fingers:—

> "The most tolerable sort of Revenge, is for those wrongs which there is no Law to remedy: But then, let a man take heed, the Revenge be such, as there is no law to punish: Else, a man's Enemy, is still before hand, and it is two for one. Some, when they take Revenge, are Desirous the party should know, whence it cometh. This is the more Generous. For the Delight seemeth to be, not so much in doing the Hurt, as in making the Party repent: But Base and Crafty Cowards are like the Arrow that flyeth in the Dark. Cosmus, Duke of Florence, had a Desperate Saying against Perfidious or Neglecting Friends, as if these wrongs were unpardonable. You shall reade (saith he) that we are commanded to forgive our Enemies: But you never read, that we are commanded, to forgive our Friends.

"Is he not a rare fellow?"

"Who?" said I.

"Francis Bacon, who screwed his wit to his philosophy, like a hammer-head to its handle, and knocked a nail in at every blow. How many of our friends round about here would be picking oakum now if they had made a gospel of that quotation?"

"You mean they take no heed that the Law may punish for that for which it gives no remedy?"

"Precisely; and specifically as to revenge. The criminal, from the murderer to the petty pilferer, is actuated solely by the spirit of vengeance—vengeance blind and speechless—towards a system that forces him into a position quite outside his natural instincts."

"As to that, we have left Nature in the thicket. It is hopeless hunting for her now."

"We hear her breathing sometimes, my friend. Otherwise Her Majesty's prison locks would rust. But, I grant you, we have grown so unfamiliar with her that we call her simplest manifestations *super*natural nowadays."

"That reminds me. I visited F—— this afternoon. The man was in a queer way—not foxing, in my opinion. Hysteria, probably."

"Oh! What was the matter with him?"

"The form it took was some absurd prejudice about the next cell—number 47, He swore it was not empty—was quite upset about it—said there was some infernal influence at work in his neighbourhood. Nerves, he finds, I suppose, may revenge themselves on one who has made a habit of playing tricks with them. To satisfy him, I asked Johnson to open the door of the next cell—"

"Well?"

"He refused."

"It is closed by my orders."

"That settles it, of course. The manner of Johnson's refusal was a bit uncivil, but—"

He had been looking at me intently all this time—so intently that I was conscious of a little embarrassment and confusion. His mouth was set like a dash between brackets, and his eyes glistened. Now his features relaxed, and he gave a short high neigh of a laugh.

"My dear fellow, you must make allowances for the rough old lurcher. He was a soldier. He is all cut and measured out to the regimental pattern. With him Major Shrike, like the king, can do no wrong. Did I ever tell you he served under me in India? He did; and, moreover, I saved his life there."

"In an engagement?"

"Worse—from the bite of a snake. It was a mere question of will. I told him to wake and walk, and he did. They had thought him already in *rigor mortis*; and, as for him—well, his devotion to me since has been single to the last degree."

"That's as it should be."

"To be sure. And he's quite in my confidence. You must pass over the old beggar's churlishness."

I laughed an assent. And then an odd thing happened. As I spoke, I had walked over to a bookcase on the opposite side of the room to that on which my host stood. Near this bookcase hung a mirror—an oblong affair, set in brass *repoussé* work—on the wall; and, happening to glance into it as I approached, I caught sight of the Major's reflection as he turned his face to follow my movement.

I say "turned his face"—a formal description only. What met my startled gaze was an image of some nameless horror—of features grooved, and battered, and shapeless, as if they had been torn by a wild beast.

I gave a little indrawn gasp and turned about. There stood the Major, plainly himself, with a pleasant smile on his face.

"What's up?" said he.

He spoke abstractedly, pulling at his cigar; and I answered rudely, "That's a damned bad looking-glass of yours!"

"I didn't know there was anything wrong with it," he said, still abstracted and apart. And, indeed, when by sheer mental effort I forced myself to look again, there stood my companion as he stood in the room.

I gave a tremulous laugh, muttered something or nothing, and fell to examining the books in the case. But my fingers shook a trifle as I aimlessly pulled out one volume after another.

"Am *I* getting fanciful?" I thought—"I whose business it is to give practical account of every bugbear of the nerves. Bah! My liver must be out of order. A speck of bile in one's eye may look a flying dragon."

I dismissed the folly from my mind, and set myself resolutely to inspecting the books marshalled before me. Roving amongst them, I pulled out, entirely at random, a thin, worn duodecimo, that was thrust well back at a shelf end, as if it shrank from comparison with its prosperous and portly neighbours. Nothing but chance impelled me to the choice; and I don't know to this day what the ragged volume was about. It opened naturally at a marker that lay in it—a folded slip of paper, yellow with age; and glancing at this, a printed name caught my eye.

With some stir of curiosity, I spread the slip out. It was a title-page to a volume, of poems, presumably; and the author was James Shrike.

I uttered an exclamation, and turned, book in hand.

"An author!" I said. "You an author, Major Shrike!"

To my surprise, he snapped round upon me with something like a glare of fury on his face. This the more startled me as I believed I had reason to regard him as a man whose principles of conduct had long disciplined a temper that was naturally hasty enough.

Before I could speak to explain, he had come hurriedly across the room and had rudely snatched the paper out of my hand.

"How did this get—" he began; then in a moment came to himself, and apologized for his ill manners.

"I thought every scrap of the stuff had been destroyed," he said, and tore the page into fragments. "It is an ancient effusion, doctor—perhaps the greatest folly of my life; but it's something of a sore subject with me, and I shall be obliged if you'll not refer to it again."

He courted my forgiveness so frankly that the matter passed without embarrassment; and we had our game and spent a genial evening together. But memory of the queer little scene stuck in my mind, and I could not forbear pondering it fitfully.

Surely here was a new side-light that played upon my friend and superior a little fantastically.

Conscious of a certain vague wonder in my mind, I was traversing the prison, lost in thought, after my sociable evening with the Governor, when the fact that dim light was issuing from the open door of cell number 49 brought me to myself and to a pause in the corridor outside.

Then I saw that something was wrong with the cell's inmate, and that my services were required.

The medium was struggling on the floor, in what looked like an epileptic fit, and Johnson and another warder were holding him from doing an injury to himself.

The younger man welcomed my appearance with relief.

"Heerd him guggling," he said, "and thought as something were up. You come timely, sir."

More assistance was procured, and I ordered the prisoner's removal to the infirmary. For a minute, before following him, I was left alone with Johnson.

"It came to a climax, then?" I said, looking the man steadily in the face.

"He may be subject to 'em, sir," he replied, evasively.

I walked deliberately up to the closed door of the adjoining cell, which was the last on that side of the corridor. Huddled against the massive end wall, and half imbedded in it, as it seemed, it lay in a certain shadow, and bore every sign of dust and disuse.

Looking closely, I saw that the trap in the door was not only firmly bolted, but *screwed into its socket*.

I turned and said to the warder quietly,—

"Is it long since this cell was in use?"

"You're very fond of asking questions," he answered doggedly.

It was evident he would baffle me by impertinence rather than yield a confidence. A queer insistence had seized me—a strange desire to know more about this mysterious chamber. But, for all my curiosity, I flushed at the man's tone.

"You have your orders," I said sternly, "and do well to hold by them. I doubt, nevertheless, if they include impertinence to your superiors."

"I look straight on my duty, sir," he said, a little abashed. "I don't wish to give offence."

He did not, I feel sure. He followed his instinct to throw me off the scent, that was all.

I strode off in a fume, and after attending F—— in the infirmary, went promptly to my own quarters.

I was in an odd frame of mind, and for long tramped my sitting-room to and fro, too restless to go to bed, or, as an alternative, to settle down to a book. There was a welling up in my heart of some emotion that I could neither trace nor define. It seemed neighbour to terror, neighbour to an intense fainting pity, yet was not distinctly either of these. Indeed, where was cause for one, or the subject of the other? F—— might have endured mental sufferings which it was only human to help to end, yet F—— was a swindling rogue, who, once relieved, merited no further consideration.

It was not on him my sentiments were wasted. Who, then, was responsible for them?

There is a very plain line of demarcation between the legitimate spirit of inquiry and mere apish curiosity. I could recognise it, I have no doubt, as a rule, yet in my then mood, under the influence of a kind of morbid seizure, inquisitiveness took me by the throat. I could not whistle my mind from the chase of a certain graveyard will-o'-the-wisp; and on it went stumbling and floundering through bog and mire, until it fell into a state of collapse, and was useful for nothing else.

I went to bed and to sleep without difficulty, but I was conscious of myself all the time, and of a shadowless horror that seemed to come stealthily out of corners and to bend over and look at me, and to be nothing but a curtain or a hanging coat when I started and stared.

Over and over again this happened, and my temperature rose by leaps, and suddenly I saw that if I failed to assert myself, and promptly, fever would lap me in a consuming fire. Then in a moment I broke into a profuse perspiration, and sank exhausted into delicious unconsciousness.

Morning found me restored to vigour, but still with the maggot of curiosity boring in my brain. It worked there all day, and for many subsequent days, and at last it seemed as if my every faculty were honeycombed with its ramifications. Then "this will not do," I thought, but still the tunnelling process went on.

At first I would not acknowledge to myself what all this mental to-do was about. I was ashamed of my new development, in fact, and nervous, too, in a degree of what it might reveal in the matter of moral degeneration; but gradually, as the curious devil mastered me, I grew into such harmony with it that I could shut my eyes no longer to the true purpose of its insistence. It was the *closed cell* about which my thoughts hovered like crows circling round carrion.

"In the dead waste and middle" of a certain night I awoke with a strange, quick recovery of consciousness. There was the passing of a single expiration, and I had been asleep and was awake. I had gone to bed with no sense of premonition or of resolve in a particular direction; I sat up a monomaniac. It was as if, swelling in the silent hours, the tumour of curiosity had come to a head, and in a moment it was necessary to operate upon it.

I make no excuse for my then condition. I am convinced I was the victim of some undistinguishable force, that I was an agent under the control of the supernatural, if you like. Some thought had been in my mind of late that in my position it was my duty to unriddle the mystery of the closed cell. This was a sop timidly held out to and rejected by my better reason. I sought—and I knew it in my heart—solution of the puzzle, because it was a puzzle with an atmosphere that vitiated my moral fibre. Now, suddenly, I knew I must act, or, by forcing self-control, imperil my mind's stability.

All strung to a sort of exaltation, I rose noiselessly and dressed myself with rapid, nervous hands. My every faculty was focussed upon a solitary point. Without and around there was nothing but shadow and uncertainty. I seemed conscious only of a shaft of light, as it were, traversing the darkness and globing itself in a steady disc of radiance on a lonely door.

Slipping out into the great echoing vault of the prison in stockinged feet, I sped with no hesitation of purpose in the direction of the corridor that was my goal. Surely some resolute Providence guided and encompassed me, for no meeting with the night patrol occurred at any point to embarrass or deter me. Like a ghost myself, I flitted along the stone flags of the passages, hardly waking a murmur from them in my progress.

Without, I knew, a wild and stormy wind thundered on the walls of the prison. Within, where the very atmosphere was self-contained, a cold and solemn peace held like an irrevocable judgment.

I found myself as if in a dream before the sealed door that had for days harassed my waking thoughts. Dim light from a distant gas jet made a patch of yellow upon one of its panels; the rest was buttressed with shadow.

A sense of fear and constriction was upon me as I drew softly from my pocket a screwdriver I had brought with me. It never occurred to me, I swear, that the quest was no business of mine, and that even now I could withdraw from it, and no one be the wiser. But I was afraid—I was afraid. And there was not even the negative comfort of knowing that the neighbouring cell was tenanted. It gaped like a ghostly garret next door to a deserted house.

What reason had I to be there at all, or, being there, to fear? I can no more explain than tell how it was that I, an impartial follower of my vocation, had allowed myself to be tricked by that in the nerves I had made it my interest to study and combat in others.

My hand that held the tool was cold and wet. The stiff little shriek of the first screw, as it turned at first uneasily in its socket, sent a jarring thrill through me. But I persevered, and it came out readily by-and-by, as did the four or five others that held the trap secure.

Then I paused a moment; and, I confess, the quick pant of fear seemed to come grey from my lips. There were sounds about me—the deep breathing of imprisoned men; and I envied the sleepers their hard-wrung repose.

At last, in one access of determination, I put out my hand, and sliding back the bolt, hurriedly flung open the trap. An acrid whiff of dust assailed my nostrils as I stepped back a pace and stood expectant of anything—or nothing. What did I wish, or dread, or foresee? The complete absurdity of my behaviour was revealed to me in a moment. I could shake off the incubus here and now, and be a sane man again.

I giggled, with an actual ring of self-contempt in my voice, as I made a forward movement to close the aperture. I advanced my face to it, and inhaled the sluggish air that stole forth, and—God in heaven!

I had staggered back with that cry in my throat, when I felt fingers like iron clamps close on my arm and hold it. The grip, more than the face I turned to look upon in my surging terror, was forcibly human.

It was the warder Johnson who had seized me, and my heart bounded as I met the cold fury of his eyes.

"Prying!" he said, in a hoarse, savage whisper. "So you will, will you? And now let the devil help you!"

It was not this fellow I feared, though his white face was set like a demon's; and in the thick of my terror I made a feeble attempt to assert my authority.

"Let me go!" I muttered. "What! you dare?"

In his frenzy he shook my arm as a terrier shakes a rat, and, like a dog, he held on, daring me to release myself.

For the moment an instinct half-murderous leapt in me. It sank and was overwhelmed in a slough of some more secret emotion.

"Oh!" I whispered, collapsing, as it were, to the man's fury, even pitifully deprecating it. "What is it? What's there? It drew me—something unnameable."

He gave a snapping laugh like a cough. His rage waxed second by second. There was a maniacal suggestiveness in it; and not much longer, it was evident, could he have it under control. I saw it run and congest in his eyes; and, on the instant of its accumulation, he tore at me with a sudden wild strength, and drove me up against the very door of the secret cell.

The action, the necessity of self-defence, restored me to some measure of dignity and sanity.

"Let me go, you ruffian!" I cried, struggling to free myself from his grasp.

It was useless. He held me madly. There was no beating him off: and, so holding me, he managed to produce a single key from one of his pockets, and to slip it with a rusty clang into the lock of the door.

"You dirty, prying civilian!" he panted at me, as he swayed this way and that with the pull of my body. "You shall have your wish, by G——! You want to see inside, do you? Look, then!"

He dashed open the door as he spoke, and pulled me violently into the opening. A great waft of the cold, dank air came at us, and with it—what?

The warder had jerked his dark lantern from his belt, and now—an arm of his still clasped about one of mine—snapped the slide open.

"Where is it?" he muttered, directing the disc of light round and about the floor of the cell. I ceased struggling. Some counter influence was raising an odd curiosity in me.

"Ah!" he cried, in a stifled voice, "there you are, my friend!"

He was setting the light slowly travelling along the stone flags close by the wall over against us, and now, so guiding it, looked askance at me with a small, greedy smile.

"Follow the light, sir," he whispered jeeringly.

I looked, and saw twirling on the floor, in the patch of radiance cast by the lamp, *a little eddy of dust*, it seemed. This eddy was never still, but went circling in that stagnant place without apparent cause or influence; and, as it circled, it moved slowly on by wall and corner, so that presently in its progress it must reach us where we stood.

Now, draughts will play queer freaks in quiet places, and of this trifling phenomenon I should have taken little note ordinarily. But, I must say at once, that as I gazed upon the odd moving thing my heart seemed to fall in upon itself like a drained artery.

"Johnson!" I cried, "I must get out of this. I don't know what's the matter, or—Why do you hold me? D———n it! man, let me go; let me go, I say!"

As I grappled with him he dropped the lantern with a crash and flung his arms violently about me.

"You don't!" he panted, the muscles of his bent and rigid neck seeming actually to cut into my shoulder-blade. "You don't, by G———! You came of your own accord, and now you shall take your bellyful!"

It was a struggle for life or death, or, worse, for life and reason. But I was young and wiry, and held my own, if I could do little more. Yet there was something to combat beyond the mere brute strength of the man I struggled with, for I fought in an atmosphere of horror unexplainable, and I knew that inch by inch the *thing* on the floor was circling round in our direction.

Suddenly in the breathing darkness I felt it close upon us, gave one mortal yell of fear, and, with a last despairing fury, tore myself from the encircling arms, and sprang into the corridor without. As I plunged and leapt, the warder clutched at me, missed, caught a foot on the edge of the door, and, as the latter whirled to with a clap, fell heavily at my feet in a fit. Then, as I stood staring down upon him, steps sounded along the corridor and the voices of scared men hurrying up.

Ill and shaken, and, for the time, little in love with life, yet fearing death as I had never dreaded it before, I spent the rest of that horrible night huddled between my crumpled sheets, fearing to look forth, fearing to think, wild only to be far away, to be housed in some green and innocent hamlet, where I might forget the madness and the terror in learning to walk the unvext paths of placid souls. I had not fairly knocked under until alone with my new dread familiar. That unction I could lay to my heart, at least. I had done the manly part by the stricken warder, whom I had attended to his own home, in a row of little tenements that stood south of the prison walls. I had replied to all inquiries with some dignity and spirit, attributing my ruffled condition to an assault on the part of Johnson, when he was already under the shadow of his seizure. I had directed his removal, and grudged him no professional attention that it was in my power to bestow. But afterwards, locked into my room, my whole nervous system broke up like a trodden ant-hill, leaving me conscious of nothing but an aimless scurrying terror

AN EDDY ON THE FLOOR

and the black swarm of thoughts, so that I verily fancied my reason would give under the strain.

Yet I had more to endure and to triumph over.

Near morning I fell into a troubled sleep, throughout which the drawn twitch of muscle seemed an accent on every word of ill-omen I had ever spelt out of the alphabet of fear. If my body rested, my brain was an open chamber for any toad of ugliness that listed to "sit at squat" in.

Suddenly I woke to the fact that there was a knocking at my door—that there had been for some little time.

I cried, "Come in!" finding a weak restorative in the mere sound of my own human voice; then, remembering the key was turned, bade the visitor wait until I could come to him.

Scrambling, feeling dazed and white-livered, out of bed, I opened the door, and met one of the warders on the threshold. The man looked scared, and his lips, I noticed, were set in a somewhat boding fashion.

"Can you come at once, sir?" he said. "There's summat wrong with the Governor."

"Wrong? What's the matter with him?"

"Why,"—he looked down, rubbed an imaginary protuberance smooth with his foot, and glanced up at me again with a quick, furtive expression,— "he's got his face set in the grating of 47, and danged if a man Jack of us can get him to move or speak."

I turned away, feeling sick. I hurriedly pulled on coat and trousers, and hurriedly went off with my summoner. Reason was all absorbed in a wildest phantasy of apprehension.

"Who found him?" I muttered, as we sped on.

"Vokins see him go down the corridor about half after eight, sir, and see him give a start like when he noticed the trap open. It's never been so before in my time. Johnson must ha' done it last night, before he were took."

"Yes, yes."

"The man said the Governor went to shut it, it seemed, and to draw his face to'ards the bars in so doin'. Then he see him a-lookin' through, as he thought; but nat'rally it weren't no business of his'n, and he went off about his work. But when he come anigh agen, fifteen minutes later, there were the Governor in the same position; and he got scared over it, and called out to one or two of us."

"Why didn't one of you ask the Major if anything was wrong?"

"Bless you! we did; and no answer. And we pulled him, compatible with discipline, but—"

"But what?"

"He's stuck."

"Stuck!"

"See for yourself, sir. That's all I ask."

I did, a moment later. A little group was collected about the door of cell 47, and the members of it spoke together in whispers, as if they were frightened men. One young fellow, with a face white in patches, as if it had been floured, slid from them as I approached, and accosted me tremulously.

"Don't go anigh, sir. There's something wrong about the place."

I pulled myself together, forcibly beating down the excitement reawakened by the associations of the spot. In the discomfiture of others' nerves I found my own restoration.

"Don't be an ass!" I said, in a determined voice, "There's nothing here that can't be explained. Make way for me, please!"

They parted and let me through, and I saw him. He stood, spruce, frock-coated, dapper, as he always was, with his face pressed against and *into* the grill, and either hand raised and clenched tightly round a bar of the trap. His posture was as of one caught and striving frantically to release himself; yet the narrowness of the interval between the rails precluded so extravagant an idea. He stood quite motionless—taut and on the strain, as it were—and nothing of his face was visible but the back ridges of his jaw-bones, showing white through a bush of red whiskers.

"Major Shrike!" I rapped out, and, allowing myself no hesitation, reached forth my hand and grasped his shoulder. The body vibrated under my touch, but he neither answered nor made sign of hearing me. Then I pulled at him forcibly, and ever with increasing strength. His fingers held like steel braces. He seemed glued to the trap, like Theseus to the rock.

Hastily I peered round, to see if I could get glimpse of his face. I noticed enough to send me back with a little stagger.

"Has none of you got a key to this door?" I asked, reviewing the scared faces about me, than which my own was no less troubled, I feel sure.

"Only the Governor, sir," said the warder who had fetched me. "There's not a man but him amongst us that ever seen this opened."

He was wrong there, I could have told him; but held my tongue, for obvious reasons.

"I want it opened. Will one of you feel in his pockets?"

Not a soul stirred. Even had not sense of discipline precluded, that of a certain inhuman atmosphere made fearful creatures of them all.

AN EDDY ON THE FLOOR

"Then," said I, "I must do it myself."

I turned once more to the stiff-strung figure, had actually put hand on it, when an exclamation from Vokins arrested me.

"There's a key—there, sir!" he said—"stickin' out yonder between its feet."

Sure enough there was—Johnson's, no doubt, that had been shot from its socket by the clapping to of the door, and afterwards kicked aside by the warder in his convulsive struggles.

I stooped, only too thankful for the respite, and drew it forth. I had seen it but once before, yet I recognised it at a glance.

Now, I confess, my heart felt ill as I slipped the key into the wards, and a sickness of resentment at the tyranny of Fate in making me its helpless minister surged up in my veins. Once, with my fingers on the iron loop, I paused, and ventured a fearful side glance at the figure whose crookt elbow almost touched my face; then, strung to the high pitch of inevitability, I shot the lock, pushed at the door, and in the act, made a back leap into the corridor.

Scarcely, in doing so, did I look for the totter and collapse outwards of the rigid form. I had expected to see it fall away, face down, into the cell, as its support swung from it. Yet it was, I swear, as if *something* from within had relaxed its grasp and given the fearful dead man a swinging push outwards as the door opened.

It went on its back, with a dusty slap on the stone flags, and from all its spectators—me included—came a sudden drawn sound, like wind in a keyhole.

What can I say, or how describe it? A dead thing it was—but the face!

Barred with livid scars where the grating rails had crossed it, the rest seemed to have been worked and kneaded into a mere featureless plate of yellow and expressionless flesh.

And it was this I had seen in the glass!

There was an interval following the experience above narrated, during which a certain personality that had once been mine was effaced or suspended, and I seemed a passive creature, innocent of the least desire of independence. It was not that I was actually ill or actually insane. A merciful Providence set my finer wits slumbering, that was all, leaving me a sufficiency of the grosser faculties that were necessary to the right ordering of my behaviour.

I kept to my room, it is true, and even lay a good deal in bed; but this was more to satisfy the busy scruples of a *locum tenens*—a practitioner of the neighbourhood, who came daily to the prison to officiate in my absence—than to cosset a complaint that in its inactivity was purely negative. I could review what had happened with a calmness as profound as if I had read of it in a book. I could have wished to continue my duties, indeed, had the power of insistence remained to me. But the saner medicus was acute where I had gone blunt, and bade me to the restful course. He was right. I was mentally stunned, and had I not slept off my lethargy, I should have gone mad in an hour—leapt at a bound, probably, from inertia to flaming lunacy.

I remembered everything, but through a fluffy atmosphere, so to speak. It was as if I looked on bygone pictures through ground glass that softened the ugly outlines.

Sometimes I referred to these to my substitute, who was wise to answer me according to my mood; for the truth left me unruffled, whereas an obvious evasion of it would have distressed me.

"Hammond," I said one day, "I have never yet asked you. How did I give my evidence at the inquest?"

"Like a doctor and a sane man."

"That's good. But it was a difficult course to steer. You conducted the *post-mortem*. Did any peculiarity in the dead man's face strike you?"

"Nothing but this: that the excessive contraction of the bicipital muscles had brought the features into such forcible contact with the bars as to cause bruising and actual abrasion. He must have been dead some little time when you found him."

"And nothing else? You noticed nothing else in his face—a sort of obliteration of what makes one human, I mean?"

"Oh, dear, no! nothing but the painful constriction that marks any ordinary fatal attack of *angina pectoris*.—There's a rum breach of promise case in the paper to-day. You should read it; it'll make you laugh."

I had no more inclination to laugh than to sigh; but I accepted the change of subject with an equanimity now habitual to me.

One morning I sat up in bed, and knew that consciousness was wide awake in me once more. It had slept, and now rose refreshed, but trembling. Looking back, all in a flutter of new responsibility, along the misty path by way of which I had recently loitered, I shook with an awful thankfulness at sight of the pitfalls I had skirted and escaped—of the demons my witlessness had baffled.

The joy of life was in my heart again, but chastened and made pitiful by experience.

Hammond noticed the change in me directly he entered, and congratulated me upon it.

"Go slow at first, old man," he said. "You've fairly sloughed the old skin; but give the sun time to toughen the new one. Walk in it at present, and be content."

I was, in great measure, and I followed his advice. I got leave of absence, and ran down for a month in the country to a certain house we wot of, where kindly ministration to my convalescence was only one of the many blisses to be put to an account of rosy days.

> Then did my love awake,
> Most like a lily-flower,
> And as the lovely queene of heaven,
> So shone shee in her bower.

Ah, me! ah, me! when was it? A year ago, or two-thirds of a lifetime? Alas! "Age with stealing steps hath clawde me with his crowch." And will the yews root in *my* heart, I wonder?

I was well, sane, recovered, when one morning, towards the end of my visit, I received a letter from Hammond, enclosing a packet addressed to me, and jealously sealed and fastened. My friend's communication ran as follows:—

> There died here yesterday afternoon a warder, Johnson—he who had that apoplectic seizure, you will remember, the night before poor Shrike's exit. I attended him to the end, and, being alone with him an hour before the finish, he took the enclosed from under his pillow, and a solemn oath from me that I would forward it direct to you, sealed as you will find it, and permit no other soul to examine or even touch it. I acquit myself of the charge, but, my dear fellow, with an uneasy sense of the responsibility I incur in thus possibly suggesting to you a retrospect of events which you had much best consign to the limbo of the—not unexplainable, but not worth trying to explain. It was patent from what I have gathered that you were in an overstrung and excitable condition at that time, and that your temporary collapse was purely nervous in its character. It seems there was some nonsense abroad in the prison about a certain cell, and that there were fools who thought fit to associate Johnson's attack and the other's death with the opening of that cell's door. I have given the new Governor a tip, and he has stopped all that. We have examined the cell in company, and found it, as one might suppose, a very ordinary chamber. The two men died perfectly natural deaths, and there is the last to be said on the subject. I mention it only from the fear

that enclosed may contain some allusion to the rubbish, a perusal of which might check the wholesome convalescence of your thoughts. If you take my advice, you will throw the packet into the fire unread. At least, if you do examine it, postpone the duty till you feel yourself absolutely impervious to any mental trickery, and—bear in mind that you are a worthy member of a particularly matter-of-fact and unemotional profession.

I smiled at the last clause, for I was now in a condition to feel a rather warm shame over my erst weak-knee'd collapse before a sheet and an illuminated turnip. I took the packet to my bedroom, shut the door, and sat myself down by the open window. The garden lay below me, and the dewy meadows beyond. In the one, bees were busy ruffling the ruddy gillyflowers and April stocks; in the other, the hedge twigs were all frosted with Mary buds, as if Spring had brushed them with the fleece of her wings in passing.

I fetched a sigh of content as I broke the seal of the packet and brought out the enclosure. Somewhere in the garden a little sardonic laugh was clipt to silence. It came from groom or maid, no doubt; yet it thrilled me with an odd feeling of uncanniness, and I shivered slightly.

"Bah!" I said to myself determinedly. "There is a shrewd nip in the wind, for all the show of sunlight"; and I rose, pulled down the window, and resumed my seat.

Then in the closed room, that had become deathly quiet by contrast, I opened and read the dead man's letter.

> Sir,—I hope you will read what I here put down. I lay it on you as a solemn injunction, for I am a dying man, and I know it. And to who is my death due, and the Governor's death, if not to you, for your pryin' and curiosity, as surely as if you had drove a nife through our harts? Therefore, I say, Read this, and take my burden from me, for it has been a burden; and now it is right that you that interfered should have it on your own mortal shoulders. The Major is dead and I am dying, and in the first of my fit it went on in my head like cimbells that the trap was left open, and that if he passed he would look in and *it* would get him. For he knew not fear, neither would he submit to bullying by God or devil.
>
> Now I will tell you the truth, and Heaven quit you of your responsibility in our destruction.

There wasn't another man to me like the Governor in all the countries of the world. Once he brought me to life after doctors had given me up for dead; but he willed it, and I lived; and ever afterwards I loved him as a dog loves its master. That was in the Punjab; and I came home to England with him, and was his servant when he got his appointment to the jail here. I tell you he was a proud and fierce man, but under control and tender to those he favoured; and I will tell you also a strange thing about him. Though he was a soldier and an officer, and strict in discipline as made men fear and admire him, his heart at bottom was all for books, and literature, and such-like gentle crafts. I had his confidence, as a man gives his confidence to his dog, and before me sometimes he unbent as he never would before others. In this way I learnt the bitter sorrow of his life. He had once hoped to be a poet, acknowledged as such before the world. He was by natur' an idelist, as they call it, and God knows what it meant to him to come out of the woods, so to speak, and sweat in the dust of cities; but he did it, for his will was of tempered steel. He buried his dreams in the clouds and came down to earth greatly resolved, but with one undying hate. It is not good to hate as he could, and worse to be hated by such as him; and I will tell you the story, and what it led to.

It was when he was a subaltern that he made up his mind to the plunge. For years he had placed all his hopes and confidents in a book of verses he had wrote, and added to, and improved during that time. A little encouragement, a little word of praise, was all he looked for, and then he was ready to buckle to again, profitin' by advice, and do better. He put all the love and beauty of his heart into that book, and at last, after doubt, and anguish, and much diffidents, he published it and give it to the world. Sir, it fell what they call still-born from the press. It was like a green leaf flutterin' down in a dead wood. To a proud and hopeful man, bubblin' with music, the pain of neglect, when he come to realize it, was terrible. But nothing was said, and there was nothing to say. In silence he had to endure and suffer.

But one day, during maneuvers, there came to the camp a greyfaced man, a newspaper correspondent, and young Shrike knocked up a friendship with him. Now how it come about I cannot tell, but so it did that this skip-kennel wormed the lad's sorrow out of him, and his confidents, swore he'd been damnabilly used, and that when he got back he'd crack up the book himself in his own paper. He was a fool for his pains, and a serpent in his cruelty. The notice come out as promised, and, my God! the author was laughed and mocked at from beginning to end. Even confidentses he had given to the creature was twisted to his ridicule, and his very appearance joked over. And the mess got wind of it, and made a rare story for the dog days.

He bore it like a soldier, and that he became heart and liver from the moment. But he put something to the account of the grey-faced man and locked it up in his breast.

He come across him again years afterwards in India, and told him very politely that he hadn't forgotten him, and didn't intend to. But he was anigh losin' sight of him there for ever and a day, for the creature took cholera, or what looked like it, and rubbed shoulders with death and the devil before he pulled through. And he come across him again over here, and that was the last of him, as you shall see presently.

Once, after I knew the Major (he were Captain then), I was a-brushin' his coat, and he stood a long while before the glass. Then he twisted upon me, with a smile on his mouth, and says he,—

"The dog was right, Johnson: this isn't the face of a poet. I was a presumtious ass, and born to cast up figgers with a pen behind my ear."

"Captain," I says, "if you was skinned, you'd look like any other man without his. The quality of a soul isn't expressed by a coat."

"Well," he answers, "my soul's pretty clean-swept, I think, save for one Bluebeard chamber in it that's been kep' locked ever so many years. It's nice and dirty by this time, I expect," he says. Then the grin comes on his mouth again. "I'll open it some day," he says, "and look. There's something in it about comparing me to a dancing dervish, with the wind in my petticuts. Perhaps I'll get the chance to set somebody else dancing by-and-by."

He did, and took it, and the Bluebeard chamber come to be opened in this very jail.

It was when the system was lying fallow, so to speak, and the prison was deserted. Nobody was there but him and me and the echoes from the empty courts. The contract for restoration hadn't been signed, and for months, and more than a year, we lay idle, nothing bein' done.

Near the beginnin' of this period, one day comes, for the third time of the Major's seein' him, the grey-faced man. "Let bygones be bygones," he says. "I was a good friend to you, though you didn't know it; and now, I expect, you're in the way to thank me."

"I am," says the Major.

"Of course," he answers. "Where would be your fame and reputation as one of the leadin' prison reformers of the day if you had kep' on in that riming nonsense?"

"Have you come for my thanks?" says the Governor.

"I've come," says the grey-faced man, "to examine and report upon your system."

"For your paper?"

"Possibly; but to satisfy myself of its efficacy, in the first instance."

"You aren't commissioned, then?"

"No; I come on my own responsibility."

"Without consultation with any one?"

"Absolutely without. I haven't even a wife to advise me," he says, with a yellow grin. What once passed for cholera had set the bile on his skin like paint, and he had caught a manner of coughing behind his hand like a toast-master.

"I know," says the Major, looking him steady in the face, "that what you say about me and my affairs is sure to be actuated by conscientious motives."

"Ah," he answers. "You're sore about that review still, I see."

"Not at all," says the Major; "and, in proof, I invite you to be my guest for the night, and to-morrow I'll show you over the prison and explain my system."

The creature cried, "Done!" and they set to and discussed jail matters in great earnestness. I couldn't guess the Governor's intentions, but, somehow, his manner troubled me. And yet I can remember only one point of his talk. He were always dead against making public show of his birds. "They're there for reformation, not ignimony," he'd say. Prisons in the old days were often, with the asylum and the work'us, made the holiday show-places of towns. I've heard of one Justice of the Peace, up North, who, to save himself trouble, used to sign a lot of blank orders for leave to view, so that applicants needn't bother him when they wanted to go over. They've changed all that, and the Governor were instrumental in the change.

"It's against my rule," he said that night, "to exhibit to a stranger without a Government permit; but, seein' the place is empty, and for old remembrance' sake, I'll make an exception in your favour, and you shall learn all I can show you of the inside of a prison."

Now this was natural enough; but I was uneasy.

He treated his guest royally; so much that when we assembled the next mornin' for the inspection, the grey-faced man were shaky as a wet dog. But the Major were all set prim and dry, like the soldier he was.

We went straight away down corridor B, and at cell 47 we stopped.

"We will begin our inspection here," said the Governor. "Johnson, open the door."

I had the keys of the row, fitted in the right one, and pushed open the door.

"After you, sir," said the Major; and the creature walked in, and he shut the door on him.

I think he smelt a rat at once, for he began beating on the wood and calling out to us. But the Major only turned round to me with his face like a stone.

"Take that key from the bunch," he said, "and give it to me."

I obeyed, all in a tremble, and he took and put it in his pocket.

"My God, Major!" I whispered, "what are you going to do with him?"

"Silence, sir!" he said. "How dare you question your superior officer!"

And the noise inside grew louder.

The Governor, he listened to it a moment like music; then he unbolted and flung open the trap, and the creature's face came at it like a wild beast's.

"Sir," said the Major to it, "you can't better understand my system than by experiencing it. What an article for your paper you could write already—almost as pungint a one as that in which you ruined the hopes and prospects of a young cockney poet."

The man mouthed at the bars. He was half-mad, I think, in that one minute.

"Let me out!" he screamed. "This is a hideous joke! Let me out!"

"When you are quite quiet—deathly quiet," said the Major, "you shall come out. Not before"; and he shut the trap in its face very softly.

"Come, Johnson, march!" he said, and took the lead, and we walked out of the prison.

I was like to faint, but I dared not disobey, and the man's screeching followed us all down the empty corridors and halls, until we shut the first great door on it.

It may have gone on for hours, alone in that awful emptiness. The creature was a reptile, but the thought sickened my heart.

And from that hour till his death, five months later, he rotted and maddened in his dreadful tomb.

There was more, but I pushed the ghastly confession from me at this point in uncontrollable loathing and terror. Was it possible—possible, that injured vanity could so falsify its victim's every tradition of decency?

"Oh!" I muttered, "what a disease is ambition! Who takes one step towards it puts his foot on Alsirat!"

It was minutes before my shocked nerves were equal to a resumption of the task; but at last I took it up again, with a groan.

I don't think at first I realized the full mischief the Governor intended to do. At least, I hoped he only meant to give the man a good fright and then let him go. I might have known better. How could he ever release him without ruining himself?

The next morning he summoned me to attend him. There was a strange new look of triumph in his face, and in his hand he held a heavy hunting-crop. I pray to God he acted in madness, but my duty and obedience was to him.

"There is sport toward, Johnson," he said. "My dervish has got to dance."

I followed him quiet. We listened when I opened the jail door, but the place was silent as the grave. But from the cell, when we reached it, came a low, whispering sound.

The Governor slipped the trap and looked through.

"All right," he said, and put the key in the door and flung it open.

He were sittin' crouched on the ground, and he looked up at us vacant-like. His face were all fallen down, as it were, and his mouth never ceased to shake and whisper.

The Major shut the door and posted me in a corner. Then he moved to the creature with his whip.

"Up!" he cried. "Up, you dervish, and dance to us!" and he brought the thong with a smack across his shoulders.

The creature leapt under the blow, and then to his feet with a cry, and the Major whipped him till he danced. All round the cell he drove him, lashing and cutting—and again, and many times again, until the poor thing rolled on the floor whimpering and sobbing. I shall have to give an account of this some day. I shall have to whip my master with a red-hot serpent round the blazing furnace of the pit, and I shall do it with agony, because here my love and my obedience was to him.

When it was finished, he bade me put down food and drink that I had brought with me, and come away with him; and we went, leaving him rolling on the floor of the cell, and shut him alone in the empty prison until we should come again at the same time to-morrow.

So day by day this went on, and the dancing three or four times a week, until at last the whip could be left behind, for the man would scream and begin to dance at the mere turning of the key in the lock. And he danced for four months, but not the fifth.

Nobody official came near us all this time. The prison stood lonely as a deserted ruin where dark things have been done.

Once, with fear and trembling, I asked my master how he would account for the inmate of 47 if he was suddenly called upon by authority to open the cell; and he answered, smiling,—

"I should say it was my mad brother. By his own account, he showed me a brother's love, you know. It would be thought a liberty; but the authorities, I think, would stretch a point for me. But if I got sufficient notice, I should clear out the cell."

I asked him how, with my eyes rather than my lips, and he answered me only with a look.

And all this time he was, outside the prison, living the life of a good man—helping the needy, ministering to the poor. He even entertained occasionally, and had more than one noisy party in his house.

But the fifth month the creature danced no more. He was a dumb, silent animal then, with matted hair and beard; and when one entered he would only look up at one pitifully, as if he said, "My long punishment is nearly ended." How it came that no inquiry was ever made about him I know not, but none ever was. Perhaps he was one of the wandering gentry that nobody ever knows where they are next. He was unmarried, and had apparently not told of his intended journey to a soul.

And at the last he died in the night. We found him lying stiff and stark in the morning, and scratched with a piece of black crust on a stone of the wall these strange words: "An Eddy on the Floor." Just that—nothing else.

Then the Governor came and looked down, and was silent. Suddenly he caught me by the shoulder.

"Johnson," he cried, "if it was to do again, I would do it! I repent of nothing. But he has paid the penalty, and we call quits. May he rest in peace!"

"Amen!" I answered low. Yet I knew our turn must come for this.

We buried him in quicklime under the wall where the murderers lie, and I made the cell trim and rubbed out the writing, and the Governor locked all up and took away the key. But he locked in more than he bargained for.

For months the place was left to itself, and neither of us went anigh 47. Then one day the workmen was to be put in, and the Major he took me round with him for a last examination of the place before they come.

He hesitated a bit outside a particular cell; but at last he drove in the key and kicked open the door.

"My God!" he says, "he's dancing still!"

My heart was thumpin', I tell you, as I looked over his shoulder. What did we see? What you well understand, sir; but, for all it was no more than that, we knew as well as if it was shouted in our ears that it was him, dancin'. It went round by the walls and drew towards us, and as it stole near I screamed out, "An Eddy on the Floor!" and seized and dragged the Major out and clapped to the door behind us.

"Oh!" I said, "in another moment it would have had us."

He looked at me gloomily.

"Johnson," he said, "I'm not to be frighted or coerced. He may dance, but he shall dance alone. Get a screwdriver and some screws and fasten up this trap. No one from this time looks into this cell."

I did as he bid me, sweatin'; and I swear all the time I wrought I dreaded a hand would come through the trap and clutch mine.

On one pretex' or another, from that day till the night you meddled with it, he kep' that cell as close shut as a tomb. And he went his ways, discardin' the past from that time forth. Now and again a over-sensitive prisoner in the next cell would complain of feelin' uncomfortable. If possible, he would be removed to another; if not, he was damd for his fancies. And so it might be goin' on to now, if you hadn't pried and interfered. I don't blame you at this moment, sir. Likely you were an instrument in the hands of Providence; only, as the instrument, you must now take the burden of the truth on your own shoulders. I am a dying man, but I cannot die till I have confessed. Per'aps you may find it in your hart some day to give up a prayer for me—but it must be for the Major as well.

Your obedient servant,
J. Johnson

What comment of my own can I append to this wild narrative? Professionally, and apart from personal experiences, I should rule it the composition of an epileptic. That a noted journalist, nameless as he was and is to me, however nomadic in habit, could disappear from human ken, and his fellows rest content to leave him unaccounted for, seems a tax upon credulity so stupendous that I cannot seriously endorse the statement.

Yet, also—there *is* that little matter of my personal experience.

The Haunted Baronet

J. Sheridan Le Fanu

I. The George and Dragon

THE PRETTY LITTLE TOWN OF GOLDEN FRIARS—STANDING BY THE MARGIN OF the lake, hemmed round by an amphitheatre of purple mountain, rich in tint and furrowed by ravines, high in air, when the tall gables and narrow windows of its ancient greystone houses, and the tower of the old church, from which every evening the curfew still rings, show like silver in the moonbeams, and the black elms that stand round throw moveless shadows upon the short level grass—is one of the most singular and beautiful sights I have ever seen.

There it rises, "as from the stroke of the enchanter's wand," looking so light and filmy, that you could scarcely believe it more than a picture reflected on the thin mist of night.

On such a still summer night the moon shone splendidly upon the front of the George and Dragon, the comfortable greystone inn of Golden Friars, with the grandest specimen of the old inn-sign, perhaps, left in England. It looks right across the lake; the road that skirts its margin running by the steps of the hall-door, opposite to which, at the other side of the road, between two great posts, and framed in a fanciful wrought-iron border splendid with gilding, swings the famous sign of St. George and the Dragon, gorgeous with colour and gold.

In the great room of the George and Dragon, three or four of the old *habitués* of that cozy lounge were refreshing a little after the fatigues of the day.

This is a comfortable chamber, with an oak wainscot; and whenever in summer months the air is sharp enough, as on the present occasion, a fire helped to light it up; which fire, being chiefly wood, made a pleasant broad flicker on panel and ceiling, and yet did not make the room too hot.

On one side sat Doctor Torvey, the doctor of Golden Friars, who knew the weak point of every man in the town, and what medicine agreed with each inhabitant—a fat gentleman, with a jolly laugh and an appetite for all sorts of news, big and little, and who liked a pipe, and made a tumbler of punch at about this hour, with a bit of lemon-peel in it. Beside him sat William Peers, a thin old gentleman, who had lived for more than thirty years in India, and was quiet and benevolent, and the last man in Golden Friars who wore a pigtail. Old Jack Amerald, an ex-captain of the navy, with his short stout leg on a chair, and its wooden companion beside it, sipped his grog, and bawled in the old-fashioned navy way, and called his friends his "hearties." In the middle, opposite the hearth, sat deaf Tom Hollar, always placid, and smoked his pipe, looking serenely at the fire. And the landlord of the George and Dragon every now and then strutted in, and sat down in the high-backed wooden arm-chair, according to the old-fashioned republican ways of the place, and took his share in the talk gravely, and was heartily welcome.

"And so Sir Bale is coming home at last," said the Doctor. "Tell us any more you heard since."

"Nothing," answered Richard Turnbull, the host of the George. "Nothing to speak of; only 'tis certain sure, and so best; the old house won't look so dowly now."

"Twyne says the estate owes a good capful o' money by this time, hey?" said the Doctor, lowering his voice and winking.

"Weel, they do say he's been nout at dow. I don't mind saying so to *you*, mind, sir, where all's friends together; but he'll get that right in time."

"More like to save here than where he is," said the Doctor with another grave nod.

"He does very wisely," said Mr. Peers, having blown out a thin stream of smoke, "and creditably, to pull-up in time. He's coming here to save a little, and perhaps he'll marry; and it is the more creditable, if, as they say, he dislikes the place, and would prefer staying where he is."

And having spoken thus gently, Mr. Peers resumed his pipe cheerfully.

"No, he don't like the place; that is, I'm told he *didn't*," said the innkeeper.

"He *hates* it," said the Doctor with another dark nod.

"And no wonder, if all's true I've heard," cried old Jack Amerald. "Didn't he drown a woman and her child in the lake?"

"Hollo! my dear boy, don't let them hear you say that; you're all in the clouds."

"By Jen!" exclaimed the landlord after an alarmed silence, with his mouth and eyes open, and his pipe in his hand, "why, sir, I pay rent for the house up there. I'm thankful—dear knows, I *am* thankful—we're all to ourselves!"

Jack Amerald put his foot on the floor, leaving his wooden leg in its horizontal position, and looked round a little curiously.

"Well, if it wasn't him, it was some one else. I'm sure it happened up at Mardykes. I took the bearings on the water myself from Glads Scaur to Mardykes Jetty, and from the George and Dragon sign down here—down to the white house under Forrick Fells. I could fix a buoy over the very spot. Some one here told me the bearings, I'd take my oath, where the body was seen; and yet no boat could ever come up with it; and that was queer, you know, so I clapt it down in my log."

"Ay, sir, there *was* some flummery like that, Captain," said Turnbull; "for folk will be gabbin'. But 'twas his grandsire was talked o', not him; and 'twould play the hangment wi' me doun here, if 'twas thought there was stories like that passin' in the George and Dragon."

"Well, his grandfather; 'twas all one to him, I take it."

"There never was no proof, Captain, no more than smoke; and the family up at Mardykes wouldn't allow the king to talk o' them like that, sir; for though they be lang deod that had most right to be angered in the matter, there's none o' the name but would be half daft to think 'twas still believed, and he full out as mich as any. Not that I need care more than another, though they do say he's a bit frowsy and short-waisted; for he can't shouther me out o' the George while I pay my rent, till nine hundred and ninety-nine year be rin oot; and a man, be he ne'er sa het, has time to cool before then. But there's no good quarrellin' wi' teathy folk; and it may lie in his way to do the George mony an ill turn, and mony a gude one; an' it's only fair to say it happened a long way before he was born, and there's no good in vexin' him; and I lay ye a pound, Captain, the Doctor hods wi' me."

The Doctor, whose business was also sensitive, nodded; and then he said, "But for all that, the story's old, Dick Turnbull—older than you or I, my jolly good friend."

"And best forgotten," interposed the host of the George.

"Ay, best forgotten; but that it's not like to be," said the Doctor, plucking up courage. "Here's our friend the Captain has heard it; and the mistake he has made shows there's one thing worse than its being quite remembered, and that is, its being *half* remembered. We can't stop people talking; and a story like that will see us all off the hooks, and be in folks' mouths, still, as strong as ever."

"Ay; and now I think on it, 'twas Dick Harman that has the boat down there—an old tar like myself—that told me that yarn. I was trying for pike, and he pulled me over the place, and that's how I came to hear it. I say, Tom, my hearty, serve us out another glass of brandy, will you?" shouted the Captain's voice as the waiter crossed the room; and that florid and grizzled naval hero clapped his leg again on the chair by its wooden companion, which he was wont to call his jury-mast.

"Well, I do believe it will be spoke of longer than we are like to hear," said the host, "and I don't much matter the story, if it baint told o' the wrong man." Here he touched his tumbler with the spoon, indicating by that little ring that Tom, who had returned with the Captain's grog, was to replenish it with punch. "And Sir Bale is like to be a friend to this house. I don't see no reason why he shouldn't. The George and Dragon has bin in our family ever since the reign of King Charles the Second. It was William Turnbull in that time, which they called it the Restoration, he taking the lease from Sir Tony Mardykes that was then. They was but knights then. They was made baronets first in the reign of King George the Second; you may see it in the list of baronets and the nobility. The lease was made to William Turnbull, which came from London; and he built the stables, which they was out o' repair, as you may read to this day in the lease; and the house has never had but one sign since—the George and Dragon, it is pretty well known in England—and one name to its master. It has been owned by a Turnbull from that day to this, and they have not been counted bad men." A murmur of applause testified the assent of his guests. "They has been steady churchgoin' folk, and brewed good drink, and maintained the best o' characters, hereaways and farther off too, though 'tis I, Richard Turnbull, that says it; and while they pay their rent, no man has power to put them out; for their title's as good to the George and Dragon, and the two fields, and the croft, and the grazing o' their kye on the green, as Sir Bale Mardykes to the Hall up there and estate. So 'tis nout to me, except in the way o' friendliness, what the family may think o' me; only the George and they has always been kind and friendly, and I don't want to break the old custom."

"Well said, Dick!" exclaimed Doctor Torvey; "I own to your conclusion; but there ain't a soul here but ourselves—and we're all friends, and you are your own master—and, hang it, you'll tell us that story about the drowned woman, as you heard it from your father long ago."

"Ay, do, and keep us to our liquor, my hearty!" cried the Captain.

Mr. Peers looked his entreaty; and deaf Mr. Hollar, having no interest in the petition, was at least a safe witness, and, with his pipe in his lips, a cozy piece of furniture.

Richard Turnbull had his punch beside him; he looked over his shoulder. The door was closed, the fire was cheery, and the punch was fragrant, and all friendly faces about him. So said he:

"Gentlemen, as you're pleased to wish it, I don't see no great harm in it; and at any rate, 'twill prevent mistakes. It is more than ninety years since. My father was but a boy then; and many a time I have heard him tell it in this very room."

And looking into his glass he mused, and stirred his punch slowly.

II. The Drowned Woman

"It ain't much of a homminy," said the host of the George. "I'll not keep you long over it, gentlemen. There was a handsome young lady, Miss Mary Feltram o' Cloostedd by name. She was the last o' that family; and had gone very poor. There's but the walls o' the house left now; grass growing in the hall, and ivy over the gables; there's no one livin' has ever hard tell o' smoke out o' they chimblies. It stands on t'other side o' the lake, on the level wi' a deal o' a'ad trees behint and aside it at the gap o' the clough, under the pike o' Maiden Fells. Ye may see it wi' a spyin'-glass from the boat-bield at Mardykes Hall."

"I've been there fifty times," said the Doctor.

"Well there was dealin's betwixt the two families; and there's good and bad in every family; but the Mardykes, in them days, was a wild lot. And when old Feltram o' Cloostedd died, and the young lady his daughter was left a ward o' Sir Jasper Mardykes—an ill day for her, poor lass!—twenty year older than her he was, an' more; and nothin' about him, they say, to make anyone like or love him, ill-faur'd and little and dow."

"Dow—that's gloomy," Doctor Torvey instructed the Captain aside.

"But they do say, they has an old blud-stean ring in the family that has a charm in't; and happen how it might, the poor lass fell in love wi' him. Some said they was married. Some said it hang'd i' the bell-ropes, and never had the priest's blessing; but anyhow, married or no, there was talk enough amang the folk, and out o' doors she would na budge. And there was two wee barns; and she prayed him hard to confess the marriage, poor thing! But t'was a bootlese bene, and he would not allow they should bear his name, but their mother's; he was a hard man, and hed the bit in his teeth, and went his ain gait. And having tired of her, he took in his head to marry a lady of the Barnets, and it behoved him to be shut o' her and her children; and so she nor them was seen no more at Mardykes Hall. And the eldest, a boy, was left in care of my grandfather's father here in the George."

"That queer Philip Feltram that's travelling with Sir Bale so long is a descendant of his?" said the Doctor.

"Grandson," observed Mr. Peers, removing his pipe for a moment; "and is the last of that stock."

"Well, no one could tell where she had gone to. Some said to distant parts, some said to the madhouse, some one thing, some another; but neither she nor the barn was ever seen or spoke to by the folk at Mardykes in life again. There was one Mr. Wigram that lived in them times down at Moultry, and had sarved, like the Captain here, in the king's navy in his day; and early of a morning down he comes to the town for a boat, sayin' he was looking towards Snakes Island through his spyin'-glass, and he seen a woman about a hundred and fifty yards outside of it; the Captain here has heard the bearings right enough. From her hips upwards she was stark and straight out o' the water, and a baby in her arms. Well, no one else could see it, nor he neither, when they went down to the boat. But next morning he saw the same thing, and the boatman saw it too; and they rowed for it, both pulling might and main; but after a mile or so they could see it no more, and gave over. The next that saw it was the vicar, I forget his name now—but he was up the lake to a funeral at Mortlock Church; and coming back with a bit of a sail up, just passin' Snakes Island, what should they hear on a sudden but a wowl like a death-cry, shrill and bleak, as made the very blood hoot in their veins; and looking along the water not a hundred yards away, saw the same grizzled sight in the moonlight; so they turned the tiller, and came near enough to see her face—blea it was, and drenched wi' water—and she was above the lake to her middle, stiff as a post, holdin' the weeny barn out to them, and flyrin' [smiling scornfully] on them as they drew nigh her. They were half-frighted, not knowing what to make of it; but passing as close as the boatman could bring her side, the vicar stretched over the gunwale to catch her, and she bent forward, pushing the dead bab forward; and as she did, on a sudden she gave a yelloch that scared them, and they saw her no more. 'Twas no livin' woman, for she couldn't rise that height above the water, as they well knew when they came to think; and knew it was a dobby they saw; and ye may be sure they didn't spare prayer and blessin', and went on their course straight before the wind; for neither would a-took the worth o' all the Mardykes to look sich a freetin' i' the face again. 'Twas seen another time by market-folk crossin' fra Gyllenstan in the self-same place; and Snakes Island got a bad neam, and none cared to go nar it after nightfall."

"Do you know anything of that Feltram that has been with him abroad?" asked the Doctor.

"They say he's no good at anything—a harmless mafflin; he was a long gaumless gawky when he went awa," said Richard Turnbull. "The Feltrams and the Mardykes was sib, ye know; and that made what passed in the misfortune o' that young lady spoken of all the harder; and this young man ye speak of is a grandson o' the lad that was put here in care o' my grandfather."

"*Great*-grandson. His father was grandson," said Mr. Peers; "he held a commission in the army and died in the West Indies. This Philip Feltram is the last o' that line—illegitimate, you know, it is held—and the little that remained of the Feltram property went nearly fourscore years ago to the Mardykes, and this Philip is maintained by Sir

Bale; it is pleasant, notwithstanding all the stories one hears, gentlemen, that the only thing we know of him for certain should be so creditable to his kindness."

"To be sure," acquiesced Mr. Turnbull.

While they talked the horn sounded, and the mail-coach drew up at the door of the George and Dragon to set down a passenger and his luggage.

Dick Turnbull rose and went out to the hall with careful bustle, and Doctor Torvey followed as far as the door, which commanded a view of it, and saw several trunks cased in canvas pitched into the hall, and by careful Tom and a boy lifted one on top of the other, behind the corner of the banister. It would have been below the dignity of his cloth to go out and read the labels on these, or the Doctor would have done otherwise, so great was his curiosity.

III. Philip Feltram

The new guest was now in the hall of the George, and Doctor Torvey could hear him talking with Mr. Turnbull. Being himself one of the dignitaries of Golden Friars, the Doctor, having regard to first impressions, did not care to be seen in his post of observation; and closing the door gently, returned to his chair by the fire, and in an under-tone informed his cronies that there was a new arrival in the George, and he could not hear, but would not wonder if he were taking a private room; and he seemed to have trunks enough to build a church with.

"Don't be too sure we haven't Sir Bale on board," said Amerald, who would have followed his crony the Doctor to the door—for never was retired naval hero of a village more curious than he—were it not that his wooden leg made a distinct pounding on the floor that was inimical, as experience had taught him, to mystery.

"That can't be," answered the Doctor; "Charley Twyne knows everything about it, and has a letter every second day; and there's no chance of Sir Bale before the tenth; this is a tourist, you'll find. I don't know what the d——l keeps Turnbull; he knows well enough we are all naturally willing to hear who it is."

"Well, he won't trouble us here, I bet ye"; and catching deaf Mr. Hollar's eye, the Captain nodded, and pointed to the little table beside him, and made a gesture imitative of the rattling of a dice-box; at which that quiet old gentleman also nodded sunnily; and up got the Captain and conveyed the backgammon-box to the table, near Hollar's elbow, and the two worthies were soon sinc-ducing and catre-acing, with the pleasant clatter that accompanies that ancient game. Hollar had thrown sizes and made his double point, and the honest Captain, who could stand many things better than Hollar's throwing such throws so early in the evening, cursed his opponent's luck and sneered at his play, and called the company to witness, with a distinctness which a stranger to smiling Hollar's deafness would have thought hardly civil; and just at this moment the door opened, and Richard Turnbull showed his new guest into the room, and ushered him to a vacant seat near the other corner of the table before the fire.

The stranger advanced slowly and shyly, with something a little deprecatory in his air, to which a lathy figure, a slight stoop, and a very gentle and even heartbroken look in his pale long face, gave a more marked character of shrinking and timidity.

He thanked the landlord aside, as it were, and took his seat with a furtive glance round, as if he had no right to come in and intrude upon the happiness of these honest gentlemen.

He saw the Captain scanning him from under his shaggy grey eyebrows while he was pretending to look only at his game; and the Doctor was able to recount to Mrs. Torvey when he went home every article of the stranger's dress.

It was odd and melancholy as his peaked face.

He had come into the room with a short black cloak on, and a rather tall foreign felt hat, and a pair of shiny leather gaiters or leggings on his thin legs; and altogether presented a general resemblance to the conventional figure of Guy Fawkes.

Not one of the company assembled knew the appearance of the Baronet. The Doctor and old Mr. Peers remembered something of his looks; and certainly they had no likeness, but the reverse, to those presented by the new-comer. The Baronet, as now described by people who had chanced to see him, was a dark man, not above the middle size, and with a certain decision in his air and talk; whereas this person was tall, pale, and in air and manner feeble. So this broken trader in the world's commerce, with whom all seemed to have gone wrong, could not possibly be he.

Presently, in one of his stealthy glances, the Doctor's eye encountered that of the stranger, who was by this time drinking his tea—a thin and feminine liquor little used in that room.

The stranger did not seem put out; and the Doctor, interpreting his look as a permission to converse, cleared his voice, and said urbanely,

"We have had a little frost by night, down here, sir, and a little fire is no great harm—it is rather pleasant, don't you think?"

The stranger bowed acquiescence with a transient wintry smile, and looked gratefully on the fire.

"This place is a good deal admired, sir, and people come a good way to see it; you have been here perhaps before?"

"Many years ago."

Here was another pause.

THE HAUNTED BARONET

"Places change imperceptibly—in detail, at least—a good deal," said the Doctor, making an effort to keep up a conversation that plainly would not go on of itself; "and people too; population shifts—there's an old fellow, sir, they call *Death*."

"And an old fellow they call the *Doctor*, that helps him," threw in the Captain humorously, allowing his attention to get entangled in the conversation, and treating them to one of his tempestuous ha-ha-ha's.

"We are expecting the return of a gentleman who would be a very leading member of our little society down here," said the Doctor, not noticing the Captain's joke. "I mean Sir Bale Mardykes. Mardykes Hall is a pretty object from the water, sir, and a very fine old place."

The melancholy stranger bowed slightly, but rather in courtesy to the relator, it seemed, than that the Doctor's lore interested him much.

"And on the opposite side of the lake," continued Doctor Torvey, "there is a building that contrasts very well with it—the old house of the Feltrams—quite a ruin now, at the mouth of the glen—Cloostedd House, a very picturesque object."

"Exactly opposite," said the stranger dreamily, but whether in the tone of acquiescence or interrogatory, the Doctor could not be quite sure.

"That was one of our great families down here that has disappeared. It has dwindled down to nothing."

"Duce ace," remarked Mr. Hollar, who was attending to his game.

"While others have mounted more suddenly and amazingly still," observed gentle Mr. Peers, who was great upon county genealogies.

"Sizes!" thundered the Captain, thumping the table with an oath of disgust.

"And Snakes Island is a very pretty object; they say there used to be snakes there," said the Doctor, enlightening the visitor.

"Ah! that's a mistake," said the dejected guest, making his first original observation. "It should be spelt *Snaiks*. In the old papers it is called Sen-aiks Island from the seven oaks that grew in a clump there."

"Hey? that's very curious, egad! I daresay," said the Doctor, set right thus by the stranger, and eyeing him curiously.

"Very true, sir," observed Mr. Peers; "three of those oaks, though, two of them little better than stumps, are there still; and Clewson of Heckleston has an old document—"

Here, unhappily, the landlord entered the room in a fuss, and walking up to the stranger, said, "The chaise is at the door, Mr. Feltram, and the trunks up, sir."

Mr. Feltram rose quietly and took out his purse, and said,

"I suppose I had better pay at the bar?"

"As you like best, sir," said Richard Turnbull.

Mr. Feltram bowed all round to the gentlemen, who smiled, ducked or waved their hands; and the Doctor fussily followed him to the hall-door, and welcomed him back to Golden Friars—there was real kindness in this welcome—and proffered his broad brown hand, which Mr. Feltram took; and then he plunged into his chaise, and the door being shut, away he glided, chaise, horses, and driver, like shadows, by the margin of the moonlighted lake, towards Mardykes Hall.

And after a minute's stand upon the steps, looking along the shadowy track of the chaise, they returned to the glow of the room, in which a pleasant perfume of punch still prevailed; and beside Mr. Philip Feltram's deserted tea-things, the host of the George enlightened his guests by communicating freely the little he had picked up. The principal fact he had to tell was, that Sir Bale adhered strictly to his original plan, and was to arrive on the tenth. A few days would bring them to that, and the nine-days wonder run its course and lose its interest. But in the meantime, all Golden Friars was anxious to see what Sir Bale Mardykes was like.

IV. The Baronet Appears

As the candles burn blue and the air smells of brimstone at the approach of the Evil One, so, in the quiet and healthy air of Golden Friars, a depressing and agitating influence announced the coming of the long-absent Baronet.

From abroad, no good whatever had been at any time heard of him, and a great deal that was, in the ears of simple folk living in that unsophisticated part of the world, vaguely awful.

Stories that travel so far, however, lose something of their authority, as well as definiteness, on the way; there was always room for charity to suggest a mistake or exaggeration; and if good men turned up their hands and eyes after a new story, and ladies of experience, who knew mankind, held their heads high and looked grim and mysterious at mention of his name, nevertheless an interval of silence softened matters a little, and the sulphureous perfume dissipated itself in time.

Now that Sir Bale Mardykes had arrived at the Hall, there were hurried consultations held in many households. And though he was tried and sentenced by drum-head over some austere hearths, as a rule the law of gravitation prevailed, and the greater house drew the lesser about it, and county people within the visiting radius paid their respects at the Hall.

The Reverend Martin Bedel, the then vicar of Golden Friars, a stout short man, with a mulberry-coloured face and small gray eyes, and taciturn habits, called and entered the drawing-room at Mardykes Hall, with his fat and garrulous wife on his arm.

The drawing-room has a great projecting Tudor window looking out on the lake, with its magnificent back-ground of furrowed and purple mountains.

Sir Bale was not there, and Mrs. Bedel examined the pictures, and ornaments, and the books, making such remarks as she saw fit; and then she looked out of the window, and admired the prospect. She wished to stand well with the Baronet, and was in a mood to praise everything.

You may suppose she was curious to see him, having heard for years such strange tales of his doings.

She expected the hero of a brilliant and wicked romance; and listened for the step of the truant Lovelace who was to fulfil her idea of manly beauty and fascination.

She sustained a slight shock when he did appear.

Sir Bale Mardykes was, as she might easily have remembered, a middle-aged man—and he looked it. He was not even an imposing-looking man for his time of life: he was of about the middle height, slightly made, and dark featured. She had expected something of the gaiety and animation of Versailles, and an evident cultivation of the art of pleasing. What she did see was a remarkable gravity, not to say gloom, of countenance—the only feature of which that struck her being a pair of large dark-grey eyes, that were cold and earnest. His manners had the ease of perfect confidence; and his talk and air were those of a person who might have known how to please, if it were worth the trouble, but who did not care two-pence whether he pleased or not.

He made them each a bow, courtly enough, but there was no smile—not even an affectation of cordiality. Sir Bale, however, was chatty, and did not seem to care much what he said, or what people thought of him; and there was a suspicion of sarcasm in what he said that the rustic literality of good Mrs. Bedel did not always detect.

"I believe I have not a clergyman but *you*, sir, within any reasonable distance?"

"Golden Friars *is* the nearest," said Mrs. Bedel, answering, as was her pleasure on all practicable occasions, for her husband. "And southwards, the nearest is Wyllarden—and by a bird's flight that is thirteen miles and a half, and by the road more than nineteen—twenty, I may say, by the road. Ha, ha, ha! it is a long way to look for a clergyman."

"Twenty miles of road to carry you thirteen miles across, hey? The road-makers lead you a pretty dance here; those gentlemen know how to make money, and like to show people the scenery from a variety of points. No one likes a straight road but the man who pays for it, or who, when he travels, is brute enough to wish to get to his journey's end."

"That is so true, Sir Bale; one never cares if one is not in a hurry. That's what Martin thinks—don't we, Martin?—And then, you know, coming home is the time you *are* in a hurry—when you are thinking of your cup of tea and the children; and *then*, you know, you have the fall of the ground all in your favour."

"It's well to have anything in your favour in this place. And so there are children?"

"A good many," said Mrs. Bedel, with a proud and mysterious smile, and a nod; "you wouldn't guess how many."

"Not I; I only wonder you did not bring them all."

"That's very good-natured of you, Sir Bale, but all could not come at *one* bout; there are—tell him, Martin—ha, ha, ha! there are eleven."

"It must be very cheerful down at the vicarage," said Sir Bale graciously; and turning to the vicar he added, "But how unequally blessings are divided! You have eleven, and I not one—that I'm aware of."

"And then, in that direction straight before you, you have the lake, and then the fells; and five miles from the foot of the mountain at the other side, before you reach Fottrell—and that is twenty-five miles by the road—"

"Dear me! how far apart they are set! My gardener told me this morning that asparagus grows very thinly in this part of the world. How thinly clergymen grow also down here—in one sense," he added politely, for the vicar was stout.

"We were looking out of the window—we amused ourselves that way before you came—and your view is certainly the very best anywhere round this side; your view of the lake and the fells—what mountains they are, Sir Bale!"

"'Pon my soul, they are! I wish I could blow them asunder with a charge of duck-shot, and I shouldn't be stifled by them long. But I suppose, as we can't get rid of them, the next best thing is to admire them. We are pretty well married to them, and there is no use in quarrelling."

"I know you don't think so, Sir Bale, ha, ha, ha! You wouldn't take a good deal and spoil Mardykes Hall."

"You can't get a mouthful or air, or see the sun of a morning, for those frightful mountains," he said with a peevish frown at them.

"Well, the lake at all events—that you *must* admire, Sir Bale?"

"No ma'am, I don't admire the lake. I'd drain the lake if I could—I hate the lake. There's nothing so gloomy as a lake pent up among barren mountains. I can't conceive what possessed my people to build our house down here, at the edge of a lake; unless it was the fish, and precious fish it is—pike! I don't know how people digest it—*I* can't. I'd as soon think of eating a watchman's pike."

"I thought that having travelled so much abroad, you would have acquired a great liking for that kind of scenery, Sir Bale; there is a great deal of it on the Continent, ain't there?" said Mrs. Bedel. "And the boating."

"Boating, my dear Mrs. Bedel, is the dullest of all things; don't you think so? Because a boat looks very pretty from the shore, we fancy the shore must look very pretty from a boat; and when we try it, we find we have only got down into a pit and can see nothing rightly. For my part I hate boating, and I hate the water; and I'd rather have my house, like Haworth, at the edge of a moss, with good wholesome peat to look at, and an open horizon—savage and stupid and bleak as all that is—than be suffocated among impassable mountains, or upset in a black lake and drowned like a kitten. O, there's luncheon in the next room; won't you take some?"

V. Mrs. Julaper's Room

Sir Bale Mardykes being now established in his ancestral house, people had time to form conclusions respecting him. It must be allowed he was not popular. There was, perhaps, in his conduct something of the caprice of contempt. At all events his temper and conduct were uncertain, and his moods sometimes violent and insulting.

With respect to but one person was his conduct uniform, and that was Philip Feltram. He was a sort of aide-de-camp near Sir Bale's person, and chargeable with all the commissions and offices which could not be suitably intrusted to a mere servant. But in many respects he was treated worse than any servant of the Baronet's. Sir Bale swore at him, and cursed him; laid the blame of everything that went wrong in house, stable, or field upon his shoulders; railed at him, and used him, as people said, worse than a dog.

Why did Feltram endure this contumelious life? What could he do but endure it? was the answer. What was the power that induced strong soldiers to put off their jackets and shirts, and present their hands to be tied up, and tortured for hours, it might be, under the scourge, with an air of ready volition? The moral coercion of despair; the result of an unconscious calculation of chances which satisfies them that it is ultimately better to do all that, bad as it is, than try the alternative. These unconscious calculations are going on every day with each of us, and the results embody themselves in our lives; and no one knows that there has been a process and a balance struck, and that what they see, and very likely blame, is by the fiat of an invisible but quite irresistible power.

A man of spirit would rather break stones on the highway than eat that bitter bread, was the burden of every man's song on Feltram's bondage. But he was not so sure that even the stone-breaker's employment was open to him, or that he could break stones well enough to retain it on a fair trial. And he had other ideas of providing for himself, and a different alternative in his mind.

Good-natured Mrs. Julaper, the old housekeeper at Mardykes Hall, was kind to Feltram, as to all others who lay in her way and were in affliction.

She was one of those good women whom Nature provides to receive the burden of other people's secrets, as the reeds did long ago, only that no chance wind could steal them away, and send them singing into strange ears.

You may still see her snuggery in Mardykes Hall, though the housekeeper's room is now in a different part of the house.

Mrs. Julaper's room was in the oldest quarter of that old house. It was wainscoted, in black panels, up to the ceiling, which was stuccoed over in the fanciful diagrams of James the First's time. Several dingy portraits, banished from time to time from other statelier rooms, found a temporary abode in this quiet spot, where they had come finally to settle and drop out of remembrance. There is a lady in white satin and a ruff; a gentleman whose legs have faded out of view, with a peaked beard, and a hawk on his wrist. There is another in a black periwig lost in the dark background, and with a steel cuirass, the gleam of which out of the darkness strikes the eye, and a scarf is dimly discoverable across it. This is that foolish Sir Guy Mardykes, who crossed the Border and joined Dundee, and was shot through the temple at Killiecrankie and whom more prudent and whiggish scions of the Mardykes family removed forthwith from his place in the Hall, and found a retirement here, from which he has not since emerged.

At the far end of this snug room is a second door, on opening which you find yourself looking down upon the great kitchen, with a little balcony before you, from which the housekeeper used to issue her commands to the cook, and exercise a sovereign supervision.

There is a shelf on which Mrs Julaper had her Bible, her *Whole Duty of Man*, and her *Pilgrim's Progress*; and, in a file beside them, her books of housewifery, and among them volumes of MS. recipes, cookery-books, and some too on surgery and medicine, as practised by the Ladies Bountiful of the Elizabethan age, for which an antiquarian would nowadays give an eye or a hand.

Gentle half-foolish Philip Feltram would tell the story of his wrongs, and weep and wish he was dead; and kind Mrs. Julaper, who remembered him a child, would comfort him with cold pie and cherry-brandy, or a cup of coffee, or some little dainty.

"O, ma'am, I'm tired of my life. What's the good of living, if a poor devil is never let alone, and called worse names than a dog? Would not it be better, Mrs. Julaper, to be dead? Wouldn't it be better, ma'am? I think so; I think it night and day. I'm always thinking the same thing. I don't care, I'll just tell him what I think, and have it off my mind. I'll tell him I can't live and bear it longer."

"There now, don't you be frettin'; but just sip this, and remember you're not to judge a friend by a wry word. He does not mean it, not he. They all had a rough side to their tongue now and again; but no one minded that. I don't, nor you needn't, no more than other folk; for the tongue, be it never so bitin', it can't draw blood, mind ye, and hard words break no bones; and I'll make a cup o' tea—ye like a cup o' tea—and we'll take a cup together, and ye'll chirp up a bit, and see how pleasant and ruddy the sun shines on the lake this evening."

She was patting him gently on the shoulder, as she stood slim and stiff in her dark silk by his chair, and her rosy little face smiled down on him. She was, for an old woman, wonderfully pretty still. What a delicate skin she must have had! The wrinkles were etched upon it with so fine a needle, you scarcely could see them a little way off; and as she smiled her cheeks looked fresh and smooth as two ruddy little apples.

"Look out, I say," and she nodded towards the window, deep set in the thick wall. "See how bright and soft everything looks in that pleasant light; *that's* better, child, than the finest picture man's hand ever painted yet, and God gives it us for nothing; and how pretty Snakes Island glows up in that light!"

The dejected man, hardly raising his head, followed with his eyes the glance of the old woman, and looked mournfully through the window.

"That island troubles me, Mrs. Julaper."

"Everything troubles you, my poor goose-cap. I'll pull your lug for ye, child, if ye be so dowly"; and with a mimic pluck the good-natured old housekeeper pinched his ear and laughed.

"I'll go to the still-room now, where the water's boiling, and I'll make a cup of tea; and if I find ye so dow when I come back, I'll throw it all out o' the window, mind."

It was indeed a beautiful picture that Feltram saw in its deep frame of old masonry. The near part of the lake was flushed all over with the low western light; the more distant waters lay dark in the shadow of the mountains; and against this shadow of purple the rocks on Snakes Island, illuminated by the setting sun, started into sharp clear yellow.

But this beautiful view had no charm—at least, none powerful enough to master the latent horror associated with its prettiest feature—for the weak and dismal man who was looking at it; and being now alone, he rose and leant on the window, and looked out, and then with a kind of shudder clutching his hands together, and walking distractedly about the room.

Without his perceiving, while his back was turned, the housekeeper came back; and seeing him walking in this distracted way, she thought to herself, as he leant again upon the window:

"Well, it *is* a burning shame to worrit any poor soul into that state. Sir Bale was always down on someone or something, man or beast; there always was something he hated, and could never let alone. It was not pretty; it was his nature. Happen, poor fellow, he could not help it; but so it was."

A maid came in and set the tea-things down; and Mrs. Julaper drew her sad guest over by the arm, and made him sit down, and she said: "What has a man to do, frettin' in that way? By Jen, I'm ashamed o' ye, Master Philip! Ye like three lumps o' sugar, I think, and—look cheerful, ye must!—a good deal o' cream?"

"You're so kind, Mrs. Julaper, you're so cheery. I feel quite comfortable after awhile when I'm with you; I feel quite happy," and he began to cry.

She understood him very well by this time and took no notice, but went on chatting gaily, and made his tea as he liked it; and he dried his tears hastily, thinking she had not observed.

So the clouds began to clear. This innocent fellow liked nothing better than a cup of tea and a chat with gentle and cheery old Mrs. Julaper, and a talk in which the shadowy old times which he remembered as a child emerged into sunlight and lived again.

When he began to feel better, drawn into the kindly old times by the tinkle of that harmless old woman's tongue, he said:

"I sometimes think I would not so much mind—I should not care so much—if my spirits were not so depressed, and I so agitated. I suppose I am not quite well."

"Well, tell me what's wrong, child, and it's odd but I have a recipe on the shelf there that will do you good."

"It is not a matter of that sort I mean; though I'd rather have you than any doctor, if I needed medicine, to prescribe for me."

Mrs. Julaper smiled in spite of herself, well pleased; for her skill in pharmacy was a point on which the good lady prided herself, and was open to flattery, which, without intending it, the simple fellow administered.

"No, I'm well enough; I can't say I ever was better. It is only, ma'am, that I have such dreams—you have no idea."

"There are dreams and dreams, my dear: there's some signifies no more than the babble of the lake down there on the pebbles, and there's others that has a meaning; there's dreams that is but vanity, and there's dreams that is good, and dreams that is bad. Lady Mardykes—heavens be her bed this day! that's his grandmother I mean—was very sharp for reading dreams. Take another cup of tea. Dear me! what a noise the crows keep aboon our heads, going home! and how high they wing it!—that's a sure sign of fine weather. An' what do you dream about? Tell me your dream, and I may show you it's a good one, after all. For many a dream is ugly to see and ugly to tell, and a good dream, with a happy meaning, for all that."

VI. The Intruder

"Well, Mrs. Julaper, dreams I've dreamed like other people, old and young; but this, ma'am, has taken a fast hold of me," said Mr. Feltram dejectedly, leaning back in his chair and looking down with his hands in his pockets. "I think, Mrs. Julaper, it is getting into me. I think it's like possession."

"Possession, child! what do you mean?"

"I think there is something trying to influence me. Perhaps it is the way fellows go mad; but it won't let me alone. I've seen it three times, think of that!"

"Well, dear, and what *have* ye seen?" she asked, with an uneasy cheerfulness, smiling, with eyes fixed steadily upon him; for the idea of a madman—even gentle Philip in that state—was not quieting.

"Do you remember the picture, full-length, that had no frame—the lady in the white-satin saque—she was beautiful, *funeste*," he added, talking more to himself; and then more distinctly to Mrs. Julaper again—"in the white-satin saque; and with the little mob cap and blue ribbons to it, and a bouquet in her fingers; that was—that—you know who she was?"

"That was your great-grandmother, my dear," said Mrs. Julaper, lowering her eyes. "It was a dreadful pity it was spoiled. The boys in the pantry had it for a year there on the table for a tray, to wash the glasses on and the like. It was a shame; that was the prettiest picture in the house, with the gentlest, rosiest face."

"It ain't so gentle or rosy now, I can tell you," said Philip. "As fixed as marble; with thin lips, and a curve at the nostril. Do you remember the woman that was found dead in the clough, when I was a boy, that the gipsies murdered, it was thought,—a cruel-looking woman?"

"Agoy! Master Philip, dear! ye would not name that terrible-looking creature with the pretty, fresh, kindly face!"

"Faces change, you see; no matter what she's like; it's her talk that frightens me. She wants to make use of me; and, you see, it is like getting a share in my mind, and a voice in my thoughts, and a command over me gradually; and it is just one idea, as straight as a line of light across the lake—see what she's come to. O Lord, help me!"

"Well, now, don't you be talkin' like that. It is just a little bit dowly and troubled, because the master says a wry word now and then; and so ye let your spirits go down, don't ye see, and all sorts o' fancies comes into your head."

"There's no fancy in my head," he said with a quick look of suspicion; "only you asked me what I dreamed. I don't care if all the world knew. I dreamed I went down a flight of steps under the lake, and got a message. There are no steps near Snakes Island, we all know that," and he laughed chillily. "I'm out of spirits, as you say; and—and—O dear! I wish—Mrs. Julaper—I wish I was in my coffin, and quiet."

"Now that's very wrong of you, Master Philip; you should think of all the blessings you have, and not be makin' mountains o' molehills; and those little bits o' temper Sir Bale shows, why, no one minds 'em—that is, to take 'em to heart like you do, don't ye see?"

"I daresay; I suppose, Mrs. Julaper, you are right. I'm unreasonable often, I know," said gentle Philip Feltram. "I daresay I make too much of it; I'll try. I'm his secretary, and I know I'm not so bright as he is, and it is natural he should sometimes be a little impatient; I ought to be more reasonable, I'm sure. It is all that thing that has been disturbing me—I mean fretting, and, I think, I'm not quite well; and—and letting myself think too much of vexations. It's my own fault, I'm sure, Mrs. Julaper; and I know I'm to blame."

"That's quite right, that's spoken like a wise lad; only I don't say you're to blame, nor no one; for folk can't help frettin' sometimes, no more than they can help a headache—none but a mafflin would say that—and I'll not deny but he has dowly ways when the fit's on him, and he frumps us all round, if such be his humour. But who is there hasn't his faults? We must bear and forbear, and take what we get and be cheerful. So chirp up, my lad; Philip, didn't I often ring the a'd rhyme in your ear long ago?

> "Be always as merry as ever you can,
> For no one delights in a sorrowful man.

"So don't ye be gettin' up off your chair like that, and tramping about the room wi' your hands in your pockets, looking out o' this window, and staring out o' that, and sighing and crying, and looking so black-ox-trodden, 'twould break a body's heart to see you. Ye must be cheery; and happen you're hungry, and don't know it. I'll tell the cook to grill a hot bit for ye."

"But I'm not hungry, Mrs. Julaper. How kind you are! dear me, Mrs. Julaper, I'm not worthy of it; I don't deserve half your kindness. I'd have been heartbroken long ago, but for you."

"And I'll make a sup of something hot for you; you'll take a rummer-glass of punch—you must."

"But I like the tea better; I do, indeed, Mrs. Julaper."

"Tea is no drink for a man when his heart's down. It should be something with a leg in it, lad; something hot that will warm your courage for ye, and set your blood a-dancing, and make ye talk brave and merry; and will you have a bit of a broil first? No? Well then, you'll have a drop o' punch?—ye sha'n't say no."

And so, all resistance overpowered, the consolation of Philip Feltram proceeded.

A gentler spirit than poor Feltram, a more good-natured soul than the old housekeeper, were nowhere among the children of earth.

Philip Feltram, who was reserved enough elsewhere, used to come into her room and cry, and take her by both hands piteously, standing before her and looking down in her face, while tears ran deviously down his cheeks.

"Did you ever know such a case? was there ever a fellow like *me*? did you ever *know* such a thing? You know what I am, Mrs. Julaper, and who I am. They call me Feltram; but Sir Bale knows as well as I that my true name is not that. I'm Philip Mardykes; and another fellow would make a row about it, and claim his name and his rights, as she is always croaking in my ear I ought. But you know that is not reasonable. My grandmother was married; she was the true Lady Mardykes; *think* what it was to see a woman like that turned out of doors, and her children robbed of their name. O, ma'am, you *can't* think it; unless you were me, you couldn't—you couldn't—you couldn't!"

"Come, come, Master Philip, don't you be taking on so; and ye mustn't be talking like that, d'ye mind? You know he wouldn't stand that; and it's an old story now, and there's naught can be proved concerning it; and what I think is this—I wouldn't wonder the poor lady was beguiled. But anyhow she surely thought she was his lawful wife; and though the law may hev found a flaw somewhere—and I take it 'twas so—yet sure I am she was an honourable lady. But where's the use of stirring that old sorrow? or how can ye prove aught? and the dead hold their peace, you know; dead mice, they say, feels no cold; and dead folks are past fooling. So don't you talk like that; for stone walls have ears, and ye might say that ye couldn't *un*say; and death's day is doom's day. So leave all in the keeping of God; and, above all, never lift hand when ye can't strike."

"Lift my hand! O, Mrs. Julaper, you couldn't think that; you little know me; I did not mean that; I never dreamed of hurting Sir Bale. Good heavens! Mrs. Julaper, you couldn't think that! It all comes of my poor impatient temper, and complaining as I do, and my misery; but O, Mrs. Julaper, you could not think I ever meant to trouble him by law, or any other annoyance! I'd like to see a stain removed from my family, and my name restored; but to touch his property, O, no!—O, no! that never entered my mind, by heaven! that never entered my mind, Mrs. Julaper. I'm not cruel; I'm not rapacious; I don't care for money; don't you know that, Mrs. Julaper? O, surely you won't think me capable of attacking the man whose bread I have eaten so long! I never dreamed of it; I should hate myself. Tell me you don't believe it; O, Mrs. Julaper, say you don't!"

And the gentle feeble creature burst into tears and good Mrs. Julaper comforted him with kind words; and he said,

"Thank you, ma'am; thank you. God knows I would not hurt Bale, nor give him one uneasy hour. It is only this: that I'm—I'm so miserable; and I'm only casting in my mind where to turn to, and what to do. So little a thing would be enough, and then I shall leave Mardykes. I'll go; not in any anger, Mrs. Julaper—don't think that; but I can't stay, I must be gone."

"Well, now, there's nothing yet, Master Philip, to fret you like that. You should not be talking so wild-like. Master Bale has his sharp word and his short temper now and again; but I'm sure he likes you. If he didn't, he'd a-said so to me long ago. I'm sure he likes you well."

"Hollo! I say, who's there? Where the devil's Mr. Feltram?" called the voice of the baronet, at a fierce pitch, along the passage.

"La! Mr. Feltram, it's him! Ye'd better run to him," whispered Mrs. Julaper.

"D—n me! does nobody hear? Mrs. Julaper! Hollo! ho! house, there! ho! D—n me, will nobody answer?"

And Sir Bale began to slap the wainscot fast and furiously with his walking-cane with a clatter like a harlequin's lath in a pantomime.

Mrs. Julaper, a little paler than usual, opened her door, and stood with the handle in her hand, making a little curtsey, enframed in the door-case; and Sir Bale, being in a fume, when he saw her, ceased whacking the panels of the corridor, and stamped on the floor, crying,

"Upon my soul, ma'am, I'm glad to see you! Perhaps you can tell me where Feltram is?"

"He is in my room, Sir Bale. Shall I tell him you want him, please?"

"Never mind; thanks," said the Baronet. "I've a tongue in my head"; marching down the passage to the housekeeper's room, with his cane clutched hard, glaring savagely, and with his teeth fast set, like a fellow advancing to beat a vicious horse that has chafed his temper.

VII. The Bank Note

Sir Bale brushed by the housekeeper as he strode into her sanctuary, and there found Philip Feltram awaiting him dejectedly, but with no signs of agitation.

If one were to judge by the appearance the master of Mardykes presented, very grave surmises as to impending violence would have suggested themselves; but though he clutched his cane so hard that it quivered in his grasp, he had no notion of committing the outrage of a blow. The Baronet was unusually angry notwithstanding, and stopping short about three steps away, addressed Feltram with a pale face and gleaming eyes. It was quite plain that there was something very exciting upon his mind.

"I've been looking for you, Mr. Feltram; I want a word or two, if you have done your—your—whatever it is." He whisked the point of his stick towards the modest tea-tray. "I should like five minutes in the library."

The Baronet was all this time eyeing Feltram with a hard suspicious gaze, as if he expected to read in his face the shrinkings and trepidations of guilt; and then turning suddenly on his heel he led the way to his library—a good long march, with a good many turnings. He walked very fast, and was not long in getting there. And as Sir Bale reached the hearth, on which was smouldering a great log of wood, and turned about suddenly, facing the door, Philip Feltram entered.

The Baronet looked oddly and stern—so oddly, it seemed to Feltram, that he could not take his eyes off him, and returned his grim and somewhat embarrassed gaze with a stare of alarm and speculation.

And so doing, his step was shortened, and grew slow and slower, and came quite to a stop before he had got far from the door—a wide stretch of that wide floor still intervening between him and Sir Bale, who stood upon the hearthrug, with his heels together and his back to the fire, cane in hand, like a drill-sergeant, facing him.

"Shut that door, please; that will do; come nearer now. I don't want to bawl what I have to say. Now listen."

The Baronet cleared his voice and paused, with his eyes upon Feltram.

"It is only two or three days ago," said he, "that you said you wished you had a hundred pounds. Am I right?"

"Yes; I think so."

"*Think?* you know it, sir, devilish well. You said that you wished to get away. I have nothing particular to say against that, more especially now. Do you understand what I say?"

"Understand, Sir Bale? I do, sir—quite."

"I daresay *quite*," he repeated with an angry sneer. "Here, sir, is an odd coincidence: you want a hundred pounds, and you can't earn it, and you can't borrow it—there's another way, it seems—but I have got it—a Bank-of-England note of £100—locked up in that desk"; and he poked the end of his cane against the brass lock of it viciously. "There it is, and there are the papers you work at; and there are two keys—I've got one and you have the other—and devil another key in or out of the house has any one living. Well, do you begin to see? Don't mind. I don't want any d——d lying about it."

Feltram was indeed beginning to see that he was suspected of something very bad, but exactly what, he was not yet sure; and being a man of that unhappy temperament which shrinks from suspicion, as others do from detection, he looked very much put out indeed.

"Ha, ha! I think we do begin to see," said Sir Bale savagely. "It's a bore, I know, troubling a fellow with a story that he knows before; but I'll make mine short. When I take my key, intending to send the note to pay the crown and quit-rents that you know—you—you—no matter—you know well enough must be paid, I open it so—and so—and look *there*, where I left it, for my note; and the note's gone—you understand, the note's *gone*!"

Here was a pause, during which, under the Baronet's hard insulting eye, poor Feltram winced, and cleared his voice, and essayed to speak, but said nothing.

"It's gone, and we know where. Now, Mr. Feltram, *I* did not steal that note, and no one but you and I have access to this desk. You wish to go away, and I have no objection to that—but d——n me if you take away that note with you; and you may as well produce it now and here, as hereafter in a worse place."

"O, my good heaven!" exclaimed poor Feltram at last. "I'm very ill."

"So you are, of course. It takes a stiff emetic to get all that money off a fellow's stomach; and it's like parting with a tooth to give up a bank-note. Of course you're ill, but that's no sign of innocence, and I'm no fool. You had better give the thing up quietly."

"May my Maker strike me——"

"So He will, you d——d rascal, if there's justice in heaven, unless you produce the money. I don't want to hang you. I'm willing to let you off if you'll let me, but I'm cursed if I let my note off along with you; and unless you give it up forthwith, I'll get a warrant and have you searched, pockets, bag, and baggage."

"Lord! am I awake?" exclaimed Philip Feltram.

"Wide awake, and so am I," replied Sir Bale. "You don't happen to have got it about you?"

"God forbid, sir! O, Sir—O, Sir Bale—why, Bale, *Bale*, it's impossible! You *can't* believe it. When did I ever wrong you? You know me since I was not higher than the table, and—and—"

He burst into tears.

"Stop your snivelling, sir, and give up the note. You know devilish well I can't spare it; and I won't spare you if you put me to it. I've said my say."

Sir Bale signed towards the door; and like a somnambulist, with dilated gaze and pale as death, Philip Feltram, at his wit's end, went out of the room. It was not till he had again reached the housekeeper's door that he recollected in what direction he was going. His shut hand was pressed with all his force to his heart, and the first breath he was conscious of was a deep wild sob or two that quivered from his heart as he looked from the lobby-window upon a landscape which he did not see.

All he had ever suffered before was mild in comparison with this dire paroxysm. Now, for the first time, was he made acquainted with his real capacity for pain, and how near he might be to madness and yet retain intellect enough to weigh every scruple, and calculate every chance and consequence, in his torture.

Sir Bale, in the meantime, had walked out a little more excited than he would have allowed. He was still convinced that Feltram had stolen the note, but not quite so certain as he had been. There were things in his manner that confirmed, and others that perplexed, Sir Bale.

The Baronet stood upon the margin of the lake, almost under the evening shadow of the house, looking towards Snakes Island. There were two things about Mardykes he specially disliked.

One was Philip Feltram, who, right or wrong, he fancied knew more than was pleasant of his past life.

The other was the lake. It was a beautiful piece of water, his eye, educated at least in the excellences of landscape-painting, acknowledged. But although he could pull a good oar, and liked other lakes, to this particular sheet of water there lurked within him an insurmountable antipathy. It was engendered by a variety of associations.

There is a faculty in man that will acknowledge the unseen. He may scout and scare religion from him; but if he does, superstition perches near. His boding was made-up of omens, dreams, and such stuff as he most affected to despise, and there fluttered at his heart a presentiment and disgust.

His foot was on the gunwale of the boat, that was chained to its ring at the margin; but he would not have crossed that water in it for any reason that man could urge.

What was the mischief that sooner or later was to befall him from that lake, he could not define; but that some fatal danger lurked there, was the one idea concerning it that had possession of his fancy.

He was now looking along its still waters, towards the copse and rocks of Snakes Island, thinking of Philip Feltram; and the yellow level sunbeams touched his dark features, that bore a saturnine resemblance to those of Charles II., and marked sharply their firm grim lines, and left his deep-set eyes in shadow.

Who has the happy gift to seize the present, as a child does, and live in it? Who is not often looking far off for his happiness, as Sidney Smith says, like a man looking for his hat when it is upon his head? Sir Bale was brooding over his double hatred, of Feltram and of the lake. It would have been better had he struck down the raven that croaked upon his shoulder, and listened to the harmless birds that were whistling all round among the branches in the golden sunset.

VIII. Feltram's Plan

This horror of the beautiful lake, which other people thought so lovely, was, in that mind which affected to scoff at the unseen, a distinct creation of downright superstition.

The nursery tales which had scared him in his childhood were founded on the tragedy of Snakes Island, and haunted him with an unavowed persistence still. Strange dreams untold had visited him, and a German conjuror, who had made some strangely successful vaticinations, had told him that his worst enemy would come up to him from a lake. He had heard very nearly the same thing from a fortune-teller in France; and once at Lucerne, when he was waiting alone in his room for the hour at which he had appointed to go upon the lake, all being quiet, there came to the window, which was open, a sunburnt, lean, wicked face. Its ragged owner leaned his arm on the window-frame, and with his head in the room, said in his patois, "Ho! waiting are you? You'll have enough of the lake one day. Don't you mind watching; they'll send when you're wanted"; and twisting his yellow face into a malicious distortion, he went on.

This thing had occurred so suddenly, and chimed-in so oddly with his thoughts, which were at that moment at distant Mardykes and the haunted lake, that it disconcerted him. He laughed, he looked out of the window. He would have given that fellow money to tell him why he said that. But there was no good in looking for the scamp; he was gone.

A memory not preoccupied with that lake and its omens, and a presentiment about himself, would not have noted such things. But *his* mind they touched indelibly; and he was ashamed of his childish slavery, but could not help it.

The foundation of all this had been laid in the nursery, in the winter's tales told by its fireside, and which seized upon his fancy and his fears with a strange congeniality.

There is a large bedroom at Mardykes Hall, which tradition assigns to the lady who had perished tragically in the lake. Mrs. Julaper was sure of it; for her aunt, who died a very old woman twenty years before, remembered the time of the lady's death, and when she grew to woman's estate had opportunity in abundance; for the old people who surrounded her could remember forty years farther back, and tell everything connected with the old house in beautiful Miss Feltram's time.

This large old-fashioned room, commanding a view of Snakes Island, the fells, and the lake—somewhat vast and gloomy, and furnished in a stately old fashion—was said to be haunted, especially when the wind blew from the direction of Golden Friars, the point from which it blew on the night of her death in the lake; or when the sky was overcast, and thunder rolled among the lofty fells, and lightning gleamed on the wide sheet of water.

It was on a night like this that a lady visitor, who long after that event occupied, in entire ignorance of its supernatural character, that large room; and being herself a lady of a picturesque turn, and loving the grander melodrama of Nature, bid her maid leave the shutters open, and watched the splendid effects from her bed, until, the storm being still distant, she fell asleep.

It was travelling slowly across the lake, and it was the deep-mouthed clangour of its near approach that startled her, at dead of night, from her slumber, to witness the same phenomena in the tremendous loudness and brilliancy of their near approach.

At this magnificent spectacle she was looking with the awful ecstasy of an observer in whom the sense of danger is subordinated to that of the sublime, when she saw suddenly at the window a woman, whose long hair and dress seemed drenched with water. She was gazing in with a look of terror, and was shaking the sash of the window with vehemence. Having stood there for a few seconds, and before the lady, who beheld all this from her bed, could make up her mind what to do, the storm-beaten figure, wringing her hands, seemed to throw herself backward, and was gone.

Possessed with the idea that she had seen some poor woman overtaken in the storm, who, failing to procure admission there, had gone round to some of the many doors of the mansion, and obtained an entry there, she again fell asleep.

It was not till the morning, when she went to her window to look out upon the now tranquil scene, that she discovered what, being a stranger to the house, she had quite forgotten, that this room was at a great height—some thirty feet—from the ground.

Another story was that of good old Mr. Randal Rymer, who was often a visitor at the house in the late Lady Mardykes' day. In his youth he had been a campaigner; and now that he was a preacher he maintained his hardy habits, and always slept, summer and winter, with a bit of his window up. Being in that room in his bed, and after a short sleep lying awake, the moon shining softly through the window, there passed by that aperture into the room a figure dressed, it seemed to him, in grey that was nearly white. It passed straight to the hearth, where was an expiring wood fire; and cowering over it with outstretched hands, it appeared to be gathering what little heat was to be had. Mr. Rymer, amazed and awestruck, made a movement in his bed; and the figure looked round, with large eyes that in the moonlight looked like melting snow, and stretching its long arms up the chimney, they and the figure itself seemed to blend with the smoke, and so pass up and away.

Sir Bale, I have said, did not like Feltram. His father, Sir William, had left a letter creating a trust, it was said, in favour of Philip Feltram. The document had been found with the will, addressed to Sir Bale in the form of a letter.

"That is mine," said the Baronet, when it dropped out of the will; and he slipped it into his pocket, and no one ever saw it after.

But Mr. Charles Twyne, the attorney of Golden Friars, whenever he got drunk, which was pretty often, used to tell his friends with a grave wink that he knew a thing or two about that letter. It gave Philip Feltram two hundred a-year, charged on Harfax. It was only a direction. It made Sir Bale a trustee, however; and having made away with the "letter," the Baronet had been robbing Philip Feltram ever since.

Old Twyne was cautious, even in his cups, in his choice of an audience, and was a little enigmatical in his revelations. For he was afraid of Sir Bale, though he hated him for employing a lawyer who lived seven miles away, and was a rival. So people were not quite sure whether Mr. Twyne was telling lies or truth, and the principal fact that corroborated his story was Sir Bale's manifest hatred of his secretary. In fact, Sir Bale's retaining him in his house, detesting him as he seemed to do, was not easily to be accounted for, except on the principle of a tacit compromise—a miserable compensation for having robbed him of his rights.

The battle about the bank-note proceeded. Sir Bale certainly had doubts, and vacillated; for moral evidence made powerfully in favour of poor Feltram, though the evidence of circumstance made as powerfully against him. But Sir Bale admitted suspicion easily, and in weighing probabilities would count a virtue very lightly against temptation and opportunity; and whatever his doubts might sometimes be, he resisted and quenched them, and never let that ungrateful scoundrel Philip Feltram so much as suspect their existence.

For two days Sir Bale had not spoken to Feltram. He passed by on stair and passage, carrying his head high, and with a thundrous countenance, rolling conclusions and revenges in his soul.

Poor Feltram all this time existed in one long agony. He would have left Mardykes, were it not that he looked vaguely to some just power—to chance itself—against this hideous imputation. To go with this indictment ringing in his ears, would amount to a confession and flight.

Mrs. Julaper consoled him with might and main. She was a sympathetic and trusting spirit, and knew poor Philip Feltram, in her simplicity, better than the shrewdest profligate on earth could have known him. She cried with him in his misery. She was fired with indignation by these suspicions, and still more at what followed.

Sir Bale showed no signs of relenting. It might have been that he was rather glad of so unexceptionable an opportunity of getting rid of Feltram, who, people thought, knew something which it galled the Baronet's pride that he should know.

The Baronet had another shorter and sterner interview with Feltram in his study. The result was, that unless he restored the missing note before ten o'clock next morning, he should leave Mardykes.

To leave Mardykes was no more than Philip Feltram, feeble as he was of will, had already resolved. But what was to become of him? He did not very much care, if he could find any calling, however humble, that would just give him bread.

There was an old fellow and his wife (an ancient dame), who lived at the other side of the lake, on the old territories of the Feltrams, and who, from some tradition of loyalty, perhaps, were fond of poor Philip Feltram. They lived somewhat high up on the fells—about as high as trees would grow—and those which were clumped about their rude dwelling were nearly the last you passed in your ascent of the mountain. These people had a multitude of sheep and goats, and lived in their airy solitude a pastoral and simple life, and were childless. Philip Feltram was hardy and active, having passed his early days among that arduous scenery. Cold and rain did not trouble him; and these people being wealthy in their way, and loving him, would be glad to find him employment of that desultory pastoral kind which would best suit him.

This vague idea was the only thing resembling a plan in his mind.

When Philip Feltram came to Mrs. Julaper's room, and told her that he had made up his mind to leave the house forthwith—to cross the lake to the Cloostedd side in Tom Marlin's boat, and then to make his way up the hill alone to Trebeck's lonely farmstead, Mrs. Julaper was overwhelmed.

"Ye'll do no such thing to-night, anyhow. You're not to go like that. Ye'll come into the small room here, where he can't follow; and we'll sit down and talk it over a bit, and ye'll find 'twill all come straight; and this will be no night, anyhow, for such a march. Why, man, 'twould take an hour and more to cross the lake, and then a long uphill walk before ye could reach Trebeck's place; and if the night should fall while you were still on the mountain, ye might lose your life among the rocks. It can't be 'tis come to that yet; and the call was in the air, I'm told, all yesterday, and distant thunder to-day, travelling this way over Blarwyn Fells; and 'twill be a night no one will be out, much less on the mountain side."

IX. The Crazy Parson

Mrs. Julaper had grown weather-wise, living for so long among this noble and solitary scenery, where people must observe Nature or else nothing—where signs of coming storm or change are almost local, and record themselves on particular cliffs and mountain-peaks, or in the mists, or in mirrored tints of the familiar lake, and are easily learned or remembered. At all events, her presage proved too true.

The sun had set an hour and more. It was dark; and an awful thunder-storm, whose march, like the distant reverberations of an invading army, had been faintly heard beyond the barriers of Blarwyn Fells throughout the afternoon, was near them now, and had burst in deep-mouthed battle among the ravines at the other side, and over the broad lake, that glared like a sheet of burnished steel under its flashes of dazzling blue. Wild and fitful blasts sweeping down the hollows and cloughs of the fells of Golden Friars agitated the lake, and bent the trees low, and whirled away their sere leaves in melancholy drift in their tremendous gusts. And from the window, looking on a scene enveloped in more than the darkness of the night, you saw in the pulsations of the lightning, before "the speedy gleams the darkness swallowed," the tossing trees and the flying foam and eddies on the lake.

In the midst of the hurlyburly, a loud and long knocking came at the hall-door of Mardykes. How long it had lasted before a chance lull made it audible I do not know.

There was nothing picturesquely poor, any more than there were evidences of wealth, anywhere in Sir Bale Mardykes' household. He had no lack of servants, but they were of an inexpensive and homely sort; and the hall-door being opened by the son of an old tenant on the estate—the tempest beating on the other side of the house, and comparative shelter under the gables at the front—he saw standing before him, in the agitated air, a thin old man, who muttering, it might be, a benediction, stepped into the hall, and displayed long silver tresses, just as the storm had blown them, ascetic and eager features, and a pair of large light eyes that wandered wildly. He was dressed in threadbare black; a pair of long leather gaiters, buckled high above his knee, protecting his thin shanks through moss and pool; and the singularity of his appearance was heightened by a wide-leafed felt hat, over which he had tied his handkerchief, so as to bring the leaf of it over his ears, and to secure it from being whirled from his head by the storm.

This odd and storm-beaten figure—tall, and a little stooping, as well as thin—was not unknown to the servant, who saluted him with something of fear as well as of respect as he bid him reverently welcome, and asked him to come in and sit by the fire.

"Get you to your master, and tell him I have a message to him from one he has not seen for two-and-forty years."

As the old man, with his harsh old voice, thus spoke, he unknotted his handkerchief and bet the rain-drops from his hat upon his knee.

The servant knocked at the library-door, where he found Sir Bale.

"Well, what's the matter?" cried Sir Bale sharply, from his chair before the fire, with angry eyes looking over his shoulder.

"Here's 't sir cumman, Sir Bale," he answered.

"Sir," or "the Sir," is still used as the clergyman's title in the Northumbrian counties.

"What sir?"

"Sir Hugh Creswell, if you please, Sir Bale."

"Ho!—mad Creswell?—O, the crazy parson. Well, tell Mrs. Julaper to let him have some supper—and—and to let him have a bed in some suitable place. That's what he wants. These mad fellows know what they are about."

"No, Sir Bale Mardykes, that is not what he wants," said the loud wild voice of the daft sir over the servant's shoulder. "Often has Mardykes Hall given me share of its cheer and its shelter and the warmth of its fire; and I bless the house that has been an inn to the wayfarer of the Lord. But to-night I go up the lake to Pindar's Bield, three miles on; and there I rest and refresh—not here."

"And why not *here*, Mr. Creswell?" asked the Baronet; for about this crazy old man, who preached in the fields, and appeared and disappeared so suddenly in the orbit of his wide and unknown perambulations of those northern and border counties, there was that sort of superstitious feeling which attaches to the mysterious and the good—an idea that it was lucky to harbour and dangerous to offend him. No one knew whence he came or whither he went. Once in a year, perhaps, he might appear at a lonely farmstead door among the fells, salute the house, enter, and be gone in the morning. His life was austere; his piety enthusiastic, severe, and tinged with the craze which inspired among the rustic population a sort of awe.

"I'll not sleep at Mardykes to-night; neither will I eat, nor drink, nor sit me down—no, nor so much as stretch my hands to the fire. As the man of God came out of Judah to king Jeroboam, so come I to you, sent by a vision, to bear a warning; and as he said, 'If thou wilt give me half thy house, I will not go in with thee, neither will I eat bread nor drink water in this place,' so also say I."

"Do as you please," said Sir Bale, a little sulkily. "Say your say; and you are welcome to stay or go, if go you will on so mad a night as this."

"Leave us," said Creswell, beckoning the servant back with his thin hands; "what I have to say is to your master."

The servant went, in obedience to a gesture from Sir Bale, and shut the door.

The old man drew nearer to the Baronet, and lowering his loud stern voice a little, and interrupting his discourse from time to time, to allow the near thunder-peals to subside, he said,

"Answer me, Sir Bale—what is this that has chanced between you and Philip Feltram?"

The Baronet, under the influence of that blunt and peremptory demand, told him shortly and sternly enough.

"And of all these facts you are sure, else ye would not blast your early companion and kinsman with the name of thief?"

"I *am* sure," said Sir Bale grimly.

"Unlock that cabinet," said the old man with the long white locks.

"I've no objection," said Sir Bale; and he did unlock an old oak cabinet that stood, carved in high relief with strange figures and gothic grotesques, against the wall, opposite the fireplace. On opening it there were displayed a system of little drawers and pigeon-holes such as we see in more modern escritoires.

"Open that drawer with the red mark of a seal upon it," continued Hugh Creswell, pointing to it with his lank finger.

Sir Bale did so; and to his momentary amazement, and even consternation, there lay the missing note, which now, with one of those sudden caprices of memory which depend on the laws of suggestion and association, he remembered having placed there with his own hand.

"That is it," said old Creswell with a pallid smile, and fixing his wild eyes on the Baronet. The smile subsided into a frown, and said he: "Last night I slept near Haworth Moss; and your father came to me in a dream, and said: 'My son Bale accuses Philip of having stolen a bank-note from his desk. He forgets that he himself placed it in his cabinet. Come with me.' I was, in the spirit, in this room; and he led me to this cabinet, which he opened; and in that drawer he showed me that note. 'Go,' said he, 'and tell him to ask Philip Feltram's pardon, else he will but go in weakness to return in power'; and he said that which it is not lawful to repeat. My message is told. Now a word from myself," he added sternly. "The dead, through my lips, has spoken, and under God's thunder and lightning his words have found ye. Why so uppish wi' Philip Feltram? See how ye threaped, and yet were wrong. He's no tazzle—he's no taggelt. *Mine ye* ask his pardon. Ye must change, or he will no taggelt. Go, in weakness, come in power: mark ye the words. 'Twill make a peal that will be heard in toon and desert, in the swirls o' the mountain, through pikes and valleys, and mak' a waaly man o' thee."

The old man with these words, uttered in the broad northern dialect of his common speech, strode from the room and shut the door. In another minute he was forth into the storm, pursuing what remained of his long march to Pindar's Bield.

"Upon my soul!" said Sir Bale, recovering from his sort of stun which the sudden and strange visit had left, "that's a cool old fellow! Come to rate me and teach me my own business in my own house!" and he rapped out a fierce oath. "Change his mind or no, here he sha'n't stay to-night—not an hour."

Sir Bale was in the lobby in a moment, and thundered to his servants:

"I say, put that fool out of the door—put him out by the shoulder, and never let him put his foot inside it more!"

But the old man's yea was yea, and his nay nay. He had quite meant what he said; and, as I related, was beyond the reach of the indignity of extrusion.

Sir Bale on his return shut his door as violently as if it were in the face of the old prophet.

"Ask Feltram's pardon, by Jove! For what? Why, any jury on earth would have hanged him on half the evidence; and I, like a fool, was going to let him off with his liberty and my hundred pound-note! Ask his pardon indeed!"

Still there were misgivings in his mind; a consciousness that he did owe explanation and apology to Feltram, and an insurmountable reluctance to undertake either. The old dislike—a contempt mingled with fear—not any fear of his malevolence, a fear only of his carelessness and folly; for, as I have said, Feltram knew many things, it was believed, of the Baronet's Continental and Asiatic life, and had even gently remonstrated with him upon the dangers into which he was running. A simple fellow like Philip Feltram is a dangerous depository of a secret. This Baronet was proud, too; and the mere possession of his secrets by Feltram was an involuntary insult, which Sir Bale could not forgive. He wished him far away; and except for the recovery of his bank-note, which he could ill spare, he was sorry that this suspicion was cleared up.

The thunder and storm were unabated; it seemed indeed that they were growing wilder and more awful.

He opened the window-shutter and looked out upon that sublimest of scenes; and so intense and magnificent were its phenomena, that Sir Bale, for a while, was absorbed in this contemplation.

When he turned about, the sight of his £100 note, still between his finger and thumb, made him smile grimly.

The more he thought of it, the clearer it was that he could not leave matters exactly as they were. Well, what should he do? He would send for Mrs. Julaper, and tell her vaguely that he had changed his mind about Feltram, and that he might continue to stay at Mardykes Hall as usual. That would suffice. She could speak to Feltram.

He sent for her; and soon, in the lulls of the great uproar without, he could hear the jingle of Mrs. Julaper's keys and her light tread upon the lobby.

"Mrs. Julaper," said the Baronet, in his dry careless way, "Feltram may remain; your eloquence has prevailed. What have you been crying about?" he asked, observing that his housekeeper's usually cheerful face was, in her own phrase, "all cried."

"It is too late, sir; he's gone."

"And when did he go?" asked Sir Bale, a little put out. "He chose an odd evening, didn't he? So like him!"

"He went about half an hour ago; and I'm very sorry, sir; it's a sore sight to see the poor lad going from the place he was reared in, and a hard thing, sir; and on such a night, above all."

"No one asked him to go to-night. Where is he gone to?"

"I don't know, I'm sure; he left my room, sir, when I was upstairs; and Janet saw him pass the window not ten minutes after Mr. Creswell left the house."

"Well, then, there's no good, Mrs. Julaper, in thinking more about it; he has settled the matter his own way; and as he so ordains it—amen, say I. Good-night."

X. Adventure in Tom Marlin's Boat

Philip Feltram was liked very well—a gentle, kindly, and very timid creature, and, before he became so heart-broken, a fellow who liked a joke or a pleasant story, and could laugh heartily. Where will Sir Bale find so unresisting and respectful a butt and retainer? and whom will he bully now?

Something like remorse was worrying Sir Bale's heart a little; and the more he thought on the strange visit of Hugh Creswell that night, with its unexplained menace, the more uneasy he became.

The storm continued; and even to him there seemed something exaggerated and inhuman in the severity of his expulsion on such a night. It was his own doing, it was true; but would people believe that? and would he have thought of leaving Mardykes at all if it had not been for his kinsman's cruelty? Nay, was it not certain that if Sir Bale had done as Hugh Creswell had urged him, and sent for Feltram forthwith, and told him how all had been cleared up, and been a little friendly with him, he would have found him still in the house?—for he had not yet gone for ten minutes after Creswell's departure, and thus, all that was to follow might have been averted. But it was now too late, and Sir Bale would let the affair take its own course.

Below him, outside the window at which he stood ruminating, he heard voices mingling with the storm. He could with tolerable certainty perceive, looking into the obscurity, that there were three men passing close under it, carrying some very heavy burden among them.

He did not know what these three black figures in the obscurity were about. He saw them pass round the corner of the building toward the front, and in the lulls of the storm could hear their gruff voices talking.

We have all experienced what a presentiment is, and we all know with what an intuition the faculty of observation is sometimes heightened. It was such an apprehension as sometimes gives its peculiar horror to a dream—a sort of knowledge that what those people were about was in a dreadful way connected with his own fate.

He watched for a time, thinking that they might return; but they did not. He was in a state of uncomfortable suspense.

"If they want me, they won't have much trouble in finding me, nor any scruple, egad, in plaguing me; they never have."

Sir Bale returned to his letters, a score of which he was that night getting off his conscience—an arrear which would not have troubled him had he not ceased, for two or three days, altogether to employ Philip Feltram, who had been accustomed to take all that sort of drudgery off his hands.

All the time he was writing now he had a feeling that the shadows he had seen pass under his window were machinating some trouble for him, and an uneasy suspense made him lift his eyes now and then to the door, fancying sounds and footsteps; and after a resultless wait he would say to himself, "If any one is coming, why the devil don't he come?" and then he would apply himself again to his letters.

But on a sudden he heard good Mrs. Julaper's step trotting along the lobby, and the tiny ringing of her keys.

Here was news coming; and the Baronet stood up looking at the door, on which presently came a hurried rapping; and before he had answered, in the midst of a long thunder-clap that suddenly broke, rattling over the house, the good woman opened the door in great agitation, and cried with a tremulous uplifting of her hands.

"O, Sir Bale! O, la, sir! here's poor dear Philip Feltram come home dead!"

Sir Bale stared at her sternly for some seconds.

"Gome, now, do be distinct," said Sir Bale; "what has happened?"

"He's lying on the sofer in the old still-room. You never saw—my God!—O, sir—what is life?"

"D——n it, can't you cry by-and-by, and tell me what's the matter *now*?"

"A bit o' fire there, as luck would have it; but what is hot or cold now? La, sir, they're all doin' what they can; he's drowned, sir, and Tom Warren is on the gallop down to Golden Friars for Doctor Torvey."

"*Is* he drowned, or is it only a ducking? Come, bring me to the place. Dead men don't usually want a fire, or consult doctors. I'll see for myself."

So Sir Bale Mardykes, pale and grim, accompanied by the light-footed Mrs. Julaper, strode along the passages, and was led by her into the old still-room, which had ceased to be used for its original purpose. All the servants in the house were now collected there, and three men also who lived by the margin of the lake; one of them thoroughly drenched, with rivulets of water still trickling from his sleeves, water along the wrinkles and pockets of his waistcoat and from the feet of his trousers, and pumping and oozing from his shoes, and streaming from his hair down the channels of his cheeks like a continuous rain of tears.

The people drew back a little as Sir Bale entered with a quick step and a sharp pallid frown on his face. There was a silence as he stooped over Philip Feltram, who lay on a low bed next the wall, dimly lighted by two or three candles here and there about the room.

He laid his hand, for a moment, on his cold wet breast.

Sir Bale knew what should be done in order to give a man in such a case his last chance for life. Everybody was speedily put in motion. Philip's drenched clothes were removed, hot blankets enveloped him, warming-pans and hot bricks lent their aid; he was placed at the prescribed angle, so that the water flowed freely from his mouth. The old expedient for inducing artificial breathing was employed, and a lusty pair of bellows did duty for his lungs.

But these helps to life, and suggestions to nature, availed not. Forlorn and peaceful lay the features of poor Philip Feltram; cold and dull to the touch; no breath through the blue lips; no sight in the fish-like eyes; pulseless and cold in the midst of all the hot bricks and warming-pans about him.

At length, everything having been tried, Sir Bale, who had been directing, placed his hand within the clothes, and laid it silently on Philip's shoulder and over his heart; and after a little wait, he shook his head, and looking down on his sunken face, he said,

"I am afraid he's gone. Yes, he's gone, poor fellow! And bear you this in mind, all of you; Mrs. Julaper there can tell you more about it. She knows that it was certainly in no compliance with my wish that he left the house to-night: it was his own obstinate perversity, and perhaps—I forgive him for it—a wish in his unreasonable resentment to throw some blame upon this house, as having refused him shelter on such a night; than which imputation nothing can be more utterly false. Mrs. Julaper there knows how welcome he was to stay the night; but he would not; he had made up his mind, it seems, without telling any person. Had he told you, Mrs. Julaper?"

"No, sir," sobbed Mrs. Julaper from the centre of a pocket-handkerchief in which her face was buried.

"Not a human being: an angry whim of his own. Poor Feltram! and here's the result," said the Baronet. "We have done our best—done everything. I don't think the doctor, when he comes, will say that anything has been omitted; but all won't do. Does any one here know how it happened?"

Two men knew very well—the man who had been ducked, and his companion, a younger man, who was also in the still-room, and had lent a hand in carrying Feltram up to the house.

Tom Marlin had a queer old stone tenement by the edge of the lake just under Mardykes Hall. Some people said it was the stump of an old tower that had once belonged to Mardykes Castle, of which in the modern building scarcely a relic was discoverable.

This Tom Marlin had an ancient right of fishing in the lake, where he caught pike enough for all Golden Friars; and keeping a couple of boats, he made money beside by ferrying passengers over now and then. This fellow, with a furrowed face and shaggy eyebrows, bald at top, but with long grizzled locks falling upon his shoulders, said,

"He wer wi' me this mornin', sayin' he'd want t' boat to cross the lake in, but he didn't say what hour; and when it came on to thunder and blow like this, ye guess I did not look to see him to-night. Well, my wife was just lightin' a pig-tail—tho' light enough and to spare there was in the lift already—when who should come clatterin' at the latch-pin in the blow o' thunder and wind but Philip, poor lad, himself; and an ill hour for him it was. He's been some time in ill fettle, though he was never frowsy, not he, but always kind and dooce, and canty once, like anither; and he asked me to tak the boat across the lake at once to the Clough o' Cloostedd at t'other side. The woman took the pet and wodn't hear o't; and, 'Dall me, if I go to-night,' quoth I. But he would not be put off so, not he; and dingdrive he went to it, cryin' and putrein' ye'd a-said, poor fellow, he was wrang i' his garrets a'most. So at long last I bethought me, there's nout o' a sea to the north o' Snakes Island, so I'll pull him by that side—for the storm is blowin' right up by Golden Friars, ye mind—and when we get near the point, thinks I, he'll see wi' his een how the lake is, and gie it up. For I liked him, poor lad; and seein' he'd set his heart on't, I wouldn't vex nor frump him wi' a no. So down we three—myself, and Bill there, and Philip Feltram—come to the boat; and we pulled out, keeping Snakes Island atwixt us and the wind. 'Twas smooth water wi' us, for 'twas a scug there, but white enough was all beyont the point; and passing the finger-stone, not forty fathom from the shore o' the island, Bill and me pullin' and he sittin' in the stern, poor lad, up he rises, a bit rabblin' to himself, wi' his hands lifted so.

"'Look a-head!' says I, thinkin' something was comin' atort us.

"But 'twasn't that. The boat was quiet, for while we looked, oo'er our shouthers, oo'er her bows, we didn't pull, so she lay still; and lookin' back again on Philip, he was rabblin' on all the same.

"It's nobbut a prass wi' himsel', poor lad,' thinks I.

"But that wasn't it neither; for I sid something white come out o' t' water, by the gunwale, like a hand. By Jen! and he leans oo'er and tuk it; and he sagged like, and so it drew him in, under the mere, before I cud du nout. There was nout to thraa tu him, and no time; down he went, and I followed; and thrice I dived before I found him, and brought him up by the hair at last; and there he is, poor lad! and all one if he lay at the bottom o' t' mere."

As Tom Marlin ended his narrative—often interrupted by the noise of the tempest without, and the peals of thunder that echoed awfully above, like the chorus of a melancholy ballad—the sudden clang of the hall-door bell, and a more faintly-heard knocking, announced a new arrival.

XI. Sir Bale's Dream

It was Doctor Torvey who entered the old still-room now, buttoned-up to the chin in his greatcoat, and with a muffler of many colours wrapped partly over that feature.

"Well!—hey? So poor Feltram's had an accident?"

The Doctor was addressing Sir Bale, and getting to the bedside as he pulled off his gloves.

"I see you've been keeping him warm—that's right; and a considerable flow of water from his mouth; turn him a little that way. Hey? O, ho!" said the Doctor, as he placed his hand upon Philip, and gently stirred his limbs. "It's more than an hour since this happened. I'm afraid there's very little to be done now"; and in a lower tone, with his hand on poor Philip Feltram's arm, and so down to his fingers, he said in Sir Bale Mardykes' ear, with a shake of his head,

"Here, you see, poor fellow, here's the cadaveric stiffness; it's very melancholy, but it's all over, he's gone; there's no good trying any more. Come here, Mrs. Julaper. Did you ever see any one dead? Look at his eyes, look at his mouth. You ought to have known that, with half an eye. And you know," he added again confidentially in Sir Bale's ear, "trying any more *now* is all my eye."

Then after a few more words with the Baronet, and having heard his narrative, he said from time to time, "Quite right; nothing could be better; capital practice, sir," and so forth. And at the close of all this, amid the sobs of kind Mrs. Julaper and the general whimpering of the humbler handmaids, the Doctor standing by the bed, with his knuckles on the coverlet, and a glance now and then on the dead face beside him, said—by way of "quieting men's minds," as the old tract-writers used to say—a few words to the following effect:

"Everything has been done here that the most experienced physician could have wished. Everything has been done in the best way. I don't know anything that has not been done, in fact. If I had been here myself, I don't know—hot bricks—salt isn't a bad thing. I don't know, I say, that anything of any consequence has been omitted." And looking at the body, "You see," and he drew the fingers a little this way and that, letting them return, as they stiffly did, to their former attitude, "you may be sure that the poor gentleman was quite dead by the time he arrived here. So, since he was laid there, nothing has been lost by delay. And, Sir Bale, if you have any directions to send to Golden Friars, sir, I shall be most happy to undertake your message."

"Nothing, thanks; it is a melancholy ending, poor fellow! You must come to the study with me, Doctor Torvey, and talk a little bit more; and—very sad, doctor—and you must have a glass of sherry, or some port—the port used not to be bad here; I don't take it—but very melancholy it is—bring some port and sherry; and, Mrs. Julaper, you'll be good enough to see that everything that should be done here is looked to; and let Marlin and the men have supper and something to drink. You have been too long in your wet clothes, Marlin."

So, with gracious words all round, he led the Doctor to the library where he had been sitting, and was affable and hospitable, and told him his own version of all that had passed between him and Philip Feltram, and presented himself in an amiable point of view, and pleased the Doctor with his port and flatteries—for he could not afford to lose anyone's good word just now; and the Doctor was a bit of a gossip, and in most houses in that region, in one character or another, every three months in the year.

So in due time the Doctor drove back to Golden Friars, with a high opinion of Sir Bale, and higher still of his port, and highest of all of himself: in the best possible humour with the world, not minding the storm that blew in his face, and which he defied in good-humoured mock-heroics spoken in somewhat thick accents, and regarding the thunder and lightning as a lively gala of fireworks; and if there had been a chance of finding his cronies still in the George and Dragon, he would have been among them forthwith, to relate the tragedy of the night, and tell what a good fellow, after all, Sir Bale was; and what a fool, at best, poor Philip Feltram.

But the George was quiet for that night. The thunder rolled over voiceless chambers; and the lights had been put out within the windows, on whose multitudinous small panes the lightning glared. So the Doctor went home to Mrs. Torvey, whom he charmed into good-humoured curiosity by the tale of wonder he had to relate.

Sir Bale's qualms were symptomatic of something a little less sublime and more selfish than conscience. He was not sorry that Philip Feltram was out of the way. His lips might begin to babble inconveniently at any time, and why should not his mouth be stopped? and what stopper so effectual as that plug of clay which fate had introduced? But he did not want to be charged with the odium of the catastrophe. Every man cares something for the opinion of his fellows. And seeing that Feltram had been well liked, and that his death had excited a vehement commiseration, Sir Bale did not wish it to be said that he had made the house too hot to hold him, and had so driven him to extremity.

Sir Bale's first agitation had subsided. It was now late, he had written many letters, and he was tired. It was not wonderful, then, that having turned his lounging-chair to the fire, he should have fallen asleep in it, as at last he did.

The storm was passing gradually away by this time. The thunder was now echoing among the distant glens and gorges of Daulness Fells, and the angry roar and gusts of the tempest were subsiding into the melancholy soughing and piping that soothe like a lullaby.

Sir Bale therefore had his unpremeditated sleep very comfortably, except that his head was hanging a little uneasily; which, perhaps, helped him to this dream.

It was one of those dreams in which the continuity of the waking state that immediately preceded it seems unbroken; for he thought that he was sitting in the chair which he occupied, and in the room where he actually was. It seemed to him that he got up, took a candle in his hand, and went through the passages to the old still-room where Philip

Feltram lay. The house seemed perfectly still. He could hear the chirp of the crickets faintly from the distant kitchen, and the tick of the clock sounded loud and hollow along the passage. In the old still-room, as he opened the door, was no light, except what was admitted from the candle he carried. He found the body of poor Philip Feltram just as he had left it—his gentle face, saddened by the touch of death, was turned upwards, with white lips: with traces of suffering fixed in its outlines, such as caused Sir Bale, standing by the bed, to draw the coverlet over the dead man's features, which seemed silently to upbraid him. "Gone in weakness!" said Sir Bale, repeating the words of the "daft sir," Hugh Creswell; as he did so, a voice whispered near him, with a great sigh, "Come in power!" He looked round, in his dream, but there was no one; the light seemed to fail, and a horror slowly overcame him, especially as he thought he saw the figure under the coverlet stealthily beginning to move. Backing towards the door, for he could not take his eyes off it, he saw something like a huge black ape creep out at the foot of the bed; and springing at him, it griped him by the throat, so that he could not breathe; and a thousand voices were instantly round him, holloaing, cursing, laughing in his ears; and in this direful plight he waked.

Was it the ring of those voices still in his ears, or a real shriek, and another, and a long peal, shriek after shriek, swelling madly through the distant passages, that held him still, freezing in the horror of his dream?

I will tell you what this noise was.

XII. Marcella Bligh and Judith Wale Keep Watch

After his bottle of port with Sir Bale, the Doctor had gone down again to the room where poor Philip Feltram lay.

Mrs. Julaper had dried her eyes, and was busy by this time; and two old women were making all their arrangements for a night-watch by the body, which they had washed, and, as their phrase goes, "laid out" in the humble bed where it had lain while there was still a hope that a spark sufficient to rekindle the fire of life might remain. These old women had points of resemblance: they were lean, sallow, and wonderfully wrinkled, and looked each malign and ugly enough for a witch.

Marcella Bligh's thin hooked nose was now like the beak of a bird of prey over the face of the drowned man, upon whose eyelids she was placing penny-pieces, to keep them from opening; and her one eye was fixed on her work, its sightless companion showing white in its socket, with an ugly leer.

Judith Wale was lifting the pail of hot water with which they had just washed the body. She had long lean arms, a hunched back, a great sharp chin sunk on her hollow breast, and small eyes restless as a ferret's; and she clattered about in great bowls of shoes, old and clouted, that were made for a foot as big as two of hers.

The Doctor knew these two old women, who were often employed in such dismal offices.

"How does Mrs. Bligh? See me with half an eye? Hey—that's rhyme, isn't it?—And, Judy lass—why, I thought you lived nearer the town—here making poor Mr. Feltram's last toilet. You have helped to dress many a poor fellow for his last journey. Not a bad notion of drill either—they stand at attention stiff and straight enough in the sentry-box. Your recruits do you credit, Mrs. Wale."

The Doctor stood at the foot of the bed to inspect, breathing forth a vapour of very fine old port, his hands in his pockets, speaking with a lazy thickness, and looking so comfortable and facetious, that Mrs. Julaper would have liked to turn him out of the room.

But the Doctor was not unkind, only extremely comfortable. He was a good-natured fellow, and had thought and care for the living, but not a great deal of sentiment for the dead, whom he had looked in the face too often to be much disturbed by the spectacle.

"You'll have to keep that bandage on. You should be sharp; you should know all about it, girl, by this time, and not let those muscles stiffen. I need not tell you the mouth shuts as easily as this snuff-box, if you only take it in time.—I suppose, Mrs. Julaper, you'll send to Jos Fringer for the poor fellow's outfit. Fringer is a very proper man—there ain't a properer und-aker in England. I always re-mmend Fringer—in Church-street in Golden Friars. You know Fringer, I daresay."

"I can't say, sir, I'm sure. That will be as Sir Bale may please to direct," answered Mrs. Julaper.

"You've got him very straight—straighter than I thought you could; but the large joints were not so stiff. A very little longer wait, and you'd hardly have got him into his coffin. He'll want a vr-r-ry long one, poor lad. Short cake is life, ma'am. Sad thing this. They'll open their eyes, I promise you, down in the town. 'Twill be cool enough, I'd shay, affre all th-thunr-thunnle, you know. I think I'll take a nip, Mrs. Jool-fr, if you wouldn't mine makin' me out a thimmle-ful bran-band-bran-rand-andy, eh, Mishs Joolfr?"

And the Doctor took a chair by the fire; and Mrs. Julaper, with a dubious conscience and dry hospitality, procured the brandy-flask and wine-glass, and helped the physician in a thin hesitating stream, which left him ample opportunity to cry "Hold—enough!" had he been so minded. But that able physician had no confidence, it would seem, in any dose under a bumper, which he sipped with commendation, and then fell asleep with the firelight on his face—to tender-hearted Mrs. Julaper's disgust—and snored with a sensual disregard of the solemnity of his situation; until with a profound nod, or rather dive, toward the fire, he awoke, got up and shook his ears with a kind of start, and standing with his back to the fire, asked for his muffler and horse; and so took his leave also of the weird sisters, who were still pottering about the body, with croak and whisper, and nod and ogle. He took his leave also of good Mrs. Julaper, who was completing arrangements with teapot and kettle, spiced elderberry wine, and other comforts, to support them through their proposed vigil. And finally, in a sort of way, he took his leave of the body, with a long business-like stare, from the foot of the bed, with his short hands stuffed into his pockets. And so, to Mrs. Julaper's relief, this unseemly doctor, speaking thickly, departed.

And now, the Doctor being gone, and all things prepared for the "wake" to be observed by withered Mrs. Bligh of the one eye, and yellow Mrs. Wale of the crooked back, the house grew gradually still. The thunder had by this time died into the solid boom of distant battle, and the fury of the gale had subsided to the long sobbing wail that is charged with so eerie a melancholy. Within all was stirless, and the two old women, each a "Mrs." by courtesy, who had not much to thank Nature or the world for, sad and cynical, and in a sort outcasts told off by fortune to these sad and grizzly services, sat themselves down by the fire, each perhaps feeling unusually at home in the other's society; and in this soured and forlorn comfort, trimming their fire, quickening the song of the kettle to a boil, and waxing polite and chatty; each treating the other with that deprecatory and formal courtesy which invites a return in kind, and both growing strangely happy in this little world of their own, in the unusual and momentary sense of an importance and consideration which were delightful.

The old still-room of Mardykes Hall is an oblong room wainscoted. From the door you look its full length to the wide stone-shafted Tudor window at the other end. At your left is the ponderous mantelpiece, supported by two spiral stone pillars; and close to the door at the right was the bed in which the two crones had just stretched poor Philip Feltram, who lay as still as an uncoloured wax-work, with a heavy penny-piece on each eye, and a bandage under his jaw, making his mouth look stern. And the two old ladies over their tea by the fire conversed agreeably, compared their rheumatisms and other ailments wordily, and talked of old times, and early recollections, and of sick-beds they had attended, and corpses that "you would not know, so pined and windered" were they; and others so fresh and canny, you'd say the dead had never looked so bonny in life.

Then they began to talk of people who grew tall in their coffins, of others who had been buried alive, and of others who walked after death. Stories as true as holy writ.

"Were you ever down by Hawarth, Mrs. Bligh—hard by Dalworth Moss?" asked crook-backed Mrs. Wale, holding her spoon suspended over her cup.

"Neea whaar sooa far south, Mrs. Wale, ma'am; but ma father was off times down thar cuttin' peat."

"Ah, then ye'll not a kenned farmer Dykes that lived by the Lin-tree Scaur. 'Tweer I that laid him out, poor aad fellow, and a dow man he was when aught went cross wi' him; and he cursed and sweared, twad gar ye dodder to hear him. They said he was a hard man wi' some folk; but he kep a good house, and liked to see plenty, and many a time when I was swaimous about my food, he'd clap t' meat on ma plate, and mak' me eat ma fill. Na, na—there was good as well as bad in farmer Dykes. It was a year after he deed, and Tom Ettles was walking home, down by the Birken Stoop one night, and not a soul nigh, when he sees a big ball, as high as his knee, whirlin' and spangin' away before him on the road. What it wer he could not think; but he never consayted there was a freet or a bo thereaway; so he kep near it, watching every spang and turn it took, till it ran into the gripe by the roadside. There was a gravel pit just there, and Tom Ettles wished to take another gliff at it before he went on. But when he keeked into the pit, what should he see but a man atoppa a horse that could not get up or on: and says he, 'I think ye be at a dead-lift there, gaffer.' And wi' the word, up looks the man, and who sud it be but farmer Dykes himsel; and Tom Ettles saw him plain eneugh, and kenned the horse too for Black Captain, the farmer's aad beast, that broke his leg and was shot two years and more before the farmer died. 'Ay,' says farmer Dykes, lookin' very bad; 'forsett-and-backsett, ye'll tak me oot, Tom Ettles, and clap ye doun behint me quick, or I'll claw ho'd o' thee.' Tom felt his hair risin' stiff on his heed, and his tongue so fast to the roof o' his mouth he could scarce get oot a word; but says he, 'If Black Jack can't do it o' noo, he'll ne'er do't and carry double.' 'I ken my ain business best,' says Dykes. 'If ye gar me gie ye a look, 'twill gie ye the creepin's while ye live; so git ye doun, Tom'; and with that the dobby lifts its neaf, and Tom saw there was a red light round horse and man, like the glow of a peat fire. And says Tom, 'In the name o' God, ye'll let me pass'; and with the word the gooast draws itsel' doun, all a-creaked, like a man wi' a sudden pain; and Tom Ettles took to his heels more deed than alive."

They had approached their heads, and the story had sunk to that mysterious murmur that thrills the listener, when in the brief silence that followed they heard a low odd laugh near the door.

In that direction each lady looked aghast, and saw Feltram sitting straight up in the bed, with the white bandage in his hand, and as it seemed, for one foot was below the coverlet, near the floor, about to glide forth.

Mrs. Bligh, uttering a hideous shriek, clutched Mrs. Wale, and Mrs. Wale, with a scream as dreadful, gripped Mrs. Bligh; and quite forgetting their somewhat formal politeness, they reeled and tugged, wrestling towards the window, each struggling to place her companion between her and the 'dobby,' and both uniting in a direful peal of yells.

This was the uproar which had startled Sir Bale from his dream, and was now startling the servants from theirs.

XIII. The Mist on the Mountain

Doctor Torvey was sent for early next morning, and came full of wonder, learning and scepticism. Seeing is believing, however; and there was Philip Feltram living, and soon to be, in all bodily functions, just as usual.

"Upon my soul, Sir Bale, I couldn't have believed it, if I had not seen it with my eyes," said the Doctor impressively, while sipping a glass of sherry in the "breakfast parlour," as the great panelled and pictured room next the dining-room was called. "I don't think there is any similar case on record—no pulse, no more than the poker; no respiration, by Jove, no more than the chimney-piece; as cold as a lead image in the garden there. Well, you'll say all that might possibly be fallacious; but what will you say to the cadaveric stiffness? Old Judy Wale can tell you; and my friend Marcella—Monocula would be nearer the mark—Mrs. Bligh, she knows all those common, and I may say up to this, infallible, signs of death, as well as I do. There is no mystery about them; they'll depose to the literality of the symptoms. You heard how they gave tongue. Upon my honour, I'll send the whole case up to my old chief, Sir Hervey Hansard, to London. You'll hear what a noise it will make among the profession. There never was—and it ain't too much to say there never *will* be—another case like it."

During this lecture, and a great deal more, Sir Bale leaned back in his chair, with his legs extended, his heels on the ground, and his arms folded, looking sourly up in the face of a tall lady in white satin, in a ruff, and with a bird on her hand, who smiled down superciliously from her frame on the Baronet. Sir Bale seemed a little bit high and dry with the Doctor.

"You physicians are unquestionably," he said, "a very learned profession."

The Doctor bowed.

"But there's just one thing you know nothing about—"

"Eh? What's that?" inquired Doctor Torvey.

"Medicine," answered Sir Bale. "I was aware you never knew what was the matter with a sick man; but I didn't know, till now, that you couldn't tell when he was dead."

"Ha, ha!—well—ha, ha!—*yes*—well, you see, you—ha, ha!—you certainly have me there. But it's a case without a parallel—it is, upon my honour. You'll find it will not only be talked about, but written about; and, whatever papers appear upon it, will come to me; and I'll take care, Sir Bale, you shall have an opportunity of reading them."

"Of which I shan't avail myself," answered Sir Bale. "Take another glass of sherry, Doctor."

The Doctor made his acknowledgments and filled his glass, and looked through the wine between him and the window.

"Ha, ha!—see there, your port, Sir Bale, gives a fellow such habits—looking for the beeswing, by Jove. It isn't easy, in one sense at least, to get your port out of a fellow's head when once he has tasted it."

But if the honest Doctor meant a hint for a glass of that admirable bin, it fell pointless; and Sir Bale had no notion of making another libation of that precious fluid in honour of Doctor Torvey.

"And I take it for granted," said Sir Bale, "that Feltram will do very well; and, should anything go wrong, I can send for you—unless he should die again; and in that case I think I shall take my own opinion."

So he and the Doctor parted.

Sir Bale, although he did not consult the Doctor on his own case, was not particularly well. "That lonely place, those frightful mountains, and that damp black lake"—which features in the landscape he cursed all round—"are enough to give any man blue devils; and when a fellow's spirits go, he's all gone. That's why I'm dyspeptic—that and those d——d debts—and the post, with its flight of croaking and screeching letters from London. I wish there was no post here. I wish it was like Sir Amyrald's time, when they shot the York mercer that came to dun him, and no one ever took anyone to task about it; and now they can pelt you at any distance they please through the post; and fellows lose their spirits and their appetite and any sort of miserable comfort that is possible in this odious abyss."

Was there gout in Sir Bale's case, or "vapours"? I know not what the faculty would have called it; but Sir Bale's mode of treatment was simply to work off the attack by long and laborious walking.

This evening his walk was upon the Fells of Golden Friars—long after the landscape below was in the eclipse of twilight, the broad bare sides and angles of these gigantic uplands were still lighted by the misty western sun.

There is no such sense of solitude as that which we experience upon the silent and vast elevations of great mountains. Lifted high above the level of human sounds and habitations, among the wild expanses and colossal features of Nature, we are thrilled in our loneliness with a strange fear and elation—an ascent above the reach of life's vexations or companionship, and the tremblings of a wild and undefined misgiving. The filmy disc of the moon had risen in the east, and was already faintly silvering the shadowy scenery below, while yet Sir Bale stood in the mellow light of the western sun, which still touched also the summits of the opposite peaks of Morvyn Fells.

Sir Bale Mardykes did not, as a stranger might, in prudence, hasten his descent from the heights at which he stood while yet a gleam of daylight remained to him. For he was, from his boyhood, familiar with those solitary regions; and, beside this, the thin circle of the moon, hung in the eastern sky, would brighten as the sunlight sank, and hang like a lamp above his steps.

There was in the bronzed and resolute face of the Baronet, lighted now in the parting beams of sunset, a resemblance to that of Charles the Second—not our "merry" ideal, but the more energetic and saturnine face which the portraits have preserved to us.

He stood with folded arms on the side of the slope, admiring, in spite of his prejudice, the unusual effects of a view so strangely lighted—the sunset tints on the opposite peaks, lost in the misty twilight, now deepening lower down into a darker shade, through which the outlines of the stone gables and tower of Golden Friars and the light of fire or candle in their windows were dimly visible.

As he stood and looked, his more distant sunset went down, and sudden twilight was upon him, and he began to remember the beautiful Homeric picture of a landscape coming out, rock and headland, in the moonlight.

There had hung upon the higher summits, at his right, a heavy fold of white cloud, which on a sudden broke, and, like the smoke of artillery, came rolling down the slopes toward him. Its principal volume, however, unfolded itself in a mighty flood down the side of the mountain towards the lake; and that which spread towards and soon enveloped the ground on which he stood was by no means so dense a fog. A thick mist enough it was; but still, to a distance of twenty or thirty yards, he could discern the outline of a rock or scaur, but not beyond it.

There are few sensations more intimidating than that of being thus enveloped on a lonely mountain-side, which, like this one, here and there breaks into precipice.

There is another sensation, too, which affects the imagination. Overtaken thus on the solitary expanse, there comes a new chill and tremour as this treacherous medium surrounds us, through which unperceived those shapes which fancy conjures up might approach so near and bar our path.

From the risk of being reduced to an actual standstill he knew he was exempt. The point from which the wind blew, light as it was, assured him of that. Still the mist was thick enough seriously to embarrass him. It had overtaken him as he was looking down upon the lake; and he now looked to his left, to try whether in that direction it was too thick to permit a view of the nearest landmarks. Through this white film he saw a figure standing only about five-and-twenty steps away, looking down, as it seemed, in precisely the same direction as he, quite motionless, and standing like a shadow projected upon the smoky vapour. It was the figure of a slight tall man, with his arm extended, as if pointing to a remote object, which no mortal eye certainly could discern through the mist. Sir Bale gazed at this figure, doubtful whether he were in a waking dream, unable to conjecture whence it had come; and as he looked, it moved, and was almost instantly out of sight.

He descended the mountain cautiously. The mist was now thinner, and through the haze he was beginning to see objects more distinctly, and, without danger, to proceed at a quicker pace. He had still a long walk by the uplands towards Mardykes Hall before he descended to the level of the lake.

The mist was still quite thick enough to circumscribe his view and to hide the general features of the landscape; and well was it, perhaps, for Sir Bale that his boyhood had familiarised him with the landmarks on the mountain-side.

He had made nearly four miles on his solitary homeward way, when, passing under a ledge of rock which bears the name of the Cat's Skaitch, he saw the same figure in the short cloak standing within some thirty or forty yards of him—the thin curtain of mist, through which the moonlight touched it, giving to it an airy and unsubstantial character.

Sir Bale came to a standstill. The man in the short cloak nodded and drew back, and was concealed by the angle of the rock.

Sir Bale was now irritated, as men are after a start, and shouting to the stranger to halt, he "slapped" after him, as the northern phrase goes, at his best pace. But again he was gone, and nowhere could he see him, the mist favouring his evasion.

Looking down the fells that overhang Mardykes Hall, the mountain-side dips gradually into a glen, which, as it descends, becomes precipitous and wooded. A footpath through this ravine conducts the wayfarer to the level ground that borders the lake; and by this dark pass Sir Bale Mardykes strode, in comparatively clear air, along the rocky path dappled with moonlight.

As he emerged upon the lower ground he again encountered the same figure. It approached. It was Philip Feltram.

XIV. A New Philip Feltram

The Baronet had not seen Feltram since his strange escape from death. His last interview with him had been stern and threatening; Sir Bale dealing with appearances in the spirit of an incensed judge, Philip Feltram lamenting in the submission of a helpless despair.

Feltram was full in the moonlight now, standing erect, and smiling cynically on the Baronet.

There was that in the bearing and countenance of Feltram that disconcerted him more than the surprise of the sudden meeting.

He had determined to meet Feltram in a friendly way, whenever that not very comfortable interview became inevitable. But he was confused by the suddenness of Feltram's appearance; and the tone, cold and stern, in which he had last spoken to him came first, and he spoke in it after a brief silence.

"I fancied, Mr. Feltram, you were in your bed; I little expected to find you here. I think the Doctor gave very particular directions, and said that you were to remain perfectly quiet."

"But I know more than the Doctor," replied Feltram, still smiling unpleasantly.

"I think, sir, you would have been better in your bed," said Sir Bale loftily.

"Come, come, come, come!" exclaimed Philip Feltram contemptuously.

"It seems to me," said Sir Bale, a good deal astonished, "you rather forget yourself."

"Easier to forget oneself, Sir Bale, than to forgive others, at times," replied Philip Feltram in his unparalleled mood.

"That's the way fools knock themselves up," continued Sir Bale. "You've been walking ever so far—away to the Fells of Golden Friars. It was you whom I saw there. What d——d folly! What brought you there?"

"To observe you," he replied.

"And have you walked the whole way there and back again? How did you get there?"

"Pooh! how did I come—how did you come—how did the fog come? From the lake, I suppose. We all come up, and then down." So spoke Philip Feltram, with serene insolence.

"You are pleased to talk nonsense," said Sir Bale.

"Because I like it—with a *meaning*."

Sir Bale looked at him, not knowing whether to believe his eyes and ears. He did not know what to make of him.

"I had intended speaking to you in a conciliatory way; you seem to wish to make that impossible"—Philip Feltram's face wore its repulsive smile;— "and in fact I don't know what to make of you, unless you are ill; and ill you well may be. You can't have walked much less than twelve miles."

"Wonderful effort for me!" said Feltram with the same sneer.

"Rather surprising for a man so nearly drowned," answered Sir Bale Mardykes.

"A dip: you don't like the lake, sir; but I do. And so it is: as Antaeus touched the earth, so I the water, and rise refreshed."

"I think you'd better get in and refresh there. I meant to tell you that all the unpleasantness about that bank-note is over."

"Is it?"

"Yes. It has been recovered by Mr. Creswell, who came here last night. I've got it, and you're not to blame," said Sir Bale.

"But some one *is* to blame," observed Mr. Feltram, smiling still.

"Well, *you* are not, and that ends it," said the Baronet peremptorily.

"Ends it? Really, how good! how very good!"

Sir Bale looked at him, for there was something ambiguous and even derisive in the tone of Feltram's voice.

But before he could quite make up his mind, Feltram spoke again.

"Everything is settled about you and me?"

"There is nothing to prevent your staying at Mardykes now," said Sir Bale graciously.

"I shall be with you for two years, and then I go on my travels," answered Feltram, with a saturnine and somewhat wild look around him.

"Is he going mad?" thought the Baronet.

"But before I go, I'm to put you in a way of paying off your mortgages. That is my business here."

Sir Bale looked at him sharply. But now there was not the unpleasant smile, but the darkened look of a man in secret pain.

"You shall know it all by and by."

And without more ceremony, and with a darkening face, Philip Feltram made his way under the boughs of the thick oaks that grew there, leaving on Sir Bale's mind an impression that he had been watching some one at a distance, and had gone in consequence of a signal.

In a few seconds he followed in the same direction, halloaing after Feltram; for he did not like the idea of his wandering about the country by moonlight, or possibly losing his life among the precipices, and bringing a new discredit upon his house. But no answer came; nor could he in that thick copse gain sight of him again.

When Sir Bale reached Mardykes Hall he summoned Mrs. Julaper, and had a long talk with her. But she could not say that there appeared anything amiss with Philip Feltram; only he seemed more reserved, and as if he was brooding over something he did not intend to tell.

"But, you know, Sir Bale, what happened might well make a thoughtful man of him. If he's ever to think of Death, it should be after looking him so hard in the face; and I'm not ashamed to say, I'm glad to see he has grace to take the lesson, and I hope his experiences may be sanctified to him, poor fellow! Amen."

"Very good song, and very well sung," said Sir Bale; "but it doesn't seem to me that he has been improved, Mrs. Julaper. He seems, on the contrary, in a queer temper and anything but a heavenly frame of mind; and I thought I'd ask you, because if he is ill—I mean feverish—it might account for his eccentricities, as well as make it necessary to send after him, and bring him home, and put him to bed. But I suppose it is as you say,—his adventure has upset him a little, and he'll sober in a day or two, and return to his old ways."

But this did not happen. A change, more comprehensive than at first appeared, had taken place, and a singular alteration was gradually established.

He grew thin, his eyes hollow, his face gradually forbidding.

His ways and temper were changed: he was a new man with Sir Bale; and the Baronet after a time, people said, began to grow afraid of him. And certainly Feltram had acquired an extraordinary influence over the Baronet, who a little while ago had regarded and treated him with so much contempt.

XV. The Purse of Gold

The Baronet was very slightly known in his county. He had led a reserved and inhospitable life. He was pressed upon by heavy debts; and being a proud man, held aloof from society and its doings. He wished people to understand that he was nursing his estate; but somehow the estate did not thrive at nurse. In the country other people's business is admirably well known; and the lord of Mardykes was conscious, perhaps, that his neighbours knew as well he did, that the utmost he could do was to pay the interest charged upon it, and to live in a frugal way enough.

The lake measures some four or five miles across, from the little jetty under the walls of Mardykes Hall to Cloostedd.

Philip Feltram, changed and morose, loved a solitary row upon the lake; and sometimes, with no one to aid him in its management, would take the little sailboat and pass the whole day upon those lonely waters.

Frequently he crossed to Cloostedd; and mooring the boat under the solemn trees that stand reflected in that dark mirror, he would disembark and wander among the lonely woodlands, as people thought, cherishing in those ancestral scenes the memory of ineffaceable injuries, and the wrath and revenge that seemed of late to darken his countenance, and to hold him always in a moody silence.

One autumnal evening Sir Bale Mardykes was sourly ruminating after his solitary meal. A very red sun was pouring its last low beams through the valley at the western extremity of the lake, across its elsewhere sombre waters, and touching with a sudden and blood-red tint the sail of the skiff in which Feltram was returning from his lonely cruise.

"Here comes my domestic water-fiend," sneered Sir Bale, as he lay back in his cumbrous arm-chair. "Cheerful place, pleasant people, delicious fate! The place alone has been enough to set that fool out of his little senses, d——n him!"

Sir Bale averted his eyes, and another subject not pleasanter entered his mind. He was thinking of the races that were coming off next week at Heckleston Downs, and what sums of money might be made there, and how hard it was that he should be excluded by fortune from that brilliant lottery.

"Ah, Mrs. Julaper, is that you?"

Mrs. Julaper, who was still at the door, curtsied, and said, "I came, Sir Bale, to see whether you'd please to like a jug of mulled claret, sir."

"Not I, my dear. I'll take a mug of beer and my pipe; that homely solace better befits a ruined gentleman."

"H'm, sir; you're not that, Sir Bale; you're no worse than half the lords and great men that are going. I would not hear another say that of you, sir."

"That's very kind of you, Mrs. Julaper; but you won't call *me* out for backbiting myself, especially as it is true, d——d true, Mrs. Julaper! Look ye; there never was a Mardykes here before but he could lay his hundred or his thousand pounds on the winner of the Heckleston Cup; and what could I bet? Little more than that mug of beer I spoke of. It was my great-grandfather who opened the course on the Downs of Heckleston, and now *I* can't show there! Well, what must I do? Grin and bear it, that's all. If you please, Mrs. Julaper, I will have that jug of claret you offered. I want spice and hot wine to keep me alive; but I'll smoke my pipe first, and in an hour's time it will do."

When Mrs. Julaper was gone, he lighted his pipe, and drew near the window, through which he looked upon the now fading sky and the twilight landscape.

He smoked his pipe out, and by that time it had grown nearly dark. He was still looking out upon the faint outlines of the view, and thinking angrily what a little bit of luck at the races would do for many a man who probably did not want it half so much as he. Vague and sombre as his thoughts were, they had, like the darkening landscape outside, shape enough to define their general character. Bitter and impious they were—as those of egotistic men naturally are in suffering. And after brooding, and muttering by fits and starts, he said:

"How many tens and hundreds of thousands of pounds will change hands at Heckleston next week; and not a shilling in all the change and shuffle will stick to me! How many a fellow would sell himself, like Dr. Faustus, just for the knowledge of the name of the winner! But he's no fool, and does not buy his own."

Something caught his eye; something moving on the wall. The fire was lighted, and cast a flickering and gigantic shadow upward; the figure of a man standing behind Sir Bale Mardykes, on whose shoulder he placed a lean hand. Sir Bale turned suddenly about, and saw Philip Feltram. He was looking dark and stern, and did not remove his hand from his shoulder as he peered into the Baronet's face with his deep-set mad eyes.

"Ha, Philip, upon my soul!" exclaimed Sir Bale, surprised. "How time flies! It seems only this minute since I saw the boat a mile and a half away from the shore. Well—yes; there has been time; it is dark now. Ha, ha! I assure you, you startled me. Won't you take something? Do. Shall I touch the bell?"

"You have been troubled about those mortgages. I told you I should pay them off, I thought."

Here there was a pause, and Sir Bale looked hard in Feltram's face. If he had been in his ordinary spirits, or perhaps in some of his haunts less solitary than Mardykes, he would have laughed; but here he had grown unlike himself, gloomy and credulous, and was, in fact, a nervous man.

Sir Bale smiled, and shook his head dismally.

"It is very kind of you, Feltram; the idea shows a kindly disposition. I know you would do me a kindness if you could."

As Sir Bale, each looking in the other's eyes, repeated in this sentence the words "kind," "kindly," "kindness," a smile lighted Feltram's face with at each word an intenser light; and Sir Bale grew sombre in its glare; and when he had done speaking, Feltram's face also on a sudden darkened.

"I have found a fortune-teller in Cloostedd Wood. Look here."

And he drew from his pocket a leathern purse, which he placed on the table in his hand; and Sir Bale heard the pleasant clink of coin in it.

"A fortune-teller! You don't mean to say she gave you that?" said Sir Bale.

Feltram smiled again, and nodded.

"It *was* the custom to give the fortune-teller a trifle. It is a great improvement making *her* fee you," observed Sir Bale, with an approach to his old manner.

"He put that in my hand with a message," said Feltram.

"He? O, then it was a male fortune-teller!"

"Gipsies go in gangs, men and women. *He* might lend, though *she* told fortunes," said Feltram.

"It's the first time I ever heard of gipsies lending money"; and he eyed the purse with a whimsical smile.

With his lean fingers still holding it, Feltram sat down at the table. His face contracted as if in cunning thought, and his chin sank upon his breast as he leaned back.

"I think," continued Sir Bale, "ever since they were spoiled, the Egyptians have been a little shy of lending, and leave that branch of business to the Hebrews."

"What would you give to know, now, the winner at Heckleston races?" said Feltram suddenly, raising his eyes.

"Yes; that would be worth something," answered Sir Bale, looking at him with more interest than the incredulity he affected would quite warrant.

"And this money I have power to lend you, to make your game."

"Do you mean that really?" said Sir Bale, with a new energy in tone, manner, and features.

"That's heavy; there are some guineas there," said Feltram with a dark smile, raising the purse in his hand a little, and letting it drop upon the table with a clang.

"There is *something* there, at all events," said Sir Bale.

Feltram took the purse by the bottom, and poured out on the table a handsome pile of guineas.

"And do you mean to say you got all that from a gipsy in Cloostedd Wood?"

"A friend, who is—*myself*," answered Philip Feltram.

"Yourself! Then it is yours—*you* lend it?" said the Baronet, amazed; for there was no getting over the heap of guineas, and the wonder was pretty equal whence they had come.

"Myself, and not myself," said Feltram oracularly; "as like as voice and echo, man and shadow."

Had Feltram in some of his solitary wanderings and potterings lighted upon hidden treasure? There was a story of two Feltrams of Cloostedd, brothers, who had joined the king's army and fought at Marston Moor, having buried in Cloostedd Wood a great deal of gold and plate and jewels. They had, it was said, intrusted one tried servant with the secret; and that servant remained at home. But by a perverse fatality the three witnesses had perished within a month: the two brothers at Marston Moor; and the confidant, of fever, at Cloostedd. From that day forth treasure-seekers had from time to time explored the woods of Cloostedd; and many a tree of mark was dug beside, and the earth beneath many a stone and scar and other landmark in that solitary forest was opened by night, until hope gradually died out, and the tradition had long ceased to prompt to action, and had become a story and nothing more.

The image of the nursery-tale had now recurred to Sir Bale after so long a reach of years; and the only imaginable way, in his mind, of accounting for penniless Philip Feltram having all that gold in his possession was that, in some of his lonely wanderings, chance had led him to the undiscovered hoard of the two Feltrams who had died in the great civil wars.

"Perhaps those gipsies you speak of found the money where you found them; and in that case, as Cloostedd Forest, and all that is in it is my property, their sending it to me is more like my servant's handing me my hat and stick when I'm going out, than making me a present."

"You will not be wise to rely upon the law, Sir Bale, and to refuse the help that comes unasked. But if you like your mortgages as they are, keep them; and if you like my terms as they are, take them; and when you have made up your mind, let me know."

Philip Feltram dropped the heavy purse into his capacious coat-pocket, and walked, muttering, out of the room.

XVI. The Message from Cloostedd

"Come back, Feltram; come back, Philip!" cried Sir Bale hastily. "Let us talk, can't we? Come and talk this odd business over a little; you must have mistaken what I meant; I should like to hear all about it."

"All is not much, sir," said Philip Feltram, entering the room again, the door of which he had half closed after him. "In the forest of Cloostedd I met to-day some people, one of whom can foretell events, and told me the names of the winners of the first three races at Heckleston, and gave me this purse, with leave to lend you so much money as you care to stake upon the races. I take no security; you shan't be troubled; and you'll never see the lender, unless you seek him out."

"Well, those are not bad terms," said Sir Bale, smiling wistfully at the purse, which Feltram had again placed upon the table.

"No, not bad," repeated Feltram, in the harsh low tone in which he now habitually spoke.

"You'll tell me what the prophet said about the winners; I should like to hear their names."

"The names I shall tell you if you walk out with me," said Feltram.

"Why not here?" asked Sir Bale.

"My memory does not serve me here so well. Some people, in some places, though they be silent, obstruct thought. Come, let us speak," said Philip Feltram, leading the way.

Sir Bale, with a shrug, followed him.

By this time it was dark. Feltram was walking slowly towards the margin of the lake; and Sir Bale, more curious as the delay increased, followed him, and smiled faintly as he looked after his tall, gaunt figure, as if, even in the dark, expressing a ridicule which he did not honestly feel, and the expression of which, even if there had been light, there was no one near enough to see.

When he reached the edge of the lake, Feltram stooped, and Sir Bale thought that his attitude was that of one who whispers to and caresses a reclining person. What he fancied was a dark figure lying horizontally in the shallow water, near the edge, turned out to be, as he drew near, no more than a shadow on the elsewhere lighter water; and with his change of position it had shifted and was gone, and Philip Feltram was but dabbling his hand this way and that in the water, and muttering faintly to himself. He rose as the Baronet drew near, and standing upright, said,

"I like to listen to the ripple of the water among the grass and pebbles; the tongue and lips of the lake are lapping and whispering all along. It is the merest poetry; but you are so romantic, you excuse me."

There was an angry curve in Feltram's eyebrows, and a cynical smile, and something in the tone which to the satirical Baronet was almost insulting. But even had he been less curious, I don't think he would have betrayed his mortification; for an odd and unavowed influence which he hated was gradually establishing in Feltram an ascendency which sometimes vexed and sometimes cowed him.

"You are not to tell," said Feltram, drawing near him in the dusk. "The secret is yours when you promise."

"Of course I promise," said Sir Bale. "If I believed it, you don't think I could be such an ass as to tell it; and if I didn't believe it, I'd hardly take the trouble."

Feltram stooped, and dipping the hollow of his hand in the water, he raised it full, and said he, "Hold out your hand—the hollow of your hand—like this. I divide the water for a sign—share to me and share to you." And he turned his hand, so as to pour half the water into the hollow palm of Sir Bale, who was smiling, with some uneasiness mixed in his mockery.

"Now, you promise to keep all secrets respecting the teller and the finder, be that who it may?"

"Yes, I promise," said Sir Bale.

"Now do as I do," said Feltram. And he shed the water on the ground, and with his wet fingers touched his forehead and his breast; and then he joined his hand with Sir Bale's, and said, "Now you are my safe man."

Sir Bale laughed. "That's the game they call 'grand mufti,'" said he.

"Exactly; and means nothing," said Feltram, "except that some day it will serve you to remember by. And now the names. Don't speak; listen—you may break the thought else. The winner of the first is *Beeswing*; of the second, *Falcon*; and of the third, *Lightning*."

He had stood for some seconds in silence before he spoke; his eyes were closed; he seemed to bring up thought and speech with difficulty, and spoke faintly and drowsily, both his hands a little raised, and the fingers extended, with the groping air of a man who moves in the dark. In this odd way, slowly, faintly, with many a sigh and scarcely audible groan, he gradually delivered his message and was silent. He stood, it seemed, scarcely half awake, muttering indistinctly and sighing to himself. You would have said that he was exhausted and suffering, like a man at his last hour resigning himself to death.

At length he opened his eyes, looked round a little wildly and languidly, and with another great sigh sat down on a large rock that lies by the margin of the lake, and sighed heavily again and again. You might have fancied that he was a second time recovering from drowning.

Then he got up, and looked drowsily round again, and sighed like a man worn out with fatigue, and was silent.

Sir Bale did not care to speak until he seemed a little more likely to obtain an answer. When that time came, he said, "I wish, for the sake of my believing, that your list was a little less incredible. Not one of the horses you name is the least likely; not one of them has a chance."

"So much the better for you; you'll get what odds you please. You had better seize your luck; on Tuesday Beeswing runs," said Feltram. "When you want money for the purpose, I'm your banker—here is your bank."

He touched his breast, where he had placed the purse, and then he turned and walked swiftly away.

Sir Bale looked after him till he disappeared in the dark. He fluctuated among many surmises about Feltram. Was he insane, or was he practising an imposture? or was he fool enough to believe the predictions of some real gipsies? and had he borrowed this money, which in Sir Bale's eyes seemed the greatest miracle in the matter, from those thriving shepherd mountaineers, the old Trebecks, who, he believed, were attached to him? Feltram had, he thought, borrowed it as if for himself; and having, as Sir Bale in his egotism supposed, "a sneaking regard" for him, had meant the loan for his patron, and conceived the idea of his using his revelations for the purpose of making his fortune. So, seeing no risk, and the temptation being strong, Sir Bale resolved to avail himself of the purse, and use his own judgment as to what horse to back.

About eleven o'clock Feltram, unannounced, walked, with his hat still on, into Sir Bale's library, and sat down at the opposite side of his table, looking gloomily into the Baronet's face for a time.

"Shall you want the purse?" he asked at last.

"Certainly; I always want a purse," said Sir Bale energetically.

"The condition is, that you shall back each of the three horses I have named. But you may back them for much or little, as you like, only the sum must not be less than five pounds in each hundred which this purse contains. That is the condition, and if you violate it, you will make some powerful people very angry, and you will feel it. Do you agree?"

"Of course; five pounds in the hundred—certainly; and how many hundreds are there?"

"Three."

"Well, a fellow with luck may win something with three hundred pounds, but it ain't very much."

"Quite enough, if you use it aright."

"Three hundred pounds," repeated the Baronet, as he emptied the purse, which Feltram had just placed in his hand, upon the table; and contemplating them with grave interest, he began telling them off in little heaps of five-and-twenty each. He might have thanked Feltram, but he was thinking more of the guineas than of the grizzly donor.

"Ay," said he, after a second counting, "I think there *are* exactly three hundred. Well, so you say I must apply three times five—fifteen of these. It is an awful pity backing those queer horses you have named; but if I must make the sacrifice, I must, I suppose?" he added, with a hesitating inquiry in the tone.

"If you don't, you'll rue it," said Feltram coldly, and walked away.

"Penny in pocket's a merry companion," says the old English proverb, and Sir Bale felt in better spirits and temper than he had for many a day as he replaced the guineas in the purse.

It was long since he had visited either the race-course or any other place of amusement. Now he might face his kind without fear that his pride should be mortified, and dabble in the fascinating agitations of the turf once more.

"Who knows how this little venture may turn out?" he thought. "It is time the luck should turn. My last summer in Germany, my last winter in Paris—d——n me, I'm owed something. It's time I should win a bit."

Sir Bale had suffered the indolence of a solitary and discontented life imperceptibly to steal upon him. It would not do to appear for the first time on Heckleston Lea with any of those signs of negligence which, in his case, might easily be taken for poverty. All his appointments, therefore, were carefully looked after; and on the Monday following, he, followed by his groom, rode away for the Saracen's Head at Heckleston, where he was to put up, for the races that were to begin on the day following, and presented as handsome an appearance as a peer in those days need have cared to show.

XVII. On the Course—Beeswing, Falcon, and Lightning

As he rode towards Golden Friars, through which his route lay, in the early morning light, in which the mists of night were clearing, he looked back towards Mardykes with a hope of speedy deliverance from that hated imprisonment, and of a return to the continental life in which he took delight. He saw the summits and angles of the old building touched with the cheerful beams, and the grand old trees, and at the opposite side the fells dark, with their backs towards the east; and down the side of the wooded and precipitous clough of Feltram, the light, with a pleasant contrast against the beetling purple of the fells, was breaking in the faint distance. On the lake he saw the white speck that indicated the sail of Philip Feltram's boat, now midway between Mardykes and the wooded shores of Cloostedd.

"Going on the same errand," thought Sir Bale, "I should not wonder. I wish him the same luck. Yes, he's going to Cloostedd Forest. I hope he may meet his gipsies there—the Trebecks, or whoever they are."

And as a momentary sense of degradation in being thus beholden to such people smote him, "Well," thought he, "who knows? Many a fellow will make a handsome sum of a poorer purse than this at Heckleston. It will be a light matter paying them then."

Through Golden Friars he rode. Some of the spectators who did not like him, wondered audibly at the gallant show, hoped it was paid for, and conjectured that he had ridden out in search of a wife. On the whole, however, the appearance of their Baronet in a smarter style than usual was popular, and accepted as a change to the advantage of the town.

Next morning he was on the race-course of Heckleston, renewing old acquaintance and making himself as agreeable as he could—an object, among some people, of curiosity and even interest. Leaving the carriage-sides, the hoods and bonnets, Sir Bale was soon among the betting men, deep in more serious business.

How did he make his book? He did not break his word. He backed Beeswing, Falcon, and Lightning. But it must be owned not for a shilling more than the five guineas each, to which he stood pledged. The odds were forty-five to one against Beeswing, sixty to one against Lightning, and fifty to one against Falcon.

"A pretty lot to choose!" exclaimed Sir Bale, with vexation. "As if I had money so often, that I should throw it away!"

The Baronet was testy thinking over all this, and looked on Feltram's message as an impertinence and the money as his own.

Let us now see how Sir Bale Mardykes' pocket fared.

Sulkily enough at the close of the week he turned his back on Heckleston race-course, and took the road to Golden Friars.

He was in a rage with his luck, and by no means satisfied with himself; and yet he had won something. The result of the racing had been curious. In the three principal races the favourites had been beaten: one by an accident, another on a technical point, and the third by fair running. And what horses had won? The names were precisely those which the "fortune-teller" had predicted.

Well, then, how was Sir Bale in pocket as he rode up to his ancestral house of Mardykes, where a few thousand pounds would have been very welcome? He had won exactly 775 guineas; and had he staked a hundred instead of five on each of the names communicated by Feltram, he would have won 15,500 guineas.

He dismounted before his hall-door, therefore, with the discontent of a man who had lost nearly 15,000 pounds. Feltram was upon the steps, and laughed dryly.

"What do you laugh at?" asked Sir Bale tartly.

"You've won, haven't you?"

"Yes, I've won; I've won a trifle."

"On the horses I named?"

"Well, yes; it so turned out, by the merest accident."

Feltram laughed again dryly, and turned away.

Sir Bale entered Mardykes Hall, and was surly. He was in a much worse mood than before he had ridden to Heckleston. But after a week or so ruminating upon the occurrence, he wondered that Feltram spoke no more of it. It was undoubtedly wonderful. There had been no hint of repayment yet, and he had made some hundreds by the loan; and, contrary to all likelihood, the three horses named by the unknown soothsayer had won. Who was this gipsy? It would be worth bringing the soothsayer to Mardykes, and giving his people a camp on the warren, and all the poultry they could catch, and a pig or a sheep every now and then. Why, that seer was worth the philosopher's stone, and could make Sir Bale's fortune in a season. Some one else would be sure to pick him up if he did not.

So, tired of waiting for Feltram to begin, he opened the subject one day himself. He had not seen him for two or three days; and in the wood of Mardykes he saw his lank figure standing among the thick trees, upon a little knoll, leaning on a staff which he sometimes carried with him in his excursions up the mountains.

"Feltram!" shouted Sir Bale.

Feltram turned and beckoned. Sir Bale muttered, but obeyed the signal.

"I brought you here, because you can from this point with unusual clearness today see the opening of the Clough of Feltram at the other side, and the clump of trees, where you will find the way to reach the person about whom you are always thinking."

"Who said I am always thinking about him?" said the Baronet angrily; for he felt like a man detected in a weakness, and resented it.

"*I* say it, because I *know* it; and *you* know it also. See that clump of trees standing solitary in the hollow? Among them, to the left, grows an ancient oak. Cut in its bark are two enormous letters: H—F; so large and bold, that the rugged furrows of the oak bark fail to obscure them, although they are ancient and spread by time. Standing against the trunk of this great tree, with your back to these letters, you are looking up the Glen or Clough of Feltram, that opens northward, where stands Cloostedd Forest spreading far and thick. Now, how do you find our fortune-teller?"

"That is exactly what I wish to know," answered Sir Bale; "because, although I can't, of course, believe that he's a witch, yet he has either made the most marvellous fluke I've heard of, or else he has got extraordinary sources of information; or perhaps he acts partly on chance, partly on facts. Be it which you please, I say he's a marvellous fellow; and I should like to see him, and have a talk with him; and perhaps he could arrange with me. I should be very glad to make an arrangement with him to give me the benefit of his advice about any matter of the same kind again."

"I think he's willing to see you; but he's a fellow with a queer fancy and a pig-head. He'll not come here; you must go to him; and approach him his own way too, or you may fail to find him. On these terms he invites you."

Sir Bale laughed.

"He knows his value, and means to make his own terms."

"Well, there's nothing unfair in that; and I don't see that I should dispute it. How is one to find him?"

"Stand, as I told you, with your back to those letters cut in the oak. Right before you lies an old Druidic altar-stone. Cast your eye over its surface, and on some part of it you are sure to see a black stain about the size of a man's head. Standing, as I suppose you, against the oak, that stain, which changes its place from day to day, will give you the line you must follow through the forest in order to light upon him. Take carefully from it such trees or objects as will guide you; and when the forest thickens, do the best you can to keep to the same line. You are sure to find him."

"You'll come, Feltram. I should lose myself in that wilderness, and probably fail to discover him," said Sir Bale; "and I really wish to see him."

"When two people wish to meet, it is hard if they don't. I can go with you a bit of the way; I can walk a little through the forest by your side, until I see the small flower that grows peeping here and there, that always springs where those people walk; and when I begin to see that sign, I must leave you. And, first, I'll take you across the lake."

"By Jove, you'll do no such thing!" said Sir Bale hastily.

"But that is the way he chooses to be approached," said Philip Feltram.

"I have a sort of feeling about that lake; it's the one childish spot that is left in my imagination. The nursery is to blame for it—old stories and warnings; and I can't think of that. I should feel I had invoked an evil omen if I did. I know it is all nonsense; but we are queer creatures, Feltram. I must only ride there."

"Why, it is five-and-twenty miles round the lake to that; and after all were done, he would not see you. He knows what he's worth, and he'll have his own way," answered Feltram. "The sun will soon set. See that withered branch, near Snakes Island, that looks like fingers rising from the water? When its points grow tipped with red, the sun has but three minutes more to live."

"That is a wonder which I can't see; it is too far away."

"Yes, the lake has many signs; but it needs sight to see them," said Feltram.

"So it does," said the Baronet; "more than most men have got. I'll ride round, I say; and I make my visit, for this time, my own way."

"You'll not find him, then; and he wants his money. It would be a pity to vex him."

"It was to you he lent the money," said Sir Bale.

"Yes."

"Well, you are the proper person to find him out and pay him," urged Sir Bale.

"Perhaps so; but he invites you; and if you don't go, he may be offended, and you may hear no more from him."

"We'll try. When can you go? There are races to come off next week, for once and away, at Langton. I should not mind trying my luck there. What do you say?"

"I know nothing about it. What can I say?"

"You can go there and pay him, and ask the same question—what horses, I mean, are to win. All the county are to be there; and plenty of money will change hands."

"I'll try," said Feltram.

"When will you go?"

"To-morrow," he answered.

"I have an odd idea, Feltram, that you are really going to pay off those cursed mortgages."

He laid his hand with at least a gesture of kindness on the thin arm of Feltram, who coldly answered,

"So have I"; and walked down the side of the little knoll and away, without another word or look.

XVIII. On the Lake, at Last

Next day Philip Feltram crossed the lake; and Sir Bale, seeing the boat on the water, guessed its destination, and watched its progress with no little interest, until he saw it moored and its sail drop at the rude pier that affords a landing at the Clough of Feltram. He was now satisfied that Philip had actually gone to seek out the "cunning man" and gather hints for the next race.

When that evening Feltram returned, and, later still, entered Sir Bale's library, the master of Mardykes was gladder to see his face and more interested about his news than he would have cared to confess.

Philip Feltram did not affect unconsciousness of that anxiety, but, with great directness, proceeded to satisfy it.

"I was in Cloostedd Forest to-day, nearly all day—and found the old gentleman in a wax. He did not ask me to drink, nor show me any kindness. He was huffed because you would not take the trouble to cross the lake to speak to him yourself. He took the money you sent him and counted it over, and dropped it into his pocket;

and he called you hard names enough and to spare; but I brought him round, and at last he did talk."

"And what did he say?"

"He said that the estate of Mardykes would belong to a Feltram."

"He might have said something more likely," said Sir Bale sourly. "Did he say anything more?"

"Yes. He said the winner at Langton Lea would be Silver Bell."

"Any other name?"

"No."

"Silver Bell? Well, that's not so odd as the last. Silver Bell stands high in the list. He has a good many backers—long odds in his favour against most of the field. I should not mind backing Silver Bell."

The fact is, that he had no idea of backing any other horse from the moment he heard the soothsayer's prediction. He made up his mind to no half measures this time. He would go in to win something handsome.

He was in great force and full of confidence on the race course. He had no fears for the result. He bet heavily. There was a good margin still untouched of the Mardykes estate; and Sir Bale was a good old name in the county. He found a ready market for his offers, and had soon staked—such is the growing frenzy of that excitement—about twenty thousand pounds on his favourite, and stood to win seven.

He did not win, however. He lost his twenty thousand pounds.

And now the Mardykes estate was in imminent danger. Sir Bale returned, having distributed IOUs and promissory notes in all directions about him—quite at his wit's end.

Feltram was standing—as on the occasion of his former happier return—on the steps of Mardykes Hall, in the evening sun, throwing eastward a long shadow that was lost in the lake. He received him, as before, with a laugh.

Sir Bale was too much broken to resent this laugh as furiously as he might, had he been a degree less desperate.

He looked at Feltram savagely, and dismounted.

"Last time you would not trust him, and this time he would not trust you. He's huffed, and played you false."

"It was not he. I should have backed that d———d horse in any case," said Sir Bale, grinding his teeth. "What a witch you have discovered! One thing is true, perhaps. If there was a Feltram rich enough, he might have the estate now; but there ain't. They are all beggars. So much for your conjurer."

"He may make amends to you, if you make amends to him."

"He! Why, what can that wretched impostor do? D———n me, I'm past helping now."

"Don't you talk so," said Feltram. "Be civil. You must please the old gentleman. He'll make it up. He's placable when it suits him. Why not go to him his own way? I hear you are nearly ruined. You must go and make it up."

"Make it up! With whom? With a fellow who can't make even a guess at what's coming? Why should I trouble my head about him more?"

"No man, young or old, likes to be frumped. Why did you cross his fancy? He won't see you unless you go to him as he chooses."

"If he waits for that, he may wait till doomsday. I don't choose to go on that water—and cross it I won't," said Sir Bale.

But when his distracting reminders began to pour in upon him, and the idea of dismembering what remained of his property came home to him, his resolution faltered.

"I say, Feltram, what difference can it possibly make to him if I choose to ride round to Cloostedd Forest instead of crossing the lake in a boat?"

Feltram smiled darkly, and answered.

"I can't tell. Can you?"

"Of course I can't—I say I can't; besides, what audacity of a fellow like that presuming to prescribe to me! Utterly ludicrous! And he can't predict—do you really think or believe, Feltram, that he can?"

"I know he can. I know he misled you on purpose. He likes to punish those who don't respect his will; and there is a reason in it, often quite clear—not ill-natured. Now you see he compels you to seek him out, and when you do, I think he'll help you through your trouble. He said he would."

"Then you have seen him since?"

"Yesterday. He has put a pressure on you; but he means to help you."

"If he means to help me, let him remember I want a banker more than a seer. Let him give me a lift, as he did before. He must lend me money."

"He'll not stick at that. When he takes up a man, he carries him through."

"The races of Byermere—I might retrieve at them. But they don't come off for a month nearly; and what is a man like me to do in the meantime?"

"Every man should know his own business best. I'm not like you," said Feltram grimly.

Now Sir Bale's trouble increased, for some people were pressing. Something like panic supervened; for it happened that land was bringing just then a bad price, and more must be sold in consequence.

"All I can tell them is, I am selling land. It can't be done in an hour. I'm selling enough to pay them all twice over. Gentlemen used to be able to wait till a man sold his acres for payment. D——n them! do they want my body, that they can't let me alone for five minutes?"

The end of it was, that before a week Sir Bale told Feltram that he would go by boat, since that fellow insisted on it; and he did not very much care if he were drowned.

It was a beautiful autumnal day. Everything was bright in that mellowed sun, and the deep blue of the lake was tremulous with golden ripples; and crag and peak and scattered wood, faint in the distance, came out with a filmy distinctness on the fells in that pleasant light.

Sir Bale had been ill, and sent down the night before for Doctor Torvey. He was away with a patient. Now, in the morning, he had arrived inopportunely. He met Sir Bale as he issued from the house, and had a word with him in the court, for he would not turn back.

"Well," said the Doctor, after his brief inspection, "you ought to be in your bed; that's all I can say. You are perfectly mad to think of knocking about like this. Your pulse is at a hundred and ten; and, if you go across the lake and walk about Cloostedd, you'll be raving before you come back."

Sir Bale told him, apologetically, as if his life were more to his doctor than to himself, that he would take care not to fatigue himself, and that the air would do him good, and that in any case he could not avoid going; and so they parted.

Sir Bale took his seat beside Feltram in the boat, the sail was spread, and, bending to the light breeze that blew from Golden Friars, she glided from the jetty under Mardykes Hall, and the eventful voyage had begun.

XIX. Mystagogus

The sail was loosed, the boat touched the stone step, and Feltram sprang out and made her fast to the old iron ring. The Baronet followed. So! he had ventured upon that water without being drowned. He looked round him as if in a dream. He had not been there since his childhood. There were no regrets, no sentiment, no remorse; only an odd return of the associations and fresh feelings of boyhood, and a long reach of time suddenly annihilated.

The little hollow in which he stood; the three hawthorn trees at his right; every crease and undulation of the sward, every angle and crack in the lichen-covered rock at his feet, recurred with a sharp and instantaneous recognition to his memory.

"Many a time your brother and I fished for hours together from that bank there, just where the bramble grows. That bramble has not grown an inch ever since, not a leaf altered; we used to pick blackberries off it, with our rods stuck in the bank—it was later in the year than now—till we stript it quite bare after a day or two. The steward used to come over—they were marking timber for cutting and we used to stay here while they rambled through the wood, with an axe marking the trees that were to come down. I wonder whether the big old boat is still anywhere. I suppose she was broken up, or left to rot; I have not seen her since we came home. It was in the wood that lies at the right—the other wood is called the forest; they say in old times it was eight miles long, northward up the shore of the lake, and full of deer; with a forester, and a reeve, and a verderer, and all that. Your brother was older than you; he went to India, or the Colonies; is he living still?"

"I care not."

"That's good-natured, at all events; but do you know?"

"Not I; and what matter? If he's living, I warrant he has his share of the curse, the sweat of his brow and his bitter crust; and if he is dead, he's dust or worse, he's rotten, and smells accordingly."

Sir Bale looked at him; for this was the brother over whom, only a year or two ago, Philip used to cry tears of pathetic longing. Feltram looked darkly in his face, and sneered with a cold laugh.

"I suppose you mean to jest?" said Sir Bale.

"Not I; it is the truth. It is what you'd say, if you were honest. If he's alive, let him keep where he is; and if he's dead, I'll have none of him, body or soul. Do you hear that sound?"

"Like the wind moaning in the forest?"

"Yes."

"But I feel no wind. There's hardly a leaf stirring."

"I think so," said Feltram. "Come along."

And he began striding up the gentle slope of the glen, with many a rock peeping through its sward, and tufted ferns and furze, giving a wild and neglected character to the scene; the background of which, where the glen loses itself in a distant turn, is formed by its craggy and wooded side.

Up they marched, side by side, in silence, towards that irregular clump of trees, to which Feltram had pointed from the Mardykes side.

As they approached, it showed more scattered, and two or three of the trees were of grander dimensions than in the distance they had appeared; and as they walked, the broad valley of Cloostedd Forest opened grandly on their left, studding the sides of the valley with solitary trees or groups, which thickened as it descended to the broad level, in parts nearly three miles wide, on which stands the noble forest of Cloostedd, now majestically reposing in the stirless air, gilded and flushed with the melancholy tints of autumn.

I am now going to relate wonderful things; but they rest on the report, strangely consistent, it is true, of Sir Bale Mardykes. That all his senses, however, were sick and feverish, and his brain not quite to be relied on at that moment, is a fact of which sceptics have a right to make all they please and can.

Startled at their approach, a bird like a huge mackaw bounced from the boughs of the trees, and sped away, every now and then upon the ground, toward the shelter of the forest, fluttering and hopping close by the side of the little brook which, emerging from the forest, winds into the glen, and beside the course of which Sir Bale and Philip Feltram had ascended from the margin of the lake.

It fluttered on, as if one of its wings were hurt, and kept hopping and bobbing and flying along the grass at its swiftest, screaming all the time discordantly.

"That must be old Mrs. Amerald's bird, that got away a week ago," said Sir Bale, stopping and looking after it. "Was not it a mackaw?"

"No," said Feltram; "that was a grey parrot; but there are stranger birds in Cloostedd Forest, for my ancestors collected all that would live in our climate, and were at pains to find them the food and shelter they were accustomed to until they grew hardy—that is how it happens."

"By Jove, that's a secret worth knowing," said Sir Bale. "That would make quite a feature. What a fat brute that bird was! and green and dusky-crimson and yellow; but its head is white—age, I suspect; and what a broken beak—hideous bird! splendid plumage; something between a mackaw and a vulture."

Sir Bale spoke jocularly, but with the interest of a bird-fancier; a taste which, when young, he had indulged; and for the moment forgot his cares and the object of his unwonted excursion.

A moment after, a lank slim bird, perfectly white, started from the same boughs, and winged its way to the forest.

"A kite, I think; but its body is a little too long, isn't it?" said Sir Bale again, stopping and looking after its flight also.

"A foreign kite, I daresay?" said Feltram.

All this time there was hopping near them a jay, with the tameness of a bird accustomed to these solitudes. It peered over its slender wing curiously at the visitors; pecking here and nodding there; and thus hopping, it made a circle round them more than once. Then it fluttered up, and perched on a bough of the old oak, from the deep labyrinth of whose branches the other birds had emerged; and from thence it flew down and lighted on the broad druidic stone, that stood like a cyclopean table on its sunken stone props, before the snakelike roots of the oak.

Across this it hopped conceitedly, as over a stage on which it figured becomingly; and after a momentary hesitation, with a little spring, it rose and winged its way in the same direction which the other birds had taken, and was quickly lost in thick forest to the left.

"Here," said Feltram, "this is the tree."

"I remember it well! A gigantic trunk; and, yes, those marks; but I never before read them as letters. Yes, H.F., so they are—very odd I should not have remarked them. They are so large, and so strangely drawn-out in some places, and filled-in in others, and distorted, and the moss has grown about them; I don't wonder I took them for natural cracks and chasms in the bark," said Sir Bale.

"Very like," said Feltram.

Sir Bale had remarked, ever since they had begun their walk from the shore, that Feltram seemed to undergo a gloomy change. Sharper, grimmer, wilder grew his features, and shadow after shadow darkened his face wickedly.

The solitude and grandeur of the forest, and the repulsive gloom of his companion's countenance and demeanour, communicated a tone of anxiety to Sir Bale; and they stood still, side by side, in total silence for a time, looking toward the forest glades; between themselves and which, on the level sward of the valley, stood many a noble tree and fantastic group of forked birch and thorn, in the irregular formations into which Nature had thrown them.

"Now you stand between the letters. Cast your eyes on the stone," said Feltram suddenly, and his low stern tones almost startled the Baronet.

Looking round, he perceived that he had so placed himself that his point of vision was exactly from between the two great letters, now half-obliterated, which he had been scrutinizing just as he turned about to look toward the forest of Cloostedd.

"Yes, so I am," said Sir Bale.

There was within him an excitement and misgiving, akin to the sensation of a man going into battle, and which corresponded with the pale and sombre frown which Feltram wore, and the manifest change which had come upon him.

"Look on the stone steadily for a time, and tell me if you see a black mark, about the size of your hand, anywhere upon its surface," said Feltram.

Sir Bale affected no airs of scepticism now; his imagination was stirred, and a sense of some unknown reality at the bottom of that which he had affected to treat before as illusion, inspired a strange interest in the experiment.

"Do you see it?" asked Feltram.

Sir Bale was watching patiently, but he had observed nothing of the kind.

Sharper, darker, more eager grew the face of Philip Feltram, as his eyes traversed the surface of that huge horizontal block.

"Now?" asked Feltram again.

No, he had seen nothing.

Feltram was growing manifestly uneasy, angry almost; he walked away a little, and back again, and then two or three times round the tree, with his hands shut, and treading the ground like a man trying to warm his feet, and so impatiently he returned, and looked again on the stone.

Sir Bale was still looking, and very soon said, drawing his brows together and looking hard,

"Ha!—yes—hush. There it is, by Jove!—wait—yes—there; it is growing quite plain."

It seemed not as if a shadow fell upon the stone, but rather as if the stone became semi-transparent, and just under its surface was something dark—a hand, he thought it—and darker and darker it grew, as if coming up toward the surface, and after some little wavering, it fixed itself movelessly, pointing, as he thought, toward the forest.

"It looks like a hand," said he. "By Jove, it *is* a hand—pointing towards the forest with a finger."

"Don't mind the finger; look only on that black blurred mark, and from the point where you stand, taking that point for your direction, look to the forest. Take some tree or other landmark for an object, enter the forest there, and pursue the same line, as well as you can, until you find little flowers with leaves like wood-sorrel, and with tall stems and a red blossom, not larger than a drop, such as you have not seen before, growing among the trees, and follow wherever they seem to grow thickest, and there you will find him."

All the time that Feltram was making this little address, Sir Bale was endeavouring to fix his route by such indications as Feltram described; and when he had succeeded in quite establishing the form of a peculiar tree—a melancholy ash, one huge limb of which had been blasted by lightning, and its partly stricken arm stood high and barkless, stretching its white fingers, as it were, into the forest, and signing the way for him—

"I have it now," said he. "Come Feltram, you'll come a bit of the way with me."

Feltram made no answer, but slowly shook his head, and turned and walked away, leaving Sir Bale to undertake his adventure alone.

The strange sound they had heard from the midst of the forest, like the rumble of a storm or the far-off trembling of a furnace, had quite ceased. Not a bird was hopping on the grass, or visible on bough or in the sky. Not a living creature was in sight—never was stillness more complete, or silence more oppressive.

It would have been ridiculous to give way to the old reluctance which struggled within him. Feltram had strode down the slope, and was concealed by a screen of bushes from his view. So quite alone, and full of an interest quite new to him, he set out in quest of his adventures.

XX. The Haunted Forest

Sir Bale Mardykes walked in a straight line, by bush and scaur, over the undulating ground, to the blighted ash-tree; and as he approached it, its withered bough stretched more gigantically into the air, and the forest seemed to open where it pointed.

He passed it by, and in a few minutes had lost sight of it again, and was striding onward under the shadow of the forest, which already enclosed him. He was directing his march with all the care he could, in exactly that line which, according to Feltram's rule, had been laid down for him. Now and then, having, as soldiers say, taken an object, and fixed it well in his memory, he would pause and look about him.

As a boy he had never entered the wood so far; for he was under a prohibition, lest he should lose himself in its intricacies, and be benighted there. He had often heard that the wood was haunted, and that too would, when a boy, have deterred him. It was on this account that the scene was so new to him, and that he cared so often to stop and look about him. Here and there a vista opened, exhibiting the same utter desertion, and opening farther perspectives through the tall stems of the trees faintly visible in the solemn shadow. No flowers could he see, but once or twice a wood anemone, and now and then a tiny grove of wood-sorrel.

Huge oak-trees now began to mingle and show themselves more and more frequently among the other timber; and gradually the forest became a great oak wood unintruded upon by any less noble tree. Vast trunks curving outwards to the roots, and expanding again at the branches, stood like enormous columns, striking out their groining boughs, with the dark vaulting of a crypt.

As he walked under the shadow of these noble trees, suddenly his eye was struck by a strange little flower, nodding quite alone by the knotted root of one of those huge trees.

He stooped and picked it up, and as he plucked it, with a harsh scream just over his head, a large bird with heavy beating wings broke away from the midst of the branches. He could not see it, but he fancied the scream was like that of the huge mackaw whose ill-poised flight he had watched. This conjecture was but founded on the odd cry he had heard.

The flower was a curious one—a stem fine as a hair supported a little bell, that looked like a drop of blood, and never ceased trembling. He walked on, holding this in his fingers; and soon he saw another of the same odd type, then another at a shorter distance, then one a little to the right and another to the left, and farther on a little group, and at last the dark slope was all over trembling with these little bells, thicker and thicker as he descended a gentle declivity to the bank of the little brook, which flowing through the forest loses itself in the lake. The low murmur of this forest stream was almost the first sound, except the shriek of the bird that startled him a little time ago, which had disturbed the profound silence of the wood since he entered it. Mingling with the faint sound of the brook, he now heard a harsh human voice calling words at intervals, the purport of which he could not yet catch; and walking on, he saw seated upon the grass, a strange figure, corpulent, with a great hanging nose, the whole face glowing like copper. He was dressed in a bottle-green cut-velvet coat, of the style of Queen Anne's reign, with a dusky crimson waistcoat, both overlaid with broad and tarnished gold lace, and his silk stockings on thick swollen legs, with great buckled shoes, straddling on the grass, were rolled up over his knees to his short breeches. This ill-favoured old fellow, with a powdered wig that came down to his shoulders, had a dice-box in each hand, and was apparently playing his left against his right, and calling the throws with a hoarse cawing voice.

Raising his black piggish eyes, he roared to Sir Bale, by name, to come and sit down, raising one of his dice-boxes, and then indicating a place on the grass opposite to him.

Now Sir Bale instantly guessed that this was the man, gipsy, warlock, call him what he might, of whom he had come in search. With a strange feeling of curiosity, disgust, and awe, he drew near. He was resolved to do whatever this old man required of him, and to keep him, this time, in good humour.

Sir Bale did as he bid him, and sat down; and taking the box he presented, they began throwing turn about, with three dice, the copper-faced old man teaching him the value of the throws, as he proceeded, with many a curse and oath; and when he did not like a throw, grinning with a look of such real fury, that the master of Mardykes almost expected him to whip out his sword and prick him through as he sat before him.

After some time spent at this play, in which guineas passed now this way, now that, chucked across the intervening patch of grass, or rather moss, that served them for a green cloth, the old man roared over his shoulder,

"Drink"; and picking up a long-stemmed conical glass which Sir Bale had not observed before, he handed it over to the Baronet; and taking another in his fingers, he held it up, while a very tall slim old man, dressed in a white livery, with powdered hair and cadaverous face, which seemed to run out nearly all into a long thin hooked nose, advanced with a flask in each hand. Looking at the unwieldly old man, with his heavy nose, powdered head, and all the bottle-green, crimson, and gold about him, and the long slim serving man, with sharp beak, and white from head to heel, standing by him, Sir Bale was forcibly reminded of the great old macaw and the long and slender kite, whose colours they, after their fashion, reproduced, with something, also indescribable, of the air and character of the birds. Not standing on ceremony, the old fellow held up his own glass first, which the white lackey filled from the flask, and then he filled Sir Bale's glass.

It was a large glass, and might have held about half a pint; and the liquor with which the servant filled it was something of the colour of an opal, and circles of purple and gold seemed to be spreading continually outward from the centre, and running inward from the rim, and crossing one another, so as to form a beautiful rippling net-work.

"I drink to your better luck next time," said the old man, lifting his glass high, and winking with one eye, and leering knowingly with the other; "and you know what I mean."

Sir Bale put the liquor to his lips. Wine? Whatever it was, never had he tasted so delicious a flavour. He drained it to the bottom, and placing it on the grass beside him, and looking again at the old dicer, who was also setting down his glass, he saw, for the first time, the graceful figure of a young woman seated on the grass. She was dressed in deep mourning, had a black hood carelessly over her head, and, strangely, wore a black mask, such as are used at masquerades. So much of her throat and chin as he could see were beautifully white; and there was a prettiness in her air and figure which made him think what a beautiful creature she in all likelihood was. She was reclining slightly against the burly man in bottle-green and gold, and her arm was round his neck, and her slender white hand showed itself over his shoulder.

"Ho! my little Geaiette," cried the old fellow hoarsely; "it will be time that you and I should get home.—So, Bale Mardykes, I have nothing to object to you this time; you've crossed the lake, and you've played with me and won and lost, and drank your glass like a jolly companion, and now we know one another; and an acquaintance is made that will last. I'll let you go, and you'll come when I call for you. And now you'll want to know what horse will win next month at Rindermere races.—Whisper me, lass, and I'll tell him."

So her lips, under the black curtain, crept close to his ear, and she whispered.

"It will be Rainbow," said the old man harshly. "And now make your best speed out of the forest, or I'll set my black dogs after you, ho, ho, ho! and they may chance to pull you down. Away!"

He cried this last order with a glare so black, and so savage a shake of his huge fist, that Sir Bale, merely making his general bow to the group, clapped his hat on his head, and hastily began his retreat; but the same discordant voice yelled after him:

"You'll want that, you fool; pick it up." And there came hurtling after and beside him a great leather bag, stained, and stuffed with a heavy burden, and bounding by him it stopped with a little wheel that brought it exactly before his feet.

He picked it up, and found it heavy.

Turning about to make his acknowledgments, he saw the two persons in full retreat; the profane old scoundrel in the bottle-green limping and stumbling, yet bowling along at a wonderful rate, with many a jerk and reel, and the slender lady in black gliding away by his side into the inner depths of the forest.

So Sir Bale, with a strange chill, and again in utter solitude, pursued his retreat, with his burden, at a swifter pace, and after an hour or so, had recovered the point where he had entered the forest, and passing by the druidic stone and the mighty oak, saw down the glen at his right, standing by the edge of the lake, Philip Feltram, close to the bow of the boat.

XXI. Rindermere

Feltram looked grim and agitated when Sir Bale came up to him, as he stood on the flat-stone by which the boat was moored.

"You found him?" said he.

"Yes."

"The lady in black was there?"

"She was."

"And you played with him?"

"Yes."

"And what is that in your hand?"

"A bag of something, I fancy money; it is heavy; he threw it after me. We shall see just now; let us get away."

"He gave you some of his wine to drink?" said Feltram, looking darkly in his face; but there was a laugh in his eyes.

"Yes; of course I drank it; my object was to please him."

"To be sure."

The faint wind that carried them across the lake had quite subsided by the time they had reached the side where they now were.

There was now not wind enough to fill the sail, and it was already evening.

"Give me an oar; we can pull her over in little more than an hour," said Sir Bale; "only let us get away."

He got into the boat, sat down, and placed the leather bag with its heavy freightage at his feet, and took an oar. Feltram loosed the rope and shoved the boat off; and taking his seat also, they began to pull together, without another word, until, in about ten minutes, they had got a considerable way off the Cloostedd shore.

The leather bag was too clumsy a burden to conceal; besides, Feltram knew all about the transaction, and Sir Bale had no need to make a secret. The bag was old and soiled, and tied about the "neck" with a long leather thong, and it seemed to have been sealed with red wax, fragments of which were still sticking to it.

He got it open, and found it full of guineas.

"Halt!" cried Sir Bale, delighted, for he had half apprehended a trick upon his hopes; "gold it is, and a lot of it, by Jove!"

Feltram did not seem to take the slightest interest in the matter. Sulkily and drowsily he was leaning with his elbow on his knee, and it seemed thinking of something far away. Sir Bale could not wait to count them any longer. He reckoned them on the bench, and found two thousand.

It took some time; and when he had got them back into the leather bag, and tied them up again, Feltram, with a sudden start, said sharply,

"Come, take your oar—unless you like the lake by night; and see, a wind will soon be up from Golden Friars!"

He cast a wild look towards Mardykes Hall and Snakes Island, and applying himself to his oar, told Sir Bale to take his also; and nothing loath, the Baronet did so.

It was slow work, for the boat was not built for speed; and by the time they had got about midway, the sun went down, and twilight and the melancholy flush of the sunset tints were upon the lake and fells.

"Ho! here comes the breeze—up from Golden Friars," said Feltram; "we shall have enough to fill the sails now. If you don't fear spirits and Snakes Island, it is all the better for us it should blow from that point. If it blew from Mardykes now, it would be a stiff pull for you and me to get this tub home."

Talking as if to himself, and laughing low, he adjusted the sail and took the tiller, and so, yielding to the rising breeze, the boat glided slowly toward still distant Mardykes Hall.

The moon came out, and the shore grew misty, and the towering fells rose like sheeted giants; and leaning on the gunwale of the boat, Sir Bale, with the rush and gurgle of the water on the boat's side sounding faintly in his ear, thought of his day's adventure, which seemed to him like a dream—incredible but for the heavy bag that lay between his feet.

As they passed Snakes Island, a little mist, like a fragment of a fog, seemed to drift with them, and Sir Bale fancied that whenever it came near the boat's side she made a dip, as if strained toward the water; and Feltram always put out his hand, as if waving it from him, and the mist seemed to obey the gesture; but returned again and again, and the same thing always happened.

It was three weeks after, that Sir Bale, sitting up in his bed, very pale and wan, with his silk night-cap nodding on one side, and his thin hand extended on the coverlet, where the doctor had been feeling his pulse, in his darkened room, related all the wonders of this day to Doctor Torvey. The doctor had attended him through a fever which followed immediately upon his visit to Cloostedd.

"And, my dear sir, by Jupiter, can you really believe all that delirium to be sober fact?" said the doctor, sitting by the bedside, and actually laughing.

"I can't help believing it, because I can't distinguish in any way between all that and everything else that actually happened, and which I must believe. And, except that this is more wonderful, I can find no reason to reject it, that does not as well apply to all the rest."

"Come, come, my dear sir, this will never do—nothing is more common. These illusions accompanying fever frequently antedate the attack, and the man is actually raving before he knows he is ill."

"But what do you make of that bag of gold?"

"Some one has lent it. You had better ask all about it of Feltram when you can see him; for in speaking to me he seemed to know all about it, and certainly did not seem to think the matter at all out of the commonplace. It is just like that fisherman's story, about the hand that drew Feltram into the water on the night that he was nearly drowned. Every one can see what that was. Why of course it was simply the reflection of his own hand in the water, in that vivid lightning. When you have been out a little and have gained strength you will shake off these dreams."

"I should not wonder," said Sir Bale.

It is not to be supposed that Sir Bale reported all that was in his memory respecting his strange vision, if such it was, at Cloostedd. He made a selection of the incidents, and threw over the whole adventure an entirely accidental character, and described the money which the old man had thrown to him as amounting to a purse of five guineas, and mentioned nothing of the passages which bore on the coming race.

Good Doctor Torvey, therefore, reported only that Sir Bale's delirium had left two or three illusions sticking in his memory.

But if they were illusions, they survived the event of his recovery, and remained impressed on his memory with the sharpness of very recent and accurately observed fact.

He was resolved on going to the races of Rindermere, where, having in his possession so weighty a guarantee as the leather purse, he was determined to stake it all boldly on Rainbow—against which horse he was glad to hear there were very heavy odds.

The race came off. One horse was scratched, another bolted, the rider of a third turned out to have lost a buckle and three half-pence and so was an ounce and a half under weight, a fourth knocked down the post near Rinderness churchyard, and was held to have done it with his left instead of his right knee, and so had run at the wrong side. The result was that Rainbow came in first, and I should be afraid to say how much Sir Bale won. It was a sum that paid off a heavy debt, and left his affairs in a much more manageable state.

From this time Sir Bale prospered. He visited Cloostedd no more; but Feltram often crossed to that lonely shore as heretofore, and it is believed conveyed to him messages which guided his betting. One thing is certain, his luck never deserted him. His debts disappeared; and his love of continental life seemed to have departed. He became content with Mardykes Hall, laid out money on it, and although he never again cared to cross the lake, he seemed to like the scenery.

In some respects, however, he lived exactly the same odd and unpopular life. He saw no one at Mardykes Hall. He practised a very strict reserve. The neighbours laughed at and disliked him, and he was voted, whenever any accidental contact arose, a very disagreeable man; and he had a shrewd and ready sarcasm that made them afraid of him, and himself more disliked.

Odd rumours prevailed about his household. It was said that his old relations with Philip Feltram had become reversed; and that he was as meek as a mouse, and Feltram the bully now. It was also said that Mrs. Julaper had one Sunday evening when she drank tea at the Vicar's, told his good lady very mysteriously, and with many charges of secrecy, that Sir Bale was none the better of his late-found wealth; that he had a load upon his spirits, that he was afraid of Feltram, and so was every one else, more or less, in the house; that he was either mad or worse; and that it was an eerie dwelling, and strange company, and she should be glad herself of a change.

Good Mrs. Bedel told her friend Mrs. Torvey; and all Golden Friars heard all this, and a good deal more, in an incredibly short time.

All kinds of rumours now prevailed in Golden Friars, connecting Sir Bale's successes on the turf with some mysterious doings in Cloostedd Forest. Philip Feltram laughed when he heard these stories—especially when he heard the story that a supernatural personage had lent the Baronet a purse full of money.

"You should not talk to Doctor Torvey so, sir," said he grimly; "he's the greatest tattler in the town. It was old Farmer Trebeck, who could buy and sell us all down here, who lent that money. Partly from good-will, but not without acknowledgment. He has my hand for the first, not worth much, and yours to a bond for the two thousand guineas you brought home with you. It seems strange you should not remember that venerable and kind old farmer whom you talked with so long that day. His grandson, who expects to stand well in his will, being a trainer in Lord Varney's stables, has sometimes a tip to give, and he is the source of your information."

"By Jove, I must be a bit mad, then, that's all," said Sir Bale, with a smile and a shrug.

Philip Feltram moped about the house, and did precisely what he pleased. The change which had taken place in him became more and more pronounced. Dark and stern he always looked, and often malignant. He was like a man possessed of one evil thought which never left him.

There was, besides, the good old Gothic superstition of a bargain or sale of the Baronet's soul to the arch-fiend. This was, of course, very cautiously whispered in a place where he had influence. It was only a coarser and directer version of a suspicion, that in a more credulous generation penetrated a level of society quite exempt from such follies in our day.

One evening at dusk, Sir Bale, sitting after his dinner in his window, saw the tall figure of Feltram, like a dark streak, standing movelessly by the lake. An unpleasant feeling moved him, and then an impatience. He got up, and having primed himself with two glasses of brandy, walked down to the edge of the lake, and placed himself beside Feltram.

"Looking down from the window," said he, nerved with his Dutch courage, "and seeing you standing like a post, do you know what I began to think of?"

Feltram looked at him, but answered nothing.

"I began to think of taking a wife—*marrying*."

Feltram nodded. The announcement had not produced the least effect.

"Why the devil will you make me so uncomfortable! Can't you be like yourself—what you *were*, I mean? I won't go on living here alone with you. I'll take a wife, I tell you. I'll choose a good church-going woman, that will have every man, woman, and child in the house on their marrowbones twice a day, morning and evening, and three times on Sundays. How will you like that?"

"Yes, you will be married," said Feltram, with a quiet decision which chilled Sir Bale, for he had by no means made up his mind to that desperate step.

Feltram slowly walked away, and that conversation ended.

Now an odd thing happened about this time. There was a family of Feltram—county genealogists could show how related to the vanished family of Cloostedd—living at that time on their estate not far from Carlisle. Three co-heiresses now represented it. They were great beauties—the belles of their county in their day.

One was married to Sir Oliver Haworth of Haworth, a great family in those times. He was a knight of the shire, and had refused a baronetage, and, it was said, had his eye on a peerage. The other sister was married to Sir William Walsingham, a wealthy baronet; and the third and youngest, Miss Janet, was still unmarried, and at home at Cloudesly Hall, where her aunt, Lady Harbottle, lived with her, and made a dignified chaperon.

Now it so fell out that Sir Bale, having business at Carlisle, and knowing old Lady Harbottle, paid his respects at Cloudesly Hall; and being no less than five-and-forty years of age, was for the first time in his life, seriously in love.

Miss Janet was extremely pretty—a fair beauty with brilliant red lips and large blue eyes, and ever so many pretty dimples when she talked and smiled. It was odd, but not perhaps against the course of nature, that a man, though so old as he, and quite *blasé*, should fall at last under that fascination.

But what are we to say of the strange infatuation of the young lady? No one could tell why she liked him. It was a craze. Her family were against it, her intimates, her old nurse—all would not do; and the oddest thing was, that he seemed to take no pains to please her. The end of this strange courtship was that he married her; and she came home to Mardykes Hall, determined to please everybody, and to be the happiest woman in England.

With her came a female cousin, a good deal her senior, past thirty—Gertrude Mainyard, pale and sad, but very gentle, and with all the prettiness that can belong to her years.

This young lady has a romance. Her hero is far away in India; and she, content to await his uncertain return with means to accomplish the hope of their lives, in that frail chance has long embarked all the purpose and love of her life.

When Lady Mardykes came home, a new leaf was, as the phrase is, turned over. The neighbours and all the country people were willing to give the Hall a new trial. There was visiting and returning of visits; and young Lady Mardykes was liked and admired. It could not indeed have been otherwise. But here the improvement in the relations of Mardykes

Hall with other homes ceased. On one excuse or another Sir Bale postponed or evaded the hospitalities which establish intimacies. Some people said he was jealous of his young and beautiful wife. But for the most part his reserve was set down to the old inhospitable cause, some ungenial defect in his character; and in a little time the tramp of horses and roll of carriage-wheels were seldom heard up or down the broad avenue of Mardykes Hall.

Sir Bale liked this seclusion; and his wife, "so infatuated with her idolatry of that graceless old man," as surrounding young ladies said, that she was well content to forego the society of the county people for a less interrupted enjoyment of that of her husband. "What she could see in him" to interest or amuse her so, that for his sake she was willing to be "buried alive in that lonely place," the same critics were perpetually wondering.

A year and more passed thus; for the young wife, happily—*very* happily indeed, had it not been for one topic on which she and her husband could not agree. This was Philip Feltram; and an odd quarrel it was.

XXII. Sir Bale is Frightened

To Feltram she had conceived, at first sight, a horror. It was not a mere antipathy; fear mingled largely in it. Although she did not see him often, this restless dread grew upon her so, that she urged his dismissal upon Sir Bale, offering to provide, herself, for him a handsome annuity, charged on that part of her property which, by her marriage settlement, had remained in her power. There was a time when Sir Bale was only too anxious to get rid of him. But that was changed now. Nothing could now induce the Baronet to part with him. He at first evaded and resisted quietly. But, urged with a perseverance to which he was unused, he at last broke into fury that appalled her, and swore that if he was worried more upon the subject, he would leave her and the country, and see neither again. This exhibition of violence affrighted her all the more by reason of the contrast; for up to this he had been an uxorious husband. Lady Mardykes was in hysterics, and thoroughly frightened, and remained in her room for two or three days. Sir Bale went up to London about business, and was not home for more than a week. This was the first little squall that disturbed the serenity of their sky.

This point, therefore, was settled; but soon there came other things to sadden Lady Mardykes. There occurred a little incident, soon after Sir Bale's return from London, which recalled the topic on which they had so nearly quarrelled.

Sir Bale had a dressing-room, remote from the bedrooms, in which he sat and read and sometimes smoked. One night, after the house was all quiet, the Baronet being still up, the bell of this dressing-room rang long and furiously. It was such a peal as a person in extreme terror might ring. Lady Mardykes, with her maid in her room, heard it; and in great alarm she ran in her dressing-gown down the gallery to Sir Bale's room. Mallard the butler had already arrived, and was striving to force the door, which was secured. It gave way just as she reached it, and she rushed through.

Sir Bale was standing with the bell-rope in his hand, in the extremest agitation, looking like a ghost; and Philip Feltram was sitting in his chair, with a dark smile fixed upon him. For a minute she thought he had attempted to assassinate his master. She could not otherwise account for the scene.

There had been nothing of the kind, however; as her husband assured her again and again, as she lay sobbing on his breast, with her arms about his neck.

"To her dying hour," she afterwards said to her cousin, "she never could forget the dreadful look in Feltram's face."

No explanation of that scene did she ever obtain from Sir Bale, nor any clue to the cause of the agony that was so powerfully expressed in his countenance. Thus much only she learned from him, that Feltram had sought that interview for the purpose of announcing his departure, which was to take place within the year.

"You are not sorry to hear that. But if you knew all, you might. Let the curse fly where it may, it will come back to roost. So, darling, let us discuss him no more. Your wish is granted, *dis iratis*."

Some crisis, during this interview, seemed to have occurred in the relations between Sir Bale and Feltram. Henceforward they seldom exchanged a word; and when they did speak, it was coldly and shortly, like men who were nearly strangers.

One day in the courtyard, Sir Bale seeing Feltram leaning upon the parapet that overlooks the lake, approached him, and said in a low tone,

"I've been thinking if we—that is, I—do owe that money to old Trebeck, it is high time I should pay it. I was ill, and had lost my head at the time; but it turned out luckily, and it ought to be paid. I don't like the idea of a bond turning up, and a lot of interest."

"The old fellow meant it for a present. He is richer than you are; he wished to give the family a lift. He has destroyed the bond, I believe, and in no case will he take payment."

"No fellow has a right to force his money on another," answered Sir Bale. "I never asked him. Besides, as you know, I was not really myself, and the whole thing seems to me quite different from what you say it was; and, so far as my brain is concerned, it was all a phantasmagoria; but, you say, it was he."

"Every man is accountable for what he intends and for what he *thinks* he does," said Feltram cynically.

"Well, I'm accountable for dealing with that wicked old dicer I *thought* I saw—isn't that it? But I must pay old Trebeck all the same, since the money was his. Can you manage a meeting?"

"Look down here. Old Trebeck has just landed; he will sleep to-night at the George and Dragon, to meet his cattle in the morning at Golden Friars fair. You can speak to him yourself."

So saying Feltram glided away, leaving Sir Bale the task of opening the matter to the wealthy farmer of Cloostedd Fells.

A broad night of steps leads down from the courtyard to the level of the jetty at the lake: and Sir Bale descended, and accosted the venerable farmer, who was bluff, honest, and as frank as a man can be who speaks a *patois* which hardly a living man but himself can understand.

Sir Bale asked him to come to the Hall and take luncheon; but Trebeck was in haste. Cattle had arrived which he wanted to look at, and a pony awaited him on the road, hard by, to Golden Friars; and the old fellow must mount and away.

Then Sir Bale, laying his hand upon his arm in a manner that was at once lofty and affectionate, told in his ears the subject on which he wished to be understood.

The old farmer looked hard at him, and shook his head and laughed in a way that would have been insupportable in a house, and told him, "I hev narra bond o' thoine, mon."

"I know how that is; so does Philip Feltram."

"Well?"

"Well, I must replace the money."

The old man laughed again, and in his outlandish dialect told him to wait till he asked him. Sir Bale pressed it, but the old fellow put it off with outlandish banter; and as the Baronet grew testy, the farmer only waxed more and more hilarious, and at last, mounting his shaggy pony, rode off, still laughing, at a canter to Golden Friars; and when he reached Golden Friars, and got into the hall of the George and Dragon, he asked Richard Turnbull with a chuckle if he ever knew a man refuse an offer of money, or a man want to pay who did not owe; and inquired whether the Squire down at Mardykes Hall mightn't be a bit "wrang in t' garrets." All this, however, other people said, was intended merely to conceal the fact that he really had, through sheer loyalty, lent the money, or rather bestowed it, thinking the old family in jeopardy, and meaning a gift, was determined to hear no more about it. I can't say; I only know people held, some by one interpretation, some by another.

As the caterpillar sickens and changes its hue when it is about to undergo its transformation, so an odd change took place in Feltram. He grew even more silent and morose; he seemed always in an agitation and a secret rage. He used to walk through the woodlands on the slopes of the fells above Mardykes, muttering to himself, picking up the rotten sticks with which the ground was strewn, breaking them in his hands, and hurling them from him, and stamping on the earth as he paced up and down.

One night a thunder-storm came on, the wind blowing gently up from Golden Friars. It was a night black as pitch, illuminated only by the intermittent glare of the lightning. At the foot of the stairs Sir Bale met Feltram, whom he had not seen for some days. He had his cloak and hat on.

"I am going to Cloostedd to-night," he said, "and if all is as I expect, I sha'n't return. We remember all, you and I." And he nodded and walked down the passage.

Sir Bale knew that a crisis had happened in his own life. He felt faint and ill, and returned to the room where he had been sitting. Throughout that melancholy night he did not go to his bed.

In the morning he learned that Marlyn, who had been out late, saw Feltram get the boat off, and sail towards the other side. The night was so dark that he could only see him start; but the wind was light and coming up the lake, so that without a tack he could easily make the other side. Feltram did not return. The boat was found fast to the ring at Cloostedd landing-place.

Lady Mardykes was relieved, and for a time was happier than ever. It was different with Sir Bale; and afterwards her sky grew dark also.

XXIII. A Lady in Black

Shortly after this, there arrived at the George and Dragon a stranger. He was a man somewhat past forty, embrowned by distant travel, and, his years considered, wonderfully good-looking. He had good eyes; his dark-brown hair had no sprinkling of gray in it; and his kindly smile showed very white and even teeth. He made inquiries about neighbours, especially respecting Mardykes Hall; and the answers seemed to interest him profoundly. He inquired after Philip Feltram, and shed tears when he heard that he was no longer at Mardykes Hall, and that Trebeck or other friends could give him no tidings of him.

And then he asked Richard Turnbull to show him to a quiet room; and so, taking the honest fellow by the hand, he said,

"Mr. Turnbull, don't you know me?"

"No, sir," said the host of the George and Dragon, after a puzzled stare, "I can't say I do, sir."

The stranger smiled a little sadly, and shook his head: and with a gentle laugh, still holding his hand in a very friendly way, he said, "I should have known you anywhere, Mr. Turnbull—anywhere on earth or water. Had you turned up on the Himalayas, or in a junk on the Canton river, or as a dervish in the mosque of St. Sophia, I should have recognised my old friend, and asked what news from Golden Friars. But of course I'm changed. You were a little my senior; and one advantage among many you have over your juniors is that you don't change as we do. I have played many a game of hand-ball in the inn-yard of the George, Mr. Turnbull. You often wagered a pot of ale on my play; you used to say I'd make the best player of fives, and the best singer of a song, within ten miles round the meer. You used to have me behind the bar when I was a boy, with more of an appetite than I have now. I was then at Mardykes Hall, and used to go back in old Marlin's boat. Is old Marlyn still alive?"

"Ay, that—he—is," said Turnbull slowly, as he eyed the stranger again carefully. "I don't know who you can be, sir, unless you are—the boy—William Feltram. La! he was seven or eight years younger than Philip. But, lawk!—Well—By Jen, and *be* you Willie Feltram? But no, you can't!"

"Ay, Mr. Turnbull, that very boy—Willie Feltram—even he, and no other; and now you'll shake hands with me, not so formally, but like an old friend."

"Ay, that I will," said honest Richard Turnbull, with a great smile, and a hearty grasp of his guest's hand; and they both laughed together, and the younger man's eyes, for he was an affectionate fool, filled up with tears.

"And I want you to tell me this," said William, after they had talked a little quietly, "now that there is no one to interrupt us, what has become of my brother Philip? I heard from a friend an account of his health that has caused me unspeakable anxiety."

"His health was not bad; no, he was a hardy lad, and liked a walk over the fells, or a pull on the lake; but he was a bit daft, every one said, and a changed man; and, in troth, they say the air o' Mardykes don't agree with every one, no more than him. But that's a tale that's neither here nor there."

"Yes," said William, "that was what they told me—his mind affected. God help and guard us! I have been unhappy ever since; and if I only knew it was well with poor Philip, I think I should be too happy. And where is Philip now?"

"He crossed the lake one night, having took leave of Sir Bale. They thought he was going to old Trebeck's up the Fells. He likes the Feltrams, and likes the folk at Mardykes Hall—though those two families was not always o'er kind to one another. But Trebeck seed nowt o' him, nor no one else; and what has gone wi' him no one can tell."

"I heard that also," said William with a deep sigh. "But I hoped it had been cleared up by now, and something happier been known of the poor fellow by this time. I'd give a great deal to know—I don't know what I *would* not give to know—I'm so unhappy about him. And now, my good old friend, tell your people to get me a chaise, for I must go to Mardykes Hall; and, first, let me have a room to dress in."

At Mardykes Hall a pale and pretty lady was looking out, alone, from the stone-shafted drawing-room window across the courtyard and the balustrade, on which stood many a great stone cup with flowers, whose leaves were half shed and gone with the winds—emblem of her hopes. The solemn melancholy of the towering fells, the ripple of the lonely lake, deepened her sadness.

The unwonted sound of carriage-wheels awoke her from her reverie.

Before the chaise reached the steps, a hand from its window had seized the handle, the door was thrown open, and William Feltram jumped out.

She was in the hall, she knew not how; and, with a wild scream and a sob, she threw herself into his arms.

Here at last was an end of the long waiting, the dejection which had reached almost the point of despair. And like two rescued from shipwreck, they clung together in an agony of happiness.

William had come back with no very splendid fortune. It was enough, and only enough, to enable them to marry. Prudent people would have thought it, very likely, too little. But he was now home in England, with health unimpaired by his long sojourn in the East, and with intelligence and energies improved by the discipline of his arduous struggle with fortune. He reckoned, therefore, upon one way or other adding something to their income; and he knew that a few hundreds a year would make them happier than hundreds of thousand could other people.

It was five years since they had parted in France, where a journey of importance to the Indian firm, whose right hand he was, had brought him.

The refined tastes that are supposed to accompany gentle blood, his love of art, his talent for music and drawing, had accidentally attracted the attention of the little travelling-party which old Lady Harbottle chaperoned. Miss Janet, now Lady Mardykes, learning that his name was Feltram, made inquiry through a common friend, and learned what interested her still more about him. It ended in an acquaintance, which his manly and gentle nature and his entertaining qualities soon improved into an intimacy.

Feltram had chosen to work his own way, being proud, and also prosperous enough to prevent his pride, in this respect, from being placed under too severe a pressure of temptation. He heard not from but of his brother, through a friend in London, and more lately from Gertrude, whose account of him was sad and even alarming.

When Lady Mardykes came in, her delight knew no bounds. She had already formed a plan for their future, and was not to be put off—William Feltram was to take the great grazing farm that belonged to the Mardykes estate; or, if he preferred it, to farm it for her, sharing the profits. She wanted something to interest her, and this was just the thing. It was hardly half-a-mile away, up the lake, and there was such a comfortable house and garden, and she and Gertrude could be as much together as ever almost; and, in fact, Gertrude and her husband could be nearly always at Mardykes Hall.

So eager and entreating was she, that there was no escape. The plan was adopted immediately on their marriage, and no happier neighbours for a time were ever known.

But was Lady Mardykes content? was she even exempt from the heartache which each mortal thinks he has all to himself? The longing of her life was for children; and again and again had her hopes been disappointed.

One tiny pretty little baby indeed was born, and lived for two years, and then died; and none had come to supply its place and break the childless silence in the great old nursery. That was her sorrow; a greater one than men can understand.

Another source of grief was this: that Sir Bale Mardykes conceived a dislike to William Feltram that was unaccountable. At first suppressed, it betrayed itself negatively only; but with time it increased; and in the end the Baronet made little secret of his wish to get rid of him. Many and ingenious were the annoyances he contrived; and at last he told his wife plainly that he wished William Feltram to find some other abode for himself.

Lady Mardykes pleaded earnestly, and even with tears; for if Gertrude were to leave the neighbourhood, she well knew how utterly solitary her own life would become.

Sir Bale at last vouchsafed some little light as to his motives. There was an old story, he told her, that his estate would go to a Feltram. He had an instinctive distrust of that family. It was a feeling not given him for nothing; it might be the means of defeating their plotting and strategy. Old Trebeck, he fancied, had a finger in it. Philip Feltram had told him that Mardykes was to pass away to a Feltram. Well, they might conspire; but he would take what care he could that the estate should not be stolen from his family. He did not want his wife stript of her jointure, or his children, if he had any, left without bread.

All this sounded very like madness; but the idea was propounded by Philip Feltram. His own jealousy was at bottom founded on superstition which he would not avow and could hardly define. He bitterly blamed himself for having permitted William Feltram to place himself where he was.

In the midst of these annoyances William Feltram was seriously thinking of throwing up the farm, and seeking similar occupation somewhere else.

One day, walking alone in the thick wood that skirts the lake near his farm, he was discussing this problem with himself; and every now and then he repeated his question, "Shall I throw it up, and give him the lease back if he likes?" On a sudden he heard a voice near him say:

"Hold it, you fool!—hold hard, you fool!—hold it, you fool!"

The situation being lonely, he was utterly puzzled to account for the interruption, until on a sudden a huge parrot, green, crimson, and yellow, plunged from among the boughs over his head to the ground, and partly flying, and partly hopping and tumbling along, got lamely, but swiftly, out of sight among the thick underwood; and he could neither start it nor hear it any more. The interruption reminded him of that which befel Robinson Crusoe. It was more singular, however; for he owned no such bird; and its strangeness impressed the omen all the more.

He related it when he got home to his wife; and as people when living a solitary life, and also suffering, are prone to superstition, she did not laugh at the adventure, as in a healthier state of spirits, I suppose, she would.

They continued, however, to discuss the question together; and all the more industriously as a farm of the same kind, only some fifteen miles away, was now offered to all bidders, under another landlord. Gertrude, who felt Sir Bale's unkindness all the more that she was a distant cousin of his, as it had proved on comparing notes, was very strong in favour of the change, and had been urging it with true feminine ingenuity and persistence upon her husband. A very singular dream rather damped her ardour, however, and it appeared thus:

She had gone to her bed full of this subject; and she thought, although she could not remember having done so, had fallen asleep. She was still thinking, as she had been all the day, about leaving the farm. It seemed to her that she was quite awake, and a candle burning all the time in the room, awaiting the return of her husband, who was away at the fair near Haworth; she saw the interior of the room distinctly. It was a sultry night, and a little bit of the window was raised. A very slight sound in that direction attracted her attention; and to her surprise she saw a jay hop upon the window-sill, and into the room.

Up sat Gertrude, surprised and a little startled at the visit of so large a bird, without presence of mind for the moment even to frighten it away, and staring at it, as they say, with all her eyes. A sofa stood at the foot of the bed; and under this the bird swiftly hopped. She extended her hand now to take the bell-rope at the left side of the bed, and in doing so displaced the curtains, which were open only at the foot. She was amazed there to see a lady dressed entirely in black, and with the old-fashioned hood over her head. She was young and pretty, and looked kindly at her, but with now and then a slight contraction of lips and eyebrows that indicates pain. This little twitching was momentary, and recurred, it seemed, about once or twice in a minute.

How it was that she was not frightened on seeing this lady, standing like an old friend at her bedside, she could not afterwards understand. Some influence besides the kindness of her look prevented any sensation of terror at the time. With a very white hand the young lady in black held a white handkerchief pressed to her bosom at the top of her bodice.

"Who are you?" asked Gertrude.

"I am a kinswoman, although you don't know me; and I have come to tell you that you must not leave Faxwell" (the name of the place) "or Janet. If you go, I will go with you; and I can make you fear me."

Her voice was very distinct, but also very faint, with something undulatory in it, that seemed to enter Gertrude's head rather than her ear.

Saying this she smiled horribly, and, lifting her handkerchief, disclosed for a moment a great wound in her breast, deep in which Gertrude saw darkly the head of a snake writhing.

Hereupon she uttered a wild scream of terror, and, diving under the bed-clothes, remained more dead than alive there, until her maid, alarmed by her cry, came in, and having searched the room, and shut the window at her desire, did all in her power to comfort her.

If this was a nightmare and embodied only by a form of expression which in some states belongs to the imagination, a leading idea in the controversy in which her mind had long been employed, it had at least the effect of deciding her against leaving Faxwell. And so that point was settled; and unpleasant relations continued between the tenants of the farm and the master of Mardykes Hall.

To Lady Mardykes all this was very painful, although Sir Bale did not insist upon making a separation between his wife and her cousin. But to Mardykes Hall that cousin came no more. Even Lady Mardykes thought it better to see her at Faxwell than to risk a meeting in the temper in which Sir Bale then was. And thus several years passed.

No tidings of Philip Feltram were heard; and, in fact, none ever reached that part of the world; and if it had not been highly improbable that he could have drowned himself in the lake without his body sooner or later having risen to the surface, it would have been concluded that he had either accidentally or by design made away with himself in its waters.

Over Mardykes Hall there was a gloom—no sound of children's voices was heard there, and even the hope of that merry advent had died out.

This disappointment had no doubt helped to fix in Sir Bale's mind the idea of the insecurity of his property, and the morbid fancy that William Feltram and old Trebeck were conspiring to seize it; than which, I need hardly say, no imagination more insane could have fixed itself in his mind.

In other things, however, Sir Bale was shrewd and sharp, a clear and rapid man of business, and although this was a strange whim, it was not so unnatural in a man who was by nature so prone to suspicion as Sir Bale Mardykes.

During the years, now seven, that had elapsed since the marriage of Sir Bale and Miss Janet Feltram, there had happened but one event, except the death of their only child, to place them in mourning. That was the decease of Sir William Walsingham, the husband of Lady Mardykes' sister. She now lived in a handsome old dower-house at Islington, and being wealthy, made now and then an excursion to Mardykes Hall, in which she was sometimes accompanied by her sister Lady Haworth. Sir Oliver being a Parliament-man was much in London and deep in politics and intrigue, and subject, as convivial rogues are, to occasional hard hits from gout.

But change and separation had made no alteration in these ladies' mutual affections, and no three sisters were ever more attached.

Was Lady Mardykes happy with her lord? A woman so gentle and loving as she, is a happy wife with any husband who is not an absolute brute. There must have been, I suppose, some good about Sir Bale. His wife was certainly deeply attached to him. She admired his wisdom, and feared his inflexible will, and altogether made of him a domestic idol. To acquire this enviable position, I suspect there must be something not essentially disagreeable about a man. At all events, what her neighbours good-naturedly termed her infatuation continued, and indeed rather improved by time.

XXIV. An Old Portrait

Sir Bale—whom some remembered a gay and convivial man, not to say a profligate one—had grown to be a very gloomy man indeed. There was something weighing upon his mind; and I daresay some of the good gossips of Golden Friars, had there been any materials for such a case, would have believed that Sir Bale had murdered Philip Feltram, and was now the victim of the worm and fire of remorse.

The gloom of the master of the house made his very servants gloomy, and the house itself looked sombre, as if it had been startled with strange and dismal sights.

Lady Mardykes was something of an artist. She had lighted lately, in an out-of-the-way room, upon a dozen or more old portraits. Several of these were full-lengths; and she was—with the help of her maid, both in long aprons, amid sponges and basins, soft handkerchiefs and varnish-pots and brushes—busy in removing the dust and smoke-stains, and in laying-on the varnish, which brought out the colouring, and made the transparent shadows yield up their long-buried treasures of finished detail.

Against the wall stood a full-length portrait as Sir Bale entered the room; having for a wonder, a word to say to his wife.

"O," said the pretty lady, turning to him in her apron, and with her brush in her hand, "we are in such in pickle, Munnings and I, we have been cleaning these old pictures. Mrs. Julaper says they are the pictures that came from Cloostedd Hall long ago. They were buried in dust in the dark room in the clock-tower. Here is such a characteristic one. It has a long powdered wig—George the First or Second, I don't know which—and such a combination of colours, and such a face. It seems starting out of the canvas, and all but speaks. Do look; that is, I mean, Bale, if you can spare time."

Sir Bale abstractedly drew near, and looked over his wife's shoulder on the full-length portrait that stood before him; and as he did so a strange expression for a moment passed over his face.

The picture represented a man of swarthy countenance, with signs of the bottle glowing through the dark skin; small fierce pig eyes, a rather flat pendulous nose, and a grim forbidding mouth, with a large wart a little above it. On the head hung one of those full-bottomed powdered wigs that look like a cloud of cotton-wadding; a lace cravat was about his neck; he wore short black-velvet breeches with stockings rolled over them, a bottle-green coat of cut velvet and a crimson waistcoat with long flaps; coat and waistcoat both heavily laced with gold. He wore a sword, and leaned upon a crutch-handled cane, and his figure and aspect indicated a swollen and gouty state. He could not be far from sixty. There was uncommon force in this fierce and forbidding-looking portrait. Lady Mardykes said,

"What wonderful dresses they wore! How like a fine magic-lantern figure he looks! What gorgeous colouring! it looks like the plumage of a mackaw; and what a claw his hand is! and that huge broken beak of a nose! Isn't he like a wicked old mackaw?"

"Where did you find that?" asked Sir Bale.

Surprised at his tone, she looked round, and was still more surprised at his looks.

"I told you, dear Bale, I found them in the clock-tower. I hope I did right; it was not wrong bringing them here? I ought to have asked. Are you vexed, Bale?"

"Vexed! not I. I only wish it was in the fire. I must have seen that picture when I was a child. I hate to look at it. I raved about it once, when I was ill. I don't know who it is; I don't remember when I saw it. I wish you'd tell them to burn it."

"It is one of the Feltrams," she answered. "'Sir Hugh Feltram' is on the frame at the foot; and old Mrs. Julaper says he was the father of the unhappy lady who was said to have been drowned near Snakes Island."

"Well, suppose he is; there's nothing interesting in that. It is a disgusting picture. I connect it with my illness; and I think it is the kind of thing that would make any one half mad, if they only looked at it often enough. Tell them to burn it; and come away, come to the next room; I can't say what I want here."

Sir Bale seemed to grow more and more agitated the longer he remained in the room. He seemed to her both frightened and furious; and taking her a little roughly by the wrist, he led her through the door.

When they were in another apartment alone, he again asked the affrighted lady who had told her that picture was there, and who told her to clean it.

She had only the truth to plead. It was, from beginning to end, the merest accident.

"If I thought, Janet, that you were taking counsel of others, talking me over, and trying clever experiments—" he stopped short with his eyes fixed on hers with black suspicion.

His wife's answer was one pleading look, and to burst into tears.

Sir Bale let-go her wrist, which he had held up to this; and placing his hand gently on her shoulder, he said,

"You must not cry, Janet; I have given you no excuse for tears. I only wished an answer to a very harmless question; and I am sure you would tell me, if by any chance you have lately seen Philip Feltram; he is capable of arranging all that. No one knows him as I do. There, you must not cry any more; but tell me truly, has he turned up? is he at Faxwell?"

She denied all this with perfect truth; and after a hesitation of some time, the matter ended. And as soon as she and he were more themselves, he had something quite different to tell her.

"Sit down, Janet; sit down, and forget that vile picture and all I have been saying. What I came to tell you, I think you will like; I am sure it will please you."

And with this little preface he placed his arm about her neck, and kissed her tenderly. She certainly was pleased; and when his little speech was over, she, smiling, with her tears still wet upon her cheeks, put her arms round her husband's neck, and in turn kissed him with the ardour of gratitude, kissed him affectionately; again and again thanking him all the time.

It was no great matter, but from Sir Bale Mardykes it was something quite unusual. Was it a sudden whim? What was it? Something had prompted Sir Bale, early in that dark shrewd month of December, to tell his wife that he wished to call together some of his county acquaintances, and to fill his house for a week or so, as near Christmas as she could get them to come. He wished her sisters—Lady Haworth (with her husband) and the Dowager Lady Walsingham—to be invited for an early day, before the coming of the other guests, so that she might enjoy their society for a little time quietly to herself before the less intimate guests should assemble.

Glad was Lady Mardykes to hear the resolve of her husband, and prompt to obey. She wrote to her sisters to beg them to arrange to come, together, by the tenth or twelfth of the month, which they accordingly arranged to do. Sir Oliver, it was true, could not be of the party. A minister of state was drinking the waters at Bath; and Sir Oliver thought it would do him no harm to sip a little also, and his fashionable doctor politely agreed, and "ordered" to those therapeutic springs the knight of the shire, who was "consumedly vexed" to lose the Christmas with that jolly dog, Bale, down at Mardykes Hall. But a fellow must have a stomach for his Christmas pudding, and politics takes it out of a poor gentleman deucedly; and health's the first thing, egad!

So Sir Oliver went down to Bath, and I don't know that he tippled much of the waters, but he did drink the burgundy of that haunt of the ailing; and he had the honour of making a fourth not unfrequently in the secretary of state's whist-parties.

It was about the 8th of December when, in Lady Walsingham's carriage, intending to post all the way, that lady, still young, and Lady Haworth, with all the servants that were usual in such expeditions in those days, started from the great Dower House at Islington in high spirits.

Lady Haworth had not been very well—low and nervous; but the clear frosty sun, and the pleasant nature of the excursion, raised her spirits to the point of enjoyment; and expecting nothing but happiness and gaiety—for, after all, Sir Bale was but one of a large party, and even he could make an effort and be agreeable as well as hospitable on occasion—they set out on their northward expedition. The journey, which is a long one, they had resolved to break into a four days' progress; and the inns had been written to, bespeaking a comfortable reception.

XXV. Through the Wall

On the third night they put-up at the comfortable old inn called the Three Nuns. With an effort they might easily have pushed on to Mardykes Hall that night, for the distance is not more than five-and-thirty miles. But, considering her sister's health, Lady Walsingham in planning their route had resolved against anything like a forced march.

Here the ladies took possession of the best sitting-room; and, notwithstanding the fatigue of the journey, Lady Haworth sat up with her sister till near ten o'clock, chatting gaily about a thousand things.

Of the three sisters, Lady Walsingham was the eldest. She had been in the habit of taking the command at home; and now, for advice and decision, her younger sisters, less prompt and courageous than she, were wont, whenever in her neighbourhood, to throw upon her all the cares and agitations of determining what was best to be done in small things and great. It is only fair to say, in addition, that this submission was not by any means exacted; it was the deference of early habit and feebler will, for she was neither officious nor imperious.

It was now time that Lady Haworth, a good deal more fatigued than her sister, should take leave of her for the night.

Accordingly they kissed and bid each other good-night; and Lady Walsingham, not yet disposed to sleep, sat for some time longer in the comfortable room where they had taken tea, amusing the time with the book that had, when conversation flagged, beguiled the weariness of the journey. Her sister had been in her room nearly an hour, when she became herself a little sleepy. She had lighted her candle, and was going to ring for her maid, when, to her surprise, the door opened, and her sister Lady Haworth entered in a dressing-gown, looking frightened.

"My darling Mary!" exclaimed Lady Walsingham, "what is the matter? Are you well?"

"Yes, darling," she answered, "quite well; that is, I don't know what is the matter—I'm frightened." She paused, listening, with her eyes turned towards the wall. "O, darling Maud, I am so frightened! I don't know what it can be."

"You must not be agitated, darling; there's nothing. You have been asleep, and I suppose you have had a dream. Were you asleep?"

Lady Haworth had caught her sister fast by the arm with both hands, and was looking wildly in her face.

"Have *you* heard nothing?" she asked, again looking towards the wall of the room, as if she expected to hear a voice through it.

"Nonsense, darling; you are dreaming still. Nothing; there has been nothing to hear. I have been awake ever since; if there had been anything to hear, I could not have missed it. Come, sit down. Sip a little of this water; you are nervous, and over-tired; and tell me plainly, like a good little soul, what is the matter; for nothing has happened here; and you ought to know that the Three Nuns is the quietest house in England; and I'm no witch, and if you won't tell me what's the matter, I can't divine it."

"Yes, of course," said Mary, sitting down, and glancing round her wildly. "I don't hear it now; *you* don't?"

"Do, my dear Mary, tell me what you mean," said Lady Walsingham kindly but firmly.

Lady Haworth was holding the still untasted glass of water in her hand.

"Yes, I'll tell you; I have been so frightened! You are right; I had a dream, but I can scarcely remember anything of it, except the very end, when I wakened. But it was not the dream; only it was connected with what terrified me so. I was so tired when I went to bed, I thought I should have slept soundly; and indeed I fell asleep immediately; and I must have slept quietly for a good while. How long is it since I left you?"

"More than an hour."

"Yes, I must have slept a good while; for I don't think I have been ten minutes awake. How my dream began I don't know. I remember only that gradually it came to this: I was standing in a recess in a panelled gallery; it was lofty, and, I thought, belonged to a handsome but old-fashioned house. I was looking straight towards the head of a wide staircase, with a great oak banister. At the top of the stairs, as near to me, about, as that window there, was a thick short column of oak, on top of which was a candlestick. There was no other light but from that one candle; and there was a lady standing beside it, looking down the stairs, with her back turned towards me; and from her gestures I should have thought speaking to people on a lower lobby, but whom from my place I could not see. I soon perceived that this lady was in great agony of mind; for she beat her breast and wrung her hands every now and then, and wagged her head slightly from side to side, like a person in great distraction. But one word she said I could not hear. Nor when she struck her hand on the banister, or stamped, as she seemed to do in her pain, upon the floor, could I hear any sound. I found myself somehow waiting upon this lady, and was watching her with awe and sympathy. But who she was I knew not, until turning towards me I plainly saw Janet's face, pale and covered with tears, and with such a look of agony as—O God!—I can never forget."

"Pshaw! Mary darling, what is it but a dream! I have had a thousand more startling; it is only that you are so nervous just now."

"But that is not all—nothing; what followed is so dreadful; for either there is something very horrible going on at Mardykes, or else I am losing my reason," said Lady Haworth in increasing agitation. "I wakened instantly in great alarm, but I suppose no more than I have felt a hundred times on awakening from a frightful dream. I sat up in my bed; I was thinking of ringing for Winnefred, my heart was beating so, but feeling better soon I changed my mind. All this time I heard a faint sound of a voice, as if coming through a thick wall. It came from the wall at the left side of my bed, and I fancied was that of some woman lamenting in a room separated from me by that thick partition. I could only perceive that it was a sound of crying mingled with ejaculations of misery, or fear, or entreaty. I listened with a painful curiosity, wondering who it could be, and what could have happened in the neighbouring rooms of the house; and as I looked and listened, I could distinguish my own name, but at first nothing more. That, of course, might have been an accident; and I knew there were many Marys in the world besides myself. But it made me more curious; and a strange thing struck me, for I was now looking at that very wall through which the sounds were coming. I saw that there was a window in it. Thinking that the rest of the wall might nevertheless be covered by another room, I drew the curtain of it and looked out. But there is no such thing. It is the outer wall the entire way along. And it is equally impossible of the other wall, for it is to the front of the house, and has two windows in it; and the wall that the head of my bed stands against has the gallery outside it all the way; for I remarked that as I came to you."

"Tut, tut, Mary darling, nothing on earth is so deceptive as sound; this and fancy account for everything."

"But hear me out; I have not told you all. I began to hear the voice more clearly, and at last quite distinctly. It was Janet's, and she was conjuring you by name, as well as me, to come to her to Mardykes, without delay, in her extremity; yes, *you*, just as vehemently as me. It was Janet's voice. It still seemed separated by the wall, but I heard every syllable now; and I never heard voice or words of such anguish. She was imploring of us to come on, without a moment's delay, to Mardykes; and crying that, if we were not with her, she should go mad."

"Well, darling," said Lady Walsingham, "you see I'm included in this invitation as well as you, and should hate to disappoint Janet just as much; and I do assure you, in the morning you will laugh over this fancy with me; or rather, she will laugh over it with us, when we get to Mardykes. What you do want is rest, and a little sal-volatile."

So saying she rang the bell for Lady Haworth's maid. Having comforted her sister, and made her take the nervous specific she recommended, she went with her to her room; and taking possession of the arm-chair by the fire, she told her that she would keep her company until she was asleep, and remain long enough to be sure that the sleep was not likely to be interrupted. Lady Haworth had not been ten minutes in her bed, when she raised herself with a start to her elbow, listening with parted lips and wild eyes, her trembling fingers behind her ears. With an exclamation of horror, she cried,

"There it is again, upbraiding us! I can't stay longer."

She sprang from the bed, and rang the bell violently.

"Maud," she cried in an ecstasy of horror, "nothing shall keep me here, whether you go or not. I will set out the moment the horses are put to. If you refuse to come,

Maud, mind the responsibility is yours—listen!" and with white face and starting eyes she pointed to the wall. "Have you ears; don't you hear?"

The sight of a person in extremity of terror so mysterious, might have unnerved a ruder system than Lady Walsingham's. She was pale as she replied; for under certain circumstances those terrors which deal with the supernatural are more contagious than any others. Lady Walsingham still, in terms, held to her opinion; but the panic had touched her, and although she tried to smile, her face showed it.

"Well, dear Mary," she said, "as you will have it so, I see no good in resisting you longer. Here, it is plain, your nerves will not suffer you to rest. Let us go then, in heaven's name; and when you get to Mardykes Hall you will be relieved."

All this time Lady Haworth was getting on her things, with the careless hurry of a person about to fly for her life; and Lady Walsingham issued her orders for horses, and the general preparations for resuming the journey.

It was now between ten and eleven; but the servant who rode armed with them, according to the not unnecessary usage of the times, thought that with a little judicious bribing of postboys they might easily reach Mardykes Hall before three o'clock in the morning.

When the party set forward again, Lady Haworth was comparatively tranquil. She no longer heard the unearthly mimickry of her sister's voice; there remained only the fear and suspense which that illusion or visitation had produced.

Her sister, Lady Walsingham, after a brief effort to induce something like conversation, became silent. A thin sheet of snow had covered the darkened landscape, and some light flakes were still dropping. Lady Walsingham struck her repeater often in the dark, and inquired the distances frequently. She was anxious to get over the ground, though by no means fatigued. Something of the anxiety that lay heavy at her sister's heart had touched her own.

XXVI. Perplexed

The roads even then were good, and very good horses the posting-houses turned out; so that by dint of extra pay the rapid rate of travelling undertaken by the servant was fully accomplished in the first two or three stages.

While Lady Walsingham was continually striking her repeater in her ear, and as they neared their destination, growing in spite of herself more anxious, her sister's uneasiness showed itself in a less reserved way; for, cold as it was, with snowflakes actually dropping, Lady Haworth's head was perpetually out at the window, and when she drew it up, sitting again in her place, she would audibly express her alarms, and apply to her sister for consolation and confidence in her suspense.

Under its thin carpet of snow, the pretty village of Golden Friars looked strangely to their eyes. It had long been fast asleep, and both ladies were excited as they drew up at the steps of the George and Dragon, and with bell and knocker roused the slumbering household.

What tidings awaited them here? In a very few minutes the door was opened, and the porter staggered down, after a word with the driver, to the carriage-window, not half awake.

"Is Lady Mardykes well?" demanded Lady Walsingham.

"Is Sir Bale well?"

"Are all the people at Mardykes Hall quite well?"

With clasped hands Lady Haworth listened to the successive answers to these questions which her sister hastily put. The answers were all satisfactory. With a great sigh and a little laugh, Lady Walsingham placed her hand affectionately on that of her sister; who, saying, "God be thanked!" began to weep.

"When had you last news from Mardykes?" asked Lady Walsingham.

"A servant was down here about four o'clock."

"O! no one since?" said she in a disappointed tone.

No one had been from the great house since, but all were well then.

"They are early people, you know, dear; and it is dark at four, and that is as late as they could well have heard, and nothing could have happened since—very unlikely. We have come very fast; it is only a few minutes past two, darling."

But each felt the chill and load of their returning anxiety.

While the people at the George were rapidly getting a team of horses to, Lady Walsingham contrived a moment for an order from the other window to her servant, who knew Golden Friars perfectly, to knock-up the people at Doctor Torvey's, and to inquire whether all were well at Mardykes Hall.

There he learned that a messenger had come for Doctor Torvey at ten o'clock, and that the Doctor had not returned since. There was no news, however, of any one's being ill; and the Doctor himself did not know what he was wanted about. While Lady Haworth was talking to her maid from the window next the steps, Lady Walsingham was, unobserved, receiving this information at the other.

It made her very uncomfortable.

In a few minutes more, however, with a team of fresh horses, they were again rapidly passing the distance between them and Mardykes Hall.

About two miles on, their drivers pulled-up, and they heard a voice talking with them from the roadside. A servant from the Hall had been sent with a note for Lady Walsingham, and had been ordered, if necessary, to ride the whole way to the Three Nuns to deliver it. The note was already in Lady Walsingham's hand; her sister sat beside her, and with the corner of the open note in her fingers, she read it breathlessly at the same time by the light of a carriage-lamp which the man held to the window. It said:

> My dearest love—my darling sister—dear sisters both!—in God's name, lose not a moment. I am so overpowered and *terrified*. I cannot explain; I can only implore of you to come with all the haste you can make. Waste no time, darlings. I hardly understand what I write. Only this, dear sisters; I feel that my reason will desert me, unless you come soon. You will not fail me now. Your poor distracted
>
> JANET

The sisters exchanged a pale glance, and Lady Haworth grasped her sister's hand.

"Where is the messenger?" asked Lady Walsingham.

A mounted servant came to the window.

"Is any one ill at home?" she asked.

"No, all were well—my lady, and Sir Bale—no one sick."

"But the Doctor was sent for; what was that for?"

"I can't say, my lady."

"You are quite certain that no one—think—*no* one is ill?"

"There is no one ill at the Hall, my lady, that I have heard of."

"Is Lady Mardykes, my sister, still up?"

"Yes, my lady; and her maid is with her."

"And Sir Bale, are you certain he is quite well?"

"Sir Bale is quite well, my lady; he has been busy settling papers to-night, and was as well as usual."

"That will do, thanks," said the perplexed lady; and to her own servant she added, "On to Mardykes Hall with all the speed they can make. I'll pay them well, tell them."

And in another minute they were gliding along the road at a pace which the muffled beating of the horses' hoofs on the thin sheet of snow that covered the road showed to have broken out of the conventional trot, and to resemble something more like a gallop.

And now they were under the huge trees, that looked black as hearse-plumes in contrast with the snow. The cold gleam of the lake in the moon which had begun to shine out now met their gaze; and the familiar outline of Snakes Island, its solemn timber bleak and leafless, standing in a group, seemed to watch Mardykes Hall with a dismal observation across the water. Through the gate and between the huge files of trees the carriage seemed to fly; and at last the steaming horses stood panting, nodding and snorting, before the steps in the courtyard.

There was a light in an upper window, and a faint light in the hall, the door of which was opened; and an old servant came down and ushered the ladies into the house.

XXVII. The Hour

Lightly they stepped over the snow that lay upon the broad steps, and entering the door saw the dim figure of their sister, already in the large and faintly-lighted hall. One candle in the hand of her scared maid, and one burning on the table, leaving the distant parts of that great apartment in total darkness, touched the figures with the odd sharp lights in which Schalken delights; and a streak of chilly moonlight, through the open door, fell upon the floor, and was stretched like a white sheet at her feet. Lady Mardykes, with an exclamation of agitated relief, threw her arms, in turn, round the necks of her sisters, and hugging them, kissed them again and again, murmuring her thanks, calling them her "blessed sisters," and praising God for his mercy in having sent them to her in time, and altogether in a rapture of agitation and gratitude.

Taking them each by a hand, she led them into a large room, on whose panels they could see the faint twinkle of the tall gilded frames, and the darker indication of the old portraits, in which that interesting house abounds. The moonbeams, entering obliquely through the Tudor stone-shafts of the window and thrown upon the floor, reflected an imperfect light; and the candle which the maid who followed her mistress held in her hand shone dimly from the sideboard, where she placed it. Lady Mardykes told her that she need not wait.

"They don't know; they know only that we are in some great confusion; but—God have mercy on me!—nothing of the reality. Sit down, darlings; you are tired."

She sat down between them on a sofa, holding a hand of each. They sat opposite the window, through which appeared the magnificent view commanded from the front of the house: in the foreground the solemn trees of Snakes Island, one great branch stretching upward, bare and moveless, from the side, like an arm raised to heaven in wonder or in menace towards the house; the lake, in part swept by the icy splendour of the moon, trembling with a dazzling glimmer, and farther off lost in blackness; the Fells rising from a base of gloom, into ribs and peaks white with snow, and looking against the pale sky, thin and transparent as a haze. Right across to the storied woods of Cloostedd, and the old domains of the Feltrams, this view extended.

Thus alone, their mufflers still on, their hands clasped in hers, they breathlessly listened to her strange tale.

Connectedly told it amounted to this:

Sir Bale seemed to have been relieved of some great anxiety about the time when, ten days before, he had told her to invite her friends to Mardykes Hall. This morning he had gone out for a walk with Trevor, his under-steward, to talk over some plans about thinning the woods at this side; and also to discuss practically a proposal, lately made by a wealthy merchant, to take a very long lease, on advantageous terms to Sir Bale as he thought, of the old park and chase of Cloostedd, with the intention of building there, and making it once more a handsome residence.

In the improved state of his spirits, Sir Bale had taken a shrewd interest in this negotiation; and was actually persuaded to cross the lake that morning with his adviser, and to walk over the grounds with him.

Sir Bale had seemed unusually well, and talked with great animation. He was more like a young man who had just attained his majority, and for the first time grasped his estates, than the grim elderly Baronet who had been moping about Mardykes, and as much afraid as a cat of the water, for so many years.

As they returned to the boat, at the roots of that same scathed elm whose barkless bough had seemed, in his former visit to this old wood, to beckon him from a distance, like a skeleton arm, to enter the forest, he and his companion on a sudden missed an old map of the grounds which they had been consulting.

"We must have left it in the corner tower of Cloostedd House, which commands that view of the grounds, you remember; it would not do to lose it. It is the most accurate thing we have. I'll sit down here and rest a little till you come back."

The man was absent little more than twenty minutes. When he returned, he found that Sir Bale had changed his position, and was now walking to and fro, around and about, in what, at a distance, he fancied was mere impatience, on the open space a couple of hundred paces nearer to the turn in the valley towards the boat. It was not impatience. He was very much agitated. He looked pale, and he took his companion's arm—a thing he had never thought of doing before—and said,

"Let us away quickly. I've something to tell at home,—and I forgot it."

Not another word did Sir Bale exchange with his companion. He sat in the stern of the boat, gloomy as a man about to glide under traitor's-gate. He entered his house in the same sombre and agitated state. He entered his library, and sat for a long time as if stunned.

At last he seemed to have made-up his mind to something; and applied himself quietly and diligently to arranging papers, and docketing some and burning others. Dinner-time arrived. He sent to tell Lady Mardykes that he should not join her at dinner, but would see her afterwards.

"It was between eight and nine," she continued, "I forget the exact time, when he came to the tower drawing-room where I was. I did not hear his approach. There is a stone stair, with a thick carpet on it. He told me he wished to speak to me there. It is an out-of-the-way place—a small old room with very thick walls, and there is a double door, the inner one of oak—I suppose he wished to guard against being overheard.

"There was a look in his face that frightened me; I saw he had something dreadful to tell. He looked like a man on whom a lot had fallen to put some one to death," said Lady Mardykes. "O, my poor Bale! my husband, my husband! he knew what it would be to me."

Here she broke into the wildest weeping, and it was some time before she resumed.

"He seemed very kind and very calm," she said at last; "he said but little; and, I think, these were his words: 'I find, Janet, I have made a great miscalculation—I thought my hour of danger had passed. We have been many years together, but a parting must sooner or later be, and my time has come.'

"I don't know what I said. I would not have so much minded—for I could not have believed, if I had not seen him—but there was that in his look and tone which no one could doubt.

"'I shall die before to-morrow morning,' he said. 'You must command yourself, Janet; it can't be altered now.'

"'O, Bale,' I cried nearly distracted, 'you would not kill yourself!'

"'Kill myself! poor child! no, indeed,' he said; 'it is simply that I shall die. No violent death—nothing but the common subsidence of life—I have made up my mind; what happens to everybody can't be so very bad; and millions of worse men than I die every year. You must not follow me to my room, darling; I shall see you by and by.'

"His language was collected and even cold; but his face looked as if it was cut in stone; you never saw, in a dream, a face like it."

Lady Walsingham here said, "I am certain he is ill; he's in a fever. You must not distract and torture yourself about his predictions. You sent for Doctor Torvey; what did he say?"

"I could not tell him all."

"O, no; I don't mean that; they'd only say he was mad, and we little better for minding what he says. But did the Doctor see him? and what did he say of his health?"

"Yes; he says there is nothing wrong—no fever—nothing whatever. Poor Bale has been so kind; he saw him to please me," she sobbed again wildly. "I wrote to implore of him. It was my last hope, strange as it seems; and O, would to God I could think it! But there is nothing of that kind. Wait till you have seen him. There is a frightful calmness about all he says and does; and his directions are all so clear, and his mind so perfectly collected, it is quite impossible."

And poor Lady Mardykes again burst into a frantic agony of tears.

XXVIII. Sir Bale in the Gallery

"Now, Janet darling, you are yourself low and nervous, and you treat this fancy of Bale's as seriously as he does himself. The truth is, he is a hypochondriac, as the doctors say; and you will find that I am right; he will be quite well in the morning, and I daresay a little ashamed of himself for having frightened his poor little wife as he has. I will sit up with you. But our poor Mary is not, you know, very strong; and she ought to lie down and rest a little. Suppose you give me a cup of tea in the drawing-room. I will run up to my room and get these things off, and meet you in the drawing-room; or, if you like it better, you can sit with me in my own room; and for goodness' sake let us have candles enough and a bright fire; and I promise you, if you will only exert your own good sense, you shall be a great deal more cheerful in a very little time."

Lady Walsingham's address was kind and cheery, and her air confident. For a moment a ray of hope returned, and her sister Janet acknowledged at least the possibility of her theory. But if confidence is contagious, so also is panic; and Lady Walsingham experienced a sinking of the heart which she dared not confess to her sister, and vainly strove to combat.

Lady Walsingham went up with her sister Mary, and having seen her in her room, and spoken again to her in the same cheery tone in which she had lectured her sister Lady Mardykes, she went on; and having taken possession of her own room, and put off her cloaks and shawls, she was going downstairs again, when she heard Sir Bale's voice, as he approached along the gallery, issuing orders to a servant, as it seemed, exactly in his usual tone.

She turned, with a strange throb at her heart, and met him.

A little sterner, a little paler than usual he looked; she could perceive no other change. He took her hand kindly and held it, as with dilated eyes he looked with a dark inquiry for a moment in her face. He signed to the servant to go on, and said, "I'm glad you have come, Maud. You have heard what is to happen; and I don't know how Janet could have borne it without your support. You did right to come; and you'll stay with her for a day or two, and take her away from this place as soon as you can."

She looked at him with the embarrassment of fear. He was speaking to her with the calmness of a leave-taking in the pressroom—the serenity that overlies the greatest awe and agony of which human nature is capable.

"I am glad to see you, Bale," she began, hardly knowing what she said, and she stopped short.

"You are come, it turns out, on a sad mission," he resumed; "you find all about to change. Poor Janet! it is a blow to her. I shall not live to see to-morrow's sunshine."

"Come," she said, startled, "you must not talk so. No, Bale, you have no right to speak so; you can have no reason to justify it. It is cruel and wicked to trifle with your wife's feelings. If you are under a delusion, you must make an effort and shake it off, or, at least, cease to talk of it. You are not well; I know by your looks you are ill; but I am very certain we shall see you much better by to-morrow, and still better the day following."

"No, I'm not ill, sister. Feel that pulse, if you doubt me; there is no fever in it. I never was more perfectly in health; and yet I know that before the clock, that has just struck three, shall have struck five, I, who am talking to you, shall be dead."

Lady Walsingham was frightened, and her fear irritated her.

"I have told you what I think and believe," she said vehemently. "I think it wrong and cowardly of you to torture my poor sister with your whimsical predictions. Look into your own mind, and you will see you have absolutely no reason to support what you say. How *can* you inflict all this agony upon a poor creature foolish enough to love you as she does, and weak enough to believe in your idle dreams?"

"Stay, sister; it is not a matter to be debated so. If to-morrow I can hear you, it will be time enough to upbraid me. Pray return now to your sister; she needs all you can do for her. She is much to be pitied; her sufferings afflict me. I shall see you and her again before my death. It would have been more cruel to leave her unprepared. Do all in your power to nerve and tranquillise her. What is past cannot now be helped."

He paused, looking hard at her, as if he had half made up his mind to say something more. But if there was a question of the kind, it was determined in favour of silence.

He dropped her hand, turned quickly, and left her.

XXIX. Dr. Torvey's Opinion

When Lady Walsingham reached the head of the stairs, she met her maid, and from her learned that her sister, Lady Mardykes, was downstairs in the same room. On approaching, she heard her sister Mary's voice talking with her, and found them together. Mary, finding that she could not sleep, had put on her clothes again, and come down to keep her sister company. The room looked more comfortable now. There were candles lighted, and a good fire burnt in the grate; tea-things stood on a little table near the fire, and the two sisters were talking, Lady Mardykes appearing more collected, and only they two in the room.

"Have you seen him, Maud?" cried Lady Mardykes, rising and hastily approaching her the moment she entered.

"Yes, dear; and talked with him, and—"

"Well?"

"And I think very much as I did before. I think he is nervous, he says he is not ill; but he is nervous and whimsical, and as men always are when they happen to be out of sorts, very positive; and of course the only thing that can quite undeceive him is the lapse of the time he has fixed for his prediction, as it is sure to pass without any tragic result of any sort. We shall then all see alike the nature of his delusion."

"O, Maud, if I were only sure you thought so! if I were sure you really had hopes! Tell me, Maud, for God's sake, what you really think."

Lady Walsingham was a little disconcerted by the unexpected directness of her appeal.

"Come, darling, you must not be foolish," she said; "we can only talk of impressions, and we are imposed upon by the solemnity of his manner, and the fact that he evidently believes in his own delusion; every one does believe in his own delusion—there is nothing strange in that."

"O, Maud darling, I see you are not convinced; you are only trying to comfort me. You have no hope—none, none, none!" and she covered her face with her hands, and wept again convulsively.

Lady Walsingham was silent for a moment, and then with an effort said, as she placed her hand on her sister's arm, "You see, dear Janet, there is no use in my saying the same thing over and over again; an hour or two will show who is right. Sit down again, and be like yourself. My maid told me that you had sent to the parlour for Doctor Torvey; he must not find you so. What would he think? Unless you mean to tell him of Bale's strange fancy; and a pretty story that would be to set afloat in Golden Friars. I think I hear him coming."

So, in effect, he was. Doctor Torvey—with the florid gravity of a man who, having just swallowed a bottle of port, besides some glasses of sherry, is admitted to the presence of ladies whom he respects—entered the room, made what he called his "leg and his compliments," and awaited the ladies' commands.

"Sit down, Doctor Torvey," said Lady Walsingham, who in the incapacity of her sister undertook the doing of the honours. "My sister, Lady Mardykes, has got it into her head somehow that Sir Bale is ill. I have been speaking to him; he certainly does not look very well, but he says he is quite well. Do you think him well?—that is, we know you don't think there is anything of importance amiss—but she wishes to know whether you think him *perfectly* well."

The Doctor cleared his voice and delivered his lecture, a little thickly at some words, upon Sir Bale's case; the result of which was that it was no case at all; and that if he would only live something more of a country gentleman's life, he would be as well as any man could desire—as well as any man, gentle or simple, in the country.

"The utmost I should think of doing for him would be, perhaps, a little quinine, nothing mo'—shurely—he is really and toory a very shoun' shtay of health."

Lady Walsingham looked encouragingly at her sister and nodded.

"I've been shen' for, La'y Walsh—Walse—Walsing—*ham*; old Jack Amerald—he likshe his glass o' port," he said roguishly, "and shuvversh accord'n'ly," he continued, with a compassionating paddle of his right hand; "one of thoshe aw—odd feels in his stomach; and as I have pretty well done all I can man-n'ge down here, I must be off, ye shee. Wind up from Golden Friars, and a little flutter ovv zhnow, thazh all"; and with some remarks about the extreme cold of the weather, and the severity of their night journey, and many respectful and polite parting speeches, the Doctor took his leave; and they soon heard the wheels of his gig and the tread of his horse, faint and muffled from the snow in the court-yard, and the Doctor, who had connected that melancholy and agitated household with the outer circle of humanity, was gone.

There was very little snow falling, half-a-dozen flakes now and again, and their flight across the window showed, as the Doctor had in a manner boasted, that the wind was in his face as he returned to Golden Friars. Even these desultory snow-flakes ceased, at times, altogether; and returning, as they say, "by fits and starts," left for long intervals the landscape, under the brilliant light of the moon, in its wide white shroud. The curtain of the great window had not been drawn. It seemed to Lady Walsingham that the moonbeams had grown more dazzling, that Snakes Island was nearer and more distinct, and the outstretched arm of the old tree looked bigger and angrier, like the uplifted arm of an assassin, who draws silently nearer as the catastrophe approaches.

Cold, dazzling, almost repulsive in this intense moonlight and white sheeting, the familiar landscape looked in the eyes of Lady Walsingham. The sisters gradually grew more and more silent, an unearthly suspense overhung them all, and Lady Mardykes rose every now and then and listened at the open door for step or voice in vain. They all were overpowered by the intenser horror that seemed gathering around them. And thus an hour or more passed.

XXX. Hush!

Pale and silent those three beautiful sisters sat. The horrible quietude of a suspense that had grown all but insupportable oppressed the guests of Lady Mardykes, and something like the numbness of despair had reduced her to silence, the dreadful counterfeit of peace.

Sir Bale Mardykes on a sudden softly entered the room. Reflected from the floor near the window, the white moonlight somehow gave to his fixed features the character of a smile. With a warning gesture, as he came in, he placed his finger to his lips, as if to enjoin silence; and then, having successively pressed the hands of his two sisters-in-law, he stooped over his almost fainting wife, and twice pressed her cold forehead with his lips; and so, without a word, he went softly from the room.

Some seconds elapsed before Lady Walsingham, recovering her presence of mind, with one of the candlesticks from the table in her hand, opened the door and followed.

She saw Sir Bale mount the last stair of the broad flight visible from the hall, and candle in hand turn the corner of the massive banister, and as the light thrown from his candle showed, he continued, without hurry, to ascend the second flight.

With the irrepressible curiosity of horror she continued to follow him at a distance.

She saw him enter his own private room, and close the door, and in a moment she thought she heard him lock it within.

Continuing to follow she placed herself noiselessly at the door of the apartment, and in breathless silence, with a throbbing heart, listened for what should pass within.

She distinctly heard Sir Bale pace the floor up and down for some time, and then, after a pause, a sound as if some one had thrown himself heavily on the bed. A silence followed, during which her sisters, who had followed more timidly, joined her. She warned them with a look and gesture to be silent.

Lady Haworth stood a little behind, her white lips moving, and her hands clasped in a silent agony of prayer. Lady Mardykes leaned against the massive oak door-case.

With her hand raised to her ear, and her lips parted, Lady Walsingham listened for some seconds—for a minute, two minutes, three. At last, losing heart, she seized the handle in her panic, and turned it sharply. The door was locked on the inside, but some one close to it said from within, "Hush, hush!"

Much alarmed now, the same lady knocked violently at the door. No answer was returned.

She knocked again more violently, and shook the door with all her fragile force. It was something of horror in her countenance as she did so, that, no doubt, terrified Lady Mardykes, who with a loud and long scream sank in a swoon upon the floor.

The servants, alarmed by these sounds, were speedily in the gallery. Lady Mardykes was carried to her room, and laid upon her bed; her sister, Lady Haworth, accompanying her. In the meantime the door was forced. Sir Bale Mardykes was found stretched upon his bed.

Those who have once seen it, will not mistake the aspect of death. Here, in Sir Bale

Mardykes' room, in his bed, in his clothes, is a stranger, grim and awful; in a few days to be insupportable, and to pass alone into the prison-house, and to be seen no more.

Where is Sir Bale Mardykes now, whose roof-tree and whose place at board and bed will know him no more? Here lies a chap-fallen, fish-eyed image, chilling already into clay, and stiffening in every joint.

There is a marble monument in the pretty church of Golden Friars. It stands at the left side of what antiquarians call "the high altar." Two pillars at each end support an arch with several armorial bearings on as many shields sculptured above. Beneath, on a marble flooring raised some four feet, with a cornice round, lies Sir Bale Mardykes, of Mardykes Hall, ninth Baronet of that ancient family, chiseled in marble with knee-breeches and buckled-shoes, and *ailles de pigeon*, and single-breasted coat and long waist-coat, ruffles and sword, such as gentlemen wore about the year 1770, and bearing a strong resemblance to the features of the second Charles. On the broad marble which forms the background is inscribed an epitaph, which has perpetuated to our times the estimate formed by his "inconsolable widow," the Dowager Lady Mardykes, of the virtues and accomplishments of her deceased lord.

Lady Walsingham would have qualified two or three of the more highly-coloured hyperboles, at which the Golden Friars of those days sniffed and tittered. They don't signify now; there is no contemporary left to laugh or whisper. And if there be not much that is true in the letter of that inscription, it at least perpetuates something that *is* true—that wonderful glorificaion of partisanship, the affection of an idolising wife.

Lady Mardykes, a few days after the funeral, left Mardykes Hall for ever. She lived a great deal with her sister, Lady Walsingham; and died, as a line cut at the foot of Sir Bale Mardykes' epitaph records, in the year 1790; her remains being laid beside those of her beloved husband in Golden Friars.

The estates had come to Sir Bale Mardykes free of entail. He had been pottering over a will, but it was never completed, nor even quite planned; and after much doubt and scrutiny, it was at last ascertained that, in default of a will and of issue, a clause in the marriage-settlement gave the entire estates to the Dowager Lady Mardykes.

By her will she bequeathed the estates to "her cousin, also a kinsman of the late Sir Bale Mardykes her husband," William Feltram, on condition of his assuming the name and arms of Mardykes, the arms of Feltram being quartered in the shield.

Thus was oddly fulfilled the prediction which Philip Feltram had repeated, that the estates of Mardykes were to pass into the hands of a Feltram.

About the year 1795 the baronetage was revived, and William Feltram enjoyed the title for fifteen years, as Sir William Mardykes.

How Love Came to Professor Guildea

ROBERT S. HICHENS

I

Dull people often wondered how it came about that Father Murchison and Professor Frederic Guildea were intimate friends. The one was all faith, the other all scepticism. The nature of the Father was based on love. He viewed the world with an almost childlike tenderness above his long, black cassock; and his mild, yet perfectly fearless, blue eyes seemed always to be watching the goodness that exists in humanity, and rejoicing at what they saw. The Professor, on the other hand, had a hard face like a hatchet, tipped with an aggressive black goatee beard. His eyes were quick, piercing and irreverent. The lines about his small, thin-lipped mouth were almost cruel. His voice was harsh and dry, sometimes, when he grew energetic, almost soprano. It fired off words with a sharp and clipping utterance. His habitual manner was one of distrust and investigation. It was impossible to suppose that, in his busy life, he found any time for love, either of humanity in general or of an individual.

Yet his days were spent in scientific investigations which conferred immense benefits upon the world.

Both men were celibates. Father Murchison was a member of an Anglican order which forbade him to marry. Professor Guildea had a poor opinion of most things, but especially of women. He had formerly held a post as lecturer at Birmingham. But when his fame as a discoverer grew he removed to London. There, at a lecture he gave in the East End, he first met Father Murchison. They spoke a few words. Perhaps the bright intelligence of the priest appealed to the man of science, who was inclined, as a rule, to regard the clergy with some contempt. Perhaps the transparent sincerity of this devotee, full of common sense, attracted him. As he was leaving the hall he abruptly asked the Father to call on him at his house in Hyde Park Place. And the Father, who seldom went into the West End, except to preach, accepted the invitation.

"When will you come?" said Guildea.

He was folding up the blue paper on which his notes were written in a tiny, clear hand. The leaves rustled drily in accompaniment to his sharp, dry voice.

"On Sunday week I am preaching in the evening at St. Saviour's, not far off," said the Father.

"I don't go to church."

"No," said the Father, without any accent of surprise or condemnation.

"Come to supper afterwards?"

"Thank you. I will."

"What time will you come?"

The Father smiled.

"As soon as I have finished my sermon. The service is at six-thirty."

"About eight then, I suppose. Don't make the sermon too long. My number in Hyde Park Place is a hundred. Good-night to you."

He snapped an elastic band round his papers and strode off without shaking hands.

On the appointed Sunday, Father Murchison preached to a densely crowded congregation at St. Saviour's. The subject of his sermon was sympathy, and the comparative uselessness of man in the world unless he can learn to love his neighbour as himself. The sermon was rather long, and when the preacher, in his flowing, black cloak, and his hard, round hat, with a straight brim over which hung the ends of a black cord, made his way towards the Professor's house, the hands of the illuminated clock disc at the Marble Arch pointed to twenty minutes past eight.

The Father hurried on, pushing his way through the crowd of standing soldiers, chattering women and giggling street boys in their Sunday best. It was a warm April night, and, when he reached number 100, Hyde Park Place, he found the Professor bareheaded on his doorstep, gazing out towards the Park railings, and enjoying the soft, moist air, in front of his lighted passage.

"Ha, a long sermon!" he exclaimed. "Come in."

"I fear it was," said the Father, obeying the invitation. "I am that dangerous thing—an extempore preacher."

"More attractive to speak without notes, if you can do it. Hang your hat and coat—oh, cloak—here. We'll have supper at once. This is the dining-room."

He opened a door on the right and they entered a long, narrow room, with a gold paper and a black ceiling, from which hung an electric lamp with a gold-coloured shade. In the room stood a small oval table with covers laid for two. The Professor rang the bell. Then he said,

"People seem to talk better at an oval table than at a square one."

"Really. Is that so?"

"Well, I've had precisely the same party twice, once at a square table, once at an oval table. The first dinner was a dull failure, the second a brilliant success. Sit down, won't you?"

"How d'you account for the difference?" said the Father, sitting down, and pulling the tail of his cassock well under him.

"H'm. I know how you'd account for it."

"Indeed. How then?"

"At an oval table, since there are no corners, the chain of human sympathy—the electric current, is much more complete. Eh! Let me give you some soup."

"Thank you."

The Father took it, and, as he did so, turned his beaming blue eyes on his host. Then he smiled.

"What!" he said, in his pleasant, light tenor voice. "You do go to church sometimes, then?"

"To-night is the first time for ages. And, mind you, I was tremendously bored."

The Father still smiled, and his blue eyes gently twinkled.

"Dear, dear!" he said, "what a pity!"

"But not by the sermon," Guildea added. "I don't pay a compliment. I state a fact. The sermon didn't bore me. If it had, I should have said so, or said nothing."

"And which would you have done?"

The Professor smiled almost genially.

"Don't know," he said. "What wine d'you drink?"

"None, thank you. I'm a teetotaller. In my profession and *milieu* it is necessary to be one. Yes, I will have some soda water. I think you would have done the first."

"Very likely, and very wrongly. You wouldn't have minded much."

"I don't think I should."

They were intimate already. The Father felt most pleasantly at home under the black ceiling. He drank some soda water and seemed to enjoy it more than the Professor enjoyed his claret.

"You smile at the theory of the chain of human sympathy, I see," said the Father. "Then what is your explanation of the failure of your square party with corners, the success of your oval party without them?"

"Probably on the first occasion the wit of the assembly had a chill on his liver, while on the second he was in perfect health. Yet, you see, I stick to the oval table."

"And that means—"

"Very little. By the way, your omission of any allusion to the notorious part liver plays in love was a serious one to-night."

"Your omission of any desire for close human sympathy in your life is a more serious one."

"How can you be sure I have no such desire?"

"I divine it. Your look, your manner, tell me it is so. You were disagreeing with my sermon all the time I was preaching. Weren't you?"

"Part of the time."

The servant changed the plates. He was a middle-aged, blond, thin man, with a stony white face, pale, prominent eyes, and an accomplished manner of service. When he had left the room the Professor continued,

"Your remarks interested me, but I thought them exaggerated."

"For instance?"

"Let me play the egoist for a moment. I spend most of my time in hard work, very hard work. The results of this work, you will allow, benefit humanity."

"Enormously," assented the Father, thinking of more than one of Guildea's discoveries.

"And the benefit conferred by this work, undertaken merely for its own sake, is just as great as if it were undertaken because I loved my fellow man and sentimentally desired to see him more comfortable than he is at present. I'm as useful precisely in my present condition of—in my present non-affectional condition—as I should be if I were as full of gush as the sentimentalists who want to get murderers out of prison, or to put a premium on tyranny—like Tolstoi—by preventing the punishment of tyrants."

"One may do great harm with affection; great good without it. Yes, that is true. Even *le bon motif* is not everything, I know. Still I contend that, given your powers, you would be far more useful in the world with sympathy, affection for your kind, added to them than as you are. I believe even that you would do still more splendid work."

The Professor poured himself out another glass of claret.

"You noticed my butler?" he said.

"I did."

"He's a perfect servant. He makes me perfectly comfortable. Yet he has no feeling of liking for me. I treat him civilly. I pay him well. But I never think about him, or concern myself with him as a human being. I know nothing of his character except what I read of it in his last master's letter. There are, you may say, no truly human relations between us. You would affirm that his work would be better done if I had made him personally like me as man—of any class—can like man—of any other class?"

"I should, decidedly."

"I contend that he couldn't do his work better than he does it at present."

"But if any crisis occurred?"

"What?"

"Any crisis, change in your condition. If you needed his help, not only as a man and a butler, but as a man and a brother? He'd fail you then, probably. You would never get from your servant that finest service which can only be prompted by an honest affection."

"You have finished?"

"Quite."

"Let us go upstairs then. Yes, those are good prints. I picked them up in Birmingham when I was living there. This is my workroom."

They came into a double room lined entirely with books, and brilliantly, rather hardly, lit by electricity. The windows at one end looked on to the Park, at the other on to the garden of a neighbouring house. The door by which they entered was concealed from the inner and smaller room by the jutting wall of the outer room, in which stood a huge writing-table loaded with letters, pamphlets and manuscripts. Between the two windows of the inner room was a cage in which a large, grey parrot was clambering, using both beak and claws to assist him in his slow and meditative peregrinations.

"You have a pet," said the Father, surprised.

"I possess a parrot," the Professor answered, drily, "I got him for a purpose when I was making a study of the imitative powers of birds, and I have never got rid of him. A cigar?"

"Thank you."

They sat down. Father Murchison glanced at the parrot. It had paused in its journey, and, clinging to the bars of its cage, was regarding them with attentive round eyes that looked deliberately intelligent, but by no means sympathetic. He looked away from it to Guildea, who was smoking, with his head thrown back, his sharp, pointed chin, on which the small black beard bristled, upturned. He was moving his under lip up and down rapidly. This action caused the beard to stir and look peculiarly aggressive. The Father suddenly chuckled softly.

"Why's that?" cried Guildea, letting his chin drop down on his breast and looking at his guest sharply.

"I was thinking it would have to be a crisis indeed that could make you cling to your butler's affection for assistance."

Guildea smiled too.

"You're right. It would. Here he comes."

The man entered with coffee. He offered it gently, and retired like a shadow retreating on a wall.

"Splendid, inhuman fellow," remarked Guildea.

"I prefer the East End lad who does my errands in Bird Street," said the Father. "I know all his worries. He knows some of mine. We are friends. He's more noisy than your man. He even breathes hard when he is specially solicitous, but he would do more for me than put the coals on my fire, or black my square-toed boots."

"Men are differently made. To me the watchful eye of affection would be abominable."

"What about that bird?"

The Father pointed to the parrot. It had got up on its perch and, with one foot uplifted in an impressive, almost benedictory, manner, was gazing steadily at the Professor.

"That's the watchful eye of imitation, with a mind at the back of it, desirous of reproducing the peculiarities of others. No, I thought your sermon to-night very fresh, very clever. But I have no wish for affection. Reasonable liking, of course, one desires," he tugged sharply at his beard, as if to warn himself against sentimentality,— "but anything more would be most irksome, and would push me, I feel sure, towards cruelty. It would also hamper one's work."

"I don't think so."

"The sort of work I do. I shall continue to benefit the world without loving it, and it will continue to accept the benefits without loving me. That's all as it should be."

He drank his coffee. Then he added, rather aggressively:

"I have neither time nor inclination for sentimentality."

When Guildea let Father Murchison out, he followed the Father on to the doorstep and stood there for a moment. The Father glanced across the damp road into the Park.

"I see you've got a gate just opposite you," he said idly.

"Yes. I often slip across for a stroll to clear my brain. Good-night to you. Come again some day."

"With pleasure. Good-night."

The Priest strode away, leaving Guildea standing on the step.

Father Murchison came many times again to number one hundred Hyde Park Place. He had a feeling of liking for most men and women whom he knew, and of tenderness for all, whether he knew them or not, but he grew to have a special sentiment towards Guildea. Strangely enough, it was a sentiment of pity. He pitied this hard-working, eminently successful man of big brain and bold heart, who never seemed depressed, who never wanted assistance, who never complained of the twisted skein of life or faltered in his progress along its way. The Father pitied Guildea, in fact, because Guildea wanted so little. He had told him so, for the intercourse of the two men, from the beginning, had been singularly frank.

One evening, when they were talking together, the Father happened to speak of one of the oddities of life, the fact that those who do not want things often get them, while those who seek them vehemently are disappointed in their search.

"Then I ought to have affection poured upon me," said Guildea, smiling rather grimly. "For I hate it."

"Perhaps some day you will."

"I hope not, most sincerely."

Father Murchison said nothing for a moment. He was drawing together the ends of the broad band round his cassock. When he spoke he seemed to be answering someone.

"Yes," he said slowly, "yes, that *is* my feeling—pity."

"For whom?" said the Professor.

Then, suddenly, he understood. He did not say that he understood, but Father Murchison felt, and saw, that it was quite unnecessary to answer his friend's question. So Guildea, strangely enough, found himself closely acquainted with a man—his opposite in all ways,—who pitied him.

The fact that he did not mind this, and scarcely ever thought about it, shows perhaps as clearly as anything could the peculiar indifference of his nature.

II

One Autumn evening, a year and a half after Father Murchison and the Professor had first met, the Father called in Hyde Park Place and enquired of the blond and stony butler—his name was Pitting—whether his master was at home.

"Yes, sir," replied Pitting. "Will you please come this way?"

He moved noiselessly up the rather narrow stairs, followed by the Father, tenderly opened the library door, and in his soft, cold voice, announced:

"Father Murchison."

Guildea was sitting in an armchair, before a small fire. His thin, long-fingered hands lay outstretched upon his knees, his head was sunk down on his chest. He appeared to be pondering deeply. Pitting very slightly raised his voice.

"Father Murchison to see you, sir," he repeated.

The Professor jumped up rather suddenly and turned sharply round as the Father came in.

"Oh," he said. "It's you, is it? Glad to see you. Come to the fire."

The Father glanced at him and thought him looking unusually fatigued.

"You don't look well to-night," the Father said.

"No?"

"You must be working too hard. That lecture you are going to give in Paris is bothering you?"

"Not a bit. It's all arranged. I could deliver it to you at this moment verbatim. Well, sit down."

The Father did so, and Guildea sank once more into his chair and stared hard into the fire without another word. He seemed to be thinking profoundly. His friend did not interrupt him, but quietly lit a pipe and began to smoke reflectively. The eyes of Guildea were fixed upon the fire. The Father glanced about the room, at the walls of soberly bound books, at the crowded writing-table, at the windows, before which hung heavy, dark-blue curtains of old brocade, at the cage, which stood between them. A green baize covering was thrown over it. The Father wondered why. He had never seen Napoleon—so the parrot was named—covered up at night before. While he was looking at the baize, Guildea suddenly jerked up his head, and, taking his hands from his knees and clasping them, said abruptly:

"D'you think I'm an attractive man?"

Father Murchison jumped. Such a question coming from such a man astounded him.

"Bless me!" he ejaculated. "What makes you ask? Do you mean attractive to the opposite sex?"

"That's what I don't know," said the Professor gloomily, and staring again into the fire. "That's what I don't know."

The Father grew more astonished.

"Don't know!" he exclaimed.

And he laid down his pipe.

"Let's say—d'you think I'm attractive, that there's anything about me which might draw a—a human being, or an animal, irresistibly to me?"

"Whether you desired it or not?"

"Exactly—or—no, let us say definitely—if I did not desire it."

Father Murchison pursed up his rather full, cherubic lips, and little wrinkles appeared about the corners of his blue eyes.

"There might be, of course," he said, after a pause. "Human nature is weak, engagingly weak, Guildea. And you're inclined to flout it. I could understand a certain class of lady—the lion-hunting, the intellectual lady, seeking you. Your reputation, your great name"

"Yes, yes," Guildea interrupted, rather irritably—"I know all that, I know."

He twisted his long hands together, bending the palms outwards till his thin, pointed fingers cracked. His forehead was wrinkled in a frown.

"I imagine," he said,—he stopped and coughed drily, almost shrilly—"I imagine it would be very disagreeable to be liked, to be run after—that is the usual expression, isn't it—by anything one objected to."

And now he half turned in his chair, crossed his legs one over the other, and looked at his guest with an unusual, almost piercing interrogation.

"Anything?" said the Father.

"Well—well, anyone. I imagine nothing could be more unpleasant."

"To you—no," answered the Father. "But—forgive me, Guildea, I cannot conceive you permitting such intrusion. You don't encourage adoration."

Guildea nodded his head gloomily.

"I don't," he said, "I don't. That's just it. That's the curious part of it, that I—"

He broke off deliberately, got up and stretched.

"I'll have a pipe, too," he said.

He went over to the mantelpiece, got his pipe, filled it and lighted it. As he held the match to the tobacco, bending forward with an inquiring expression, his eyes fell upon the green baize that covered Napoleon's cage. He threw the match into the grate, and puffed at the pipe as he walked forward to the cage. When he reached it he put out his hand, took hold of the baize and began to pull it away. Then suddenly he pushed it back over the cage.

"No," he said, as if to himself, "no."

He returned rather hastily to the fire and threw himself once more into his armchair.

"You're wondering," he said to Father Murchison. "So am I. I don't know at all what to make of it. I'll just tell you the facts and you must tell me what you think of them. The night before last, after a day of hard work—but no harder than usual—I went to the front door to get a breath of air. You know I often do that."

"Yes, I found you on the doorstep when I first came here."

"Just so. I didn't put on hat or coat. I just stood on the step as I was. My mind, I remember, was still full of my work. It was rather a dark night, not very dark. The hour was about eleven, or a quarter past. I was staring at the Park, and presently I found that my eyes were directed towards somebody who was sitting, back to me, on one of the benches. I saw the person—if it was a person,—through the railings."

"If it was a person!" said the Father. "What do you mean by that?"

"Wait a minute. I say that because it was too dark for me to know. I merely saw some blackish object on the bench, rising into view above the level of the back of the seat. I couldn't say it was man, woman or child. But something there was, and I found that I was looking at it."

"I understand."

"Gradually, I also found that my thoughts were becoming fixed upon this thing or person. I began to wonder, first, what it was doing there; next, what it was thinking; lastly, what it was like."

"Some poor creature without a home, I suppose," said the Father.

"I said that to myself. Still, I was taken with an extraordinary interest about this object, so great an interest that I got my hat and crossed the road to go into the Park. As you know, there's an entrance almost opposite to my house. Well, Murchison, I crossed the road, passed through the gate in the railings, went up to the seat, and found that there was—nothing on it."

"Were you looking at it as you walked?"

"Part of the time. But I removed my eyes from it just as I passed through the gate, because there was a row going on a little way off, and I turned for an instant in that direction. When I saw that the seat was vacant I was seized by a most absurd sensation of disappointment, almost of anger. I stopped and looked about me to see if anything was moving away, but I could see nothing. It was a cold night and misty, and there were few people about. Feeling, as I say, foolishly and unnaturally disappointed, I retraced my steps to this house. When I got here I discovered that during my short absence I had left the hall door open—half open."

"Rather imprudent in London."

"Yes. I had no idea, of course, that I had done so, till I got back. However, I was only away three minutes or so."

"Yes."

"It was not likely that anybody had gone in."

"I suppose not."

"Was it?"

"Why do you ask me that, Guildea?"

"Well, well!"

"Besides, if anybody had gone in on your return you'd have caught him, surely."

Guildea coughed again. The Father, surprised, could not fail to recognise that he was nervous and that his nervousness was affecting him physically.

"I must have caught cold that night," he said, as if he had read his friend's thought and hastened to contradict it. Then he went on:

"I entered the hall, or passage, rather."

He paused again. His uneasiness was becoming very apparent.

"And you did catch somebody?" said the Father.

Guildea cleared his throat.

"That's just it," he said, "now we come to it. I'm not imaginative, as you know."

"You certainly are not."

"No, but hardly had I stepped into the passage before I felt certain that somebody had got into the house during my absence. I felt convinced of it, and not only that, I also felt convinced that the intruder was the very person I had dimly seen sitting upon the seat in the Park. What d'you say to that?"

"I begin to think you are imaginative."

"H'm! It seemed to me that the person— the occupant of the seat—and I, had simultaneously formed the project of interviewing each other, had simultaneously set out to put that project into execution. I became so certain of this that I walked hastily upstairs into this room, excepting to find the visitor awaiting me. But there was no one. I then came down again and went into the dining-room. No one. I was actually astonished. Isn't that odd?"

"Very," said the Father, quite gravely.

The Professor's chill and gloomy manner, and uncomfortable, constrained appearance kept away the humour that might well have lurked round the steps of such a discourse.

"I went upstairs again," he continued, "sat down and thought the matter over. I resolved to forget it, and took up a book. I might perhaps have been able to read, but suddenly I thought I noticed—"

He stopped abruptly. Father Murchison observed that he was staring towards the green baize that covered the parrot's cage.

"But that's nothing," he said. "Enough that I couldn't read. I resolved to explore the house. You know how small it is, how easily one can go all over it. I went all over it. I went into every room without exception. To the servants, who were having supper, I made some excuse. They were surprised at my advent, no doubt."

"And Pitting?"

"Oh, he got up politely when I came in, stood while I was there, but never said a word. I muttered 'don't disturb yourselves,' or something of the sort, and came out. Murchison, I found nobody new in the house—yet I returned to this room entirely convinced that somebody had entered while I was in the Park."

"And gone out again before you came back?"

"No, had stayed, and was still in the house."

"But, my dear Guildea," began the Father, now in great astonishment. "Surely—"

"I know what you want to say—what I should want to say in your place. Now, do wait. I am also convinced that this visitor has not left the house and is at this moment in it."

He spoke with evident sincerity, with extreme gravity. Father Murchison looked him full in the face, and met his quick, keen eyes.

"No," he said, as if in reply to an uttered question: "I'm perfectly sane, I assure you. The whole matter seems almost as incredible to me as it must to you. But, as you know, I never quarrel with facts, however strange. I merely try to examine into them thoroughly. I have already consulted a doctor and been pronounced in perfect bodily health."

He paused, as if expecting the Father to say something.

"Go on, Guildea," he said, "you haven't finished."

"No. I felt that night positive that somebody had entered the house, and remained in it, and my conviction grew. I went to bed as usual, and, contrary to my expectation, slept as well as I generally do. Yet directly I woke up yesterday morning I knew that my household had been increased by one."

"May I interrupt you for one moment? How did you know it?"

"By my mental sensation. I can only say that I was perfectly conscious of a new presence within my house, close to me."

"How very strange," said the Father. "And you feel absolutely certain that you are not overworked? Your brain does not feel tired? Your head is quite clear?"

"Quite. I was never better. When I came down to breakfast that morning I looked sharply into Pitting's face. He was as coldly placid and inexpressive as usual. It was evident to me that his mind was in no way distressed. After breakfast I sat down to work, all the time ceaselessly conscious of the fact of this intruder upon my privacy. Nevertheless, I laboured for several hours, waiting for any development that might occur to clear away the mysterious obscurity of this event. I lunched. About half-past two I was obliged to go out to attend a lecture. I therefore, took my coat and hat, opened my door, and stepped on to the pavement. I was instantly aware that I was no longer intruded upon, and this although I was now in the street, surrounded by people. Consequently, I felt certain that the thing in my house must be thinking of me, perhaps even spying upon me."

"Wait a moment," interrupted the Father. "What was your sensation? Was it one of fear?"

"Oh, dear no. I was entirely puzzled—as I am now—and keenly interested, but not in any way alarmed. I delivered my lecture with my usual ease and returned home in the evening. On entering the house again I was perfectly conscious that the intruder was still there. Last night I dined alone and spent the hours after dinner in reading a scientific work in which I was deeply interested. While I read, however, I never for one moment lost the knowledge that some mind—very attentive to me—was within hail of mine. I will say more than this—the sensation constantly increased, and, by the time I got up to go to bed, I had come to a very strange conclusion."

"What? What was it?"

"That whoever—or whatever—had entered my house during my short absence in the Park was more than interested in me."

"More than interested in you?"

"Was fond, or was becoming fond, of me."

"Oh!" exclaimed the Father. "Now I understand why you asked me just now whether I thought there was anything about you that might draw a human being or an animal irresistibly to you."

"Precisely. Since I came to this conclusion, Murchison, I will confess that my feeling of strong curiosity has become tinged with another feeling."

"Of fear?"

"No, of dislike, of irritation. No—not fear, not fear."

As Guildea repeated unnecessarily this asseveration he looked again towards the parrot's cage.

"What is there to be afraid of in such a matter?" he added. "I'm not a child to tremble before bogies."

In saying the last words he raised his voice sharply; then he walked quickly to the cage, and, with an abrupt movement, pulled the baize covering from it. Napoleon was disclosed, apparently dozing upon his perch with his head held slightly on one side. As the light reached him, he moved, ruffled the feathers about his neck, blinked his eyes, and began slowly to sidle to and fro, thrusting his head forward and drawing it back with an air of complacent, though rather unmeaning, energy. Guildea stood by the cage, looking at him closely, and indeed with an attention that was so intense as to be remarkable, almost unnatural.

"How absurd these birds are!" he said at length, coming back to the fire.

"You have no more to tell me?" asked the Father.

"No. I am still aware of the presence of something in my house. I am still conscious of its close attention to me. I am still irritated, seriously annoyed—I confess it—by that attention."

"You say you are aware of the presence of something at this moment?"

"At this moment—yes."

"Do you mean in this room, with us, now?"

"I should say so—at any rate, quite near us."

Again he glanced quickly, almost suspiciously, towards the cage of the parrot. The bird was sitting still on its perch now. Its head was bent down and cocked sideways, and it appeared to be listening attentively to something.

"That bird will have the intonations of my voice more correctly than ever by to-morrow morning," said the Father, watching Guildea closely with his mild blue eyes. "And it has always imitated me very cleverly."

The Professor started slightly.

"Yes," he said. "Yes, no doubt. Well, what do you make of this affair?"

"Nothing at all. It is absolutely inexplicable. I can speak quite frankly to you, I feel sure."

"Of course. That's why I have told you the whole thing."

"I think you must be over-worked, overstrained, without knowing it."

"And that the doctor was mistaken when he said I was all right?"

"Yes."

Guildea knocked his pipe out against the chimney piece.

"It may be so," he said, "I will not be so unreasonable as to deny the possibility, although I feel as well as I ever did in my life. What do you advise then?"

"A week of complete rest away from London, in good air."

"The usual prescription. I'll take it. I'll go to-morrow to Westgate and leave Napoleon to keep house in my absence."

For some reason, which he could not explain to himself, the pleasure which Father Murchison felt in hearing the first part of his friend's final remark was lessened, was almost destroyed, by the last sentence.

He walked towards the City that night, deep in thought, remembering and carefully considering the first interview he had with Guildea in the latter's house a year and a half before.

On the following morning Guildea left London.

III

Father Murchison was so busy a man that he had little time for brooding over the affairs of others. During Guildea's week at the sea, however, the Father thought about him a great deal, with much wonder and some dismay. The dismay was soon banished, for the mild-eyed priest was quick to discern weakness in himself, quicker still to drive it forth as a most undesirable inmate of the soul. But the wonder remained. It was destined to a crescendo. Guildea had left London on a Thursday. On a Thursday he returned, having previously sent a note to Father Murchison to mention that he was leaving Westgate at a certain time. When his train ran in to Victoria Station, at five o'clock in the evening, he was surprised to see the cloaked figure of his friend standing upon the grey platform behind a line of porters.

"What, Murchison!" he said. "You here! Have you seceded from your order that you are taking this holiday?"

They shook hands.

"No," said the Father. "It happened that I had to be in this neighbourhood to-day, visiting a sick person. So I thought I would meet you."

"And see if I were still a sick person, eh?"

The Professor glanced at him kindly, but with a dry little laugh.

"Are you?" replied the Father gently, looking at him with interest. "No, I think not. You appear very well."

The sea air had, in fact, put some brownish red into Guildea's always thin cheeks. His keen eyes were shining with life and energy, and he walked forward in his loose grey suit and fluttering overcoat with a vigour that was noticeable, carrying easily in his left hand his well-filled Gladstone bag.

The Father felt completely reassured.

"I never saw you look better," he said.

"I never was better. Have you an hour to spare?"

"Two."

"Good. I'll send my bag up by cab, and we'll walk across the Park to my house and have a cup of tea there. What d'you say?"

"I shall enjoy it."

They walked out of the station yard, past the flower girls and newspaper sellers towards Grosvenor Place.

"And you have had a pleasant time?" the Father said.

"Pleasant enough, and lonely. I left my companion behind me in the passage at Number 100, you know."

"And you'll not find him there now, I feel sure."

"H'm!" ejaculated Guildea. "What a precious weakling you think me, Murchison."

As he spoke he strode forward more quickly as if moved to emphasise his sensation of bodily vigour.

"A weakling—no. But anyone who uses his brain as persistently as you do yours must require an occasional holiday."

"And I required one very badly, eh?"

"You required one, I believe."

"Well, I've had it. And now we'll see."

The evening was closing in rapidly. They crossed the road at Hyde Park Corner, and entered the Park, in which were a number of people going home from work; men in corduroy trousers, caked with dried mud, and carrying tin cans slung over their shoulders, and flat panniers, in which lay their tools. Some of the younger ones talked loudly or whistled shrilly as they walked.

"Until the evening," murmured Father Murchison to himself.

"What?" asked Guildea.

"I was only quoting the last words of the text, which seems written upon life, especially upon the life of pleasure: 'Man goeth forth to his work, and to his labour.'"

"Ah, those fellows are not half bad fellows to have in an audience. There were a lot of them at the lecture I gave when I first met you, I remember. One of them tried to heckle me. He had a red beard. Chaps with red beards are always hecklers. I laid him low on that occasion. Well, Murchison, and now we're going to see."

"What?"

"Whether my companion has departed."

"Tell me—do you feel any expectation of— well—of again thinking something is there?"

"How carefully you choose language. No, I merely wonder."

"You have no apprehension?"

"Not a scrap. But I confess to feeling curious."

"Then the sea air hasn't taught you to recognise that the whole thing came from overstrain."

"No," said Guildea, very drily.

He walked on in silence for a minute. Then he added:

"You thought it would?"

"I certainly thought it might."

"Make me realise that I had a sickly, morbid, rotten imagination—heh? Come now, Murchison, why not say frankly that you packed me off to Westgate to get rid of what you considered an acute form of hysteria?"

The Father was quite unmoved by this attack.

"Come now, Guildea," he retorted, "what did you expect me to think? I saw no indication of hysteria in you. I never have. One would suppose you the last man likely to have such a malady. But which is more natural—for me to believe in your hysteria or in the truth of such a story as you told me?"

"You have me there. No, I mustn't complain. Well, there's no hysteria about me now, at any rate."

"And no stranger in your house, I hope."

Father Murchison spoke the last words with earnest gravity, dropping the half-bantering tone —which they had both assumed.

"You take the matter very seriously, I believe," said Guildea, also speaking more gravely.

"How else can I take it? You wouldn't have me laugh at it when you tell it me seriously?"

"No. If we find my visitor still in the house, I may even call upon you to exorcise it. But first I must do one thing."

"And that is?"

"Prove to you, as well as to myself, that it is still there."

"That might be difficult," said the Father, considerably surprised by Guildea's matter-of-fact tone.

"I don't know. If it has remained in my house I think I can find a means. And I shall not be at all surprised if it is still there—despite the Westgate air."

In saying the last words the Professor relapsed into his former tone of dry chaff. The Father could not quite make up his mind whether Guildea was feeling unusually grave or unusually gay. As the two men drew near to Hyde Park Place their conversation died away and they walked forward silently in the gathering darkness.

"Here we are!" said Guildea at last.

He thrust his key into the door, opened it and let Father Murchison into the passage, following him closely and banging the door.

"Here we are!" he repeated in a louder voice.

The electric light was turned on in anticipation of his arrival. He stood still and looked round.

"We'll have some tea at once," he said. "Ah, Pitting!"

The pale butler, who had heard the door bang, moved gently forward from the top of the stairs that led to the kitchen, greeted his master respectfully, took his coat and Father Murchison's cloak, and hung them on two pegs against the wall.

"All's right, Pitting? All's as usual?" said Guildea.

"Quite so, sir."

"Bring us up some tea to the library."

"Yes, sir."

Pitting retreated. Guildea waited till he had disappeared, then opened the dining-room door, put his head into the room and kept it there for a moment, standing perfectly still. Presently he drew back into the passage, shut the door, and said,

"Let's go upstairs."

Father Murchison looked at him enquiringly, but made no remark. They ascended the stairs and came into the library. Guildea glanced rather sharply round. A fire was burning on the hearth. The blue curtains were drawn. The bright gleam of the strong electric light fell on the long rows of books, on the writing table—very orderly in consequence of Guildea's holiday—and on the uncovered cage of the parrot. Guildea went up to the cage. Napoleon was sitting humped up on his perch with his feathers ruffled. His long toes, which looked as if they were covered with crocodile skin, clung to the bar. His round and blinking eyes were filmy, like old eyes. Guildea stared at the bird very hard, and then clucked with his tongue against his teeth. Napoleon shook himself, lifted one foot, extended his toes, sidled along the perch to the bars nearest to the Professor and thrust his head against them. Guildea scratched it with his forefinger two or three times, still gazing attentively at the parrot; then he returned to the fire just as Pitting entered with the tea-tray.

Father Murchison was already sitting in an arm chair on one side of the fire. Guildea took another chair and began to pour out tea, as Pitting left the room closing the door gently behind him. The Father sipped his tea, found it hot and set the cup down on a little table at his side.

"You're fond of that parrot, aren't you?" he asked his friend.

"Not particularly. It's interesting to study sometimes. The parrot mind and nature are peculiar."

"How long have you had him?"

"About four years. I nearly got rid of him just before I made your acquaintance. I'm very glad now I kept him."

"Are you? Why is that?"

"I shall probably tell you in a day or two."

The Father took his cup again. He did not press Guildea for an immediate explanation, but when they had both finished their tea he said:

"Well, has the sea-air had the desired effect?"

"No," said Guildea.

The Father brushed some crumbs from the front of his cassock and sat up higher in his chair.

"Your visitor is still here?" he asked, and his blue eyes became almost ungentle and piercing as he gazed at his friend.

"Yes," answered Guildea, calmly.

"How do you know it, when did you know it —when you looked into the dining-room just now?"

"No. Not until I came into this room. It welcomed me here."

"Welcomed you! In what way?"

"Simply by being here, by making me feel that it is here, as I might feel that a man was if I came into the room when it was dark."

He spoke quietly, with perfect composure in his usual dry manner.

"Very well," the Father said, "I shall not try to contend against your sensation, or to explain it away. Naturally, I am in amazement."

"So am I. Never has anything in my life surprised me so much. Murchison, of course I cannot expect you to believe more than that I honestly suppose—imagine, if you like—that there is some intruder here, of what kind I am totally unaware. I cannot expect you to believe that there really is anything. If you were in my place, I in yours, I should certainly consider you the victim of some nervous delusion. I could not do otherwise. But—wait. Don't condemn me as a hysteria patient, or as a madman, for two or three days. I feel convinced that—unless I am indeed unwell, a mental invalid, which I don't think is possible—I shall be able very shortly to give you some proof that there is a newcomer in my house."

"You don't tell me what kind of proof?"

"Not yet. Things must go a little farther first. But, perhaps even to-morrow I may be able to explain myself more fully. In the meanwhile, I'll say this, that if, eventually, I can't bring any kind of proof that I'm not dreaming I'll let you take me to any doctor you like, and I'll resolutely try to adopt your present view—that I'm suffering from an absurd delusion. That is your view of course?"

Father Murchison was silent for a moment. Then he said, rather doubtfully:

"It ought to be."

"But isn't it?" asked Guildea, surprised.

"Well, you know, your manner is enormously convincing. Still, of course, I doubt. How can I do otherwise? The whole thing must be fancy."

The Father spoke as if he were trying to recoil from a mental position he was being forced to take up.

"It must be fancy," he repeated.

"I'll convince you by more than my manner, or I'll not try to convince you at all," said Guildea.

When they parted that evening, he said,

"I'll write to you in a day or two probably. I think the proof I am going to give you has been accumulating during my absence. But I shall soon know."

Father Murchison was extremely puzzled as he sat on the top of the omnibus going homeward.

IV

In two days' time he received a note from Guildea asking him to call, if possible, the same evening. This he was unable to do as he had an engagement to fulfil at some East End gathering. The following day was Sunday. He wrote saying he would come on the Monday, and got a wire shortly afterwards: "Yes, Monday come to dinner seven-thirty Guildea." At half-past seven he stood on the doorstep of Number 100.

Pitting let him in.

"Is the Professor quite well, Pitting?" the Father inquired as he took off his cloak.

"I believe so, sir. He has not made any complaint," the butler formally replied. "Will you come upstairs, sir?"

Guildea met them at the door of the library. He was very pale and sombre, and shook hands carelessly with his friend.

"Give us dinner," he said to Pitting.

As the butler retired, Guildea shut the door rather cautiously. Father Murchison had never before seen him look so disturbed.

"You're worried, Guildea," the Father said. "Seriously worried."

"Yes, I am. This business is beginning to tell on me a good deal."

"Your belief in the presence of something here continues then?"

"Oh, dear, yes. There's no sort of doubt about the matter. The night I went across the road into the Park something got into the house, though what the devil it is I can't yet find out. But now, before we go down to dinner, I'll just tell you something about that proof I promised you. You remember?"

"Naturally."

"Can't you imagine what it might be."

Father Murchison moved his head to express a negative reply.

"Look about the room," said Guildea. "What do you see?"

The Father glanced round the room, slowly and carefully.

"Nothing unusual. You do not mean to tell me there is any appearance of—"

"Oh, no, no, there's no conventional, white-robed, cloud-like figure. Bless my soul, no! I haven't fallen so low as that."

He spoke with considerable irritation.

"Look again."

Father Murchison looked at him, turned in the direction of his fixed eyes and saw the grey parrot clambering in its cage, slowly and persistently.

"What?" he said, quickly. "Will the proof come from there?"

The Professor nodded. "I believe so," he said. "Now let's go down to dinner. I want some food badly."

They descended to the dining-room. While they ate and Pitting waited upon them, the Professor talked about birds, their habits, their curiosities, their fears and their powers of imitation. He had evidently studied this subject with the thoroughness that was characteristic of him in all that he did.

"Parrots," he said presently, "are extraordinarily observant. It is a pity that their means of reproducing what they see are so limited. If it were not so, I have little doubt that their echo of gesture would be as remarkable as their echo of voice often is."

"But hands are missing."

"Yes. They do many things with their heads, however. I once knew an old woman near Goring on the Thames. She was afflicted with the palsy. She held her head perpetually sideways and it trembled, moving from right to left. Her sailor son brought her home a parrot from one of his voyages. It used to reproduce the old woman's palsied movement of the head exactly. Those grey parrots are always on the watch."

Guildea said the last sentence slowly and deliberately, glancing sharply over his wine at Father Murchison, and, when he had spoken it, a sudden light of comprehension dawned in the Priest's mind. He opened his lips to make a swift remark. Guildea turned his bright eyes towards Pitting, who at the moment was tenderly bearing a cheese meringue from the lift that connected the dining-room with the lower regions. The Father closed his lips again. But presently, when the butler had placed some apples on the table, had meticulously arranged the decanters, brushed away the crumbs and evaporated, he said, quickly,

"I begin to understand. You think Napoleon is aware of the intruder?"

"I know it. He has been watching my visitant ever since the night of that visitant's arrival."

Another flash of light came to the Priest.

"That was why you covered him with green baize one evening?"

"Exactly. An act of cowardice. His behaviour was beginning to grate upon my nerves."

Guildea pursed up his thin lips and drew his brows down, giving to his face a look of sudden pain.

"But now I intend to follow his investigations," he added, straightening his features. "The week I wasted at Westgate was not wasted by him in London, I can assure you. Have an apple."

"No, thank you; no, thank you."

The Father repeated the words without knowing that he did so. Guildea pushed away his glass.

"Let us come upstairs, then."

"No, thank you," reiterated the Father.

"Eh?"

"What am I saying?" exclaimed the Father, getting up. "I was thinking over this extraordinary affair."

"Ah, you're beginning to forget the hysteria theory?"

They walked out into the passage.

"Well, you are so very practical about the whole matter."

"Why not? Here's something very strange and abnormal come into my life. What should I do but investigate it closely and calmly?"

"What, indeed?"

The Father began to feel rather bewildered, under a sort of compulsion which seemed laid upon him to give earnest attention to a matter that ought to strike him— so he felt—as entirely absurd. When they came into the library his eyes immediately turned, with profound curiosity, towards the parrot's cage. A slight smile curled the Professor's lips. He recognised the effect he was producing upon his friend. The Father saw the smile.

"Oh, I'm not won over yet," he said in answer to it.

"I know. Perhaps you may be before the evening is over. Here comes the coffee. After we have drunk it we'll proceed to our experiment. Leave the coffee, Pitting, and don't disturb us again."

"No, sir."

"I won't have it black to-night," said the Father, "plenty of milk, please. I don't want my nerves played upon."

"Suppose we don't take coffee at all?" said Guildea. "If we do you may trot out the theory that we are not in a perfectly normal condition. I know you, Murchison, devout Priest and devout sceptic."

The Father laughed and pushed away his cup.

"Very well, then. No coffee."

"One cigarette, and then to business."

The grey blue smoke curled up.

"What are we going to do?" said the Father.

He was sitting bolt upright as if ready for action. Indeed there was no suggestion of repose in the attitudes of either of the men.

"Hide ourselves, and watch Napoleon. By the way—that reminds me."

He got up, went to a corner of the room, picked up a piece of green baize and threw it over the cage.

"I'll pull that off when we are hidden."

"And tell me first if you have had any manifestation of this supposed presence during the last few days?"

"Merely an increasingly intense sensation of something here, perpetually watching me, perpetually attending to all my doings."

"Do you feel that it follows you about?"

"Not always. It was in this room when you arrived. It is here now—I feel. But, in going down to dinner, we seemed to get away from it. The conclusion is that it remained here. Don't let us talk about it just now."

They spoke of other things till their cigarettes were finished. Then, as they threw away the smouldering ends, Guildea said,

"Now, Murchison, for the sake of this experiment, I suggest that we should conceal ourselves behind the curtains on either side of the cage, so that the bird's attention may not be drawn towards us and so distracted from that which we want to know more about. I will pull away the green baize when we are hidden. Keep perfectly still, watch the bird's proceedings, and tell me afterwards how you feel about them, how you explain them. Tread softly."

The Father obeyed, and they stole towards the curtains that fell before the two windows. The Father concealed himself behind those on the left of the cage, the Professor behind those on the right. The latter, as soon as they were hidden, stretched out his arm, drew the baize down from the cage, and let it fall on the floor.

The parrot, which had evidently fallen asleep in the warm darkness, moved on its perch as the light shone upon it, ruffled the feathers round its throat, and lifted first one foot and then the other. It turned its head round on its supple, and apparently elastic, neck, and, diving its beak into the down upon its back, made some searching investigations with, as it seemed, a satisfactory result, for it soon lifted its head again, glanced around its cage, and began to address itself to a nut which had been fixed between the bars for its refreshment. With its curved beak it felt and tapped the nut, at first gently, then with severity. Finally it plucked the nut from the bars, seized it with its rough, gray toes, and, holding it down firmly on the perch, cracked it and pecked out its contents, scattering some on the floor of the cage and letting the fractured shell fall into the china bath that was fixed against the bars. This accomplished, the bird paused meditatively, extended one leg backwards, and went through an elaborate process of wing-stretching that made it look as if it were lopsided and deformed. With its head reversed, it again applied itself to a subtle and exhaustive search among the feathers of its wing. This time its investigation seemed interminable, and Father Murchison had time to realise the absurdity of the whole position, and to wonder why he had lent himself to it. Yet he did not find his sense of humour laughing at it. On the contrary, he was smitten by a sudden gust of horror. When he was talking to his friend and watching him, the Professor's manner, generally so calm, even so prosaic, vouched for the truth of his story and the well-adjusted balance of his mind. But when he was hidden this was not so. And Father Murchison, standing behind his curtain, with his eyes upon the unconcerned Napoleon, began to whisper to himself the word—madness, with a quickening sensation of pity and of dread.

The parrot sharply contracted one wing, ruffled the feathers around its throat again, then extended its other leg backwards, and proceeded to the cleaning of its other wing. In the still room the dry sound of the feathers being spread was distinctly audible. Father Murchison saw the blue curtains behind which Guildea stood tremble slightly, as if a breath of wind had come through the window they shrouded. The clock in the far room chimed, and a coal dropped into the grate, making a noise like dead leaves stirring abruptly on hard ground. And again a gust of pity and of dread swept over the Father. It seemed to him that he had behaved very foolishly, if not wrongly, in encouraging what must surely be the strange dementia of his friend. He ought to have declined to lend himself to a proceeding that, ludicrous, even childish in itself, might well be dangerous in the encouragement it gave to a diseased expectation. Napoleon's protruding leg, extended wing and twisted neck, his busy and unconscious devotion to the arrangement of his person, his evident sensation of complete loneliness, most comfortable solitude, brought home with vehemence to the Father the undignified buffoonery of his conduct; the more piteous buffoonery of his friend. He seized the curtains with his hands and was about to thrust them aside and issue forth when an abrupt movement of the parrot stopped him. The bird, as if sharply attracted by something, paused in its pecking, and, with its head still bent backward and twisted sideways on its neck, seemed to listen intently. Its round eye looked glistening and strained like the eye of a disturbed pigeon. Contracting its wing, it lifted its head and sat for a moment erect on its perch, shifting its feet mechanically up and down, as if a dawning excitement produced in it an uncontrollable desire of movement. Then it thrust its head forward in the direction of the further room and remained perfectly still. Its attitude so strongly suggested the concentration of its attention on something immediately before it that Father Murchison instinctively stared about the room, half expecting to see Pitting advance softly, having entered through the hidden door. He did not come, and there was no sound in the chamber. Nevertheless, the parrot was obviously getting excited and increasingly attentive. It bent its head lower and lower, stretching out its neck until, almost falling from the perch, it half extended its wings, raising them slightly from its back, as if about to take flight, and fluttering them rapidly up and down. It continued this fluttering movement for what seemed to the Father an immense time. At length, raising its wings as far as possible, it dropped them slowly and deliberately down to its back, caught hold of the edge of its bath with its beak, hoisted itself on to the floor of the cage, waddled to the bars, thrust its head against them, and stood quite still in the exact attitude it always assumed when its head was being scratched by the Professor. So complete was the suggestion of this delight conveyed by the bird that Father Murchison felt as if he saw a white finger gently pushed among the soft feathers of its head, and he was seized by a most strong conviction that something, unseen by him but seen and welcomed by Napoleon, stood immediately before the cage.

The parrot presently withdrew its head, as if the coaxing finger had been lifted from it, and its pronounced air of acute physical enjoyment faded into one of marked attention and alert curiosity. Pulling itself up by the bars it climbed again upon its perch, sidled to the left side of the cage, and began apparently to watch something with profound interest. It bowed its head oddly, paused for a moment, then bowed its head again. Father Murchison found himself conceiving—from this elaborate movement of the head—a distinct idea of a personality. The bird's proceedings suggested extreme sentimentality combined with that sort of weak determination which is often the most persistent. Such weak determination is a very common attribute of persons who are partially idiotic. Father Murchison was moved to think of these poor creatures who will often, so strangely and unreasonably, attach themselves with persistence to those who love them least. Like many priests, he had had some experience of them, for the amorous idiot is peculiarly sensitive to the attraction of preachers. This bowing movement of the parrot recalled to his memory a terrible, pale woman who for a time haunted all churches in which he ministered, who was perpetually endeavouring to catch his eye, and who always bent her head with an obsequious and cunningly conscious smile when she did so. The parrot went on bowing, making a short pause between each genuflection, as if it waited for a signal to be given that called into play its imitative faculty.

"Yes, yes, it's imitating an idiot," Father Murchison caught himself saying as he watched. "A love-sick idiot."

And he looked again about the room, but saw nothing; except the furniture, the dancing fire, and the serried ranks of the books. Presently the parrot ceased from bowing, and assumed the concentrated and stretched attitude of one listening very keenly. He opened his beak, showing his black tongue, shut it, then opened it again. The Father thought he was going to speak, but he remained silent, although it was obvious that he was trying to bring out something. He bowed again two or three times, paused, and then, again opening his beak, made some remark. The Father could not distinguish any words, but the voice was sickly and disagreeable, a cooing and, at the same time, querulous voice, like a woman's, he thought. And he put his ear nearer to the curtain, listening with almost feverish attention. The bowing was resumed, but this time Napoleon added to it a sidling movement, affectionate and affected, like the movement of a silly and eager thing, nestling up to someone, or giving someone a gentle and furtive nudge. Again the Father thought of that terrible, pale woman who had haunted churches. Several times he had come upon her waiting for him after evening services. Once she had hung her head smiling, had lolled out her tongue and pushed against him sideways in the dark. He remembered how his flesh had shrunk from the poor thing, the sick loathing of her that he could not banish by remembering that her mind was all astray. The parrot paused, listened, opened his beak, and again said something in the same dove-like, amorous voice, full of sickly suggestion and yet hard, even dangerous, in its intonation. A loathsome voice, the Father thought it. But this time, although he heard the voice more distinctly than before, he could not make up his mind whether it was like a woman's voice or a man's—or perhaps a child's. It seemed to be a human voice, and yet oddly sexless. In order to resolve his doubt he withdrew into the darkness of the curtains, ceased to watch Napoleon and simply listened with keen attention, striving to forget that he was listening to a bird, and to imagine that he was overhearing a human being in conversation. After two or three minutes' silence the voice spoke again, and at some length, apparently repeating several times an affectionate series of ejaculations with a cooing emphasis that was unutterably mawkish and offensive. The sickliness of the voice, its falling intonations and its strange indelicacy, combined with a die-away softness and meretricious refinement, made the Father's flesh creep. Yet he could not distinguish any words, nor could he decide on the voice's sex or age. One thing alone he was certain of as he stood still in the darkness,—that such a sound could only proceed from something peculiarly loathsome, could only express a personality unendurably abominable to him, if not to everybody. The voice presently failed, in a sort of husky gasp, and there was a prolonged silence. It was broken by the Professor, who suddenly pulled away the curtains that hid the Father and said to him:

"Come out now, and look."

The Father came into the light, blinking, glanced towards the cage, and saw Napoleon poised motionless on one foot with his head under his wing. He appeared to be asleep. The Professor was pale, and his mobile lips were drawn into an expression of supreme disgust.

"Faugh!" he said.

He walked to the windows of the further room, pulled aside the curtains and pushed the glass up, letting in the air. The bare trees were visible in the grey gloom outside. Guildea leaned out for a minute drawing the night air into his lungs. Presently he turned round to the Father, and exclaimed abruptly,

"Pestilent! Isn't it?"

"Yes—most pestilent."

"Ever hear anything like it?"

"Not exactly."

"Nor I. It gives me nausea, Murchison, absolute physical nausea."

He closed the window and walked uneasily about the room.

"What d'you make of it?" he asked, over his shoulder.

"How d'you mean exactly?"

"Is it man's, woman's, or child's voice?"

"I can't tell, I can't make up my mind."

"Nor I."

"Have you heard it often?"

"Yes, since I returned from Westgate. There are never any words that I can distinguish. What a voice!"

He spat into the fire.

"Forgive me," he said, throwing himself down in a chair. "It turns my stomach—literally."

"And mine," said the Father, truly.

"The worst of it is," continued Guildea, with a high, nervous accent, "that there's no brain with it, none at all—only the cunning of idiotcy."

The Father started at this exact expression of his own conviction by another.

"Why d'you start like that?" asked Guildea, with a quick suspicion which showed the unnatural condition of his nerves.

"Well, the very same idea had occurred to me."

"What?"

"That I was listening to the voice of something idiotic."

"Ah! That's the devil of it, you know, to a man like me. I could fight against brain—but this!"

He sprang up again, poked the fire violently, then stood on the hearth-rug with his back to it, and his hands thrust into the high pockets of his trousers.

"That's the voice of the thing that's got into my house," he said. "Pleasant, isn't it?"

And now there was really horror in his eyes, and in his voice.

"I must get it out," he exclaimed. "I must get it out. But how?"

He tugged at his short black beard with a quivering hand.

"How?" he continued. "For what is it? Where is it?"

"You feel it's here—now?"

"Undoubtedly. But I couldn't tell you in what part of the room."

He stared about, glancing rapidly at everything.

"Then you consider yourself haunted?" said Father Murchison.

He, too, was much moved and disturbed, although he was not conscious of the presence of anything near them in the room.

"I have never believed in any nonsense of that kind, as you know," Guildea answered. "I simply state a fact which I cannot understand, and which is beginning to be very painful to me. There is something here. But whereas most so-called hauntings have been described to me as inimical, what I am conscious of is that I am admired, loved, desired. This is distinctly horrible to me, Murchison, distinctly horrible."

Father Murchison suddenly remembered the first evening he had spent with Guildea, and the latter's expression almost of disgust, at the idea of receiving warm affection from anyone. In the light of that long ago conversation the present event seemed supremely strange, and almost like a punishment for an offence committed by the Professor against humanity. But, looking up at his friend's twitching face, the Father resolved not to be caught in the net of his hideous belief.

"There can be nothing here," he said. "It's impossible."

"What does that bird imitate, then?"

"The voice of someone who has been here."

"Within the last week then. For it never spoke like that before, and mind, I noticed that it was watching and striving to imitate something before I went away, since the night that I went into the Park, only since then."

"Somebody with a voice like that must have been here while you were away," Father Murchison repeated, with a gentle obstinacy.

"I'll soon find out."

Guildea pressed the bell. Pitting stole in almost immediately.

"Pitting," said the Professor, speaking in a high, sharp voice, "did anyone come into this room during my absence at the sea?"

"Certainly not, sir, except the maids—and me, sir."

"Not a soul? You are certain?"

"Perfectly certain, sir."

The cold voice of the butler sounded surprised, almost resentful. The Professor flung out his hand towards the cage.

"Has the bird been here the whole time?"

"Yes, sir."

"He was not moved, taken elsewhere, even for a moment?"

Pitting's pale face began to look almost expressive, and his lips were pursed.

"Certainly not, sir."

"Thank you. That will do."

The butler retired, moving with a sort of ostentatious rectitude. When he had reached the door, and was just going out, his master called,

"Wait a minute, Pitting."

The butler paused. Guildea bit his lips, tugged at his beard uneasily two or three times, and then said,

"Have you noticed—er—the parrot talking lately in a—a very peculiar, very disagreeable voice?"

"Yes, sir—a soft voice like, sir."

"Ha! Since when?"

"Since you went away, sir. He's always at it."

"Exactly. Well, and what did you think of it?"

"Beg pardon, sir?"

"What do you think about his talking in this voice?"

"Oh, that it's only his play, sir."

"I see. That's all, Pitting."

The butler disappeared and closed the door noiselessly behind him.

Guildea turned his eyes on his friend.

"There, you see! " he ejaculated.

"It's certainly very odd," said the Father. "Very odd indeed. You are certain you have no maid who talks at all like that?"

"My dear Murchison! Would you keep a servant with such a voice about you for two days?"

"No."

"My housemaid has been with me for five years, my cook for seven. You've heard Pitting speak. The three of them make up my entire household. A parrot never speaks in a voice it has not heard. Where has it heard that voice?"

"But we hear nothing?"

"No. Nor do we see anything. But it does. It feels something too. Didn't you observe it presenting its head to be scratched?"

"Certainly it seemed to be doing so."

"It was doing so."

Father Murchison said nothing. He was full of increasing discomfort that almost amounted to apprehension.

"Are you convinced?" said Guildea, rather irritably.

"No. The whole matter is very strange. But till I hear, see, or feel—as you do—the presence of something, I cannot believe."

"You mean that you will not?"

"Perhaps. Well, it is time I went." Guildea did not try to detain him, but said, as he let him out,

"Do me a favour, come again to-morrow night."

The Father had an engagement. He hesitated, looked into the Professor's face and said,

"I will. At nine I'll be with you. Good-night."

When he was on the pavement he felt relieved.

He turned round, saw Guildea stepping into his passage, and shivered.

V

Father Murchison walked all the way home to Bird Street that night. He required exercise after the strange and disagreeable evening he had spent, an evening upon which he looked back already as a man look's back upon a nightmare. In his ears, as he walked, sounded the gentle and intolerable voice. Even the memory of it caused him physical discomfort. He tried to put it from him, and to consider the whole matter calmly. The Professor had offered his proof that there was some strange presence in his house. Could any reasonable man accept such proof? Father Murchison told himself that no reasonable man could accept it. The parrot's proceedings were, no doubt, extraordinary. The bird had succeeded in producing an extraordinary illusion of an invisible presence in the room. But that there really was such a presence the Father insisted on denying to himself. The devoutly religious, those who believe implicitly in the miracles recorded in the Bible, and who regulate their lives by the messages they suppose themselves to receive directly from the Great Ruler of a hidden World, are seldom inclined to accept any notion of supernatural intrusion into the affairs of daily life. They put it from them with anxious determination. They regard it fixedly as hocus-pocus, childish if not wicked.

Father Murchison inclined to the normal view of the devoted churchman. He was determined to incline to it. He could not—so he now told himself—accept the idea that his friend was being supernaturally punished for his lack of humanity, his deficiency in affection, by being obliged to endure the love of some horrible thing, which could not be seen, heard, or handled. Nevertheless, retribution did certainly seem to wait upon Guildea's condition. That which he had unnaturally dreaded and shrunk from in his thought he seemed to be now forced unnaturally to suffer. The Father prayed for his friend that night before the little, humble altar in the barely-furnished, cell-like chamber where he slept.

On the following evening, when he called in Hyde Park Place, the door was opened by the housemaid, and Father Murchison mounted the stairs, wondering what had become of Pitting. He was met at the library door by Guildea and was painfully struck by the alteration in his appearance. His face was ashen in hue, and there were lines beneath his eyes. The eyes themselves looked excited and horribly forlorn. His hair and dress were disordered and his lips twitched continually, as if he were shaken by some acute nervous apprehension.

"What has become of Pitting?" asked the Father, grasping Guildea's hot and feverish hand.

"He has left my service."

"Left your service!" exclaimed the Father in utter amazement.

"Yes, this afternoon."

"May one ask why?"

"I'm going to tell you. It's all part and parcel of this—this most odious business. You remember once discussing the relations men ought to have with their servants?"

"Ah!" cried the Father, with a flash of inspiration. "The crisis has occurred?"

"Exactly," said the Professor, with a bitter smile. "The crisis has occurred. I called upon Pitting to be a man and a brother. He responded by declining the invitation. I upbraided him. He gave me warning. I paid him his wages and told him he could go at once. And he has gone. What are you looking at me like that for?"

"I didn't know," said Father Murchison, hastily dropping his eyes, and looking away. "Why," he added. "Napoleon is gone too."

"I sold him to-day to one of those shops in Shaftesbury Avenue."

"Why?"

"He sickened me with his abominable imitation of—his intercourse with—well, you know what he was at last night. Besides, I have no further need of his proof to tell me I am not dreaming. And, being convinced as I now am, that all I have thought to have happened has actually happened, I care very little about convincing others. Forgive me for saying so, Murchison, but I am now certain that my anxiety to make you believe in the presence of something here really arose from some faint doubt on that subject—within myself. All doubt has now vanished."

"Tell me why."

"I will."

Both men were standing by the fire. They continued to stand while Guildea went on,

"Last night I felt it."

"What?" cried the Father.

"I say that last night, as I was going upstairs to bed, I felt something accompanying me and nestling up against me."

"How horrible!" exclaimed the Father, involuntarily.

Guildea smiled drearily.

"I will not deny the horror of it. I cannot, since I was compelled to call on Pitting for assistance."

"But—tell me—what was it, at least what did it seem to be?"

"It seemed to be a human being. It seemed, I say; and what I mean exactly is that the effect upon me was rather that of human contact than of anything else. But I could see nothing, hear nothing. Only, three times, I felt this gentle, but determined, push against me, as if to coax me and to attract my attention. The first time it happened I was on the landing outside this room, with my foot on the first stair. I will confess to you, Murchison, that I bounded upstairs like one pursued. That is the shameful truth. Just as I was about to enter my bedroom, however, I felt the thing entering with me, and, as I have said, squeezing, with loathsome, sickening tenderness, against my side. Then—"

He paused, turned towards the fire, and leaned his head on his arm. The Father was greatly moved by the strange helplessness and despair of the attitude. He laid his hand affectionately on Guildea's shoulder.

"Then?"

Guildea lifted his head. He looked painfully abashed.

"Then, Murchison, I am ashamed to say I broke down, suddenly, unaccountably, in a way I should have thought wholly impossible to me. I struck out with my hands to thrust the thing away. It pressed more closely to me. The pressure, the contact became unbearable to me. I shouted out for Pitting. I—I believe I must have cried—'Help.'"

"He came, of course?"

"Yes, with his usual soft, unemotional quiet. His calm—its opposition to my excitement of disgust and horror—must, I suppose, have irritated me. I was not myself, no, no!"

He stopped abruptly. Then—

"But I need hardly tell you that," he added, with most piteous irony.

"And what did you say to Pitting?"

"I said that he should have been quicker. He begged my pardon. His cold voice really maddened me, and I burst out into some foolish, contemptible diatribe, called him a machine, taunted him, then—as I felt that loathsome thing nestling once more to me—begged him to assist me, to stay with me, not to leave me alone—I meant in the company of my tormentor. Whether he was frightened, or whether he was angry at my unjust and violent manner and speech a moment before, I don't know. In any case he answered that he was engaged as a butler, and not to sit up all night with people. I suspect he thought I had taken too much to drink. No doubt that was it. I believe I swore at him as a coward—I! This morning he said he wished to leave my service. I gave him a month's wages, a good character as a butler, and sent him off at once."

"But the night? How did you pass it?"

"I sat up all night."

"Where? In your bedroom?"

"Yes—with the door open—to let it go."

"You felt that it stayed?"

"It never left me for a moment, but it did not touch me again. When it was light I took a bath, lay down for a little while, but did not close my eyes. After breakfast I had the explanation with Pitting and paid him. Then I came up here. My nerves were in a very shattered condition. Well, I sat down, tried to write, to think. But the silence was broken in the most abominable manner."

"How?"

"By the murmur of that appalling voice, that voice of a love-sick idiot, sickly but determined. Ugh!"

He shuddered in every limb. Then he pulled himself together, assumed, with a self-conscious effort, his most determined, most aggressive, manner, and added:

"I couldn't stand that. I had come to the end of my tether; so I sprang up, ordered a cab to be called, seized the cage and drove with it to a bird shop in Shaftesbury Avenue. There I sold the parrot for a trifle. I think, Murchison, that I must have been nearly mad then, for, as I came out of the wretched shop, and stood for an instant on the pavement among the cages of rabbits, guinea-pigs, and puppy dogs, I laughed aloud. I felt as if a load was lifted from my shoulders, as if in selling that voice I had sold the cursed thing that torments me. But when I got back to the house it was here. It's here now. I suppose it will always be here."

He shuffled his feet on the rug in front of the fire.

"What on earth am I to do?" he said. "I'm ashamed of myself, Murchison, but—but I suppose there are things in the world that certain men simply can't endure. Well, I can't endure this, and there's an end of the matter."

He ceased. The Father was silent. In presence of this extraordinary distress he did not know what to say. He recognised the uselessness of attempting to comfort Guildea, and he sat with his eyes turned, almost moodily, to the ground. And while he sat there he tried to give himself to the influences within the room, to feel all that was within it. He even, half-unconsciously, tried to force his imagination to play tricks with him. But he remained totally unaware of any third person with them. At length he said,

"Guildea, I cannot pretend to doubt the reality of your misery here. You must go away, and at once. When is your Paris lecture?"

"Next week. In nine days from now."

"Go to Paris to-morrow then, you say you have never had any consciousness that this—this thing pursued you beyond your own front door!"

"Never—hitherto."

"Go to-morrow morning. Stay away till after your lecture. And then let us see if the affair is at an end. Hope, my dear friend, hope."

He had stood up. Now he clasped the Professor's hand.

"See all your friends in Paris. Seek distractions. I would ask you also to seek— other help."

He said the last words with a gentle, earnest gravity and simplicity that touched Guildea, who returned his handclasp almost warmly.

"I'll go," he said. "I'll catch the ten o'clock train, and to-night I'll sleep at an hotel, at the Grosvenor—that's close to the station. It will be more convenient for the train."

As Father Murchison went home that night he kept thinking of that sentence: "It will be more convenient for the train." The weakness in Guildea that had prompted its utterance appalled him.

VI

No letter came to Father Murchison from the Professor during the next few days, and this silence reassured him, for it seemed to betoken that all was well. The day of the lecture dawned, and passed. On the following morning, the Father eagerly opened the Times, and scanned its pages to see if there were any report of the great meeting of scientific men which Guildea had addressed. He glanced up and down the columns with anxious eyes, then suddenly his hands stiffened as they held the sheets. He had come upon the following paragraph:

> "We regret to announce that Professor Frederic Guildea was suddenly seized with severe illness yesterday evening while addressing a scientific meeting in Paris. It was observed that he looked very pale and nervous when he rose to his feet. Nevertheless, he spoke in French fluently for about a quarter of an hour. Then he appeared to become uneasy. He faltered and glanced about like a man apprehensive, or in severe distress. He even stopped once or twice, and seemed unable to go on, to remember what he wished to say. But, pulling himself together with an obvious effort, he continued to address the audience. Suddenly, however, he paused again, edged furtively along the platform, as if pursued by something which he feared, struck out with his hands, uttered a loud, harsh cry and fainted. The sensation in the hall was indescribable. People rose from their seats. Women screamed, and, for a moment, there was a veritable panic. It is feared that the Professor's mind must have temporarily given way owing to overwork. We understand that he will return to England as soon as possible, and we sincerely hope that necessary rest and quiet will soon have the desired effect, and that he will be completely restored to health and enabled to prosecute further the investigations which have already so benefited the world."

The Father dropped the paper, hurried out into Bird Street, sent a wire of inquiry to Paris, and received the same day the following reply: "Returning to-morrow. Please call evening. Guildea." On that evening the Father called in Hyde Park Place, was at once admitted, and found Guildea sitting by the fire in the library, ghastly pale, with a heavy rug over his knees. He looked like a man emaciated by a long and severe illness, and in his wide open eyes there was an expression of fixed horror. The Father started at the sight of him, and could scarcely refrain from crying out. He was beginning to express his sympathy when Guildea stopped him with a trembling gesture.

"I know all that," Guildea said, "I know. This Paris affair—" He faltered and stopped.

"You ought never to have gone," said the Father. "I was wrong. I ought not to have advised your going. Your were not fit."

"I was perfectly fit," he answered, with the irritability of sickness. "But I was—I was accompanied by that abominable thing."

He glanced hastily round him, shifted his chair and pulled the rug higher over his knees. The Father wondered why he was thus wrapped up. For the fire was bright and red and the night was not very cold.

"I was accompanied to Paris," he continued, pressing his upper teeth upon his lower lip.

He paused again, obviously striving to control himself. But the effort was vain. There was no resistance in the man. He writhed in his chair and suddenly burst forth in a tone of hopeless lamentation.

"Murchison, this being, thing—whatever it is— no longer leaves me even for a moment. It will not stay here unless I am here, for it loves me, persistently, idiotically. It accompanied me to Paris, stayed with me there, pursued me to the lecture hall, pressed against me, caressed me while I was speaking. It has returned with me here. It is here now"—he uttered a sharp cry—"now, as I sit here with you. It is nestling up to me, fawning upon me, touching my hands. Man, man, can't you feel that it is here?"

"No," the Father answered truly.

"I try to protect myself from its loathsome contact," Guildea continued, with fierce excitement, clutching the thick rug with both hands. "But nothing is of any avail against it. Nothing. What is it? What can it be? Why should it have come to me that night?"

"Perhaps as a punishment," said the Father, with a quick softness.

"For what?"

"You hated affection. You put human feelings aside with contempt. You had, you desired to have, no love for anyone. Nor did you desire to receive any love from anything. Perhaps this is a punishment."

Guildea stared into his face.

"D'you believe that?" he cried.

"I don't know," said the Father. "But it may be so. Try to endure it, even to welcome it. Possibly then the persecution will cease."

"I know it means me no harm," Guildea exclaimed, "it seeks me out of affection. It was led to me by some amazing attraction which I exercise over it ignorantly. I know that. But to a man of my nature that is the ghastly part of the matter. If it would hate me, I could bear it. If it would attack me, if it would try to do me some dreadful harm, I should become a man again. I should be braced to fight against it. But this gentleness, this abominable solicitude, this brainless worship of an idiot, persistent, sickly, horribly physical, I cannot endure. What does it want of me? What would it demand of me? It nestles to me. It leans against me. I feel its touch, like the touch of a feather, trembling about my heart, as if it sought to number my pulsations, to find out the inmost secrets of my impulses and desires. No privacy is left to me." He sprang up excitedly. "I cannot withdraw," he cried, "I cannot be alone, untouched, unworshipped, unwatched for even one-half second. Murchison, I am dying of this, I am dying."

He sank down again in his chair, staring apprehensively on all sides, with the passion of some blind man, deluded in the belief that by his furious and continued effort he will attain sight. The Father knew well that he sought to pierce the veil of the invisible, and have knowledge of the thing that loved him.

"Guildea," the Father said, with insistent earnestness, "try to endure this—do more—try to give this thing what it seeks."

"But it seeks my love."

"Learn to give it your love and it may go, having received what it came for."

"T'sh! You talk as a priest. Suffer your persecutors. Do good to them that despitefully use you. You talk as a priest."

"As a friend I spoke naturally, indeed, right out of my heart. The idea suddenly came to me that all this,—truth or seeming, it doesn't matter which,—may be some strange form of lesson. I have had lessons—painful ones. I shall have many more. If you could welcome—"

"I can't! I can't!" Guildea cried fiercely. "Hatred! I can give it that—always that, nothing but that—hatred, hatred."

He raised his voice, glared into the emptiness of the room, and repeated, "Hatred!"

As he spoke the waxen pallor of his cheeks increased, until he looked like a corpse with living eyes. The Father feared that he was going to collapse and faint, but suddenly he raised himself upon his chair and said, in a high and keen voice, full of suppressed excitement:

"Murchison, Murchison!"

"Yes. What is it?"

An amazing ecstasy shone in Guildea's eyes.

"It wants to leave me," he cried. "It wants to go! Don't lose a moment! Let it out! The window—the window!"

The Father, wondering, went to the near window, drew aside the curtains and pushed it open. The branches of the trees in the garden creaked drily in the light wind. Guildea leaned forward on the arms of his chair. There was silence for a moment. Then Guildea, speaking in a rapid whisper, said,

"No, no. Open this door—open the hall door. I feel—I feel that it will return the way it came. Make haste—ah, go!"

The Father obeyed—to soothe him, hurried to the door and opened it wide. Then he glanced back at Guildea. He was standing up, bent forward. His eyes were glaring with eager expectation, and, as the Father turned, he made a furious gesture towards the passage with his thin hands.

The Father hastened out and down the stairs. As he descended in the twilight he fancied he heard a slight cry from the room behind him, but he did not pause. He flung the hall door open, standing back against the wall. After waiting a moment—to satisfy Guildea, he was about to close the door again, and had his hand on it, when he was attracted irresistibly to look forth towards the park. The night was lit by a young moon, and, gazing through the railings, his eyes fell upon a bench beyond them.

Upon this bench something was sitting, huddled together very strangely.

The Father remembered instantly Guildea's description of that former night, that night of Advent, and a sensation of horror-stricken curiosity stole through him.

Was there then really something that had indeed come to the Professor? And had it finished its work, fulfilled its desire and gone back to its former existence?

The Father hesitated a moment in the doorway. Then he stepped out resolutely and crossed the road, keeping his eyes fixed upon this black or dark object that leaned so strangely upon the bench. He could not tell yet what it was like, but he fancied it was unlike anything with which his eyes were acquainted. He reached the opposite path, and was about to pass through the gate in the railings, when his arm was brusquely grasped. He started, turned round, and saw a policeman eyeing him suspiciously.

"What are you up to?" said the policeman.

The Father was suddenly aware that he had no hat upon his head, and that his appearance, as he stole forward in his cassock, with his eyes intently fixed upon the bench in the Park, was probably unusual enough to excite suspicion.

"It's all right, policeman," he answered, quickly, thrusting some money into the constable's hand.

Then, breaking from him, the Father hurried towards the bench, bitterly vexed at the interruption. When he reached it nothing was there. Guildea's experience had been almost exactly repeated and, filled with unreasonable disappointment, the Father returned to the house, entered it, shut the door and hastened up the narrow stairway into the library.

On the hearthrug, close to the fire, he found Guildea lying with his head lolled against the armchair from which he had recently risen. There was a shocking expression of terror on his convulsed face. On examining him the Father found that he was dead.

The doctor, who was called in, said that the cause of death was failure of the heart.

When Father Murchison was told this, he murmured:

"Failure of the heart! It was that then!"

He turned to the doctor and said:

"Could it have been prevented?"

The doctor drew on his gloves and answered:

"Possibly, if it had been taken in time. Weakness of the heart requires a great deal of care. The Professor was too much absorbed in his work. He should have lived very differently."

The Father nodded.

"Yes, yes," he said, sadly.

The Phantom 'Rickshaw

RUDYARD KIPLING

> May no ill dreams disturb my rest,
> Nor Powers of Darkness me molest.
> *Evening Hymn*

One of the few advantages that India has over England is a great Knowability. After five years' service a man is directly or indirectly acquainted with the two or three hundred Civilians in his Province, all the Messes of ten or twelve Regiments and Batteries, and some fifteen hundred other people of the non-official caste. In ten years his knowledge should be doubled, and at the end of twenty he knows, or knows something about, every Englishman in the Empire, and may travel anywhere and everywhere without paying hotel-bills.

Globe-trotters who expect entertainment as a right, have, even within my memory, blunted this open-heartedness, but none the less to-day, if you belong to the Inner Circle and are neither a Bear nor a Black Sheep, all houses are open to you, and our small world is very, very kind and helpful.

Rickett of Kamartha stayed with Polder of Kumaon some fifteen years ago. He meant to stay two nights, but was knocked down by rheumatic fever, and for six weeks disorganized Polder's establishment, stopped Polder's work, and nearly died in Polder's bedroom. Polder behaves as though he had been placed under eternal obligation by Rickett, and yearly sends the little Ricketts a box of presents and toys. It is the same everywhere. The men who do not take the trouble to conceal from you their opinion that you are an incompetent ass, and the women who blacken your character and misunderstand your wife's amusements, will work themselves to the bone in your behalf if you fall sick or into serious trouble.

Heatherlegh, the Doctor, kept, in addition to his regular practice, a hospital on his private account—an arrangement of loose boxes for Incurables, his friend called it—but it was really a sort of fitting-up shed for craft that had been damaged by stress of weather. The weather in India is often sultry, and since the tale of bricks is always a fixed quantity, and the only liberty allowed is permission to work overtime and get no thanks, men occasionally break down and become as mixed as the metaphors in this sentence.

Heatherlegh is the dearest doctor that ever was, and his invariable prescription to all his patients is, "lie low, go slow, and keep cool." He says that more men are killed by overwork than the importance of this world justifies. He maintains that overwork slew Pansay, who died under his hands about three years ago. He has, of course, the right to speak authoritatively, and he laughs at my theory that there was a crack in Pansay's head and a little bit of the Dark World came through and pressed him to death. "Pansay went off the handle," says Heatherlegh, "after the stimulus of long leave at Home. He may or he may not have behaved like a blackguard to Mrs. Keith-Wessington. My notion is that the work of the Katabundi Settlement ran him off his legs, and that he took to brooding and making much of an ordinary P. & O. flirtation. He certainly was engaged to Miss Mannering, and she certainly broke off the engagement. Then he took a feverish chill and all that nonsense about ghosts developed. Overwork started his illness, kept it alight, and killed him poor devil. Write him off to the System—one man to take the work of two and a half men."

I do not believe this. I used to sit up with Pansay sometimes when Heatherlegh was called out to patients, and I happened to be within claim. The man would make me most unhappy by describing in a low, even voice, the procession that was always passing at the bottom of his bed. He had a sick man's command of language. When he recovered I suggested that he should write out the whole affair from beginning to end, knowing that ink might assist him to ease his mind. When little boys have learned a new bad word they are never happy till they have chalked it up on a door. And this also is Literature.

He was in a high fever while he was writing, and the blood-and-thunder Magazine diction he adopted did not calm him. Two months afterward he was reported fit for duty, but, in spite of the fact that he was urgently needed to help an undermanned Commission stagger through a deficit, he preferred to die; vowing at the last that he was hag-ridden. I got his manuscript before he died, and this is his version of the affair, dated 1885:—

My doctor tells me that I need rest and change of air. It is not improbable that I shall get both ere long—rest that neither the red-coated messenger nor the mid-day gun can break, and change of air far beyond that which any homeward-bound steamer can give me. In the meantime I am resolved to stay where I am; and, in flat defiance of my doctor's orders, to take all the world into my confidence. You shall learn for yourselves the precise nature of my malady; and shall, too, judge for yourselves whether any man born of woman on this weary earth was ever so tormented as I.

Speaking now as a condemned criminal might speak ere the drop-bolts are drawn, my story, wild and hideously improbable as it may appear, demands at least attention. That it will ever receive credence I utterly disbelieve. Two months ago I should have scouted as mad or drunk the man who had dared tell me the like. Two months ago I was the happiest man in India. To-day, from Peshawar to the sea, there is no one more wretched. My doctor and I are the only two who know this. His explanation is, that my brain, digestion, and eyesight are all slightly affected; giving rise to my frequent and persistent "delusions." Delusions, indeed! I call him a fool; but he attends me still with the same unwearied smile, the same bland professional manner, the same neatly trimmed red whiskers, till I begin to suspect that I am an ungrateful, evil-tempered invalid. But you shall judge for yourselves.

Three years ago it was my fortune—my great misfortune—to sail from Gravesend to Bombay, on return from long leave, with one Agnes Keith-Wessington, wife of an officer on the Bombay side. It does not in the least concern you to know what manner of woman she was. Be content with the knowledge that, ere the voyage had ended, both she and I were desperately and unreasoningly in love with one another. Heaven knows that I can make the admission now without one particle of vanity. In matters of this sort there is always one who gives and another who accepts. From the first day of our ill-omened attachment, I was conscious that Agnes's passion was a stronger, a more dominant, and—if I may use the expression—a purer sentiment than mine. Whether she recognized the fact then, I do not know. Afterward it was bitterly plain to both of us.

Arrived at Bombay in the spring of the year, we went our respective ways, to meet no more for the next three or four months, when my leave and her love took us both to Simla. There we spent the season together; and there my fire of straw burned itself out to a pitiful end with the closing year. I attempt no excuse. I make no apology. Mrs. Wessington had given up much for my sake, and was prepared to give up all. From my own lips, in August, 1882, she learned that I was sick of her presence, tired of her company, and weary of the sound of her voice. Ninety-nine women out of a hundred would have wearied of me as I wearied of them; seventy-five of that number would have promptly avenged themselves by active and obtrusive flirtation with other men. Mrs. Wessington was the hundredth. On her neither my openly expressed aversion nor the cutting brutalities with which I garnished our interviews had the least effect.

"Jack, darling!" was her one eternal cuckoo cry: "I'm sure it's all a mistake—a hideous mistake; and we'll be good friends again some day. *Please* forgive me, Jack, dear."

I was the offender, and I knew it. That knowledge transformed my pity into passive endurance, and, eventually, into blind hate—the same instinct, I suppose, which prompts a man to savagely stamp on the spider he has but half killed. And with this hate in my bosom the season of 1882 came to an end.

Next year we met again at Simla—she with her monotonous face and timid attempts at reconciliation, and I with loathing of her in every fibre of my frame. Several times I could not avoid meeting her alone; and on each occasion her words were identically the same. Still the unreasoning wail that it was all a "mistake"; and still the hope of eventually "making friends." I might have seen had I cared to look, that that hope only was keeping her alive. She grew more wan and thin month by month. You will agree with me, at least, that such conduct would have driven any one to despair. It was uncalled for; childish; unwomanly. I maintain that she was much to blame. And again, sometimes, in the black, fever-stricken night-watches, I have begun to think that I might have been a little kinder to her. But that really *is* a "delusion." I could not have continued pretending to love her when I didn't; could I? It would have been unfair to us both.

Last year we met again—on the same terms as before. The same weary appeal, and the same curt answers from my lips. At least I would make her see how wholly wrong and hopeless were her attempts at resuming the old relationship. As the season wore on, we fell apart—that is to say, she found it difficult to meet me, for I had other and more absorbing interests to attend to. When I think it over quietly in my sick-room, the season of 1884 seems a confused nightmare wherein light and shade were fantastically intermingled—my courtship of little Kitty Mannering; my hopes, doubts, and fears; our long rides together; my trembling avowal of attachment; her reply; and now and again a vision of a white face flitting by in the 'rickshaw with the black and white liveries I once watched for so earnestly; the wave of Mrs. Wessington's gloved hand; and, when she met me alone, which was but seldom, the irksome monotony of her appeal. I loved Kitty Mannering; honestly, heartily loved her, and with my love for her grew my hatred for Agnes. In August Kitty and I were engaged. The next day I met those accursed "magpie" *jhampanies* at the back of Jakko, and, moved by some passing sentiment of pity, stopped to tell Mrs. Wessington everything. She knew it already.

"So I hear you're engaged, Jack dear." Then, without a moment's pause:—"I'm sure it's all a mistake—a hideous mistake. We shall be as good friends some day, Jack, as we ever were."

My answer might have made even a man wince. It cut the dying woman before me like the blow of a whip. "Please forgive me, Jack; I didn't mean to make you angry; but it's true, it's true!"

And Mrs. Wessington broke down completely. I turned away and left her to finish her journey in peace, feeling, but only for a moment or two, that I had been an unutterably mean hound. I looked back, and saw that she had turned her 'rickshaw with the idea, I suppose, of overtaking me.

The scene and its surroundings were photographed on my memory. The rain-swept sky (we were at the end of the wet weather), the sodden, dingy pines, the muddy road, and the black powder-riven cliffs formed a gloomy background against which the black and white liveries of the *jhampanies,* the yellow-paneled 'rickshaw and Mrs. Wessington's down-bowed golden head stood out clearly. She was holding her handkerchief in her left hand and was leaning back exhausted against the 'rickshaw cushions. I turned my horse up a bypath near the Sanjowlie Reservoir and literally ran away. Once I fancied I heard a faint call of "Jack!" This may have been imagination. I never stopped to verify it. Ten minutes later I came across Kitty on horseback; and, in the delight of a long ride with her, forgot all about the interview.

A week later Mrs. Wessington died, and the inexpressible burden of her existence was removed from my life. I went Plainsward perfectly happy. Before three months were over I had forgotten all about her, except that at times the discovery of some of her old letters reminded me unpleasantly of our bygone relationship. By January I had disinterred what was left of our correspondence from among my scattered belongings and had burned it. At the beginning of April of this year, 1885, I was at Simla—semideserted Simla—once more, and was deep in lover's talks and walks with Kitty. It was decided that we should be married at the end of June. You will understand, therefore, that, loving Kitty as I did, I am not saying too much when I pronounce myself to have been, at that time, the happiest man in India.

Fourteen delightful days passed almost before I noticed their flight. Then, aroused to the sense of what was proper among mortals circumstanced as we were, I pointed out to Kitty that an engagement ring was the outward and visible sign of her dignity as an engaged girl; and that she must forthwith come to Hamilton's to be measured for one. Up to that moment, I give you my word, we had completely forgotten so trivial a matter. To Hamilton's we accordingly went on the 15th of April, 1885. Remember that—whatever my doctor may say to the contrary—I was then in perfect health, enjoying a well-balanced mind and an *absolutely* tranquil spirit. Kitty and I entered Hamilton's shop together, and there, regardless of the order of affairs,

I measured Kitty for the ring in the presence of the amused assistant. The ring was a sapphire with two diamonds. We then rode out down the slope that leads to the Combermere Bridge and Peliti's shop.

While my Waler was cautiously feeling his way over the loose shale, and Kitty was laughing and chattering at my side—while all Simla, that is to say as much of it as had then come from the Plains, was grouped round the Reading-room and Peliti's veranda,—I was aware that some one, apparently at a vast distance, was calling me by my Christian name. It struck me that I had heard the voice before, but when and where I could not at once determine. In the short space it took to cover the road between the path from Hamilton's shop and the first plank of the Combermere Bridge I had thought over half a dozen people who might have committed such a solecism, and had eventually decided that it must have been singing in my ears. Immediately opposite Peliti's shop my eye was arrested by the sight of four *jhampanies* in "magpie" livery, pulling a yellow-paneled, cheap, bazar 'rickshaw. In a moment my mind flew back to the previous season and Mrs. Wessington with a sense of irritation and disgust. Was it not enough that the woman was dead and done with, without her black and white servitors reappearing to spoil the day's happiness? Whoever employed them now I thought I would call upon, and ask as a personal favor to change her *jhampanies'* livery. I would hire the men myself, and, if necessary, buy their coats from off their backs. It is impossible to say here what a flood of undesirable memories their presence evoked.

"Kitty," I cried, "there are poor Mrs. Wessington's *jhampanies* turned up again! I wonder who has them now?"

Kitty had known Mrs. Wessington slightly last season, and had always been interested in the sickly woman.

"What? Where?" she asked. "I can't see them anywhere."

Even as she spoke her horse, swerving from a laden mule, threw himself directly in front of the advancing 'rickshaw. I had scarcely time to utter a word of warning when, to my unutterable horror, horse and rider passed *through* men and carriage as if they had been thin air.

"What's the matter?" cried Kitty; "what made you call out so foolishly, Jack? If I *am* engaged I don't want all creation to know about it. There was lots of space between the mule and the veranda; and, if you think I can't ride—There!"

Whereupon wilful Kitty set off, her dainty little head in the air, at a hand-gallop in the direction of the Band-stand; fully expecting, as she herself afterward told me, that I should follow her. What was the matter? Nothing indeed. Either that I was mad or drunk, or that Simla was haunted with devils. I reined in my impatient cob, and turned round. The 'rickshaw had turned too, and now stood immediately facing me, near the left railing of the Combermere Bridge.

"Jack! Jack, darling!" (There was no mistake about the words this time: they rang through my brain as if they had been shouted in my ear.) "It's some hideous mistake, I'm sure. *Please* forgive me, Jack, and let's be friends again."

The 'rickshaw-hood had fallen back, and inside, as I hope and pray daily for the death I dread by night, sat Mrs. Keith-Wessington, handkerchief in hand, and golden head bowed on her breast.

How long I stared motionless I do not know. Finally, I was aroused by my syce taking the Waler's bridle and asking whether I was ill. From the horrible to the commonplace is but a step. I tumbled off my horse and dashed, half fainting, into Peliti's for a glass of cherry-brandy. There two or three couples were gathered round the coffee-tables discussing the gossip of the day. Their trivialities were more comforting to me just then than the consolations of religion could have been. I plunged into the midst of the conversation at once; chatted, laughed, and jested with a face (when I caught a glimpse of it in a mirror) as white and drawn as that of a corpse. Three or four men noticed my condition; and, evidently setting it down to the results of over-many pegs, charitably endeavoured to draw me apart from the rest of the loungers. But I refused to be led away. I wanted the company of my kind—as a child rushes into the midst of the dinner-party after a fright in the dark. I must have talked for about ten minutes or so, though it seemed an eternity to me, when I heard Kitty's clear voice outside inquiring for me. In another minute she had entered the shop, prepared to roundly upbraid me for failing so signally in my duties. Something in my face stopped her.

"Why, Jack," she cried, "what *have* you been doing? What *has* happened? Are you ill?" Thus driven into a direct lie, I said that the sun had been a little too much for me. It was close upon five o'clock of a cloudy April afternoon, and the sun had been hidden all day. I saw my mistake as soon as the words were out of my mouth: attempted to recover it; blundered hopelessly and followed Kitty in a regal rage, out of doors, amid the smiles of my acquaintances. I made some excuse (I have forgotten what) on the score of my feeling faint; and cantered away to my hotel, leaving Kitty to finish the ride by herself.

In my room I sat down and tried calmly to reason out the matter. Here was I, Theobald Jack Pansay, a well-educated Bengal Civilian in the year of grace, 1885, presumably sane, certainly healthy, driven in terror from my sweetheart's side by the apparition of a woman who had been dead and buried eight months ago. These were facts that I could not blink. Nothing was further from my thought than any memory of Mrs. Wessington when Kitty and I left Hamilton's shop. Nothing was more utterly commonplace than the stretch of wall opposite Peliti's. It was broad daylight. The road was full of people; and yet here, look you, in defiance of every law of probability, in direct outrage of Nature's ordinance, there had appeared to me a face from the grave.

Kitty's Arab had gone *through* the 'rickshaw: so that my first hope that some woman marvellously like Mrs. Wessington had hired the carriage and the coolies with their old livery was lost. Again and again I went round this treadmill of thought; and again and again gave up baffled and in despair. The voice was as inexplicable as the apparition. I had originally some wild notion of confiding it all to Kitty; of begging her to marry me at once; and in her arms defying the ghostly occupant of the 'rickshaw. "After all," I argued, "the presence of the 'rickshaw is in itself enough to prove the existence of a spectral illusion. One may see ghosts of men and women, but surely never of coolies and carriages. The whole thing is absurd. Fancy the ghost of a hill-man!"

Next morning I sent a penitent note to Kitty, imploring her to overlook my strange conduct of the previous afternoon. My Divinity was still very wroth, and a personal apology was necessary. I explained, with a fluency born of night-long pondering over a falsehood, that I had been attacked with sudden palpitation of the heart—the result of indigestion. This eminently practical solution had its effect; and Kitty and I rode out that afternoon with the shadow of my first lie dividing us.

Nothing would please her save a canter round Jakko. With my nerves still unstrung from the previous night I feebly protested against the notion, suggesting Observatory Hill, Jutogh, the Boileaugunge road—anything rather than the Jakko round. Kitty was angry and a little hurt: so I yielded from fear of provoking further misunderstanding, and we set out together toward Chota Simla. We walked a greater part of the way, and, according to our custom, cantered from a mile or so below the Convent to the stretch of level road by the Sanjowlie Reservoir. The wretched horses appeared to fly, and my heart beat quicker and quicker as we neared the crest of the ascent. My mind had been full of Mrs. Wessington all the afternoon; and every inch of the Jakko road bore witness to our old-time walks and talks. The bowlders were full of it; the pines sang it aloud overhead; the rain-fed torrents giggled and chuckled unseen over the shameful story; and the wind in my ears chanted the iniquity aloud.

As a fitting climax, in the middle of the level men call the Ladies' Mile the Horror was awaiting me. No other 'rickshaw was in sight—only the four black and white *jhampanies,* the yellow-paneled carriage, and the golden head of the woman within—all apparently just as I had left them eight months and one fortnight ago! For an instant I fancied that Kitty *must* see what I saw—we were so marvellously sympathetic in all things. Her next words undeceived me—"Not a soul in sight! Come along, Jack, and

I'll race you to the Reservoir buildings!" Her wiry little Arab was off like a bird, my Waler following close behind, and in this order we dashed under the cliffs. Half a minute brought us within fifty yards of the 'rickshaw. I pulled my Waler and fell back a little. The 'rickshaw was directly in the middle of the road; and once more the Arab passed through it, my horse following. "Jack! Jack dear! *Please* forgive me," rang with a wail in my ears, and, after an interval:—"It's all a mistake, a hideous mistake!"

I spurred my horse like a man possessed. When I turned my head at the Reservoir works, the black and white liveries were still waiting—patiently waiting—under the grey hillside, and the wind brought me a mocking echo of the words I had just heard. Kitty bantered me a good deal on my silence throughout the remainder of the ride. I had been talking up till then wildly and at random. To save my life I could not speak afterward naturally, and from Sanjowlie to the Church wisely held my tongue.

I was to dine with the Mannerings that night, and had barely time to canter home to dress. On the road to Elysium Hill I overheard two men talking together in the dusk.—"It's a curious thing," said one, "how completely all trace of it disappeared. You know my wife was insanely fond of the woman ('never could see anything in her myself), and wanted me to pick up her old 'rickshaw and coolies if they were to be got for love or money. Morbid sort of fancy I call it; but I've got to do what the *Memsahib* tells me. Would you believe that the man she hired it from tells me that all four of the men—they were brothers—died of cholera on the way to Hardwar, poor devils, and the 'rickshaw has been broken up by the man himself. 'Told me he never used a dead *Memsahib's* 'rickshaw. 'Spoilt his luck. Queer notion, wasn't it? Fancy poor little Mrs. Wessington spoiling any one's luck except her own!" I laughed aloud at this point; and my laugh jarred on me as I uttered it. So there *were* ghosts of 'rickshaws after all, and ghostly employments in the other world! How much did Mrs. Wessington give her men? What were their hours? Where did they go?

And for visible answer to my last question I saw the infernal Thing blocking my path in the twilight. The dead travel fast, and by short cuts unknown to ordinary coolies. I laughed aloud a second time and checked my laughter suddenly, for I was afraid I was going mad. Mad to a certain extent I must have been, for I recollect that I reined in my horse at the head of the 'rickshaw, and politely wished Mrs. Wessington "Good-evening." Her answer was one I knew only too well. I listened to the end; and replied that I had heard it all before, but should be delighted if she had anything further to say. Some malignant devil stronger than I must have entered into me that evening, for I have a dim recollection of talking the commonplaces of the day for five minutes to the Thing in front of me.

"Mad as a hatter, poor devil—or drunk. Max, try and get him to come home."

Surely *that* was not Mrs. Wessington's voice! The two men had overheard me speaking to the empty air, and had returned to look after me. They were very kind and considerate, and from their words evidently gathered that I was extremely drunk. I thanked them confusedly and cantered away to my hotel, there changed, and arrived at the Mannerings' ten minutes late. I pleaded the darkness of the night as an excuse; was rebuked by Kitty for my unlover-like tardiness; and sat down.

The conversation had already become general; and under cover of it, I was addressing some tender small talk to my sweetheart when I was aware that at the further end of the table a short red-whiskered man was describing, with much broidery, his encounter with a mad unknown that evening.

A few sentences convinced me that he was repeating the incident of half an hour ago. In the middle of the story he looked round for applause, as professional story-tellers do, caught my eye, and straightway collapsed. There was a moment's awkward silence, and the red-whiskered man muttered something to the effect that he had "forgotten the rest," thereby sacrificing a reputation as a good story teller which he had built up for six seasons past. I blessed him from the bottom of my heart, and—went on with my fish.

In the fulness of time that dinner came to an end; and with genuine regret I tore myself away from Kitty—as certain as I was of my own existence that It would be waiting for me outside the door. The red-whiskered man, who had been introduced to me as Doctor Heatherlegh, of Simla, volunteered to bear me company as far as our roads lay together. I accepted his offer with gratitude.

My instinct had not deceived me. It lay in readiness in the Mall, and, in what seemed devilish mockery of our ways, with a lighted head-lamp. The red-whiskered man went to the point at once, in a manner that showed he had been thinking over it all dinner time.

"I say, Pansay, what the deuce was the matter with you this evening on the Elysium road?" The suddenness of the question wrenched an answer from me before I was aware.

"That!" said I, pointing to It.

"*That* may be either D. T. or Eyes for aught I know. Now you don't liquor. I saw as much at dinner, so it can't be *D. T.* There's nothing whatever where you're pointing, though you're sweating and trembling with fright like a scared pony. Therefore, I conclude that it's Eyes. And I ought to understand all about them. Come along home with me. I'm on the Blessington lower road."

To my intense delight the 'rickshaw instead of waiting for us kept about twenty yards ahead—and this, too whether we walked, trotted, or cantered. In the course of that long night ride I had told my companion almost as much as I have told you here.

"Well, you've spoiled one of the best tales I've ever laid tongue to," said he, "but I'll forgive you for the sake of what you've gone through. Now come home and do what I tell you; and when I've cured you, young man, let this be a lesson to you to steer clear of women and indigestible food till the day of your death."

The 'rickshaw kept steady in front; and my red-whiskered friend seemed to derive great pleasure from my account of its exact whereabouts.

"Eyes, Pansay—all Eyes, Brain, and Stomach. And the greatest of these three is Stomach. You've too much conceited Brain, too little Stomach, and thoroughly unhealthy Eyes. Get your Stomach straight and the rest follows. And all that's French for a liver pill. I'll take sole medical charge of you from this hour! for you're too interesting a phenomenon to be passed over."

By this time we were deep in the shadow of the Blessington lower road and the 'rickshaw came to a dead stop under a pine-clad, over-hanging shale cliff. Instinctively I halted too, giving my reason. Heatherlegh rapped out an oath.

"Now, if you think I'm going to spend a cold night on the hillside for the sake of a stomach-*cum*-Brain-*cum*-Eye illusion . . . Lord, ha' mercy! What's that?"

There was a muffled report, a blinding smother of dust just in front of us, a crack, the noise of rent boughs, and about ten yards of the cliff-side—pines, undergrowth, and all—slid down into the road below, completely blocking it up. The uprooted trees swayed and tottered for a moment like drunken giants in the gloom, and then fell prone among their fellows with a thunderous crash. Our two horses stood motionless and sweating with fear. As soon as the rattle of falling earth and stone had subsided, my companion muttered:—"Man, if we'd gone forward we should have been ten feet deep in our graves by now. 'There are more things in heaven and earth'. . . . Come home, Pansay, and thank God. I want a peg badly."

We retraced our way over the Church Ridge, and I arrived at Dr. Heatherlegh's house shortly after midnight.

His attempts toward my cure commenced almost immediately, and for a week I never left his sight. Many a time in the course of that week did I bless the good-fortune which had thrown me in contact with Simla's best and kindest doctor. Day by day my spirits grew lighter and more equable. Day by day, too, I became more and more inclined to fall in with Heatherlegh's "spectral illusion" theory, implicating eyes, brain, and stomach. I wrote to Kitty, telling her that a slight sprain caused by a fall from my horse kept me indoors for a few days; and that I should be recovered before she had time to regret my absence.

Heatherlegh's treatment was simple to a degree. It consisted of liver pills, cold-water baths, and strong exercise, taken in the dusk or at early dawn—for, as he sagely observed:—"A man with a sprained ankle doesn't walk a dozen miles a day, and your young woman might be wondering if she saw you."

At the end of the week, after much examination of pupil and pulse, and strict injunctions as to diet and pedestrianism, Heatherlegh dismissed me as brusquely as he had taken charge of me. Here is his parting benediction: "Man, I can certify to your mental cure, and that's as much as to say I've cured most of your bodily ailments. Now, get your traps out of this as soon as you can; and be off to make love to Miss Kitty."

I was endeavoring to express my thanks for his kindness. He cut me short.

"Don't think I did this because I like you. I gather that you've behaved like a black-guard all through. But, all the same, you're a phenomenon, and as queer a phenomenon as you are a blackguard. No!"—checking me a second time—"not a rupee, please. Go out and see if you can find the eyes-brain-and-stomach business again. I'll give you a lakh for each time you see it."

Half an hour later I was in the Mannerings' drawing-room with Kitty—drunk with the intoxication of present happiness and the foreknowledge that I should never more be troubled with Its hideous presence. Strong in the sense of my new-found security, I proposed a ride at once; and, by preference, a canter round Jakko.

Never had I felt so well, so overladen with vitality and mere animal spirits, as I did on the afternoon of the 30th of April. Kitty was delighted at the change in my appearance, and complimented me on it in her delightfully frank and outspoken manner. We left the Manner-ings' house together, laughing and talking, and cantered along the Chota Simla road as of old.

I was in haste to reach the Sanjowlie Reservoir and there make my assurance doubly sure. The horses did their best, but seemed all too slow to my impatient mind. Kitty was astonished at my boisterousness. "Why, Jack!" she cried at last, "you are behaving like a child. What are you doing?"

We were just below the Convent, and from sheer wantonness I was making my Waler plunge and curvet across the road as I tickled it with the loop of my riding-whip.

"Doing?" I answered; "nothing, dear. That's just it. If you'd been doing nothing for a week except lie up, you'd be as riotous as I."

> "Singing and murmuring in your feastful mirth,
>   Joying to feel yourself alive;
> Lord over Nature, Lord of the visible Earth,
>   Lord of the senses five."

My quotation was hardly out of my lips before we had rounded the corner above the Convent; and a few yards further on could see across to Sanjowlie. In the centre of the level road stood the black and white liveries, the yellow-paneled 'rickshaw, and Mrs. Keith-Wessington. I pulled up, looked, rubbed my eyes, and, I believe must have said something. The next thing I knew was that I was lying face downward on the road with Kitty kneeling above me in tears.

"Has it gone, child!" I gasped. Kitty only wept more bitterly.

"Has what gone, Jack dear? what does it all mean? There must be a mistake somewhere, Jack. A hideous mistake." Her last words brought me to my feet—mad—raving for the time being.

"Yes, there *is* a mistake somewhere," I repeated, "a hideous mistake. Come and look at It."

I have an indistinct idea that I dragged Kitty by the wrist along the road up to where It stood, and implored her for pity's sake to speak to It; to tell It that we were betrothed; that neither Death nor Hell could break the tie between us; and Kitty only knows how much more to the same effect. Now and again I appealed passionately to the Terror in the 'rickshaw to bear witness to all I had said, and to release me from a torture that was killing me. As I talked I suppose I must have told Kitty of my old relations with Mrs. Wessington, for I saw her listen intently with white face and blazing eyes.

"Thank you, Mr. Pansay," she said, "that's *quite* enough. *Syce ghora láo.*"

The syces, impassive as Orientals always are, had come up with the recaptured horses; and as Kitty sprang into her saddle I caught hold of the bridle, entreating her to hear me out and forgive. My answer was the cut of her riding-whip across my face from mouth to eye, and a word or two of farewell that even now I cannot write down. So I judged, and judged rightly, that Kitty knew all; and I staggered back to the side of the 'rickshaw. My face was cut and bleeding, and the blow of the riding-whip had raised a livid blue wheal on it. I had no self-respect. Just then, Heatherlegh, who must have been following Kitty and me at a distance, cantered up.

"Doctor," I said, pointing to my face, "here's Miss Mannering's signature to my order of dismissal and . . . I'll thank you for that lakh as soon as convenient."

Heatherlegh's face, even in my abject misery, moved me to laughter.

"I'll stake my professional reputation"—he began.

"Don't be a fool," I whispered. "I've lost my life's happiness and you'd better take me home."

As I spoke the 'rickshaw was gone. Then I lost all knowledge of what was passing. The crest of Jakko seemed to heave and roll like the crest of a cloud and fall in upon me.

Seven days later (on the 7th of May, that is to say) I was aware that I was lying in Heatherlegh's room as weak as a little child. Heatherlegh was watching me intently from behind the papers on his writing-table. His first words were not encouraging; but I was too far spent to be much moved by them.

"Here's Miss Kitty has sent back your letters. You corresponded a good deal, you young people. Here's a packet that looks like a ring, and a cheerful sort of a note from Mannering Papa, which I've taken the liberty of reading and burning. The old gentleman's not pleased with you."

"And Kitty?" I asked, dully.

"Rather more drawn than her father from what she says. By the same token you must have been letting out any number of queer reminiscences just before I met you. 'Says that a man who would have behaved to a woman as you did to Mrs. Wessington ought to kill himself out of sheer pity for his kind. She's a hot-headed little virago, your mash. 'Will have it too that you were suffering from *D. T.* when that row on the Jakko road turned up. 'Says she'll die before she ever speaks to you again."

I groaned and turned over to the other side.

"Now you've got your choice, my friend. This engagement has to be broken off; and the Mannerings don't want to be too hard on you. Was it broken through *D. T.* or epileptic fits? Sorry I can't offer you a better exchange unless you'd prefer hereditary insanity. Say the word and I'll tell 'em it's fits. All Simla knows about that scene on the Ladies' Mile. Come! I'll give you five minutes to think over it."

During those five minutes I believe that I explored thoroughly the lowest circles of the Inferno which it is permitted man to tread on earth. And at the same time I myself was watching myself faltering through the dark labyrinths of doubt, misery, and utter despair. I wondered, as Heatherlegh in his chair might have wondered, which dreadful alternative I should adopt. Presently I heard myself answering in a voice that I hardly recognized—

"They're confoundedly particular about morality in these parts. Give 'em fits, Heatherlegh, and my love. Now let me sleep a bit longer."

Then my two selves joined, and it was only I (half crazed, devil-driven I) that tossed in my bed, tracing step by step the history of the past month.

"But I am in Simla," I kept repeating to myself. "I, Jack Pansay, am in Simla and there are no ghosts here. It's unreasonable of that woman to pretend there are. Why couldn't Agnes have left me alone? I never did her any harm. It might just as well have been me as Agnes. Only I'd never have come back on purpose to kill *her*. Why can't I be left alone—left alone and happy?"

It was high noon when I first awoke: and the sun was low in the sky before I slept—slept as the tortured criminal sleeps on his rack, too worn to feel further pain.

Next day I could not leave my bed. Heatherlegh told me in the morning that he had received an answer from Mr. Mannering, and that, thanks to his (Heatherlegh's) friendly offices, the story of my affliction had traveled through the length and breadth of Simla, where I was on all sides much pitied.

"And that's rather more than you deserve," he concluded, pleasantly, "though the Lord knows you've been going through a pretty severe mill. Never mind; we'll cure you yet, you perverse phenomenon."

I declined firmly to be cured. "You've been much too good to me already, old man," said I; "but I don't think I need trouble you further."

In my heart I knew that nothing Heatherlegh could do would lighten the burden that had been laid upon me.

With that knowledge came also a sense of hopeless, impotent rebellion against the unreasonableness of it all. There were scores of men no better than I whose punishments had at least been reserved for another world; and I felt that it was bitterly, cruelly unfair that I alone should have been singled out for so hideous a fate. This mood would in time give place to another where it seemed that the 'rickshaw and I were the only realities in a world of shadows; that Kitty was a ghost; that Mannering, Heatherlegh, and all the other men and women I knew were all ghosts; and the great, grey hills themselves but vain shadows devised to torture me. From mood to mood I tossed backward and forward for seven weary days; my body growing daily stronger and stronger, until the bedroom looking-glass told me that I had returned to everyday life, and was as other men once more. Curiously enough my face showed no signs of the struggle I had gone through. It was pale indeed, but as expression-less and commonplace as ever. I had expected some permanent alteration—visible evidence of the disease that was eating me away. I found nothing.

On the 15th of May, I left Heatherlegh's house at eleven o'clock in the morning; and the instinct of the bachelor drove me to the Club. There I found that every man knew my story as told by Heatherlegh, and was, in clumsy fashion, abnormally kind and attentive. Nevertheless I recognized that for the rest of my natural life I should be among but not of my fellows; and I envied very bitterly indeed the laughing coolies on the Mall below. I lunched at the Club, and at four o'clock wandered aimlessly down the Mall in the vague hope of meeting Kitty. Close to the Band-stand the black and white liveries joined me; and I heard Mrs. Wessington's old appeal at my side. I had been expecting this ever since I came out; and was only surprised at her delay. The phantom 'rickshaw and I went side by side along the Chota Simla road in silence. Close to the bazar, Kitty and a man on horseback overtook and passed us. For any sign she gave I might have been a dog in the road. She did not even pay me the compliment of quickening her pace; though the rainy afternoon had served for an excuse.

So Kitty and her companion, and I and my ghostly Light-o'-Love, crept round Jakko in couples. The road was streaming with water; the pines dripped like roof-pipes on the rocks below, and the air was full of fine, driving rain. Two or three times I found myself saying to myself almost aloud: "I'm Jack Pansay on leave at Simla—*at Simla!* Every-day, ordinary Simla. I mustn't forget that—I mustn't forget that." Then I would try to recollect some of the gossip I had heard at the Club: the prices of So-and-So's horses—anything, in fact, that related to the work-a-day Anglo-Indian world I knew so well. I even repeated the multiplication-table rapidly to myself, to make quite sure that I was not taking leave of my senses. It gave me much comfort; and must have prevented my hearing Mrs. Wessington for a time.

Once more I wearily climbed the Convent slope and entered the level road. Here Kitty and the man started off at a canter, and I was left alone with Mrs. Wessington. "Agnes," said I, "will you put back your hood and tell me what it all means?" The hood dropped noiselessly, and I was face to face with my dead and buried mistress. She was wearing the dress in which I had last seen her alive; carried the same tiny handkerchief in her right hand; and the same card-case in her left. (A woman eight months dead with a card-case!) I had to pin myself down to the multiplication-table, and to set both hands on the stone parapet of the road, to assure myself that that at least was real.

"Agnes," I repeated, "for pity's sake tell me what it all means." Mrs. Wessington leaned forward, with that odd, quick turn of the head I used to know so well, and spoke.

If my story had not already so madly overleaped the bounds of all human belief I should apologize to you now. As I know that no one—no, not even Kitty, for whom it is written as some sort of justification of my conduct—will believe me, I will go on. Mrs. Wessington spoke and I walked with her from the Sanjowlie road to the turning below the Commander-in-Chief's house as I might walk by the side of any living woman's 'rickshaw, deep in conversation. The second and most tormenting of my moods of sickness had suddenly laid hold upon me, and like the Prince in Tennyson's poem, "I seemed to move amid a world of ghosts." There had been a garden-party at the Commander-in-Chief's, and we two joined the crowd of homeward-bound folk. As I saw them then it seemed that *they* were the shadows—impalpable, fantastic shadows—that divided for Mrs. Wessington's 'rickshaw to pass through. What we said during the course of that weird interview I cannot—indeed, I dare not—tell.

Heatherlegh's comment would have been a short laugh and a remark that I had been "mashing a brain-eye-and-stomach chimera." It was a ghastly and yet in some indefinable way a marvellously dear experience. Could it be possible, I wondered, that I was in this life to woo a second time the woman I had killed by my own neglect and cruelty?

I met Kitty on the homeward road—a shadow among shadows.

If I were to describe all the incidents of the next fortnight in their order, my story would never come to an end; and your patience would be exhausted. Morning after morning and evening after evening the ghostly 'rickshaw and I used to wander through Simla together. Wherever I went there the four black and white liveries followed me and bore me company to and from my hotel. At the Theatre I found them amid the crowd or yelling *jhampanies*; outside the Club veranda, after a long evening of whist; at the Birthday Ball, waiting patiently for my reappearance; and in broad daylight when I went calling. Save that it cast no shadow, the 'rickshaw was in every respect as real to look upon as one of wood and iron. More than once, indeed, I have had to check myself from warning some hard-riding friend against cantering over it. More than once I have walked down the Mall deep in conversation with Mrs. Wessington to the unspeakable amazement of the passers-by.

Before I had been out and about a week I learned that the "fit" theory had been discarded in favour of insanity. However, I made no change in my mode of life. I called, rode, and dined out as freely as ever. I had a passion for the society of my kind which I had never felt before; I hungered to be among the realities of life; and at the same time I felt vaguely unhappy when I had been separated too long from my ghostly companion. It would be almost impossible to describe my varying moods from the 15th of May up to to-day.

The presence of the 'rickshaw filled me by turns with horror, blind fear, a dim sort of pleasure, and utter despair. I dared not leave Simla; and I knew that my stay there was killing me. I knew, moreover, that it was my destiny to die slowly and a little every day. My only anxiety was to get the penance over as quietly as might be. Alternately I hungered for a sight of Kitty and watched her outrageous flirtations with my successor—to speak more accurately, my successors—with amused interest. She was as much out of my life as I was out of hers. By day I wandered with Mrs. Wessington almost content. By night I implored Heaven to let me return to the world as I used to know it. Above all these varying moods lay the sensation of dull, numbing wonder that the Seen and the Unseen should mingle so strangely on this earth to hound one poor soul to its grave.

August 27.—Heatherlegh has been indefatigable in his attendance on me; and only yesterday told me that I ought to send in an application for sick leave. An application to escape the company of a phantom! A request that the Government would graciously permit me to get rid of five ghosts and an airy 'rickshaw by going to England! Heatherlegh's proposition moved me to almost hysterical laughter. I told him that I should await the end quietly at Simla; and I am sure that the end is not far off. Believe me that I dread its advent more than any word can say; and I torture myself nightly with a thousand speculations as to the manner of my death.

Shall I die in my bed decently and as an English gentleman should die; or, in one last walk on the Mall, will my soul be wrenched from me to take its place for ever and ever by the side of that ghastly phantasm? Shall I return to my old lost allegiance in the next world, or shall I meet Agnes loathing her and bound to her side through all eternity? Shall we two hover over the scene of our lives till the end of Time? As the day of my death draws nearer, the intense horror that all living flesh feels toward escaped spirits from beyond the grave grows more and more powerful. It is an awful thing to go down quick among the dead with scarcely one-half of your life completed. It is a thousand times more awful to wait as I do in your midst, for I know not what unimaginable terror. Pity me, at least on the score of my "delusion," for I know you will never believe what I have written here. Yet as surely as ever a man was done to death by the Powers of Darkness I am that man.

In justice, too, pity her. For as surely as ever woman was killed by man, I killed Mrs. Wessington. And the last portion of my punishment is ever now upon me.

The Three Sisters

W. W. Jacobs

Thirty years ago on a wet autumn evening the household of Mallett's Lodge was gathered round the death-bed of Ursula Mallow, the eldest of the three sisters who inhabited it. The dingy moth-eaten curtains of the old wooden bedstead were drawn apart, the light of a smoking oil-lamp falling upon the hopeless countenance of the dying woman as she turned her dull eyes upon her sisters. The room was in silence except for an occasional sob from the youngest sister, Eunice. Outside the rain fell steadily over the steaming marshes.

"Nothing is to be changed, Tabitha," gasped Ursula to the other sister, who bore a striking likeness to her although her expression was harder and colder; "this room is to be locked up and never opened."

"Very well," said Tabitha brusquely, "though I don't see how it can matter to you then."

"It does matter," said her sister with startling energy. "How do you know, how do I know that I may not sometimes visit it? I have lived in this house so long I am certain that I shall see it again. I *will* come back. Come back to watch over you both and see that no harm befalls you."

"You are talking wildly," said Tabitha, by no means moved at her sister's solicitude for her welfare. "Your mind is wandering; you know that I have no faith in such things."

Ursula sighed, and beckoning to Eunice, who was weeping silently at the bedside, placed her feeble arms around her neck and kissed her.

"Do not weep, dear," she said feebly. "Perhaps it is best so. A lonely woman's life is scarce worth living. We have no hopes, no aspirations; other women have had happy husbands and children, but we in this forgotten place have grown old together. I go first, but you must soon follow."

Tabitha, comfortably conscious of only forty years and an iron frame, shrugged her shoulders and smiled grimly.

"I go first," repeated Ursula in a new and strange voice as her heavy eyes slowly closed, "but I will come for each of you in turn, when your lease of life runs out. At that moment I will be with you to lead your steps whither I now go."

As she spoke the flickering lamp went out suddenly as though extinguished by a rapid hand, and the room was left in utter darkness. A strange suffocating noise issued from the bed, and when the trembling women had relighted the lamp, all that was left of Ursula Mallow was ready for the grave.

That night the survivors passed together. The dead woman had been a firm believer in the existence of that shadowy borderland which is said to form an unhallowed link between the living and the dead, and even the stolid Tabitha, slightly unnerved by the events of the night, was not free from certain apprehensions that she might have been right.

With the bright morning their fears disappeared. The sun stole in at the window, and seeing the poor earthworn face on the pillow so touched it and glorified it that only its goodness and weakness were seen, and the beholders came to wonder how they could ever have felt any dread of aught so calm and peaceful. A day or two passed, and the body was transferred to a massive coffin long regarded as the finest piece of work of its kind ever turned out of the village carpenter's workshop. Then a slow and melancholy cortege headed by four bearers wound its solemn way across the marshes to the family vault in the grey old church, and all that was left of Ursula was placed by the father and mother who had taken that self-same journey some thirty years before.

To Eunice as they toiled slowly home the day seemed strange and Sabbath-like, the flat prospect of marsh wilder and more forlorn than usual, the roar of the sea more depressing. Tabitha had no such fancies. The bulk of the dead woman's property had been left to Eunice, and her avaricious soul was sorely troubled and her proper sisterly feelings of regret for the deceased sadly interfered with in consequence.

"What are you going to do with all that money, Eunice?" she asked as they sat at their quiet tea.

"I shall leave it as it stands," said Eunice slowly. "We have both got sufficient to live upon, and I shall devote the income from it to supporting some beds in a children's hospital."

"If Ursula had wished it to go to a hospital," said Tabitha in her deep tones, "she would have left the money to it herself. I wonder you do not respect her wishes more."

"What else can I do with it then?" inquired Eunice.

"Save it," said the other with gleaming eyes, "save it."

Eunice shook her head.

"No," said she, "it shall go to the sick children, but the principal I will not touch, and if I die before you it shall become yours and you can do what you like with it."

"Very well," said Tabitha, smothering her anger by a strong effort; "I don't believe that was what Ursula meant you to do with it, and I don't believe she will rest quietly in the grave while you squander the money she stored so carefully."

"What do you mean?" asked Eunice with pale lips. "You are trying to frighten me; I thought that you did not believe in such things."

Tabitha made no answer, and to avoid the anxious inquiring gaze of her sister, drew her chair to the fire, and folding her gaunt arms, composed herself for a nap.

For some time life went on quietly in the old house. The room of the dead woman, in accordance with her last desire, was kept firmly locked, its dirty windows forming a strange contrast to the prim cleanliness of the others. Tabitha, never very talkative, became more taciturn than ever, and stalked about the house and the neglected garden like an unquiet spirit, her brow roughened into the deep wrinkles suggestive of much thought. As the winter came on, bringing with it the long dark evenings, the old house became more lonely than ever, and an air of mystery and dread seemed to hang over it and brood in its empty rooms and dark corridors. The deep silence of night was broken by strange noises for which neither the wind nor the rats could be held accountable. Old Martha, seated in her distant kitchen, heard strange sounds upon the stairs, and once, upon hurrying to them, fancied that she saw a dark figure squatting upon the landing, though a subsequent search with candle and spectacles failed to discover anything. Eunice was disturbed by several vague incidents, and, as she suffered from a complaint of the heart, rendered very ill by them. Even Tabitha admitted a strangeness about the house, but, confident in her piety and virtue, took no heed of it, her mind being fully employed in another direction.

Since the death of her sister all restraint upon her was removed, and she yielded herself up entirely to the stern and hard rules enforced by avarice upon its devotees. Her house-keeping expenses were kept rigidly separate from those of Eunice and her food limited to the coarsest dishes, while in the matter of clothes, the old servant was by far the better dressed. Seated alone in her bedroom this uncouth, hard-featured creature revelled in her possessions, grudging even the expense of the candle-end which enabled her to behold them. So completely did this passion change her that both Eunice and Martha became afraid of her, and lay awake in their beds night after night trembling at the chinking of the coins at her unholy vigils.

One day Eunice ventured to remonstrate. "Why don't you bank your money, Tabitha?" she said; "it is surely not safe to keep such large sums in such a lonely house."

"Large sums!" repeated the exasperated Tabitha, "large sums! what nonsense is this? You know well that I have barely sufficient to keep me."

"It's a great temptation to housebreakers," said her sister, not pressing the point. "I made sure last night that I heard somebody in the house."

"Did you?" said Tabitha, grasping her arm, a horrible look on her face. "So did I. I thought they went to Ursula's room, and I got out of bed and went on the stairs to listen."

"Well?" said Eunice faintly, fascinated by the look on her sister's face.

"There was *something* there," said Tabitha slowly. "I'll swear it, for I stood on the landing by her door and listened; something scuffling on the floor round and round the room. At first I thought it was the cat, but when I went up there this morning the door was still locked, and the cat was in the kitchen."

"Oh, let us leave this dreadful house," moaned Eunice.

"What!" said her sister grimly; "afraid of poor Ursula? Why should you be? Your own sister who nursed you when you were a babe, and who perhaps even now comes and watches over your slumbers."

"Oh!" said Eunice, pressing her hand to her side, "if I saw her I should die. I should think that she had come for me as she said she would. O God! have mercy on me, I am dying."

She reeled as she spoke, and before Tabitha could save her, sank senseless to the floor.

"Get some water," cried Tabitha, as old Martha came hurrying up the stairs, "Eunice has fainted."

The old woman, with a timid glance at her, retired, reappearing shortly afterwards with the water, with which she proceeded to restore her much-loved mistress to her senses. Tabitha, as soon as this was accomplished, stalked off to her room, leaving her sister and Martha sitting drearily enough in the small parlour, watching the fire and conversing in whispers.

It was clear to the old servant that this state of things could not last much longer, and she repeatedly urged her mistress to leave a house so lonely and so mysterious. To her great delight Eunice at length consented, despite the fierce opposition of her sister, and at the mere idea of leaving gained greatly in health and spirits. A small but comfortable house was hired in Morville, and arrangements made for a speedy change.

It was the last night in the old house, and all the wild spirits of the marshes, the wind and the sea seemed to have joined forces for one supreme effort. When the wind dropped, as it did at brief intervals, the sea was heard moaning on the distant beach, strangely mingled with the desolate warning of the bell-buoy as it rocked to the waves. Then the wind rose again, and the noise of the sea was lost in the fierce gusts which, finding no obstacle on the open marshes, swept with their full fury upon the house by the creek. The strange voices of the air shrieked in its chimneys, windows rattled, doors slammed, and even the very curtains seemed to live and move.

Eunice was in bed, awake. A small night-light in a saucer of oil shed a sickly glare upon the worm-eaten old furniture, distorting the most innocent articles into ghastly shapes. A wilder gust than usual almost deprived her of the protection afforded by that poor light, and she lay listening fearfully to the creakings and other noises on the stairs, bitterly regretting that she had not asked Martha to sleep with her. But it was not too late even now. She slipped hastily to the floor, crossed to the huge wardrobe, and was in the very act of taking her dressing-gown from its peg when an unmistakable footfall was heard on the stairs. The robe dropped from her shaking fingers, and with a quickly beating heart she regained her bed.

The sounds ceased and a deep silence followed, which she herself was unable to break although she strove hard to do so. A wild gust of wind shook the windows and nearly extinguished the light, and when its flame had regained its accustomed steadiness she saw that the door was slowly opening, while the huge shadow of a hand blotted the papered wall. Still her tongue refused its office. The door flew open with a crash, a cloaked figure entered and, throwing aside its coverings, she saw with a horror past all expression the napkin-bound face of the dead Ursula smiling terribly at her. In her last extremity she raised her faded eyes above for succour, and then as the figure noiselessly advanced and laid its cold hand upon her brow, the soul of Eunice Mallow left its body with a wild shriek and made its way to the Eternal.

Martha, roused by the cry, and shivering with dread, rushed to the door and gazed in terror at the figure which stood leaning over the bedside. As she watched, it slowly removed the cowl and the napkin and exposed the fell face of Tabitha, so strangely contorted between fear and triumph that she hardly recognized it.

"Who's there?" cried Tabitha in a terrible voice as she saw the old woman's shadow on the wall.

"I thought I heard a cry," said Martha, entering. "Did anybody call?"

"Yes, Eunice," said the other, regarding her closely. "I, too, heard the cry, and hurried to her. What makes her so strange? Is she in a trance?"

"Ay," said the old woman, falling on her knees by the bed and sobbing bitterly, "the trance of death. Ah, my dear, my poor lonely girl, that this should be the end of it! She has died of fright," said the old woman, pointing to the eyes, which even yet retained their horror. "She has seen something *devilish*."

Tabitha's gaze fell. "She has always suffered with her heart," she muttered; "the night has frightened her; it frightened me."

She stood upright by the foot of the bed as Martha drew the sheet over the face of the dead woman.

"First Ursula, then Eunice," said Tabitha, drawing a deep breath. "I can't stay here. I'll dress and wait for the morning."

She left the room as she spoke, and with bent head proceeded to her own. Martha remained by the bedside, and gently closing the staring eyes, fell on her knees, and prayed long and earnestly for the departed soul. Overcome with grief and fear she remained with bowed head until a sudden sharp cry from Tabitha brought her to her feet.

"Well," said the old woman, going to the door.

"Where are you?" cried Tabitha, somewhat reassured by her voice.

"In Miss Eunice's bedroom. Do you want anything?"

"Come down at once. Quick! I am unwell."

Her voice rose suddenly to a scream. "Quick! For God's sake! Quick, or I shall go mad. *There is some strange woman in the house.*"

The old woman stumbled hastily down the dark stairs. "What is the matter?" she cried, entering the room. "Who is it? What do you mean?"

"I saw it," said Tabitha, grasping her convulsively by the shoulder. "I was coming to you when I saw the figure of a woman in front of me going up the stairs. Is it—can it be Ursula come for the soul of Eunice, as she said she would?"

"Or for yours?" said Martha, the words coming from her in some odd fashion, despite herself.

Tabitha, with a ghastly look, fell cowering by her side, clutching tremulously at her clothes. "Light the lamps," she cried hysterically. "Light a fire, make a noise; oh, this dreadful darkness! Will it never be day!"

"Soon, soon," said Martha, overcoming her repugnance and trying to pacify her. "When the day comes you will laugh at these fears."

"I murdered her," screamed the miserable woman, "I killed her with fright. Why did she not give me the money? 'Twas no use to her. Ah! *Look there!*"

Martha, with a horrible fear, followed her glance to the door, but saw nothing.

"It's Ursula," said Tabitha from between her teeth. "Keep her off! Keep her off!"

The old woman, who by some unknown sense seemed to feel the presence of a third person in the room, moved a step forward and stood before her. As she did so Tabitha waved her arms as though to free herself from the touch of a detaining hand, half rose to her feet, and without a word fell dead before her.

At this the old woman's courage forsook her, and with a great cry she rushed from the room, eager to escape from this house of death and mystery. The bolts of the great door were stiff with age, and strange voices seemed to ring in her ears as she strove wildly to unfasten them. Her brain whirled. She thought that the dead in their distant rooms called to her, and that a devil stood on the step outside laughing and holding the door against her. Then with a supreme effort she flung it open, and heedless of her night-clothes passed into the bitter night. The path across the marshes was lost in the darkness, but she found it; the planks over the ditches slippery and narrow, but she crossed them in safety, until at last, her feet bleeding and her breath coming in great gasps, she entered the village and sank down more dead than alive on a cottage door-step.

The Ghost-Ship

Richard Middleton

Fairfield is a little village lying near the Portsmouth Road about half-way between London and the sea. Strangers who find it by accident now and then, call it a pretty, old-fashioned place; we who live in it and call it home don't find anything very pretty about it, but we should be sorry to live anywhere else. Our minds have taken the shape of the inn and the church and the green, I suppose. At all events we never feel comfortable out of Fairfield.

Of course the Cockneys, with their vasty houses and noise-ridden streets, can call us rustics if they choose, but for all that Fairfield is a better place to live in than London. Doctor says that when he goes to London his mind is bruised with the weight of the houses, and he was a Cockney born. He had to live there himself when he was a little chap, but he knows better now. You gentlemen may laugh—perhaps some of you come from London way—but it seems to me that a witness like that is worth a gallon of arguments.

Dull? Well, you might find it dull, but I assure you that I've listened to all the London yarns you have spun tonight, and they're absolutely nothing to the things that happen at Fairfield. It's because of our way of thinking and minding our own business. If one of your Londoners were set down on the green of a Saturday night when the ghosts of the lads who died in the war keep tryst with the lasses who lie in the church-yard, he couldn't help being curious and interfering, and then the ghosts would go somewhere where it was quieter. But we just let them come and go and don't make any fuss, and in consequence Fairfield is the ghostiest place in all England. Why, I've seen a headless man sitting on the edge of the well in broad daylight, and the children playing about his feet as if he were their father. Take my word for it, spirits know when they are well off as much as human beings.

Still, I must admit that the thing I'm going to tell you about was queer even for our part of the world, where three packs of ghost-hounds hunt regularly during the season, and blacksmith's great-grandfather is busy all night shoeing the dead gentlemen's horses. Now that's a thing that wouldn't happen in London, because of their interfering ways, but blacksmith he lies up aloft and sleeps as quiet as a lamb. Once

THE GHOST-SHIP

when he had a bad head he shouted down to them not to make so much noise, and in the morning he found an old guinea left on the anvil as an apology. He wears it on his watch-chain now. But I must get on with my story; if I start telling you about the queer happenings at Fairfield I'll never stop.

It all came of the great storm in the spring of '97, the year that we had two great storms. This was the first one, and I remember it very well, because I found in the morning that it had lifted the thatch of my pigsty into the widow's garden as clean as a boy's kite. When I looked over the hedge, widow—Tom Lamport's widow that was—was prodding for her nasturtiums with a daisy-grubber. After I had watched her for a little I went down to the "Fox and Grapes" to tell landlord what she had said to me. Landlord he laughed, being a married man and at ease with the sex. "Come to that," he said, "the tempest has blowed something into my field. A kind of a ship I think it would be."

I was surprised at that until he explained that it was only a ghost-ship and would do no hurt to the turnips. We argued that it had been blown up from the sea at Portsmouth, and then we talked of something else. There were two slates down at the parsonage and a big tree in Lumley's meadow. It was a rare storm.

I reckon the wind had blown our ghosts all over England. They were coming back for days afterwards with foundered horses and as footsore as possible, and they were so glad to get back to Fairfield that some of them walked up the street crying like little children. Squire said that his great-grandfather's great-grandfather hadn't looked so dead-beat since the battle of Naseby, and he's an educated man.

What with one thing and another, I should think it was a week before we got straight again, and then one afternoon I met the landlord on the green and he had a worried face. "I wish you'd come and have a look at that ship in my field," he said to me; "it seems to me it's leaning real hard on the turnips. I can't bear thinking what the missus will say when she sees it."

I walked down the lane with him, and sure enough there was a ship in the middle of his field, but such a ship as no man had seen on the water for three hundred years, let alone in the middle of a turnip-field. It was all painted black and covered with carvings, and there was a great bay window in the stern for all the world like the Squire's drawing-room. There was a crowd of little black cannon on deck and looking out of her port-holes, and she was anchored at each end to the hard ground. I have seen the wonders of the world on picture-postcards, but I have never seen anything to equal that.

"She seems very solid for a ghost-ship," I said, seeing the landlord was bothered.

"I should say it's a betwixt and between," he answered, puzzling it over, "but it's going to spoil a matter of fifty turnips, and missus she'll want it moved." We went up to her and touched the side, and it was as hard as a real ship. "Now there's folks in England would call that very curious," he said.

Now I don't know much about ships, but I should think that that ghost-ship weighed a solid two hundred tons, and it seemed to me that she had come to stay, so that I felt sorry for landlord, who was a married man. "All the horses in Fairfield won't move her out of my turnips," he said, frowning at her.

Just then we heard a noise on her deck, and we looked up and saw that a man had come out of her front cabin and was looking down at us very peaceably. He was dressed in a black uniform set out with rusty gold lace, and he had a great cutlass by his side in a brass sheath. "I'm Captain Bartholomew Roberts," he said, in a gentleman's voice, "put in for recruits. I seem to have brought her rather far up the harbour."

"Harbour!" cried landlord; "why, you're fifty miles from the sea."

Captain Roberts didn't turn a hair. "So much as that, is it?" he said coolly. "Well, it's of no consequence."

Landlord was a bit upset at this. "I don't want to be unneighbourly," he said, "but I wish you hadn't brought your ship into my field. You see, my wife sets great store on these turnips."

The captain took a pinch of snuff out of a fine gold box that he pulled out of his pocket, and dusted his fingers with a silk handkerchief in a very genteel fashion. "I'm only here for a few months," he said; "but if a testimony of my esteem would pacify your good lady I should be content," and with the words he loosed a great gold brooch from the neck of his coat and tossed it down to landlord.

Landlord blushed as red as a strawberry. "I'm not denying she's fond of jewellery," he said, "but it's too much for half a sackful of turnips." And indeed it was a handsome brooch.

The captain laughed. "Tut, man," he said, "it's a forced sale, and you deserve a good price. Say no more about it"; and nodding good-day to us, he turned on his heel and went into the cabin. Landlord walked back up the lane like a man with a weight off his mind. "That tempest has blowed me a bit of luck," he said; "the missus will be much pleased with that brooch. It's better than blacksmith's guinea, any day."

Ninety-seven was Jubilee year, the year of the second Jubilee, you remember, and we had great doings at Fairfield, so that we hadn't much time to bother about the ghost-ship though anyhow it isn't our way to meddle in things that don't concern us. Landlord, he saw his tenant once or twice when he was hoeing his turnips and passed the time of day, and landlord's wife wore her new brooch to church every Sunday. But we didn't mix much with the ghosts at any time, all except an idiot lad there was in the

THE GHOST-SHIP

village, and he didn't know the difference between a man and a ghost, poor innocent! On Jubilee Day, however, somebody told Captain Roberts why the church bells were ringing, and he hoisted a flag and fired off his guns like a loyal Englishman. 'Tis true the guns were shotted, and one of the round shot knocked a hole in Farmer Johnstone's barn, but nobody thought much of that in such a season of rejoicing.

It wasn't till our celebrations were over that we noticed that anything was wrong in Fairfield. 'Twas shoemaker who told me first about it one morning at the "Fox and Grapes." "You know my great great-uncle?" he said to me.

"You mean Joshua, the quiet lad," I answered, knowing him well.

"Quiet!" said shoemaker indignantly. "Quiet you call him, coming home at three o'clock every morning as drunk as a magistrate and waking up the whole house with his noise."

"Why, it can't be Joshua!" I said, for I knew him for one of the most respectable young ghosts in the village.

"Joshua it is," said shoemaker; "and one of these nights he'll find himself out in the street if he isn't careful."

This kind of talk shocked me, I can tell you, for I don't like to hear a man abusing his own family, and I could hardly believe that a steady youngster like Joshua had taken to drink. But just then in came butcher Aylwin in such a temper that he could hardly drink his beer. "The young puppy! the young puppy!" he kept on saying; and it was some time before shoemaker and I found out that he was talking about his ancestor that fell at Senlac.

"Drink?" said shoemaker hopefully, for we all like company in our misfortunes, and butcher nodded grimly.

"The young noodle," he said, emptying his tankard.

Well, after that I kept my ears open, and it was the same story all over the village. There was hardly a young man among all the ghosts of Fairfield who didn't roll home in the small hours of the morning the worse for liquor. I used to wake up in the night and hear them stumble past my house, singing outrageous songs. The worst of it was that we couldn't keep the scandal to ourselves and the folk at Greenhill began to talk of "sodden Fairfield" and taught their children to sing a song about us:

Sodden Fairfield, sodden Fairfield, has no use for bread-and-butter,
Rum for breakfast, rum for dinner, rum for tea, and rum for supper!

We are easy-going in our village, but we didn't like that.

Of course we soon found out where the young fellows went to get the drink, and landlord was terribly cut up that his tenant should have turned out so badly, but his wife wouldn't hear of parting with the brooch, so that he couldn't give the Captain notice to quit. But as time went on, things grew from bad to worse, and at all hours of the day you would see those young reprobates sleeping it off on the village green. Nearly every afternoon a ghost-wagon used to jolt down to the ship with a lading of rum, and though the older ghosts seemed inclined to give the Captain's hospitality the go-by, the youngsters were neither to hold nor to bind.

So one afternoon when I was taking my nap I heard a knock at the door, and there was parson looking very serious, like a man with a job before him that he didn't altogether relish. "I'm going down to talk to the Captain about all this drunkenness in the village, and I want you to come with me," he said straight out.

I can't say that I fancied the visit much, myself, and I tried to hint to parson that as, after all, they were only a lot of ghosts it didn't very much matter.

"Dead or alive, I'm responsible for the good conduct," he said, "and I'm going to do my duty and put a stop to this continued disorder. And you are coming with me John Simmons." So I went, parson being a persuasive kind of man.

We went down to the ship, and as we approached her I could see the Captain tasting the air on deck. When he saw parson he took off his hat very politely and I can tell you that I was relieved to find that he had a proper respect for the cloth. Parson acknowledged his salute and spoke out stoutly enough. "Sir, I should be glad to have a word with you."

"Come on board, sir; come on board," said the Captain, and I could tell by his voice that he knew why we were there. Parson and I climbed up an uneasy kind of ladder, and the Captain took us into the great cabin at the back of the ship, where the bay-window was. It was the most wonderful place you ever saw in your life, all full of gold and silver plate, swords with jewelled scabbards, carved oak chairs, and great chests that look as though they were bursting with guineas. Even parson was surprised, and he did not shake his head very hard when the Captain took down some silver cups and poured us out a drink of rum. I tasted mine, and I don't mind saying that it changed my view of things entirely. There was nothing betwixt and between about that rum, and I felt that it was ridiculous to blame the lads for drinking too much of stuff like that. It seemed to fill my veins with honey and fire.

Parson put the case squarely to the Captain, but I didn't listen much to what he said; I was busy sipping my drink and looking through the window at the fishes swimming to and fro over landlord's turnips. Just then it seemed the most natural thing in the world that they should be there, though afterwards, of course, I could see that that proved it was a ghost-ship.

But even then I thought it was queer when I saw a drowned sailor float by in the thin air with his hair and beard all full of bubbles. It was the first time I had seen anything quite like that at Fairfield.

All the time I was regarding the wonders of the deep parson was telling Captain Roberts how there was no peace or rest in the village owing to the curse of drunkenness, and what a bad example the youngsters were setting to the older ghosts. The Captain listened very attentively, and only put in a word now and then about boys being boys and young men sowing their wild oats. But when parson had finished his speech he filled up our silver cups and said to parson, with a flourish, "I should be sorry to cause trouble anywhere where I have been made welcome, and you will be glad to hear that I put to sea to-morrow night. And now you must drink me a prosperous voyage." So we all stood up and drank the toast with honour, and that noble rum was like hot oil in my veins.

After that Captain showed us some of the curiosities he had brought back from foreign parts, and we were greatly amazed, though afterwards I couldn't clearly remember what they were. And then I found myself walking across the turnips with parson, and I was telling him of the glories of the deep that I had seen through the window of the ship. He turned on me severely. "If I were you, John Simmons," he said, "I should go straight home to bed." He has a way of putting things that wouldn't occur to an ordinary man, has parson, and I did as he told me.

Well, next day it came on to blow, and it blew harder and harder, till about eight o'clock at night I heard a noise and looked out into the garden. I dare say you won't believe me, it seems a bit tall even to me, but the wind had lifted the thatch of my pigsty into the widow's garden a second time. I thought I wouldn't wait to hear what widow had to say about it, so I went across the green to the "Fox and Grapes," and the wind was so strong that I danced along on tiptoe like a girl at the fair. When I got to the inn landlord had to help me shut the door; it seemed as though a dozen goats were pushing against it to come in out of the storm.

"It's a powerful tempest," he said, drawing the beer. "I hear there's a chimney down at Dickory End."

"It's a funny thing how these sailors know about the weather," I answered. "When Captain said he was going to-night, I was thinking it would take a capful of wind to carry the ship back to sea, but now here's more than a capful."

"Ah, yes," said landlord, "it's to-night he goes true enough, and, mind you, though he treated me handsome over the rent, I'm not sure it's a loss to the village. I don't hold with gentrice who fetch their drink from London instead of helping local traders to get their living."

"But you haven't got any rum like his," I said, to draw him out.

His neck grew red above his collar, and I was afraid I'd gone too far; but after a while he got his breath with a grunt.

"John Simmons," he said, "if you've come down here this windy night to talk a lot of fool's talk, you've wasted a journey."

Well, of course, then I had to smooth him down with praising his rum, and Heaven forgive me for swearing it was better than Captain's. For the like of that rum no living lips have tasted save mine and parson's. But somehow or other I brought landlord round, and presently we must have a glass of his best to prove its quality.

"Beat that if you can!" he cried, and we both raised our glasses to our mouths, only to stop half-way and look at each other in amaze. For the wind that had been howling outside like an outrageous dog had all of a sudden turned as melodious as the carol-boys of a Christmas Eve.

"Surely that's not my Martha," whispered landlord; Martha being his great-aunt that lived in the loft overhead.

We went to the door, and the wind burst it open so that the handle was driven clean into the plaster of the wall. But we didn't think about that at the time; for over our heads, sailing very comfortably through the windy stars, was the ship that had passed the summer in landlord's field. Her portholes and her bay-window were blazing with lights, and there was a noise of singing and fiddling on her decks. "He's gone," shouted landlord above the storm, "and he's taken half the village with him!" I could only nod in answer, not having lungs like bellows of leather.

In the morning we were able to measure the strength of the storm, and over and above my pigsty there was damage enough wrought in the village to keep us busy. True it is that the children had to break down no branches for the firing that autumn, since the wind had strewn the woods with more than they could carry away. Many of our ghosts were scattered abroad, but this time very few came back, all the young men having sailed with Captain; and not only ghosts, for a poor half-witted lad was missing, and we reckoned that he had stowed himself away or perhaps shipped as cabin-boy, not knowing any better.

What with the lamentations of the ghost-girls and the grumbling of families who had lost an ancestor, the village was upset for a while, and the funny thing was that it was the folk who had complained most of the carryings-on of the youngsters, who made most noise now that they were gone. I hadn't any sympathy with shoemaker or butcher, who ran about saying how much they missed their lads, but it made me grieve to hear the poor bereaved girls calling their lovers by name on the village green at nightfall. It didn't seem fair to me that they should have lost their men a second time, after giving up life in order to join them, as like as not. Still, not even a spirit can be sorry for ever, and after a few months we made up our mind that the folk who had sailed in the ship were never coming back, and we didn't talk about it any more.

And then one day, I dare say it would be a couple of years after, when the whole business was quite forgotten, who should come trapesing along the road from Portsmouth but the daft lad who had gone away with the ship, without waiting till he was dead to become a ghost. You never saw such a boy as that in all your life. He had a great rusty cutlass hanging to a string at his waist, and he was tattooed all over in fine colours, so that even his face looked like a girl's sampler. He had a handkerchief in his hand full of foreign shells and old-fashioned pieces of small money, very curious, and he walked up to the well outside his mother's house and drew himself a drink as if he had been nowhere in particular.

The worst of it was that he had come back as soft-headed as he went, and try as we might we couldn't get anything reasonable out of him. He talked a lot of gibberish about keel-hauling and walking the plank and crimson murders—things which a decent sailor should know nothing about, so that it seemed to me that for all his manners Captain had been more of a pirate than a gentleman mariner. But to draw sense out of that boy was as hard as picking cherries off a crab-tree. One silly tale he had that he kept on drifting back to, and to hear him you would have thought that it was the only thing that happened to him in his life. "We was at anchor," he would say, "off an island called the Basket of Flowers, and the sailors had caught a lot of parrots and we were teaching them to swear. Up and down the decks, up and down the decks, and the language they used was dreadful. Then we looked up and saw the masts of the Spanish ship outside the harbour. Outside the harbour they were, so we threw the parrots into the sea and sailed out to fight. And all the parrots were drownded in the sea and the language they used was dreadful." That's the sort of boy he was, nothing but silly talk of parrots when we asked him about the fighting. And we never had a chance of teaching him better, for two days after he ran away again, and hasn't been seen since.

That's my story, and I assure you that things like that are happening at Fairfield all the time. The ship has never come back, but somehow as people grow older they seem to think that one of these windy nights she'll come sailing in over the hedges with all the lost ghosts on board. Well, when she comes, she'll be welcome. There's one ghost-lass that has never grown tired of waiting for her lad to return. Every night you'll see her out on the green, straining her poor eyes with looking for the mast-lights among the stars. A faithful lass you'd call her, and I'm thinking you'd be right.

Landlord's field wasn't a penny the worse for the visit, but they do say that since then the turnips that have been grown in it have tasted of rum.

The Roll-Call of the Reef

ARTHUR QUILLER-COUCH

"Yes, sir," said my host the quarryman, reaching down the relics from their hook in the wall over the chimney-piece; "they've hung there all my time, and most of my father's. The women won't touch 'em; they're afraid of the story. So here they'll dangle, and gather dust and smoke, till another tenant comes and tosses 'em out o' doors for rubbish. Whew! 'tis coarse weather."

He went to the door, opened it, and stood studying the gale that beat upon his cottage front, straight from the Manacle Reef. The rain drove past him into the kitchen, aslant like threads of gold silk in the shine of the wreckwood fire. Meanwhile by the same firelight I examined the relics on my knee. The metal of each was tarnished out of knowledge. But the trumpet was evidently an old cavalry trumpet, and the threads of its parti-coloured sling, though frayed and dusty, still hung together. Around the side-drum, beneath its cracked brown varnish, I could hardly trace a royal coat-of-arms, and a legend running—*Per Mare per Terram*—the motto of the Marines. Its parchment, though coloured and scented with wood-smoke, was limp and mildewed; and I began to tighten up the straps—under which the drumsticks had been loosely thrust—with the idle purpose of trying if some music might be got out of the old drum yet.

But as I turned it on my knee, I found the drum attached to the trumpet-sling by a curious barrel-shaped padlock, and paused to examine this. The body of the lock was composed of half a dozen brass rings, set accurately edge to edge; and, rubbing the brass with my thumb, I saw that each of the six had a series of letters engraved around it.

I knew the trick of it, I thought. Here was one of those word-padlocks, once so common; only to be opened by getting the rings to spell a certain word, which the dealer confides to you.

My host shut and barred the door, and came back to the hearth.

"'Twas just such a wind—east by south—that brought in what you've got between your hands. Back in the year 'nine it was; my father has told me the tale a score o' times. You're twisting round the rings, I see. But you'll never guess the word. Parson Kendall, he made the word, and locked down a couple o' ghosts in their graves with it; and when his time came, he went to his own grave and took the word with him."

"Whose ghosts, Matthew?"

"You want the story, I see, sir. My father could tell it better than I can. He was a young man in the year 'nine, unmarried at the time, and living in this very cottage just as I be. That's how he came to get mixed up with the tale."

He took a chair, lit a short pipe, and unfolded the story in a low musing voice, with his eyes fixed on the dancing violet flames.

"Yes, he'd ha' been about thirty year old in January, of the year 'nine. The storm got up in the night o' the twenty-first o' that month. My father was dressed and out long before daylight; he never was one to 'bide in bed, let be that the gale by this time was pretty near lifting the thatch over his head. Besides which, he'd fenced a small 'taty-patch that winter, down by Lowland Point, and he wanted to see if it stood the night's work. He took the path across Gunner's Meadow—where they buried most of the bodies afterwards. The wind was right in his teeth at the time, and once on the way (he's told me this often) a great strip of ore-weed came flying through the darkness and fetched him a slap on the cheek like a cold hand. But he made shift pretty well till he got to Lowland, and then had to drop upon his hands and knees and crawl, digging his fingers every now and then into the shingle to hold on, for he declared to me that the stones, some of them as big as a man's head, kept rolling and driving past till it seemed the whole foreshore was moving westward under him. The fence was gone, of course; not a stick left to show where it stood; so that, when first he came to the place, he thought he must have missed his bearings. My father, sir, was a very religious man; and if he reckoned the end of the world was at hand—there in the great wind and night, among the moving stones—you may believe he was certain of it when he heard a gun fired, and, with the same, saw a flame shoot up out of the darkness to windward, making a sudden fierce light in all the place about. All he could find to think or say was, 'The Second Coming—The Second Coming! The Bridegroom cometh, and the wicked He will toss like a ball into a large country!' and being already upon his knees, he just bowed his head and 'bided, saying this over and over.

"But by'm-by, between two squalls, he made bold to lift his head and look, and then by the light—a bluish colour 'twas—he saw all the coast clear away to Manacle Point, and off the Manacles, in the thick of the weather, a sloop-of-war with top-gallants housed, driving stern foremost towards the reef. It was she, of course, that was burning the flare. My father could see the white streak and the ports of her quite plain as she rose to it, a little outside the breakers, and he guessed easy enough that her captain had just managed to wear ship, and was trying to force her nose to the sea with the help of her small bower anchor and the scrap or two of canvas that hadn't yet been blown out of her. But while he looked, she fell off, giving her broadside to it foot by foot, and drifting back on the breakers around Carn dû and the Varses. The rocks lie so thick thereabouts, that 'twas a toss up which she struck first; at any rate, my father couldn't tell at the time, for just then the flare died down and went out.

"Well, sir, he turned then in the dark and started back for Coverack to cry the dismal tidings—though well knowing ship and crew to be past any hope; and as he turned, the wind lifted him and tossed him forward 'like a ball,' as he'd been saying, and homeward along the foreshore. As you know, 'tis ugly work, even by daylight, picking your way among the stones there, and my father was prettily knocked about at first in the dark. But by this 'twas nearer seven than six o'clock, and the day spreading. By the time he reached North Corner, a man could see to read print; hows'ever, he looked neither out to sea nor towards Coverack, but headed straight for the first cottage—the same that stands above North Corner to-day. A man named Billy Ede lived there then, and when my father burst into the kitchen bawling, 'Wreck! wreck!' he saw Billy Ede's wife, Ann, standing there in her clogs, with a shawl over her head, and her clothes wringing wet.

"'Save the chap!' says Billy Ede's wife, Ann. 'What d' 'ee mean by crying stale fish at that rate?'

"'But 'tis a wreck, I tell 'ee. I've a-zeed 'n!'

"'Why, so 'tis,' says she, 'and I've a-zeed 'n too; and so has everyone with an eye in his head.'

"And with that she pointed straight over my father's shoulder, and he turned; and there, close under Dolor Point, at the end of Coverack town, he saw another wreck washing, and the point black with people, like emmets, running to and fro in the morning light. While he stood staring at her, he heard a trumpet sounded on board, the notes coming in little jerks, like a bird rising against the wind; but faintly, of course, because of the distance and the gale blowing—though this had dropped a little.

"'She's a transport,' said Billy Ede's wife, Ann, 'and full of horse soldiers, fine long men. When she struck they must ha' pitched the hosses over first to lighten the ship, for a score of dead hosses had washed in afore I left, half an hour back. An' three or four soldiers, too—fine long corpses in white breeches and jackets of blue and gold. I held the lantern to one. Such a straight young man!'

"My father asked her about the trumpeting.

"'That's the queerest bit of all. She was burnin' a light when me an' my man joined the crowd down there. All her masts had gone; whether they carried away, or were cut away to ease her, I don't rightly know. Anyway, there she lay 'pon the rocks with her decks bare. Her keelson was broke under her and her bottom sagged and stove, and she had just settled down like a sitting hen—just the leastest list to starboard; but a man could stand there easy. They had rigged up ropes across her, from bulwark to bulwark, an' beside these the men were mustered, holding on like grim death whenever the sea made a clean breach over them, an' standing up like heroes as soon as it passed. The captain an' the officers were clinging to the rail of the quarter-deck, all in their golden uniforms, waiting for the end as if 'twas King George they expected. There was no way to help, for she lay right beyond cast of line, though our folk tried it fifty times. And beside them clung a trumpeter, a whacking big man, an' between the heavy seas he would lift his trumpet with one hand, and blow a call; and every time he blew, the men gave a cheer. There' (she says)'—hark 'ee now—there he goes agen! But you won't hear no cheering any more, for few are left to cheer, and their voices weak. Bitter cold the wind is, and I reckon it numbs their grip o' the ropes, for they were dropping off fast with every sea when my man sent me home to get his breakfast. Another wreck, you say? Well, there's no hope for the tender dears, if 'tis the Manacles. You'd better run down and help yonder; though 'tis little help that any man can give. Not one came in alive while I was there. The tide's flowing, an' she won't hold together another hour, they say.'

"Well, sure enough, the end was coming fast when my father got down to the point. Six men had been cast up alive, or just breathing—a seaman and five troopers. The seaman was the only one that had breath to speak; and while they were carrying him into the town, the word went round that the ship's name was the *Despatch*, transport, homeward bound from Corunna, with a detachment of the 7th Hussars, that had been fighting out there with Sir John Moore. The seas had rolled her farther over by this time, and given her decks a pretty sharp slope; but a dozen men still held on, seven by the ropes near the ship's waist, a couple near the break of the poop, and three on the quarter-deck. Of these three my father made out one to be the skipper; close by him clung an officer in full regimentals—his name, they heard after, was Captain Duncanfield; and last came the tall trumpeter; and if you'll believe me, the fellow was making shift there, at the very last, to blow '*God Save the King*.' What's more, he got to '*Send us victorious*' before an extra big sea came bursting across and washed them off the deck—every man but one of the pair beneath the poop—and *he* dropped his hold before the next wave; being stunned, I reckon. The others went out of sight at once, but the trumpeter—being, as I said, a powerful man as well as a tough swimmer—rose like a duck, rode out a couple of breakers, and came in on the crest of the third. The folks looked to see him broke like an egg at their feet; but when the smother cleared, there he was, lying face downward on a ledge below them; and one of the men that happened to have a rope round him—I forget the fellow's name, if I ever heard it—jumped down and grabbed him by the ankle as he began to slip back. Before the next big sea, the pair were hauled high enough to be out of harm, and another heave brought them up to grass. Quick work; but master trumpeter wasn't quite dead; nothing worse than a cracked head and three staved ribs. In twenty minutes or so they had him in bed, with the doctor to tend him."

"Now was the time—nothing being left alive upon the transport—for my father to tell of the sloop he'd seen driving upon the Manacles. And when he got a hearing, though the most were set upon salvage, and believed a wreck in the hand, so to say, to be worth half a dozen they couldn't see, a good few volunteered to start off with him and have a look. They crossed Lowland Point; no ship to be seen on the Manacles, nor anywhere upon the sea. One or two was for calling my father a liar. 'Wait till we come to Dean Point,' said he. Sure enough, on the far side of Dean Point, they found the sloop's mainmast washing about with half a dozen men lashed to it—men in red jackets—every mother's son drowned and staring; and a little farther on, just under the Dean, three or four bodies cast up on the shore, one of them a small drummer-boy, side-drum and all; and, near by, part of a ship's gig, with 'H.M.S. *Primrose*' cut on the stern-board. From this point on, the shore was littered thick with wreckage and dead bodies—the most of them Marines in uniform; and in Godrevy Cove, in particular, a heap of furniture from the captain's cabin, and amongst it a water-tight box, not much damaged, and full of papers; by which, when it came to be examined next day, the wreck was easily made out to be the *Primrose*, of eighteen guns, outward bound from Portsmouth, with a fleet of transports for the Spanish War—thirty sail, I've heard, but I've never heard what became of them. Being handled by merchant skippers, no doubt they rode out the gale and reached the Tagus safe and sound. Not but what the captain of the *Primrose* (Mein was his name) did quite right to try and club-haul his vessel when he found himself under the land: only he never ought to have got there if he took proper soundings. But it's easy talking.

"The *Primrose*, sir, was a handsome vessel—for her size, one of the handsomest in the King's service—and newly fitted out at Plymouth Dock. So the boys had brave pickings from her in the way of brass-work, ship's instruments, and the like, let alone some barrels of stores not much spoiled. They loaded themselves with as much as they could carry, and started for home, meaning to make a second journey before the preventive men got wind of their doings and came to spoil the fun. But as my father was passing back under the Dean, he happened to take a look over his shoulder at the bodies there. 'Hullo,' says he, and dropped his gear: 'I do believe there's a leg moving!' And, running fore, he stooped over the small drummer-boy that I told you about. The poor little chap was lying there, with his face a mass of bruises and his eyes closed: but he had shifted one leg an inch or two, and was still breathing. So my father pulled out a knife and cut him free from his drum—that was lashed on to him with a double turn of Manilla rope—and took him up and carried him along here, to this very room that we're sitting in. He lost a good deal by this, for when he went back to fetch his bundle the preventive men had got hold of it, and were thick as thieves along the foreshore; so that 'twas only by paying one or two to look the other way that he picked up anything worth carrying off: which you'll allow to be hard, seeing that he was the first man to give news of the wreck."

"Well, the inquiry was held, of course, and my father gave evidence; and for the rest they had to trust to the sloop's papers: for not a soul was saved besides the drummer-boy, and he was raving in a fever, brought on by the cold and the fright. And the seamen and the five troopers gave evidence about the loss of the *Despatch*. The tall trumpeter, too, whose ribs were healing, came forward and kissed the Book; but somehow his head had been hurt in coming ashore, and he talked foolish-like, and 'twas easy seen he would never be a proper man again. The others were taken up to Plymouth, and so went their ways; but the trumpeter stayed on in Coverack; and King George, finding he was fit for nothing, sent him down a trifle of a pension after a while—enough to keep him in board and lodging, with a bit of tobacco over.

"Now the first time that this man—William Tallifer, he called himself—met with the drummer-boy, was about a fortnight after the little chap had bettered enough to be allowed a short walk out of doors, which he took, if you please, in full regimentals. There never was a soldier so proud of his dress. His own suit had shrunk a brave bit with the salt water; but into ordinary frock an' corduroys he declared he would not get—not if he had to go naked the rest of his life; so my father, being a good-natured man and handy with the needle, turned to and repaired damages with a piece or two of scarlet cloth cut from the jacket of one of the drowned Marines. Well, the poor little chap chanced to be standing, in this rig-out, down by the gate of Gunner's Meadow, where they had buried two score and over of his comrades. The morning was a fine one, early in March month; and along came the cracked trumpeter, likewise taking a stroll.

"'Hullo!' says he; 'good mornin'! And what might you be doin' here?'

"'I was a-wishin',' says the boy, 'I had a pair o' drum-sticks. Our lads were buried yonder without so much as a drum tapped or a musket fired; and that's not Christian burial for British soldiers.'

"'Phut!' says the trumpeter, and spat on the ground; 'a parcel of Marines!'

"The boy eyed him a second or so, and answered up: 'If I'd a tab of turf handy, I'd bung it at your mouth, you greasy cavalryman, and learn you to speak respectful of your betters. The Marines are the handiest body of men in the service.'

"The trumpeter looked down on him from the height of six foot two, and asked: 'Did they die well?'

"'They died very well. There was a lot of running to and fro at first, and some of the men began to cry, and a few to strip off their clothes. But when the ship fell off for the last time, Captain Mein turned and said something to Major Griffiths, the commanding officer on board, and the Major called out to me to beat to quarters. It might have been for a wedding, he sang it out so cheerful. We'd had word already that 'twas to be parade order, and the men fell in as trim and decent as if they were going to church. One or two even tried to shave at the last moment. The Major wore his medals. One of the seamen, seeing I had hard work to keep the drum steady—the sling being a bit loose for me and the wind what you remember—lashed it tight with a piece of rope; and that saved my life afterwards, a drum being as good as a cork until 'tis stove. I kept beating away until every man was on deck; and then the Major formed them up and told them to die like British soldiers, and the chaplain read a prayer or two—the boys standin' all the while like rocks, each man's courage keeping up the others'. The chaplain was in the middle of a prayer when she struck. In ten minutes she was gone. That was how they died, cavalryman.'

"'And that was very well done, drummer of the Marines. What's your name?'

"'John Christian.'

"'Mine is William George Tallifer, trumpeter, of the 7th Light Dragoons—the Queen's Own. I played "*God Save the King*" while our men were drowning. Captain Duncanfield told me to sound a call or two, to put them in heart; but that matter of "*God Save the King*" was a notion of my own. I won't say anything to hurt the feelings of a Marine, even if he's not much over five-foot tall; but the Queen's Own Hussars is a tearin' fine regiment. As between horse and foot, 'tis a question o' which gets the chance. All the way from Sahagun to Corunna 'twas we that took and gave the knocks—at Mayorga and Rueda, and Bennyventy.' (The reason, sir, I can speak the names so pat is that my father learnt 'em by heart afterwards from the trumpeter, who was always talking about Mayorga and Rueda and Bennyventy.) 'We made the rear-guard, under General Paget, and drove the French every time; and all the infantry did was to sit about in wine-shops till we whipped 'em out, an' steal an' straggle an' play the tom-fool in general. And when it came to a stand-up fight at Corunna, 'twas the horse, or the best part of it, that had to stay sea-sick aboard the transports, an' watch the infantry in the thick o' the caper. Very well they behaved, too; 'specially the 4th Regiment, an' the 42nd Highlanders an' the

Dirty Half-Hundred. Oh, ay; they're decent regiments, all three. But the Queen's Own Hussars is a tearin' fine regiment. So you played on your drum when the ship was goin' down? Drummer John Christian, I'll have to get you a new pair o' drum-sticks for that.'

"Well, sir, it appears that the very next day the trumpeter marched into Helston, and got a carpenter there to turn him a pair of box-wood drum-sticks for the boy. And this was the beginning of one of the most curious friendships you ever heard tell of. Nothing delighted the pair more than to borrow a boat off my father and pull out to the rocks where the *Primrose* and the *Despatch* had struck and sunk; and on still days 'twas pretty to hear them out there off the Manacles, the drummer playing his tattoo—for they always took their music with them—and the trumpeter practising calls, and making his trumpet speak like an angel. But if the weather turned roughish, they'd be walking together and talking; leastwise, the youngster listened while the other discoursed about Sir John's campaign in Spain and Portugal, telling how each little skirmish befell; and of Sir John himself, and General Baird and General Paget, and Colonel Vivian, his own commanding officer, and what kind of men they were; and of the last bloody stand-up at Corunna, and so forth, as if neither could have enough.

"But all this had to come to an end in the late summer; for the boy, John Christian, being now well and strong again, must go up to Plymouth to report himself. 'Twas his own wish (for I believe King George had forgotten all about him), but his friend wouldn't hold him back. As for the trumpeter, my father had made an arrangement to take him on as a lodger as soon as the boy left; and on the morning fixed for the start, he was up at the door here by five o'clock, with his trumpet slung by his side, and all the rest of his kit in a small valise. A Monday morning it was, and after breakfast he had fixed to walk with the boy some way on the road towards Helston, where the coach started. My father left them at breakfast together, and went out to meat the pig, and do a few odd morning jobs of that sort. When he came back, the boy was still at table, and the trumpeter standing here by the chimney-place with the drum and trumpet in his hands, hitched together just as they be at this moment.

"'Look at this,' he says to my father, showing him the lock; 'I picked it up off a starving brass-worker in Lisbon, and it is not one of your common locks that one word of six letters will open at any time. There's *janius* in this lock; for you've only to make the rings spell any six-letter word you please, and snap down the lock upon that, and never a soul can open it—not the maker, even—until somebody comes along that knows the word you snapped it on. Now, Johnny here's goin', and he leaves his drum behind him; for, though he can make pretty music on it, the parchment sags in wet weather, by reason of the sea-water getting at it; an' if he carries it to Plymouth, they'll only condemn it and give him another. And, as for me, I shan't have the heart to put lip to the trumpet any more when Johnny's gone. So we've chosen a word together, and locked 'em together upon that; and, by your leave, I'll hang 'em here together on the hook over your fireplace. Maybe Johnny'll come back; maybe not. Maybe, if he comes, I'll be dead an' gone, an' he'll take 'em apart an' try their music for old sake's sake. But if he never comes, nobody can separate 'em; for nobody beside knows the word. And if you marry and have sons, you can tell 'em that here are tied together the souls of Johnny Christian, drummer of the Marines, and William George Tallifer, once trumpeter of the Queen's Own Hussars. Amen.'

"With that he hung the two instruments 'pon the hook there; and the boy stood up and thanked my father and shook hands; and the pair went forth of the door, towards Helston.

"Somewhere on the road they took leave of one another; but nobody saw the parting, nor heard what was said between them. About three in the afternoon the trumpeter came walking back over the hill; and by the time my father came home from the fishing, the cottage was tidied up and the tea ready, and the whole place shining like a new pin. From that time for five years he lodged here with my father, looking after the house and tilling the garden; and all the while he was steadily failing, the hurt in his head spreading, in a manner, to his limbs. My father watched the feebleness growing on him, but said nothing. And from first to last neither spake a word about the drummer, John Christian; nor did any letter reach them, nor word of his doings.

"The rest of the tale you'm free to believe, sir, or not, as you please. It stands upon my father's words, and he always declared he was ready to kiss the Book upon it before judge and jury. He said, too, that he never had the wit to make up such a yarn; and he defied anyone to explain about the lock, in particular, by any other tale. But you shall judge for yourself.

"My father said that about three o'clock in the morning, April fourteenth of the year 'fourteen, he and William Tallifer were sitting here, just as you and I, sir, are sitting now. My father had put on his clothes a few minutes before, and was mending his spiller by the light of the horn lantern, meaning to set off before daylight to haul the trammel. The trumpeter hadn't been to bed at all. Towards the last he mostly spent his nights (and his days, too) dozing in the elbow-chair where you sit at this minute. He was dozing then (my father said), with his chin dropped forward on his chest, when a knock sounded upon the door, and the door opened, and in walked an upright young man in scarlet regimentals.

"He had grown a brave bit, and his face was the colour of wood-ashes; but it was the drummer, John Christian. Only his uniform was different from the one he used to wear, and the figures '38' shone in brass upon his collar.

"The drummer walked past my father as if he never saw him, and stood by the elbow-chair and said:

"'Trumpeter, trumpeter, are you one with me?'

"And the trumpeter just lifted the lids of his eyes, and answered, 'How should I not be one with you, drummer Johnny—Johnny boy? The men are patient. 'Till you come, I count; while you march, I mark time; until the discharge comes.'

"'The discharge has come to-night,' said the drummer, 'and the word is Corunna no longer'; and stepping to the chimney-place, he unhooked the drum and trumpet, and began to twist the brass rings of the lock, spelling the word aloud, so—C-O-R-U-N-A. When he had fixed the last letter, the padlock opened in his hand.

"'Did you know, trumpeter, that when I came to Plymouth they put me into a line regiment?'

"'The 38th is a good regiment,' answered the old Hussar, still in his dull voice. 'I went back with them from Sahagun to Corunna. At Corunna they stood in General Fraser's division, on the right. They behaved well.'

"'But I'd fain see the Marines again,' says the drummer, handing him the trumpet; 'and you—you shall call once more for the Queen's Own. Matthew,' he says, suddenly, turning on my father—and when he turned, my father saw for the first time that his scarlet jacket had a round hole by the breast-bone, and that the blood was welling there—'Matthew, we shall want your boat.'

"Then my father rose on his legs like a man in a dream, while they two slung on, the one his drum, and t'other his trumpet. He took the lantern, and went quaking before them down to the shore, and they breathed heavily behind him; and they stepped into his boat, and my father pushed off.

"'Row you first for Dolor Point,' says the drummer. So my father rowed them out past the white houses of Coverack to Dolor Point, and there, at a word, lay on his oars. And the trumpeter, William Tallifer, put his trumpet to his mouth and sounded the *Revelly*. The music of it was like rivers running.

"'They will follow,' said the drummer. 'Matthew, pull you now for the Manacles.'

"So my father pulled for the Manacles, and came to an easy close outside Carn dû. And the drummer took his sticks and beat a tattoo, there by the edge of the reef; and the music of it was like a rolling chariot.

"'That will do,' says he, breaking off; 'they will follow. Pull now for the shore under Gunner's Meadow.'

"Then my father pulled for the shore, and ran his boat in under Gunner's Meadow. And they stepped out, all three, and walked up to the meadow. By the gate the drummer halted and began his tattoo again, looking out towards the darkness over the sea.

"And while the drum beat, and my father held his breath, there came up out of the sea and the darkness a troop of many men, horse and foot, and formed up among the graves; and others rose out of the graves and formed up—drowned Marines with bleached faces, and pale Hussars riding their horses, all lean and shadowy. There was no clatter of hoofs or accoutrements, my father said, but a soft sound all the while, like the beating of a bird's wing, and a black shadow lying like a pool about the feet of all. The drummer stood upon a little knoll just inside the gate, and beside him the tall trumpeter, with hand on hip, watching them gather; and behind them both my father, clinging to the gate. When no more came, the drummer stopped playing, and said, 'Call the roll.'

"Then the trumpeter stepped towards the end man of the rank and called, 'Troop-Sergeant-Major Thomas Irons!' and the man in a thin voice answered 'Here!'

"'Troop-Sergeant-Major Thomas Irons, how is it with you?'

"The man answered, 'How should it be with me? When I was young, I betrayed a girl; and when I was grown, I betrayed a friend; and for these things I must pay. But I died as a man ought. God save the King!'

"The trumpeter called to the next man, 'Trooper Henry Buckingham!' and the next man answered, 'Here!'

"'Trooper Henry Buckingham, how is it with you?'

"'How should it be with me? I was a drunkard, and I stole, and in Lugo, in a wine-shop, I knifed a man. But I died as a man should. God save the King!'

"So the trumpeter went down the line; and when he had finished, the drummer took it up, hailing the dead Marines in their order. Each man answered to his name, and each man ended with 'God save the King!' When all were hailed, the drummer stepped back to his mound, and called:

"'It is well. You are content, and we are content to join you. Wait yet a little while.'

"With this he turned and ordered my father to pick up the lantern, and lead the way back. As my father picked it up, he heard the ranks of dead men cheer and call, 'God save the King!' all together, and saw them waver and fade back into the dark, like a breath fading off a pane.

"But when they came back here to the kitchen, and my father set the lantern down, it seemed they'd both forgot about him. For the drummer turned in the lantern-light—and my father could see the blood still welling out of the hole in his breast—and took the trumpet-sling from around the other's neck, and locked drum and trumpet together again, choosing the letters on the lock very carefully. While he did this he said:

"'The word is no more Corunna, but Bayonne. As you left out an "n" in Corunna, so must I leave out an "n" in Bayonne.' And before snapping the padlock, he spelt out the word slowly—'B-A-Y-O-N-E.' After that, he used no more speech; but turned and hung the two instruments back on the hook; and then took the trumpeter by the arm; and the pair walked out into the darkness, glancing neither to right nor left.

"My father was on the point of following, when he heard a sort of sigh behind him; and there, sitting in the elbow-chair, was the very trumpeter he had just seen walk out by the door! If my father's heart jumped before, you may believe it jumped quicker now. But after a bit, he went up to the man asleep in the chair, and put a hand upon him. It was the trumpeter in flesh and blood that he touched; but though the flesh was warm, the trumpeter was dead.

"Well, sir, they buried him three days after; and at first my father was minded to say nothing about his dream (as he thought it). But the day after the funeral, he met Parson Kendall coming from Helston market: and the parson called out: 'Have 'ee heard the news the coach brought down this mornin'?' 'What news?' says my father. 'Why, that peace is agreed upon.' 'None too soon,' says my father. 'Not soon enough for our poor lads at Bayonne,' the parson answered. 'Bayonne!' cries my father, with a jump. 'Why, yes'; and the parson told him all about a great sally the French had made on the night of April 13th. 'Do you happen to know if the 38th Regiment was engaged?' my father asked. 'Come, now,' said Parson Kendall, 'I didn't know you was so well up in the campaign. But, as it happens, I *do* know that the 38th was engaged, for 'twas they that held a cottage and stopped the French advance.'

"Still my father held his tongue; and when, a week later, he walked into Helston and bought a *Mercury* off the Sherborne rider, and got the landlord of the 'Angel' to spell out the list of killed and wounded, sure enough, there among the killed was Drummer John Christian, of the 38th Foot.

"After this, there was nothing for a religious man but to make a clean breast. So my father went up to Parson Kendall and told the whole story. The parson listened, and put a question or two, and then asked:

"'Have you tried to open the lock since that night?'

"'I han't dared to touch it,' says my father.

"'Then come along and try.' When the parson came to the cottage here, he took the things off the hook and tried the lock. 'Did he say "*Bayonne*"? The word has seven letters.'

"'Not if you spell it with one "n" as *he* did,' says my father.

"The parson spelt it out—B-A-Y-O-N-E. 'Whew!' says he, for the lock had fallen open in his hand.

"He stood considering it a moment, and then he says, 'I tell you what. I shouldn't blab this all round the parish, if I was you. You won't get no credit for truth-telling, and a miracle's wasted on a set of fools. But if you like, I'll shut down the lock again upon a holy word that no one but me shall know, and neither drummer nor trumpeter, dead nor alive, shall frighten the secret out of me.'

"'I wish to gracious you would, parson,' said my father.

"The parson chose the holy word there and then, and shut the lock back upon it, and hung the drum and trumpet back in their place. He is gone long since, taking the word with him. And till the lock is broken by force, nobody will ever separate those twain."

The Captain of the Pole-Star

Arthur Conan Doyle

[Being an extract from the singular journal of John M'Alister Ray, student of medicine.]

SEPTEMBER 11TH.—LAT. 81° 40' N.; LONG. 2° E. STILL LYING-TO AMID ENORMOUS ICE fields. The one which stretches away to the north of us, and to which our ice-anchor is attached, cannot be smaller than an English county. To the right and left unbroken sheets extend to the horizon. This morning the mate reported that there were signs of pack ice to the southward. Should this form of sufficient thickness to bar our return, we shall be in a position of danger, as the food, I hear, is already running somewhat short. It is late in the season, and the nights are beginning to reappear. This morning I saw a star twinkling just over the fore-yard, the first since the beginning of May. There is considerable discontent among the crew, many of whom are anxious to get back home to be in time for the herring season, when labour always commands a high price upon the Scotch coast. As yet their displeasure is only signified by sullen countenances and black looks, but I heard from the second mate this afternoon that they contemplated sending a deputation to the Captain to explain their grievance. I much doubt how he will receive it, as he is a man of fierce temper, and very sensitive about anything approaching to an infringement of his rights. I shall venture after dinner to say a few words to him upon the subject. I have always found that he will tolerate from me what he would resent from any other member of the crew. Amsterdam Island, at the north-west corner of Spitzbergen, is visible upon our starboard quarter—a rugged line of volcanic rocks, intersected by white seams, which represent glaciers. It is curious to think that at the present moment there is probably no human being nearer to us than the Danish settlements in the south of Greenland—a good nine hundred miles as the crow flies. A captain takes a great responsibility upon himself when he risks his vessel under such circumstances. No whaler has ever remained in these latitudes till so advanced a period of the year.

9 P.M.—I have spoken to Captain Craigie, and though the result has been hardly satisfactory, I am bound to say that he listened to what I had to say very quietly and even deferentially. When I had finished he put on that air of iron determination which I have frequently observed upon his face, and paced rapidly backwards and forwards across the narrow cabin for some minutes. At first I feared that I had seriously offended him, but he dispelled the idea by sitting down again, and putting his hand upon my arm with a gesture which almost amounted to a caress. There was a depth of tenderness too in his wild dark eyes which surprised me considerably. "Look here, Doctor," he said, "I'm sorry I ever took you—I am indeed—and I would give fifty pounds this minute to see you standing safe upon the Dundee quay. It's hit or miss with me this time. There are fish to the north of us. How dare you shake your head, sir, when I tell you I saw them blowing from the masthead?"—this in a sudden burst of fury, though I was not conscious of having shown any signs of doubt. "Two-and-twenty fish in as many minutes as I am a living man, and not one under ten foot.[1] Now, Doctor, do you think I can leave the country when there is only one infernal strip of ice between me and my fortune? If it came on to blow from the north to-morrow we could fill the ship and be away before the frost could catch us. If it came on to blow from the south—well, I suppose the men are paid for risking their lives, and as for myself it matters but little to me, for I have more to bind me to the other world than to this one. I confess that I am sorry for *you*, though. I wish I had old Angus Tait who was with me last voyage, for he was a man that would never be missed, and you—you said once that you were engaged, did you not?"

"Yes," I answered, snapping the spring of the locket which hung from my watch-chain, and holding up the little vignette of Flora.

"Curse you!" he yelled, springing out of his seat, with his very beard bristling with passion. "What is your happiness to me? What have I to do with her that you must dangle her photograph before my eyes?" I almost thought that he was about to strike me in the frenzy of his rage, but with another imprecation he dashed open the door of the cabin and rushed out upon deck, leaving me considerably astonished at his extraordinary violence. It is the first time that he has ever shown me anything but courtesy and kindness. I can hear him pacing excitedly up and down overhead as I write these lines.

I should like to give a sketch of the character of this man, but it seems presumptuous to attempt such a thing upon paper, when the idea in my own mind is at best a vague and uncertain one. Several times I have thought that I grasped the clue which might explain it, but only to be disappointed by his presenting himself in some new light which

---

1 A whale is measured among whalers not by the length of its body, but by the length of its whalebone.

would upset all my conclusions. It may be that no human eye but my own shall ever rest upon these lines, yet as a psychological study I shall attempt to leave some record of Captain Nicholas Craigie.

A man's outer case generally gives some indication of the soul within. The Captain is tall and well-formed, with dark, handsome face, and a curious way of twitching his limbs, which may arise from nervousness, or be simply an outcome of his excessive energy. His jaw and whole cast of countenance is manly and resolute, but the eyes are the distinctive feature of his face. They are of the very darkest hazel, bright and eager, with a singular mixture of recklessness in their expression, and of something else which I have sometimes thought was more allied with horror than any other emotion. Generally the former predominated, but on occasions, and more particularly when he was thoughtfully inclined, the look of fear would spread and deepen until it imparted a new character to his whole countenance. It is at these times that he is most subject to tempestuous fits of anger, and he seems to be aware of it, for I have known him lock himself up so that no one might approach him until his dark hour was passed. He sleeps badly, and I have heard him shouting during the night, but his cabin is some little distance from mine, and I could never distinguish the words which he said.

This is one phase of his character, and the most disagreeable one. It is only through my close association with him, thrown together as we are day after day, that I have observed it. Otherwise he is an agreeable companion, well-read and entertaining, and as gallant a seaman as ever trod a deck. I shall not easily forget the way in which he handled the ship when we were caught by a gale among the loose ice at the beginning of April. I have never seen him so cheerful, and even hilarious, as he was that night, as he paced backwards and forwards upon the bridge amid the flashing of the lightning and the howling of the wind. He has told me several times that the thought of death was a pleasant one to him, which is a sad thing for a young man to say; he cannot be much more than thirty, though his hair and moustache are already slightly grizzled. Some great sorrow must have overtaken him and blighted his whole life. Perhaps I should be the same if I lost my Flora—God knows! I think if it were not for her that I should care very little whether the wind blew from the north or the south to-morrow. There, I hear him come down the companion, and he has locked himself up in his room, which shows that he is still in an unamiable mood. And so to bed, as old Pepys would say, for the candle is burning down (we have to use them now since the nights are closing in), and the steward has turned in, so there are no hopes of another one.

September 12th.—Calm, clear day, and still lying in the same position. What wind there is comes from the south-east, but it is very slight. Captain is in a better humour, and apologised to me at breakfast for his rudeness. He still looks somewhat distrait, however, and retains that wild look in his eyes which in a Highlander would mean that he was "fey"—at least so our chief engineer remarked to me, and he has some reputation among the Celtic portion of our crew as a seer and expounder of omens.

It is strange that superstition should have obtained such mastery over this hard-headed and practical race. I could not have believed to what an extent it is carried had I not observed it for myself. We have had a perfect epidemic of it this voyage, until I have felt inclined to serve out rations of sedatives and nerve-tonics with the Saturday allowance of grog. The first symptom of it was that shortly after leaving Shetland the men at the wheel used to complain that they heard plaintive cries and screams in the wake of the ship, as if something were following it and were unable to overtake it. This fiction has been kept up during the whole voyage, and on dark nights at the beginning of the seal-fishing it was only with great difficulty that men could be induced to do their spell. No doubt what they heard was either the creaking of the rudder-chains, or the cry of some passing sea-bird. I have been fetched out of bed several times to listen to it, but I need hardly say that I was never able to distinguish anything unnatural. The men, however, are so absurdly positive upon the subject that it is hopeless to argue with them. I mentioned the matter to the Captain once, but to my surprise he took it very gravely, and indeed appeared to be considerably disturbed by what I told him. I should have thought that he at least would have been above such vulgar delusions.

All this disquisition upon superstition leads me up to the fact that Mr. Manson, our second mate, saw a ghost last night—or, at least, says that he did, which of course is the same thing. It is quite refreshing to have some new topic of conversation after the eternal routine of bears and whales which has served us for so many months. Manson swears the ship is haunted, and that he would not stay in her a day if he had any other place to go to. Indeed the fellow is honestly frightened, and I had to give him some chloral and bromide of potassium this morning to steady him down. He seemed quite indignant when I suggested that he had been having an extra glass the night before, and I was obliged to pacify him by keeping as grave a countenance as possible during his story, which he certainly narrated in a very straight-forward and matter-of-fact way.

"I was on the bridge," he said, "about four bells in the middle watch, just when the night was at its darkest. There was a bit of a moon, but the clouds were blowing across it so that you couldn't see far from the ship. John M'Leod, the harpooner, came aft from the foc's'le-head and reported a strange noise on the starboard bow. I went forrard and we both heard it, sometimes like a bairn crying and sometimes like a wench in pain. I've been seventeen years to the country and I never heard seal, old or young, make a sound like that. As we were standing there on the foc'sle-head the moon came out from behind a cloud, and we both saw a sort of white figure moving across the ice field in the same direction that we had heard the cries. We lost sight of it for a while, but it came back on the port bow, and we could just make it out like a shadow on the ice. I sent a hand aft for the rifles, and M'Leod and I went down on to the pack, thinking that maybe it might be a bear. When we got on the ice I lost sight of M'Leod, but I pushed on in the direction where I could still hear the cries. I followed them for a mile or maybe more, and then running round a hummock I came right on to the top of it standing and waiting for me seemingly. I don't know what it was. It wasn't a bear any way. It was tall and white and straight, and if it wasn't a man nor a woman, I'll stake my davy it was something worse. I made for the ship as hard as I could run, and precious glad I was to find myself aboard. I signed articles to do my duty by the ship, and on the ship I'll stay, but you don't catch me on the ice again after sundown."

That is his story, given as far as I can in his own words. I fancy what he saw must, in spite of his denial, have been a young bear erect upon its hind legs, an attitude which they often assume when alarmed. In the uncertain light this would bear a resemblance to a human figure, especially to a man whose nerves were already somewhat shaken. Whatever it may have been, the occurrence is unfortunate, for it has produced a most unpleasant effect upon the crew. Their looks are more sullen than before, and their discontent more open. The double grievance of being debarred from the herring fishing and of being detained in what they choose to call a haunted vessel, may lead them to do something rash. Even the harpooners, who are the oldest and steadiest among them, are joining in the general agitation.

Apart from this absurd outbreak of superstition, things are looking rather more cheerful. The pack which was forming to the south of us has partly cleared away, and the water is so warm as to lead me to believe that we are lying in one of those branches of the gulf-stream which run up between Greenland and Spitzbergen. There are numerous small Medusse and sealemons about the ship, with abundance of shrimps, so that there is every possibility of "fish" being sighted. Indeed one was seen blowing about dinner-time, but in such a position that it was impossible for the boats to follow it.

September 13th.—Had an interesting conversation with the chief mate, Mr. Milne, upon the bridge. It seems that our Captain is as great an enigma to the seamen, and even to the owners of the vessel, as he has been to me. Mr. Milne tells me that when the ship is paid off, upon returning from a voyage, Captain Craigie disappears, and is not seen again until the approach of another season, when he walks quietly into the office of the company, and asks whether his services will be required. He has no friend in Dundee, nor does any one pretend to be acquainted with his early history. His position depends entirely upon his skill as a seaman, and the name for courage and coolness which he had earned in the capacity of mate, before being entrusted with a separate command. The unanimous opinion seems to be that he is not a Scotchman, and that his name is an assumed one. Mr. Milne thinks that he has devoted himself to whaling simply for the reason that it is the most dangerous occupation which he could select, and that he courts death in every possible manner. He mentioned several instances of this, one of which is rather curious, if true. It seems that on one occasion he did not put in an appearance at the office, and a substitute had to be selected in his place. That was at the time of the last Russian and Turkish war. When he turned up again next spring he had a puckered wound in the side of his neck which he used to endeavour to conceal with his cravat. Whether the mate's inference that he had been engaged in the war is true or not I cannot say. It was certainly a strange coincidence.

The wind is veering round in an easterly direction, but is still very slight. I think the ice is lying closer than it did yesterday. As far as the eye can reach on every side there is one wide expanse of spotless white, only broken by an occasional rift or the dark shadow of a hummock. To the south there is the narrow lane of blue water which is our sole means of escape, and which is closing up every day. The Captain is taking a heavy responsibility upon himself. I hear that the tank of potatoes has been finished, and even the biscuits are running short, but he preserves the same impassible countenance, and spends the greater part of the day at the crow's nest, sweeping the horizon with his glass. His manner is very variable, and he seems to avoid my society, but there has been no repetition of the violence which he showed the other night.

7:30 P.M.—My deliberate opinion is that we are commanded by a madman. Nothing else can account for the extraordinary vagaries of Captain Craigie. It is fortunate that I have kept this journal of our voyage, as it will serve to justify us in case we have to put him under any sort of restraint, a step which I should only consent to as a last resource. Curiously enough it was he himself who suggested lunacy and not mere eccentricity as the secret of his strange conduct. He was standing upon the bridge about an hour ago, peering as usual through his glass, while I was walking up and down the quarterdeck. The majority of the men were below at their tea, for the watches have not been regularly kept of late. Tired of walking, I leaned against the bulwarks, and admired the mellow glow cast by the sinking sun upon the great ice fields which surround us. I was suddenly aroused from the reverie into which I had fallen by a hoarse voice at my elbow, and starting round I found that the Captain had descended and was standing by my side. He was staring out over the ice with an expression in which horror, surprise, and something approaching to joy were contending for the mastery. In spite of the cold, great drops of perspiration were coursing down his forehead, and he was evidently fearfully excited. His limbs twitched like those of a man upon the verge of an epileptic fit, and the lines about his mouth were drawn and hard.

"Look!" he gasped, seizing me by the wrist, but still keeping his eyes upon the distant ice, and moving his head slowly in a horizontal direction, as if following some object which was moving across the field of vision. "Look! There, man, there! Between the hummocks! Now coming out from behind the far one! You see her—you *must* see her! There still! Flying from me, by God, flying from me—and gone!"

He uttered the last two words in a whisper of concentrated agony which shall never fade from my remembrance. Clinging to the ratlines he endeavoured to climb up upon the top of the bulwarks as if in the hope of obtaining a last glance at the departing object. His strength was not equal to the attempt, however, and he staggered back against the saloon skylights, where he leaned panting and exhausted. His face was so livid that I expected him to become unconscious, so lost no time in leading him down the companion, and stretching him upon one of the sofas in the cabin. I then poured him out some brandy, which I held to his lips, and which had a wonderful effect upon him, bringing the blood back into his white face and steadying his poor shaking limbs. He raised himself up upon his elbow, and looking round to see that we were alone, he beckoned to me to come and sit beside him.

"You saw it, didn't you?" he asked, still in the same subdued awesome tone so foreign to the nature of the man.

"No, I saw nothing."

His head sank back again upon the cushions. "No, he wouldn't without the glass," he murmured. "He couldn't. It was the glass that showed her to me, and then the eyes of love—the eyes of love. I say, Doc, don't let the steward in! He'll think I'm mad. Just bolt the door, will you!"

I rose and did what he had commanded.

He lay quiet for a while, lost in thought apparently, and then raised himself up upon his elbow again, and asked for some more brandy.

"You don't think I am, do you, Doc?" he asked, as I was putting the bottle back into the after-locker. "Tell me now, as man to man, do you think that I am mad?"

"I think you have something on your mind," I answered, "which is exciting you and doing you a good deal of harm."

"Right there, lad!" he cried, his eyes sparkling from the effects of the brandy. "Plenty on my mind—plenty! But I can work out the latitude and the longitude, and I can handle my sextant and manage my logarithms. You couldn't prove me mad in a court of law, could you, now?" It was curious to hear the man lying back and coolly arguing out the question of his own sanity.

"Perhaps not," I said; "but still I think you would be wise to get home as soon as you can, and settle down to a quiet life for a while."

"Get home, eh?" he muttered, with a sneer upon his face. "One word for me and two for yourself, lad. Settle down with Flora—pretty little Flora. Are bad dreams signs of madness?"

"Sometimes," I answered.

"What else? What would be the first symptoms?"

"Pains in the head, noises in the ears flashes before the eyes, delusions"—

"Ah! what about them?" he interrupted. "What would you call a delusion?"

"Seeing a thing which is not there is a delusion."

"But she *was* there!" he groaned to himself. "She *was* there!" and rising, he unbolted the door and walked with slow and uncertain steps to his own cabin, where I have no doubt that he will remain until to-morrow morning. His system seems to have received a terrible shock, whatever it may have been that he imagined himself to have seen. The man becomes a greater mystery every day, though I fear that the solution which he has himself suggested is the correct one, and that his reason is affected. I do not think that a guilty conscience has anything to do with his behaviour. The idea is a popular one among the officers, and, I believe, the crew; but I have seen nothing to support it. He has not the air of a guilty man, but of one who has had terrible usage at the hands of fortune, and who should be regarded as a martyr rather than a criminal.

The wind is veering round to the south to-night. God help us if it blocks that narrow pass which is our only road to safety! Situated as we are on the edge of the main Arctic pack, or the "barrier" as it is called by the whalers, any wind from the north has the effect of shredding out the ice around us and allowing our escape, while a wind from the south blows up all the loose ice behind us and hems us in between two packs. God help us, I say again!

September 14th.—Sunday, and a day of rest. My fears have been confirmed, and the thin strip of blue water has disappeared from the southward. Nothing but the great motionless ice fields around us, with their weird hummocks and fantastic pinnacles. There is a deathly silence over their wide expanse which is horrible. No lapping of the waves now, no cries of seagulls or straining of sails, but one deep universal silence in which the murmurs of the seamen, and the creak of their boots upon the white shining deck, seem discordant and out of place. Our only visitor was an Arctic fox, a rare animal upon the pack, though common enough upon the land. He did not come near the ship, however, but after surveying us from a distance fled rapidly across the ice. This was curious conduct, as they generally know nothing of man, and being of an inquisitive nature, become so familiar that they are easily captured. Incredible as it may seem, even this little incident produced a bad effect upon the crew. "Yon puir beastie kens mair, ay, an' sees mair nor you nor me!" was the comment of one of the leading harpooners, and the others nodded their acquiescence. It is vain to attempt to argue against such puerile superstition. They have made up their minds that there is a curse upon the ship, and nothing will ever persuade them to the contrary.

The Captain remained in seclusion all day except for about half an hour in the afternoon, when he came out upon the quarterdeck. I observed that he kept his eye fixed upon the spot where the vision of yesterday had appeared, and was quite prepared for another outburst, but none such came. He did not seem to see me although I was standing close beside him. Divine service was read as usual by the chief engineer. It is a curious thing that in whaling vessels the Church of England Prayer-book is always employed, although there is never a member of that Church among either officers or crew. Our men are all Roman Catholics or Presbyterians, the former predominating. Since a ritual is used which is foreign to both, neither can complain that the other is preferred to them, and they listen with all attention and devotion, so that the system has something to recommend it.

A glorious sunset, which made the great fields of ice look like a lake of blood. I have never seen a finer and at the same time more weird effect. Wind is veering round. If it will blow twenty-four hours from the north all will yet be well.

September 15th.—To-day is Flora's birthday. Dear lass! it is well that she cannot see her boy, as she used to call me, shut up among the ice fields with a crazy captain and a few weeks' provisions. No doubt she scans the shipping list in the *Scotsman* every morning to see if we are reported from Shetland. I have to set an example to the men and look cheery and unconcerned; but God knows, my heart is very heavy at times.

The thermometer is at nineteen Fahrenheit to-day. There is but little wind, and what there is comes from an unfavourable quarter. Captain is in an excellent humour; I think he imagines he has seen some other omen or vision, poor fellow, during the night, for he came into my room early in the morning, and stooping down over my bunk, whispered, "It wasn't a delusion, Doc; it's all right!" After breakfast he asked me to find out how much food was left, which the second mate and I proceeded to do. It is even less than we had expected. Forward they have half a tank full of biscuits, three barrels of salt meat, and a very limited supply of coffee beans and sugar. In the after-hold and lockers there are a good many luxuries, such as tinned salmon, soups, haricot mutton, but they will go a very short way among a crew of fifty men. There are two barrels of flour in the store-room, and an unlimited supply of tobacco. Altogether there is about enough to keep the men on half rations for eighteen or twenty days—certainly not more. When we reported the state of things to the Captain, he ordered all hands to be piped, and addressed them from the quarterdeck. I never saw him to better advantage. With his tall, well-knit figure, and dark animated face, he seemed a man born to command, and he discussed the situation in a cool sailor-like way which showed that while appreciating the danger he had an eye for every loophole of escape.

"My lads," he said, "no doubt you think I brought you into this fix, if it is a fix, and maybe some of you feel bitter against me on account of it. But you must remember that for many a season no ship that comes to the country has brought in as much oil-money as the old *Pole-Star*, and every one of you has had his share of it. You can leave your wives behind you in comfort while other poor fellows come back to find their lasses on the parish. If you have to thank me for the one you have to thank me for the other, and we may call it quits. We've tried a bold venture before this and succeeded, so now that we've tried one and failed we've no cause to cry out about it. If the worst comes to the worst, we can make the land across the ice, and lay in a stock of seals which will keep us alive until the spring. It won't come to that, though, for you'll see the Scotch coast again before three weeks are out. At present every man must go on half rations, share and share alike, and no favour to any. Keep up your hearts and you'll pull through this as you've pulled through many a danger before." These few simple words of his had a wonderful effect upon the crew. His former unpopularity was forgotten, and the old harpooner whom I have already mentioned for his superstition, led off three cheers, which were heartily joined in by all hands.

September 16th.—The wind has veered round to the north during the night, and the ice shows some symptoms of opening out. The men are in a good humour in spite of the short allowance upon which they have been placed. Steam is kept up in the engine-room, that there may be no delay should an opportunity for escape present itself. The Captain is in exuberant spirits, though he still retains that wild "fey" expression which I have already remarked upon. This burst of cheerfulness puzzles me more than his former gloom. I cannot understand it. I think I mentioned in an early part of this journal that one of his oddities is that he never permits any person to enter his cabin, but insists upon making his own bed, such as it is, and performing every other office for himself. To my surprise he handed me the key to-day and requested me to go down there and take the time by his chronometer while he measured the altitude of the sun at noon. It is a bare little room, containing a washing-stand and a few books, but little else in the way of luxury, except some pictures upon the walls. The majority of these are small cheap oleographs, but there was one water-colour sketch of the head of a young lady which arrested my attention. It was evidently a portrait, and not one of those fancy types of female beauty which sailors particularly affect. No artist could have evolved from his own mind such a curious mixture of character and weakness. The languid, dreamy eyes, with their drooping lashes, and the broad, low brow, unruffled by thought or care, were in strong contrast with the clean-cut, prominent jaw, and the resolute set of the lower lip. Underneath it in one of the corners was written, "M. B., æt. 19." That any one in the short space of nineteen years of existence could develop such strength of will as was stamped upon her face seemed to me at the time to be well-nigh incredible. She must have been an extraordinary woman. Her features have thrown such a glamour over me that, though I had but a fleeting glance at them, I could, were I a draughtsman, reproduce them line for line upon this page of the journal. I wonder what part she has played in our Captain's life. He has hung her picture at the end of his berth, so that his eyes continually rest upon it. Were he a less reserved man I should make some remark upon the subject. Of the other things in his cabin there was nothing worthy of mention—uniform coats, a camp-stool, small looking-glass, tobacco-box, and numerous pipes, including an oriental hookah—which, by-the-bye, gives some colour to Mr. Milne's story about his participation in the war, though the connection may seem rather a distant one.

11:20 p.m.—Captain just gone to bed after a long and interesting conversation on general topics. When he chooses he can be a most fascinating companion, being remarkably well-read, and having the power of expressing his opinion forcibly without appearing to be dogmatic. I hate to have my intellectual toes trod upon. He spoke about the nature of the soul, and sketched out the views of Aristotle and Plato upon the subject in a masterly manner. He seems to have a leaning for metempsychosis and the doctrines of Pythagoras. In discussing them we touched upon modern spiritualism, and I made some joking allusion to the impostures of Slade, upon which, to my surprise, he warned me most impressively against confusing the innocent with the guilty, and argued that it would be as logical to brand Christianity as an error because Judas, who professed that religion, was a villain. He shortly afterwards bade me good-night and retired to his room.

The wind is freshening up, and blows steadily from the north. The nights are as dark now as they are in England. I hope to-morrow may set us free from our frozen fetters.

September 17th.—The Bogie again. Thank Heaven that I have strong nerves! The superstition of these poor fellows, and the circumstantial accounts which they give, with the utmost earnestness and self-conviction, would horrify any man not accustomed to their ways. There are many versions of the matter, but the sum-total of them all is that something uncanny has been flitting round the ship all night, and that Sandie M'Donald of Peterhead and "lang" Peter Williamson of Shetland saw it, as also did Mr. Milne on the bridge—so, having three witnesses, they can make a better case of it than the second mate did. I spoke to Milne after breakfast, and told him that he should be above such nonsense, and that as an officer he ought to set the men a better example. He shook his weather-beaten head ominously, but answered with characteristic caution, "Mebbe aye, mebbe na, Doctor," he said; "I didna ca' it a ghaist. I canna' say I preen my faith in sea-bogles an' the like, though there's a mony as claims to ha' seen a' that and waur. I'm no easy feared, but maybe your ain bluid would run a bit cauld, mun, if instead o' speerin' aboot it in daylicht ye were wi' me last night, an' seed an awfu' like shape, white an' gruesome, whiles here, whiles there, an' it greetin' and ca'ing in the darkness like a bit lambie that hae lost its mither. Ye would na' be sae ready to put it a' doon to auld wives' clavers then, I'm thinkin'." I saw it was hopeless to reason with him, so contented myself with begging him as a personal favour to call me up the next time the spectre appeared—a request to which he acceded with many ejaculations expressive of his hopes that such an opportunity might never arise.

As I had hoped, the white desert behind us has become broken by many thin streaks of water which intersect it in all directions. Our latitude to-day was 80° 52' N., which shows that there is a strong southerly drift upon the pack. Should the wind continue favourable it will break up as rapidly as it formed. At present we can do nothing but smoke and wait and hope for the best. I am rapidly becoming a fatalist. When dealing with such uncertain factors as wind and ice a man can be nothing else. Perhaps it was the wind and sand of the Arabian deserts which gave the minds of the original followers of Mahomet their tendency to bow to kismet.

These spectral alarms have a very bad effect upon the Captain. I feared that it might excite his sensitive mind, and endeavoured to conceal the absurd story from him, but unfortunately he overheard one of the men making an allusion to it, and insisted upon being informed about it. As I had expected, it brought out all his latent lunacy in an exaggerated form. I can hardly believe that this is the same man who discoursed philosophy last night with the most critical acumen and coolest judgment. He is pacing backwards and forwards upon the quarterdeck like a caged tiger, stopping now and again to throw out his hands with a yearning gesture, and stare impatiently out over the ice. He keeps up a continual mutter to himself, and once he called out, "But a little time, love—but a little time!" Poor fellow, it is sad to see a gallant seaman and accomplished gentleman reduced to such a pass, and to think that imagination and delusion can cow a mind to which real danger was but the salt of life. Was ever a man in such a position as I, between a demented captain and a ghost-seeing mate? I sometimes think I am the only really sane man aboard the vessel—except perhaps the second engineer, who is a kind of ruminant, and would care nothing for all the fiends in the Red Sea so long as they would leave him alone and not disarrange his tools.

The ice is still opening rapidly, and there is every probability of our being able to make a start to-morrow morning. They will think I am inventing when I tell them at home all the strange things that have befallen me.

12 p.m.—I have been a good deal startled, though I feel steadier now, thanks to a stiff glass of brandy. I am hardly myself yet, however, as this handwriting will testify. The fact is, that I have gone through a very strange experience, and am beginning to doubt whether I was justified in branding every one on board as madmen because they professed to have seen things which did not seem reasonable to my understanding. Pshaw! I am a fool to let such a trifle unnerve me; and yet, coming as it does after all these alarms, it has an additional significance, for I cannot doubt either Mr. Manson's story or that of the mate, now that I have experienced that which I used formerly to scoff at.

After all it was nothing very alarming—a mere sound, and that was all. I cannot expect that any one reading this, if any one ever should read it, will sympathise with my feelings, or realise the effect which it produced upon me at the time. Supper was over, and I had gone on deck to have a quiet pipe before turning in. The night was very dark—so dark that, standing under the quarter-boat, I was unable to see the officer upon the bridge. I think I have already mentioned the extraordinary silence which prevails in these frozen seas. In other parts of the world, be they ever so barren, there is some slight vibration of the air—some faint hum, be it from the distant haunts of men, or from the leaves of the trees, or the wings of the birds, or even the faint rustle of the grass that covers the ground. One may not actively perceive the sound, and yet if it were withdrawn it would be missed. It is only here in these Arctic seas that stark, unfathomable stillness obtrudes itself upon you in all its gruesome reality. You find your tympanum straining to catch some little murmur, and dwelling eagerly upon every accidental sound within the vessel. In this state I was leaning against the bulwarks when there arose from the ice almost directly underneath me a cry, sharp and shrill, upon the silent air of the night, beginning, as it seemed to me, at a note such as prima donna never reached, and mounting from that ever higher and higher until it culminated in a long wail of agony, which might have been the last cry of a lost soul. The ghastly scream is still ringing in my ears. Grief, unutterable grief, seemed to be expressed in it, and a great longing, and yet through it all there was an occasional wild note of exultation. It shrilled out from close beside me, and yet as I glared into the darkness I could discern nothing. I waited some little time, but without hearing any repetition of the sound, so I came below, more shaken than I have ever been in my life before. As I came down the companion I met Mr. Milne coming up to relieve the watch. "Weel, Doctor," he said, "maybe that's auld wives' clavers tae? Did ye no hear it skirling? Maybe that's a supersteetion? What d'ye think o't noo?" I was obliged to apologise to the honest fellow, and acknowledge that I was as puzzled by it as he was. Perhaps to-morrow things may look different. At present I dare hardly write all that I think. Reading it again in days to come, when I have shaken off all these associations, I should despise myself for having been so weak.

September 18th.—Passed a restless and uneasy night, still haunted by that strange sound. The Captain does not look as if he had had much repose either, for his face is haggard and his eyes bloodshot. I have not told him of my adventure of last night, nor shall I. He is already restless and excited, standing up, sitting down, and apparently utterly unable to keep still.

A fine lead appeared in the pack this morning, as I had expected, and we were able to cast off our ice-anchor, and steam about twelve miles in a west-sou'-westerly direction. We were then brought to a halt by a great floe as massive as any which we have left behind us. It bars our progress completely, so we can do nothing but anchor again and wait until it breaks up, which it will probably do within twenty-four hours, if the wind holds. Several bladder-nosed seals were seen swimming in the water, and one was shot, an immense creature more than eleven feet long. They are fierce, pugnacious animals, and are said to be more than a match for a bear. Fortunately they are slow and clumsy in their movements, so that there is little danger in attacking them upon the ice.

The Captain evidently does not think we have seen the last of our troubles, though why he should take a gloomy view of the situation is more than I can fathom, since every one else on board considers that we have had a miraculous escape, and are sure now to reach the open sea.

"I suppose you think it's all right now, Doctor?" he said, as we sat together after dinner.

"I hope so," I answered.

"We mustn't be too sure—and yet no doubt you are right. We'll all be in the arms of our own true loves before long, lad, won't we? But we mustn't be too sure—we mustn't be too sure."

He sat silent a little, swinging his leg thoughtfully backwards and forwards. "Look here," he continued; "it's a dangerous place this, even at its best—a treacherous, dangerous place. I have known men cut off very suddenly in a land like this. A slip would do it sometimes—a single slip, and down you go through a crack, and only a bubble on the green water to show where it was that you sank. It's a queer thing," he continued with a nervous laugh, "but all the years I've been in this country I never once thought of making a will—not that I have anything to leave in particular, but still when a man is exposed to danger he should have everything arranged and ready—don't you think so?"

"Certainly," I answered, wondering what on earth he was driving at.

"He feels better for knowing it's all settled," he went on. "Now if anything should ever befall me, I hope that you will look after things for me. There is very little in the cabin, but such as it is I should like it to be sold, and the money divided in the same proportion as the oil-money among the crew. The chronometer I wish you to keep yourself as some slight remembrance of our voyage. Of course all this is a mere precaution, but I thought I would take the opportunity of speaking to you about it. I suppose I might rely upon you if there were any necessity?"

"Most assuredly," I answered; "and since you are taking this step, I may as well"—

"You! you!" he interrupted. "*You're* all right. What the devil is the matter with *you*? There, I didn't mean to be peppery, but I don't like to hear a young fellow, that has hardly began life, speculating about death. Go up on deck and get some fresh air into your lungs instead of talking nonsense in the cabin, and encouraging me to do the same."

The more I think of this conversation of ours the less do I like it. Why should the man be settling his affairs at the very time when we seem to be emerging from all danger? There must be some method in his madness. Can it be that he contemplates suicide? I remember that upon one occasion he spoke in a deeply reverent manner of the heinousness of the crime of self-destruction. I shall keep my eye upon him, however, and though I cannot obtrude upon the privacy of his cabin, I shall at least make a point of remaining on deck as long as he stays up.

Mr. Milne pooh-poohs my fears, and says it is only the "skipper's little way." He himself takes a very rosy view of the situation. According to him we shall be out of the ice by the day after to-morrow, pass Jan Meyen two days after that, and sight Shetland in little more than a week. I hope he may not be too sanguine. His opinion may be fairly balanced against the gloomy precautions of the Captain, for he is an old and experienced seaman, and weighs his words well before uttering them.

The long-impending catastrophe has come at last. I hardly know what to write about it. The Captain is gone. He may come back to us again alive, but I fear me—I fear me. It is now seven o'clock of the morning of the 19th of September. I have spent the whole night traversing the great ice-floe in front of us with a party of seamen in the hope of coming upon some trace of him, but in vain. I shall try to give some account of the circumstances which attended upon his disappearance. Should any one ever chance to read the words which I put down, I trust they will remember that I do not write from conjecture or from hearsay, but that I, a sane and educated man, am describing accurately what actually occurred before my very eyes. My inferences are my own, but I shall be answerable for the facts.

The Captain remained in excellent spirits after the conversation which I have recorded. He appeared to be nervous and impatient, however, frequently changing his position, and moving his limbs in an aimless choreic way which is characteristic of him at times. In a quarter of an hour he went upon deck seven times, only to descend after a few hurried paces. I followed him each time, for there was something about his face which confirmed my resolution of not letting him out of my sight. He seemed to observe the effect which his movements had produced, for he endeavoured by an over-done hilarity, laughing boisterously at the very smallest of jokes, to quiet my apprehensions.

After supper he went on to the poop once more, and I with him. The night was dark and very still, save for the melancholy soughing of the wind among the spars. A thick cloud was coming up from the northwest, and the ragged tentacles which it threw out in front of it were drifting across the face of the moon, which only shone now and again through a rift in the wrack. The Captain paced rapidly backwards and forwards, and then seeing me still dogging him, he came across and hinted that he thought I should be better below—which, I need hardly say, had the effect of strengthening my resolution to remain on deck.

I think he forgot about my presence after this, for he stood silently leaning over the taffrail, and peering out across the great desert of snow, part of which lay in shadow, while part glittered mistily in the moonlight. Several times I could see by his movements that he was referring to his watch, and once he muttered a short sentence, of which I could only catch the one word "ready." I confess to having felt an eerie feeling creeping over me as I watched the loom of his tall figure through the darkness, and noted how completely he fulfilled the idea of a man who is keeping a tryst. A tryst with whom? Some vague perception began to dawn upon me as I pieced one fact with another, but I was utterly unprepared for the sequel.

By the sudden intensity of his attitude I felt that he saw something. I crept up behind him. He was staring with an eager questioning gaze at what seemed to be a wreath of mist, blown swiftly in a line with the ship. It was a dim, nebulous body, devoid of shape, sometimes more, sometimes less apparent, as the light fell on it. The moon was dimmed in its brilliancy at the moment by a canopy of thinnest cloud, like the coating of an anemone.

"Coming, lass, coming," cried the skipper, in a voice of unfathomable tenderness and compassion, like one who soothes a beloved one by some favour long looked for, and as pleasant to bestow as to receive.

What followed happened in an instant. I had no power to interfere. He gave one spring to the top of the bulwarks, and another which took him on to the ice, almost to the feet of the pale misty figure. He held out his hands as if to clasp it, and so ran into the darkness with outstretched arms and loving words. I still stood rigid and motionless, straining my eyes after his retreating form, until his voice died away in the distance. I never thought to see him again, but at that moment the moon shone out brilliantly through a chink in the cloudy heaven, and illuminated the great field of ice. Then I saw his dark figure already a very long way off, running with prodigious speed across the frozen plain. That was the last glimpse which we caught of him—perhaps the last we ever shall. A party was organised to follow him, and I accompanied them, but the men's hearts were not in the work, and nothing was found. Another will be formed within a few hours. I can hardly believe I have not been dreaming, or suffering from some hideous nightmare, as I write these things down.

7:30 p.m.—Just returned dead beat and utterly tired out from a second unsuccessful search for the Captain. The floe is of enormous extent, for though we have traversed at least twenty miles of its surface, there has been no sign of its coming to an end. The frost has been so severe of late that the overlying snow is frozen as hard as granite, otherwise we might have had the footsteps to guide us. The crew are anxious that we should cast off and steam round the floe and so to the southward, for the ice has opened up during the night, and the sea is visible upon the horizon. They argue that Captain Craigie is certainly dead, and that we are all risking our lives to no purpose by remaining when we have an opportunity of escape. Mr. Milne and I have had the greatest difficulty in persuading them to wait until to-morrow night, and have been compelled to promise that we will not under any circumstances delay our departure longer than that. We propose therefore to take a few hours' sleep, and then to start upon a final search.

September 20th, evening.—I crossed the ice this morning with a party of men exploring the southern part of the floe, while Mr. Milne went off in a northerly direction.

We pushed on for ten or twelve miles without seeing a trace of any living thing except a single bird, which fluttered a great way over our heads, and which by its flight I should judge to have been a falcon. The southern extremity of the ice field tapered away into a long narrow spit which projected out into the sea. When we came to the base of this promontory, the men halted, but I begged them to continue to the extreme end of it, that we might have the satisfaction of knowing that no possible chance had been neglected.

We had hardly gone a hundred yards before M'Donald of Peterhead cried out that he saw something in front of us, and began to run. We all got a glimpse of it and ran too. At first it was only a vague darkness against the white ice, but as we raced along together it took the shape of a man, and eventually of the man of whom we were in search. He was lying face downwards upon a frozen bank. Many little crystals of ice and feathers of snow had drifted on to him as he lay, and sparkled upon his dark seaman's jacket. As we came up some wandering puff of wind caught these tiny flakes in its vortex, and they whirled up into the air, partially descended again, and then, caught once more in the current, sped rapidly away in the direction of the sea. To my eyes it seemed but a snow-drift, but many of my companions averred that it started up in the shape of a woman, stooped over the corpse and kissed it, and then hurried away across the floe. I have learned never to ridicule any man's opinion, however strange it may seem. Sure it is that Captain Nicholas Craigie had met with no painful end, for there was a bright smile upon his blue pinched features, and his hands were still outstretched as though grasping at the strange visitor which had summoned him away into the dim world that lies beyond the grave.

We buried him the same afternoon with the ship's ensign around him, and a thirty-two pound shot at his feet. I read the burial service, while the rough sailors wept like children, for there were many who owed much to his kind heart, and who showed now the affection which his strange ways had repelled during his lifetime. He went off the grating with a dull, sullen splash, and as I looked into the green water I saw him go down, down, down until he was but a little flickering patch of white hanging upon the outskirts of eternal darkness. Then even that faded away, and he was gone. There he shall lie, with his secret and his sorrows and his mystery all still buried in his breast, until that great day when the sea shall give up its dead, and Nicholas Craigie come out from among the ice with the smile upon his face, and his stiffened arms outstretched in greeting. I pray that his lot may be a happier one in that life than it has been in this.

I shall not continue my journal. Our road to home lies plain and clear before us, and the great ice field will soon be but a remembrance of the past. It will be some time before I get over the shock produced by recent events. When I began this record of our voyage I little thought of how I should be compelled to finish it. I am writing these final words in the lonely cabin, still starting at times and fancying I hear the quick nervous step of the dead man upon the deck above me. I entered his cabin to-night, as was my duty, to make a list of his effects in order that they might be entered in the official log. All was as it had been upon my previous visit, save that the picture which I have described as having hung at the end of his bed had been cut out of its frame, as with a knife, and was gone. With this last link in a strange chain of evidence I close my diary of the voyage of the *Pole-Star*.

[NOTE by Dr. John M'Alister Ray, senior.—I have read over the strange events connected with the death of the Captain of the *Pole-Star*, as narrated in the journal of my son. That everything occurred exactly as he describes it I have the fullest confidence, and, indeed, the most positive certainty, for I know him to be a strong-nerved and unimaginative man, with the strictest regard for veracity. Still, the story is, on the face of it, so vague and so improbable, that I was long opposed to its publication. Within the last few days, however, I have had independent testimony upon the subject which throws a new light upon it. I had run down to Edinburgh to attend a meeting of the British Medical Association, when I chanced to come across Dr. P———, an old college chum of mine, now practising at Saltash, in Devonshire. Upon my telling him of this experience of my son's, he declared to me that he was familiar with the man, and proceeded, to my no small surprise, to give me a description of him, which tallied remarkably well with that given in the journal, except that he depicted him as a younger man. According to his account, he had been engaged to a young lady of singular beauty residing upon the Cornish coast. During his absence at sea his betrothed had died under circumstances of peculiar horror.]

The Cigarette Case

Oliver Onions

"A cigarette, Loder?" I said, offering my case. For the moment Loder was not smoking; for long enough he had not been talking.

"Thanks," he replied, taking not only the cigarette, but the case also. The others went on talking; Loder became silent again; but I noticed that he kept my cigarette case in his hand, and looked at it from time to time with an interest that neither its design nor its costliness seemed to explain. Presently I caught his eye.

"A pretty case," he remarked, putting it down on the table. "I once had one exactly like it."

I answered that they were in every shop window.

"Oh yes," he said, putting aside any question of rarity. . . . "I lost mine."

"Oh? . . ."

He laughed. "Oh, that's all right—I got it back again—don't be afraid I'm going to claim yours. But the way I lost it—found it—the whole thing—was rather curious. I've never been able to explain it. I wonder if you could?"

I answered that I certainly couldn't till I'd heard it, whereupon Loder, taking up the silver case again and holding it in his hand as he talked, began:

"This happened in Provence, when I was about as old as Marsham there—and every bit as romantic. I was there with Carroll—you remember poor old Carroll and what a blade of a boy he was—as romantic as four Marshams rolled into one. (Excuse me, Marsham, won't you? It's a romantic tale, you see, or at least the setting is.) . . . We were in Provence, Carroll and I; twenty-four or thereabouts; romantic, as I say; and—and this happened.

"And it happened on the top of a whole lot of other things, you must understand, the things that do happen when you're twenty-four. If it hadn't been Provence, it would have been somewhere else, I suppose, nearly, if not quite as good; but this was Provence, that smells (as you might say) of twenty-four as it smells of argelasse and wild lavender and broom. . . .

"We'd had the dickens of a walk of it, just with knapsacks—had started somewhere in the Ardèche and tramped south through the vines and almonds and olives—Montélimar, Orange, Avignon, and a fortnight at that blanched skeleton of a town, Les Baux. We'd nothing to do, and had gone just where we liked, or rather just where Carroll had liked; and Carroll had had the *De Bello Gallico* in his pocket, and had had a notion, I fancy, of taking in the whole ground of the Roman conquest —I remember he lugged me off to some place or other, Pourrières I believe its name was, because—I forget how many thousands—were killed in a river-bed there, and they stove in the water-casks so that if the men wanted water they'd have to go forward and fight for it. And then we'd gone on to Arles, where Carroll had fallen in love with everything that had a bow of black velvet in her hair, and after that Tarascon, Nîmes, and so on, the usual round—I won't bother you with that. In a word, we'd had two months of it, eating almonds and apricots from the trees, watching the women at the communal washing-fountains under the dark plane-trees, singing *Magali* and the *Qué Cantes*, and Carroll yarning away all the time about Caesar and Vercingetorix and Dante, and trying to learn Provençal so that he could read the stuff in the *Journal des Félibriges* that he'd never have looked at if it had been in English. . . .

"Well, we got to Darbisson. We'd run across some young chap or other—Rangon his name was—who was a vine-planter in those parts, and Rangon had asked us to spend a couple of days with him, with him and his mother, if we happened to be in the neighbourhood. So as we might as well happen to be there as anywhere else, we sent him a postcard and went. This would be in June or early in July. All day we walked across a plain of vines, past hurdles of wattled *cannes* and great wind-screens of velvety cypresses, sixty feet high, all white with dust on the north side of 'em, for the mistral was having its three-days' revel, and it whistled and roared through the *cannes* till scores of yards of 'em at a time were bowed nearly to the earth. A roaring day it was, I remember. . . . But the wind fell a little late in the afternoon, and we were poring over what it had left of our Ordnance Survey—like fools, we'd got the unmounted paper maps instead of the linen ones—when Rangon himself found us, coming out to meet us in a very badly turnedout trap. He drove us back himself, through Darbisson, to the house, a mile and a half beyond it, where he lived with his mother.

"He spoke no English, Rangon didn't, though, of course, both French and Provençal; and as he drove us, there was Carroll, using him as a Franco-Provençal dictionary, peppering him with questions about the names of things in the patois—I beg its pardon, the language—though there's a good deal of my eye and Betty Martin about that, and I fancy this Félibrige business will be in a good many pieces when Frédéric Mistral is under that Court-of-Love pavilion arrangement he's had put up for himself in the graveyard at Maillanne. If the language has got to go, well, it's got to go, I suppose; and while I personally don't want to give it a kick, I rather sympathise with the Government. Those jaunts of a Sunday out to Les Baux, for instance, with paper lanterns and Bengal fire and a fellow spouting O blanche *Venus d'Arles*—they're well enough, and compare favourably with our Bank Holidays and Sunday League picnics, but . . . but that's nothing to do with my tale after all. . . . So he drove on, and by the time we got to Rangon's house Carroll had learned the greater part of *Magali*. . . .

"As you, no doubt, know, it's a restricted sort of life in some respects that a young *vigneron* lives in those parts, and it was as we reached the house that Rangon remembered something— or he might have been trying to tell us as we came along for all I know, and not been able to get a word in edgeways for Carroll and his Provençal. It seemed that his mother was away from home for some days—apologies of the most profound, of course; our host was the soul of courtesy, though he did try to get at us a bit later. . . . We expressed our polite regrets, naturally; but I didn't quite see at first what difference it made. I only began to see when Rangon, with more apologies, told us that we should have to go back to Darbisson for dinner. It appeared that when Madame Rangon went away for a few days she dispersed the whole of the female side of her establishment also, and she'd left her son with nobody to look after him except an old man we'd seen in the yard mending one of these double-cylindered sulphur-sprinklers they clap across the horse's back and drive between the rows of vines. . . . Rangon explained all this as we stood in the hall drinking an *apéritif*—a hall crowded with oak furniture and photographs and a cradle-like bread-crib and doors opening to right and left to the other rooms of the ground floor. He had also, it seemed, to ask us to be so infinitely obliging as to excuse him for one hour after dinner—our postcard had come unexpectedly, he said, and already he had made an appointment with his agent about the *vendange* for the coming autumn. . . . We begged him, of course, not to allow us to interfere with his business in the slightest degree. He thanked us a thousand times.

"'But though we dine in the village, we will take our own wine with us,' he said, 'a wine *surfin*—one of my wines—you shall see—'

"Then he showed us round his place—I forget how many hundreds of acres of vines, and into the great building with the presses and pumps and casks and the huge barrel they call the thunderbolt—and about seven o'clock we walked back to Darbisson to dinner, carrying our wine with us. I think the restaurant we dined in was the only one in the place, and our gaillard of a host—he was a straight-backed, well-set-up chap, with rather fine eyes—did us on the whole pretty well. His wine certainly was good stuff, and set our tongues going. . . .

"A moment ago I said a fellow like Rangon leads a restricted sort of life in those parts. I saw this more clearly as dinner went on. We dined by an open window, from which we could see the stream with the planks across it where the women washed clothes during the day and assembled in the evening for gossip. There were a dozen or so of them there as we dined, laughing and chatting in low tones—they all seemed pretty—it was quickly falling dusk—all the girls are pretty then, and are quite conscious of it—you know, Marsham. Behind them, at the end of the street, one of these great cypress wind-screens showed black against the sky, a ragged edge something like the line the needle draws on a rainfall chart; and you could only tell whether they were men or women under the plantains by their voices rippling and chattering and suddenly a deeper note. . . . Once I heard a muffled scuffle and a sound like a kiss. . . . It was then that Rangon's little trouble came out. . . .

"It seemed that he didn't know any girls—wasn't allowed to know any girls. The girls of the village were pretty enough, but you see how it was—he'd a position to keep up—appearances to maintain—couldn't be familiar during the year with the girls who gathered his grapes for him in the autumn. . . . And as soon as Carroll gave him a chance, *he* began to ask *us* questions, about England, English girls, the liberty they had, and so on.

"Of course, we couldn't tell him much he hadn't heard already, but that made no difference; he could stand any amount of that, our strapping young *vigneron*; and he asked us questions by the dozen, that we both tried to answer at once. And his delight and envy! . . . What! In England did the young men see the young women of their own class without restraint—the sisters of their friends *même*—even at the house? Was it permitted that they drank tea with them in the afternoon, or went without invitation to pass the *soirée*? . . . He had all the later Prévosts in his room, he told us (I don't doubt he had the earlier ones also); Prévost and the Disestablishment between them must be playing the mischief with the convent system of education for young girls; and our young man was—what d'you call it?—'Co-ed'–co-educationalist—by Jove, yes! . . . He seemed to marvel that we should have left a country so blessed as England to visit his dusty, wild-lavender-smelling, girl-less Provence. . . . You don't know half your luck, Marsham. . . .

"Well, we talked after this fashion—we'd left the dining-room of the restaurant and had planted ourselves on a bench outside with Rangon between us—when Rangon suddenly looked at his watch and said it was time he was off to see this agent of his. Would we take a walk, he asked us, and meet him again there? he said. . . . But as his agent lived in the direction of his own home, we said we'd meet him at the house in an hour or so. Off he went, envying every Englishman who stepped, I don't doubt. . . . I told you how old—how young—we were. . . . Heigho! . . .

"Well, off goes Rangon, and Carroll and I got up, stretched ourselves, and took a walk. We walked a mile or so, until it began to get pretty dark, and then turned; and it was as we came into the blackness of one of these cypress hedges that the thing I'm telling you of happened. The hedge took a sharp turn at that point; as we came round the angle we saw a couple of women's figures hardly more than twenty yards ahead—don't know how they got there so suddenly, I'm sure; and that same moment I found my foot on something small and white and glimmering on the grass.

"I picked it up. It was a handkerchief—a woman's—embroidered—

"The two figures ahead of us were walking in our direction; there was every probability that the handkerchief belonged to one of them; so we stepped out. . . .

"At my 'Pardon, madame,' and lifted hat one of the figures turned her head; then, to my surprise, she spoke in English—cultivated English. I held out the handkerchief. It belonged to the elder lady of the two, the one who had spoken, a very gentle-voiced old lady, older by very many years than her companion. She took the handkerchief and thanked me. . . .

"Somebody—Sterne, isn't it?—says that Englishmen don't travel to see Englishmen. I don't know whether he'd stand to that in the case of Englishwomen; Carroll and I didn't. . . . We were walking rather slowly along, four abreast across the road; we asked permission to introduce ourselves, did so, and received some name in return which, strangely enough, I've entirely forgotten—I only remember that the ladies were aunt and niece, and lived at Darbisson. They shook their heads when I mentioned M. Rangon's name and said we were visiting him. They didn't know him. . . .

"I'd never been in Darbisson before, and I haven't been since, so I don't know the map of the village very well. But the place isn't very big, and the house at which we stopped in twenty minutes or so is probably there yet. It had a large double door—a double door in two senses, for it was a big *porte-cochère* with a smaller door inside it, and an iron grille shutting in the whole. The gentle-voiced old lady had already taken a key from her reticule and was thanking us again for the little service of the handkerchief; then, with the little gesture one makes when one has found oneself on the point of omitting a courtesy, she gave a little musical laugh.

"'But,' she said with a little movement of invitation, 'one sees so few compatriots here—if you have the time to come in and smoke a cigarette . . . also the cigarette,' she added, with another rippling laugh, 'for we have few callers, and live alone—'

"Hastily as I was about to accept, Carroll was before me, professing a nostalgia for the sound of the English tongue that made his recent protestations about Provençal a shameless hypocrisy. Persuasive young rascal, Carroll was—poor chap. . . . So the elder lady opened the grille and the wooden door beyond it, and we entered.

"By the light of the candle which the younger lady took from a bracket just within the door we saw that we were in a handsome hall or vestibule; and my wonder that Rangon had made no mention of what was apparently a considerable establishment was increased by the fact that its tenants must be known to be English and could be seen to be entirely charming. I couldn't understand it, and I'm afraid hypotheses rushed into my head that cast doubts on the Rangons—you know—whether they were all right. We knew nothing about our young planter, you see. . . .

"I looked about me. There were tubs here and there against the walls, gaily painted, with glossy-leaved aloes and palms in them—one of the aloes, I remember, was flowering; a little fountain in the middle made a tinkling noise; we put our caps on a carved and gilt console table; and before us rose a broad staircase with shallow steps of spotless stone and a beautiful wrought-iron handrail. At the top of the staircase were more palms and aloes, and double doors painted in a clear grey.

"We followed our hostesses up the staircase. I can hear yet the sharp clean click our boots made on that hard shiny stone—see the lights of the candle gleaming on the handrail. . . . The young girl—she was not much more than a girl-pushed at the doors, and we went in.

"The room we entered was all of a piece with the rest for rather old-fashioned fineness. It was large, lofty, beautifully kept. Carroll went round for Miss . . . whatever her name was . . . lighting candles in sconces; and as the flames crept up they glimmered on a beautifully polished floor, which was bare except for an Eastern rug here and there. The elder lady had sat down in a gilt chair, Louis Fourteenth I should say, with a striped rep of the colour of a petunia; and I really don't know—don't smile, Smith—what induced me to lead her to it by the finger-tips, bending over her hand for a moment as she sat down. There was an old tambour-frame behind her chair, I remember, and a vast oval mirror with clustered candle-brackets filled the greater part of the farther wall, the brightest and clearest glass I've ever seen. . . ."

He paused, looking at my cigarette case, which he had taken into his hand again. He smiled at some recollection or other, and it was a minute or so before he continued.

"I must admit that I found it a little annoying, after what we'd been talking about at dinner an hour before, that Rangon wasn't with us. I still couldn't understand how he could have neighbours so charming without knowing about them, but I didn't care to insist on this to the old lady, who for all I knew might have her own reasons for keeping to herself. And, after all, it was our place to return Rangon's hospitality in London if he ever came there, not, so to speak, on his own doorstep.... So presently I forgot all about Rangon, and I'm pretty sure that Carroll, who was talking to his companion of some Félibrige junketing or other and having the air of Gounod's *Mireille* hummed softly over to him, didn't waste a thought on him either. Soon Carroll—you remember what a pretty crooning, humming voice he had—soon Carroll was murmuring what they call 'seconds,' but so low that the sound hardly came across the room; and I came in with a soft bass note from time to time. No instrument, you know; just an unaccompanied murmur no louder than an Æolian harp; and it sounded infinitely sweet and plaintive and—what shall I say?—weak—attenuated—faint—'pale' you might almost say—in that formal, rather old-fashioned *salon*, with that great clear oval mirror throwing back the still flames of the candles in the sconces on the walls. Outside the wind had now fallen completely; all was very quiet; and suddenly in a voice not much louder than a sigh, Carroll's companion was singing *Oft in the Stilly Night*— you know it...."

He broke off again to murmur the beginning of the air. Then, with a little laugh for which we saw no reason, he went on again:

"Well, I'm not going to try to convince you of such a special and delicate thing as the charm of that hour—it wasn't more than an hour—it would be all about an hour we stayed. Things like that just have to be said and left; you destroy them the moment you begin to insist on them; we've every one of us had experiences like that, and don't say much about them. I was as much in love with my old lady as Carroll evidently was with his young one—I can't tell you why—being in love has just to be taken for granted too, I suppose ... Marsham understands.... We smoked our cigarettes, and sang again, once more filling that clear-painted, quiet apartment with a murmuring no louder than if a light breeze found that the bells of a bed of flowers were really bells and played on 'em. The old lady moved her fingers gently on the round table by the side of her chair ... oh, infinitely pretty it was.... Then Carroll wandered off into the *Qué Cantes*—awfully pretty—'It is not for myself I sing, but for my friend who is near me'—and I can't tell you how like four old friends we were, those two so oddly met ladies and Carroll and myself.... And so to *Oft in the Stilly Night* again....

"But for all the sweetness and the glamour of it, we couldn't stay on indefinitely, and I wondered what time it was, but didn't ask—anything to do with clocks and watches would have seemed a cold and mechanical sort of thing just then.... And when presently we both got up neither Carroll nor I asked to be allowed to call again in the morning to thank them for a charming hour. . . . And they seemed to feel the same as we did about it. There was no 'hoping that we should meet again in London'—neither an au revoir nor a good-bye—just a tacit understanding that that hour should remain isolated, accepted like a good gift without looking the gift-horse in the mouth, single, unattached to any hours before or after— I don't know whether you see what I mean. . . . Give me a match somebody. . . .

"And so we left, with no more than looks exchanged and finger-tips resting between the back of our hands and our lips for a moment. We found our way out by ourselves, down that shallow-stepped staircase with the handsome handrail, and let ourselves out of the double door and grille, closing it softly. We made for the village without speaking a word. . . . Heigho! . . ."

Loder had picked up the cigarette case again, but for all the way his eyes rested on it I doubt whether he really saw it. I'm pretty sure he didn't; I knew when he did by the glance he shot at me, as much as to say "I see you're wondering where the cigarette case comes in." . . . He resumed with another little laugh.

"Well," he continued, "we got back to Rangon's house. I really don't blame Rangon for the way he took it when we told him, you know—he thought we were pulling his leg, of course, and he wasn't having any; not he l There were no English ladies in Darbisson, he said. . . . We told him as nearly as we could just where the house was—we weren't very precise, I'm afraid, for the village had been in darkness as we had come through it, and I had to admit that the cypress hedge I tried to describe where we'd met our friends was a good deal like other cypress hedges—and, as I say, Rangon wasn't taking any. I myself was rather annoyed that he should think we were returning his hospitality by trying to get at him, and it wasn't very easy either to explain in my French and Carroll's Provençal that we were going to let the thing stand as it was and weren't going to call on our charming friends again. . . . The end of it was that Rangon just laughed and yawned. . . .

"'I knew it was good, my wine,' he said, 'but—' a shrug said the rest. 'Not so good as all that,' he meant. . . .

"Then he gave us our candles, showed us to our rooms, shook hands, and marched off to his own room and the Prévosts.

"I dreamed of my old lady half the night.

"After coffee the next morning I put my hand into my pocket for my cigarette case and didn't find it. I went through all my pockets, and then I asked Carroll if he'd got it.

"'No,' he replied. . . . 'Think you left it behind at that place last night!'

"'Yes; did you?' Rangon popped in with a twinkle.

"I went through all my pockets again. No cigarette case. . . .

"Of course, it was possible that I'd left it behind, and I was annoyed again. I didn't want to go back, you see. . . . But, on the other hand, I didn't want to lose the case—it was a present—and Rangon's smile nettled me a good deal, too. It was both a challenge to our truthfulness and a testimonial to that very good wine of his. . . .

"'Might have done,' I grunted. . . . 'Well, in that case we'll go and get it.'

"'If one tried the restaurant first—?' Rangon suggested, smiling again.

"'By all means,' said I stuffily, though I remembered having the case after we'd left the restaurant.

"We were round at the restaurant by half-past nine. The case wasn't there. I'd known jolly well beforehand it wasn't, and I saw Rangon's mouth twitching with amusement.

"'So we now seek the abode of these English ladies, *hein?*' he said.

"'Yes,' said I; and we left the restaurant and strode through the village by the way we'd taken the evening before. . . .

"That *vigneron's* smile became more and more irritating to me. . . . 'It is then the *next* village?' he said presently, as we left the last house and came out into the open plain.

"We went back. . . .

"I was irritated because we were two to one, you see, and Carroll backed me up. 'A double door, with a grille in front of it,' he repeated for the fiftieth time. . . . Rangon merely replied that it wasn't our good faith he doubted. He didn't actually use the word 'drunk'. . . .

"'*Mais tiens,*' he said suddenly, trying to conceal his mirth. '*Si c'est possible* . . . *si c'est possible* . . . a double door with a grille But perhaps that I know it, the domicile of these so elusive ladies. . . . Come this way.'

"He took us back along a plantain-groved street, and suddenly turned up an alley that was little more than two gutters and a crack of sky overhead between two broken-tiled roofs. It was a dilapidated, deserted *ruelle*, and I was positively angry when Rangon pointed to a blistered old *porte-cochère* with a half-unhinged railing in front of it.

"'Is it that, your house?' he asked.

"'No,' says I, and 'No,' says Carroll . . . and off we started again. . . .

"But another half-hour brought us back to the same place, and Carroll scratched his head.

"'Who lives there, anyway?' he said, glowering at the *porte-cochère*, chin forward, hands in pockets.

"'Nobody,' says Rangon, as much as to say 'look at it!' 'M'sieu then meditates taking it?' . . .

THE CIGARETTE CASE

"Then I struck in, quite out of temper by this time.

"'How much would the rent be?' I asked, as if I really thought of taking the place just to get back at him.

"He mentioned something ridiculously small in the way of francs.

"'One might at least see the place,' says I. 'Can the key be got?'

"He bowed. The key was at the baker's, not a hundred yards away, he said. . . .

"We got the key. It was the key of the inner wooden door—that grid of rusty iron didn't need one—it came clean off its single hinge when Carroll touched it. Carroll opened, and we stood for a moment motioning to one another to step in. Then Rangon went in first, and I heard him murmur 'Pardon, Mesdames'. . . .

"Now this is the odd part. We passed into a sort of vestibule or hall, with a burst lead pipe in the middle of a dry tank in the centre of it. There was a broad staircase rising in front of us to the first floor, and double doors just seen in the half-light at the head of the stairs. Old tubs stood against the walls, but the palms and aloes in them were dead—only a cabbage-stalk or two—and the rusty hoops lay on the ground about them. One tub had come to pieces entirely and was no more than a heap of staves on a pile of spilt earth. And everywhere, everywhere was dust—the floor was an inch deep in dust and old plaster that muffled our footsteps, cobwebs hung like old dusters on the walls, a regular goblin's tatter of cobwebs draped the little bracket inside the door, and the wrought-iron of the hand-rail was closed up with webs in which not even a spider moved. The whole thing was preposterous. . . .

"'It is possible that for even a less rental—' Rangon murmured, dragging his forefinger across the hand-rail and leaving an inch-deep furrow. . . .

"'Come upstairs,' said I suddenly. . . .

"Up we went. All was in the same state there. A clutter of stuff came down as I pushed at the double doors of the *salon*, and I had to strike a stinking French sulphur match to see into the room at all. Underfoot was like walking on thicknesses of flannel, and except where we put our feet the place was as printless as a snowfield— dust, dust, unbroken grey dust. My match burned down. . . .

"'Wait a minute—I've a *bougie*,' said Carroll, and struck the wax match. . . .

"There were the old sconces, with never a candle-end in them. There was the large oval mirror. but hardly reflecting Carroll's match for the dust on it. And the broken chairs were there, all giltless, and the rickety old round table. . . .

"But suddenly I darted forward. Something new and bright on the table twinkled with the light of Carroll's match. The match went out, and by the time Carroll had lighted another I had stopped. I wanted Rangon to see what was on the table. . . .

"'You'll see by my footprints how far from that table *I've* been,' I said. 'Will you pick it up?'

"And Rangon, stepping forward, picked up from the middle of the table—my cigarette case."

Loder had finished. Nobody spoke. For quite a minute nobody spoke, and then Loder himself broke the silence, turning to me.

"Make anything of it?" he said. I lifted my eyebrows. "Only your *vigneron*'s explanation—" I began, but stopped again, seeing that wouldn't do.

"*Any*body make anything of it?" said Loder, turning from one to another.

I gathered from Smith's face that he thought *one* thing might be made of it—namely, that Loder had invented the whole tale. But even Smith didn't speak.

"Were any English ladies ever found to have lived in the place—murdered, you know-bodies found and all that?" young Marsham asked diffidently, yearning for an obvious completeness.

"Not that we could ever learn," Loder replied. "We made inquiries too. . . . So you all give it up? Well, so do I. . . ."

And he rose. As he walked to the door, myself following him to get his hat and stick, I heard him humming softly the lines—they are from *Oft in the Stilly Night*—

> "I seem like one who treads alone
> Some banquet-hall deserted,
> Whose guests are fled, whose garlands dead,
> And all but he—departed!"

A Curious Experience

Mrs. Henry Wood

WHAT I AM ABOUT TO TELL OF TOOK PLACE DURING THE LAST YEAR OF JOHN Whitney's life, now many years ago. We could never account for it, or understand it: but it occurred (at least, so far as our experience of it went) just as I relate it.

It was not the custom for schools to give a long holiday at Easter then: one week at most. Dr. Frost allowed us from the Thursday in Passion week, to the following Thursday; and many of the boys spent it at school.

Easter was late that year, and the weather lovely. On the Wednesday in Easter week, the Squire and Mrs. Todhetley drove over to spend the day at Whitney Hall, Tod and I being with them. Sir John and Lady Whitney were beginning to be anxious about John's health—their eldest son. He had been ailing since the previous Christmas, and he seemed to grow thinner and weaker. It was so perceptible when he got home from school this Easter, that Sir John put himself into a flurry (he was just like the Squire in that and in many another way), and sent an express to Worcester for Henry Carden, asking him to bring Dr. Hastings with him. They came. John wanted care, they said, and they could not discover any specific disease at present. As to his returning to school, they both thought that question might be left with the boy himself. John told them he should prefer to go back, and laughed a little at this fuss being made over him: he should soon be all right, he said; people were apt to lose strength more or less in the spring. He was sixteen then, a slender, upright boy, with a delicate, thoughtful face, dreamy, grey-blue eyes and brown hair, and he was ever gentle, sweet-tempered, and considerate. Sir John related to the Squire what the doctors had said, avowing that he could not "make much out of it."

In the afternoon, when we were out-of-doors on the lawn in the hot sunshine, listening to the birds singing and the cuckoo calling, Featherston came in, the local doctor, who saw John nearly every day. He was a tall, grey, hard-worked man, with a face of care. After talking a few moments with John and his mother, he turned to the rest of us on the grass. The Squire and Sir John were sitting on a garden bench, some wine and lemonade on a little table between them. Featherston shook hands.

"Will you take some?" asked Sir John.

"I don't mind a glass of lemonade with a dash of sherry in it," answered Featherston, lifting his hat to rub his brow. "I have been walking beyond Goose Brook and back, and upon my word it is as hot as midsummer."

"Ay, it is," assented Sir John. "Help yourself, doctor."

He filled a tumbler with what he wanted, brought it over to the opposite bench, and sat down by Mrs. Todhetley. John and his mother were at the other end of it; I sat on the arm. The rest of them, with Helen and Anna, had gone strolling away; to the North Pole, for all we knew.

"John still says he shall go back to school," began Lady Whitney, to Featherston.

"Ay; to-morrow's the day, isn't it, John? Black Thursday, some of you boys call it."

"I like school," said John.

"Almost a pity, though," continued Featherston, looking up and about him. "To be out at will all day in this soft air, under the blue skies and the sunbeams, might be of more benefit to you, Master John, than being cooped up in a close school-room."

"You hear, John!" cried Lady Whitney. "I wish you would persuade him to take a longer rest at home, Mr. Featherston!"

Mr. Featherston stooped for his tumbler, which he had lodged on the smooth grass, and took another drink before replying. "If you and John would follow my advice, Lady Whitney, I'd give it."

"Yes?" cried she, all eagerness.

"Take John somewhere for a fortnight, and let him go back to school at the end," said the surgeon. "That would do him good."

"Why, of course it would," called out Sir John, who had been listening. "And I say it shall be done. John, my boy, you and your mother shall go to the seaside—to Aberystwith."

"Well, I don't think I should quite say that, Sir John," said Featherston again. "The seaside would be all very well in this warm weather; but it may not last, it may change to cold and frost. I should suggest one of the inland watering-places, as they are called: where there's a Spa, and a Pump Room, and a Parade, and lots of gay company. It would be lively for him, and a thorough change."

"What a nice idea!" cried Lady Whitney, who was the most unsophisticated woman in the world. "Such as Pumpwater."

"Such as Pumpwater: the very place," agreed Featherston. "Well, were I you, my lady, I would try it for a couple of weeks. Let John take a companion with him; one of his schoolfellows. Here's Johnny Ludlow: he might do."

"I'd rather have Johnny Ludlow than any one," said John.

Remarking that his time was up, for a patient waited for him, and that he must leave us to settle the question, Featherston took his departure. But it appeared to be settled already.

"Johnny can go," spoke up the Squire. "The loss of a fortnight's lessons is not much, compared with doing a little service to a friend. Charming spots are those inland watering-places, and Pumpwater is about the best of them all."

"We must take lodgings," said Lady Whitney presently, when they had done expatiating upon the gauds and glories of Pumpwater. "To stay at an hotel would be so noisy; and expensive besides."

"I know of some," cried Mrs. Todhetley, in sudden thought. "If you could get into Miss Gay's rooms, you would be well off. Do you remember them?"—turning to the Squire. "We stayed at her house on our way from—"

"Why, bless me, to be sure I do," he interrupted. "Somebody had given us Miss Gay's address, and we drove straight to it to see if she had rooms at liberty; she had, and took us in at once. We were so comfortable there that we stayed at Pumpwater three days instead of two."

It was hastily decided that Mrs. Todhetley should write to Miss Gay, and she went indoors to do so. All being well, Lady Whitney meant to start on Saturday.

Miss Gay's answer came punctually, reaching Whitney Hall on Friday morning. It was addressed to Mrs. Todhetley, but Lady Whitney, as had been arranged, opened it. Miss Gay wrote that she should be much pleased to receive Lady Whitney. Her house, as it chanced, was then quite empty; a family, who had been with her six weeks, had just left: so Lady Whitney might take her choice of the rooms, which she would keep vacant until Saturday. In conclusion, she begged Mrs. Todhetley to notice that her address was changed. The old house was too small to accommodate the many kind friends who patronized her, and she had moved into a larger house, superior to the other and in the best position.

Thus all things seemed to move smoothly for our expedition; and we departed by train on the Saturday morning for Pumpwater.

It was a handsome house, standing in the high-road, between the parade and the principal street, and rather different from the houses on each side of it, inasmuch as that it was detached and had a narrow slip of gravelled ground in front. In fact, it looked too large and handsome for a lodging-house; and Lady Whitney, regarding it from the fly which had brought us from the station, wondered whether the driver had made a mistake. It was built of red-brick, with white stone facings; the door, set in a pillared portico, stood in the middle, and three rooms, each with a bay-window, lay one above another on both sides.

But in a moment we saw it was all right. A slight, fair woman, in a slate silk gown, came out and announced herself as Miss Gay. She had a mild, pleasant voice, and a mild, pleasant face, with light falling curls, the fashion then for every one, and she wore a lace cap, trimmed with pink. I took to her and to her face at once.

"I am glad to be here," said Lady Whitney, cordially, in answer to Miss Gay's welcome. "Is there any one who can help with the luggage? We have not brought either man or maid-servant."

"Oh dear, yes, my lady. Please let me show you indoors, and then leave all to me. Susannah! Oh, here you are, Susannah! Where's Charity?—my cousin and chief help-mate, my lady."

A tall, dark person, about Miss Gay's own age, which might be forty, wearing brown ribbon in her hair and a purple bow at her throat, dropped a curtsy to Lady Whitney. This was Susannah. She looked strong-minded and capable. Charity, who came running up the kitchen-stairs, was a smiling young woman-servant, with a coarse apron tied round her, and red arms bared to the elbow.

There were four sitting-rooms on the ground-floor: two in front, with their large bay-windows; two at the back, looking out upon some bright, semi-public gardens.

"A delightful house!" exclaimed Lady Whitney to Miss Gay, after she had looked about a little. "I will take one of these front-rooms for our sitting-room," she added, entering, haphazard, the one on the right of the entrance-hall, and putting down her bag and parasol. "This one, I think, Miss Gay."

"Very good, my lady. And will you now be pleased to walk upstairs and fix upon the bedrooms."

Lady Whitney seemed to fancy the front of the house. "This room shall be my son's; and I should like to have the opposite one for myself," she said, rather hesitatingly, knowing they must be the two best chambers of all. "Can I?"

Miss Gay seemed quite willing. We were in the room over our sitting-room on the right of the house looking to the front. The objection, if it could be called one, came from Susannah.

"You can have the other room, certainly, my lady; but I think the young gentleman would find this one noisy, with all the carriages and carts that pass by, night and morning. The back-rooms are much more quiet."

"But I like noise," put in John; "it seems like company to me. If I could do as I would, I'd never sleep in the country."

"One of the back-rooms is very lively, sir; it has a view of the turning to the Pump Room," persisted Susannah, a sort of suppressed eagerness in her tone; and it struck me that she did not want John to have this front-chamber. "I think you would like it best."

"No," said John, turning round from the window, out of which he had been looking, "I will have this. I shall like to watch the shops down that turning opposite, and the people who go into them."

No more was said. John took this chamber, which was over our sitting-room, Lady Whitney had the other front-chamber, and I had a very good one at the back of John's. And thus we settled down.

Pumpwater is a nice place, as you would know if I gave its proper name, bright and gay, and our house was in the best of situations. The principal street, with its handsome shops, lay to our right; the Parade, leading to the Spa and Pump Room, to our left, and company and carriages were continually passing by. We visited some of the shops and took a look at the Pump Room.

In the evening, when tea was over, Miss Gay came in to speak of the breakfast. Lady Whitney asked her to sit down for a little chat. She wanted to ask about the churches.

"What a very nice house this is!" again observed Lady Whitney presently: for the more she saw of it, the better she found it. "You must pay a high rent for it, Miss Gay."

"Not so high as your ladyship might think," was the answer; "not high at all for what it is. I paid sixty pounds for the little house I used to be in, and I pay only seventy for this."

"Only seventy!" echoed Lady Whitney, in surprise. "How is it you get it so cheaply?"

A waggonette, full of people, was passing just then; Miss Gay seemed to want to watch it by before she answered. We were sitting in the dusk with the blinds up.

"For one thing, it had been standing empty for some time, and I suppose Mr. Bone, the agent, was glad to have my offer," replied Miss Gay, who seemed to be as fond of talking as any one else is, once set on. "It had belonged to a good old family, my lady, but they got embarrassed and put it up for sale some six or seven years ago. A Mr. Calson bought it. He had come to Pumpwater about that time from foreign lands; and he and his wife settled down in the house. A puny, weakly little woman she was, who seemed to get weaklier instead of stronger, and in a year or two she died. After her death her husband grew ill; he went away for change of air, and died in London; and the house was left to a little nephew living over in Australia."

"And has the house been vacant ever since?" asked John.

"No, sir. At first it was let furnished, then unfurnished. But it had been vacant some little time when I applied to Mr. Bone. I concluded he thought it better to let it at a low rent than for it to stand empty."

"It must cost you incessant care and trouble, Miss Gay, to conduct a house like this—when you are full," remarked Lady Whitney.

"It does," she answered. "One's work seems never done—and I cannot, at that, give satisfaction to all. Ah, my lady, what a difference there is in people!—you would never think it. Some are so kind and considerate to me, so anxious not to give trouble unduly, and so satisfied with all I do that it is a pleasure to serve them: while others make gratuitous work and trouble from morning till night, and treat me as if I were just a dog under their feet. Of course when we are full I have another servant in, two sometimes."

"Even that must leave a great deal for yourself to do and see to."

"The back is always fitted to the burden," sighed Miss Gay. "My father was a farmer in this county, as his ancestors had been before him, farming his three hundred acres of land, and looked upon as a man of substance. My mother made the butter, saw to the poultry, and superintended her household generally: and we children helped her. Farmers' daughters then did not spend their days in playing the piano and doing fancy work, or expect to be waited upon like ladies born."

"They do now, though," said Lady Whitney.

"So I was ready to turn my hand to anything when hard times came—not that I had thought I should have to do it," continued Miss Gay. "But my father's means dwindled down. Prosperity gave way to adversity. Crops failed; the stock died off; two of my brothers fell into trouble and it cost a mint of money to extricate them. Altogether, when father died, but little of his savings remained to us. Mother took a house in the town here, to let lodgings, and I came with her. She is dead, my lady, and I am left."

The silent tears were running down poor Miss Gay's cheeks.

"It is a life of struggle, I am sure," spoke Lady Whitney, gently. "And not deserved, Miss Gay."

"But there's another life to come," spoke John, in a half-whisper, turning to Miss Gay from the large bay-window. "None of us will be overworked *there*."

Miss Gay stealthily wiped her cheeks. "I do not repine," she said, humbly. "I have been enabled to rub on and keep my head above water, and to provide little comforts for mother in her need; and I gratefully thank God for it."

The bells of the churches, ringing out at eight o'clock, called us up in the morning. Lady Whitney was downstairs, first. I next. Susannah, who waited upon us, had brought up the breakfast. John followed me in.

"I hope you have slept well, my boy," said Lady Whitney, kissing him. "I have."

"So have I," I put in.

"Then you and the mother make up for me, Johnny," he said; "for I have not slept at all."

"Oh, John!" exclaimed his mother.

"Not a wink all night long," added John. "I can't think what was the matter with me."

Susannah, then stooping to take the sugar-basin out of the side-board, rose, turned sharply round and fixed her eyes on John. So curious an expression was on her face that I could but notice it.

"Do you not think it was the noise, sir?" she said to him. "I knew that room would be too noisy for you."

"Why, the room was as quiet as possible," he answered. "A few carriages rolled by last night—and I liked to hear them; but that was all over before midnight; and I have heard none this morning."

"Well, sir, I'm sure you would be more comfortable in a back-room," contended Susannah.

"It was a strange bed," said John. "I shall sleep all the sounder to-night."

Breakfast was half over when John found he had left his watch upstairs, on the drawers. I went to fetch it.

The door was open, and I stepped to the drawers, which stood just inside. Miss Gay and Susannah were making the bed and talking, too busy to see or hear me. A lot of things lay on the white cloth, and at first I could not see the watch.

"He declares he has not slept at all; *not at all*," Susannah was saying with emphasis. "If you had only seconded me yesterday, Harriet, they need not have had this room. But you never made a word of objection; you gave in at once."

"Well, I saw no reason to make it," said Miss Gay, mildly. "If I were to give in to your fancies, Susannah, I might as well shut up the room. Visitors must get used to it."

The watch had been partly hidden under one of John's neckties. I caught it up and decamped.

We went to church after breakfast. The first hymn sung was that one beginning, "Brief life."

> Brief life is here our portion;
> Brief sorrow, short-lived care:
> The life that knows no ending,
> The tearless life, is *there*.

As the verses went on, John touched my elbow: "Miss Gay," he whispered; his eyelashes moist with the melody of the music. I have often thought since that we might have seen by these very moods of John—his thoughts bent upon heaven more than upon earth—that his life was swiftly passing.

There's not much to tell of that Sunday. We dined in the middle of the day; John fell asleep after dinner; and in the evening we attended church again. And I think every one was ready for bed when bedtime came. I know I was.

Therefore it was all the more surprising when, the next morning, John said he had again not slept.

"What, not at all!" exclaimed his mother.

"No, not at all. As I went to bed, so I got up—sleepless."

"I never heard of such a thing!" cried Lady Whitney. "Perhaps, John, you were too tired to sleep?"

"Something of that sort," he answered. "I felt both tired and sleepy when I got into bed; particularly so. But I had no sleep: not a wink. I could not lie still, either; I was frightfully restless all night; just as I was the night before. I suppose it can't be the bed?"

"Is the bed not comfortable?" asked his mother.

"It seems as comfortable a bed as can be when I first lie down in it. And then I grow restless and uneasy."

"It must be the restlessness of extreme fatigue," said Lady Whitney. "I fear the journey was rather too much for you my dear."

"Oh, I shall be all right as soon as I can sleep, mamma."

We had a surprise that morning. John and I were standing before a tart-shop, our eyes glued to the window, when a voice behind us called out, "Don't they look nice, boys!" Turning round, there stood Henry Carden of Worcester, arm-in-arm with a little white-haired gentleman. Lady Whitney, in at the fishmonger's next door, came out while he was shaking hands with us.

"Dear me!—is it you?" she cried to Mr. Carden.

"Ay," said he in his pleasant manner, "here am I at Pumpwater! Come all this way to spend a couple of days with my old friend: Dr. Tambourine," added the surgeon, introducing him to Lady Whitney. Any way, that was the name she understood him to say. John thought he said Tamarind, and I Carrafin. The street was noisy.

The doctor seemed to be chatty and courteous, a gentleman of the old school. He said his wife should do herself the honour of calling upon Lady Whitney if agreeable; Lady Whitney replied that it would be. He and Mr. Carden, who would be starting for Worcester by train that afternoon, walked with us up the Parade to the Pump Room. How a chance meeting like this in a strange place makes one feel at home in it!

The name turned out to be Parafin. Mrs. Parafin called early in the afternoon, on her way to some entertainment at the Pump Room: a chatty, pleasant woman, younger than her husband. He had retired from practice, and they lived in a white villa outside the town.

And what with looking at the shops, and parading up and down the public walks, and the entertainment at the Pump Room, to which we went with Mrs. Parafin, and all the rest of it, we felt uncommonly sleepy when night came, and were beginning to regard Pumpwater as a sort of Eden.

"Johnny, have you slept?"

I was brushing my hair at the glass, under the morning sun, when John Whitney, half-dressed, and pale and languid, opened my door and thus accosted me.

"Yes; like a top. Why? Is anything the matter, John?"

"See here," said he, sinking into the easy-chair by the fireplace, "it is an odd thing, but I have again not slept. I *can't* sleep."

I put my back against the dressing-table and stood looking down at him, brush in hand. Not slept again! It *was* an odd thing.

"But what can be the reason, John?"

"I am beginning to think it must be the room."

"How can it be the room?"

"I don't know. There's nothing the matter with the room that I can see; it seems well-ventilated; the chimney's not stopped up. Yet this is the third night that I cannot get to sleep in it."

"But *why* can you not get to sleep?" I persisted.

"I say I don't know why. Each night I have been as sleepy as possible; last night I could hardly undress I was so sleepy; but no sooner am I in bed than sleep goes right away from me. Not only that: I grow terribly restless."

Weighing the problem this way and that, an idea struck me.

"John, do you think it is nervousness?"

"How can it be? I never was nervous in my life."

"I mean this: not sleeping the first night, you may have got nervous about it the second and third."

He shook his head. "I have been nothing of the kind, Johnny. But look here: I hardly see what I am to do. I cannot go on like this without sleep; yet, if I tell the mother again, she'll say the air of the place does not suit me and run away from it—"

"Suppose we change rooms to-night, John?" I interrupted. "I can't think but you would sleep here. If you do not, why, it must be the air of Pumpwater, and the sooner you are out of it the better."

"You wouldn't mind changing rooms for one night?" he said, wistfully.

"Mind! Why, I shall be the gainer. Yours is the better room of the two."

At that it was settled; nothing to be said to any one about the bargain. We did not want to be kidnapped out of Pumpwater—and Lady Whitney had promised us a night at the theatre.

Two or three more acquaintances were made, or found out, that day. Old Lady Scott heard of us, and came to call on Lady Whitney; they used to be intimate. She introduced some people at the Pump Room. Altogether, it seemed that we should not lack society.

Night came; and John and I went upstairs together. He undressed in his own room, and I in mine; and then we made the exchange. I saw him into my bed and wished him a good-night.

"Good-night, Johnny," he answered. "I hope you will sleep."

"Little doubt of that, John. I always sleep when I have nothing to trouble me. A very good-night to *you*."

I had nothing to trouble me, and I was as sleepy as could be; and yet, I did not and could not sleep. I lay quiet as usual after getting into bed, yielding to the expected sleep, and I shut my eyes and never thought but it was coming.

Instead of that, came restlessness. A strange restlessness quite foreign to me, persistent and unaccountable. I tossed and turned from side to side, and I had not had a wink of sleep at day dawn, nor any symptom of it. Was I growing nervous? Had I let the feeling creep over me that I had suggested to John? No; not that I was aware of. What could it be?

Unrefreshed and weary, I got up at the usual hour, and stole silently into the other room. John was in a deep sleep, his calm face lying still upon the pillow. Though I made no noise, my presence awoke him.

"Oh, Johnny!" he exclaimed, "I have had *such* a night."

"Bad?"

"No; *good*. I went to sleep at once and never woke till now. It has done me a world of good. And you?"

"I? Oh well, I don't think I slept quite as well as I did here; it was a strange bed," I answered, carelessly.

The next night the same plan was carried out, he taking my bed; I his. And again John slept through it, while I *did not sleep at all*. I said nothing about it: John Whitney's comfort was of more importance than mine.

The third night came. This night we had been to the theatre, and had laughed ourselves hoarse, and been altogether delighted. No sooner was I in bed, and feeling dead asleep, than the door slowly opened and in came Lady Whitney, a candle in one hand, a wineglass in the other.

"John, my dear," she began, "your tonic was forgotten this evening. I think you had better take it now. Featherston said, you know— Good gracious!" she broke off. "Why, it is Johnny!"

I could hardly speak for laughing, her face presented such a picture of astonishment. Sitting up in bed, I told her all; there was no help for it: that we had exchanged beds, John not having been able to sleep in this one.

"And do you sleep well in it?" she asked.

"No, not yet. But I feel very sleepy to-night, dear Lady Whitney."

"Well, you are a good lad, Johnny, to do this for him; and to say nothing about it," she concluded, as she went away with the candle and the tonic.

Dead sleepy though I was, I could not get to sleep. It would be simply useless to try to describe my sensations. Each succeeding night they had been more marked. A strange, discomforting restlessness pervaded me; a feeling of uneasiness, I could not tell why or wherefore. I saw nothing uncanny, I heard nothing; nevertheless, I felt just as though some uncanny presence was in the room, imparting a sense of semi-terror. Once or twice, when I nearly dozed off from sheer weariness, I started up in real terror, wide awake again, my hair and face damp with a nameless fear.

I told this at breakfast, in answer to Lady Whitney's questions: John confessed that precisely the same sensations had attacked him the three nights he lay in the bed. Lady Whitney declared she never heard the like; and she kept looking at us alternately, as if doubting what could be the matter with us, or whether we had taken scarlet-fever.

On this morning, Friday, a letter came from Sir John, saying that Featherston was coming to Pumpwater. Anxious on the score of his son, he was sending Featherston to see him, and take back a report. "I think he would stay a couple of days if you made it convenient to entertain him, and it would be a little holiday for the poor hard-worked man," wrote Sir John, who was just as kind-hearted as his wife.

"To be sure I will," said Lady Whitney. "He shall have that room; I dare say he won't say he cannot sleep in it: it will be more comfortable for him than getting a bed at an hotel. Susannah shall put a small bed into the back-room for Johnny. And when Featherston is gone, I will take the room myself. I am not like you two silly boys—afraid of lying awake."

Mr. Featherston arrived late that evening, with his grey face of care and his thin frame. He said he could hardly recall the time when he had had as much as two days' holiday, and thanked Lady Whitney for receiving him. That night John and I occupied the back-room, having conducted Featherston in state to the front, with two candles; and both of us slept excellently well.

At breakfast Featherston began talking about the air. He had always believed Pumpwater to have a rather soporific air, but supposed he must be mistaken. Any way, it had kept him awake; and it was not a little that did that for him.

"Did you not sleep well?" asked Lady Whitney.

"I did not sleep at all; did not get a wink of it all night long. Never mind," he added with a good-natured laugh, "I shall sleep all the sounder to-night."

But he did not. The next morning (Sunday) he looked grave and tired, and ate his breakfast almost in silence. When we had finished, he said he should like, with Lady Whitney's permission, to speak to the landlady. Miss Gay came in at once: in a light fresh print gown and black silk apron.

"Ma'am," began Featherston, politely, "something is wrong with that bedroom overhead. What is it?"

"Something wrong, sir?" repeated Miss Gay, her meek face flushing. "Wrong in what way, sir?"

"I don't know," answered Featherston; "I thought perhaps you could tell me: any way, it ought to be seen to. It is something that scares away sleep. I give you my word, ma'am, I never had two such restless nights in succession in all my life. Two such *strange* nights. It was not only that sleep would not come near me; that's nothing uncommon you may say; but I lay in a state of uneasy, indescribable restlessness. I have examined the room again this morning, and I can see nothing to induce it, yet a cause there must undoubtedly be. The paper is not made of arsenic, I suppose?"

"The paper is pale pink, sir," observed Miss Gay. "I fancy it is the green papers that have arsenic in them."

"Ay; well. I think there must be poison behind the paper; in the paste, say," went on Featherston. "Or perhaps another paper underneath has arsenic in it?"

Miss Gay shook her head, as she stood with her hand on the back of a chair. Lady Whitney had asked her to sit down, but she declined. "When I came into the house six months ago, that room was re-papered, and I saw that the walls were thoroughly scraped. If you think there's anything—anything in the room that prevents people sleeping, and—and could point out what it is, I'm sure, sir, I should be glad to remedy it," said Miss Gay, with uncomfortable hesitation.

But this was just what Featherston, for all he was a doctor, could not point out. That something was amiss with the room, he felt convinced, but he had not discovered what it was, or how it could be remedied.

A CURIOUS EXPERIENCE

• 465 •

"After lying in torment half the night, I got up and lighted my candle," said he. "I examined the room and opened the window to let the cool breeze blow in. I could find nothing likely to keep me awake, no stuffed-up chimney, no accumulation of dust, and I shut the window and got into bed again. I was pretty cool by that time and reckoned I should sleep. Not a bit of it, ma'am. I lay more restless than ever, with the same unaccountable feeling of discomfort and depression upon me. Just as I had felt the night before."

"I am very sorry, sir," sighed Miss Gay, taking her hand from the chair to depart. "If the room is close, or anything of that—"

"But it is not close, ma'am. I don't know what it is. And I'm sure I hope you will be able to find it out, and get it remedied," concluded Featherston as she withdrew.

We then told him of our experience, John's and mine. It amazed him. "What an extraordinary thing!" he exclaimed. "One would think the room was haunted."

"Do you believe in haunted rooms, sir?" asked John.

"Well, I suppose such things are," he answered. "Folks say so. If haunted houses exist, why not haunted rooms?"

"It must lie in the Pumpwater air," said Lady Whitney, who was too practical to give in to haunted regions, "and I am very sorry you should have had your two nights' rest spoilt by it, Mr. Featherston. I will take the room myself: nothing keeps me awake."

"Did you ever see a ghost, sir?" asked John.

"No, never. But I know those who have seen them; and I cannot disbelieve what they say. One such story in particular is often in my mind; it was a very strange one."

"Won't you tell it us, Mr. Featherston?"

The doctor only laughed in answer. But after we came out of church, when he was sitting with me and John on the Parade, he told it. And I only wish I had space to relate it here.

He left Pumpwater in the afternoon, and Lady Whitney had the room prepared for her use at once, John moving into hers. So that I had mine to myself again, and the little bed was taken out of it.

The next day was Monday. When Lady Whitney came down in the morning the first thing she told us was, that she had not slept. All the curious symptoms of restless disturbance, of inward agitation, which we had experienced, had visited her.

"I will not give in, my dears," she said, bravely. "It may be, you know, that what I had heard against the room took all sleep out of me, though I was not conscious of it; so I shall keep to it. I must say it is a most comfortable bed."

She "kept" to the room until the Wednesday; three nights in all; getting no sleep. Then she gave in. Occasionally during the third night, when she was dropping asleep from exhaustion, she was startled up from it in sudden terror: terror of she knew not what. Just as it had been with me and with John. On the Wednesday morning she told Susannah that they must give her the back-room opposite mine, and we would abandon that front-room altogether.

"It is just as though there were a ghost in the room," she said to Susannah.

"Perhaps there is, my lady," was Susannah's cool reply.

On the Friday evening Dr. and Mrs. Parafin came in to tea. Our visit would end on the morrow. The old doctor held John before him in the lamplight, and decided that he looked better—that the stay had done him good.

"I am sure it has," assented Lady Whitney. "Just at first I feared he was going backward: but that must have been owing to the sleepless nights."

"Sleepless nights!" echoed the doctor, in a curious tone.

"For the first three nights of our stay here, he never slept; *never slept at all.* After that—"

"Which room did he occupy?" interrupted the doctor, breathlessly. "Not the one over this?"

"Yes, it was. Why? Do you know anything against it?" questioned Lady Whitney, for she saw Dr. and Mrs. Parafin exchange glances.

"Only this: that I have heard of other people who were unable to sleep in that room," he answered.

"But what can be amiss with the room, Dr. Parafin?"

"Ah," said he, "there you go beyond me. It is, I believe, a fact, a singular fact, that there is something or other in the room which prevents people from sleeping. Friends of ours who lived in the house before Miss Gay took it, ended by shutting the room up."

"Is it haunted, sir?" I asked. "Mr. Featherston thought it might be."

He looked at me and smiled, shaking his head. Mrs. Parafin nodded hers, as much as to say *It is.*

"No one has been able to get any sleep in that room since the Calsons lived here," said Mrs. Parafin, dropping her voice.

"How very strange!" cried Lady Whitney. "One might think murder had been done in it."

Mrs. Parafin coughed significantly. "The wife died in it," she said. "Some people thought her husband had—had—had at least hastened her death—"

"Hush, Matty!" interposed the doctor, warningly. "It was all rumour, all talk. Nothing was proved—or attempted to be."

"Perhaps there existed no proof," returned Mrs. Parafin. "And if there had—who was there to take it up? She was in her grave, poor woman, and he was left flourishing, master of himself and every one about him. Any way, Thomas, be that as it may, you cannot deny that the room has been like a haunted room since."

Dr. Parafin laughed lightly, objecting to be serious; men are more cautious than women. "I cannot deny that people find themselves unable to sleep in the room; I never heard that it was 'haunted' in any other way," he added, to Lady Whitney. "But there—let us change the subject; we can neither alter the fact nor understand it."

After they left us, Lady Whitney said she should like to ask Miss Gay what her experience of the room had been. But Miss Gay had stepped out to a neighbour's, and Susannah stayed to talk in her place. She could tell us more about it, she said, than Miss Gay.

"I warned my cousin she would do well not to take this house," began Susannah, accepting the chair to which Lady Whitney pointed. "But it is a beautiful house for letting, as you see, my lady, and that and the low rent tempted her. Besides, she did not believe the rumour about the room; she does not believe it fully yet, though it is beginning to worry her: she thinks the inability to sleep must lie in the people themselves."

"It has been an uncanny room since old Calson's wife died in it, has it not, Susannah?" said John, as if in jest. "I suppose he did not murder her?"

"*I think he did*," whispered Susannah.

The answer sounded so ghostly that it struck us all into silence.

Susannah resumed. "Nobody *knew*: but one or two suspected. The wife was a poor, timid, gentle creature, worshipping the very ground her husband trod on, yet always in awe of him. She lay in the room, sick, for many many months before she died. Old Sarah—"

"What was her illness?" interrupted Lady Whitney.

"My lady, that is more than I can tell you, more, I fancy, than any one could have told. Old Sarah would often say to me that she did not believe there was any great sickness, only he made it out there was, and persuaded his wife so. He could just wind her round his little finger. The person who attended on her was one Astrea, quite a heathenish name I used to think, and a heathenish woman too; she was copper-coloured, and came with them from abroad. Sarah was in the kitchen, and there was only a man besides. I lived housekeeper at that time with an old lady on the Parade, and I looked in here from time to time to ask after the mistress. Once I was invited by Mr. Calson upstairs to see her, she lay in the room over this; the one that nobody can now sleep in. She looked so pitiful!—her poor, pale, patient face down deep in the pillow. Was she better, I asked; and what was it that ailed her. She thought it was not much beside weakness, she answered, and that she felt a constant nausea; and she was waiting for the warm weather: her dear husband assured her she would be better when that came."

"Was he kind to her, Susannah?"

"He seemed to be, Master Johnny; very kind and attentive indeed. He would sit by the hour together in her room, and give her her medicine, and feed her when she grew too weak to feed herself, and sit up at night with her. A doctor came to see her occasionally; it was said he could not find much the matter with her but debility, and that she seemed to be wasting away. Well, she died, my lady; died quietly in that room; and Calson ordered a grand funeral."

"So did Jonas Chuzzlewit," breathed John.

"Whispers got afloat when she was under ground—not before—that there had been something wrong about her death, that she had not come by it fairly, or by the illness either," continued Susannah. "But they were not spoken openly; under the rose, as may be said; and they died away. Mr. Calson continued to live in the house as before; but he became soon ill. Real sickness, his was, my lady, whatever his wife's might have been. His illness was chiefly on the nerves; he grew frightfully thin; and the setting-in of some grave inward complaint was suspected: so if he did act in any ill manner to his wife it seemed he would not reap long benefit from it. All the medical men in Pumpwater were called to him in succession; but they could not cure him. He kept growing thinner and thinner till he was like a walking shadow. At last he shut up his house and went to London for advice; and there he died, fourteen months after the death of his wife."

"How long was the house kept shut up?" asked Lady Whitney, as Susannah paused.

"About two years, my lady. All his property was willed away to the little son of his brother, who lived over in Australia. Tardy instructions came from thence to Mr. Jermy the lawyer to let the house furnished, and Mr. Jermy put it into the hands of Bone the house-agent. A family took it, but they did not stay: then another family took it, and they did not stay. Each party went to Bone and told him that something was the matter with one of the rooms and nobody could sleep in it. After that, the furniture was sold off, and some people took the house by the year. They did not remain in it six months. Some other people took it then, and they stayed the year, but it was known that they shut up that room. Then the house stayed empty. My cousin, wanting a better house than the one she was in, cast many a longing eye towards it; finding it did not let, she went to Bone and asked him what the rent would be. Seventy pounds to her, he said; and she took it. Of course she had heard about the room, but she did not believe it; she thought, as Mr. Featherston said the other morning, that something must be wrong with the paper, and she had the walls scraped and cleaned and a fresh paper put on."

"And since then—have your lodgers found anything amiss with the room?" questioned Lady Whitney.

"I am bound to say they have, my lady. It has been the same story with them all—not able to get to sleep in it. One gentleman, an old post-captain, after trying it a few nights, went right away from Pumpwater, swearing at the air. But the most singular experience we have had was that of two little girls. They were kept in that room for two nights, and each night they cried and screamed all night long, calling out that they were frightened. Their mother could not account for it; they were not at all timid children, she said, and such a thing had never happened with them before. Altogether, taking one thing with another, I fear, my lady, that something *is* wrong with the room. Miss Gay sees it now: but she is not superstitious, and she asks *what* it can be."

Well, that was Susannah's tale: and we carried it away with us on the morrow.

Sir John Whitney found his son looking all the better for his visit to Pumpwater. Temporarily he was so. Temporarily only; not materially: for John died before the year was out.

Have I heard anything of the room since, you would like to ask. Yes, a little. Some eighteen months later, I was halting at Pumpwater for a few hours with the Squire, and ran to the house to see Miss Gay. But the house was empty. A black board stood in front with big white letters on it TO BE LET. Miss Gay had moved into another house facing the Parade.

"It was of no use my trying to stay in it," she said to me, shaking her head. "I moved into the room myself, Master Johnny, after you and my Lady Whitney left, and I am free to confess that I could not sleep. I had Susannah in, and she could not sleep; and, in short, we had to go out of it again. So I shut the room up, sir, until the year had expired, and then I gave up the house. It has not been let since, and people say it is falling into decay."

"Was anything ever *seen* in the room, Miss Gay?"

"Nothing," she answered, "or heard either; nothing whatever. The room is as nice a room as could be wished for in all respects, light, large, cheerful, and airy; and yet nobody can get to sleep in it. I shall never understand it, sir."

I'm sure I never shall. It remains one of those curious experiences that cannot be solved in this world. But it is none the less true.

The Story of the Inexperienced Ghost

H. G. Wells

THE SCENE AMIDST WHICH CLAYTON TOLD HIS LAST STORY COMES BACK VERY vividly to my mind. There he sat, for the greater part of the time, in the corner of the authentic settle by the spacious open fire, and Sanderson sat beside him smoking the Broseley clay that bore his name. There was Evans, and that marvel among actors, Wish, who is also a modest man. We had all come down to the Mermaid Club that Saturday morning, except Clayton, who had slept there overnight—which indeed gave him the opening of his story. We had golfed until golfing was invisible; we had dined, and we were in that mood of tranquil kindliness when men will suffer a story. When Clayton began to tell one, we naturally supposed he was lying. It may be that indeed he was lying—of that the reader will speedily be able to judge as well as I. He began, it is true, with an air of matter-of-fact anecdote, but that we thought was only the incurable artifice of the man.

"I say!" he remarked, after a long consideration of the upward rain of sparks from the log that Sanderson had thumped, "you know I was alone here last night?"

"Except for the domestics," said Wish.

"Who sleep in the other wing," said Clayton. "Yes. Well—" He pulled at his cigar for some little time as though he still hesitated about his confidence. Then he said, quite quietly, "I caught a ghost!"

"Caught a ghost, did you?" said Sanderson. "Where is it?"

And Evans, who admires Clayton immensely and has been four weeks in America, shouted, "*Caught* a ghost, did you, Clayton? I'm glad of it! Tell us all about it right now."

Clayton said he would in a minute, and asked him to shut the door.

He looked apologetically at me. "There's no eavesdropping of course, but we don't want to upset our very excellent service with any rumours of ghosts in the place.

There's too much shadow and oak panelling to trifle with that. And this, you know, wasn't a regular ghost. I don't think it will come again—ever."

"You mean to say you didn't keep it?" said Sanderson.

"I hadn't the heart to," said Clayton.

And Sanderson said he was surprised.

We laughed, and Clayton looked aggrieved. "I know," he said, with the flicker of a smile, "but the fact is it really *was* a ghost, and I'm as sure of it as I am that I am talking to you now. I'm not joking. I mean what I say."

Sanderson drew deeply at his pipe, with one reddish eye on Clayton, and then emitted a thin jet of smoke more eloquent than many words.

Clayton ignored the comment. "It is the strangest thing that has ever happened in my life. You know, I never believed in ghosts or anything of the sort, before, ever; and then, you know, I bag one in a corner; and the whole business is in my hands."

He meditated still more profoundly, and produced and began to pierce a second cigar with a curious little stabber he affected.

"You talked to it?" asked Wish.

"For the space, probably, of an hour."

"Chatty?" I said, joining the party of the sceptics.

"The poor devil was in trouble," said Clayton, bowed over his cigar-end and with the very faintest note of reproof.

"Sobbing?" some one asked.

Clayton heaved a realistic sigh at the memory. "Good Lord!" he said; "yes." And then, "Poor fellow! yes."

"Where did you strike it?" asked Evans, in his best American accent.

"I never realised," said Clayton, ignoring him, "the poor sort of thing a ghost might be," and he hung us up again for a time, while he sought for matches in his pocket and lit and warmed to his cigar.

"I took an advantage," he reflected at last.

We were none of us in a hurry. "A character," he said, "remains just the same character for all that it's been disembodied. That's a thing we too often forget. People with a certain strength or fixity of purpose may have ghosts of a certain strength and fixity of purpose—most haunting ghosts, you know, must be as one-idea'd as monomaniacs and as obstinate as mules to come back again and again. This poor creature wasn't." He suddenly looked up rather queerly, and his eye went round the room. "I say it," he said, "in all kindliness, but that is the plain truth of the case. Even at the first glance he struck me as weak."

He punctuated with the help of his cigar.

"I came upon him, you know, in the long passage. His back was towards me and I saw him first. Right off I knew him for a ghost. He was transparent and whitish; clean through his chest I could see the glimmer of the little window at the end. And not only his physique but his attitude struck me as being weak. He looked, you know, as though he didn't know in the slightest whatever he meant to do. One hand was on the panelling and the other fluttered to his mouth. Like—*so*!"

"What sort of physique?" said Sanderson.

"Lean. You know that sort of young man's neck that has two great flutings down the back, here and here—so! And a little, meanish head with scrubby hair—And rather bad ears. Shoulders bad, narrower than the hips; turndown collar, ready-made short jacket, trousers baggy and a little frayed at the heels. That's how he took me. I came very quietly up the staircase. I did not carry a light, you know—the candles are on the landing table and there is that lamp—and I was in my list slippers, and I saw him as I came up. I stopped dead at that—taking him in. I wasn't a bit afraid. I think that in most of these affairs one is never nearly so afraid or excited as one imagines one would be. I was surprised and interested. I thought, 'Good Lord! Here's a ghost at last! And I haven't believed for a moment in ghosts during the last five-and-twenty years.'"

"Um," said Wish.

"I suppose I wasn't on the landing a moment before he found out I was there. He turned on me sharply, and I saw the face of an immature young man, a weak nose, a scrubby little moustache, a feeble chin. So for an instant we stood—he looking over his shoulder at me and regarded one another. Then he seemed to remember his high calling. He turned round, drew himself up, projected his face, raised his arms, spread his hands in approved ghost fashion—came towards me. As he did so his little jaw dropped, and he emitted a faint, drawn-out 'Boo.' No, it wasn't—not a bit dreadful. I'd dined. I'd had a bottle of champagne, and being all alone, perhaps two or three—perhaps even four or five—whiskies, so I was as solid as rocks and no more frightened than if I'd been assailed by a frog. 'Boo!' I said. 'Nonsense. You don't belong to *this* place. What are you doing here?'

"I could see him wince. 'Boo-oo,' he said.

"'Boo—be hanged! Are you a member?' I said; and just to show I didn't care a pin for him I stepped through a corner of him and made to light my candle. 'Are you a member?' I repeated, looking at him sideways.

"He moved a little so as to stand clear of me, and his bearing became crestfallen. 'No,' he said, in answer to the persistent interrogation of my eye; 'I'm not a member—I'm a ghost.'

"'Well, that doesn't give you the run of the Mermaid Club. Is there any one you want to see, or anything of that sort?' and doing it as steadily as possible for fear that he should mistake the carelessness of whisky for the distraction of fear, I got my candle alight. I turned on him, holding it. 'What are you doing here?' I said.

"He had dropped his hands and stopped his booing, and there he stood, abashed and awkward, the ghost of a weak, silly, aimless young man. 'I'm haunting,' he said.

"'You haven't any business to,' I said in a quiet voice.

"'I'm a ghost,' he said, as if in defence.

"'That may be, but you haven't any business to haunt here. This is a respectable private club; people often stop here with nursemaids and children, and, going about in the careless way you do, some poor little mite could easily come upon you and be scared out of her wits. I suppose you didn't think of that?'

"'No, sir,' he said, 'I didn't.'

"'You should have done. You haven't any claim on the place, have you? Weren't murdered here, or anything of that sort?'

"'None, sir; but I thought as it was old and oak-panelled—'

"'That's *no* excuse.' I regarded him firmly. 'Your coming here is a mistake,' I said, in a tone of friendly superiority. I feigned to see if I had my matches, and then looked up at him frankly. 'If I were you I wouldn't wait for cock-crow—I'd vanish right away.'

"He looked embarrassed. 'The fact *is*, sir—' he began.

"'I'd vanish,' I said, driving it home.

"'The fact is, sir, that—somehow—I can't.'

"'You *can't?*'

"'No, sir. There's something I've forgotten. I've been hanging about here since midnight last night, hiding in the cupboards of the empty bedrooms and things like that. I'm flurried. I've never come haunting before, and it seems to put me out.'

"'Put you out?'

"'Yes, sir. I've tried to do it several times, and it doesn't come off. There's some little thing has slipped me, and I can't get back.'

"That, you know, rather bowled me over. He looked at me in such an abject way that for the life of me I couldn't keep up quite the high, hectoring vein I had adopted. 'That's queer,' I said, and as I spoke I fancied I heard some one moving about down below. 'Come into my room and tell me more about it,' I said. 'I didn't, of course, understand this,' and I tried to take him by the arm. But, of course, you might as well have tried to take hold of a puff of smoke! I had forgotten my number, I think; anyhow, I remember going into several bedrooms—it was lucky I was the only soul in that wing—until I saw my traps. 'Here we are,' I said, and sat down in the arm-chair; 'sit down and tell me all about it. It seems to me you have got yourself into a jolly awkward position, old chap.'

"Well, he said he wouldn't sit down! he'd prefer to flit up and down the room if it was all the same to me. And so he did, and in a little while we were deep in a long and serious talk. And presently, you know, something of those whiskies and sodas evaporated out of me, and I began to realise just a little what a thundering rum and weird business it was that I was in. There he was, semi-transparent—the proper conventional phantom, and noiseless except for his ghost of a voice—flitting to and fro in that nice, clean, chintz-hung old bedroom. You could see the gleam of the copper candlesticks through him, and the lights on the brass fender, and the corners of the framed engravings on the wall, and there he was telling me all about this wretched little life of his that had recently ended on earth. He hadn't a particularly honest face, you know, but being transparent, of course, he couldn't avoid telling the truth."

"Eh?" said Wish, suddenly sitting up in his chair.

"What?" said Clayton.

"Being transparent—couldn't avoid telling the truth—I don't see it," said Wish.

"*I* don't see it," said Clayton, with inimitable assurance. "But it *is* so, I can assure you nevertheless. I don't believe he got once a nail's breadth off the Bible truth. He told me how he had been killed—he went down into a London basement with a candle to look for a leakage of gas—and described himself as a senior English master in a London private school when that release occurred."

"Poor wretch!" said I.

"That's what I thought, and the more he talked the more I thought it. There he was, purposeless in life and purposeless out of it. He talked of his father and mother and his schoolmaster, and all who had ever been anything to him in the world, meanly. He had been too sensitive, too nervous; none of them had ever valued him properly or understood him, he said. He had never had a real friend in the world, I think; he had never had a success. He had shirked games and failed examinations. 'It's like that with some people,' he said; 'whenever I got into the examination-room or anywhere everything seemed to go.' Engaged to be married of course—to another over-sensitive person, I suppose—when the indiscretion with the gas escape ended his affairs. 'And where are you now?' I asked. 'Not in—?'

"He wasn't clear on that point at all. The impression he gave me was of a sort of vague, intermediate state, a special reserve for souls too non-existent for anything so positive as either sin or virtue. *I* don't know. He was much too egotistical and unobservant to give me any clear idea of the kind of place, kind of country, there is on the Other Side of Things. Wherever he was, he seems to have fallen in with a set of kindred spirits: ghosts of weak Cockney young men, who were on a footing of Christian names, and among these there was certainly a lot of talk about 'going haunting' and things like that. Yes—going haunting! They seemed to think 'haunting' a tremendous adventure, and most of them funked it all the time. And so primed, you know, he had come."

"But really!" said Wish to the fire.

"These are the impressions he gave me, anyhow," said Clayton, modestly. "I may, of course, have been in a rather uncritical state, but that was the sort of background he gave to himself. He kept flitting up and down, with his thin voice going talking, talking about his wretched self, and never a word of clear, firm statement from first to last. He was thinner and sillier and more pointless than if he had been real and alive. Only then, you know, he would not have been in my bedroom here—if he *had* been alive. I should have kicked him out."

"Of course," said Evans, "there *are* poor mortals like that."

"And there's just as much chance of their having ghosts as the rest of us," I admitted.

"What gave a sort of point to him, you know, was the fact that he did seem within limits to have found himself out. The mess he had made of haunting had depressed him terribly. He had been told it would be a 'lark'; he had come expecting it to be a 'lark,' and here it was, nothing but another failure added to his record! He proclaimed himself an utter out-and-out failure. He said, and I can quite believe it, that he had never tried to do anything all his life that he hadn't made a perfect mess of—and through all the wastes of eternity he never would. If he had had sympathy, perhaps—. He paused at that, and stood regarding me. He remarked that, strange as it might seem to me, nobody, not any one, ever, had given him the amount of sympathy I was doing now. I could see what he wanted straight away, and I determined to head him off at once. I may be a brute, you know, but being the Only Real Friend, the recipient of the confidences of one of these egotistical weaklings, ghost or body, is beyond my physical endurance. I got up briskly. 'Don't you brood on these things too much,' I said. 'The thing you've got to do is to get out of this get out of this—sharp. You pull yourself together and *try*.' 'I can't,' he said. 'You try,' I said, and try he did."

"Try!" said Sanderson. "*How?*"

"Passes," said Clayton.

"Passes?"

"Complicated series of gestures and passes with the hands. That's how he had come in and that's how he had to get out again. Lord! what a business I had!"

"But how could *any* series of passes——?" I began.

"My dear man," said Clayton, turning on me and putting a great emphasis on certain words, "you want *everything* clear. *I* don't know *how*. All I know is that you *do*—that *he* did, anyhow, at least. After a fearful time, you know, he got his passes right and suddenly disappeared."

"Did you," said Sanderson, slowly, "observe the passes?"

"Yes," said Clayton, and seemed to think. "It was tremendously queer," he said. "There we were, I and this thin vague ghost, in that silent room, in this silent, empty inn, in this silent little Friday-night town. Not a sound except our voices and a faint panting he made when he swung. There was the bedroom candle, and one candle on the dressing-table alight, that was all—sometimes one or other would flare up into a tall, lean, astonished flame for a space. And queer things happened. 'I can't,' he said; 'I shall never—!' And suddenly he sat down on a little chair at the foot of the bed and began to sob and sob. Lord! what a harrowing, whimpering thing he seemed!

"'You pull yourself together,' I said, and tried to pat him on the back, and . . . my confounded hand went through him! By that time, you know, I wasn't nearly so—massive as I had been on the landing. I got the queerness of it full. I remember snatching back my hand out of him, as it were, with a little thrill, and walking over to the dressing-table. 'You pull yourself together,' I said to him, 'and try.' And in order to encourage and help him I began to try as well."

"What!" said Sanderson, "the passes?"

"Yes, the passes."

"But——" I said, moved by an idea that eluded me for a space.

"This is interesting," said Sanderson, with his finger in his pipe-bowl. "You mean to say this ghost of yours gave away—"

"Did his level best to give away the whole confounded barrier? *Yes*."

"He didn't," said Wish; "he couldn't. Or you'd have gone there too."

"That's precisely it," I said, finding my elusive idea put into words for me.

"That *is* precisely it," said Clayton, with thoughtful eyes upon the fire.

For just a little while there was silence.

"And at last he did it?" said Sanderson.

"At last he did it. I had to keep him up to it hard, but he did it at last—rather suddenly. He despaired, we had a scene, and then he got up abruptly and asked me to go through the whole performance, slowly, so that he might see. 'I believe,' he said, 'if I could *see* I should spot what was wrong at once.' And he did. '*I* know,' he said. 'What do you know?' said I. '*I* know,' he repeated. Then he said, peevishly, 'I *can't* do it if you look at me—I really *can't*; it's been that, partly, all along. I'm such a nervous fellow that you put me out.' Well, we had a bit of an argument. Naturally I wanted to see; but he was as obstinate as a mule, and suddenly I had come over as tired as a dog—he tired me out. 'All right,' I said, '*I* won't look at you,' and turned towards the mirror, on the wardrobe, by the bed.

"He started off very fast. I tried to follow him by looking in the looking-glass, to see just what it was had hung. Round went his arms and his hands, so, and so, and so, and then with a rush came to the last gesture of all—you stand erect and open out your arms—and so, don't you know, he stood. And then he didn't! He didn't! He wasn't! I wheeled round from the looking-glass to him. There was nothing, I was alone, with the flaring candles and a staggering mind. What had happened? Had anything happened? Had I been dreaming? . . . And then, with an absurd note of finality about it, the clock upon the landing discovered the moment was ripe for striking *one*. So!—Ping! And I was as grave and sober as a judge, with all my champagne and whisky gone into the vast serene. Feeling queer, you know—confoundedly *queer*! Queer! Good Lord!"

He regarded his cigar-ash for a moment. "That's all that happened," he said.

"And then you went to bed?" asked Evans.

"What else was there to do?"

I looked Wish in the eye. We wanted to scoff, and there was something, something perhaps in Clayton's voice and manner, that hampered our desire.

"And about these passes?" said Sanderson.

"I believe I could do them now."

"Oh!" said Sanderson, and produced a pen-knife and set himself to grub the dottel out of the bowl of his clay.

"Why don't you do them now?" said Sanderson, shutting his pen-knife with a click.

"That's what I'm going to do," said Clayton.

"They won't work," said Evans.

"If they do——" I suggested.

"You know, I'd rather you didn't," said Wish, stretching out his legs.

"Why?" asked Evans.

"I'd rather he didn't," said Wish.

"But he hasn't got 'em right," said Sanderson, plugging too much tobacco in his pipe.

"All the same, I'd rather he didn't," said Wish.

We argued with Wish. He said that for Clayton to go through those gestures was like mocking a serious matter. "But you don't believe——?" I said. Wish glanced at

Clayton, who was staring into the fire, weighing something in his mind. "I do—more than half, anyhow, I do," said Wish.

"Clayton," said I, "you're too good a liar for us. Most of it was all right. But that disappearance... happened to be convincing. Tell us, it's a tale of cock and bull."

He stood up without heeding me, took the middle of the hearthrug, and faced me. For a moment he regarded his feet thoughtfully, and then for all the rest of the time his eyes were on the opposite wall, with an intent expression. He raised his two hands slowly to the level of his eyes and so began. . . .

Now, Sanderson is a Freemason, a member of the lodge of the Four Kings, which devotes itself so ably to the study and elucidation of all the mysteries of Masonry past and present, and among the students of this lodge Sanderson is by no means the least. He followed Clayton's motions with a singular interest in his reddish eye. "That's not bad," he said, when it was done. "You really do, you know, put things together, Clayton, in a most amazing fashion. But there's one little detail out."

"I know," said Clayton. "I believe I could tell you which."

"Well?"

"This," said Clayton, and did a queer little twist and writhing and thrust of the hands.

"Yes."

"That, you know, was what *he* couldn't get right," said Clayton. "But how do *you*—?"

"Most of this business, and particularly how you invented it, I don't understand at all," said Sanderson, "but just that phase—I do." He reflected. "These happen to be a series of gestures—connected with a certain branch of esoteric Masonry. Probably you know. Or else—*How?*" He reflected still further. "I do not see I can do any harm in telling you just the proper twist. After all, if you know, you know; if you don't, you don't."

"I know nothing," said Clayton, "except what the poor devil let out last night."

"Well, anyhow," said Sanderson, and placed his churchwarden very carefully upon the shelf over the fireplace. Then very rapidly he gesticulated with his hands.

"So?" said Clayton, repeating.

"So," said Sanderson, and took his pipe in hand again.

"Ah, *now*," said Clayton, "I can do the whole thing—right."

He stood up before the waning fire and smiled at us all. But I think there was just a little hesitation in his smile. "If I begin—" he said.

"I wouldn't begin," said Wish.

THE STORY OF THE INEXPERIENCED GHOST

"It's all right!" said Evans. "Matter is indestructible. You don't think any jiggery-pokery of this sort is going to snatch Clayton into the world of shades. Not it! You may try, Clayton, so far as I'm concerned, until your arms drop off at the wrists."

"I don't believe that," said Wish, and stood up and put his arm on Clayton's shoulder. "You've made me half believe in that story somehow, and I don't want to see the thing done!"

"Goodness!" said I, "here's Wish frightened!"

"I am," said Wish, with real or admirably feigned intensity. "I believe that if he goes through these motions right he'll *go*."

"He'll not do anything of the sort," I cried. "There's only one way out of this world for men, and Clayton is thirty years from that. Besides... And such a ghost! Do you think—?"

Wish interrupted me by moving. He walked out from among our chairs and stopped beside the table and stood there. "Clayton," he said, "you're a fool."

Clayton, with a humorous light in his eyes, smiled back at him. "Wish," he said, "is right and all you others are wrong. I shall go. I shall get to the end of these passes, and as the last swish whistles through the air, Presto!—this hearthrug will be vacant, the room will be blank amazement, and a respectably dressed gentleman of fifteen stone will plump into the world of shades. I'm certain. So will you be. I decline to argue further. Let the thing be tried."

"*No,*" said Wish, and made a step and ceased, and Clayton raised his hands once more to repeat the spirit's passing.

By that time, you know, we were all in a state of tension—largely because of the behaviour of Wish. We sat all of us with our eyes on Clayton—I, at least, with a sort of tight, stiff feeling about me as though from the back of my skull to the middle of my thighs my body had been changed to steel. And there, with a gravity that was imperturbably serene, Clayton bowed and swayed and waved his hands and arms before us. As he drew towards the end one piled up, one tingled in one's teeth. The last gesture, I have said, was to swing the arms out wide open, with the face held up. And when at last he swung out to this closing gesture I ceased even to breathe. It was ridiculous, of course, but you know that ghost-story feeling. It was after dinner, in a queer, old shadowy house. Would he, after all—?

There he stood for one stupendous moment, with his arms open and his upturned face, assured and bright, in the glare of the hanging lamp. We hung through that moment as if it were an age, and then came from all of us something that was half a sigh of infinite relief and half a reassuring "*No!*" For visibly—he wasn't going. It was all nonsense.

He had told an idle story, and carried it almost to conviction, that was all! . . . And then in that moment the face of Clayton changed.

It changed. It changed as a lit house changes when its lights are suddenly extinguished. His eyes were suddenly eyes that were fixed, his smile was frozen on his lips, and he stood there still. He stood there, very gently swaying.

That moment, too, was an age. And then, you know, chairs were scraping, things were falling, and we were all moving. His knees seemed to give, and he fell forward, and Evans rose and caught him in his arms. . . .

It stunned us all. For a minute I suppose no one said a coherent thing. We believed it, yet could not believe it. . . . I came out of a muddled stupefaction to find myself kneeling beside him, and his vest and shirt were torn open, and Sanderson's hand lay on his heart. . . .

Well—the simple fact before us could very well wait our convenience; there was no hurry for us to comprehend. It lay there for an hour; it lies athwart my memory, black and amazing still, to this day. Clayton had, indeed, passed into the world that lies so near to and so far from our own, and he had gone thither by the only road that mortal man may take. But whether he did indeed pass there by that poor ghost's incantation, or whether he was stricken suddenly by apoplexy in the midst of an idle tale—as the coroner's jury would have us believe—is no matter for my judging; it is just one of those inexplicable riddles that must remain unsolved until the final solution of all things shall come. All I certainly know is that, in the very moment, in the very instant, of concluding those passes, he changed, and staggered, and fell down before us—dead!

The Ghosts

Lord Dunsany

THE ARGUMENT THAT I HAD WITH MY BROTHER IN HIS GREAT LONELY HOUSE WILL scarcely interest my readers. Not those, at least, whom I hope may be attracted by the experiment that I undertook, and by the strange things that befell me in that hazardous region into which so lightly and so ignorantly I allowed my fancy to enter. It was at Oneleigh that I had visited him.

Now Oneleigh stands in a wide isolation, in the midst of a dark gathering of old whispering cedars. They nod their heads together when the North Wind comes, and nod again and agree, and furtively grow still again, and say no more awhile. The North Wind is to them like a nice problem among wise old men; they nod their heads over it, and mutter about it all together. They know much, those cedars, they have been there so long. Their grandsires knew Lebanon, and the grandsires of these were the servants of the King of Tyre and came to Solomon's court. And amidst these black-haired children of grey-headed Time stood the old house of Oneleigh. I know not how many centuries had lashed against it their evanescent foam of years; but it was still unshattered, and all about it were the things of long ago, as cling strange growths to some sea-defying rock. Here, like the shells of long-dead limpets, was armour that men encased themselves in long ago; here, too, were tapestries of many colours, beautiful as seaweed; no modern flotsam ever drifted hither, no early Victorian furniture, no electric light. The great trade routes that littered the years with empty meat tins and cheap novels were far from here. Well, well, the centuries will shatter it and drive its fragments on to distant shores. Meanwhile, while it yet stood, I went on a visit there to my brother, and we argued about ghosts. My brother's intelligence on this subject seemed to me to be in need of correction. He mistook things imagined for things having an actual existence; he argued that second-hand evidence of persons having seen ghosts proved ghosts to exist. I said that even if they had seen ghosts, this was no proof at all; nobody believes that there are red rats, though there is plenty of first-hand evidence of men having seen them in delirium. Finally, I said I would see ghosts myself, and continue to argue against their actual existence. So I collected a handful of cigars and drank several cups of very strong tea, and went without my dinner, and retired into a room where there was dark oak and all the chairs were covered with tapestry; and my brother went to bed bored with our argument, and trying hard to dissuade me from making myself uncomfortable. All the way up the old stairs as I stood at the bottom of them, and as his candle went winding up and up, I heard him still trying to persuade me to have supper and go to bed.

It was a windy winter, and outside the cedars were muttering I know not what about; but I think that they were Tories of a school long dead, and were troubled about something new. Within, a great damp log upon the fireplace began to squeak and sing, and struck up a whining tune, and a tall flame stood up over it and beat time, and all the shadows crowded round and began to dance. In distant corners old masses of darkness sat still like chaperones and never moved. Over there, in the darkest part of the room, stood a door that was always locked. It led into the hall, but no one ever used it; near that door something had happened once of which the family are not proud. We do not speak of it. There in the firelight stood the venerable forms of the old chairs; the hands that had made their tapestries lay far beneath the soil, the needles with which they wrought were many separate flakes of rust. No one wove now in that old room—no one but the assiduous ancient spiders who, watching by the deathbed of the things of yore, worked shrouds to hold their dust. In shrouds about the cornices already lay the heart of the oak wainscot that the worm had eaten out.

Surely at such an hour, in such a room, a fancy already excited by hunger and strong tea might see the ghosts of former occupants. I expected nothing less. The fire flickered and the shadows danced, memories of strange historic things rose vividly in my mind; but midnight chimed solemnly from a seven-foot clock, and nothing happened. My imagination would not be hurried, and the chill that is with the small hours had come upon me, and I had nearly abandoned myself to sleep, when in the hall adjoining there arose the rustling of silk dresses that I had waited for and expected. Then there entered two by two the high-born ladies and their gallants of Jacobean times. They were little more than shadows—very dignified shadows, and almost indistinct; but you have all read ghost stories before, you have all seen in museums the dresses of those times—there is little need to describe them; they entered, several of them, and sat down on the old chairs, perhaps a little carelessly considering the value of the tapestries. Then the rustling of their dresses ceased.

Well—I had seen ghosts, and was neither frightened nor convinced that ghosts existed. I was about to get up out of my chair and go to bed, when there came a sound of pattering in the hall, a sound of bare feet coming over the polished floor, and every now and then a foot would slip and I heard claws scratching along the wood as some four-footed thing lost and regained its balance. I was not frightened, but uneasy. The pattering came straight towards the room that I was in, then I heard the sniffing of expectant nostrils; perhaps "uneasy" was not the most suitable word to describe my feelings then. Suddenly a herd of black creatures larger than bloodhounds came galloping in; they had large pendulous ears, their noses were to the ground sniffing, they went up to the lords and ladies of long ago and fawned about them disgustingly. Their eyes were horribly bright, and ran down to great depths. When I looked into them I knew suddenly what these creatures were, and I was afraid. They were the sins, the filthy, immortal sins of those courtly men and women.

How demure she was, the lady that sat near me on an old-world chair—how demure she was, and how fair, to have beside her with its jowl upon her lap a sin with such cavernous red eyes, a clear case of murder. And you, yonder lady with the golden hair, surely not you—and yet that fearful beast with the yellow eyes slinks from you to yonder courtier there, and whenever one drives it away it slinks back to the other. Over there a lady tries to smile as she strokes the loathsome furry head of another's sin, but one of her own is jealous and intrudes itself under her hand. Here sits an old nobleman with his grandson on his knee, and one of the great black sins of the grandfather is licking the child's face and has made the child its own. Sometimes a ghost would move and seek another chair, but always his pack of sins would move behind him. Poor ghosts, poor ghosts! how many flights they must have attempted for two hundred years from their hated sins, how many excuses they must have given for their presence, and the sins were with them still—and still unexplained. Suddenly one of them seemed to scent my living blood, and bayed horribly, and all the others left their ghosts at once and dashed up to the sin that had given tongue. The brute had picked up my scent near the door by which I had entered, and they moved slowly nearer to me sniffing along the floor, and uttering every now and then their fearful cry. I saw that the whole thing had gone too far. But now they had seen me, now they were all about me, they sprang up trying to reach my throat; and whenever their claws touched me, horrible thoughts came into my mind and unutterable desires dominated my heart. I planned bestial things as these creatures leaped around me, and planned them with a masterly cunning. A great red-eyed murder was among the foremost of those furry things from whom I feebly strove to defend my throat. Suddenly it seemed to me good that I should kill my brother. It seemed important to me that I should not risk being punished. I knew where a revolver was kept; after I had shot him, I would dress the body up and put flour on the face like a man that had been acting as a ghost. It would be very simple. I would say that he had frightened me—and the servants had heard us talking about ghosts. There were one or two trivialities that would have to be arranged, but nothing escaped my mind. Yes, it seemed to me very good that I should kill my brother as I looked into the red depths of this creature's eyes. But one last effort as they dragged me down—"If two straight lines cut one another," I said, "the opposite angles are equal. Let AB, CD, cut one another at E, then the angles CEA, CEB equal two right angles (prop. xiii.). Also CEA, AED equal two right angles."

I moved towards the door to get the revolver; a hideous exultation arose among the beasts. "But the angle CEA is common, therefore AED equals CEB. In the same way CEA equals DEB. *Q.E.D.*" It was proved. Logic and reason re-established themselves in my mind, there were no dark hounds of sin, the tapestried chairs were empty. It seemed to me an inconceivable thought that a man should murder his brother.

In Kropfsberg Keep

Ralph Adams Cram

To the traveller from Innsbrück to Munich, up the lovely valley of the silver Inn, many castles appear, one after another, each on its beetling cliff or gentle hill—appear and disappear, melting into the dark fir trees that grow so thickly on every side—Laneck, Lichtwer, Ratholtz, Tratzberg, Matzen, Kropfsberg, gathering close around the entrance to the dark and wonderful Zillerthal.

But to us—Tom Rendel and myself—there are two castles only: not the gorgeous and princely Ambras, nor the noble old Tratzberg, with its crowded treasures of solemn and splendid mediævalism; but little Matzen, where eager hospitality forms the new life of a never-dead chivalry, and Kropfsberg, ruined, tottering, blasted by fire and smitten with grievous years—a dead thing, and haunted—full of strange legends, and eloquent of mystery and tragedy.

We were visiting the von C——s at Matzen, and gaining our first wondering knowledge of the courtly, cordial castle life in the Tyrol—of the gentle and delicate hospitality of noble Austrians. Brixleg had ceased to be but a mark on a map, and had become a place of rest and delight, a home for homeless wanderers on the face of Europe, while Schloss Matzen was a synonym for all that was gracious and kindly and beautiful in life. The days moved on in a golden round of riding and driving and shooting: down to Landl and Thiersee for chamois, across the river to the magic Achensee, up the Zillerthal, across the Schmerner Joch, even to the railway station at Steinach. And in the evenings after the late dinners in the upper hall where the sleepy hounds leaned against our chairs looking at us with suppliant eyes, in the evenings when the fire was dying away in the hooded fireplace in the library, stories. Stories, and legends, and fairy tales, while the stiff old portraits changed countenance constantly under the flickering firelight, and the sound of the drifting Inn came softly across the meadows far below.

If ever I tell the Story of Schloss Matzen, then will be the time to paint the too inadequate picture of this fair oasis in the desert of travel and tourists and hotels; but just now it is Kropfsberg the Silent that is of greater importance, for it was only in Matzen that the story was told by Fräulein E——, the gold-haired niece of Frau von C——, one hot evening in July, when we were sitting in the great west window of the drawing-room after a long ride up the Stallenthal. All the windows were open to catch the faint wind, and we had sat for a long time watching the Otzethaler Alps turn rose-color over distant Innsbrück, then deepen to violet as the sun went down and the white mists rose slowly until Lichtwer and Laneck and Kropfsberg rose like craggy islands in a silver sea.

And this is the story as Fräulein E—— told it to us—the Story of Kropfsberg Keep.

A great many years ago, soon after my grandfather died, and Matzen came to us, when I was a little girl, and so young that I remember nothing of the affair except as something dreadful that frightened me very much, two young men who had studied painting with my grandfather came down to Brixleg from Munich, partly to paint, and partly to amuse themselves—"ghost-hunting" as they said, for they were very sensible young men and prided themselves on it, laughing at all kinds of "superstition," and particularly at that form which believed in ghosts and feared them. They had never seen a real ghost, you know, and they belonged to a certain set of people who believed nothing they had not seen themselves—which always seemed to me *very* conceited. Well, they knew that we had lots of beautiful castles here in the "lower valley," and they assumed, and rightly, that every castle has at least *one* ghost story connected with it, so they chose this as their hunting ground, only the game they sought was ghosts, not chamois. Their plan was to visit every place that was supposed to be haunted, and to meet every reputed ghost, and prove that it really was no ghost at all.

There was a little inn down in the village then, kept by an old man named Peter Rosskopf, and the two young men made this their headquarters. The very first night they began to draw from the old innkeeper all that he knew of legends and ghost stories connected with Brixleg and its castles, and as he was a most garrulous old gentleman he filled them with the wildest delight by his stories of the ghosts of the castles about the mouth of the Zillerthal. Of course the old man believed every word he said, and you can imagine his horror and amazement when, after telling his guests the particularly blood-curdling story of Kropfsberg and its haunted keep, the elder of the two boys, whose surname I have forgotten, but whose Christian name was Rupert, calmly said, "Your story is most satisfactory: we will sleep in Kropfsberg Keep to-morrow night, and you must provide us with all that we may need to make ourselves comfortable."

The old man nearly fell into the fire. "What for a blockhead are you?" he cried, with big eyes. "The keep is haunted by Count Albert's ghost, I tell you!"

"That is why we are going there to-morrow night; we wish to make the acquaintance of Count Albert."

"But there was a man stayed there once, and in the morning he was dead."

"Very silly of him; there are two of us, and we carry revolvers."

"But it's a *ghost*, I tell you," almost screamed the innkeeper; "are ghosts afraid of firearms?"

"Whether they are or not, we are *not* afraid of *them*."

Here the younger boy broke in—he was named Otto von Kleist. I remember the name, for I had a music teacher once by that name. He abused the poor old man shamefully; told him that they were going to spend the night in Kropfsberg in spite of Count Albert and Peter Rosskopf, and that he might as well make the most of it and earn his money with cheerfulness.

In a word, they finally bullied the old fellow into submission, and when the morning came he set about preparing for the suicide, as he considered it, with sighs and mutterings and ominous shakings of the head.

You know the condition of the castle now,—nothing but scorched walls and crumbling piles of fallen masonry. Well, at the time I tell you of, the keep was still partially preserved. It was finally burned out only a few years ago by some wicked boys who came over from Jenbach to have a good time. But when the ghost hunters came, though the two lower floors had fallen into the crypt, the third floor remained. The peasants said it *could* not fall, but that it would stay until the Day of Judgment, because it was in the room above that the wicked Count Albert sat watching the flames destroy the great castle and his imprisoned guests, and where he finally hung himself in a suit of armor that had belonged to his mediæval ancestor, the first Count Kropfsberg.

No one dared touch him, and so he hung there for twelve years, and all the time venturesome boys and daring men used to creep up the turret steps and stare awfully through the chinks in the door at that ghostly mass of steel that held within itself the body of a murderer and suicide, slowly returning to the dust from which it was made. Finally it disappeared, none knew whither, and for another dozen years the room stood empty but for the old furniture and the rotting hangings.

So, when the two men climbed the stairway to the haunted room, they found a very different state of things from what exists now. The room was absolutely as it was left the night Count Albert burned the castle, except that all trace of the suspended suit of armor and its ghastly contents had vanished.

No one had dared to cross the threshold, and I suppose that for forty years no living thing had entered that dreadful room.

On one side stood a vast canopied bed of black wood, the damask hangings of which were covered with mould and mildew. All the clothing of the bed was in perfect order, and on it lay a book, open, and face downward. The only other furniture in the room consisted of several old chairs, a carved oak chest, and a big inlaid table covered with books and papers, and on one corner two or three bottles with dark solid sediment at the bottom, and a glass, also dark with the dregs of wine that had been poured out almost half a century before. The tapestry on the walls was green with mould, but hardly torn or otherwise defaced, for although the heavy dust of forty years lay on everything the room had been preserved from further harm. No spider web was to be seen, no trace of nibbling mice, not even a dead moth or fly on the sills of the diamond-paned windows; life seemed to have shunned the room utterly and finally.

The men looked at the room curiously, and, I am sure, not without some feelings of awe and unacknowledged fear; but, whatever they may have felt of instinctive shrinking, they said nothing, and quickly set to work to make the room passably inhabitable. They decided to touch nothing that had not absolutely to be changed, and therefore they made for themselves a bed in one corner with the mattress and linen from the inn. In the great fireplace they piled a lot of wood on the caked ashes of a fire dead for forty years, turned the old chest into a table, and laid out on it all their arrangements for the evening's amusement: food, two or three bottles of wine, pipes and tobacco, and the chess-board that was their inseparable travelling companion.

All this they did themselves: the innkeeper would not even come within the walls of the outer court; he insisted that he had washed his hands of the whole affair, the silly dunderheads might go to their death their own way. *He* would not aid and abet them. One of the stable boys brought the basket of food and the wood and the bed up the winding stone stairs, to be sure, but neither money nor prayers nor threats would bring him within the walls of the accursed place, and he stared fearfully at the hare-brained boys as they worked around the dead old room preparing for the night that was coming so fast.

At length everything was in readiness, and after a final visit to the inn for dinner Rupert and Otto started at sunset for the Keep. Half the village went with them, for Peter Rosskopf had babbled the whole story to an open-mouthed crowd of wondering men and women, and as to an execution the awe-struck crowd followed the two boys dumbly, curious to see if they surely would put their plan into execution. But none went farther than the outer doorway of the stairs, for it was already growing twilight. In absolute silence they watched the two foolhardy youths with their lives in their hands enter the terrible Keep, standing like a tower in the midst of the piles of stones that had once formed walls joining it with the mass of the castle beyond.

IN KROPFSBERG KEEP

When a moment later a light showed itself in the high windows above, they sighed resignedly and went their ways, to wait stolidly until morning should come and prove the truth of their fears and warnings.

In the mean time the ghost hunters built a huge fire, lighted their many candles, and sat down to await developments. Rupert afterwards told my uncle that they really felt no fear whatever, only a contemptuous curiosity, and they ate their supper with good appetite and an unusual relish. It was a long evening. They played many games of chess, waiting for midnight. Hour passed after hour, and nothing occurred to interrupt the monotony of the evening. Ten, eleven, came and went—it was almost midnight. They piled more wood in the fireplace, lighted new candles, looked to their pistols—and waited. The clocks in the village struck twelve; the sound coming muffled through the high, deep-embrasured windows. Nothing happened, nothing to break the heavy silence; and with a feeling of disappointed relief they looked at each other and acknowledged that they had met another rebuff.

Finally they decided that there was no use in sitting up and boring themselves any longer, they had much better rest; so Otto threw himself down on the mattress, falling almost immediately asleep. Rupert sat a little longer, smoking, and watching the stars creep along behind the shattered glass and the bent leads of the lofty windows; watching the fire fall together, and the strange shadows move mysteriously on the mouldering walls. The iron hook in the oak beam, that crossed the ceiling midway, fascinated him, not with fear, but morbidly. So, it was from that hook that for twelve years, twelve long years of changing summer and winter, the body of Count Albert, murderer and suicide, hung in its strange casing of mediæval steel; moving a little at first, and turning gently while the fire died out on the hearth, while the ruins of the castle grew cold, and horrified peasants sought for the bodies of the score of gay, reckless, wicked guests whom Count Albert had gathered in Kropfsberg for a last debauch, gathered to their terrible and untimely death. What a strange and fiendish idea it was, the young, handsome noble who had ruined himself and his family in the society of the splendid debauchees, gathering them all together, men and women who had known only love and pleasure, for a glorious and awful riot of luxury, and then, when they were all dancing in the great ballroom, locking the doors and burning the whole castle about them, the while he sat in the great keep listening to their screams of agonized fear, watching the fire sweep from wing to wing until the whole mighty mass was one enormous and awful pyre, and then, clothing himself in his great-great-grandfather's armor, hanging himself in the midst of the ruins of what had been a proud and noble castle. So ended a great family, a great house.

But that was forty years ago.

He was growing drowsy; the light flickered and flared in the fireplace; one by one the candles went out; the shadows grew thick in the room. Why did that great iron hook stand out so plainly? why did that dark shadow dance and quiver so mockingly behind it?—why—But he ceased to wonder at anything. He was asleep.

It seemed to him that he woke almost immediately; the fire still burned, though low and fitfully on the hearth. Otto was sleeping, breathing quietly and regularly; the shadows had gathered close around him, thick and murky; with every passing moment the light died in the fireplace; he felt stiff with cold. In the utter silence he heard the clock in the village strike two. He shivered with a sudden and irresistible feeling of fear, and abruptly turned and looked towards the hook in the ceiling.

Yes, It was there. He knew that It would be. It seemed quite natural, he would have been disappointed had he seen nothing; but now he knew that the story was true, knew that he was wrong, and that the dead *do* sometimes return to earth, for there, in the fast-deepening shadow, hung the black mass of wrought steel, turning a little now and then, with the light flickering on the tarnished and rusty metal. He watched it quietly; he hardly felt afraid; it was rather a sentiment of sadness and fatality that filled him, of gloomy forebodings of something unknown, unimaginable. He sat and watched the thing disappear in the gathering dark, his hand on his pistol as it lay by him on the great chest. There was no sound but the regular breathing of the sleeping boy on the mattress.

It had grown absolutely dark; a bat fluttered against the broken glass of the window. He wondered if he was growing mad, for—he hesitated to acknowledge it to himself—he heard music; far, curious music, a strange and luxurious dance, very faint, very vague, but unmistakable.

Like a flash of lightning came a jagged line of fire down the blank wall opposite him, a line that remained, that grew wider, that let a pale cold light into the room, showing him now all its details—the empty fireplace, where a thin smoke rose in a spiral from a bit of charred wood, the mass of the great bed, and, in the very middle, black against the curious brightness, the armored man, or ghost, or devil, standing, not suspended, beneath the rusty hook. And with the rending of the wall the music grew more distinct, though sounding still very, very far away.

Count Albert raised his mailed hand and beckoned to him; then turned, and stood in the riven wall.

Without a word, Rupert rose and followed him, his pistol in hand. Count Albert passed through the mighty wall and disappeared in the unearthly light. Rupert followed mechanically. He felt the crushing of the mortar beneath his feet, the roughness of the jagged wall where he rested his hand to steady himself.

The keep rose absolutely isolated among the ruins, yet on passing through the wall Rupert found himself in a long, uneven corridor, the floor of which was warped and sagging, while the walls were covered on one side with big faded portraits of an inferior quality, like those in the corridor that connects the Pitti and Uffizzi in Florence. Before him moved the figure of Count Albert—a black silhouette in the ever-increasing light. And always the music grew stronger and stranger, a mad, evil, seductive dance that bewitched even while it disgusted.

In a final blaze of vivid, intolerable light, in a burst of hellish music that might have come from Bedlam, Rupert stepped from the corridor into a vast and curious room where at first he saw nothing, distinguished nothing but a mad, seething whirl of sweeping figures, white, in a white room, under white light, Count Albert standing before him, the only dark object to be seen. As his eyes grew accustomed to the fearful brightness, he knew that he was looking on a dance such as the damned might see in hell, but such as no living man had ever seen before.

Around the long, narrow hall, under the fearful light that came from nowhere, but was omnipresent, swept a rushing stream of unspeakable horrors, dancing insanely, laughing, gibbering hideously; the dead of forty years. White, polished skeletons, bare of flesh and vesture, skeletons clothed in the dreadful rags of dried and rattling sinews, the tags of tattering grave-clothes flaunting behind them. These were the dead of many years ago. Then the dead of more recent times, with yellow bones showing only here and there, the long and insecure hair of their hideous heads writhing in the beating air. Then green and gray horrors, bloated and shapeless, stained with earth or dripping with spattering water; and here and there white, beautiful things, like chiselled ivory, the dead of yesterday, locked it may be, in the mummy arms of rattling skeletons.

Round and round the cursed room, a swaying, swirling maelstrom of death, while the air grew thick with miasma, the floor foul with shreds of shrouds, and yellow parchment, clattering bones, and wisps of tangled hair.

And in the very midst of this ring of death, a sight not for words nor for thought, a sight to blast forever the mind of the man who looked upon it: a leaping, writhing dance of Count Albert's victims, the score of beautiful women and reckless men who danced to their awful death while the castle burned around them, charred and shapeless now, a living charnel-house of nameless horror.

Count Albert, who had stood silent and gloomy, watching the dance of the damned, turned to Rupert, and for the first time spoke.

"We are ready for you now; dance!"

A prancing horror, dead some dozen years, perhaps, flaunted from the rushing river of the dead, and leered at Rupert with eyeless skull.

"Dance!"

Rupert stood frozen, motionless.

"Dance!"

His hard lips moved. "Not if the devil came from hell to make me."

Count Albert swept his vast two-handed sword into the fœtid air while the tide of corruption paused in its swirling, and swept down on Rupert with gibbering grins.

The room, and the howling dead, and the black portent before him circled dizzily around, as with a last effort of departing consciousness he drew his pistol and fired full in the face of Count Albert.

Perfect silence, perfect darkness; not a breath, not a sound: the dead stillness of a long-sealed tomb. Rupert lay on his back, stunned, helpless, his pistol clenched in his frozen hand, a smell of powder in the black air. Where was he? Dead? In hell? He reached his hand out cautiously; it fell on dusty boards. Outside, far away, a clock struck three. Had he dreamed? Of course; but how ghastly a dream! With chattering teeth he called softly—

"Otto!"

There was no reply, and none when he called again and again. He staggered weakly to his feet, groping for matches and candles. A panic of abject terror came on him; the matches were gone! He turned towards the fireplace: a single coal glowed in the white ashes. He swept a mass of papers and dusty books from the table, and with trembling hands cowered over the embers, until he succeeded in lighting the dry tinder. Then he piled the old books on the blaze, and looked fearfully around.

No: It was gone—thank God for that; the hook was empty.

But why did Otto sleep so soundly; why did he not awake?

He stepped unsteadily across the room in the flaring light of the burning books, and knelt by the mattress.

So they found him in the morning, when no one came to the inn from Kropfsberg Keep, and the quaking Peter Rosskopf arranged a relief party—found him kneeling beside the mattress where Otto lay, shot in the throat and quite dead.

The Lost Stradivarius

J. Meade Falkner

Letter from Miss Sophia Maltravers to her Nephew, Sir Edward Maltravers, then a Student at Christ Church, Oxford.

13 Pauncefort Buildings, Bath
Oct. 21, 1867

My Dear Edward,

It was your late father's dying request that certain events which occurred in his last years should be communicated to you on your coming of age. I have reduced them to writing, partly from my own recollection, which is, alas! still too vivid, and partly with the aid of notes taken at the time of my brother's death. As you are now of full age, I submit the narrative to you. Much of it has necessarily been exceedingly painful to me to write, but at the same time I feel it is better that you should hear the truth from me than garbled stories from others who did not love your father as I did.

Your loving Aunt,
Sophia Maltravers

To Sir Edward Maltravers, Bart.

MISS SOPHIA MALTRAVERS' STORY

I

Your father, John Maltravers, was born in 1820 at Worth, and succeeded his father and mine, who died when we were still young children. John was sent to Eton in due course, and in 1839, when he was nineteen years of age, it was determined that he should go to Oxford. It was intended at first to enter him at Christ Church; but Dr. Sarsdell, who visited us at Worth in the summer of 1839, persuaded Mr. Thoresby, our guardian, to send him instead to Magdalen Hall. Dr. Sarsdell was himself Principal of that institution, and represented that John, who then exhibited some symptoms of delicacy, would meet with more personal attention under his care than he could hope to do in so large a college as Christ Church. Mr. Thoresby, ever solicitous for his ward's welfare, readily waived other considerations in favour of an arrangement which he considered conducive to John's health, and he was accordingly matriculated at Magdalen Hall in the autumn of 1839.

Dr. Sarsdell had not been unmindful of his promise to look after my brother, and had secured him an excellent first-floor sitting-room, with a bedroom adjoining, having an aspect towards New College Lane.

I shall pass over the first two years of my brother's residence at Oxford, because they have nothing to do with the present story. They were spent, no doubt, in the ordinary routine of work and recreation common in Oxford at that period.

From his earliest boyhood he had been passionately devoted to music, and had attained a considerable proficiency on the violin. In the autumn term of 1841 he made the acquaintance of Mr. William Gaskell, a very talented student at New College, and also a more than tolerable musician. The practice of music was then very much less common at Oxford than it has since become, and there were none of those societies existing which now do so much to promote its study among undergraduates. It was therefore a cause of much gratification to the two young men, and it afterwards became a strong bond of friendship, to discover that one was as devoted to the pianoforte as was the other to the violin. Mr. Gaskell, though in easy circumstances, had not a pianoforte in his rooms, and was pleased to use a fine instrument by D'Almaine that John had that term received as a birthday present from his guardian.

From that time the two students were thrown much together, and in the autumn term of 1841 and Easter term of 1842 practised a variety of music in John's rooms, he taking the violin part and Mr. Gaskell that for the pianoforte.

It was, I think, in March 1842 that John purchased for his rooms a piece of furniture which was destined afterwards to play no unimportant part in the story I am narrating. This was a very large and low wicker chair of a form then coming into fashion in Oxford, and since, I am told, become a familiar object of most college rooms. It was cushioned with a gaudy pattern of chintz, and bought for new of an upholsterer at the bottom of the High Street.

Mr. Gaskell was taken by his uncle to spend Easter in Rome, and obtaining special leave from his college to prolong his travels, did not return to Oxford till three weeks of the summer term were passed and May was well advanced. So impatient was he to see his friend that he would not let even the first evening of his return pass without coming round to John's rooms. The two young men sat without lights until the night was late; and Mr. Gaskell had much to narrate of his travels, and spoke specially of the beautiful music which he had heard at Easter in the Roman churches. He had also had lessons on the piano from a celebrated professor of the Italian style, but seemed to have been particularly delighted with the music of the seventeenth-century composers, of whose works he had brought back some specimens set for piano and violin.

It was past eleven o'clock when Mr. Gaskell left to return to New College; but the night was unusually warm, with a moon near the full, and John sat for some time in a cushioned window-seat before the open sash thinking over what he had heard about the music of Italy. Feeling still disinclined for sleep, he lit a single candle and began to turn over some of the musical works which Mr. Gaskell had left on the table. His attention was especially attracted to an oblong book, bound in soiled vellum, with a coat of arms stamped in gilt upon the side. It was a manuscript copy of some early suites by Graziani for violin and harpsichord, and was apparently written at Naples in the year 1744, many years after the death of that composer. Though the ink was yellow and faded, the transcript had been accurately made, and could be read with tolerable comfort by an advanced musician in spite of the antiquated notation.

Perhaps by accident, or perhaps by some mysterious direction which our minds are incapable of appreciating, his eye was arrested by a suite of four movements with a *basso continuo*, or figured bass, for the harpsichord. The other suites in the book were only distinguished by numbers, but this one the composer had dignified with the name of "l'Areopagita." Almost mechanically John put the book on his music-stand, took his violin from its case, and after a moment's tuning stood up and played the first movement, a lively *Coranto*. The light of the single candle burning on the table was scarcely sufficient to illumine the page; the shadows hung in the creases of the leaves, which had grown into those wavy folds sometimes observable in books made of thick paper and remaining long shut; and it was with difficulty that he could read what he was playing. But he felt the strange impulse of the old-world music urging him forward, and did not even pause to light the candles which stood ready in their sconces on either side of the desk. The *Coranto* was followed by a *Sarabanda*, and the *Sarabanda* by a *Gagliarda*. My brother stood playing, with his face turned to the window, with the room and the large wicker chair of which I have spoken behind him. The *Gagliarda* began with a bold and lively air, and as he played the opening bars, he heard behind him a creaking of the wicker chair. The sound was a perfectly familiar one—as of some person placing a hand on either arm of the chair preparatory to lowering himself into it, followed by another as of the same person being leisurely seated. But for the tones of the violin, all was silent, and the creaking of the chair was strangely distinct. The illusion was so complete that my brother stopped playing suddenly, and turned round expecting that some late friend of his had slipped in unawares, being attracted by the sound of the violin, or that Mr. Gaskell himself had returned. With the cessation of the music an absolute stillness fell upon all; the light of the single candle scarcely reached the darker corners of the room, but fell directly on the wicker chair and showed it to be perfectly empty. Half amused, half vexed with himself at having without reason interrupted his music, my brother returned to the *Gagliarda*; but some impulse induced him to light the candles in the sconces, which gave an illumination more adequate to the occasion. The *Gagliarda* and the last movement, a *Minuetto*, were finished, and John closed the book, intending, as it was now late, to seek his bed. As he shut the pages a creaking of the wicker chair again attracted his attention, and he heard distinctly sounds such as would be made by a person raising himself from a sitting posture. This time, being less surprised, he could more aptly consider the probable causes of such a circumstance, and easily arrived at the conclusion that there must be in the wicker chair osiers responsive to certain notes of the violin, as panes of glass in church windows are observed to vibrate in sympathy with certain tones of the organ. But while this argument approved itself to his reason, his imagination was but half convinced; and he could not but be impressed with the fact that the second creaking of the chair had been coincident with his shutting the music-book; and, unconsciously, pictured to himself some strange visitor waiting until the termination of the music, and then taking his departure.

His conjectures did not, however, either rob him of sleep or even disturb it with dreams, and he woke the next morning with a cooler mind and one less inclined to fantastic imagination. If the strange episode of the previous evening had not entirely vanished from his mind, it seemed at least fully accounted for by the acoustic explanation to which I have alluded above. Although he saw Mr. Gaskell in the course of the morning, he did not think it necessary to mention to him so trivial a circumstance, but made with him an appointment to sup together in his own rooms that evening, and to amuse themselves afterwards by essaying some of the Italian music.

It was shortly after nine that night when, supper being finished, Mr. Gaskell seated himself at the piano and John tuned his violin. The evening was closing in; there had been heavy thunder-rain in the afternoon, and the moist air hung now heavy and steaming, while across it there throbbed the distant vibrations of the tenor bell at Christ Church. It was tolling the customary 101 strokes, which are rung every night in term-time as a signal for closing the college gates. The two young men enjoyed themselves for some while, playing first a suite by Cesti, and then two early sonatas by Buononcini. Both of them were sufficiently expert musicians to make reading at sight a pleasure rather than an effort; and Mr. Gaskell especially was well versed in the theory of music, and in the correct rendering of the *basso continuo*. After the Buononcini Mr. Gaskell took up the oblong copy of Graziani, and turning over its leaves, proposed that they should play the same suite which John had performed by himself the previous evening. His selection was apparently perfectly fortuitous, as my brother had purposely refrained from directing his attention in any way to that piece of music. They played the *Coranto* and the *Sarabanda*, and in the singular fascination of the music John had entirely forgotten the episode of the previous evening, when, as the bold air of the *Gagliarda* commenced, he suddenly became aware of the same strange creaking of the wicker chair that he had noticed on the first occasion. The sound was identical, and so exact was its resemblance to that of a person sitting down that he stared at the chair, almost wondering that it still appeared empty. Beyond turning his head sharply for a moment to look round, Mr. Gaskell took no notice of the sound; and my brother, ashamed to betray any foolish interest or excitement, continued the *Gagliarda*, with its repeat. At its conclusion Mr. Gaskell stopped before proceeding to the minuet, and turning the stool on which he was sitting round towards the room, observed, "How very strange, Johnnie,"—for these young men were on terms of sufficient intimacy to address each other in a familiar style,—"How very strange! I thought I heard some one sit down in that chair when we began the *Gagliarda*. I looked round quite expecting to see some one had come in. Did you hear nothing?"

"It was only the chair creaking," my brother answered, feigning an indifference which he scarcely felt. "Certain parts of the wicker-work seem to be in accord with musical notes and respond to them; let us continue with the *Minuetto*."

Thus they finished the suite, Mr. Gaskell demanding a repetition of the *Gagliarda*, with the air of which he was much pleased. As the clocks had already struck eleven, they determined not to play more that night; and Mr. Gaskell rose, blew out the sconces, shut the piano, and put the music aside. My brother has often assured me that he was quite prepared for what followed, and had been almost expecting it; for as the books were put away, a creaking of the wicker chair was audible, exactly similar to that which he had heard when he stopped playing on the previous night. There was a moment's silence; the young men looked involuntarily at one another, and then Mr. Gaskell said, "I cannot understand the creaking of that chair; it has never done so before, with all the music we have played. I am perhaps imaginative and excited with the fine airs we have heard to-night, but I have an impression that I cannot dispel that something has been sitting listening to us all this time, and that now when the concert is ended it has got up and gone." There was a spirit of raillery in his words, but his tone was not so light as it would ordinarily have been, and he was evidently ill at ease.

"Let us try the *Gagliarda* again," said my brother; "it is the vibration of the opening notes which affects the wicker-work, and we shall see if the noise is repeated." But Mr. Gaskell excused himself from trying the experiment, and after some desultory conversation, to which it was evident that neither was giving any serious attention, he took his leave and returned to New College.

II

I shall not weary you, my dear Edward, by recounting similar experiences which occurred on nearly every occasion that the young men met in the evenings for music. The repetition of the phenomenon had accustomed them to expect it. Both professed to be quite satisfied that it was to be attributed to acoustical affinities of vibration between the wicker-work and certain of the piano wires, and indeed this seemed the only explanation possible. But, at the same time, the resemblance of the noises to those caused by a person sitting down in or rising from a chair was so marked, that even their frequent recurrence never failed to make a strange impression on them. They felt a reluctance to mention the matter to their friends, partly from a fear of being themselves laughed at, and partly to spare from ridicule a circumstance to which each perhaps, in spite of himself, attached some degree of importance. Experience soon convinced them that the first noise as of one sitting down never occurred unless the *Gagliarda* of the "Areopagita" was played, and that this noise being once heard, the second only followed it when they ceased playing for the evening. They met every night, sitting later with the lengthening summer evenings, and every night, as by some tacit understanding, played the "Areopagita" suite before parting. At the opening bars of the *Gagliarda* the creaking of the chair occurred spontaneously with the utmost regularity. They seldom spoke even to one another of the subject; but one night, when John was putting away his violin after a long evening's music without having played the "Areopagita," Mr. Gaskell, who had risen from the pianoforte, sat down again as by a sudden impulse and said—

"Johnnie, do not put away your violin yet. It is near twelve o'clock and I shall get shut out, but I cannot stop to-night without playing the *Gagliarda*. Suppose that all our theories of vibration and affinity are wrong, suppose that there really comes here night by night some strange visitant to hear us, some poor creature whose heart is bound up in that tune; would it not be unkind to send him away without the hearing of that piece which he seems most to relish? Let us not be ill-mannered, but humour his whim; let us play the *Gagliarda*."

They played it with more vigour and precision than usual, and the now customary sound of one taking his seat at once ensued. It was that night that my brother, looking steadfastly at the chair, saw, or thought he saw, there some slight obscuration, some penumbra, mist, or subtle vapour which, as he gazed, seemed to struggle to take human form. He ceased playing for a moment and rubbed his eyes, but as he did so all dimness vanished and he saw the chair perfectly empty. The pianist stopped also at the cessation of the violin, and asked what ailed him.

"It is only that my eyes were dim," he answered.

"We have had enough for to-night," said Mr. Gaskell; "let us stop. I shall be locked out." He shut the piano, and as he did so the clock in New College tower struck twelve. He left the room running, but was late enough at his college door to be reported, admonished with a fine against such late hours, and confined for a week to college; for being out after midnight was considered, at that time at least, a somewhat serious offence.

Thus for some days the musical practice was compulsorily intermitted, but resumed on the first evening after Mr. Gaskell's term of confinement was expired. After they had performed several suites of Graziani, and finished as usual with the "Areopagita," Mr. Gaskell sat for a time silent at the instrument, as though thinking with himself, and then said—

"I cannot say how deeply this old-fashioned music affects me. Some would try to persuade us that these suites, of which the airs bear the names of different dances, were always written rather as a musical essay and for purposes of performance than for persons to dance to, as their names would more naturally imply. But I think these critics are wrong at least in some instances. It is to me impossible to believe that such a melody, for instance, as the *Giga* of Corelli which we have played, was not written for actual purposes of dancing. One can almost hear the beat of feet upon the floor, and I imagine that in the time of Corelli the practice of dancing, while not a whit inferior in grace, had more of the tripudistic or beating character than is now esteemed consistent with a correct ball-room performance. The *Gagliarda* too, which we play now so constantly, possesses a singular power of assisting the imagination to picture or reproduce such scenes as those which it no doubt formerly enlivened. I know not why, but it is constantly identified in my mind with some revel which I have perhaps seen in a picture, where several couples are dancing a licentious measure in a long room lit by a number of silver sconces of the debased model common at the end of the seventeenth century. It is probably a reminiscence of my late excursion that gives to these dancers in my fancy the olive skin, dark hair, and bright eyes of the Italian type; and they wear dresses of exceedingly rich fabric and elaborate design. Imagination is whimsical enough to paint for me the character of the room itself, as having an arcade of arches running down one side alone, of the fantastic and paganised Gothic of the Renaissance. At the end is a gallery or balcony for the musicians, which on its coved front has a florid coat of arms of foreign heraldry. The shield bears, on a field *or*, a cherub's head blowing on three lilies—a blazon I have no doubt seen somewhere in my travels, though I cannot recollect where. This scene, I say, is so nearly connected in my brain with the *Gagliarda*, that scarcely are its first notes sounded ere it presents itself to my eyes with a vividness which increases every day. The couples advance, set, and recede, using free and licentious gestures which my imagination should be ashamed to recall. Amongst so many foreigners, fancy pictures, I know not in the least why, the presence of a young man of an English type of face, whose features, however, always elude my mind's attempt to fix them. I think that the opening subject of this *Gagliarda* is a superior composition to the rest of it, for it is only during the first sixteen bars that the vision of bygone revelry presents itself to me. With the last note of the sixteenth bar a veil is drawn suddenly across the scene, and with a sense almost of some catastrophe it vanishes. This I attribute to the fact that the second subject must be inferior in conception to the first, and by some sense of incongruity destroys the fabric which the fascination of the preceding one built up."

My brother, though he had listened with interest to what Mr. Gaskell had said, did not reply, and the subject was allowed to drop.

III

It was in the same summer of 1842, and near the middle of June, that my brother John wrote inviting me to come to Oxford for the Commemoration festivities. I had been spending some weeks with Mrs. Temple, a distant cousin of ours, at their house of Royston in Derbyshire, and John was desirous that Mrs. Temple should come up to Oxford and chaperone her daughter Constance and myself at the balls and various other entertainments which take place at the close of the summer term. Owing to Royston being some two hundred miles from Worth Maltravers, our families had hitherto seen little of one another, but during my present visit I had learned to love Mrs. Temple, a lady of singular sweetness of disposition, and had contracted a devoted attachment to her daughter Constance. Constance Temple was then eighteen years of age, and to great beauty united such mental graces and excellent traits of character as must ever appear to reasoning persons more enduringly valuable than even the highest personal attractions. She was well read and witty, and had been trained in those principles of true religion which she afterwards followed with devoted consistency in the self-sacrifice and resigned piety of her too short life. In person, I may remind you, my dear Edward, since death removed her ere you were of years to appreciate either her appearance or her qualities, she was tall, with a somewhat long and oval face, with brown hair and eyes.

Mrs. Temple readily accepted Sir John Maltravers' invitation. She had never seen Oxford herself, and was pleased to afford us the pleasure of so delightful an excursion. John had secured convenient rooms for us above the shop of a well-known printseller in High Street, and we arrived in Oxford on Friday evening, June 18, 1842. I shall not dilate to you on the various Commemoration festivities, which have probably altered little since those days, and with which you are familiar. Suffice it to say that my brother had secured us admission to every entertainment, and that we enjoyed our visit as only youth with its keen sensibilities and uncloyed pleasures can. I could not help observing that John was very much struck by the attractions of Miss Constance Temple, and that she for her part, while exhibiting no unbecoming forwardness, certainly betrayed no aversion to him. I was greatly pleased both with my own powers of observation which had enabled me to discover so important a fact, and also with the circumstance itself. To a romantic girl of nineteen it appeared high time that a brother of twenty-two should be at least preparing some matrimonial project; and my friend was so good and beautiful that it seemed impossible that I should ever obtain a more lovable sister or my brother a better wife. Mrs. Temple could not refuse her sanction to such a scheme; for while their mental qualities seemed eminently compatible, John was in his own right master of Worth Maltravers, and her daughter sole heiress of the Royston estates.

The Commemoration festivities terminated on Wednesday night with a grand ball at the Music-Room in Holywell Street. This was given by a Lodge of University Freemasons, and John was there with Mr. Gaskell—whose acquaintance we had made with much gratification—both wearing blue silk scarves and small white aprons. They introduced us to many other of their friends similarly adorned, and these important and mysterious insignia sat not amiss with their youthful figures and boyish faces. After a long and pleasurable programme, it was decided that we should prolong our visit till the next evening, leaving Oxford at half-past ten o'clock at night and driving to Didcot, there to join the mail for the west. We rose late the next morning and spent the day rambling among the old colleges and gardens of the most beautiful of English cities. At seven o'clock we dined together for the last time at our lodgings in High Street, and my brother proposed that before parting we should enjoy the fine evening in the gardens of St. John's College. This was at once agreed to, and we proceeded thither, John walking on in front with Constance and Mrs. Temple, and I following with Mr. Gaskell. My companion explained that these gardens were esteemed the most beautiful in the University, but that under ordinary circumstances it was not permitted to strangers to walk there of an evening. Here he quoted some Latin about "aurum per medios ire satellites," which I smilingly made as if I understood, and did indeed gather from it that John had bribed the porter to admit us. It was a warm and very still night, without a moon, but with enough of fading light to show the outlines of the garden front. This long low line of buildings built in Charles I.'s reign looked so exquisitely beautiful that I shall never forget it, though I have not since seen its oriel windows and creeper-covered walls. There was a very heavy dew on the broad lawn, and we walked at first only on the paths. No one spoke, for we were oppressed by the very beauty of the scene, and by the sadness which an imminent parting from friends and from so sweet a place combined to cause. John had been silent and depressed the whole day, nor did Mr. Gaskell himself seem inclined to conversation. Constance and my brother fell a little way behind, and Mr. Gaskell asked me to cross the lawn if I was not afraid of the dew, that I might see the garden front to better advantage from the corner. Mrs. Temple waited for us on the path, not wishing to wet her feet. Mr. Gaskell pointed out the beauties of the perspective as seen from his vantage-point, and we were fortunate in hearing the sweet descant of nightingales for which this garden has ever been famous. As we stood silent and listening, a candle was lit in a small oriel at the end, and the light showing the tracery of the window added to the picturesqueness of the scene.

Within an hour we were in a landau driving through the still warm lanes to Didcot. I had seen that Constance's parting with my brother had been tender, and I am not sure that she was not in tears during some part at least of our drive; but I did not observe her closely, having my thoughts elsewhere.

Though we were thus being carried every moment further from the sleeping city, where I believe that both our hearts were busy, I feel as if I had been a personal witness of the incidents I am about to narrate, so often have I heard them from my brother's lips. The two young men, after parting with us in the High Street, returned to their respective colleges. John reached his rooms shortly before eleven o'clock. He was at once sad and happy—sad at our departure, but happy in a new-found world of delight which his admiration for Constance Temple opened to him. He was, in fact, deeply in love with her, and the full flood of a hitherto unknown passion filled him with an emotion so overwhelming that his ordinary life seemed transfigured. He moved, as it were, in an ether superior to our mortal atmosphere, and a new region of high resolves and noble possibilities spread itself before his eyes. He slammed his heavy outside door (called an "oak") to prevent anyone entering and flung himself into the window-seat. Here he sat for a long time, the sash thrown up and his head outside, for he was excited and feverish. His mental exaltation was so great and his thoughts of so absorbing an interest that he took no notice of time, and only remembered afterwards that the scent of a syringa-bush was borne up to him from a little garden-patch opposite, and that a bat had circled slowly up and down the lane, until he heard the clocks striking three. At the same time the faint light of dawn made itself felt almost imperceptibly; the classic statues on the roof of the schools began to stand out against the white sky, and a faint glimmer to penetrate the darkened room. It glistened on the varnished top of his violin-case lying on the table, and on a jug of toast-and-water placed there by his college servant or scout every night before he left. He drank a glass of this mixture, and was moving towards his bedroom door when a sudden thought struck him. He turned back, took the violin from its case, tuned it, and began to play the "Areopagita" suite. He was conscious of that mental clearness and vigour which not unfrequently comes with the dawn to those who have sat watching or reading through the night: and his thoughts were exalted by the effect which the first consciousness of a deep passion causes in imaginative minds. He had never played the suite with more power; and the airs, even without the piano part, seemed fraught with a meaning hitherto unrealised. As he began the *Gagliarda* he heard the wicker chair creak; but he had his back towards it, and the sound was now too familiar to him to cause him even to look round. It was not till he was playing the repeat that he became aware of a new and overpowering sensation. At first it was a vague feeling, so often experienced by us all, of not being alone. He did not stop playing, and in a few seconds the impression of a presence in the room other than his own became so strong that he was actually afraid to look round. But in another moment he felt that at all hazards he must see what or who this presence was. Without stopping he partly turned and partly looked over his shoulder. The silver light of early morning was filling the room, making the various objects appear of less bright colour than usual, and giving to everything a pearl-grey neutral tint. In this cold but clear light he saw seated in the wicker chair the figure of a man.

In the first violent shock of so terrifying a discovery, he could not appreciate such details as those of features, dress, or appearance. He was merely conscious that with him, in a locked room of which he knew himself to be the only human inmate, there sat something which bore a human form. He looked at it for a moment with a hope, which he felt to be vain, that it might vanish and prove a phantom of his excited imagination, but still it sat there. Then my brother put down his violin, and he used to assure me that a horror overwhelmed him of an intensity which he had previously believed impossible. Whether the image which he saw was subjective or objective, I cannot pretend to say: you will be in a position to judge for yourself when you have finished this narrative. Our limited experience would lead us to believe that it was a phantom conjured up by some unusual condition of his own brain; but we are fain to confess that there certainly do exist in nature phenomena such as baffle human reason; and it is possible that, for some hidden purposes of Providence, permission may occasionally be granted to those who have passed from this life to assume again for a time the form of their earthly tabernacle. We must, I say, be content to suspend our judgment on such matters; but in this instance the subsequent course of events is very difficult to explain, except on the supposition that there was then presented to my brother's view the actual bodily form of one long deceased. The dread which took possession of him was due, he has more than once told me when analysing his feelings long afterwards, to two predominant causes. Firstly, he felt that mental dislocation which accompanies the sudden subversion of preconceived theories, the sudden alteration of long habit, or even the occurrence of any circumstance beyond the walk of our daily experience. This I have observed myself in the perturbing effect which a sudden death, a grievous accident, or in recent years the declaration of war, has exercised upon all except the most lethargic or the most determined minds. Secondly, he experienced the profound self-abasement or mental annihilation caused by the near conception of a being of a superior order. In the presence of an existence wearing, indeed, the human form, but of attributes widely different from and superior to his own, he felt the combined reverence and revulsion which even the noblest wild animals exhibit when brought for the first time face to face with man. The shock was so great that I feel persuaded it exerted an effect on him from which he never wholly recovered.

After an interval which seemed to him interminable, though it was only of a second's duration, he turned his eyes again to the occupant of the wicker chair. His faculties had so far recovered from the first shock as to enable him to see that the figure was that of a man perhaps thirty-five years of age and still youthful in appearance. The face was long and oval, the hair brown, and brushed straight off an exceptionally high forehead. His complexion was very pale or bloodless. He was clean shaven, and his finely cut mouth, with compressed lips, wore something of a sneering smile. His general expression was unpleasing, and from the first my brother felt as by intuition that there was present some malign and wicked influence. His eyes were not visible, as he kept them cast down, resting his head on his hand in the attitude of one listening. His face and even his dress were impressed so vividly upon John's mind, that he never had any difficulty in recalling them to his imagination; and he and I had afterwards an opportunity of verifying them in a remarkable manner. He wore a long cut-away coat of green cloth with an edge of gold embroidery, and a white satin waistcoat figured with rose-sprigs, a full cravat of rich lace, knee-breeches of buff silk, and stockings of the same. His shoes were of polished black leather with heavy silver buckles, and his costume in general recalled that worn a century ago. As my brother gazed at him, he got up, putting his hands on the arms of the chair to raise himself, and causing the creaking so often heard before. The hands forced themselves on my brother's notice: they were very white, with the long delicate fingers of a musician. He showed a considerable height; and still keeping his eyes on the floor, walked with an ordinary gait towards the end of the bookcase at the side of the room farthest from the window. He reached the bookcase, and then John suddenly lost sight of him. The figure did not fade gradually, but went out, as it were, like the flame of a suddenly extinguished candle.

The room was now filled with the clear light of the summer morning: the whole vision had lasted but a few seconds, but my brother knew that there was no possibility of his having been mistaken, that the mystery of the creaking chair was solved, that he had seen the man who had come evening by evening for a month past to listen to the rhythm of the *Gagliarda*. Terribly disturbed, he sat for some time half dreading and half expecting a return of the figure; but all remained unchanged: he saw nothing, nor did he dare to challenge its reappearance by playing again the *Gagliarda*, which seemed to have so strange an attraction for it. At last, in the full sunlight of a late June morning at Oxford, he heard the steps of early pedestrians on the pavement below his windows, the cry of a milkman, and other sounds which showed the world was awake. It was after six o'clock, and going to his bedroom he flung himself on the outside of the bed for an hour's troubled slumber.

IV

When his servant called him about eight o'clock my brother sent a note to Mr. Gaskell at New College, begging him to come round to Magdalen Hall as soon as might be in the course of the morning. His summons was at once obeyed, and Mr. Gaskell was with him before he had finished breakfast. My brother was still much agitated, and at once told him what had happened the night before, detailing the various circumstances with minuteness, and not even concealing from him the sentiments which he entertained towards Miss Constance Temple. In narrating the appearance which he had seen in the chair, his agitation was still so excessive that he had difficulty in controlling his voice.

Mr. Gaskell heard him with much attention, and did not at once reply when John had finished his narration. At length he said, "I suppose many friends would think it right to affect, even if they did not feel, an incredulity as to what you have just told me. They might consider it more prudent to attempt to allay your distress by persuading you that what you have seen has no objective reality, but is merely the phantasm of an excited imagination; that if you had not been in love, had not sat up all night, and had not thus overtaxed your physical powers, you would have seen no vision. I shall not argue thus, for I am as certainly convinced as of the fact that we sit here, that on all the nights when we have played this suite called the 'Areopagita,' there has been some one listening to us, and that you have at length been fortunate or unfortunate enough to see him."

"Do not say fortunate," said my brother; "for I feel as though I shall never recover from last night's shock."

"That is likely enough," Mr. Gaskell answered, coolly; "for as in the history of the race or individual, increased culture and a finer mental susceptibility necessarily impair the brute courage and powers of endurance which we note in savages, so any supernatural vision such as you have seen must be purchased at the cost of physical reaction. From the first evening that we played this music, and heard the noises mimicking so closely the sitting down and rising up of some person, I have felt convinced that causes other than those which we usually call natural were at work, and that we were very near the manifestation of some extraordinary phenomenon."

"I do not quite apprehend your meaning."

"I mean this," he continued, "that this man or spirit of a man has been sitting here night after night, and that we have not been able to see him, because our minds are dull and obtuse. Last night the elevating force of a strong passion, such as that which you have confided to me, combined with the power of fine music, so exalted your mind that you became endowed, as it were, with a sixth sense, and suddenly were enabled to see that which had previously been invisible. To this sixth sense music gives, I believe, the key. We are at present only on the threshold of such a knowledge of that art as will enable us to use it eventually as the greatest of all humanising and educational agents. Music will prove a ladder to the loftier regions of thought; indeed I have long found for myself that I cannot attain to the highest range of my intellectual power except when hearing good music. All poets, and most writers of prose, will say that their thought is never so exalted, their sense of beauty and proportion never so just, as when they are listening either to the artificial music made by man, or to some of the grander tones of nature, such as the roar of a western ocean, or the sighing of wind in a clump of firs. Though I have often felt on such occasions on the very verge of some high mental discovery, and though a hand has been stretched forward as it were to rend the veil, yet it has never been vouchsafed me to see behind it. This you no doubt were allowed in a measure to do last night. You probably played the music with a deeper intuition than usual, and this, combined with the excitement under which you were already labouring, raised you for a moment to the required pitch of mental exaltation."

"It is true," John said, "that I never felt the melody so deeply as when I played it last night."

"Just so," answered his friend; "and there is probably some link between this air and the history of the man whom you saw last night; some fatal power in it which enables it to exert an attraction on him even after death. For we must remember that the influence of music, though always powerful, is not always for good. We can scarcely doubt that as certain forms of music tend to raise us above the sensuality of the animal, or the more degrading passion of material gain, and to transport us into the ether of higher thought, so other forms are directly calculated to awaken in us luxurious emotions, and to whet those sensual appetites which it is the business of a philosopher not indeed to annihilate or to be ashamed of, but to keep rigidly in check. This possibility of music to effect evil as well as good I have seen recognised, and very aptly expressed in some beautiful verses by Mr. Keble which I have just read:—

> "Cease, stranger, cease those witching notes,
>   The art of syren choirs;
> Hush the seductive voice that floats
>   Across the trembling wires.
>
> "Music's ethereal power was given
>   Not to dissolve our clay,
> But draw Promethean beams from heaven
>   To purge the dross away."

"They are fine lines," said my brother, "but I do not see how you apply your argument to the present instance."

"I mean," Mr. Gaskell answered, "that I have little doubt that the melody of this *Gagliarda* has been connected in some manner with the life of the man you saw last night. It is not unlikely, either, that it was a favourite air of his whilst in the flesh, or even that it was played by himself or others at the moment of some crisis in his history. It is possible that such connection may be due merely to the innocent pleasure the melody gave him in life; but the nature of the music itself, and a peculiar effect it has upon my own thoughts, induce me to believe that it was associated with some occasion when he either fell into great sin or when some evil fate, perhaps even death itself, overtook him. You will remember I have told you that this air calls up to my mind a certain scene of Italian revelry in which an Englishman takes part. It is true that I have never been able to fix his features in my mind, nor even to say exactly how he was dressed. Yet now some instinct tells me that it is this very man whom you saw last night. It is not for us to attempt to pierce the mystery which veils from our eyes the secrets of an after-death existence; but I can scarcely suppose that a spirit entirely at rest would feel so deeply the power of a certain melody as to be called back by it to his old haunts like a dog by his master's whistle. It is more probable that there is some evil history connected with the matter, and this, I think, we ought to consider if it be possible to unravel."

My brother assenting, he continued, "When this man left you, Johnnie, did he walk to the door?"

"No; he made for the side wall, and when he reached the end of the bookcase I lost sight of him."

Mr. Gaskell went to the bookcase and looked for a moment at the titles of the books, as though expecting to see something in them to assist his inquiries; but finding apparently no clue, he said—

"This is the last time we shall meet for three months or more; let us play the *Gagliarda* and see if there be any response."

My brother at first would not hear of this, showing a lively dread of challenging any reappearance of the figure he had seen: indeed he felt that such an event would probably fling him into a state of serious physical disorder. Mr. Gaskell, however, continued to press him, assuring him that the fact of his now being no longer alone should largely allay any fear on his part, and urging that this would be the last opportunity they would have of playing together for some months.

At last, being overborne, my brother took his violin, and Mr. Gaskell seated himself at the pianoforte. John was very agitated, and as he commenced the *Gagliarda* his hands trembled so that he could scarcely play the air. Mr. Gaskell also exhibited some nervousness, not performing with his customary correctness. But for the first time the charm failed: no noise accompanied the music, nor did anything of an unusual character occur. They repeated the whole suite, but with a similar result.

Both were surprised, but neither had any explanation to offer. My brother, who at first dreaded intensely a repetition of the vision, was now almost disappointed that nothing had occurred; so quickly does the mood of man change.

After some further conversation the young men parted for the Long Vacation—John returning to Worth Maltravers and Mr. Gaskell going to London, where he was to pass a few days before he proceeded to his home in Westmorland.

V

John spent nearly the whole of this summer vacation at Worth Maltravers. He had been anxious to pay a visit to Royston; but the continued and serious illness of Mrs. Temple's sister had called her and Constance to Scotland, where they remained until the death of their relative allowed them to return to Derbyshire in the late autumn. John and I had been brought up together from childhood. When he was at Eton we had always spent the holidays at Worth, and after my dear mother's death, when we were left quite alone, the bonds of our love were naturally drawn still closer. Even after my brother went to Oxford, at a time when most young men are anxious to enjoy a new-found liberty, and to travel or to visit friends in their vacation, John's ardent affection for me and for Worth Maltravers kept him at home; and he was pleased on most occasions to make me the partner of his thoughts and of his pleasures. This long vacation of 1842 was, I think, the happiest of our lives. In my case I know it was so, and I think it was happy also for him; for none could guess that the small cloud seen in the distance like a man's hand was afterwards to rise and darken all his later days. It was a summer of brilliant and continued sunshine; many of the old people said that they could never recollect so fine a season, and both fruit and crops were alike abundant. John hired a small cutter-yacht, the *Palestine*, which he kept in our little harbour of Encombe, and in which he and I made many excursions, visiting Weymouth, Lyme Regis, and other places of interest on the south coast.

In this summer my brother confided to me two secrets,—his love for Constance Temple, which indeed was after all no secret, and the history of the apparition which he had seen. This last filled me with inexpressible dread and distress. It seemed cruel and unnatural that any influence so dark and mysterious should thus intrude on our bright life, and from the first I had an impression which I could not entirely shake off, that any such appearance or converse of a disembodied spirit must portend misfortune, if not worse, to him who saw or heard it. It never occurred to me to combat or to doubt the reality of the vision; he believed that he had seen it, and his conviction was enough to convince me. He had meant, he said, to tell no one, and had given a promise to Mr. Gaskell to that effect; but I think that he could not bear to keep such a matter in his own breast, and within the first week of his return he made me his confidant. I remember, my dear Edward, the look everything wore on that sad night when he first told me what afterwards proved so terrible a secret. We had dined quite alone, and he had been moody and depressed all the evening. It was a chilly night, with some fret blowing up from the sea. The moon showed that blunted and deformed appearance which she assumes a day or two past the full, and the moisture in the air encircled her with a stormy-looking halo. We had stepped out of the dining-room windows on to the little terrace looking down towards Smedmore and Encombe. The glaucous shrubs that grow in between the balusters were wet and dripping with the salt breath of the sea, and we could hear the waves coming into the cove from the west. After standing a minute I felt chill, and proposed that we should go back to the billiard-room, where a fire was lit on all except the warmest nights. "No," John said, "I want to tell you something, Sophy," and then we walked on to the old boat summer-house. There he told me everything. I cannot describe to you my feelings of anguish and horror when he told me of the appearance of the man. The interest of the tale was so absorbing to me that I took no note of time, nor of the cold night air, and it was only when it was all finished that I felt how deadly chill it had become. "Let us go in, John," I said; "I am cold and feel benumbed."

But youth is hopeful and strong, and in another week the impression had faded from our minds, and we were enjoying the full glory of midsummer weather, which I think only those know who have watched the blue sea come rippling in at the foot of the white chalk cliffs of Dorset.

I had felt a reluctance even so much as to hear the air of the *Gagliarda*, and though he had spoken to me of the subject on more than one occasion, my brother had never offered to play it to me. I knew that he had the copy of Graziani's suites with him at Worth Maltravers, because he had told me that he had brought it from Oxford; but I had never seen the book, and fancied that he kept it intentionally locked up. He did not, however, neglect the violin, and during the summer mornings, as I sat reading or working on the terrace, I often heard him playing to himself in the library. Though he had never even given me any description of the melody of the *Gagliarda*, yet I felt certain that he not infrequently played it. I cannot say how it was; but from the moment that I heard him one morning in the library performing an air set in a curiously low key, it forced itself upon my attention, and I knew, as it were by instinct, that it must be the *Gagliarda* of the "Areopagita." He was using a *sordino* and playing it very softly; but I was not mistaken. One wet afternoon in October, only a week before the time of his leaving us to return to Oxford for the autumn term, he walked into the drawing-room where I was sitting, and proposed that we should play some music together. To this I readily agreed. Though but a mediocre performer, I have always taken much pleasure in the use of the pianoforte, and esteemed it an honour whenever he asked me to play with him, since my powers as a musician were so very much inferior to his. After we had played several pieces, he took up an oblong music-book bound in white vellum, placed it upon the desk of the pianoforte, and proposed that we should play a suite by Graziani. I knew that he meant the "Areopagita," and begged him at once not to ask me to play it. He rallied me lightly on my fears, and said it would much please him to play it, as he had not heard the pianoforte part since he had left Oxford three months ago. I saw that he was eager to perform it, and being loath to disoblige so kind a brother during the last week of his stay at home, I at length overcame my scruples and set out to play it. But I was so alarmed at the possibility of any evil consequences ensuing, that when we commenced the *Gagliarda* I could scarcely find my notes. Nothing in any way unusual, however, occurred; and being reassured by this, and feeling an irresistible charm in the music, I finished the suite with more appearance of ease. My brother, however, was, I fear, not satisfied with my performance, and compared it, very possibly, with that of Mr. Gaskell, to which it was necessarily much inferior, both through weakness of execution and from my insufficient knowledge of the principles of the *basso continuo*. We stopped playing, and John stood looking out of the window across the sea, where the sky was clearing low down under the clouds. The sun went down behind Portland in a fiery glow which cheered us after a long day's rain. I had taken the copy of Graziani's suites off the desk, and was holding it on my lap turning over the old foxed and yellow pages. As I closed it a streak of evening sunlight fell across the room and lighted up a coat of arms stamped in gilt on the cover. It was much faded and would ordinarily have been hard to make out; but the ray of strong light illumined it, and in an instant I recognised the same shield which Mr. Gaskell had pictured to himself as hanging on the musicians' gallery of his phantasmal dancing-room. My brother had often recounted to me this effort of his friend's imagination, and here I saw before me the same florid foreign blazon, a cherub's head blowing on three lilies on a gold field. This discovery was not only of interest, but afforded me much actual relief; for it accounted rationally for at least one item of the strange story. Mr. Gaskell had no doubt noticed at some time this shield stamped on the outside of the book, and bearing the impression of it unconsciously in his mind, had reproduced it in his imagined revels. I said as much to my brother, and he was greatly interested, and after examining the shield agreed that this was certainly a probable solution of that part of the mystery. On the 12th of October John returned to Oxford.

VI

My brother told me afterwards that more than once during the summer vacation he had seriously considered with himself the propriety of changing his rooms at Magdalen Hall. He had thought that it might thus be possible for him to get rid at once of the memory of the apparition, and of the fear of any reappearance of it. He could either have moved into another set of rooms in the Hall itself, or else gone into lodgings in the town—a usual proceeding, I am told, for gentlemen near the end of their course at Oxford. Would to God that he had indeed done so! but with the supineness which has, I fear, my dear Edward, been too frequently a characteristic of our family, he shrank from the trouble such a course would involve, and the opening of the autumn term found him still in his old rooms. You will forgive me for entering here on a very brief description of your father's sitting-room. It is, I think, necessary for the proper understanding of the incidents that follow. It was not a large room, though probably the finest in the small buildings of Magdalen Hall, and panelled from floor to ceiling with oak which successive generations had obscured by numerous coats of paint. On one side were two windows having an aspect on to New College Lane, and fitted with deep cushioned seats in the recesses. Outside these windows there were boxes of flowers, the brightness of which formed in the summer term a pretty contrast to the grey and crumbling stone, and afforded pleasure at once to the inmate and to passers-by. Along nearly the whole length of the wall opposite to the windows, some tenant in years long past had had mahogany book-shelves placed, reaching to a height of perhaps five feet from the floor. They were handsomely made in the style of the eighteenth century and pleased my brother's taste. He had always exhibited a partiality for books, and the fine library at Worth Maltravers had no doubt contributed to foster his tastes in that direction. At the time of which I write he had formed a small collection for himself at Oxford, paying particular attention to the bindings, and acquiring many excellent specimens of that art, principally I think, from Messrs. Payne & Foss, the celebrated London booksellers.

Towards the end of the autumn term, having occasion one cold day to take down a volume of Plato from its shelf, he found to his surprise that the book was quite warm. A closer examination easily explained to him the reason—namely, that the flue of a chimney, passing behind one end of the bookcase, sensibly heated not only the wall itself, but also the books in the shelves. Although he had been in his rooms now near three years, he had never before observed this fact; partly, no doubt, because the books in these shelves were seldom handled, being more for show as specimens of bindings than for practical use. He was somewhat annoyed at this discovery, fearing lest such a heat, which in moderation is beneficial to books, might through its excess warp the leather or otherwise injure the bindings. Mr. Gaskell was sitting with him at the time of the discovery, and indeed it was for his use that my brother had taken down the volume of Plato. He strongly advised that the bookcase should be moved, and suggested that it would be better to place it across that end of the room where the pianoforte then stood.

They examined it and found that it would easily admit of removal, being, in fact, only the frame of a bookcase, and showing at the back the painted panelling of the wall. Mr. Gaskell noted it as curious that all the shelves were fixed and immovable except one at the end, which had been fitted with the ordinary arrangement allowing its position to be altered at will. My brother thought that the change would improve the appearance of his rooms, besides being advantageous for the books, and gave instructions to the college upholsterer to have the necessary work carried out at once.

The two young men had resumed their musical studies, and had often played the "Areopagita" and other music of Graziani since their return to Oxford in the Autumn. They remarked, however, that the chair no longer creaked during the *Gagliarda*—and, in fact, that no unusual occurrence whatever attended its performance. At times they were almost tempted to doubt the accuracy of their own remembrances, and to consider as entirely mythical the mystery which had so much disturbed them in the summer term. My brother had also pointed out to Mr. Gaskell my discovery that the coat of arms on the outside of the music-book was identical with that which his fancy portrayed on the musicians' gallery. He readily admitted that he must at some time have noticed and afterwards forgotten the blazon on the book, and that an unconscious reminiscence of it had no doubt inspired his imagination in this instance. He rebuked my brother for having agitated me unnecessarily by telling me at all of so idle a tale; and was pleased to write a few lines to me at Worth Maltravers, felicitating me on my shrewdness of perception, but speaking banteringly of the whole matter.

On the evening of the 14th of November my brother and his friend were sitting talking in the former's room. The position of the bookcase had been changed on the morning of that day, and Mr. Gaskell had come round to see how the books looked when placed at the end instead of at the side of the room. He had applauded the new arrangement, and the young men sat long over the fire, with a bottle of college port and a dish of medlars which I had sent my brother from our famous tree in the Upper Croft at Worth Maltravers. Later on they fell to music, and played a variety of pieces, performing also the "Areopagita" suite. Mr. Gaskell before he left complimented John on the improvement which the alteration in the place of the bookcase had made in his room, saying, "Not only do the books in their present place very much enhance the general appearance of the room, but the change seems to me to have affected also a marked acoustical improvement. The oak panelling now exposed on the side of the room has given a resonant property to the wall which is peculiarly responsive to the tones of your violin. While you were playing the *Gagliarda* to-night, I could almost have imagined that someone in an adjacent room was playing the same air with a *sordino*, so distinct was the echo."

Shortly after this he left.

My brother partly undressed himself in his bedroom, which adjoined, and then returning to his sitting-room, pulled the large wicker chair in front of the fire, and sat there looking at the glowing coals, and thinking perhaps of Miss Constance Temple. The night promised to be very cold, and the wind whistled down the chimney, increasing the comfortable sensation of the clear fire. He sat watching the ruddy reflection of the firelight dancing on the panelled wall, when he noticed that a picture placed where the end of the bookcase formerly stood was not truly hung, and needed adjustment. A picture hung askew was particularly offensive to his eyes, and he got up at once to alter it. He remembered as he went up to it that at this precise spot four months ago he had lost sight of the man's figure which he saw rise from the wicker chair, and at the memory felt an involuntary shudder. This reminiscence probably influenced his fancy also in another direction; for it seemed to him that very faintly, as though played far off, and with the *sordino*, he could hear the air of the *Gagliarda*. He put one hand behind the picture to steady it, and as he did so his finger struck a very slight projection in the wall. He pulled the picture a little to one side, and saw that what he had touched was the back of a small hinge sunk in the wall, and almost obliterated with many coats of paint. His curiosity was excited, and he took a candle from the table and examined the wall carefully. Inspection soon showed him another hinge a little further up, and by degrees he perceived that one of the panels had been made at some time in the past to open, and serve probably as the door of a cupboard. At this point he assured me that a feverish anxiety to re-open this cupboard door took possession of him, and that the intense excitement filled his mind which we experience on the eve of a discovery which we fancy may produce important results. He loosened the paint in the cracks with a penknife, and attempted to press open the door; but his instrument was not adequate to such a purpose, and all his efforts remained ineffective. His excitement had now reached an overmastering pitch; for he anticipated, though he knew not why, some strange discovery to be made in this sealed cupboard. He looked round the room for some weapon with which to force the door, and at length with his penknife cut away sufficient wood at the joint to enable him to insert the end of the poker in the hole. The clock in the New College Tower struck one at the exact moment when with a sharp effort he thus forced open the door. It appeared never to have had a fastening, but merely to have been stuck fast by the accumulation of paint. As he bent it slowly back upon the rusted hinges his heart beat so fast that he could scarcely catch his breath, though he was conscious all the while of a ludicrous aspect of his position, knowing that it was most probable that the cavity within would be found empty. The cupboard was small but very deep, and in the obscure light seemed at first to contain nothing except a small heap of dust and cobwebs. His sense of disappointment was keen as he thrust his hand into it, but changed again in a moment to breathless interest on feeling something solid in what he had imagined to be only an accumulation of mould and dirt. He snatched up a candle, and holding this in one hand, with the other pulled out an object from the cupboard and put it on the table, covered as it was with the curious drapery of black and clinging cobwebs which I have seen adhering to bottles of old wine. It lay there between the dish of medlars and the decanter, veiled indeed with thick dust as with a mantle, but revealing beneath it the shape and contour of a violin.

VII

John was excited at his discovery, and felt his thoughts confused in a manner that I have often experienced myself on the unexpected receipt of news interesting me deeply, whether for pleasure or pain. Yet at the same time he was half amused at his own excitement, feeling that it was childish to be moved over an event so simple as the finding of a violin in an old cupboard. He soon collected himself and took up the instrument, using great care, as he feared lest age should have rendered the wood brittle or rotten. With some vigorous puffs of breath and a little dusting with a handkerchief he removed the heavy outer coating of cobwebs, and began to see more clearly the delicate curves of the body and of the scroll. A few minutes' more gentle handling left the instrument sufficiently clean to enable him to appreciate its chief points. Its seclusion from the outer world, which the heavy accumulation of dust proved to have been for many years, did not seem to have damaged it in the least; and the fact of a chimney-flue passing through the wall at no great distance had no doubt conduced to maintain the air in the cupboard at an equable temperature. So far as he was able to judge, the wood was as sound as when it left the maker's hands; but the strings were of course broken, and curled up in little tangled knots. The body was of a light-red colour, with a varnish of peculiar lustre and softness. The neck seemed rather longer than ordinary, and the scroll was remarkably bold and free.

The violin which my brother was in the habit of using was a fine *Pressenda*, given to him on his fifteenth birthday by Mr. Thoresby, his guardian. It was of that maker's later and best period, and a copy of the Stradivarius model. John took this from its case and laid it side by side with his new discovery, meaning to compare them for size and form. He perceived at once that while the model of both was identical, the superiority of the older violin in every detail was so marked as to convince him that it was undoubtedly an instrument of exceptional value. The extreme beauty of its varnish impressed him vividly, and though he had never seen a genuine Stradivarius, he felt a conviction gradually gaining on him that he stood in the presence of a masterpiece of that great maker. On looking into the interior he found that surprisingly little dust had penetrated into it, and by blowing through the sound-holes he soon cleared it sufficiently to enable him to discern a label. He put the candle close to him, and held the violin up so that a little patch of light fell through the sound-hole on to the label. His heart leapt with a violent pulsation as he read the characters, "*Antonius Stradiuarius Cremonensis faciebat*, 1704." Under ordinary circumstances it would naturally be concluded that such a label was a forgery, but the conditions were entirely altered in the case of a violin found in a forgotten cupboard, with proof so evident of its having remained there for a very long period.

He was not at that time as familiar with the history of the fiddles of the great maker as he, and indeed I also, afterwards became. Thus he was unable to decide how far the exact year of its manufacture would determine its value as compared with other specimens of Stradivarius. But although the Pressenda he had been used to play on was always considered a very fine instrument both in make and varnish, his new discovery so far excelled it in both points as to assure him that it must be one of the Cremonese master's greatest productions.

He examined the violin minutely, scrutinising each separate feature, and finding each in turn to be of the utmost perfection, so far as his knowledge of the instrument would enable him to judge. He lit more candles that he might be able better to see it, and holding it on his knees, sat still admiring it until the dying fire and increasing cold warned him that the night was now far advanced. At last, carrying it to his bedroom, he locked it carefully into a drawer and retired for the night.

He woke next morning with that pleasurable consciousness of there being some reason for gladness, which we feel on waking in seasons of happiness, even before our reason, locating it, reminds us what the actual source of our joy may be. He was at first afraid lest his excitement, working on the imagination, should have led him on the previous night to overestimate the fineness of the instrument, and he took it from the drawer half expecting to be disappointed with its daylight appearance. But a glance sufficed to convince him of the unfounded nature of his suspicions. The various beauties which he had before observed were enhanced a hundredfold by the light of day, and he realised more fully than ever that the instrument was one of altogether exceptional value.

And now, my dear Edward, I shall ask your forgiveness if in the history I have to relate any observation of mine should seem to reflect on the character of your late father, Sir John Maltravers. And I beg you to consider that your father was also my dear and only brother, and that it is inexpressibly painful to me to recount any actions of his which may not seem becoming to a noble gentleman, as he surely was. I only now proceed because, when very near his end, he most strictly enjoined me to narrate these circumstances to you fully when you should come of age. We must humbly remember that to God alone belongs judgment, and that it is not for poor mortals to decide what is right or wrong in certain instances for their fellows, but that each should strive most earnestly to do his own duty.

Your father entirely concealed from me the discovery he had made. It was not till long afterwards that I had it narrated to me, and I only obtained a knowledge of this and many other of the facts which I am now telling you at a date much subsequent to their actual occurrence.

He explained to his servant that he had discovered and opened an old cupboard in the panelling, without mentioning the fact of his having found anything in it, but merely asking him to give instructions for the paint to be mended and the cupboard put into a usable state. Before he had finished a very late breakfast Mr. Gaskell was with him, and it has been a source of lasting regret to me that my brother concealed also from his most intimate and trusted friend the discovery of the previous night. He did, indeed, tell him that he had found and opened an old cupboard in the panelling, but made no mention of there having been anything within. I cannot say what prompted him to this action; for the two young men had for long been on such intimate terms that the one shared almost as a matter of course with the other any pleasure or pain which might fall to his lot. Mr. Gaskell looked at the cupboard with some interest, saying afterwards, "I know now, Johnnie, why the one shelf of the bookcase which stood there was made movable when all the others were fixed. Some former occupant used the cupboard, no doubt, as a secret receptacle for his treasures, and masked it with the book-shelves in front. Who knows what he kept in here, or who he was! I should not be surprised if he were that very man who used to come here so often to hear us play the 'Areopagita,' and whom you saw that night last June. He had the one shelf made, you see, to move so as to give him access to this cavity on occasion: then when he left Oxford, or perhaps died, the mystery was forgotten, and with a few times of painting the cracks closed up."

Mr. Gaskell shortly afterwards took his leave as he had a lecture to attend, and my brother was left alone to the contemplation of his new-found treasure. After some consideration he determined that he would take the instrument to London, and obtain the opinion of an expert as to its authenticity and value. He was well acquainted with the late Mr. George Smart, the celebrated London dealer, from whom his guardian, Mr. Thoresby, had purchased the Pressenda violin which John commonly used. Besides being a dealer in valuable instruments, Mr. Smart was a famous collector of Stradivarius fiddles, esteemed one of the first authorities in Europe in that domain of art, and author of a valuable work of reference in connection with it. It was to him, therefore, that my brother decided to submit the violin, and he wrote a letter to Mr. Smart saying that he should give himself the pleasure of waiting on him the next day on a matter of business. He then called on his tutor, and with some excuse obtained leave to journey to London the next morning. He spent the rest of the day in very carefully cleaning the violin, and noon of the next saw him with it, securely packed, in Mr. Smart's establishment in Bond Street.

Mr. Smart received Sir John Maltravers with deference, demanded in what way he could serve him; and on hearing that his opinion was required on the authenticity of a violin, smiled somewhat dubiously and led the way into a back parlour.

"My dear Sir John," he said, "I hope you have not been led into buying any instrument by a faith in its antiquity. So many good copies of instruments by famous makers and bearing their labels are now afloat, that the chances of obtaining a genuine fiddle from an unrecognised source are quite remote; of hundreds of violins submitted to me for opinion, I find that scarce one in fifty is actually that which it represents itself to be. In fact the only safe rule," he added as a professional commentary, "is never to buy a violin unless you obtain it from a dealer with a reputation to lose, and are prepared to pay a reasonable price for it."

My brother had meanwhile unpacked the violin and laid it on the table. As he took from it the last leaf of silver paper he saw Mr. Smart's smile of condescension fade, and assuming a look of interest and excitement, he stepped forward, took the violin in his hands, and scrutinised it minutely. He turned it over in silence for some moments, looking narrowly at each feature, and even applying the test of a magnifying-glass. At last he said with an altered tone, "Sir John, I have had in my hands nearly all the finest productions of Stradivarius, and thought myself acquainted with every instrument of note that ever left his workshop; but I confess myself mistaken, and apologise to you for the doubt which I expressed as to the instrument you had brought me. This violin is of the great master's golden period, is incontestably genuine, and finer in some respects than any Stradivarius that I have ever seen, not even excepting the famous *Dolphin* itself. You need be under no apprehension as to its authenticity: no connoisseur could hold it in his hand for a second and entertain a doubt on the point."

My brother was greatly pleased at so favourable a verdict, and Mr. Smart continued—

"The varnish is of that rich red which Stradivarius used in his best period after he had abandoned the yellow tint copied by him at first from his master Amati. I have never seen a varnish thicker or more lustrous, and it shows on the back that peculiar shading to imitate wear which we term 'breaking up.' The purfling also is of an unsurpassable excellence. Its execution is so fine that I should recommend you to use a magnifying-glass for its examination."

So he ran on, finding from moment to moment some new beauties to admire.

My brother was at first anxious lest Mr. Smart should ask him whence so extraordinary an instrument came, but he saw that the expert had already jumped to a conclusion in the matter. He knew that John had recently come of age, and evidently supposed that he had found the violin among the heirlooms of Worth Maltravers. John allowed Mr. Smart to continue in this misconception, merely saying that he had discovered the instrument in an old cupboard, where he had reason to think it had remained hidden for many years.

"Are there no records attached to so splendid an instrument?" asked Mr. Smart. "I suppose it has been with your family a number of years. Do you not know how it came into their possession?"

I believe this was the first occasion on which it had occurred to John to consider what right he had to the possession of the instrument. He had been so excited by its discovery that the question of ownership had never hitherto crossed his mind. The unwelcome suggestion that it was not his after all, that the College might rightfully prefer a claim to it, presented itself to him for a moment; but he set it instantly aside, quieting his conscience with the reflection that this at least was not the moment to make such a disclosure.

He fenced with Mr. Smart's inquiry as best he could, saying that he was ignorant of the history of the instrument, but not contradicting the assumption that it had been a long time in his family's possession.

"It is indeed singular," Mr. Smart continued, "that so magnificent an instrument should have lain buried so long; that even those best acquainted with such matters should be in perfect ignorance of its existence. I shall have to revise the list of famous instruments in the next edition of my 'History of the Violin,' and to write," he added smiling, "a special paragraph on the 'Worth Maltravers Stradivarius.'"

After much more, which I need not narrate, Mr. Smart suggested that the violin should be left with him that he might examine it more at leisure, and that my brother should return in a week's time, when he would have the instrument opened, an operation which would be in any case advisable. "The interior," he added, "appears to be in a strictly original state, and this I shall be able to ascertain when opened. The label is perfect, but if I am not mistaken I can see something higher up on the back which appears like a second label. This excites my interest, as I know of no instance of an instrument bearing two labels."

To this proposal my brother readily assented, being anxious to enjoy alone the pleasure of so gratifying a discovery as that of the undoubted authenticity of the instrument.

As he thought over the matter more at leisure, he grew anxious as to what might be the import of the second label in the violin of which Mr. Smart had spoken. I blush to say that he feared lest it might bear some owner's name or other inscription proving that the instrument had not been so long in the Maltravers family as he had allowed Mr. Smart to suppose. So within so short a time it was possible that Sir John Maltravers of Worth should dread being detected, if not in an absolute falsehood, at least in having by his silence assented to one.

During the ensuing week John remained in an excited and anxious condition. He did little work, and neglected his friends, having his thoughts continually occupied with the strange discovery he had made. I know also that his sense of honour troubled him, and that he was not satisfied with the course he was pursuing. The evening of his return from London he went to Mr. Gaskell's rooms at New College, and spent an hour conversing with him on indifferent subjects. In the course of their talk he proposed to his friend as a moral problem the question of the course of action to be taken were one to find some article of value concealed in his room. Mr. Gaskell answered unhesitatingly that he should feel bound to disclose it to the authorities. He saw that my brother was ill at ease, and with a clearness of judgment which he always exhibited, guessed that he had actually made some discovery of this sort in the old cupboard in his rooms. He could not divine, of course, the exact nature of the object found, and thought it might probably relate to a hoard of gold; but insisted with much urgency on the obligation to at once disclose anything of this kind. My brother, however, misled, I fear, by that feeling of inalienable right which the treasure-hunter experiences over the treasure, paid no more attention to the advice of his friend than to the promptings of his own conscience, and went his way.

From that day, my dear Edward, he began to exhibit a spirit of secretiveness and reserve entirely alien to his own open and honourable disposition, and also saw less of Mr. Gaskell. His friend tried, indeed, to win his confidence and affection in every way in his power; but in spite of this the rift between them widened insensibly, and my brother lost the fellowship and counsel of a true friend at a time when he could ill afford to be without them.

He returned to London the ensuing week, and met Mr. George Smart by appointment in Bond Street. If the expert had been enthusiastic on a former occasion, he was ten times more so on this. He spoke in terms almost of rapture about the violin. He had compared it with two magnificent instruments in the collection of the late Mr. James Loding, then the finest in Europe; and it was admittedly superior to either, both in the delicate markings of its wood and singularly fine varnish. "Of its tone," he said, "we cannot, of course, yet pronounce with certainty, but I am very sure that its voice will not belie its splendid exterior. It has been carefully opened, and is in a strangely perfect condition. Several persons eminently qualified to judge unite with me in considering that it has been exceedingly little played upon, and admit that never has so intact an interior been seen. The scroll is exceptionally bold and original. Although undoubtedly from the hand of the great master, this is of a pattern entirely different and distinct from any that have ever come under my observation."

He then pointed out to my brother that the side lines of the scroll were unusually deeply cut, and that the front of it projected far more than is common with such instruments.

"The most remarkable feature," he concluded, "is that the instrument bears a double label. Besides the label which you have already seen bearing '*Antonius Stradiuarius Cremonensis faciebat,*' with the date of his most splendid period, 1704, so clearly that the ink seems scarcely dry, there is another smaller one higher up on the back which I will show you."

He took the violin apart and showed him a small label with characters written in faded ink. "That is the writing of Antonio Stradivarius himself, and is easily recognisable, though it is much firmer than a specimen which I once saw, written in extreme old age, and giving his name and the date 1736. He was then ninety-two, and died in the following year. But this, as you will see, does not give his name, but merely the two words '*Porphyrius philosophus.*' What this may refer to I cannot say: it is beyond my experience. My friend Mr. Calvert has suggested that Stradivarius may have dedicated this violin to the pagan philosopher, or named it after him; but this seems improbable. I have, indeed, heard of two famous violins being called 'Peter' and 'Paul,' but the instances of such naming are very rare; and I believe it to be altogether without precedent to find a name attached thus on a label.

"In any case, I must leave this matter to your ingenuity to decipher. Neither the sound-post nor the bass-bar have ever been moved, and you see here a Stradivarius violin wearing exactly the same appearance as it once wore in the great master's workshop, and in exactly the same condition; yet I think the belly is sufficiently strong to stand modern stringing. I should advise you to leave the instrument with me for some little while, that I may give it due care and attention and ensure its being properly strung."

My brother thanked him and left the violin with him, saying that he would instruct him later by letter to what address he wished it sent.

VIII

Within a few days after this the autumn term came to an end, and in the second week of December John returned to Worth Maltravers for the Christmas vacation. His advent was always a very great pleasure to me, and on this occasion I had looked forward to his company with anticipation keener than usual, as I had been disappointed of the visit of a friend and had spent the last month alone. After the joy of our first meeting had somewhat sobered, it was not long before I remarked a change in his manner, which puzzled me. It was not that he was less kind to me, for I think he was even more tenderly forbearing and gentle than I had ever known him, but I had an uneasy feeling that some shadow had crept in between us. It was the small cloud rising in the distance that afterwards darkened his horizon and mine. I missed the old candour and open-hearted frankness that he had always shown; and there seemed to be always something in the background which he was trying to keep from me. It was obvious that his thoughts were constantly elsewhere, so much so that on more than one occasion he returned vague and incoherent answers to my questions. At times I was content to believe that he was in love, and that his thoughts were with Miss Constance Temple; but even so, I could not persuade myself that his altered manner was to be thus entirely accounted for. At other times a dazed air, entirely foreign to his bright disposition, which I observed particularly in the morning, raised in my mind the terrible suspicion that he was in the habit of taking some secret narcotic or other deleterious drug.

We had never spent a Christmas away from Worth Maltravers, and it had always been a season of quiet joy for both of us. But under these altered circumstances it was a great relief and cause of thankfulness to me to receive a letter from Mrs. Temple inviting us both to spend Christmas and New Year at Royston. This invitation had upon my brother precisely the effect that I had hoped for. It roused him from his moody condition, and he professed much pleasure in accepting it, especially as he had never hitherto been in Derbyshire.

There was a small but very agreeable party at Royston, and we passed a most enjoyable fortnight. My brother seemed thoroughly to have shaken off his indisposition; and I saw my fondest hopes realised in the warm attachment which was evidently springing up between him and Miss Constance Temple.

Our visit drew near its close, and it was within a week of John's return to Oxford. Mrs. Temple celebrated the termination of the Christmas festivities by giving a ball on Twelfth-night, at which a large party were present, including most of the county families. Royston was admirably adapted for such entertainments, from the number and great size of its reception-rooms. Though Elizabethan in date and external appearance, succeeding generations had much modified and enlarged the house; and an ancestor in the middle of the last century had built at the back an enormous hall after the classic model, and covered it with a dome or cupola. In this room the dancing went forward. Supper was served in the older hall in the front, and it was while this was in progress that a thunderstorm began. The rarity of such a phenomenon in the depth of winter formed the subject of general remark; but though the lightning was extremely brilliant, being seen distinctly through the curtained windows, the storm appeared to be at some distance, and, except for one peal, the thunder was not loud. After supper dancing was resumed, and I was taking part in a polka (called, I remember, the "*King Pippin*"), when my partner pointed out that one of the footmen wished to speak with me. I begged him to lead me to one side, and the servant then informed me that my brother was ill. Sir John, he said, had been seized with a fainting fit, but had been got to bed, and was being attended by Dr. Empson, a physician who chanced to be present among the visitors.

I at once left the hall and hurried to my brother's room. On the way I met Mrs. Temple and Constance, the latter much agitated and in tears. Mrs. Temple assured me that Dr. Empson reported favourably of my brother's condition, attributing his faintness to over-exertion in the dancing-room. The medical man had got him to bed with the assistance of Sir John's valet, had given him a quieting draught, and ordered that he should not be disturbed for the present. It was better that I should not enter the room; she begged that I would kindly comfort and reassure Constance, who was much upset, while she herself returned to her guests.

I led Constance to my bedroom, where there was a bright fire burning, and calmed her as best I could. Her interest in my brother was evidently very real and unaffected, and while not admitting her partiality for him in words, she made no effort to conceal her sentiments from me. I kissed her tenderly, and bade her narrate the circumstances of John's attack.

It seemed that after supper they had gone upstairs into the music-room, and he had himself proposed that they should walk thence into the picture-gallery, where they would better be able to see the lightning, which was then particularly vivid. The picture-gallery at Royston is a very long, narrow, and rather low room, running the whole length of the south wing, and terminating in a large Tudor oriel or flat bay window looking east. In this oriel they had sat for some time watching the flashes, and the wintry landscape revealed for an instant and then plunged into outer blackness. The gallery itself was not illuminated, and the effect of the lightning was very fine.

There had been an unusually bright flash accompanied by that single reverberating peal of thunder which I had previously noticed. Constance had spoken to my brother, but he had not replied, and in a moment she saw that he had swooned. She summoned aid without delay, but it was some short time before consciousness had been restored to him.

She had concluded this narrative, and sat holding my hand in hers. We were speculating on the cause of my brother's illness, thinking it might be due to over-exertion, or to sitting in a chilly atmosphere as the picture-gallery was not warmed, when Mrs. Temple knocked at the door and said that John was now more composed and desired earnestly to see me.

On entering my brother's bedroom I found him sitting up in bed wearing a dressing-gown. Parnham, his valet, who was arranging the fire, left the room as I came in. A chair stood at the head of the bed and I sat down by him. He took my hand in his and without a word burst into tears. "Sophy," he said, "I am so unhappy, and I have sent for you to tell you of my trouble, because I know you will be forbearing to me. An hour ago all seemed so bright I was sitting in the picture-gallery with Constance, whom I love dearly. We had been watching the lightning, till the thunder had grown fainter and the storm seemed past. I was just about to ask her to become my wife when a brighter flash than all the rest burst on us, and I saw—I saw, Sophy, standing in the gallery as close to me as you are now—I saw—that man I told you about at Oxford; and then this faintness came on me."

"Whom do you mean?" I said, not understanding what he spoke of, and thinking for a moment he referred to someone else. "Did you see Mr. Gaskell?"

"No, it was not he; but that dead man whom I saw rising from my wicker chair the night you went away from Oxford."

You will perhaps smile at my weakness, my dear Edward, and indeed I had at that time no justification for it; but I assure you that I have not yet forgotten, and never shall forget, the impression of overwhelming horror which his words produced upon me. It seemed as though a fear which had hitherto stood vague and shadowy in the background, began now to advance towards me, gathering more distinctness as it approached. There was to me something morbidly terrible about the apparition of this man at such a momentous crisis in my brother's life, and I at once recognised that unknown form as being the shadow which was gradually stealing between John and myself. Though I feigned incredulity as best I might, and employed those arguments or platitudes which will always be used on such occasions, urging that such a phantom could only exist in a mind disordered by physical weakness, my brother was not deceived by my words, and perceived in a moment that I did not even believe in them myself.

"Dearest Sophy," he said, with a much calmer air, "let us put aside all dissimulation. I *know* that what I have to-night seen, and that what I saw last summer at Oxford, are *not* phantoms of my brain; and I believe that you too in your inmost soul are convinced of this truth. Do not, therefore, endeavour to persuade me to the contrary. If I am not to believe the evidence of my senses, it were better at once to admit my madness—and I know that I am not mad. Let us rather consider what such an appearance can portend, and who the man is who is thus presented. I cannot explain to you why this appearance inspires me with so great a revulsion. I can only say that in its presence I seem to be brought face to face with some abysmal and repellent wickedness. It is not that the form he wears is hideous. Last night I saw him exactly as I saw him at Oxford—his face waxen pale, with a sneering mouth, the same lofty forehead, and hair brushed straight up so as almost to appear standing on end. He wore the same long coat of green cloth and white waistcoat. He seemed as if he had been standing listening to what we said, though we had not seen him till this bright flash of lightning made him manifest. You will remember that when I saw him at Oxford his eyes were always cast down, so that I never knew their colour. This time they were wide open; indeed he was looking full at us, and they were a light brown and very brilliant."

I saw that my brother was exciting himself, and was still weak from his recent swoon. I knew, too, that any ordinary person of strong mind would say at once that his brain wandered, and yet I had a dreadful conviction all the while that what he told me was the truth. All I could do was to beg him to calm himself, and to reflect how vain such fancies must be. "We must trust, dear John," I said, "in God. I am sure that so long as we are not living in conscious sin, we shall never be given over to any evil power; and I know my brother too well to think that he is doing anything he knows to be evil. If there be evil spirits, as we are taught there are, we are taught also that there are good spirits stronger than they, who will protect us."

So I spoke with him a little while, until he grew calmer; and then we talked of Constance and of his love for her. He was deeply pleased to hear from me how she had shown such obvious signs of interest in his illness, and sincere affection for him. In any case, he made me promise that I would never mention to her either what he had seen this night or last summer at Oxford.

It had grown late, and the undulating beat of the dances, which had been distinctly sensible in his room—even though we could not hear any definite noise—had now ceased. Mrs. Temple knocked at the door as she went to bed and inquired how he did, giving him at the same time a kind message of sympathy from Constance, which afforded him much gratification. After she had left I prepared also to retire; but before going he begged me to take a prayer-book lying on the table, and to read aloud a collect which he pointed out. It was that for the second Sunday in Lent, and evidently well known to him. As I read it the words seemed to bear a new and deeper significance, and my heart repeated with fervour the petition for protection from those "evil thoughts which may assault and hurt the soul." I bade him good night and went away very sorrowful. Parnham, at John's request, had arranged to sleep on a sofa in his master's bedroom.

I rose betimes the next morning and inquired at my brother's room how he was. Parnham reported that he had passed a restless night, and on entering a little later I found him in a high fever, slightly delirious, and evidently not so well as when I saw him last. Mrs. Temple, with much kindness and forethought, had begged Dr. Empson to remain at Royston for the night, and he was soon in attendance on his patient. His verdict was sufficiently grave: John was suffering from a sharp access of brain-fever; his condition afforded cause for alarm; he could not answer for any turn his sickness might take. You will easily imagine how much this intelligence affected me; and Mrs. Temple and Constance shared my anxiety and solicitude. Constance and I talked much with one another that morning. Unaffected anxiety had largely removed her reserve, and she spoke openly of her feelings towards my brother, not concealing her partiality for him. I on my part let her understand how welcome to me would be any union between her and John, and how sincerely I should value her as a sister.

It was a wild winter's morning, with some snow falling and a high wind. The house was in the disordered condition which is generally observable on the day following a ball or other important festivity. I roamed restlessly about, and at last found my way to the picture-gallery, which had formed the scene of John's adventure on the previous night. I had never been in this part of the house before, as it contained no facilities for heating, and so often remained shut in the winter months. I found a listless pleasure in admiring the pictures which lined the walls, most of them being portraits of former members of the family, including the famous picture of Sir Ralph Temple and his family, attributed to Holbein. I had reached the end of the gallery and sat down in the oriel watching the snow-flakes falling sparsely, and the evergreens below me waving wildly in the sudden rushes of the wind. My thoughts were busy with the events of the previous evening,—with John's illness, with the ball,—and I found myself humming the air of a waltz that had caught my fancy. At last I turned away from the garden scene towards the gallery, and as I did so my eyes fell on a remarkable picture just opposite to me.

It was a full-length portrait of a young man, life-size, and I had barely time to appreciate even its main features when I knew that I had before me the painted counterfeit of my brother's vision. The discovery caused me a violent shock, and it was with an infinite repulsion that I recognised at once the features and dress of the man whom John had seen rising from the chair at Oxford. So accurately had my brother's imagination described him to me, that it seemed as if I had myself seen him often before. I noted each feature, comparing them with my brother's description, and finding them all familiar and corresponding exactly. He was a man still in the prime of life. His features were regular and beautifully modelled; yet there was something in his face that inspired me with a deep aversion, though his brown eyes were open and brilliant. His mouth was sharply cut, with a slight sneer on the lips, and his complexion of that extreme pallor which had impressed itself deeply on my brother's imagination and my own.

After the first intense surprise had somewhat subsided, I experienced a feeling of great relief, for here was an extraordinary explanation of my brother's vision of last night. It was certain that the flash of lightning had lit up this ill-starred picture, and that to his predisposed fancy the painted figure had stood forth as an actual embodiment. That such an incident, however startling, should have been able to fling John into a brain-fever, showed that he must already have been in a very low and reduced state, on which excitement would act much more powerfully than on a more robust condition of health. A similar state of weakness, perturbed by the excitement of his passion for Constance Temple, might surely also have conjured up the vision which he thought he saw the night of our leaving Oxford in the summer. These thoughts, my dear Edward, gave me great relief; for it seemed a comparatively trivial matter that my brother should be ill, even seriously ill, if only his physical indisposition could explain away the supernatural dread which had haunted us for the past six months. The clouds were breaking up. It was evident that John had been seriously unwell for some months; his physical weakness had acted on his brain; and I had lent colour to his wandering fancies by being alarmed by them, instead of rejecting them at once or gently laughing them away as I should have done. But these glad thoughts took me too far, and I was suddenly brought up by a reflection that did not admit of so simple an explanation. If the man's form my brother saw at Oxford were merely an effort of disordered imagination, how was it that he had been able to describe it exactly like that represented in this picture? He had never in his life been to Royston, therefore he could have no image of the picture impressed unconsciously on or hidden away in his mind. Yet his description had never varied. It had been so close as to enable me to produce in my fancy a vivid representation of the man he had seen; and here I had before me the features and dress exactly reproduced. In the presence of a coincidence so extraordinary reason stood confounded, and I knew not what to think. I walked nearer to the picture and scrutinised it closely.

The dress corresponded in every detail with that which my brother had described the figure as wearing at Oxford: a long cut-away coat of green cloth with an edge of gold embroidery, a white satin waistcoat with sprigs of embroidered roses, gold-lace at the pocket-holes, buff silk knee-breeches, and low down on the finely modelled neck a full cravat of rich lace. The figure was posed negligently against a fluted stone pedestal or short column on which the left elbow leant, and the right foot was crossed lightly over the left. His shoes were of polished black leather with heavy silver buckles, and the whole costume was very old-fashioned, and such as I had only seen worn at fancy dress balls. On the foot of the pedestal was the painter's name, "BATTONI pinxit, Romæ, 1750." On the top of the pedestal, and under his left elbow, was a long roll apparently of music, of which one end, unfolded, hung over the edge.

For some minutes I stood still gazing at this portrait which so much astonished me, but turned on hearing footsteps in the gallery, and saw Constance, who had come to seek for me.

"Constance," I said, "whose portrait is this? It is a very striking picture, is it not?"

"Yes, it is a splendid painting, though of a very bad man. His name was Adrian Temple, and he once owned Royston. I do not know much about him, but I believe he was very wicked and very clever. My mother would be able to tell you more. It is a picture we none of us like, although so finely painted; and perhaps because he was always pointed out to me from childhood as a bad man, I have myself an aversion to it. It is singular that when the very bright flash of lightning came last night while your brother John and I were sitting here, it lit this picture with a dazzling glare that made the figure stand out so strangely as to seem almost alive. It was just after that I found that John had fainted."

The memory was not a pleasant one for either of us and we changed the subject. "Come," I said, "let us leave the gallery, it is very cold here."

Though I said nothing more at the time, her words had made a great impression on me. It was so strange that, even with the little she knew of this Adrian Temple, she should speak at once of his notoriously evil life, and of her personal dislike to the picture. Remembering what my brother had said on the previous night, that in the presence of this man he felt himself brought face to face with some indescribable wickedness, I could not but be surprised at the coincidence. The whole story seemed to me now to resemble one of those puzzle pictures or maps which I have played with as a child, where each bit fits into some other until the outline is complete. It was as if I were finding the pieces one by one of a bygone history, and fitting them to one another until some terrible whole should be gradually built up and stand out in its complete deformity.

Dr. Empson spoke gravely of John's illness, and entertained without reluctance the proposal of Mrs. Temple, that Dr. Dobie, a celebrated physician in Derby, should be summoned to a consultation. Dr. Dobie came more than once, and was at last able to report an amendment in John's condition, though both the doctors absolutely forbade anyone to visit him, and said that under the most favourable circumstances a period of some weeks must elapse before he could be moved.

Mrs. Temple invited me to remain at Royston until my brother should be sufficiently convalescent to be moved; and both she and Constance, while regretting the cause, were good enough to express themselves pleased that accident should detain me so long with them.

As the reports of the doctors became gradually more favourable, and our minds were in consequence more free to turn to other subjects, I spoke to Mrs. Temple one day about the picture, saying that it interested me, and asking for some particulars as to the life of Adrian Temple.

"My dear child," she said, "I had rather that you should not exhibit any curiosity as to this man, whom I wish that we had not to call an ancestor. I know little of him myself, and indeed his life was of such a nature as no woman, much less a young girl, would desire to be well acquainted with. He was, I believe, a man of remarkable talent, and spent most of his time between Oxford and Italy, though he visited Royston occasionally, and built the large hall here, which we use as a dancing-room. Before he was twenty wild stories were prevalent as to his licentious life, and by thirty his name was a by-word among sober and upright people. He had constantly with him at Oxford and on his travels a boon companion called Jocelyn, who aided him in his wickednesses, until on one of their Italian tours Jocelyn left him suddenly and became a Trappist monk. It was currently reported that some wild deed of Adrian Temple had shocked even him, and so outraged his surviving instincts of common humanity that he was snatched as a brand from the burning and enabled to turn back even in the full tide of his wickedness. However that may be, Adrian went on in his evil course without him, and about four years after disappeared. He was last heard of in Naples, and it is believed that he succumbed during a violent outbreak of the plague which took place in Italy in the autumn of 1752. That is all I shall tell you of him, and indeed I know little more myself. The only good trait that has been handed down concerning him is that he was a masterly musician, performing admirably upon the violin, which he had studied under the illustrious Tartini himself. Yet even his art of music, if tradition speaks the truth, was put by him to the basest of uses."

I apologised for my indiscretion in asking her about an unpleasant subject, and at the same time thanked her for what she had seen fit to tell me, professing myself much interested, as indeed I really was.

"Was he a handsome man?"

"That is a girl's question," she answered, smiling. "He is said to have been very handsome; and indeed his picture, painted after his first youth was past, would still lead one to suppose so. But his complexion was spoiled, it is said, and turned to deadly white by certain experiments, which it is neither possible nor seemly for us to understand. His face is of that long oval shape of which all the Temples are proud, and he had brown eyes: we sometimes tease Constance, saying she is like Adrian."

It was indeed true, as I remembered after Mrs. Temple had pointed it out, that Constance had a peculiarly long and oval face. It gave her, I think, an air of staid and placid beauty, which formed in my eyes, and perhaps in John's also, one of her greatest attractions.

"I do not like even his picture," Mrs. Temple continued, "and strange tales have been narrated of it by idle servants which are not worth repeating. I have sometimes thought of destroying it; but my late husband, being a Temple, would never hear of this, or even of removing it from its present place in the gallery; and I should be loath to do anything now contrary to his wishes, once so strongly expressed. It is, besides, very perfect from an artistic point of view, being painted by Battoni, and in his happiest manner."

I could never glean more from Mrs. Temple; but what she told me interested me deeply. It seemed another link in the chain, though I could scarcely tell why, that Adrian Temple should be so great a musician and violinist. I had, I fancy, a dim idea of that malign and outlawed spirit sitting alone in darkness for a hundred years, until he was called back by the sweet tones of the Italian music, and the lilt of the "Areopagita" that he had loved so long ago.

IX

John's recovery, though continuous and satisfactory, was but slow; and it was not until Easter, which fell early, that his health was pronounced to be entirely re-established. The last few weeks of his convalescence had proved to all of us a time of thankful and tranquil enjoyment. If I may judge from my own experience, there are few epochs in our life more favourable to the growth of sentiments of affection and piety, or more full of pleasurable content, than is the period of gradual recovery from serious illness. The chastening effect of our recent sickness has not yet passed away, and we are at once grateful to our Creator for preserving us, and to our friends for the countless acts of watchful kindness which it is the peculiar property of illness to evoke.

No mother ever nursed a son more tenderly than did Mrs. Temple nurse my brother, and before his restoration to health was complete the attachment between him and Constance had ripened into a formal betrothal. Such an alliance was, as I have before explained, particularly suitable, and its prospect afforded the most lively pleasure to all those concerned. The month of March had been unusually mild, and Royston being situated in a valley, as is the case with most houses of that date, was well sheltered from cold winds. It had, moreover, a south aspect, and as my brother gradually gathered strength, Constance and he and I would often sit out of doors in the soft spring mornings. We put an easy-chair with many cushions for him on the gravel by the front door, where the warmth of the sun was reflected from the red brick walls, and he would at times read aloud to us while we were engaged with our crochet-work. Mr. Tennyson had just published anonymously a first volume of poems, and the sober dignity of his verse well suited our frame of mind at that time. The memory of those pleasant spring mornings, my dear Edward, has not yet passed away, and I can still smell the sweet moist scent of the violets, and see the bright colours of the crocus-flowers in the parterres in front of us.

John's mind seemed to be gathering strength with his body. He had apparently flung off the cloud which had overshadowed him before his illness, and avoided entirely any reference to those unpleasant events which had been previously so constantly in his thoughts. I had, indeed, taken an early opportunity of telling him of my discovery of the picture of Adrian Temple, as I thought it would tend to show him that at least the last appearance of this ghostly form admitted of a rational explanation. He seemed glad to hear of this, but did not exhibit the same interest in the matter that I had expected, and allowed it at once to drop. Whether through lack of interest, or from a lingering dislike to revisit the spot where he was seized with illness, he did not, I believe, once enter the picture-gallery before he left Royston.

I cannot say as much for myself. The picture of Adrian Temple exerted a curious fascination over me, and I constantly took an opportunity of studying it. It was, indeed, a beautiful work; and perhaps because John's recovery gave a more cheerful tone to my thoughts, or perhaps from the power of custom to dull even the keenest antipathies, I gradually got to lose much of the feeling of aversion which it had at first inspired. In time the unpleasant look grew less unpleasing, and I noticed more the beautiful oval of the face, the brown eyes, and the fine chiselling of the features. Sometimes, too, I felt a deep pity for so clever a gentleman who had died young, and whose life, were it ever so wicked, must often have been also lonely and bitter.

More than once I had been discovered by Mrs. Temple or Constance sitting looking at the picture, and they had gently laughed at me, saying that I had fallen in love with Adrian Temple.

One morning in early April, when the sun was streaming brightly through the oriel, and the picture received a fuller light than usual, it occurred to me to examine closely the scroll of music painted as hanging over the top of the pedestal on which the figure leant. I had hitherto thought that the signs depicted on it were merely such as painters might conventionally use to represent a piece of musical notation. This has generally been the case, I think, in such pictures as I have ever seen in which a piece of music has been introduced. I mean that while the painting gives a general representation of the musical staves, no attempt is ever made to paint any definite notes such as would enable an actual piece to be identified. Though, as I write this, I do remember that on the monument to Handel in Westminster Abbey there is represented a musical scroll similar to that in Adrian Temple's picture, but actually sculptured with the opening phrase of the majestic melody, "I know that my Redeemer liveth."

On this morning, then, at Royston I thought I perceived that there were painted on the scroll actual musical staves, bars, and notes; and my interest being excited, I stood upon a chair so as better to examine them. Though time had somewhat obscured this portion of the picture as with a veil or film, yet I made out that the painter had intended to depict some definite piece of music. In another moment I saw that the air represented consisted of the opening bars of the *Gagliarda* in the suite by Graziani with which my brother and I were so well acquainted. Though I believe that I had not seen the volume of music in which that piece was contained more than twice, yet the melody was very familiar to me, and I had no difficulty whatever in making myself sure that I had here before me the air of the *Gagliarda* and none other. It was true that it was only roughly painted, but to one who knew the tune there was no room left for doubt.

Here was a new cause, I will not say for surprise, but for reflection. It might, of course, have been merely a coincidence that the artist should have chosen to paint in this picture this particular piece of music; but it seemed more probable that it had actually been a favourite air of Adrian Temple, and that he had chosen deliberately to have it represented with him. This discovery I kept entirely to myself, not thinking it wise to communicate it to my brother, lest by doing so I might reawaken his interest in a subject which I hoped he had finally dismissed from his thoughts.

In the second week of April the happy party at Royston was dispersed, John returning to Oxford for the summer term, Mrs. Temple making a short visit to Scotland, and Constance coming to Worth Maltravers to keep me company for a time.

It was John's last term at Oxford. He expected to take his degree in June, and his marriage with Constance Temple had been provisionally arranged for the September following. He returned to Magdalen Hall in the best of spirits, and found his rooms looking cheerful with well-filled flower-boxes in the windows. I shall not detain you with any long narration of the events of the term, as they have no relation to the present history. I will only say that I believe my brother applied himself diligently to his studies, and took his amusement mostly on horseback, riding two horses which he had had sent to him from Worth Maltravers.

About the second week after his return he received a letter from Mr. George Smart to the effect that the Stradivarius violin was now in complete order. Subsequent examination, Mr. Smart wrote, and the unanimous verdict of connoisseurs whom he had consulted, had merely confirmed the views he had at first expressed—namely, that the violin was of the finest quality, and that my brother had in his possession a unique and intact example of Stradivarius's best period. He had had it properly strung; and as the bass-bar had never been moved, and was of a stronger nature than that usual at the period of its manufacture, he had considered it unnecessary to replace it. If any signs should become visible of its being inadequate to support the tension of modern stringing, another could be easily substituted for it at a later date. He had allowed a young German *virtuoso* to play on it, and though this gentleman was one of the first living performers, and had had an opportunity of handling many splendid instruments, he assured Mr. Smart that he had never performed on one that could in any way compare with this. My brother wrote in reply thanking him, and begging that the violin might be sent to Magdalen Hall.

The pleasant musical evenings, however, which John had formerly been used to spend in the company of Mr. Gaskell were now entirely prætermitted. For though there was no cause for any diminution of friendship between them, and though on Mr. Gaskell's part there was an ardent desire to maintain their former intimacy, yet the two young men saw less and less of one another, until their intercourse was confined to an accidental greeting in the street. I believe that during all this time my brother played very frequently on the Stradivarius violin, but always alone. Its very possession seemed to have engendered from the first in his mind a secretive tendency which, as I have already observed, was entirely alien to his real disposition. As he had concealed its discovery from his sister, so he had also from his friend, and Mr. Gaskell remained in complete ignorance of the existence of such an instrument.

On the evening of its arrival from London, John seems to have carefully unpacked the violin and tried it with a new bow of Tourte's make which he had purchased of Mr.

Smart. He had shut the heavy outside door of his room before beginning to play, so that no one might enter unawares; and he told me afterwards that though he had naturally expected from the instrument a very fine tone, yet its actual merits so far exceeded his anticipations as entirely to overwhelm him. The sound issued from it in a volume of such depth and purity as to give an impression of the passages being chorded, or even of another violin being played at the same time. He had had, of course, no opportunity of practising during his illness, and so expected to find his skill with the bow somewhat diminished; but he perceived, on the contrary, that his performance was greatly improved, and that he was playing with a mastery and feeling of which he had never before been conscious. While attributing this improvement very largely to the beauty of the instrument on which he was performing, yet he could not but believe that by his illness, or in some other unexplained way, he had actually acquired a greater freedom of wrist and fluency of expression, with which reflection he was not a little elated. He had had a lock fixed on the cupboard in which he had originally found the violin, and here he carefully deposited it on each occasion after playing, before he opened the outer door of his room.

So the summer term passed away. The examinations had come in their due time, and were now over. Both the young men had submitted themselves to the ordeal, and while neither would of course have admitted as much to anyone else, both felt secretly that they had no reason to be dissatisfied with their performance. The results would not be published for some weeks to come. The last night of the term had arrived, the last night too of John's Oxford career. It was near nine o'clock, but still quite light, and the rich orange glow of sunset had not yet left the sky. The air was warm and sultry, as on that eventful evening when just a year ago he had for the first time seen the figure or the illusion of the figure of Adrian Temple. Since that time he had played the "Areopagita" many, many times; but there had never been any reappearance of that form, nor even had the once familiar creaking of the wicker chair ever made itself heard. As he sat alone in his room, thinking with a natural melancholy that he had seen the sun set for the last time on his student life, and reflecting on the possibilities of the future and perhaps on opportunities wasted in the past, the memory of that evening last June recurred strongly to his imagination, and he felt an irresistible impulse to play once more the "Areopagita." He unlocked the now familiar cupboard and took out the violin, and never had the exquisite gradations of colour in its varnish appeared to greater advantage than in the soft mellow light of the fading day. As he began the *Gagliarda* he looked at the wicker chair, half expecting to see a form he well knew seated in it; but nothing of the kind ensued, and he concluded the "Areopagita" without the occurrence of any unusual phenomenon.

It was just at its close that he heard some one knocking at the outer door. He hurriedly locked away the violin and opened the "oak." It was Mr. Gaskell. He came in rather awkwardly, as though not sure whether he would be welcomed.

"Johnnie," he began, and stopped.

The force of ancient habit sometimes, dear nephew, leads us unwittingly to accost those who were once our friends by a familiar or nick-name long after the intimacy that formerly justified it has vanished. But sometimes we intentionally revert to the use of such a name, not wishing to proclaim openly, as it were, by a more formal address that we are no longer the friends we once were. I think this latter was the case with Mr. Gaskell as he repeated the familiar name.

"Johnnie, I was passing down New College Lane, and heard the violin from your open windows. You were playing the 'Areopagita,' and it all sounded so familiar to me that I thought I must come up. I am not interrupting you, am I?"

"No, not at all," John answered.

"It is the last night of our undergraduate life, the last night we shall meet in Oxford as students. To-morrow we make our bow to youth and become men. We have not seen much of each other this term at any rate, and I daresay that is my fault. But at least let us part as friends. Surely our friends are not so many that we can afford to fling them lightly away."

He held out his hand frankly, and his voice trembled a little as he spoke—partly perhaps from real emotion, but more probably from the feeling of reluctance which I have noticed men always exhibit to discovering any sentiment deeper than those usually deemed conventional in correct society. My brother was moved by his obvious wish to renew their former friendship, and grasped the proffered hand.

There was a minute's pause, and then the conversation was resumed, a little stiffly at first, but more freely afterwards. They spoke on many indifferent subjects, and Mr. Gaskell congratulated John on the prospect of his marriage, of which he had heard. As he at length rose up to take his departure, he said, "You must have practised the violin diligently of late, for I never knew anyone make so rapid progress with it as you have done. As I came along I was spellbound by your music. I never before heard you bring from the instrument so exquisite a tone: the chorded passages were so powerful that I believed there had been another person playing with you. Your Pressenda is certainly a finer instrument than I ever imagined."

My brother was pleased with Mr. Gaskell's compliment, and the latter continued, "Let me enjoy the pleasure of playing with you once more in Oxford; let us play the 'Areopagita.'"

And so saying he opened the pianoforte and sat down.

John was turning to take out the Stradivarius when he remembered that he had never even revealed its existence to Mr. Gaskell, and that if he now produced it an explanation must follow. In a moment his mood changed, and with less geniality he excused himself, somewhat awkwardly, from complying with the request, saying that he was fatigued.

Mr. Gaskell was evidently hurt at his friend's altered manner, and without renewing his petition rose at once from the pianoforte, and after a little forced conversation took his departure. On leaving he shook my brother by the hand, wished him all prosperity in his marriage and after-life, and said, "Do not entirely forget your old comrade, and remember that if at any time you should stand in need of a true friend, you know where to find him!"

John heard his footsteps echoing down the passage and made a half-involuntary motion towards the door as if to call him back, but did not do so, though he thought over his last words then and on a subsequent occasion.

X

The summer was spent by us in the company of Mrs. Temple and Constance, partly at Royston and partly at Worth Maltravers. John had again hired the cutter-yacht *Palestine*, and the whole party made several expeditions in her. Constance was entirely devoted to her lover; her life seemed wrapped up in his; she appeared to have no existence except in his presence.

I can scarcely enumerate the reasons which prompted such thoughts, but during these months I sometimes found myself wondering if John still returned her affection as ardently as I knew had once been the case. I can certainly call to mind no single circumstance which could justify me in such a suspicion. He performed punctiliously all those thousand little acts of devotion which are expected of an accepted lover; he seemed to take pleasure in perfecting any scheme of enjoyment to amuse her; and yet the impression grew in my mind that he no longer felt the same heart-whole love to her that she bore him, and that he had himself shown six months earlier. I cannot say, my dear Edward, how lively was the grief that even the suspicion of such a fact caused me, and I continually rebuked myself for entertaining for a moment a thought so unworthy, and dismissed it from my mind with reprobation. Alas! ere long it was sure again to make itself felt. We had all seen the Stradivarius violin; indeed it was impossible for my brother longer to conceal it from us, as he now played continually on it. He did not recount to us the story of its discovery, contenting himself with saying that he had become possessed of it at Oxford. We imagined naturally that he had purchased it; and for this I was sorry, as I feared Mr. Thoresby, his guardian, who had given him some years previously an excellent violin by Pressenda, might feel hurt at seeing his present so unceremoniously laid aside. None of us were at all intimately acquainted with the fancies of fiddle-collectors, and were consequently quite ignorant of the enormous value that fashion attached to so splendid an instrument. Even had we known, I do not think that we should have been surprised at John purchasing it; for he had recently come of age, and was in possession of so large a fortune as would amply justify him in such an indulgence had he wished to gratify it. No one, however, could remain unaware of the wonderful musical qualities of the instrument. Its rich and melodious tones would commend themselves even to the most unmusical ear, and formed a subject of constant remark. I noticed also that my brother's knowledge of the violin had improved in a very perceptible manner, for it was impossible to attribute the great beauty and power of his present performance entirely to the excellence of the instrument he was using. He appeared more than ever devoted to the art, and would shut himself up in his room alone for two or more hours together for the purpose of playing the violin—a habit which was a source of sorrow to Constance, for he would never allow her to sit with him on such occasions, as she naturally wished to do.

So the summer fled. I should have mentioned that in July, after going up to complete the *viva-voce* part of their examination, both Mr. Gaskell and John received information that they had obtained "first-classes." The young men had, it appears, done excellently well, and both had secured a place in that envied division of the first-class which was called "above the line." John's success proved a source of much pleasure to us all, and mutual congratulations were freely exchanged. We were pleased also at Mr. Gaskell's high place, remembering the kindness which he had shown us at Oxford in the previous year. I desired to send him my compliments and felicitations when he should next be writing to him. I did not doubt that my brother would return Mr. Gaskell's congratulations, which he had already received: he said, however, that his friend had given no address to which he could write, and so the matter dropped.

On the 1st of September John and Constance Temple were married. The wedding took place at Royston, and by John's special desire (with which Constance fully agreed) the ceremony was of a strictly private and unpretentious nature. The newly married pair had determined to spend their honeymoon in Italy, and left for the Continent in the forenoon.

Mrs. Temple invited me to remain with her for the present at Royston, which I was very glad to do, feeling deeply the loss of a favourite brother, and looking forward with dismay to six weeks of loneliness which must elapse before I should again see him and my dearest Constance.

We received news of our travellers about a fortnight afterwards, and then heard from them at frequent intervals. Constance wrote in the best of spirits, and with the keenest appreciation. She had never travelled in Switzerland or Italy before and all was enchantingly novel to her. They had journeyed through Basle to Lucerne, spending a few days in that delightful spot, and thence proceeding by the Simplon Pass to Lugano and the Italian lakes. Then we heard that they had gone further south than had been at first contemplated; they had reached Rome, and were intending to go on to Naples.

After the first few weeks we neither of us received any more letters from John. It was always Constance who wrote, and even her letters grew very much less frequent than had at first been the case. This was perhaps natural, as the business of travel no doubt engrossed their thoughts. But ere long we both perceived that the letters of our dear girl were more constrained and formal than before. It was as if she was writing now rather to comply with a sense of duty than to give vent to the light-hearted gaiety and naïve enjoyment which breathed in every line of her earlier communications. So at least it seemed to us, and again the old suspicion presented itself to my mind, and I feared that all was not as it should be.

Naples was to be the turning-point of their travels, and we expected them to return to England by the end of October. November had arrived, however, and we still had no intimation that their return journey had commenced or was even decided on. From John there was no word, and Constance wrote less often than ever. John, she said, was enraptured with Naples and its surroundings; he devoted himself much to the violin, and though she did not say so, this meant, I knew, that she was often left alone. For her own part, she did not think that a continued residence in Italy would suit her health; the sudden changes of temperature tried her, and people said that the airs rising in the evening from the bay were unwholesome.

Then we received a letter from her which much alarmed us. It was written from Naples and dated October 25. John, she said, had been ailing of late with nervousness and insomnia. On Wednesday, two days before the date of her letter, he had suffered all day from a strange restlessness, which increased after they had retired for the evening. He could not sleep and had dressed again, telling her he would walk a little in the night air to compose himself. He had not returned till near six in the morning, and then was so deadly pale and seemed so exhausted that she insisted on his keeping to his bed till she could get medical advice. The doctors feared that he had been attacked by some strange form of malarial fever, and said he needed much care. Our anxiety was, however, at least temporarily relieved by the receipt of later tidings which spoke of John's recovery; but November drew to a close without any definite mention of their return having reached us.

That month is always, I think, a dreary one in the country. It has neither the brilliant tints of October, nor the cosy jollity of mid-winter with its Christmas joys to alleviate it. This year it was more gloomy than usual. Incessant rain had marked its close, and the Roy, a little brook which skirted the gardens not far from the house, had swollen to unusual proportions. At last one wild night the flood rose so high as to completely cover the garden terraces, working havoc in the parterres, and covering the lawns with a thick coat of mud. Perhaps this gloominess of nature's outer face impressed itself in a sense of apprehension on our spirits, and it was with a feeling of more than ordinary pleasure and relief that early in December we received a letter dated from Laon, saying that our travellers were already well advanced on their return journey, and expected to be in England a week after the receipt by us of this advice. It was, as usual, Constance who wrote. John begged, she said, that Christmas might be spent at Worth Maltravers, and that we would at once proceed thither to see that all was in order against their return. They reached Worth about the middle of the month, and were, I need not say, received with the utmost affection by Mrs. Temple and myself.

In reply to our inquiries John professed that his health was completely restored; but though we could indeed discern no other signs of any special weakness, we were much shocked by his changed appearance. He had completely lost his old healthy and sun-burnt complexion, and his face, though not thin or sunken, was strangely pale. Constance assured us that though in other respects he had apparently recovered, he had never regained his old colour from the night of his attack of fever at Naples.

I soon perceived that her own spirits were not so bright as was ordinarily the case with her; and she exhibited none of the eagerness to narrate to others the incidents of travel which is generally observable in those who have recently returned from a journey. The cause of this depression was, alas! not difficult to discover, for John's former abstraction and moodiness seemed to have returned with an increased force. It was a source of infinite pain to Mrs. Temple, and perhaps even more so to me, to observe this sad state of things. Constance never complained, and her affection towards her husband seemed only to increase in the face of difficulties. Yet the matter was one which could not be hid from the anxious eyes of loving kinswomen, and I believe that it was the consciousness that these altered circumstances could not but force themselves upon our notice that added poignancy to my poor sister's grief. While not markedly neglecting her, my brother had evidently ceased to take that pleasure in her company which might reasonably have been expected in any case under the circumstances of a recent marriage, and a thousand times more so when his wife was so loving and beautiful a creature as Constance Temple. He appeared little except at meals, and not even always at lunch, shutting himself up for the most part in his morning-room or study and playing continually on the violin. It was in vain that we attempted even by means of his music to win him back to a sweeter mood. Again and again I begged him to allow me to accompany him on the pianoforte, but he would never do so, always putting me off with some excuse. Even when he sat with us in the evening, he spoke little, devoting himself for the most part to reading. His books were almost always Greek or Latin, so that I am ignorant of the subjects of his study; but he was content that either Constance or I should play on the pianoforte, saying that the melody, so far from distracting his attention, helped him rather to appreciate what he was reading. Constance always begged me to allow her to take her place at the instrument on these occasions, and would play to him sometimes for hours without receiving a word of thanks, being eager even in this unreciprocated manner to testify her love and devotion to him.

Christmas Day, usually so happy a season, brought no alleviation of our gloom. My brother's reserve continually increased, and even his longest-established habits appeared changed. He had been always most observant of his religious duties, attending divine service with the utmost regularity whatever the weather might be, and saying that it was a duty a landed proprietor owed as much to his tenantry as himself to set a good example in such matters. Ever since our earliest years he and I had gone morning and afternoon on Sundays to the little church of Worth, and there sat together in the Maltravers chapel where so many of our name had sat before us. Here their monuments and achievements stood about us on every side, and it had always seemed to me that with their name and property we had inherited also the obligation to continue those acts of piety, in the practice of which so many of them had lived and died. It was, therefore, a source of surprise and great grief to me when on the Sunday after his return my brother omitted all religious observances, and did not once attend the parish church. He was not present with us at breakfast, ordering coffee and a roll to be taken to his private sitting-room. At the hour at which we usually set out for church I went to his room to tell him that we were all dressed and waiting for him. I tapped at the door, but on trying to enter found it locked. In reply to my message he did not open the door, but merely begged us to go on to church, saying he would possibly follow us later. We went alone, and I sat anxiously in our seat with my eyes fixed on the door, hoping against hope that each late comer might be John, but he never came. Perhaps this will appear to you, Edward, a comparatively trivial circumstance (though I hope it may not), but I assure you that it brought tears to my eyes. When I sat in the Maltravers chapel and thought that for the first time my dear brother had preferred in an open way his convenience or his whim to his duty, and had of set purpose neglected to come to the house of God, I felt a bitter grief that seemed to rise up in my throat and choke me. I could not think of the meaning of the prayers nor join in the singing: and all the time that Mr. Butler, our clergyman, was preaching, a verse of a little piece of poetry which I learnt as a girl was running in my head:—

> How easy are the paths of ill;
>   How steep and hard the upward ways;
> A child can roll the stone down hill
>   That breaks a giant's arm to raise.

It seemed to me that our loved one had set his foot upon the downward slope, and that not all the efforts of those who would have given their lives to save him could now hold him back.

It was even worse on Christmas Day. Ever since we had been confirmed John and I had always taken the Sacrament on that happy morning, and after service he had distributed the Maltravers dole in our chapel. There are given, as you know, on that day to each of twelve old men £5 and a green coat, and a like sum of money with a blue cloth dress to as many old women. These articles of dress are placed on the altar-tomb of Sir Esmoun de Maltravers, and have been thence distributed from days immemorial by the head of our house. Ever since he was twelve years old it had been my pride to watch my handsome brother doing this deed of noble charity, and to hear the kindly words he added with each gift.

Alas! alas! it was all different this Christmas. Even on this holy day my brother did not approach either the altar or the house of God. Till then Christmas had always seemed to me to be a day given us from above, that we might see even while on earth a faint glimpse of that serenity and peaceful love which will hereafter gild all days in heaven. Then covetous men lay aside their greed and enemies their rancour, then warm hearts grow warmer, and Christians feel their common brotherhood. I can scarcely imagine any man so lost or guilty as not to experience on that day some desire to turn back to the good once more, as not to recognise some far-off possibility of better things. It was thoughts free and happy such as these that had previously come into my heart in the service of Christmas Day, and been particularly associated with the familiar words that we all love so much. But that morning the harmonies were all jangled: it seemed as though some evil spirit was pouring wicked thoughts into my ear; and even while children sang "Hark the herald angels," I thought I could hear through it all a melody which I had learnt to loathe, the *Gagliarda* of the "Areopagita."

Poor Constance! Though her veil was down, I could see her tears, and knew her thoughts must be sadder even than mine: I drew her hand towards me, and held it as I would a child's. After the service was over a new trial awaited us. John had made no arrangement for the distribution of the dole. The coats and dresses were all piled ready on Sir Esmoun's tomb, and there lay the little leather pouches of money, but there was no one to give them away. Mr. Butler looked puzzled, and approaching us, said he feared Sir John was ill—had he made no provision for the distribution? Pride kept back the tears which were rising fast, and I said my brother was indeed unwell, that it would be better for Mr. Butler to give away the dole, and that Sir John would himself visit the recipients during the week. Then we hurried away, not daring to watch the distribution of the dole, lest we should no longer be able to master our feelings, and should openly betray our agitation.

From one another we no longer attempted to conceal our grief. It seemed as though we had all at once resolved to abandon the farce of pretending not to notice John's estrangement from his wife, or of explaining away his neglectful and unaccountable treatment of her.

I do not think that three poor women were ever so sad on Christmas Day before as were we on our return from church that morning. None of us had seen my brother, but about five in the afternoon Constance went to his room, and through the locked door begged piteously to see him. After a few minutes he complied with her request and opened the door. The exact circumstances of that interview she never revealed to me, but I knew from her manner when she returned that something she had seen or heard had both grieved and frightened her. She told me only that she had flung herself in an agony of tears at his feet, and kneeling there, weary and broken-hearted, had begged him to tell her if she had done aught amiss, had prayed him to give her back his love. To all this he answered little, but her entreaties had at least such an effect as to induce him to take his dinner with us that evening. At that meal we tried to put aside our gloom, and with feigned smiles and cheerful voices, from which the tears were hardly banished, sustained a weary show of conversation and tried to wile away his evil mood. But he spoke little; and when Foster, my father's butler, put on the table the three-handled Maltravers' loving-cup that he had brought up Christmas by Christmas for thirty years, my brother merely passed it by without a taste. I saw by Foster's face that the master's malady was no longer a secret even from the servants.

I shall not harass my own feelings nor yours, my dear Edward, by entering into further details of your father's illness, for such it was obvious his indisposition had become. It was the only consolation, and that was a sorry one, that we could use with Constance, to persuade her that John's estrangement from her was merely the result or manifestation of some physical infirmity. He obviously grew worse from week to week, and his treatment of his wife became colder and more callous. We had used all efforts to persuade him to take a change of air—to go to Royston for a month, and place himself under the care of Dr. Dobie. Mrs. Temple had even gone so far as to write privately to this physician, telling him as much of the case as was prudent, and asking his advice. Not being aware of the darker sides of my brother's ailment, Dr. Dobie replied in a less serious strain than seemed to us convenient, but recommended in any case a complete change of air and scene.

It was, therefore, with no ordinary pleasure and relief that we heard my brother announce quite unexpectedly one morning in March that he had made up his mind to seek change, and was going to leave almost immediately for the Continent. He took his valet Parnham with him, and quitted Worth one morning before lunch, bidding us an unceremonious adieu, though he kissed Constance with some apparent tenderness. It was the first time for three months, she confessed to me afterwards, that he had shown her even so ordinary a mark of affection; and her wounded heart treasured up what she hoped would prove a token of returning love. He had not proposed to take her with him, and even had he done so, we should have been reluctant to assent, as signs were not wanting that it might have been imprudent for her to undertake foreign travel at that period.

For nearly a month we had no word of him. Then he wrote a short note to Constance from Naples, giving no news, and indeed, scarce speaking of himself at all, but mentioning as an address to which she might write if she wished, the Villa de Angelis at Posilipo. Though his letter was cold and empty, yet Constance was delighted to get it, and wrote henceforth herself nearly every day, pouring out her heart to him, and retailing such news as she thought would cheer him.

XI

A month later Mrs. Temple wrote to John warning him of the state in which Constance now found herself, and begging him to return at least for a few weeks in order that he might be present at the time of her confinement. Though it would have been in the last degree unkind, or even inhuman, that a request of this sort should have been refused, yet I will confess to you that my brother's recent strangeness had prepared me for behaviour on his part however wild; and it was with a feeling of extreme relief that I heard from Mrs. Temple a little later that she had received a short note from John to say that he was already on his return journey. I believe Mrs. Temple herself felt as I did in the matter, though she said nothing.

When he returned we were all at Royston, whither Mrs. Temple had taken Constance to be under Dr. Dobie's care. We found John's physical appearance changed for the worse. His pallor was as remarkable as before, but he was visibly thinner; and his strange mental abstraction and moodiness seemed little if any abated. At first, indeed, he greeted Constance kindly or even affectionately. She had been in a terrible state of anxiety as to the attitude he would assume towards her, and this mental strain affected prejudicially her very delicate bodily condition. His kindness, of an ordinary enough nature indeed, seemed to her yearning heart a miracle of condescending love, and she was transported with the idea that his affection to her, once so sincere, was indeed returning. But I grieve to say that his manner thawed only for a very short time, and ere long he relapsed into an attitude of complete indifference. It was as if his real, true, honest, and loving character had made one more vigorous effort to assert itself,—as though it had for a moment broken through the hard and selfish crust that was forming around him; but the blighting influence which was at work proved seemingly too strong for him to struggle against, and riveted its chains again upon him with a weight heavier than before. That there was some malefic influence, mental or physical, thus working on him, no one who had known him before could for a moment doubt. But while Mrs. Temple and I readily admitted this much, we were entirely unable even to form a conjecture as to its nature. It is true that Mrs. Temple's fancy suggested that Constance had some rival in his affections; but we rejected such a theory almost before it was proposed, feeling that it was inherently improbable, and that, had it been true, we could not have remained entirely unaware of the circumstances which had conduced to such a state of things. It was this inexplicable nature of my brother's affliction that added immeasurably to our grief. If we could only have ascertained its cause we might have combated it; but as it was, we were fighting in the dark, as against some enemy who was assaulting us from an obscurity so thick that we could not see his form. Of any mental trouble we thus knew nothing, nor could we say that my brother was suffering from any definite physical ailment, except that he was certainly growing thinner.

Your birth, my dear Edward, followed very shortly. Your poor mother rallied in an unusually short time, and was filled with rapture at the new treasure which was thus given as a solace to her afflictions. Your father exhibited little interest at the event, though he sat nearly half an hour with her one evening, and allowed her even to stroke his hair and caress him as in time long past. Although it was now the height of summer he seldom left the house, sitting much and sleeping in his own room, where he had a field-bed provided for him, and continually devoting himself to the violin.

One evening near the end of July we were sitting after dinner in the drawing-room at Royston, having the French windows looking on to the lawn open, as the air was still oppressively warm. Though things were proceeding as indifferently as before, we were perhaps less cast down than usual, for John had taken his dinner with us that evening. This was a circumstance now, alas! sufficiently uncommon, for he had nearly all his meals served for him in his own rooms. Constance, who was once more downstairs, sat playing at the pianoforte, performing chiefly melodies by Scarlatti or Bach, of which old-fashioned music she knew her husband to be most fond. A later fashion, as you know, has revived the cultivation of these composers, but at the time of which I write their works were much less commonly known. Though she was more than a passable musician, he would not allow her to accompany him; indeed he never now performed at all on the violin before us, reserving his practice entirely for his own chamber. There was a pause in the music while coffee was served. My brother had been sitting in an easy-chair apart reading some classical work during his wife's performance, and taking little notice of us. But after a while he put down his book and said, "Constance, if you will accompany me, I will get my violin and play a little while." I cannot say how much his words astonished us. It was so simple a matter for him to say, and yet it filled us all with an unspeakable joy. We concealed our emotion till he had left the room to get his instrument, then Constance showed how deeply she was gratified by kissing first her mother and then me, squeezing my hand but saying nothing. In a minute he returned, bringing his violin and a music-book. By the soiled vellum cover and the shape I perceived instantly that it was the book containing the "Areopagita." I had not seen it for near two years, and was not even aware that it was in the house, but I knew at once that he intended to play that suite. I entertained an unreasoning but profound aversion to its melodies, but at that moment I would have welcomed warmly that or any other music, so that he would only choose once more to show some thought for his neglected wife. He put the book open at the "Areopagita" on the desk of the pianoforte, and asked her to play it with him. She had never seen the music before, though I believe she was not unacquainted with the melody, as she had heard him playing it by himself, and once heard, it was not easily forgotten.

They began the "Areopagita" suite, and at first all went well. The tone of the violin, and also, I may say with no undue partiality, my brother's performance, were so marvellously fine that though our thoughts were elsewhere when, the music commenced, in a few seconds they were wholly engrossed in the melody, and we sat spellbound. It was as if the violin had become suddenly endowed with life, and was singing to us in a mystical language more deep and awful than any human words. Constance was comparatively unused to the figuring of the *basso continuo*, and found some trouble in reading it accurately, especially in manuscript; but she was able to mask any difficulty she may have had until she came to the *Gagliarda*. Here she confessed to me her thoughts seemed against her will to wander, and her attention became too deeply riveted on her husband's performance to allow her to watch her own. She made first one slight fault, and then growing nervous, another, and another. Suddenly John stopped and said brusquely, "Let Sophy play, I cannot keep time with you." Poor Constance! The tears came swiftly to my own eyes when I heard him speak so thoughtlessly to her, and I was almost provoked to rebuke him openly. She was still weak from her recent illness; her nerves were excited by the unusual pleasure she felt in playing once more with her husband, and this sudden shattering of her hopes of a renewed tenderness proved more than she could bear: she put her head between her hands upon the keyboard and broke into a paroxysm of tears.

We both ran to her; but while we were attempting to assuage her grief, John shut his violin into its case, took the music-book under his arm, and left the room without saying a word to any of us, not even to the weeping girl, whose sobs seemed as though they would break her heart.

We got her put to bed at once, but it was some hours before her convulsive sobbing ceased. Mrs. Temple had administered to her a soothing draught of proved efficacy, and after sitting with her till after one o'clock, I left her at last dozing off to sleep, and myself sought repose. I was quite wearied out with the weight of my anxiety, and with the crushing bitterness of seeing my dearest Constance's feelings so wounded. Yet in spite, or rather perhaps on account of my trouble, my head had scarcely touched my pillow ere I fell into a deep sleep.

A room in the south wing had been converted for the nonce into a nursery, and for the convenience of being near her infant Constance now slept in a room adjoining. As this portion of the house was somewhat isolated, Mrs. Temple had suggested that I should keep her daughter company, and occupy a room in the same passage, only removed a few doors, and this I had accordingly done. I was aroused from my sleep that night by some one knocking gently on the door of my bedroom; but it was some seconds before my thoughts became sufficiently awake to allow me to remember where I was. There was some moonlight, but I lighted a candle, and looking at my watch saw that it was two o'clock. I concluded that either Constance or her baby was unwell, and that the nurse needed my assistance. So I left my bed, and moving to the door, asked softly who was there. It was, to my surprise, the voice of Constance that replied, "O Sophy, let me in."

In a second I had opened the door, and found my poor sister wearing only her night-dress, and standing in the moonlight before me.

She looked frightened and unusually pale in her white dress and with the cold gleam of the moon upon her. At first I thought she was walking in her sleep, and perhaps rehearsing again in her dreams the troubles which dogged her waking footsteps. I took her gently by the arm, saying, "Dearest Constance, come back at once to bed; you will take cold."

She was not asleep, however, but made a motion of silence, and said in a terrified whisper, "Hush; do you hear nothing?" There was something so vague and yet so mysterious in the question and in her evident perturbation that I was infected too by her alarm. I felt myself shiver, as I strained my ear to catch if possible the slightest sound. But a complete silence pervaded everything: I could hear nothing.

"Can you hear it?" she said again. All sorts of images of ill presented themselves to my imagination: I thought the baby must be ill with croup, and that she was listening for some stertorous breath of anguish; and then the dread came over me that perhaps her sorrows had been too much for her, and that reason had left her seat. At that thought the marrow froze in my bones.

"Hush," she said again; and just at that moment, as I strained my ears, I thought I caught upon the sleeping air a distant and very faint murmur.

"Oh, what is it, Constance?" I said. "You will drive me mad"; and while I spoke the murmur seemed to resolve itself into the vibration, felt almost rather than heard, of some distant musical instrument. I stepped past her into the passage. All was deadly still, but I could perceive that music was being played somewhere far away; and almost at the same minute my ears recognised faintly but unmistakably the *Gagliarda* of the "Areopagita."

I have already mentioned that for some reason which I can scarcely explain, this melody was very repugnant to me. It seemed associated in some strange and intimate way with my brother's indisposition and moral decline. Almost at the moment that I had heard it first two years ago, peace seemed to have risen up and left our house, gathering her skirts about her, as we read that the angels left the Temple at the siege of Jerusalem. And now it was even more detestable to my ears, recalling as it did too vividly the cruel events of the preceding evening.

"John must be sitting up playing," I said.

"Yes," she answered; "but why is he in this part of the house, and why does he always play *that* tune?"

It was if some irresistible attraction drew us towards the music. Constance took my hand in hers and we moved together slowly down the passage. The wind had risen, and though there was a bright moon, her beams were constantly eclipsed by driving clouds. Still there was light enough to guide us, and I extinguished the candle. As we reached the end of the passage the air of the *Gagliarda* grew more and more distinct.

Our passage opened on to a broad landing with a balustrade, and from one side of it ran out the picture-gallery which you know.

I looked at Constance significantly. It was evident that John was playing in this gallery. We crossed the landing, treading carefully and making no noise with our naked feet, for both of us had been too excited even to think of putting on shoes.

We could now see the whole length of the gallery. My poor brother sat in the oriel window of which I have before spoken. He was sitting so as to face the picture of Adrian Temple, and the great windows of the oriel flung a strong light on him. At times a cloud hid the moon, and all was plunged in darkness; but in a moment the cold light fell full on him, and we could trace every feature as in a picture. He had evidently not been to bed, for he was fully dressed, exactly as he had left us in the drawing-room five hours earlier when Constance was weeping over his thoughtless words. He was playing the violin, playing with a passion and reckless energy which I had never seen, and hope never to see again. Perhaps he remembered that this spot was far removed from the rest of the house, or perhaps he was careless whether any were awake and listening to him or not; but it seemed to me that he was playing with a sonorous strength greater than I had thought possible for a single violin. There came from his instrument such a volume and torrent of melody as to fill the gallery so full, as it were, of sound that it throbbed and vibrated again. He kept his eyes fixed on something at the opposite side of the gallery; we could not indeed see on what, but I have no doubt at all that it was the portrait of Adrian Temple. His gaze was eager and expectant, as though he were waiting for something to occur which did not.

I knew that he had been growing thin of late, but this was the first time I had realised how sunk were the hollows of his eyes and how haggard his features had become. It may have been some effect of moonlight which I do not well understand, but his fine-cut face, once so handsome, looked on this night worn and thin like that of an old man. He never for a moment ceased playing. It was always one same dreadful melody, the *Gagliarda* of the "Areopagita," and he repeated it time after time with the perseverance and apparent aimlessness of an automaton.

He did not see us, and we made no sign, standing afar off in silent horror at that nocturnal sight. Constance clutched me by the arm: she was so pale that I perceived it even in the moonlight. "Sophy," she said, "he is sitting in the same place as on the first night when he told me how he loved me." I could answer nothing, my voice was frozen in me. I could only stare at my brother's poor withered face, realising then for the first time that he must be mad, and that it was the haunting of the *Gagliarda* that had made him so.

We stood there I believe for half an hour without speech or motion, and all the time that sad figure at the end of the gallery continued its performance. Suddenly he stopped, and an expression of frantic despair came over his face as he laid down the violin and buried his head in his hands. I could bear it no longer. "Constance," I said, "come back to bed. We can do nothing," So we turned and crept away silently as we had come. Only as we crossed the landing Constance stopped, and looked back for a minute with a heart-broken yearning at the man she loved. He had taken his hands from his head, and she saw the profile of his face clear cut and hard in the white moonlight.

It was the last time her eyes ever looked upon it.

She made for a moment as if she would turn back and go to him, but her courage failed her, and we went on. Before we reached her room we heard in the distance, faintly but distinctly, the burden of the *Gagliarda*.

XII

The next morning, my maid brought me a hurried note written in pencil by my brother. It contained only a few lines, saying that he found that his continued sojourn at Royston was not beneficial to his health, and had determined to return to Italy. If we wished to write, letters would reach him at the Villa de Angelis: his valet Parnham was to follow him thither with his baggage as soon as it could be got together. This was all; there was no word of adieu even to his wife.

We found that he had never gone to bed that night. But in the early morning he had himself saddled his horse *Sentinel* and ridden in to Derby, taking the early mail thence to London. His resolve to leave Royston had apparently been arrived at very suddenly, for so far as we could discover, he had carried no luggage of any kind. I could not help looking somewhat carefully round his room to see if he had taken the Stradivarius violin. No trace of it or even of its case was to be seen, though it was difficult to imagine how he could have carried it with him on horseback. There was, indeed, a locked travelling-trunk which Parnham was to bring with him later, and the instrument might, of course, have been in that; but I felt convinced that he had actually taken it with him in some way or other, and this proved afterwards to have been the case.

I shall draw a veil, my dear Edward, over the events which immediately followed your father's departure. Even at this distance of time the memory is too inexpressibly bitter to allow me to do more than briefly allude to them.

A fortnight after John's departure, we left Royston and removed to Worth, wishing to get some sea-air, and to enjoy the late summer of the south coast. Your mother seemed entirely to have recovered from her confinement, and to be enjoying as good health as could be reasonably expected under the circumstances of her husband's indisposition. But suddenly one of those insidious maladies which are incidental to women in her condition seized upon her. We had hoped and believed that all such period of danger was already happily past; but, alas! it was not so, and within a few hours of her first seizure all realised how serious was her case. Everything that human skill can do under such conditions was done, but without avail. Symptoms of blood-poisoning showed themselves, accompanied with high fever, and within a week she was in her coffin.

Though her delirium was terrible to watch, yet I thank God to this day, that if she was to die, it pleased Him to take her while in an unconscious condition. For two days before her death she recognised no one, and was thus spared at least the sadness of passing from life without one word of kindness or even of reconciliation from her unhappy husband.

The communication with a place so distant as Naples was not then to be made under fifteen or twenty days, and all was over before we could hope that the intelligence even of his wife's illness had reached John. Both Mrs. Temple and I remained at Worth in a state of complete prostration, awaiting his return. When more than a month had passed without his arrival, or even a letter to say that he was on his way, our anxiety took a new turn, as we feared that some accident had befallen him, or that the news of his wife's death, which would then be in his hands, had so seriously affected him as to render him incapable of taking any action. To repeated subsequent communications we received no answer; but at last, to a letter which I wrote to Parnham, the servant replied, stating that his master was still at the Villa de Angelis, and in a condition of health little differing from that in which he left Royston, except that he was now slightly paler if possible and thinner. It was not till the end of November that any word came from him, and then he wrote only one page of a sheet of note-paper to me in pencil, making no reference whatever to his wife's death, but saying that he should not return for Christmas, and instructing me to draw on his bankers for any moneys that I might require for household purposes at Worth.

I need not tell you the effect that such conduct produced on Mrs. Temple and myself; you can easily imagine what would have been your own feelings in such a case. Nor will I relate any other circumstances which occurred at this period, as they would have no direct bearing upon my narrative. Though I still wrote to my brother at frequent intervals, as not wishing to neglect a duty, no word from him ever came in reply.

About the end of March, indeed, Parnham returned to Worth Maltravers, saying that his master had paid him a half-year's wages in advance, and then dispensed with his services. He had always been an excellent servant, and attached to the family, and I was glad to be able to offer him a suitable position with us at Worth until his master should return. He brought disquieting reports of John's health, saying that he was growing visibly weaker. Though I was sorely tempted to ask him many questions as to his master's habits and way of life, my pride forbade me to do so. But I heard incidentally from my maid that Parnham had told her Sir John was spending money freely in alterations at the Villa de Angelis, and had engaged Italians to attend him, with which his English valet was naturally much dissatisfied.

So the spring passed and the summer was well advanced.

On the last morning of July I found waiting for me on the breakfast-table an envelope addressed in my brother's hand. I opened it hastily. It only contained a few words, which I have before me as I write now. The ink is a little faded and yellow, but the impression it made is yet vivid as on that summer morning.

> MY DEAREST SOPHY (it began),—Come to me here at once, if possible, or it may be too late. I want to see you. They say that I am ill, and too weak to travel to England.—Your loving brother,
>
> JOHN

There was a great change in the style, from the cold and conventional notes that he had hitherto sent at such long intervals; from the stiff "Dear Sophia" and "Sincerely yours" to which, I grieve to say, I had grown accustomed. Even the writing itself was altered. It was more the bold boyish hand he wrote when first he went to Oxford, than the smaller cramped and classic character of his later years. Though it was a little matter enough, God knows, in comparison with his grievous conduct, yet it touched me much that he should use again the once familiar "Dearest Sophy," and sign himself "my loving brother." I felt my heart go out towards him; and so strong is woman's affection for her own kin, that I had already forgotten any resentment and reprobation in my great pity for the poor wanderer, lying sick perhaps unto death and alone in a foreign land.

I took his note at once to Mrs. Temple. She read it twice or thrice, trying to take in the meaning of it. Then she drew me to her and, kissing me, said, "Go to him at once, Sophy. Bring him back to Worth; try to bring him back to the right way."

I ordered my things to be packed, determining to drive to Southampton and take train thence to London; and at the same time Mrs. Temple gave instructions that all should be prepared for her own return to Royston within a few days. I knew she did not dare to see John after her daughter's death.

I took my maid with me, and Parnham to act as courier. At London we hired a carriage for the whole journey, and from Calais posted direct to Naples. We took the short route by Marseilles and Genoa, and travelled for seventeen days without intermission, as my brother's note made me desirous of losing no time on the way. I had never been in Italy before; but my anxiety was such that my mind was unable to appreciate either the beauty of the scenery or the incidents of travel. I can, in fact, remember nothing of our journey now, except the wearisome and interminable jolting over bad roads and the insufferable heat. It was the middle of August in an exceptionally warm summer, and after passing Genoa the heat became almost tropical. There was no relief even at night, for the warm air hung stagnant and suffocating, and the inside of my travelling coach was often like a furnace.

We were at last approaching the conclusion of our journey, and had left Rome behind us. The day that we set out from Aversa was the hottest that I have ever felt, the sun beating down with an astonishing power even in the early hours, and the road being thick with a white and blinding dust. It was soon after midnight that our carriage began rattling over the great stone blocks with which the streets of Naples are paved. The suburbs that we at first passed through were, I remember, in darkness and perfect quiet; but after traversing the heart of the city and reaching the western side, we suddenly found ourselves in the midst of an enormous and very dense crowd. There were lanterns everywhere, and interminable lanes of booths, whose proprietors were praising their wares with loud shouts; and here acrobats, jugglers, minstrels, black-vested priests, and blue-coated soldiers mingled with a vast crowd whose numbers at once arrested the progress of the carriage. Though it was so late of a Sunday night, all seemed here awake and busy as at noonday. Oil-lamps with reeking fumes of black smoke flung a glare over the scene, and the discordant cries and chattering conversation united in so deafening a noise as to make me turn faint and giddy, wearied as I already was with long travelling. Though I felt that intense eagerness and expectation which the approaching termination of a tedious journey inspires, and was desirous of pushing forward with all imaginable despatch, yet here our course was sadly delayed. The horses could only proceed at the slowest of foot-paces, and we were constantly brought to a complete stop for some minutes before the post-boy could force a passage through the unwilling crowd. This produced a feeling of irritation, and despair of ever reaching my destination; and the mirth and careless hilarity of the people round us chafed with bitter contrast on my depressed spirits. I inquired from the post-boy what was the origin of so great a commotion, and understood him to say in reply that it was a religious festival held annually in honour of "Our Lady of the Grotto." I cannot, however, conceive of any truly religious person countenancing such a gathering, which seemed to me rather like the unclean orgies of a heathen deity than an act of faith of Christian people. This disturbance occasioned us so serious a delay, that as we were climbing the steep slope leading up to Posilipo it was already three in the morning and the dawn was at hand.

After mounting steadily for a long time we began to rapidly descend, and just as the sun came up over the sea we arrived at the Villa de Angelis. I sprang from the carriage, and passing through a trellis of vines, reached the house. A man-servant was in waiting, and held the door open for me; but he was an Italian, and did not understand me when I asked in English where Sir John Maltravers was. He had evidently, however, received instructions to take me at once to my brother, and led the way to an inner part of the house. As we proceeded I heard the sound of a rich alto voice singing very sweetly to a mandoline some soothing or religious melody. The servant pulled aside a heavy curtain and I found myself in my brother's room. An Italian youth sat on a stool near the door, and it was he who had been singing. At a few words from John, addressed to him in his own language, he set down his mandoline and left the room, pulling to the curtain and shutting a door behind it.

The room looked directly on to the sea: the villa was, in fact, built upon rocks at the foot of which the waves lapped. Through two folding windows which opened on to a balcony the early light of the summer morning streamed in with a rosy flush. My brother sat on a low couch or sofa, propped up against a heap of pillows, with a rug of brilliant colours flung across his feet and legs. He held out his arms to me, and I ran to him; but even in so brief an interval I had perceived that he was terribly weak and wasted.

All my memories of his past faults had vanished and were dead in that sad aspect of his worn features, and in the conviction which I felt, even from the first moment, that he had but little time longer to remain with us. I knelt by him on the floor, and with my arms round his neck, embraced him tenderly, not finding any place for words, but only sobbing in great anguish. Neither of us spoke, and my weariness from long travel and the strangeness of the situation caused me to feel that paralysing sensation of doubt as to the reality of the scene, and even of my own existence, which all, I believe, have experienced at times of severe mental tension. That I, a plain English girl, should be kneeling here beside my brother in the Italian dawn; that I should read, as I believed, on his young face the unmistakable image and superscription of death; and reflect that within so few months he had married, had wrecked his home, that my poor Constance was no more;—these things seemed so unrealisable that for a minute I felt that it must all be a nightmare, that I should immediately wake with the fresh salt air of the Channel blowing through my bedroom window at Worth, and find I had been dreaming. But it was not so; the light of day grew stronger and brighter, and even in my sorrow the panorama of the most beautiful spot on earth, the Bay of Naples, with Vesuvius lying on the far side, as seen then from these windows, stamped itself for ever on my mind. It was unreal as a scene in some brilliant dramatic spectacle, but, alas! no unreality was here. The flames of the candles in their silver sconces waxed paler and paler, the lines and shadows on my brother's face grew darker, and the pallor of his wasted features showed more striking in the bright rays of the morning sun.

XIII

I had spent near a week at the Villa de Angelis. John's manner to me was most tender and affectionate; but he showed no wish to refer to the tragedy of his wife's death and the sad events which had preceded it, or to attempt to explain in any way his own conduct in the past. Nor did I ever lead the conversation to these topics; for I felt that even if there were no other reason, his great weakness rendered it inadvisable to introduce such subjects at present, or even to lead him to speak at all more than was actually necessary. I was content to minister to him in quiet, and infinitely happy in his restored affection. He seemed desirous of banishing from his mind all thoughts of the last few months, but spoke much of the years before he had gone to Oxford, and of happy days which we had spent together in our childhood at Worth Maltravers. His weakness was extreme, but he complained of no particular malady except a short cough which troubled him at night.

I had spoken to him of his health, for I could see that his state was such as to inspire anxiety, and begged that he would allow me to see if there was an English doctor at Naples who could visit him. This he would not assent to, saying that he was quite content with the care of an Italian doctor who visited him almost daily, and that he hoped to be able, under my escort, to return within a very short time to England.

"I shall never be much better, dear Sophy," he said one day. "The doctor tells me that I am suffering from some sort of consumption, and that I must not expect to live long. Yet I yearn to see Worth once more, and to feel again the west winds blowing in the evening across from Portland, and smell the thyme on the Dorset downs. In a few days I hope perhaps to be a little stronger, and I then wish to show you a discovery which I have made in Naples. After that you may order them to harness the horses, and carry me back to Worth Maltravers."

I endeavoured to ascertain from Signor Baravelli, the doctor, something as to the actual state of his patient; but my knowledge of Italian was so slight that I could neither make him understand what I would be at, nor comprehend in turn what he replied, so that this attempt was relinquished. From my brother himself I gathered that he had begun to feel his health much impaired as far back as the early spring, but though his strength had since then gradually failed him, he had not been confined to the house until a month past. He spent the day and often the night reclining on his sofa and speaking little. He had apparently lost the taste for the violin which had once absorbed so much of his attention; indeed I think the bodily strength necessary for its performance had probably now failed him. The Stradivarius instrument lay near his couch in its case; but I only saw the latter open on one occasion, I think, and was deeply thankful that John no longer took the same delight as heretofore in the practice of this art,—not only because the mere sound of his violin was now fraught to me with such bitter memories, but also because I felt sure that its performance had in some way which I could not explain a deleterious effect upon himself. He exhibited that absence of vitality which is so often noticeable in those who have not long to live, and on some days lay in a state of semi-lethargy from which it was difficult to rouse him. But at other times he suffered from a distressing restlessness which forbade him to sit still even for a few minutes, and which was more painful to watch than his lethargic stupor. The Italian boy, of whom I have already spoken, exhibited an untiring devotion to his master which won my heart. His name was Raffaelle Carotenuto, and he often sang to us in the evening, accompanying himself on the mandoline. At nights, too, when John could not sleep, Raffaelle would read for hours till at last his master dozed off. He was well educated, and though I could not understand the subject he read, I often sat by and listened, being charmed with his evident attachment to my brother and with the melodious intonation of a sweet voice.

My brother was nervous apparently in some respects, and would never be left alone even for a few minutes; but in the intervals while Raffaelle was with him I had ample opportunity to examine and appreciate the beauties of the Villa de Angelis. It was built, as I have said, on some rocks jutting into the sea, just before coming to the Capo di Posilipo as you proceed from Naples. The earlier foundations were, I believe, originally Roman, and upon them a modern villa had been constructed in the eighteenth century, and to this again John had made important additions in the past two years. Looking down upon the sea from the windows of the villa, one could on calm days easily discern the remains of Roman piers and moles lying below the surface of the transparent water; and the tufa-rock on which the house was built was burrowed with those unintelligible excavations of a classic date so common in the neighbourhood. These subterranean rooms and passages, while they aroused my curiosity, seemed at the same time so gloomy and repellent that I never explored them. But on one sunny morning, as I walked at the foot of the rocks by the sea, I ventured into one of the larger of these chambers, and saw that it had at the far end an opening leading apparently to an inner room. I had walking with me an old Italian female servant who took a motherly interest in my proceedings, and who, relying principally upon a very slight knowledge of English, had constituted herself my body-guard. Encouraged by her presence, I penetrated this inner room and found that it again opened in turn into another, and so on until we had passed through no less than four chambers.

They were all lighted after a fashion through vent-holes which somewhere or other reached the outer air, but the fourth room opened into a fifth which was unlighted. My companion, who had been showing signs of alarm and an evident reluctance to proceed further, now stopped abruptly and begged me to return. It may have been that her fear communicated itself to me also, for on attempting to cross the threshold and explore the darkness of the fifth cell, I was seized by an unreasoning panic and by the feeling of undefined horror experienced in a nightmare. I hesitated for an instant, but my fear became suddenly more intense, and springing back, I followed my companion, who had set out to run back to the outer air. We never paused until we stood panting in the full sunlight by the sea. As soon as the maid had found her breath, she begged me never to go there again, explaining in broken English that the caves were known in the neighbourhood as the "Cells of Isis," and were reputed to be haunted by demons. This episode, trifling as it may appear, had so great an effect upon me that I never again ventured on to the lower walk which ran at the foot of the rocks by the sea.

In the house above, my brother had built a large hall after the ancient Roman style, and this, with a dining-room and many other chambers, were decorated in the fashion of those discovered at Pompeii. They had been furnished with the utmost luxury, and the beauty of the paintings, furniture, carpets, and hangings was enhanced by statues in bronze and marble. The villa, indeed, and its fittings were of a kind to which I was little used, and at the same time of such beauty that I never ceased to regard all as a creation of an enchanter's wand, or as the drop-scene to some drama which might suddenly be raised and disappear from my sight. The house, in short, together with its furniture, was, I believe, intended to be a reproduction of an ancient Roman villa, and had something about it repellent to my rustic and insular ideas. In the contemplation of its perfection I experienced a curious mental sensation, which I can only compare to the physical oppression produced on some persons by the heavy and cloying perfume of a bouquet of gardenias or other too highly scented exotics.

In my brother's room was a medieval reproduction in mellow alabaster of a classic group of a dolphin encircling a Cupid. It was, I think, the fairest work of art I ever saw, but it jarred upon my sense of propriety that close by it should hang an ivory crucifix. I would rather, I think, have seen all things material and pagan entirely, with every view of the future life shut out, than have found a medley of things sacred and profane, where the emblems of our highest hopes and aspirations were placed in insulting indifference side by side with the embodied forms of sensuality. Here, in this scene of magical beauty, it seemed to me for a moment that the years had rolled back, that Christianity had still to fight with a *living* Paganism, and that the battle was not yet won. It was the same all through the house; and there were many other matters which filled me with regret, mingled with vague and apprehensive surmises which I shall not here repeat.

At one end of the house was a small library, but it contained few works except Latin and Greek classics. I had gone thither one day to look for a book that John had asked for, when in turning out some drawers I found a number of letters written from Worth by my lost Constance to her husband. The shock of being brought suddenly face to face with a handwriting that evoked memories at once so dear and sad was in itself a sharp one; but its bitterness was immeasurably increased by the discovery that not one of these envelopes had ever been opened. While that dear heart, now at rest, was pouring forth her love and sorrow to the ears that should have been above all others ready to receive them, her letters, as they arrived, were flung uncared for, unread, even unopened, into any haphazard receptacle.

The days passed one by one at the Villa de Angelis with but little incident, nor did my brother's health either visibly improve or decline. Though the weather was still more than usually warm, a grateful breeze came morning and evening from the sea and tempered the heat so much as to render it always supportable. John would sometimes in the evening sit propped up with cushions on the trellised balcony looking towards Baia, and watch the fishermen setting their nets. We could hear the melody of their deep-voiced songs carried up on the night air. "It was here, Sophy," my brother said, as we sat one evening looking on a scene like this,— "It was here that the great epicure Pollio built himself a famous house, and called it by two Greek words meaning a 'truce to care,' from which our name of Posilipo is derived. It was his *sans-souci*, and here he cast aside his vexations; but they were lighter than mine. Posilipo has brought no cessation of care to me. I do not think I shall find any truce this side the grave; and beyond, who knows?"

This was the first time John had spoken in this strain, and he seemed stirred to an unusual activity, as though his own words had suddenly reminded him how frail was his state. He called Raffaelle to him and despatched him on an errand to Naples. The next morning he sent for me earlier than usual, and begged that a carriage might be ready by six in the evening, as he desired to drive into the city. I tried at first to dissuade him from his project, urging him to consider his weak state of health. He replied that he felt somewhat stronger, and had something that he particularly wished me to see in Naples. This done, it would be better to return at once to England: he could, he thought, bear the journey if we travelled by very short stages.

XIV

Shortly after six o'clock in the evening we left the Villa de Angelis. The day had been as usual cloudlessly serene; but a gentle sea-breeze, of which I have spoken, rose in the afternoon and brought with it a refreshing coolness. We had arranged a sort of couch in the landau with many cushions for my brother, and he mounted into the carriage with more ease than I had expected. I sat beside him, with Raffaelle facing me on the opposite seat. We drove down the hill of Posilipo through the ilex-trees and tamarisk-bushes that then skirted the sea, and so into the town. John spoke little except to remark that the carriage was an easy one. As we were passing through one of the principal streets he bent over to me and said, "You must not be alarmed if I show you to-day a strange sight. Some women might perhaps be frightened at what we are going to see; but my poor sister has known already so much of trouble that a light thing like this will not affect her." In spite of his encomiums upon my supposed courage, I felt alarmed and agitated by his words. There was a vagueness in them which frightened me, and bred that indefinite apprehension which is often infinitely more terrifying than the actual object which inspires it. To my inquiries he would give no further response than to say that he had whilst at Posilipo made some investigations in Naples leading to a strange discovery, which he was anxious to communicate to me. After traversing a considerable distance, we had penetrated apparently into the heart of the town. The streets grew narrower and more densely thronged; the houses were more dirty and tumbledown, and the appearance of the people themselves suggested that we had reached some of the lower quarters of the city. Here we passed through a further network of small streets of the name of which I took no note, and found ourselves at last in a very dark and narrow lane called the *Via del Giardino*. Although my brother had, so far as I had observed, given no orders to the coachman, the latter seemed to have no difficulty in finding his way, driving rapidly in the Neapolitan fashion, and proceeding direct as to a place with which he was already familiar.

In the Via del Giardino the houses were of great height, and overhung the street so as nearly to touch one another. It seemed that this quarter had been formerly inhabited, if not by the aristocracy, at least by a class very much superior to that which now lived there; and many of the houses were large and dignified, though long since parcelled out into smaller tenements. It was before such a house that we at last brought up. Here must have been at one time a house or palace of some person of distinction, having a long and fine façade adorned with delicate pilasters, and much florid ornamentation of the Renaissance period. The ground-floor was divided into a series of small shops, and its upper storeys were evidently peopled by sordid families of the lowest class. Before one of these little shops, now closed and having its windows carefully blocked with boards, our carriage stopped. Raffaelle alighted, and taking a key from his pocket unlocked the door, and assisted John to leave the carriage. I followed, and directly we had crossed the threshold, the boy locked the door behind us, and I heard the carriage drive away.

We found ourselves in a narrow and dark passage, and as soon as my eyes grew accustomed to the gloom I perceived there was at the end of it a low staircase leading to some upper room, and on the right a door which opened into the closed shop. My brother moved slowly along the passage, and began to ascend the stairs. He leant with one hand on Raffaelle's arm, taking hold of the balusters with the other. But I could see that to mount the stairs cost him considerable effort, and he paused frequently to cough and get his breath again. So we reached a landing at the top, and found ourselves in a small chamber or magazine directly over the shop. It was quite empty except for a few broken chairs, and appeared to be a small loft formed by dividing what had once been a high room into two storeys, of which the shop formed the lower. A long window, which had no doubt once formed one of several in the walls of this large room, was now divided across its width by the flooring, and with its upper part served to light the loft, while its lower panes opened into the shop. The ceiling was, in consequence of these alterations, comparatively low, but though much mutilated, retained evident traces of having been at one time richly decorated, with the raised mouldings and pendants common in the sixteenth century. At one end of the loft was a species of coved and elaborately carved dado, of which the former use was not obvious; but the large original room had without doubt been divided in length as Well as in height, as the lath-and-plaster walls at either end of the loft had evidently been no part of the ancient structure.

My brother sat down in one of the old chairs, and seemed to be collecting his strength before speaking. My anxiety was momentarily increasing, and it was a great relief when he began, talking in a low voice as one that had much to say and wished to husband his strength.

"I do not know whether you will recollect my having told you of something Mr. Gaskell once said about the music of Graziani's 'Areopagita' suite. It had always, he used to say, a curious effect upon his imagination, and the melody of the *Gagliarda* especially called up to his thoughts in some strange way a picture of a certain hall where people were dancing. He even went so far as to describe the general appearance of the room itself, and of the persons who were dancing there."

"Yes," I answered, "I remember your telling me of this"; and indeed my memory had in times past so often rehearsed Mr. Gaskell's description that, although I had not recently thought of it, its chief features immediately returned to my mind.

"He described it," my brother continued, "as a long hall with an arcade of arches running down one side, of the fantastic Gothic of the Renaissance. At the end was a gallery or balcony for the musicians, which on its front carried a coat of arms."

I remembered this perfectly and told John so, adding that the shield bore a cherub's head fanning three lilies on a golden field.

"It is strange," John went on, "that the description of a scene which our friend thought a mere effort of his own imagination has impressed itself so deeply on both our minds. But the picture which he drew was more than a fancy, for we are at this minute in the very hall of his dream."

I could not gather what my brother meant, and thought his reason was failing him; but he continued, "This miserable floor on which we stand has of course been afterwards built in; but you see above you the old ceiling, and here at the end was the musicians' gallery with the shield upon its front."

He pointed to the carved and white-washed dado which had hitherto so puzzled me. I stepped up to it, and although the lath-and-plaster partition wall was now built around it, it was clear that its curved outline might very easily, as John said, have formed part of the front of a coved gallery. I looked closer at the relief-work which had adorned it. Though the edges were all rubbed off, and the mouldings in some cases entirely removed, I could trace without difficulty a shield in the midst; and a more narrow inspection revealed underneath the whitewash, which had partly peeled away, enough remnants of colour to show that it had certainly been once painted gold and borne a cherub's head with three lilies.

"That is the shield of the old Neapolitan house of Doma-Cavalli," my brother continued; "they bore a cherub's head fanning three lilies on a shield or. It was in the balcony behind this shield, long since blocked up as you see, that the musicians sat on that ball night of which Gaskell dreamt. From it they looked down on the hall below where dancing was going forward, and I will now take you downstairs that you may see if the description tallies."

So saying, he raised himself, and descending the stairs with much less difficulty than he had shown in mounting them, flung open the door which I had seen in the passage and ushered us into the shop on the ground-floor. The evening light had now faded so much that we could scarcely see even in the passage, and the shop having its windows barricaded with shutters, was in complete darkness. Raffaelle, however, struck a match and lit three half-burnt candles in a tarnished sconce upon the wall.

The shop had evidently been lately in the occupation of a wine-seller, and there were still several empty wooden wine-butts, and some broken flasks on shelves. In one corner I noticed that the earth which formed the floor had been turned up with spades. There was a small heap of mould, and a large flat stone was thus exposed below the surface. This stone had an iron ring attached to it, and seemed to cover the aperture of a well, or perhaps a vault. At the back of the shop, and furthest from the street, were two lofty arches separated by a column in the middle, from which the outside casing had been stripped.

To these arches John pointed and said, "That is a part of the arcade which once ran down the whole length of the hall. Only these two arches are now left, and the fine marbles which doubtless coated the outside of this dividing pillar have been stripped off. On a summer's night about one hundred years ago dancing was going on in this hall. There were a dozen couples dancing a wild step such as is never seen now. The tune that the musicians were playing in the gallery above was taken from the 'Areopagita' suite of Graziani. Gaskell has often told me that when he played it the music brought with it to his mind a sense of some impending catastrophe, which culminated at the end of the first movement of the *Gagliarda*. It was just at that moment, Sophy, that an Englishman who was dancing here was stabbed in the back and foully murdered."

I had scarcely heard all that John had said, and had certainly not been able to take in its import; but without waiting to hear if I should say anything, he moved across to the uncovered stone with the ring in it. Exerting a strength which I should have believed entirely impossible in his weak condition, he applied to the stone a lever which lay ready at hand. Raffaelle at the same time seized the ring, and so they were able between them to move the covering to one side sufficiently to allow access to a small staircase which thus appeared to view. The stair was a winding one, and once led no doubt to some vaults below the ground-floor. Raffaelle descended first, taking in his hand the sconce of three candles, which he held above his head so as to fling a light down the steps. John went next, and then I followed, trying to support my brother if possible with my hand. The stairs were very dry, and on the walls there was none of the damp or mould which fancy usually associates with a subterraneous vault. I do not know what it was I expected to see, but I had an uneasy feeling that I was on the brink of some evil and distressing discovery. After we had descended about twenty steps we could see the entry to some vault or underground room, and it was just at the foot of the stairs that I saw something lying, as the light from the candles fell on it from above. At first I thought it was a heap of dust or refuse, but on looking closer it seemed rather a bundle of rags. As my eyes penetrated the gloom, I saw there was about it some tattered cloth of a faded green tint, and almost at the same minute I seemed to trace under the clothes the lines or dimensions of a human figure. For a moment I imagined it was some poor man lying face downwards and bent up against the wall. The idea of a man or of a dead body being there shocked me violently, and I cried to my brother, "Tell me, what is it?" At that instant the light from Raffaelle's candles fell in a somewhat different direction. It lighted up the white bowl of a human skull, and I saw that what I had taken for a man's form was instead that of a clothed skeleton. I turned faint and sick for an instant, and should have fallen had it not been for John, who put his arm about me and sustained me with an unexpected strength.

"God help us!" I exclaimed, "let us go. I cannot bear this; there are foul vapours here; let us get back to the outer air."

He took me by the arm, and pointing at the huddled heap, said, "Do you know whose bones those are? That is Adrian Temple. After it was all over, they flung his body down the steps, dressed in the clothes he wore."

At that name, uttered in so ill-omened a place, I felt a fresh access of terror. It seemed as though the soul of that wicked man must be still hovering over his unburied remains, and boding evil to us all. A chill crept over me, the light, the walls, my brother, and Raffaelle all swam round, and I sank swooning on the stairs.

When I returned fully to my senses we were in the landau again making our way back to the Villa de Angelis.

XV

The next morning my health and strength were entirely restored to me, but my brother, on the contrary, seemed weak and exhausted from his efforts of the previous night. Our return journey to the Villa de Angelis had passed in complete silence. I had been too much perturbed to question him on the many points relating to the strange events as to which I was still completely in the dark, and he on his side had shown no desire to afford me any further information. When I saw him the next morning he exhibited signs of great weakness, and in response to an effort on my part to obtain some explanation of the discovery of Adrian Temple's body, avoided an immediate reply, promising to tell me all he knew after our return to Worth Maltravers.

I pondered over the last terrifying episode very frequently in my own mind, and as I thought more deeply of it all, it seemed to me that the outlines of some evil history were piece by piece developing themselves, that I had almost within my grasp the clue that would make all plain, and that had eluded me so long. In that dim story Adrian Temple, the music of the *Gagliarda,* my brother's fatal passion for the violin, all seemed to have some mysterious connection, and to have conspired in working John's mental and physical ruin. Even the Stradivarius violin bore a part in the tragedy, becoming, as it were, an actively malignant spirit, though I could not explain how, and was yet entirely unaware of the manner in which it had come into my brother's possession.

I found that John was still resolved on an immediate return to England. His weakness, it is true, led me to entertain doubts as to how he would support so long a journey; but at the same time I did not feel justified in using any strong efforts to dissuade him from his purpose. I reflected that the more wholesome air and associations of England would certainly re-invigorate both body and mind, and that any extra strain brought about by the journey would soon be repaired by the comforts and watchful care with which we could surround him at Worth Maltravers.

So the first week in October saw us once more with our faces set towards England. A very comfortable swinging-bed or hammock had been arranged for John in the travelling carriage, and we determined to avoid fatigue as much as possible by dividing our journey into very short stages. My brother seemed to have no intention of giving up the Villa de Angelis. It was left complete with its luxurious furniture, and with all his servants, under the care of an Italian *maggior-duomo*. I felt that as John's state of health forbade his entertaining any hope of an immediate return thither, it would have been much better to close entirely his Italian house. But his great weakness made it impossible for him to undertake the effort such a course would involve, and even if my own ignorance of the Italian tongue had not stood in the way, I was far too eager to get my invalid back to Worth to feel inclined to import any further delay, while I should myself adjust matters which were after all comparatively trifling. As Parnham was now ready to discharge his usual duties of valet, and as my brother seemed quite content that he should do so, Raffaelle was of course to be left behind. The boy had quite won my heart by his sweet manners, combined with his evident affection to his master, and in making him understand that he was now to leave us, I offered him a present of a few pounds as a token of my esteem. He refused, however, to touch this money, and shed tears when he learnt that he was to be left in Italy, and begged with many protestations of devotion that he might be allowed to accompany us to England. My heart was not proof against his entreaties, supported by so many signs of attachment, and it was agreed, therefore, that he should at least attend us as far as Worth Maltravers. John showed no surprise at the boy being with us; indeed I never thought it necessary to explain that I had originally purposed to leave him behind.

Our journey, though necessarily prolonged by the shortness of its stages, was safely accomplished. John bore it as well as I could have hoped, and though his body showed no signs of increased vigour, his mind, I think, improved in tone, at any rate for a time. From the evening on which he had shown me the terrible discovery in the Via del Giardino he seemed to have laid aside something of his care and depression. He now exhibited little trace of the moroseness and selfishness which had of late so marred his character; and though he naturally felt severely at times the fatigue of travel, yet we had no longer to dread any relapse into that state of lethargy or stupor which had so often baffled every effort to counteract it at Posilipo. Some feeling of superstitious aversion had prompted me to give orders that the Stradivarius violin should be left behind at Posilipo. But before parting my brother asked for it, and insisted that it should be brought with him, though I had never heard him play a note on it for many weeks. He took an interest in all the petty episodes of travel, and certainly appeared to derive more entertainment from the journey than was to have been anticipated in his feeble state of health.

To the incidents of the evening spent in the Via del Giardino he made no allusion of any kind, nor did I for my part wish to renew memories of so unpleasant a nature. His only reference occurred one Sunday evening as we were passing a small graveyard near Genoa. The scene apparently turned his thoughts to that subject, and he told me that he had taken measures before leaving Naples to ensure that the remains of Adrian Temple should be decently interred in the cemetery of Santa Bibiana. His words set me thinking again, and unsatisfied curiosity prompted me strongly to inquire of him how he had convinced himself that the skeleton at the foot of the stairs was indeed that of Adrian Temple. But I restrained myself, partly from a reliance on his promise that he would one day explain the whole story to me, and partly being very reluctant to mar the enjoyment of the peaceful scenes through which we were passing, by the introduction of any subjects so jarring and painful as those to which I have alluded.

We reached London at last, and here we stopped a few days to make some necessary arrangements before going down to Worth Maltravers. I had urged upon John during the journey that immediately on his arrival in London he should obtain the best English medical advice as to his own health. Though he at first demurred, saying that nothing more was to be done, and that he was perfectly satisfied with the medicine given him by Dr. Baravelli, which he continued to take, yet by constant entreaty I prevailed upon him to accede to so reasonable a request. Dr. Frobisher, considered at that time the first living authority on diseases of the brain and nerves, saw him on the morning after our arrival. He was good enough to speak with me at some length after seeing my brother, and to give me many hints and recipes whereby I might be better enabled to nurse the invalid.

Sir John's condition, he said, was such as to excite serious anxiety. There was, indeed, no brain mischief of any kind to be discovered, but his lungs were in a state of advanced disease, and there were signs of grave heart affection. Yet he did not bid me to despair, but said that with careful nursing life might certainly be prolonged, and even some measure of health in time restored. He asked me more than once if I knew of any trouble or worry that preyed upon Sir John's mind. Were there financial difficulties; had he been subjected to any mental shock; had he received any severe fright? To all this I could only reply in the negative. At the same time I told Dr. Frobisher as much of John's history as I considered pertinent to the question. He shook his head gravely, and recommended that Sir John should remain for the present in London, under his own constant supervision. To this course my brother would by no means consent. He was eager to proceed at once to his own house, saying that if necessary we could return again to London for Christmas. It was therefore agreed that we should go down to Worth Maltravers at the end of the week.

Parnham had already left us for Worth in order that he might have everything ready against his master's return, and when we arrived we found all in perfect order for our reception. A small morning-room next to the library, with a pleasant south aspect and opening on to the terrace, had been prepared for my brother's use, so that he might avoid the fatigue of mounting stairs, which Dr. Frobisher considered very prejudicial in his present condition. We had also purchased in London a chair fitted with wheels, which enabled him to be moved, or, if he were feeling equal to the exertion, to move himself, without difficulty, from room to room.

His health, I think, improved; very gradually, it is true, but still sufficiently to inspire me with hope that he might yet be spared to us. Of the state of his mind or thoughts I knew little, but I could see that he was at times a prey to nervous anxiety. This showed itself in the harassed look which his pale face often wore, and in his marked dislike to being left alone. He derived, I think, a certain pleasure from the quietude and monotony of his life at Worth, and perhaps also from the consciousness that he had about him loving and devoted hearts. I say hearts, for every servant at Worth was attached to him, remembering the great consideration and courtesy of his earlier years, and grieving to see his youthful and once vigorous frame reduced to so sad a strait. Books he never read himself, and even the charm of Raffaelle's reading seemed to have lost its power; though he never tired of hearing the boy sing, and liked to have him sit by his chair even when his eyes were shut and he was apparently asleep. His general health seemed to me to change but little either for better or worse. Dr. Frobisher had led me to expect some such a sequel. I had not concealed from him that I had at times entertained suspicions as to my brother's sanity; but he had assured me that they were totally unfounded, that Sir John's brain was as clear as his own. At the same time he confessed that he could not account for the exhausted vitality of his patient,—a condition which he would under ordinary circumstances have attributed to excessive study or severe trouble. He had urged upon me the pressing necessity for complete rest, and for much sleep. My brother never even incidentally referred to his wife, his child, or to Mrs. Temple, who constantly wrote to me from Royston, sending kind messages to John, and asking how he did. These messages I never dared to give him, fearing to agitate him, or retard his recovery by diverting his thoughts into channels which must necessarily be of a painful character. That he should never even mention her name, or that of Lady Maltravers, led me to wonder sometimes if one of those curious freaks of memory which occasionally accompany a severe illness had not entirely blotted out from his mind the recollection of his marriage and of his wife's death. He was unable to consider any affairs of business, and the management of the estate remained as it had done for the last two years in the hands of our excellent agent, Mr. Baker.

But one evening in the early part of December he sent Raffaelle about nine o'clock, saying he wished to speak to me. I went to his room, and without any warning he began at once, "You never show me my boy now, Sophy; he must be grown a big child, and I should like to see him." Much startled by so unexpected a remark, I replied that the child was at Royston under the care of Mrs. Temple, but that I knew that if it pleased him to see Edward she would be glad to bring him down to Worth. He seemed gratified with this idea, and begged me to ask her to do so, desiring that his respects should be at the same time conveyed to her. I almost ventured at that moment to recall his lost wife to his thoughts, by saying that his child resembled her strongly; for your likeness at that time, and even now, my dear Edward, to your poor mother was very marked. But my courage failed me, and his talk soon reverted to an earlier period, comparing the mildness of the month to that of the first winter which he spent at Eton. His thoughts, however, must, I fancy, have returned for a moment to the days when he first met your mother, for he suddenly asked, "Where is Gaskell? Why does he never come to see me?" This brought quite a new idea to my mind. I fancied it might do my brother much good to have by him so sensible and true a friend as I knew Mr. Gaskell to be. The latter's address had fortunately not slipped from my memory, and I put all scruples aside and wrote by the next mail to him, setting forth my brother's sad condition, saying that I had heard John mention his name, and begging him on my own account to be so good as to help us if possible and come to us in this hour of trial. Though he was so far off as Westmorland, Mr. Gaskell's generosity brought him at once to our aid, and within a week he was installed at Worth Maltravers, sleeping, in the library, where we had arranged a bed at his own desire, so that he might be near his sick friend.

His presence was of the utmost assistance to us all. He treated John at once with the tenderness of a woman and the firmness of a clever and strong man. They sat constantly together in the mornings, and Mr. Gaskell told me John had not shown with him the same reluctance to talk freely of his married life as he had discovered with me. The tenor of his communications I cannot guess, nor did I ever ask; but I knew that Mr. Gaskell was much affected by them.

John even amused himself now at times by having Mr. Baker into his rooms of a morning, that the management of the estate might be discussed with his friend; and he also expressed his wish to see the family solicitor, as he desired to draw his will. Thinking that any diversion of this nature could not but be beneficial to him, we sent to Dorchester for our solicitor, Mr. Jeffreys, who together with his clerk spent three nights at Worth, and drew up a testament for my brother.

So time went on, and the year was drawing to a close.

It was Christmas Eve, and I had gone to bed shortly after twelve o'clock, having an hour earlier bid good night to John and Mr. Gaskell. The long habit of watching with, or being in charge of an invalid at night, had made my ears extraordinarily quick to apprehend even the slightest murmur. It must have been, I think, near three in the morning when I found myself awake and conscious of some unusual sound. It was low and far off, but I knew instantly what it was, and felt a choking sensation of fear and horror, as if an icy hand had gripped my throat, on recognising the air of the *Gagliarda*. It was being played on the violin, and a long way off, but I knew that tune too well to permit of my having any doubt on the subject.

Any trouble or fear becomes, as you will some day learn, my dear nephew, immensely intensified and exaggerated at night. It is so, I suppose, because our nerves are in an excited condition, and our brain not sufficiently awake to give a due account of our foolish imaginations. I have myself many times lain awake wrestling in thought with difficulties which in the hours of darkness seemed insurmountable, but with the dawn resolved themselves into merely trivial inconveniences. So on this night, as I sat up in bed looking into the dark, with the sound of that melody in my ears, it seemed as if something too terrible for words had happened; as though the evil spirit, which we had hoped was exorcised, had returned with others sevenfold more wicked than himself, and taken up his abode again with my lost brother. The memory of another night rushed to my mind when Constance had called me from my bed at Royston, and we had stolen together down the moonlit passages with the lilt of that wicked music vibrating on the still summer air. Poor Constance! She was in her grave now; yet *her* troubles at least were over, but here, as by some bitter irony, instead of carol or sweet symphony, it was the *Gagliarda* that woke me from my sleep on Christmas morning.

I flung my dressing-gown about me, and hurried through the corridor and down the stairs which led to the lower storey and my brother's room. As I opened my bedroom door the violin ceased suddenly in the middle of a bar. Its last sound was not a musical note, but rather a horrible scream, such as I pray I may never hear again. It was a sound such as a wounded beast might utter. There is a picture I have seen of Blake's, showing the soul of a strong wicked man leaving his body at death. The spirit is flying out through the window with awful staring eyes, aghast at the desolation into which it is going. If in the agony of dissolution such a lost soul could utter a cry, it would, I think, sound like the wail which I heard from the violin that night.

Instantly all was in absolute stillness. The passages were silent and ghostly in the faint light of my candle; but as I reached the bottom of the stairs I heard the sound of other footsteps, and Mr. Gaskell met me. He was fully dressed, and had evidently not been to bed. He took me kindly by the hand and said, "I feared you might be alarmed by the sound of music. John has been walking in his sleep; he had taken out his violin and was playing on it in a trance. Just as I reached him something in it gave way, and the discord caused by the slackened strings roused him at once. He is awake now and has returned to bed. Control your alarm for his sake and your own. It is better that he should not know you have been awakened."

He pressed my hand and spoke a few more reassuring words, and I went back to my room still much agitated, and yet feeling half ashamed for having shown so much anxiety with so little reason.

That Christmas morning was one of the most beautiful that I ever remember. It seemed as though summer was so loath to leave our sunny Dorset coast that she came back on this day to bid us adieu before her final departure. I had risen early and had partaken of the Sacrament at our little church. Dr. Butler had recently introduced this early service, and though any alteration of time-honoured customs in such matters might not otherwise have met with my approval, I was glad to avail myself of the privilege on this occasion, as I wished in any case to spend the later morning with my brother. The singular beauty of the early hours, and the tranquillising effect of the solemn service brought back serenity to my mind, and effectually banished from it all memories of the preceding night. Mr. Gaskell met me in the hall on my return, and after greeting me kindly with the established compliments of the day, inquired after my health, and hoped that the disturbance of my slumber on the previous night had not affected me injuriously. He had good news for me: John seemed decidedly better, was already dressed, and desired, as it was Christmas morning, that we would take our breakfast with him in his room.

To this, as you may imagine, I readily assented. Our breakfast party passed off with much content, and even with some quiet humour, John sitting in his easy-chair at the head of the table and wishing us the compliments of the season. I found laid in my place a letter from Mrs. Temple greeting us all (for she knew Mr. Gaskell was at Worth), and saying that she hoped to bring little Edward to us at the New Year. My brother seemed much pleased at the prospect of seeing his son, and though perhaps it was only imagination, I fancied he was particularly gratified that Mrs. Temple herself was to pay us a visit. She had not been to Worth since the death of Lady Maltravers.

Before we had finished breakfast the sun beat on the panes with an unusual strength and brightness. His rays cheered us all, and it was so warm that John first opened the windows, and then wheeled his chair on to the walk outside. Mr. Gaskell brought him a hat and mufflers, and we sat with him on the terrace basking in the sun. The sea was still and glassy as a mirror, and the Channel lay stretched before us like a floor of moving gold. A rose or two still hung against the house, and the sun's rays reflected from the red sandstone gave us a December morning more mild and genial than many June days that I have known in the north. We sat for some minutes without speaking, immersed in our own reflections and in the exquisite beauty of the scene.

The stillness was broken by the bells of the parish church ringing for the morning service. There were two of them, and their sound, familiar to us from childhood, seemed like the voices of old friends. John looked at me and said with a sigh, "I should like to go to church. It is long since I was there. You and I have always been on Christmas mornings, Sophy, and Constance would have wished it had she been with us."

His words, so unexpected and tender, filled my eyes with tears; not tears of grief, but of deep thankfulness to see my loved one turning once more to the old ways. It was the first time I had heard him speak of Constance, and that sweet name, with the infinite pathos of her death, and of the spectacle of my brother's weakness, so overcame me that I could not speak. I only pressed his hand and nodded. Mr. Gaskell, who had turned away for a minute, said he thought John would take no harm in attending the morning service provided the church were warm. On this point I could reassure him, having found it properly heated even in the early morning.

Mr. Gaskell was to push John's chair, and I ran off to put on my cloak, with my heart full of profound thankfulness for the signs of returning grace so mercifully vouchsafed to our dear sufferer on this happy day. I was ready dressed and had just entered the library when Mr. Gaskell stepped hurriedly through the window from the terrace. "John has fainted!" he said. "Run for some smelling salts and call Parnham!"

There was a scene of hurried alarm, giving place ere long to terrified despair. Parnham mounted a horse and set off at a wild gallop to Swanage to fetch Dr. Bruton; but an hour before he returned we knew the worst. My brother was beyond the aid of the physician: his wrecked life had reached a sudden term!

I have now, dear Edward, completed the brief narrative of some of the facts attending the latter years of your father's life. The motive which has induced me to commit them to writing has been a double one. I am anxious to give effect as far as may be to the desire expressed most strongly to Mr. Gaskell by your father, that you should be put in possession of these facts on your coming of age. And for my own part I think it better that you should thus hear the plain truth from me, lest you should be at the mercy of haphazard reports, which might at any time reach you from ignorant or interested sources. Some of the circumstances were so remarkable that it is scarcely possible to suppose that they were not known, and most probably frequently discussed, in so large an establishment as that of Worth Maltravers. I even have reason to believe that exaggerated and absurd stories were current at the time of Sir John's death, and I should be grieved to think that such foolish tales might by any chance reach your ear without your having any sure means of discovering where the truth lay. God knows how grievous it has been to me to set down on paper some of the facts that I have here narrated. You as a dutiful son will reverence the name even of a father whom you never knew; but you must remember that his sister did more; she loved him with a single-hearted devotion, and it still grieves her to the quick to write anything which may seem to detract from his memory. Only, above all things, let us speak the truth. Much of what I have told you needs, I feel, further explanation, but this I cannot give, for I do not understand the circumstances. Mr. Gaskell, your guardian, will, I believe, add to this account a few notes of his own, which may tend to elucidate some points, as he is in possession of certain facts of which I am still ignorant.

MR. GASKELL'S NOTE

I have read what Miss Maltravers has written, and have but little to add to it. I can give no explanation that will tally with all the facts or meet all the difficulties involved in her narrative. The most obvious solution of some points would be, of course, to suppose that Sir John Maltravers was insane. But to anyone who knew him as intimately as I did, such an hypothesis is untenable; nor, if admitted, would it explain some of the strangest incidents. Moreover, it was strongly negatived by Dr. Frobisher, from whose verdict in such matters there was at the time no appeal, by Dr. Dobie, and by Dr. Bruton, who had known Sir John from his infancy. It is possible that towards the close of his life he suffered occasionally from hallucination, though I could not positively affirm even so much; but this was only when his health had been completely undermined by causes which are very difficult to analyse.

When I first knew him at Oxford he was a strong man physically as well as mentally; open-hearted, and of a merry and genial temperament. At the same time he was, like most cultured persons—and especially musicians,—highly strung and excitable. But at a certain point in his career his very nature seemed to change; he became reserved, secretive, and saturnine. On this moral metamorphosis followed an equally startling physical change. His robust health began to fail him, and although there was no definite malady which doctors could combat, he went gradually from bad to worse until the end came.

The commencement of this extraordinary change coincided, I believe, almost exactly with his discovery of the Stradivarius violin; and whether this was, after all, a mere coincidence or something more it is not easy to say. Until a very short time before his death neither Miss Maltravers nor I had any idea how that instrument had come into his possession, or I think something might perhaps have been done to save him.

Though towards the end of his life he spoke freely to his sister of the finding of the violin, he only told her half the story, for he concealed from her entirely that there was anything else in the hidden cupboard at Oxford. But as a matter of fact, he had found there also two manuscript books containing an elaborate diary of some years of a man's life. That man was Adrian Temple, and I believe that in the perusal of this diary must be sought the origin of John Maltravers's ruin. The manuscript was beautifully written in a clear but cramped eighteenth century hand, and gave the idea of a man writing with deliberation, and wishing to transcribe his impressions with accuracy for further reference. The style was excellent, and the minute details given were often of high antiquarian interest; but the record throughout was marred by gross licence. Adrian Temple's life had undoubtedly so definite an influence on Sir John's that a brief outline of it, as gathered from his diaries, is necessary for the understanding of what followed.

Temple went up to Oxford in 1737. He was seventeen years old, without parents, brothers, or sisters; and he possessed the Royston estates in Derbyshire, which were then, as now, a most valuable property. With the year 1738 his diaries begin, and though then little more than a boy, he had tasted every illicit pleasure that Oxford had to offer. His temptations were no doubt great; for besides being wealthy he was handsome, and had probably never known any proper control, as both his parents had died when he was still very young. But in spite of other failings, he was a brilliant scholar, and on taking his degree, was made at once a fellow of St. John's. He took up his abode in that College in a fine set of rooms looking on to the gardens, and from this period seems to have used Royston but little, living always either at Oxford or on the Continent. He formed at this time the acquaintance of one Jocelyn, whom he engaged as companion and amanuensis. Jocelyn was a man of talent, but of irregular life, and was no doubt an accomplice in many of Temple's excesses. In 1743 they both undertook the so-called "grand tour," and though it was not his first visit, it was then probably that Temple first felt the fascination of pagan Italy,—a fascination which increased with every year of his after-life.

On his return from foreign travel he found himself among the stirring events of 1745. He was an ardent supporter of the Pretender, and made no attempt to conceal his views. Jacobite tendencies were indeed generally prevalent in the College at the time, and had this been the sum of his offending, it is probable that little notice would have been taken by the College authorities. But his notoriously wild life told against the young man, and certain dark suspicions were not easily passed over. After the *fiasco* of the Rebellion Dr. Holmes, then President of the College, seems to have made a scapegoat of Temple. He was deprived of his fellowship, and though not formally expelled, such pressure was put upon him as resulted in his leaving St. John's and removing to Magdalen Hall. There his great wealth evidently secured him consideration, and he was given the best rooms in the Hall, that very set looking on to New College Lane which Sir John Maltravers afterwards occupied.

In the first half of the eighteenth century the romance of the middle ages, though dying, was not dead, and the occult sciences still found followers among the Oxford towers. From his early years Temple's mind seems to have been set strongly towards mysticism of all kinds, and he and Jocelyn were versed in the jargon of the alchemist and astrologer, and practised according to the ancient rules. It was his reputation as a necromancer, and the stories current of illicit rites performed in the garden-rooms at St. John's, that contributed largely to his being dismissed from that College. He had also become acquainted with Francis Dashwood, the notorious Lord le Despencer, and many a winter's night saw him riding through the misty Thames meadows to the door of the sham Franciscan abbey. In his diaries were more notices than one of the "Franciscans" and the nameless orgies of Medmenham.

He was devoted to music. It was a rare enough accomplishment then, and a rarer thing still to find a wealthy landowner performing on the violin. Yet so he did, though he kept his passion very much to himself, as fiddling was thought lightly of in those days. His musical skill was altogether exceptional, and he was the first possessor of the Stradivarius violin which afterwards fell so unfortunately into Sir John's hands. This violin Temple bought in the autumn of 1738, on the occasion of a first visit to Italy. In that year died the nonagenarian Antonius Stradivarius, the greatest violin-maker the world has ever seen. After Stradivarius's death the stock of fiddles in his shop was sold by auction. Temple happened to be travelling in Cremona at the time with a tutor, and at the auction he bought that very instrument which we afterwards had cause to know so well. A note in his diary gave its cost at four louis, and said that a curious history attached to it. Though it was of his golden period, and probably the finest instrument he ever made, Stradivarius would never sell it, and it had hung for more than thirty years in his shop. It was said that from some whim as he lay dying he had given orders that it should be burnt; but if that were so, the instructions were neglected, and after his death it came under the hammer. Adrian Temple from the first recognised the great value of the instrument. His notes show that he only used it on certain special occasions, and it was no doubt for its better protection that he devised the hidden cupboard where Sir John eventually found it.

The later years of Temple's life were spent for the most part in Italy. On the Scoglio di Venere, near Naples, he built the Villa de Angelis, and there henceforth passed all except the hottest months of the year. Shortly after the completion of the villa Jocelyn left him suddenly, and became a Carthusian monk. A caustic note in his diary hinted that even this foul parasite was shocked into the austerest form of religion by something he had seen going forward. At Naples Temple's dark life became still darker. He dallied, it is true, with Neo-Platonism, and boasts that he, like Plotinus, had twice passed the circle of the nous and enjoyed the fruition of the deity; but the ideals of even that easy doctrine grew in his evil life still more miserably debased. More than once in the manuscript he made mention by name of the *Gagliarda* of Graziani as having been played at pagan mysteries which these enthusiasts revived at Naples, and the air had evidently impressed itself deeply on his memory. The last entry in his diary is made on the 16th of December, 1752. He was then in Oxford for a few days, but shortly afterwards returned to Naples. The accident of his having just completed a second volume, induced him, no doubt, to leave it behind him in the secret cupboard. It is probable that he commenced a third, but if so it was never found.

In reading the manuscript I was struck with the author's clear and easy style, and found the interest of the narrative increase rather than diminish. At the same time its study was inexpressibly painful to me. Nothing could have supported me in my determination to thoroughly master it but the conviction that if I was to be of any real assistance to my poor friend Maltravers, I must know as far as possible every circumstance connected with his malady. As it was, I felt myself breathing an atmosphere of moral contagion during the perusal of the manuscript, and certain passages have since returned at times to haunt me in spite of all efforts to dislodge them from my memory. When I came to Worth at Miss Maltravers's urgent invitation, I found my friend Sir John terribly altered. It was not only that he was ill and physically weak, but he had entirely lost the manner of youth, which, though indefinable, is yet so appreciable, and draws so sharp a distinction between the first period of life and middle age. But the most striking feature of his illness was the extraordinary pallor of his complexion, which made his face resemble a subtle counterfeit of white wax rather than that of a living man. He welcomed me undemonstratively, but with evident sincerity; and there was an entire absence of the constraint which often accompanies the meeting again of friends whose cordial relations have suffered interruption. From the time of my arrival at Worth until his death we were constantly together; indeed I was much struck by the almost childish dislike which he showed to be left alone even for a few moments. As night approached this feeling became intensified. Parnham slept always in his master's room; but if anything called the servant away even for a minute, he would send for Carotenuto or myself to be with him until his return. His nerves were weak; he started violently at any unexpected noise, and above all, he dreaded being in the dark. When night fell he had additional lamps brought into his room, and even when he composed himself to sleep, insisted on a strong light being kept by his bedside.

I had often read in books of people wearing a "hunted" expression, and had laughed at the phrase as conventional and unmeaning. But when I came to Worth I knew its truth; for if any face ever wore a hunted—I had almost written a haunted—look, it was the white face of Sir John Maltravers. His air seemed that of a man who was constantly expecting the arrival of some evil tidings, and at times reminded me painfully of the guilty expectation of a felon who knows that a warrant is issued for his arrest.

During my visit he spoke to me frequently about his past life, and instead of showing any reluctance to discuss the subject, seemed glad of the opportunity of disburdening his mind. I gathered from him that the reading of Adrian Temple's memoirs had made a deep impression on his mind, which was no doubt intensified by the vision which he thought he saw in his rooms at Oxford, and by the discovery of the portrait at Royston. Of those singular phenomena I have no explanation to offer.

The romantic element in his disposition rendered him peculiarly susceptible to the fascination of that mysticism which breathed through Temple's narrative. He told me that almost from the first time he read it he was filled with a longing to visit the places and to revive the strange life of which it spoke. This inclination he kept at first in check, but by degrees it gathered strength enough to master him.

There is no doubt in my mind that the music of the *Gagliarda* of Graziani helped materially in this process of mental degradation. It is curious that Michael Prætorius in the "Syntagma musicum" should speak of the Galliard generally as an "invention of the devil, full of shameful and licentious gestures and immodest movements," and the singular melody of the *Gagliarda* in the "Areopagita" suite certainly exercised from the first a strange influence over me. I shall not do more than touch on the question here, because I see Miss Maltravers has spoken of it at length, and will only say, that though since the day of Sir John's death I have never heard a note of it, the air is still fresh in my mind, and has at times presented itself to me unexpectedly, and always with an unwholesome effect. This I have found happen generally in times of physical depression, and the same air no doubt exerted a similar influence on Sir John, which his impressionable nature rendered from the first more deleterious to him.

I say this advisedly, because I am sure that if some music is good for man and elevates him, other melodies are equally bad and enervating. An experience far wider than any we yet possess is necessary to enable us to say how far this influence is capable of extension. How far, that is, the mind may be directed on the one hand to ascetic abnegation by the systematic use of certain music, or on the other to illicit and dangerous pleasures by melodies of an opposite tendency. But this much is, I think, certain, that after a comparatively advanced standard of culture has once been attained, music is the readiest if not the only key which admits to the yet narrower circle of the highest imaginative thought.

On the occasion for travel afforded him by his honeymoon, an impulse which he could not at the time explain, but which after-events have convinced me was the haunting suggestion of the *Gagliarda*, drove him to visit the scenes mentioned so often in Temple's diary. He had always been an excellent scholar, and a classic of more than ordinary ability. Rome and Southern Italy filled him with a strange delight. His education enabled him to appreciate to the full what he saw; he peopled the stage with the figures of the original actors, and tried to assimilate his thought to theirs. He began reading classical literature widely, no longer from the scholarly but the literary standpoint. In Rome he spent much time in the librarians' shops, and there met with copies of the numerous authors of the later empire and of those Alexandrine philosophers which are rarely seen in England. In these he found a new delight and fresh food for his mysticism.

Such study, if carried to any extent, is probably dangerous to the English character, and certainly was to a man of Maltravers's romantic sympathies. This reading produced in time so real an effect upon his mind that if he did not definitely abandon Christianity, as I fear he did, he at least adulterated it with other doctrines till it became to him Neo-Platonism. That most seductive of philosophies, which has enthralled so many minds from Proclus and Julian to Augustine and the Renaissancists, found an easy convert in John Maltravers. Its passionate longing for the vague and undefined good, its tolerance of æsthetic impressions, the pleasant superstitions of its dynamic pantheism, all touched responsive chords in his nature. His mind, he told me, became filled with a measureless yearning for the old culture of pagan philosophy, and as the past became clearer and more real, so the present grew dimmer, and his thoughts were gradually weaned entirely from all the natural objects of affection and interest which should otherwise have occupied them. To what a terrible extent this process went on, Miss Maltravers's narrative shows. Soon after reaching Naples he visited the Villa de Angelis, which Temple had built on the ruins of a sea-house of Pomponius. The later building had in its turn become dismantled and ruinous, and Sir John found no difficulty in buying the site outright. He afterwards rebuilt it on an elaborate scale, endeavouring to reproduce in its equipment the luxury of the later empire. I had occasion to visit the house more than once in my capacity of executor, and found it full of priceless works of art, which, though neither so difficult to procure at that time nor so costly as they would be now, were yet sufficiently valuable to have necessitated an unjustifiable outlay.

The situation of the building fostered his infatuation for the past. It lay between the Bay of Naples and the Bay of Baia, and from its windows commanded the same exquisite view which had charmed Cicero and Lucullus, Severus and the Antonines. Hard by stood Baia, the princely seaside resort of the empire. That most luxurious and wanton of all cities of antiquity survived the cataclysms of ages, and only lost its civic continuity and became the ruined village of to-day in the sack of the fifteenth century. But a continuity of wickedness is not so easily broken, and those who know the spot best say that it is still instinct with memories of a shameful past.

For miles along that haunted coast the foot cannot be put down except on the ruins of some splendid villa, and over all there broods a spirit of corruption and debasement actually sensible and oppressive. Of the dawns and sunsets, of the noonday sun tempered by the sea-breeze and the shade of scented groves, those who have been there know the charm, and to those who have not no words can describe it. But there are malefic vapours rising from the corpse of a past not altogether buried, and most cultivated Englishmen who tarry there long feel their influence as did John Maltravers. Like so many *decepti deceptores* of the Neo-Platonic school, he did not practise the abnegation enjoined by the very cult he professed to follow. Though his nature was far too refined, I believe, ever to sink into the sensualism revealed in Temple's diaries, yet it was through the gratification of corporeal tastes that he endeavoured to achieve the divine *extasis*; and there were constantly lavish and sumptuous entertainments at the villa, at which strange guests were present.

In such a nightmare of a life it was not to be expected that any mind would find repose, and Maltravers certainly found none. All those cares which usually occupy men's minds, all thoughts of wife, child, and home were, it is true, abandoned; but a wild unrest had hold of him, and never suffered him to be at ease. Though he never told me as much, yet I believe he was under the impression that the form which he had seen at Oxford and Royston had reappeared to him on more than one subsequent occasion. It must have been, I fancy, with a vague hope of "laying" this spectre that he now set himself with eagerness to discover where or how Temple had died. He remembered that Royston tradition said he had succumbed at Naples in the plague of 1752, but an idea seized him that this was not the case; indeed I half suspect his fancy unconsciously pictured that evil man as still alive. The methods by which he eventually discovered the skeleton, or learnt the episodes which preceded Temple's death, I do not know. He promised to tell me some day at length, but a sudden death prevented his ever doing so. The facts as he narrated them, and as I have little doubt they actually occurred, were these: Adrian Temple, after Jocelyn's departure, had made a confidant of one Palamede Domacavalli, a scion of a splendid Parthenopean family of that name. Palamede had a palace in the heart of Naples, and was Temple's equal in age and also in his great wealth. The two men became boon companions, associated in all kinds of wickedness and excess. At length Palamede married a beautiful girl named Olimpia Aldobrandini, who was also of the noblest lineage; but the intimacy between him and Temple was not interrupted. About a year subsequent to this marriage dancing was going on after a splendid banquet in the great hall of the Palazzo Domacavalli. Adrian, who was a favoured guest, called to the musicians in the gallery to play the "Areopagita" suite, and danced it with Olimpia, the wife of his host. The *Gagliarda* was reached but never finished, for near the end of the second movement Palamede from behind drove a stiletto into his friend's heart. He had found out that day that Adrian had not spared even Olimpia's honour.

I have endeavoured to condense into a connected story the facts learnt piecemeal from Sir John in conversation. To a certain extent they supplied, if not an explanation, at least an account of the change that had come over my friend. But only to a certain extent; there the explanation broke down and I was left baffled. I could imagine that a life of unwholesome surroundings and disordered studies might in time produce such a loss of mental tone as would lead in turn to moral *acolasia*, sensual excess, and physical ruin. But in Sir John's case the cause was not adequate; he had, so far as I know, never wholly given the reins to sensuality, and the change was too abrupt and the breakdown of body and mind too complete to be accounted for by such events as those of which he had spoken.

I had, too, an uneasy feeling, which grew upon me the more I saw of him, that while he spoke freely enough on certain topics, and obviously meant to give a complete history of his past life, there was in reality something in the background which he always kept from my view. He was, it seemed, like a young man asked by an indulgent father to disclose his debts in order that they may be discharged, who, although he knows his parent's leniency, and that any debt not now disclosed will be afterwards but a weight upon his own neck, yet hesitates for very shame to tell the full amount, and keeps some items back. So poor Sir John kept something back from me his friend, whose only aim was to afford him consolation and relief, and whose compassion would have made me listen without rebuke to the narration of the blackest crimes. I cannot say how much this conviction grieved me. I would most willingly have given my all, my very life, to save my friend and Miss Maltravers's brother; but my efforts were paralysed by the feeling that I did not know what I had to combat, that some evil influence was at work on him which continually evaded my grasp. Once or twice it seemed as though he were within an ace of telling me all; once or twice, I believe, he had definitely made up his mind to do so; but then the mood changed, or more probably his courage failed him.

It was on one of these occasions that he asked me, somewhat suddenly, whether I thought that a man could by any conscious act committed in the flesh take away from himself all possibility of repentance and ultimate salvation. Though, I trust, a sincere Christian, I am nothing of a theologian, and the question touching on a topic which had not occurred to my mind since childhood, and which seemed to savour rather of medieval romance than of practical religion, took me for a moment aback. I hesitated for an instant, and then replied that the means of salvation offered man were undoubtedly so sufficient as to remove from one truly penitent the guilt of any crime however dark. My hesitation had been but momentary; but Sir John seemed to have noticed it, and sealed his lips to any confession, if he had indeed intended to make any, by changing the subject abruptly. This question naturally gave me food for serious reflection and anxiety. It was the first occasion on which he appeared to me to be undoubtedly suffering from definite hallucination, and I was aware that any illusions connected with religion are generally most difficult to remove. At the same time, anything of this sort was the more remarkable in Sir John's case, as he had, so far as I knew, for a considerable time entirely abandoned the Christian belief.

Unable to elicit any further information from him, and being thus thrown entirely upon my own resources, I determined that I would read through again the whole of Temple's diaries. The task was a very distasteful one, as I have already explained, but I hoped that a second reading might perhaps throw some light on the dark misgiving that was troubling Sir John. I read the manuscript again with the closest attention. Nothing, however, of any importance seemed to have escaped me on the former occasions, and I had reached nearly the end of the second volume when a comparatively slight matter arrested my attention. I have said that the pages were all carefully numbered, and the events of each day recorded separately; even where Temple had found nothing of moment to notice on a given day, he had still inserted the date with the word *nil* written against it. But as I sat one evening in the library at Worth after Sir John had gone to bed, and was finally glancing through the days of the months in Temple's diary to make sure that all were complete, I found one day was missing. It was towards the end of the second volume, and the day was the 23d of October in the year 1752. A glance at the numbering of the pages revealed the fact that three leaves had been entirely removed, and that the pages numbered 349 to 354 were not to be found. Again I ran through the diaries to see whether there were any leaves removed in other places, but found no other single page missing. All was complete except at this one place, the manuscript beautifully written, with scarcely an error or erasure throughout. A closer examination showed that these leaves had been cut out close to the back, and the cut edges of the paper appeared too fresh to admit of this being done a century ago. A very short reflection convinced me, in fact, that the excision was not likely to have been Temple's, and that it must have been made by Sir John.

My first intention was to ask him at once what the lost pages had contained, and why they had been cut out. The matter might be a mere triviality which he could explain in a moment. But on softly opening his bedroom door I found him sleeping, and Parnham (whom the strong light always burnt in the room rendered more wakeful) informed me that his master had been in a deep sleep for more than an hour. I knew how sorely his wasted energies needed such repose, and stepped back to the library without awaking him. A few minutes before, I had been feeling sleepy at the conclusion of my task, but now all wish for sleep was suddenly banished and a painful wakefulness took its place. I was under a species of mental excitement which reminded me of my feelings some years before at Oxford on the first occasion of our ever playing the *Gagliarda* together, and an idea struck me with the force of intuition that in these three lost leaves lay the secret of my friend's ruin.

I turned to the context to see whether there was anything in the entries preceding or following the lacuna that would afford a clue to the missing passage. The record of the few days immediately preceding the 23d of October was short and contained nothing of any moment whatever. Adrian and Jocelyn were alone together at the Villa de Angelis. The entry on the 22d was very unimportant and apparently quite complete, ending at the bottom of page 348. Of the 23d there was, as I have said, no record at all, and the entry for the 24th began at the top of page 355. This last memorandum was also brief, and written when the author was annoyed by Jocelyn leaving him.

The defection of his companion had been apparently entirely unexpected. There was at least no previous hint of any such intention. Temple wrote that Jocelyn had left the Villa de Angelis that day and taken up his abode with the Carthusians of San Martino. No reason for such an extraordinary change was given; but there was a hint that Jocelyn had professed himself shocked at something that had happened. The entry concluded with a few bitter remarks: "*So farewell to my holy anchoret; and if I cannot speed him with a leprosie as one Elisha did his servant, yet at least he went out from my presence with a face as white as snow.*"

I had read this sentence more than once before without its attracting other than a passing attention. The curious expression, that Jocelyn had gone out from his presence with a face as white as snow, had hitherto seemed to me to mean nothing more than that the two men had parted in violent anger, and that Temple had abused or bullied his companion. But as I sat alone that night in the library the words seemed to assume an entirely new force, and a strange suspicion began to creep over me.

I have said that one of the most remarkable features of Sir John's illness was his deadly pallor. Though I had now spent some time at Worth, and had been daily struck by this lack of colour, I had never before remembered in this connection that a strange paleness had also been an attribute of Adrian Temple, and was indeed very clearly marked in the picture painted of him by Battoni. In Sir John's account, moreover, of the vision which he thought he had seen in his rooms at Oxford, he had always spoken of the white and waxen face of his spectral visitant. The family tradition of Royston said that Temple had lost his colour in some deadly magical experiment, and a conviction now flashed upon me that Jocelyn's face "as white as snow" could refer only to this same unnatural pallor, and that he too had been smitten with it as with the mark of the beast.

In a drawer of my despatch-box, I kept by me all the letters which the late Lady Maltravers had written home during her ill-fated honeymoon. Miss Maltravers had placed them in my hands in order that I might be acquainted with every fact that could at all elucidate the progress of Sir John's malady. I remembered that in one of these letters mention was made of a sharp attack of fever in Naples, and of her noticing in him for the first time this singular pallor. I found the letter again without difficulty and read it with a new light. Every line breathed of surprise and alarm. Lady Maltravers feared that her husband was very seriously ill. On the Wednesday, two days before she wrote, he had suffered all day from a strange restlessness, which had increased after they had retired in the evening. He could not sleep and had dressed again, saying he would walk a little in the night air to compose himself. He had not returned till near six in the morning, and then seemed so exhausted that he had since been confined to his bed. He was terribly pale, and the doctors feared he had been attacked by some strange fever.

The date of the letter was the 25th of October, fixing the night of the 23d as the time of Sir John's first attack. The coincidence of the date with that of the day missing in Temple's diary was significant, but it was not needed now to convince me that Sir John's ruin was due to something that occurred on that fatal night at Naples.

The question that Dr. Frobisher had asked Miss Maltravers when he was first called to see her brother in London returned to my memory with an overwhelming force. "Had Sir John been subjected to any mental shock; had he received any severe fright?" I knew now that the question should have been answered in the affirmative, for I felt as certain as if Sir John had told me himself that he had received a violent shock, probably some terrible fright, on the night of the 23d of October. What the nature of that shock could have been my imagination was powerless to conceive, only I knew that whatever Sir John had done or seen, Adrian Temple and Jocelyn had done or seen also a century before and at the same place. That horror which had blanched the face of all three men for life had fallen perhaps with a less overwhelming force on Temple's seasoned wickedness, but had driven the worthless Jocelyn to the cloister, and was driving Sir John to the grave.

These thoughts as they passed through my mind filled me with a vague alarm. The lateness of the hour, the stillness and the subdued light, made the library in which I sat seem so vast and lonely that I began to feel the same dread of being alone that I had observed so often in my friend. Though only a door separated me from his bedroom, and I could hear his deep and regular breathing, I felt as though I must go in and waken him or Parnham to keep me company and save me from my own reflections. By a strong effort I restrained myself, and sat down to think the matter over and endeavour to frame some hypothesis that might explain the mystery. But it was all to no purpose. I merely wearied myself without being able to arrive at even a plausible conjecture, except that it seemed as though the strange coincidence of date might point to some ghastly charm or incantation which could only be carried out on one certain night of the year.

It must have been near morning when, quite exhausted, I fell into an uneasy slumber in the arm-chair where I sat. My sleep, however brief, was peopled with a succession of fantastic visions, in which I continually saw Sir John, not ill and wasted as now, but vigorous and handsome as I had known him at Oxford, standing beside a glowing brazier and reciting words I could not understand, while another man with a sneering white face sat in a corner playing the air of the *Gagliarda* on a violin. Parnham woke me in my chair at seven o'clock; his master, he said, was still sleeping easily.

I had made up my mind that as soon as he awoke I would inquire of Sir John as to the pages missing from the diary; but though my expectation and excitement were at a high pitch, I was forced to restrain my curiosity, for Sir John's slumber continued late into the day. Dr. Bruton called in the morning, and said that this sleep was what the patient's condition most required, and was a distinctly favourable symptom; he was on no account to be disturbed. Sir John did not leave his bed, but continued dozing all day till the evening. When at last he shook off his drowsiness, the hour was already so late that, in spite of my anxiety, I hesitated to talk with him about the diaries, lest I should unduly excite him before the night.

As the evening advanced he became very uneasy, and rose more than once from his bed. This restlessness, following on the repose of the day, ought perhaps to have made me anxious, for I have since observed that when death is very near an apprehensive unrest often sets in both with men and animals. It seems as if they dreaded to resign themselves to sleep, lest as they slumber the last enemy should seize them unawares. They try to fling off the bedclothes, they sometimes must leave their beds and walk. So it was with poor John Maltravers on his last Christmas Eve. I had sat with him grieving for his disquiet until he seemed to grow more tranquil, and at length fell asleep. I was sleeping that night in his room instead of Parnham, and tired with sitting up through the previous night, I flung myself, dressed as I was, upon the bed. I had scarcely dozed off, I think, before the sound of his violin awoke me. I found he had risen from his bed, had taken his favourite instrument, and was playing in his sleep. The air was the *Gagliarda* of the "Areopagita" suite, which I had not heard since we had played it last together at Oxford, and it brought back with it a crowd of far-off memories and infinite regrets. I cursed the sleepiness which had overcome me at my watchman's post, and allowed Sir John to play once more that melody which had always been fraught with such evil for him; and I was about to wake him gently when he was startled from sleep by a strange accident. As I walked towards him the violin seemed entirely to collapse in his hands, and, as a matter of fact, the belly then gave way and broke under the strain of the strings. As the strings slackened, the last note became an unearthly discord. If I were superstitious I should say that some evil spirit then went out of the violin, and broke in his parting throes the wooden tabernacle which had so long sheltered him. It was the last time the instrument was ever used, and that hideous chord was the last that Maltravers ever played.

I had feared that the shock of waking thus suddenly from sleep would have a very prejudicial effect upon the sleep-walker, but this seemed not to be the case. I persuaded him to go back at once to bed, and in a few minutes he fell asleep again. In the morning he seemed for the first time distinctly better; there was indeed something of his old self in his manner. It seemed as though the breaking of the violin had been an actual relief to him; and I believe that on that Christmas morning his better instincts woke, and that his old religious training and the associations of his boyhood then made their last appeal. I was pleased at such a change, however temporary it might prove. He wished to go to church, and I determined that again I would subdue my curiosity and defer the questions I was burning to put till after our return from the morning service. Miss Maltravers had gone indoors to make some preparation, Sir John was in his wheel-chair on the terrace, and I was sitting by him in the sun. For a few moments he appeared immersed in silent thought, and then bent over towards me till his head was close to mine, and said, "Dear William, there is something I must tell you. I feel I cannot even go to church till I have told you all." His manner shocked me beyond expression. I knew that he was going to tell me the secret of the lost pages, but instead of wishing any longer to have my curiosity satisfied, I felt a horrible dread of what he might say next. He took my hand in his and held it tightly, as a man who was about to undergo severe physical pain and sought the consolation of a friend's support. Then he went on—"You will be shocked at what I am going to tell you; but listen, and do not give me up: You must stand by me and comfort me and help me to turn again." He paused for a moment and continued—"It was one night in October, when Constance and I were at Naples. I took that violin and went by myself to the ruined villa on the Scoglio di Venere." He had been speaking with difficulty. His hand clutched mine convulsively, but still I felt it trembling, and I could see the moisture standing thick on his forehead. At this point the effort seemed too much for him and he broke off. "I cannot go on, I cannot tell you, but you can read it for yourself. In that diary which I gave you there are some pages missing." The suspense was becoming intolerable to me, and I broke in, "Yes, yes,

I know; you cut them out. Tell me where they are," He went on—"Yes, I cut them out lest they should possibly fall into anyone's hands unaware. But before you read them you must swear, as you hope for salvation, that you will never try to do what is written in them. Swear this to me now, or I never can let you see them." My eagerness was too great to stop now to discuss trifles, and to humour him I swore as desired. He had been speaking with a continual increasing effort; he cast a hurried and fearful glance round as though he expected to see someone listening, and it was almost in a whisper that he went on, "You will find them in—" His agitation had become most painful to watch, and as he spoke the last words a convulsion passed over his face, and speech failing him, he sank back on his pillow. A strange fear took hold of me. For a moment I thought there were others on the terrace beside myself, and turned round expecting to see Miss Maltravers returned; but we were still alone. I even fancied that just as Sir John spoke his last words I felt something brush swiftly by me. He put up his hands, beating the air with a most painful gesture, as though he were trying to keep off an antagonist who had gripped him by the throat, and made a final struggle to speak. But the spasm was too strong for him; a dreadful stillness followed, and he was gone.

There is little more to add; for Sir John's guilty secret perished with him. Though I was sure from his manner that the missing leaves were concealed somewhere at Worth, and though as executor I caused the most diligent search to be made, no trace of them was afterwards found; nor did any circumstance ever transpire to fling further light upon the matter. I must confess that I should have felt the discovery of these pages as a relief; for though I dreaded what I might have had to read, yet I was more anxious lest, being found at a later period and falling into other hands, they should cause a recrudescence of that plague which had blighted Sir John's life.

Of the nature of the events which took place on that night at Naples I can form no conjecture. But as certain physical sights have ere now proved so revolting as to unhinge the intellect, so I can imagine that the mind may in a state of extreme tension conjure up to itself some form of moral evil so hideous as metaphysically to sear it: and this, I believe, happened in the case both of Adrian Temple and of Sir John Maltravers.

It is difficult to imagine the accessories used to produce the mental excitation in which alone such a presentment of evil could become imaginable. Fancy and legend, which have combined to represent as possible appearances of the supernatural, agree also in considering them as more likely to occur at certain times and places than at others; and it is possible that the missing pages of the diary contained an account of the time, place, and other conditions chosen by Temple for some deadly experiment. Sir John most probably re-enacted the scene under precisely similar conditions, and the effect on his overwrought imagination was so vivid as to upset the balance of his mind. The time chosen was no doubt the night of the 23d of October, and I cannot help thinking that the place was one of those evil-looking and ruinous sea-rooms which had so terrifying an effect on Miss Maltravers. Temple may have used on that night one of the medieval incantations, or possibly the more ancient invocation of the Isiac rite with which a man of his knowledge and proclivities would certainly be familiar. The accessories of either are sufficiently hideous to weaken the mind by terror, and so prepare it for a belief in some frightful apparition. But whatever was done, I feel sure that the music of the *Gagliarda* formed part of the ceremonial.

Medieval philosophers and theologians held that evil is in its essence so horrible that the human mind, if it could realise it, must perish at its contemplation. Such realisation was by mercy ordinarily withheld, but its possibility was hinted in the legend of the *Visio Malefica*. The *Visio Beatifica* was, as is well known, that vision of the Deity or realisation of the perfect Good which was to form the happiness of heaven, and the reward of the sanctified in the next world. Tradition says that this vision was accorded also to some specially elect spirits even in this life, as to Enoch, Elijah, Stephen, and Jerome. But there was a converse to the Beatific Vision in the *Visio Malefica*, or presentation of absolute Evil, which was to be the chief torture of the damned, and which, like the Beatific Vision, had been made visible in life to certain desperate men. It visited Esau, as was said, when he found no place for repentance, and Judas, whom it drove to suicide. Cain saw it when he murdered his brother, and legend relates that in his case, and in that of others, it left a physical brand to be borne by the body to the grave. It was supposed that the Malefic Vision, besides being thus spontaneously presented to typically abandoned men, had actually been purposely called up by some few great adepts, and used by them to blast their enemies. But to do so was considered equivalent to a conscious surrender to the powers of evil, as the vision once seen took away all hope of final salvation.

Adrian Temple would undoubtedly be cognisant of this legend, and the lost experiment may have been an attempt to call up the Malefic Vision. It is but a vague conjecture at the best, for the tree of the knowledge of Evil bears many sorts of poisonous fruit, and no one can give full account of the extravagances of a wayward fancy.

Conjointly with Miss Sophia, Sir John appointed me his executor and guardian of his only son. Two months later we had lit a great fire in the library at Worth. In it, after the servants were gone to bed, we burnt the book containing the "Areopagita" of Graziani, and the Stradivarius fiddle. The diaries of Temple I had already destroyed, and wish that I could as easily blot out their foul and debasing memories from my mind.

I shall probably be blamed by those who would exalt art at the expense of everything else, for burning a unique violin. This reproach I am content to bear. Though I am not unreasonably superstitious, and have no sympathy for that potential pantheism to which Sir John Maltravers surrendered his intellect, yet I felt so great an aversion to this violin that I would neither suffer it to remain at Worth, nor pass into other hands. Miss Sophia was entirely at one with me on this point. It was the same feeling which restrains any except fools or braggarts from wishing to sleep in "haunted" rooms, or to live in houses polluted with the memory of a revolting crime. No sane mind believes in foolish apparitions, but fancy may at times bewitch the best of us. So the Stradivarius was burnt. It was, after all, perhaps not so serious a matter, for, as I have said, the bass-bar had given way. There had always been a question whether it was strong enough to resist the strain of modern stringing. Experience showed at last that it was not. With the failure of the bass-bar the belly collapsed, and the wood broke across the grain in so extraordinary a manner as to put the fiddle beyond repair, except as a curiosity. Its loss, therefore, is not to be so much regretted. Sir Edward has been brought up to think more of a cricket-bat than of a violin-bow; but if he wishes at any time to buy a Stradivarius, the fortunes of Worth and Royston, nursed through two long minorities, will certainly justify his doing so.

Miss Sophia and I stood by and watched the holocaust. My heart misgave me for a moment when I saw the mellow red varnish blistering off the back, but I put my regret resolutely aside. As the bright flames jumped up and lapped it round, they flung a red glow on the scroll. It was wonderfully wrought, and differed, as I think Miss Maltravers has already said, from any known example of Stradivarius. As we watched it, the scroll took form, and we saw what we had never seen before, that it was cut so that the deep lines in a certain light showed as the profile of a man. It was a wizened little paganish face, with sharp-cut features and a bald head. As I looked at it I knew at once (and a cameo has since confirmed the fact) that it was a head of Porphyry. Thus the second label found in the violin was explained and Sir John's view confirmed, that Stradivarius had made the instrument for some Neo-Platonist enthusiast who had dedicated it to his master Porphyrius.

A year after Sir John's death I went with Miss Maltravers to Worth church to see a plain slab of slate which we had placed over her brother's grave. We stood in bright sunlight in the Maltravers chapel, with the monuments of that splendid family about us. Among them were the altar-tomb of Sir Esmoun, and the effigies of more than one Crusader. As I looked on their knightly forms, with their heads resting on their tilting helms, their faces set firm, and their hands joined in prayer, I could not help envying them that full and unwavering faith for which they had fought and died. It seemed to stand out in such sharp contrast with our latter-day sciolism and half-believed creeds, and to be flung into higher relief by the dark shadow of John Maltravers's ruined life. At our feet was the great brass of one Sir Roger de Maltravers. I pointed out the end of the inscription to my companion— "Cvjvs animæ, atqve animabvs omnivm fidelvm defvnctorvm, atqve nostris animabvs qvvm ex hac lvce transiverimvs, propitietvr Devs." Though no Catholic, I could not refuse to add a sincere Amen. Miss Sophia, who is not ignorant of Latin, read the inscription after me. "Ex hac luce," she said, as though speaking to herself, "out of this light; alas! alas! for some the light is darkness."

Keeping His Promise

ALGERNON BLACKWOOD

It was eleven o'clock at night, and young Marriott was locked into his room, cramming as hard as he could cram. He was a "Fourth Year Man" at Edinburgh University and he had been ploughed for this particular examination so often that his parents had positively declared they could no longer supply the funds to keep him there.

His rooms were cheap and dingy, but it was the lecture fees that took the money. So Marriott pulled himself together at last and definitely made up his mind that he would pass or die in the attempt, and for some weeks now he had been reading as hard as mortal man can read. He was trying to make up for lost time and money in a way that showed conclusively he did not understand the value of either. For no ordinary man—and Marriott was in every sense an ordinary man—can afford to drive the mind as he had lately been driving his, without sooner or later paying the cost.

Among the students he had few friends or acquaintances, and these few had promised not to disturb him at night, knowing he was at last reading in earnest. It was, therefore, with feelings a good deal stronger than mere surprise that he heard his doorbell ring on this particular night and realised that he was to have a visitor. Some men would simply have muffled the bell and gone on quietly with their work. But Marriott was not this sort. He was nervous. It would have bothered and pecked at his mind all night long not to know who the visitor was and what he wanted. The only thing to do, therefore, was to let him in—and out again—as quickly as possible.

The landlady went to bed at ten o'clock punctually, after which hour nothing would induce her to pretend she heard the bell, so Marriott jumped up from his books with an exclamation that augured ill for the reception of his caller, and prepared to let him in with his own hand.

The streets of Edinburgh town were very still at this late hour—it was late for Edinburgh—and in the quiet neighbourhood of F—— Street, where Marriott lived on the third floor, scarcely a sound broke the silence. As he crossed the floor, the bell rang a second time, with unnecessary clamour, and he unlocked the door and passed into the little hallway with considerable wrath and annoyance in his heart at the insolence of the double interruption.

"The fellows all know I'm reading for this exam. Why in the world do they come to bother me at such an unearthly hour?"

The inhabitants of the building, with himself, were medical students, general students, poor Writers to the Signet, and some others whose vocations were perhaps not so obvious. The stone staircase, dimly lighted at each floor by a gas-jet that would not turn above a certain height, wound down to the level of the street with no pretence at carpet or railing. At some levels it was cleaner than at others. It depended on the landlady of the particular level.

The acoustic properties of a spiral staircase seem to be peculiar. Marriott, standing by the open door, book in hand, thought every moment the owner of the footsteps would come into view. The sound of the boots was so close and so loud that they seemed to travel disproportionately in advance of their cause. Wondering who it could be, he stood ready with all manner of sharp greetings for the man who dared thus to disturb his work. But the man did not appear. The steps sounded almost under his nose, yet no one was visible.

A sudden queer sensation of fear passed over him—a faintness and a shiver down the back. It went, however, almost as soon as it came, and he was just debating whether he would call aloud to his invisible visitor, or slam the door and return to his books, when the cause of the disturbance turned the corner very slowly and came into view.

It was a stranger. He saw a youngish man short of figure and very broad. His face was the colour of a piece of chalk and the eyes, which were very bright, had heavy lines underneath them. Though the cheeks and chin were unshaven and the general appearance unkempt, the man was evidently a gentleman, for he was well dressed and bore himself with a certain air. But, strangest of all, he wore no hat, and carried none in his hand; and although rain had been falling steadily all the evening, he appeared to have neither overcoat nor umbrella.

A hundred questions sprang up in Marriott's mind and rushed to his lips, chief among which was something like "Who in the world are you?" and "What in the name of heaven do you come to me for?" But none of these questions found time to express themselves in words, for almost at once the caller turned his head a little so that the gas light in the hall fell upon his features from a new angle. Then in a flash Marriott recognised him.

"Field! Man alive! Is it you?" he gasped.

The Fourth Year Man was not lacking in intuition, and he perceived at once that here was a case for delicate treatment. He divined, without any actual process of thought, that the catastrophe often predicted had come at last, and that this man's father had turned him out of the house. They had been at a private school together years before, and though they had hardly met once since, the news had not failed to reach him from time to time with considerable detail, for the family lived near his own and between certain of the sisters there was great intimacy. Young Field had gone wild later, he remembered hearing about it all—drink, a woman, opium, or something of the sort—he could not exactly call to mind.

"Come in," he said at once, his anger vanishing. "There's been something wrong, I can see. Come in, and tell me all about it and perhaps I can help—" He hardly knew what to say, and stammered a lot more besides. The dark side of life, and the horror of it, belonged to a world that lay remote from his own select little atmosphere of books and dreamings. But he had a man's heart for all that.

He led the way across the hall, shutting the front door carefully behind him, and noticed as he did so that the other, though certainly sober, was unsteady on his legs, and evidently much exhausted. Marriott might not be able to pass his examinations, but he at least knew the symptoms of starvation—acute starvation, unless he was much mistaken—when they stared him in the face.

"Come along," he said cheerfully, and with genuine sympathy in his voice. "I'm glad to see you. I was going to have a bite of something to eat, and you're just in time to join me."

The other made no audible reply, and shuffled so feebly with his feet that Marriott took his arm by way of support. He noticed for the first time that the clothes hung on him with pitiful looseness. The broad frame was literally hardly more than a frame. He was as thin as a skeleton. But, as he touched him, the sensation of faintness and dread returned. It only lasted a moment, and then passed off, and he ascribed it not unnaturally to the distress and shock of seeing a former friend in such a pitiful plight.

"Better let me guide you. It's shamefully dark—this hall. I'm always complaining," he said lightly, recognising by the weight upon his arm that the guidance was sorely needed, "but the old cat never does anything except promise." He led him to the sofa, wondering all the time where he had come from and how he had found out the address. It must be at least seven years since those days at the private school when they used to be such close friends.

"Now, if you'll forgive me for a minute," he said, "I'll get supper ready—such as it is. And don't bother to talk. Just take it easy on the sofa. I see you're dead tired. You can tell me about it afterwards, and we'll make plans."

The other sat down on the edge of the sofa and stared in silence, while Marriott got out the brown loaf, scones, and huge pot of marmalade that Edinburgh students always keep in their cupboards. His eyes shone with a brightness that suggested drugs, Marriott thought, stealing a glance at him from behind the cupboard door. He did not like yet to take a full square look. The fellow was in a bad way, and it would have been so like an examination to stare and wait for explanations. Besides, he was evidently almost too exhausted to speak. So, for reasons of delicacy—and for another reason as well which he could not exactly formulate to himself—he let his visitor rest apparently unnoticed, while he busied himself with the supper. He lit the spirit lamp to make cocoa, and when the water was boiling he drew up the table with the good things to the sofa, so that Field need not have even the trouble of moving to a chair.

"Now, let's tuck in," he said, "and afterwards we'll have a pipe and a chat. I'm reading for an exam, you know, and I always have something about this time. It's jolly to have a companion."

He looked up and caught his guest's eyes directed straight upon his own. An involuntary shudder ran through him from head to foot. The face opposite him was deadly white and wore a dreadful expression of pain and mental suffering.

"By Gad!" he said, jumping up, "I quite forgot. I've got some whisky somewhere. What an ass I am. I never touch it myself when I'm working like this."

He went to the cupboard and poured out a stiff glass which the other swallowed at a single gulp and without any water. Marriott watched him while he drank it, and at the same time noticed something else as well—Field's coat was all over dust, and on one shoulder was a bit of cobweb. It was perfectly dry; Field arrived on a soaking wet night without hat, umbrella, or overcoat, and yet perfectly dry, even dusty. Therefore he had been under cover. What did it all mean? Had he been hiding in the building...?

It was very strange. Yet he volunteered nothing; and Marriott had pretty well made up his mind by this time that he would not ask any questions until he had eaten and slept. Food and sleep were obviously what the poor devil needed most and first—he was pleased with his powers of ready diagnosis—and it would not be fair to press him till he had recovered a bit.

They ate their supper together while the host carried on a running one-sided conversation, chiefly about himself and his exams and his "old cat" of a landlady, so that the guest need not utter a single word unless he really wished to—which he evidently did not! But, while he toyed with his food, feeling no desire to eat, the other ate voraciously. To see a hungry man devour cold scones, stale oatcake, and brown bread laden with marmalade was a revelation to this inexperienced student who had never known what it was to be without at least three meals a day. He watched in spite of himself, wondering why the fellow did not choke in the process.

But Field seemed to be as sleepy as he was hungry. More than once his head dropped and he ceased to masticate the food in his mouth. Marriott had positively to shake him before he would go on with his meal. A stronger emotion will overcome a weaker, but this struggle between the sting of real hunger and the magical opiate of overpowering sleep was a curious sight to the student, who watched it with mingled astonishment and alarm. He had heard of the pleasure it was to feed hungry men, and watch them eat, but he had never actually witnessed it, and he had no idea it was like this. Field ate like an animal—gobbled, stuffed, gorged. Marriott forgot his reading, and began to feel something very much like a lump in his throat.

"Afraid there's been awfully little to offer you, old man," he managed to blurt out when at length the last scone had disappeared, and the rapid, one-sided meal was at an end. Field still made no reply, for he was almost asleep in his seat. He merely looked up wearily and gratefully.

"Now you must have some sleep, you know," he continued, "or you'll go to pieces. I shall be up all night reading for this blessed exam. You're more than welcome to my bed. To-morrow we'll have a late breakfast and—and see what can be done—and make plans—I'm awfully good at making plans, you know," he added with an attempt at lightness.

Field maintained his "dead sleepy" silence, but appeared to acquiesce, and the other led the way into the bedroom, apologising as he did so to this half-starved son of a baronet—whose own home was almost a palace—for the size of the room. The weary guest, however, made no pretence of thanks or politeness. He merely steadied himself on his friend's arm as he staggered across the room, and then, with all his clothes on, dropped his exhausted body on the bed. In less than a minute he was to all appearances sound asleep.

For several minutes Marriott stood in the open door and watched him; praying devoutly that he might never find himself in a like predicament, and then fell to wondering what he would do with his unbidden guest on the morrow. But he did not stop long to think, for the call of his books was imperative, and happen what might, he must see to it that he passed that examination.

Having again locked the door into the hall, he sat down to his books and resumed his notes on *materia medica* where he had left off when the bell rang. But it was difficult for some time to concentrate his mind on the subject. His thoughts kept wandering to the picture of that white-faced, strange-eyed fellow, starved and dirty, lying in his clothes and boots on the bed. He recalled their schooldays together before they had drifted apart, and how they had vowed eternal friendship—and all the rest of it. And now! What horrible straits to be in. How could any man let the love of dissipation take such hold upon him?

But one of their vows together Marriott, it seemed, had completely forgotten. Just now, at any rate, it lay too far in the background of his memory to be recalled.

Through the half-open door—the bedroom led out of the sitting-room and had no other door—came the sound of deep, long-drawn breathing, the regular, steady breathing of a tired man, so tired that, even to listen to it made Marriott almost want to go to sleep himself.

"He needed it," reflected the student, "and perhaps it came only just in time!"

Perhaps so; for outside the bitter wind from across the Forth howled cruelly and drove the rain in cold streams against the window-panes, and down the deserted streets. Long before Marriott settled down again properly to his reading, he heard distantly, as it were, through the sentences of the book, the heavy, deep breathing of the sleeper in the next room.

A couple of hours later, when he yawned and changed his books, he still heard the breathing, and went cautiously up to the door to look round.

At first the darkness of the room must have deceived him, or else his eyes were confused and dazzled by the recent glare of the reading lamp. For a minute or two he could make out nothing at all but dark lumps of furniture, the mass of the chest of drawers by the wall, and the white patch where his bath stood in the centre of the floor.

Then the bed came slowly into view. And on it he saw the outline of the sleeping body gradually take shape before his eyes, growing up strangely into the darkness, till it stood out in marked relief—the long black form against the white counterpane.

He could hardly help smiling. Field had not moved an inch. He watched him a moment or two and then returned to his books. The night was full of the singing voices of the wind and rain. There was no sound of traffic; no hansoms clattered over the cobbles, and it was still too early for the milk carts. He worked on steadily and conscientiously, only stopping now and again to change a book, or to sip some of the poisonous stuff that kept him awake and made his brain so active, and on these occasions Field's breathing was always distinctly audible in the room. Outside, the storm continued to howl, but inside the house all was stillness. The shade of the reading lamp threw all the light upon the littered table, leaving the other end of the room in comparative darkness. The bedroom door was exactly opposite him where he sat. There was nothing to disturb the worker, nothing but an occasional rush of wind against the windows, and a slight pain in his arm.

This pain, however, which he was unable to account for, grew once or twice very acute. It bothered him; and he tried to remember how, and when, he could have bruised himself so severely, but without success.

At length the page before him turned from yellow to grey, and there were sounds of wheels in the street below. It was four o'clock. Marriott leaned back and yawned prodigiously. Then he drew back the curtains. The storm had subsided and the Castle Rock was shrouded in mist. With another yawn he turned away from the dreary outlook and prepared to sleep the remaining four hours till breakfast on the sofa. Field was still breathing heavily in the next room, and he first tip-toed across the floor to take another look at him.

Peering cautiously round the half-opened door his first glance fell upon the bed now plainly discernible in the grey light of morning. He stared hard. Then he rubbed his eyes. Then he rubbed his eyes again and thrust his head farther round the edge of the door. With fixed eyes he stared harder still, and harder.

But it made no difference at all. He was staring into an empty room.

The sensation of fear he had felt when Field first appeared upon the scene returned suddenly, but with much greater force. He became conscious, too, that his left arm was throbbing violently and causing him great pain. He stood wondering, and staring, and trying to collect his thoughts. He was trembling from head to foot.

By a great effort of the will he left the support of the door and walked forward boldly into the room.

There, upon the bed, was the impress of a body, where Field had lain and slept. There was the mark of the head on the pillow, and the slight indentation at the foot of the bed where the boots had rested on the counterpane. And there, plainer than ever—for he was closer to it—was *the breathing*!

Marriott tried to pull himself together. With a great effort he found his voice and called his friend aloud by name!

"Field! Is that you? Where are you?"

There was no reply; but the breathing continued without interruption, coming directly from the bed. His voice had such an unfamiliar sound that Marriott did not care to repeat his questions, but he went down on his knees and examined the bed above and below, pulling the mattress off finally, and taking the coverings away separately one by one. But though the sounds continued there was no visible sign of Field, nor was there any space in which a human being, however small, could have concealed itself. He pulled the bed out from the wall, but the sound *stayed where it was*. It did not move with the bed.

Marriott, finding self-control a little difficult in his weary condition, at once set about a thorough search of the room. He went through the cupboard, the chest of drawers, the little alcove where the clothes hung—everything. But there was no sign of anyone. The small window near the ceiling was closed; and, anyhow, was not large enough to let a cat pass. The sitting-room door was locked on the inside; he could not have got out that way. Curious thoughts began to trouble Marriott's mind, bringing in their train unwelcome sensations. He grew more and more excited; he searched the bed again till it resembled the scene of a pillow fight; he searched both rooms, knowing all the time it was useless,—and then he searched again. A cold perspiration broke out all over his body; and the sound of heavy breathing, all this time, never ceased to come from the corner where Field had lain down to sleep.

Then he tried something else. He pushed the bed back exactly into its original position—and himself lay down upon it just where his guest had lain. But the same instant he sprang up again in a single bound. The breathing was close beside him, almost on his cheek, and between him and the wall! Not even a child could have squeezed into the space.

He went back into his sitting-room, opened the windows, welcoming all the light and air possible, and tried to think the whole matter over quietly and clearly. Men who read too hard, and slept too little, he knew were sometimes troubled with very vivid hallucinations. Again he calmly reviewed every incident of the night; his accurate sensations; the vivid details; the emotions stirred in him; the dreadful feast—no single hallucination could ever combine all these and cover so long a period of time. But with less satisfaction he thought of the recurring faintness, and curious sense of horror that had once or twice come over him, and then of the violent pains in his arm. These were quite unaccountable.

Moreover, now that he began to analyse and examine, there was one other thing that fell upon him like a sudden revelation: *During the whole time Field had not actually uttered a single word!* Yet, as though in mockery upon his reflections, there came ever from that inner room the sound of the breathing, long-drawn, deep, and regular. The thing was incredible. It was absurd.

Haunted by visions of brain fever and insanity, Marriott put on his cap and macintosh and left the house. The morning air on Arthur's Seat would blow the cobwebs from his brain; the scent of the heather, and above all, the sight of the sea. He roamed over the wet slopes above Holyrood for a couple of hours, and did not return until the exercise had shaken some of the horror out of his bones, and given him a ravening appetite into the bargain.

As he entered he saw that there was another man in the room, standing against the window with his back to the light. He recognised his fellow-student Greene, who was reading for the same examination.

"Read hard all night, Marriott," he said, "and thought I'd drop in here to compare notes and have some breakfast. You're out early?" he added, by way of a question. Marriott said he had a headache and a walk had helped it, and Greene nodded and said "Ah!" But when the girl had set the steaming porridge on the table and gone out again, he went on with rather a forced tone, "Didn't know you had any friends who drank, Marriott?"

This was obviously tentative, and Marriott replied drily that he did not know it either.

"Sounds just as if some chap were 'sleeping it off' in there, doesn't it, though?" persisted the other, with a nod in the direction of the bedroom, and looking curiously at his friend. The two men stared steadily at each other for several seconds, and then Marriott said earnestly—

"Then you hear it too, thank God!"

"Of course I hear it. The door's open. Sorry if I wasn't meant to."

"Oh, I don't mean that," said Marriott, lowering his voice. "But I'm awfully relieved. Let me explain. Of course, if you hear it too, then it's all right; but really it frightened me more than I can tell you. I thought I was going to have brain fever, or something, and you know what a lot depends on this exam. It always begins with sounds, or visions, or some sort of beastly hallucination, and I—"

"Rot!" ejaculated the other impatiently. "What *are* you talking about?"

"Now, listen to me, Greene," said Marriott, as calmly as he could, for the breathing was still plainly audible, "and I'll tell you what I mean, only don't interrupt." And thereupon he related exactly what had happened during the night, telling everything, even down to the pain in his arm. When it was over he got up from the table and crossed the room.

"You hear the breathing now plainly, don't you?" he said. Greene said he did. "Well, come with me, and we'll search the room together." The other, however, did not move from his chair.

"I've been in already," he said sheepishly; "I heard the sounds and thought it was you. The door was ajar—so I went in."

Marriott made no comment, but pushed the door open as wide as it would go. As it opened, the sound of breathing grew more and more distinct.

"*Someone* must be in there," said Greene under his breath.

"*Someone* is in there, but *where*?" said Marriott. Again he urged his friend to go in with him. But Greene refused point-blank; said he had been in once and had searched the room and there was nothing there. He would not go in again for a good deal.

They shut the door and retired into the other room to talk it all over with many pipes. Greene questioned his friend very closely, but without illuminating result, since questions cannot alter facts.

"The only thing that ought to have a proper, a logical, explanation is the pain in my arm," said Marriott, rubbing that member with an attempt at a smile. "It hurts so infernally and aches all the way up. I can't remember bruising it, though."

"Let me examine it for you," said Greene. "I'm awfully good at bones in spite of the examiners' opinion to the contrary." It was a relief to play the fool a bit, and Marriott took his coat off and rolled up his sleeve.

"By George, though, I'm bleeding!" he exclaimed. "Look here! What on earth's this?"

On the forearm, quite close to the wrist, was a thin red line. There was a tiny drop of apparently fresh blood on it. Greene came over and looked closely at it for some minutes. Then he sat back in his chair, looking curiously at his friend's face.

"You've scratched yourself without knowing it," he said presently.

"There's no sign of a bruise. It must be something else that made the arm ache."

Marriott sat very still, staring silently at his arm as though the solution of the whole mystery lay there actually written upon the skin.

"What's the matter? I see nothing very strange about a scratch," said Greene, in an unconvincing sort of voice. "It was your cuff links probably. Last night in your excitement—"

But Marriott, white to the very lips, was trying to speak. The sweat stood in great beads on his forehead. At last he leaned forward close to his friend's face.

"Look," he said, in a low voice that shook a little. "Do you see that red mark? I mean *underneath* what you call the scratch?"

Greene admitted he saw something or other, and Marriott wiped the place clean with his handkerchief and told him to look again more closely.

"Yes, I see," returned the other, lifting his head after a moment's careful inspection. "It looks like an old scar."

"It *is* an old scar," whispered Marriott, his lips trembling. "*Now* it all comes back to me."

"All what?" Greene fidgeted on his chair. He tried to laugh, but without success. His friend seemed bordering on collapse.

"Hush! Be quiet, and—I'll tell you," he said. "*Field made that scar.*"

For a whole minute the two men looked each other full in the face without speaking.

"Field made that scar!" repeated Marriott at length in a louder voice.

"Field! You mean—last night?"

"No, not last night. Years ago—at school, with his knife. And I made a scar in his arm with mine." Marriott was talking rapidly now.

"We exchanged drops of blood in each other's cuts. He put a drop into my arm and I put one into his—"

"In the name of heaven, what for?"

"It was a boys' compact. We made a sacred pledge, a bargain. I remember it all perfectly now. We had been reading some dreadful book and we swore to appear to one another—I mean, whoever died first swore to show himself to the other. And we sealed the compact with each other's blood. I remember it all so well—the hot summer afternoon in the playground, seven years ago—and one of the masters caught us and confiscated the knives—and I have never thought of it again to this day—"

"And you mean—" stammered Greene.

But Marriott made no answer. He got up and crossed the room and lay down wearily upon the sofa, hiding his face in his hands.

Greene himself was a bit non-plussed. He left his friend alone for a little while, thinking it all over again. Suddenly an idea seemed to strike him. He went over to where Marriott still lay motionless on the sofa and roused him. In any case it was better to face the matter, whether there was an explanation or not. Giving in was always the silly exit.

"I say, Marriott," he began, as the other turned his white face up to him. "There's no good being so upset about it. I mean—if it's all an hallucination we know what to do. And if it isn't—well, we know what to think, don't we?"

"I suppose so. But it frightens me horribly for some reason," returned his friend in a hushed voice. "And that poor devil—"

"But, after all, if the worst is true and—and that chap *has* kept his promise—well, he has, that's all, isn't it?"

Marriott nodded.

"There's only one thing that occurs to me," Greene went on, "and that is, are you quite sure that—that he really ate like that—I mean that he actually *ate anything at all?*" he finished, blurting out all his thought.

Marriott stared at him for a moment and then said he could easily make certain. He spoke quietly. After the main shock no lesser surprise could affect him.

"I put the things away myself," he said, "after we had finished. They are on the third shelf in that cupboard. No one's touched 'em since."

He pointed without getting up, and Greene took the hint and went over to look.

"Exactly," he said, after a brief examination; "just as I thought. It was partly hallucination, at any rate. The things haven't been touched. Come and see for yourself."

Together they examined the shelf. There was the brown loaf, the plate of stale scones, the oatcake, all untouched. Even the glass of whisky Marriott had poured out stood there with the whisky still in it.

"You were feeding—no one," said Greene "Field ate and drank nothing. He was not there at all!"

"But the breathing?" urged the other in a low voice, staring with a dazed expression on his face.

Greene did not answer. He walked over to the bedroom, while Marriott followed him with his eyes. He opened the door, and listened. There was no need for words. The sound of deep, regular breathing came floating through the air. There was no hallucination about that, at any rate. Marriott could hear it where he stood on the other side of the room.

Greene closed the door and came back. "There's only one thing to do," he declared with decision. "Write home and find out about him, and meanwhile come and finish your reading in my rooms. I've got an extra bed."

"Agreed," returned the Fourth Year Man; "there's no hallucination about that exam; I must pass that whatever happens."

And this was what they did.

It was about a week later when Marriott got the answer from his sister. Part of it he read out to Greene—

"It is curious," she wrote, "that in your letter you should have enquired after Field. It seems a terrible thing, but you know only a short while ago Sir John's patience became exhausted, and he turned him out of the house, they say without a penny. Well, what do you think? He has killed himself. At least, it looks like suicide. Instead of leaving the house, he went down into the cellar and simply starved himself to death. . . . They're trying to suppress it, of course, but I heard it all from my maid, who got it from their footman. . . . They found the body on the 14th and the doctor said he had died about twelve hours before. . . . He was dreadfully thin. . . ."

"Then he died on the 13th," said Greene.

Marriott nodded.

"That's the very night he came to see you."

Marriott nodded again.

The Moonlit Road

Ambrose Bierce

I. Statement of Joel Hetman, Jr.

I AM THE MOST UNFORTUNATE OF MEN. RICH, RESPECTED, FAIRLY WELL EDUCATED and of sound health—with many other advantages usually valued by those having them and coveted by those who have them not—I sometimes think that I should be less unhappy if they had been denied me, for then the contrast between my outer and my inner life would not be continually demanding a painful attention. In the stress of privation and the need of effort I might sometimes forget the somber secret ever baffling the conjecture that it compels.

I am the only child of Joel and Julia Hetman. The one was a well-to-do country gentleman, the other a beautiful and accomplished woman to whom he was passionately attached with what I now know to have been a jealous and exacting devotion. The family home was a few miles from Nashville, Tennessee, a large, irregularly built dwelling of no particular order of architecture, a little way off the road, in a park of trees and shrubbery.

At the time of which I write I was nineteen years old, a student at Yale. One day I received a telegram from my father of such urgency that in compliance with its unexplained demand I left at once for home. At the railway station in Nashville a distant relative awaited me to apprise me of the reason for my recall: my mother had been barbarously murdered—why and by whom none could conjecture, but the circumstances were these:

My father had gone to Nashville, intending to return the next afternoon. Something prevented his accomplishing the business in hand, so he returned on the same night, arriving just before the dawn. In his testimony before the coroner he explained that having no latchkey and not caring to disturb the sleeping servants, he had, with no clearly defined intention, gone round to the rear of the house. As he turned an angle of the building, he heard a sound as of a door gently closed, and saw in the darkness, indistinctly, the figure of a man, which instantly disappeared among the trees of the lawn. A hasty pursuit and brief search of the grounds in the belief that the trespasser was some one secretly visiting a servant proving fruitless, he entered at the unlocked door and mounted the stairs to my mother's chamber. Its door was open, and stepping into black darkness he fell headlong over some heavy object on the floor. I may spare myself the details; it was my poor mother, dead of strangulation by human hands!

Nothing had been taken from the house, the servants had heard no sound, and excepting those terrible finger-marks upon the dead woman's throat—dear God! that I might forget them!—no trace of the assassin was ever found.

I gave up my studies and remained with my father, who, naturally, was greatly changed. Always of a sedate, taciturn disposition, he now fell into so deep a dejection that nothing could hold his attention, yet anything—a footfall, the sudden closing of a door—aroused in him a fitful interest; one might have called it an apprehension. At any small surprise of the senses he would start visibly and sometimes turn pale, then relapse into a melancholy apathy deeper than before. I suppose he was what is called a "nervous wreck." As to me, I was younger then than now—there is much in that. Youth is Gilead, in which is balm for every wound. Ah, that I might again dwell in that enchanted land! Unacquainted with grief, I knew not how to appraise my bereavement; I could not rightly estimate the strength of the stroke.

One night, a few months after the dreadful event, my father and I walked home from the city. The full moon was about three hours above the eastern horizon; the entire countryside had the solemn stillness of a summer night; our footfalls and the ceaseless song of the katydids were the only sound aloof. Black shadows of bordering trees lay athwart the road, which, in the short reaches between, gleamed a ghostly white. As we approached the gate to our dwelling, whose front was in shadow, and in which no light shone, my father suddenly stopped and clutched my arm, saying, hardly above his breath:

"God! God! what is that?"

"I hear nothing," I replied.

"But see—see!" he said, pointing along the road, directly ahead.

I said: "Nothing is there. Come, father, let us go in—you are ill."

He had released my arm and was standing rigid and motionless in the center of the illuminated roadway, staring like one bereft of sense. His face in the moonlight showed a pallor and fixity inexpressibly distressing. I pulled gently at his sleeve, but he had forgotten my existence. Presently he began to retire backward, step by step, never for an instant removing his eyes from what he saw, or thought he saw. I turned half round to follow, but stood irresolute. I do not recall any feeling of fear, unless a sudden chill was its physical manifestation. It seemed as if an icy wind had touched my face and enfolded my body from head to foot; I could feel the stir of it in my hair.

At that moment my attention was drawn to a light that suddenly streamed from an upper window of the house: one of the servants, awakened by what mysterious premonition of evil who can say, and in obedience to an impulse that she was never able to name, had lit a lamp. When I turned to look for my father he was gone, and in all the years that have passed no whisper of his fate has come across the borderland of conjecture from the realm of the unknown.

II. State of Caspar Grattan

To-day I am said to live; to-morrow, here in this room, will lie a senseless shape of clay that all too long was I. If anyone lift the cloth from the face of that unpleasant thing it will be in gratification of a mere morbid curiosity. Some, doubtless, will go further and inquire, "Who was he?" In this writing I supply the only answer that I am able to make—Caspar Grattan. Surely, that should be enough. The name has served my small need for more than twenty years of a life of unknown length. True, I gave it to myself, but lacking another I had the right. In this world one must have a name; it prevents confusion, even when it does not establish identity. Some, though, are known by numbers, which also seem inadequate distinctions.

One day, for illustration, I was passing along a street of a city, far from here, when I met two men in uniform, one of whom, half pausing and looking curiously into my face, said to his companion, "That man looks like 767." Something in the number seemed familiar and horrible. Moved by an uncontrollable impulse, I sprang into a side street and ran until I fell exhausted in a country lane.

I have never forgotten that number, and always it comes to memory attended by gibbering obscenity, peals of joyless laughter, the clang of iron doors. So I say a name, even if self-bestowed, is better than a number. In the register of the potter's field I shall soon have both. What wealth!

Of him who shall find this paper I must beg a little consideration. It is not the history of my life; the knowledge to write that is denied me. This is only a record of broken and apparently unrelated memories, some of them as distinct and sequent as brilliant beads upon a thread, others remote and strange, having the character of crimson dreams with interspaces blank and black—witch-fires glowing still and red in a great desolation.

Standing upon the shore of eternity, I turn for a last look landward over the course by which I came. There are twenty years of footprints fairly distinct, the impressions of bleeding feet. They lead through poverty and pain, devious and unsure, as of one staggering beneath a burden—

> Remote, unfriended, melancholy, slow.

Ah, the poet's prophecy of Me—how admirable, how dreadfully admirable!

Backward beyond the beginning of this *via dolorosa*—this epic of suffering with episodes of sin—I see nothing clearly; it comes out of a cloud. I know that it spans only twenty years, yet I am an old man.

One does not remember one's birth—one has to be told. But with me it was different; life came to me full-handed and dowered me with all my faculties and powers. Of a previous existence I know no more than others, for all have stammering intimations that may be memories and may be dreams. I know only that my first consciousness was of maturity in body and mind—a consciousness accepted without surprise or conjecture. I merely found myself walking in a forest, half-clad, footsore, unutterably weary and hungry. Seeing a farmhouse, I approached and asked for food, which was given me by one who inquired my name. I did not know, yet knew that all had names. Greatly embarrassed, I retreated, and night coming on, lay down in the forest and slept.

The next day I entered a large town which I shall not name. Nor shall I recount further incidents of the life that is now to end—a life of wandering, always and everywhere haunted by an overmastering sense of crime in punishment of wrong and of terror in punishment of crime. Let me see if I can reduce it to narrative.

I seem once to have lived near a great city, a prosperous planter, married to a woman whom I loved and distrusted. We had, it sometimes seems, one child, a youth of brilliant parts and promise. He is at all times a vague figure, never clearly drawn, frequently altogether out of the picture.

One luckless evening it occurred to me to test my wife's fidelity in a vulgar, common-place way familiar to everyone who has acquaintance with the literature of fact and fiction. I went to the city, telling my wife that I should be absent until the following afternoon. But I returned before daybreak and went to the rear of the house, purposing to enter by a door with which I had secretly so tampered that it would seem to lock, yet not actually fasten. As I approached it, I heard it gently open and close, and saw a man steal away into the darkness. With murder in my heart, I sprang after him, but he had vanished without even the bad luck of identification. Sometimes now I cannot even persuade myself that it was a human being.

Crazed with jealousy and rage, blind and bestial with all the elemental passions of insulted manhood, I entered the house and sprang up the stairs to the door of my wife's chamber. It was closed, but having tampered with its lock also, I easily entered and despite the black darkness soon stood by the side of her bed. My groping hands told me that although disarranged it was unoccupied.

"She is below," I thought, "and terrified by my entrance has evaded me in the darkness of the hall."

With the purpose of seeking her I turned to leave the room, but took a wrong direction—the right one! My foot struck her, cowering in a corner of the room. Instantly my hands were at her throat, stifling a shriek, my knees were upon her struggling body; and there in the darkness, without a word of accusation or reproach, I strangled her till she died!

There ends the dream. I have related it in the past tense, but the present would be the fitter form, for again and again the somber tragedy reenacts itself in my consciousness—over and over I lay the plan, I suffer the confirmation, I redress the wrong. Then all is blank; and afterward the rains beat against the grimy window-panes, or the snows fall upon my scant attire, the wheels rattle in the squalid streets where my life lies in poverty and mean employment. If there is ever sunshine I do not recall it; if there are birds they do not sing.

There is another dream, another vision of the night. I stand among the shadows in a moonlit road. I am aware of another presence, but whose I cannot rightly determine. In the shadow of a great dwelling I catch the gleam of white garments; then the figure of a woman confronts me in the road—my murdered wife! There is death in the face; there are marks upon the throat. The eyes are fixed on mine with an infinite gravity which is not reproach, nor hate, nor menace, nor anything less terrible than recognition. Before this awful apparition I retreat in terror—a terror that is upon me as I write. I can no longer rightly shape the words. See! they—

Now I am calm, but truly there is no more to tell: the incident ends where it began—in darkness and in doubt.

Yes, I am again in control of myself: "the captain of my soul." But that is not respite; it is another stage and phase of expiation. My penance, constant in degree, is mutable in kind: one of its variants is tranquillity. After all, it is only a life-sentence. "To Hell for life"—that is a foolish penalty: the culprit chooses the duration of his punishment. To-day my term expires.

To each and all, the peace that was not mine.

III. Statement of the Late Julia Hetman, Through the Medium Bayrolles

I had retired early and fallen almost immediately into a peaceful sleep, from which I awoke with that indefinable sense of peril which is, I think, a common experience in that other, earlier life. Of its unmeaning character, too, I was entirely persuaded, yet that did not banish it. My husband, Joel Hetman, was away from home; the servants slept in another part of the house. But these were familiar conditions; they had never before distressed me. Nevertheless, the strange terror grew so insupportable that conquering my reluctance to move I sat up and lit the lamp at my bedside. Contrary to my expectation this gave me no relief; the light seemed rather an added danger, for I reflected that it would shine out under the door, disclosing my presence to whatever evil thing might lurk outside. You that are still in the flesh, subject to horrors of the imagination, think what a monstrous fear that must be which seeks in darkness security from malevolent existences of the night. That is to spring to close quarters with an unseen enemy—the strategy of despair!

Extinguishing the lamp I pulled the bed-clothing about my head and lay trembling and silent, unable to shriek, forgetful to pray. In this pitiable state I must have lain for what you call hours—with us there are no hours, there is no time.

At last it came—a soft, irregular sound of footfalls on the stairs! They were slow, hesitant, uncertain, as of something that did not see its way; to my disordered reason all the more terrifying for that, as the approach of some blind and mindless malevolence to which is no appeal. I even thought that I must have left the hall lamp burning and the groping of this creature proved it a monster of the night. This was foolish and inconsistent with my previous dread of the light, but what would you have? Fear has no brains; it is an idiot. The dismal witness that it bears and the cowardly counsel that it whispers are unrelated. We know this well, we who have passed into the Realm of Terror, who skulk in eternal dusk among the scenes of our former lives, invisible even to ourselves and one another, yet hiding forlorn in lonely places; yearning for speech with our loved ones, yet dumb, and as fearful of them as they of us. Sometimes the disability is removed, the law suspended: by the deathless power of love or hate we break the spell—we are seen by those whom we would warn, console, or punish. What form we seem to them to bear we know not; we know only that we terrify even those whom we most wish to comfort, and from whom we most crave tenderness and sympathy.

Forgive, I pray you, this inconsequent digression by what was once a woman. You who consult us in this imperfect way—you do not understand. You ask foolish questions about things unknown and things forbidden. Much that we know and could impart in our speech is meaningless in yours. We must communicate with you through a stammering intelligence in that small fraction of our language that you yourselves can speak. You think that we are of another world. No, we have knowledge of no world but yours, though for us it holds no sunlight, no warmth, no music, no laughter, no song of birds, nor any companionship. O God! what a thing it is to be a ghost, cowering and shivering in an altered world, a prey to apprehension and despair!

No, I did not die of fright: the Thing turned and went away. I heard it go down the stairs, hurriedly, I thought, as if itself in sudden fear. Then I rose to call for help. Hardly had my shaking hand found the doorknob when-merciful heaven!—I heard it returning. Its footfalls as it remounted the stairs were rapid, heavy and loud; they shook the house. I fled to an angle of the wall and crouched upon the floor. I tried to pray. I tried to call the name of my dear husband. Then I heard the door thrown open. There was an interval of unconsciousness, and when I revived I felt a strangling clutch upon my throat—felt my arms feebly beating against something that bore me backward—felt my tongue thrusting itself from between my teeth! And then I passed into this life.

No, I have no knowledge of what it was. The sum of what we knew at death is the measure of what we know afterward of all that went before. Of this existence we know many things, but no new light falls upon any page of that; in memory is written all of it that we can read. Here are no heights of truth overlooking the confused landscape of that dubitable domain. We still dwell in the Valley of the Shadow, lurk in its desolate places, peering from brambles and thickets at its mad, malign inhabitants. How should we have new knowledge of that fading past?

What I am about to relate happened on a night. We know when it is night, for then you retire to your houses and we can venture from our places of concealment to move unafraid about our old homes, to look in at the windows, even to enter and gaze upon your faces as you sleep. I had lingered long near the dwelling where I had been so cruelly changed to what I am, as we do while any that we love or hate remain. Vainly I had sought some method of manifestation, some way to make my continued existence and my great love and poignant pity understood by my husband and son. Always if they slept they would wake, or if in my desperation I dared approach them when they were awake, would turn toward me the terrible eyes of the living, frightening me by the glances that I sought from the purpose that I held.

On this night I had searched for them without success, fearing to find them; they were nowhere in the house, nor about the moonlit lawn. For, although the sun is lost to us forever, the moon, full-orbed or slender, remains to us. Sometimes it shines by night, sometimes by day, but always it rises and sets, as in that other life.

I left the lawn and moved in the white light and silence along the road, aimless and sorrowing. Suddenly I heard the voice of my poor husband in exclamations of astonishment, with that of my son in reassurance and dissuasion; and there by the shadow of a group of trees they stood—near, so near! Their faces were toward me, the eyes of the elder man fixed upon mine. He saw me—at last, at last, he saw me! In the consciousness of that, my terror fled as a cruel dream. The death-spell was broken: Love had conquered Law! Mad with exultation I shouted—I *must* have shouted, "He sees, he sees: he will understand!" Then, controlling myself, I moved forward, smiling and consciously beautiful, to offer myself to his arms, to comfort him with endearments, and, with my son's hand in mine, to speak words that should restore the broken bonds between the living and the dead.

Alas! alas! his face went white with fear, his eyes were as those of a hunted animal. He backed away from me, as I advanced, and at last turned and fled into the wood—whither, it is not given to me to know. To my poor boy, left doubly desolate, I have never been able to impart a sense of my presence. Soon he, too, must pass to this Life Invisible and be lost to me forever.

The House with the Brick-Kiln

E. F. Benson

THE HAMLET OF TREVOR MAJOR LIES VERY LONELY AND SEQUESTERED IN A HOLlow below the north side of the south downs that stretch westward from Lewes, and run parallel with the coast. It is a hamlet of some three or four dozen inconsiderable houses and cottages much girt about with trees, but the big Norman church and the manor house which stands a little outside the village are evidence of a more conspicuous past. This latter, except for a tenancy of rather less than three weeks, now four years ago, has stood unoccupied since the summer of 1896, and though it could be taken at a rent almost comically small, it is highly improbable that either of its last tenants, even if times were very bad, would think of passing a night in it again. For myself—I was one of the tenants—I would far prefer living in a workhouse to inhabiting those low-pitched oak-panelled rooms, and I would sooner look from my garret windows on to the squalor and grime of Whitechapel than from the diamond-shaped and leaded panes of the Manor of Trevor Major on to the boskage of its cool thickets, and the glimmering of its clear chalk-stream where the quick trout glance among the waving water-weeds and over the chalk and gravel of its sliding rapids.

It was the news of these trout that led Jack Singleton and myself to take the house for the month between mid-May and mid-June, but as I have already mentioned a short three weeks was all the time we passed there, and we had more than a week of our tenancy yet unexpired when we left the place, though on the very last afternoon we enjoyed the finest dry-fly fishing that has ever fallen to my lot. Singleton had originally seen the advertisement of the house in a Sussex paper, with the statement that there was good dry-fly fishing belonging to it, but it was with but faint hopes of the reality of the dry-fly fishing that we went down to look at the place, since we had before this so often inspected depopulated ditches which were offered to the unwary under high-sounding titles. Yet after a half-hour's stroll by the stream, we went straight back to the agent, and before nightfall had taken it for a month with option of renewal.

We arrived accordingly from town at about five o'clock on a cloudless afternoon in May, and through the mists of horror that now stand between me and the remembrance of what occurred later, I cannot forget the exquisite loveliness of the impression then conveyed. The garden, it is true, appeared to have been for years untended; weeds half-choked the gravel paths, and the flower-beds were a congestion of mingled wild and cultivated vegetations. It was set in a wall of mellowed brick, in which snap-dragon and stone-crop had found an anchorage to their liking, and beyond that there stood sentinel a ring of ancient pines in which the breeze made music as of a distant sea. Outside that the ground sloped slightly downwards in a bank covered with a jungle of wild-rose to the stream that ran round three sides of the garden, and then followed a meandering course through the two big fields which lay towards the village. Over all this we had fishing-rights; above, the same rights extended for another quarter of a mile to the arched bridge, over which there crossed the road which led to the house. In this field above the house on the fourth side, where the ground had been embanked to carry the road, stood a brick-kiln in a ruinous state. A shallow pit, long overgrown with tall grasses and wild field-flowers, showed where the clay had been digged.

The house itself was long and narrow; entering, you passed direct into a square panelled hall, on the left of which was the dining-room which communicated with the passage leading to the kitchen and offices. On the right of the hall were two excellent sitting-rooms looking out, the one on to the gravel in front of the house, the other on to the garden. From the first of these you could see, through the gap in the pines by which the road approached the house, the brick-kiln of which I have already spoken. An oak staircase went up from the hall, and round it ran a gallery on to which the three principal bedrooms opened. These were commensurate with the dining-room and the two sitting-rooms below. From this gallery there led a long narrow passage shut off from the rest of the house by a red-baize door, which led to a couple more guestrooms and the servant's quarters.

Jack Singleton and I share the same flat in town, and we had sent down in the morning Franklyn and his wife, two old and valued servants, to get things ready at Trevor Major, and procure help from the village to look after the house, and Mrs. Franklyn with her stout comfortable face all wreathed in smiles opened the door to us. She had had some previous experience of the "comfortable quarters" which go with fishing, and had come down prepared for the worst, but found it all of the best. The kitchen-boiler was not furred; hot and cold water were laid on in the most convenient fashion, and could be obtained from taps that neither stuck nor leaked. Her husband, it appeared, had gone into the village to buy a few necessaries, and she brought up tea for us, and then went upstairs to the two rooms over the dining-room and bigger sitting-room, which we had chosen for our bedrooms, to unpack. The doors of these were exactly opposite one another to right and left of the gallery, and Jack who chose the bedroom above the sitting-room had thus a smaller room, above the second sitting-room, unoccupied, next his and opening out from it.

We had a couple of hours' fishing before dinner, each of us catching three or four brace of trout, and came back in the dusk to the house. Franklyn had returned from the village from his errand, reported that he had got a woman to come in to do housework in the mornings, and mentioned that our arrival had seemed to arouse a good deal of interest. The reason for this was obscure; he could only tell us that he was questioned a dozen times as to whether we really intended to live in the house, and his assurance that we did produced silence and a shaking of heads. But the country-folk of Sussex are notable for their silence and chronic attitude of disapproval, and we put this down to local idiosyncrasy.

The evening was exquisitely warm, and after dinner we pulled out a couple of basket-chairs on to the gravel by the front door, and sat for an hour or so, while the night deepened in throbs of gathering darkness. The moon was not risen and the ring of pines cut off much of the pale starlight, so that when we went in, allured by the shining of the lamp in the sitting-room, it was curiously dark for a clear night in May. And at that moment of stepping from the darkness into the cheerfulness of the lighted house, I had a sudden sensation, to which, during the next fortnight, I became almost accustomed, of there being something unseen and unheard and dreadful near me. In spite of the warmth, I felt myself shiver, and concluded instantly that I had sat out-of-doors long enough, and without mentioning it to Jack, followed him into the smaller sitting-room in which we had scarcely yet set foot. It like the hall was oak-panelled, and in the panels hung some half-dozen of water-colour sketches, which we examined, idly at first, and then with growing interest, for they were executed with extraordinary finish and delicacy, and each represented some aspect of the house or garden. Here you looked up the gap in the fir-trees into a crimson sunset; here the garden, trim and carefully tended, dozed beneath some languid summer noon; here an angry wreath of storm-cloud brooded over the meadow where the trout-stream ran grey and leaden below a threatening sky, while another, the most careful and arresting of all, was a study of the brick-kiln. In this, alone of them all, was there a human figure; a man, dressed in grey, peered into the open door from which issued a fierce red glow. The figure was painted with miniature-like elaboration; the face was in profile, and represented a youngish man, clean-shaven with a long aquiline nose and singularly square chin. The sketch was long and narrow in shape, and the chimney of the kiln appeared against a dark sky. From it there issued a thin streamer of grey smoke.

Jack looked at this with attention.

"What a horrible picture," he said, "and how beautifully painted. I feel as if it meant something, as if it was a representation of something that happened, not a mere sketch. By Jove!—" He broke off suddenly, and went in turn to each of the other pictures.

"That's a queer thing," he said. "See if you notice what I mean."

With the brick-kiln rather vividly impressed on my mind, it was not difficult to see what he had noticed. In each of the pictures appeared the brick-kiln, chimney and all, now seen faintly between trees, now in full view, and in each the chimney was smoking.

"And the odd part is that from the garden side, you can't really see the kiln at all," observed Jack, "it's hidden by the house, and yet the artist F. A., as I see by his signature, puts it in just the same."

"What do you make of that?" I asked.

"Nothing. I suppose he had a fancy for brick-kilns. Let's have a game of picquet."

A fortnight of our three weeks passed without incident, except that again and again the curious feeling of something dreadful being close at hand was present in my mind. In a way, as I said, I got used to it, but on the other hand the feeling itself seemed to gain in poignancy. Once just at the end of the fortnight I mentioned it to Jack.

"Odd you should speak of it," he said, "because I've felt the same. When do you feel it! Do you feel it now for instance?"

"We were again sitting out after dinner, and as he spoke I felt it with far greater intensity than ever before. And at the same moment the house-door which had been closed, though probably not latched, swung gently open, letting out a shaft of light from the hall, and as gently swung to again, as if something had stealthily entered.

"Yes," I said. "I felt it then. I only feel it in the evening. It was rather bad that time."

Jack was silent a moment.

"Funny thing the door opening and shutting like that," he said.

"Let's go indoors."

We got up and I remember seeing at that moment that the windows of my bedroom were lit; Mrs. Franklyn probably was making things ready for the night. Simultaneously, as we crossed the gravel, there came from just inside the house the sound of a hurried footstep on the stairs, and entering we found Mrs. Franklyn in the hall, looking rather white and startled.

"Anything wrong?" I asked.

She took two or three quick breaths before she answered:

"No, sir," she said, "at least nothing that I can give an account of. I was tidying up in your room, and I thought you came in. But there was nobody, and it gave me a turn. I left my candle there; I must go up for it."

I waited in the hall a moment, while she again ascended the stairs, and passed along the gallery to my room. At the door, which I could see was open, she paused, not entering.

"What is the matter?" I asked from below.

"I left the candle alight," she said, "and it's gone out."

Jack laughed.

"And you left the door and window open," said he.

"Yes, sir, but not a breath of wind is stirring," said Mrs. Franklyn, rather faintly.

This was true, and yet a few moments ago the heavy hall-door had swung open and back again. Jack ran upstairs.

"We'll brave the dark together, Mrs. Franklyn," he said.

He went into my room, and I heard the sound of a match struck. Then through the open door came the light of the rekindled candle and simultaneously I heard a bell ring in the servant's quarters. In a moment came steps, and Franklyn appeared.

"What bell was that?" I asked.

"Mr. Jack's bedroom, sir," he said.

I felt there was a marked atmosphere of nerves about for which there was really no adequate cause. All that had happened of a disturbing nature was that Mrs. Franklyn had thought I had come into my bedroom, and had been startled by finding I had not. She had then left the candle in a draught, and it had been blown out. As for a bell ringing, that, even if it had happened, was a very innocuous proceeding.

"Mouse on a wire," I said. "Mr. Jack is in my room this moment lighting Mrs. Franklyn's candle for her."

Jack came down at this juncture, and we went into the sitting-room. But Franklyn apparently was not satisfied, for we heard him in the room above us, which was Jack's bedroom, moving about with his slow and rather ponderous tread. Then his steps seemed to pass into the bedroom adjoining, and we heard no more.

I remember feeling hugely sleepy that night, and went to bed earlier than usual, to pass rather a broken night with stretches of dreamless sleep interspersed with startled awakenings, in which I passed very suddenly into complete consciousness. Sometimes the house was absolutely still, and the only sound to be heard was the sighing of the night breeze outside in the pines, but sometimes the place seemed full of muffled movements, and once I could have sworn that the handle of my door turned. That required verification, and I lit my candle, but found that my ears must have played me false. Yet even as I stood there, I thought I heard steps just outside, and with a considerable qualm, I must confess, I opened the door and looked out. But the gallery was quite empty, and the house quite still. Then from Jack's room opposite I heard a sound that was somehow comforting, the snorts of the snorer, and I went back to bed and slept again, and when next I woke, morning was already breaking in red lines on the horizon, and the sense of trouble that had been with me ever since last evening had gone.

Heavy rain set in after lunch next day, and as I had arrears of letter-writing to do, and the water was soon both muddy and rising, I came home alone about five, leaving Jack still sanguine by the stream, and worked for a couple of hours sitting at a writing-table in the room overlooking the gravel at the front of the house, where hung the water-colours. By seven I had finished, and just as I got up to light candles, since it was already dusk, I saw, as I thought, Jack's figure emerge from the bushes that bordered the path to the stream, on to the space in front of the house. Then instantaneously and with a sudden queer sinking of the heart, quite unaccountable, I saw that it was not Jack at all, but a stranger. He was only some six yards from the window, and after pausing there a moment he came close up to the window, so that his face nearly touched the glass, looking intently at me. In the light from the freshly-kindled candles I could distinguish his features with great clearness, but though, as far as I knew, I had never seen him before, there was something familiar about both his face and figure. He appeared to smile at me, but the smile was one of inscrutable evil and malevolence, and immediately he walked on, straight towards the house-door opposite him, and out of sight of the sitting-room window.

Now, little though I liked the look of the man, he was, as I have said, familiar to my eye, and I went out into the hall, since he was clearly coming to the front-door, to open it to him and learn his business. So without waiting for him to ring, I opened it, feeling sure I should find him on the step. Instead, I looked out into the empty gravel-sweep, the heavy-falling rain, the thick dusk. And even as I looked, I felt something that I could not see push by me through the half-opened door and pass into the house. Then the stairs creaked, and a moment after a bell rang.

Franklyn is the quickest man to answer a bell I have ever seen, and next instant he passed me going upstairs. He tapped at Jack's door, entered, and then came down again.

"Mr. Jack still out, sir?" he asked.

"Yes. His bell ringing again?"

"Yes, sir," said Franklyn, quite imperturbably.

I went back into the sitting-room, and soon Franklyn brought a lamp. He put it on the table above which hung the careful and curious picture of the brick-kiln, and then with a sudden horror I saw why the stranger on the gravel outside had been so familiar to me. In all respects he resembled the figure that peered into the kiln; it was more than a resemblance, it was an identity. And what had happened to this man who had inscrutably and evilly smiled at me! And what had pushed in through the half-closed door?

At that moment I saw the face of Fear; my mouth went dry, and I heard my heart leaping and cracking in my throat. That face was only turned on me for a moment, and then away again, but I knew it to be the genuine thing; not apprehension, not foreboding, not a feeling of being startled, but Fear, cold Fear. And then though nothing had occurred to assuage the Fear, it passed, and a certain sort of reason usurped—for so I must say—its place. I had certainly seen somebody on the gravel outside the house; I had supposed he was going to the front-door. I had opened it, and found he had not come to the front-door. Or—and once again the terror resurged—had the invisible pushing thing been that which I had seen outside? And if so, what was it? And how came it that the face and figure of the man I had seen was the same as that which was so scrupulously painted in the picture of the brick-kiln?

I set myself to argue down the Fear for which there was no more foundation than this, this and the repetition of the ringing bell, and my belief is that I did so. I told myself, till I believed it, that a man—a human man—had been walking across the gravel outside, and that he had not come to the front-door but had gone, as he might easily have done, up the drive into the high-road. I told myself that it was mere fancy that was the cause of the belief that Something had pushed in by me, and as for the ring of the bell, I said to myself, as was true, that this had happened before. And I must ask the reader to believe also that I argued these things away, and looked no longer on the face of Fear itself. I was not comfortable, but I fell short of being terrified.

I sat down again by the window looking on to the gravel in front of the house, and finding another letter that asked, though it did not demand an answer, proceeded to occupy myself with it. Straight in front led the drive through the gap in the pines, and passed through the field where lay the brick-kiln. In a pause of page-turning I looked up and saw something unusual about it; at the same moment an unusual smell came to my nostril. What I saw was smoke coming out of the chimney of the kiln, what I smelt was the odour of roasting meat. The wind—such as there was—set from the kiln to the house. But as far as I knew the smell of roast meat probably came from the kitchen where dinner, so I supposed, was cooking. I had to tell myself this: I wanted reassurance, lest the face of Fear should look whitely on me again.

Then there came a crisp step on the gravel, a rattle at the front-door, and Jack came in.

"Good sport," he said, "you gave up too soon."

And he went straight to the table above which hung the picture of the man at the brick-kiln, and looked at it. Then there was silence; and eventually I spoke, for

THE HOUSE WITH THE BRICK-KILN

I wanted to know one thing.

"Seen anybody?" I asked.

"Yes. Why do you ask?"

"Because I have also; the man in that picture." Jack came and sat down near me.

"It's a ghost, you know," he said. "He came down to the river about dusk and stood near me for an hour. At first I thought he was—was real, and I warned him that he had better stand further off if he didn't want to be hooked. And then it struck me he wasn't real, and I cast, well, right through him, and about seven he walked up towards the house."

"Were you frightened?"

"No. It was so tremendously interesting. So you saw him here too. Whereabouts?"

"Just outside. I think he is in the house now."

Jack looked round.

"Did you see him come in?" he asked.

"No, but I felt him. There's another queer thing too; the chimney of the brick-kiln is smoking."

Jack looked out of the window. It was nearly dark but the wreathing smoke could just be seen.

"So it is," he said, "fat, greasy smoke. I think I'll go up and see what's on. Come too!"

"I think not," I said.

"Are you frightened? It isn't worth while. Besides, it is so tremendously interesting."

Jack came back from his little expedition still interested. He had found nothing stirring at the kiln, but though it was then nearly dark the interior was faintly luminous, and against the black of the sky he could see a wisp of thick white smoke floating northwards. But for the rest of the evening we neither heard nor saw anything of abnormal import, and the next day ran a course of undisturbed hours. Then suddenly a hellish activity was manifested.

That night, while I was undressing for bed, I heard a bell ring furiously, and I thought I heard a shout also. I guessed where the ring came from, since Franklyn and his wife had long ago gone to bed, and went straight to Jack's room. But as I tapped at the door I heard his voice from inside calling loud to me. "Take care," it said, "he's close to the door."

A sudden qualm of blank fear took hold of me, but mastering it as best I could, I opened the door to enter, and once again something pushed softly by me, though I saw nothing.

Jack was standing by his bed, half-undressed. I saw him wipe his forehead with the back of his hand.

"He's been here again," he said. "I was standing just here, a minute ago, when I found him close by me. He came out of the inner room, I think. Did you see what he had in his hand?"

"I saw nothing."

"It was a knife; a great long carving knife. Do you mind my sleeping on the sofa in your room to-night? I got an awful turn then. There was another thing too. All round the edge of his clothes, at his collar and at his wrists, there were little flames playing, little white licking flames."

But next day, again, we neither heard nor saw anything, nor that night did the sense of that dreadful presence in the house come to us. And then came the last day. We had been out till it was dark, and as I said, had a wonderful day among the fish. On reaching home we sat together in the sitting-room, when suddenly from overhead came a tread of feet, a violent pealing of the bell, and the moment after yell after yell as of someone in mortal agony. The thought occurred to both of us that this might be Mrs. Franklyn in terror of some fearful sight, and together we rushed up and sprang into Jack's bedroom.

The doorway into the room beyond was open, and just inside it we saw the man bending over some dark huddled object. Though the room was dark we could see him perfectly, for a light stale and impure seemed to come from him. He had again a long knife in his hand, and as we entered he was wiping it on the mass that lay at his feet. Then he took it up, and we saw what it was, a woman with head nearly severed. But it was not Mrs. Franklyn.

And then the whole thing vanished, and we were standing looking into a dark and empty room. We went downstairs without a word, and it was not till we were both in the sitting-room below that Jack spoke.

"And he takes her to the brick-kiln," he said rather unsteadily. "I say, have you had enough of this house? I have. There is hell in it."

About a week later Jack put into my hand a guidebook to Sussex open at the description of Trevor Major, and I read:

"Just outside the village stands the picturesque manor house, once the home of the artist and notorious murderer, Francis Adam. It was here he killed his wife, in a fit, it is believed, of groundless jealousy, cutting her throat and disposing of her remains by burning them in a brick-kiln. Certain charred fragments found six months afterwards led to his arrest and execution."

So I prefer to leave the house with the brick-kiln and the pictures signed F. A. to others.

The Wind in the Rose-Bush

Mary E. Wilkins Freeman

Ford Village has no railroad station, being on the other side of the river from Porter's Falls, and accessible only by the ford which gives it its name, and a ferry line.

The ferry-boat was waiting when Rebecca Flint got off the train with her bag and lunch basket. When she and her small trunk were safely embarked she sat stiff and straight and calm in the ferry-boat as it shot swiftly and smoothly across stream. There was a horse attached to a light country wagon on board, and he pawed the deck uneasily. His owner stood near, with a wary eye upon him, although he was chewing, with as dully reflective an expression as a cow. Beside Rebecca sat a woman of about her own age, who kept looking at her with furtive curiosity; her husband, short and stout and saturnine, stood near her. Rebecca paid no attention to either of them. She was tall and spare and pale, the type of a spinster, yet with rudimentary lines and expressions of matronhood. She all unconsciously held her shawl, rolled up in a canvas bag, on her left hip, as if it had been a child. She wore a settled frown of dissent at life, but it was the frown of a mother who regarded life as a froward child, rather than as an overwhelming fate.

The other woman continued staring at her; she was mildly stupid, except for an over-developed curiosity which made her at times sharp beyond belief. Her eyes glittered, red spots came on her flaccid cheeks; she kept opening her mouth to speak, making little abortive motions. Finally she could endure it no longer; she nudged Rebecca boldly.

"A pleasant day," said she.

Rebecca looked at her and nodded coldly.

"Yes, very," she assented.

"Have you come far?"

"I have come from Michigan."

"Oh!" said the woman, with awe. "It's a long way," she remarked presently.

"Yes, it is," replied Rebecca, conclusively.

Still the other woman was not daunted; there was something which she determined to know, possibly roused thereto by a vague sense of incongruity in the other's appearance. "It's a long ways to come and leave a family," she remarked with painful slyness.

"I ain't got any family to leave," returned Rebecca shortly.

"Then you ain't—"

"No, I ain't."

"Oh!" said the woman.

Rebecca looked straight ahead at the race of the river.

It was a long ferry. Finally Rebecca herself waxed unexpectedly loquacious. She turned to the other woman and inquired if she knew John Dent's widow who lived in Ford Village. "Her husband died about three years ago," said she, by way of detail.

The woman started violently. She turned pale, then she flushed; she cast a strange glance at her husband, who was regarding both women with a sort of stolid keenness.

"Yes, I guess I do," faltered the woman finally.

"Well, his first wife was my sister," said Rebecca with the air of one imparting important intelligence.

"Was she?" responded the other woman feebly. She glanced at her husband with an expression of doubt and terror, and he shook his head forbiddingly.

"I'm going to see her, and take my niece Agnes home with me," said Rebecca.

Then the woman gave such a violent start that she noticed it.

"What is the matter?" she asked.

"Nothin', I guess," replied the woman, with eyes on her husband, who was slowly shaking his head, like a Chinese toy.

"Is my niece sick?" asked Rebecca with quick suspicion.

"No, she ain't sick," replied the woman with alacrity, then she caught her breath with a gasp.

"When did you see her?"

"Let me see; I ain't seen her for some little time," replied the woman. Then she caught her breath again.

"She ought to have grown up real pretty, if she takes after my sister. She was a real pretty woman," Rebecca said wistfully.

"Yes, I guess she did grow up pretty," replied the woman in a trembling voice.

"What kind of a woman is the second wife?"

The woman glanced at her husband's warning face. She continued to gaze at him while she replied in a choking voice to Rebecca:

"I—guess she's a nice woman," she replied. "I—don't know, I—guess so. I—don't see much of her."

"I felt kind of hurt that John married again so quick," said Rebecca; "but I suppose he wanted his house kept, and Agnes wanted care. I wasn't so situated that I could take her when her mother died. I had my own mother to care for, and I was school-teaching. Now mother has gone, and my uncle died six months ago and left me quite a little property, and I've given up my school, and I've come for Agnes. I guess she'll be glad to go with me, though I suppose her stepmother is a good woman, and has always done for her."

The man's warning shake at his wife was fairly portentous.

"I guess so," said she.

"John always wrote that she was a beautiful woman," said Rebecca.

Then the ferry-boat grated on the shore.

John Dent's widow had sent a horse and wagon to meet her sister-in-law. When the woman and her husband went down the road, on which Rebecca in the wagon with her trunk soon passed them, she said reproachfully:

"Seems as if I'd ought to have told her, Thomas."

"Let her find it out herself," replied the man. "Don't you go to burnin' your fingers in other folks' puddin', Maria."

"Do you s'pose she'll see anything?" asked the woman with a spasmodic shudder and a terrified roll of her eyes.

"See!" returned her husband with stolid scorn. "Better be sure there's anything to see."

"Oh, Thomas, they say—"

"Lord, ain't you found out that what they say is mostly lies?"

"But if it should be true, and she's a nervous woman, she might be scared enough to lose her wits," said his wife, staring uneasily after Rebecca's erect figure in the wagon disappearing over the crest of the hilly road.

"Wits that so easy upset ain't worth much," declared the man. "You keep out of it, Maria."

Rebecca in the meantime rode on in the wagon, beside a flaxen-headed boy, who looked, to her understanding, not very bright. She asked him a question, and he paid no attention. She repeated it, and he responded with a bewildered and incoherent grunt. Then she let him alone, after making sure that he knew how to drive straight.

They had traveled about half a mile, passed the village square, and gone a short distance beyond, when the boy drew up with a sudden Whoa! before a very prosperous-looking house. It had been one of the aboriginal cottages of the vicinity, small and white, with a roof extending on one side over a piazza, and a tiny "L" jutting out in the rear, on the right hand. Now the cottage was transformed by dormer windows, a bay window on the piazzaless side, a carved railing down the front steps, and a modern hard-wood door.

"Is this John Dent's house?" asked Rebecca.

The boy was as sparing of speech as a philosopher. His only response was in flinging the reins over the horse's back, stretching out one foot to the shaft, and leaping out of the wagon, then going around to the rear for the trunk. Rebecca got out and went toward the house. Its white paint had a new gloss; its blinds were an immaculate apple green; the lawn was trimmed as smooth as velvet, and it was dotted with scrupulous groups of hydrangeas and cannas.

"I always understood that John Dent was well-to-do," Rebecca reflected comfortably. "I guess Agnes will have considerable. I've got enough, but it will come in handy for her schooling. She can have advantages."

The boy dragged the trunk up the fine gravel-walk, but before he reached the steps leading up to the piazza, for the house stood on a terrace, the front door opened and a fair, frizzled head of a very large and handsome woman appeared. She held up her black silk skirt, disclosing voluminous ruffles of starched embroidery, and waited for Rebecca. She smiled placidly, her pink, double-chinned face widened and dimpled, but her blue eyes were wary and calculating. She extended her hand as Rebecca climbed the steps.

"This is Miss Flint, I suppose," said she.

"Yes, ma'am," replied Rebecca, noticing with bewilderment a curious expression compounded of fear and defiance on the other's face.

"Your letter only arrived this morning," said Mrs. Dent, in a steady voice. Her great face was a uniform pink, and her china-blue eyes were at once aggressive and veiled with secrecy.

"Yes, I hardly thought you'd get my letter," replied Rebecca. "I felt as if I could not wait to hear from you before I came. I supposed you would be so situated that you could have me a little while without putting you out too much, from what John used to write me about his circumstances, and when I had that money so unexpected I felt as if I must come for Agnes. I suppose you will be willing to give her up. You know she's my own blood, and of course she's no relation to you, though you must have got attached to her. I know from her picture what a sweet girl she must be, and John always said she looked like her own mother, and Grace was a beautiful woman, if she was my sister."

Rebecca stopped and stared at the other woman in amazement and alarm. The great handsome blonde creature stood speechless, livid, gasping, with her hand to her heart, her lips parted in a horrible caricature of a smile.

THE WIND IN THE ROSE-BUSH

"Are you sick!" cried Rebecca, drawing near. "Don't you want me to get you some water!"

Then Mrs. Dent recovered herself with a great effort. "It is nothing," she said. "I am subject to—spells. I am over it now. Won't you come in, Miss Flint?"

As she spoke, the beautiful deep-rose colour suffused her face, her blue eyes met her visitor's with the opaqueness of turquoise—with a revelation of blue, but a concealment of all behind.

Rebecca followed her hostess in, and the boy, who had waited quiescently, climbed the steps with the trunk. But before they entered the door a strange thing happened. On the upper terrace close to the piazza-post, grew a great rose-bush, and on it, late in the season though it was, one small red, perfect rose.

Rebecca looked at it, and the other woman extended her hand with a quick gesture. "Don't you pick that rose!" she brusquely cried.

Rebecca drew herself up with stiff dignity.

"I ain't in the habit of picking other folks' roses without leave," said she.

As Rebecca spoke she started violently, and lost sight of her resentment, for something singular happened. Suddenly the rose-bush was agitated violently as if by a gust of wind, yet it was a remarkably still day. Not a leaf of the hydrangea standing on the terrace close to the rose trembled.

"What on earth—" began Rebecca, then she stopped with a gasp at the sight of the other woman's face. Although a face, it gave somehow the impression of a desperately clutched hand of secrecy.

"Come in!" said she in a harsh voice, which seemed to come forth from her chest with no intervention of the organs of speech. "Come into the house. I'm getting cold out here."

"What makes that rose-bush blow so when there isn't any wind?" asked Rebecca, trembling with vague horror, yet resolute.

"I don't see as it is blowing," returned the woman calmly. And as she spoke, indeed, the bush was quiet.

"It was blowing," declared Rebecca.

"It isn't now," said Mrs. Dent. "I can't try to account for everything that blows out-of-doors. I have too much to do."

She spoke scornfully and confidently, with defiant, unflinching eyes, first on the bush, then on Rebecca, and led the way into the house.

"It looked queer," persisted Rebecca, but she followed, and also the boy with the trunk.

Rebecca entered an interior, prosperous, even elegant, according to her simple ideas. There were Brussels carpets, lace curtains, and plenty of brilliant upholstery and polished wood.

"You're real nicely situated," remarked Rebecca, after she had become a little accustomed to her new surroundings and the two women were seated at the tea-table.

Mrs. Dent stared with a hard complacency from behind her silver-plated service. "Yes, I be," said she.

"You got all the things new?" said Rebecca hesitatingly, with a jealous memory of her dead sister's bridal furnishings.

"Yes," said Mrs. Dent; "I was never one to want dead folks' things, and I had money enough of my own, so I wasn't beholden to John. I had the old duds put up at auction. They didn't bring much."

"I suppose you saved some for Agnes. She'll want some of her poor mother's things when she is grown up," said Rebecca with some indignation.

The defiant stare of Mrs. Dent's blue eyes waxed more intense. "There's a few things up garret," said she.

"She'll be likely to value them," remarked Rebecca. As she spoke she glanced at the window. "Isn't it most time for her to be coming home?" she asked.

"Most time," answered Mrs. Dent carelessly; "but when she gets over to Addie Slocum's she never knows when to come home."

"Is Addie Slocum her intimate friend?"

"Intimate as any."

"Maybe we can have her come out to see Agnes when she's living with me," said Rebecca wistfully. "I suppose she'll be likely to be homesick at first."

"Most likely," answered Mrs. Dent.

"Does she call you mother?" Rebecca asked.

"No, she calls me Aunt Emeline," replied the other woman shortly. "When did you say you were going home?"

"In about a week, I thought, if she can be ready to go so soon," answered Rebecca with a surprised look.

She reflected that she would not remain a day longer than she could help after such an inhospitable look and question.

"Oh, as far as that goes," said Mrs. Dent, "it wouldn't make any difference about her being ready. You could go home whenever you felt that you must, and she could come afterward."

"Alone?"

"Why not? She's a big girl now, and you don't have to change cars."

"My niece will go home when I do, and not travel alone; and if I can't wait here for her, in the house that used to be her mother's and my sister's home, I'll go and board somewhere," returned Rebecca with warmth.

"Oh, you can stay here as long as you want to. You're welcome," said Mrs. Dent.

Then Rebecca started. "There she is!" she declared in a trembling, exultant voice. Nobody knew how she longed to see the girl.

"She isn't as late as I thought she'd be," said Mrs. Dent, and again that curious, subtle change passed over her face, and again it settled into that stony impassiveness.

Rebecca stared at the door, waiting for it to open. "Where is she?" she asked presently.

"I guess she's stopped to take off her hat in the entry," suggested Mrs. Dent.

Rebecca waited. "Why don't she come? It can't take her all this time to take off her hat."

For answer Mrs. Dent rose with a stiff jerk and threw open the door.

"Agnes!" she called. "Agnes!" Then she turned and eyed Rebecca. "She ain't there."

"I saw her pass the window," said Rebecca in bewilderment.

"You must have been mistaken."

"I know I did," persisted Rebecca.

"You couldn't have."

"I did. I saw first a shadow go over the ceiling, then I saw her in the glass there"—she pointed to a mirror over the sideboard opposite—"and then the shadow passed the window."

"How did she look in the glass?"

"Little and light-haired, with the light hair kind of tossing over her forehead."

"You couldn't have seen her."

"Was that like Agnes?"

"Like enough; but of course you didn't see her. You've been thinking so much about her that you thought you did."

"You thought *you* did."

"I thought I saw a shadow pass the window, but I must have been mistaken. She didn't come in, or we would have seen her before now. I knew it was too early for her to get home from Addie Slocum's, anyhow."

When Rebecca went to bed Agnes had not returned. Rebecca had resolved that she would not retire until the girl came, but she was very tired, and she reasoned with herself that she was foolish. Besides, Mrs. Dent suggested that Agnes might go to the church social with Addie Slocum. When Rebecca suggested that she be sent for and told that her aunt had come, Mrs. Dent laughed meaningly.

"I guess you'll find out that a young girl ain't so ready to leave a sociable, where there's boys, to see her aunt," said she.

"She's too young," said Rebecca incredulously and indignantly.

"She's sixteen," replied Mrs. Dent; "and she's always been great for the boys."

"She's going to school four years after I get her before she thinks of boys," declared Rebecca.

"We'll see," laughed the other woman.

After Rebecca went to bed, she lay awake a long time listening for the sound of girlish laughter and a boy's voice under her window; then she fell asleep.

The next morning she was down early. Mrs. Dent, who kept no servants, was busily preparing breakfast.

"Don't Agnes help you about breakfast?" asked Rebecca.

"No, I let her lay," replied Mrs. Dent shortly.

"What time did she get home last night?"

"She didn't get home."

"What?"

"She didn't get home. She stayed with Addie. She often does."

"Without sending you word?"

"Oh, she knew I wouldn't worry."

"When will she be home?"

"Oh, I guess she'll be along pretty soon."

Rebecca was uneasy, but she tried to conceal it, for she knew of no good reason for uneasiness. What was there to occasion alarm in the fact of one young girl staying overnight with another? She could not eat much breakfast. Afterward she went out on the little piazza, although her hostess strove furtively to stop her.

"Why don't you go out back of the house? It's real pretty—a view over the river," she said.

"I guess I'll go out here," replied Rebecca. She had a purpose: to watch for the absent girl.

Presently Rebecca came hustling into the house through the sitting-room, into the kitchen where Mrs. Dent was cooking.

"That rose-bush!" she gasped.

Mrs. Dent turned and faced her.

"What of it?"

"It's a-blowing."

"What of it?"

"There isn't a mite of wind this morning."

Mrs. Dent turned with an inimitable toss of her fair head. "If you think I can spend my time puzzling over such nonsense as—" she began, but Rebecca interrupted her with a cry and a rush to the door.

"There she is now!" she cried. She flung the door wide open, and curiously enough a breeze came in and her own gray hair tossed, and a paper blew off the table to the floor with a loud rustle, but there was nobody in sight.

"There's nobody here," Rebecca said.

She looked blankly at the other woman, who brought her rolling-pin down on a slab of pie-crust with a thud.

"I didn't hear anybody," she said calmly.

"*I saw somebody pass that window!*"

"You were mistaken again."

"I *know* I saw somebody."

"You couldn't have. Please shut that door."

Rebecca shut the door. She sat down beside the window and looked out on the autumnal yard, with its little curve of footpath to the kitchen door.

"What smells so strong of roses in this room?" she said presently. She sniffed hard.

"I don't smell anything but these nutmegs."

"It is not nutmeg."

"I don't smell anything else."

"Where do you suppose Agnes is?"

"Oh, perhaps she has gone over the ferry to Porter's Falls with Addie. She often does. Addie's got an aunt over there, and Addie's got a cousin, a real pretty boy."

"You suppose she's gone over there?"

"Mebbe. I shouldn't wonder."

"When should she be home?"

"Oh, not before afternoon."

Rebecca waited with all the patience she could muster. She kept reassuring herself, telling herself that it was all natural, that the other woman could not help it, but she made up her mind that if Agnes did not return that afternoon she should be sent for.

When it was four o'clock she started up with resolution. She had been furtively watching the onyx clock on the sitting-room mantel; she had timed herself. She had said that if Agnes was not home by that time she should demand that she be sent for. She rose and stood before Mrs. Dent, who looked up coolly from her embroidery.

"I've waited just as long as I'm going to," she said. "I've come 'way from Michigan to see my own sister's daughter and take her home with me. I've been here ever since yesterday—twenty-four hours—and I haven't seen her. Now I'm going to. I want her sent for."

Mrs. Dent folded her embroidery and rose.

"Well, I don't blame you," she said. "It is high time she came home. I'll go right over and get her myself."

Rebecca heaved a sigh of relief. She hardly knew what she had suspected or feared, but she knew that her position had been one of antagonism if not accusation, and she was sensible of relief.

"I wish you would," she said gratefully, and went back to her chair, while Mrs. Dent got her shawl and her little white head-tie. "I wouldn't trouble you, but I do feel as if I couldn't wait any longer to see her," she remarked apologetically.

"Oh, it ain't any trouble at all," said Mrs. Dent as she went out. "I don't blame you; you have waited long enough."

Rebecca sat at the window watching breathlessly until Mrs. Dent came stepping through the yard alone. She ran to the door and saw, hardly noticing it this time, that the rose-bush was again violently agitated, yet with no wind evident elsewhere.

"Where is she?" she cried.

Mrs. Dent laughed with stiff lips as she came up the steps over the terrace. "Girls will be girls," said she. "She's gone with Addie to Lincoln. Addie's got an uncle who's conductor on the train, and lives there, and he got 'em passes, and they're goin' to stay to Addie's Aunt Margaret's a few days. Mrs. Slocum said Agnes didn't have time to come over and ask me before the train went, but she took it on herself to say it would be all right, and—"

"Why hadn't she been over to tell you?" Rebecca was angry, though not suspicious. She even saw no reason for her anger.

"Oh, she was putting up grapes. She was coming over just as soon as she got the black off her hands. She heard I had company, and her hands were a sight. She was holding them over sulphur matches."

"You say she's going to stay a few days?" repeated Rebecca dazedly.

"Yes; till Thursday, Mrs. Slocum said."

"How far is Lincoln from here?"

"About fifty miles. It'll be a real treat to her. Mrs. Slocum's sister is a real nice woman."

"It is goin' to make it pretty late about my goin' home."

"If you don't feel as if you could wait, I'll get her ready and send her on just as soon as I can," Mrs. Dent said sweetly.

"I'm going to wait," said Rebecca grimly.

The two women sat down again, and Mrs. Dent took up her embroidery.

"Is there any sewing I can do for her?" Rebecca asked finally in a desperate way. "If I can get her sewing along some—"

Mrs. Dent arose with alacrity and fetched a mass of white from the closet. "Here," she said, "if you want to sew the lace on this nightgown. I was going to put her to it, but she'll be glad enough to get rid of it. She ought to have this and one more before she goes. I don't like to send her away without some good underclothing."

Rebecca snatched at the little white garment and sewed feverishly.

That night she wakened from a deep sleep a little after midnight and lay a minute trying to collect her faculties and explain to herself what she was listening to. At last she discovered that it was the then popular strains of "The Maiden's Prayer" floating up through the floor from the piano in the sitting-room below. She jumped up, threw a shawl over her nightgown, and hurried downstairs trembling. There was nobody in the sitting-room; the piano was silent. She ran to Mrs. Dent's bedroom and called hysterically:

"Emeline! Emeline!"

"What is it?" asked Mrs. Dent's voice from the bed. The voice was stern, but had a note of consciousness in it.

"Who—who was that playing 'The Maiden's Prayer' in the sitting-room, on the piano?"

"I didn't hear anybody."

"There was some one."

"I didn't hear anything."

"I tell you there was some one. But—*there ain't anybody there.*"

"I didn't hear anything."

"I did—somebody playing 'The Maiden's Prayer' on the piano. Has Agnes got home? *I want to know.*"

"Of course Agnes hasn't got home," answered Mrs. Dent with rising inflection. "Be you gone crazy over that girl? The last boat from Porter's Falls was in before we went to bed. Of course she ain't come."

"I heard—"

"You were dreaming."

"I wasn't; I was broad awake."

Rebecca went back to her chamber and kept her lamp burning all night.

The next morning her eyes upon Mrs. Dent were wary and blazing with suppressed excitement. She kept opening her mouth as if to speak, then frowning, and setting her lips hard. After breakfast she went upstairs, and came down presently with her coat and bonnet.

"Now, Emeline," she said, "I want to know where the Slocums live."

Mrs. Dent gave a strange, long, half-lidded glance at her. She was finishing her coffee. "Why?" she asked.

"I'm going over there and find out if they have heard anything from her daughter and Agnes since they went away. I don't like what I heard last night."

"You must have been dreaming."

"It don't make any odds whether I was or not. Does she play 'The Maiden's Prayer' on the piano? I want to know."

"What if she does? She plays it a little, I believe. I don't know. She don't half play it, anyhow; she ain't got an ear."

"That wasn't half played last night. I don't like such things happening. I ain't superstitious, but I don't like it. I'm going. Where do the Slocums live?"

"You go down the road over the bridge past the old grist mill, then you turn to the left; it's the only house for half a mile. You can't miss it. It has a barn with a ship in full sail on the cupola."

"Well, I'm going. I don't feel easy."

About two hours later Rebecca returned. There were red spots on her cheeks. She looked wild. "I've been there," she said, "and there isn't a soul at home. Something *has* happened."

"What has happened?"

"I don't know. Something. I had a warning last night. There wasn't a soul there. They've been sent for to Lincoln."

"Did you see anybody to ask?" asked Mrs. Dent with thinly concealed anxiety.

"I asked the woman that lives on the turn of the road. She's stone deaf. I suppose you know. She listened while I screamed at her to know where the Slocums were, and then she said, 'Mrs. Smith don't live here.' I didn't see anybody on the road, and that's the only house. What do you suppose it means?"

"I don't suppose it means much of anything," replied Mrs. Dent coolly. "Mr. Slocum is conductor on the railroad, and he'd be away anyway, and Mrs. Slocum often goes early when he does, to spend the day with her sister in Porter's Falls. She'd be more likely to go away than Addie."

"And you don't think anything has happened?" Rebecca asked with diminishing distrust before the reasonableness of it.

"Land, no!"

Rebecca went upstairs to lay aside her coat and bonnet. But she came hurrying back with them still on.

"Who's been in my room?" she gasped. Her face was pale as ashes.

Mrs. Dent also paled as she regarded her.

"What do you mean?" she asked slowly.

"I found when I went upstairs that—little nightgown of—Agnes's on—the bed, laid out. It was—*laid out*. The sleeves were folded across the bosom, and there was that little red rose between them. Emeline, what is it? Emeline, what's the matter? Oh!"

Mrs. Dent was struggling for breath in great, choking gasps. She clung to the back of a chair. Rebecca, trembling herself so she could scarcely keep on her feet, got her some water.

As soon as she recovered herself Mrs. Dent regarded her with eyes full of the strangest mixture of fear and horror and hostility.

"What do you mean talking so?" she said in a hard voice.

"It *is there*."

"Nonsense. You threw it down and it fell that way."

"It was folded in my bureau drawer."

"It couldn't have been."

"Who picked that red rose?"

"Look on the bush," Mrs. Dent replied shortly.

Rebecca looked at her; her mouth gaped. She hurried out of the room. When she came back her eyes seemed to protrude. (She had in the meantime hastened upstairs, and come down with tottering steps, clinging to the banisters.)

"Now I want to know what all this means?" she demanded.

"What what means?"

"The rose is on the bush, and it's gone from the bed in my room! Is this house haunted, or what?"

"I don't know anything about a house being haunted. I don't believe in such things. Be you crazy?" Mrs. Dent spoke with gathering force. The colour flashed back to her cheeks.

"No," said Rebecca shortly. "I ain't crazy yet, but I shall be if this keeps on much longer. I'm going to find out where that girl is before night."

Mrs. Dent eyed her.

"What be you going to do?"

"I'm going to Lincoln."

A faint triumphant smile overspread Mrs. Dent's large face.

"You can't," said she; "there ain't any train."

"No train?"

"No; there ain't any afternoon train from the Falls to Lincoln."

"Then I'm going over to the Slocums' again to-night."

However, Rebecca did not go; such a rain came up as deterred even her resolution, and she had only her best dresses with her. Then in the evening came the letter from the Michigan village which she had left nearly a week ago. It was from her cousin, a single woman, who had come to keep her house while she was away. It was a pleasant unexciting letter enough, all the first of it, and related mostly how she missed Rebecca; how she hoped she was having pleasant weather and kept her health; and how her friend, Mrs. Greenaway, had come to stay with her since she had felt lonesome the first night in the house; how she hoped Rebecca would have no objections to this, although nothing had been said about it, since she had not realized that she might be nervous alone. The cousin was painfully conscientious, hence the letter. Rebecca smiled in spite of her disturbed mind as she read it, then her eye caught the postscript. That was in a different hand, purporting to be written by the friend, Mrs. Hannah Greenaway, informing her that the cousin had fallen down the cellar stairs and broken her hip, and was in a dangerous condition, and begging Rebecca to return at once, as she herself was rheumatic and unable to nurse her properly, and no one else could be obtained.

Rebecca looked at Mrs. Dent, who had come to her room with the letter quite late; it was half-past nine, and she had gone upstairs for the night.

"Where did this come from?" she asked.

"Mr. Amblecrom brought it," she replied.

"Who's he?"

"The postmaster. He often brings the letters that come on the late mail. He knows I ain't anybody to send. He brought yours about your coming. He said he and his wife came over on the ferry-boat with you."

"I remember him," Rebecca replied shortly. "There's bad news in this letter."

Mrs. Dent's face took on an expression of serious inquiry.

"Yes, my Cousin Harriet has fallen down the cellar stairs—they were always dangerous—and she's broken her hip, and I've got to take the first train home to-morrow."

"You don't say so. I'm dreadfully sorry."

"No, you ain't sorry!" said Rebecca, with a look as if she leaped. "You're glad. I don't know why, but you're glad. You've wanted to get rid of me for some reason ever since I came. I don't know why. You're a strange woman. Now you've got your way, and I hope you're satisfied."

"How you talk."

Mrs. Dent spoke in a faintly injured voice, but there was a light in her eyes.

"I talk the way it is. Well, I'm going to-morrow morning, and I want you, just as soon as Agnes Dent comes home, to send her out to me. Don't you wait for anything. You pack what clothes she's got, and don't wait even to mend them, and you buy her ticket. I'll leave the money, and you send her along. She don't have to change cars. You start her off, when she gets home, on the next train!"

"Very well," replied the other woman. She had an expression of covert amusement.

"Mind you do it."

"Very well, Rebecca."

Rebecca started on her journey the next morning. When she arrived, two days later, she found her cousin in perfect health. She found, moreover, that the friend had not written the postscript in the cousin's letter. Rebecca would have returned to Ford Village the next morning, but the fatigue and nervous strain had been too much for her. She was not able to move from her bed. She had a species of low fever induced by anxiety and fatigue. But she could write, and she did, to the Slocums, and she received no answer. She also wrote to Mrs. Dent; she even sent numerous telegrams, with no response. Finally she wrote to the postmaster, and an answer arrived by the first possible mail. The letter was short, curt, and to the purpose. Mr. Amblecrom, the postmaster, was a man of few words, and especially wary as to his expressions in a letter.

> Dear madam (he wrote) your favour rec'ed. No Slocums in Ford's Village. All dead. Addie ten years ago, her mother two years later, her father five. House vacant. Mrs. John Dent said to have neglected stepdaughter. Girl was sick. Medicine not given. Talk of taking action. Not enough evidence. House said to be haunted. Strange sights and sounds. Your niece, Agnes Dent, died a year ago, about this time.
>
> Yours truly,
> THOMAS AMBLECROM

An Episode of Cathedral History

M. R. James

THERE WAS ONCE A LEARNED GENTLEMAN WHO WAS DEPUTED TO EXAMINE AND report upon the archives of the Cathedral of Southminster. The examination of these records demanded a very considerable expenditure of time: hence it became advisable for him to engage lodgings in the city: for though the Cathedral body were profuse in their offers of hospitality, Mr. Lake felt that he would prefer to be master of his day. This was recognized as reasonable. The Dean eventually wrote advising Mr. Lake, if he were not already suited, to communicate with Mr. Worby, the principal Verger, who occupied a house convenient to the church and was prepared to take in a quiet lodger for three or four weeks. Such an arrangement was precisely what Mr. Lake desired. Terms were easily agreed upon, and early in December, like another Mr. Datchery (as he remarked to himself), the investigator found himself in the occupation of a very comfortable room in an ancient and "cathedraly" house.

One so familiar with the customs of Cathedral churches, and treated with such obvious consideration by the Dean and Chapter of this Cathedral in particular, could not fail to command the respect of the Head Verger. Mr. Worby even acquiesced in certain modifications of statements he had been accustomed to offer for years to parties of visitors. Mr. Lake, on his part, found the Verger a very cheery companion, and took advantage of any occasion that presented itself for enjoying his conversation when the day's work was over.

One evening, about nine o'clock, Mr. Worby knocked at his lodger's door. "I've occasion," he said, "to go across to the Cathedral, Mr. Lake, and I think I made you a promise when I did so next I would give you the opportunity to see what it looks like at night time. It is quite fine and dry outside, if you care to come."

"To be sure I will; very much obliged to you, Mr. Worby, for thinking of it, but let me get my coat."

"Here it is, sir, and I've another lantern here that you'll find advisable for the steps, as there's no moon."

"Any one might think we were Jasper and Durdles, over again, mightn't they," said Lake, as they crossed the close, for he had ascertained that the Verger had read *Edwin Drood*.

"Well, so they might," said Mr. Worby, with a short laugh, "though I don't know whether we ought to take it as a compliment. Odd ways, I often think, they had at that Cathedral, don't it seem so to you, sir? Full choral matins at seven o'clock in the morning all the year round. Wouldn't suit our boys' voices nowadays, and I think there's one or two of the men would be applying for a rise if the Chapter was to bring it in—particular the alltoes."

They were now at the south-west door. As Mr. Worby was unlocking it, Lake said, "Did you ever find anybody locked in here by accident?"

"Twice I did. One was a drunk sailor; however he got in I don't know. I s'pose he went to sleep in the service, but by the time I got to him he was praying fit to bring the roof in. Lor'! what a noise that man did make! said it was the first time he'd been inside a church for ten years, and blest if ever he'd try it again. The other was an old sheep: them boys it was, up to their games. That was the last time they tried it on, though. There, sir now you see what we look like; our late Dean used now and again to bring parties in, but he preferred a moonlight night, and there was a piece of verse he'd coat to 'em, relating to a Scotch cathedral, I understand; but I don't know; I almost think the effect's better when it's all dark-like. Seems to add to the size and heighth. Now if you won't mind stopping somewhere in the nave while I go up into the choir where my business lays, you'll see what I mean."

Accordingly Lake waited, leaning against a pillar, and watched the light wavering along the length of the church, and up the steps into the choir, until it was intercepted by some screen or other furniture, which only allowed the reflection to be seen on the piers and roof. Not many minutes had passed before Worby reappeared at the door of the choir and by waving his lantern signalled to Lake to rejoin him.

"I suppose it *is* Worby, and not a substitute," thought Lake to himself, as he walked up the nave. There was, in fact, nothing untoward. Worby showed him the papers which he had come to fetch out of the Dean's stall, and asked him what he thought of the spectacle: Lake agreed that it was well worth seeing. "I suppose," he said, as they walked towards the altar-steps together, "that you're too much used to going about here at night to feel nervous—but you must get a start every now and then, don't you, when a book falls down or a door swings to."

"No, Mr. Lake, I can't say I think much about noises, not nowadays: I'm much more afraid of finding an escape of gas or a burst in the stove pipes than anything else. Still there have been times, years ago. Did you notice that plain altar-tomb there—fifteenth century we say it is, I don't know if you agree to that? Well, if you didn't look at it, just come back and give it a glance, if you'd be so good." It was on the north side of the choir, and rather awkwardly placed: only about three feet from the enclosing stone screen. Quite plain, as the Verger had said, but for some ordinary stone panelling. A metal cross of some size on the northern side (that next to the screen) was the solitary feature of any interest.

Lake agreed that it was not earlier than the Perpendicular period: "but," he said, "unless it's the tomb of some remarkable person, you'll forgive me for saying that I don't think it's particularly noteworthy."

"Well, I can't say as it is the tomb of anybody noted in 'istory," said Worby, who had a dry smile on his face, "for we don't own any record whatsoever of who it was put up to. For all that, if you've half an hour to spare, sir, when we get back to the house, Mr. Lake, I could tell you a tale about that tomb. I won't begin on it now; it strikes cold here, and we don't want to be dawdling about all night."

"Of course I should like to hear it immensely."

"Very well, sir, you shall. Now if I might put a question to you," he went on, as they passed down the choir aisle, "in our little local guide—and not only there, but in the little book on our Cathedral in the series—you'll find it stated that this portion of the building was erected previous to the twelfth century. Now of course I should be glad enough to take that view, but—mind the step, sir—but, I put it to you—does the lay of the stone 'ere in this portion of the wall (which he tapped with his key) does it to your eye carry the flavour of what you might call Saxon masonry? No? I thought not; no more it does to me: now, if you'll believe me, I've said as much to those men— one's the librarian of our Free Libry here, and the other came down from London on purpose—fifty times, if I have once, but I might just as well have talked to that bit of stonework. But there it is, I suppose every one's got their opinions."

The discussion of this peculiar trait of human nature occupied Mr. Worby almost up to the moment when he and Lake re-entered the former's house. The condition of the fire in Lake's sitting-room led to a suggestion from Mr. Worby that they should finish the evening in his own parlour. We find them accordingly settled there some short time afterwards.

Mr. Worby made his story a long one, and I will not undertake to tell it wholly in his own words, or in his own order. Lake committed the substance of it to paper immediately after hearing it, together with some few passages of the narrative which had fixed themselves *verbatim* in his mind; I shall probably find it expedient to condense Lake's record to some extent.

Mr. Worby was born, it appeared, about the year 1828. His father before him had been connected with the Cathedral, and likewise his grandfather. One or both had been choristers, and in later life both had done work as mason and carpenter respectively about the fabric. Worby himself, though possessed, as he frankly acknowledged, of an indifferent voice, had been drafted into the choir at about ten years of age.

It was in 1840 that the wave of the Gothic revival smote the Cathedral of Southminster. "There was a lot of lovely stuff went then, sir," said Worby, with a sigh. "My father couldn't hardly believe it when he got his orders to clear out the choir. There was a new dean just come in—Dean Burscough it was—and my father had been 'prenticed to a good firm of joiners in the city, and knew what good work was when he saw it. Crool it was, he used to say: all that beautiful wainscot oak, as good as the day it was put up, and garlands-like of foliage and fruit, and lovely old gilding work on the coats of arms and the organ pipes. All went to the timber yard—every bit except some little pieces worked up in the Lady Chapel, and 'ere in this overmantel. Well—I may be mistook, but I say our choir never looked as well since. Still there was a lot found out about the history of the church, and no doubt but what it did stand in need of repair. There were very few winters passed but what we'd lose a pinnicle." Mr. Lake expressed his concurrence with Worby's views of restoration, but owns to a fear about this point lest the story proper should never be reached. Possibly this was perceptible in his manner.

Worby hastened to reassure him, "Not but what I could carry on about that topic for hours at a time, and do do when I see my opportunity. But Dean Burscough he was very set on the Gothic period, and nothing would serve him but everything must be made agreeable to that. And one morning after service he appointed for my father to meet him in the choir, and he came back after he'd taken off his robes in the vestry, and he'd got a roll of paper with him, and the verger that was then brought in a table, and they begun spreading it out on the table with prayer books to keep it down, and my father helped 'em, and he saw it was a picture of the inside of a choir in a Cathedral; and the Dean—he was a quick spoken gentleman—he says, 'Well, Worby, what do you think of that?' 'Why,' says my father, 'I don't think I 'ave the pleasure of knowing that view. Would that be Hereford Cathedral, Mr. Dean?' 'No, Worby,' says the Dean, 'that's Southminster Cathedral as we hope to see it before many years.' 'In-deed, sir,' says my father, and that was all he did say—leastways to the Dean—but he used to tell me he felt really faint in himself when he looked round our choir as I can remember it, all comfortable and furnished-like, and then see this nasty little dry picter, as he called it, drawn out by some London architect. Well, there I am again. But you'll see what I mean if you look at this old view."

Worby reached down a framed print from the wall. "Well, the long and the short of it was that the Dean he handed over to my father a copy of an order of the Chapter that he was to clear out every bit of the choir—make a clean sweep—ready for the new work that was being designed up in town, and he was to put it in hand as soon as ever he could get the breakers together. Now then, sir, if you look at that view, you'll see where the pulpit used to stand: that's what I want you to notice, if you please." It was, indeed, easily seen; an unusually large structure of timber with a domed sounding-board, standing at the east end of the stalls on the north side of the choir, facing the bishop's throne. Worby proceeded to explain that during the alterations, services were held in the nave, the members of the choir being thereby disappointed of an anticipated holiday, and the organist in particular incurring the suspicion of having wilfully damaged the mechanism of the temporary organ that was hired at considerable expense from London.

The work of demolition began with the choir screen and organ loft, and proceeded gradually eastwards, disclosing, as Worby said, many interesting features of older work. While this was going on, the members of the Chapter were, naturally, in and about the choir a great deal, and it soon became apparent to the elder Worby—who could not help overhearing some of their talk—that, on the part of the senior Canons especially, there must have been a good deal of disagreement before the policy now being carried out had been adopted. Some were of opinion that they should catch their deaths of cold in the return-stalls, unprotected by a screen from the draughts in the nave: others objected to being exposed to the view of persons in the choir aisles, especially, they said, during the sermons, when they found it helpful to listen in a posture which was liable to misconstruction. The strongest opposition, however, came from the oldest of the body, who up to the last moment objected to the removal of the pulpit. "You ought not to touch it, Mr. Dean," he said with great emphasis one morning, when the two were standing before it: "you don't know what mischief you may do." "Mischief? it's not a work of any particular merit, Canon." "Don't call me Canon," said the old man with great asperity, "that is, for thirty years I've been known as Dr. Ayloff, and I shall be obliged, Mr. Dean, if you would kindly humour me in that matter. And as to the pulpit (which I've preached from for thirty years, though I don't insist on that) all I'll say is, I *know* you're doing wrong in moving it." "But what sense could there be, my dear Doctor, in leaving it where it is, when we're fitting up the rest of the choir in a totally different *style*? What reason could be given—apart from the look of the thing?" "Reason! reason!" said old Dr. Ayloff; "if you young men—if I may say so without any disrespect, Mr. Dean—if you'd only listen to reason a little, and not be always asking for it, we should get on better. But there, I've said my say." The old gentleman hobbled off, and as it proved, never entered the Cathedral again. The season—it was a hot summer—turned sickly on a sudden. Dr. Ayloff was one of the first to go, with some affection of the muscles of the thorax, which took him painfully at night. And at many services the number of choirmen and boys was very thin.

Meanwhile the pulpit had been done away with. In fact, the sounding-board (part of which still exists as a table in a summer-house in the palace garden) was taken down within an hour or two of Dr. Ayloff's protest. The removal of the base—not effected without considerable trouble—disclosed to view, greatly to the exultation of the restoring party, an altar-tomb—the tomb, of course, to which Worby had attracted Lake's attention that same evening. Much fruitless research was expended in attempts to identify the occupant; from that day to this he has never had a name put to him. The structure had been most carefully boxed in under the pulpit-base, so that such slight ornament as it possessed was not defaced; only on the north side of it there was what looked like an injury; a gap between two of the slabs composing the side. It might be two or three inches across. Palmer, the mason, was directed to fill it up in a week's time, when he came to do some other small jobs near that part of the choir.

The season was undoubtedly a very trying one. Whether the church was built on a site that had once been a marsh, as was suggested, or for whatever reason, the residents in its immediate neighbourhood had, many of them, but little enjoyment of the exquisite sunny days and the calm nights of August and September. To several of the older people—Dr. Ayloff, among others, as we have seen—the summer proved downright fatal, but even among the younger, few escaped either a sojourn in bed for a matter of weeks, or at the least, a brooding sense of oppression, accompanied by hateful nightmares. Gradually there formulated itself a suspicion—which grew into a conviction—that the alterations in the Cathedral had something to say in the matter. The widow of a former old verger, a pensioner of the Chapter of Southminster, was visited by dreams, which she retailed to her friends, of a shape that slipped out of the little door of the south transept as the dark fell in, and flitted—taking a fresh direction every night—about the close, disappearing for a while in house after house, and finally emerging again when the night sky was paling. She could see nothing of it, she said, but that it was a moving form: only she had an impression that when it returned to the church, as it seemed to do in the end of the dream, it turned its head: and then, she could not tell why, but she thought it had red eyes. Worby remembered hearing the old lady tell this dream at a tea-party in the house of the chapter clerk. Its recurrence might, perhaps, he said, be taken as a symptom of approaching illness; at any rate before the end of September the old lady was in her grave.

The interest excited by the restoration of this great church was not confined to its own county. One day that summer an F.S.A., of some celebrity, visited the place. His business was to write an account of the discoveries that had been made, for the Society of Antiquaries, and his wife, who accompanied him, was to make a series of illustrative drawings for his report. In the morning she employed herself in making a general sketch of the choir; in the afternoon she devoted herself to details. She first drew the newly exposed altar-tomb, and when that was finished, she called her husband's attention to a beautiful piece of diaper-ornament on the screen just behind it, which had, like the tomb itself, been completely concealed by the pulpit. Of course, he said, an illustration of that must be made; so she seated herself on the tomb and began a careful drawing which occupied her till dusk.

Her husband had by this time finished his work of measuring and description, and they agreed that it was time to be getting back to their hotel. "You may as well brush my skirt, Frank," said the lady, "it must have got covered with dust, I'm sure." He obeyed dutifully; but, after a moment, he said, "I don't know whether you value this dress particularly, my dear, but I'm inclined to think it's seen its best days. There's a great bit of it gone." "Gone? Where?" said she. "I don't know where it's gone, but it's off at the bottom edge behind here." She pulled it hastily into sight, and was horrified to find a jagged tear extending some way into the substance of the stuff; very much, she said, as if a dog had rent it away. The dress was, in any case, hopelessly spoilt, to her great vexation, and though they looked everywhere, the missing piece could not be found. There were many ways, they concluded, in which the injury might have come about, for the choir was full of old bits of woodwork with nails sticking out of them. Finally, they could only suppose that one of these had caused the mischief, and that the workmen, who had been about all day, had carried off the particular piece with the fragment of dress still attached to it.

It was about this time, Worby thought, that his little dog began to wear an anxious expression when the hour for it to be put into the shed in the back yard approached. (For his mother had ordained that it must not sleep in the house.) One evening, he said, when he was just going to pick it up and carry it out, it looked at him "like a Christian, and waved its 'and, I was going to say—well, you know 'ow they do carry on sometimes, and the end of it was I put it under my coat, and 'uddled it upstairs—and I'm afraid I as good as deceived my poor mother on the subject. After that the dog acted very artful with 'iding itself under the bed for half-an-hour or more before bed-time came, and we worked it so as my mother never found out what we'd done." Of course Worby was glad of its company anyhow, but more particularly when the nuisance that is still remembered in Southminster as "the crying" set in.

"Night after night," said Worby, "that dog seemed to know it was coming; he'd creep out, he would, and snuggle into the bed and cuddle right up to me shivering, and when the crying come he'd be like a wild thing, shoving his head under my arm, and I was fully near as bad. Six or seven times we'd hear it, not more, and when he'd dror out his 'ed again I'd know it was over for that night. What was it like, sir? Well, I never heard but one thing that seemed to hit it off. I happened to be playing about in the Close, and there was two of the Canons met and said 'Good morning' one to another. 'Sleep well last night?' says one—it was Mr. Henslow that one, and Mr. Lyall was the other—'Can't say I did,' says Mr. Lyall, 'rather too much of Isaiah 34:14 for me.' '34:14,' says Mr. Henslow, 'what's that?' 'You call yourself a Bible reader!' says Mr. Lyall. (Mr. Henslow, you must know, he was one of what used to be termed Simeon's lot—pretty much what we should call the Evangelical party.) 'You go and look it up.' I wanted to know what he was getting at myself, and so off I ran home and got out my own Bible, and there it was: 'the satyr shall cry to his fellow.' Well, I thought, is that what we've been listening to these past nights? and I tell you it made me look over my shoulder a time or two. Of course I'd asked my father and mother about what it could be before that, but they both said it was most likely cats: but they spoke very short, and I could see they was troubled. My word! that was a noise—'ungry-like, as if it was calling after some one that wouldn't come. If ever you felt you wanted company, it would be when you was waiting for it to begin again. I believe two or three nights there was men put on to watch in different parts of the Close; but they all used to get together in one corner, the nearest they could to the High Street, and nothing came of it.

"Well, the next thing was this. Me and another of the boys—he's in business in the city now as a grocer, like his father before him—we'd gone up in the Close after morning service was over, and we heard old Palmer the mason bellowing to some of his men. So we went up nearer, because we knew he was a rusty old chap and there might be some fun going. It appears Palmer'd told this man to stop up the chink in that old tomb. Well, there was this man keeping on saying he'd done it the best he could, and there was Palmer carrying on like all possessed about it. 'Call that making a job of it?' he says. 'If you had your rights you'd get the sack for this. What do you suppose I pay you your wages for? What do you suppose I'm going to say to the Dean and Chapter when they come round, as come they may do any time, and see where you've been bungling about covering the 'ole place with mess and plaster and Lord knows what?' 'Well, master, I done the best I could,' says the man; 'I don't know no more than what you do 'ow it come to fall out this way. I tamped it right in the 'ole,' he says, 'and now it's fell out,' he says, 'I never see.'

"'Fell out?' says old Palmer, 'why it's nowhere near the place. Blowed out, you mean,' and he picked up a bit of plaster, and so did I, that was laying up against the screen, three or four feet off, and not dry yet; and old Palmer he looked at it curious-like, and then he turned round on me and he says, 'Now then, you boys, have you been up to some of your games here?' 'No,' I says, 'I haven't, Mr. Palmer; there's none of us been about here till just this minute,' and while I was talking the other boy, Evans, he got looking in through the chink, and I heard him draw in his breath, and he came away sharp and up to us, and says he, 'I believe there's something in there. I saw something shiny.' 'What! I daresay,' says old Palmer; 'Well, I ain't got time to stop about there. You, William, you go off and get some more stuff and make a job of it this time; if not, there'll be trouble in my yard,' he says.

"So the man he went off, and Palmer too, and us boys stopped behind, and I says to Evans, 'Did you really see anything in there?' 'Yes,' he says, 'I did indeed.' So then I says, 'Let's shove something in and stir it up.' And we tried several of the bits of wood that was laying about, but they were all too big. Then Evans he had a sheet of music he'd brought with him, an anthem or a service, I forget which it was now, and he rolled it up small and shoved it in the chink; two or three times he did it, and nothing happened. 'Give it me, boy,' I said, and I had a try. No, nothing happened. Then, I don't know why I thought of it, I'm sure, but I stooped down just opposite the chink and put my two fingers in my mouth and whistled—you know the way—and at that I seemed to think I heard something stirring, and I says to Evans, 'Come away,' I says; 'I don't like this.' 'Oh, rot,' he says, 'Give me that roll,' and he took it and shoved it in. And I don't think ever I see any one go so pale as he did. 'I say, Worby,' he says, 'it's caught, or else some one's got hold of it.' 'Pull it out or leave it,' I says, 'Come and let's get off.' So he gave a good pull, and it came away. Leastways most of it did, but the end was gone. Torn off it was, and Evans looked at it for a second and then he gave a sort of a croak and let it drop, and we both made off out of there as quick as ever we could. When we got outside Evans says to me, 'Did you see the end of that paper.' 'No,' I says, 'only it was torn.' 'Yes, it was,' he says, 'but it was wet too, and black!' Well, partly because of the fright we had, and partly because that music was wanted in a day or two, and we knew there'd be a set-out about it with the organist, we didn't say nothing to any one else, and I suppose the workmen they swept up the bit that was left along with the rest of the rubbish. But Evans, if you were to ask him this very day about it, he'd stick to it he saw that paper wet and black at the end where it was torn."

After that the boys gave the choir a wide berth, so that Worby was not sure what was the result of the mason's renewed mending of the tomb. Only he made out from fragments of conversation dropped by the workmen passing through the choir that some difficulty had been met with, and that the governor—Mr. Palmer to wit—had tried his own hand at the job. A little later, he happened to see Mr. Palmer himself knocking at the door of the Deanery and being admitted by the butler. A day or so after that, he gathered from a remark his father let fall at breakfast that something a little out of the common was to be done in the Cathedral after morning service on the morrow. "And I'd just as soon it was to-day," his father added, "I don't see the use of running risks." "'Father,' I says, 'what are you going to do in the Cathedral to-morrow?' and he turned on me as savage as I ever see him—he was a wonderful good-tempered man as a general thing, my poor father was. 'My lad,' he says, 'I'll trouble you not to go picking up your elders' and betters' talk: it's not manners and it's not straight. What I'm going to do or not going to do in the Cathedral to-morrow is none of your business: and if I catch sight of you hanging about the place to-morrow after your work's done, I'll send you home with a flea in your ear. Now you mind that.' Of course I said I was very sorry and that, and equally of course I went off and laid my plans with Evans. We knew there was a stair up in the corner of the transept which you can get up to the triforium, and in them days the door to it was pretty well always open, and even if it wasn't we knew the key usually laid under a bit of matting hard by. So we made up our minds we'd be putting away music and that, next morning while the rest of the boys was clearing off, and then slip up the stairs and watch from the triforium if there was any signs of work going on.

"Well, that same night I dropped off asleep as sound as a boy does, and all of a sudden the dog woke me up, coming into the bed, and thought I, now we're going to get it sharp, for he seemed more frightened than usual. After about five minutes sure enough came this cry. I can't give you no idea what it was like; and so near too—nearer than I'd heard it yet—and a funny thing, Mr. Lake, you know what a place this Close is for an echo, and particular if you stand this side of it. Well, this crying never made no sign of an echo at all. But, as I said, it was dreadful near this night; and on the top of the start I got with hearing it, I got another fright; for I heard something rustling outside in the passage. Now to be sure I thought I was done; but I noticed the dog seemed to perk up a bit, and next there was some one whispered outside the door, and I very near laughed out loud, for I knew it was my father and mother that had got out of bed with the noise. 'Whatever is it?' says my mother. 'Hush! I don't know,' says my father, excited-like, 'don't disturb the boy. I hope he didn't hear nothing.'

"So, me knowing they were just outside, it made me bolder, and I slipped out of bed across to my little window—giving on the Close—but the dog he bored right down to the bottom of the bed—and I looked out. First go off I couldn't see anything.

Then right down in the shadow under a buttress I made out what I shall always say was two spots of red—a dull red it was—nothing like a lamp or a fire, but just so as you could pick 'em out of the black shadow. I hadn't but just sighted 'em when it seemed we wasn't the only people that had been disturbed, because I see a window in a house on the left-hand side become lighted up, and the light moving. I just turned my head to make sure of it, and then looked back into the shadow for those two red things, and they were gone, and for all I peered about and stared, there was not a sign more of them. Then come my last fright that night—something come against my bare leg—but that was all right: that was my little dog had come out of bed, and prancing about, making a great to-do, only holding his tongue, and me seeing he was quite in spirits again, I took him back to bed and we slept the night out!

"Next morning I made out to tell my mother I'd had the dog in my room, and I was surprised, after all she'd said about it before, how quiet she took it. 'Did you?' she says. 'Well, by good rights you ought to go without your breakfast for doing such a thing behind my back: but I don't know as there's any great harm done, only another time you ask my permission, do you hear?' A bit after that I said something to my father about having heard the cats again. '*Cats*,' he says, and he looked over at my poor mother, and she coughed and he says, 'Oh! ah! yes, cats. I believe I heard 'em myself.'

"That was a funny morning altogether: nothing seemed to go right. The organist he stopped in bed, and the minor Canon he forgot it was the 19th day and waited for the *Venite*; and after a bit the deputy he set off playing the chant for evensong, which was a minor; and then the Decani boys were laughing so much they couldn't sing, and when it came to the anthem the solo boy he got took with the giggles, and made out his nose was bleeding, and shoved the book at me what hadn't practised the verse and wasn't much of a singer if I had known it. Well, things was rougher, you see, fifty years ago, and I got a nip from the counter-tenor behind me that I remembered.

"So we got through somehow, and neither the men nor the boys weren't by way of waiting to see whether the Canon in residence—Mr. Henslow it was—would come to the vestries and fine 'em, but I don't believe he did: for one thing I fancy he'd read the wrong lesson for the first time in his life, and knew it. Anyhow Evans and me didn't find no difficulty in slipping up the stairs as I told you, and when we got up we laid ourselves down flat on our stomachs where we could just stretch our heads out over the old tomb, and we hadn't but just done so when we heard the verger that was then, first shutting the iron porch-gates and locking the south-west door, and then the transept door, so we knew there was something up, and they meant to keep the public out for a bit.

"Next thing was, the Dean and the Canon come in by their door on the north, and then I see my father, and old Palmer, and a couple of their best men, and Palmer stood a talking for a bit with the Dean in the middle of the choir. He had a coil of rope and the men had crows. All of 'em looked a bit nervous. So there they stood talking, and at last I heard the Dean say, 'Well, I've no time to waste, Palmer. If you think this'll satisfy Southminster people, I'll permit it to be done; but I must say this, that never in the whole course of my life have I heard such arrant nonsense from a practical man as I have from you. Don't you agree with me, Henslow?' As far as I could hear Mr. Henslow said something like 'Oh! well we're told, aren't we, Mr. Dean, not to judge others?' and the Dean he gave a kind of sniff, and walked straight up to the tomb, and took his stand behind it with his back to the screen, and the others they come edging up rather gingerly. Henslow, he stopped on the south side and scratched on his chin, he did. Then the Dean spoke up: 'Palmer,' he says, 'which can you do easiest, get the slab off the top, or shift one of the side slabs?'

"Old Palmer and his men they pottered about a bit looking round the edge of the top slab and sounding the sides on the south and east and west and everywhere but the north. Henslow said something about it being better to have a try at the south side, because there was more light and more room to move about in. Then my father, who'd been watching of them, went round to the north side, and knelt down and felt of the slab by the chink, and he got up and dusted his knees and says to the Dean: 'Beg pardon, Mr. Dean, but I think if Mr. Palmer'll try this here slab he'll find it'll come out easy enough. Seems to me one of the men could prize it out with his crow by means of this chink.' 'Ah! thank you, Worby,' says the Dean; 'that's a good suggestion. Palmer, let one of your men do that, will you?'

"So the man come round, and put his bar in and bore on it, and just that minute when they were all bending over, and we boys got our heads well out over the edge of the triforium, there come a most fearful crash down at the west end of the choir, as if a whole stack of big timber had fallen down a flight of stairs. Well, you can't expect me to tell you everything that happened all in a minute. Of course there was a terrible commotion. I heard the slab fall out, and the crowbar on the floor, and I heard the Dean say 'Good God!'

"When I looked down again I saw the Dean tumbled over on the floor, the men was making off down the choir, Henslow was just going to help the Dean up, Palmer was going to stop the men, as he said afterwards, and my father was sitting on the altar step with his face in his hands. The Dean he was very cross. 'I wish to goodness you'd look where you're coming to, Henslow,' he says. 'Why you should all take to your heels when a stick of wood tumbles down I cannot imagine,' and all Henslow could do, explaining he was right away on the other side of the tomb, would not satisfy him.

"Then Palmer came back and reported there was nothing to account for this noise and nothing seemingly fallen down, and when the Dean finished feeling of himself they gathered round—except my father, he sat where he was—and some one lighted up a bit of candle and they looked into the tomb. 'Nothing there,' says the Dean, 'what did I tell you? Stay! here's something. What's this: a bit of music paper, and a piece of torn stuff—part of a dress it looks like. Both quite modern—no interest whatever. Another time perhaps you'll take the advice of an educated man'—or something like that, and off he went, limping a bit, and out through the north door, only as he went he called back angry to Palmer for leaving the door standing open. Palmer called out 'Very sorry, sir,' but he shrugged his shoulders, and Henslow says, 'I fancy Mr. Dean's mistaken. I closed the door behind me, but he's a little upset.' Then Palmer says, 'Why, where's Worby?' and they saw him sitting on the step and went up to him. He was recovering himself, it seemed, and wiping his forehead, and Palmer helped him up on to his legs, as I was glad to see.

"They were too far off for me to hear what they said, but my father pointed to the north door in the aisle, and Palmer and Henslow both of them looked very surprised and scared. After a bit, my father and Henslow went out of the church, and the others made what haste they could to put the slab back and plaster it in. And about as the clock struck twelve the Cathedral was opened again and us boys made the best of our way home.

"I was in a great taking to know what it was had given my poor father such a turn, and when I got in and found him sitting in his chair taking a glass of spirits, and my mother standing looking anxious at him, I couldn't keep from bursting out and making confession where I'd been. But he didn't seem to take on, not in the way of losing his temper. 'You was there, was you? Well did you see it?' 'I see everything, father,' I said, 'except when the noise came.' 'Did you see what it was knocked the Dean over?' he says, 'that what come out of the monument? You didn't? Well, that's a mercy.' 'Why, what was it, father?' I said. 'Come, you must have seen it,' he says. '*Didn't* you see? A thing like a man, all over hair, and two great eyes to it?'

"Well, that was all I could get out of him that time, and later on he seemed as if he was ashamed of being so frightened, and he used to put me off when I asked him about it. But years after, when I was got to be a grown man, we had more talk now and again on the matter, and he always said the same thing. 'Black it was,' he'd say, 'and a mass of hair, and two legs, and the light caught on its eyes.'

"Well, that's the tale of that tomb, Mr. Lake; it's one we don't tell to our visitors, and I should be obliged to you not to make any use of it till I'm out of the way. I doubt Mr. Evans'll feel the same as I do, if you ask him."

This proved to be the case. But over twenty years have passed by, and the grass is growing over both Worby and Evans; so Mr. Lake felt no difficulty about communicating his notes—taken in 1890—to me. He accompanied them with a sketch of the tomb and a copy of the short inscription on the metal cross which was affixed at the expense of Dr. Lyall to the centre of the northern side. It was from the Vulgate of Isaiah xxxiv., and consisted merely of the three words—

IBI CUBAVIT LAMIA.

Thurnley Abbey

Perceval Landon

Three years ago I was on my way out to the East, and as an extra day in London was of some importance, I took the Friday evening mail-train to Brindisi instead of the usual Thursday morning Marseilles express. Many people shrink from the long forty-eight-hour train journey through Europe, and the subsequent rush across the Mediterranean on the nineteen-knot *Isis* or *Osiris*; but there is really very little discomfort on either the train or the mail-boat, and unless there is actually nothing for me to do, I always like to save the extra day and a half in London before I say goodbye to her for one of my longer tramps. This time—it was early, I remember, in the shipping season, probably about the beginning of September—there were few passengers, and I had a compartment in the P. & O. Indian express to myself all the way from Calais. All Sunday I watched the blue waves dimpling the Adriatic, and the pale rosemary along the cuttings; the plain white towns, with their flat roofs and their bold "duomos," and the grey-green gnarled olive orchards of Apulia. The journey was just like any other. We ate in the dining-car as often and as long as we decently could. We slept after luncheon; we dawdled the afternoon away with yellow-backed novels; sometimes we exchanged platitudes in the smoking-room, and it was there that I met Alastair Colvin.

Colvin was a man of middle height, with a resolute, well-cut jaw; his hair was turning grey; his moustache was sun-whitened, otherwise he was clean-shaven—obviously a gentleman, and obviously also a pre-occupied man. He had no great wit. When spoken to, he made the usual remarks in the right way, and I dare say he refrained from banalities only because he spoke less than the rest of us; most of the time he buried himself in the Wagonlit Company's Time-table, but seemed unable to concentrate his attention on any one page of it. He found that I had been over the Siberian railway, and for a quarter of an hour he discussed it with me. Then he lost interest in it, and rose to go to his compartment. But he came back again very soon, and seemed glad to pick up the conversation again.

Of course this did not seem to me to be of any importance. Most travellers by train become a trifle infirm of purpose after thirty-six hours' rattling. But Colvin's restless way I noticed in somewhat marked contrast with the man's personal importance and dignity; especially ill suited was it to his finely made large hand with strong, broad, regular nails and its few lines. As I looked at his hand I noticed a long, deep, and recent scar of ragged shape. However, it is absurd to pretend that I thought anything was unusual. I went off at five o'clock on Sunday afternoon to sleep away the hour or two that had still to be got through before we arrived at Brindisi.

Once there, we few passengers transhipped our hand baggage, verified our berths—there were only a score of us in all—and then, after an aimless ramble of half an hour in Brindisi, we returned to dinner at the Hôtel International, not wholly surprised that the town had been the death of Virgil. If I remember rightly, there is a gaily painted hall at the International—I do not wish to advertise anything, but there is no other place in Brindisi at which to await the coming of the mails—and after dinner I was looking with awe at a trellis overgrown with blue vines, when Colvin moved across the room to my table. He picked up *Il Secolo*, but almost immediately gave up the pretence of reading it. He turned squarely to me and said:

"Would you do me a favour?"

One doesn't do favours to stray acquaintances on Continental expresses without knowing something more of them than I knew of Colvin. But I smiled in a noncommittal way, and asked him what he wanted. I wasn't wrong in part of my estimate of him; he said bluntly:

"Will you let me sleep in your cabin on the *Osiris*?" And he coloured a little as he said it.

Now, there is nothing more tiresome than having to put up with a stable-companion at sea, and I asked him rather pointedly:

"Surely there is room for all of us?" I thought that perhaps he had been partnered off with some mangy Levantine, and wanted to escape from him at all hazards.

Colvin, still somewhat confused, said: "Yes; I am in a cabin by myself. But you would do me the greatest favour if you would allow me to share yours."

This was all very well, but, besides the fact that I always sleep better when alone, there had been some recent thefts on board English liners, and I hesitated, frank and honest and self-conscious as Colvin was. Just then the mail-train came in with a clatter and a rush of escaping steam, and I asked him to see me again about it on the boat when we started. He answered me curtly—I suppose he saw the mistrust in my manner—"I am a member of White's and the Beefsteak." I smiled to myself as he said it, but I remembered in a moment that the man—if he were really what he claimed to be, and I make no doubt that he was—must have been sorely put to it before he urged the fact as a guarantee of his respectability to a total stranger at a Brindisi hotel.

That evening, as we cleared the red and green harbour-lights of Brindisi, Colvin explained. This is his story in his own words:

"When I was travelling in India some years ago, I made the acquaintance of a youngish man in the Woods and Forests. We camped out together for a week, and I found him a pleasant companion. John Broughton was a light-hearted soul when off duty, but a steady and capable man in any of the small emergencies that continually arise in that department. He was liked and trusted by the natives, and though a trifle over-pleased with himself when he escaped to civilisation at Simla or Calcutta, Broughton's future was well assured in Government service, when a fair-sized estate was unexpectedly left to him, and he joyfully shook the dust of the Indian plains from his feet and returned to England. For five years he drifted about London. I saw him now and then. We dined together about every eighteen months, and I could trace pretty exactly the gradual sickening of Broughton with a merely idle life. He then set out on a couple of long voyages, returned as restless as before, and at last told me that he had decided to marry and settle down at his place, Thurnley Abbey, which had long been empty. He spoke about looking after the property and standing for his constituency in the usual way. Vivien Wilde, his fiancée, had, I suppose, begun to take him in hand. She was a pretty girl with a deal of fair hair and rather an exclusive manner; deeply religious in a narrow school, she was still kindly and high-spirited, and I thought that Broughton was in luck. He was quite happy and full of information about his future.

"Among other things, I asked him about Thurnley Abbey. He confessed that he hardly knew the place. The last tenant, a man called Clarke, had lived in one wing for fifteen years and seen no one. He had been a miser and a hermit. It was the rarest thing for a light to be seen at the Abbey after dark. Only the barest necessities of life were ordered, and the tenant himself received them at the side-door. His one half-caste man-servant, after a month's stay in the house, had abruptly left without warning, and had returned to the Southern States. One thing Broughton complained bitterly about: Clarke had wilfully spread the rumour among the villagers that the Abbey was haunted, and had even condescended to play childish tricks with spirit-lamps and salt in order to scare trespassers away at night. He had been detected in the act of this tomfoolery, but the story spread, and no one, said Broughton, would venture near the house except in broad daylight. The hauntedness of Thurnley Abbey was now, he said with a grin, part of the gospel of the countryside, but he and his young wife were going to change all that. Would I propose myself any time I liked? I, of course, said I would, and equally, of course, intended to do nothing of the sort without a definite invitation.

"The house was put in thorough repair, though not a stick of the old furniture and tapestry were removed. Floors and ceilings were relaid; the roof was made watertight again, and the dust of half a century was scoured out. He showed me some photographs of the place. It was called an Abbey, though as a matter of fact it had been only the infirmary of the long-vanished Abbey of Clouster some five miles away. The larger part of the building remained as it had been in pre-Reformation days, but a wing had been added in Jacobean times, and that part of the house had been kept in something like repair by Mr. Clarke. He had in both the ground and first floors set a heavy timber door, strongly barred with iron, in the passage between the earlier and the Jacobean parts of the house, and had entirely neglected the former. So there had been a good deal of work to be done.

"Broughton, whom I saw in London two or three times about this period, made a deal of fun over the positive refusal of the workmen to remain after sundown. Even after the electric light had been put into every room, nothing would induce them to remain, though, as Broughton observed, electric light was death on ghosts. The legend of the Abbey's ghosts had gone far and wide, and the men would take no risks. They went home in batches of five and six, and even during the daylight hours there was an inordinate amount of talking between one and another, if either happened to be out of sight of his companion. On the whole, though nothing of any sort or kind had been conjured up even by their heated imaginations during their five months' work upon the Abbey, the belief in the ghosts was rather strengthened than otherwise in Thurnley because of the men's confessed nervousness, and local tradition declared itself in favour of the ghost of an immured nun.

"'Good old nun!' said Broughton.

"I asked him whether in general he believed in the possibility of ghosts, and, rather to my surprise, he said that he couldn't say he entirely disbelieved in them. A man in India had told him one morning in camp that he believed that his mother was dead in England, as her vision had come to his tent the night before. He had not been alarmed, but had said nothing, and the figure vanished again. As a matter of fact, the next possible dak-walla brought on a telegram announcing the mother's death. 'There the thing was,' said Broughton.

"But at Thurnley he was practical enough. He roundly cursed the idiotic selfishness of Clarke, whose silly antics had caused all the inconvenience. At the same time, he couldn't refuse to sympathise to some extent with the ignorant workmen.

"'My own idea,' said he, 'is that if a ghost ever does come in one's way, one ought to speak to it.'

"I agreed. Little as I knew of the ghost world and its conventions, I had always remembered that a spook was in honour bound to wait to be spoken to. It didn't seem much to do, and I felt that the sound of one's own voice would at any rate reassure oneself as to one's wakefulness. But there are few ghosts outside Europe—few, that is, that a white man can see—and I had never been troubled with any. However, as I have said, I told Broughton that I agreed.

"So the wedding took place, and I went to it in a tall hat which I bought for the occasion, and the new Mrs. Broughton smiled very nicely at me afterwards. As it had to happen, I took the Orient Express that evening and was not in England again for nearly six months. Just before I came back I got a letter from Broughton. He asked if I could see him in London or come to Thurnley, as he thought I should be better able to help him than anyone else he knew. His wife sent a nice message to me at the end, so I was reassured about at least one thing. I wrote from Budapest that I would come and see him at Thurnley two days after my arrival in London, and as I sauntered out of the Pannonia into the Kerepesi Utcza to post my letters, I wondered of what earthly service I could be to Broughton. I had been out with him after tiger on foot, and I could imagine few men better able at a pinch to manage their own business. However, I had nothing to do, so after dealing with some small accumulations of business during my absence, I packed a kit-bag and departed to Euston.

"I was met by Broughton's great limousine at Thurnley Road station, and after a drive of nearly seven miles we echoed through the sleepy streets of Thurnley village, into which the main gates of the park thrust themselves, splendid with pillars and spread-eagles and tom-cats rampant atop of them. I never was a herald, but I know that the Broughtons have the right to supporters—Heaven knows why! From the gates a quadruple avenue of beech-trees led inwards for a quarter of a mile. Beneath them a neat strip of fine turf edged the road and ran back until the poison of the dead beech-leaves killed it under the trees. There were many wheel-tracks on the road, and a comfortable little pony trap jogged past me laden with a country parson and his wife and daughter. Evidently there was some garden party going on at the Abbey. The road dropped away to the right at the end of the avenue, and I could see the Abbey across a wide pasturage and a broad lawn thickly dotted with guests.

"The end of the building was plain. It must have been almost mercilessly austere when it was first built, but time had crumbled the edges and toned the stone down to an orange-lichened grey wherever it showed behind its curtain of magnolia, jasmine, and ivy. Farther on was the three-storied Jacobean house, tall and handsome. There had not been the slightest attempt to adapt the one to the other, but the kindly ivy had glossed over the touching-point. There was a tall flèche in the middle of the building, surmounting a small bell tower. Behind the house there rose the mountainous verdure of Spanish chestnuts all the way up the hill.

"Broughton had seen me coming from afar, and walked across from his other guests to welcome me before turning me over to the butler's care. This man was sandy-haired and rather inclined to be talkative. He could, however, answer hardly any questions about the house; he had, he said, only been there three weeks. Mindful of what Broughton had told me, I made no inquiries about ghosts, though the room into which I was shown might have justified anything. It was a very large low room with oak beams projecting from the white ceiling. Every inch of the walls, including the doors, was covered with tapestry, and a remarkably fine Italian fourpost bedstead, heavily draped, added to the darkness and dignity of the place. All the furniture was old, well made, and dark. Underfoot there was a plain green pile carpet, the only new thing about the room except the electric light fittings and the jugs and basins. Even the looking-glass on the dressing-table was an old pyramidal Venetian glass set in heavy repoussé frame of tarnished silver.

"After a few minutes' cleaning up, I went downstairs and out upon the lawn, where I greeted my hostess. The people gathered there were of the usual country type, all anxious to be pleased and roundly curious as to the new master of the Abbey. Rather to my surprise, and quite to my pleasure, I rediscovered Glenham, whom I had known well in old days in Barotseland: he lived quite close, as, he remarked with a grin, I ought to have known. 'But,' he added, 'I don't live in a place like this.' He swept his hand to the long, low lines of the Abbey in obvious admiration, and then, to my intense interest, muttered beneath his breath, 'Thank God!' He saw that I had overheard him, and turning to me said decidedly, 'Yes, thank God I said, and I meant I wouldn't live at the Abbey for all Broughton's money.'

"'But surely,' I demurred, 'you know that old Clarke was discovered in the very act of setting light on his bug-a-boos?'

"Glenham shrugged his shoulders. 'Yes, I know about that. But there is something wrong with the place still. All I can say is that Broughton is a different man since he has lived there. I don't believe that he will remain much longer. But—you're staying here?—Well, you'll hear all about it to-night. There's a big dinner, I understand.' The conversation turned off to old reminiscences, and Glenham soon after had to go.

"Before I went to dress that evening I had twenty minutes' talk with Broughton in his library. There was no doubt that the man was altered, gravely altered. He was nervous and fidgety, and I found him looking at me only when my eye was off him. I naturally asked him what he wanted of me. I told him I would do anything I could, but that I couldn't conceive what he lacked that I could provide. He said with a lustreless smile that there was, however, something, and that he would tell me the following morning. It struck me that he was somehow ashamed of himself, and perhaps ashamed of the part he was asking me to play. However, I dismissed the subject from my mind and went up to dress in my palatial room. As I shut the door a draught blew out the Queen of Sheba from the wall, and I noticed that the tapestries were not fastened to the wall at the bottom. I have always held very practical views about spooks, and it has often seemed to me that the slow waving in firelight of loose tapestry upon a wall would account for ninety-nine per cent. of the stories one hears. Certainly the dignified undulation of this lady with her attendants and huntsmen—one of whom was untidily cutting the throat of a fallow deer upon the very steps on which King Solomon, a grey-faced Flemish nobleman with the order of the Golden Fleece, awaited his fair visitor—gave colour to my hypothesis.

"Nothing much happened at dinner. The people were very much like those of the garden party. A young woman next me seemed anxious to know what was being read in London. As she was far more familiar than I with the most recent magazines and literary supplements, I found salvation in being myself instructed in the tendencies of modern fiction. All true art, she said, was shot through and through with melancholy. How vulgar were the attempts at wit that marked so many modern books! From the beginning of literature it had always been tragedy that embodied the highest attainment of every age. To call such works morbid merely begged the question. No thoughtful man—she looked sternly at me through the steel rim of her glasses—could fail to agree with me. Of course, as one would, I immediately and properly said that I slept with Pett Ridge and Jacobs under my pillow at night, and that if Jorrocks weren't quite so large and cornery, I would add him to the company. She hadn't read any of them, so I was saved—for a time. But I remember grimly that she said that the dearest wish of her life was to be in some awful and soul-freezing situation of horror, and I remember that she dealt hardly with the hero of Nat Paynter's vampire story, between nibbles at her brown-bread ice. She was a cheerless soul, and I couldn't help thinking that if there were many such in the neighbourhood, it was not surprising that old Glenham had been stuffed with some nonsense or other about the Abbey. Yet nothing could well have been less creepy than the glitter of silver and glass, and the subdued lights and cackle of conversation all round the dinner-table.

"After the ladies had gone I found myself talking to the rural dean. He was a thin, earnest man, who at once turned the conversation to old Clarke's buffooneries. But, he said, Mr. Broughton had introduced such a new and cheerful spirit, not only into the Abbey, but, he might say, into the whole neighbourhood, that he had great hopes that the ignorant superstitions of the past were from henceforth destined to oblivion. Thereupon his other neighbour, a portly gentleman of independent means and position, audibly remarked 'Amen,' which damped the rural dean, and we talked to partridges past, partridges present, and pheasants to come. At the other end of the table Broughton sat with a couple of his friends, red-faced hunting men. Once I noticed that they were discussing me, but I paid no attention to it at the time. I remembered it a few hours later.

"By eleven all the guests were gone, and Broughton, his wife, and I were alone together under the fine plaster ceiling of the Jacobean drawing-room. Mrs. Broughton talked about one or two of the neighbours, and then, with a smile, said that she knew I would excuse her, shook hands with me, and went off to bed. I am not very good at analysing things, but I felt that she talked a little uncomfortably and with a suspicion of effort, smiled rather conventionally, and was obviously glad to go. These things seem trifling enough to repeat, but I had throughout the faint feeling that everything was not quite square. Under the circumstances, this was enough to set me wondering what on earth the service could be that I was to render—wondering also whether the whole business were not some ill-advised jest in order to make me come down from London for a mere shooting-party.

"Broughton said little after she had gone. But he was evidently labouring to bring the conversation round to the so-called haunting of the Abbey. As soon as I saw this, of course I asked him directly about it. He then seemed at once to lose interest in the matter. There was no doubt about it: Broughton was somehow a changed man, and to my mind he had changed in no way for the better. Mrs. Broughton seemed no sufficient cause. He was clearly very fond of her, and she of him. I reminded him that he was going to tell me what I could do for him in the morning, pleaded my journey, lighted a candle, and went upstairs with him. At the end of the passage leading into the old house he grinned weakly and said, 'Mind, if you see a ghost, do talk to it; you said you would.' He stood irresolutely a moment and then turned away. At the door of his dressing-room he paused once more: 'I'm here,' he called out, 'if you should want anything. Good night,' and he shut the door.

"I went along the passage to my room, undressed, switched on a lamp beside my bed, read a few pages of *The Jungle Book*, and then, more than ready for sleep, turned the light off and went fast asleep.

*****

"Three hours later I woke up. There was not a breath of wind outside. There was not even a flicker of light from the fireplace. As I lay there, an ash tinkled slightly as it cooled, but there was hardly a gleam of the dullest red in the grate. An owl cried among the silent Spanish chestnuts on the slope outside. I idly reviewed the events of the day, hoping that I should fall off to sleep again before I reached dinner. But at the end I seemed as wakeful as ever. There was no help for it. I must read my *Jungle Book* again till I felt ready to go off, so I fumbled for the pear at the end of the cord that hung down inside the bed, and I switched on the bedside lamp. The sudden glory dazzled me for a moment. I felt under my pillow for my book with half-shut eyes. Then, growing used to the light, I happened to look down to the foot of my bed.

"I can never tell you really when happened then. Nothing I could ever confess in the most abject words could even faintly picture to you what I felt. I know that my heart stopped dead, and my throat shut automatically. In one instinctive movement I crouched back up against the head-boards of the bed, staring at the horror. The movement set my heart going again, and the sweat dripped from every pore. I am not a particularly religious man, but I had always believed that God would never allow any supernatural appearance to present itself to man in such a guise and in such circumstances that harm, either bodily or mental, could result to him. I can only tell you that at the moment both my life and my reason rocked unsteadily on their seats."

The other *Osiris* passengers had gone to bed. Only he and I remained leaning over the starboard railing, which rattled uneasily now and then under the fierce vibration of the over-engined mail-boat. Far over, there were the lights of a few fishing-smacks riding out the night, and a great rush of white combing and seething water fell out and away from us overside.

At last Colvin went on:

"Leaning over the foot of my bed, looking at me, was a figure swathed in a rotten and tattered veiling. This shroud passed over the head, but left both eyes and the right side of the face bare. It then followed the line of the arm down to where the hand grasped the bed-end. The face was not entirely that of a skull, though the eyes and the flesh of the face were totally gone. There was a thin, dry skin drawn tightly over the features, and there was some skin left on the hand. One wisp of hair crossed the forehead. It was perfectly still. I looked at it, and it looked at me, and my brains turned dry and hot in my head. I had still got the pear of the electric lamp in my hand, and I played idly with it; only I dared not turn the light out again. I shut my eyes, only to open them in a hideous terror the same second. The thing had not moved. My heart was thumping, and the sweat cooled me as it evaporated. Another cinder tinkled in the grate, and a panel creaked in the wall.

"My reason failed me. For twenty minutes, or twenty seconds, I was able to think of nothing else but this awful figure, till there came, hurtling through the empty channels of my senses, the remembrances that Broughton and his friends had discussed me furtively at dinner. The dim possibility of its being a hoax stole gratefully into my unhappy mind, and once there, one's pluck came creeping back along a thousand tiny veins. My first sensation was one of blind unreasoning thankfulness that my brain was going to stand the trial. I am not a timid man, but the best of us needs some human handle to steady him in time of extremity, and in this faint but growing hope that after all it might be only a brutal hoax, I found the fulcrum that I needed. At last I moved.

"How I managed to do it I cannot tell you, but with one spring towards the foot of the bed I got within arm's-length and struck out one fearful blow with my fist at the thing. It crumbled under it, and my hand was cut to the bone. With a sickening revulsion after my terror, I dropped half-fainting across the end of the bed. So it was merely a foul trick after all. No doubt the trick had been played many a time before: no doubt Broughton and his friends had had some large bet among themselves as to what I should do when I discovered the gruesome thing. From my state of abject terror I found myself transported into an insensate anger. I shouted curses upon Broughton. I dived rather than climbed over the bed-end of the sofa. I tore at the robed skeleton—how well the whole thing had been carried out, I thought—I broke the skull against the floor, and stamped upon its dry bones. I flung the head away under the bed, and rent the brittle bones of the trunk in pieces. I snapped the thin thigh-bones across my knee, and flung them in different directions. The shin-bones I set up against a stool and broke with my heel. I raged like a Berserker against the loathly thing, and stripped the ribs from the backbone and slung the breastbone against the cupboard. My fury increased as the work of destruction went on. I tore the frail rotten veil into twenty pieces, and the dust went up over everything, over the clean blotting-paper and the silver inkstand. At last my work was done. There was but a raffle of broken bones and strips of parchment and crumbling wool. Then, picking up a piece of the skull—it was the cheek and temple bone of the right side, I remember—I opened the door and went down the passage to Broughton's dressing-room. I remember still how my sweat-dripping pyjamas clung to me as I walked. At the door I kicked and entered.

"Broughton was in bed. He had already turned the light on and seemed shrunken and horrified. For a moment he could hardly pull himself together. Then I spoke. I don't know what I said. Only I know that from a heart full and over-full with hatred and contempt, spurred on by shame of my own recent cowardice, I let my tongue run on. He answered nothing. I was amazed at my own fluency. My hair still clung lankily to my wet temples, my hand was bleeding profusely, and I must have looked a strange sight. Broughton huddled himself up at the head of the bed just as I had. Still he made no answer, no defence. He seemed preoccupied with something besides my reproaches, and once or twice moistened his lips with his tongue. But he could say nothing though he moved his hands now and then, just as a baby who cannot speak moves its hands.

"At last the door into Mrs. Broughton's rooms opened and she came in, white and terrified. 'What is it? What is it? Oh, in God's name! what is it?' she cried again and again, and then she went up to her husband and sat on the bed in her night-dress, and the two faced me. I told her what the matter was. I spared her husband not a word for her presence there. Yet he seemed hardly to understand. I told the pair that I had spoiled their cowardly joke for them. Broughton looked up.

"'I have smashed the foul thing into a hundred pieces,' I said. Broughton licked his lips again and his mouth worked. 'By God!' I shouted, 'it would serve you right if I thrashed you within an inch of your life. I will take care that not a decent man or woman of my acquaintance ever speaks to you again. And there,' I added, throwing the broken piece of the skull upon the floor beside his bed, 'there is a souvenir for you, of your damned work to-night!'

"Broughton saw the bone, and in a moment it was his turn to frighten me. He squealed like a hare caught in a trap. He screamed and screamed till Mrs. Broughton, almost as bewildered as myself, held on to him and coaxed him like a child to be quiet. But Broughton—and as he moved I thought that ten minutes ago I perhaps looked as terribly ill as he did—thrust her from him, and scrambled out of bed on to the floor, and still screaming put out his hand to the bone. It had blood on it from my hand. He paid no attention to me whatever. In truth I said nothing. This was a new turn indeed to the horrors of the evening. He rose from the floor with the bone in his hand and stood silent. He seemed to be listening. 'Time, time, perhaps,' he muttered, and almost at the same moment fell at full length on the carpet, cutting his head against the fender. The bone flew from his hand and came to rest near the door. I picked Broughton up, haggard and broken, with blood over his face. He whispered hoarsely and quickly, 'Listen, listen!' We listened.

"After ten seconds' utter quiet, I seemed to hear something. I could not be sure, but at last there was no doubt. There was a quiet sound as one moving along the passage. Little regular steps came towards us over the hard oak flooring. Broughton moved to where his wife sat, white and speechless, on the bed, and pressed her face into his shoulder.

"Then, the last thing that I could see as he turned the light out, he fell forward with his own head pressed into the pillow of the bed. Something in their company, something in their cowardice, helped me, and I faced the open doorway of the room, which was outlined fairly clearly against the dimly lighted passage. I put out one hand and touched Mrs. Broughton's shoulder in the darkness. But at the last moment I too failed. I sank on my knees and put my face in the bed. Only, we all heard. The footsteps came to the door and there they stopped. The piece of bone was lying a yard inside the door. There was a rustle of moving stuff, and the thing was in the room. Mrs. Broughton was silent: I could hear Broughton's voice praying, muffled in the pillow: I was cursing my own cowardice. Then the steps moved out again on the oak boards of the passage, and I heard the sounds dying away. In a flash of remorse I went to the door and looked out. At the end of the corridor I thought I saw something that moved away. A moment later the passage was empty. I stood with my forehead against the jamb of the door almost physically sick.

"'You can turn the light on,' I said, and there was an answering flare. There was no bone at my feet. Mrs. Broughton had fainted. Broughton was almost useless, and it took me ten minutes to bring her to. Broughton only said one thing worth remembering. For the most part he went on muttering prayers. But I was glad afterwards to recollect that he had said that thing. He said in a colourless voice, half as a question, half as a reproach, 'You didn't speak to her.'

"We spent the remainder of the night together. Mrs. Broughton actually fell off into a kind of sleep before dawn, but she suffered so horribly in her dreams that I shook her into consciousness again. Never was dawn so long in coming. Three or four times Broughton spoke to himself. Mrs. Broughton would then just tighten her hold on his arm, but she could say nothing. As for me, I can honestly say that I grew worse as the hours passed and the light strengthened. The two violent reactions had battered down my steadiness of view, and I felt that the foundations of my life had been built upon the sand. I said nothing, and after binding up my hand with a towel, I did not move. It was better so. They helped me and I helped them, and we all three knew that our reason had gone very near to ruin that night. At last, when the light came in pretty strongly, and the birds outside were chattering and singing, we felt that we must do something. Yet we never moved. You might have thought that we should particularly dislike being found as we were by the servants: yet nothing of that kind mattered a straw, and an overpowering listlessness bound us as we sat, until Chapman, Broughton's man, actually knocked and opened the door. None of us moved. Broughton, speaking hardly and stiffly, said, 'Chapman, you can come back in five minutes.' Chapman, was a discreet man, but it would have made no difference to us if he had carried his news to the 'room' at once.

"We looked at each other and I said I must go back. I meant to wait outside till Chapman returned. I simply dared not re-enter my bedroom alone. Broughton roused himself and said that he would come with me. Mrs. Broughton agreed to remain in her own room for five minutes if the blinds were drawn up and all the doors left open.

"So Broughton and I, leaning stiffly one against the other, went down to my room. By the morning light that filtered past the blinds we could see our way, and I released the blinds. There was nothing wrong with the room from end to end, except smears of my own blood on the end of the bed, on the sofa, and on the carpet where I had torn the thing to pieces."

Colvin had finished his story. There was nothing to say. Seven bells stuttered out from the fo'c'sle, and the answering cry wailed through the darkness. I took him downstairs.

"Of course I am much better now, but it is a kindness of you to let me sleep in your cabin."

The Searcher of the End House

WILLIAM HOPE HODGSON

It was still evening, as I remember, and the four of us, Jessop, Arkwright, Taylor and I, looked disappointedly at Carnacki, where he sat silent in his great chair.

We had come in response to the usual card of invitation, which—as you know—we have come to consider as a sure prelude to a good story; and now, after telling us the short incident of the Three Straw Platters, he had lapsed into a contented silence, and the night not half gone, as I have hinted.

However, as it chanced, some pitying fate jogged Carnacki's elbow, or his memory, and he began again, in his queer level way:—

"The 'Straw Platters' business reminds me of the 'Searcher' Case, which I have sometimes thought might interest you. It was some time ago, in fact a deuce of a long time ago, that the thing happened; and my experience of what I might term 'curious' things was very small at that time.

"I was living with my mother, when it occurred, in a small house just outside of Appledorn, on the South Coast. The house was the last of a row of detached cottage-villas, each house standing in its own garden; and very dainty little places they were, very old, and most of them smothered in roses; and all with those quaint old leaded windows, and doors of genuine oak. You must try to picture them for the sake of their complete niceness.

"Now I must remind you at the beginning, that my mother and I had lived in that little house for two years; and in the whole of that time there had not been a single peculiar happening to worry us.

"And then, something happened.

"It was about two o'clock one morning, as I was finishing some letters, that I heard the door of my mother's bedroom open, and she came to the top of the stairs, and knocked on the banisters.

"'All right, dear,' I called; for I suppose she was merely reminding me that I should have been in bed long ago; then I heard her go back to her room, and I hurried my work, for fear she should lie awake, until she heard me safe up to my room.

"When I was finished, I lit my candle, put out the lamp, and went upstairs. As I came opposite the door of my mother's room, I saw that it was open, called good-night to her, very softly, and asked whether I should close the door. As there was no answer, I knew that she had dropped off to sleep again, and I closed the door very gently, and turned into my room, just across the passage. As I did so, I experienced a momentary, half-aware sense of a faint, peculiar, disagreeable odour in the passage; but it was not until the following night that I *realised* I had noticed a smell that offended me. You follow me? It is so often like that—one suddenly *knows* a thing that really recorded itself on one's consciousness, perhaps a year before.

"The next morning at breakfast, I mentioned casually to my mother that she had 'dropped-off,' and I had shut the door for her. To my surprise, she assured me she had never been out of her room. I reminded her about the two raps she had given upon the banister; but she still was certain I must be mistaken; and in the end I teased her, saying she had grown so accustomed to my bad habit of sitting up late, that she had come to call me in her sleep. Of course, she denied this, and I let the matter drop; but I was more than a little puzzled, and did not know whether to believe my own explanation, or to take the mater's, which was to put the noises down to the mice, and the open door to the fact that she couldn't have properly latched it, when she went to bed. I suppose, away in the subconscious part of me, I had a stirring of less reasonable thoughts; but certainly, I had no real uneasiness at that time.

"The next night there came a further development. About two-thirty a.m., I heard my mother's door open, just as on the previous night, and immediately afterward she rapped sharply, on the banister, as it seemed to me. I stopped my work and called up that I would not be long. As she made no reply, and I did not hear her go back to bed, I had a quick sense of wonder whether she might not be doing it in her sleep, after all, just as I had said.

"With the thought, I stood up, and taking the lamp from the table, began to go towards the door, which was open into the passage. It was then I got a sudden nasty sort of thrill; for it came to me, all at once, that my mother never knocked, when I sat up too late; she always called. You will understand I was not really frightened in any way; only vaguely uneasy, and pretty sure she must really be doing the thing in her sleep.

"I went quickly up the stairs, and when I came to the top, my mother was not there; but her door was open. I had a bewildered sense though believing she must have gone quietly back to bed, without my hearing her. I entered her room and found her sleeping quietly and naturally; for the vague sense of trouble in me was sufficiently strong to make me go over to look at her.

"When I was sure that she was perfectly right in every way, I was still a little bothered; but much more inclined to think my suspicion correct and that she had gone quietly back to bed in her sleep, without knowing what she had been doing. This was the most reasonable thing to think, as you must see.

"And then it came to me, suddenly, that vague, queer, mildewy smell in the room; and it was in that instant I became aware I had smelt the same strange, uncertain smell the night before in the passage.

"I was definitely uneasy now, and began to search my mother's room; though with no aim or clear thought of anything, except to assure myself that there was nothing in the room. All the time, you know, I never expected really to find anything; only my uneasiness had to be assured.

"In the middle of my search my mother woke up, and of course I had to explain. I told her about her door opening, and the knocks on the banister, and that I had come up and found her asleep. I said nothing about the smell, which was not very distinct; but told her that the thing happening twice had made me a bit nervous, and possibly fanciful, and I thought I would take a look round, just to feel satisfied.

"I have thought since that the reason I made no mention of the smell, was not only that I did not want to frighten my mother, for I was scarcely that myself; but because I had only a vague half-knowledge that I associated the smell with fancies too indefinite and peculiar to bear talking about. You will understand that I am able now to analyse and put the thing into words; but then I did not even know my chief reason for saying nothing; let alone appreciate its possible significance.

"It was my mother, after all, who put part of my vague sensations into words:—

"'What a disagreeable smell!' she exclaimed, and was silent a moment, looking at me. Then:— 'You feel there's something wrong?' still looking at me, very quietly but with a little, nervous note of questioning expectancy.

"'I don't know,' I said. 'I can't understand it, unless you've really been walking about in your sleep.'

"'The smell,' she said.

"'Yes,' I replied. 'That's what puzzles me too. I'll take a walk through the house; but I don't suppose it's anything.'

"I lit her candle, and taking the lamp, I went through the other bedrooms, and afterwards all over the house, including the three underground cellars, which was a little trying to the nerves, seeing that I was more nervous than I would admit.

"Then I went back to my mother, and told her there was really nothing to bother about; and, you know, in the end, we talked ourselves into believing it was nothing.

My mother would not agree that she might have been sleep-walking; but she was ready to put the door opening down to the fault of the latch, which certainly snicked very lightly. As for the knocks, they might be the old warped woodwork of the house cracking a bit, or a mouse rattling a piece of loose plaster. The smell was more difficult to explain; but finally we agreed that it might easily be the queer night-smell of the moist earth, coming in through the open window of my mother's room, from the back garden, or — for that matter — from the little churchyard beyond the big wall at the bottom of the garden.

"And so we quietened down, and finally I went to bed, and to sleep.

"I think this is certainly a lesson on the way we humans can delude ourselves; for there was not one of these explanations that my reason could really accept. Try to imagine yourself in the same circumstances, and you will see how absurd our attempts to explain the happenings really were.

"In the morning, when I came down to breakfast, we talked it all over again, and whilst we agreed that it was strange, we also agreed that we had begun to imagine funny things in the backs of our minds, which now we felt half ashamed to admit. This is very strange when you come to look into it; but very human.

"And then that night again my mother's door was slammed once more just after midnight. I caught up the lamp, and when I reached her door, I found it shut. I opened it quickly, and went in, to find my mother lying with her eyes open, and rather nervous; having been waked by the bang of the door. But what upset me more than anything, was the fact that there was a disgusting smell in the passage and in her room.

"Whilst I was asking her whether she was all right, a door slammed twice downstairs; and you can imagine how it made me feel. My mother and I looked at one another; and then I lit her candle, and taking the poker from the fender, went downstairs with the lamp, beginning to feel really nervous. The culminative effect of so many queer happenings was getting hold of me; and all the apparently reasonable explanations seemed futile.

"The horrible smell seemed to be very strong in the downstairs passage; also in the front room and the cellars; but chiefly in the passage. I made a very thorough search of the house, and when I had finished, I knew that all the lower windows and doors were properly shut and fastened, and that there was no living thing in the house, beyond our two selves. Then I went up to my mother's room again, and we talked the thing over for an hour or more, and in the end came to the conclusion that we might, after all, be reading too much into a number of little things; but, you know, inside of us, we did not believe this.

"Later, when we had talked ourselves into a more comfortable state of mind, I said good night, and went off to bed; and presently managed to get to sleep.

"In the early hours of the morning, whilst it was still dark, I was waked by a loud noise. I sat up in bed, and listened. And from downstairs, I heard:—bang, bang, bang, one door after another being slammed; at least, that is the impression the sounds gave to me.

"I jumped out of bed, with the tingle and shiver of sudden fright on me; and at the same moment, as I lit my candle, my door was pushed slowly open; I had left it unlatched, so as not to feel that my mother was quite shut off from me.

"'Who's there?' I shouted out, in a voice twice as deep as my natural one, and with a queer breathlessness, that sudden fright so often gives one. 'Who's there?'

"Then I heard my mother saying:—

"'It's me, Thomas. Whatever is happening downstairs?'

"She was in the room by this, and I saw she had her bedroom poker in one hand, and her candle in the other. I could have smiled at her, had it not been for the extraordinary sounds downstairs.

"I got into my slippers, and reached down an old sword-bayonet from the wall; then I picked up my candle, and begged my mother not to come; but I knew it would be little use, if she had made up her mind; and she had, with the result that she acted as a sort of rearguard for me, during our search. I know, in some ways, I was very glad to have her with me, as you will understand.

"By this time, the door-slamming had ceased, and there seemed, probably because of the contrast, to be an appalling silence in the house. However, I led the way, holding my candle high, and keeping the sword-bayonet very handy. Downstairs we found all the doors wide open; although the outer doors and the windows were closed all right. I began to wonder whether the noises had been made by the doors after all. Of one thing only were we sure, and that was, there was no living thing in the house, beside ourselves, while everywhere throughout the house, there was the taint of that disgusting odour.

"Of course it was absurd to try to make-believe any longer. There was something strange about the house; and as soon as it was daylight, I set my mother to packing; and soon after breakfast, I saw her off by train.

"Then I set to work to try to clear up the mystery. I went first to the landlord, and told him all the circumstances. From him, I found that twelve or fifteen years back, the house had got rather a curious name from three or four tenants; with the result that it had remained empty a long while; in the end he had let it at a low rent to a Captain Tobias, on the one condition that he should hold his tongue, if he saw anything peculiar. The landlord's idea—as he told me frankly—was to free the house from these tales of 'something queer,' by keeping a tenant in it, and then to sell it for the best price he could get.

"However, when Captain Tobias left, after a ten years' tenancy, there was no longer any talk about the house; so when I offered to take it on a five years' lease, he had jumped at the offer. This was the whole story; so he gave me to understand. When I pressed him for details of the supposed peculiar happenings in the house, all those years back, he said the tenants had talked about a woman who always moved about the house at night. Some tenants never saw anything; but others would not stay out the first month's tenancy.

"One thing the landlord was particular to point out, that no tenant had ever complained about knockings, or door slamming. As for the smell, he seemed positively indignant about it; but why, I don't suppose he knew himself, except that he probably had some vague feeling that it was an indirect accusation on my part that the drains were not right.

"In the end, I suggested that he should come down and spend the night with me. He agreed at once, especially as I told him I intended to keep the whole business quiet, and try to get to the bottom of the curious affair; for he was anxious to keep the rumour of the haunting from getting about.

"About three o'clock that afternoon, he came down, and we made a thorough search of the house, which, however, revealed nothing unusual. Afterwards, the landlord made one or two tests, which showed him the drainage was in perfect order; after that we made our preparations for sitting up all night.

"First, we borrowed two policemen's dark lanterns from the station near by, and where the superintendent and I were friendly; and as soon as it was really dusk, the landlord went up to his house for his gun. I had the sword-bayonet I have told you about; and when the landlord got back, we sat talking in my study until nearly midnight.

"Then we lit the lanterns and went upstairs. We placed the lanterns, gun and bayonet handy on the table; then I shut and sealed the bedroom doors; afterwards we took our seats, and turned off the lights.

"From then, until two o'clock, nothing happened; but a little after two, as I found by holding my watch near the faint glow of the closed lanterns, I had a time of extraordinary nervousness; and I bent towards the landlord, and whispered to him that I had a queer feeling something was about to happen, and to be ready with his lantern; at the same time I reached out towards mine. In the very instant I made this movement, the darkness which filled the passage seemed to become suddenly of a dull violet colour; not, as if a light had been shone; but as if the natural blackness of the night had changed colour. And then, coming through this violet night, through this violet-coloured gloom, came a little naked Child, running. In an extraordinary way, the Child seemed not to be distinct from the surrounding gloom; but almost as if it were a concentration of that extraordinary atmosphere; as if that gloomy colour which had changed the night, came from the Child. It seems impossible to make clear to you; but try to understand it.

"The Child went past me, running, with the natural movement of the legs of a chubby human child, but in an absolute and inconceivable silence. It was a very small Child, and must have passed under the table; but I saw the Child through the table, as if it had been only a slightly darker shadow than the coloured gloom. In the same instant, I saw that a fluctuating glimmer of violet light outlined the metal of the gun-barrels and the blade of the sword-bayonet, making them seem like faint shapes of glimmering light, floating unsupported where the table-top should have shown solid.

"Now, curiously, as I saw these things, I was subconsciously aware that I heard the anxious breathing of the landlord, quite clear and laboured, close to my elbow, where he waited nervously with his hands on the lantern. I realised in that moment that he saw nothing; but waited in the darkness, for my warning to come true.

"Even as I took heed of these minor things, I saw the Child jump to one side, and hide behind some half-seen object, that was certainly nothing belonging to the passage. I stared, intently, with a most extraordinary thrill of expectant wonder, with fright making goose-flesh of my back. And even as I stared, I solved for myself the less important problem of what the two black clouds were that hung over a part of the table. I think it very curious and interesting, the double working of the mind, often so much more apparent during times of stress. The two clouds came from two faintly shining shapes, which I knew must be the metal of the lanterns; and the things that looked black to the sight with which I was then seeing, could be nothing else but what to normal human sight is known as light. This phenomenon I have always remembered. I have twice seen a somewhat similar thing; in the Dark Light Case and in that trouble of Maaetheson's, which you know about.

"Even as I understood this matter of the lights, I was looking to my left, to understand why the Child was hiding. And suddenly, I heard the landlord shout out:— 'The Woman!' But I saw nothing. I had a disagreeable sense that something repugnant was near to me, and I was aware in the same moment that the landlord was gripping my arm in a hard, frightened grip. Then I was looking back to where the Child had hidden. I saw the Child peeping out from behind its hiding-place, seeming to be looking up the passage;

but whether in fear I could not tell. Then it came out, and ran headlong away, through the place where should have been the wall of my mother's bedroom; but the Sense with which I was seeing these things, showed me the wall only as a vague, upright shadow, unsubstantial. And immediately the child was lost to me, in the dull violet gloom. At the same time, I felt the landlord press back against me, as if something had passed close to him; and he called out again, a hoarse sort of cry:—'The Woman! The Woman!' and turned the shade clumsily from off his lantern. But I had seen no Woman; and the passage showed empty, as he shone the beam of his light jerkily to and fro; but chiefly in the direction of the doorway of my mother's room.

"He was still clutching my arm, and had risen to his feet; and now, mechanically and almost slowly, I picked up my lantern and turned on the light. I shone it, a little dazedly, at the seals upon the doors; but none were broken; then I sent the light to and fro, up and down the passage; but there was nothing; and I turned to the landlord, who was saying something in a rather incoherent fashion. As my light passed over his face, I noted, in a dull sort of way, that he was drenched with sweat.

"Then my wits became more handleable, and I began to catch the drift of his words:—'Did you see her? Did you see her?' he was saying, over and over again; and then I found myself telling him, in quite a level voice, that I had not seen any Woman. He became more coherent then, and I found that he had seen a Woman come from the end of the passage, and go past us; but he could not describe her, except that she kept stopping and looking about her, and had even peered at the wall, close beside him, as if looking for something. But what seemed to trouble him most, was that she had not seemed to see him at all. He repeated this so often, that in the end I told him, in an absurb sort of way, that he ought to be very glad she had not. What did it all mean? was the question; somehow I was not so frightened, as utterly bewildered. I had seen less then, than since; but what I had seen, had made me feel adrift from my anchorage of Reason.

"What did it mean? He had seen a Woman, searching for something. I had not seen this Woman. *I* had seen a Child, running away, and hiding from Something or Someone. *He* had not seen the Child, or the other things—only the Woman. And *I* had not seen her. What did it all mean?

"I had said nothing to the landlord about the Child. I had been too bewildered, and I realised that it would be futile to attempt an explanation. He was already stupid with the thing he had seen; and not the kind of man to understand. All this went through my mind as we stood there, shining the lanterns to and fro. All the time, intermingled with a streak of practical reasoning, I was questioning myself, what did it all mean? What was the Woman searching for; what was the Child running from?

"Suddenly, as I stood there, bewildered and nervous, making random answers to the landlord, a door below was violently slammed, and directly I caught the horrible reek of which I have told you.

"'There!' I said to the landlord, and caught his arm, in my turn. 'The Smell! Do you smell it?'

"He looked at me so stupidly that in a sort of nervous anger, I shook him.

"'Yes,' he said, in a queer voice, trying to shine the light from his shaking lantern at the stair-head.

"'Come on!' I said, and picked up my bayonet; and he came, carrying his gun awkwardly. I think he came, more because he was afraid to be left alone, than because he had any pluck left, poor beggar. I never sneer at that kind of funk, at least very seldom; for when it takes hold of you, it makes rags of your courage.

"I led the way downstairs, shining my light into the lower passage, and afterwards at the doors to see whether they were shut; for I had closed and latched them, placing a corner of a mat against each door, so I should know which had been opened.

"I saw at once that none of the doors had been opened; then I threw the beam of my light down alongside the stairway, in order to see the mat I had placed against the door at the top of the cellar stairs. I got a horrid thrill; for the mat was flat! I paused a couple of seconds, shining my light to and fro in the passage, and holding fast to my courage, I went down the stairs.

"As I came to the bottom step, I saw patches of wet all up and down the passage. I shone my lantern on them. It was the imprint of a wet foot on the oilcloth of the passage; not an ordinary footprint, but a queer, soft, flabby, spreading imprint, that gave me a feeling of extraordinary horror.

"Backward and forward I flashed the light over the impossible marks and saw them everwhere. Suddenly I noticed that they led to each of the closed doors. I felt something touch my back, and glanced round swiftly, to find the landlord had come close to me, almost pressing against me, in his fear.

"'It's all right,' I said, but in a rather breathless whisper, meaning to put a little courage into him; for I could feel that he was shaking through all his body. Even then as I tried to get him steadied enough be of some use, his gun went off with a tremendous bang. He jumped, and yelled with sheer terror; and I swore because of the shock.

"'Give it to me for God's sake!' I said, and slipped the gun from his hand; and in the same instant there was a sound of running steps up the garden path, and immediately the flash of a bull's-eye lantern upon the fan-light over the front door. Then the door was tried, and directly afterwards there came a thunderous knocking, which told me a policeman had heard the shot.

"I went to the door, and opened it. Fortunately the constable knew me, and when I had beckoned him in, I was able to explain matters in a very short time. While doing this, Inspector Johnstone came up the path, having missed the officer, and seeing lights and the open door. I told him as briefly as possible what had occurred, and did not mention the Child or the Woman; for it would have seem too fantastic for him to notice. I showed him the queer, wet footprints and how they went towards the closed doors. I explained quickly about the mats, and how that the one against the cellar door was flat, which showed the door had been opened.

"The inspector nodded, and told the constable to guard the door at the top of the cellar stairs. He then asked the hall lamp to be lit, after which he took the policeman's lantern, and led the way into the front room. He paused with the door wide open, and threw the light all round; then he jumped into the room, and looked behind the door; there was no one there; but all over the polished oak floor, between the scattered rugs, went the marks of those horrible spreading footprints; and the room permeated with the horrible odour.

"The inspector searched the room carefully, and then went into the middle room, using the same precautions. There was nothing in the middle room, or in the kitchen or pantry; but everywhere went the wet footmarks through all the rooms, showing plainly wherever there were woodwork or oilcloth; and always there was the smell.

"The inspector ceased from his search of the rooms, and spent a minute in trying whether the mats would really fall flat when the doors were open, or merely ruckle up in a way as to appear they had been untouched; but in each case, the mats fell flat, and remained so.

"'Extraordinary!' I heard Johnstone mutter to himself. And then he went towards the cellar door. He had inquired at first whether there were windows to the cellar, and when he learned there was no way out, except by the door, he had left this part of the search to the last.

"As Johnstone came up to the door, the policeman made a motion of salute, and said something in a low voice; and something in the tone made me flick my light across him. I saw then that the man was very white, and he looked strange and bewildered.

"'What?' said Johnstone impatiently. 'Speak up!'

"'A woman come along 'ere, sir, and went throught this 'ere door,' said the constable, clearly, but with a curious monotonous intonation that is sometimes heard from an unintelligent man.

"'Speak up!' shouted the inspector.

"'A woman come along and went through this 'ere door,' repeated the man, monotonously.

"The inspector caught the man by the shoulder, and deliberately sniffed his breath.

"'No!' he said. And then sarcastically:—'I hope you held the door open politely for the lady.'

"'The door weren't opened, sir,' said the man, simply.

"'Are you mad—' began Johnstone.

"'No,' broke in the landlord's voice from the back. Speaking steadily enough. 'I saw the Woman upstairs.' It was evident that he had got back his control again.

"'I'm afraid, Inspector Johnstone,' I said, 'that there's more in this than you think. I certainly saw some very extraordinary things upstairs.'

"The inspector seemed about to say something; but instead, he turned again to the door, and flashed his light down and round about the mat. I saw then that the strange, horrible footmarks came straight up to the cellar door; and the last print showed under the door; yet the policeman said the door had not been opened.

"And suddenly, without any intention, or realisation of what I was saying, I asked the landlord:—

"'What were the feet like?'

"I received no answer; for the inspector was ordering the constable to open the cellar door, and the man was not obeying. Johnstone repeated the order, and at last, in a queer automatic way, the man obeyed, and pushed the door open. The loathsome smell beat up at us, in a great wave of horror, and the inspector came backward a step.

"'My God!' he said, and went forward again, and shone his light down the steps; but there was nothing visible, only that on each step showed the unnatural footprints.

"The inspector brought the beam of the light vividly on the top step; and there, clear in the light, there was something small, moving. The inspector bent to look, and the policeman and I with him. I don't want to disgust you; but the thing we looked at was a maggot. The policeman backed suddenly out of the doorway:

"'The churchyard,' he said, '... at the back of the 'ouse.'

"'Silence!' said Johnstone, with a queer break in the word, and I knew that at last he was frightened. He put his lantern into the doorway, and shone it from step to step, following the footprints down into the darkness; then he stepped back from the open doorway, and we all gave back with him. He looked round, and I had a feeling that he was looking for a weapon of some kind.

"'Your gun,' I said to the landlord, and he brought it from the front hall, and passed it over to the inspector, who took it and ejected the empty shell from the right barrel. He held out his hand for a live cartridge, which the landlord brought from his pocket. He loaded the gun and snapped the breech. He turned to the constable:—

"'Come on,' he said, and moved towards the cellar doorway.

"'I ain't comin', sir,' said the policeman, very white in the face.

"With a sudden blaze of passion, the inspector took the man by the scruff and hove him bodily down into the darkness, and he went downward, screaming. The inspector followed him instantly, with his lantern and the gun; and I after the inspector, with the bayonet ready. Behind me, I heard the landlord.

"At the bottom of the stairs, the inspector was helping the policeman to his feet, where he stood swaying a moment, in a bewildered fashion; then the inspector went into the front cellar, and his man followed him in stupid fashion; but evidently no longer with any thought of running away from the horror.

"We all crowded into the front cellar, flashing our lights to and fro. Inspector Johnstone was examining the floor, and I saw that the footmarks went all round the cellar, into all the corners, and across the floor. I thought suddenly of the Child that was running away from Something. Do you see the thing that I was seeing vaguely?

"We went out of the cellar in a body, for there was nothing to be found. In the next cellar, the footprints went everywhere in that queer erratic fashion, as of someone searching for something, or following some blind scent.

"In the third cellar the prints ended at the shallow well that had been the old water-supply of the house. The well was full to the brim, and the water so clear that the pebbly bottom was plainly to be seen, as we shone the lights into the water. The search came to an abrupt end, and we stood about the well, looking at one another, in an absolute, horrible silence.

"Johnstone made another examination of the footprints; then he shone his light again into the clear shallow water, searching each inch of the plainly seen bottom; but there was nothing there. The cellar was full of the dreadful smell; and everyone stood silent, except for the constant turning of the lamps to and fro around the cellar.

"The inspector looked up from his search of the well, and nodded quietly across at me, with his sudden acknowledgment that our belief was now his belief, the smell in the cellar seemed to grow more dreadful, and to be, as it were, a menace—the material expression that some monstrous thing was there with us, invisible.

"'I think—' began the inspector, and shone his light towards the stairway; and at this the constable's restraint went utterly, and he ran for the stairs, making a queer sound in his throat.

"The landlord followed, at a quick walk, and then the inspector and I. He waited a single instant for me, and we went up together, treading on the same steps, and with our lights held backwards. At the top, I slammed and locked the stair door, and wiped my forehead, and my hands were shaking.

"The inspector asked me to give his man a glass of whisky, and then he sent him on his beat. He stayed a short while with the landlord and me, and it was arranged that he would join us again the following night and watch the Well with us from midnight until daylight. Then he left us, just as the dawn was coming in. The landlord and I locked up the house, and went over to his place for a sleep.

"In the afternoon, the landlord and I returned to the house, to make arrangements for the night. He was very quiet, and I felt he was to be relied on, now that he had been 'salted,' as it were, with his fright of the previous night.

"We opened all the doors and windows, and blew the house through very thoroughly; and in the meanwhile, we lit the lamps in the house, and took them into the cellars, where we set them all about, so as to have light everywhere. Then we carried down three chairs and a table, and set them in the cellar where the well was sunk. After that, we stretched thin piano wire across the cellar, about nine inches from the floor, at such a height that it should catch anything moving about in the dark.

"When this was done, I went through the house with the landlord, and sealed every window and door in the place, excepting only the front door and the door at the top of the cellar stairs.

"Meanwhile, a local wire-smith was making something to my order; and when the landlord and I had finished tea at his house, we went down to see how the smith was getting on. We found the thing complete. It looked rather like a huge parrot's cage, without any bottom, of very heavy gage wire, and stood about seven feet high and was four feet in diameter. Fortunately, I remembered to have it made longitudinally in two halves, or else we should never have got it through the doorways and down the cellar stairs.

"I told the wire-smith to bring the cage up to the house so he could fit the two halves rigidly together. As we returned, I called in at an iron-monger's, where I bought some thin hemp rope and an iron rack-pulley, like those used in Lancashire for hauling up the ceiling clothes-racks, which you will find in every cottage. I bought also a couple of pitchforks.

"'We shan't want to touch it,' I said to the landlord; and he nodded, rather white all at once.

"As soon as the cage arrived and had been fitted together in the cellar, I sent away the smith; and the landlord and I suspended it over the well, into which it fitted easily. After a lot of trouble, we managed to hang it so perfectly central from the rope over the iron pulley, that when hoisted to the ceiling and dropped, it went every time plunk into the well, like a candle-extinguisher. When we had it finally arranged, I hoisted it up once more, to the ready position, and made the rope fast to a heavy wooden pillar, which stood in the middle of the cellar.

"By ten o'clock, I had everything arranged, with the two pitchforks and the two police-lanterns; also some whisky and sandwiches. Underneath the table I had several buckets full of disinfectant.

"A little after eleven o'clock, there was a knock at the front door, and when I went, I found Inspector Johnstone had arrived, and brought with him one of his plain-clothes men. You will understand how pleased I was to see there would be this addition to our watch; for he looked a tough, nerveless man, brainy and collected; and one I should have picked to help us with the horrible job I felt pretty sure we should have to do that night.

"When the inspector and the detective had entered, I shut and locked the front door; then, while the inspector held the light, I sealed the door carefully, with tape and wax. At the head of the cellar stairs, I shut and locked that door also, and sealed it in the same way.

"As we entered the cellar, I warned Johnstone and his man to be careful not to fall over the wires; and then, as I saw his surprise at my arrangements, I began to explain my ideas and intentions, to all of which he listened with strong approval. I was pleased to see also that the detective was nodding his head, as I talked, in a way that showed he appreciated all my precautions.

"As he put his lantern down, the inspector picked up one of the pitchforks, and balanced it in his hand; he looked at me, and nodded.

"'The best thing,' he said. 'I only wish you'd got two more.'

"Then we all took our seats, the detective getting a washing-stool from the corner of the cellar. From then, until a quarter to twelve, we talked quietly, whilst we made a light supper of whisky and sandwiches; after which, we cleared everything off the table, excepting the lanterns and the pitchforks. One of the latter, I handed to the inspector; the other I took myself, and then, having set my chair so as to be handy to the rope which lowered the cage into the well, I went round the cellar and put out every lamp.

"I groped my way to my chair, and arranged the pitchfork and the dark lantern ready to my hand; after which I suggested that everyone should keep an absolute silence throughout the watch. I asked, also, that no lantern should be turned on, until I gave the word.

"I put my watch on the table, where a faint glow from my lantern made me able to see the time. For an hour nothing happened, and everyone kept an absolute silence, except for an occasional uneasy movement.

"About half-past one, however, I was conscious again of the same extraordinary and peculiar nervousness, which I had felt on the previous night. I put my hand out quickly, and eased the hitched rope from around the pillar. The inspector seemed aware of the movement; for I saw the faint light from his lantern, move a little, as if he had suddenly taken hold of it, in readiness.

"A minute later, I noticed there was a change in the colour of the night in the cellar, and it grew slowly violet-tinted upon my eyes. I glanced to and fro, quickly, in the new darkness, and even as I looked, I was conscious that the violet colour deepened. In the direction of the well, but seeming to be at a great distance, there was, as it were, a nucleus to the change; and the nucleus came swiftly toward us, appearing to come from a great space, almost in a single moment. It came near, and I saw again that it was a little naked Child, running, and seeming to be *of* the violet night in which it ran.

"The Child came with a natural running movement, exactly as I described it before; but in a silence so peculiarly intense, that it was as if it brought the silence with it. About half-way between the well and the table, the Child turned swiftly, and looked back at something invisible to me; and suddenly it went down into a crouching attitude, and seemed to be hiding behind something that showed vaguely; but there was nothing there, except the bare floor of the cellar; nothing, I mean, of our world.

"I could hear the breathing of the three other men, with a wonderful distinctness; and also the tick of my watch upon the table seemed to sound as loud and as slow as the tick of an old grandfather's clock. Someway I knew that none of the others saw what I was seeing.

"Abruptly, the landlord, who was next to me, let out his breath with a little hissing sound; I knew then that something was visible to him. There came a creak from the table, and I had a feeling that the inspector was leaning forward, looking at something that I could not see. The landlord reached out his hand through the darkness, and fumbled a moment to catch my arm:—

"'The Woman!' he whispered, close to my ear. 'Over by the well.'

"I stared hard in that direction; but saw nothing, except that the violet colour of the cellar seemed a little duller just there.

"I looked back quickly to the vague place where the Child was hiding. I saw it was peering back from its hiding-place. Suddenly it rose and ran straight for the middle of the table, which showed only as vague shadow half-way between my eyes and the unseen floor. As the Child ran under the table, the steel prongs of my pitchfork glimmered with a violet, fluctuating light. A little way off, there showed high up in the gloom, the vaguely shining outline of the other fork, so I knew the inspector had it raised in his hand, ready. There was no doubt but that he saw something. On the table, the metal of the five lanterns shone with the same strange glow; and about each lantern there was a little cloud of absolute blackness, where the phenomenon that is light to our natural eyes, came through the fittings; and in this complete darkness, the metal of each lantern showed plain, as might a cat's-eye in a nest of black cotton wool.

"Just beyond the table, the Child paused again, and stood, seeming to oscillate a little upon its feet, which gave the impression that it was lighter and vaguer than a thistle-down; and yet, in the same moment, another part of me seemed to know that it was to me, as something that might be beyond thick, invisible glass, and subject to conditions and forces that I was unable to comprehend.

"The Child was looking back again, and my gaze went the same way. I stared across the cellar, and saw the cage hanging clear in the violet light, every wire and tie outlined with its glimmering; above it there was a little space of gloom, and then the dull shining of the iron pulley which I had screwed into the ceiling.

"I stared in a bewildered way round the cellar; there were thin lines of vague fire crossing the floor in all directions; and suddenly I remembered the piano wire that the landlord and I had stretched. But there was nothing else to be seen, except that near the table there were indistinct glimmerings of light, and at the far end the ouline of a dull-glowing revolver, evidently in the detective's pocket. I remember a sort of subconscious satisfaction, as I settled the point in a queer automatic fashion. On the table, near to me, there was a little shapeless collection of the light; and this I knew, after an instant's consideration, to be the steel portions of my watch.

"I had looked several times at the Child, and round at the cellar, whilst I was decided these trifles; and had found it still in that attitude of hiding from something. But now, suddenly, it ran clear away into the distance, and was nothing more than a slightly deeper coloured nucleus far away in the strange coloured atmosphere.

"The landlord gave out a queer little cry, and twisted over against me, as if to avoid something. From the inspector there came a sharp breathing sound, as if he had been suddenly drenched with cold water. Then suddenly the violet colour went out of the night, and I was conscious of the nearness of something monstrous and repugnant.

"There was a tense silence, and the blackness of the cellar seemed absolute, with only the faint glow about each of the lanterns on the table. Then, in the darkness and the silence, there came a faint tinkle of water from the well, as if something were rising noiselessly out of it, and the water running back with a gentle tinkling. In the same instant, there came to me a sudden waft of the awful smell.

"I gave a sharp cry of warning to the inspector, and loosed the rope. There came instantly the sharp splash of the cage entering the water; and then, with a stiff, frightened movement, I opened the shutter of my lantern, and shone the light at the cage, shouting to the others to do the same.

"As my light struck the cage, I saw that about two feet of it projected from the top of the well, and there was something protruding up out of the water, into the cage. I stared, with a feeling that I recognised the thing; and then, as the other lanterns were opened, I saw that it was a leg of mutton. The thing was held by a brawny fist and arm, that rose out of the water. I stood utterly bewildered, watching to see what was coming. In a moment there rose into view a great bearded face, that I felt for one quick instant was the face of a drowned man, long dead. Then the face opened at the mouth part, and spluttered and coughed. Another big hand came into view, and wiped the water from the eyes, which blinked rapidly, and then fixed themselves into a stare at the lights.

"From the detective there came a sudden shout:—

"'Captain Tobias!' he shouted, and the inspector echoed him; and instantly burst into loud roars of laughter.

"The inspector and the detective ran across the cellar to the cage; and I followed, still bewildered. The man in the cage was holding the leg of mutton as far away from him, as possible, and holding his nose.

"'Lift thig dam trap, quig!' he shouted in a stifled voice; but the inspector and the detective simply doubled before him, and tried to hold their noses, whilst they laughed, and the light from their lanterns went dancing all over the place.

"'Quig! quig!' said the man in the cage, still holding his nose, and trying to speak plainly.

"Then Johnstone and the detective stopped laughing, and lifted the cage. The man in the well threw the leg across the cellar, and turned swiftly to go down into the well; but the officers were too quick for him, and had him out in a twinkling. Whilst they held him, dripping upon the floor, the inspector jerked his thumb in the direction of the offending leg, and the landlord, having harpooned it with one of the pitchforks, ran with it upstairs and so into the open air.

"Meanwhile, I had given the man from the well a stiff tot of whisky; for which he thanked me with a cheerful nod, and having emptied the glass at a draught, held his hand for the bottle, which he finished, as if it had been so much water.

"As you will remember, it was a Captain Tobias who had been the previous tenant; and this was the very man, who had appeared from the well. In the course of the talk that followed, I learned the reason for Captain Tobias leaving the house; he had been wanted by the police for smuggling. He had undergone imprisonment; and had been released only a couple of weeks earlier.

"He had returned to find new tenants in his old home. He had entered the house through the well, the walls of which were not continued to the bottom (this I will deal with later); and gone up by a little stairway in the cellar wall, which opened at the top through a panel beside my mother's bedroom. This panel was opened, by revolving the left doorpost of the bedroom door, with the result that the bedroom door always became unlatched, in the process of opening the panel.

"The captain complained, without any bitterness, that the panel had warped, and that each time he opened it, it made a cracking noise. This had been evidently what I mistook for raps. He would not give his reason for entering the house; but it was pretty obvious that he had hidden something, which he wanted to get. However, as he found it impossible to get into the house, without the risk of being caught, he decided to try to drive us out, relying on the bad reputation of the house, and his own artistic efforts as a ghost. I must say he succeeded. He intended then to rent the house again, as before; and would then, of course have plenty of time to get whatever he had hidden. The house suited him admirably; for there was a passage—as he showed me afterwards—connecting the dummy well with the crypt of the church beyond the garden wall; and these, in turn, were connected with certain caves in the cliffs, which went down to the beach beyond the church.

"In the course of his talk, Captain Tobias offered to take the house off my hands; and as this suited me perfectly, for I was about stalled with it, and the plan also suited the landlord, it was decided that no steps should be taken against him; and that the whole business should be hushed up.

"I asked the captain whether there was really anything queer about the house; whether he had ever seen anything. He said yes, that he had twice seen a Woman going about the house. We all looked at one another, when the captain said that. He told us she never bothered him, and that he had only seen her twice, and on each occasion it had followed a narrow escape from the Revenue people.

"Captain Tobias was an observant man; he had seen how I had placed the mats against the doors; and after entering the rooms, and walking all about them, so as to leave the foot-marks of an old pair of wet woollen slippers everywhere, he had deliberately put the mats back as he found them.

"The maggot which had dropped from his disgusting leg of mutton had been an accident, and beyond even his horrible planning. He was hugely delighted to learn how it had affected us.

"The mouldy smell I had noticed was from the little closed stairway, when the captain opened the panel. The door slamming was also another of his contributions.

"I come now to the end of the captain's ghost-play; and to the difficulty of trying to explain the other peculiar things. In the first place, it was obvious there was something genuinely strange in the house; which made itself manifest as a Woman. Many different people had seen this Woman, under differing circumstances, so it is impossible to put the thing down to fancy; at the same time it must seem extraordinary that I should have lived two years in the house, and seen nothing; whilst the policeman saw the Woman, before he had been there twenty minutes; the landlord, the detective, and the inspector all saw her.

"I can only surmise that fear was in every case the key, as I might say, which opened the senses to the presence of the Woman. The policeman was a highly-strung man, and when he became frightened, was able to see the Woman. The same reasoning applies all round. I saw nothing, until I became really frightened; then I saw, not the Woman; but a Child, running away from Something or Someone. However, I will touch on that later. In short, until a very strong degree of fear was present, no one was affected by the Force which made Itself evident, as a Woman. My theory explains why some tenants were never aware of anything strange in the house, whilst others left immediately. The more sensitive they were, the less would be the degree of fear necessary to make them aware of the Force present in the house.

"The peculiar shining of all the metal objects in the cellar, had been visible only to me. The cause, naturally I do not know; neither do I know why I, alone, was able to see the shining."

"The Child," I asked. "Can you explain that part at all? Why you didn't see the Woman, and why they didn't see the Child. Was it merely the same Force, appearing differently to different people?"

"No," said Carnacki, "I can't explain that. But I am quite sure that the Woman and the Child were not only two complete and different entities; but even they were each not in quite the same planes of existence.

"To give you a root-idea, however, it is held in the Sigsand MS. that a child 'still-born' is 'Snatyched back bye thee Haggs.' This is crude; but may yet contain an elemental truth. Yet, before I make this clearer, let me tell you a thought that has often been made. It may be that physical birth is but a secondary process; and that prior to the possibility, the Mother-Spirit searches for, until it finds, the small Element—the primal Ego or child's soul. It may be that a certain waywardness would cause such to strive to evade capture by the Mother-Spirit. It may have been such a thing as this, that I saw. I have always tried to think so; but it is impossible to ignore the sense of repulsion that I felt when the unseen Woman went past me. This repulsion carries forward the idea suggested in the Sigsand MS., that a still-born child is thus, because its ego or spirit has been snatched back by the 'Hags.' In other words, by certain of the Monstrosities of the Outer Circle. The thought is inconceivably terrible, and probably the more so because it is so fragmentary. It leaves us with the conception of a child's soul adrift half-way between two lives, and running through Eternity from Something incredible and inconceivable (because not understood) to our senses.

"The thing is beyond further discussion; for it is futile to attempt to discuss a thing, to any purpose, of which one has a knowledge so fragmentary as this. There is one thought, which is often mine. Perhaps there is a Mother Spirit—"

"And the well?" said Arkwright. "How did the captain get in from the other side?"

"As I said before," answered Carnacki. "The side walls of the well did not reach to the bottom; so that you had only to dip down into the water, and come up again on the other side of the wall, under the cellar floor, and so climb into the passage. Of course, the water was the same height on both sides of the walls. Don't ask me who made the well-entrance or the little stairway; for I don't know. The house was very old, as I have told you; and that sort of thing was useful in the old days."

"And the Child," I said, coming back to the thing which chiefly interested me. "You would say that the birth must have occurred in that house; and in this way, one might suppose that the house to have become *en rapport*, if I can use the word in that way, with the Forces that produced the tragedy?"

"Yes," replied Carnacki. "This is, supposing we take the suggestion of the Sigsand MS., to account for the phenomenon."

"There may be other houses—I began.

"There are," said Carnacki; and stood up.

"Out you go," he said, genially, using the recognised formula. And in five minutes we were on the Embankment, going thoughtfully to our various homes.

The Shadowy Third

Ellen Glasgow

When the call came I remember that I turned from the telephone in a romantic flutter. Though I had spoken only once to the great surgeon, Roland Maradick, I felt on that December afternoon that to speak to him only once—to watch him in the operating-room for a single hour—was an adventure which drained the color and the excitement from the rest of life. After all these years of work on typhoid and pneumonia cases, I can still feel the delicious tremor of my young pulses; I can still see the winter sunshine slanting through the hospital windows over the white uniforms of the nurses.

"He didn't mention me by name. Can there be a mistake?" I stood, incredulous yet ecstatic, before the superintendent of the hospital.

"No, there isn't a mistake. I was talking to him before you came down." Miss Hemphill's strong face softened while she looked at me. She was a big, resolute woman, a distant Canadian relative of my mother's, and the kind of nurse, I had discovered in the month since I had come up from Richmond, that Northern hospital boards, if not Northern patients, appear instinctively to select. From the first, in spite of her hardness, she had taken a liking—I hesitate to use the word "fancy" for a preference so impersonal—to her Virginia cousin. After all, it isn't every Southern nurse, just out of training, who can boast a kinswoman in the superintendent of a New York hospital. If experience was what I needed, Miss Hemphill, I judged, was abundantly prepared to supply it.

"And he made you understand positively that he meant me?" The thing was so wonderful that I simply couldn't believe it.

"He asked particularly for the nurse who was with Miss Hudson last week when he operated. I think he didn't even remember that you had a name—this isn't the South, you know, where people still regard nurses as human, not as automata. When I asked if he meant Miss Randolph, he repeated that he wanted the nurse who had been with Miss Hudson. She was small, he said, and cheerful-looking. This, of course, might apply to one or two others, but none of these was with Miss Hudson. Miss Maupin, the only nurse, except you, who went near her, is large and heavy."

"Then I suppose it is really true?" My pulses were tingling. "And I am to be there at six o'clock?"

"Not a minute later. The day nurse goes off duty at that hour, and Mrs. Maradick is never left by herself for an instant."

"It is her mind, isn't it? And that makes it all the stranger that he should select me, for I have had so few mental cases."

"So few cases of any kind." Miss Hemphill was smiling, and when she smiled I wondered if the other nurses would know her. "By the time you have gone through the treadmill in New York, Margaret, you will have lost a good many things besides your inexperience. I wonder how long you will keep your sympathy and your imagination? After all, wouldn't you have made a better novelist than a nurse?"

"I can't help putting myself into my cases. I suppose one ought not to?"

"It isn't a question of what one ought to do, but of what one must. When you are drained of every bit of sympathy and enthusiasm and have got nothing in return for it, not even thanks, you will understand why I try to keep you from wasting yourself."

"But surely in a case like this—for Doctor Maradick?"

"Oh, well, of course—for Doctor Maradick?" She must have seen that I implored her confidence, for, after a minute, she let fall almost carelessly a gleam of light on the situation. "It is a very sad case when you think what a charming man and a great surgeon Doctor Maradick is."

Above the starched collar of my uniform I felt the blood leap in bounds to my cheeks. "I have spoken to him only once," I murmured, "but he is charming, and, oh, so kind and handsome, isn't he?"

"His patients adore him."

"Oh, yes, I've seen that. Every one hangs on his visits." Like the patients and the other nurses, I, also, had come by delightful, if imperceptible, degrees to hang on the daily visits of Doctor Maradick. He was, I suppose, born to be a hero to women. Fate had selected him for the role, and it would have been sheer impertinence for a mortal to cross wills with the invisible Powers. From my first day in his hospital, from the moment when I watched, through closed shutters, while he stepped out of his car, I have never doubted that he was assigned to the great part in the play. If I had been ignorant of his spell—of the charm he exercised over his hospital—I should have felt it in the waiting hush, like a drawn breath, which followed his ring at the door and preceded his imperious footstep on the stairs. My first impression of him, even after the terrible events of the next year, records a memory that is both careless and splendid. At that moment, when, gazing through the chinks in the shutters, I watched him, in his coat of dark fur, cross the pavement over the pale streaks of sunshine, I knew beyond any doubt—I knew with a sort of infallible prescience—that my fate was irretrievably bound with his in the future. I knew this, I repeat, though Miss Hemphill would still insist that my foreknowledge was merely a sentimental gleaning from indiscriminate novels. But it wasn't only first love, impressionable as my kinswoman believed me to be. It wasn't only the way he looked, handsome as he was. Even more than his appearance—more than the shining dark of his eyes, the silvery brown of his hair, the dusky glow in his face—even more than his charm and his magnificence, I think, the beauty and sympathy in his voice won my heart. It was a voice, I heard some one say afterward, that ought always to speak poetry.

So you will see why—if you do not understand at the beginning, I can never hope to make you believe impossible things!—so you will see why I accepted the call when it came as an imperative summons. I couldn't have stayed away after he sent for me. However much I may have tried not to go, I know that in the end I must have gone. In those days, while I was still hoping to write novels, I used to talk a great deal about "destiny" (I have learned since then how silly all such talk is), and I suppose it was my "destiny" to be caught in the web of Roland Maradick's personality. But I am not the first nurse to grow love-sick about a doctor who never gave her a thought.

"I am glad you got the call, Margaret. It may mean a great deal to you. Only try not to be too emotional about it." I remember that Miss Hemphill was holding a bit of rose-geranium in her hand while she spoke—one of the patients had given it to her from a pot she kept in her room, and the scent of the flower is still in my nostrils—or my memory. Since then—oh, long since then—I have wondered if she also had been caught in the web.

"I wish I knew more about the case." I was clearly pressing for light. "Have you ever seen Mrs. Maradick?"

"Oh, dear, yes. They have been married only a little over a year, and in the beginning she used to come sometimes to the hospital and wait outside while the doctor made his visits. She was a very sweet-looking woman then—not exactly pretty, but fair and slight, with the loveliest smile, I think, I have ever seen. In those first months she was so much in love that we used to laugh about it among ourselves. To see her face light up when the doctor came out of the hospital and crossed the pavement to his car, was as good as a play. We never got tired watching her—I wasn't superintendent then, so I had more time to look out of the window while I was on day duty. Once or twice she brought her little girl in to see one of the patients. The child was so much like her that you would have known them anywhere for mother and daughter."

I had heard that Mrs. Maradick was a widow, with one child, when she first met the doctor, and I asked now, still seeking an illumination I had not found: "There was a great deal of money, wasn't there?"

"A great fortune. If she hadn't been so attractive, people would have said, I suppose, that Doctor Maradick married her for her money. Only," she appeared to make an effort of memory, "I believe I've heard somehow that it was all left in trust away from Mrs. Maradick if she married again. I can't, to save my life, remember just how it was; but it was a queer will, I know, and Mrs. Maradick wasn't to come into the money unless the child didn't live to grow up. The pity of it—"

A young nurse came into the office to ask for something—the keys, I think, of the operating-room, and Miss Hemphill broke off inconclusively as she hurried out of the door. I was sorry that she left off just when she did. Poor Mrs. Maradick! Perhaps I was too emotional, but even before I saw her I had begun to feel her pathos and her strangeness.

My preparations took only a few minutes. In those days I always kept a suitcase packed and ready for sudden calls; and it was not yet six o'clock when I turned from 10th Street into Fifth Avenue, and stopped for a minute, before ascending the steps, to look at the house in which Doctor Maradick lived. A fine rain was falling, and I remember thinking, as I turned the corner, how depressing the weather must be for Mrs. Maradick. It was an old house, with damp-looking walls (though that may have been because of the rain) and a spindle-shaped iron railing which ran up the stone steps to the black door, where I noticed a dim flicker through the old-fashioned fan-light. Afterward I discovered that Mrs. Maradick had been born in the house—her maiden name was Calloran—and that she had never wanted to live anywhere else. She was a woman—this I found out when I knew her better—of strong attachments to both persons and places; and though Doctor Maradick had tried to persuade her to move up-town after her marriage, she had clung, against his wishes, to the old house in lower Fifth Avenue. I dare say she was obstinate about it in spite of her gentleness and her passion for the doctor. Those sweet, soft women, especially when they have always been rich, are sometimes amazingly obstinate. I have nursed so many of them since—women with strong affections and weak intellects—that I have come to recognize the type as soon as I set eyes upon it.

My ring at the bell was answered after a little delay, and when I entered the house I saw that the hall was quite dark except for the waning glow from an open fire which burned in the library. When I gave my name, and added that I was the night nurse, the servant appeared to think my humble presence unworthy of illumination. He was an old negro butler, inherited perhaps from Mrs. Maradick's mother, who, I learned afterward, had been from South Carolina; and while he passed me on his way up the staircase, I heard him vaguely muttering that he "wan't gwinter tu'n on dem lights twel de chile had done playin'."

To the right of the hall, the soft glow drew me into the library, and crossing the threshold timidly I stooped to dry my wet coat by the fire. As I bent there, meaning to start up at the first sound of a footstep, I thought how cosy the room was after the damp walls outside to which some bared creepers were clinging; and I was watching pleasantly the strange shapes and patterns the firelight made on the old Persian rug, when the lamps of a slowly turning motor flashed on me through the white shades at the window. Still dazzled by the glare, I looked round in the dimness and saw a child's ball of red and blue rubber roll toward me out of the gloom of one of the adjoining rooms. A moment later, while I made a vain attempt to capture the toy as it spun past me, a little girl darted airily, with peculiar lightness and grace, through the doorway, and stopped quickly, as if in surprise at the sight of a stranger. She was a small child—so small and slight that her footsteps made no sound on the polished floor of the threshold; and I remember thinking while I looked at her that she had the gravest and sweetest face I had ever seen. She couldn't—I decided this afterward—have been more than six or seven, yet she stood there with a curious prim dignity, like the dignity of a very old person, and gazed up at me with enigmatical eyes. She was dressed in Scotch plaid, with a bit of red ribbon in her hair, which was cut in a fringe over her forehead and hung very straight to her shoulders. Charming as she was, from her uncurled brown hair to the white socks and black slippers on her little feet, I recall most vividly the singular look in her eyes, which appeared in the shifting light to be of an indeterminate color. For the odd thing about this look was that it was not the look of childhood at all. It was the look of profound experience, of bitter knowledge.

"Have you come for your ball?" I asked; but while the friendly question was still on my lips, I heard the servant returning. Even in my haste I made a second ineffectual grasp at the plaything, which rolled, with increased speed, away from me into the dusk of the drawing-room. Then, as I raised my head, I saw that the child also had slipped from the room; and without looking after her I followed the old negro into the pleasant study above, where the great surgeon awaited me.

Ten years ago, before hard nursing had taken so much out of me, I blushed very easily, and I was aware at the moment when I crossed Doctor Maradick's study that my cheeks were the color of peonies. Of course, I was a fool—no one knows this better than

I do—but I had never been alone, even for an instant, with him before, and the man was more than a hero to me, he was—there isn't any reason now why I should blush over the confession—almost a god. At that age I was mad about the wonders of surgery, and Roland Maradick in the operating-room was magician enough to have turned an older and more sensible head than mine. Added to his great reputation and his marvellous skill, he was, I am sure of this, the most splendid-looking man, even at forty-five, that one could imagine. Had he been ungracious—had he been positively rude to me, I should still have adored him, but when he held out his hand, and greeted me in the charming way he had with women, I felt that I would have died for him. It is no wonder that a saying went about the hospital that every woman he operated on fell in love with him. As for the nurses—well, there wasn't a single one of them who had escaped his spell—not even Miss Hemphill, who could scarcely have been a day under fifty.

"I am glad you could come, Miss Randolph. You were with Miss Hudson last week when I operated?"

I bowed. To save my life I couldn't have spoken without blushing the redder.

"I noticed your bright face at the time. Brightness, I think, is what Mrs. Maradick needs. She finds her day nurse depressing." His eyes rested so kindly upon me that I have suspected since that he was not entirely unaware of my worship. It was a small thing, heaven knows, to flatter his vanity—a nurse just out of a training-school—but to some men no tribute is too insignificant to give pleasure.

"You will do your best, I am sure." He hesitated an instant—just long enough for me to perceive the anxiety beneath the genial smile on his face—and then added gravely: "We wish to avoid, if possible, having to send her away for treatment."

I could only murmur in response, and after a few carefully chosen words about his wife's illness, he rang the bell and directed the maid to take me up-stairs to my room. Not until I was ascending the stairs to the third story did it occur to me that he had really told me nothing. I was as perplexed about the nature of Mrs. Maradick's malady as I had been when I entered the house.

I found my room pleasant enough. It had been arranged—by Doctor Maradick's request, I think—that I was to sleep in the house, and after my austere little bed at the hospital I was agreeably surprised by the cheerful look of the apartment into which the maid led me. The walls were papered in roses, and there were curtains of flowered chintz at the window, which looked down on a small formal garden at the rear of the house. This the maid told me, for it was too dark for me to distinguish more than a marble fountain and a fir-tree, which looked old, though I afterward learned that it was replanted almost every season.

In ten minutes I had slipped into my uniform and was ready to go to my patient; but for some reason—to this day I have never found out what it was that turned her against me at the start—Mrs. Maradick refused to receive me. While I stood outside her door I heard the day nurse trying to persuade her to let me come in. It wasn't any use, however, and in the end I was obliged to go back to my room and wait until the poor lady got over her whim and consented to see me. That was long after dinner—it must have been nearer eleven than ten o'clock—and Miss Peterson was quite worn out by the time she came to fetch me.

"I'm afraid you'll have a bad night," she said as we went down-stairs together. That was her way, I soon saw, to expect the worst of everything and everybody.

"Does she often keep you up like this?"

"Oh, no, she is usually very considerate. I never knew a sweeter character. But she still has this hallucination—"

Here again, as in the scene with Doctor Maradick, I felt that the explanation had only deepened the mystery. Mrs. Maradick's hallucination, whatever form it assumed, was evidently a subject for evasion and subterfuge in the household. It was on the tip of my tongue to ask, "What is her hallucination?"—but before I could get the words past my lips we had reached Mrs. Maradick's door, and Miss Peterson motioned me to be silent. As the door opened a little way to admit me, I saw that Mrs. Maradick was already in bed, and that the lights were out except for a night-lamp burning on a candle-stand beside a book and a carafe of water.

"I won't go in with you," said Miss Peterson in a whisper; and I was on the point of stepping over the threshold when I saw the little girl, in the dress of Scotch plaid, slip by me from the dusk of the room into the electric light of the hall. She held a doll in her arms, and as she went by she dropped a doll's work-basket in the doorway. Miss Peterson must have picked up the toy, for when I turned in a minute to look for it I found that it was gone. I remember thinking that it was late for a child to be up—she looked delicate, too—but, after all, it was no business of mine, and four years in a hospital had taught me never to meddle in affairs that do not concern me. There is nothing a nurse learns quicker than not to try to put the world to rights in a day.

When I crossed the floor to the chair by Mrs. Maradick's bed, she turned over on her side and looked at me with the sweetest and saddest smile.

"You are the new night nurse," she said in a gentle voice; and from the moment she spoke I knew that there was nothing hysterical or violent about her mania—or hallucination, as they called it. "They told me your name, but I have forgotten it."

"Randolph—Margaret Randolph." I liked her from the start, and I think she must have seen it.

"You look very young, Miss Randolph."

"I am twenty-two, but I suppose I don't look quite my age. People usually think I am younger."

For a minute she was silent, and while I settled myself in the chair by the bed I thought how strikingly she resembled the little girl I had seen first in the afternoon, and then leaving her room a few moments ago. They had the same small, heart-shaped faces, colored ever so faintly; the same straight, soft hair, between brown and flaxen; and the same large, grave eyes, set very far apart under arched eyebrows. What surprised me most, however, was that they both looked at me with that enigmatical and vaguely wondering expression—only in Mrs. Maradick's face the vagueness seemed to change now and then to a definite fear—a flash, I had almost said, of startled horror.

I sat quite still in my chair, and until the time came for Mrs. Maradick to take her medicine not a word passed between us. Then, when I bent over her with the glass in my hand, she raised her head from the pillow and said in a whisper of suppressed intensity:

"You look kind. I wonder if you could have seen my little girl?"

As I slipped my arm under the pillow I tried to smile cheerfully down on her. "Yes, I've seen her twice. I'd know her anywhere by her likeness to you."

A glow shone in her eyes, and I thought how pretty she must have been before illness took the life and animation out of her features. "Then I know you're good." Her voice was so strained and low that I could barely hear it. "If you weren't good you couldn't have seen her."

I thought this queer enough, but all I answered was: "She looked delicate to be sitting up so late."

A quiver passed over her thin features, and for a minute I thought she was going to burst into tears. As she had taken the medicine, I put the glass back on the candle-stand and, bending over the bed, smoothed the straight brown hair, which was as fine and soft as spun silk, back from her forehead. There was something about her—I don't know what it was—that made you love her as soon as she looked at you.

"She always had that light and airy way, though she was never sick a day in her life," she answered calmly after a pause. Then, groping for my hand, she whispered passionately: "You must not tell him—you must not tell any one that you have seen her!"

"I mustn't tell any one?" Again I had the impression that had come to me first in Doctor Maradick's study, and afterward with Miss Peterson on the staircase, that I was seeking a gleam of light in the midst of obscurity.

"Are you sure there isn't any one listening—that there isn't any one at the door?" she asked, pushing aside my arm and sitting up among the pillows.

"Quite, quite sure. They have put out the lights in the hall."

"And you will not tell him? Promise me that you will not tell him." The startled horror flashed from the vague wonder of her expression. "He doesn't like her to come back, because he killed her."

"Because he killed her!" Then it was that light burst on me in a blaze. So this was Mrs. Maradick's hallucination! She believed that her child was dead—the little girl I had seen with my own eyes leaving her room; and she believed that her husband—the great surgeon we worshipped in the hospital—had murdered her. No wonder they veiled the dreadful obsession in mystery! No wonder that even Miss Peterson had not dared to drag the horrid thing out into the light! It was the kind of hallucination one simply couldn't stand having to face.

"There is no use telling people things that nobody believes," she resumed slowly, still holding my hand in a grasp that would have hurt me if her fingers had not been so fragile. "Nobody believes that he killed her. Nobody believes that she comes back every day to the house. Nobody believes—and yet you saw her—"

"Yes, I saw her—but why should your husband have killed her?" I spoke soothingly, as one would speak to a person who was quite mad; yet she was not mad, I could have sworn this while I looked at her.

For a moment she moaned inarticulately, as if the horror of her thought were too great to pass into speech. Then she flung out her thin, bare arm with a wild gesture.

"Because he never loved me!" she said. "He never loved me!"

"But he married you," I urged gently after a moment in which I stroked her hair. "If he hadn't loved you, why should he have married you?"

"He wanted the money—my little girl's money. It all goes to him when I die."

"But he is rich himself. He must make a fortune from his profession."

"It isn't enough. He wanted millions." She had grown stern and tragic. "No, he never loved me. He loved some one else from the beginning—before I knew him."

It was quite useless, I saw, to reason with her. If she wasn't mad, she was in a state of terror and despondency so black that it had almost crossed the borderline into madness. I thought once of going up-stairs and bringing the child down from her nursery; but, after a moment's thought, I realized that Miss Peterson and Doctor Maradick must have long ago tried all these measures. Clearly, there was nothing to do except soothe and quiet her as much as I could; and this I did until she dropped into a light sleep which lasted well into the morning.

By seven o'clock I was worn out—not from work, but from the strain on my sympathy—and I was glad, indeed, when one of the maids came in to bring me an early cup of coffee. Mrs. Maradick was still sleeping—it was a mixture of bromide and chloral I had given her—and she did not wake until Miss Peterson came on duty an hour or two later. Then, when I went down-stairs, I found the dining-room deserted except for the old house-keeper, who was looking over the silver. Doctor Maradick, she explained to me presently, had his breakfast served in the morning-room on the other side of the house.

"And the little girl? Does she take her meals in the nursery?"

She threw me a startled glance. Was it, I questioned afterward, one of distrust or apprehension?

"There isn't any little girl. Haven't you heard?"

"Heard? No. Why, I saw her only yesterday."

The look she gave me—I was sure of it now—was full of alarm.

"The little girl—she was the sweetest child I ever saw—died just two months ago of pneumonia."

"But she couldn't have died." I was a fool to let this out, but the shock had completely unnerved me. "I tell you I saw her yesterday."

The alarm in her face deepened. "That is Mrs. Maradick's trouble. She believes that she still sees her."

"But don't you see her?" I drove the question home bluntly.

"No." She set her lips tightly. "I never see anything."

So I had been wrong, after all, and the explanation, when it came, only accentuated the terror. The child was dead—she had died of pneumonia two months ago—and yet I had seen her, with my own eyes, playing ball in the library; I had seen her slipping out of her mother's room, with her doll in her arms.

"Is there another child in the house? Could there be a child belonging to one of the servants?" A gleam had shot through the fog in which I was groping.

"No, there isn't any other. The doctors tried bringing one once, but it threw the poor lady into such a state she almost died of it. Besides, there wouldn't be any other child as quiet and sweet-looking as Dorothea. To see her skipping along in her dress of Scotch plaid used to make me think of a fairy, though they say that fairies wear nothing but white or green."

"Has any one else seen her—the child, I mean—any of the servants?"

"Only old Gabriel, the colored butler, who came with Mrs. Maradick's mother from South Carolina. I've heard that negroes often have a kind of second sight— though I don't know that that is just what you would call it. But they seem to believe in the supernatural by instinct, and Gabriel is so old and doty—he does no work except answer the door-bell and clean the silver—that nobody pays much attention to anything that he sees—"

"Is the child's nursery kept as it used to be?"

"Oh, no. The doctor had all the toys sent to the children's hospital. That was a great grief to Mrs. Maradick; but Doctor Brandon thought, and all the nurses agreed with him, that it was best for her not to be allowed to keep the room as it was when Dorothea was living."

"Dorothea? Was that the child's name?"

"Yes, it means the gift of God, doesn't it? She was named after the mother of Mrs. Maradick's first husband, Mr. Ballard. He was the grave, quiet kind—not the least like the doctor."

I wondered if the other dreadful obsession of Mrs. Maradick's had drifted down through the nurses or the servants to the housekeeper; but she said nothing about it, and since she was, I suspected, a garrulous person, I thought it wiser to assume that the gossip had not reached her.

A little later, when breakfast was over and I had not yet gone up-stairs to my room, I had my first interview with Doctor Brandon, the famous alienist who was in charge of the case. I had never seen him before, but from the first moment that I looked at him I took his measure, almost by intuition. He was, I suppose, honest enough—I have always granted him that, bitterly as I have felt toward him. It wasn't his fault that he lacked red blood in his brain, or that he had formed the habit, from long association with abnormal phenomena, of regarding all life as a disease. He was the sort of physician—every nurse will understand what I mean—who deals instinctively with groups instead of with individuals. He was long and solemn and very round in the face; and I hadn't talked to him ten minutes before I knew he had been educated in Germany, and that he had learned over there to treat every emotion as a pathological manifestation. I used to wonder what he got out of life—what any one got out of life who had analyzed away everything except the bare structure.

When I reached my room at last, I was so tired that I could barely remember either the questions Doctor Brandon had asked or the directions he had given me. I fell asleep, I know, almost as soon as my head touched the pillow; and the maid who came to inquire if I wanted luncheon decided to let me finish my nap. In the afternoon, when she returned with a cup of tea, she found me still heavy and drowsy. Though I was used to night nursing, I felt as if I had danced from sunset to daybreak. It was fortunate, I reflected, while I drank my tea, that every case didn't wear on one's sympathies as acutely as Mrs. Maradick's hallucination had worn on mine.

Through the day, of course, I did not see Doctor Maradick, but at seven o'clock, when I came up from my early dinner on my way to take the place of Miss Peterson, who had kept on duty an hour later than usual, he met me in the hall and asked me to come into his study. I thought him handsomer than ever in his evening clothes, with a white flower in his buttonhole. He was going to some public dinner, the housekeeper told me, but, then, he was always going somewhere. I believe he didn't dine at home a single evening that winter.

"Did Mrs. Maradick have a good night?" He had closed the door after us, and, turning now with the question, he smiled kindly, as if he wished to put me at ease in the beginning.

"She slept very well after she took the medicine. I gave her that at eleven o'clock."

For a minute he regarded me silently, and I was aware that his personality—his charm—had been focussed upon me. It was almost as if I stood in the centre of converging rays of light, so vivid was my impression of him.

"Did she allude in any way to her—to her hallucination?" he asked.

How the warning reached me—what invisible waves of sense-perception transmitted the message—I have never known; but while I stood there, facing the splendor of the doctor's presence, every intuition cautioned me that the time had come when I must take sides in the household. While I stayed there I must stand either with Mrs. Maradick or against her.

"She talked quite rationally," I replied after a moment.

"What did she say?"

"She told me how she was feeling, that she missed her child, and that she walked a little every day about her room."

His face changed—how, I could not at first determine.

"Have you seen Doctor Brandon?"

"He came this morning to give me his directions."

"He thought her less well to-day. He has even advised me to send her to Rosedale."

I have never, even in secret, tried to account for Doctor Maradick. He may have been sincere. I tell only what I know—not what I believe or imagine—and the human is sometimes as inscrutable, as inexplicable, as the supernatural.

While he watched me I was conscious of an inner struggle, as if opposing angels warred somewhere in the depths of my being. When at last I made my decision, I was acting less from reason, I knew, than in obedience to the pressure of some secret current of thought. Heaven knows, even then, the man held me captive while I defied him.

"Doctor Maradick," I lifted my eyes for the first time frankly to his, "I believe that your wife is as sane as I am—or as you are."

He started. "Then she did not talk freely to you?"

"She may be mistaken, unstrung, piteously distressed in mind"—I brought this out with emphasis—"but she is not—I am willing to stake my future on it—a fit subject for an asylum. It would be foolish—it would be cruel to send her to Rosedale."

"Cruel, you say?" A troubled look crossed his face, and his voice grew very gentle. "You do not imagine that I could be cruel to her?"

"No, I do not think that." My voice also had softened.

"We will let things go on as they are. Perhaps Doctor Brandon may have some other suggestion to make." He drew out his watch and compared it with the clock—nervously, I observed, as if his action were a screen for his discomfiture or his perplexity. "I must be going now. We will speak of this again in the morning."

But in the morning we did not speak of it, and during the month that I nursed Mrs. Maradick I was not called again into her husband's study. When I met him in the hall or on the staircase, which was seldom, he was as charming as ever; yet, in spite of his courtesy, I had a persistent feeling that he had taken my measure on that evening, and that he had no further use for me.

As the days went by Mrs. Maradick seemed to grow stronger. Never, after our first night together, had she mentioned the child to me; never had she alluded by so much as a word to her dreadful charge against her husband. She was like any other woman recovering from a great sorrow, except that she was sweeter and gentler. It is no wonder that every one who came near her loved her; for there was a mysterious loveliness about her like the mystery of light, not of darkness. She was, I have always thought, as much of an angel as it is possible for a woman to be on this earth. And yet, angelic as she was, there were times when it seemed to me that she both hated and feared her husband. Though he never entered her room while I was there, and I never heard his name on her lips until an hour before the end, still I could tell by the look of terror in her face whenever his step passed down the hall that her very soul shivered at his approach.

During the whole month I did not see the child again, though one night, when I came suddenly into Mrs. Maradick's room, I found a little garden, such as children make out of pebbles and bits of box, on the window-sill. I did not mention it to Mrs. Maradick, and a little later, as the maid lowered the shades, I noticed that the garden had vanished. Since then I have often wondered if the child were invisible only to the rest of us, and if her mother still saw her. But there was no way of finding out except by questioning, and Mrs. Maradick was so well and patient that I hadn't the heart to question. Things couldn't have been better with her than they were, and I was beginning to tell myself that she might soon go out for an airing, when the end came suddenly.

It was a mild January day—the kind of day that brings the foretaste of spring in the middle of winter, and when I came down-stairs in the afternoon, I stopped a minute by the window at the end of the hall to look down on the box maze in the garden. There was an old fountain, bearing two laughing boys in marble, in the centre of the gravelled walk, and the water, which had been turned on that morning for Mrs. Maradick's pleasure, sparkled now like silver as the sunlight splashed over it. I had never before felt the air quite so soft and springlike in January; and I thought, as I gazed down on the garden, that it would be a good idea for Mrs. Maradick to go out and bask for an hour or so in the sunshine. It seemed strange to me that she was never allowed to get any fresh air except the air that came through her windows.

When I went into her room, however, I found that she had no wish to go out. She was sitting, wrapped in shawls, by the open window, which looked down on the fountain; and as I entered she glanced up from a little book she was reading. A pot of daffodils stood on the window-sill—she was very fond of flowers and we tried always to keep some growing in her room.

"Do you know what I was reading, Miss Randolph?" she asked in her soft voice; and then she read aloud a verse while I went over to the candle-stand to measure out a dose of medicine.

"'If thou hast two loaves of bread, sell one and buy daffodils, for bread nourisheth the body, but daffodils delight the soul.' That is very beautiful, don't you think so?"

I said "Yes," that it was beautiful; and then I asked her if she wouldn't go down-stairs and walk about in the garden?

"He wouldn't like it," she answered; and it was the first time she had mentioned her husband to me since the night I came to her. "He doesn't want me to go out."

I tried to laugh her out of the idea; but it was no use, and after a few minutes I gave up and began talking of other things. Even then it did not occur to me that her fear of Doctor Maradick was anything but a fancy. I could see, of course, that she wasn't out of her head; but sane persons, I knew, sometimes have unaccountable prejudices, and I accepted her dislike as a mere whim or aversion. I did not understand then, and—I may as well confess this before the end comes—I do not understand any better to-day. I am writing down the things I actually saw, and I repeat that I have never had the slightest twist in the direction of the miraculous.

The afternoon slipped away while we talked—she talked brightly when any subject came up that interested her—and it was the last hour of day—that grave, still hour when the movement of life seems to droop and falter for a few precious minutes—that brought us the thing I had dreaded silently since my first night in the house. I remember that I had risen to close the window, and was leaning out for a breath of the mild air, when there was the sound of steps, consciously softened in the hall outside, and Doctor Brandon's usual knock fell on my ears. Then, before I could cross the room, the door opened, and the doctor entered with Miss Peterson. The day nurse, I knew, was a stupid woman; but she had never appeared to me so stupid, so armored and incased in her professional manner, as she did at that moment.

"I am glad to see that you have been taking the air." As Doctor Brandon came over to the window, I wondered maliciously what devil of contradictions had made him a distinguished specialist in nervous diseases.

"Who was the other doctor you brought this morning?" asked Mrs. Maradick gravely; and that was all I ever heard about the visit of the second alienist.

"Some one who is anxious to cure you." He dropped into a chair beside her and patted her hand with his long, pale fingers. "We are so anxious to cure you that we want to send you away to the country for a fortnight or so. Miss Peterson has come to help you get ready, and I've kept my car waiting for you. There couldn't be a nicer day for a little trip, could there?"

The moment had come at last. I knew at once what he meant, and so did Mrs. Maradick. A wave of color flowed and ebbed in her thin cheeks, and I felt her body quiver when I moved from the window and put my arms on her shoulders. I was aware again, as I had been aware that evening in Doctor Maradick's study, of a current of thought that beat from the air around into my brain. Though it cost me my career as a nurse and my reputation for sanity, I knew that I must obey that invisible warning.

"You are going to take me to an asylum," said Mrs. Maradick.

He made some foolish denial or evasion; but before he had finished I turned from Mrs. Maradick and faced him impulsively. In a nurse this was flagrant rebellion, and I realized that the act wrecked my professional future. Yet I did not care—I did not hesitate. Something stronger than I was driving me on.

"Doctor Brandon," I said, "I beg you—I implore you to wait until to-morrow. There are things I must tell you."

A queer look came into his face, and I understood, even in my excitement, that he was mentally deciding in which group he should place me—to which class of morbid manifestations I must belong.

"Very well, very well, we will hear everything," he replied soothingly; but I saw him glance at Miss Peterson, and she went over to the wardrobe for Mrs. Maradick's fur coat and hat.

Suddenly, without warning, Mrs. Maradick threw the shawls away from her, and stood up. "If you send me away," she said, "I shall never come back. I shall never live to come back."

The gray of twilight was just beginning, and while she stood there, in the dusk of the room, her face shone out as pale and flower-like as the daffodils on the window-sill. "I cannot go away!" she cried in a sharper voice. "I cannot go away from my child!"

I saw her face clearly; I heard her voice; and then—the horror of the scene sweeps back over me!—I saw the door slowly open and the little girl run across the room to her mother. I saw her lift her little arms, and I saw the mother stoop and gather her to her bosom. So closely locked were they in that passionate embrace that their forms seemed to mingle in the gloom that enveloped them.

"After this can you doubt?" I threw out the words almost savagely—and then, when I turned from the mother and child to Doctor Brandon and Miss Peterson, I knew breathlessly—oh, there was a shock in the discovery!—that they were blind to the child. Their blank faces revealed the consternation of ignorance, not of conviction. They had seen nothing except the vacant arms of the mother and the swift, erratic gesture with which she stooped to embrace some phantasmal presence. Only my vision—and I have asked myself since if the power of sympathy enabled me to penetrate the web of material fact and see the spiritual form of the child—only my vision was not blinded by the clay through which I looked.

"After this can you doubt?" Doctor Brandon had flung my words back to me. Was it his fault, poor man, if life had granted him only the eyes of flesh? Was it his fault if he could see only half of the thing there before him?

But they couldn't see, and since they couldn't see I realized that it was useless to tell them. Within an hour they took Mrs. Maradick to the asylum; and she went quietly, though when the time came for parting from me she showed some faint trace of feeling. I remember that at the last, while we stood on the pavement, she lifted her black veil, which she wore for the child, and said: "Stay with her, Miss Randolph, as long as you can. I shall never come back."

Then she got into the car and was driven off, while I stood looking after her with a sob in my throat. Dreadful as I felt it to be, I didn't, of course, realize the full horror of it, or I couldn't have stood there quietly on the pavement. I didn't realize it, indeed, until several months afterward when word came that she had died in the asylum. I never knew what her illness was, though I vaguely recall that something was said about "heart failure"—a loose enough term. My own belief is that she died simply of the terror of life.

To my surprise Doctor Maradick asked me to stay on as his office nurse after his wife went to Rosedale; and when the news of her death came there was no suggestion of my leaving. I don't know to this day why he wanted me in the house. Perhaps he thought I should have less opportunity to gossip if I stayed under his roof; perhaps he still wished to test the power of his charm over me. His vanity was incredible in so great a man. I have seen him flush with pleasure when people turned to look at him in the street, and I know that he was not above playing on the sentimental weaknesses of his patients. But he was magnificent, heaven knows! Few men, I imagine, have been the objects of so many foolish infatuations.

The next summer Doctor Maradick went abroad for two months, and while he was away I took my vacation in Virginia. When we came back the work was heavier than ever—his reputation by this time was tremendous—and my days were so crowded with appointments, and hurried flittings to emergency cases, that I had scarcely a minute left in which to remember poor Mrs. Maradick. Since the afternoon when she went to the asylum the child had not been seen in the house; and at last I was beginning to persuade myself that the little figure had been an optical illusion—the effect of shifting lights in the gloom of the old rooms—not the apparition I had once believed it to be. It does not take long for a phantom to fade from the memory—especially when one leads the active and methodical life I was forced into that winter. Perhaps—who knows?—(I remember telling myself) the doctors may have been right, after all, and the poor lady may have actually been out of her mind. With this view of the past, my judgment of Doctor Maradick insensibly altered. It ended, I think, in my acquitting him altogether. And then, just as he stood clear and splendid in my verdict of him, the reversal came so precipitately that I grow breathless now whenever I try to live it over again. The violence of the next turn in affairs left me, I often fancy, with a perpetual dizziness of the imagination.

It was in May that we heard of Mrs. Maradick's death, and exactly a year later, on a mild and fragrant afternoon, when the daffodils were blooming in patches around the old fountain in the garden, the housekeeper came into the office, where I lingered over some accounts, to bring me news of the doctor's approaching marriage.

"It is no more than we might have expected," she concluded rationally. "The house must be lonely for him—he is such a sociable man. But I can't help feeling," she brought out slowly after a pause in which I felt a shiver pass over me, "I can't help feeling that it is hard for that other woman to have all the money poor Mrs. Maradick's first husband left her."

"There is a great deal of money, then?" I asked curiously.

"A great deal." She waved her hand, as if words were futile to express the sum. "Millions and millions!"

"They will give up this house, of course?"

"That's done already, my dear. There won't be a brick left of it by this time next year. It's to be pulled down and an apartment-house built on the ground."

Again the shiver passed over me. I couldn't bear to think of Mrs. Maradick's old home falling to pieces.

"You didn't tell me the name of the bride," I said. "Is she some one he met while he was in Europe?"

"Dear me, no! She is the very lady he was engaged to before he married Mrs. Maradick, only she threw him over, so people said, because he wasn't rich enough. Then she married some lord or prince from over the water; but there was a divorce, and now she has turned again to her old lover. He is rich enough now, I guess, even for her!"

It was all perfectly true, I suppose; it sounded as plausible as a story out of a newspaper; and yet while she told me I was aware of a sinister, an impalpable hush in the atmosphere. I was nervous, no doubt; I was shaken by the suddenness with which the housekeeper had sprung her news on me; but as I sat there I had quite vividly an impression that the old house was listening—that there was a real, if invisible, presence somewhere in the room or the garden. Yet, when an instant afterward I glanced through the long window which opened down to the brick terrace, I saw only the faint sunshine over the deserted garden, with its maze of box, its marble fountain, and its patches of daffodils.

The housekeeper had gone—one of the servants, I think, came for her—and I was sitting at my desk when the words of Mrs. Maradick on that last evening floated into my mind. The daffodils brought her back to me; for I thought, as I watched them growing, so still and golden in the sunshine, how she would have enjoyed them. Almost unconsciously I repeated the verse she had read to me.

"If thou hast two loaves of bread, sell one and buy daffodils"—and it was at that very instant, while the words were on my lips, that I turned my eyes to the box maze and saw the child skipping rope along the gravelled path to the fountain. Quite distinctly, as clear as day, I saw her come, with what children call the dancing step, between the low box borders to the place where the daffodils bloomed by the fountain. From her straight brown hair to her frock of Scotch plaid and her little feet, which twinkled in white socks and black slippers over the turning rope, she was as real to me as the ground on which she trod or the laughing marble boys under the splashing water. Starting up from my chair, I made a single step to the terrace. If I could only reach her—only speak to her—I felt that I might at last solve the mystery. But with my first call, with the first flutter of my dress on the terrace, the airy little form melted into the dusk of the maze. Not a breath stirred the daffodils, not a shadow passed over the sparkling flow of the water; yet, weak and shaken in every nerve, I sat down on the brick step of the terrace and burst into tears. I must have known that something terrible would happen before they pulled down Mrs. Maradick's home.

The doctor dined out that night. He was with the lady he was going to marry, the housekeeper told me; and it must have been almost midnight when I heard him come in and go up-stairs to his room. I was down-stairs because I had been unable to sleep, and the book I wanted to finish I had left that afternoon in the office. The book—I can't remember what it was—had seemed to me very exciting when I began it in the morning; but after the visit of the child I found the romantic novel as dull as a treatise on nursing. It was impossible for me to follow the lines, and I was on the point of giving up and going to bed, when Doctor Maradick opened the front door with his latch-key and went up the staircase. "There can't be a bit of truth in it." I thought over and over again as I listened to his even step ascending the stairs. "There can't be a bit of truth in it." And yet, though I assured myself that "there couldn't be a bit of truth in it," I shrank, with a creepy sensation, from going through the house to my room in the third story. I was tired out after a hard day, and my nerves must have reacted morbidly to the silence and the darkness. For the first time in my life I knew what it was to be afraid of the unknown, of the invisible; and while I bent over my book, in the glare of the electric light, I became conscious presently that I was straining my senses for some sound in the spacious emptiness of the rooms overhead. The noise of a passing motor-car in the street jerked me back from the intense hush of expectancy; and I can recall the wave of relief that swept over me as I turned to my book again and tried to fix my distracted mind on its pages.

I was still sitting there when the telephone on my desk rang, with what seemed to my overwrought nerves a startling abruptness, and the voice of the superintendent told me hurriedly that Doctor Maradick was needed at the hospital. I had become so accustomed to these emergency calls in the night that I felt reassured when I had rung up the doctor in his room and had heard the hearty sound of his response. He had not yet undressed, he said, and would come down immediately while I ordered back his car, which must just have reached the garage.

"I'll be with you in five minutes!" he called as cheerfully as if I had summoned him to his wedding.

I heard him cross the floor of his room; and before he could reach the head of the staircase, I opened the door and went out into the hall in order that I might turn on the light and have his hat and coat waiting. The electric button was at the end of the hall, and as I moved toward it, guided by the glimmer that fell from the landing above, I instinctively lifted my eyes to the staircase, which climbed dimly, with its slender mahogany balustrade, as far as the third story. Then it was, at the very moment when the doctor, humming gayly, began his quick descent of the steps, that I distinctly saw—I will swear to this on my death-bed—a child's skipping-rope lying loosely coiled, as if it had dropped from a careless little hand, in the bend of the staircase. With a spring I had reached the electric button, flooding the hall with light; but as I did so, while my arm was still outstretched behind me, I heard the humming voice change to a cry of surprise or terror, and the figure on the staircase tripped heavily and stumbled with groping hands into emptiness. The scream of warning died in my throat while I watched him pitch forward down the long flight of stairs to the floor at my feet. Even before I bent over him, before I wiped the blood from his brow and felt for his silent heart, I knew that he was dead.

Something—it may have been, as the world believes, a misstep in the dimness, or it may have been, as I am ready to bear witness, a phantasmal judgment—something had killed him at the very moment when he most wanted to live.

Kerfol

Edith Wharton

I

"You ought to buy it," said my host; "it's just the place for a solitary-minded devil like you. And it would be rather worth while to own the most romantic house in Brittany. The present people are dead broke, and it's going for a song—you ought to buy it."

It was not with the least idea of living up to the character my friend Lanrivain ascribed to me (as a matter of fact, under my unsociable exterior I have always had secret yearnings for domesticity) that I took his hint one autumn afternoon and went to Kerfol. My friend was motoring over to Quimper on business: he dropped me on the way, at a cross-road on a heath, and said: "First turn to the right and second to the left. Then straight ahead till you see an avenue. If you meet any peasants, don't ask your way. They don't understand French, and they would pretend they did and mix you up. I'll be back for you here by sunset—and don't forget the tombs in the chapel."

I followed Lanrivain's directions with the hesitation occasioned by the usual difficulty of remembering whether he had said the first turn to the right and second to the left, or the contrary. If I had met a peasant I should certainly have asked, and probably been sent astray; but I had the desert landscape to myself, and so stumbled on the right turn and walked on across the heath till I came to an avenue. It was so unlike any other avenue I have ever seen that I instantly knew it must be *the* avenue. The grey-trunked trees sprang up straight to a great height and then interwove their pale-grey branches in a long tunnel through which the autumn light fell faintly. I know most trees by name, but I haven't to this day been able to decide what those trees were. They had the tall curve of elms, the tenuity of poplars, the ashen colour of olives under a rainy sky; and they stretched ahead of me for half a mile or more without a break in their arch. If ever I saw an avenue that unmistakably led to something, it was the avenue at Kerfol. My heart beat a little as I began to walk down it.

Presently the trees ended and I came to a fortified gate in a long wall. Between me and the wall was an open space of grass, with other grey avenues radiating from it. Behind the wall were tall slate roofs mossed with silver, a chapel belfry, the top of a keep. A moat filled with wild shrubs and brambles surrounded the place; the drawbridge had been replaced by a stone arch, and the portcullis by an iron gate. I stood for a long time on the hither side of the moat, gazing about me, and letting the influence of the place sink in. I said to myself: "If I wait long enough, the guardian will turn up and show me the tombs—" and I rather hoped he wouldn't turn up too soon.

I sat down on a stone and lit a cigarette. As soon as I had done it, it struck me as a puerile and portentous thing to do, with that great blind house looking down at me, and all the empty avenues converging on me. It may have been the depth of the silence that made me so conscious of my gesture. The squeak of my match sounded as loud as the scraping of a brake, and I almost fancied I heard it fall when I tossed it onto the grass. But there was more than that: a sense of irrelevance, of littleness, of childish bravado, in sitting there puffing my cigarette-smoke into the face of such a past.

I knew nothing of the history of Kerfol—I was new to Brittany, and Lanrivain had never mentioned the name to me till the day before—but one couldn't as much as glance at that pile without feeling in it a long accumulation of history. What kind of history I was not prepared to guess: perhaps only the sheer weight of many associated lives and deaths which gives a kind of majesty to all old houses. But the aspect of Kerfol suggested something more—a perspective of stern and cruel memories stretching away, like its own grey avenues, into a blur of darkness.

Certainly no house had ever more completely and finally broken with the present. As it stood there, lifting its proud roofs and gables to the sky, it might have been its own funeral monument. "Tombs in the chapel? The whole place is a tomb!" I reflected. I hoped more and more that the guardian would not come. The details of the place, however striking, would seem trivial compared with its collective impressiveness; and I wanted only to sit there and be penetrated by the weight of its silence.

"It's the very place for you!" Lanrivain had said; and I was overcome by the almost blasphemous frivolity of suggesting to any living being that Kerfol was the place for him. "Is it possible that any one could *not* see—?" I wondered. I did not finish the thought: what I meant was undefinable. I stood up and wandered toward the gate. I was beginning to want to know more; not to *see* more—I was by now so sure it was not a question of seeing—but to feel more: feel all the place had to communicate. "But to get in one will have to rout out the keeper," I thought reluctantly, and hesitated. Finally I crossed the bridge and tried the iron gate. It yielded, and I walked under the tunnel formed by the thickness of the *chemin de ronde*. At the farther end, a wooden barricade had been laid across the entrance, and beyond it I saw a court enclosed in noble architecture. The main building faced me; and I now discovered that one half was a mere ruined front, with gaping windows through which the wild growths of the moat and the trees of the park were visible. The rest of the house was still in its robust beauty. One end abutted on the round tower, the other on the small traceried chapel, and in an angle of the building stood a graceful well-head adorned with mossy urns. A few roses grew against the walls, and on an upper window-sill I remember noticing a pot of fuchsias.

My sense of the pressure of the invisible began to yield to my architectural interest. The building was so fine that I felt a desire to explore it for its own sake. I looked about the court, wondering in which corner the guardian lodged. Then I pushed open the barrier and went in. As I did so, a little dog barred my way. He was such a remarkably beautiful little dog that for a moment he made me forget the splendid place he was defending. I was not sure of his breed at the time, but have since learned that it was Chinese, and that he was of a rare variety called the "Sleeve-dog." He was very small and golden brown, with large brown eyes and a ruffled throat: he looked rather like a large tawny chrysanthemum. I said to myself: "These little beasts always snap and scream, and somebody will be out in a minute."

The little animal stood before me, forbidding, almost menacing: there was anger in his large brown eyes. But he made no sound, he came no nearer. Instead, as I advanced, he gradually fell back, and I noticed that another dog, a vague rough brindled thing, had limped up. "There'll be a hubbub now," I thought; for at the same moment a third dog, a long-haired white mongrel, slipped out of a doorway and joined the others. All three stood looking at me with grave eyes; but not a sound came from them. As I advanced they continued to fall back on muffled paws, still watching me. "At a given point, they'll all charge at my ankles: it's one of the dodges that dogs who live together put up on one," I thought. I was not much alarmed, for they were neither large nor formidable. But they let me wander about the court as I pleased, following me at a little distance—always the same distance—and always keeping their eyes on me. Presently I looked across at the ruined facade, and saw that in one of its window-frames another dog stood: a large white pointer with one brown ear. He was an old grave dog, much more experienced than the others; and he seemed to be observing me with a deeper intentness.

"I'll hear from *him*," I said to myself; but he stood in the empty window-frame, against the trees of the park, and continued to watch me without moving. I looked back at him for a time, to see if the sense that he was being watched would not rouse him.

Half the width of the court lay between us, and we stared at each other silently across it. But he did not stir, and at last I turned away. Behind me I found the rest of the pack, with a newcomer added: a small black greyhound with pale agate-coloured eyes. He was shivering a little, and his expression was more timid than that of the others. I noticed that he kept a little behind them. And still there was not a sound.

I stood there for fully five minutes, the circle about me—waiting, as they seemed to be waiting. At last I went up to the little golden-brown dog and stooped to pat him. As I did so, I heard myself laugh. The little dog did not start, or growl, or take his eyes from me—he simply slipped back about a yard, and then paused and continued to look at me. "Oh, hang it!" I exclaimed aloud, and walked across the court toward the well.

As I advanced, the dogs separated and slid away into different corners of the court. I examined the urns on the well, tried a locked door or two, and up and down the dumb facade; then I faced about toward the chapel. When I turned I perceived that all the dogs had disappeared except the old pointer, who still watched me from the empty window-frame. It was rather a relief to be rid of that cloud of witnesses; and I began to look about me for a way to the back of the house. "Perhaps there'll be somebody in the garden," I thought. I found a way across the moat, scrambled over a wall smothered in brambles, and got into the garden. A few lean hydrangeas and geraniums pined in the flower-beds, and the ancient house looked down on them indifferently. Its garden side was plainer and severer than the other: the long granite front, with its few windows and steep roof, looked like a fortress-prison. I walked around the farther wing, went up some disjointed steps, and entered the deep twilight of a narrow and incredibly old box-walk. The walk was just wide enough for one person to slip through, and its branches met overhead. It was like the ghost of a box-walk, its lustrous green all turning to the shadowy greyness of the avenues. I walked on and on, the branches hitting me in the face and springing back with a dry rattle; and at length I came out on the grassy top of the *chemin de ronde*. I walked along it to the gate-tower, looking down into the court, which was just below me. Not a human being was in sight; and neither were the dogs. I found a flight of steps in the thickness of the wall and went down them; and when I emerged again into the court, there stood the circle of dogs, the golden-brown one a little ahead of the others, the black greyhound shivering in the rear.

"Oh, hang it—you uncomfortable beasts, you!" I exclaimed, my voice startling me with a sudden echo. The dogs stood motionless, watching me. I knew by this time that they would not try to prevent my approaching the house, and the knowledge left me free to examine them. I had a feeling that they must be horribly cowed to be so silent and inert. Yet they did not look hungry or ill-treated. Their coats were smooth and they were not thin, except the shivering greyhound. It was more as if they had lived a long time with people who never spoke to them or looked at them: as though the silence of the place had gradually benumbed their busy inquisitive natures. And this strange passivity, this almost human lassitude, seemed to me sadder than the misery of starved and beaten animals. I should have liked to rouse them for a minute, to coax them into a game or a scamper; but the longer I looked into their fixed and weary eyes the more preposterous the idea became. With the windows of that house looking down on us, how could I have imagined such a thing? The dogs knew better: *they* knew what the house would tolerate and what it would not. I even fancied that they knew what was passing through my mind, and pitied me for my frivolity. But even that feeling probably reached them through a thick fog of listlessness. I had an idea that their distance from me was as nothing to my remoteness from them. In the last analysis, the impression they produced was that of having in common one memory so deep and dark that nothing that had happened since was worth either a growl or a wag.

"I say," I broke out abruptly, addressing myself to the dumb circle, "do you know what you look like, the whole lot of you? You look as if you'd seen a ghost—that's how you look! I wonder if there *is* a ghost here, and nobody but you left for it to appear to?" The dogs continued to gaze at me without moving . . .

It was dark when I saw Lanrivain's motor lamps at the cross-roads—and I wasn't exactly sorry to see them. I had the sense of having escaped from the loneliest place in the whole world, and of not liking loneliness—to that degree—as much as I had imagined I should. My friend had brought his solicitor back from Quimper for the night, and seated beside a fat and affable stranger I felt no inclination to talk of Kerfol. . . .

But that evening, when Lanrivain and the solicitor were closeted in the study, Madame de Lanrivain began to question me in the drawing-room.

"Well—are you going to buy Kerfol?" she asked, tilting up her gay chin from her embroidery.

"I haven't decided yet. The fact is, I couldn't get into the house," I said, as if I had simply postponed my decision, and meant to go back for another look.

"You couldn't get in? Why, what happened? The family are mad to sell the place, and the old guardian has orders—"

"Very likely. But the old guardian wasn't there."

"What a pity! He must have gone to market. But his daughter—?"

"There was nobody about. At least I saw no one."

"How extraordinary! Literally nobody?"

"Nobody but a lot of dogs—a whole pack of them—who seemed to have the place to themselves."

Madame de Lanrivain let the embroidery slip to her knee and folded her hands on it. For several minutes she looked at me thoughtfully.

"A pack of dogs—you *saw* them?"

"Saw them? I saw nothing else!"

"How many?" She dropped her voice a little. "I've always wondered—"

I looked at her with surprise: I had supposed the place to be familiar to her. "Have you never been to Kerfol?" I asked.

"Oh, yes: often. But never on that day."

"What day?"

"I'd quite forgotten—and so had Hervé, I'm sure. If we'd remembered, we never should have sent you today—but then, after all, one doesn't half believe that sort of thing, does one?"

"What sort of thing?" I asked, involuntarily sinking my voice to the level of hers. Inwardly I was thinking: "I *knew* there was something. . . ."

Madame de Lanrivain cleared her throat and produced a reassuring smile. "Didn't Hervé tell you the story of Kerfol? An ancestor of his was mixed up in it. You know every Breton house has its ghost-story; and some of them are rather unpleasant."

"Yes—but those dogs?" I insisted.

"Well, those dogs are the ghosts of Kerfol. At least, the peasants say there's one day in the year when a lot of dogs appear there; and that day the keeper and his daughter go off to Morlaix and get drunk. The women in Brittany drink dreadfully." She stooped to match a silk; then she lifted her charming inquisitive Parisian face: "Did you *really* see a lot of dogs? There isn't one at Kerfol," she said.

II

Lanrivain, the next day, hunted out a shabby calf volume from the back of an upper shelf of his library.

"Yes—here it is. What does it call itself? *A History of the Assizes of the Duchy of Brittany. Quimper,* 1702. The book was written about a hundred years later than the Kerfol affair; but I believe the account is transcribed pretty literally from the judicial records. Anyhow, it's queer reading. And there's a Hervé de Lanrivain mixed up in it—not exactly *my* style, as you'll see. But then he's only a collateral. Here, take the book up to bed with you. I don't exactly remember the details; but after you've read it I'll bet anything you'll leave your light burning all night!"

I left my light burning all night, as he had predicted; but it was chiefly because, till near dawn, I was absorbed in my reading. The account of the trial of Anne de Cornault, wife of the lord of Kerfol, was long and closely printed. It was, as my friend had said, probably an almost literal transcription of what took place in the court-room; and the trial lasted nearly a month. Besides, the type of the book was detestable. . . .

At first I thought of translating the old record. But it is full of wearisome repetitions, and the main lines of the story are forever straying off into side issues. So I have tried to disentangle it, and give it here in a simpler form. At times, however, I have reverted to the text because no other words could have conveyed so exactly the sense of what I felt at Kerfol; and nowhere have I added anything of my own.

III

It was in the year 16— that Yves de Cornault, lord of the domain of Kerfol, went to the *pardon* of Locronan to perform his religious duties. He was a rich and powerful noble, then in his sixty-second year, but hale and sturdy, a great horseman and hunter and a pious man. So all his neighbours attested. In appearance he seems to have been short and broad, with a swarthy face, legs slightly bowed from the saddle, a hanging nose and broad hands with black hairs on them. He had married young and lost his wife and son soon after, and since then had lived alone at Kerfol. Twice a year he went to Morlaix, where he had a handsome house by the river, and spent a week or ten days there; and occasionally he rode to Rennes on business. Witnesses were found to declare that during these absences he led a life different from the one he was known to lead at Kerfol, where he busied himself with his estate, attended mass daily, and found his only amusement in hunting the wild boar and water-fowl. But these rumours are not particularly relevant, and it is certain that among people of his own class in the neighbourhood he passed for a stern and even austere man, observant of his religious obligations, and keeping strictly to himself. There was no talk of any familiarity with the women on his estate, though at that time the nobility were very free with their peasants. Some people said he had never looked at a woman since his wife's death; but such things are hard to prove, and the evidence on this point was not worth much.

Well, in his sixty-second year, Yves de Cornault went to the *pardon* at Locronan, and saw there a young lady of Douarnenez, who had ridden over pillion behind her father to do her duty to the saint. Her name was Anne de Barrigan, and she came of good old Breton stock, but much less great and powerful than that of Yves de Cornault;

and her father had squandered his fortune at cards, and lived almost like a peasant in his little granite manor on the moors. . . . I have said I would add nothing of my own to this bald statement of a strange case; but I must interrupt myself here to describe the young lady who rode up to the lych-gate of Locronan at the very moment when the Baron de Cornault was also dismounting there. I take my description from a faded drawing in red crayon, sober and truthful enough to be by a late pupil of the Clouets, which hangs in Lanrivain's study, and is said to be a portrait of Anne de Barrigan. It is unsigned and has no mark of identity but the initials A. B., and the date 16—, the year after her marriage. It represents a young woman with a small oval face, almost pointed, yet wide enough for a full mouth with a tender depression at the corners. The nose is small, and the eyebrows are set rather high, far apart, and as lightly pencilled as the eyebrows in a Chinese painting. The forehead is high and serious, and the hair, which one feels to be fine and thick and fair, drawn off it and lying close like a cap. The eyes are neither large nor small, hazel probably, with a look at once shy and steady. A pair of beautiful long hands are crossed below the lady's breast . . .

The chaplain of Kerfol, and other witnesses, averred that when the Baron came back from Locronan he jumped from his horse, ordered another to be instantly saddled, called to a young page come with him, and rode away that same evening to the south. His steward followed the next morning with coffers laden on a pair of pack mules. The following week Yves de Cornault rode back to Kerfol, sent for his vassals and tenants, and told them he was to be married at All Saints to Anne de Barrigan of Douarnenez. And on All Saints' Day the marriage took place.

As to the next few years, the evidence on both sides seems to show that they passed happily for the couple. No one was found to say that Yves de Cornault had been unkind to his wife, and it was plain to all that he was content with his bargain. Indeed, it was admitted by the chaplain and other witnesses for the prosecution that the young lady had a softening influence on her husband, and that he became less exacting with his tenants, less harsh to peasants and dependents, and less subject to the fits of gloomy silence which had darkened his widow-hood. As to his wife, the only grievance her champions could call up in her behalf was that Kerfol was a lonely place, and that when her husband was away on business at Rennes or Morlaix—whither she was never taken—she was not allowed so much as to walk in the park unaccompanied. But no one asserted that she was unhappy, though one servant-woman said she had surprised her crying, and had heard her say that she was a woman accursed to have no child, and nothing in life to call her own. But that was a natural enough feeling in a wife attached to her husband; and certainly it must have been a great grief to Yves de Cornault that she gave him no son. Yet he never made her feel her childlessness as a reproach—she herself admits this in her evidence—but seemed to try to make her forget it by showering gifts and favours on her. Rich though he was, he had never been open-handed; but nothing was too fine for his wife, in the way of silks or gems or linen, or whatever else she fancied. Every wandering merchant was welcome at Kerfol, and when the master was called away he never came back without bringing his wife a handsome present—something curious and particular—from Morlaix or Rennes or Quimper. One of the waiting-women gave, in cross-examination, an interesting list of one year's gifts, which I copy. From Morlaix, a carved ivory junk, with Chinamen at the oars, that a strange sailor had brought back as a votive offering for Notre Dame de la Clarte, above Ploumanac'h; from Quimper, an embroidered gown, worked by the nuns of the Assumption; from Rennes, a silver rose that opened and showed an amber Virgin with a crown of garnets; from Morlaix, again, a length of Damascus velvet shot with gold, bought of a Jew from Syria; and for Michaelmas that same year, from Rennes, a necklet or bracelet of round stones—emeralds and pearls and rubies—strung like beads on a gold wire. This was the present that pleased the lady best, the woman said. Later on, as it happened, it was produced at the trial, and appears to have struck the Judges and the public as a curious and valuable jewel.

The very same winter, the Baron absented himself again, this time as far as Bordeaux, and on his return he brought his wife something even odder and prettier than the bracelet. It was a winter evening when he rode up to Kerfol and, walking into the hall, found her sitting listlessly by the fire, her chin on her hand, looking into the fire. He carried a velvet box in his hand and, setting it down on the hearth, lifted the lid and let out a little golden-brown dog.

Anne de Cornault exclaimed with pleasure as the little creature bounded toward her. "Oh, it looks like a bird or a butterfly!" she cried as she picked it up; and the dog put its paws on her shoulders and looked at her with eyes "like a Christian's." After that she would never have it out of her sight, and petted and talked to it as if it had been a child—as indeed it was the nearest thing to a child she was to know. Yves de Cornault was much pleased with his purchase. The dog had been brought to him by a sailor from an East India merchantman, and the sailor had bought it of a pilgrim in a bazaar at Jaffa, who had stolen it from a nobleman's wife in China: a perfectly permissible thing to do, since the pilgrim was a Christian and the nobleman a heathen doomed to hellfire. Yves de Cornault had paid a long price for the dog, for they were beginning to be in demand at the French court, and the sailor knew he had got hold of a good thing; but Anne's pleasure was so great that, to see her laugh and play with the little animal, her husband would doubtless have given twice the sum.

* * * * *

So far, all the evidence is at one, and the narrative plain sailing; but now the steering becomes difficult. I will try to keep as nearly as possible to Anne's own statements; though toward the end, poor thing. . . .

Well, to go back. The very year after the little brown dog was brought to Kerfol, Yves de Cornault, one winter night, was found dead at the head of a narrow flight of stairs leading down from his wife's rooms to a door opening on the court. It was his wife who found him and gave the alarm, so distracted, poor wretch, with fear and horror—for his blood was all over her—that at first the roused household could not make out what she was saying, and thought she had gone suddenly mad. But there, sure enough, at the top of the stairs lay her husband, stone dead, and head foremost, the blood from his wounds dripping down to the steps below him. He had been dreadfully scratched and gashed about the face and throat, as if with a dull weapon; and one of his legs had a deep tear in it which had cut an artery, and probably caused his death. But how did he come there, and who had murdered him?

His wife declared that she had been asleep in her bed, and hearing his cry had rushed out to find him lying on the stairs; but this was immediately questioned. In the first place, it was proved that from her room she could not have heard the struggle on the stairs, owing to the thickness of the walls and the length of the intervening passage; then it was evident that she had not been in bed and asleep, since she was dressed when she roused the house, and her bed had not been slept in. Moreover, the door at the bottom of the stairs was ajar, and it was noticed by the chaplain (an observant man) that the dress she wore was stained with blood about the knees, and that there were traces of small blood-stained hands low down on the staircase walls, so that it was conjectured that she had really been at the postern-door when her husband fell and, feeling her way up to him in the darkness on her hands and knees, had been stained by his blood dripping down on her. Of course it was argued on the other side that the blood-marks on her dress might have been caused by her kneeling down by her husband when she rushed out of her room; but there was the open door below, and the fact that the fingermarks in the staircase all pointed upward.

The accused held to her statement for the first two days, in spite of its improbability; but on the third day word was brought to her that Hervé de Lanrivain, a young nobleman of the neighbourhood, had been arrested for complicity in the crime. Two or three witnesses thereupon came forward to say that it was known throughout the country that Lanrivain had formerly been on good terms with the lady of Cornault; but that he had been absent from Brittany for over a year, and people had ceased to associate their names. The witnesses who made this statement were not of a very reputable sort. One was an old herb-gatherer suspected of witch-craft, another a drunken clerk from a neighbouring parish, the third a half-witted shepherd who could be made to say anything; and it was clear that the prosecution was not satisfied with its case, and would have liked to find more definite proof of Lanrivain's complicity than the statement of the herb-gatherer, who swore to having seen him climbing the wall of the park on the night of the murder. One way of patching out incomplete proofs in those days was to put some sort of pressure, moral or physical, on the accused person. It is not clear what pressure was put on Anne de Cornault; but on the third day, when she was brought into court, she "appeared weak and wandering," and after being encouraged to collect herself and speak the truth, on her honour and the wounds of her Blessed Redeemer, she confessed that she had in fact gone down the stairs to speak with Hervé de Lanrivain (who denied everything), and had been surprised there by the sound of her husband's fall. That was better; and the prosecution rubbed its hands with satisfaction. The satisfaction increased when various dependents living at Kerfol were induced to say—with apparent sincerity—that during the year or two preceding his death their master had once more grown uncertain and irascible, and subject to the fits of brooding silence which his household had learned to dread before his second marriage. This seemed to show that things had not been going well at Kerfol; though no one could be found to say that there had been any signs of open disagreement between husband and wife.

Anne de Cornault, when questioned as to her reason for going down at night to open the door to Hervé de Lanrivain, made an answer which must have sent a smile around the court. She said it was because she was lonely and wanted to talk with the young man. Was this the only reason? she was asked; and replied: "Yes, by the Cross over your Lordships' heads." "But why at midnight?" the court asked. "Because I could see him in no other way." I can see the exchange of glances across the ermine collars under the Crucifix.

Anne de Cornault, further questioned, said that her married life had been extremely lonely: "desolate" was the word she used. It was true that her husband seldom spoke harshly to her; but there were days when he did not speak at all. It was true that he had never struck or threatened her; but he kept her like a prisoner at Kerfol, and when he rode away to Morlaix or Quimper or Rennes he set so close a watch on her that she could not pick a flower in the garden without having a waiting-woman at her heels. "I am no Queen, to need such honours," she once said to him; and he had answered that a man who has a treasure does not leave the key in the lock when he goes out. "Then take me with you," she urged; but to this he said that towns were pernicious places, and young wives better off at their own firesides.

"But what did you want to say to Hervé de Lanrivain?" the court asked; and she answered: "To ask him to take me away."

"Ah—you confess that you went down to him with adulterous thoughts?"

"No."

"Then why did you want him to take you away?"

"Because I was afraid for my life."

"Of whom were you afraid?"

"Of my husband."

"Why were you afraid of your husband?"

"Because he had strangled my little dog."

Another smile must have passed around the court-room: in days when any nobleman had a right to hang his peasants—and most of them exercised it—pinching a pet animal's wind-pipe was nothing to make a fuss about.

At this point one of the Judges, who appears to have had a certain sympathy for the accused, suggested that she should be allowed to explain herself in her own way; and she thereupon made the following statement.

The first years of her marriage had been lonely; but her husband had not been unkind to her. If she had had a child she would not have been unhappy; but the days were long, and it rained too much.

It was true that her husband, whenever he went away and left her, brought her a handsome present on his return; but this did not make up for the loneliness. At least nothing had, till he brought her the little brown dog from the East: after that she was much less unhappy. Her husband seemed pleased that she was so fond of the dog; he gave her leave to put her jewelled bracelet around its neck, and to keep it always with her.

One day she had fallen asleep in her room, with the dog at her feet, as his habit was. Her feet were bare and resting on his back. Suddenly she was waked by her husband: he stood beside her, smiling not unkindly.

"You look like my great-grandmother, Juliane de Cornault, lying in the chapel with her feet on a little dog," he said.

The analogy sent a chill through her, but she laughed and answered: "Well, when I am dead you must put me beside her, carved in marble, with my dog at my feet."

"Oho—we'll wait and see," he said, laughing also, but with his black brows close together. "The dog is the emblem of fidelity."

"And do you doubt my right to lie with mine at my feet?"

"When I'm in doubt I find out," he answered. "I am an old man," he added, "and people say I make you lead a lonely life. But I swear you will have your monument if you earn it."

"And I swear to be faithful," she returned, "if only for the sake of having my little dog at my feet."

Not long afterward he went on business to the Quimper Assizes; and while he was away his aunt, the widow of a great nobleman of the duchy, came to spend a night at Kerfol on her way to the *pardon* of Ste. Barbe. She was a woman of great piety and consequence, and much respected by Yves de Cornault, and when she proposed to Anne to go with her to Ste. Barbe no one could object, and even the chaplain declared himself in favour of the pilgrimage. So Anne set out for Ste. Barbe, and there for the first time she talked with Hervé de Lanrivain. He had come once or twice to Kerfol with his father, but she had never before exchanged a dozen words with him. They did not talk for more than five minutes now: it was under the chestnuts, as the procession was coming out of the chapel. He said: "I pity you," and she was surprised, for she had not supposed that any one thought her an object of pity. He added: "Call for me when you need me," and she smiled a little, but was glad afterward, and thought often of the meeting.

She confessed to having seen him three times afterward: not more. How or where she would not say—one had the impression that she feared to implicate some one. Their meetings had been rare and brief; and at the last he had told her that he was starting the next day for a foreign country, on a mission which was not without peril and might keep him for many months absent. He asked her for a remembrance, and she had none to give him but the collar about the little dog's neck. She was sorry afterward that she had given it, but he was so unhappy at going that she had not had the courage to refuse.

Her husband was away at the time. When he returned a few days later he picked up the little dog to pet it, and noticed that its collar was missing. His wife told him that the dog had lost it in the undergrowth of the park, and that she and her maids had hunted a whole day for it. It was true, she explained to the court, that she had made the maids search for the necklet—they all believed the dog had lost it in the park. . . .

Her husband made no comment, and that evening at supper he was in his usual mood, between good and bad: you could never tell which. He talked a good deal, describing what he had seen and done at Rennes; but now and then he stopped and looked hard at her; and when she went to bed she found her little dog strangled on her pillow. The little thing was dead, but still warm; she stooped to lift it, and her distress turned to horror when she discovered that it had been strangled by twisting twice round its throat the necklet she had given to Lanrivain.

The next morning at dawn she buried the dog in the garden, and hid the necklet in her breast. She said nothing to her husband, then or later, and he said nothing to her; but that day he had a peasant hanged for stealing a faggot in the park, and the next day he nearly beat to death a young horse he was breaking.

Winter set in, and the short days passed, and the long nights, one by one; and she heard nothing of Hervé de Lanrivain. It might be that her husband had killed him; or merely that he had been robbed of the necklet. Day after day by the hearth among the spinning maids, night after night alone on her bed, she wondered and trembled. Sometimes at table her husband looked across at her and smiled; and then she felt sure that Lanrivain was dead. She dared not try to get news of him, for she was sure her husband would find out if she did: she had an idea that he could find out anything. Even when a witch-woman who was a noted seer, and could show you the whole world in her crystal, came to the castle for a night's shelter, and the maids flocked to her, Anne held back.

The winter was long and black and rainy. One day, in Yves de Cornault's absence, some gypsies came to Kerfol with a troop of performing dogs. Anne bought the smallest and cleverest, a white dog with a feathery coat and one blue and one brown eye. It seemed to have been ill-treated by the gypsies, and clung to her plaintively when she took it from them. That evening her husband came back, and when she went to bed she found the dog strangled on her pillow.

After that she said to herself that she would never have another dog; but one bitter cold evening a poor lean greyhound was found whining at the castle-gate, and she took him in and forbade the maids to speak of him to her husband. She hid him in a room that no one went to, smuggled food to him from her own plate, made him a warm bed to lie on and petted him like a child.

Yves de Cornault came home, and the next day she found the greyhound strangled on her pillow. She wept in secret, but said nothing, and resolved that even if she met a dog dying of hunger she would never bring him into the castle; but one day she found a young sheep-dog, a brindled puppy with good blue eyes, lying with a broken leg in the snow of the park. Yves de Cornault was at Rennes, and she brought the dog in, warmed and fed it, tied up its leg and hid it in the castle till her husband's return. The day before, she gave it to a peasant woman who lived a long way off, and paid her handsomely to care for it and say nothing; but that night she heard a whining and scratching at her door, and when she opened it the lame puppy, drenched and shivering, jumped up on her with little sobbing barks. She hid him in her bed, and the next morning was about to have him taken back to the peasant woman when she heard her husband ride into the court. She shut the dog in a chest and went down to receive him. An hour or two later, when she returned to her room, the puppy lay strangled on her pillow. . . .

After that she dared not make a pet of any other dog; and her loneliness became almost unendurable. Sometimes, when she crossed the court of the castle, and thought no one was looking, she stopped to pat the old pointer at the gate. But one day as she was caressing him her husband came out of the chapel; and the next day the old dog was gone. . . .

This curious narrative was not told in one sitting of the court, or received without impatience and incredulous comment. It was plain that the Judges were surprised by its puerility, and that it did not help the accused in the eyes of the public. It was an odd tale, certainly; but what did it prove? That Yves de Cornault disliked dogs, and that his wife, to gratify her own fancy, persistently ignored this dislike. As for pleading this trivial disagreement as an excuse for her relations—whatever their nature—with her supposed accomplice, the argument was so absurd that her own lawyer manifestly regretted having let her make use of it, and tried several times to cut short her story. But she went on to the end, with a kind of hypnotized insistence, as though the scenes she evoked were so real to her that she had forgotten where she was and imagined herself to be re-living them.

At length the Judge who had previously shown a certain kindness to her said (leaning forward a little, one may suppose, from his row of dozing colleagues): "Then you would have us believe that you murdered your husband because he would not let you keep a pet dog?"

"I did not murder my husband."

"Who did, then? Hervé de Lanrivain?"

"No."

"Who then? Can you tell us?"

"Yes, I can tell you. The dogs—" At that point she was carried out of the court in a swoon.

It was evident that her lawyer tried to get her to abandon this line of defense. Possibly her explanation, whatever it was, had seemed convincing when she poured it out to him in the heat of their first private colloquy; but now that it was exposed to the cold daylight of judicial scrutiny, and the banter of the town, he was thoroughly ashamed of it, and would have sacrificed her without a scruple to save his professional reputation. But the obstinate Judge—who perhaps, after all, was more inquisitive than kindly—evidently wanted to hear the story out, and she was ordered, the next day, to continue her deposition.

She said that after the disappearance of the old watch-dog nothing particular happened for a month or two. Her husband was much as usual: she did not remember any special incident. But one evening a pedlar woman came to the castle and was selling trinkets to the maids. She had no heart for trinkets, but she stood looking on while the women made their choice. And then, she did not know how, but the pedlar coaxed her into buying for herself an odd pear-shaped pomander with a strong scent in it—she had once seen something of the kind on a gypsy woman. She had no desire for the pomander, and did not know why she had bought it. The pedlar said that whoever wore it had the power to read the future; but she did not really believe that, or care much either. However, she bought the thing and took it up to her room, where she sat turning it about in her hand. Then the strange scent attracted her and she began to wonder what kind of spice was in the box. She opened it and found a grey bean rolled in a strip of paper; and on the paper she saw a sign she knew, and a message from Hervé de Lanrivain, saying that he was at home again and would be at the door in the court that night after the moon had set. . . .

She burned the paper and then sat down to think. It was nightfall, and her husband was at home. . . . She had no way of warning Lanrivain, and there was nothing to do but to wait. . . .

At this point I fancy the drowsy court-room beginning to wake up. Even to the oldest hand on the bench there must have been a certain aesthetic relish in picturing the feelings of a woman on receiving such a message at nightfall from a man living twenty miles away, to whom she had no means of sending a warning. . . .

She was not a clever woman, I imagine; and as the first result of her cogitation she appears to have made the mistake of being, that evening, too kind to her husband. She could not ply him with wine, according to the traditional expedient, for though he drank heavily at times he had a strong head; and when he drank beyond its strength it was because he chose to, and not because a woman coaxed him. Not his wife, at any rate—she was an old story by now. As I read the case, I fancy there was no feeling for her left in him but the hatred occasioned by his supposed dishonour.

At any rate, she tried to call up her old graces; but early in the evening he complained of pains and fever, and left the hall to go up to the closet where he sometimes slept. His servant carried him a cup of hot wine, and brought back word that he was sleeping and not to be disturbed; and an hour later, when Anne lifted the tapestry and listened at his door, she heard his loud regular breathing. She thought it might be a feint, and stayed a long time barefooted in the cold passage, her ear to the crack; but the breathing went on too steadily and naturally to be other than that of a man in a sound sleep. She crept back to her room reassured, and stood in the window watching the moon set through the trees of the park. The sky was misty and starless, and after the moon went down the night was pitch black. She knew the time had come, and stole along the passage, past her husband's door—where she stopped again to listen to his breathing—to the top of the stairs. There she paused a moment, and assured herself that no one was following her; then she began to go down the stairs in the darkness. They were so steep and winding that she had to go very slowly, for fear of stumbling. Her one thought was to get the door unbolted, tell Lanrivain to make his escape, and hasten back to her room. She had tried the bolt earlier in the evening, and managed to put a little grease on it; but nevertheless, when she drew it, it gave a squeak . . . not loud, but it made her heart stop; and the next minute, overhead, she heard a noise. . . .

"What noise?" the prosecution interposed.

"My husband's voice calling out my name and cursing me."

"What did you hear after that?"

"A terrible scream and a fall."

"Where was Hervé de Lanrivain at this time?"

"He was standing outside in the court. I just made him out in the darkness. I told him for God's sake to go, and then I pushed the door shut."

"What did you do next?"

"I stood at the foot of the stairs and listened."

"What did you hear?"

"I heard dogs snarling and panting." (Visible discouragement of the bench, boredom of the public, and exasperation of the lawyer for the defense. Dogs again—! But the inquisitive Judge insisted.)

"What dogs?"

She bent her head and spoke so low that she had to be told to repeat her answer: "I don't know."

"How do you mean—you don't know?"

"I don't know what dogs. . . ."

The Judge again intervened: "Try to tell us exactly what happened. How long did you remain at the foot of the stairs?"

"Only a few minutes."

"And what was going on meanwhile overhead?"

"The dogs kept on snarling and panting. Once or twice he cried out. I think he moaned once. Then he was quiet."

"Then what happened?"

"Then I heard a sound like the noise of a pack when the wolf is thrown to them—gulping and lapping."

(There was a groan of disgust and repulsion through the court, and another attempted intervention by the distracted lawyer. But the inquisitive Judge was still inquisitive.)

"And all the while you did not go up?"

"Yes—I went up then—to drive them off."

"The dogs?"

"Yes."

"Well—?"

"When I got there it was quite dark. I found my husband's flint and steel and struck a spark. I saw him lying there. He was dead."

"And the dogs?"

"The dogs were gone."

"Gone—where to?"

"I don't know. There was no way out—and there were no dogs at Kerfol."

She straightened herself to her full height, threw her arms above her head, and fell down on the stone floor with a long scream. There was a moment of confusion in the court-room. Some one on the bench was heard to say: "This is clearly a case for the ecclesiastical authorities"—and the prisoner's lawyer doubtless jumped at the suggestion.

After this, the trial loses itself in a maze of cross-questioning and squabbling. Every witness who was called corroborated Anne de Cornault's statement that there were no dogs at Kerfol: had been none for several months. The master of the house had taken a dislike to dogs, there was no denying it. But, on the other hand, at the inquest, there had been long and bitter discussion as to the nature of the dead man's wounds. One of the surgeons called in had spoken of marks that looked like bites. The suggestion of witchcraft was revived, and the opposing lawyers hurled tomes of necromancy at each other.

At last Anne de Cornault was brought back into court—at the instance of the same Judge—and asked if she knew where the dogs she spoke of could have come from. On the body of her Redeemer she swore that she did not. Then the Judge put his final question: "If the dogs you think you heard had been known to you, do you think you would have recognized them by their barking?"

"Yes."

"Did you recognize them?"

"Yes."

"What dogs do you take them to have been?"

"My dead dogs," she said in a whisper. . . . She was taken out of court, not to reappear there again. There was some kind of ecclesiastical investigation, and the end of the business was that the Judges disagreed with each other, and with the ecclesiastical committee, and that Anne de Cornault was finally handed over to the keeping of her husband's family, who shut her up in the keep of Kerfol, where she is said to have died many years later, a harmless madwoman.

So ends her story. As for that of Hervé de Lanrivain, I had only to apply to his collateral descendant for its subsequent details. The evidence against the young man being insufficient, and his family influence in the duchy considerable, he was set free, and left soon afterward for Paris. He was probably in no mood for a worldly life, and he appears to have come almost immediately under the influence of the famous M. Arnauld d'Andilly and the gentlemen of Port Royal. A year or two later he was received into their Order, and without achieving any particular distinction he followed its good and evil fortunes till his death some twenty years later. Lanrivain showed me a portrait of him by a pupil of Philippe de Champaigne: sad eyes, an impulsive mouth and a narrow brow. Poor Hervé de Lanrivain: it was a grey ending. Yet as I looked at his stiff and sallow effigy, in the dark dress of the Jansenists, I almost found myself envying his fate. After all, in the course of his life two great things had happened to him: he had loved romantically, and he must have talked with Pascal. . . .

The Turn of the Screw

Henry James

The story had held us, round the fire, sufficiently breathless, but except the obvious remark that it was gruesome, as on Christmas Eve in an old house a strange tale should essentially be, I remember no comment uttered till somebody happened to note it as the only case he had met in which such a visitation had fallen on a child. The case, I may mention, was that of an apparition in just such an old house as had gathered us for the occasion—an appearance, of a dreadful kind, to a little boy sleeping in the room with his mother and waking her up in the terror of it; waking her not to dissipate his dread and soothe him to sleep again, but to encounter also herself, before she had succeeded in doing so, the same sight that had shocked him. It was his observation that drew from Douglas—not immediately, but later in the evening—a reply that had the interesting consequence to which I call attention. Some one else told a story not particularly effective, which I saw he was not following. This I took for a sign that he had himself something to produce and that we should only have to wait. We waited in fact till two nights later; but that same evening, before we scattered, he brought out what was in his mind.

"I quite agree—in regard to Griffin's ghost, or whatever it was—that its appearing first to the little boy, at so tender an age, adds a particular touch. But it's not the first occurrence of its charming kind that I know to have been concerned with a child. If the child gives the effect another turn of the screw, what do you say to *two* children—?"

"We say of course," somebody exclaimed, "that two children give two turns! Also that we want to hear about them."

I can see Douglas there before the fire, to which he had got up to present his back, looking down at this converser with his hands in his pockets. "Nobody but me, till now, has ever heard. It's quite too horrible." This was naturally declared by several voices to give the thing the utmost price, and our friend, with quiet art, prepared his triumph by turning his eyes over the rest of us and going on: "It's beyond everything. Nothing at all that I know touches it."

"For sheer terror?" I remember asking.

He seemed to say it wasn't so simple as that; to be really at a loss how to qualify it. He passed his hand over his eyes, made a little wincing grimace. "For dreadful—dreadfulness!"

"Oh how delicious!" cried one of the women.

He took no notice of her; he looked at me, but as if, instead of me, he saw what he spoke of. "For general uncanny ugliness and horror and pain."

"Well then," I said, "just sit right down and begin."

He turned round to the fire, gave a kick to a log, watched it an instant. Then as he faced us again: "I can't begin. I shall have to send to town." There was a unanimous groan at this, and much reproach; after which, in his preoccupied way, he explained. "The story's written. It's in a locked drawer—it has not been out for years. I could write to my man and enclose the key; he could send down the packet as he finds it." It was to me in particular that he appeared to propound this—appeared almost to appeal for aid not to hesitate. He had broken a thickness of ice, the formation of many a winter; had had his reasons for a long silence. The others resented postponement, but it was just his scruples that charmed me. I adjured him to write by the first post and to agree with us for an early hearing; then I asked him if the experience in question had been his own. To this his answer was prompt. "Oh thank God, no!"

"And is the record yours? You took the thing down?"

"Nothing but the impression. I took that *here*"—he tapped his heart. "I've never lost it."

"Then your manuscript—?"

"Is in old faded ink and in the most beautiful hand." He hung fire again. "A woman's. She has been dead these twenty years. She sent me the pages in question before she died." They were all listening now, and of course there was somebody to be arch, or at any rate to draw the inference. But if he put the inference by without a smile it was also without irritation. "She was a most charming person, but she was ten years older than I. She was my sister's governess," he quietly said. "She was the most agreeable woman I've ever known in her position; she'd have been worthy of any whatever. It was long ago, and this episode was long before. I was at Trinity, and I found her at home on my coming down the second summer I was much there that year—it was a beautiful one; and we had, in her off-hours, some strolls and talks in the garden—talks in which she struck me as awfully clever and nice. Oh yes; don't grin: I liked her extremely and am glad to this day to think she liked me too. If she hadn't she wouldn't have told me. She had never told any one. It wasn't simply that she said so, but that I knew she hadn't. I was sure; I could see. You'll easily judge why when you hear."

"Because the thing had been such a scare?"

He continued to fix me. "You'll easily judge," he repeated: "*you* will."

I fixed him too. "I see. She was in love."

He laughed for the first time. "You *are* acute. Yes, she was in love. That is she *had* been. That came out—she couldn't tell her story without its coming out. I saw it, and she saw I saw it; but neither of us spoke of it. I remember the time and the place—the corner of the lawn, the shade of the great beeches and the long hot summer afternoon. It wasn't a scene for a shudder; but oh—!" He quitted the fire and dropped back into his chair.

"You'll receive the packet Thursday morning?" I said.

"Probably not till the second post."

"Well then; after dinner—"

"You'll all meet me here?" He looked us round again. "Isn't anybody going?" It was almost the tone of hope.

"Everybody will stay!"

"*I* will—and *I* will!" cried the ladies whose departure had been fixed. Mrs. Griffin, however, expressed the need for a little more light. "Who was it she was in love with?"

"The story will tell," I took upon myself to reply.

"Oh I can't wait for the story!"

"The story *won't* tell," said Douglas; "not in any literal vulgar way."

"More's the pity then. That's the only way I ever understand."

"Won't *you* tell, Douglas?" somebody else enquired.

He sprang to his feet again. "Yes—to-morrow. Now I must go to bed. Good-night." And, quickly catching up a candlestick, he left us slightly bewildered. From our end of the great brown hall we heard his step on the stair; whereupon Mrs. Griffin spoke. "Well, if I don't know who she was in love with I know who *he* was."

"She was ten years older," said her husband.

"*Raison de plus*—at that age! But it's rather nice, his long reticence."

"Forty years!" Griffin put in.

"With this outbreak at last."

"The outbreak," I returned, "will make a tremendous occasion of Thursday night"; and every one so agreed with me that in the light of it we lost all attention for everything else. The last story, however incomplete arid like the mere opening of a serial, had been told; we handshook and "candlestuck," as somebody said, and went to bed.

I knew the next day that a letter containing the key had, by the first post, gone off to his London apartments; but in spite of—or perhaps just on account of—the eventual diffusion of this knowledge we quite let him alone till after dinner, till such an hour of the evening in fact as might best accord with the kind of emotion on which our hopes were fixed. Then he became as communicative as we could desire, and indeed gave us his best reason for being so. We had it from him again before the fire in the hall, as we had had our mild wonders of the previous night. It appeared that the narrative he had promised to read us really required for a proper intelligence a few words of prologue. Let me say here distinctly, to have done with it, that this narrative, from an exact transcript of my own made much later, is what I shall presently give. Poor Douglas, before his death—when it was in sight—committed to me the manuscript that reached him on the third of these days and that, on the same spot, with immense effect, he began to read to our hushed little circle on the night of the fourth. The departing ladies who had said they would stay didn't, of course, thank heaven, stay: they departed, in consequence of arrangements made, in a rage of curiosity, as they professed, produced by the touches with which he had already worked us up. But that only made his little final auditory more compact and select, kept it, round the hearth, subject to a common thrill.

The first of these touches conveyed that the written statement took up the tale at a point after it had, in a manner, begun. The fact to be in possession of was therefore that his old friend, the youngest of several daughters of a poor country parson, had at the age of twenty, on taking service for the first time hi the schoolroom, come up to London, in trepidation, to answer in person an advertisement that had already placed her in brief correspondence with the advertiser. This person proved, on her presenting herself for judgement at a house in Harley Street that impressed her as vast and imposing—this prospective patron proved a gentleman, a bachelor in the prime of life, such a figure as had never risen, save in a dream or an old novel, before a fluttered anxious girl out of a Hampshire vicarage. One could easily fix his type; it never, happily, dies out. He was handsome and bold and pleasant, off-hand and gay and kind. He struck her, inevitably, as gallant and splendid, but what took her most of all and gave her the courage she afterwards showed was that he put the whole thing to her as a favour, an obligation he should gratefully incur. She figured him as rich, but as fearfully extravagant—saw him all in a glow of high fashion, of good looks, of expensive habits, of charming ways with women. He had for his town residence a big house filled with the spoils of travel and the trophies of the chase; but it was to his country home, an old family place in Essex, that he wished her immediately to proceed.

He had been left, by the death of his parents in India, guardian to a small nephew and a small niece, children of a younger, a military brother whom he had lost two years before. These children were, by the strangest of chances for a man in his position—a lone man without the right sort of experience or a grain of patience—very heavy on his hands. It had all been a great worry and, on his own part doubtless, a series of blunders, but he immensely pitied the poor chicks and had done all he could; had in particular sent them down to his other house, the proper place for them being of course the country, and kept them there from the first with the best people he could find to look after them, parting even with his own servants to wait on them and going down himself, whenever he might, to see how they were doing. The awkward thing was that they had practically no other relations and that his own affairs took up all his time. He had put them in possession of Bly, which was healthy and secure, and had placed at the head of their little establishment—but belowstairs only—an excellent woman, Mrs. Grose, whom he was sure his visitor would like and who had formerly been maid to his mother. She was now housekeeper and was also acting for the time as superintendent to the little girl, of whom, without children of her own, she was by good luck extremely fond. There were plenty of people to help, but of course the young lady who should go down as governess would be in supreme authority. She would also have, in holidays, to look after the small boy, who had been for a term at school—young as he was to be sent, but what else could be done?—and who, as the holidays were about to begin, would be back from one day to the other. There had been for the two children at first a young lady whom they had had the misfortune to lose. She had done for them quite beautifully—she was a most respectable person—till her death, the great awkwardness of which had, precisely, left no alternative but the school for little Miles. Mrs. Grose, since then, in the way of manners and things, had done as she could for Flora; and there were, further, a cook, a housemaid, a dairywoman, an old pony, an old groom and an old gardener, all likewise thoroughly respectable.

So far had Douglas presented his picture when some one put a question. "And what did the former governess die of? Of so much respectability?"

Our friend's answer was prompt. "That will come out. I don't anticipate."

"Pardon me—I thought that was just what you *are* doing."

"In her successor's place," I suggested, "I should (have wished to learn if the office brought with it—"

"Necessary danger to life?" Douglas completed my thought. "She did wish to learn, and she did learn. You shall hear to-morrow what she learnt. Meanwhile of course the prospect struck her as slightly grim. She was young, untried, nervous: it was a vision of serious duties and little company, of really great loneliness. She hesitated—took a couple of days to consult and consider. But the salary offered much exceeded her modest measure, and on a second interview she faced the music, she engaged." And Douglas, with this, made a pause that, for the benefit of the company, moved me to throw in—

"The moral of which was of course the seduction exercised by the splendid young man. She succumbed to it."

He got up and, as he had done the night before, went to the fire, gave a stir to a log with his foot, then stood a moment with his back to us. "She saw him only twice."

"Yes, but that's just the beauty of her passion."

A little to my surprise, on this, Douglas turned round to me. "It *was* the beauty of it. There were others," he went on, "who hadn't succumbed. He told her frankly all his difficulty—that for several applicants the conditions had been prohibitive. They were somehow simply afraid. It sounded dull—it sounded strange; and all the more so because of his main condition."

"Which was—?"

"That she should never trouble him—but never, never: neither appeal nor complain nor write about anything; only meet all questions herself, receive all moneys from his solicitor, take the whole thing over and let him alone. She promised to do this, and she mentioned to me that when, for a moment, disburdened, delighted, he held her hand, thanking her for the sacrifice, she already felt rewarded."

"But was that all her reward?" one of the ladies asked.

"She never saw him again."

"Oh!" said the lady; which, as our friend immediately again left us, was the only other word of importance contributed to the subject till, the next night, by the corner of the hearth, in the best chair, he opened the faded red cover of a thin old-fashioned gilt-edged album. The whole thing took indeed more nights than one, but on the first occasion the same lady put another question. "What's your title?"

"I haven't one."

"Oh *I* have!" I said. But Douglas, without heeding me, had begun to read with a fine clearness that was like a rendering to the ear of the beauty of his author's hand.

I

I remember the whole beginning as a succession of flights and drops, a little see-saw of the right throbs and the wrong. Softer rising, in town, to meet his appeal I had at all events a couple of very bad days—found all my doubts bristle again, felt indeed sure I had made a mistake. In this state of mind I spent the long hours of bumping swinging coach that carried me to the stopping-place at which I was to be met by a vehicle from the house. This convenience, I was told, had been ordered, and I found, toward the close of the June afternoon, a commodious fly in waiting for me. Driving at that hour, on a lovely day, through a country the summer sweetness of which served as a friendly welcome, my fortitude revived and, as we turned into the avenue, took a flight that was probably but a proof of the point to which it had sunk. I suppose I had expected, or had dreaded, something so dreary that what greeted me was a good surprise. I remember as a thoroughly pleasant impression the broad clear front, its open windows and fresh curtains and the pair of maids looking out; I remember the lawn and the bright flowers and the crunch of my wheels on the gravel and the clustered tree-tops over which the rooks circled and cawed in the golden sky. The scene had a greatness that made it a different affair from my own scant home, and there immediately appeared at the door, with a little girl in her hand, a civil person who dropped me as decent a curtsey as if I had been the mistress or a distinguished visitor. I had received in Harley Street a narrower notion of the place, and that, as I recalled it, made me think the proprietor still more of a gentleman, suggested that what I was to enjoy might be a matter beyond his promise.

I had no drop again till the next day, for I was carried triumphantly through the following hours by my introduction to the younger of my pupils. The little girl who accompanied Mrs. Grose affected me on the spot as a creature too charming not to make it a great fortune to have to do with her. She was the most beautiful child I had ever seen, and I afterwards wondered why my employer hadn't made more of a point to me of this. I slept little that night—I was too much excited; and this astonished me too, I recollect, remained with me, adding to my sense of the liberality with which I was treated. The large impressive room, one of the best in the house, the great state bed, as I almost felt it, the figured full draperies, the long glasses in which, for the first time, I could see myself from head to foot, all struck me—like the wonderful appeal of my small charge—as so many things thrown in. It was thrown in as well, from the first moment, that I should get on with Mrs. Grose in a relation over which, on my way, in the coach, I fear I had rather brooded. The one appearance indeed that in this early outlook might have made me shrink again was that of her being so inordinately glad to see me. I felt within half an hour that she was so glad—stout simple plain clean wholesome woman—as to be positively on her guard against showing it too much. I wondered even then a little why she should wish *not* to show it, and that, with reflexion, with suspicion, might of course have made me uneasy.

But it was a comfort that there could be no uneasiness in a connexion with anything so beatific as the radiant image of my little girl, the vision of whose angelic beauty had probably more than anything else to do with the restlessness that, before morning, made me several times rise and wander about my room to take in the whole picture

THE TURN OF THE SCREW

and prospect; to watch from my open window the faint summer dawn, to look at such stretches of the rest of the house as I could catch, and to listen, while in the fading dusk the first birds began to twitter, for the possible recurrence of a sound or two, less natural and not without but within, that I had fancied I heard. There had been a moment when I believed I recognised, faint and far, the cry of a child; there had been another when I found myself just consciously starting as at the passage, before my door, of a light footstep. But these fancies were not marked enough not to be thrown off, and it is only in the light, or the gloom, I should rather say, of other and subsequent matters that they now come back to me. To watch, teach, "form" little Flora would too evidently be the making of a happy and useful life. It had been agreed between us downstairs that after this first occasion I should have her as a matter of course at night, her small white bed being already arranged, to that end, in my room. What I had undertaken was the whole care of her, and she had remained just this last time with Mrs. Grose only as an effect of our consideration for my inevitable strangeness and her natural timidity. In spite of this timidity—which the child herself, in the oddest way in the world, had been perfectly frank and brave about, allowing it, without a sign of uncomfortable consciousness, with the deep sweet serenity indeed of one of Raphael's holy infants, to be discussed, to be imputed to her and to determine us—I felt quite sure she would presently like me. It was part of what I already liked Mrs. Grose herself for, the pleasure I could see her feel in my admiration and wonder as I sat at supper with four tall candles and with my pupil, in a high chair and a bib, brightly facing me between them over bread and milk. There were naturally things that in Flora's presence could pass between us only as prodigious and gratified looks, obscure and roundabout allusions.

"And the little boy—does he look like her? Is he too so very remarkable?"

One wouldn't, it was already conveyed between us, too grossly flatter a child. "Oh Miss, *most* remarkable. If you think well of this one!"—and she stood there with a plate in her hand, beaming at our companion, who looked from one of us to the other with placid heavenly eyes that contained nothing to check us.

"Yes; if I do—?"

"You *will* be carried away by the little gentleman!"

"Well, that, I think, is what I came for—to be carried away. I'm afraid, however," I remember feeling the impulse to add, "I'm rather easily carried away. I was carried away in London!"

I can still see Mrs. Grose's broad face as she took this in. "In Harley Street?"

"In Harley Street."

"Well, Miss, you're not the first—and you won't be the last."

"Oh I've no pretensions," I could laugh, "to being the only one. My other pupil, at any rate, as I understand, comes back to-morrow?"

"Not to-morrow—Friday, Miss. He arrives, as you did, by the coach, under care of the guard, and is to be met by the same carriage."

I forthwith wanted to know if the proper as well as the pleasant and friendly thing wouldn't therefore be that on the arrival of the public conveyance I should await him with his little sister; a proposition to which Mrs. Grose assented so heartily that I somehow took her manner as a kind of comforting pledge—never falsified, thank heaven!—that we should on every question be quite at one. Oh she was glad I was there!

What I felt the next day was, I suppose, nothing that could be fairly called a reaction from the cheer of my arrival; it was probably at the most only a slight oppression produced by a fuller measure of the scale, as I walked round them, gazed up at them, took them in, of my new circumstances. They had, as it were, an extent and mass for which I had not been prepared and in the presence of which I found myself, freshly, a little scared not less than a little proud. Regular lessons, in this agitation, certainly suffered some wrong, I reflected that my first duty was, by the gentlest arts I could contrive, to win the child into the sense of knowing me. I spent the day with her out of doors; I arranged with her, to her great satisfaction, that it should be she, she only, who might show me the place. She showed it step by step and room by room and secret by secret, with droll delightful childish talk about it and with the result, in half an hour, of our becoming tremendous friends. Young as she was I was struck, throughout our little tour, with her confidence and courage, with the way, in empty chambers and dull corridors, on crooked staircases that made me pause and even on the summit of an old machicolated square tower that made me dizzy, her morning music, her disposition to tell me so many more things than she asked, rang out and led me on. I have not seen Bly since the day I left it, and I dare say that to my present older and more informed eyes it would show a very reduced importance. But as my little conductress, with her hair of gold and her frock of blue, danced before me round corners and pattered down passages, I had the view of a castle of romance inhabited by a rosy sprite, such a place as would somehow, for diversion of the young idea, take all colour out of story-books and fairy-tales. Wasn't it just a story-book over which I had fallen a-doze and a-dream? No; it was a big ugly antique but convenient house, embodying a few features of a building still older, half-displaced and half-utilised, in which I had the fancy of our being almost as lost as a handful of passengers in a great drifting ship. Well, I was strangely at the helm!

II

This came home to me when, two days later, I drove over with Flora to meet, as Mrs. Grose said, the little gentleman; and all the more for an incident that, presenting itself the second evening, had deeply disconcerted me. The first day had been, on the whole, as I have expressed, reassuring; but I was to see it wind up to a change of note. The postbag that evening—it came late—contained a letter for me which, however, in the hand of my employer, I found to be composed but of a few words enclosing another, addressed to himself, with a seal still unbroken. "This, I recognise, is from the head-master, and the headmaster's an awful bore. Read him, please; deal with him; but mind you don't report. Not a word. I'm off!" I broke the seal with a great effort— so great a one that I was a long time coming to it; took the unopened missive at last up to my room and only attacked it just before going to bed. I had better have let it wait till morning, for it gave me a second sleepless night. With no counsel to take, the next day, I was full of distress; and it finally got so the better of me that I determined to open myself at least to Mrs. Grose.

"What does it mean? The child's dismissed his school."

She gave me a look that I remarked at the moment; then, visibly, with a quick blankness, seemed to try to take it back. "But aren't they all—?"

"Sent home—yes. But only for the holidays. Miles may never go back at all."

Consciously, under my attention, she reddened. "They won't take him?"

"They absolutely decline."

At this she raised her eyes, which she had turned from me; I saw them fill with good tears. "What has he done?"

I cast about; then I judged best simply to hand her my document—which, however, had the effect of making her, without taking it, simply put her hands behind her. She shook her head sadly. "Such things are not for me, Miss."

My counsellor couldn't read! I winced at my mistake, which I attenuated as I could, and opened the letter again to repeat it to her; then, faltering in the act and folding it up once more, I put it back in my pocket. "Is he really *bad*?"

The tears were still in her eyes. "Do the gentlemen say so?"

"They go into no particulars. They simply express their regret that it should be impossible to keep him. That can have but one meaning." Mrs. Grose listened with dumb emotion; she forbore to ask me what this meaning might be; so that, presently, to put the thing with some coherence and with the mere aid of her presence to my own mind, I went on: "That he's an injury to the others."

At this, with one of the quick turns of simple folk, she suddenly flamed up. "Master Miles!—*him* an injury?"

There was such a flood of good faith in it that, though I had not yet seen the child, my very fears made me jump to the absurdity of the idea. I found myself, to meet my friend the better, offering it, on the spot, sarcastically. "To his poor little innocent mates!"

"It's too dreadful," cried Mrs. Grose, "to say such cruel things! Why he's scarce ten years old."

"Yes, yes; it would be incredible."

She was evidently grateful for such a profession. "See him, Miss, first. *Then* believe it!" I felt forthwith a new impatience to see him; it was the beginning of a curiosity that, all the next hours, was to deepen almost to pain. Mrs. Grose was aware, I could judge, of what she had produced in me, and she followed it up with assurance. "You might as well believe it of the little lady. Bless her," she added the next moment—"*look* at her!"

I turned and saw that Flora, whom, ten minutes before, I had established in the schoolroom with a sheet of white paper, a pencil and a copy of nice "round O's," now presented herself to view at the open door. She expressed in her little way an extraordinary detachment from disagreeable duties, looking at me, however, with a great childish light that seemed to offer it as a mere result of the affection she had conceived for my person, which had rendered necessary that she should follow me. I needed nothing more than this to feel the full force of Mrs. Grose's comparison, and, catching my pupil in my arms, covered her with kisses in which there was a sob of atonement.

None the less, the rest of the day, I watched for further occasion to approach my colleague, especially as, toward evening, I began to fancy she rather sought to avoid me. I overtook her, I remember, on the staircase; we went down together and at the bottom I detained her, holding her there with a hand on her arm. "I take what you said to me at noon as a declaration that *you've* never known him to be bad."

She threw back her head; she had clearly by this time, and very honestly, adopted an attitude. "Oh never known him—I don't pretend *that*!"

I was upset again. "Then you *have* known him—?"

"Yes indeed, Miss, thank God!"

On reflexion I accepted this. "You mean that a boy who never is —?"

"Is no boy for *me*!"

I held her tighter. "You like them with the spirit to be naughty?" Then, keeping pace with her answer, "So do I!" I eagerly brought out. "But not to the degree to contaminate—"

"To contaminate?"—my big word left her at a loss.

I explained it. "To corrupt."

She stared, taking my meaning in; but it produced in her an odd laugh. "Are you afraid he'll corrupt *you*?" She put the question with such a fine bold humour that with a laugh, a little silly doubtless, to match her own, I gave way for the time to the apprehension of ridicule.

But the next day, as the hour for my drive approached, I cropped up in another place. "What was the lady who was here before?"

"The last governess? She was also young and pretty—almost as young and almost as pretty, Miss, even as you."

"Ah then I hope her youth and her beauty helped her!" I recollect throwing off. "He seems to like us young and pretty!"

"Oh he *did*," Mrs. Grose assented: "it was the way he liked every one!" She had no sooner spoken indeed than she caught herself up. "I mean that's *his* way—the master's."

I was struck. "But of whom did you speak first?"

She looked blank, but she coloured. "Why of *him*."

"Of the master?"

"Of who else?"

There was so obviously no one else that the next moment I had lost my impression of her having accidentally said more than she meant; and I merely asked what I wanted to know. "Did *she* see anything in the boy—?"

"That wasn't right? She never told me."

I had a scruple, but I overcame it. "Was she careful—particular?"

Mrs. Grose appeared to try to be conscientious. "About some things—yes."

"But not about all?"

Again she considered. "Well, Miss—she's gone. I won't tell tales."

"I quite understand your feeling," I hastened to reply; but I thought it after an instant not opposed to this concession to pursue: "Did she die here?"

"No—she went off."

I don't know what there was in this brevity of Mrs. Grose's that struck me as ambiguous. "Went off to die?" Mrs. Grose looked straight out of the window, but I felt that, hypothetically, I had a right to know what young persons engaged for Bly were expected to do. "She was taken ill, you mean, and went home?"

"She was not taken ill, so far as appeared, in this house. She left it, at the end of the year, to go home, as she said, for a short holiday, to which the time she had put in had certainly given her a right. We had then a young woman—a nursemaid who had stayed on and who was a good girl and clever; and *she* took the children altogether for the interval. But our young lady never came back, and at the very moment I was expecting her I heard from the master that she was dead."

I turned this over. "But of what?"

"He never told me! But please, Miss," said Mrs. Grose, "I must get to my work."

III

Her thus turning her back on me was fortunately not, for my just preoccupations, a snub that could check the growth of our mutual esteem. We met, after I had brought home little Miles, more intimately than ever on the ground of my stupefaction, my general emotion: so monstrous was I then ready to pronounce it that such a child as had now been revealed to me should be under an interdict. I was a little late on the scene of his arrival, and I felt, as he stood wistfully looking out for me before the door of the inn at which the coach had put him down, that I had seen him on the instant, without and within, in the great glow of freshness, the same positive fragrance of purity, in which I had from the first moment seen his little sister. He was incredibly beautiful, and Mrs. Grose had put her finger on it: everything but a sort of passion of tenderness for him was swept away by his presence. What I then and there took him to my heart for was something divine that I have never found to the same degree in any child—his indescribable little air of knowing nothing in the world but love. It would have been impossible to carry a bad name with a greater sweetness of innocence, and by the time I had got back to Bly with him I remained merely bewildered—so far, that is, as I was not outraged—by the sense of the horrible letter locked up in one of the drawers of my room. As soon as I could compass a private word with Mrs. Grose I declared to her that it was grotesque.

She promptly understood me. "You mean the cruel charge—?"

"It doesn't live an instant. My dear woman, *look* at him!"

She smiled at my pretension to have discovered his charm. "I assure you, Miss, I do nothing else! What will you say then?" she immediately added.

"In answer to the letter?" I had made up my mind. "Nothing at all."

"And to his uncle?"

I was incisive. "Nothing at all."

"And to the boy himself?"

I was wonderful. "Nothing at all."

She gave with her apron a great wipe to her mouth. "Then I'll stand by you. We'll see it out."

"We'll see it out!" I ardently echoed, giving her my hand to make it a vow.

She held me there a moment, then whisked up her apron again with her detached hand. "Would you mind, Miss, if I used the freedom—"

"To kiss me? No!" I took the good creature in my arms and after we had embraced like sisters felt still more fortified and indignant.

This at all events was for the time: a time so full that as I recall the way it went it reminds me of all the art I now need to make it a little distinct. What I look back at with amazement is the situation I accepted. I had undertaken, with my companion, to see it out, and I was under a charm apparently that could smooth away the extent and the far and difficult connexions of such an effort. I was lifted aloft on a great wave of infatuation and pity. I found it simple, in my ignorance, my confusion and perhaps my conceit, to assume that I could deal with a boy whose education for the world was all on the point of beginning. I am unable even to remember at this day what proposal I framed for the end of his holidays and the resumption of his studies. Lessons with me indeed, that charming summer, we all had a theory that he was to have; but I now feel that for weeks the lessons must have been rather my own. I learnt something—at first certainly—that had not been one of the teachings of my small smothered life; learnt to be amused, and even amusing, and not to think for the morrow. It was the first time, in a manner, that I had known space and air and freedom, all the music of summer and all the mystery of nature. And then there was consideration—and consideration was sweet. Oh it was a trap—not designed but deep—to my imagination, to my delicacy, perhaps to my vanity; to whatever in me was most excitable. The best way to picture it all is to say that I was off my guard. They gave me so little trouble—they were of a gentleness so extraordinary. I used to speculate—but even this with a dim disconnectedness—as to how the rough future (for all futures are rough!) would handle them and might bruise them. They had the bloom of health and happiness; and yet, as if I had been in charge of a pair of little grandees, of princes of the blood, for whom everything, to be right, would have to be fenced about and ordered and arranged, the only form that in my fancy the after-years could take for them was that of a romantic, a really royal extension of the garden and the park. It may be of course above all that what suddenly broke into this gives the previous time a charm of stillness—that hush in which something gathers or crouches. The change was actually like the spring of a beast.

In the first weeks the days were long; they often, at their finest, gave me what I used to call my own hour, the hour when, for my pupils, tea-time and bed-time having come and gone, I had before my final retirement a small interval alone. Much as I liked my companions this hour was the thing in the day I liked most; and I liked it best of all when, as the light faded—or rather, I should say, the day lingered and the last calls of the last birds sounded, in a flushed sky, from the old trees—I could take a turn into the grounds and enjoy, almost with a sense of property that amused and flattered me, the beauty and dignity of the place. It was a pleasure at these moments to feel myself tranquil and justified; doubtless perhaps also to reflect that by my discretion, my quiet good sense and general high propriety, I was giving pleasure—if he ever thought of it!—to the person to whose pressure I had yielded. What I was doing was what he had earnestly hoped and directly asked of me, and that I *could*, after all, do it proved even a greater joy than I had expected. I dare say I fancied myself in short a remarkable young woman and took comfort in the faith that this would more publicly appear. Well, I needed to be remarkable to offer a front to the remarkable things that presently gave their first sign.

It was plump, one afternoon, in the middle of my very hour: the children were tucked away and I had come out for my stroll. One of the thoughts that, as I don't in the least shrink now from noting, used to be with me in these wanderings was that it would be as charming as a charming story suddenly to meet some one. Some one would appear there at the turn of a path and would stand before me and smile and approve. I didn't ask more than that—I only asked that he should *know*; and the only way to be sure he knew would be to see it, and the kind light of it, in his handsome face. That was exactly present to me—by which I mean the face was—when, on the first of these occasions, at the end of a long June day, I stopped short on emerging from one of the plantations and coming into view of the house. What arrested me on the spot—and with a shock much greater than any vision had allowed for—was the sense that my imagination had, in a flash, turned real. He did stand there!—but high up, beyond the lawn and at the very top of the tower to which, on that first morning, little Flora had conducted me. This tower was one of a pair—square incongruous crenellated structures—that were distinguished, for some reason, though I could see little difference, as the new and the old. They flanked opposite ends of the house and were probably architectural absurdities, redeemed in a measure indeed by not being wholly disengaged nor of a height too pretentious, dating, in their gingerbread antiquity, from a romantic revival that was already a respectable past. I admired them, had fancies about them, for we could all profit in a degree, especially when they loomed through the dusk, by the grandeur of their actual battlements; yet it was not at such an elevation that the figure I had so often invoked seemed most in place.

It produced in me, this figure, in the clear twilight, I remember, two distinct gasps of emotion, which were, sharply, the shock of my first and that of my second surprise. My second was a violent perception of the mistake of my first: the man who met my eyes was not the person I had precipitately supposed. There came to me thus a bewilderment of vision of which, after these years, there is no living view that I can hope to give. An unknown man in a lonely place is a permitted object of fear to a young woman privately bred; and the figure that faced me was—a few more seconds assured me—as little any one else I knew as it was the image that had been in my mind. I had not seen it in Harley Street—I had not seen it anywhere. The place moreover, in the strangest way in the world, had on the instant and by the very fact of its appearance become a solitude. To me at least, making my statement here with a deliberation with which I have never made it, the whole feeling of the moment returns. It was as if, while I took in, what I did take in, all the rest of the scene had been stricken with death. I can hear again, as I write, the intense hush in which the sounds of evening dropped. The rooks stopped cawing in the golden sky and the friendly hour lost for the unspeakable minute all its voice. But there was no other change in nature, unless indeed it were a change that I saw with a stranger sharpness. The gold was still in the sky, the clearness in the air, and the man who looked at me over the battlements was as definite as a picture in a frame. That's how I thought, with extraordinary quickness, of each person he might have been and that he wasn't. We were confronted across our distance quite long enough for me to ask myself with intensity who then he was and to feel, as an effect of my inability to say, a wonder that in a few seconds more became intense.

The great question, or one of these, is afterwards, I know, with regard to certain matters, the question of how long they have lasted. Well, this matter of mine, think what you will of it, lasted while I caught at a dozen possibilities, none of which made a difference for the better, that I could see, in there having been in the house—and for how long, above all?—a person of whom I was in ignorance. It lasted while I just bridled a little with the sense of how my office seemed to require that there should be no such ignorance and no such person. It lasted while this visitant, at all events—and there was a touch of the strange freedom, as I remember, in the sign of familiarity of his wearing no hat—seemed to fix me, from his position, with just the question, just the scrutiny through the fading light, that his own presence provoked. We were too far apart to call to each other, but there was a moment at which, at shorter range, some challenge between us, breaking the hush, would have been the right result of our straight mutual stare. He was in one of the angles, the one away from the house, very erect, as it struck me, and with both hands on the ledge. So I saw him as I see the letters I form on this page; then, exactly, after a minute, as if to add to the spectacle, he slowly changed his place—passed, looking at me hard all the while, to the opposite corner of the platform. Yes, it was intense to me that during this transit he never took his eyes from me, and I can see at this moment the way his hand, as he went, moved from one of the crenellations to the next. He stopped at the other corner, but less long, and even as he turned away still markedly fixed me. He turned away; that was all I knew.

IV

It was not that I didn't wait, on this occasion, for more, since I was as deeply rooted as shaken. Was there a "secret" at Bly—a mystery of Udolpho or an insane, an unmentionable relative kept in unsuspected confinement? I can't say how long I turned it over, or how long, in a confusion of curiosity and dread, I remained where I had had my collision; I only recall that when I re-entered the house darkness had quite closed in. Agitation, in the interval, certainly had held me and driven me, for I must, in circling about the place, have walked three miles; but I was to be later on so much more overwhelmed that this mere dawn of alarm was a comparatively human chill. The most singular part of it in fact—singular as the rest had been—was the part I became, in the hall, aware of in meeting Mrs. Grose. This picture comes back to me in the general train—the impression, as I received it on my return, of the wide white panelled space, bright in the lamplight and with its portraits and red carpet, and of the good surprised look of my friend, which immediately told me she had missed me. It came to me straightway, under her contact, that, with plain heartiness, mere relieved anxiety at my appearance, she knew nothing whatever that could bear upon the incident I had there ready for her. I had not suspected in advance that her comfortable face would pull me up, and I somehow measured the importance of what I had seen by my thus finding myself hesitate to mention it. Scarce anything in the whole history seems to me so odd as this fact that my real beginning of fear was one, as I may say, with the instinct of sparing my companion. On the spot, accordingly, in the pleasant hall and with her eyes on me, I, for a reason that I couldn't then have phrased, achieved an inward revolution—offered a vague pretext for my lateness and, with the plea of the beauty of the night and of the heavy dew and wet feet, went as soon as possible to my room.

Here it was another affair; here, for many days after, it was a queer affair enough. There were hours, from day to day—or at least there were moments, snatched even from clear duties—when I had to shut myself up to think. It wasn't so much yet that I was more nervous than I could bear to be as that I was remarkably afraid of becoming so; for the truth I had now to turn over was simply and clearly the truth that I could arrive at no account whatever of the visitor with whom I had been so inexplicably and yet, as it seemed to me, so intimately concerned. It took me little time to see that I might easily sound, without forms of enquiry and without exciting remark, any domestic complication. The shock I had suffered must have sharpened all my senses; I felt sure, at the end of three days and as the result of mere closer attention, that I had not been practised upon by the servants nor made the object of any "game." Of whatever it was that I knew nothing was known around me. There was but one sane inference: some one had taken a liberty rather monstrous. That was what, repeatedly, I dipped into my room and locked the door to say to myself. We had been, collectively, subject to an intrusion; some unscrupulous traveller, curious in old houses, had made his way in unobserved, enjoyed the prospect from the best point of view and then stolen out as he came. If he had given me such a hold hard stare, that was but a part of his indiscretion. The good thing, after all, was that we should surely see no more of him.

This was not so good a thing, I admit, as not to leave me to judge that what, essentially, made nothing else much signify was simply my charming work. My charming work was just my life with Miles and Flora, and through nothing could I so like it as through feeling that to throw myself into it was to throw myself out of my trouble. The attraction of my small charges was a constant joy, leading me to wonder afresh at the vanity of my original fears, the distaste I had begun by entertaining for the probable grey prose of my office. There was to be no grey prose, it appeared, and no long grind; so how could work not be charming that presented itself as daily beauty? It was all the romance of the nursery and the poetry of the schoolroom. I don't mean by this of course that we studied only fiction and verse; I mean that I can express no otherwise the sort of interest my companions inspired. How can I describe that except by saying that instead of growing deadly used to them—and it's a marvel for a governess: I call the sisterhood to witness!—I made constant fresh discoveries. There was one direction, assuredly, in which these discoveries stopped: deep obscurity continued to cover the region of the boy's conduct at school. It had been promptly given me, I have noted, to face that mystery without a pang. Perhaps even it would be nearer the truth to say that—without a word—he himself had cleared it up. He had made the whole charge absurd. My conclusion bloomed there with the real rose-flush of his innocence: he was only too fine and fair for the little horrid unclean school-world, and he had paid a price for it. I reflected acutely that the sense of such individual differences, such superiorities of quality, always, on the part of the majority—which could include even stupid sordid head-masters—turns infallibly to the vindictive.

Both the children had a gentleness—it was their only fault, and it never made Miles a muff—that kept them (how shall I express it?) almost impersonal and certainly quite unpunishable. They were like those cherubs of the anecdote who had—morally at any rate—nothing to whack! I remember feeling with Miles in especial as if he had had, as it were, nothing to call even an infinitesimal history. We expect of a small child scant enough "antecedents," but there was in this beautiful little boy something extraordinarily sensitive, yet extraordinarily happy, that, more than in any creature of his age I have seen, struck me as beginning anew each day. He had never for a second suffered. I took this as a direct disproof of his having really been chastised. If he had been wicked he would have "caught" it, and I should have caught it by the rebound—I should have found the trace, should have felt the wound and the dishonour. I could reconstitute nothing at all, and he was therefore an angel. He never spoke of his school, never mentioned a comrade or a master; and I, for my part, was quite too much disgusted to allude to them. Of course I was under the spell, and the wonderful part is that, even at the time, I perfectly knew I was. But I gave myself up to it; it was an antidote to any pain, and I had more pains than one. I was in receipt in these days of disturbing letters from home, where things were not going well. But with this joy of my children what things in the world mattered? That was the question I used to put to my scrappy retirements. I was dazzled by their loveliness.

There was a Sunday—to get on—when it rained with such force and for so many hours that there could be no procession to church; in consequence of which, as the day declined, I had arranged with Mrs. Grose that, should the evening show improvement, we would attend together the late service. The rain happily stopped, and I prepared for our walk, which, through the park and by the good road to the village, would be a matter of twenty minutes. Coming downstairs to meet my colleague in the hall, I remembered a pair of gloves that had required three stitches and that had received them—with a publicity perhaps not edifying—while I sat with the children at their tea, served on Sundays, by exception, in that cold clean temple of mahogany and brass, the "grown-up" dining-room. The gloves had been dropped there, and I turned in to recover them. The day was grey enough, but the afternoon light still lingered, and it enabled me, on crossing the threshold, not only to recognise, on a chair near the wide window, then closed, the articles I wanted, but to become aware of a person on the other side of the window and looking straight in. One step into the room had sufficed; my vision was instantaneous; it was all there. The person looking straight in was the person who had already appeared to me. He appeared thus again with I won't say greater distinctness, for that was impossible, but with a nearness that represented a forward stride in our intercourse and made me, as I met him, catch my breath and turn cold. He was the same—he was the same, and seen, this time, as he had been seen before, from the waist up, the window, though the dining-room was on the ground floor, not going down to the terrace on which he stood. His face was close to the glass, yet the effect of this better view was, strangely, just to show me how intense the former had been. He remained but a few seconds—long enough to

THE TURN OF THE SCREW

convince me he also saw and recognised; but it was as if I had been looking at him for years and had known him always. Something, however, happened this time that had not happened before; his stare into my face, through the glass and across the room, was as deep and hard as then, but it quitted me for a moment during which I could still watch it, see it fix successively several other things. On the spot there came to me the added shock of a certitude that it was not for me he had come. He had come for some one else.

The flash of this knowledge—for it was knowledge in the midst of dread—produced in me the most extraordinary effect, starting, as I stood there, a sudden vibration of duty and courage. I say courage because I was beyond all doubt already far gone. I bounded straight out of the door again, reached that of the house, got in an instant upon the drive and, passing along the terrace as fast as I could rush, turned a corner and came full in sight. But it was in sight of nothing now—my visitor had vanished. I stopped, almost dropped, with the real relief of this; but I took in the whole scene—I gave him time to reappear. I call it time, but how long was it? I can't speak to the purpose to-day of the duration of these things. That kind of measure must have left me: they couldn't have lasted as they actually appeared to me to last. The terrace and the whole place, the lawn and the garden beyond it, all I could see of the park, were empty with a great emptiness. There were shrubberies and big trees, but I remember the clear assurance I felt that none of them concealed him. He was there or was not there: not there if I didn't see him. I got hold of this; then, instinctively, instead of returning as I had come, went to the window. It was confusedly present to me that I ought to place myself where he had stood. I did so; I applied my face to the pane and looked, as he had looked, into the room. As if, at this moment, to show me exactly what his range had been, Mrs. Grose, as I had done for himself just before, came in from the hall. With this I had the full image of a repetition of what had already occurred. She saw me as I had seen my own visitant; she pulled up short as I had done; I gave her something of the shock that I had received. She turned white, and this made me ask myself if I had blanched as much. She stared, in short, and retreated just on *my* lines, and I knew she had then passed out and come round to me and that I should presently meet her. I remained where I was, and while I waited I thought of more things than one. But there's only one I take space to mention. I wondered why *she* should be scared.

V

Oh she let me know as soon as, round the corner of the house, she loomed again into view. "What in the name of goodness is the matter—?" She was now flushed and out of breath.

I said nothing till she came quite near. "With me?" I must have made a wonderful face. "Do I show it?"

"You're as white as a sheet. You look awful."

I considered; I could meet on this, without scruple, any degree of innocence. My need to respect the bloom of Mrs. Grose's had dropped, without a rustle, from my shoulders, and if I wavered for the instant it was not with what I kept back. I put out my hand to her and she took it; I held her hard a little, liking to feel her close to me. There was a kind of support in the shy heave of her surprise. "You came for me for church, of course, but I can't go."

"Has anything happened?"

"Yes. You must know now. Did I look very queer?"

"Through this window? Dreadful!"

"Well," I said, "I've been frightened." Mrs. Grose's eyes expressed plainly that *she* had no wish to be, yet also that she knew too well her place not to be ready to share with me any marked inconvenience. Oh it was quite settled that she *must* share! "Just what you saw from the dining-room a minute ago was the effect of that. What *I* saw—just before—was much worse."

Her hand tightened. "What was it?"

"An extraordinary man. Looking in."

"What extraordinary man?"

"I haven't the least idea."

Mrs. Grose gazed round us in vain. "Then where is he gone?"

"I know still less."

"Have you seen him before?"

"Yes—once. On the old tower."

She could only look at me harder. "Do you mean he's a stranger?"

"Oh very much!"

"Yet you didn't tell me?"

"No—for reasons. But now that you've guessed—"

Mrs. Grose's round eyes encountered this charge. "Ah I haven't guessed!" she said very simply. "How can I if *you* don't imagine?"

"I don't in the very least."

"You've seen him nowhere but on the tower?"

"And on this spot just now."

Mrs. Grose looked round again. "What was he doing on the tower?"

"Only standing there and looking down at me."

She thought a minute. "Was he a gentleman?"

I found I had no need to think. "No." She gazed in deeper wonder. "No."

"Then nobody about the place? Nobody from the village?"

"Nobody—nobody. I didn't tell you, but I made sure."

She breathed a vague relief: this was, oddly, so much to the good. It only went indeed a little way. "But if he isn't a gentleman—"

"What *is* he? He's a horror."

"A horror?"

"He's—God help me if I know *what* he is!"

Mrs. Grose looked round once more; she fixed her eyes on the duskier distance and then, pulling herself together, turned to me with full inconsequence. "It's time we should be at church."

"Oh I'm not fit for church!"

"Won't it do you good?"

"It won't do *them*—!" I nodded at the house.

"The children?"

"I can't leave them now."

"You're afraid—?"

I spoke boldly. "I'm afraid of *him*."

Mrs. Grose's large face showed me, at this, for the first time, the far-away faint glimmer of a consciousness more acute: I somehow made out in it the delayed dawn of an idea I myself had not given her and that was as yet quite obscure to me. It comes back to me that I thought instantly of this as something I could get from her; and I felt it to be connected with the desire she presently showed to know more. "When was it—on the tower?"

"About the middle of the month. At this same hour."

"Almost at dark," said Mrs. Grose. "Oh no, not nearly. I saw him as I see you."

"Then how did he get in?"

"And how did he get out?" I laughed. "I had no opportunity to ask him! This evening, you see," I pursued, "he has not been able to get in."

"He only peeps?"

"I hope it will be confined to that!" She had now let go my hand; she turned away a little. I waited an instant; then I brought out: "Go to church. Goodbye. I must watch."

Slowly she faced me again. "Do you fear for them?"

We met in another long look. "Don't *you*?" Instead of answering she came nearer to the window and, for a minute, applied her face to the glass. "You see how he could see," I meanwhile went on.

She didn't move. "How long was he here?"

"Till I came out. I came to meet him."

Mrs. Grose at last turned round, and there was still more in her face. "*I* couldn't have come out."

"Neither could I!" I laughed again. "But I did come. I've my duty."

"So have I mine," she replied; after which she added: "What's he like?"

"I've been dying to tell you. But he's like nobody."

"Nobody?" she echoed.

"He has no hat." Then seeing in her face that she already, in this, with a deeper dismay, found a touch of picture, I quickly added stroke to stroke. "He has red hair, very red, close-curling, and a pale face, long in shape, with straight good features and little rather queer whiskers that are as red as his hair. His eyebrows are somehow darker; they look particularly arched and as if they might move a good deal. His eyes are sharp, strange—awfully; but I only know clearly that they're rather small and very fixed. His mouth's wide, and his lips are thin, and except for his little whiskers he's quite clean-shaven. He gives me a sort of sense of looking like an actor."

"An actor!" It was impossible to resemble one less, at least, than Mrs. Grose at that moment.

"I've never seen one, but so I suppose them. He's tall, active, erect," I continued, "but never—no, never!—a gentleman."

My companion's face had blanched as I went on; her round eyes started and her mild mouth gaped. "A gentleman?" she gasped, confounded, stupefied: "a gentleman *he*?"

"You know him then?"

She visibly tried to hold herself. "But he *is* handsome?"

I saw the way to help her. "Remarkably!"

"And dressed—?"

"In somebody's clothes. They're smart, but they're not his own."

She broke into a breathless affirmative groan. "They're the master's!"

I caught it up. "You *do* know him?"

She faltered but a second. "Quint!" she cried.

"Quint?"

"Peter Quint—his own man, his valet, when he was here!"

"When the master was?"

Gaping still, but meeting me, she pieced it all together. "He never wore his hat, but he did wear—well, there were waistcoats missed! They were both here—last year. Then the master went, and Quint was alone."

I followed, but halting a little. "Alone?"

"Alone with *us*." Then as from a deeper depth, "In charge," she added.

"And what became of him?"

She hung fire so long that I was still more mystified. "He went too," she brought out at last.

"Went where?"

Her expression, at this, became extraordinary. "God knows where! He died."

"Died?" I almost shrieked.

She seemed fairly to square herself, plant herself more firmly to express the wonder of it. "Yes. Mr. Quint's dead."

VI

It took of course more than that particular passage to place us together in presence of what we had now to live with as we could, my dreadful liability to impressions of the order so vividly exemplified, and my companion's knowledge henceforth—a knowledge half consternation and half compassion—of that liability. There had been this evening, after the revelation that left me for an hour so prostrate—there had been for either of us no attendance on any service but a little service of tears and vows, of prayers and promises, a climax to the series of mutual challenges and pledges that had straightway ensued on our retreating together to the schoolroom and shutting ourselves up there to have everything out. The result of our having everything out was simply to reduce our situation to the last rigour of its elements. She herself had seen nothing, not the shadow of a shadow, and nobody in the house but the governess was in the governess's plight; yet she accepted without directly impugning my sanity the truth as I gave it to her, and ended by showing me on this ground an awestricken tenderness, a deference to my more than questionable privilege, of which the very breath has remained with me as that of the sweetest of human charities.

What was settled between us accordingly that night was that we thought we might bear things together; and I was not even sure that in spite of her exemption it was she who had the best of the burden. I knew at this hour, I think, as well as I knew later, what I was capable of meeting to shelter my pupils; but it took me some time to be wholly sure of what my honest comrade was prepared for to keep terms with so stiff an agreement. I was queer company enough—quite as queer as the company I received; but as I trace over what we went through I see how much common ground we must have found in the one idea that, by good fortune, *could* steady us. It was the idea, the second movement, that led me straight out, as I may say, of the inner chamber of my dread. I could take the air in the court, at least, and there Mrs. Grose could join me. Perfectly can I recall now the particular way strength came to me before we separated for the night. We had gone over and over every feature of what I had seen.

"He was looking for some one else, you say—some one who was not you?"

"He was looking for little Miles." A portentous clearness now possessed me. "*That's* whom he was looking for."

"But how do you know?"

"I know, I know, I know!" My exaltation grew. "And *you* know, my dear!"

She didn't deny this, but I required, I felt, not even so much telling as that. She took it up again in a moment. "What if *he* should see him?"

"Little Miles? That's what he wants!"

She looked immensely scared again. "The child?"

"Heaven forbid! The man. He wants to appear to them." That he might was an awful conception, and yet somehow I could keep it at bay; which moreover, as we lingered there, was what I succeeded in practically proving. I had an absolute certainty that I should see again what I had already seen, but something within me said that by offering myself bravely as the sole subject of such experience, by accepting, by inviting, by surmounting it all, I should serve as an expiatory victim and guard the tranquillity of the rest of the household. The children in especial I should thus fence about and absolutely save. I recall one of the last things I said that night to Mrs. Grose.

"It does strike me that my pupils have never mentioned—!"

She looked at me hard as I musingly pulled up. "His having been here and the time they were with him?"

"The time they were with him, and his name, his presence, his history, in any way. They've never alluded to it."

"Oh the little lady doesn't remember. She never heard or knew."

"The circumstances of his death?" I thought with some intensity. "Perhaps not. But Miles would remember—Miles would know."

"Ah don't try him!" broke from Mrs. Grose.

I returned her the look she had given me. "Don't be afraid." I continued to think. "It *is* rather odd."

"That he has never spoken of him?"

"Never by the least reference. And you tell me they were 'great friends.'"

"Oh it wasn't *him*!" Mrs. Grose with emphasis declared. "It was Quint's own fancy. To play with him, I mean—to spoil him." She paused a moment; then she added: "Quint was much too free."

This gave me, straight from my vision of his face—*such* a face!—a sudden sickness of disgust. "Too free with *my* boy?"

"Too free with every one!"

I forbore for the moment to analyse this description further than by the reflexion that a part of it applied to several of the members of the household, of the half-dozen maids and men who were still of our small colony. But there was everything, for our apprehension, in the lucky fact that no discomfortable legend, no perturbation of scullions, had ever, within any one's memory, attached to the kind old place. It had neither bad name nor ill fame, and Mrs. Grose, most apparently, only desired to cling to me and to quake in silence. I even put her, the very last thing of all, to the test. It was when, at midnight, she had her hand on the schoolroom door to take leave. "I *have* it from you then—for it's of great importance—that he was definitely and admittedly bad?"

"Oh not admittedly. *I* knew it—but the master didn't."

"And you never told him?"

"Well, he didn't like tale-bearing—he hated complaints. He was terribly short with anything of that kind, and if people were all right to *him*—"

"He wouldn't be bothered with more?" This squared well enough with my impression of him: he was not a trouble-loving gentleman, nor so very particular perhaps about some of the company he himself kept. All the same, I pressed my informant. "I promise you *I* would have told!"

She felt my discrimination. "I dare say I was wrong. But really I was afraid."

"Afraid of what?"

"Of things that man could do. Quint was so clever—he was so deep."

I took this in still more than I probably showed. "You weren't afraid of anything else? Not of his effect—?"

"His effect?" she repeated with a face of anguish and waiting while I faltered.

"On innocent little precious lives. They were in your charge."

"No, they weren't in mine!" she roundly and distressfully returned. "The master believed in him and placed him here because he was supposed not to be quite in health and the country air so good for him. So he had everything to say. Yes"—she let me have it—"even about *them*."

"Them—that creature?" I had to smother a kind of howl. "And you could bear it?"

"No. I couldn't—and I can't now!" And the poor woman burst into tears.

A rigid control, from the next day, was, as I have said, to follow them; yet how often and how passionately, for a week, we came back together to the subject! Much as we had discussed it that Sunday night, I was, in the immediate later hours in especial—for it may be imagined whether I slept—still haunted with the shadow of something she had not told me. I myself had kept back nothing, but there was a word Mrs. Grose had kept back. I was sure moreover by morning that this was not from a failure of frankness, but because on every side there were fears. It seems to me indeed, in raking it all over, that by the time the morrow's sun was high I had restlessly read into the facts before us almost all the meaning they were to receive from subsequent and more cruel occurrences. What they gave me above all was just the sinister figure of the living man—the dead one would keep a while!—and of the months he had continuously passed at Bly, which, added up, made a formidable stretch. The limit of this evil time had arrived only when, on the dawn of a winter's morning, Peter Quint was found, by a labourer going to early work, stone dead on the road from the village: a catastrophe explained—superficially at least—by a visible wound to his head; such a wound as might have been produced (and as, on the final evidence, *had* been) by a fatal slip, in the dark and after leaving the public-house, on the steepish icy slope, a wrong path altogether, at the bottom of which he lay. The icy slope, the turn mistaken at night and in liquor, accounted for much—practically, in the end and after the inquest and boundless chatter, for everything; but there had been matters in his life, strange passages and perils, secret disorders, vices more than suspected, that would have accounted for a good deal more.

I scarce know how to put my story into words that shall be a credible picture of my state of mind; but I was in these days literally able to find a joy in the extraordinary flight of heroism the occasion demanded of me. I now saw that I had been asked for a service admirable and difficult; and there would be a greatness in letting it be seen—oh in the right quarter!—that I could succeed where many another girl might have failed. It was an immense help to me—I confess I rather applaud myself as I look back!—that I saw my response so strongly and so simply. I was there to protect and defend the little creatures in the world the most bereaved and the most loveable, the appeal of whose helplessness had suddenly become only too explicit, a deep constant ache of one's own engaged affection. We were cut off, really, together; we were united in our danger. They had nothing but me, and I—well, I had *them*. It was in short a magnificent chance. This chance presented itself to me in an image richly material. I was a screen—I was to stand before them. The more I saw the less they would. I began to watch them in a stifled suspense, a disguised tension, that might well, had it continued too long, have turned to something like madness. What saved me, as I now see, was that it turned to another matter altogether. It didn't last as suspense—it was superseded by horrible proofs. Proofs, I say, yes—from the moment I really took hold.

    This moment dated from an afternoon hour that I happened to spend in the grounds with the younger of my pupils alone. We had left Miles indoors, on the red cushion of a deep window-seat; he had wished to finish a book, and I had been glad to encourage a purpose so laudable in a young man whose only defect was a certain ingenuity of restlessness. His sister, on the contrary, had been alert to come out, and I strolled with her half an hour, seeking the shade, for the sun was still high and the day exceptionally warm. I was aware afresh with her, as we went, of how, like her brother, she contrived—it was the charming thing in both children—to let me alone without appearing to drop me and to accompany me without appearing to oppress. They were never importunate and yet never listless. My attention to them all really went to seeing them amuse themselves immensely without me: this was a spectacle they seemed actively to prepare and that employed me as an active admirer. I walked in a world of their invention—they had no occasion whatever to draw upon mine; so that my time was taken only with being for them some remarkable person or thing that the game of the moment required and that was merely, thanks to my superior, my exalted stamp, a happy and highly distinguished sinecure. I forget what I was on the present occasion; I only remember that I was something very important and very quiet and that Flora was playing very hard. We were on the edge of the lake, and, as we had lately begun geography, the lake was the Sea of Azof.

    Suddenly, amid these elements, I became aware that on the other side of the Sea of Azof we had an interested spectator. The way this knowledge gathered in me was the strangest thing in the world—the strangest, that is, except the very much stranger in which it quickly merged itself. I had sat down with a piece of work—for I was something or other that could sit—on the old stone bench which overlooked the pond; and in this position I began to take in with certitude and yet without direct vision the presence, a good way off, of a third person. The old trees, the thick shrubbery, made a great and pleasant shade, but it was all suffused with the brightness of the hot still hour. There was no ambiguity in anything; none whatever at least in the conviction I from one moment to another found myself forming as to what I should see straight before me and across the lake as a consequence of raising my eyes. They were attached at this juncture to the stitching in which I was engaged, and I can feel once more the spasm of my effort not to move them till I should so have steadied myself as to be able to make up my mind what to do. There was an alien object in view—a figure whose right of presence I instantly and passionately questioned. I recollect counting over perfectly the possibilities, reminding myself that nothing was more natural for instance than the appearance of one of the men about the place, or even of a messenger, a postman or a tradesman's boy, from the village. That reminder had as little effect on my practical certitude as I was conscious—still even without looking—of its having upon the character and attitude of our visitor. Nothing was more natural than that these things should be the other things they absolutely were not.

Of the positive identity of the apparition I would assure myself as soon as the small clock of my courage should have ticked out the right second; meanwhile, with an effort that was already sharp enough, I transferred my eyes straight to little Flora, who, at the moment, was about ten yards away. My heart had stood still for an instant with the wonder and terror of the question whether she too would see; and I held my breath while I waited for what a cry from her, what some sudden innocent sign either of interest or of alarm, would tell me. I waited, but nothing came; then in the first place—and there is something more dire in this, I feel, than in anything I have to relate—I was determined by a sense that within a minute all spontaneous sounds from her had dropped; and in the second by the circumstance that also within the minute she had, in her play, turned her back to the water. This was her attitude when I at last looked at her—looked with the confirmed conviction that we were still, together, under direct personal notice. She had picked up a small flat piece of wood which happened to have in it a little hole that had evidently suggested to her the idea of sticking in another fragment that might figure as a mast and make the thing a boat. This second morsel, as I watched her, she was very markedly and intently attempting to tighten in its place. My apprehension of what she was doing sustained me so that after some seconds I felt I was ready for more. Then I again shifted my eyes—I faced what I had to face.

VII

I got hold of Mrs. Grose as soon after this as I could; and I can give no intelligible account of how I fought out the interval. Yet I still hear myself cry as I fairly threw myself into her arms: "They *know*—it's too monstrous: they know, they know!"

"And what on earth—?" I felt her incredulity as she held me.

"Why all that *we* know—and heaven knows what more besides!" Then as she released me I made it out to her, made it out perhaps only now with full coherency even to myself. "Two hours ago, in the garden"—I could scarce articulate—"Flora *saw*!"

Mrs. Grose took it as she might have taken a blow in the stomach. "She has told you?" she panted.

"Not a word—that's the horror. She kept it to herself! The child of eight, *that* child!" Unutterable still for me was the stupefaction of it.

Mrs. Grose of course could only gape the wider. "Then how do you know?"

"I was there—I saw with my eyes: saw she was perfectly aware."

"Do you mean aware of *him*?"

"No—of *her*." I was conscious as I spoke that I looked prodigious things, for I got the slow reflexion of them in my companion's face. "Another person—this time; but a figure of quite as unmistakeable horror and evil: a woman in black, pale and dreadful—with such an air also, and such a face!—on the other side of the lake. I was there with the child—quiet for the hour; and in the midst of it she came."

"Came how—from where?"

"From where they come from! She just appeared and stood there—but not so near."

"And without coming nearer?"

"Oh for the effect and the feeling she might have been as close as you!"

My friend, with an odd impulse, fell back a step. "Was she some one you've never seen?"

"Never. But some one the child has. Some one *you* have." Then to show how I had thought it all out: "My predecessor—the one who died."

"Miss Jessel?"

"Miss Jessel. You don't believe me?" I pressed.

She turned right and left in her distress. "How can you be sure?"

This drew from me, in the state of my nerves, a flash of impatience. "Then ask Flora—*she's* sure!" But I had no sooner spoken than I caught myself up. "No, for God's sake *don't*! She'll say she isn't—she'll lie!"

Mrs. Grose was not too bewildered instinctively to protest. "Ah how *can* you?"

"Because I'm clear. Flora doesn't want me to know."

"It's only then to spare you."

"No, no—there are depths, depths! The more I go over it the more I see in it, and the more I see in it the more I fear. I don't know what I *don't* see, what I *don't* fear!"

Mrs. Grose tried to keep up with me. "You mean you're afraid of seeing her again?"

"Oh no; that's nothing—now!" Then I explained. "It's of *not* seeing her."

But my companion only looked wan. "I don't understand."

"Why, it's that the child may keep it up—and that the child assuredly *will*—without my knowing it."

At the image of this possibility Mrs. Grose for a moment collapsed, yet presently to pull herself together again as from the positive force of the sense of what, should we yield an inch, there would really be to give way to. "Dear, dear—we must keep our heads! And after all, if she doesn't mind it—!" She even tried a grim joke. "Perhaps she likes it!"

"Like *such* things—a scrap of an infant!"

"Isn't it just a proof of her blest innocence?" my friend bravely enquired.

She brought me, for the instant, almost round. "Oh we must clutch at *that*—we must cling to it! If it isn't a proof of what you say, it's a proof of—God knows what! For the woman's a horror of horrors."

Mrs. Grose, at this, fixed her eyes a minute on the ground; then at last raising them, "Tell me how you know," she said.

"Then you admit it's what she was?" I cried.

"Tell me how you know," my friend simply repeated.

"Know? By seeing her! By the way she looked." "At you, do you mean—so wickedly?"

"Dear me, no—I could have borne that. She gave me never a glance. She only fixed the child."

Mrs. Grose tried to see it. "Fixed her?"

"Ah with such awful eyes!"

She stared at mine as if they might really have resembled them. "Do you mean of dislike?"

"God help us, no. Of something much worse."

"Worse than dislike?"—this left her indeed at a loss.

"With a determination—indescribable. With a kind of fury of intention."

I made her turn pale. "Intention?"

"To get hold of her." Mrs. Grose—her eyes just lingering on mine—gave a shudder and walked to the window; and while she stood there looking out I completed my statement. *"That's* what Flora knows."

After a little she turned round. "The person was in black, you say?"

"In mourning—rather poor, almost shabby. But—yes—with extraordinary beauty." I now recognised to what I had at last, stroke by stroke, brought the victim of my confidence, for she quite visibly weighed this. "Oh handsome—very, very," I insisted; "wonderfully handsome. But infamous."

She slowly came back to me. "Miss Jessel—*was* infamous." She once more took my hand in both her own, holding it as tight as if to fortify me against the increase of alarm I might draw from this disclosure. "They were both infamous," she finally said.

So for a little we faced it once more together; and I found absolutely a degree of help in seeing it now so straight. "I appreciate," I said, "the great decency of your not having hitherto spoken; but the time has certainly come to give me the whole thing." She appeared to assent to this, but still only in silence; seeing which I went on: "I must have it now. Of what did she die? Come, there was something between them."

"There was everything."

"In spite of the difference—?"

"Oh of their rank, their condition"—she brought it woefully out. "*She* was a lady."

I turned it over; I again saw. "Yes—she was a lady."

"And he so dreadfully below," said Mrs. Grose.

I felt that I doubtless needn't press too hard, in such company, on the place of a servant in the scale; but there was nothing to prevent an acceptance of my companion's own measure of my predecessor's abasement. There was a way to deal with that, and I dealt; the more readily for my full vision—on the evidence—of our employer's late clever good-looking "own" man; impudent, assured, spoiled, depraved. "The fellow was a hound."

Mrs. Grose considered as if it were perhaps a little a case for a sense of shades. "I've never seen one like him. He did what he wished."

"With *her*?"

"With them all."

It was as if now in my friend's own eyes Miss Jessel had again appeared. I seemed at any rate for an instant to trace their evocation of her as distinctly as I had seen her by the pond; and I brought out with decision: "It must have been also what *she* wished!"

Mrs. Grose's face signified that it had been indeed, but she said at the same time: "Poor woman—she paid for it!"

"Then you do know what she died of?" I asked.

"No—I know nothing. I wanted not to know; I was glad enough I didn't; and I thanked heaven she was well out of this!"

"Yet you had then your idea—"

"Of her real reason for leaving? Oh yes—as to that. She couldn't have stayed. Fancy it here—for a governess! And afterwards I imagined—and I still imagine. And what I imagine is dreadful."

"Not so dreadful as what *I* do," I replied; on which I must have shown her—as I was indeed but too conscious—a front of miserable defeat. It brought out again all her compassion for me, and at the renewed touch of her kindness my power to resist broke down. I burst, as I had the other time made her burst, into tears; she took me to her motherly breast, where my lamentation overflowed. "I don't do it!" I sobbed in despair; "I don't save or shield them! It's far worse than I dreamed. They're lost!"

VIII

What I had said to Mrs. Grose was true enough: there were in the matter I had put before her depths and possibilities that I lacked resolution to sound; so that when we met once more in the wonder of it we were of a common mind about the duty of resistance to extravagant fancies. We were to keep our heads if we should keep nothing else—difficult indeed as that might be in the face of all that, in our prodigious experience, seemed least to be questioned. Late that night, while the house slept, we had another talk in my room; when she went all the way with me as to its being beyond doubt that I had seen exactly what I had seen. I found that to keep her thoroughly in the grip of this I had only to ask her how, if I had "made it up." I came to be able to give, of each of the persons appearing to me, a picture disclosing, to the last detail, their special marks—a portrait on the exhibition of which she had instantly recognised and named them. She wished, of course—small blame to her!—to sink the whole subject; and I was quick to assure her that my own interest in it had now violently taken the form of a search for the way to escape from it. I closed with her cordially on the article of the likelihood that with recurrence—for recurrence we took for granted—I should get used to my danger; distinctly professing that my personal exposure had suddenly become the least of my discomforts. It was my new suspicion that was intolerable; and yet even to this complication the later hours of the day had brought a little ease.

On leaving her, after my first outbreak, I had of course returned to my pupils, associating the right remedy for my dismay with that sense of their charm which I had already recognised as a resource I could positively cultivate and which had never failed me yet. I had simply, in other words, plunged afresh into Flora's special society and there become aware—it was almost a luxury!—that she could put her little conscious hand straight upon the spot that ached. She had looked at me in sweet speculation and then had accused me to my face of having "cried." I had supposed the ugly signs of it brushed away; but I could literally—for the time at all events—rejoice, under this fathomless charity, that they had not entirely disappeared. To gaze into the depths of blue of the child's eyes and pronounce their loveliness a trick of premature cunning was to be guilty of a cynicism in preference to which I naturally preferred to abjure my judgement and, so far as might be, my agitation. I couldn't abjure for merely wanting to, but I could repeat to Mrs. Grose—as I did there, over and over, in the small hours—that with our small friends' voices in the air, their pressure on one's heart and their fragrant faces against one's cheek, everything fell to the ground but their incapacity and their beauty. It was a pity that, somehow, to settle this once for all, I had equally to re-enumerate the signs of subtlety that, in the afternoon, by the lake, had made a miracle of my show of self-possession. It was a pity to be obliged to re-investigate the certitude of the moment itself and repeat how it had come to me as a revelation that the inconceivable communion I then surprised must have been for both parties a matter of habit. It was a pity I should have had to quaver out again the reasons for my not having, in my delusion, so much as questioned that the little girl saw our visitant even as I actually saw Mrs. Grose herself, and that she wanted, by just so much as she did thus see, to make me suppose she didn't, and at the same time, without showing anything, arrive at a guess as to whether I myself did! It was a pity I needed to recapitulate the portentous little activities by which she sought to divert my attention—the perceptible increase of movement, the greater intensity of play, the singing, the gabbling of nonsense and the invitation to romp.

Yet if I had not indulged, to prove there was nothing in it, in this review, I should have missed the two or three dim elements of comfort that still remained to me. I shouldn't for instance have been able to asseverate to my friend that I was certain—which was so much to the good—that *I* at least had not betrayed myself. I shouldn't have been prompted, by stress of need, by desperation of mind—I scarce know what to call it—to invoke such further aid to intelligence as might spring from pushing my colleague fairly to the wall. She had told me, bit by bit, under pressure, a great deal; but a small shifty spot on the wrong side of it all still sometimes brushed my brow like the wing of a bat; and I remember how on this occasion—for the sleeping house and the concentration alike of our danger and our watch seemed to help—I felt the importance of giving the last jerk to the curtain. "I don't believe anything so horrible," I recollect saying; "no, let us put it definitely, my dear, that I don't. But if I did, you know, there's a thing I should require now, just without sparing you the least bit more—oh not a scrap, come!—to get out of you. What was it you had in mind when, in our distress, before Miles came back, over the letter from his school, you said, under my insistence, that you didn't pretend for him he hadn't literally ever been 'bad'? He has *not*, truly, 'ever,' in these weeks that I myself have lived with him and so closely watched him; he has been an imperturbable little prodigy of delightful loveable goodness. Therefore you might perfectly have made the claim for him if you had not, as it happened, seen an exception to take. What was your exception, and to what passage in your personal observation of him did you refer?"

It was a straight question enough, but levity was not our note, and in any case I had before the grey dawn admonished us to separate got my answer. What my friend had had in mind proved immensely to the purpose. It was neither more nor less than the particular fact that for a period of several months Quint and the boy had been perpetually together. It was indeed the very appropriate item of evidence of her having ventured to criticise the propriety, to hint at the incongruity, of so close an alliance, and even to go so far on the subject as a frank overture to Miss Jessel would take her. Miss Jessel had, with a very high manner about it, requested her to mind her business, and the good woman had on this directly approached little Miles. What she had said to him, since I pressed, was that *she* liked to see young gentlemen not forget their station.

I pressed again, of course, the closer for that.

"You reminded him that Quint was only a base menial?"

"As you might say! And it was his answer, for one thing, that was bad."

"And for another thing?" I waited. "He repeated your words to Quint?"

"No, not that. It's just what he *wouldn't*!" she could still impress on me. "I was sure, at any rate," she added, "that he didn't. But he denied certain occasions."

"What occasions?"

"When they had been about together quite as if Quint were his tutor—and a very grand one—and Miss Jessel only for the little lady. When he had gone off with the fellow, I mean, and spent hours with him."

"He then prevaricated about it—he said he hadn't?" Her assent was clear enough to cause me to add in a moment: "I see. He lied."

"Oh!" Mrs. Grose mumbled. This was a suggestion that it didn't matter; which indeed she backed up by a further remark. "You see, after all, Miss Jessel didn't mind. She didn't forbid him."

I considered. "Did he put that to you as a justification?"

At this she dropped again. "No, he never spoke of it."

"Never mentioned her in connexion with Quint?"

She saw, visibly flushing, where I was coming out. "Well, he didn't show anything. He denied," she repeated; "he denied."

Lord, how I pressed her now! "So that you could see he knew what was between the two wretches?"

"I don't know—I don't know!" the poor woman wailed.

"You do know, you dear thing," I replied; "only you haven't my dreadful boldness of mind, and you keep back, out of timidity and modesty and delicacy, even the impression that in the past, when you had, without my aid, to flounder about in silence, most of all made you miserable. But I shall get it out of you yet! There was something in the boy that suggested to you," I continued, "his covering and concealing their relation."

"Oh he couldn't prevent—"

"Your learning the truth? I dare say! But, heavens," I fell, with vehemence, a-thinking, "what it shows that they must, to that extent, have succeeded in making of him!"

"Ah nothing that's not nice *now*!" Mrs. Grose lugubriously pleaded.

"I don't wonder you looked queer," I persisted, "when I mentioned to you the letter from his school!"

"I doubt if I looked as queer as you!" she retorted with homely force. "And if he was so bad then as that comes to, how is he such an angel now?"

"Yes indeed—and if he was a fiend at school! How, how, how? Well," I said in my torment, "you must put it to me again, though I shall not be able to tell you for some days. Only put it to me again!" I cried in a way that made my friend stare. "There are directions in which I mustn't for the present let myself go." Meanwhile I returned to her first example—the one to which she had just previously referred—of the boy's happy capacity for an occasional slip. "If Quint—on your remonstrance at the time you speak of—was a base menial, one of the things Miles said to you, I find myself guessing, was that you were another." Again her admission was so adequate that I continued: "And you forgave him that?"

"Wouldn't *you*?"

"Oh yes!" And we exchanged there, in the stillness, a sound of the oddest amusement. Then I went on: "At all events, while he was with the man—"

"Miss Flora was with the woman. It suited them all!"

It suited me too, I felt, only too well; by which I mean that it suited exactly the particular deadly view I was in the very act of forbidding myself to entertain. But I so far succeeded in checking the expression of this view that I will throw, just here, no further light on it than may be offered by the mention of my final observation to Mrs. Grose. "His having lied and been impudent are, I confess, less engaging specimens than I had hoped to have from you of the outbreak in him of the little natural man. Still," I mused, "they must do, for they make me feel more than ever that I must watch."

It made me blush, the next minute, to see in my friend's face how much more unreservedly she had forgiven him than her anecdote struck me as pointing out to my own tenderness any way to do. This was marked when, at the schoolroom door, she quitted me. "Surely you don't accuse *him*—"

"Of carrying on an intercourse that he conceals from me? Ah remember that, until further evidence, I now accuse nobody." Then before shutting her out to go by another passage to her own place, "I must just wait," I wound up.

IX

I waited and waited, and the days took as they elapsed something from my consternation. A very few of them, in fact, passing, in constant sight of my pupils, without a fresh incident, sufficed to give to grievous fancies and even to odious memories a kind of brush of the sponge. I have spoken of the surrender to their extraordinary childish grace as a thing I could actively promote in myself, and it may be imagined if I neglected now to apply at this source for whatever balm it would yield. Stranger than I can express, certainly, was the effort to struggle against my new lights. It would doubtless have been a greater tension still, however, had it not been so frequently successful. I used to wonder how my little charges could help guessing that I thought strange things about them; and the circumstance that these things only made them more interesting was not by itself a direct aid to keeping them in the dark. I trembled lest they should see that they *were* so immensely more interesting. Putting things at the worst, at all events, as in meditation I so often did, any clouding of their innocence could only be—blameless and foredoomed as they were—a reason the more for taking risks. There were moments when I knew myself to catch them up by an irresistible impulse and press them to my heart. As soon as I had done so I used to wonder—"What will they think of that? Doesn't it betray too much?" It would have been easy to get into a sad wild tangle about how much I might betray; but the real account, I feel, of the hours of peace I could still enjoy was that the immediate charm of my companions was a beguilement still effective even under the shadow of the possibility that it was studied. For if it occurred to me that I might occasionally excite suspicion by the little outbreaks of my sharper passion for them, so too I remember asking if I mightn't see a queerness in the traceable increase of their own demonstrations.

They were at this period extravagantly and preternaturally fond of me; which, after all, I could reflect, was no more than a graceful response in children perpetually bowed down over and hugged. The homage of which they were so lavish succeeded in truth for my nerves quite as well as if I never appeared to myself, as I may say, literally to catch them at a purpose in it. They had never, I think, wanted to do so many things for their poor protectress; I mean—though they got their lessons better and better, which was naturally what would please her most—in the way of diverting, entertaining, surprising her; reading her passages, telling her stories, acting her charades, pouncing out at her, in disguises, as animals and historical characters, and above all astonishing her by the "pieces" they had secretly got by heart and could interminably recite. I should never get to the bottom—were I to let myself go even now—of the prodigious private commentary, all under still more private correction, with which I in these days overscored their full hours. They had shown me from the first a facility for everything, a general faculty which, taking a fresh start, achieved remarkable flights. They got their little tasks as if they loved them; they indulged, from the mere exuberance of the gift, in the most unimposed little miracles of memory. They not only popped out at me as tigers and as

Romans, but as Shakespeareans, astronomers and navigators. This was so singularly the case that it had presumably much to do with the fact as to which, at the present day, I am at a loss for a different explanation: I allude to my unnatural composure on the subject of another school for Miles. What I remember is that I was content for the time not to open the question, and that contentment must have sprung from the sense of his perpetually striking show of cleverness. He was too clever for a bad governess, for a parson's daughter, to spoil; and the strangest if not the brightest thread in the pensive embroidery I just spoke of was the impression I might have got, if I had dared to work it out, that he was under some influence operating in his small intellectual life as a tremendous incitement.

If it was easy to reflect, however, that such a boy could postpone school, it was at least as marked that for such a boy to have been "kicked out" by a schoolmaster was a mystification without end. Let me add that in their company now—and I was careful almost never to be out of it—I could follow no scent very far. We lived in a cloud of music and affection and success and private theatricals. The musical sense in each of the children was of the quickest, but the elder in especial had a marvellous knack of catching and repeating. The schoolroom piano broke into all gruesome fancies; and when that failed there were confabulations in corners, with a sequel of one of them going out in the highest spirits in order to "come in" as something new. I had had brothers myself, and it was no revelation to me that little girls could be slavish idolaters of little boys. What surpassed everything was that there was a little boy in the world who could have for the inferior age, sex and intelligence so fine a consideration. They were extraordinarily at one, and to say that they never either quarrelled or complained is to make the note of praise coarse for their quality of sweetness. Sometimes perhaps indeed (when I dropped into coarseness) I came across traces of little understandings between them by which one of them should keep me occupied while the other slipped away. There is a naïf side, I suppose, in all diplomacy; but if my pupils practised upon me it was surely with the minimum of grossness. It was all in the other quarter that, after a lull, the grossness broke out.

I find that I really hang back; but I must take my horrid plunge. In going on with the record of what was hideous at Bly I not only challenge the most liberal faith—for which I little care; but (and this is another matter) I renew what I myself suffered, I again push my dreadful way through it to the end. There came suddenly an hour after which, as I look back, the business seems to me to have been all pure suffering; but I have at least reached the heart of it, and the straightest road out is doubtless to advance. One evening—with nothing to lead up or prepare it—I felt the cold touch of the impression that had breathed on me the night of my arrival and which, much lighter then as I have mentioned, I should probably have made little of in memory had my subsequent sojourn been less agitated. I had not gone to bed; I sat reading by a couple of candles. There was a roomful of old books at Bly—last-century fiction some of it, which, to the extent of a distinctly deprecated renown, but never to so much as that of a stray specimen, had reached the sequestered home and appealed to the unavowed curiosity of my youth. I remember that the book I had in my hand was Fielding's "Amelia"; also that I was wholly awake. I recall further both a general conviction that it was horribly late and a particular objection to looking at my watch. I figure finally that the white curtain draping, in the fashion of those days, the head of Flora's little bed, shrouded, as I had assured myself long before, the perfection of childish rest. I recollect in short that though I was deeply interested in my author I found myself, at the turn of a page and with his spell all scattered, looking straight up from him and hard at the door of my room. There was a moment during which I listened, reminded of the faint sense I had had, the first night, of there being something undefinably astir in the house, and noted the soft breath of the open casement just move the half-drawn blind. Then, with all the marks of a deliberation that must have seemed magnificent had there been any one to admire it, I laid down my book, rose to my feet and, taking a candle, went straight out of the room and, from the passage, on which my light made little impression, noiselessly closed and locked the door.

    I can say now neither what determined nor what guided me, but I went straight along the lobby, holding my candle high, till I came within sight of the tall window that presided over the great turn of the staircase. At this point I precipitately found myself aware of three things. They were practically simultaneous, yet they had flashes of succession. My candle, under a bold flourish, went out, and I perceived, by the uncovered window, that the yielding dusk of earliest morning rendered it unnecessary. Without it, the next instant, I knew that there was a figure on the stair. I speak of sequences, but I required no lapse of seconds to stiffen myself for a third encounter with Quint. The apparition had reached the landing halfway up and was therefore on the spot nearest the window, where, at sight of me, it stopped short and fixed me exactly as it had fixed me from the tower and from the garden. He knew me as well as I knew him; and so, in the cold faint twilight, with a glimmer in the high glass and another on the polish of the oak stair below, we faced each other in our common intensity. He was absolutely, on this occasion, a living detestable dangerous presence. But that was not the wonder of wonders; I reserve this distinction for quite another circumstance: the circumstance that dread had unmistakeably quitted me and that there was nothing in me unable to meet and measure him.

I had plenty of anguish after that extraordinary moment, but I had, thank God, no terror. And he knew I hadn't—I found myself at the end of an instant magnificently aware of this. I felt, in a fierce rigour of confidence, that if I stood my ground a minute I should cease—for the time at least—to have him to reckon with; and during the minute, accordingly, the thing was as human and hideous as a real interview: hideous just because it was human, as human as to have met alone, in the small hours, in a sleeping house, some enemy, some adventurer, some criminal. It was the dead silence of our long gaze at such close quarters that gave the whole horror, huge as it was, its only note of the unnatural. If I had met a murderer in such a place and at such an hour we still at least would have spoken. Something would have passed, in life, between us; if nothing had passed one of us would have moved. The moment was so prolonged that it would have taken but little more to make me doubt if even *I* were in life. I can't express what followed it save by saying that the silence itself—which was indeed in a manner an attestation of my strength—became the element into which I saw the figure disappear; in which I definitely saw it turn, as I might have seen the low wretch to which it had once belonged turn on receipt of an order, and pass, with my eyes on the villainous back that no hunch could have more disfigured, straight down the staircase and into the darkness in which the next bend was lost.

X

I remained a while at the top of the stair, but with the effect presently of understanding that when my visitor had gone, he had gone; then I returned to my room. The foremost thing I saw there by the light of the candle I had left burning was that Flora's little bed was empty; and on this I caught my breath with all the terror that, five minutes before, I had been able to resist. I dashed at the place in which I had left her lying and over which—for the small silk counterpane and the sheets were disarranged—the white curtains had been deceivingly pulled forward; then my step, to my unutterable relief, produced an answering sound: I noticed an agitation of the window-blind, and the child, ducking down, emerged rosily from the other side of it. She stood there in so much of her candour and so little of her night-gown; with her pink bare feet and the golden glow of her curls. She looked intensely grave, and I had never had such a sense of losing an advantage acquired (the thrill of which had just been so prodigious) as on my consciousness that she addressed me with a reproach—"You naughty: where *have* you been?" Instead of challenging her own irregularity I found myself arraigned and explaining. She herself explained, for that matter, with the loveliest eagerest simplicity. She had known suddenly, as she lay there, that I was out of the room, and had jumped up to see what had become of me. I had dropped, with the joy of her reappearance, back into my chair—feeling then, and then only, a little faint; and she had pattered straight over to me, thrown herself upon my knee, given herself to be held with the flame of the candle full in the wonderful little face that was still flushed with sleep. I remember closing my eyes an instant, yieldingly, consciously, as before the excess of something beautiful that shone out of the blue of her own. "You were looking for me out of the window?" I said. "You thought I might be walking in the grounds?"

"Well, you know, I thought some one was"—she never blanched as she smiled out that at me.

Oh how I looked at her now! "And did you see any one?"

"Ah *no*!" she returned almost (with the full privilege of childish inconsequence) resentfully, though with a long sweetness in her little drawl of the negative.

At that moment, in the state of my nerves, I absolutely believed she lied; and if I once more closed my eyes it was before the dazzle of the three or four possible ways in which I might take this up. One of these for a moment tempted me with such singular force that, to resist it, I must have gripped my little girl with a spasm that, wonderfully, she submitted to without a cry or a sign of fright. Why not break out at her on the spot and have it all over?—give it to her straight in her lovely little lighted face? "You see, you see, you *know* that you do and that you already quite suspect I believe it; therefore why not frankly confess it to me, so that we may at least live with it together and learn perhaps, in the strangeness of our fate, where we are and what it means?" This solicitation dropped, alas, as it came: if I could immediately have succumbed to it I might have spared myself—well, you'll see what. Instead of succumbing I sprang again to my feet, looked at her bed and took a helpless middle way. "Why did you pull the curtain over the place to make me think you were still there?"

Flora luminously considered; after which, with her little divine smile: "Because I don't like to frighten you!"

"But if I had, by your idea, gone out—?"

She absolutely declined to be puzzled; she turned her eyes to the flame of the candle as if the question were as irrelevant, or at any rate as impersonal, as Mrs. Marcet or nine-times-nine. "Oh but you know," she quite adequately answered, "that you might come back, you dear, and that you *have*!" And after a little, when she had got into bed, I had, a long time, by almost sitting on her for the retention of her hand, to show how I recognised the pertinence of my return.

You may imagine the general complexion, from that moment, of my nights. I repeatedly sat up till I didn't know when; I selected moments when my room-mate unmistakeably slept, and, stealing out, took noiseless turns in the passage. I even pushed as far as to where I had last met Quint. But I never met him there again, and I may as well say at once that I on no other occasion saw him in the house. I just missed, on the staircase, nevertheless, a different adventure. Looking down it from the top I once recognised the presence of a woman seated on one of the lower steps with her back presented to me, her body half-bowed and her head, in an attitude of woe, in her hands. I had been there but an instant, however, when she vanished without looking round at me. I knew, for all that, exactly what dreadful face she had to show; and I wondered whether, if instead of being above I had been below, I should have had the same nerve for going up that I had lately shown Quint. Well, there continued to be plenty of call for nerve. On the eleventh night after my latest encounter with that gentleman—they were all numbered now—I had an alarm that perilously skirted it and that indeed, from the particular quality of its unexpectedness, proved quite my sharpest shock. It was precisely the first night during this series that, weary with vigils, I had conceived I might again without laxity lay myself down at my old hour. I slept immediately and, as I afterwards knew, till about one o'clock; but when I woke it was to sit straight up, as completely roused as if a hand had shaken me. I had left a light burning, but it was now out, and I felt an instant certainty that Flora had extinguished it. This brought me to my feet and straight, in the darkness, to her bed, which I found she had left. A glance at the window enlightened me further, and the striking of a match completed the picture.

The child had again got up—this time blowing out the taper, and had again, for some purpose of observation or response, squeezed in behind the blind and was peering out into the night. That she now saw—as she had not, I had satisfied myself, the previous time—was proved to me by the fact that she was disturbed neither by my re-illumination nor by the haste I made to get into slippers and into a wrap. Hidden, protected, absorbed, she evidently rested on the sill—the casement opened forward—and gave herself up. There was a great still moon to help her, and this fact had counted in my quick decision. She was face to face with the apparition we had met at the lake, and could now communicate with it as she had not then been able to do. What I, on my side, had to care for was, without disturbing her, to reach, from the corridor, some other window turned to the same quarter. I got to the door without her hearing me; I got out of it, closed it and listened, from the other side, for some sound from her. While I stood in the passage I had my eyes on her brother's door, which was but ten steps off and which, indescribably, produced in me a renewal of the strange impulse that I lately spoke of as my temptation. What if I should go straight in and march to *his* window?—what if, by risking to his boyish bewilderment a revelation of my motive, I should throw across the rest of the mystery the long halter of my boldness?

This thought held me sufficiently to make me cross to his threshold and pause again. I preternaturally listened; I figured to myself what might portentously be; I wondered if his bed were also empty and he also secretly at watch. It was a deep soundless minute, at the end of which my impulse failed. He was quiet; he might be innocent; the risk was hideous; I turned away. There was a figure in the grounds—a figure prowling for a sight, the visitor with whom Flora was engaged; but it wasn't the visitor most concerned with my boy. I hesitated afresh, but on other grounds and only a few seconds; then I had made my choice. There were empty rooms enough at Bly, and it was only a question of choosing the right one. The right one suddenly presented itself to me as the lower one—though high above the gardens—in the solid corner of the house that I have spoken of as the old tower. This was a large square chamber, arranged with some state as a bedroom, the extravagant size of which made it so inconvenient that it had not for years, though kept by Mrs. Grose in exemplary order, been occupied. I had often admired it and I knew my way about in it; I had only, after just faltering at the first chill gloom of its disuse, to pass across it and unbolt in all quietness one of the shutters. Achieving this transit I uncovered the glass without a sound and, applying my face to the pane, was able, the darkness without being much less than within, to see that I commanded the right direction. Then I saw something more. The moon made the night extraordinarily penetrable and showed me on the lawn a person, diminished by distance, who stood there motionless and as if fascinated, looking up to where I had appeared— looking, that is, not so much straight at me as at something that was apparently above me. There was clearly another person above me—there was a person on the tower; but the presence on the lawn was not in the least what I had conceived and had confidently hurried to meet. The presence on the lawn—I felt sick as I made it out—was poor little Miles himself.

XI

It was not till late next day that I spoke to Mrs. Grose; the rigour with which I kept my pupils in sight making it often difficult to meet her privately: the more as we each felt the importance of not provoking—on the part of the servants quite as much as on that of the children—any suspicion of a secret flurry or of a discussion of mysteries. I drew a great security in this particular from her mere smooth aspect. There was nothing in her fresh face to pass on to others the least of my horrible confidences. She believed me, I was sure, absolutely: if she hadn't I don't know what would have become of me, for I couldn't have borne the strain alone. But she was a magnificent monument to the blessing of a want of imagination, and if she could see in our little charges nothing but their beauty and amiability, their happiness and cleverness, she had no direct communication with the sources of my trouble. If they had been at all visibly blighted or battered she would doubtless have grown, on tracing it back, haggard enough to match them; as matters stood, however, I could feel her, when she surveyed them with her large white arms folded and the habit of serenity in all her look, thank the Lord's mercy that if they were ruined the pieces would still serve. Flights of fancy gave place, in her mind, to a steady fireside glow, and I had already begun to perceive how, with the development of the conviction that—as time went on without a public accident—our young things could, after all, look out for themselves, she addressed her greatest solicitude to the sad case presented by their deputy-guardian. That, for myself, was a sound simplification: I could engage that, to the world, my face should tell no tales, but it would have been, in the conditions, an immense added worry to find myself anxious about hers.

At the hour I now speak of she had joined me, under pressure, on the terrace, where, with the lapse of the season, the afternoon sun was now agreeable; and we sat there together while before us and at a distance, yet within call if we wished, the children strolled to and fro in one of their most manageable moods. They moved slowly, in unison, below us, over the lawn, the boy, as they went, reading aloud from a story-book and passing his arm round his sister to keep her quite in touch. Mrs. Grose watched them with positive placidity; then I caught the suppressed intellectual creak with which she conscientiously turned to take from me a view of the back of the tapestry. I had made her a receptacle of lurid things, but there was an odd recognition of my superiority—my accomplishments and my function—in her patience under my pain. She offered her mind to my disclosures as, had I wished to mix a witch's broth and proposed it with assurance, she would have held out a large clean saucepan. This had become thoroughly her attitude by the time that, in my recital of the events of the night, I reached the point of what Miles had said to me when, after seeing him, at such a monstrous hour, almost on the very spot where he happened now to be, I had gone down to bring him in; choosing then, at the window, with a concentrated need of not alarming the house, rather that method than any noisier process. I had left her meanwhile in little doubt of my small hope of representing with success even to her actual sympathy my sense of the real splendour of the little inspiration with which, after I had got him into the house, the boy met my final articulate challenge. As soon as I appeared in the moonlight on the terrace he had come to me as straight as possible; on which I had taken his hand without a word and led him, through the dark spaces, up the staircase where Quint had so hungrily hovered for him, along the lobby where I had listened and trembled, and so to his forsaken room.

Not a sound, on the way, had passed between us, and I had wondered—oh *how* I had wondered!—if he were groping about in his dreadful little mind for something plausible and not too grotesque. It would tax his invention certainly, and I felt, this time, over his real embarrassment, a curious thrill of triumph. It was a sharp trap for any game hitherto successful. He could play no longer at perfect propriety, nor could he pretend to it; so how the deuce would he get out of the scrape? There beat in me indeed, with the passionate throb of this question, an equal dumb appeal as to how the deuce *I* should. I was confronted at last, as never yet, with all the risk attached even now to sounding my own horrid note. I remember in fact that as we pushed into his little chamber, where the bed had not been slept in at all and the window, uncovered to the moonlight, made the place so clear that there was no need of striking a match—I remember how I suddenly dropped, sank upon the edge of the bed from the force of the idea that he must know how he really, as they say, "had" me. He could do what he liked, with all his cleverness to help him, so long as I should continue to defer to the old tradition of the criminality of those caretakers of the young who minister to superstitions and fears. He "had" me indeed, and in a cleft stick; for who would ever absolve me, who would consent that I should go unhung, if, by the faintest tremor of an overture, I were the first to introduce into our perfect intercourse an element so dire? No, no: it was useless to attempt to convey to Mrs. Grose, just as it is scarcely less so to attempt to suggest here, how, during our short stiff brush there in the dark, he fairly shook me with admiration. I was of course thoroughly kind and merciful; never, never yet had I placed on his small shoulders hands of such tenderness as those with which, while I rested against the bed, I held him there well under fire. I had no alternative but, in form at least, to put it to him.

"You must tell me now—and all the truth. What did you go out for? What were you doing there?"

I can still see his wonderful smile, the whites of his beautiful eyes and the uncovering of his clear teeth, shine to me in the dusk. "If I tell you why, will you understand?" My heart, at this, leaped into my mouth. *Would* he tell me why? I found no sound on my lips to press it, and I was aware of answering only with a vague repeated grimacing nod. He was gentleness itself, and while I wagged my head at him he stood there more than ever a little fairy prince. It was his brightness indeed that gave me a respite. Would it be so great if he were really going to tell me? "Well," he said at last, "just exactly in order that you should do this."

"Do what?"

"Think me—for a change—*bad*!" I shall never forget the sweetness and gaiety with which he brought out the word, nor how, on top of it, he bent forward and kissed me. It was practically the end of everything. I met his kiss and I had to make, while I folded him for a minute in my arms, the most stupendous effort not to cry. He had given exactly the account of himself that permitted least my going behind it, and it was only with the effect of confirming my acceptance of it that, as I presently glanced about the room, I could say—

"Then you didn't undress at all?"

He fairly glittered in the gloom. "Not at all. I sat up and read."

"And when did you go down?"

"At midnight. When I'm bad I *am* bad!"

"I see, I see—it's charming. But how could you be sure I should know it?"

"Oh I arranged that with Flora." His answers rang out with a readiness! "She was to get up and look out."

"Which is what she did do." It was I who fell into the trap!

"So she disturbed you, and, to see what she was looking at, you also looked—you saw."

"While you," I concurred, "caught your death in the night air!"

He literally bloomed so from this exploit that he could afford radiantly to assent. "How otherwise should I have been bad enough?" he asked. Then, after another embrace, the incident and our interview closed on my recognition of all the reserves of goodness that, for his joke, he had been able to draw upon.

XII

The particular impression I had received proved in the morning light, I repeat, not quite successfully presentable to Mrs. Grose, though I re-enforced it with the mention of still another remark that he had made before we separated. "It all lies in half a dozen words," I said to her, "words that really settle the matter. 'Think, you know, what I *might* do!' He threw that off to show me how good he is. He knows down to the ground what he 'might do.' That's what he gave them a taste of at school."

"Lord, you do change!" cried my friend.

"I don't change—I simply make it out. The four, depend upon it, perpetually meet. If on either of these last nights you had been with either child you'd clearly have understood. The more I've watched and waited the more I've felt that if there were nothing else to make it sure it would be made so by the systematic silence of each. *Never,* by a slip of the tongue, have they so much as alluded to either of their old friends, any more than Miles has alluded to his expulsion. Oh yes, we may sit here and look at them, and they may show off to us there to their fill; but even while they pretend to be lost in their fairy-tale they're steeped in their vision of the dead restored to them. He's not reading to her," I declared; "they're talking of *them*—they're talking horrors! I go on, I know, as if I were crazy; and it's a wonder I'm not. What I've seen would have made *you* so; but it has only made me more lucid, made me get hold of still other things."

My lucidity must have seemed awful, but the charming creatures who were victims of it, passing and repassing in their interlocked sweetness, gave my colleague something to hold on by; and I felt how tight she held as, without stirring in the breath of my passion, she covered them still with her eyes. "Of what other things have you got hold?"

"Why of the very things that have delighted, fascinated and yet, at bottom, as I now so strangely see, mystified and troubled me. Their more than earthly beauty, their absolutely unnatural goodness. It's a game," I went on; "it's a policy and a fraud!"

"On the part of little darlings—?"

"As yet mere lovely babies? Yes, mad as that seems!" The very act of bringing it out really helped me to trace it—follow it all up and piece it all together. "They haven't been good—they've only been absent. It has been easy to live with them because they're simply leading a life of their own. They're not mine—they're not ours. They're his and they're hers!"

"Quint's and that woman's?"

"Quint's and that woman's. They want to get to them."

Oh how, at this, poor Mrs. Grose appeared to study them! "But for what?"

"For the love of all the evil that, in those dreadful days, the pair put into them. And to ply them with that evil still, to keep up the work of demons, is what brings the others back."

"Laws!" said my friend under her breath. The exclamation was homely, but it revealed a real acceptance of my further proof of what, in the bad time—for there had been a worse even than this!—must have occurred. There could have been no such justification for me as the plain assent of her experience to whatever depth of depravity I found credible in our brace of scoundrels. It was in obvious submission of memory that she brought out after a moment: "They *were* rascals! But what can they now do?" she pursued.

"Do?" I echoed so loud that Miles and Flora, as they passed at their distance, paused an instant in their walk and looked at us. "Don't they do enough?" I demanded in a lower tone, while the children, having smiled and nodded and kissed hands to us, resumed their exhibition. We were held by it a minute; then I answered: "They can destroy them!" At this my companion did turn, but the appeal she launched was a silent one, the effect of which was to make me more explicit. "They don't know as yet quite how—but they're trying hard. They're seen only across, as it were, and beyond—in strange places and on high places, the top of towers, the roof of houses, the outside of windows, the further edge of pools; but there's a deep design, on either side, to shorten the distance and overcome the obstacle: so the success of the tempters is only a question of time. They've only to keep to their suggestions of danger."

"For the children to come?"

"And perish in the attempt!" Mrs. Grose slowly got up, and I scrupulously added: "Unless, of course, we can prevent!"

Standing there before me while I kept my seat she visibly turned things over. "Their uncle must do the preventing. He must take them away."

"And who's to make him?"

She had been scanning the distance, but she now dropped on me a foolish face. "You, Miss."

"By writing to him that his house is poisoned and his little nephew and niece mad?"

"But if they *are*, Miss?"

"And if I am myself, you mean? That's charming news to be sent him by a person enjoying his confidence and whose prime undertaking was to give him no worry."

Mrs. Grose considered, following the children again. "Yes, he do hate worry. That was the great reason—"

"Why those fiends took him in so long? No doubt, though his indifference must have been awful. As I'm not a fiend, at any rate, I shouldn't take him in."

My companion, after an instant and for all answer, sat down again and grasped my arm. "Make him at any rate come to you."

I stared. "To *me*?" I had a sudden fear of what she might do. "'Him'?"

"He ought to *be* here—he ought to help."

I quickly rose and I think I must have shown her a queerer face than ever yet. "You see me asking him for a visit?" No, with her eyes on my face she evidently couldn't. Instead of it even—as a woman reads another—she could see what I myself saw: his derision, his amusement, his contempt for the breakdown of my resignation at being left alone and for the fine machinery I had set in motion to attract his attention to my slighted charms. She didn't know—no one knew—how proud I had been to serve him and to stick to our terms; yet she none the less took the measure, I think, of the warning I now gave her. "If you should so lose your head as to appeal to him for me—"

She was really frightened. "Yes, Miss?"

"I would leave, on the spot, both him and you."

XIII

It was all very well to join them, but speaking to them proved quite as much as ever an effort beyond my strength—offered, in close quarters, difficulties as insurmountable as before. This situation continued a month, and with new aggravations and particular notes, the note above all, sharper and sharper, of the small ironic consciousness on the part of my pupils. It was not, I am as sure today as I was sure then, my mere infernal imagination: it was absolutely traceable that they were aware of my predicament and that this strange relation made, in a manner, for a long time, the air in which we moved. I don't mean that they had their tongues in their cheeks or did anything vulgar, for that was not one of their dangers: I do mean, on the other hand, that the element of the unnamed and untouched became, between us, greater than any other, and that so much avoidance couldn't have been made successful without a great deal of tacit arrangement. It was as if, at moments, we were perpetually coming into sight of subjects before which we must stop short, turning suddenly out of alleys that we perceived to be blind, closing with a little bang that made us look at each other—for, like all bangs, it was something louder than we had intended—the doors we had indiscreetly opened. All roads lead to Rome, and there were times when it might have struck us that almost every branch of study or subject of conversation skirted forbidden ground. Forbidden ground was the question of the return of the dead in general and of whatever, in especial, might survive, for memory, of the friends little children had lost. There were days when I could have sworn that one of them had, with a small invisible nudge, said to the other: "She thinks she'll do it this time—but she *won't!*" To "do it" would have been to indulge for instance—and for once in a way—in some direct reference to the lady who had prepared them for my discipline. They had a delightful endless appetite for passages in my own history to which I had again and again treated them; they were in possession of everything that had ever happened to me, had had, with every circumstance, the story of my smallest adventures and of those of my brothers and sisters and of the cat and the dog at home, as well as many particulars of the whimsical bent of my father, of the furniture and arrangement of our house and of the conversation of the old women of our village. There were things enough, taking one with another, to chatter about, if one went very fast and knew by instinct when to go round. They pulled with an art of their own the strings of my invention and my memory; and nothing else perhaps, when I thought of such occasions afterwards, gave me so the suspicion of being watched from under cover. It was in any case over my life, my past and my friends alone that we could take anything like our ease; a state of affairs that led them sometimes without the least pertinence to break out into sociable reminders. I was invited—with no visible connexion—to repeat afresh Goody Gosling's celebrated *mot* or to confirm the details already supplied as to the cleverness of the vicarage pony.

It was partly at such junctures as these and partly at quite different ones that, with the turn my matters had now taken, my predicament, as I have called it, grew most sensible. The fact that the days passed for me without another encounter ought, it would have appeared, to have done something toward soothing my nerves. Since the light brush, that second night on the upper landing, of the presence of a woman at the foot of the stair, I had seen nothing, whether in or out of the house, that one had better not have seen. There was many a corner round which I expected to come upon Quint, and many a situation that, in a merely sinister way, would have favoured the appearance of Miss Jessel. The summer had turned, the summer had gone; the autumn had dropped upon Bly and had blown out half our lights. The place, with its grey sky and withered garlands, its bared spaces and scattered dead leaves, was like a theatre after the performance—all strewn with crumpled playbills. There were exactly states of the air, conditions of sound and of stillness, unspeakable impressions of the *kind* of ministering moment, that brought back to me, long enough to catch it, the feeling of the medium in which, that June evening out of doors, I had had my first sight of Quint, and in which too, at those other instants, I had, after seeing him through the window, looked for him in vain in the circle of shrubbery. I recognised the signs, the portents—I recognised the moment, the spot. But they remained unaccompanied and empty, and I continued unmolested; if unmolested one could call a young woman whose sensibility had, in the most extraordinary fashion, not declined but deepened. I had said in my talk with Mrs. Grose on that horrid scene of Flora's by the lake—and had perplexed her by so saying—that it would from that moment distress me much more to lose my power than to keep it. I had then expressed what was vividly in my mind: the truth that, whether the children really saw or not—since, that is, it was not yet definitely proved—I greatly preferred, as a safeguard, the fulness of my own exposure. I was ready to know the very worst that was to be known. What I had then had an ugly glimpse of was that my eyes might be sealed just while theirs were most opened. Well, my eyes *were* sealed, it appeared, at present—a consummation for which it seemed blasphemous not to thank God. There was, alas, a difficulty about that: I would have thanked him with all my soul had I not had in a proportionate measure this conviction of the secret of my pupils.

How can I retrace to-day the strange steps of my obsession? There were times of our being together when I would have been ready to swear that, literally, in my presence, but with my direct sense of it closed, they had visitors who were known and were welcome. Then it was that, had I not been deterred by the very chance that such an injury might prove greater than the injury to be averted, my exaltation would have broken out. "They're here, they're here, you little wretches," I would have cried, "and you can't deny it now!" The little wretches denied it with all the added volume of their sociability and their tenderness, just in the crystal depths of which—like the flash of a fish in a stream—the mockery of their advantage peeped up. The shock had in truth sunk into me still deeper than I knew on the night when, looking out either for Quint or for Miss Jessel under the stars, I had seen there the boy over whose rest I watched and who had immediately brought in with him—had straightway there turned on me—the lovely upward look with which, from the battlements above us, the hideous apparition of Quint had played. If it was a question of a scare my discovery on this occasion had scared me more than any other, and it was essentially in the scared state that I drew my actual conclusions. They harassed me so that sometimes, at odd moments, I shut myself up audibly to rehearse—it was at once a fantastic relief and a renewed despair—the manner in which I might come to the point. I approached it from one side and the other while, in my room, I flung myself about, but I always broke down in the monstrous utterance of names. As they died away on my lips I said to myself that I should indeed help them to represent something infamous if by pronouncing them I should violate as rare a little case of instinctive delicacy as any schoolroom probably had ever known. When I said to myself: "*They* have the manners to be silent, and you, trusted as you are, the baseness to speak!" I felt myself crimson and covered my face with my hands. After these secret scenes I chattered more than ever, going on volubly enough till one of our prodigious palpable hushes occurred—I can call them nothing else—the strange dizzy lift or swim (I try for terms!) into a stillness, a pause of all life, that had nothing to do with the more or less noise we at the moment might be engaged in making and that I could hear through any intensified mirth or quickened recitation or louder strum of the piano. Then it was that the others, the outsiders, were there. Though they were not angels they "passed," as the French say, causing me, while they stayed, to tremble with the fear of their addressing to their younger victims some yet more infernal message or more vivid image than they had thought good enough for myself.

What it was least possible to get rid of was the cruel idea that, whatever I had seen, Miles and Flora saw *more*—things terrible and unguessable and that sprang from dreadful passages of intercourse in the past. Such things naturally left on the surface, for the time, a chill that we vociferously denied we felt; and we had all three, with repetition, got into such splendid training that we went, each time, to mark the close of the incident, almost automatically through the very same movements. It was striking of the children at all events to kiss me inveterately with a wild irrelevance and never to fail—one or the other—of the precious question that had helped us through many a peril. "When do you think he *will* come? Don't you think we *ought* to write?"—there was nothing like that enquiry, we found by experience, for carrying off an awkwardness. "He" of course was their uncle in Harley Street; and we lived in much profusion of theory that he might at any moment arrive to mingle in our circle. It was impossible to have given less encouragement than he had administered to such a doctrine, but if we had not had the doctrine to fall back upon we should have deprived each other of some of our finest exhibitions. He never wrote to them—that may have been selfish, but it was a part of the flattery of his trust of myself; for the way in which a man pays his highest tribute to a woman is apt to be but by the more festal celebration of one of the sacred laws of his comfort. So I held that I carried out the spirit of the pledge given not to appeal to him when I let our young friends understand that their own letters were but charming literary exercises. They were too beautiful to be posted; I kept them myself; I have them all to this hour. This was a rule indeed which only added to the satiric effect of my being plied with the supposition that he might at any moment be among us. It was exactly as if our young friends knew how almost more awkward than anything else that might be for me. There appears to me moreover as I look back no note in all this more extraordinary than the mere fact that, in spite of my tension and of their triumph, I never lost patience with them. Adorable they must in truth have been, I now feel, since I didn't in these days hate them! Would exasperation, however, if relief had longer been postponed, finally have betrayed me? It little matters, for relief arrived. I call it relief though it was only the relief that a snap brings to a strain or the burst of a thunderstorm to a day of suffocation. It was at least change, and it came with a rush.

XIV

Walking to church a certain Sunday morning, I had little Miles at my side and his sister, in advance of us and at Mrs. Grose's, well in sight. It was a crisp clear day, the first of its order for some time; the night had brought a touch of frost and the autumn air, bright and sharp, made the church-bells almost gay. It was an odd accident of thought that I should have happened at such a moment to be particularly and very gratefully struck with the obedience of my little charges. Why did they never resent my inexorable, my perpetual society? Something or other had brought nearer home to me that I had all but pinned the boy to my shawl, and that in the way our companions were marshalled before me I might have appeared to provide against some danger of rebellion. I was like a gaoler with an eye to possible surprises and escapes. But all this belonged—I mean their magnificent little surrender—just to the special array of the facts that were most abysmal. Turned out for Sunday by his uncle's tailor, who had had a free hand and a notion of pretty waistcoats and of his grand little air, Miles's whole title to independence, the rights of his sex and situation, were so stamped upon him that if he had suddenly struck for freedom I should have had nothing to say. I was by the strongest of chances wondering how I should meet him when the revolution unmistakeably occurred. I call it a revolution because I now see how, with the word he spoke, the curtain rose on the last act of my dreadful drama and the catastrophe was precipitated. "Look here, my dear, you know," he charmingly said, "when in the world, please, am I going back to school?"

Transcribed here the speech sounds harmless enough, particularly as uttered in the sweet, high, casual pipe with which, at all interlocutors, but above all at his eternal governess, he threw off intonations as if he were tossing roses. There was something in them that always made one "catch," and I caught at any rate now so effectually that I stopped as short as if one of the trees of the park had fallen across the road. There was something new, on the spot, between us, and he was perfectly aware I recognised it, though to enable me to do so he had no need to look a whit less candid and charming than usual. I could feel in him how he already, from my at first finding nothing to reply, perceived the advantage he had gained. I was so slow to find anything that he had plenty of time, after a minute, to continue with his suggestive but inconclusive smile: "You know, my dear, that for a fellow to be with a lady *always*—!" His "my dear" was constantly on his lips for me, and nothing could have expressed more the exact shade of the sentiment with which I desired to inspire my pupils than its fond familiarity. It was so respectfully easy.

But oh how I felt that at present I must pick my own phrases! I remember that, to gain time, I tried to laugh, and I seemed to see in the beautiful face with which he watched me how ugly and queer I looked. "And always with the same lady?" I returned.

He neither blenched nor winked. The whole thing was virtually out between us. "Ah of course she's a jolly 'perfect' lady; but after all I'm a fellow, don't you see? who's—well, getting on."

I lingered there with him an instant ever so kindly. "Yes, you're getting on." Oh but I felt helpless!

I have kept to this day the heartbreaking little idea of how he seemed to know that and to play with it. "And you can't say I've not been awfully good, can you?"

I laid my hand on his shoulder, for though I felt how much better it would have been to walk on I was not yet quite able. "No, I can't say that, Miles."

"Except just that one night, you know—!"

"That one night?" I couldn't look as straight as he.

"Why when I went down—went out of the house."

"Oh yes. But I forget what you did it for."

"You forget?"—he spoke with the sweet extravagance of childish reproach. "Why it was just to show you I could!"

"Oh yes—you could."

"And I can again."

I felt I might perhaps after all succeed in keeping my wits about me. "Certainly. But you won't."

"No, not *that* again. It was nothing."

"It was nothing," I said. "But we must go on."

He resumed our walk with me, passing his hand into my arm. "Then when *am* I going back?"

I wore, in turning it over, my most responsible air. "Were you very happy at school?"

He just considered. "Oh I'm happy enough anywhere!"

"Well then," I quavered, "if you're just as happy here—!"

"Ah but that isn't everything! Of course *you* know a lot—"

"But you hint that you know almost as much?" I risked as he paused.

"Not half I want to!" Miles honestly professed. "But it isn't so much that."

"What is it then?"

"Well—I want to see more life."

"I see; I see." We had arrived within sight of the church and of various persons, including several of the household of Bly, on their way to it and clustered about the door to see us go in. I quickened our step; I wanted to get there before the question between us opened up much further; I reflected hungrily that he would have for more than an hour to be silent; and I thought with envy of the comparative dusk of the pew and of the almost spiritual help of the hassock on which I might bend my knees. I seemed literally to be running a race with some confusion to which he was about to reduce me, but I felt he had got in first when, before we had even entered the churchyard, he threw out—

"I want my own sort!"

It literally made me bound forward. "There aren't many of your own sort, Miles!" I laughed. "Unless perhaps dear little Flora!"

"You really compare me to a baby girl?"

This found me singularly weak. "Don't you then *love* our sweet Flora?"

"If I didn't—and you too; if I didn't—!" he repeated as if retreating for a jump, yet leaving his thought so unfinished that, after we had come into the gate, another stop, which he imposed on me by the pressure of his arm, had become inevitable. Mrs. Grose and Flora had passed into the church, the other worshippers had followed and we were, for the minute, alone among the old thick graves. We had paused, on the path from the gate, by a low oblong table-like tomb.

"Yes, if you didn't—?"

He looked, while I waited, about at the graves. "Well, you know what!" But he didn't move, and he presently produced something that made me drop straight down on the stone slab as if suddenly to rest. "Does my uncle think what *you* think?"

I markedly rested. "How do you know what I think?"

"Ah well, of course I don't; for it strikes me you never tell me. But I mean does *he* know?"

"Know what, Miles?"

"Why the way I'm going on."

I recognised quickly enough that I could make, to this enquiry, no answer that wouldn't involve something of a sacrifice of my employer. Yet it struck me that we were all, at Bly, sufficiently sacrificed to make that venial. "I don't think your uncle much cares."

Miles, on this, stood looking at me. "Then don't you think he can be made to?"

"In what way?"

"Why by his coming down."

"But who'll get him to come down?"

"*I* will!" the boy said with extraordinary brightness and emphasis. He gave me another look charged with that expression and then marched off alone into church.

XV

The business was practically settled from the moment I never followed him. It was a pitiful surrender to agitation, but my being aware of this had somehow no power to restore me. I only sat there on my tomb and read into what our young friend had said to me the fulness of its meaning; by the time I had grasped the whole of which I had also embraced, for absence, the pretext that I was ashamed to offer my pupils and the rest of the congregation such an example of delay. What I said to myself above all was that Miles had got something out of me and that the gage of it for him would be just this awkward collapse. He had got out of me that there was something I was much afraid of, and that he should probably be able to make use of my fear to gain, for his own purpose, more freedom. My fear was of having to deal with the intolerable question of the grounds of his dismissal from school, since that was really but the question of the horrors gathered behind. That his uncle should arrive to treat with me of these things was a solution that, strictly speaking, I ought now to have desired to bring on; but I could so little face the ugliness and the pain of it that I simply procrastinated and lived from hand to mouth. The boy, to my deep discomposure, was immensely in the right, was in a position to say to me: "Either you clear up with my guardian the mystery of this interruption of my studies, or you cease to expect me to lead with you a life that's so unnatural for a boy." What was so unnatural for the particular boy I was concerned with was this sudden revelation of a consciousness and a plan.

That was what really overcame me, what prevented my going in. I walked round the church, hesitating, hovering; I reflected that I had already, with him, hurt myself beyond repair. Therefore I could patch up nothing and it was too extreme an effort to squeeze beside him into the pew: he would be so much more sure than ever to pass his arm into mine and make me sit there for an hour in close mute contact with his commentary on our talk. For the first minute since his arrival I wanted to get away from him. As I paused beneath the high east window and listened to the sounds of worship I was taken with an impulse that might master me, I felt, and completely, should I give it the least encouragement. I might easily put an end to my ordeal by getting away altogether. Here was my chance; there was no one to stop me; I could give the whole thing up—turn my back and bolt. It was only a question of hurrying again, for a few preparations, to the house which the attendance at church of so many of the servants would practically have left unoccupied. No one, in short, could blame me if I should just drive desperately off. What was it to get away if I should get away only till dinner? That would be in a couple of hours, at the end of which—I had the acute prevision—my little pupils would play at innocent wonder about my non-appearance in their train.

"What *did* you do, you naughty bad thing? Why in the world, to worry us so—and take our thoughts off too, don't you know?—did you desert us at the very door?" I couldn't meet such questions nor, as they asked them, their false little lovely eyes; yet it was all so exactly what I should have to meet that, as the prospect grew sharp to me, I at last let myself go.

I got, so far as the immediate moment was concerned, away; I came straight out of the churchyard and, thinking hard, retraced my steps through the park. It seemed to me that by the time I reached the house I had made up my mind to cynical flight. The Sunday stillness both of the approaches and of the interior, in which I met no one, fairly stirred me with a sense of opportunity. Were I to get off quickly this way I should get off without a scene, without a word. My quickness would have to be remarkable, however, and the question of a conveyance was the great one to settle. Tormented, in the hall, with difficulties and obstacles, I remember sinking down at the foot of the staircase—suddenly collapsing there on the lowest step and then, with a revulsion, recalling that it was exactly where, more than a month before, in the darkness of night and just so bowed with evil things, I had seen the spectre of the most horrible of women. At this I was able to straighten myself; I went the rest of the way up; I made, in my turmoil, for the schoolroom, where there were objects belonging to me that I should have to take. But I opened the door to find again, in a flash, my eyes unsealed. In the presence of what I saw I reeled straight back upon resistance.

Seated at my own table in the clear noonday light I saw a person whom, without my previous experience, I should have taken at the first blush for some housemaid who might have stayed at home to look after the place and who, availing herself of rare relief from observation and of the schoolroom table and my pens, ink and paper, had applied herself to the considerable effort of a letter to her sweetheart. There was an effort in the way that, while her arms rested on the table, her hands, with evident weariness, supported her head; but at the moment I took this in I had already become aware that, in spite of my entrance, her attitude strangely persisted. Then it was—with the very act of its announcing itself—that her identity flared up in a change of posture. She rose, not as if she had heard me, but with an indescribable grand melancholy of indifference and detachment, and, within a dozen feet of me, stood there as my vile predecessor. Dishonoured and tragic, she was all before me; but even as I fixed and, for memory, secured it, the awful image passed away, park as midnight in her black dress, her haggard beauty and her unutterable woe, she had looked at me long enough to appear to say that her right to sit at my table was as good as mine to sit at hers. While these instants lasted indeed I had the extraordinary chill of a feeling that it was I who was the intruder. It was as a wild protest against it that, actually addressing her—"You terrible miserable woman!"—I heard myself break into a sound that, by the open door, rang through the long passage and the empty house. She looked at me as if she heard me, but I had recovered myself and cleared the air. There was nothing in the room the next minute but the sunshine and the sense that I must stay.

XVI

I had so perfectly expected the return of the others to be marked by a demonstration that I was freshly upset at having to find them merely dumb and discreet about my desertion. Instead of gaily denouncing and caressing me they made no allusion to my having failed them, and I was left, for the time, on perceiving that she too said nothing, to study Mrs. Grose's odd face. I did this to such purpose that I made sure they had in some way bribed her to silence; a silence that, however, I would engage to break down on the first private opportunity. This opportunity came before tea: I secured five minutes with her in the housekeeper's room, where, in the twilight, amid a smell of lately-baked bread, but with the place all swept and garnished, I found her sitting in pained placidity before the fire. So I see her still, so I see her best: facing the flame from her straight chair in the dusky shining room, a large clean picture of the "put away"—of drawers closed and locked and rest without a remedy.

"Oh yes, they asked me to say nothing; and to please them—so long as they were there—of course I promised. But what had happened to you?"

"I only went with you for the walk," I said. "I had then to come back to meet a friend."

She showed her surprise. "A friend—*you*?"

"Oh yes, I've a couple!" I laughed. "But did the children give you a reason?"

"For not alluding to your leaving us? Yes; they said you'd like it better. *Do* you like it better?"

My face had made her rueful. "No, I like it worse!" But after an instant I added: "Did they say why I should like it better?"

"No; Master Miles only said 'We must do nothing but what she likes!'"

"I wish indeed he would! And what did Flora say?"

"Miss Flora was too sweet. She said 'Oh of course, of course!'—and I said the same."

I thought a moment. "You were too sweet too—I can hear you all. But none the less, between Miles and me, it's now all out."

"All out?" My companion stared. "But what, Miss?"

"Everything. It doesn't matter. I've made up my mind. I came home, my dear," I went on, "for a talk with Miss Jessel."

I had by this time formed the habit of having Mrs. Grose literally well in hand in advance of my sounding that note; so that even now, as she bravely blinked under the signal of my word, I could keep her comparatively firm. "A talk! Do you mean she spoke?"

"It came to that. I found her, on my return, in the schoolroom."

"And what did she say?" I can hear the good woman still, and the candour of her stupefaction.

"That she suffers the torments—!" It was this, of a truth, that made her, as she filled out my picture, gape. "Do you mean," she faltered "—of the lost?"

"Of the lost. Of the damned. And that's why, to share them—" I faltered myself with the horror of it.

But my companion, with less imagination, kept me up. "To share them—?"

"She wants Flora." Mrs. Grose might, as I gave it to her, fairly have fallen away from me had I not been prepared. I still held her there, to show I was. "As I've told you, however, it doesn't matter."

"Because you've made up your mind? But to what?"

"To everything."

"And what do you call 'everything'?"

"Why to sending for their uncle."

"Oh Miss, in pity do," my friend broke out.

"Ah but I will, I *will*! I see it's the only way. What's 'out,' as I told you, with Miles is that if he thinks I'm afraid to—and has ideas of what he gains by that—he shall see he's mistaken. Yes, yes; his uncle shall have it here from me on the spot (and before the boy himself if necessary) that if I'm to be reproached with having done nothing again about more school—"

"Yes, Miss—" my companion pressed me.

"Well, there's that awful reason."

There were now clearly so many of these for my poor colleague that she was excusable for being vague. "But—a—which?"

"Why the letter from his old place."

"You'll show it to the master?"

"I ought to have done so on the instant."

"Oh no!" said Mrs. Grose with decision.

"I'll put it before him," I went on inexorably, "that I can't undertake to work the question on behalf of a child who has been expelled—"

"For we've never in the least known what!" Mrs. Grose declared.

"For wickedness. For what else—when he's so clever and beautiful and perfect? Is he stupid? Is he untidy? Is he infirm? Is he ill-natured? He's exquisite—so it can be only *that*; and that would open up the whole thing. After all," I said, "it's their uncle's fault. If he left here such people—!"

"He didn't really in the least know them. The fault's mine." She had turned quite pale.

"Well, you shan't suffer," I answered.

"The children shan't!" she emphatically returned.

I was silent a while; we looked at each other. "Then what am I to tell him?"

"You needn't tell him anything. *I'll* tell him."

I measured this. "Do you mean you'll write—?" Remembering she couldn't, I caught myself up. "How do you communicate?"

"I tell the bailiff. *He* writes."

"And should you like him to write our story?"

My question had a sarcastic force that I had not fully intended, and it made her after a moment inconsequently break down. The tears were again in her eyes. "Ah Miss, *you* write!"

"Well—to-night," I at last returned; and on this we separated.

XVII

I went so far, in the evening, as to make a beginning. The weather had changed back, a great wind was abroad, and beneath the lamp, in my room, with Flora at peace beside me, I sat for a long time before a blank sheet of paper and listened to the lash of the rain and the batter of the gusts. Finally I went out, taking a candle; I crossed the passage and listened a minute at Miles's door. What, under my endless obsession, I had been impelled to listen for was some betrayal of his not being at rest, and I presently caught one, but not in the form I had expected. His voice tinkled out. "I say, you there—come in." It was gaiety in the gloom!

I went in with my light and found him in bed, very wide awake but very much at his ease. "Well, what are *you* up to?" he asked with a grace of sociability in which it occurred to me that Mrs. Grose, had she been present, might have looked in vain for proof that anything was "out."

I stood over him with my candle. "How did you know I was there?"

"Why of course I heard you. Did you fancy you made no noise? You're like a troop of cavalry!" he beautifully laughed.

"Then you weren't asleep?"

"Not much! I lie awake and think."

I had put my candle, designedly, a short way off, and then, as he held out his friendly old hand to me, had sat down on the edge of his bed. "What is it," I asked, "that you think of?"

"What in the world, my dear, but *you*?"

"Ah the pride I take in your appreciation doesn't insist on that! I had so far rather you slept."

"Well, I think also, you know, of this queer business of ours."

I marked the coolness of his firm little hand. "Of what queer business, Miles?"

"Why the way you bring me up. And all the rest!"

I fairly held my breath a minute, and even from my glimmering taper there was light enough to show how he smiled up at me from his pillow. "What do you mean by all the rest?"

"Oh you know, you know!"

I could say nothing for a minute, though I felt as I held his hand and our eyes continued to meet that my silence had all the air of admitting his charge and that nothing in the whole world of reality was perhaps at that moment so fabulous as our actual relation. "Certainly you shall go back to school," I said, "if it be that that troubles you. But not to the old place—we must find another, a better. How could I know it did trouble you, this question, when you never told me so, never spoke of it at all?" His clear listening face, framed in its smooth whiteness, made him for the minute as appealing as some wistful patient in a children's hospital; and I would have given, as the resemblance came to me, all I possessed on earth really to be the nurse or the sister of charity who might have helped to cure him. Well, even as it was I perhaps might help! "Do you know you've never said a word to me about your school—I mean the old one; never mentioned it in any way?"

He seemed to wonder; he smiled with the same loveliness. But he clearly gained time; he waited, he called for guidance. "Haven't I?" It wasn't for *me* to help him—it was for the thing I had met!

Something in his tone and the expression of his face, as I got this from him, set my heart aching with such a pang as it had never yet known; so unutterably touching was it to see his little brain puzzled and his little resources taxed to play, under the spell laid on him, a part of innocence and consistency. "No, never—from the hour you came back. You've never mentioned to me one of your masters, one of your comrades, nor the least little thing that ever happened to you at school. Never, little Miles—no never—have you given me an inkling of anything that *may* have happened there. Therefore you can fancy how much I'm in the dark. Until you came out, that way, this morning, you had since the first hour I saw you scarce even made a reference to anything in your previous life. You seemed so perfectly to accept the present." It was extraordinary how my absolute conviction of his secret precocity—or whatever I might call the poison of an influence that I dared but half-phrase—made him, in spite of the faint breath of his inward trouble, appear as accessible as an older person, forced me to treat him as an intelligent equal. "I thought you wanted to go on as you are."

It struck me that at this he just faintly coloured. He gave, at any rate, like a convalescent slightly fatigued, a languid shake of his head. "I don't—I don't. I want to get away."

"You're tired of Bly?"

"Oh no, I like Bly."

"Well then—?"

"Oh *you* know what a boy wants!"

I felt I didn't know so well as Miles, and I took temporary refuge. "You want to go to your uncle?"

Again, at this, with his sweet ironic face, he made a movement on the pillow. "Ah you can't get off with that!"

I was silent a little, and it was I now, I think, who changed colour. "My dear, I don't want to get off!"

"You can't even if you do. You can't, you can't!"—he lay beautifully staring. "My uncle must come down and you must completely settle things."

"If we do," I returned with some spirit, "you may be sure it will be to take you quite away."

"Well, don't you understand that that's exactly what I'm working for? You'll have to *tell* him—about the way you've let it all drop: you'll have to tell him a tremendous lot!"

The exultation with which he uttered this helped me somehow for the instant to meet him rather more. "And how much will *you*, Miles, have to tell him? There are things he'll ask you!"

He turned it over. "Very likely. But what things?"

"The things you've never told me. To make up his mind what to do with you. He can't send you back—"

"I don't want to go back!" he broke in. "I want a new field."

He said it with admirable serenity, with positive unimpeachable gaiety; and doubtless it was that very note that most evoked for me the poignancy, the unnatural childish tragedy, of his probable reappearance at the end of three months with all this bravado and still more dishonour. It overwhelmed me now that I should never be able to bear that, and it made me let myself go. I threw myself upon him and in the tenderness of my pity I embraced him. "Dear little Miles, dear little Miles—!"

My face was close to his, and he let me kiss him, simply taking it with indulgent good humour. "Well, old lady?"

"Is there nothing—nothing at all that you want to tell me?"

He turned off a little, facing round toward the wall and holding up his hand to look at as one had seen sick children look. "I've told you—I told you this morning."

Oh I was sorry for him! "That you just want me not to worry you?"

He looked round at me now as if in recognition of my understanding him; then ever so gently, "To let me alone," he replied.

There was even a strange little dignity in it, something that made me release him, yet, when I had slowly risen, linger beside him. God knows *I* never wished to harass him, but I felt that merely, at this, to turn my back on him was to abandon or, to put it more truly, lose him. "I've just begun a letter to your uncle," I said.

"Well then, finish it!"

I waited a minute. "What happened before?" He gazed up at me again. "Before what?"

"Before you came back. And before you went away."

For some time he was silent, but he continued to meet my eyes. "What happened?"

It made me, the sound of the words, in which it seemed to me I caught for the very first time a small faint quaver of consenting consciousness—it made me drop on my knees beside the bed and seize once more the chance of possessing him. "Dear little Miles, dear little Miles, if you *knew* how I want to help you! It's only that, it's nothing but that, and I'd rather die than give you a pain or do you a wrong—I'd rather die than hurt a hair of you. Dear little Miles"—oh I brought it out now even if I *should* go too far—"I just want you to help me to save you!" But I knew in a moment after this that I had gone too far. The answer to my appeal was instantaneous, but it came in the form of an extraordinary blast and chill, a gust of frozen air and a shake of the room as great as if, in the wild wind, the casement had crashed in. The boy gave a loud high shriek which, lost in the rest of the shock of sound, might have seemed, indistinctly, though I was so close to him, a note either of jubilation or of terror. I jumped to my feet again and was conscious of darkness. So for a moment we remained, while I stared about me and saw the drawn curtains unstirred and the window still tight. "Why the candle's out!" I then cried.

"It was I who blew it, dear!" said Miles.

XVIII

The next day, after lessons, Mrs. Grose found a moment to say to me quietly: "Have you written, Miss?"

"Yes—I've written." But I didn't add—for the hour—that my letter, sealed and directed, was still in my pocket. There would be time enough to send it before the messenger should go to the village. Meanwhile there had been on the part of my pupils no more brilliant, more exemplary morning. It was exactly as if they had both had at heart to gloss over any recent little friction. They performed the dizziest feats of arithmetic, soaring quite out of *my* feeble range, and perpetrated, in higher spirits than ever, geographical and historical jokes. It was conspicuous of course in Miles in particular that he appeared to wish to show how easily he could let me down. This child, to my memory, really lives in a setting of beauty and misery that no words can translate; there was a distinction all his own in every impulse he revealed; never was a small natural creature, to the uninformed eye all frankness and freedom, a more ingenious, a more extraordinary little gentleman. I had perpetually to guard against the wonder of contemplation into which my initiated view betrayed me; to check the irrelevant gaze and discouraged sigh in which I constantly both attacked and renounced the enigma of what such a little gentleman could have done that deserved a penalty. Say that, by the dark prodigy I knew, the imagination of all evil *had* been opened up to him: all the justice within me ached for the proof that it could ever have flowered into an act.

He had never at any rate been such a little gentleman as when, after our early dinner on this dreadful day, he came round to me and asked if I shouldn't like him for half an hour to play to me. David playing to Saul could never have shown a finer sense of the occasion. It was literally a charming exhibition of tact, of magnanimity, and quite tantamount to his saying outright: "The true knights we love to read about never push an advantage too far. I know what you mean now: you mean that—to be let alone yourself and not followed up—you'll cease to worry and spy upon me, won't keep me so close to you, will let me go and come. Well, I 'come,' you see—but I don't go! There'll be plenty of time for that. I do really delight in your society and I only want to show you that I contended for a principle." It may be imagined whether I resisted this appeal or failed to accompany him again, hand in hand, to the schoolroom. He sat down at the old piano and played as he had never played; and if there are those who think he had better have been kicking a football I can only say that I wholly agree with them. For at the end of a time that under his influence I had quite ceased to measure I started up with a strange sense of having literally slept at my post. It was after luncheon, and by the schoolroom fire, and yet I hadn't really in the least slept; I had only done something much worse—I had forgotten. Where all this time was Flora? When I put the question to Miles he played on a minute before answering, and then could only say: "Why, my dear, how do *I* know?"—breaking moreover into a happy laugh which immediately after, as if it were a vocal accompaniment, he prolonged into incoherent extravagant song.

I went straight to my room, but his sister was not there; then, before going downstairs, I looked into several others. As she was nowhere about she would surely be with Mrs. Grose, whom in the comfort of that theory I accordingly proceeded in quest of. I found her where I had found her the evening before, but she met my quick challenge with blank scared ignorance. She had only supposed that, after the repast, I had carried off both the children; as to which she was quite in her right, for it was the very first time I had allowed the little girl out of my sight without some special provision. Of course now indeed she might be with the maids, so that the immediate thing was to look for her without an air of alarm. This we promptly arranged between us; but when, ten minutes later and in pursuance of our arrangement, we met in the hall, it was only to report on either side that after guarded enquiries we had altogether failed to trace her. For a minute there, apart from observation, we exchanged mute alarms, and I could feel with what high interest my friend returned me all those I had from the first given her.

"She'll be above," she presently said—"in one of the rooms you haven't searched."

"No; she's at a distance." I had made up my mind. "She has gone out."

Mrs. Grose stared. "Without a hat?"

I naturally also looked volumes. "Isn't that woman always without one?"

"She's with *her*?"

"She's with *her*!" I declared. "We must find them."

My hand was on my friend's arm, but she failed for the moment, confronted with such an account of the matter, to respond to my pressure. She communed, on the contrary, where she stood, with her uneasiness. "And where's Master Miles?"

"Oh *he's* with Quint. They'll be in the schools' room."

"Lord, Miss!" My view, I was myself aware—and therefore I suppose my tone—had never yet reached so calm an assurance.

"The trick's played," I went on; "they've successfully worked their plan. He found the most divine little way to keep me quiet while she went off."

"'Divine'?" Mrs. Grose bewilderedly echoed.

"Infernal then!" I almost cheerfully rejoined. "He has provided for himself as well. But come!"

She had helplessly gloomed at the upper regions. "You leave him—?"

"So long with Quint? Yes—I don't mind that now."

She always ended at these moments by getting possession of my hand, and in this manner she could at present still stay me. But after gasping an instant at my sudden resignation, "Because of your letter?" she eagerly brought out.

I quickly, by way of answer, felt for my letter, drew it forth, held it up, and then, freeing myself, went and laid it on the great hall-table. "Luke will take it," I said as I came back. I reached the house-door and opened it; I was already on the steps.

My companion still demurred: the storm of the night and the early morning had dropped, but the afternoon was damp and grey. I came down to the drive while she stood in the doorway. "You go with nothing on?"

"What do I care when the child has nothing? I can't wait to dress," I cried, "and if you must do so I leave you. Try meanwhile yourself upstairs."

"With *them*?" Oh on this the poor woman promptly joined me!

XIX

We went straight to the lake, as it was called at Bly, and I dare say rightly called, though it may have been a sheet of water less remarkable than my untravelled eyes supposed it. My acquaintance with sheets of water was small, and the pool of Bly, at all events on the few occasions of my consenting, under the protection of my pupils, to affront its surface in the old flat-bottomed boat moored there for our use, had impressed me both with its extent and its agitation. The usual place of embarkation was half a mile from the house, but I had an intimate conviction that, wherever Flora might be, she was not near home. She had not given me the slip for any small adventure, and, since the day of the very great one that I had shared with her by the pond, I had been aware, in our walks, of the quarter to which she most inclined. This was why I had now given to Mrs. Grose's steps so marked a direction—a direction making her, when she perceived it, oppose a resistance that showed me she was freshly mystified. "You're going to the water, Miss?—you think she's *in*—?"

"She may be, though the depth is, I believe, nowhere very great. But what I judge most likely is that she's on the spot from which, the other day, we saw together what I told you."

"When she pretended not to see—?"

"With that astounding self-possession! I've always been sure she wanted to go back alone. And now her brother has managed it for her."

Mrs. Grose still stood where she had stopped. "You suppose they really *talk* of them?"

I could meet this with an assurance! "They say things that, if we heard them, would simply appal us."

"And if she *is* there—?"

"Yes?"

"Then Miss Jessel is?"

"Beyond a doubt. You shall see."

"Oh thank you!" my friend cried, planted so firm that, taking it in, I went straight on without her. By the time I reached the pool, however, she was close behind me, and I knew that, whatever, to her apprehension, might befall me, the exposure of sticking to me struck her as her least danger. She exhaled a moan of relief as we at last came in sight of the greater part of the water without a sight of the child. There was no trace of Flora on that nearer side of the bank where my observation of her had been most startling, and none on the opposite edge, where, save for a margin of some twenty yards, a thick copse came down to the pond. This expanse, oblong in shape, was so narrow compared to its length that, with its ends out of view, it might have been taken for a scant river. We looked at the empty stretch, and then I felt the suggestion in my friend's eyes. I knew what she meant and I replied with a negative headshake.

"No, no; wait! She has taken the boat."

My companion stared at the vacant mooring-place and then again across the lake. "Then where is it?"

"Our not seeing it is the strongest of proofs. She has used it to go over, and then has managed to hide it."

"All alone—that child?"

"She's not alone, and at such times she's not a child: she's an old, old woman." I scanned all the visible shore while Mrs. Grose took again, into the queer element I offered her, one of her plunges of submission; then I pointed out that the boat might perfectly be in a small refuge formed by one of the recesses of the pool, an indentation masked, for the hither side, by a projection of the bank and by a clump of trees growing close to the water.

"But if the boat's there, where on earth's *she*?" my colleague anxiously asked.

"That's exactly what we must learn." And I started to walk further.

"By going all the way round?"

"Certainly, far as it is. It will take us but ten minutes, yet it's far enough to have made the child prefer not to walk. She went straight over."

"Laws!" cried my friend again: the chain of my logic was ever too strong for her. It dragged her at my heels even now, and when we had got halfway round—a devious tiresome process, on ground much broken and by a path choked with overgrowth— I paused to give her breath. I sustained her with a grateful arm, assuring her that she might hugely help me; and this started us afresh, so that in the course of but few minutes more we reached a point from which we found the boat to be where I had supposed it. It had been intentionally left as much as possible out of sight and was tied to one of the stakes of a fence that came, just there, down to the brink and that had been an assistance to disembarking. I recognised, as I looked at the pair of short thick oars, quite safely drawn up, the prodigious character of the feat for a little girl; but I had by this time lived too long among wonders and had panted to too many livelier measures. There was a gate in the fence, through which we passed, and that brought us after a trifling interval more into the open. Then "There she is!" we both exclaimed at once.

Flora, a short way off, stood before us on the grass and smiled as if her performance had now become complete. The next thing she did, however, was to stoop straight down and pluck—quite as if it were all she was there for—a big ugly spray of withered fern. I at once felt sure she had just come out of the copse. She waited for us, not herself taking a step, and I was conscious of the rare solemnity with which we presently approached her. She smiled and smiled, and we met; but it was all done in a silence by this time flagrantly ominous. Mrs. Grose was the first to break the spell: she threw herself on her knees and, drawing the child to her breast, clasped in a long embrace the little tender yielding body. While this dumb convulsion lasted I could only watch it—which I did the more intently when I saw Flora's face peep at me over our companion's shoulder. It was serious now—the flicker had left it; but it strengthened the pang with which I at that moment envied Mrs. Grose the simplicity of *her* relation. Still, all this while, nothing more passed between us save that Flora had let her foolish fern again drop to the ground. What she and I had virtually said to each other was that pretexts were useless now. When Mrs. Grose finally got up she kept the child's hand, so that the two were still before me; and the singular reticence of our communion was even more marked in the frank look she addressed me. "I'll be hanged," it said, "if *I'll* speak!"

It was Flora who, gazing all over me in candid wonder, was the first. She was struck with our bareheaded aspect. "Why where are your things?"

"Where yours are, my dear!" I promptly returned.

She had already got back her gaiety and appeared to take this as an answer quite sufficient. "And where's Miles?" she went on.

There was something in the small valour of it that quite finished me: these three words from her were in a flash like the glitter of a drawn blade the jostle of the cup that my hand for weeks and weeks had held high and full to the brim and that now, even before speaking, I felt overflow in a deluge. "I'll tell you if you'll tell *me*—" I heard myself say, then heard the tremor in which it broke.

"Well, what?"

Mrs. Grose's suspense blazed at me, but it was too late now, and I brought the thing out handsomely. "Where, my pet, is Miss Jessel?"

XX

Just as in the churchyard with Miles, the whole thing was upon us. Much as I had made of the fact that this name had never once, between us, been sounded, the quick smitten glare with which the child's face now received it fairly likened my breach of the silence to the smash of a pane of glass. It added to the interposing cry, as if to stay the blow, that Mrs. Grose at the same instant uttered over my violence—the shriek of a creature scared, or rather wounded, which, in turn, within a few seconds, was completed by a gasp of my own. I seized my colleague's arm. "She's there, she's there!"

Miss Jessel stood before us on the opposite bank exactly as she had stood the other time, and I remember, strangely, as the first feeling now produced in me, my thrill of joy at having brought on a proof. She was there, so I was justified; she was there, so I was neither cruel nor mad. She was there for poor scared Mrs. Grose, but she was there most for Flora; and no moment of my monstrous time was perhaps so extraordinary as that in which I consciously threw out to her—with the sense that, pale and ravenous demon as she was, she would catch and understand it—an inarticulate message of gratitude. She rose erect on the spot my friend and I had lately quitted, and there wasn't in all the long reach of her desire an inch of her evil that fell short. This first vividness of vision and emotion were things of a few seconds, during which Mrs. Grose's dazed blink across to where I pointed struck me as showing that she too at last saw, just as it carried my own eyes precipitately to the child. The revelation then of the manner in which Flora was affected startled me in truth far more than it would have done to find her also merely agitated, for direct dismay was of course not what I had expected. Prepared and on her guard as our pursuit had actually made her, she would repress every betrayal; and I was therefore at once shaken by my first glimpse of the particular one for which I had not allowed. To see her, without a convulsion of her small pink face, not even feign to glance in the direction of the prodigy I announced, but only, instead of that, turn at *me* an expression of hard still gravity, an expression absolutely new and unprecedented and that appeared to read and accuse and judge me—this was a stroke that somehow converted the little girl herself into a figure portentous. I gaped at her coolness even though my certitude of her thoroughly seeing was never greater than at that instant, and then, in the immediate need to defend myself, I called her passionately to witness. "She's there, you little unhappy thing—there, there, *there*, and you know it as well as you know me!" I had said shortly before to Mrs. Grose that she was not at these times a child, but an old, old woman, and my description of her couldn't have been more strikingly confirmed than in the way in which, for all notice of this, she simply showed me, without an expressional concession or admission, a countenance of deeper and deeper, of indeed suddenly quite fixed reprobation. I was by this time—if I can put the whole thing at all together—more appalled at what I may properly call her manner than at anything else, though it was quite simultaneously that I became aware of having Mrs. Grose also, and very formidably, to reckon with. My elder companion, the next moment, at any rate, blotted out everything but her own flushed face and her loud shocked protest, a burst of high disapproval. "What a dreadful turn, to be sure, Miss! Where on earth do you see anything?"

I could only grasp her more quickly yet, for even while she spoke the hideous plain presence stood undimmed and undaunted. It had already lasted a minute, and it lasted while I continued, seizing my colleague, quite thrusting her at it and presenting her to it, to insist with my pointing hand. "You don't see her exactly as *we* see?—you mean to say you don't now—now? She's as big as a blazing fire! Only look, dearest woman, *look*—!" She looked, just as I did, and gave me, with her deep groan of negation, repulsion, compassion—the mixture with her pity of her relief at her exemption—a sense, touching to me even then, that she would have backed me up if she had been able. I might well have needed that, for with this hard blow of the proof that her eyes were hopelessly sealed I felt my own situation horribly crumble, I felt—I saw—my livid predecessor press, from her position, on my defeat, and I took the measure, more than all, of what I should have from this instant to deal with in the astounding little attitude of Flora. Into this attitude Mrs. Grose immediately and violently entered, breaking, even while there pierced through my sense of ruin a prodigious private triumph, into breathless reassurance.

"She isn't there, little lady, and nobody's there—and you never see nothing, my sweet! How can poor Miss Jessel—when poor Miss Jessel's dead and buried? *We* know, don't we, love?"—and she appealed, blundering in, to the child. "It's all a mere mistake and a worry and a joke—and we'll go home as fast as we can!"

Our companion, on this, had responded with a strange quick primness of propriety, and they were again, with Mrs. Grose on her feet, united, as it were, in shocked opposition to me. Flora continued to fix me with her small mask of disaffection, and even at that minute I prayed God to forgive me for seeming to see that, as she stood there holding tight to our friend's dress, her incomparable childish beauty had suddenly failed, had quite vanished. I've said it already—she was literally, she was hideously hard; she had turned common and almost ugly. "I don't know what you mean. I see nobody. I see nothing. I never *have*. I think you're cruel. I don't like you!" Then, after this deliverance, which might have been that of a vulgarly pert little girl in the street, she hugged Mrs. Grose more closely and buried in her skirts the dreadful little face. In this position she launched an almost furious wail. "Take me away, take me away—oh take me away from *her*!"

"From *me*?" I panted.

"From you—from you!" she cried.

Even Mrs. Grose looked across at me dismayed; while I had nothing to do but communicate again with the figure that, on the opposite bank, without a movement, as rigidly still as if catching, beyond the interval, our voices, was as vividly there for my disaster as it was not there for my service. The wretched child had spoken exactly as if she had got from some outside source each of her stabbing little words, and I could therefore, in the full despair of all I had to accept, but sadly shake my head at her. "If I had ever doubted all my doubt would at present have gone. I've been living with the miserable truth, and now it has only too much closed round me. Of course I've lost you: I've interfered, and you've seen, under *her* dictation"—with which I faced, over the pool again, our infernal witness—"the easy and perfect way to meet it. I've done my best but I've lost you. Good-bye." For Mrs. Grose I had an imperative, an almost frantic "Go, go!" before which, in infinite distress, but mutely possessed of the little girl and clearly convinced, in spite of her blindness, that something awful had occurred and some collapse engulfed us, she retreated, by the way we had come, as fast as she could move.

Of what first happened when I was left alone I had no subsequent memory. I only knew that at the end of, I suppose, a quarter of an hour, an odorous dampness and roughness, chilling and piercing my trouble, had made me understand that I must have thrown myself, on my face, to the ground and given way to a wildness of grief. I must have lain there long and cried and wailed, for when I raised my head the day was almost done. I got up and looked a moment, through the twilight, at the grey pool and its blank haunted edge, and then I took, back to the house, my dreary and difficult course. When I reached the gate in the fence the-boat, to my surprise, was gone, so that I had a fresh reflexion to make on Flora's extraordinary command of the situation. She passed that night, by the most tacit and, I should add, were not the word so grotesque a false note, the happiest of arrangements, with Mrs. Grose. I saw neither of them on my return, but on the other hand I saw, as by an ambiguous compensation, a great deal of Miles. I saw—I can use no other phrase—so much of him that it fairly measured more than it had ever measured. No evening I had passed at Bly was to have had the portentous quality of this one; in spite of which—and in spite also of the deeper depths of consternation that had opened beneath my feet—there was literally, in the ebbing actual, an extraordinarily sweet sadness. On reaching the house I had never so much as looked for the boy; I had simply gone straight to my room to change what I was wearing and to take in, at a glance, much material testimony to Flora's rupture. Her little belongings had all been removed. When later, by the schoolroom fire, I was served with tea by the usual maid, I indulged, on the article of my other pupil, in no enquiry whatever. He had his freedom now—he might have it to the end! Well, he did have it; and it consisted—in part at least—of his coming in at about eight o'clock and sitting down with me in silence. On the removal of the tea-things I had blown out the candles and drawn my chair closer: I was conscious of a mortal coldness and felt as if I should never again be warm. So when he appeared I was sitting in the glow with my thoughts. He paused a moment by the door as if to look at me; then—as if to share them—came to the other side of the hearth and sank into a chair. We sat there in absolute stillness; yet he wanted, I felt, to be with me.

XXI

Before a new day, in my room, had fully broken, my eyes opened to Mrs. Grose, who had come to my bedside with worse news. Flora was so markedly feverish that an illness was perhaps at hand; she had passed a night of extreme unrest, a night agitated above all by fears that had for their subject not in the least her former but wholly her present governess. It was not against the possible re-entrance of Miss Jessel on the scene that she protested—it was conspicuously and passionately against mine. I was at once on my feet, and with an immense deal to ask; the more that my friend had discernibly now girded her loins to meet me afresh. This I felt as soon as I had put to her the question of her sense of the child's sincerity as against my own. "She persists in denying to you that she saw, or has ever seen, anything?"

My visitor's trouble truly was great. "Ah Miss, it isn't a matter on which I can push her! Yet it isn't either, I must say, as if I much needed to. It has made her, every inch of her, quite old."

"Oh I see her perfectly from here. She resents, for all the world like some high little personage, the imputation on her truthfulness and, as it were, her respectability. 'Miss Jessel indeed—*she*!' Ah she's 'respectable,' the chit! The impression she gave me there yesterday was, I assure you, the very strangest of all: it was quite beyond any of the others. I *did* put my foot in it! She'll never speak to me again."

Hideous and obscure as it all was, it held Mrs. Grose briefly silent; then she granted my point with a frankness which, I made sure, had more behind it. "I think, indeed, Miss, she never will. She do have a grand manner about it!"

"And that manner"—I summed it up—"is practically what's the matter with her now."

Oh that manner, I could see in my visitor's face, and not a little else besides! "She asks me every three minutes if I think you're coming in."

"I see—I see." I too, on my side, had so much more than worked it out. "Has she said to you since yesterday—except to repudiate her familiarity with anything so dreadful—a single other word about Miss Jessel?"

"Not one, Miss. And of course, you know," my friend added, "I took it from her by the lake that just then and there at least there *was* nobody."

"Rather! And naturally you take it from her still."

"I don't contradict her. What else can I do?"

"Nothing in the world! You've the cleverest little person to deal with. They've made them—their two friends, I mean—still cleverer even than nature did; for it was wondrous material to play on! Flora has now her grievance, and she'll work it to the end."

"Yes, Miss; but to *what* end?"

"Why that of dealing with me to her uncle. She'll make me out to him the lowest creature—!"

I winced at the fair show of the scene in Mrs. Grose's face; she looked for a minute as if she sharply saw them together. "And him who thinks so well of you!"

"He has an odd way—it comes over me now," I laughed, "—of proving it! But that doesn't matter. What Flora wants of course is to get rid of me."

My companion bravely concurred. "Never again to so much as look at you."

"So that what you've come to me now for," I asked, "is to speed me on my way?" Before she had time to reply, however, I had her in check. "I've a better idea—the result of my reflections. My going *would* seem the right thing, and on Sunday I was terribly near it. Yet that won't do. It's *you* who must go. You must take Flora."

My visitor, at this, did speculate. "But where in the world—?"

"Away from here. Away from *them*. Away, even most of all, now, from me. Straight to her uncle."

"Only to tell on you—?"

"No, not 'only'! To leave me, in addition, with my remedy."

She was still vague. "And what *is* your remedy?"

"Your loyalty, to begin with. And then Miles's."

She looked at me hard. "Do you think he—?"

"Won't, if he has the chance, turn on me? Yes, I venture still to think it. At all events I want to try. I venture still to think it. At all events I want to try. Get off with his sister as soon as possible and leave me with him alone." I was amazed, myself, at the spirit I had still in reserve, and therefore perhaps a trifle the more disconcerted at the way in which, in spite of this fine example of it, she hesitated. "There's one thing, of course," I went on: "they mustn't, before she goes, see each other for three seconds." Then it came over me, in spite of Flora's presumable sequestration from the instant of her return from the pool, it might already be too late. "Do you mean," I anxiously asked, "that they *have* met?"

At this she quite flushed. "Ah, Miss, I'm not such a fool as that! If I've been obliged to leave her three or four times, it has been each time with one of the maids, and at present, though she's alone, she's locked in safe. And yet—and yet!" There were too many things.

"And yet what?"

"Well, are you so sure of the little gentleman?"

"I'm not sure of anything but *you*. But I have, since last evening, a new hope. I think he wants to give me an opening. I do believe that—poor little exquisite wretch!—he wants to speak. Last evening, in the firelight and the silence, he sat with me for two hours as if it were just coming."

Mrs. Grose looked hard through the window at the grey gathering day. "And did it come?"

"No, though I waited and waited I confess it didn't, and it was without a breach of the silence, or so much as a faint allusion to his sister's condition and absence, that we at last kissed for good-night. All the same," I continued, "I can't, if her uncle sees her, consent to his seeing her brother without my having given the boy—and most of all because things have got so bad—a little more time."

My friend appeared on this ground more reluctant than I could quite understand. "What do you mean by more time?"

"Well, a day or two—really to bring it out. He'll then be on *my* side—of which you see the importance. If nothing comes I shall only fail, and you at the worst have helped me by doing on your arrival in town whatever you may have found possible." So I put it before her, but she continued for a little so lost in other reasons that I came again to her aid. "Unless indeed," I wound up, "you really want *not* to go."

I could see it, in her face, at last clear itself: she put out her hand to me as a pledge. "I'll go—I'll go. I'll go this morning."

I wanted to be very just. "If you *should* wish still to wait I'd engage she shouldn't see me."

"No, no: it's the place itself. She must leave it." She held me a moment with heavy eyes, then brought out the rest. "Your idea's the right one. I myself, Miss—"

"Well?"

"I can't stay."

The look she gave me with it made me jump at possibilities. "You mean that, since yesterday, you *have* seen—?"

She shook her head with dignity. "I've *heard*—!"

"Heard?"

"From that child—horrors! There!" she sighed with tragic relief. "On my honour, Miss, she says things—!" But at this evocation she broke down; she dropped with a sudden cry upon my sofa and, as I had seen her do before, gave way to all the anguish of it.

It was quite in another manner that I for my part let myself go. "Oh thank God!"

She sprang up again at this, drying her eyes with a groan. "'Thank God'?"

"It so justifies me!"

"It does that, Miss!"

I couldn't have desired more emphasis, but I just waited. "She's so horrible?"

I saw my colleague scarce knew how to put it. "Really shocking."

"And about me?"

"About you, Miss—since you must have it. It's beyond everything, for a young lady; and I can't think wherever she must have picked up—"

"The appalling language she applies to me? I can then!" I broke in with a laugh that was doubtless significant enough.

It only in truth left my friend still more grave. "Well, perhaps I ought to also—since I've heard some of it before! Yet I can't bear it," the poor woman went on while with the same movement she glanced, on my dressing-table, at the face of my watch. "But I must go back."

I kept her, however. "Ah if you can't bear it—!"

"How can I stop with her, you mean? Why just *for* that: to get her away. Far from this," she pursued, "far from *them*—"

"She may be different? she may be free?" I seized her almost with joy. "Then in spite of yesterday you *believe*—"

"In such doings?" Her simple description of them required, in the light of her expression, to be carried no further, and she gave me the whole thing as she had never done. "I believe."

Yes, it was a joy, and we were still shoulder to shoulder: if I might continue sure of that I should care but little what else happened. My support in the presence of disaster would be the same as it had been in my early need of confidence, and if my friend would answer for my honesty I would answer for all the rest. On the point of taking leave of her, none the less, I was to some extent embarrassed. "There's one thing of course—it occurs to me—to remember. My letter giving the alarm will have reached town before you."

I now felt still more how she had been beating about the bush and how weary at last it had made her. "Your letter won't have got there. Your letter never went."

"What then became of it?"

"Goodness knows! Master Miles—"

"Do you mean *he* took it?" I gasped.

She hung fire, but she overcame her reluctance. "I mean that I saw yesterday, when I came back with Miss Flora, that it wasn't where you had put it. Later in the evening I had the chance to question Luke, and he declared that he had neither noticed nor touched it." We could only exchange, on this, one of our deeper mutual soundings, and it was Mrs. Grose who first brought up the plumb with an almost elate "You see!"

"Yes, I see that if Miles took it instead he probably will have read it and destroyed it."

"And don't you see anything else?"

I faced her a moment with a sad smile. "It strikes me that by this time your eyes are open even wider than mine."

They proved to be so indeed, but she could still almost blush to show it. "I make out now what he must have done at school." And she gave, in her simple sharpness, an almost droll disillusioned nod. "He stole!"

I turned it over—I tried to be more judicial. "Well—perhaps."

She looked as if she found me unexpectedly calm. "He stole *letters*!"

She couldn't know my reasons for a calmness after all pretty shallow; so I showed them off as I might. "I hope then it was to more purpose than in this case! The note, at all events, that I put on the table yesterday," I pursued, "will have given him so scant an advantage—for it contained only the bare demand for an interview—that he's already much ashamed of having gone so far for so little, and that what he had on his mind last evening was precisely the need of confession." I seemed to myself for the instant to have mastered it, to see it all. "Leave us, leave us"—I was already, at the door, hurrying her off. "I'll get it out of him. He'll meet me. He'll confess. If he confesses he's saved. And if he's saved—"

"Then *you* are?" The dear woman kissed me on this, and I took her farewell. "I'll save you without him!" she cried as she went.

XXII

Yet it was when she had got off—and I missed her on the spot—that the great pinch really came. If I had counted on what it would give me to find myself alone with Miles I quickly recognised that it would give me at least a measure. No hour of my stay in fact was so assailed with apprehensions as that of my coming down to learn that the carriage containing Mrs. Grose and my younger pupil had already rolled out of the gates. Now I *was,* I said to myself, face to face with the elements, and for much of the rest of the day, while I fought my weakness, I could consider that I had been supremely rash. It was a tighter place still than I had yet turned round in; all the more that, for the first time, I could see in the aspect of others a confused reflexion of the crisis. What had happened naturally caused them all to stare; there was too little of the explained, throw out whatever we might, in the suddenness of my colleague's act. The maids and the men looked blank; the effect of which on my nerves was an aggravation until I saw the necessity of making it a positive aid. It was in short by just clutching the helm that I avoided total wreck; and I dare say that, to bear up at all, I became that morning very grand and very dry. I welcomed the consciousness that I was charged with much to do, and I caused it to be known as well that, left thus to myself, I was quite remarkably firm. I wandered with that manner, for the next hour or two, all over the place and looked, I have no doubt, as if I were ready for any onset. So, for the benefit of whom it might concern, I paraded with a sick heart.

The person it appeared least to concern proved to be, till dinner, little Miles himself. My perambulations had given me meanwhile no glimpse of him, but they had tended to make more public the change taking place in our relation as a consequence of his having at the piano, the day before, kept me, in Flora's interest, so beguiled and befooled. The stamp of publicity had of course been fully given by her confinement and departure, and the change itself was now ushered in by our non-observance of the regular custom of the schoolroom. He had already disappeared when, on my way down, I pushed open his door, and I learned below that he had breakfasted—in the presence of a couple of the maids—with Mrs. Grose and his sister. He had then gone out, as he said, for a stroll; than which nothing, I reflected, could better have expressed his frank view of the abrupt transformation in my office. What he would now permit this office to consist of was yet to be settled: there was at the least a queer relief—I mean for myself in especial—in the renouncement of one pretension. If so much had sprung to the surface I scarce put it too strongly in saying that what had perhaps sprung highest was the absurdity of our prolonging the fiction that I had anything more to teach him. It sufficiently stuck out that, by tacit little tricks in which even more than myself he carried out the care for my dignity, I had had to appeal to him to let me off straining to meet him on the ground of his true capacity. He had at any rate his freedom now; I was never to touch it again: as I had amply shown, moreover, when, on his joining me in the schoolroom the previous night, I uttered, in reference to the interval just concluded, neither challenge nor hint. I had too much, from this moment, my other ideas. Yet when he at last arrived the difficulty of applying them, the accumulations of my problem, were brought straight home to me by the beautiful little presence on which what had occurred had as yet, for the eye, dropped neither stain nor shadow.

To mark, for the house, the high state I cultivated I decreed that my meals with the boy should be served, as we called it, downstairs; so that I had been awaiting him in the ponderous pomp of the room outside the window of which I had had from Mrs. Grose, that first scared Sunday, my flash of something it would scarce have done to call light. Here at present I felt afresh—for I had felt it again and again—how my equilibrium depended on the success of my rigid will, the will to shut my eyes as tight as possible to the truth that what I had to deal with was, revoltingly, against nature. I could only get on at all by taking "nature" into my confidence and my account, by treating my monstrous ordeal as a push in a direction unusual, of course, and unpleasant, but demanding after all, for a fair front, only another turn of the screw of ordinary human virtue. No attempt, none the less, could well require more tact than just this attempt to supply, one's self, all the nature. How could I put even a little of that article into a suppression of reference to what had occurred? How on the other hand could I make a reference without a new plunge into the hideous obscure? Well, a sort of answer, after a time, had come to me, and it was so far confirmed as that I was met, incontestably, by the quickened vision of what was rare in my little companion. It was indeed as if he had found even now—as he had so often found at lessons—still some other delicate way to ease me off. Wasn't there light in the fact which, as we shared our solitude, broke out with a specious glitter it had never yet quite worn?—the fact that (opportunity aiding, precious opportunity which had now come) it would be preposterous, with a child so endowed, to forego the help one might wrest from absolute intelligence? What had his intelligence been given him for but to save him? Mightn't one, to reach his mind, risk the stretch of a stiff arm across his character? It was as if, when we were face to face in the dining-room, he had literally shown me the way. The roast mutton was on the table and I had dispensed with attendance. Miles, before he sat down, stood a moment with his hands in his pockets and looked at the joint, on which he seemed on the point of passing some humorous judgement. But what he presently produced was: "I say, my dear, is she really very awfully ill?"

"Little Flora? Not so bad but that she'll presently be better. London will set her up. Bly had ceased to agree with her. Come here and take your mutton."

He alertly obeyed me, carried the plate carefully to his seat and, when he was established, went on. "Did Bly disagree with her so terribly all at once?"

"Not so suddenly as you might think. One had seen it coming on."

"Then why didn't you get her off before?"

"Before what?"

"Before she became too ill to travel."

I found myself prompt. "She's *not* too ill to travel; she only might have become so if she had stayed. This was just the moment to seize. The journey will dissipate the influence"—oh I was grand!—"and carry it off."

"I see, I see"—Miles, for that matter, was grand too. He settled to his repast with the charming little "table manner" that, from the day of his arrival, had relieved me of all grossness of admonition. Whatever he had been expelled from school for, it wasn't for ugly feeding. He was irreproachable, as always, today; but was unmistakeably more conscious. He was discernibly trying to take for granted more things than he found, without assistance, quite easy; and he dropped into peaceful silence while he felt his situation. Our meal was of the briefest—mine a vain pretence, and I had the things immediately removed. While this was done Miles stood again with his hands in his little pockets and his back to me—stood and looked out of the wide window through which, that other day, I had seen what pulled me up. We continued silent while the maid was with us—as silent, it whimsically occurred to me, as some young couple who, on their wedding-journey, at the inn, feel shy in the presence of the waiter. He turned round only when the waiter had left us. "Well—so we're alone!"

XXIII

"Oh more or less." I imagine my smile was pale. "Not absolutely. We shouldn't like that!" I went on.

"No—I suppose we shouldn't. Of course we've the others."

"We've the others—we've indeed the others," I concurred.

"Yet even though we have them," he returned, still with his hands in his pockets and planted there in front of me, "they don't much count, do they?"

I made the best of it, but I felt wan. "It depends on what you call 'much'!"

"Yes"—with all accommodation—"everything depends!" On this, however, he faced to the window again and presently reached it with his vague restless cogitating step. He remained there a while with his forehead against the glass, in contemplation of the stupid shrubs I knew and the dull things of November. I had always my hypocrisy of "work," behind which I now gained the sofa. Steadying myself with it there as I had repeatedly done at those moments of torment that I have described as the moments of my knowing the children to be given to something from which I was barred, I sufficiently obeyed my habit of being prepared for the worst. But an extraordinary impression dropped on me as I extracted a meaning from the boy's embarrassed back—none other than the impression that I was not barred now. This inference grew in a few minutes to sharp intensity and seemed bound up with the direct perception that it was positively *he* who was. The frames and squares of the great window were a kind of image, for him, of a kind of failure. I felt that I saw him, in any case, shut in or shut out. He was admirable but not comfortable: I took it in with a throb of hope. Wasn't he looking through the haunted pane for something he couldn't see?—and wasn't it the first time in the whole business that he had known such a lapse? The first, the very first: I found it a splendid portent. It made him anxious, though he watched himself; he had been anxious all day and, even while in his usual sweet little manner he sat at table, had needed all his small strange genius to give it a gloss. When he at last turned round to meet me it was almost as if this genius had succumbed. "Well, I think I'm glad Bly agrees with *me*!"

"You'd certainly seem to have seen, these twenty-four hours, a good deal more of it than for some time before. I hope," I went on bravely, "that you've been enjoying yourself."

"Oh yes, I've been ever so far; all round about—miles and miles away. I've never been so free."

He had really a manner of his own, and I could only try to keep up with him. "Well, do you like it?"

He stood there smiling; then at last he put into two words—"Do *you*?"—more discrimination than I had ever heard two words contain. Before I had time to deal with that, however, he continued as if with the sense that this was an impertinence to be softened. "Nothing could be more charming than the way you take it, for of course if we're alone together now it's you that are alone most. But I hope," he threw in, "you don't particularly mind!"

"Having to do with you?" I asked. "My dear child, how can I help minding? Though I've renounced all claim to your company—you're so beyond me—I at least greatly enjoy it. What else should I stay on for?"

He looked at me more directly, and the expression of his face, graver now, struck me as the most beautiful I had ever found in it. "You stay on just for *that*?"

"Certainly. I stay on as your friend and from the tremendous interest I take in you till something can be done for you that may be more worth your while. That needn't surprise you." My voice trembled so that I felt it impossible to suppress the shake. "Don't you remember how I told you, when I came and sat on your bed the night of the storm, that there was nothing in the world I wouldn't do for you?"

"Yes, yes!" He, on his side, more and more visibly nervous, had a tone to master; but he was so much more successful than I that, laughing out through his gravity, he could pretend we were pleasantly jesting. "Only that, I think, was to get me to do something for *you*!"

"It was partly to get you to do something," I conceded. "But, you know, you didn't do it."

"Oh yes," he said with the brightest superficial eagerness, "you wanted me to tell you something."

"That's it. Out, straight out. What you have on your mind, you know."

"Ah then is *that* what you've stayed over for?"

He spoke with a gaiety through which I could still catch the finest little quiver of resentful passion; but I can't begin to express the effect upon me of an implication of surrender even so faint. It was as if what I had yearned for had come at last only to astonish me. "Well, yes—I may as well make a clean breast of it. It was precisely for that."

He waited so long that I supposed it for the purpose of repudiating the assumption on which my action had been founded; but what he finally said was: "Do you mean now—here?"

"There couldn't be a better place or time." He looked round him uneasily, and I had the rare—oh the queer!—impression of the very first symptom I had seen in him of the approach of immediate fear. It was as if he were suddenly afraid of me—which struck me indeed as perhaps the best thing to make him. Yet in the very pang of the effort I felt it vain to try sternness, and I heard myself the next instant so gentle as to be almost grotesque. "You want so to go out again?"

"Awfully!" He smiled at me heroically, and the touching little bravery of it was enhanced by his actually flushing with pain. He had picked up his hat, which he had brought in, and stood twirling it in a way that gave me, even as I was just nearly reaching port, a perverse horror of what I was doing. To do it in *any* way was an act of violence, for what did it consist of but the obtrusion of the idea of grossness and guilt on a small helpless creature who had been for me a revelation of the possibilities of beautiful intercourse? Wasn't it base to create for a being so exquisite a mere alien awkwardness? I suppose I now read into our situation a clearness it couldn't have had at the time, for I seem to see our poor eyes already lighted with some spark of a prevision of the anguish that was to come. So we circled about with terrors and scruples, fighters not daring to close. But it was for each other we feared! That kept us a little longer suspended and unbruised. "I'll tell you everything," Miles said—"I mean I'll tell you anything you like. You'll stay on with me, and we shall both be all right, and I *will* tell you—I will. But not now."

"Why not now?"

My insistence turned him from me and kept him once more at his window in a silence during which, between us, you might have heard a pin drop. Then he was before me again with the air of a person for whom, outside, some one who had frankly to be reckoned with was waiting. "I have to see Luke."

I had not yet reduced him to quite so vulgar a lie, and I felt proportionately ashamed. But, horrible as it was, his lies made up my truth. I achieved thoughtfully a few loops of my knitting. "Well then go to Luke, and I'll wait for what you promise. Only in return for that satisfy, before you leave me, one very much smaller request."

He looked as if he felt he had succeeded enough to be able still a little to bargain. "Very much smaller—?"

"Yes, a mere fraction of the whole. Tell me"—oh my work preoccupied me, and I was off-hand!—"if, yesterday afternoon, from the table in the hall, you took, you know, my letter."

XXIV

My grasp of how he received this suffered for a minute from something that I can describe only as a fierce split of my attention—a stroke that at first, as I sprang straight up, reduced me to the mere blind movement of getting hold of him, drawing him close and, while I just fell for support against the nearest piece of furniture, instinctively keeping him with his back to the window. The appearance was full upon us that I had already had to deal with here: Peter Quint had come into view like a sentinel before a prison. The next thing I saw was that, from outside, he had reached the window, and then I knew that, close to the glass and glaring in through it, he offered once more to the room his white face of damnation. It represents but grossly what took place within me at the sight to say that on the second my decision was made; yet I believe that no woman so overwhelmed ever in so short a time recovered her command of the *act*. It came to me in the very horror of the immediate presence that the act would be, seeing and facing what I saw and faced, to keep the boy himself unaware. The inspiration—I can call it by no other name—was that I felt how voluntarily, how transcendently, I *might*. It was like fighting with a demon for a human soul, and when I had fairly so appraised it I saw how the human soul—held out, in the tremor of my hands, at arms' length—had a perfect dew of sweat on a lovely childish forehead. The face that was close to mine was as white as the face against the glass, and out of it presently came a sound, not low nor weak, but as if from much further away, that I drank like a waft of fragrance.

"Yes—I took it."

At this, with a moan of joy, I enfolded, I drew him close; and while I held him to my breast, where I could feel in the sudden fever of his little body the tremendous pulse of his little heart, I kept my eyes on the thing at the window and saw it move and shift its posture. I have likened it to a sentinel, but its slow wheel, for a moment, was rather the prowl of a baffled beast. My present quickened courage, however, was such that, not too much to let it through, I had to shade, as it were, my flame. Meanwhile the glare of the face was again at the window, the scoundrel fixed as if to watch and wait. It was the very confidence that I might now defy him, as well as the positive certitude, by this time, of the child's unconsciousness, that made me go on. "What did you take it for?"

"To see what you said about me."

"You opened the letter?"

"I opened it."

My eyes were now, as I held him off a little again, on Miles's own face, in which the collapse of mockery showed me how complete was the ravage of uneasiness. What was prodigious was that at last, by my success, his sense was sealed and his communication stopped: he knew that he was in presence, but knew not of what, and knew still less that I also was and that I did know. And what did this strain of trouble matter when my eyes went back to the window only to see that the air was clear again and—by my personal triumph—the influence quenched? There was nothing there. I felt that the cause was mine and that I should surely get all. "And you found nothing!"—I let my elation out.

He gave the most mournful, thoughtful little headshake. "Nothing."

"Nothing, nothing!" I almost shouted in my joy.

"Nothing, nothing," he sadly repeated.

I kissed his forehead; it was drenched. "So what have you done with it?"

"I've burnt it."

"Burnt it?" It was now or never. "Is that what you did at school?"

Oh what this brought up! "At school?"

"Did you take letters?—or other things?"

"Other things?" He appeared now to be thinking of something far off and that reached him only through the pressure of his anxiety. Yet it did reach him. "Did I *steal?*"

I felt myself redden to the roots of my hair as well as wonder if it were more strange to put to a gentleman such a question or to see him take it with allowances that gave the very distance of his fall in the world. "Was it for that you mightn't go back?"

The only thing he felt was rather a dreary little surprise. "Did you know I mightn't go back?"

"I know everything."

He gave me at this the longest and strangest look. "Everything?"

"Everything. Therefore *did* you—?" But I couldn't say it again.

Miles could, very simply. "No. I didn't steal."

My face must have shown him I believed him utterly; yet my hands—but it was for pure tenderness—shook him as if to ask him why, if it was all for nothing, he had condemned me to months of torment. "What then did you do?"

He looked in vague pain all round the top of the room and drew his breath, two or three times over, as if with difficulty. He might have been standing at the bottom of the sea and raising his eyes to some faint green twilight. "Well—I said things."

"Only that?"

"They thought it was enough!"

"To turn you out for?"

Never, truly, had a person "turned out" shown so little to explain it as this little person! He appeared to weigh my question, but in a manner quite detached and almost helpless. "Well, I suppose I oughtn't."

"But to whom did you say them?"

He evidently tried to remember, but it dropped—he had lost it. "I don't know!"

He almost smiled at me in the desolation of his surrender, which was indeed practically, by this time, so complete that I ought to have left it there. But I was infatuated—I was blind with victory, though even then the very effect that was to have brought him so much nearer was already that of added separation. "Was it to everyone?" I asked.

"No; it was only to—" But he gave a sick little headshake. "I don't remember their names."

"Were they then so many?"

"No—only a few. Those I liked."

Those he liked? I seemed to float not into clearness, but into a darker obscure, and within a minute there had come to me out of my very pity the appalling alarm of his being perhaps innocent. It was for the instant confounding and bottomless, for if he *were* innocent what then on earth was I? Paralysed, while it lasted, by the mere brush of the question, I let him go a little, so that, with a deep-drawn sigh, he turned away from me again; which, as he faced toward the clear window, I suffered, feeling that I had nothing now there to keep him from. "And did they repeat what you said?" I went on after a moment.

He was soon at some distance from me, still breathing hard and again with the air, though now without anger for it, of being confined against his will. Once more, as he had done before, he looked up at the dim day as if, of what had hitherto sustained him, nothing was left but an unspeakable anxiety. "Oh yes," he nevertheless replied—"they must have repeated them. To those *they* liked," he added.

There was somehow less of it than I had expected; but I turned it over. "And these things came round—?"

"To the masters? Oh yes!" he answered very simply. "But I didn't know they'd tell."

"The masters? They didn't—they've never told. That's why I ask you."

He turned to me again his little beautiful fevered face. "Yes, it was too bad."

"Too bad?"

"What I suppose I sometimes said. To write home."

I can't name the exquisite pathos of the contradiction given to such a speech by such a speaker; I only know that the next instant I heard myself throw off with homely force: "Stuff and nonsense!" But the next after that I must have sounded stern enough. "What *were* these things?"

My sternness was all for his judge, his executioner; yet it made him avert himself again, and that movement made *me*, with a single bound and an irrepressible cry, spring straight upon him. For there again, against the glass, as if to blight his confession and stay his answer, was the hideous author of our woe—the white face of damnation. I felt a sick swim at the drop of my victory and all the return of my battle, so that the wildness of my veritable leap only served as a great betrayal. I saw him, from the midst of my act, meet it with a divination, and on the perception that even now he only guessed, and that the window was still to his own eyes free, I let the impulse flame up to convert the climax of his dismay into the very proof of his liberation. "No more, no more, no more!" I shrieked to my visitant as I tried to press him against me.

"Is she *here*?" Miles panted as he caught with his sealed eyes the direction of my words. Then as his strange "she" staggered me and, with a gasp, I echoed it, "Miss Jessel, Miss Jessel!" he with sudden fury gave me back.

I seized, stupefied, his supposition—some sequel to what we had done to Flora, but this made me only want to show him that it was better still than that. "It's not Miss Jessel! But it's at the window—straight before us. It's *there*—the coward horror, there for the last time!"

At this, after a second in which his head made the movement of a baffled dog's on a scent and then gave a frantic little shake for air and light, he was at me in a white rage, bewildered, glaring vainly over the place and missing wholly, though it now, to my sense, filled the room like the taste of poison, the wide overwhelming presence. "It's *he*?"

I was so determined to have all my proof that I flashed into ice to challenge him. "Whom do you mean by 'he'?"

"Peter Quint—you devil!" His face gave again, round the room, its convulsed supplication. "*Where?*"

They are in my ears still, his supreme surrender of the name and his tribute to my devotion. "What does he matter now, my own?—what will he *ever* matter? *I* have you," I launched at the beast, "but he has lost you for ever!" Then for the demonstration of my work, "There, *there*!" I said to Miles.

But he had already jerked straight round, stared, glared again, and seen but the quiet day. With the stroke of the loss I was so proud of he uttered the cry of a creature hurled over an abyss, and the grasp with which I recovered him might have been that of catching him in his fall. I caught him, yes, I held him—it may be imagined with what a passion; but at the end of a minute I began to feel what it truly was that I held. We were alone with the quiet day, and his little heart, dispossessed, had stopped.

Original Sources

Benson, E. F. "The House with the Brick-Kiln," *The Room in the Tower and Other Stories*. London: Mills & Boon, Limited, 1912.

Bierce, Ambrose. "The Moonlit Road," *The Collected Works of Ambrose Bierce, Volume III: Can Such Things Be?* New York: The Neale Publishing Company, 1909.

Blackwood, Algernon. "Keeping His Promise," *The Empty House*. London: Eveleigh Nash Company, 1916.

Buchan, John. "Fullcircle," *Blackwood's Magazine*, January 1920.

Bulwer-Lytton, Edward. "The Haunted and the Haunters; or, The House and the Brain," *Blackwood's Edinburgh Magazine*, August 1859.

Capes, Bernard. "An Eddy on the Floor," *At a Winter's Fire*. London: Methuen & Co., 1899.

Collins, Wilkie. "Mad Monkton," *The Queen of Hearts*. London: Chatto and Windus, 1875.

Cram, Ralph Adams. "In Kropfsberg Keep," *Black Spirits and White*. Chicago: Stone and Kimball, 1895.

Dickens, Charles. "No. 1 Branch Line—The Signal-Man," *All the Year Round*, Christmas 1866.

Doyle, Arthur Conan. "The Captain of the *Pole-Star*," *The Captain of the Polestar and Other Tales*. London: Longman's, Green, and Co., 1894.

Dunsany, Lord. "The Ghosts," *The Sword of Welleran and Other Stories*. London: George Allen & Sons, 1908.

Edwards, Amelia B. "The North Mail," *Miss Carew*. London: Hurst and Blackett, Publishers, 1865.

Falkner, J. Meade. *The Lost Stradivarius*. London: William Blackwood and Sons, 1896.

Freeman, Mary E. Wilkins. "The Wind in the Rose-Bush," *The Wind in the Rose-Bush and Other Stories of the Supernatural*. Doubleday, Page & Company, 1903.

Gaskell, Elizabeth. "The Old Nurse's Story," *Lizzie Leigh and Other Tales*. London: Chapman and Hall, 1855.

Glasgow, Ellen. "The Shadowy Third," *Scribner's Magazine*, December 1916.

Hichens, Robert S. "How Love Came to Professor Guildea," *Tongues of Conscience*. London: Methuen & Co., 1900.

Hodgson, William Hope. "The Searcher of the End House," *Carnacki the Ghost Finder*. London: Eveleigh Nash Company, 1913.

Jacobs, W. W. "The Three Sisters," *Night Watches*. New York: McKinlay, Stone & Mackenzie, 1914.

James, Henry. "The Turn of the Screw," *The Novels and Tales of Henry James, Volume IV*. New York: Charles Scribner's Sons, 1908.

James, M. R. "An Episode of Cathedral History," *A Thin Ghost and Others*. London: Edward Arnold, 1919.

Kipling, Rudyard. "The Phantom 'Rickshaw," *The Phantom 'Rickshaw and Other Tales*. Allahabad: A. H. Wheeler & Co., 1888.

Landon, Perceval. "Thurnley Abbey," *McClure's Magazine*, October 1908.

Le Fanu, J. Sheridan. "The Haunted Baronet," *Belgravia*, October 1870–January 1871.

Lee, Vernon. "Amour Dure," *Hauntings: Fantastic Stories*. London: John Lane, The Bodley Head, 1889.

Middleton, Richard. "The Ghost-Ship," *The Ghost-Ship and Other Stories*. London: T. Fisher Unwin, 1912.

Onions, Oliver. "The Cigarette Case," *Widdershins*. London: Martin Secker, 1911.

Poe, Edgar Allan. "Eleonora," *The Works of the Late Edgar Allan Poe*. New York: J. S. Redfield, 1857.

Quiller-Couch, Arthur. "The Roll-Call of the Reef," *Wandering Heath*. London: Cassell and Company Limited, 1896.

Riddell, Mrs. J. H. "A Terrible Vengeance," *Princess Sunshine and Other Stories*. London: Ward and Downey, 1899.

Wells, H. G. "The Story of the Inexperienced Ghost," *Twelve Stories and a Dream*. London: Macmillan and Co., Ltd., 1903.

Wharton, Edith. "Kerfol," *Xingu and Other Stories*. New York: Charles Scribner's Sons, 1916.

Wood, Mrs. Henry. "A Curious Experience," *Johnny Ludlow, Fourth Series*. New York: Macmillan and Co., Limited, 1901.